MW00353896

Nightlord

KNIGHTFALL

Garon Whited

Copyright © 2017 by Garon Whited.
Cover Art: "Firebrand" by R. Beaconsfield (rbeaconsfield@hotmail.com)
ISBN: 978-0-692-87416-5

This is a work of fiction. Names, characters, places and incidents either
are the product of the author's imagination or are used fictitiously, and any
resemblance to any actual persons, living or dead, events, or locales is
entirely coincidental.

"Don't mistake my kindness for weakness. I am kind to everyone, but when someone is unkind to me, weak is not what you are going to remember about me."

— Al Capone

Disclaimer

In the normal course of events, occasionally one must take a moment to pause and reflect, to take a breath—if one does such a thing—and to consider the sum of one's life. Taken as a whole, is the life in question a thing of good or evil, right or wrong, chaos or order? Do these concepts even hold any relevance when applied to life, itself? Or are they only for actions, specific and limited?

Moral questions have never been my forte. I specialize in the practical, not the philosophical, theological, or political.

Yet I wonder, sometimes... am I a good person or a bad person? I prefer to think of myself in positive terms, to believe I am a creature of principles and kindness, not some hollow shell animated by hunger, pain, and fear. Does the desire to be good make me more than a monster? Does wishing to be better mean I am less a monster than I fear? Or am I only as much a monster as any man?

There are things about myself I do not like. But can a man—or a monster— change his nature by some act of will? Or must such change, by necessity, come from some external force, some outside intervention, for good or ill? Or is it some alchemy of within and without, above and below, will and destiny? I am torn between the hope I may change for the better, and the fear I may be changed for the worse.

How am I to judge? Who am I to judge myself—or anyone? My reflection mocks me by its absence, and my shadow twists and shapes itself in ways my spirit cannot follow.

I can see myself only through the eyes of others, and I do not trust their eyes to see me as I truly am.

What Day Is It?

I hit with a splash and a thud. The water was only a few inches deep and did nothing to break my fall, but it gave me one hell of a scare before I hit bottom. I pushed myself upright and wiped scummy water from my face. The room was pitch-black, which, for me, only meant the world was black, white, and shades of grey. At least my vision told me it was between sunset and sunrise, corroborated by the absence of my heartbeat.

Five seconds later, I recognized where I was. It was my old gate room, and this was the former gate-pool I aimed for. Ten points to House Bloodsucker for a successful, if somewhat poorly-executed, escape.

And, while I'm at it, add a point to my paranoia score. I sat there in brackish, filthy water and activated my cloaking device. Which is to say I cast spells to hide myself from detection spells. It might not do any good, of course, or it might be completely unnecessary. Or it could be the only thing keeping a bunch of soul-scorched magi from tracing me and turning me into undead chowder. Regardless, I raised cloaking spells.

They tried to kill me, but I'm sort of used to that. What burned itself into me was the thought of how they wounded me, *used* me—and having used me, they tried to dispose of me like the foil wrapper off a condom, and with about as much respect.

I could list a lot of emotions appropriate to the situation, all of which I had. Most prevalent were fear and rage. Possibly rage and fear. The two were pretty well mixed.

The room was empty, unused. The water smelled and tasted awful. When I finished my cloaking work, I climbed out of the pool. I wrung myself out and dry-cleaned with a few sharp gestures. It helped I was still missing my hair. Johann enjoyed setting me on fire almost as much as I didn't.

I didn't know if Johann would pursue me immediately or if he would gather his forces before striking… or, to be fair, if he might be content with the tortures inflicted. Somehow, I doubted the last option. I killed his grandson and a number of other relatives in my breakout from the Mendoza estate. He would come after me again, I felt certain, but he might have other hobbies to distract him from doing it instantly.

Can I call this a huge misunderstanding? No, in the Mendoza Incident they came hunting for me, chasing down a vampire. The fact I'm not one of the Atlantean vampires has nothing to do with it. I'm a victim of prejudice. I'm offended. Triggered. I need a safe space. I'm sure there's some other whiny-sounding thing I could come up with, but I really don't like whining. They came after a vampire, they got one. I don't think they have any right to be angry when their would-be prey turns into a predator. That won't stop them from being angry, of course. Besides…

He's got my orb. It's helping him and he's obviously listening to it. He'll come after me. The orb will talk him into it—if it even needs to.

With some dismay, I realized my amulet was missing, as were my rings. I hoped really hard the mountain's anti-detection defenses were also in good working order. Now, where did I leave my stuff? Did Johann take it? Or did they remove my stuff in Carrillon when they were peeling clothes off me to treat electrical burns? Could go either way, I decided. Maybe I could ask Lissette or Tianna.

While I thought about my missing stuff, I searched the perimeter of the room. I didn't find a door. A moment of work with a spell and the mountain started making one for me.

I sat down on the raised lip of the pool and waited. The room obviously hadn't been used in quite some time, possibly not since I ran through a gate and T'yl destroyed it. There were no signs of the damage caused by an exploding gate, though. Good to know the mountain could fix such things.

In that quiet moment, while I waited, recent memory reared up, towered over me, and guilt fell on me like the proverbial bricks down a well.

Yes, a Lord of Night can weep. The tears are blood, and they streak down like comets with crimson tails before vanishing. We can keep it up all night, especially when we're feeling particularly sorry for ourselves.

I was used by Johann for a number of things. Tricked, tortured, lied to, manipulated... and, part and parcel of all of it, he used me to kill children. How many, I'm not certain, but even one was too many. Worse, he made it personal by finding children I *knew*. Children I liked. Even—in my self-centered, egotistical fashion—children I loved. All four of them, plus the little one. They were good kids. Kind. Helpful. Loyal. Clever. Talented. And little Olivia could barely say my alias, pronouncing it "Flad" the few times she tried.

And I killed them.

Oh, I know Johann set it up. He pushed me into being a starved, mindless killer and set me loose on a roomful of children—teleporting them in, dumping them in through the ceiling, whatever. He kept feeding me the things he knew I would never eat until I could grasp the enormity of what I'd done.

Whether or not Johann might come after me no longer mattered. He used me. He forced me to murder children. I hated him for it, as if I needed another reason. I wanted to kill him. No, I wanted to hurt him, hurt him as badly as he hurt me. I wanted to punish him. Not out of a sense of justice, either. Revenge, pure and cold and bright. I wanted him to understand pain. To understand *my* pain by possessing it for himself.

I got a grip on myself, down there in the depths of the mountain, in the dark. I was thinking like something in an orb. I know I can, but I should aspire to greater things.

But it's hard. It's so hard to think of rising above when you're knee-deep in the bloodless bodies of slain children. It's a sensation I'll never forget and—are you listening, God? —hope never to repeat.

Could I walk away from my hatred? Could I walk away from revenge disguised as justice? Every time I try to punish the wicked, something terrible results. Every time I try to do something *good*, it seems to turn around and bite me. What about giving up? What about walking away, finding some random world in the tree of infinite possibilities and simply hiding? With no idea as to my whereabouts, they could search for a thousand years and never find a clue, much less me.

Lissette could rule without my help. Seldar could be happy as a priest of Justice. Mary could steal anything she liked and live in the palace atop Karvalen. The various children of my body might or might not need a father figure, but *I* certainly wasn't a worthy role model. Firebrand could stay or go, whatever it chose. Amber and Tianna have careers as professional clergy. All I would need is Bronze and a day or so to shift from one world to the next—maybe we could keep traveling from world to world, exploring!

Oh, that sounded so good. Tempting, even. But... Lissette has problems, Seldar is trying to help me, Mary would miss me and insist on coming along, Amber and Tianna would want a way to keep in touch...

And then there's Tort. Most especially Tort.

No, I can't simply walk away. I still have to find out what happened to Tort. T'yl, too, but mostly Tort. They're both adults and capable of looking out for themselves, but it took me a long time to come to terms with loving Tort—to admit to myself how much I love Tort. I owe her better than she ever got from me. If she's alive, I have to know. At minimum, I have to know her fate and, if she isn't happy with it, change it.

That's part of why I'm staying. The other part is what happens when I close my eyes. An image is seared into my eyeballs. When I turned to look at the wall of my torture chamber, my eyes absorbed every detail. Four bloodless bodies hanging in their chains, and the fifth one, the tiny one, ripped in two. *By my hands.*

No, I have to admit it, if only to myself. I can't let Johann get away with this. I'm their Guardian Demon. Their deathly faces won't go away until I kill Johann—maybe not even then. I have a kingdom to settle, true, but also a magi family leader to kill. And I will.

Miles to go before I sleep.

The mountain built a pivot-door very quickly, for a geological pet. It doesn't start at a point and draw a line somewhere. It defines where the door is and pulls the stone of the frame away it, all the way around it, all at once. I pushed it open. A passage curved outside the door, sloping gradually up and down, and it was a long walk up before I reached a public area. I gave the mountain a spell-note to have the old gate room connected to the private passages of the palace.

People gave me funny looks as I walked through the undermountain city. I was hardly in the height of fashion. The velvety chiton and sandals Juliet conjured for me stood out like a Roman senator in Camelot, and for much the same reasons. Nobody bothered me, though. They tended mostly toward odd looks; nobody recognized me. A few of the ladies gave me interested, even flirtatious looks. I'm guessing they liked my dress. Either that, or bald guys with slightly-pointed ears are in fashion.

Luckily, there weren't a lot of people up and about. Judging by the silvery tint to the lighting, it was some ungodly, cow-milking hour of the way-too-early morning.

I went up to the lower door of the palace—essentially, the front door, rather than the long, sloping back door of the Kingsway. This was the somewhat more public entrance, rather than the King's Private Driveway. I pushed, the door opened, and I closed it behind me.

Oddly enough, I felt at home.

I barely made it up the ramp to the top door of the entryway before it started swinging open. Mary slithered through it and grabbed me, squeezing for all she was worth. I hugged her in return and wondered how long I'd been gone *this* time. After a minute, she switched from hugging to kissing, which kept me fully occupied for another minute.

Finally, she let go of me and looked me over.

"What in the name of sanity are you wearing?"

"I'm pretty sure it's called a chiton," I told her. "Kind of a short, one-shoulder toga, it was popular—"

"Stop right there. We'll get you out of the skirt and into some regular clothes. Your *de facto* council wants to talk to you about the war."

She took me by the hand and led me inside while I wondered about the war. I turn my back and everything goes to pieces. What *is* it with my life?

"How long have I been gone?"

"Sixteen days. Where have you been?"

"Summoned, captured, tortured, abused, tricked, used, offended, and deeply enraged."

"How is 'deeply enraged' different from 'angry'?"

"Scale."

"Here we go again. I remember the last time we had a talk like this. Maybe you have some examples?" she requested.

"Angry is someone getting their head ripped off with my bare hands. Deeply enraged is binding someone's soul into a mummified tongue before burying it in a demon's outhouse."

"I have a good imagination and I remember feeding in a slaughterhouse," she said, thoughtfully. "I am amazingly sorry I asked for examples."

"I've been through worse. Recently, in fact."

"Is that where you lost your beard, hair, and eyebrows?"

"Yes. Thank you for reminding me." I worked on my follicles for a moment. "Do I need the beard?"

"No. It would be best for you to look like the king they remember."

"I'll take your word for it." I started the spell; hair sprouted on my head and started to lengthen. It went much more quickly than if I had been alive—no messy biological balances to maintain, probably. We walked on while it slowly grew out.

"Where's Tianna?" I asked.

"She, Bronze, and Firebrand are guests of the Queen."

"Hold on. Define 'guests.'"

"Real guests. She's the granddaughter of the King and the other two are his personal property. Although," she added, "someone did raise the question of whether or not your laws on slavery applied to any living thing, including intelligent magical artifacts."

"Freedom is the right of anything capable of understanding the concept and desiring the state," I replied. "But Tianna, Bronze, and Firebrand are all okay?"

"Yep. Spoke with Tianna just yesterday, on the mirror. She's trying to get Lissette to see reason."

"She's trying to persuade Lissette and make her see the light. Reason isn't the anthropomorphic personification Tianna represents."

Mary was silent for several steps, apparently considering how seriously to take my remark.

"By the way," I added, "who are all these people in my house?" As we talked and walked, we passed a dozen or more individuals. They all stepped out of our path and bowed their heads until we passed by.

"I don't know them all. Some of them are Order of Shadow, some are merely members of the faithful, some are other locals, a few are immigrants from Rethven. Seldar and Dantos are acting as head honchos since nobody seems to want to follow a woman."

"Is that bitterness I hear?"

"It ain't sugar."

"I'll have a word with the two of them."

"Seldar's okay. I think his wife beat him over the head with her competence. It's the rest of these primitive idiots."

"Duly noted," I replied, but I was thinking, *Wife? Seldar has a wife? He can't be older than... Nine years older than the kid I remember.*

Immortality problems. Will I ever get used to this? Sure I will. It's just a matter of time.

We stopped by my chambers for a change of clothes. Mary selected my outfit; I wore what she picked out. She also told me to stop the hair-growing spell and she trimmed it for me. She wanted me looking dignified. I didn't have Firebrand to go with the swordbelt, but someone hung one on it while I was out. It was the lighter, elvish-style blade I'd woken up with inside the base of my statue. Still had the sharpness enchantment, too. I was glad to have it. I don't feel dressed without a sword, these days.

Is it my paranoia acting up, or am I simply used to having a sword?

The scabbard was more interesting to me. Magical monatomic edges don't sit well in normal scabbards. Last I looked, my three knights were using spells to protect the interior of their scabbards from touching the actual edge of the super-sharp blades. This scabbard had an enchantment for that, yes, but the clever bit was mechanical. A lever on the scabbard could work a mechanism to turn off-center cylinders inside the scabbard. When rotated into position, they clamped the blade along the flat, pinning it in place. When clicked into the other position, they rotated the thicker portion of the off-center cylinders away from the blade, allowing it to be drawn.

"Are you done admiring the gadget?" Mary asked. I admitted I was and locked the blade in place again. Mary watched me with a perplexed expression.

"Are you all right?"

"No."

"Sit down," she instructed, pointing at a heavy, carved chair. I did so. "Tell Mary what's wrong."

"It's going to take a while."

"I know. You can't be concise to save your life. Do it anyway."

"Don't you have a meeting scheduled for me...?"

"They're still waking up; it's at least another hour until dawn—or a couple of candle stripes. We really need a clock."

"Don't I know it."

"So talk."

Under her urging, I did. I left out no detail, not even the torture. I made sure she was especially clear on the orb's involvement, too. When I finished, she simply stared at me with an expression of horrified fascination.

"You've been tortured for all this time?" she asked, softly.

"Time runs differently between worlds," I replied, "and somewhat irregularly and possibly unpredictably. It's only been... um... three or four days? At least, over there. I kind of lost track."

"And they aren't dead?"

"*Not yet*," I said. She flinched away from me as though zapped with a cattle prod.

"What the hell was *that*?" she demanded.

"What was what?"

"Your voice. It did a thing."

"What thing?"

"The creepy monster thing!"

"What creepy monster thing?"

"You know!"

"No, I don't," I said. "What happened?"

"It... it had the quivery, echo-y reverb thing and... and... a twist on the bass control, and... something. It was... startling. Unexpected." She shivered a little, my undead lover, which told me more about my tone of voice than a six-hour lecture with slideshows. "It was kind of scary. And sexy, too."

"You have a one-track mind."

"I do not," she answered, affronted. "I have at least two."

"Oh?"

"Work and fun. Although," she admitted, "not always in that order."

"And sometimes they overlap."

"I feel sunrise starting," she replied, changing the subject. "Waterfall?"

"And then to work?"

"Eventually."

"I'm not really in the mood for that. Not even for dealing with bureaucratic nonsense. I've had a really bad time," I admitted, "and I'm more on edge than I like to think about. It's dangerous to be around me, or I'm afraid it is. I'm torn between curling up in the dark until I feel better, or plotting vengeance and carnage."

"What sorts of vengeance and carnage?" she asked, pulling me to my feet. I suffered myself to be led to the bathroom.

"I'm not sure, yet. I don't have any ideas, aside from nuking them from orbit—which might not work. Maybe cracking the planet. I'd rather not commit genocide, though. It strikes me as indiscriminate."

"I hear nuking them from orbit is the only way to be sure, but they weren't talking about magi, were they?"

"No. The magi have a spell-dome of unknown properties over their territory and it's irritated some governments. I don't know for certain, but someone may have already tried nuking them from orbit. That leaves planet-cracking, and I'm resisting the idea."

"I imagine it takes a lot of effort."

"Yeah. It's a constant temptation."

"I mean, a lot of effort to do it, not effort to resist it."

"No, it's actually pretty easy to destroy a planet. There are very few legitimate reasons to do it."

"Oh," she said, in a very small voice. I think she regretted asking.

We stepped into the waterfall. It is a measure of my mental state that all her subtle and not-so-subtle attempts to distract me failed. Maybe it had something to do with being subjected to intense and prolonged pain. Maybe it was being chained down and treated like a talking piece of meat. Maybe it was being manipulated into being a murderous monster. Maybe the trickery, the personalized deception, the galling feeling of being used so contemptuously— those could have something to do with it.

And, let's be honest, maybe it was the fear.

It's not really the fear of their power. I've met things that can pretend to be gods. I've *been* that sort of low-order deity, possibly an angelic creature, although only briefly. Johann and his family may be of a similar order of power, but they have a major weakness—physical bodies. Flesh.

People with immense power scare me. The fact I have power scares me. I live in a sea of fear and swim in the currents of terror, and I can barely dog-paddle. The best I can do is not let it bother me.

Whee.

None of this changed the fact I was disturbed on several levels. I'm only glad I was conscious of it. Being angry and afraid is something I'm used to—much too used to. But there are psychological aspects to torture I simply do not understand. I *know* my head isn't working the way it usually does and I'm not sure how it's different. I really need to keep a tight grip on myself. No snap decisions, no angry orders, no commands without thinking. Calm, cool, and controlled. I better start working on that, or take a while off to cool down.

Can I afford to wait until I feel better? Or should I rush into plans for vengeance and destruction, hoping my friends can spot any flaws? Come to that, what kind of plans can I make—or should I make? —when I know my brain isn't running at optimum?

I hate people messing with my mind, directly, indirectly, or simply as a side effect. Hate it. It alters the very thing I feel is the nature of being. It's one thing to remove body parts. Whether they grow back or not, I'm still myself, driving a flesh-vehicle which may or may not malfunction. But when people start screwing around with the guy doing the driving—the fundamental *me*....

The best decision I could make would have to do. Fortunately, I trust the judgment of the people around me. If they think it's a bad idea, I'll have to listen. Maybe they'll have some good ideas I can use as examples of how I should be thinking!

I decided to try and recover some mental and spiritual equilibrium before choosing my tactics for horrific vengeance. This plan involved finishing my shower, sitting under the waterfall, rocking back and forth in the dark, and getting a grip on myself. Mary sat with me, holding me while we rocked back and forth. I think it says something fundamental about her that she stayed with me until I settled down.

Karvalen, Saturday, February 21st

I have a council chamber.

When did I get a council chamber? Nobody told me I had a council chamber. I wasn't too clear on having a council, much less a chamber to put them in. To be fair, I try not to get in the way too much and let other people get on with the whole running-the-kingdom thing, but maybe I ought to pay more attention.

Then again, the palace in Karvalen is almost ridiculously large. I might have missed it, or the mountain might have grown one at Seldar's request. Mary pushed on the door to spin it and I wondered if we should get some more normal doors put in the place. There were lots of them in the overcity, mounted to doorframes simply by asking the mountain to hold on to the hinges. We could do that up here, too. The mountain wouldn't mind.

And I realized my mind was wandering. I made a deliberate effort to focus and put my game face on. I can sit in the dark and rock back and forth anytime; right now, it was time to pretend to be a king.

Would it help, I wonder, to have actual hats to reflect the number of metaphorical hats I have to wear? Interesting psychological question—for later.

The council chamber is more complicated than a simple open space. It has a waiting room, a couple of private rooms off to the side of the waiting room, and some other chambers off the main chamber. In the waiting room, we encountered a pair of massive, black-armored ogres. At least, that was my first impression.

They stood up as we came in, which caused the optical illusion of the room shrinking. They towered to about seven feet tall. Broad-shouldered and thick, I wondered how well they would do as walls. Pretty well, was my guess. They might also do well as asteroids or dwarf planets; they could eclipse small suns. They made me think about half-giants, basketball players turned weightlifters, and how to approach someone with so much reach. Four hundred pounds? Five hundred? Men that big might weigh as much as I do. If they were as fast as they were strong, I wouldn't want to face them during the day without a bazooka and surprise.

There followed some clicking and unlatching as they removed their helmets. It hurt me a little that I didn't recognize them instantly. The last time I saw them, they were nine years younger and considerably smaller. Back then, they didn't need to shave often, so the changes in their faces were almost as drastic. It was a good thing the super-high-tech suits of armor were enchanted to adapt to the wearer over time.

They threw the latches on their scabbards and drew swords I recognized. It hurt me a little more to realize I recognized the blades more quickly than I recognized them. Then again, the blades hadn't changed. They laid the weapons on the floor and the armored figures went to one knee, which put their heads slightly below mine.

Did I mention they were huge?

Torvil and Kammen, all grown up. Way up. And sideways. Those grow-your-own-warrior spells apparently had considerable cumulative effect. I hadn't intended them for long-term use, just as a temporary aid. If we started earlier, what kind of results would we get? Maybe we could try them on a *dazhu* and extrapolate; anyone too young wasn't allowed to volunteer for human experimentation.

"Your Majesty," Torvil said. His voice was deeper, more rumbling. Mature. No longer a teenager, but a full-grown man well into his twenties.

"I think you meant to say 'Halar,'" I corrected.

"As you say, Sire."

"What's the meaning of this?" I asked, toeing one of the blades carefully. Anything sharp on an atomic scale deserves to be treated with respect.

"We goofed," Kammen said. Technically, the word he used was *currastalt*, which is a combination of *failure* and *foolish*. The best translation might be *failure compounded with foolishness*. Goofed.

"The story I heard," I replied, "was how you stayed with me—well, with the person you thought was me, the Demon King—despite the atrocities and depravities involved. You minimized the awfulness as much as you could, as well as protected my body, for which I am duly grateful. What makes you think you failed foolishly?"

"Seldar told us how, when you broke the Oath of Kings, you freed us from our oaths as knights," Torvil answered. "Kammen and I disagreed with him. We swore. If you broke your oath—which, now that we know what truly happened, we can say you did not—well, if you break your word, is it reason to break ours? We were supposed to be... to make you a better person? To encourage you to goodness? To be good examples? All of that. Yet, Seldar reports he is not chastised for his choice."

"Makes us the wrong ones," Kammen finished.

"What makes you think there was one right choice?" I asked.

"Isn't there always?"

"I'm not going to get into that. It'll take a textbook and a philosophy professor. Instead, let's look at you guys. You were supposed to be good examples," I reassured them, "and I'm sure you were, within the limits of your capabilities. I don't remember, but I believe in you. I trust you. I'm sure you did your best."

"Are we in trouble, Boss?" Kammen asked. I expected Firebrand to pipe up, but it was still in Carrillon, probably...

"Don't call him that," Mary chimed in. "Firebrand doesn't like it."

"I can't get away with nothing," Kammen complained, but smiled as he said it. He favored Mary with an appraising look. Mary returned it, along with a sultry smile. I ignored it.

"First off, Seldar isn't in trouble," I said. "He did what he thought was right. That's one of the things about knights in my personal retinue; they have a lot more leeway for initiative. Second, he came to me and took responsibility for his actions—he didn't try to justify himself. He explained, yes, but he was also willing to accept whatever judgment I rendered.

"You two could have done similar things. You could have quit to join various clergy, or start rebellions, or just raise social awareness about the monster on the throne—if you'd thought it was called for. I trust your judgment. I trust you. You're kinder, nobler men than I will ever be, and I believe you can help me be something better than I am. So, no, you're not in trouble. You did what you thought was best, according to the principles of knighthood, as did Seldar. Thank you."

I crouched and picked up the weapons by the flat of the blades, very carefully. If I lost fingers, we could reattach them, but it would be awkward until after sunset. I held out the weapons to Torvil and Kammen.

"Don't repeat it," I told them. "You never forgot your oath."

They took the hilts, gingerly, cautious of my hands, but I didn't let go.

"While you serve me," I said, softly, "I will honor you, respect you, and ask no service of you that will bring dishonor to my house or to yours. I will heed your councils that we may find wisdom together. I will stand with you to defend those who cannot defend themselves. I will be faithful in love and loyal in friendship. I will uphold justice by being fair to all. I will forgive when asked, that my own mistakes will be forgiven."

I let go the weapons. They saluted, sheathed them, clamped them in place, and rose like avalanches in reverse.

"Now, I hear arguments beyond the door. Does it lead to my council chamber?"

"It does, Sire."

"Let's go see what the fuss is about."

Torvil and Kammen glanced at each other before locking their helmets on again. I took it as a warning.

When we entered, there was a lively discussion going on about armies, navies, negotiations, and ultimatums. There were fingers pointed, voices raised.

It's disconcerting to walk into a room and watch the whole place fall silent to stare at you. I've had it happen when bringing graded test papers to class and it's always disquieting. This was a smaller group, but their gazes seemed to have more weight. Everyone stood up.

Mary ushered me to the head of the table. I sat down. Mary sat on my left; Seldar remained standing on my right. I recognized Beltar and Dantos. The rest were unfamiliar to me. Torvil and Kammen took up station behind and to either side of me, standing like... like... like really huge guys in super-high-tech enchanted armor. There's really nothing I can compare them to. Tank turrets, maybe. Artillery pieces.

Seldar looked at the towering figures. They nodded, just slightly. I was looking at his face, so I saw the effort it took not to smile. He shifted his gaze to me.

"Sire," Seldar said. Everyone saluted.

"Be seated." They sat. "Before we get on with whatever else is planned, I presume you have a sword for me?"

"Several, Sire."

"Do you have one with you?"

"I do, Sire." He stood and brought out a sword and tackle from behind his chair. He handed it to me wordlessly. I examined it; it had the same mechanical setup in the scabbard. My suspicion was Seldar had come up with the idea—or, if someone else had the idea, he implemented it. It was only a suspicion, though.

"Do you remember your oath, Seldar?"

"My ghost will remember," he informed me, solemnly. He saluted, closed fist over his heart, and recited:

"To my King I swear loyalty and bravery. To the Crown I swear to be just and fair as far as my mortal wisdom will allow. At my King's command, I swear to grant mercy, or to withhold mercy; to take life, or to grant it; to harm those from whom my King shall lift his grace; to heal and help those upon whom my King's grace shall descend."

I didn't ask him to repeat it, only whether or not he remembered it. I had intended to ask him if his duties as a priest or reverend or minister of Justice would interfere with being a knight in the service of the King, but either it wasn't a problem or he was quitting the religion business.

"While you serve me," I replied, "I will honor you, respect you, and ask no service of you that will bring dishonor to my house or to yours. I will heed your councils that we may find wisdom together. I will stand with you to defend those who cannot defend themselves. I will be faithful in love and loyal in friendship. I will uphold justice by being fair to all. I will forgive when asked, that my own mistakes will be forgiven."

I handed him his sword. He took it, ignoring the tears streaking his cheeks, and belted it on rather than hang it behind his chair.

"You're a better man than I am, Sir Seldar," I told him. "See to it you help me improve."

"It will be my honor, Sire."

"Speaking of which, do I have a castellan?"

"Sir Dantos has been fulfilling the role, with some assistance from your...?" he trailed off, questioningly, as he gestured at Mary.

"Consort?" Mary supplied, smiling her amused smile.

"Consort," I agreed. "Very good. You are now my seneschal in Karvalen. I'm not sure how that's going to work with a Baron in residence in the city, though. I'll want you to talk to the Baron of Karvalen when you have a moment."

"I am honored, Sire."

"If you keep demonstrating all the great virtues, you're going to get honored a lot. Try to get used to it. Now, perhaps we should have introductions. I trust everyone here knows who I am?"

They acknowledged such was the case.

"Good. I know Mary, Seldar, Beltar, Dantos, Torvil, and Kammen. Around the table, please. Who are you?"

First of the four strangers was Sir Nothar, a knight to Baron Gosford. He was a handsome fellow, blue-eyed and blond-haired. He was present to represent his aged father.

Percel was the local priest of the Temple of Justice. Maybe his presence was why Seldar could be so confident about being a knight versus being a priest. Someone else could be in charge of the Temple of Justice, assuming they had one in the overcity, somewhere. Percel was a small man with a keen gaze and a way of looking at you that seemed to imply he knew what you meant, rather than what you said. Fitting, considering his career choice.

Liet rounded out our attending clergy as the representative of the Grey Lady. She was surprisingly young, no more than thirty, with a wide smile and more laugh lines than I expected. Her hair hung loose, unbraided, in the manner of young girls. I wondered what it meant in ecclesiastical circles.

The last of the attendees was Corran, the head of the Wizards' Guild in Karvalen. He was a hefty man with dark hair, a full beard, and rings on all his fingers to hold prepared spells. I doubted he could get them off; he obviously didn't miss any meals. He regarded me with interest, fingertips steepled together over his ample waistline.

"Any word on T'yl or Tort?" I asked. There was none. "All right. At least we have extra chairs in case they show up. Wait a second. Shouldn't Rendal be here? He's still in charge of the City Guard, is he not?"

"Sire," Seldar said, "Rendal is not noble, a representative of a god, nor a member of your personal advisors."

I looked at Seldar and waited, silently. He started to say something, caught himself, nodded.

"I will extend to him an invitation to join us," Seldar assured me.

"Good. Now that we have introductions out of the way...What's going on, Seldar?"

"In short, the Queen marches on Karvalen."

Well, he did keep it short.

"Perhaps you might elaborate?" I encouraged.

"When you escaped from her custody—I beg your pardon, Sire. When you departed the royal palace without making your farewells, she became convinced your visit was part of some plan. You came to her palace, achieved what you wanted—or were thwarted—and departed."

"Did anyone point out my getting struck by lightning might have had something to do with it?" I didn't add it was a precursor to stealing me. If I'd been myself at the time, rather than fried extra-crispy, could I have resisted the summons? Interesting question.

"I believe the point was made," Seldar said. "However, lacking a Court Magician, her chief advisor on matters of magic is Thomen, the Court Wizard."

"Ah."

"Exactly. It is well-known he hates you. Even so, his voice carries weight. The Queen values him."

"All right, she thinks I came to visit as part of a nefarious plot. Then I left. This is cause for war?"

"Not by itself," Seldar agreed.

"It's the murders," Corran interjected. I turned to look at him.

"What murders?"

"Coincident with your... departure... nearly a hundred children were killed in the capitol, all between the ages of one and eight years. They were all found with their throats torn out and an almost total lack of blood. All of them were likewise rumored to be yours. Doubtless, the Queen believes you are responsible. It is possible she fears for the lives of her own children, which are, of course, undeniably yours."

I didn't like the faint tone of mockery in his voice, but chose not to pursue it. Larger concerns and all that.

"And she's going to war because of this?"

"Not precisely," Seldar said, shifting in his chair. "I arrived in Karvalen by ship shortly after your disappearance from Carrillon. The lady Mary spoke with the Queen."

"Mary?" I asked, turning to her.

"She… that is, Lissette cranked up a mirror and wanted to talk to you. That was okay by me; I wanted to talk to you. She accused me of attacking the palace to get you out and I denied it. Then I accused her of imprisoning or killing you, which she denied."

"You thought she still had me, while she thought you stole me?"

"Pretty much."

"I don't suppose you mentioned I want her to rule the kingdom?"

"It didn't come up."

"And *this* is why we're throwing a war?"

"Your Majesty?" Nothar asked. "If I may?"

"By all means."

"It is my understanding," he said, "that you have been unable to follow the events of the last nine years or so—in truth, unable to fathom events during and after the wars of unification. May I ask if this is fact or fancy?"

"Fact."

"Then Your Majesty is probably unaware of the circumstances surrounding Karvalen, Mochara, and, in effect, the whole of the Eastern Marches."

"Probably."

"The old kingdom of Rethven is reunited, even expanded. It now claims—without enforcing—dominion over the lands from the mountain of Karvalen all the way to the Western Ocean, but has little real power over the cities beyond the Darkwood. It holds no dominion over the People of the Plains, of course, but regards them more favorably than in the past, a position largely reciprocated by the People, as well.

"In similar vein, the King left the lands of the Eastern Marches almost entirely in the hands of my father, the Baron Gosford, just as he has left the administration of the races that live within the Eastrange in the hands of the Duke of Vathula. We have been largely unmolested by the activities and proclivities of the Demon King, if I may use the phrase."

"I understand," I told him. "You're going somewhere with this?"

"Your Majesty, perhaps you may not know the Eastern Marches have long considered themselves the personal property of the King—you, in fact—ever since you founded the mountain of living stone. Even in the past decade, the lack of interference, the minimal taxation, the… benevolent neglect?… we enjoyed was far preferable to the direct attention Rethven endured. We therefore have a different view of the Demon King. And, with no disrespect to Your Majesty, of your royal self, since the two are not the same. During the interregnum between the disappearance of the Demon King and the return of the true King, preparations were made to dissociate ourselves from Rethven and become the Kingdom of Karvalen."

"Does Lissette know this?" I asked.

"Your Majesty, I do not know for certain. I would think not, but who can say with surety what another does *not* know?"

"Fair point. Go on."

"There is little else to say. A readiness for war sometimes encourages it. If the Queen did not know of my father's intentions, she is surely aware of them now. An army does not spring to arms overnight and ours has been slowly building for years."

"Okay. So, why isn't your father here to tell me this? Why did he send you?"

"My father is an old man, Sire, and does not travel well, even so short a way as up into the palace, here. I am also here at the request of your granddaughter, Your Majesty."

"Well, that's certainly a good reason," I agreed. "I take it the Baron Gosford is prepared to defend me—and my smaller kingdom—with every resource at his command?"

"If it is your will, Your Majesty, it will be so," he assured me. I did notice he didn't exactly answer my question.

"That's good to know. However, I'm still not quite clear on why we're having a war right *now*."

I looked around the table. Nobody met my eyes.

"Halar?" Mary asked.

"Yes?"

"It might be my fault."

"Go on."

"Well, not entirely. I mean, there were all these preparations for a war already, and a lot of suspicion, and the reputation your demon version had—"

"Factors were favorable for it, got it. What did you do?"

"It wasn't me. Well, it was Lissette and me. We… don't… really know each other. She doesn't trust me and I don't trust her. When we were talking through the mirror, she called me a liar, I called her a liar, then we called each other a few more things and she threatened me, so I threatened her…"

"So, when the Red Phone rang, you and the head of state on the other end traded insults and threats until it was time to send for the nuclear football?"

"I thought you were her prisoner! I was thinking of it more as 'that bitch has him and is going to do awful things to him.' You did warn me it was a possibility."

"I did, yes," I admitted. "I remember."

"So, I wasn't thinking of her as a head of state, only as a bitch. And…" she trailed off.

"And when the balloon went up, you realized your mistake?"

"Actually, while we were shouting at each other, she hung up in my face, which really made me mad. It wasn't until Seldar got reports about troop movements when I realized what was going on."

I rubbed my temples. I hate wars.

"All right. How long do we have before troop movements turn into military fronts?"

"They are still gathering their forces. The major concentrations are in Baret, Formia, and Tegron."

"Why?"

"Baret and Tegron are well-placed for overland travel—Baret being on the southern King's Road and the coast, Tegron bordering on Vathula and the Eastgate. Formia is farther west and on the Quaen river; it is likely a staging point for transport by sea."

"Yeah. I hear people have tried to assault Mochara by sea before."

"But now it is more commonly known why their keels shatter," Seldar pointed out. "Defensive measures will be taken to protect their ships in new and more extensive ways."

"Good point. What else did Lissette have to say?"

"As I said," Seldar continued, "I arrived shortly afterward. I did call the palace in the hope of smoothing the situation over, but the Queen did not wish to speak to me. I spoke instead with people I could trust." He nodded at the giants behind me. "Once we were mutually informed, they elected to come here."

"Our loyalty to the King is well-known," Torvil said. "We were—we are— responsible for keeping him alive. We would be of no use imprisoned under the palace or in the Knight's Tower."

"Besides," Kammen added, "this could be a good fight."

"I'm hoping it won't come to that," I told them.

What I meant by that was, "I have, in no particular order, godlike magi, an angry Master Wizard, a missing girlfriend, a trusted advisor who's vanished, an evil orb of nastiness, a public-relations disaster, and a couple of huge, steaming piles of guilt and rage to shovel. If it comes to a war, I'm either going to rip people apart in an uncontrollable fury or I'm going to hide in my bedroom, lock the door, eat ice cream, and cry until everyone goes away. I don't want to be bothered with this right now."

I don't think they noticed the subtext.

"I'll be talking with Lissette as soon as it can be arranged," I continued. "With luck, she'll see reason. And I'm sure Mary will help me out by delivering an eloquent, sincere apology to Her Majesty."

"Of course," Mary agreed. I sensed a lack of enthusiasm.

"In the meantime, Your Majesty," Nothar asked, "what are your wishes? Shall we dismantle our preparations in anticipation of peace? Or shall we continue to make ready in case the negotiations fail? And, if I may be so bold as to ask, what is your intention regarding two kingdoms, one of Rethven and one of Karvalen?"

"Remain in readiness to defend," I decided. "We won't be marching anywhere. If they insist on coming to us, well… that's their problem. Don't Karvalen and Mochara have long histories of simply minding their own business and allowing invaders to go splat whenever they visit?"

"Indeed."

"We'll keep up the tradition. As for the division of the kingdom, I'm against it, unless something drastic changes. What else?" I asked.

"Sire," Seldar said, "we also have the matter of the Church of Light."

"What about it?"

"The High Priest in Karvalen, Lotar, is still exhorting the faithful to destroy the 'evil' within the mountain. He also blames you for the deaths of Perrin, Framon, and Worval."

"I remember Perrin, and I presume Framon and Worval died from falling off the Kingsway?"

"He claims they were all 'cast down by the evil forces' dwelling here."

"I told the mountain to turn the Kingsway into a tunnel out of courtesy, to make it safer. I presume it's done?"

"It has altered substantially," Seldar said, carefully, "but I have no way of knowing if it has fulfilled its instructions."

"But is it a tunnel?"

"Yes."

"See? Safety first. Doesn't that count for anything?"

"With respect, Sire, Lord Lotar is hardly the most reasonable of men in regard to yourself." He gestured around the table. "We invited him to attend. He did not dignify our invitation with a reply."

"Yeah, that sounds typical. For the record, I didn't throw anyone off the mountain or Kingsway or whatever. If they fell, as far as I know it was accidental. Someone else might have pushed them, I suppose, but I didn't order it."

"I believe you," Corran said, suddenly.

"You do?"

"Yes. You do not strike me as the sort to rely on subterfuge and assassins. You face your enemies."

"I'd like to think so, yes," I agreed. I deliberately failed to correct him about my willingness to employ assassination and subterfuge as survival tools.

"You still claim you are not fit to be a knight?" he pressed.

"Yes. A knight needs to be a better man than I am. My goal is to be surrounded by persons of greater honor, courage, and worthiness than myself. That way, they can be good examples for me to follow. Maybe I can be a better person therefore. See how selfish I am?"

Corran shook his head and fell silent.

"At any rate," Seldar resumed, "Lord Lotar is encouraging rebellion and revolution within the realm. What do you wish done?"

"Is he doing anything besides talking?"

"Not to my knowledge."

Mary cleared her throat. Everyone looked at her. It seemed to surprise her.

"Ah, I'd like to talk to you about him. Later."

"Of course," I agreed. Then, to Seldar, "He hasn't been arming his followers or anything of the sort, has he?"

"Again, not to my knowledge."

"Then let him talk. When he gets around to something more than talking, then we'll see. And send him an invitation to dine with the King. Apparently, I'm stuck with being King until I can calm things down and make sure Lissette has everything firmly in hand." I shot a look at Nothar. "I'm going to need help with that."

"If I may ask, Your Majesty?"

"Go ahead."

"It is your intent to have a woman rule? A ruling queen?"

"It is."

"I mean no disrespect, Your Majesty, but is that wise?"

"I think so. Why do you think it might not be?"

Nothar looked uncomfortable. Several people around the table seemed disturbed, as well.

"Majesty," he began, slowly, "while I will agree to carry out whatever orders you wish to give, I suspect the elevation of a woman to such a position of power will not be met with... the... full approval of the nobles."

"That's fine," I told him. "If they don't like it, we can always get new nobles."

I left the statement hanging in the air. They took their time about absorbing it and thinking it over.

"Now," I continued, once they had a chance to digest it, "I would like to have a private word with my knights, please. And Corran—please don't go far; I would like to consult with you shortly. Can I persuade you to stay for lunch?"

Corran bowed from the neck, trying to look relaxed. Everyone rose and shuffled out. Mary paused before rising, catching my eye, clearly asking if she should go. I shrugged and she decided to leave with the rest.

I sent for breakfast and we spent the rest of the morning catching up. It wasn't a briefing, but I noticed something. Seldar treated it as a briefing, asking questions, even taking notes on—huzzah! —paper. Torvil kept a running list of my adversaries, asking about their strengths and weaknesses. Kammen only wanted to know what the other two might need in the way of help— "Does that mean we kill him?" was the most common question he asked. Dantos remained silent and expressionless, taking it all in; I think he was a little put off by the quasi-legendary nature of the people around him. He might also have been smarting a little at having Seldar promoted over him so abruptly. I made a note to address that.

They took most of the story pretty well. There were a couple of things they found fundamentally objectionable. Their King was tortured, used, abused, and deceived. These things did seem to offend them. And the incident with the bloodless children—that drew not only some sharp breaths but a few shudders. I don't think it was in horror, though. They don't seem the type to be easily horrified. No, I think they were afraid. Not of me, exactly, but of what I might do. Maybe they were concerned about some sort of back-sliding into evil ways. I admit, my desire to punish the man responsible was bordering closely on the fiendish, possibly even the diabolic.

"So, if I understand you correctly, Sire?" Seldar asked. "Our principle objectives are these. First, the Orb of Darkness, containing the essence of the Demon King. It exerts some influence on those around it and has ensnared some quite powerful wizards of another world. It must be destroyed or contained.

"Second, those same wizards, now much more powerful, will doubtless seek to do you harm, directly or indirectly. They must be dealt with, either by destroying them or forcing them to turn their attention elsewhere.

"Third, the Lady Tort, Consort to the King and Court Magician. She is missing or dead. If she is not dead, she must be found and her status ascertained.

"Fourth, T'yl, the Magician of Karvalen, is also missing or dead. His status, too, must be discovered.

"Fifth, the Kingdom of Rethven is to be placed under the unquestioned rule of Queen Lissette, removing the stigma of the Demon King from the throne and crown. And, incidentally, preventing a war between the Rethven territories and the Eastern Marches—Karvalen.

"Sixth, the murders in Carrillon must be investigated, their perpetrator discovered, and the individuals in question brought before you."

"I'd say you've summed it up," I agreed, "but there are quite a number of sub-objectives under each of those. Also, the order may be in doubt. Some of the less-prioritized things may be quick and easy to solve. By comparison, I mean. I think Lissette as the Queen comes first, while we work on others."

"Before we go any further," Torvil said, "I would like to ask something, if I may, Sire."

"Sure."

"Assuming the Queen is empowered to reign and the reins of the kingdom placed in her hands, what becomes of us? We are not knights of the Queen, after all."

"I think I would want you to watch over the royal house—the princes and princesses of Rethven. No doubt Lissette will want to pick her own bodyguards, but she may want your oversized feet to fill those mammoth shoes. Personally, I'm pretty sure I won't be sticking around the palace, nor would I be welcome. It would be nice to know someone I trust is watching out for the kids."

Torvil and Kammen looked at each other. It wasn't quite the same as Malana and Malena looking at each other, but it reminded me of them.

"It will be done," Torvil assured me. Kammen nodded grimly.

"Good. Now, which of these objectives do you three think you can handle?"

"None of them, Sire," Seldar replied. The other two nodded.

"None of them?"

"None."

"Then, if I may make so bold as to ask, what do you intend to do?"

"Keep you alive long enough for you to do so."

"Fat lot of help you are. I was hoping to hand all my problems off to you and wait for results."

Seldar smiled. Torvil smiled. Kammen grinned. Dantos remained inscrutable.

Strangely enough, that made me feel better.

"Dantos," I said.

"Yes, Sire."

"You've been running the place in my absence?"

"Yes, Sire. With help from the lady Mary and Sir Seldar."

"Very good. I've placed Seldar in charge because of his seniority and experience, but I want you to know your familiarity with the city is vital."

"The lady Mary has already made mention of it."

"Really?"

"She is often out all day or all night, and always has many questions when she returns."

"I see." I made a note to talk to Mary. What was she doing? Out enjoying the place? Or actively listening to rumors, gauging the people, polling the voters? Probably the second one.

Whups. No voters. It's an absolute monarchy. Make it "polling the peasants."

"Well," I continued, "I'm pleased she has you to consult. I'll expect you to advise Seldar, too, and to be at every meeting. There's no telling when your knowledge or opinions will be sought."

"As you wish, Sire."

"Another thing. What do you think of Nothar?"

"He is an honest man, loyal and brave. His loyalties are divided. He wishes to be loyal to his father, but he also wishes to be loyal to his king, and he wants to be loyal to his..." Dantos trailed off. "I am not sure what she is."

"Tianna?"

"Yes."

"I think we can say she's his girlfriend." Rethven doesn't really have a word for *girl-friend*. I used *amisincae,* a word from Zirafel, then had to explain it to everyone. Rethven, being somewhat short on feminism and long on chauvinism, only has a few relationship categories for ladies: children, acquaintance, betrothed, wives, widows, and dead. Women who aren't "ladies" have a couple of other possible categories, all of which have some variation on "mistress" or "prostitute." There simply aren't enough women with sufficient independence and power to have a fundamental cultural impact on a culture this static. I've often thought I could fix that. Cultural changes take time, but I'm immortal. At least, I might fix it if I ever got to stay awake and active for long enough.

"Girlfriend," Kammen repeated, as though tasting it. "I like it."

"You would," Torvil replied. He seemed half joking, half sneering.

"Just 'cause I'm the handsome one and you the ugly one—" Kammen said, serenely, but I interrupted.

"So, Dantos? Nothar will definitely be helpful as long as we don't have to cross his father's interests? And then it could be a problem?"

"I would say that is fair. He would not betray you, I think, but he would not think it wrong to also help his father, the Baron, on his own initiative, if it did not interfere with your own plans."

"That's less than I'd hope for in a knight, but more than I can expect from most people," I mused. "I can live with it. It's good to know and may be important. Thank you." Dantos bowed from the neck, accepting the implied praise.

The world bent. It twisted, in fact, as though someone grabbed it by the edges and tried to rotate it while the center remained fixed—and tried to twist me with it. I didn't know what it was, but I knew I didn't like it. Reflexively, I grabbed it right back and turned it the other way, relieving the tension on myself and, hopefully, on the fabric of space around me.

All four of my knights had swords out and were standing around me, dividing their attention between me and anything that might show up outside their perimeter. They guarded me while I wrestled with the space-time continuum and the weird ways it wanted to warp. It went on for a while—two minutes? Ten? — before whatever it was gave up.

When things settled down, Torvil asked the obvious question.

"What was that?"

"I think," I said, slowly, still gripping the edge of the table, "someone wants to see me."

"A message?'

"No, a summons. I think I resisted it."

Which made me wonder. If the astral girl-spirit hadn't lightning-blasted me, could I have done something similar with the initial summons? If not, how did I resist this attempt? Did they think with their recently-enhanced powers they could simply summon me without weakening me first? And how did they know where I was without pinpointing me with another spirit? Or was a pinpoint location required? Maybe they only needed to get the right world?

Naturally, I thought it was Johann & Family. And I knew it was a space-bending attempt to grab me. I know how a gate spell works, and this felt like the initial stages of one. The fact they could even try such a thing without a perimeter-defining locus at this end said a lot about how powerful they had become.

Assuming, of course, it wasn't someone entirely different in *this* universe. But that's another level of paranoia and problems.

It happened again. I resisted it again. Then a third, fourth, and fifth time. It wasn't easy—that is, it wasn't a casual thing, like brushing off an insect. It was more like moving a heavy piece of furniture; it involved a fair amount of effort, but the outcome wasn't really in doubt.

Inter-universal logistics being as difficult as they were, that roughed in well with my estimation of their powers. Dragging me out of this universe and into theirs wouldn't be impossible with an open nexus, and they had *four*. But why keep trying if it failed? Could they know their summons was actively counteracted, or were they unable to tell why it failed?

After the fifth attempt, they apparently gave up. Seldar provided me with a handkerchief. I proceeded to dab at sweat on my upper lip and forehead.

"Is there anything we can do?" Seldar asked.

"Not at the moment. I think they've quit for now."

"Who is it?"

"Those magi from another world, I think. I'll work on something automatic to defend me as soon as I can."

"Very good, Sire, because I do not understand what happened."

I put the handkerchief away and noticed the edge of the stone slab serving as a table. It had strange ripples in it, changes in the texture of the stone. There were odd, overlapping lines, somewhat curved, like an interference pattern or two mismatched spirals. The curves seemed to center somewhere off the table—about where I was sitting. I checked the heavy, wooden chair for ripples. Yes, it was oddly patterned, too, almost as though the grain of the wood itself was altered.

"Yeah," I agreed. "I'm not real clear on it yet, myself."

When our inner circle meeting broke up, I sent the four of them off and asked them to send in Mary. Seldar and Dantos headed out, but Torvil and Kammen remained. Seldar looked back quizzically. There was an exchange of headshake and eyebrow language before he shrugged and swung the door shut behind himself.

"Something the matter?" I asked.

"Sire," Torvil began, "we need a word in private."

I gestured, sending an arc of power into the air, then widened and rotated it until it surrounded the chamber.

"It won't last long, but if anybody breaks it to listen in, I'll know it. Talk fast."

"Sire, during the course of our duties in the Palace, we had ample opportunity to discover things, overhear things, which, while not officially part of our mandate—" Torvil began, but Kammen interrupted.

"The Queen's doing the Court Wizard. Liam is the only kid that's yours."

Torvil stared at Kammen, aghast. I merely looked at them mildly.

"Well," Kammen went on, addressing Torvil, "he said talk fast. You were blathering like Seldar."

"I hadn't intended to be so..."

"Blunt?" I supplied.

"Yes. Sire."

"It's okay. I suspected the two of them were... Anyway. I wasn't aware of the paternity business, precisely, but okay."

"Okay?"

"It's fine," I assured him. He wasn't getting it, so I reached for an excuse. "Look, Liam is the prince, right? He's mine. No problem. Lissette is the Queen and can have kids by anyone she cares about. Given that we have magic to prevent a pregnancy or stop one, if she's chosen to have children with Thomen, what do I care? They're half-royal, at least, and Thomen doesn't seem a bad choice for a father. Liam will need advisors and loyal nobility when he takes the throne. If everyone is raised as part of one big family, what's the problem?"

"That," Torvil said, "is unbelievably tolerant."

"*I'm* happy to hear it," Kammen countered, then added, "Beats the last nine years." Torvil winced.

"He has a point, Sire," Torvil admitted. "We're not really used to you being..."

"Nice," Kammen finished.

"Yeah, nice. We expected you to tear the table apart at the very least."

"I'm me again," I reminded them. "I'm not the Demon King. I'm the king you would have had if I wasn't stupid."

"Speaking for myself," Torvil began.

"We're glad you're back," Kammen finished.

"So am I. Now can I talk to Mary?"

They went to swing the door open. While Torvil pushed, Kammen ran back to me, grabbed me in a bear hug that lifted me completely off the ground, then ran after Torvil.

I think he missed me.

Mary came in a few minutes later, carrying a large, wooden tray.

"Second breakfast?" she asked, cheerily.

"This could be hobbit-forming," I replied. She winced, but sat down. We ate while we talked.

"So, tell me more about this disastrous conversation with Lissette," I prompted. Mary swallowed and sighed.

"Look, before we get into that, we need—I need—to understand a little more about the whole political marriage thing."

"Sure. What do you want to know?"

"For starters, how do you feel about Lissette? Compared to me? I need to know where I stand."

Either she was listening at the door or it was a pressing concern. Either way, it was a good question and deserved an answer. We ate in silence for a minute while I put my thoughts together. It wasn't really a matter of deciding how things stood, merely a matter of how to explain them.

"The way I see it," I said, "Lissette is the Queen. I'm the King, but I'm trying to give the kingdom to the Queen so I can walk away. The stigma of the Demon King is too much for me to handle; sticking around won't help anyone."

"And this relates... how?"

"Legally, I'm married. I'm also a king, which means—at least, from what I understand of Rethven—that I have other options besides having a wife. Consorts and concubines and so forth. While, legally, I'm married, I'm also allowed, even expected, to, uh, 'have' other women." I sighed. "Patriarchal only starts to cover this culture. Women aren't actually property, but they're right next door to it."

"I've noticed. Nobody gives *me* a hard time, though."

"Nobody? Not even people who don't know who you are?"

"You raise a good point," Mary admitted. "But chauvanists are delicious. They're like bacon with the blood still in it."

"I'm going to ask you not to elaborate," I decided. "Back to my point. As for the royal prerogative of a harem—or unreasonable facsimile—I don't fully agree with the idea, but in the cases of a purely political marriage, I can see how it's workable. The marriage cements an alliance, the children are a generational assurance of continued unity, all that stuff. It's unfair to Lissette, of course; it's a massive double standard. As a king, I can pretty much do who I please and as I please, but she's expected to be the faithful wife so as to assure the political aspects of the relationship stay solid.

"As for you, you're not a political move. While I like Lissette, I'm not in love with her. I respect her, even admire her, but I simply don't know her well enough to say I love her—although, from what little I know of her, I think I could, given time. However, since the Demon King has apparently done some awful things to her, I'm starting to think I'm not going to get a chance to apologize, much less be a model husband and father for the rest of her life."

"So, where does that leave me?"

"Officially?"

"Start there."

"Technically, a 'consort,' as we know it, is the non-royal spouse of a reigning monarch. Around here, it's anyone a member of the nobility chooses to have as an official lover. If Lissette had a lover, he would be—or she would be, I suppose, if Lissette went that way—a consort, as well. It's kind of like having a second spouse, ranking with-but-after the official spouse."

"So, what's a concubine, then?"

"Um. Less dignified. A concubine, at least in Rethven, would be a... hmm. Where a consort has an intimate relationship with the noble person, both physically and emotionally, a concubine is more like a prostitute under exclusive contract. A consort can have a headache, ask for the night off, even tell the noble what to go do with himself and get away with it. They have romantic dinners, go on picnics, read books together by the fireplace in the winter, all that sort of thing. They're friends as well as lovers, at least in theory. A concubine, on the other hand, has a job to do, and that job is to make the noble happy—and if it involves sex, a foot-rub, peeling grapes, or just lounging around in a skimpy outfit as a pretty piece of living art, that's what happens."

"A slave?"

"Not exactly. Maybe someone paid to pretend to be a slave. A concubine can quit. I think. If they couldn't before, they can now—or should. I'll have to ask about how well my anti-slavery policies have been enacted."

"Okay. Now that we have the terms defined, where do I stand?"

"Legally, you qualify as a consort. I know you better than I know Lissette and I like you more. I'm stuck being married to her; she needs the legality to rule Rethven effectively. But I plan to spend my time with you, not her—at least, if you'll let me."

Mary smiled and raised a cup in my direction.

"Hail, Halar, Demon King of Rethven. Long may you reign far away from your wife."

"I admit, I'm relieved to hear you say that."

"Why?"

"Because I was appallingly nervous this was leading up to something I wouldn't like."

Mary put her hand on mine and looked me in the eyes.

"You may be the most interesting man I know," she said, softly. "Ignoring the magical powers, you're brilliant, charming, handsome, and tireless. In some ways, relentless—it goes with being a little OCD, I think. And you're as close to an honorable man as I've ever met, regardless of what you tell your knights to motivate them. It scares them a little to have to try and live up to being better than you—and the ones I've met aren't counting the Demon King thing, just so you know. They're thinking of back when you first showed up in this mountain. And, lastly, if I'm ever in trouble, I know you'll move Heaven and Earth on your way through Hell to save me."

I didn't know what to say. While I could agree with a little of it—I can be a little obsessive, and I would go through fire and water to help her—she was way, way off on the rest. But how could I tell her she was delusional? It didn't seem like a good idea to burst her bubble, so I nodded and went back to eating.

"By the way," she added, "two other things are on my mind."

"That makes it a three-track mind, not two."

"Don't make me stab you with a fork."

"I apologize. What's on your multi-track mind?"

"First, I've been poking around town in various disguises, getting wired in and establishing my connections. Dantos has been really helpful in telling me about the place and who I should get to know or get to know about."

"Good for him. Let me know if you think he needs to be promoted."

"He needs to be promoted," she replied. "He's sharp, respectful, and he can be one smooth operator, let me tell you."

"Like him?"

"A lot. If I can sell it to his wife, can I borrow him some day while you're busy?"

"The Consort's consort? Or just to play with?"

"Jealous?"

"Not yet. But if you can get Laisa to agree, I won't argue. Want me to baby-sit Caris?"

"Maybe. I'll see what Laisa has to say about it."

"Definitely start there, but be prepared to take 'no' for an answer. What else?"

"One of the things I've discovered is the church of shiny stuff has a right bastard for a leader."

"Um. Lotar?"

"That's the local guy, only he's 'Lord Lotar.' He's not going by a religious title unless you're part of his religion—exclusively part of his religion."

"That's unusual," I observed. "Most people venerate one deity over others, but it's a personal choice and usually not exclusive. All the others get some attention based on their areas of control, too."

"It's not a purely religious thing. He has very secular aims. In my digging around, I've discovered something I think is relevant."

"Such as?"

"Did you know the mess of morons on the Kingsway were sent up there by Lotar?"

"The ones who were chanting and waving medallions at me?"

"Yes. Those."

"No, I didn't."

"He hand-picked them from among the clergy. They were the most devout he could find, I think. They were the ones who leaned toward the vows of poverty, humility, good works, and personal sacrifice."

"I did notice a shortage of shoes, now you mention it."

"I think he's using you—or tried to use you—as a way to deal with what he thinks of as an internal problem within his local branch of the Church. The goodie-no-shoes were meant to go up the Kingsway, be cast down and killed, and the holy war could begin without interference from the kinder, gentler elements."

"Huh. That makes entirely too much sense. It makes me wonder if he had anything to do with Brother Perrin falling from the Kingsway. I didn't see it, so I assumed it was an accident…"

"No idea," Mary said. "I wouldn't put it past him, though. Lacking a mass slaughter, he might be framing you for picking off individuals. Not the big splash he wanted, but still useful to him and his cronies. From what I hear, he's working with someone outside the city—he has a surprising amount of correspondence going in and out, usually at least one message a day. I think they're planning either a coup or a revolution. It might have some bearing on the troop movements in Rethven."

"How did you find this out?"

"During the day, I can fraternize with anyone," she replied, smiling prettily. "At night, I can't actually enter the building he's using as a temple—regardless of the shape, it's apparently holy ground of some sort—but I can listen from outside. I even got a megaphone and used it like an ear trumpet to help localize what I was hearing. It was surprisingly helpful."

"I imagine it would be. It would cut down on the extraneous sounds from other directions, making it easier to focus on what you aimed at."

"Yep. Try it sometime."

"I might."

"Second thing. There's an elf who wants to talk to you. Some eye candy named Salishar. She says she's an emissary from the Duke of Vathula. We didn't include her in the council meeting because nobody trusts her and she's only the messenger. She's been waiting here for you for about a week, so no rush."

"I'll see her after I have lunch with Corrin."

"I'll let her know."

"Thanks."

"Oh, and one more thing. I think Lissette has a concubine or consort or sideboy. I'm not sure."

"Oh?" I felt my eyebrows rise. "That's interesting."

"I bring it up because I don't *know*, I just suspect. I heard rumors about her and the Demon King. You might not be the father of all Lissette's children. Seeing as they're potential heirs, I suppose you might want to look into it."

"Thanks for the heads-up. It's probably Thomen, but I'll keep my ear to the wall."

"Isn't that supposed to be 'ear to the ground'?"

"We're inside a mountain. The wall *is* the ground."

"Fair point," she agreed. "I'll do my best to help. Anything you want me to find out?"

"I don't know. I'm still trying to take in the big picture and digest the details. A lot happened while I was having my autopsy and I'm not feeling completely myself, yet."

"That's hardly polite table talk."

"True. Blame it on my post-traumatic stress disorder."

"You joke about it, but maybe you're whistling past the graveyard. You have plenty of cause for PTSD."

"I know. And I'm also aware I'm not quite myself. That's why I want more time to think about things and settle down. I'm trying to take extra time and make extra-rational decisions because I know I could do terrible things if I don't stay tightly focused and controlled."

We were silent for a few minutes, getting a lot of food off the tray.

"Vlad—I mean, Halar," Mary asked, "do we know why Lissette is throwing troops this way? I mean, it's not because I was disrespectful, was it?"

"No, I'm sure that's not it. Oh, it may have been a precipitating factor or a good excuse or a last straw, but the last straw can't be blamed for the breaking of the camel's back. I'll give good odds I can talk her into calling it off."

"Really? How?"

"By giving her anything she wants. That's basically my plan."

"Oh." Mary was silent for a moment while I put plates back on the tray. "Isn't that a bit one-sided?"

"Ah, but I want her to be Queen, along with all it entails. People need to know she's in charge, ruling and reigning, and toe the line for her as they apparently did for the Demon King."

"Hmm. Okay. If you say so."

"Problem?"

"I'm not sure about it. We'll give it a good try and see if it takes."

"Fair enough. And for the meeting with the elf... I'm not in a great mood, but I think I can manage to keep my temper with Salishar. Go ahead and send her in, please. I'll handle her first, *then* have lunch with Corran. Warn her His Majesty is not in the best of tempers, would you?"

"I'll take the tray, too, Your Majesty," she said, adding a mocking lilt to her voice. I approved; I don't take my title seriously, either. I only make use of it.

Mary took the dishes away. A few minutes later, the door pivoted open again and Torvil escorted Salishar into the room. She entered with the usual uncanny, slightly-unnerving grace characteristic of elves. Waves roll up a beach in a stumbling, clumsy fashion by comparison. Wind staggers drunkenly through the autumn treetops. Comets lumber heavily through the sky, waving crazy tails at the stars. Clouds collide and grind together like children driving bumper cars. I'm either jealous or envious; I keep confusing the two. But when you add in some inhuman elven beauty I'm definitely disgusted.

Salishar drew back her hood and knelt as soon as she came through the doorway, crossing her hands before her face, palms out. I looked her over, trying to spot a weapon. Her outfit was a mix of silk and leather, all in shades of grey, with her silver hair matching the silvery trim on her garments. I didn't see anything, not even a hairpin, but the bracers on her forearms and the greaves on her shins could conceal a variety of smaller nasties. Unless they strip-searched her—which I doubted they did—they wouldn't find everything. Maybe not even then.

I decided not to dismiss Torvil. Instead, I caught his eye and nodded at the seat at the far end of the table. He escorted her there and stood behind her, sword drawn. Given the table was a slab of stone supported by two smaller slabs of stone, there was no way to throw something under the table at me. With her seat pushed hard forward, she wasn't getting up quickly unless Torvil let her.

She made no objection to any of this. She kept her hands in plain sight on top of the table. She moved slowly, even meekly. I didn't buy it. I'm a nightlord and I terrify elves because they remember the old days, when nightlords were the dark demigods of the world. But elves are unpredictable and treacherous. At least, everyone I've ever eaten seemed to think so. I haven't really seen it, myself, but maybe they're being extra cautious around the ancient evil demigod.

On the other hand, maybe I was feeling extra paranoid for some reason. Can't imagine what it would be, though.

"Welcome to Karvalen," I offered.

"It is my honor and pleasure to greet you once again, *Na'irethed zarad'na.*"

"Indeed, it is," I agreed, putting on my Egotistical Tyrant hat. "You have something to tell me?"

"I was sent to report, *Na'irethed zarad'na.*" She glanced to the side, as though to look behind her without turning her head. "Shall I do so now?" she asked, with a faint emphasis on "now."

Report. On what? By whom? Why? I wanted to ask, but it would show how much I didn't know. Was the Duke of Vathula actively serving the Demon King? Or was he aware of the deception by my darker half and simply played along? If the latter, he might be trying to find out if I was myself again. If the former, he might be disturbed to know I was myself again. Who was providing information to whom in this meeting?

Speaking of information, what could she report on? Whatever it was, she didn't think I wanted her to talk about it in front of Torvil, which told me it was unpleasant to a degree my personal guards might find objectionable. If I insisted on a report in Torvil's presence, it would tell her something—what, I'm not sure, but something.

Never give anything away to an elf.

"Torvil, would you be so good as to send for something? Wine, Salishar?"

"Yes, *Na'irethed zarad'na.*"

Torvil nodded and left the room, swinging the door closed behind him.

"Now that we're alone, stop calling me that. Address me as 'Dread Lord.' Calling me 'Master of the Lords of Shadow' is too much of a mouthful and I don't want to keep hearing it."

"Yes, Dread Lord."

"Better. Now, report," I snapped. Her hands tensed, as though trying to grip the glossy stone of the tabletop.

"Dread Lord, with your disappearance, the Duke of Vathula set into motion the contingencies you decreed. They progress."

"I see." I didn't. "Details."

"The magician T'yl has been taken and has been destroyed. His ashes have been scattered. Several agents have been dispatched to deal with the children; the process of extermination is ongoing. However, recently there have been others who interfere with the work by doing it first. In a single night, Carrillon has lost almost a hundred of those children to some agency we have not yet identified."

I am surrounded by child-murdering fiends in flesh. Is it something the Demon King arranged deliberately, or is it merely a side effect of employing bastards?

I took a minute to tell myself some things.

It's the Demon King, not Salishar, who is responsible. You can't do anything about the dead ones, but you can save the rest. Yes, you make a great guardian demon, but anyone you kill in revenge right now is only a messenger, not the one truly responsible—and the one truly responsible is in the hands of Johann. Or has Johann. Something like that.

Calm down.

I noticed Salishar wasn't speaking. She was waiting, silently, for me to say something. Her breathing was fast and shallow and I could see the rapid-fire thump of her pulse in her throat.

Goodness. I think she was frightened. I wondered if my shadow was doing something weird even though it was daytime. I chose not to look.

"Go on," I instructed, quietly.

"May I ask if it was something you performed personally, Dread Lord?"

"The murder of the children?" I asked. It was difficult to keep a straight face. She was asking the Demon King, or thought she was. Not me. I resisted the impulse to kick the slab of the tabletop through her chest.

"It was not," I told her.

"Shall we attempt to discover the party or parties responsible? Or is it of concern to you who does it so long as your command is carried out?"

I thought furiously for several seconds while trying to maintain a façade of cool deliberation. It wasn't easy. I needed the time to suppress my instant desire to leap the length of the table and put my fist through her face. I wasn't exactly at my most calm and controlled, especially after the children's bloodbath.

"What I wanted," I said, lying as well as I knew how, "was the personal satisfaction involved in being the force of life and death. This has been corrupted by someone. The entirety of the thing, the artistic merit of it, is ruined. Recall the agents; there is no point in continuing." I leaned forward and lowered my voice.

"Find out who was responsible for the incident in Carrillon. I want to know." That, at least, wasn't a lie. She seemed to grasp I was especially serious about that part; she momentarily raised her hands in the face-hiding gesture, as though saluting.

"I will see to it, Dread Lord."

"Good," I said, leaning back. "Have you more to report?"

"Yes, Dread Lord. We have attempted to locate and destroy the magician Tort in the same fashion as the magician T'yl. We have been unsuccessful. Agents did locate a body, but have since located two more. We believe them all to be decoys, not the real Tort. With this revelation, we are now concerned about the measures the magician T'yl may have taken. It is possible only decoys have been destroyed, not the magician himself."

"Obviously, this is more challenging than expected," I said, trying to sound as though I were merely musing. This was like a list of buttons marked *Do Not Push* for me. Was this deliberate on the part of the Demon King? Did he consider a time when his reign would end and prepare for it—that is, prepare contingencies to hurt and enrage me? It certainly felt like it. And, given the later manipulations by the Evil Orb, it seemed more than a possibility, maybe more than a probability.

I realized I was distracted from the conversation and returned my wandering attention to Salishar.

"Very well, continue to search. However, upon locating T'yl or Tort, take no action other than to notify me. I'll handle them personally."

"As you command, Dread Lord."

"What else?"

"His Grace the Duke of Vathula requests three more human women be impregnated. He wishes to know if you desire the women sent here for your use, or to Carrillon."

"Three more?" I repeated. "What happened to the previous ones?"

"Alas, Dread Lord, the process of changing an unborn human into an elf is arduous and long. Few survive the process. Even the early stages may prove fatal."

I knew that. Something I'd discussed with Bob a long time ago. Elves—at least, the elves of this flat world—don't reproduce. They weren't designed to be self-replicating. Apparently, their creator intended them to last forever and occasionally manufactured a few more to make up any losses. When their creator-thing went away or faded out or did whatever mythological origin creatures do, they were stuck with trying to manufacture more elves. So, they figured out a way, using unborn human babies, transforming them into elves in the womb.

It failed nine times out of ten, or some such awful statistic. But so what? They didn't care. You spend seven years working on it and it dies. Oops. Start over. Elves are immortal and they were *made* that way from the beginning. It's simply how they think—infinitely long-term.

I could stand to have a dose of that sort of patience. Maybe I need more elves in my diet.

So, now, if I could assume awful things of Bob and Salishar and the Demon King—safe bet—Bob was sending human women to the Demon King for him to impregnate. The Demon King sent them back for Bob to use in manufacturing more elves.

While I'm not a fan of genocide—elves need a way to reproduce, too, I suppose—I'm not sure what other options the elves have in avoiding extinction. Their method is, to say the least, objectionable, and I'm four-square against being involved in it. At least, I object to the idea of sending pregnant women off to die in the transformation pits, or whatever it is they do.

The implications of this never really occurred to me. It was an abstract method until I realized it's not something they might do sometime in the future. It's ongoing, persistent—they're doing it *all the time*. Which means, if I do nothing, they'll keep kidnapping pregnant women and killing them. But can I order them to stop? Will such an order stick? Or will some of them keep right on doing as they please?

Not all the elves serve me, I'm sure. They have some sort of reverence for nightlords, although I'm not sure why, exactly. I doubt it extends to racial suicide. Bob might obey the order; he has a very persuasive handprint on his chest. All the others would simply hide their activites more thoroughly.

They need a better way to reproduce. Since they're superficially similar to humans, maybe they have vestigial reproductive systems. I haven't actually dissected an elf to find out. Maybe I should. Or maybe I should just look closely without developing my vivisection skills.

Ever since the invasion of Karvalen, I've been somewhat less fond of elves.

"Tell Bob I may have a better idea," I decided.

"Dread Lord?"

"I've been thinking about a way to make this process quicker, easier, and more reliable. Put the women on hold; he won't be needing them."

"As you command, Dread Lord."

"Good. Also convey this message to... the Duke of Vathula," I said, making it clear from my tone I found the title amusing. She smiled slightly. "I require a crown of the finest workmanship, fit for a queen. Deliver it *here*, however, as I have enchantments to place upon it before it ever touches her brow." Salishar smiled, obviously thinking of the possible enchantments. I doubted we were thinking of the same ones. I once had an idea for a crown and a quantum computer core, but that would have to change, now... Where are those computer-core gems, anyway? I should find them.

"It shall be done, Dread Lord."

"You may go." I did not add, *Get out of my sight before I drink your blood and find out if I can eat the flesh of my victims.* It was daytime, but I had an urge to, quite literally, bite chunks out of her and eat them. I have the teeth for it, and she was a brutal, nasty, evil bitch who could safely be said to deserve it. If I'd had my way, she would still be embedded in a wall. Instead, she was loose and trying to find my Tort for me.

The thought saved her life. I want my Tort, and the more people looking for her for me, the better.

I've had a bad week. Did I say "bad"? How about awful? Atrocious? Appalling? I need a better word for it. And now I've got a duchy of nasty creatures run by an evil elf who is sending out death squads and assassins at the order of the Demon King. He's also capturing women for my amusement, it seems. What *else* is he doing? What else did the Demon King order? Or, rather, arrange to happen after his demise, deposition, or departure?

I really need to work on my self-control and rational behavior. Keep a grip on my already-frayed temper.

Salishar pushed back from the table and rose. She stepped out from behind the table, knelt, did her crossed-hands-in-front-of-face-thing again, and departed.

With both pivot doors closed between me and the corridor, I finally let go a piece of my frustration and rage.

Torvil came in, pushing the massive door open with one hand, the other hand carrying a tray with a bottle and two glasses. He paused for a moment and took in the situation. I ignored him in favor of working on a healing spell for my hands and feet. They were still throbbing painfully and my hands were bleeding from the abrasions, but none of my bones were broken. Maybe I'm tougher than I know.

He righted a chair and set the tray on the seat.

"Sire?"

"Present," I admitted.

"I apologize for taking so long."

"Think nothing of it. The meeting simply didn't go as long as I thought it would."

Torvil eyed the pieces of the table. It was mostly in large chunks.

"Don't worry," I told him. "It's stone. The mountain will absorb it and make a new table. A couple of days, tops."

"As you say, Sire." He picked up a piece of one of the vertical supports, about the size of a small headstone, and fitted it in place. The mountain was paying attention; the pieces joined together. He played with the jigsaw puzzle of the shattered table for a bit, deliberately not pressing me on the matter. He seemed to take the destruction in stride. I wondered how often he witnessed the aftermath of the Demon King's tantrums. The Demon King would have a much shorter temper, of course.

"Several times," he replied, when I asked about it. "They never involved his own blood, though."

"Yeah, I can imagine."

"I don't have to, Sire, and I wish I did."

"I'm sorry about that."

"So am I. But this is nothing. It's only stone. And not even wasted stone, as I can see from the way it's sticking together. Hardly worth mentioning. And I won't."

"I know, and I thank you for it. You've always been someone I could count on, Torvil. All three of you guys."

"You've been sorely missed, Sire, even though we saw you every day." He sat on another of the surviving chairs and poured wine. "Drink?"

"Normally, I do not drink… wine," I misquoted, "but today it sounds like a great idea." I took the cup and slugged it down. It was as awful as I expected, so I tried one of my new sensory-diminishing spells. The wine still tasted awful, but at least it was a diluted awful instead of concentrated.

"How else may I be of service, Sire?"

"I need to talk to Lissette."

"I'll have someone put it in motion."

"Good. And have someone come get me when it's time to have… Corrin? The wizard."

"Corran."

"Right. I'm going to have lunch with him. Set it up and send someone to get me when it's time."

"Where will you be, Sire?"

"Right here," I said, and poured another glass of that awful stuff.

"As you wish, Sire." He bowed and backed out.

I practiced brooding. It's a requirement for immortal bloodsuckers, I'm told. It's in all the brochures.

Am I a dark and tragic figure? Or am I merely some pathetic fool? Do I have to be strong enough to endure days of torture and helplessness and simply shake it off? My body can do it, sure. What about the rest of me?

A bottle of wine, a dark room, and some time alone with my thoughts seemed reasonable.

"Sire?" Torvil asked.

"I heard you coming. It's these doors. They really do make a nasty grinding sound, don't they?"

"I suppose so, Sire. They do not seem overloud to me. May I ask why it is dark?"

"I didn't feel like light, so I turned off the lighting spell."

"Of course, Sire. Are you sober enough for lunch?"

"Make a note, Torvil." I snapped my fingers and the ceiling lit up again. "I can drink a whole bottle of wine and barely feel it. Either my liver is much stronger than I thought or some other metabolic change is involved."

"Duly noted, Sire, if not understood. I'll have someone come in for the shards of the bottle."

"The mountain is already eating them. What's for lunch?"

"*Dazhu,* venison, baked *chan* fish, and a variety of things I don't pay attention to. Plants. Rinella has prepared several different dishes. Laisa and Seldar both advised her regarding the appetites involved."

"Smart lady, whoever she is. Is she in charge of the kitchens?"

"That's debatable," Torvil admitted. "Laisa seems to have prior claim, but Rinella is the better cook. They seem to have some personal arrangement, but I'm not paid enough to take sides in that war."

"Probably safest. Show me to wherever I'm supposed to be."

We walked together. People stepped aside as we approached, bowing heads until we passed. It reminded me of something in Egypt, with the pharaohs... something about the Pharaoh being a descendant of the sun-god, I think, and how normal people weren't supposed to look at him. I'm not sure how it applied here, exactly. Maybe people don't look into the darkness lest it look back? Nietzsche, anyone?

Torvil showed me to a dining room. Similar table design, but smaller, more intimate—about the size of a small dining room table instead of a conference table. Two servers were already there, waiting to pour wine, bring dishes, or remove plates. Corran rose as I came in, levering himself up from his chair with his staff.

"Your Majesty," he said, bowing, still leaning on his staff.

"Corran. Please, be seated." I took my seat as he did. Torvil took up station behind Corran, a fact which did not escape his notice. He bit his lips rather than say anything.

Lunch was served. A dozen different things hit the table within a minute, all of them steaming. No doubt they were delicious. I dialed down my sense of smell and taste and started in. Corran followed suit. I figured to get through a couple of servings before talking. He struck me as the sort who would like to eat before getting down to serious discussion.

Once we had appetizers down and entrées in front of us, I started.

"I understand you are the head of the Wizards' Guild in Karvalen."

"Yes, I am," he replied. Torvil grunted from behind him. Corran hastily added, "Your Majesty."

"How does it relate to the Wizards' Guild in Rethven?"

"Majesty?"

"Do you answer to Thomen? Or is there a guild council of all the masters of the guild? Or is there a chief wizard in each city's guildhall? How does it work?"

"With respect, Your Majesty, you are not a member of our guild."

I made no immediate reply. Instead, I thought and ate. Corran returned to his food, but seemed more conscious of my presence. Kind of like poking the sleeping bear; if you do it, you want to know if you woke it.

It wasn't good for him that I was already in a bad mood, possibly even in a fragile state of mind. It increased the risk of a sudden removal of vital organs.

I caught myself wondering if I could reach up under the ribcage and get a better angle on removing the heart. Down the throat, while visually impressive, is awkward. Under the ribs, though, might be quicker and more efficient. It's certainly quick for the victim; blood loss on that scale is measured in seconds. On the other hand, the liver is much less well-protected. It's larger, though, so it takes multiple handfuls...

"Corran," I said, "I think we need to establish something."

"Your Majesty?"

"I'm the King."

"Of this I am aware, Your Majesty."

"Moreover, I know Thomen is having an affair with the Queen."

Corran didn't react, other than to shift his expression into neutral. He also stopped eating. His eyes searched my face as I paused.

"I don't care," I went on. "Whatever Lissette wants to do, she can. She's the Queen. It's her job to rule in a just and wise manner. My job is to smite for the good of the realm whatever she deems needful of smiting. Are we clear so far?"

"I... yes, I believe so, Your Majesty."

"Good, good, good. Now, on a personal level, I'm also a dark and terrible thing that will bite your eyes out and burn you slowly to death if you fail to serve my interests." I finished by extending around fourteen inches of tongue, wrapping it about the food on the end of my fork, and drawing the bite back into my mouth. Nothing says "dark and terrible thing" like a tentacle-tongue. My teeth, aside from the fangs, are somewhat subtle.

I returned my attention to my plate, cutting small bites and chewing carefully. He didn't resume his dinner. Maybe I put him off his appetite. I let him think for a few minutes before resuming.

"Now, Corran, another question or two. Who established a formal Guild of Wizards in this kingdom?"

"You did, or so I am told."

"I did. I was there. I remember it. So, who does the Guild owe its existence to? And who does Thomen work for? To whom does he owe his allegiance?"

"The... the King and Queen."

"Right. And, like a noble in our service, those under him also owe their allegiance to the King and Queen, yes?"

"Yes," he admitted, reluctantly. Torvil shifted a bit, making some noise with his sword and belts. Corran added, "Your Majesty," in a hurry.

"So, when I ask you a question—about the structure of the Wizards' Guild, for instance—if you fail to answer it, or try to lie, or even attempt to mislead me, that's treason, isn't it?"

Corran did not reply. I didn't press him on it.

"Torvil? What's the penalty for treason?"

"To be bound in chains in a cauldron of oil, slowly brought to a boil, Sire. However, under the law, any crime punishable by death may be commutated to serving the King as dinner, at your discretion."

"Good to know. Now, Corran, one last question before we resume our conversation. Who frightens you more? Thomen? Or me?"

Corran leaned back in his chair and steepled his fingers. As he rubbed the fingertips together in small circles, I saw small discs of power forming between them.

"Don't do it," I advised. He stopped.

"Do what, Your Majesty?" he asked, innocently. Torvil drew his sword, silently. Corran didn't notice.

"You say I'm not a member of the Guild. You may be under the impression I'm not a wizard. If that's the case, you haven't paid attention to history and legend the way you should." I flicked a finger at the small discs of magical force, shattering the beginning spells.

"I see," he said. "Yes, I suppose I did not believe the legends. You've demonstrated no magical talents, only powers—like a sorcerer."

Torvil growled behind him and laid the flat of the blade on Corran's shoulder. Corran's eyes opened like terrified sphincters.

"Obviously, any being with innate abilities can be compared to a sorcerer," he added, hastily. "I apologize if the comparison is unflattering."

I picked up my eating knife and snapped it in two. Corran stared at the broken metal. It wasn't a piddly little thing like civilized diners use, but a real, solid knife. I snapped it easily, like breaking a pencil. Not our best steel, obviously. Too brittle.

"Now listen to me," I hissed, leaning forward, glaring across the table. "If I were still the Demon King people accuse me of being, you would already be dead and your soul screaming in agony for my amusement. Those were sharp little things you were conjuring; I could easily take your gesture as the beginnings of an attempt on my life—treason. You've tried to evade my questions about Thomen and the Guild—also, potentially, treasonous. I suspect you of trying to hide your knowledge of Thomen's involvement with the Queen—an attempt to deceive the King. Do I need to state the obvious?"

As I spoke, Torvil gestured sharply, a disruption spell that caused various magical functions on Corran to either pause or simply break. He then snatched Corran's staff away and made a warding gesture to keep him from connecting with it magically.

I keep forgetting the Big Three are combat wizards as well as masters of physical mayhem.

"I've had a very bad week," I went on, "so my temper and patience are both short. I gave Thomen official standing. I made him head of the Wizards' Guild. I made him Court Wizard. I can turn him into ground pork and feed him to the stray dogs in the street if it suits me—and you with him, if you keep jerking me around. Do you understand me?"

"Yes, Your Majesty," he replied, white-faced.

"Here is what you are going to do. You are going to Carrillon as a messenger, sent by the King. You are explaining, in person, to Thomen. He'll talk to me via mirror and we'll compare what you tell him to what I tell you. If I find you've lied to him about any aspect of our conversation, I'll fry your liver and *then* tear it out of you. *Do you understand me?*"

"Yes, Your Majesty!" he answered, trembling.

"I'll be calling Thomen in the morning." I snatched his eating-knife out of his hand with a gesture, then turned my attention to my food.

"Your Majesty... how will I get to Carrillon before morning?"

"Wizards are supposed to be *clever*," I countered, not looking up. "Get out of my mountain. Now!"

Torvil pulled the chair back with a sharp jerk—Corran included. Corran reached for his staff and Torvil held it away from him. Corran hesitated, as though he considered arguing, but obviously realized how much good it would do to argue with a faceless pile of armor. He left in a hurry.

I sat back in my chair, suddenly very tired. My hands were shaking. That was brutal, unpleasant, and emotional. Maybe I'm brutal, unpleasant, and emotional even when I'm consciously trying to be calm and rational.

Yeah, it's been a very bad week.

Torvil nodded at the ladies standing by to serve. They took away used dishes and replaced them with new courses. They moved very carefully, as though putting food bowls down while the tiger was busy ripping flesh off something else. One of them removed the snapped knife. Torvil put the staff in a corner and reinforced his blocking spell before speaking.

"What do you want done with this, Sire?"

"I have no idea."

"I'll deal with it, then."

"I'm sorry," I said. "I didn't mean to be so... I don't know what's gotten into me."

"On the contrary, Sire. Something has obviously gotten out of you. He's not screaming in agony while you chuckle and bite pieces off."

"Fair point. It's still not how I wanted this to go."

"You mentioned you were tortured."

"Yes."

"It can make a man short-tempered, Sire."

"You don't sound as judgmental as I expect."

"I've seen far worse things done by your hand."

"So have I," I whispered. "So have I."

Talking to people obviously wasn't a good idea. Torvil followed me around in silence. Let the kingdom fall; let the world end. I was in no shape to make good decisions.

Instead, I went to my sand table's display of the spy-satellite-spell results and looked it over. It wouldn't find Tort for me, but it would give me places to look, which I call progress. Right then, I'd take any sort of progress on anything. I needed something to go right for me.

No... I take that back. A lot of things have gone right for me. I'm incredibly lucky, both good and bad. Objectively speaking, a lot of things have worked out in my favor. At the moment, though, I wasn't feeling objective, and I needed to *feel* as though something was going right.

As with so very much in my life, the sand table was the very picture of ambivalence.

The world was laid out for me. Mountains across the width of the world formed the southern boundary. The edges of the world ran north from there, eventually curving inward like a square with two corners hammered off. Ice fields and snow occupied the northern half, farther from the path of the sun. A band of land, all around the edge, restrained the great ocean. In the west, it was the Western Sea, but it curved as it went south, becoming the Southern Sea. Hundred, possibly thousands of islands dotted it in a long, wide footprint leading to a narrower place, near the middle of the world. The waters widened again to the east for thousands of miles before the ocean veered northward again, heading into the ice—presumably the Eastern Sea. All of it the Circle Sea, or the World Ocean, surrounding the continent of which Rethven is but a tiny part.

Does the ocean run under the ice, I wonder? Or is it frozen as solid in the depths as it is over the top?

The black dots and domes of shielding spells were heavily clustered. Naturally, there would be more of them in cities, fewer of them as the population density decreased. Many of the clusters were hazy, indistinct; they had too few scan pulses go through the area from too few directions. One thing for certain, the hazy areas were blocked by long-term scrying shields. Once a scan pulse went through an area without being blocked, the temporary thing came off the map and the actual geography posted to the display.

Lesser mountains, lakes and rivers, great plains, rolling hills, all the geography of a world stood before me, scanned and mapped and laid out over half the table.

The Mountains of the Sun, the southern range, cut the table's display in half. They were a trifle fuzzy at their northern edge, where the Shining Desert met their feet, and the image resolution worsened rapidly at the edge of the range. It degraded badly enough and quickly enough so I couldn't even find the Spire of the Sun. All the other geography, including the lesser mountain ranges, were clear and sharp within the limits of the medium—that is, somewhat grainy.

Which still left half the table blank and featureless.

If the Mountains of the Sun fuzzed out scanning for some reason—magical ore? Naturally-occurring orichalcum? Singularity-powered Romulan spiders weaving anti-scanning webs? —the table would expand the apparent scale to best fit the tabletop. This seemed to indicate the orbiting scan-spells couldn't send back data pulses, but the permanent linkage between them and the mountain's triangulation points was able to keep track of them. Kind of like being able to track a satellite beacon even after losing the spy camera signal.

Which implied the world was even bigger than I thought. About twice as big, in fact. There might be a whole other half of the world beyond the Mountains of the Sun. The mountain range might not be the southern edge of the world, just the fence between two halves of it!

Would people on that side think of the Mountains of the Sun as "south"? If you go far enough away from the Mountains, far from the path of the sun, where it gets cold and icy, would they think of that as the "north"?

I worked with the sand table for a bit, trying to examine the Mountains more closely. There was definitely something wrong, there. It didn't resist my attempts to look into them, not in any way I understood. It seemed more like shining a light into a fog, or trying to tune in a radio station through intense static. Which, come to think of it, would help explain why everyone believed them to be the southern edge of the world. You can't look past the edge of the world. There's nothing there to see!

I let the sand table go back to mapping and regarded it thoughtfully. All the little dots of scrying shields—some of them large in a human scale, but still tiny on a map of the world—made me think of the power-centers in another world. They didn't have the distribution, of course, but Mary's world has been on my mind. I started visualizing lines of power between them, looking for patterns. I didn't see any, but you never know.

Does this world have ley lines? Are there power centers I could tap *here*? Or are they only on spherical worlds? Or in universes with particular magical laws?

I felt a sudden temptation to tell everyone to go to hell while I walked away, off to explore different worlds. Maybe I will. Not today.

I returned to the magic mirror. I knew about how high I could go, so I set the view for something like maximum height and looked down. A little spell-work and some panning back and forth revealed nothing. No ley lines, no lines of power, just a regular, generic magical field. Not a webwork of hidden forces, but a field, like a magnet, accessible everywhere.

But if it's like a magnet, I reasoned, *where are the magical analogues of the magnetic poles?*

This world doesn't have a magnetic field, so the people on it couldn't use it as a metaphor, a frame of reference. Has anyone ever looked at the magical field itself, before? Has anyone ever known what to look *for*? Surely, someone has wondered about the source of magic?

I didn't recall anything from my digested memories. Maybe nobody cared, as long as magic worked. Or, perhaps it was esoteric knowledge, known only by a few people who had a burning interest, or… or no one who ever tried to find out ever reported their findings.

I can think of a couple of reasons for that last one.

Still, I might need to know. There are godlike magi to deal with and maybe a hostile guild of wizards.

I stepped up the gain on my magical detection spell. I've been meaning to develop a measuring system, but I don't know how to set up a standard unit of magic. On the other hand, all I wanted at the moment was the ability to tell whether the local magical field was stronger or weaker in two areas, not get a precise measurement.

With some good cheer, I set about scrying a few dozen random spots. This gave me a rudimentary chart of variations in the field intensity. As a rule—barring some weird spots—magic gets weaker toward the north, stronger toward the south. The highest intensity is in the Shining Desert, near the middle of the Mountains of the Sun. It falls off a little to the east and west, along the range, but it falls off much more rapidly with distance northward and levels out quickly. The difference is small, not even enough to concern most spellcasters, but it's detectable, and that's good enough for me.

I didn't get to make an equation for it, but it reminded me of part of a high-intensity black-body radiation curve. The field strength increased gradually along the line from north to south—it was a barely detectable slope—and increased markedly in the Shining Desert. It skyrocketed just inside the Mountains of the Sun, where the field grew too intense to examine.

So, the Mountains of the Sun contained a huge amount of magical energy. From long exposure to sunlight, perhaps? Power radiated from the sun—and the moon, for all I know—for thousands upon thousands of years, diffusing outward through the world. Every day, it refreshed the system with a new wave of energy, "heating" the mountains up again to radiate magical force.

It's one hypothesis. I don't see a way to test it from here, though. I can't exactly pack up and head south to look, either.

Still, I wonder why one world would have ley lines and another would have a completely different energy distribution system. Difference in sources? Difference in magical laws? Difference in other laws, other physical constants, in the universe as a whole? Since there are different universes, apparently with different physical laws, how do they all relate? Admittedly, the ones I've visited are universes which permit life to exist—usually in a manner I can comprehend—but what combinations of those physical constants permit it? How do they interact with each other? Some of them are obvious, but I suspect I'm not qualified even to speculate by a dozen or thirty Ph.D.'s.

I went back to studying the shielded areas. I might not find Tort today, but I could at least start eliminating places. Knocking down a scryshield is possible, but generally regarded as rude. It's on par with bashing through a privacy fence. It takes work and it usually gets you noticed. That's why the palace scryshields don't block a scrying spell, just divert it into a complex illusion. If you don't know you've failed to look through a scryshield, you can't work on knocking it down.

On the other hand, scrying shields only work against spells projecting a sensor through them. You can look around inside the shield if you're already inside, of course. Or, if outside, you can park a scrying sensor *near* a shielded area, then treat it as though you're standing outside, looking in. To go with the fence metaphor, I can stand on a ladder and look over the fence, no problem. I just need a telescope. I still can't float my magical camera view around inside the house, but I can look in the windows, at least. It might be cheating, but I'm okay with that. I started with the isolated ones, for practice. The clusters in population centers were going to be trickier.

During the next hour, I found a number of isolated towers, ruined fortresses, mountain hideaways, and forest huts. While I couldn't put a sensor inside the shields and look around, I could passively scan for other radiations emitted. Using a spectrum shifter to scan them in infrared and other non-visible ranges allowed me to mark all of them off my list. These people and places were minding their own business—or, at least, staying out of mine—so I returned the favor once I determined Tort was not present.

A feeling of deep unease interrupted my work of Tort-finding. Something was wrong. Nothing seemed out of the ordinary in the laboratory, but the feeling persisted. It took only a moment to realize Bronze was annoyed.

Huh. Well, that's unusual, thought I.

I tried to reach out to her, to see what she saw, but our connection isn't like that, it seems. I can't use a location spell; she's better protected against that sort of thing than *I* am. Maybe with a magic mirror… no, no help from that without some idea where she was. All I could tell was Bronze was somewhere to the west. Hardly a precise measurement.

I started crafting a message spell to target Bronze. With a function to allow her to plant an impression of her location, it would then come back to me and I could magic mirror my way to her.

And I almost screamed in frustration at myself. The hammerblow of enlightenment landed squarely on my metaphorical third eye and cracked my shell of preconceptions.

Hmm. I should look into the idea of a mystical "third eye." It would explain a lot about how wizards see magic, as well as how vampires see life energy. Or would that require four eyes? I recall something about the idea of a mystical eye, or an inner eye, or whatever from my digested memories, but there are so many different magical traditions, schools of thought, methods and systems…

Back to my point. Message spells. Identifying spells. Alarm spells. All these and variations thereof require the spell to recognize certain qualities in a subject before performing an action. These don't act like radar. They're *passive* detection. They're like ears or eyeballs. They're like old-fashioned transistor radios. They don't send out a pulse to ask for identification; they only receive whatever signals are broadcast. Tune them to a specific set of signals and you get music. The radio doesn't actually go out and get it; it just tells you what it hears.

The compass-box! The magic-detecting compass-box I… borrowed… from the Etiennes. It did much the same thing. Admittedly, it was looking for power sources—much "louder" than anything else—but the principle was the same. The throne in Zirafel… even the stick I made for Tyma… Good lord, how many other examples have been staring me in the face, sticking out their tongues, mocking me all this time?

When I send a message spell to look for someone, I imprint on it a sort of psychic signature and send it to where I think the person is. It circles around, listening for the psychic radiations matching the signature. The range isn't great; it's not very sophisticated. It's like a person, wandering around, listening for someone's voice so it can deliver a letter.

Why not scale them up? Why not build a… a giant spell-dish and listen for Tort? I could build three—one on the mountain, two in the Eastrange to form an equilateral triangle, and pick up signals from anywhere in the world! Then it's just a matter of triangulation, and I've already got the best map of the world ever made!

I'm a genius. A slow genius, but I get there.

Okay. Okay. First things first. Bronze.

I put together my psychic listening device. In principle, it's easy. Think of it as a parabolic reflector to focus the emanations, much like a satellite dish, or one of those bowl-shaped solar ovens. Once I had the idea, it wasn't overwhelmingly difficult. I even had other spells that incorporated something like it in the design. It was only a matter of drastically increasing the sensitivity. Doing so took me half an hour, mostly to work out the basic structure of the prototype. It wasn't what I'd call pretty, but some cardboard and tinfoil can concentrate enough sunlight to start fires. I can develop an industrial-scale version later.

It had some bugs. I ignored the psychic screeching—static? —and got a bearing on Bronze. Of course, by then, she wasn't annoyed anymore. I still wanted to see if this would work.

Since I couldn't triangulate—all I had was a bearing—I cranked up the magic mirror, set the altitude at a couple hundred yards above ground, and scrolled the world by. It was like having a souped-up version of a drone camera. My viewpoint shot westward along the line, jiggling up and down as it went over the Eastrange, and rising slightly with distance to widen my view and allow for errors in alignment. Once on the far side of the mountains, it settled down. I noticed it was bearing slightly to my left, or south.

If Bronze was out on the coastal Kingsroad, where my bearing line crossed it would be a good place to look. I shifted my scrying sensor there and started looking along the road.

I zoomed in on a pulsing flare of fire. It didn't stand out, really, not in the daytime, but the trail of smoke was like a broad arrowhead pointing straight to it. Bronze was headed east at a moderate pace—sixty miles an hour? Moderate for Bronze, anyway. She was well outside Carrillon on the road to Tolcaren. I panned and scanned; there was nobody chasing her. When I zoomed in from altitude, I saw Tianna was aboard and had Firebrand hanging on Bronze's saddlehorn.

Well, that would simplify things. With a mirror image for targeting and a communication spell to enhance a psychic link…

Firebrand?

Boss! Where are you?

Karvalen.

And I can hear you from there? I'm impressed. Got yourself a big brain, Boss.

When it works, I countered. *I felt Bronze's annoyance. What's going on?*

Oh, Tianna's been talking with the Queen and everybody else. Your granddaughter likes you, Boss. She's been trying to explain what happened to you and what you want, at least as far as we understand it. There's been some religious stuff, too, but mostly she's been trying to break your image as a monster, blaming it all on the Demon King.

Any luck?

Yes and no. A lot of people believe her because of who—or what—she is. Lissette always starts the day unwilling to believe, but by evening is usually more willing to listen. Then, the next time they talk, it's the same thing.

Like she changes her mind overnight and goes back to her original viewpoint?

Pretty much, yeah. Then Tianna talks her out of it again. Your nest-mate isn't the most stable brain in the world, Boss.

I'm going to have a talk with Thomen. This could be him pillow-talking her around to his viewpoint, but I'm told he's directly affecting her mind. If he's doing this because he hates me, that's one thing. We can sort that out. If he's doing this because he's angling for the throne, that's another thing. Not that I would object, necessarily, to him being King, but I strongly object to his methods. I want to know his motives before I put my foot so far up his backside my toenails tickle his brainstem.

How long has this been going on? For years, as he planned a palace coup? Or is this a gentle usurpation started since the Demon King departed? Did Lissette conspire with Thomen while the Demon King was on the throne, then try to brush him off when the Demon King was gone? Or was Thomen doing something like this all along?

Well, crap. I'm going to have to institute a spy service just to find out who I need to know about, much less what they're doing!

But first things first.

So why was Bronze annoyed?

Tianna's done what she can with everyone else, but she gave up on keeping Lissette convinced. So, Tianna decided to go home. She's got duties in her temple, I hear. Thing is, Lissette didn't say I could come. She didn't say Bronze could, either.

Tianna took it into her head to ride away on Bronze with you hanging off the saddlehorn?

Pretty much, yeah. She's the granddaughter of the King and a Priestess of the Flame. Bronze and I are the personal property of the King and were willing to go with her. She didn't defy the Queen's order; she simply didn't ask permission.

And how did it go?

She didn't even kill anyone! I have issues with the way you raise your younglings, Boss. They don't seem to appreciate the value of a good torching for getting the survivors to listen. Which, when you think about it, is pretty weird, especially given who they work for!

Your advice on mammalian child-rearing is noted. Again, I have to ask... why was Bronze annoyed?

Leaving the Palace was easy enough, but the people called ahead and closed the city gates.

Let me see, I mused. *Big wooden things with iron and brass holding them together? Blocking the path of a fire-breathing, multi-ton metal horse? And a dragon-spirit in a flaming sword? And a fire-witch wizardess?*

Yes. Firebrand sounded smug. A little too smug.

Did you melt the walls?

Nope! Those are part of the mountain and it wouldn't have understood. I torched the gate, Bronze did the kicking and running, Tianna did the whole vaporize-anything-they-shoot-at-us thing, Firebrand reported. I found myself standing, hand on swordhilt.

*They **shot** at my granddaughter?*

Yep. Not sure it was orders, though—just frightened guards trying to do their job. We mostly ignored them. Tianna did something magical when a wizard did something magical, but other than that...

I didn't think she was that good a wizard.

It's easier to block stuff than it is to cast it, isn't it?

Generally, yes. Okay, I thought back. *Okay. I don't like it, but... mistakes happen. Nothing hit her?*

Do ashes count?

No. All right. I can let it go as a misunderstanding, I decided. *Panicked guards, screaming and confusion, someone launches a bolt, a few others take their cue from him... I can see that. It might be different if they'd hurt her.*

Yeah. There might be a bunch of people running screaming out of the flaming ruins of the city.

Intelligence is a survival trait, I told it. *All right. Do you need anything?*

No. We're on our way back. You might want to teach her the air-shield thing and the downhill-all-the-way spell, though.

Bronze feels happy, I argued.

She is. But she's not hurrying, just enjoying the run. The spells help even when she's goofing off.

I'll bear it in mind.

I cut the connection and turned to Torvil.

"Torvil?"

"Yes, Sire?" he asked. He was already on his feet, sword out—a response to my earlier reaction.

"Did Tort ever stay here? Did she have quarters?"

"She did, Sire, though it was but a seldom thing even in the latter days of the reign of the Demon King. She stayed near him and he did not often visit, even in secret."

"Get up to her quarters and find me something she wore—a ring, a hairpin, a cloak-clasp, whatever."

"Immediately." He shoved the door out of the way and hurried off, fishing out a pocket mirror as he went. I stopped the door in its spinning and closed it. I did debugging work on my kludged-together passive sensor spell.

Seldar came in while I was working. He wasn't stealthy about it, but he did keep quiet, for which I was grateful. He didn't clear his throat or wave, so it wasn't important enough to interrupt. I finished my mark two prototype and left it hanging, uncharged and waiting for a target.

"What's up, Seldar?"

"Sire. Torvil is on your mission and Kammen is sleeping. It falls to me to guard you."

"Oh. Yes, of course."

"With your permission, I would like to arrange an additional guard detail, as well as a runner to carry messages for you."

"I leave it in your hands, Seldar. Shouldn't you be excused from guard duty? Don't you have a palace to run?"

"Dantos is seeing to the palace and helping arrange things for me with the Baron. But yes, Sire, I do have other duties. This is why I ask for the additional guard detail. You have not yet agreed to permit us to include others in the personal guard of the King."

"Oh, right, right. Look, Seldar... skip the permission thing, okay? You're wise and you're just. You know what I'll like and what I won't. If it turns out you've started something I don't like, I'll tell you why and we can discuss it. Right now, I have a magician to find, a horse to recover, a war I don't want, a kingdom to lose, a mountain range full of nasty people to spy on, a whole family of evil magi after my head, and a granddaughter on an unauthorized field trip. You'll understand if I'm more than a little distracted."

"Of course, Sire. Is there anything I can do to help?"

"You're already taking a ton of worries off my shoulders."

"I meant with whatever you're doing now."

"Oh. Oh! Yes, actually, you can. Throw up a spell for yourself, to block detection magic." He obligingly did so. I tested my sensor; it worked. I kept getting bleed-through from other people, though. I could focus on Seldar and get a deep hum, but there was always a constant cacophony of tones and buzzes and hisses in the background. It was like listening to a faint radio station with a street full of traffic outside. It was there, but it wasn't clear.

"Okay, that's working," I told him. "Thanks. I still need to refine it some more, I think. Maybe an additional level of filtering based on other psychic characteristics? It won't help with people I don't have on file, but ought to be useful for finding people I know..."

"Sire?"

"Sorry. Thinking out loud."

"Good. I hope I will not be responsible for understanding any of that."

"Later, after I teach it to you. I'm busy inventing it."

"I see. Is there anything else I may do to assist you?"

"Got a good way to solve my other problems?"

"Not all of them, Sire, no."

"Well, then, that's—wait, what do you mean 'not *all*'?"

"I only have ideas about some of them, Sire."

I put the sensor aside and pulled two chairs closer together. I ushered him into one and took the other.

"I am all attention."

"You have mentioned a number of magi families," he began. "From what you have told me, prior to your most recent disappearance, the Fries family is the one proving difficult?"

"Yes."

"Will not the other families aid you against your enemy?"

"I doubt it. They aren't able to confront the Fries directly, not now. I suspect they won't want to have anything to do with me, either. Ancient curses, sunken continent, loss of magic, all that stuff. Long story, but they don't like nightlords."

"Not even a Lord of Night who will give them back the magic?"

"I... hmm. I'm not sure."

"As I see it, Sire, they will be subjugated under the Fries or destroyed. You can give them the power to resist their enemies."

"I made their enemies powerful," I pointed out.

"Perhaps they will see it so," Seldar admitted. "They may also welcome your offer to open the power of this... nexus?"

"Nexus, yes. This could work," I mused. "The problem is what happens afterward. I may be trading in one family of trouble for several families of trouble after the magical shootout."

"A definite threat traded for a potential threat?" he suggested.

"I'll have to look into it. But that will be later; I can't risk hitting a time distortion and disappearing right now."

"Time distortion?"

"Yeah. See, inter-universal travel is weird."

"I will take your word for it, Sire. One world is more than enough for me."

"No, you need to understand what happens, at least, if not why."

"Very well."

"See, while we're here, when a candle burns down one band, it burns down about one band everywhere else. If I'm here and you're in Carrillon, we can each light a candle and wait until it's almost burned out. We then scry on each other and see the other candle has burned about as much. Time passes the same no matter where we're standing. Right?"

"There may be exceptions, but I accept your statement as the norm."

"Good man. This similarity of time doesn't appear to hold in other universes. A candle may burn one band here, but burn ten bands there—or barely have melted the wax around the wick. I spent four days or so there, but sixteen days passed here."

I didn't go into the possibility I was in a world shockingly similar to the Rethven I knew. I just went with the assumption I was in the right universe. Everybody recognized me and there wasn't a duplicate of me. That meant it was close enough, surely. But *is* there a world exactly like Rethven, but where I (or the analog of me) went away and never returned? Are the other versions of me out there?

It's possible. Somehow, I don't like it. Still, the thing about infinity still applies. You can look through an infinite number of even numbers and never find an odd one. I need to research the rules for alternate universes. Later.

"I see," Seldar said, tugging at one ear in thought. "You have no way to tell how the ribbons of fate flutter in other worlds?"

"Not until I come back. I don't know if gate connections do anything to it, or if it's cyclical, or even if it's in constant change or periodically alters. Right now, it's random. I'll work out the pattern, if there is one."

Someday. But I didn't add that, either.

"So, your enemies may have years in which to work while we speak here?"

"Or only a few flickers of the candle may have passed since I returned."

"That would seem more likely."

"How so?"

"From the description of your escape, they were prepared to work with vast powers. Yet, how long was it between that escape and the summoning attempt? And a second attempt has not yet been made. Surely, time must flow more slowly for them while we speak here."

"Seems reasonable," I admitted. "It could go wrong very quickly, though. Remember, we don't know what causes a shift in the time differential—assuming something does—or how rapidly the ratio changes naturally."

"Then we should work quickly."

"As usual."

"Indeed."

"So, the last thing to do is go over there and discuss fighting the Fries family with other families. Got it. In the meantime, do you have any other solutions to my problems?"

"A few. Have someone run over Lotar in the street. Or have a word with his god, since I suspect Lotar is after personal power, not righteousness. His faith benefits from this, of course, for he sees his church as a vehicle to power. I would not think it meets with the full approval of his god, but I am hardly an expert in such matters. You may wish to speak with Mary about him, or see him yourself."

"Oh? Has Mary been looking him over?"

"Yes, but she has made no report to me. Doubtless she wishes to speak directly to you."

"Doubtless. I'll talk to her later and see what I learn. Don't misunderstand me; I trust your judgment. I just don't feel comfortable ordering someone's assassination without knowing he deserves it."

"I know." Seldar smiled. "It comforts me."

"Still on the lookout for the Demon King?"

"No. Merely testing to see if you are learning from the example of your knights. It is a part of my duties."

"Fair point. What else can you solve for me?"

"I am not sure I have solved anything for you," he observed.

"Maybe not, but you've got ideas. That's a few steps ahead of me."

"The Queen?"

"What about her?"

"You wish her to rule, yes?"

"Yes."

"Perhaps... you could encourage some of the less-cooperative of the lords to formally acknowledge her authority. This might smooth her path, and yours. If they fear you enough to obey your Queen, as your regent, then your goal is accomplished, is it not?"

"There's a thought. Got a list of people I should talk to?"

"I shall have one for you before morning."

"Excellent. Now, I have a question about the Duke of Vathula."

"Bob?"

"Yes. I understand he's the Duke of Vathula, and Vathula is the entire mountain range. Were you aware I—as the Demon King—made some sort of post-mortem arrangements with him? So far, I'm told T'yl is supposed to be dead as part of the arrangement. Tort should be, except they couldn't find her. They've also begun killing off my biological children, but I put a stop to it.

"Which," I continued, "leads me to an aside. *They* didn't kill and exsanguinate a hundred children in Carrillon on the night of my most recent departure. I've got them looking into it because I'd like to find out who did it and why."

"I was unaware of this," Seldar stated. "Perhaps Torvil or Kammen might know more."

"Consult with them. I want to know more about my dark elf secret police assassin death squads before I call Bob up and ask him what the hell is going on. If they're doing things on the orders of the Demon King, I probably want to stop them—but I think it unwise to just come out and ask, 'Hey, what did I order you to do?' It shows weakness, which is a very bad thing with elves, *orku, galgar,* and most other unpleasant races."

"Humans, too," Seldar added. "I will discover if there are any unusual occurrences."

"Mostly deaths, I would imagine." Seldar nodded in agreement. "I also want to know more about Thomen and his relationship with the Queen. I strongly suspect he's doing bad things to her brain and compromising her judgment. I want to know what he's doing, specifically, and why. If I have to, I'll ask him myself. Since that's likely to end badly—I'm not feeling terribly patient or emotionally stable—let's try to keep things from getting that far."

"I will begin these investigations immediately, Sire. For the works of the Vathulans, I will report as I find them. When I discover who is responsible for the night of the hundred deaths, do you wish them delivered to you? Or will you insist on being personal?"

"I'm sure the murderers were only acting under orders from someone. It wasn't personal. But I'm taking it personally."

"May I remind Your Majesty that a good king does not take anything personally?"

"Even on my best day, I'm a terrible king. But your point is well-taken. Find out who is responsible and *deal* with them."

"I shall see to it, Sire. However, I feel I should mention you—not the Demon King—are regarded as a great king, and can command the unquestioned loyalty of thousands."

"Which is why I'm trying to get out from under the crown and stick Lissette with the job."

"Aha. *Now* I understand!"

"Good. Why are you still sitting there?"

"No one has arrived to take my place as your bodyguard, Sire."

"This could get old. Really quick."

"We will try to make it as painless as possible."

Beltar chose that moment to push the door open—either excellent timing or he was listening at the door. We both turned to look. He was in his black armor. He also had a tabard on over the armor, held in place by the sash. The tabard was a uniform grey, either lead or slate-colored. My device—the sword-through-dragon arrangement—was embroidered up near the shoulder, rather than plastered all over the chest.

"My lord?"

"Hello, Beltar. Good to see you again. Do come in. We were discussing the horrors of the Demon King."

"A lengthy discussion," he agreed, entering. "I don't wish to interrupt, but if I might have a few moments?"

"Always a few moments for my knights."

"And priests?"

"Let's not get into that, please. Seldar? Does he count?"

"I am most agreeable to Lord Beltar's assumption of the duty, Sire. With your permission, I will be about my tasks."

"Go." Seldar went; Beltar sat.

"So, Beltar, what's on your mind?"

"There are a number of individuals who are nearing the borders of this life, my lord." His *my lord* was really the word *herus* (herr-OOS), from the original Imperial tongue, and was more an ecclesiastical honorific than a political one. It wasn't quite on par with directly addressing god, but it wouldn't be out of place when speaking to Sparky while she borrowed Tianna's mouth, either.

"I thought this sort of thing was handled without me."

"In a way. However, not long ago, a dark horse started coming to the houses of the dying and—"

"Yes, I know. It was Bronze, somewhat colored."

"I thought as much, especially when the priestess of the Mother of Flame began to speak of it. Now, though, the horse no longer visits. Now there exists the hope they may be found worthy of a personal escort, so they come to the Temple of Shadow. We are at a loss, my lord."

"You've tried sending them to the Temple of the Grey Lady?"

"We have. The trouble is, the Grey Lady will not end a life. She merely waits until it ends. Many who seek you out are not about to die, but are too weary of life to continue."

"Great. I'm the euthanasia specialist," I grumbled. *At least I'm not a vulture,* I reflected. *Or not as much as I feared. I'm not waiting for something to die so I can swoop down on it; they're queuing up and asking me to kill them. That's better. I'm pretty sure it's better. I hope it's better.*

"What shall I tell them?" Beltar asked, anxiously.

"Good question. Can we get them up here easily?"

"Easily? No, but arrangements can be made, if you wish it so."

"How many are we talking about?"

"Fourteen, at present."

"Hasn't Mary been doing anything with this? She knows what to do. Or did she not explain…?"

"Oh, yes, my lord. For many days, she has served as the doorway of death for those who have the strength to climb the throat of the Kingsway. The ones who come to the Temple are those who cannot make the climb, or those who revere you above all other gods. Most of those who yet remain simply hope for you to return to escort them beyond the realm of life."

*Do the divine ascension thing **one** time and you never hear the end of it,* I reflected.

"All right… let me ask this. In your opinion, how many of them want some sort of full-family ceremony? The whole farewell and funeral thing? How many are going to take a lot of my time?"

"Given opportunity, my lord, all of them." He frowned and sighed. "Lord, they will accept a swift and painless death, without fanfare, without fuss, if that is your will. But is it not meet a man should die with some feeling of significance? Of importance? The feeling his death is something of an occasion?"

I sat there and stared at him for a minute. He shifted uncomfortably and lowered his eyes.

"Beltar, have I ever told you how impressive you are?"

"You once mentioned the burden of a great potential, my lord."

"You're well on your way to living up to it," I told him. "All right. Make arrangements for them to come here. You can come up the Kingsway and arrange them in the great hall. Notify Dantos and work with him to set it up. They can bring their families, but warn them the ceremony will not start until after dark and they will *not* be staying overnight—up the Kingsway and back down again before dawn. Got it?"

"I do, my lord. You are most gracious."

"I'm a self-centered, arrogant jerk who doesn't want to waste all night hurrying down into the city for a circumstance of pomp and ceremony before hurrying home again."

"You will forgive me, my lord, if I do not believe you. While your reasoning might serve to dissuade others, you forget I believe in you, as you believe in me."

I stood up and turned back to my sand table. He stood up when I did.

"That will be all, Beltar. I've got work to do," I told him, trying to keep my voice level.

"Yes, my King," he replied. I heard the door grind shut. I dabbed at my eyes—the sand from the sand table must have irritated them.

Torvil brought me a selection of items from Tort's chambers. A little jewelry, a staff—probably a spare, judging by the spells in it—some pieces of clothing, a stuffed doll, and a comb. There was a spell on the comb to destroy any hair it collected, but not the hair it combed. It was a good piece of work.

I remembered the doll. I gave it to her shortly before I left to have a showdown with Tobias and the Devourer at the Edge of the World. What was it doing here? If she almost never came to Karvalen, why leave it here? To keep it away from the Demon King? Or to keep it safe until he was banished? She might have simply left it behind, but I won't believe that.

Torvil's armor had a nasty burn mark across the chest, stretching up to the helmet, discoloring part of the face shield. It was repairing itself, but it would be a while before he could see to his right at all clearly.

"What happened?"

"Defensive spell on a small box, Sire. I thought I had it counteracted, but I was wrong."

"Is it gone?"

"No. It fired off one charge."

"Obviously, whatever is in the box isn't supposed to be disturbed."

"I figured it out on my own, Sire."

I took the items and arranged them. The tricky bit, from my point of view, was using any residual signature left on items to enhance my memory of Tort. Dialing in a precise signature would help increase the range at which I could detect it—the more precise I was, the less static I would get, hence the better the signal-to-noise ratio would be, effectively increasing the range... It's a radio thing.

I spent much of the afternoon meditating, remembering Tort. It's a strange thing, going through memories like old photo albums, each picture alive and moving, a window to the past, while looking for the pieces a person leaves behind. Tiny bits of someone, scattered through my mind, living inside me in a way very different from the ones I've eaten.

A million people died inside me, but how many live? Tort does. Dead or alive, some part of her is left in me, alive and smiling, because I remember her. Her hand touches mine, her voice speaks to me, her lips meet my cheek. I can smell her hair as we hold each other, feel its softness as it attacks me, make sputtering noises as I try to get it out of my mouth. Late at night, and I sit beside her and hold her hand—I cannot leave; she holds my hand too tightly, even in sleep. She slips into my workroom, places food on a table, and slips out again, not wishing to disturb me. An assassin fries in the rain, Tort's face twisted into lines of fury and fear, lightning snaking from her fingers like sizzling snakes. She cradles my head in her arms, murmuring softly, telling me the things I need to hear. We stand together, power surging around us, each supporting the other as we prepare a spell.

She falls, sliding down the half-rotted wood, and lands in my arms. She is startled and in pain, but she is not afraid. I see a little girl. She sees her angel. She cries in the night, afraid of the things in her dreams, and so sleeps between me and Tamara, no longer afraid. She rides my hip, listening, watching, quiet and attentive. She sees me prepare to depart and asks if I will return.

How many memories do I have of her? Not enough, not for me. What I do have may be enough for this. Each of them is a fraction of her, a trace of her soul, and I write it, inscribe it, weave it into the structure of my spell like stamping letters of fire into steel.

Is that what souls are? Do they start as pure, untainted energy, only to be changed and patterned by the other energies around us? Like organic matter, taken in, digested, turned into flesh and blood and given to reproduce, forming a body that grows and changes. Does the forming body absorb the energy of souls, concentrate it? Is it imprinted, altered, changed by the souls around it?

I can see them, handle them, move them around or destroy them, but I do not understand them. Maybe that's what being a god is about, and why I will never truly be one.

The *ding!* of a message spell didn't interrupt me, but I was aware of it. I finished my transcription of Tort into the sensor and sealed it before answering.

Tianna sent me a message. They were not far west of the Eastrange and she wanted me to call as soon as was convenient. Well, the sun was going down, so... did she remember to bring her call-forwarded mini-mirror? I'd have to check.

As we headed for my quarters, I realized I needed more security spells. Anyone who knew me could use passive sensors to target me. A new brain-bunker would be a good idea, too. A whole host of things really needed to be cast... but each of those was, in some way, an inconvenience. If I blocked my own emanations, message spells and other passive seeking spells would be unable to find me, for example. There's always a trade-off between security and convenience. Maybe I could set up a receptionist spell—or simply get a person to be a receptionist. Back in the Old Days, when Zirafel was one-half the heart of the Empire, they relied on people more than spells. Now, I think, I'm starting to understand why.

I set my small mirror on a shelf as the sunset started. Unlike an electronic phone, mirrors don't short out under waterfalls. I angled it for a headshot of me and manipulated it to reach Tianna's mirror.

The lady who answered was unfamiliar to me. She looked startled. Well, I was, too.

"Sorry," I said. "Wrong mirror." I didn't know I could misdial a mirror. I hung up and tried again. She answered again.

"I'm doubly sorry," I said. "I'm trying to reach Tianna, but I keep getting this mirror."

"You have the right of it, Your Majesty. This is the mirror in the Temple of Flame."

"Oh! My mistake. I wasn't aware she—no, she did mention something about other priestesses. I don't think we've met."

"I am Sheena, Your Majesty."

"Pleased to meet you. I wasn't aware anyone could be a priestess without red hair?"

"Dark hair is not a bar to service, Your Majesty. One of the Goddess' children is needed for a high priestess, but others also serve." She twiddled with a lock of her loose hair. "I may flatter myself in thinking my own has grown highlights of reddish hue."

"Could be," I agreed. "Well, I learn something new every night. I don't suppose you could connect me with my granddaughter?"

"I am sorry, Your Majesty, but my magical training is only enough to operate some devices."

"Can you reach her on your mirror?"

"No, but I can speak to her through the flames."

"Hmm. Not exactly what I had in mind. I've got an idea. If it doesn't work, I'll call you back."

"As you wish, Your Majesty."

That was refreshing. She didn't scream and hang up in my face, which says good things about how I'm viewed in Karvalen. No, on second thought, it says good things about how I'm viewed in the Temple of Flame. I still don't know much about the day-to-day goings-on of the man on the street. I spend too much of my time in palaces, temples, and meetings.

We hung up and I finished my waterfall. Mary came in to help; this did not make things go faster. As we toweled off, she turned serious.

"It's nice of you to allow those people up here."

"It is?"

"You have no idea what I'm talking about."

"Sure I do. There are people up here," I said. She smacked me with a towel.

"The ones who want a personal escort into the land of the dead?" she prompted.

"Oh! Right, right. I remember. Are they all set up in the great hall?"

"They're setting things up. Dantos is a good organizer, but it'll still be a while."

"Good. I have things to do."

"Pity you didn't have this attitude earlier."

"I've been busy."

"Too busy. Can I schedule some time in the morning? Or are you still, you know...?"

"I'm feeling much better. Accomplishing things always makes me feel better. I'm still going to pick a fight with Johann and kill him with a cheese grater, but I don't feel like hiding under the bed anymore."

"Good. I'd much rather you were on it."

"Two-track mind," I accused.

"Yes. And on the other track, we need to talk about Lotar."

"Can I answer my page from Tianna, first?"

"Of course. Lotar's only a power-hungry religious leader with a fanatical cult following. He'll wait."

"Sometimes, your sarcasm borders on brutal honesty."

"I really am good."

"I promise to listen to the Lotar thing after the Tianna thing and the not-yet-dead-people thing."

"That's fair. And we get a morning to ourselves?"

"I can't promise, but I can promise to try."

"You're lucky I'm an old woman. A younger one would be all pouty and disappointed."

"You're lucky I'm an old man. A younger one would have promised anyway."

"Touché."

"Later, if I can find the time."

Mary came with me to the workroom. I had to go through the Rube Goldberg process of letting Bronze know I was looking for her, letting Firebrand translate, and have Tianna ready her pocket mirror for a call. Eventually, we did manage to get a mirror connection between my main mirror and her pocket one.

For the record, we only managed it because it already had a call-forwarding spell on it for receiving calls. The typical magic mirror enchantment isn't built for calling nonmagical mirrors. Even most of the mirrors used for scrying aren't magic mirrors, merely mirrors upon which a spell is cast. This is the trouble with magic. It's hard to build a factory to produce "generic" magic items. They may each use the same spell, but magical objects are hand-crafted, one-off, purpose-built things. They don't roll off an assembly line.

"I'm getting you your own mirror," I grumbled, once Tianna's image appeared.

"I have this one."

"A permanent one. A small one, fully enchanted, and capable of making a connection through the Palace scrying defenses. I went through way too much just to track you down."

"You could have called the one at the Temple," Tianna advised. "They would have notified me and I would have called you back. Just have a candle or something handy."

A whole series of conversations through fire—between universes, no less—came back to me in a lump.

Well, thought I, *now I feel stupid.*

"Good idea. I'll remember that," I told her. "All right, what's on your mind?"

"Granddad, do you remember how Lissette didn't want us to leave?"

"I'm not sure about what she wants versus what Thomen wants, but yes, I recall."

"There's an army in our way. Two, actually."

"Define 'in the way,' please."

"We headed for Baret along the southern Kingsroad, the coast road. There's a lot of people camped out around Baret. Rather than try and skirt them to get into the mountains, we decided to see if the Vathula Pass was any better. It is, but not much. There are only two thousand men, give or take, camped out in front of the city of Vathula, itself, but Vathula is locked up and the army has drawn its lines. It doesn't look like a formal siege, just a... a blocking force. I don't know if they're there to stop us or to prevent anything from coming out of the pass."

I knew there were armies headed this way. It didn't occur to me they might be *in* the way! If Tianna performed a breakout, however mild, from the royal palace, someone might have sent word ahead. Walking into camp—or blazing through it at a hundred miles an hour—might trigger whatever preparations they'd made in the last several hours. Going face-first into an army isn't usually the preferred way of going about things.

I should know. I've done it. But I'm less breakable than most people, as well as dumber. Case in point, I should have seen this coming.

My reply was somewhat profane. Tianna clucked her tongue reprovingly.

"Language. You're being a bad example, Grandfather."

"I'm a blood-sucking monster who devours the souls of the living," I countered.

"You're still supposed to demonstrate proper decorum around your grandchildren."

"Fine. 'Poop.' Satisfied?"

"It'll do. So, how do I get home?"

"Just looking over your shoulder, it looks as though you're in a wooded area. Do you have anything you can build into an archway? One big enough to ride through?"

"I'm not sure. Why?"

"I'll open a gate."

"Direct," she observed. "I was thinking you might know a secret road through the mountains, since you get along with rocks so well."

That sparked a memory. When I examined the mountain, its roots and branches, I had an intimate knowledge of where it ran and how. Coming back to myself, I remembered it only dimly. Yes, there was a way under the mountains— more than one, in fact. The details were faded into obscurity, but the general knowledge was there.

"I think there is," I admitted. "Tell you what. You work on an archway of some sort. I'll look into the roads. When I call back, you'll either ride home or simply step through."

"All right. What's involved in this arch-building of which you speak?"

"All we need is the physical representation to define the locus."

"Perhaps you might put it in normal-people terms?"

"We need a shape big enough for the two of you."

"I'm fairly sure we can do that."

"See you in a bit."

We signed off and I turned to one wall. Mary laid a hand on my arm.

"Before you do the weird thing where you plug a rock into your brain, maybe we should handle the passers-on? The rock thing is not only creepy, but it takes a while."

"Oh. Yes, of course."

We headed for the great hall.

"Can I ask you a question?" Mary began.

"Always."

"Maybe it's not really a question."

"Okay, ask me the statement."

"What I *mean*," she said, thumping me in the arm, "is… well… you're kind of attached to your granddaughter, right?"

"Yes."

"I was expecting you to go off and fight your way through an army. I mean, you've been a little short-tempered today, and I've heard a lot of legends in the past couple of weeks."

"I'm not going to ask what you've heard. I've heard a few, and they always seem bigger than I remember."

"The legends are pretty impressive," she admitted. "Did you really eat a hundred thousand elves when they invaded the mountain?"

"No. Mostly it was *orku* and *galgar*. It was only around fifteen elves, I think, and I imprisoned them in the basement, sealing them in stone except for food-related openings—input and output. See what I mean?"

"Yes. Although I'm not sure it makes me feel any different."

"My point is, legends grow with the telling. And no, I don't feel like tackling an army, especially when there's no reason to. I hope to resolve this peacefully and let everyone go home. Besides, Tianna isn't in any danger. She's got Bronze and Firebrand with her, as well as her training as a fire-witch and as a wizard. She's probably got Sparky watching out for her, too. She might be safer than *I* am. If it comes down to cases, she might be the safest person in the world.

"Besides," I added, "I'm a complete wash as a protector. Guardian angel isn't my field at all. I'm awful at it. Guardian demon, on the other hand, I think I've got down. If anything happens to Tianna, there will be new legends. Scary legends. Legends the locals won't know how to exaggerate. But I'm also deliberately trying to be more thoughtful and self-controlled right now because I know I'm not as calm and centered as I should be. So, unless something actually *happens* to her—or Amber, or you—I will make an effort to be a cool, calm, rational being rather than an enraged badger on meth."

"Fair enough. It's just… sometimes I realize I don't always get how you think. I'm tempted to say I don't understand you."

"I can imagine how frustrating that must be."

"No, you can't."

"Hey, I don't understand me and I live in this skull."

"You raise a valid point. Hold on."

We stopped in the hall and she made sure I was presentable. She had me deactivate my disguise spell; the dark skin, the black eyes—people expected them. Mary brushed my hair back over my ears to make them visible, as well.

"Smile. Show your teeth. And don't call attention to your ears, just display them. They add another subtle level of exotic and wicked to your features."

I simply followed her instructions. She pushed the pivot-door open and stood aside, hands clasped, head bowed. I entered. Thanks to her, I made an entrance.

The great hall was full of people—hundreds, maybe in the low thousands. They packed the floor and crowded the balcony, leaving only enough space for the musicians in the gallery and an aisle down the middle of the hall. There was also a roped-off area in front of the steps leading up to the throne. The people waiting for their escort were nowhere to be seen. The quartet of musicians were playing something with a serious, somber air to it until the door ground open. They stopped playing and the room went silent. Everyone looked at me. I think everyone held their breath.

I was torn. I didn't want to be here, but since I had to be, I wanted better regalia. If I have to play the part of a king, I should have the right costume. I didn't want to be on stage in the first place, but I should do it right. People want ceremony and spectacle, or maybe some spectacle with their ceremony. Sometimes it's rude to be brutally practical.

Note for the future: Wear the costume.

As I entered, everyone knelt, including the line of black-armored, red-sashed giants just inside the rope. I didn't make any comments; this was a ceremony. Instead, I looked at Dantos. He ushered me up toward the dragon's-head throne. I didn't argue. He choreographed this so I wouldn't have to. It was only fair to do it the way he planned it.

The main door swung grandly open. A group of people came in, carrying a stretcher and a withered old man on it. They advanced with measured tread while the musicians played something slow. The whole thing reminded me of pallbearers at a funeral.

They set the stretcher down on the highest step—the steps are easily wide enough—and backed away. I looked at Dantos and he nodded. That didn't help me. I wanted to ask him what I was supposed to do, since this was his show. So, I asked Firebrand to ask him and remembered Firebrand was with Tianna. Dammit.

Well, I was here to be a psychopomp. A lethal psychopomp. I took a wild guess at my next move.

I moved forward and down, sitting on a lower step of the dais and beside the old man. His name was Teselo. We spoke for a bit while I asked him what he liked best about his life, what he was proudest of, what made him happy at various times. He finally explained what was wrong with him and asked to be relieved. I explained how I was willing. He held up a bony old hand and told me/asked me to please go ahead. So, I did.

I picked him up, carefully, gently, and held him on my lap like a child, cradling his head and shoulders on one arm. I lowered my head as I ran lines of tendrils through him, tracing out the paths of his spirit, drinking in the colors of his soul. By the time my teeth met his flesh, the bright places within were empty, gone, vanished into the night. Blood flowed as I bit and soon the body was as empty of blood as it was of soul.

When I looked up, the knights were still standing there, unmoved. Teselo's relatives prostrated themselves, faces down on the floor, hands clasped and extended toward me. The crowd was pressed back against the far wall as though trying to push through it. I wondered if anyone could breathe, they were packed so tightly.

On impulse, I looked behind me. The light in the great hall is from the firepits and some magical lights up near the reflective, gold-leaf ceiling. The light was too ambient, too scattered, to make real shadows. My shadow, like any shadows in the room, should have been a dim, indistinct thing on the floor.

Mine stood behind me like an inky cloth, stretched over throne and wall, towering twenty feet high. It had *wings*, outspread, but drew them in as it shrank down toward normalcy again.

As soon as I figure out how, it and I are going to have a talk.

I laid Teselo's empty body on his stretcher and beckoned his family to take it away. I had to tell them aloud; none of them were willing to look at me. Eventually, they did approach—skittishly, I'd say. It helped when I moved back onto the throne, away from the body. Once they started walking away, the musicians picked up again, and the next person's pallbearers started in. There was a minor traffic jam as people squeezed aside, clearing the way, but it was only a delay. Nobody dropped anyone.

It occurred to me to wonder, just then, what they did with the bodies. I remember having to bury Jon, then dig him up again for the fire-worshipper cremation ceremony. What do people do with the bodies around here? What do the plainsmen do? The *viksagi*? What do they do in Carrillon? I'm usually only involved in events leading up to the funeral, not the actual funeral.

Fourteen people came up to me, and fourteen times I got to feel both elated at helping and sad at a leavetaking. It's an intimate, personal thing, escorting someone out of their flesh. It's very different, that willing departure, from killing someone who tries to kill me. It's almost like saying goodbye to a friend, except whoever it is doesn't really leave. These people become a part of me in some way, a different way. I'm not sure how, but it feels more... I don't know.

And, every single time, the throne-end of the great hall was engulfed in shadow—my shadow—as they left their bodies behind. Why? I don't know. I don't know why blood crawls over to me or why my eyes are black or the precise mechanism by which I misplaced my nighttime reflection. Of all the things I know little about, me, myself, and I top the list. At least the people in the hall stopped compressing at the far end. After the fourth or fifth time, they started to realize it was a harmless manifestation... well, harmless to them. Probably. At least it didn't harm them. They grew accustomed to it and that was good enough.

I sat down on the nose of the dragon throne while the last of the departures was taken down the steps. I felt elated and sad, energized and weary. It was a feeling of great intensity and grand contradictions. I sat there as the crowd flowed away, like water draining from the hall. The knights on duty closed doors behind people and shut the place up. One guy in plain, steel armor worked with them.

When they were done, they came and knelt before me.

"Who is this?" I asked, indicating the steel-clad gentleman.

"My lord," Dantos said, kneeling and doing the fist-on-floor thing. "He is Lanval. During the wars of reunification, he acquitted himself with courage, honor, and skill on the field. He is one of many knighted by the Demon King into the Order of the Sword, but we believe him to be a worthy addition to the Order of Shadow."

"Do the rest of you say so?" I asked, looking at the kneeling knights.

One by one, they unbuckled swords and laid them on the lowest step of the dais.

"We do," they said, more or less in unison.

Clearly, they meant it. Whoever this Lanval guy was, he impressed them, and anyone who can do that impresses me.

I descended to the black-clad knight on my left and picked up his sheathed sword.

"What is your oath?" I asked. He recited it again. I nodded and moved on to the next, on down the line, picking up swords as I went. When I came to Lanval, I had a dozen swords cradled in one arm, kind of like the flowers of a particularly dangerous beauty pageant winner. I held out my hand and he placed his sword in it.

Everyone held their breath. Sometimes I like to be dramatic. It was night, so I took the opportunity to search his heart, see what kind of man he was. He convinced a dozen good men he was someone they wanted to serve with—men I trusted, men with ideals, men with honor—but if I can fool people into thinking I'm a king, people are easily fooled. The colors of your soul never lie.

Surprisingly, I agreed with their assessment. I don't know what he did on the field or what his skills were, but he was a good man. That was enough.

"What is your oath?" I asked him, and the world breathed again. He recited it and I couldn't help but see the blaze of his spirit as he did so.

Then I recited *my* oath as I walked back down the line and handed back each sword.

I dismissed them. They bowed and departed, all but Dantos. I gestured for him to wait and he did. I climbed back on the throne and hurried to ask my mountain some questions. Yes, there were ways under the mountains. The southern road and the road through the pass were both wide, easy roads to travel, but they were also thick stone over buried tunnels. Down the length and breadth of the kingdom, everywhere there was a road of stone, the Kingsroad, there was a tunnel through the solid rock beneath it. Well, once you grow a road, extending it down, thickening it, really isn't much of a trick.

A secret highway for the Demon King, perhaps? A way to get around without being seen? He could travel through a tunnel, pop out through a secret door in any city, and spy, scare, or kill anyone he pleased.

On the other hand, there was an accessway connected to the palace in Karvalen. I could walk into the palace in Carrillon and never see the sky. I could walk to Crag Keep and never get mud on my boots. If I cared to let the world know about my secret highway network, I could march an army from Karvalen to Vathula, or Carrillon, or even to far-distant Lyraneyn and no one would see it coming until men were pouring into the city streets.

I didn't care to use it. It strikes me as a handy thing to have, but only useful as long as it's a closely-held secret.

I speeded up to a more human timescale and stepped down from the throne. Dantos was still with me, waiting patiently while I appeared to nap. He moved to kneel and fist-on-floor before me.

"Get up. And stop doing that when we're alone."

"Yes, my lord."

"Good. First thing: You did a fantastic job putting all this together. Well done."

"I thank Your Majesty," he said, and added something in the language of the plains tribes.

"What was that?" I asked. "I didn't have a translation spell running."

"It is hard to put in Rethven, Sire. 'When the darkness is content, the night is swift?' 'When the darkness does not hunger, the hours of the night flow by quickly and without worry?'"

"'When the dark doesn't eat you, it's a good night'?" I asked. He flashed a rare smile.

"Yes, my lord."

"I like the first one better," I told him. "Now, what time is it?"

"The moon will reach midheaven in less than a band of the candle."

"Thanks. I don't see anyone else around. Are you on bodyguard detail?"

"Yes, my lord."

"Right. To the gate-cave, Robin!"

"Robin?"

"I'll try the joke again for Mary. She'll get it. Come on."

We went to the new, upstairs gate room the mountain made for me—I really need to relocate and consolidate my gate rooms. I have the new one with my makeshift gate, but the old gate room is still down there. Maybe I should have a gate room for guests and one for my personal use. Although, now that I think of it, I suppose I do.

As I entered, I noticed a change in the walls. They were still where I left them—which, all things considered, isn't the most certain thing in the universe. They were developing lines, crystalline veins of some sort. The lines formed a radial pattern around the gate. The gate itself wasn't part of the wall, of course; the mountain doesn't like having bits of itself enchanted. But the glittering lines in the wall centered on an area the size of the gate and radiated outward from the edge of it.

Quartz? Something crystalline, certainly. Did the mountain pick up on the fact I needed crystals to store power for my temporary gate? Was it that sensitive and responsive? The fact it could produce veins of crystals wasn't too surprising.

It regularly supplies all sorts of subterranean and mineral substances, from water to coal to gold. It's even given me diamonds.

Were those veins of crystal projecting from the wall a bit, as though being squeezed out of the stone? I thought they might be. Upon close examination, it seemed several dozen individual crystals were growing, but maybe these were projections of one giant crystal instead of lots of little ones.

Which gave me an idea. I put some instructions in a spell and slid it into the rock. Soon, we should have a big crystal in the center and a constellation of smaller ones around it. One crystal can house more than one spell, but it's complicated to do and the spells have to be simple. But you crack a crystal and you ruin everything in it. If we're going to use these to power a gate, having multiple batteries is better than one big battery. Less efficient, yes, but much more failure-tolerant.

Pleased as I was to have a much longer-lasting gate, this interfered with my idea to move it down to the old gate room. The mountain would have to start over. Would it be easier to get people to move all the miscellaneous stuff to another room and call it my workroom or laboratory, instead? Probably. Upper gate room, lower gate room and a more mundane magical workroom... okay. I mentioned it to Dantos and he assured me it would be taken care of. I immediately felt more organized.

I wonder how long *that* will last.

I went through the whole where-are-you routine to hunt down Tianna on the mirror next to the gate. Once I had a lock, I regarded her handiwork. She found two trees fairly close together, trimmed away some lower limbs, and bent branches toward each other. It wasn't exactly an archway, but it was roughly the right shape and right size. I connected to her mirror and her face swam into focus.

"Grandfather?"

"Yep. Ready to come home?"

"Yes, I think so. Have you looked at my construction?"

"I have. I think it should work beautifully. Just get on Bronze and hang on for dear life. She's going to make a sudden leap forward when the gate opens. Got it?"

"Whenever you are ready."

She hung up, but I watched through the magic mirror, centering the point of view inside the makeshift archway. The mirror connection should act as a guide for the gate spell, making it certain to establish the connection in the right spot. Who knows? It might even make it less power-intensive. I've done that sort of thing before, but I wasn't in a position to get a good gauge of power consumption.

Bronze kicked divots in the ground for starting-blocks; I knew she was ready. Since this was only a spell-enhanced archway—not an enchanted Gate, merely an archway with a spell on it—I pushed some personal energy into it to save as much of the gem-charge as possible. The image flushed and swirled away in the mirror, as though I looked down into a whirlpool of silver light. The whirling image faded as I watched and the archway filled with a long tunnel of whirling brightness, reaching for the destination. The idea struck me that maybe I should have the mirror on the wall behind the gate.

The far-distant image of a wooded area, huge horse, red-haired rider—all of it snapped forward, leaving only a doorway from one place to another. I expected it. Dantos backed away quickly, pressing against a wall. Not a bad idea, really, considering what happened next.

Bronze sprang through the now-stable opening. I couldn't hear her hooves, thanks to her enchanted bracelets, but I felt the rapid-fire thunder in the floor. She didn't skid a bit, either. I'm proud of those enchantments.

On the other hand, like Dantos, I was suddenly rather pleased to be standing to one side. There are advantages to having the mirror beside the gate, rather than behind it. If I put it behind the gate, I'll wind up blocking the door every time I open it. Bronze wouldn't run me over, but it would take more time, and time is power. Ask any Gallifreyan.

The instant Bronze was through, I cut the power to the active portions of the spell. The view through the gate shredded, disintegrated, vanished. Not bad from a power consumption standpoint. Since the spell's power wasn't fully expended, it could be used again. With the existing charge in the archway's embedded crystals, we could do that several times more before burning up the existing spell. Mirror connections do help. I resolved to make sure the archway's crystals stayed charged, at least until I could get around to putting in a permanent enchantment to replace the spell.

Tianna dismounted and handed me Firebrand. We all exchanged greetings— Firebrand telepathically, Tianna by hugging me, and Bronze by lowering her head to be hugged. I skritched Bronze with my talons since she was the only one who could enjoy it.

"Grandfather," Tianna began, "we have a problem."

"Another one?"

"I'm serious!"

"So am I. Go ahead, tell me about it."

"Thomen is doing something to the Queen. I think he's controlling her."

"This is not news to me."

I told her that, Firebrand said. *I told her I told you, but—*

"You didn't tell him what we found out," Tianna countered.

Well, no, but—

"Hold it. I'm on a schedule, here. What's the story with Thomen and the Queen?"

"What I've been able to find out—"

What we found out, Firebrand insisted.

"Shut up," Tianna advised, and Firebrand did. Impressive. "What *we* have been able to find out is this. During the reign of the Demon King, Lissette had a number of miscarriages, but most people don't know it. They think she's had perfectly normal pregnancies, aside from the demon-spawn rumors. What they don't know is *Thomen*, in his office as the Queen's Physician, killed the unborn children."

I think I managed to restrain myself rather well. I doubt there was anything more than a twitch around one eye, really. Oh, and my fangs didn't want to retract. Other than that, I don't think I showed any sign of my instant desire to murder Thomen by drowning him in scorpions.

"Before I get all bent out of shape," I said, carefully, "did you determine if this was Lissette's idea or Thomen's? If he did it without Lissette's approval, that's one thing. If he obeyed the orders of his Queen, that's quite another."

"Surely, that doesn't matter? He murdered the unborn!"

"I'm not going to get into an abortion debate with you. I want to figure out who to have the debate with. Do I need to find Thomen and explain to him why what he did to the Queen and her unborn children was wrong? Or do I need to acknowledge he was doing as he was ordered and have my discussion with the Queen, herself?"

"Oh," Tianna replied. "I hadn't thought of it in that light." She thought for several seconds. "I have to say it's not exactly clear. What is clear is the children she's had since then."

"The ones after Liam?"

"That's right. They're all Thomen's children!"

"Okay."

There was a long silence.

"Grandfather?"

"Yes, Tianna?"

"I just told you your wife has several children by another man."

"Again, was it her idea?"

"I don't think so."

"Now I'm interested. Tell me more."

"Firebrand?" she said, encouraging it.

I spent a lot of time on the Demon King's hip, Boss. I didn't spend a lot of time around Lissette or Thomen while this was going on. I have, now. I know you don't much like how I hear what people are thinking, but it's the only way I can talk to them. I hear stuff because people's minds are always muttering to themselves. Okay?

"I understand. It's how you are. I'm used to it."

Okay. With that out of the way, I've been listening a lot while Tianna does the talking. People pay a lot of attention to what they're saying when she asks searching questions. They pay less attention to governing their thoughts. Usually, they think about a lot of things—what to say, what not to say, how to say it, and so on. That's how I know Lissette isn't altogether there. Pieces of her thinking are... walled off? Closed. It's like someone decided what things she can think about, or... no, it's more like there are things she's not allowed to think about.

"What's the difference?"

I'm not sure how to explain it. If I told you to only think about eating, sleeping, and raiding villages for gold, you couldn't think about mating, right? But if I told you **not** *to think about attacking a magician's tower, you could think about anything else—even the tower, or the magician, just not about attacking the tower.*

"It's an exclusion set, rather than an inclusive one. Got it."

Uh, sure. Whatever you say, Boss. But the person doing it—

"Thomen."

Only one I can see doing it, Boss. His own think-parts are harder to sort out, what with being a professional wizard and all. He knows he's doing something wrong and it scares him, but he's doing it anyway. What I think happened is he told Lissette about her demon-spawn and somehow convinced her to get rid of them. Then, since a complete lack of any children would be suspicious to the Demon King, he also convinced her to substitute his kids for the Demon King's.

"I can kind of see his point," I admitted. "And, to be perfectly frank, if he loves Lissette enough to take such a massive risk—and vice-versa—I'm prepared to look the other way. I've said it before and I'll say it again: It's a political marriage, not a romantic one. I'm not even too keen on the whole succession thing. If the Queen has a child, the child is in line for the throne. End of story."

"That's… you can do that?" Tianna asked.

"My goal, here, is to *not be King*," I reminded her. "What I want to set up is a Royal House—if there's a King, he rules; if not, the Queen rules. The succession is through the line of Queens, but selected by the King."

"Huh."

"You sound amazed."

"You sound crazy."

"But a good crazy, I hope."

"I'm not sure you can get the nobles to take that."

"I'm sure the survivors will think it a fantastic way to run a kingdom."

I'm behind you all the way on this, Boss!

"You stay out of it," Tianna snapped. "Grandfather, are you sure this is the right way to… to…"

"No, I'm not. But it's the only way I can think of to keep me from being pinned between a crown and a throne! The kingdom doesn't need the Demon King; it doesn't need me. It needs a stable monarchy and competent rulers who view the responsibilities of kingship as a duty, not a privilege. When you get a politician who thinks being in charge is a goal, rather than a duty, you have lousy politicians."

"I see your point, but it's such a drastic change from the way it's supposed to be done—"

"It's a new deal," I advised. "There wasn't a real king for close to ninety years. This is how we're going to do it."

"If you say so, I'll back you, but you're going to have troubles."

"When don't I? But, speaking of troubles, I see I have a lot to ask Thomen about."

"Yes."

"Here's the thing. Yes, it looks kind of like he's a traitorous, usurper-ous, power-hungry weasel. But could he be an honest, upright individual who started out as the Queen's Physician, became her lover, and is continuing to shield her mind from the horror of her own memories at being the wife of the Demon King?"

"That's an awfully generous thought."

"Yes, it is, and I know it!" I snapped. I caught myself and rubbed my forehead. "I'm sorry. I'm tempery. Yes, I'm reaching, and I know it. I'm overcompensating for a huge desire to go out and kill something—anything. So, let me reach for my misplaced optimism and take the benefit of the vague doubt, will you?"

"Of course, Grandfather. Especially when you put it like that."

"Thank you. Firebrand? How about it? Could Thomen be a good guy, here?"

I... Boss, there's too much in Lissette's head I can't get to. I don't know. I can't call it one way or another. It could be good, having stuff hidden away from her in her own mind. On the other hand, it could as easily be a suppression of anything that would contradict... well, whatever Thomen wants to tell her. He could be saving her sanity or using her ruthlessly. I can't tell, and that's all there is to it.

"Don't forget," Tianna replied, "we were hunted the whole way home."

"Explain that."

"I was blocking location attempts all along the way. It was a non-stop thing, pecking at my spells, trying to find us. It couldn't have been just Thomen. It required dozens of people. What they would have done if they found me—found us—I don't know. Someone went to a lot of effort to locate us, though. If we hadn't been moving at Bronze speeds, they might have succeeded. She got us far away quickly enough that I could hide us without wearing myself out."

"Doesn't Sparky give you a vitality boost?"

"Yes. We're talking about a *lot* of power I had to block, Gramps. Once we were outside Carrillon, they started piling on, trying to find us. They had to know we were on the road to Tolcaren, but I can only assume they needed to get a precise location. The only reasons to do that are to communicate or to hit someone like a nail. When I realized what was happening, we took some of the lesser roads and did a little cross-country traveling, too, before we got back on the Kingsroad."

"Lesser roads?"

"The ones that aren't straight paths of stone? Dirt tracks through lesser towns and villages. Those roads."

"Oh. Okay." I thought about the implications of the constant pinging for Tianna's location. "I think I need to talk to Thomen."

"I'd say so!"

"Good thing I already scheduled a call."

"Already?" Her eyebrows went up. "My, you're an awfully clever grandfather."

"Yes. And sometimes—once in a great while—a little bit lucky. We'll see how it goes."

"Good. I'd like to be there for the conversation. Right now, though, can I borrow Bronze to get me to the Temple of Flame in a hurry? It's a long walk and I've been away much longer than I should."

"By all means, go handle your religion."

"Wow. That's irony."

"It is?"

"One god telling me to go handle the affairs of another." Tianna's smile was dazzling.

"Because you're my granddaughter—"

"And, therefore, quasi-divine?" she interjected. I ignored this.

"—I'm going to ignore that. Just remember I gave up being a god." I didn't add anything about how my alternative was apparently madness and death. Nor did I mention my knowledge of energy-state beings. They aren't gods, merely non-physical entities feeding off the projected energies of mankind.

"If you say so," she agreed.

"I'll send word... no, on second thought, I'll try to conference you in from the temple."

"Conference?"

"When I'm talking with Thomen, I should be able to rig it so you can see and hear us both, but we won't see you. It'll be like sitting in the room without the need to leave the temple. How's that sound?"

"Wonderful!" She stood on tiptoe and kissed my cheek. "You're sweet, Grandfather."

"Only to the people who deserve it. Off you go." I buckled on Firebrand while Bronze curled a foreleg back as a step for Tianna. Good thing I raised the ceilings in the halls. Dantos started opening the door while Tianna mounted. Bronze waited politely for him to finish, rather than shoving it open herself. Very mannerly, my horse. Dantos pivoted it slowly shut again after they left.

Mary came in a few minutes later. She and Dantos traded greetings. I was busy, laying the basic power-storing enchantment in the crystals oozing out of the walls. The mountain could hold them and move them into their proper places by manipulating the stone in which they were embedded. It wouldn't be able to increase their size once I put the power matrix into the crystals, but it could always produce more crystals.

"I saw Tianna and Bronze. I take it everything is in good shape?"

"Yes and no."

"As usual?"

"Pretty much. Tianna's fine, but Lissette may be the victim of post-traumatic stress disorder—"

"I hear it's going around."

"—or she may be mind-controlled by the Evil Wizard acting as her Grand Vizier."

"That's rather cliché, isn't it?" she asked, cocking her head to the side. I noticed she changed her hair color again, this time to an inky black. She also wore it in a braid.

"Yes, it is, but even the clichés have a grain of truth to them. That's why the become clichés. And what's with your hair?"

"I like it black."

"I mean the braid."

"I'm not married."

"Well, no, I suppose not. But why not put it in a ponytail?"

"Either you're trying to get my goat or you're legitimately asking. Which is it?"

"I don't understand," I admitted.

"Ah. So you really don't know?"

"Know what?"

"A ponytail is for prostitutes," Mary informed me.

"Seriously?"

"Well, maybe I should call them 'working women.' Loose hair is for children, braids for unmarried girls, and that *wriage*-thing for married women. Ponytails, however, are generally worn by women for hire. Remember, this place doesn't view women the same way. You can hire a girl to do your laundry, rub your feet, cook your meals—and she's a 'working woman' in that sense. But a woman on the street asking if you want a good time? She has her hair in a ponytail, too." Mary cocked her head at me, puzzled. "I'm surprised you don't know that."

"How would I?" I countered. "Most of my encounters with society are in a meeting, running through crowds, or killing people."

"Not the ideal learning environment," she agreed.

"Welcome to my life."

"Speaking of which, how's the morning looking?"

"Well, I expect to talk to Thomen... but he'll wait until I'm good and ready for it. I have a number of things I should be doing."

"Am I one of them?"

"Thank you for reminding me. Yes. Of course you are."

"Just making sure." She moved up beside me and put an arm around my waist. "Working on a project, I see."

"Always."

"Am I going to have to keep poking you to remind you I'm here?"

"I hope not. I'm trying to toss this whole king thing back into the laps of people who can do it better. If I get my way, eventually I'll have a nice, quiet spot with easy access to dinner, a huge library, and a workroom for anything I want to accidentally blow up. Until then," I told her, turning to put my arms around her, "yes, you might need to poke me and remind me you're there once in a while."

"All right. I hope your quiet little spot has other fun stuff. I like reading as much as the next girl, but I also need to get out and do things."

"I'll add it to the list. In the meantime, do you and Firebrand want to help me?"

"With what?"

"I'm thinking I should take a nap before I start making major decisions about the upcoming war, Thomen, Johann, and Tort." I grimaced. "I don't want to, but you pointed out I probably should sleep every so often. Maybe you're right. I don't think I can afford to be wrong about it. But I also don't like it, and I'm more than half afraid if I do sleep, something awful will sneak up on me."

"That's what you want Firebrand and I to help with?"

"Yes. Dantos can keep an eye out for immediate, physical threats. You and Firebrand can watch for magical and mental ones."

"I'm not much of a wizardette, yet."

"All you have to do is wake me up if something starts knocking on my defenses." I grinned at her. "I'm not sleeping outside a protective circle."

"Seems reasonable. Okay. I'll watch you sleep."

"Dantos? When is your shift over?"

"Dawn, my lord."

"Just checking. Let's head to bed."

We went up to the royal snooze room and I laid out an Ascension Sphere. It's not a perfect defense, but against anything done remotely, it was a fantastic start. Inside it, I put up a more standard blocking and containment spell; nothing gets in, nothing gets out. At least, nothing immaterial.

Mary and Dantos watched me set all this up on the slab serving as a bed. When I started laying out furs and blankets again, Dantos spoke up.

"My lord? Shall I wait outside? Or do you wish me to remain in the room?"

"Please remain. Although, if you want to post someone outside the door, go ahead. I leave it up to you."

Dantos bowed slightly in acknowledgement. He fished out a small mirror and called for backup.

Mary accepted a sheathed Firebrand and sat down inside the Ascension Sphere, folding her legs together and laying Firebrand across her knees.

"So, how does an undead get a nap?" she asked. "Isn't sleep a thing for mortals?"

"Yes. But I've got a plan. You'll see."

"Okay."

Once we had everything laid out—including me—I stepped into my headspace. There, I checked the trapdoor to the basement and made sure it was still bolted tight. With that done, I sat down at my desk, tried to relax, and slowly started dimming the lights.

It seemed to work. At any rate, when the lights went out, so did I.

A thousand paths, each branching in all directions. Footsteps on each line, each a strand of destiny, marching in unison, feet tromping like metronomes in perfect time, all advancing together. Here I am, everywhere, stomping forward, regardless of which path I take, almost heedless, because I take them all. Every path, every branch, I am there, splitting to follow every way.

Rarely, paths intersect, merging again. There I merge, as well, becoming myself, and continue. We are a line drawn across all the possibilities, creeping forward relentlessly down branching roads which never end.

I realize this is not quite true. Some paths do end. They simply stop, although I do not. At each such end, my relentless march carries me beyond the path and I topple, tumble, twisting down into darkness, still marching. Before me, there are many paths, and many of those have endings. A culling, a trimming of this tangled hedge of possibility, it seems. A place where the line of us will lose so many ways.

Beyond, the paths which continue branch and branch again, filling the empty spaces. When I reach them, I will split again, and again, and again, down all the myriad ways.

Can I go back and divert those selves who would venture down dead-end roads? Merge them again on some longer trail, lead them back? No, there is no way to turn around, no going back, no returning. Can I even shout? Can I call out to the others of myself, the might-have-beens, the never-were, the could-have-happened?

It is strange, being one of these and seeing us all. Being oneself and being outside, looking in. Inside, I am as helpless as all the rest, rushing headlong or dragging feet, yet moving inexorably forward. Outside, I see all the lines, all the others who are me, our paths, our destinies, our decisions.

I open my mouth to warn me, for many are coming to places final, to turns or twists or branches where there is no other way but all the way and to the end.

What do I say? Are there words for it? I cannot comprehend myself at this moment. All I know is I cry out, I speak. I listen and heed. New branches form to connect final ways to other ways, but the ends remain. I split, I divide, I take all paths, as always, and for every self diverted to a safer course, another tumbles into oblivion.

Sunday, February 22nd

The sunrise woke me like falling out of bed into a pool of hot water. I jerked upright, sweating, shaking.

"That sounded like a doozy," Mary commented.

It was, Firebrand assured her.

I ignored both of them as I got a grip on myself. It's not an easy thing to go from weird omniscient psychic dream state to mortal solidity. It takes a minute to get one's bearings. It took me closer to two.

Once I felt more grounded and oriented, I hugged my knees and closed my eyes, reviewing what I'd dreamed, trying to understand the vision. Offhand, I could see several possible ways to interpret it, along with a lot of inevitability and futility. If the point of it was to say every decision could lead to an infinite series of decisions, and no matter what decisions I made, an alternate me made another, then it was a lousy point. If it was about the inevitability of destiny and the illusion of free will, ditto.

This is another reason I have issues with sleep. My dreams make no sense whatsoever.

I opened my eyes. Dantos was still by the door. Mary still sat cross-legged with Firebrand on her lap.

"Shower?" she prompted. I didn't need another prompting. I felt sticky already.

We cleaned up as the sunrise continued. Mary encouraged me in a not-at-all subtle fashion to take the morning off. I was already planning on it, but she knows I forget things.

When we came out of the bathroom, Firebrand was hanging on a wall and Dantos, or his replacement, was nowhere to be seen. Someone had brought in a lot of food and arranged the trays neatly on the slab serving as a writing-desk. My guess was Mary already made arrangements. I hoped those arrangements included exceptions for emergencies.

After that, Mary took my mind off my nightmares.

Boss? Firebrand asked, during a lull.

What?

There's a debate about whether or not to disturb you.

I can hear them talking through the door, but it's faint and I haven't had attention to spare. What's the deal?

Lissette denounced the Demon King for drinking the blood of children—the hundred or so kids, I think—and declared war. Ships have set sail from Formia and the armies around Baret are marching east along the southern Kingsroad.

Is anyone doing anything about it?

I dunno. Seldar's giving orders and people are doing what he tells them. Does that count?

It most certainly does. Do we have an estimate on how long it'll be until the army gets to Mochara?

Three or four days, they tell me. Something about armies taking more time than someone walking. Which is weird, since it's a bunch of guys walking, you know? You'd think—

Yes, it is odd, I interrupted. *Do we know when the ships arrive?*

About the same time, maybe a little sooner. Weather and ocean stuff.

Got it. It can wait another hour or two.

Seriously, Boss?

Seriously. Mary wanted a morning; I said I would. Besides, Seldar will have a report for me by then and some idea of how my own powers might best be employed. He'll have a much better idea of what strategy we should use. I'll be happy to listen to it and approve. Right now, he's busy. I'll bother him later.

You're taking this not-be-king thing a little seriously, aren't you?

Seldar's high on my list of alternates.

You really aren't kidding?

I'm really not kidding.

Okay. If you say so, Boss.

I sighed and stretched. Mary raised her head from my chest and smiled at me. She blew a lock of hair away from her face and grinned at me.

"Firebrand?" she asked.

"How could you tell?"

"You tensed up."

"Oh. Yes. Can I have a minute to put some instructions into a rock?"

"I'll pop into the bathroom for a minute. Don't eat all the red berries; I like those."

"*Shulua* berries," I informed her, listening to what my mouth said. It was news to me. "They're sweeter when they're fresh. These are well-preserved, though."

"Good to know. I still don't want you to eat them all."

"Perish the thought."

She skipped into the bathroom and I put some instructions into a spell.

The road along the coast clung, for the most part, to the mountainsides facing the sea. On the north side it was generally a wall of rock; the south side was usually a descending slope of variable steepness, from straight down to about thirty degrees, often ending in either a ravine or heaving sea, depending on the time of day and the height of the tide.

Huh. The sun of this world goes down and vanishes as it passes the horizon. It reappears on the other side of the world to rise for the morning. It isn't a celestial body in the sense of a star or planet. It's an energy manifestation in a magical universe. Does it affect the tide?

How about the moon? Is it really a moon? Or is it something else again? It seems to orbit the world on the same time interval as the sun, only as an opposite—the sun sets as the moon rises, and vice-versa. Is that by design or merely a coincidence? Does the moon actually affect the tides? I've never paid much attention because I've never cared much for ships, sailing or otherwise. But if I knew how the tides worked, it might give me insight into the things influencing them.

Crap. I may need to be more nautical and I hate boats. No, on second thought, I don't. I hate oceans, sinking, and drowning. Boats are okay.

Anyway, the Kingsroad along the southern coast.

I imprinted the instructions and slid the spell into the rock face nearest me. The mountain started changing the road. It immediately began to narrow as the rock wall inched slowly into the right-of-way. The surface of the road tilted, ever so slowly, toward the sea-side. The road surface started developing speed bumps two or three feet apart, rising up in humps, sinking down in dips, making it progressively more difficult, minute by minute, to roll a wagon over. The two bridges started to change shape, the road surface rising in the center and dropping off on both sides like the peak of a roof. Places where the road ran under an overhang, the ceiling started to lower, growing downward, decreasing the clearance.

The mountain seemed almost gleeful to have something to do. Come to think of it, it enjoyed my instructions about the Kingsway, too. I think it likes having large projects, but I have no idea why. I would think it would prefer to sit contentedly, like a... well, like a rock. But what do I know?

None of this would happen quickly. They'd notice the dips first, of course. If they were smart, they'd turn around and hurry back before they ever caught on to the tilting of the road or the narrowing of it. If they weren't smart, the army, strung out along the road in the mountains, would find their road gradually disappearing from under their feet. Hopefully, everyone would go back to their staging area around Baret.

Hmm. Mental note: Call the Baron of Baret and see how he's doing. He might be inadvertently besieged by a force he wants nothing to do with.

Mary came out of the bathroom, finger-combing her hair into a semblance of order.

"Breakfast?"

"Absolutely."

We had breakfast and went back to bed.

Mary seemed reasonably happy about the morning. I admit, it was a good morning. It helped my morale, certainly, and moreso since I insisted she trim her fingernails before we started. Thinking ahead pays off.

By the time we cleaned up, dressed, and made ourselves presentable, there were a number of people waiting to see me. We came out of the bedroom and Kammen handed me a stack of messages.

"What's this?"

"Everyone wants to see you, Sire. We got a buncha guys headed here."

"Yes, I know. Lissette declared war."

"You know?" Kammen asked.

"I have good ears."

Hey, don't I get any credit? Firebrand asked.

I don't want to admit you listen in on people. Keeping it in the realm of "That's just how it talks" keeps people from looking at you as though you're riffling through their brains.

But I don't. It doesn't work like that.

And I'm not the Demon King.

So? What's that got to do with... oh.

"You knew a war started?" Mary asked.

"Sure. A little after breakfast."

"Why didn't you tell me?"

"It would have ruined our morning." I turned to Kammen again. "Please let Seldar know I'm available. As for the rest of these," I said, thumping the papers, "if it's not a personal matter—personal to me—tell them to take it up with Seldar or Dantos."

"Gotcha, Sire."

"Good. Now, I'm going to call Thomen and see if I can sort this out."

"Can it wait a bit?"

"For?"

"Seldar. He really wants to see you."

"All right. I suppose I should find out what's going on in more detail... and he may want to sit in on the conversation. I'll be in the workroom."

"I'll let him know," Kammen said, and drew out a small mirror. He spoke with Seldar while we relocated. I wound up following Kammen. Dantos had already set up the new workroom, separate from the new gate room.

Once there, I called Tianna. I didn't want to talk to her so much as to work on her mirror and mine so they could act like an extension phones. She blew me a kiss through the mirror and went back to doing whatever fire-priestesses do. Mary got a lesson in mirror communications while I worked on the spells.

Something made a ripping, wet sort of sound, like tearing flesh. I held my spell-work stable for a moment and looked over my shoulder.

It was big, about eight feet tall, and shaped vaguely like an old-fashioned beehive. It was greenish-blue, splotchy, and covered with tentacles. The tentacles were about as long as it was tall and arranged radially, emerging from each level of the "beehive" in decreasing numbers as they ascended. Each tentacle seemed covered in eyes, at least at first. The eyes were open and looking around as the tentacles writhed. Then the eyeballs opened to reveal needle-like teeth and extend long, sharp tongues. Each eyeball-mouth-thing emitted a screech in a slightly different note, grating on the nerves and raising hackles.

Mary screamed. I didn't blame her a bit; I felt like screaming, too.

Kammen, on the other hand, didn't seem to care if it was screaming, screeching, writhing, flailing, or begging for help. It appeared, unannounced, in the presence of the King. Like a computer following instructions, he attacked. *Condition:* it appears unannounced. *Action:* kill it. Kammen killed it.

He started by charging into it, sword out, and buried the blade in the thick, tough hide of the thing. Tentacles immediately snapped around him, smothering him in coils. The next thing I saw was the tip of his blade emerging from the top of the thing as he sliced upward from the entry wound. A few more swipes and pieces of the thing fell away, thrashing madly on the floor. This freed him well enough to remove tentacles in much the same manner as trimming a hedge, followed by carving a ham. Ichor went everywhere, splattering and stinking like wet dung and industrial waste. At least it didn't sizzle.

Kammen stood there, his armor dripping bluish-black fluid, and regarded the writhing pieces. A few quick swipes and they were very small writhing pieces. He finished up with a spell, a wiping gesture to remove foreign material from his armor and weapon. Then, with perfect aplomb, he resumed his place by the door.

Elapsed time: six seconds.

Holy crap on a cracker.

"I'll have someone get the bits and burn 'em, Sire." He sounded about as excited as my grandmother over her morning cup of tea. Which, even if it's a particularly good cup of tea, still isn't too excited.

"Yes," I said, and tried to keep my voice from shaking. "Yes, do that."

"What *was* that?" Mary asked, almost whispered.

"I have no idea. Probably something from Johann. Since he couldn't drag me away, he's probably sending presents."

"Wherever it is he shops, promise me we'll never, ever go there."

One of the bits of tentacle opened its eye and screeched at us. Kammen stomped it with a *splat!*

"I promise."

Mary, Tianna, and I tested the new mirror system. I'm glad we did; it didn't work on the first try. Tianna got sound, but all she could see was a huge, flaming eye. I found the problem and fixed it, then she got vision but no sound. It was a fight to make it work, but it was a fight I could win. The two used different sorts of transmission. The vision was a light-emitting function while the sound was more of a psychic thing, yet they both fed off the same information feed from remote mirrors. Most everyone else uses a solely psychic technique in which only the actual user can receive sensory impressions. This makes the mirrors useless as displays. Mine generally work more like televisions. Admittedly, mine are more complicated to make and definitely more energy-intensive, but they can be treated like actual images, not merely psychic visions.

Mary and I were both glad to have a problem to solve. Some of the monster-bits were still wriggling. It disturbed me greatly to realize some of the bits were also fighting and eating other bits. Firebrand poured fire over a few; luckily, they burned normally, giving off a sickly-sweet smell not unlike some high-explosive residues. It made me wonder if the smell was toxic. As a precaution, I magically guided the smoke up through an exhaust vent.

A squad of people with buckets, tongs, and mops came in to deal with the monster remains. After subduing some of the larger portions, they took them away to be burned. I cautioned them about not touching it or breathing the smoke. We'll see if anything awful happens.

Most Things simply dissolve once you kill them. The Things from beyond the world do, anyway. Every time I've killed one, it collapses in on itself, liquefies, and evaporates.

This wasn't a Thing-thing, merely a physical thing. It was a biological organism. It adhered to world-rules even after it died, rather than simply ceasing to exist. It was made of matter—presumably matter as I understood matter—and had all the problems a physical creature does, which definitely includes Kammen and high-speed vivisection.

So who sent it? And it surely was sent. Even *I* don't have random monsters teleporting into my vicinity as a *coincidence*.

My money was on Johann. Thomen might like the idea, but he'd have to find such a monster (problematic), precisely locate me (difficult in the extreme, at the moment), then transport his creature through both the city and palace defenses (unlikely, bordering on impossible). I simply couldn't see it happening. Johann, on the other hand, is looking past the city defenses, not through them. He's on another plane of existence and the city shields don't prevent interuniversal transportation.

I should fix that. I should build some permanent enchanted items to take care of my more mundane magical defenses, too. I should also get on the stick and start negotiating with other families of magi to help me out. Time is ticking, although it's hard to tell how fast.

As for where he found a monster, I don't know. I can make a couple of guesses. He could have looked into other universes, picked the first ugly thing he saw, and dragged it home to play with me. He could have conjured up a physical creature from someone's nightmare. What I would probably have done, if I had all the power at his disposal, was to start with a living creature and transform it into a monster. A squid, maybe, or some particularly unpleasant sea creature.

Just three options, and those off the top of my head. I'm sure there are more.

Seldar came in as they were mopping up the last of it. I noticed while they didn't wizard up the mess, but they did magically clean the mops, draining all the water and goo into the bucket. Interesting. Less power-intensive but more time-consuming. That does seem to be the usual trade-off.

"Sire."

"Seldar. How's the war?"

"On its way. I beg your pardon for my tardiness. I was engaged in discussion—"

"Hold it. No excuses. You are doing *your job*. I don't keep track of what you're doing; if it's important, go do it. I can wait."

"You are a most unfair monarch, Sire."

"I am?"

"How can I use you as an excuse to free myself from unpleasant meetings if you take such an attitude?"

Mary snickered. I sneered at her.

"All right, I'll take the blame. It'll be our secret. Right?"

"Right, Sire."

"Absolutely," Mary added.

You got it, Boss! Firebrand said.

"Whatever," Kammen rumbled.

"I'm surrounded by snark," I observed.

"But no boojums," Mary said. "I like your Seldar. Can I have one?"

"Ask his wife," I advised. "Where's Dantos, Seldar?"

"With Rendal, reviewing the city wall and its defenses. They know the people here better than I do."

"Fair enough. Do you want to brief me before or after I try to talk Thomen into talking Lissette into calling the whole thing off?"

"If I may ask, what plans do you have in the event he will not do so, Sire?"

"Well, the way I see it, there are a few possibilities. Try and follow me on my thinking and correct me where my thinking's stinking. I figure I can stop the war by handing over everything to Lissette and walking away. You want the marbles? Here you go; I'm done playing this game. That sort of thing. I'm working up to it anyway, but there are complications.

"One of those complications is the question of whether or not Thomen is treating her for post-traumatic stress or if he's doing nasty things to her mind and controlling her. I'm going to have to see for myself before I'll believe the results. I need to know she's not some pawn under the thumb of the wizard who would be king."

"I find it doubtful they will permit you—which is to say, the Demon King—in the presence of the Queen, much less allow you to examine her mind," Seldar pointed out.

"Right, which makes things more difficult. If he's a good guy, Thomen deserves thanks, not the alternative."

"What is the alternative?"

"I'm thinking I try to kill him. Of course, it didn't work out so well the last time I went off to kill someone. I'm sure he's spent a good little while preparing for my attempt."

"I would."

"You're not helping. However, I did come up with an alternative to killing him."

"Which is?"

"Got a coin on you?"

"Of course." He fumbled at his belt pouch and drew out a handful of change.

"What's the biggest value coin? Got one of those?"

"Here." He handed me an octagonal gold coin. It was about an inch across from side to side, rather thick, and looked struck rather than molded or carved. On the front of it, somebody did a terrible job of capturing my likeness; I looked noble, bordering on handsome. It was probably copied from some statue.

"How many of these would it take to buy... oh, say, a large merchant vessel? A full-sized, brand-new ship?"

"Ships are exceedingly expensive," he informed me. "Each one is twenty or thirty thousand, depending on a number of factors."

"When I announce I want Thomen dead and I will give a *hundred* thousand of these to the person who kills him, what will happen?"

Mary let out a low whistle. Seldar's eyebrows went up and his eyes went wide.

"You once mentioned," I told him, "that I'm a king and I don't have to do everything myself. I could pay people to do this, couldn't I?"

"Do we *have* a hundred thousand to spend?" Seldar asked.

"Yes."

"I would say... it would be... difficult. For Thomen. It might encourage him to kill you quickly, however, and so remove the reward."

"A good thought. I'll have to find someone to hold it and administrate it for me. That way, even if I die, the reward stands."

"Who could do such a thing without earning a death-mark from Thomen?"

"I'm thinking Bob would do it. It would appeal to his sense of humor, I think."

"He has one?"

"A dark and twisted one, but yes."

"Very well. Shall I send word, Sire?'

"Not so fast. We haven't established if he's a good guy, merely misguided, or an evil overlord in the making. I'm ninety percent sure he's a brain-twisting would-be usurper, but I have to be certain. It matters."

"Of course, Sire."

"So, now that I've told you what I'm thinking, what do you have for me?"

"I have spoken with a number of individuals in Carrillon, all of them Order of Shadow. They are asking questions, discreetly, about Thomen, the Queen, and their relationship. So far, my investigations agree with yours. It is probable he is using her, but I cannot prove it as a fact."

"Well, keep looking. What else?"

"Troop movements. The Temple of Shadow has the table of vision in their undervaults. Their best estimate of the force on the south road is fifteen thousand infantry, two thousand archers—counting crossbowmen—a hundred wizards, five hundred horse archers, two thousand heavy cavalry, and perhaps a hundred knights."

"The Order of Shadow has my original sand table? Is that where it went?"

"Yes, Sire," Seldar replied, surprised. "It is yours, is it not?"

"Yes, but why didn't Tort take it?" Then the answer hit me.

"Because the Demon King would have it," Seldar and I said, in unison.

"A better question," I continued, "is why didn't he want it? He could have moved it to Carrillon."

"I am not privy to that, but if I may offer a guess?"

"Go for it."

"I think Tort may have lied to him about the feasibility of transporting it. It *is* a table of stone and quite large. She might even have lied to him about it being part of the mountain."

"That could work. What else do the shadows have?"

"They have the spirit-stone—your crystal warrior—kept in the Temple. It is my understanding they have the room where a knight is given his armor, somehow, and have claimed it as theirs. I do not have the details."

"Probably a hidden passage to the room and all other access blocked off," I mused. "The mountain might even have moved the whole room, I suppose. Fair enough. Back to our troop movements. Any sign of other troops?"

"Not in the main army. If it matters, there appear to be no religious contingents other than the Lord of Light."

"That's not surprising. They don't like other gods."

"Very true, Sire."

"By the way, what's the difference between heavy cavalry and knights?" The words he used were *equitanae* and *armania*. The first specifically meant some sort of horse-mounted combatant while the second was less specific about the method of fighting.

"Training and equipment, Sire. The cavalry are dangerous, but they are not as skillful nor as well equipped as a knight. Knights will fight from horseback, on foot—anywhere and everywhere. Cavalry are mounted warriors used for swift response, flanking maneuvers, and breakthrough attacks."

"Got it. Go on."

"Eighteen ships have set sail from Formia. The two forces appear to be timing their arrival at Mochara."

"What's on the boats?"

"We are not certain. The ships are much better protected than the army. This leads me to believe the ships carry much of the magical forces. I also believe this to be the case because of prior difficulties in assaulting Mochara by sea, or landing troops anywhere along the coast within any reasonable distance. Down the coast, the keels tend to shatter. Closer to the city, the ships erupt in flames. Knowing this, I would send my heaviest magical defenses with the ships to prevent disaster."

"Seems reasonable. By the way, send someone to find Flim, down in Mochara. Ask him if he would be good enough to receive me early this evening."

Seldar made a notation, nodding.

"The ultimate strategy of these two forces, Sire, is still in question. I can understand sending the wizards on ships. One does not march wizards anywhere if you expect them to be well-rested—much more important for wizards than for most other troops."

"I agree."

"It is possible they will attempt to regroup and form a cohesive force before attacking. It is also possible they will attempt to attack on two fronts."

"You assume they're going after Mochara?"

"They must. The ships cannot rise to the canals, nor could they sail along them. Moreover, the army dares not leave Mochara at its back." He paused, frowning and rubbing his jaw. "They could march on Karvalen while the ships engaged Mochara, threatening it with invasion to prevent a relieving force, but this would dangerously and needlessly divide their armies. I would not do it."

"Sound thinking," I agreed. "Good strategy dictates wise action. This makes professional soldiers somewhat predictable. The problem is, the world is full of amateurs."

"Of course, Sire."

"A bit of good news, though. I don't think the army will be joining us."

"Sire?"

I explained what I did to the road. Seldar bit his lips to hide his smile. Mary didn't bother; she grinned as though trying to fade from view. I even heard Kammen chortle in his helmet.

"So we're likely to have several boatloads of wizards," I concluded, "assuming they don't decide to call it off."

"They might," Seldar said. "I would."

"And if they don't?"

"When attacked, we fight."

There was really nothing for anyone to say after that. I changed the subject.

"All right. Who wants to join me in a conversation with Thomen?" Everyone volunteered. "Figures. Okay. I'll do the talking. If anyone has something to tell me, pass me a note. I'd rather not have an open discussion while he's watching. We need to present a picture of unity and certitude."

"Sire?"

"Yes, Seldar?"

"May I suggest only one chair be visible? You should sit casually, as though this is merely a minor matter, while the rest of us stand behind you as though awaiting your attention."

"Good thinking." We arranged ourselves in front of the mirror. I called Tianna and she settled in to observe. I dialed the palace in Carrillon. A nice young lady answered it and didn't even bother to ask my business; she sent a messenger and offered to entertain me on her *duzan-kin*.

They've invented "hold" music.

I told her to play; I'd never seen one before. It looked like a square, wooden pipe, open at both ends, with five strings mounted on the top. She plucked the strings with one hand and slid fingertips back and forth to vary the pitch and chord it. I couldn't tell if she was good or not. She was obviously nervous and I'm as competent a judge of music as I am of Precambrian art.

Yes, I know when the Precambrian Era was. That's what makes it funny.

Thomen waved a hand and dismissed her, moving into view and seating himself.

"I've been expecting this call," he said.

"I did tell Corran to tell you."

"Yes, you did."

Awkward silence.

"Well? What did he say?" I asked. "I'd like to make sure he told you what he was supposed to."

"He says a great many things. The gist of it was that you want to see Lissette ruling Rethven."

"Pretty much."

"I'm for it," Thomen agreed. "You, however, do not need to be involved."

"I'm listening."

"You are a plague on the people of Rethven."

"I'm still listening."

"What more need be said?"

"Well, I can think of a few points we should cover. First, before I surrender my crown and throne, I need to know Lissette is healthy, sane, and free of any magical influence." I saw Thomen stiffen as I said it. "Second, I need to be sure the nobles of the realm will acknowledge her authority. If we can accomplish those two things, I'll happily throw a feast in the Palace of Carrillon, invite all the nobles to watch me passing along the crown, and vanish thereafter. What do you think?"

"I think you are deceitful and cannot be trusted. You are the Demon King and likely lying." He glance flicked behind me. "Those automata behind you prove nothing. They are either controlled or deceived. You are a child-murderer and a monster. You will never see Lissette nor sit on the throne again."

Mary put a hand on my arm, gently. I glanced down and saw my knuckles were white on the arm of the chair. With great deliberation, I relaxed.

"So," I said, swallowed, and started over. "So, Thomen, what you're saying is I should annihilate Carrillon, declare a new capitol, find a new queen, and produce a new heir. In twenty years, I can have a worthy heir and turn the kingdom over to him or her. That should be my plan?"

"You have no chance of that," Thomen sneered. "Between us stands an army greater than any since the days of Zirafel. With, I might add, more magic at our command than you could muster in a year."

"I see. Well. That's certainly one opinion."

"It is my estimation, based on years of observation."

"Well, that settles it, then. I know Lissette would prefer to die than to live as a wizard's puppet. I'll arrange for the city to be destroyed immediately. Good day." I reached out toward the mirror, as though to shut it off. Thomen stopped me.

"Wait!"

"Wait? How long? Long enough for you to escape my wrath? That would involve waiting for you to die of natural causes. That's not going to happen."

"What do you mean, 'destroy'?"

"I mean I will smite the city with fire and thunder the likes of which the world has never seen. The blow I will strike risks cracking the world in two, but it's a fairly small risk. The city, however, will vanish utterly. Where once there was a city, there will be a circular lake at the new mouth of the Dormer river. The city and everything in it will be reduced to ashes and dust in a blast so profound the people in Karvalen will look up and see the cloud of it rising beyond the mountains."

I don't know what the people behind me were doing, but Thomen looked at them, then at me, and licked his lips.

"You can't do that."

"People keep *saying* that to me," I observed, leaning forward and smiling my best Evil Bastard smile. It's a good smile. I think it's the teeth that really sell it. They're subtle, but they add a little touch of predatory to make it especially unnerving. "I don't know why. It's almost as though they're challenging me to prove I *can*. Is that what you're doing? Are you *challenging* me to destroy Carrillon, Thomen?"

"Such power is not found in mortal hands."

I sat back, put my elbows on the arms of the chair, extended my fangs, and deliberately, slowly, began drumming my fingertips against each other. I clicked my fingernails together to emphasize my point.

"Yes," I agreed. "*Mortals* don't have such power."

Technically true. I didn't know any mortals who knew the trick to it. Once you know matter is a kind of highly-compressed, sticky energy, though... As for Thomen, I let him wonder if I was implying nightlords might have such an ability, or if my brief stint as a demigod might have given me some sort of smiting authority.

Thomen turned the mirror away for a moment. I let out a huge breath and resettled myself in the chair. When I looked at the others, Kammen was smiling and Mary looked worried.

Mary is concerned you might have a nuke up your sleeve. The other two are sure you can do what you say. They don't know how, but they believe it.

Good to know. I see Seldar isn't especially cheerful. Seldar looked concerned and was scribbling a note.

He wants to know when you're going to start negotiating.

Aren't I?

He thinks you're just threatening and demanding. Very kingly. Not very diplomatic, though.

He has a point, I agreed, thinking it over. I nodded at Seldar and he handed me the note. Yes, it said basically what Firebrand already told me.

Thomen turned the mirror back again. I put on my game face.

"Before we resume," I said, "allow me to take this opportunity to apologize." Thomen looked startled, then suspicious. "I've been demanding and ordering and suchlike. I shouldn't be. It's one of the reasons I don't want to be King. I apologize for being unpleasant and discourteous."

"That's very gracious," Thomen allowed. "I accept your apology, although it does not move me. I have consulted with my advisors and we do not believe you can do what you threaten. I will not agree."

"I understand, but hear me out. The smiting of cities is the stick. Rude and unpleasant. Let me try the carrot."

"Carrot? Stick?"

"Don't you people know the story? Nevermind. I've offered a penalty for not working with me. Now let me offer a reward."

"A reward." His suspicious expression deepened. "I'm listening."

"I think I've made clear what I want. Yes?"

"Yes."

"If I get what I want, I'm prepared to give you things."

"Such as?"

"If Lissette is alive and well, I'll place her on the throne, the crown on her head, the royal regalia all over her, the works. Then I'll abdicate in her favor. She'll be the sole monarch of the kingdom. She can then marry whomever she chooses. Anything between you and her then becomes moot—not only to me, but to the people, as well. Whatever arrangement you two come to is your affair. I'll be off somewhere else and won't care. How does that sound?"

"I think," he said, slowly, "you are trying to buy time. You know my forces are advancing on you; you know I can defeat you. You are trying to persuade me to recall them so you can hatch some plot, form some alliance—something. Why else would you go to such lengths?"

"Because, right here, right now, we can change the course of the future."

"Oh?"

"If we go on as we are, thousands will die. Most of your soldiers—most of mine, too—don't want to fight."

I ignored the muffled snort from Kammen.

"They march because we order it," I went on. "There's no need for any of this. We can keep it from happening. If you truly care about Lissette, as I hope you do, you can get what you want without bloodshed and death. I'm willing to work with you on it. I can get what I want, too, if you'll work with me. This doesn't have to end badly."

"Yes, it does," he countered, leaning forward suddenly. "You have to die. Permanently. You are a plague and an abomination—and I'm not even talking about your blood! *You* are a terrible thing, upsetting the traditions of a thousand years, muddying the water of class and station. You are ruining everything about this kingdom, twisting it, making it into a seething cauldron of chaos. People don't know their place. Nobles watch the other nobles, maneuvering for power and prestige. Peasants dream of rising above themselves. Women dare to speak in the presence of men! You even want one to *rule!* Everyone is looking at anyone higher and wondering how to take their place.

"You started this with your words, with your school of letters and numbers, with the temptation of ambition for the common man. It's worst in Karvalen, and I thank the gods you never encouraged it to spread to this side of the mountains! You have to die, your cities have to die, and your ideas *must* die—crushed out utterly, like a coal beneath a bootheel!"

We glared at each other through the magic glass for several seconds. I counted silently to ten in English, Rethven, and German. Thomen sat there, gripping the arms of his chair, red-faced and angry.

"I see. Well. You've certainly clarified your position."

"I have."

"Just to make sure I understand you correctly? Lissette must not rule. I have to die. The cities of Karvalen and Mochara must be destroyed, mostly because they're full of people with the ambition to try and be something other than whatever their social position allows. Does that cover it?"

"I'd say so," Thomen agreed, slowly settling back in his seat.

"Okay. Now we know where we stand," I told him, trying to keep my voice mild. It wasn't easy. My temper has been ruined.

"And where do you stand on all this?" he asked.

"I'm going to have to think about my response. I told you what I want. You told me what you want. Now I have to figure out how to give you what you deserve."

I hung up on him.

"Sire?" Seldar asked.

"What?" I snapped.

"A word?"

"Fine, but make it fast. Everybody else, out. I'm going to need some alone time."

They didn't argue. I heard some whispering from Firebrand—thoughts not directed at me. Everyone but Seldar left the room. I wasn't sure if I was going to break anything or not, but I didn't want to find out with people in the room. My feelings have been a little less nailed down ever since the Johann Incident.

"Make it quick, please."

"Halar?"

I blinked, startled out of my black mood for a moment. He never calls me that.

"Yes?"

"What are you?"

"I don't understand the question."

"I thought not," he agreed. "Do you at least understand I love you, my King?"

"Yes," I agreed, slowly. "Yes, I think I understand it in the way you mean it. And I think it fair to say, in the same spirit, I love you, Seldar. If you were my son, I would be proud to say so. Is that close to what you mean?"

"It is," he agreed, nodding. "And I would be proud to claim you as my father. Having said so, I trust you will understand how much it pains me to do this," he added , and he smacked me, open-handed, across the face, rocking my head to the side.

I froze in that position, hands cracking the chair arms under my grip. Long, slow, deep breaths and no other movement, none, until I had as good a grip on myself as I did on the chair. It wasn't likely, but I tried.

Firebrand said, as though across a great distance, *Fangs, Boss. Fangs.* It continued, very quietly, as though psychically tip-toeing through a minefield, *Your fangs are out, and you'll never forgive yourself if you accidentally kill Seldar!*

Slowly, I turned my head and regarded him. With Firebrand to remind me, I tried, but couldn't seem to retract my fangs. I did manage to let go of the chair arms, noting, in passing, I had to pull my fingernails out of the wood.

"If anyone else had done that," I said, slowly, "they would probably be dead."

"Yes, Sire, and rightly so. My life is forfeit. But I must do as my conscience dictates—I must do what, in my mortal wisdom, seems right to me."

"So you must," I agreed, still speaking slowly and trying not to show the storm inside. Those fangs are really annoying at times. "*Explain,*" I ordered, and Seldar flinched.

The flinch is what helped the most. *Seldar flinched.* Seldar. Seldar, for one instant, showed fear. Fear of *me.*

It hurt, and it made me want to fix it, want to protect him from whatever made him afraid. Whatever it was, it would find me standing between it and Seldar, and it was going to have to go through me to get him.

When I realized I was the thing making him afraid, and my anger turned inward instead of outward.

"Are you a god?" he asked. "Are you a man? A Thing from beyond the world? I need to know. What are you? Demon, nightlord, wizard, or king? I *deserve* to know, because the one I serve is a king. I thought I served a king. I meant to, but I am having difficulty in finding my King. I saw him turn into a creature of horror, the Demon King, and I could not bear it. Now I see him again, less horrifying, but lacking the certain something which made him a king. Made him *my* King.

"So I have to ask: What are you? Are you some impostor, warming my King's chair until you can arrange for the Queen to rule? Or are you the true King? *My* King? I must know."

I sat there and thought about it, hating myself, hating being a king, hating my life, hating everyone and everything. By God, I felt like an angsty teenager again.

"All right, you've asked your question. I agree you deserve an answer. And I'll give you one the moment I understand the question. As it stands, I'm not sure what you're asking."

"How can I make it more clear?"

"First, what brought all this on? What made you decide I needed a smack across the chops?"

"You heard the traitor Thomen?"

"I did."

"You agree he is a traitor?"

"Oh, yes. He's made his position very clear."

"Has he?" Seldar snapped.

"Yes," I agreed, surprised. "My only concern now is how to deal with him. For that, I need to understand how Lissette feels about him."

"And that, Sire, is why I feel the urge to hit you again," he replied, hands flexing into fists. "And again. Until you cease to spiral into stupidity."

"Please don't. Explain, instead."

"Did you not hear Thomen? He spoke of troops, and ships, and forces, did he not?"

"He did. So? I'm well aware they're on their way."

"Whose forces are they? No, wait," he said, holding up a hand. "Whose forces did he *say* they were?"

"Why, they... he said..." I trailed off as my memory played back parts of the conversation.

*...you know **my** forces... persuade **me** to recall them...*

"...they were *his* forces," I finished, softly. "Not the Queen's forces, not the kingdom's armies, but *his*."

"With all the other evidence, do you need anything further to make a decision? Or will you continue to be hesitant, uncertain, overcautious, even cowardly in your decision-making?"

I sat there for a bit, thinking. When Seldar lectures me on how I'm being a lousy commander-in-chief, I need to listen. Come to that, I *am* a lousy commander-in-chief, so I need all the help I can get.

"You've brought it to my attention. Now get out."

Seldar did the one-knee, fist-on-floor thing and departed. I turned off the light and sat there, in the dark, thinking. Somehow, I feel more comfortable in the dark.

At least I've finally got the hang of this brooding thing.

One good thing about brooding, it involves thinking. That's kind of the point to brooding. I gave serious thought to a number of things, most of which needed to be done immediately if not sooner. I need to find Tort. I need to stop a fleet. I need to kill Thomen. I need to put Lissette on the throne. I need to rip Johann's face off and shove his head in a bucket of vinegar. I need to talk to a family of magi—probably the Etiennes; they seemed like decent people. Maybe the Stuarts, if I could appeal to their self-interest... blah, blah, blah, all the stuff on my To-Do List.

But Seldar raised a point. Have I been acting like a king? I've never been anything great, as far as kings go, but have I been especially goofy? Probably, if Seldar is willing to smack me across the face to get his point across. That's either profound courage or total desperation.

With Seldar, my money is on the courage. He may be the bravest man I know.

And I didn't see the smack coming, that's for sure. He's grown up a lot. The kid I knew would have followed me to the underworld and never asked if we were coming back. I think I like the grown Seldar even better than the too-serious youngster, right cross and all.

Ever since I've been back, I've been trying to soft-pedal the whole King thing. I want people to look to Lissette, not me. But if I'm not being much of a king, how can I hand her my authority? To be free of the crown, I have to put it on, first... and if Thomen is controlling the Queen, she *can't* rule. I have to. Then I have to put Lissette in a position to rule, which means I have to fix the damned political system, which is oxymoronic.

I've probably said it before, but it bears repeating. Politics. From the Latin *poly*, meaning *many,* and *tics,* meaning *blood-sucking parasites.*

That may be incorrect, but it's not wrong.

So, what to do? Answer: Something. Anything. Progress treats depression. Success, however small a dose, is my drug of choice for treating despair. And a king doesn't dither and vacillate; he acts. I've been... I don't know. Seldar had trouble putting it into words, so how am I going to do better? I think I know what I need to do, though. If I can at least act... decisive? Resolute? Determined? Purposeful! That's the word. If I can act like I have a purpose, have a plan, maybe it'll be catching.

I'm afraid to do things which might end badly, might cause innocents to be hurt. I've done it so many times before.

The risk, though, goes with being King. And, whatever else I'm going to do, I have to be King. For a little while, at least. Time to put on my invisible crown— maybe my real one, too—straighten my tie, grab my lapels, stand up straight, and act like I know what I'm doing.

I really wish I did.

I turned on the lights and did a little spell-work. The mountain has veins of metal and other minerals it squeezes out of its structure. Lower down, in the forges, it does this with iron and coal, possibly some other metals—I haven't checked recently. Higher up, in what I used to think of the metals room, it does this mainly with gold and silver—the royal treasury. I looked in on it earlier and it appeared to have stopped when thirty or forty pounds of the stuff accumulated. My message spell for the mountain restarted the process and set a higher limit. I might need a hundred thousand pieces of gold in the near future.

I wonder where they keep the stamping thing for making coins? Or do they just hammer them out by hand?

With the money sorted out, I opened the door. Mary and Kammen were waiting. Seldar was nowhere to be seen.

"Seldar?"

"Off doing the organizing and operations thing," Mary replied.

"Did he say if he was avoiding me?"

"No. Why?"

"He made a very pointed point, and one I disliked as much as I appreciated."

"That's weird, even for you," Mary observed.

"I know."

"He said you might want him, though, and he'll be in your council chamber for a few hours."

"Good man."

"I'll say. If he wasn't married, I'd have to seriously consider taking him on as a substitute for when you're busy."

"Noted. I have a lot to do."

"That was my point," she agreed. "But, since I can't have a Seldar of my own, can I help?"

"Yes. You were going to tell me something about Lotar."

"Oh, yes!" she said, clapping her hands in delight. "He's *definitely* out to get you!"

"This is news on Mars, maybe, but not to me."

"But the details, my doofus dear, the details. Someone you may know broke into the building they're using as a temple—during the day—and stole a fair amount of his private correspondence. You'll never guess who he's been negotiating with."

"Thomen."

"Aww."

"Sorry."

"Yes, he was negotiating with Thomen. From what I've read, Lotar was ordered to base himself here by someone higher up—a patriarch of the church, something called the *deveas* of the Lord of Light."

"*Deveas* is sort of like a direct agent for the deity. God's spokesman. Amber would probably be Sparky's."

"And Beltar is yours?"

"Wash your mouth out," I suggested. She giggled and continued.

"Anyway, on this side of the Eastrange, the church could hope to avoid the Demon King's notice. When the King vanished, Lotar started pushing a major move into Rethven. Little cults all over the place geared up into actual churches and sent missionaries—or evangelists or whatever they're called—into any town or city lacking a franchise. When you reappeared, he started talking things over with Thomen about giving religious support in exchange for official sanction."

"Official sanction? The local religions don't need to be fill out a form. They just *are*."

"Lotar's negotiating for acknowledgment as the state religion."

I sat down and rubbed my temples. When I first arrived in Rethven, almost a century ago, the place was ruled by a king, had the Church of Light for a state religion, a failure of the dynasty, corruption in the church, a demonic Thing posing as their deity, and the organized hunting of vampires.

Everything could revert to that in amazingly short order. We were practically there already.

Is this how the world works? Or is it human nature? Which, of course, leads me back to my usual dilemma: I'm trying to change things without fully understanding how those changes will cause other changes. Like a little boy throwing a rock into a pond, I make ripples. Stopping the ripples is as futile as throwing in more rocks to make ripples to cancel out other ripples. It doesn't work.

And I'm still throwing rocks. Am I irresponsible, stupid, or too egotistical to care? Maybe they have their system and should be left alone. Have your kingdom, your church, your crazy vampire-hunting club. If you'll leave me out of it, I'll leave you alone, too.

No, that won't work. Religious fanatics on a holy mission never compromise, and if they do, they're lying about it.

"All right," I said, finally. "What did Lotar promise?"

"According to his latest letters—well, Thomen's latest letters—"

"Wait a second. Why is Thomen talking to Lotar via messenger? Why not use a magic mirror?"

"Sire?" Kammen offered.

"Yes, Kammen?"

"I can answer that one."

"By all means. It's not often I actually get answers."

"Two reasons. Lotar don't trust wizards and magicians. None of the Lighters do. The Hand uses 'em for stuff, if they swear to the Lord of Light, but there's no love for any of 'em. And makin' a mirror's a tough job. Some wizards will sell you one, sure, but it'll be days of work to make it."

"Seriously?" I asked. "It's not so hard."

"I'm the best of us three, Sire, at makin' mirrors and such," Kammen pointed out, "so I oughtta know. With all the respect due you, you ain't the best judge of what's hard for mortals."

"Well, no. I suppose not. But making a matched set of mirrors only takes an hour or so, at most."

"For you, Sire. You're a more than half-demon Thing with the powers of the gods, remember? And Thomen, he's the Guildmaster, but he's still a wizard. He hasn't done the magician thing for the higher magic, or whatever it is, and magicians take a couple days to put magic in a mirror. Like the rest of us, Thomen can't handle big powers without a lot of painted lines and chanting and helpers. He also don't gulp down souls and stuff them into things, neither."

"I do not—"

AHEM, Firebrand said.

"—usually—"

That's better.

"—do that sort of thing," I finished. I remembered the dragon-spirit, of course. Come to think of it, there was also the incident with Linnaeus, taking a little bit of his soul and enchanting it into the three instruments for him... and the tendrils of power I put into the blades for my first three knights, Torvil, Kammen, and Seldar. And a small herd of sheep when I attacked the Hand compound in Telen with a tornado...

"Don't matter," Kammen rumbled on. "Thomen's just a wizard when all's said and done. Making magic mirrors ain't something he does lightly. Nobody does. Nobody mortal. Most people don't send even messages anywhere, ever.

Sometimes rich people send letters. *We* use mirrors because you set a whole slew of 'em up for us."

"All right. So, from his point of view, he has good reason to communicate by letter. Question answered, and well done, Kammen."

"Pleasure to be of service, Sire."

"You were saying, Mary?"

"According to his latest letters, Thomen will get the most devout and faithful of the priests and under-priests in old Rethven seconded to him for the war. When the attack comes, the rest of the faithful will work from within to open the gates, create diversions, and so forth, in both Mochara and Karvalen. In return, Thomen agrees to reinstate the Church of Light as the state religion of Rethven."

"He can't do that."

"I don't see how anyone will stop him."

"No, I mean he's not the King. He can't do that."

"I didn't see anything about it in the papers I stole, but I'd guess he plans to be King after you're gone. Presumably, he can arrange for a marriage to Lissette whenever you're out of the way."

"That would follow," I mused. "Okay. Kammen?"

"Sire."

"Get whoever is next on bodyguard rotation on deck; you need to find Dantos. The two of you are going to get knights you trust and arrest Lotar."

"As you command, Sire." He saluted and grabbed his pocket mirror, calling for backup.

"Mary, you've done a spectacular job, and I'm going to have to find some way to express my thanks. I'll probably need handcuffs, but at least a rope. In the meantime, can I ask you to do a similarly-spectacular and dangerous job?"

"Does it involve breaking and entering?"

"Possibly. It certainly involves sneaking."

"Tell me more, my love, for you interest me strangely."

"How would you like to negotiate with and assist a house or three of magi?"

"How does that involve sneaking?"

"Without being noticed or caught by a much more powerful house of magi."

"Now it's getting interesting."

"My problem with Johann is I simply can't face him directly. He's too powerful on his home ground and there's no way to make him leave it. Thomen, on the other hand... I think I can deal with Thomen as soon as I figure out some details. But Johann worries me in another way. There's the time differential between universes. Time is passing over there, maybe faster, maybe slower, and Johann isn't sitting on his hands. He's either taking over the world or consolidating his power or plotting to do nasty things to me, possibly all at once. The tentacle-thing that showed up was probably his."

"Why do you think so? If you don't mind my asking."

"It wasn't demonic. It wasn't a Thing from beyond the world, outside the firmament. It was a biological organism. Around here, when someone sends something to kill me, it's a Thing. That, all by itself, tells me it isn't someone local."

"Oh."

"So I need someone to go back to your world and be my... negotiator? Ambassador? I don't know the word," I admitted. Mary nodded, thoughtfully.

"And I'm the only person—aside from yourself—who knows the place well enough to get by," she said, still nodding, one finger twirling a lock of hair while she thought.

"Well... yes. I'd rather keep you here to help me; I don't like dividing forces. As it is, if Johann is dumping nasty things into *this* world, he could wind up helping the local opposition without even knowing it. I don't need to be in the middle of an attack on the palace in Carrillon when a two-ton landshark surfaces behind me."

"I see the problem. And this needs to happen in a hurry?"

"That's the real issue. I don't know, and it worries me. Time could be going by faster over there. Even if it's going slower, there's a lot to get in motion. I can't fight on multiple fronts like this, especially with the logistics problems involved in inter-universal conflicts. I need to be two people, maybe three or four, and I haven't figured out how to do that."

"Yet. But the possibilities boggle the mind!" she added, smiling brilliantly.

"Yes, they do," I admitted, and paused to consider her smile. "You're not thinking what I'm thinking, are you?"

Mary bit her lower lip and looked at me through lowered lashes.

"No, that's not what I was thinking," I said. "But if I ever do manage to duplicate myself, I'm sure you'll have suggestions."

"Oh, I have all sorts of ideas already."

"I'm sure you do. But, back to my point? If we can get the other magi to engage the Fries family, that could be important here as well as there."

"All right. I'm on board. Assuming the other magi will listen, you want me to tell them... what?"

"At the moment, just sound them out. By now, I'm pretty sure they know how powerful Johann is. Do they want to serve him, fight him, hide from him, or what? Are they willing to face him if they have help? What do they know about the situation we don't? That sort of thing."

"I presume you're willing to help them."

"Oh, yes! Don't tell them I can open a nexus; if they don't already know it, I don't want them to. I'm afraid I'd have every house of magi in the world trying to get their own nexus and their own dome of power over their personal magical kingdom."

"Surely, they wouldn't all act like Johann."

"No, but Johann did. I don't want to tempt them with phenomenal cosmic power. I also don't want them blaming me for Johann."

"Another excellent point. What do you plan to do to help? They'll want to know."

"I'll provide magical energy so they can attack Johann effectively. Yes, I'll open up a nexus, but don't tell them how I'll provide it."

"Gotcha. I can do this. They'll also want to know what you get out of this."

"The enemy of my enemy is my friend. I want to kill Johann and his magically-enhanced family."

"Seems doable," Mary said, nodding. "I can pitch that, but I'm going to need some stuff."

"Already thinking about it. I'll be working on it today, possibly later tonight." I turned as the door opened. Torvil came in, exchanged salutes with Kammen, and took over guard duty. Kammen hurried off.

"Perfect! Torvil, show me to Tort's quarters. I'm looking for some gems she used to have. Or maybe T'yl's quarters. I'm not sure who had them last."

"Can I come?" Mary asked.

"I'd rather meet you. Could you run up to our quarters and find Diogenes?"

"You mean your computer drive?"

"Yes, please."

"What on earth for?"

"We're not on Earth," I pointed out, "and I'd rather show you."

"You better bring a lot of rope when I get back from this business trip," she warned. "I plan to put up quite a fight."

"I'll have some straps made. *Dazhu* leather is stronger than you'd think."

"Deal." She skipped off and Torvil led me to Tort's chambers.

I liked them. Not very lived-in, though. This wasn't her residence. This was someplace she occasionally inhabited. It had the feel of a backup apartment, a crash pad, a place to go when you don't want to go home. Maybe a vacation cabin, something that only sees use every other year or so. I'm not sure why I had such a feeling, though. A lot of close work with Tort's psychic resonance, maybe? I could be oversensitive to impressions she left behind. Come to that, I could just be oversensitive.

Whatever, it was only a feeling. I turned my attention to searching the place. Torvil cautioned me about a particular box. I left it alone for the moment and searched for the quantum computer cores. I didn't see them, so I did a quick spell to scan for them. Still no sign of them.

Which left me with a heavily-warded and sealed box.

Under normal circumstances, I wouldn't go through Tort's stuff, especially anything as heavily protected as this. The magic on it was of a different order than the type I was familiar with. It reminded me of some of the magician-class things Tort and T'yl did—spells I didn't understand, like flying, phasing through walls, and so on. I could tell some of what the wards on the box did, but the mechanism of action was something of a mystery.

I'm one hell of a wizard, but as a magician I need a lot of work.

Fortunately, I didn't see the need to open it. All I wanted was to find out whether or not the gems were in it. So I x-rayed and radar scanned it. I put a spectrum-shifting spell on either side of the box, shone a light at the upshifting side and looked at it through the downshifting side.

Nope, no computer cores. What it did have was a trio of large, heavy keys. All I saw were silhouettes, so I couldn't be sure, but I suspected they were keys salvaged from the ruins of Telen. Magical keys the Church of Light—well, the Hand—used to open gates to my world.

It was immensely tempting to bash the box open on the spot. I resisted it; I didn't feel like dealing with whatever unpleasantness the wards did. Besides, T'yl used one of the things in his attempt to send me home and he *still* missed!

Obviously, they weren't foolproof. Or maybe they needed to be used in particular ways. Regardless, these three weren't going anywhere. They'd been left alone for months, possibly years.

I asked the mountain to hide the box for me. It started sinking into the floor. That would work.

We moved on to T'yl's rooms.

These looked much more… lived-in. I don't want to call T'yl a slob. I'm not sure what else to call him, though. Don't misunderstand; his rooms and everything in them were clean. No dust, no dirt, no grime, nothing. But the blankets and furs on the bed-platform were in a bunch. Scrolls and books were stacked haphazardly where they weren't in piles. Several plates were scattered around the room—cleaned of any trace of food, to be sure, but still implying a rather lackadaisical housekeeping. I can understand why no one entered the professional magician's rooms to clear away dishes, but I would have thought his animated suit of armor could stack the mess in neater piles.

Come to that, where is that suit of armor? Tort might still have it, I suppose.

There was no way I intended to search the chaos by hand. I went straight to my sensor spell. It registered hits, so I started digging. I came across his flying carpet, the magical rope I salvaged from the assault force that attacked Karvalen, a number of animated image crystals—video recordings, basically. Yes, I found his porn stash, which told me a lot more about him than I really wanted to know—and some magical underwear. Enchanted socks, shorts, that sort of thing, made to keep the wearer warm or cool, dry and clean. I also found several regular crystals—nonmagical, but high quality—as well as the computer crystals.

T'yl never truly understood what they were, but he knew I valued them. He went to the trouble of having a box made with little niches and velvet lining. Very thoughtful. Of course, then he put it down somewhere and forgot about it. It was pressed up against a heap of scrolls, keeping the pile of them stable.

The box contained eight crystals, quantum computer cores salvaged from a post-apocalyptic world with advanced computer technology. I brought back a dozen. Did they break some? Did they find a use for them? I know they tried to put me in one when the initial stages of my exorcism went wrong. Are they good for containing spirits you don't want wandering off?

Hurray! More questions I can't answer.

I tried to ignore the angry feeling. I don't like not knowing, but you'd think I'd be used to it by now. I'm probably a little more sensitive than usual, these days. I know I'm getting better, but will I ever be back to my old self? I'll never again be the mild-mannered professor who poured students out of the car and onto their various lawns, but maybe I can be less of a rage-monster.

In some ways, it would be easier to turn green and wake up somewhere else, afterward. People would know when to run, at least, and I wouldn't feel so responsible for the mess. I think.

Another quick scan of the room failed to find any magical keys. Which doesn't mean there weren't any, only that they didn't show up on a scan. They might be in another heavily-warded, magically-sealed box… buried under a pile of stuff. I couldn't take time to put the room in order and inventory the place. If there were more keys, I'd find them later.

With the box of crystals in hand, I headed back to my workroom. There were a lot of things to do.

Mary was already waiting. Diogenes was on a table.

"Thanks. Now, let's get you set up."

"In what way?"

"Versatility, wealth, and stealthiness. And a letter of introduction."

"Have you a plan?"

"I know a family of magi who seem exceedingly polite. Two, actually, but only one of them strikes me as trustworthy. The Etienne family seem like reasonable people; the Wilmont family would probably sell us out if they could get a good enough price. If push comes to shove, we might try the Stuarts."

"The Etienne family... they're in France?" Mary asked.

"Yep. Avignon, if I remember the return address right. Will that be a problem?"

"Bien sûr que non. Je peux me débrouiller assez bien."

I looked at her for a moment while she grinned at me.

She said it won't be a problem, Firebrand translated. *She's sure she can get by.*

You know, I almost understood her?

"I'm sure you can," I told Mary. "Remind me to eat some more French."

"Delicious."

"I wasn't asking for an evaluation."

"Your loss. Anything else I need to do?"

I hesitated for several seconds. I had an idea, but I didn't like my idea.

"Mary, we don't know how things have gone over there. It may have been minutes or years. The world may have barely changed, or there might be craters with a bluish glow at night. If the world is even remotely functional—economically, that is—I want you to get a yacht."

"I've always wanted my own yacht. Don't you hate boats, though?"

"No, I simply despise their tendency to sink when I get on them. But get the yacht—something seagoing, with engines; I'm no sailor. Wait, can you sail?"

"I spent several of my pre-college summers on a sailing yacht."

"Figures," I said, disgusted.

"But I'm by no means a professional. I know what I'm doing, sort of, but we'll want something you and I can drive. Where do you want to go in it? Or do you want it as a floating hideout?"

"We need something we can take all over the world, preferably without refueling."

"That's called an expedition yacht. They make all sorts with a wide variety of power and propulsion. I'll see what I can find."

"I'd favor endurance over comfort. I'll get you a list of specialty equipment, too."

"Speaking of equipment, what have you got for me, Q?"

"First off, Jane Bond, we get you the usual sort of stuff. Clothes, money—mostly gold and gems—a letter to the Etiennes, and your weapons. I'll enchant something to keep you off the magical detection radar. I'm not sure we can risk inter-universal messages; Johann might notice gate activity, especially if we keep doing it. We may have to rely on rendezvous points. Once we're daylit on this side and not likely to fry by accident, I hit the big gate, drop you off in France, and you do your thing."

"Assuming you open it and we don't see a boiling wasteland?"

"Exactly. Or a ton of death-squad goons taking aim at our portal."

"Okay. What do you want, exactly, from the Etiennes?"

"I'd like to know how they feel about Johann and his magical Kingdom of the Dome. If they're against it, I'd also like to know if they're willing to help me out when I try to turn Johann into pâté de foie grouch."

"Sounds good. Any ideas on how they can help?"

"The very first thing is to get suggestions, because I have no idea what they *can* do. I'm prepared to pay for any help, but first see if they're willing to come at this from the standpoint of allies, rather than mercenaries for hire."

"Ah, yes. Appeal to their self-interest first, then greed."

"I knew you'd understand."

"What if they want to have an open nexus of their own?"

"Again, it's a last resort, assuming they even know about opening a nexus. I don't really relish the idea of unleashing more soulless monsters of enormous power on the world. I'd rather not, if it can be avoided."

"Do I need to know how to do the nexus thing?"

"Remember seeing the process?"

"I watched. There's no way I can do it."

"Step inside; we'll go over the spell. If you think you need to open a nexus, you should be able to."

"No, I don't think so. Your tendrils are big, angry things. My tendril is more delicate, as befits my feminine nature."

"More vicious and quick instead of brutal and strong?"

"Exactly! See, that's one reason I like you so much. You get me."

"Come inside," I countered. "You've got a spell to learn."

"No way," she countered, shaking her head. "I'm not going into a coven's lair with that kind of knowledge in my head. They might pry my skull open to get it out. Besides, I'm certain it wouldn't do any good. I *can't* do it, not even if I do learn the spells."

"Really? Does it seem so difficult?"

Mary laid a gentle hand on my arm. I cocked my head at her.

"Halar, one of your more adorable failings is your complete and utter lack of perspective. You don't have a sense of scale, much less a clue, do you?"

"I had a clue, once, but I put it in a box so I wouldn't lose it. As soon as I find the box, I'll let you know."

"I'm serious. You really don't understand how dangerously powerful you are, do you? How people look at you and see something so fiendishly terrifying they would rather jump into a swimming pool of angry rattlesnakes than attract your attention?"

"Sure I do. I'm a monster, a king, and I know all sorts of dangerous spells—"

"Sweetheart?" she interrupted. I stopped and blinked at her.

"Yes? Dear?"

"What's the most difficult and powerful spell you know?"

"That's easy. Gate spells. Awful things, especially the full version. You can use an abbreviated form of one for point-to-point within a single world, but crossing—"

"Stop talking. Now, this full gate spell. How many people do you know who can cast it?"

"Uh... me?"

"Could you teach it to someone?"

"Of course."

"And could that someone cast it?"

"Sure. Magicians in Zirafel even built a permanent gate with the complicated version. Why, I don't know. Even modern magicians have an extremely simplified version for local movement. Of course, they don't have to account for the rotation of a spherical world or the change in orientation when—"

"But," Mary cut me off, "this short and simple version is something the average magician just fires up and uses?"

"Well... no. It's usually something they spend several days enchanting and charging. They don't cast the spell directly because of the complexity and power demands of—"

"Then how do you manage?" she interrupted.

"Oh, I'm a vampire. I have an enormous capacity for channeling energies. My flesh doesn't boil away like mortal flesh does, so it can handle higher loads. I've also spent a lot of time in an Ascension Sphere, accidentally training up to endure higher powers. And there was an incident with the temporary transmogrification to a higher plane of existence, but I managed to get out of that."

Mary nodded, looking expectant.

"And?" I asked.

Mary shook her head, sighing.

"I think you may not be equipped to understand."

"There are a lot of things like that," I admitted. "I still can't tell the difference between eggshell and off-white. I think it's a guy thing."

"Just take my word for it. You're much more terrifying than you suspect, and I shouldn't know the spell. All right?"

"Well... if you're sure?"

"I'm sure. Trust me."

"I can do that."

Torvil shoved open the door while we were talking and stuck his head into the room.

"Sire?"

"What's the trouble, Torvil?"

"Sire, the high priest of the lights has been arrested and is waiting."

"Oh, excellent! Where is he?"

"In the dungeons, Sire."

I took a moment to absorb that.

"I have dungeons?"

"Indeed, Sire," he assured me. I gave Mary a sidelong look.

"I have dungeons," I told her, raising my eyebrows. Mary poked me in the ribs. I rubbed the sudden sore spot.

"Keep your mind on business," she advised.

"I didn't think I'd ever hear that from you. I mean, *dungeons*."

She poked me again. I resolved to keep my mind on business.

"Well, I guess I should go see the dungeons. Is he the only prisoner?" I asked. Torvil chuckled.

"Have you ordered anyone else arrested, Sire?"

"Good point."

The dungeons in question aren't part of the palace proper, but they are in the undercity. They serve as holding cells for use by the city guard. To reach the dungeons, one goes through chambers used by the city guard, in fact—I'd call it a police station. Under normal circumstances, the cops are all over the station, effectively guarding the dungeons, and today there was also a sizable contingent of people in black, fancy armor. The black armor came in two sorts, average (for the grey sashes) and ridiculously big (for the red).

Everyone in black came to attention and drew swords, saluting. Everyone else either did the hands-over face thing or the fist-on-floor thing. Mary seemed quite pleased and held on to my arm.

"Torvil?" I asked, quietly.

"Sire?"

"How many of these people are my knights?"

"Several. The big ones, red sashes."

"And the rest?"

"Temple of Shadow. Grey sashes."

"Why did we involve them?"

"You said to get people I could trust. Dantos didn't think the knights of the local baron fit the bill for something this sensitive, so I got volunteers from the Temple. They aren't your *personal* knights—you didn't knight them—but they've taken the vow before the Lord of Shadows and they're under Lord Beltar's command."

"Ah."

I gave them an empty-handed salute and they resheathed weapons. One of the regular-sized figures came over to me, went to one knee, and did the thing Salishar did, the cross-hands-over-the-face thing, before putting a fist on the floor.

"Your Majesty, I am Ariander, priest of the Temple of Shadow, First Blade of the Order." I noticed his name started with a vowel, a *gata* indicator, but I didn't feel like chasing that rabbit just at the moment.

"Pleased to meet you. Get up. Where's the prisoner?"

"If Your Majesty will follow me?" He rose and led the way. A tide of armored figures flowed aside. It was like parting a deep sea of ink. We went into the chambers behind the guard offices, passed by the equivalent of minimum-security, went through medium-security, and finally came to the maximum-security holding cells—the dungeon.

It was a long, wide hallway with a path on one side and a number of pivot-doors in a row on the other. Most were open; one was bolted to keep it closed. I looked down through an open one. Below it was a square pit, smooth-sided, fifteen to twenty feet deep, about ten feet across. The floor was a slant, smoothly sloped from one wall to another. A small trickle of water dribbled down the deeper side; it drained through a narrow crack at the bottom. There was no furniture, nowhere to sit, and no toilet. If the prisoner was thirsty, licking water off the wall was the only option. It was also poorly ventilated and probably colder than most places under the mountain.

Yeah, this wasn't someplace you wanted to stay. It was someplace you stayed because someone really wanted you to. Someone who didn't like you.

As we went to the closed floor-door, I saw a hole in it, about two inches in diameter.

"What's the hole in the door for?" I asked.

"Air and gruel."

Apparently, the plan was to never remove a prisoner once confined. None of these weenie ideas about exercise time or yard time or any of that. This was an oubliette.

Ariander threw the two bolts holding the pivot door closed. A light touch started the carefully-balanced stone swinging. He stopped it when it reached a vertical position. I conjured a light and shone it down.

A middle-aged fellow in some rather dirty robes glared up at me. From the looks of him, he recently had a nosebleed. Other than that, he didn't seem hurt. His feet were braced against the wall on the deeper side as he reclined on the cold, sloping floor. He sat up as the light hit him.

"You can't keep me here!" he shouted. "I am the High Priest of the Light!"

"What is it with people? They keep telling me I can't do things when the evidence clearly points the other way."

"I will be delivered from this dank confinement and deliver vengeance *sevenfold* upon you!"

"Can you swim?" I asked.

"What?" he asked, confused. "What's that got to do with anything?"

"If I can't keep you here, I suppose I should lock the door and flood the pit. So, before you start telling me what I can and can't do, maybe you should consider what I *will* do."

"Hearken to me, filth! You are an abomination of life and all things pure! You shall be cast down and condemned to the darkness of the underworld—"

I pushed the pivot-door so it swung closed and waited for the screaming to die down. A quick word to one of the armored gentlemen accompanying us and a couple of buckets of water were brought in. They poured the water down the gruel-hole. The screaming changed pitch, from angry to panicky. After four buckets of water, I called a halt to it and nodded to have them pivot the door open again.

A wet, frightened, and angry priest looked up at me. His comment was remarkably profane, involving as it did my mother, a scorpion, and a pile of feces. I figured he had cause to be upset, so I didn't take him seriously. Mary suppressed a smile and turned away. Torvil simply stood there, inscrutable in his helmet.

"Yes, surely," I agreed, "but at least my mother knows who my father was. Now, if you can cut out the religious rhetoric and profanity, I'd like to discuss the political future of the kingdom of Rethven. Hold it!" I snapped, as he opened his mouth. "Before you say *one more word*, understand this: I'm in no mood for screwing around. For every pious mouthing you spit out, I will remove something from your body. Starting with toes and moving up one joint at a time. Once we get to your hips, I'll start over on the fingertips. And before you tell me I can't do that, consider the difference between 'can't,' and 'I don't want you to.' And look where you're standing."

I glared at him. He glared back.

"Now," I said, more softly, "I'm going to have you brought before me. Use the time to consider what you can realistically get away with and how many body parts you're prepared to lose in finding out."

I turned to Ariander.

"Put him in chains and bring him to the great hall," I said, speaking loudly enough for Lotar to hear me. "If he gives you any trouble at all, beat him unconscious and drag him by the chains."

"As Your Majesty commands."

A wee bit touchy, Boss?

I've only met two priests of this light-god who I like, I replied, *and both of them are dead. The rest of them killed women I loved and hunted me. One of them made deals with magicians, demons, and even one of the other so-called gods of this world. The last time I encountered their deity, it was being eaten from within by a demon who wanted to shatter the firmament and let the Things Beyond into the world. So, yeah, I might be a little less nice to them than a diplomatic, tactful king really should be.*

I understand. I'm not sure most other people will. They'll just see the Demon King again, Boss.

Damn! You're right. I have to be **nice** *all the time, don't I?*

Yeah. Slow walk back to the palace while you cool down?

I would, but I don't have the time. Too much to do and I need to set stuff up in the great hall.

We left the guard station and headed back up. Torvil led the way, but Mary stopped me in a ladderway. She grabbed my head and kissed me, hard. When she let me breathe again, I asked my question.

"What was that for?"

"For the bit in the dungeons. That was the man I was looking for."

"Lotar?"

"Not what I meant, moron," she countered, running fingers through my hair. "If you weren't busy being a powerful, confident ruler, I'd have your domineering butt up in the bedroom for the rest of the day."

"There's something not quite right about your statement."

"Yes. You're busy. Pity."

We chased after Torvil, who waited when he realized we stopped. He didn't come back for us, though—quite the soul of discretion.

We took all the shortcuts back up. Mary went off to do whatever Mary does when she's not baby-sitting me. I didn't ask.

Instead, I grabbed crystals and set them up around the throne end of the room, embedding them in the walls. Torvil helped; he kept them pressed in place while the mountain slowly slurped around them, mounting them in place. Given the tree/vine motif of the metallic veins in the walls, I think they blended it quite well—rare fruits, or something. A little spell-work to set them up and I was ready for Lotar.

Naturally, Lotar wasn't there, yet. Torvil checked on their progress. Someone decided to take him outside and up the Kingsway, rather than travel up inside the mountain. Oh, well. I hadn't intended to make such a public production out of it, but his arrest was probably news everywhere already. We still had some time to wait.

I was on a roll and didn't feel like sitting around. I took Torvil back to the workroom and started setting up my Tort-detector. We picked up another knight, there. His name was Gilam and he was from the Temple of Shadow. Seldar picked him as one of the additional guards for the King. Frankly, I thought of him as some fresh-faced kid. He may have been a full-grown, well-trained knight, but he still looked the part of the eager-beaver sidekick who gets killed in the second act to establish how awful the villain is. His job was to follow Torvil around and learn the drill.

Poor guy. If he thought of me in religious terms, he was going to be amazingly disappointed. I hoped I could keep him alive long enough to get away from me and any unexpected meteor strikes in my vicinity.

Once I powered up my newest Tort-detecting spell, I started searching. It wasn't rocket science. All I did was stand behind the spell's dish and swing it in a very slow circle, listening intently for a clear, steady tone—the resonance between the signature built into it and the signals it received.

Three hundred and sixty degrees of scan and all I got was static.

Damn.

Well, should I be surprised? If Tort is dead, I won't find her. However, since she's alive—I choose to believe she's alive—and I don't know how she managed it, she *must* be more clever than I. She's concealed herself from this form of detection as well. She's a professional, after all, while I'm merely a talented dabbler in the dark arts.

It still pissed me off. Torvil sensed it and escorted Gilam out of the room to give me some privacy. I didn't thank him; I was too frustrated to speak. This was a huge disappointment, and the way it hit me shocked me. Of course, I know why it bothered me so much. I'm still fragile after… well, everything. Knowing I'm fragile and why still doesn't help, though. In some ways, it makes things worse, because I know I'm stronger than this, even though I'm not, and it frustrates me further, causing a spiral of emotional chaos.

I got a grip on myself and deliberately calmed down. I settled to the floor and did my best to breathe and center myself. No Tort. Fine. Maybe Sir Sedrick had something by now. Probably not, but I could call him on his mirror and ask what he discovered. I did so, apologizing for the brief conversation and for pestering him for a report.

"Think nothing of it, Your Majesty," replied his image in the mirror. "I have discovered few clues, and most of those regarding your other magician, T'yl. I have some evidence he is a prisoner of the Duke of Vathula."

"I just got a report from there about how they killed him."

"Yes, I've heard that. I've heard how they killed him on two different occasions. This makes me think they did not do so at all, but were deceived."

I recalled the remains I found that were supposed to be Tort. If she could construct a duplicate to attract assassins and assaults, why couldn't T'yl? And, if you do that, you want to defend them... but not too hard. Just hard enough to convince someone he got the target.

"I've seen some things to make me think you're right," I admitted. "Anything on Tort at all?"

"Not since the Demon King went to Karvalen. I suspect she had some sort of plans already laid, rather than a sudden urge to hide. It does not do to run from an immortal. It attracts their attention."

"I know her. She definitely planned it out in meticulous detail."

"Then I will continue to investigate."

"Thank you. Need any help?"

"Not at present. I shall continue to seek your Tort and T'yl."

"Thank you for all your efforts, Sir Sedrick."

"It is a dream of every Hero to rescue a kidnapped lady at the behest of a king. Thank you, Your Majesty."

We signed off and I headed back to the main hall. It was time to browbeat the clergyman.

The main doors opened. I was already on the throne, ankles crossed on the dragon's nose. Torvil stood on my right and the new guy, Gilam, on my left. The firepits were burning brightly and throwing light all over the golden ceiling, illuminating the whole room. The side doors were closed, with guards outside to keep them that way.

Surrounding Lotar, forty men in black armor came in through the main doors. He was cleaner than I recalled, but wearing chains. He was also walking on his own feet. Maybe my comment about beating him unconscious and dragging him encouraged cooperation. It boded well for our future relations.

The rest of the floor was clear, but up in the gallery, people packed together along the rail. The Demon King summoned the High Priest. This should be a good show.

Witnesses were a good thing, at least for the first part of My Nefarious Plan.

The escort stopped at the foot of the dais and parted enough to let Lotar forward. He didn't have a lot of choice; the men behind him pushed him until he was on the lowest step.

"Good afternoon," I offered. "Do you have anything to say for yourself?"

I waited patiently while he launched into his diatribe about "creature of evil," "Demon King," "son of the Lord of Darkness," and so forth. Knights shifted restlessly behind him, clearly ready to turn him into cutlets on the spot. I sat back on my not-too-uncomfortable chunk of rock and smiled, waiting for Lotar to wind down. So far, he was being perfectly predictable, which suited me. Besides, I was trying to work a couple of small, special-effects sorts of spells while he rambled on.

When he finally ran down—I think he ran out of religious insults and wasn't willing to stoop to simple vulgarities in public—I uncrossed my ankles and leaned forward.

"Now that you've made your position abundantly clear, to me and to everyone present, it seems you have absolutely no tolerance for me. At all. In any way. Am I correct?"

Naturally, this set him off again. I waited until he was through; it was a much shorter outburst.

"Leave us," I commanded. "Seal the doors. Lotar and I will speak alone." I nodded at Torvil and then at Gilam. Torvil frowned, eyed Lotar, and eyed me. I nodded at him again, so he took Gilam with him as he left. Everyone filed out in a reasonably orderly fashion. We waited some more, the guards closed the doors, and the room grew quiet.

"Okay, Lotar; we're alone."

"Kill me if you will, creature of evil! It matters not that no one sees—my death will be on your hands!"

"I'm surprisingly okay with that. It's the duty of my kind to escort important people out of the world when their time comes, but I'll stoop to helping you. Not today, though."

"You will not kill me?" I wasn't sure if he was more surprised or disappointed.

"That's correct. See, here's the deal. I know you and I aren't going to get along. Your Church has a long history of being unpleasant to nightlords and nothing I can do will change it. I've got a history of being unpleasant to the Hand—a sect within your Church—and, by my standards, for good reason. We're not going to agree on much."

"Except that."

"Pretty much. However, can we agree hunting nightlords through magical gates has been… shall we say… less than wonderfully successful?"

Lotar thought about it, trying to see where I was going.

"Perhaps."

"If you hadn't been opening gates and hunting for us in other worlds, you would never have come to my attention. I wouldn't be here. True?"

"True."

"Then I'll make you a deal."

"No."

"You haven't even heard it."

"I will not bargain with one whose very blood is corrupted by the outer darkness!"

I sighed and counted to thirteen. Ten wasn't enough.

"Here's a dilemma for you," I said. "What do you do when what you want is the same thing I want? If you say a certain man needs to die and I attempt to kill him, do you stop me?"

"I…" he began, and stopped, perplexed. Then he rallied. "I will not stoop to debate—"

"Hear me out, because that's kind of the situation we're in. Of course, if you don't want to listen, I'll publish these," I added, and tossed him the folio of letters. He picked it up and opened it, flipping through them.

"Where did you get these?" he demanded.

"I'm a king. People talk to me. They bring me things. They give me presents. Especially if they think it will help them in some way. I won't say who gave them to me, but do you know anyone who might benefit if your involvement in these matters was revealed?"

"No one will believe this," he said, but I thought I detected a smattering of doubt. "These are not proof."

"Proof? Who said anything about proof? What matters is what people believe, isn't it? Don't you deal in belief? You don't care about ultimate truth as long as people can be made to believe what you want."

Lotar was silent for several seconds, thinking quickly. He glanced backward.

"Make a move toward a firepit and I'll disembowel you," I said, calmly. He shrugged. I doubt the chains on his wrists and ankles were the deciding factor. He closed the folio, and threw it back to me. I put it in the mouth of the dragon throne, sliding it between two of the teeth.

"What do you want?" Lotar asked.

"To give you a chance at everything you want."

"I don't understand."

"Right now, you're guilty of treason. As the leader of your Church, you've made a deal with Thomen, backing him in his bid for the throne. From a religious standpoint, it's your holy war against the Demon King. From a political standpoint, it's a chance to regain, at a stroke, the influence you once had in Rethven—for your Church, of course. And, as the leader of the Church in Rethven, it will put you on par with Thomen when he's crowned King." I paused as a thought struck me.

"You're planning doing the crowning, too, as part of the deal to make him King," I guessed. "It will add another layer of Church authority, being seen to hold the power to crown a king, make him official. And all that is on the way to a ruling religion, supplanting temporal authority. And, of course, one with you at the top." Lotar kept eye contact, never flinching, and his face stayed in perfect neutral. That was enough to convince me my guesses were right.

"As I said, what do you want?"

"I'm willing to offer you a counterproposal. Recall your faithful followers from their holy war. Wait until the political infighting is over. Then evangelize and missionary-ize all you want. If your religion is destined to be the one true right and only way, then you'll eventually win. In the meantime, you, personally, will have at least a moderate amount of power and wealth, all the comforts you might desire. I won't interfere with you as long as you don't interfere with me.

"Alternatively, you can continue to back Thomen. Go down that road and you risk everything. *Everything.* First off, I'll immediately have a night of the long knives; everyone wearing a medallion of the light will die, tonight, and vanish from the face of the world. No one will know what happens to them. No one will ever see or hear anything. They'll simply fall off the edge of the world, never to be seen again.

"The only exception will be you. You will go back into a deep pit, there to live out your long, miserable life in darkness and in filth until it pleases me to drag you out—old, withered, and blind—and present you to your god as the man who provoked me to destroy his worshippers. Do you think he'll be pleased to see you? I don't."

"You're saying I can support you or support Thomen?"

"No, I'm saying you can support Thomen or stay out of it."

"You're not asking for my support?"

"Of course not! You can't make such a deal and I know it. All I want is for you to stop meddling. I don't want your religion—or any other—involved with politics in the first place." I shrugged. "But you can do whatever you please. We're not making a deal. We're not negotiating. I'm telling you what the consequences will be."

Lotar paced back and forth, chains clinking slightly, hands clasped together before him, eyes on the floor. I wondered what was going through his head.

You want me to look, Boss?

Not really. I wouldn't subject you to a snake-pit like that.

"You say if I support Thomen—"

"The usurper."

"—Thomen, the usurper, you will declare war on my faith."

"No. I'll simply kill all the priests I ever find. Incidentally, what did happen to Perrin? I know I didn't throw him off the Kingsway."

"His death is irrelevant."

"I disagree. I've already taken the blame for it. I think I deserve to know. Besides, if you tell me, I'll be more kindly disposed toward you. Considering where you're standing, my goodwill is a pearl beyond price."

Lotar sneered at me.

"Perrin was a naïve fool, believing only in the power of his faith, not in the power of the Church. I sent him up to face you, but you sent him back. Thomen was clever enough to anticipate your move; his servants in the Wizards' Guild made sure Perrin did not come down the Kingsway."

"That makes perfect sense. Perrin was an obstacle—or his kind of priest is an obstacle—to the temporal power of the Church. Do you have a lot of those?" Another thought struck me. "Or is that part of the deal with Thomen? You send the most faithful and, as you put it, naïve of the priesthood to fight in a war. That either breaks them of their naïveté or gets them killed. Maybe more of the latter than the former. Is that part of the deal?"

"I will not discuss internal affairs of the Church with you."

"I suppose it's really none of my business how you kill each other off," I agreed. "Back to the main point: Are you planning to continue being a vexation to me? Or are you going to keep your nose out of the political arena and stick to outmaneuvering the faiths of other gods?"

"If I choose to challenge your rule? I spend the rest of my life in a dungeon pit?"

"Yes."

"But if I withdraw my support of Thomen—yes, yes, the usurper—you will leave me alone?"

"You'll be leaving me alone, staying out of my business. I'll return the favor and stay out of yours. I will give you my word on it, if you like, but I doubt you think it's worth anything."

"And if we come into conflict with the Temple of Shadow or the Temple of Flame?"

"Conflict all you like, but in my kingdom, bloodshed and other violence is the province of the King. You can persuade the people to worship; you can ask, offer, or cajole. But you don't force anyone into a religion, you don't muster troops, and you don't kill people simply for disagreeing."

"I reject your proposal."

We looked at each other for several seconds.

"May I ask why?" I asked, gently.

"You are a dark thing and cannot be trusted."

"That's it?"

"People are fools, as well. They cannot be trusted to do what is right. They must be taken in hand and made to see the truth of the Light. They must follow the right path, even if, in their stupidity, they refuse it. I will see it done, no matter what. It is my duty and my right as Rethven's Patriarch of the Light."

"How will you do all this from a dungeon pit?"

"I don't believe you will do that, either. You are not a complete fool. Too many already know of my arrest. Even now, the Church must be gathering the faithful. They will come for me, a never-ending horde of believers, until you are cast down and destroyed."

"Kind of like when you sent a lot of your faithful to kill the Demon King several months ago? Right here, in this very mountain. Oh! Was that an attempt to kill the Demon King? Or just a way to reduce the true faithful by attrition? Or both?"

"You say the Demon King was not truly you, do you not? It was a possessing spirit?" he asked, smugly.

"You have a point. I suppose I can't hold the attempt against you. But now? Won't an open attack on the proper king damage the Church? And what about your letters? Don't you think the nobility of Rethven will take a dim view of your interference?"

"I am worth it. Without me, the Church in Rethven is nothing. I am the leader; I am the Patriarch of Rethven and answer only to the *deveas* of the true Church. The letters are nothing; you cannot prove they are mine. More, trying to discredit me with them will only help me ferret out those fools whose faith in me is weaker than their faith in the Light. To do so will only add to my power. I will purge those who do not follow me unquestioningly. Under my guidance, my Church will ascend again to its rightful place, commanding the obedience of all who live and breathe within this kingdom, making the power of my Church absolute. Then may I cleanse the world in light!"

"Oh. In that case, you are free to go."

"What?"

"Go. Get out. Beat it. Scram. You're cluttering up my throne room and I have things to do. The door is behind you."

"You're... letting me go?"

"Of course. Who do you think I am? The Demon King? I'm me again, no longer possessed by the monster."

I reached out with a sharp gesture and yanked his medallion into my hand. It was more effort than I let on—during the day, my ability to move things with my mind is rather weak—but I wanted this for the theatrics.

Story of my life, sort of. All the really cool-looking moves are harder than they seem.

The medallion's chain flipped up over his head and the thing sailed through the air to my hand. I held it there, on my palm, and moved it a bit to reflect the light. I wanted it very visible, both for witnesses and to worry Lotar.

"See? Not a trace of smoke," I observed.

"Give it back!" he demanded, taking a step up toward the throne.

"No, I don't think so," I said, putting it on. "I rather like it. Solid gold, is it?"

"Of course! And it is a holy thing, not to be touched by the likes of you!"

I flicked it a couple of times where it hung on my chest.

"It doesn't seem to mind. But, as I said, you can go."

"Give it back!" he repeated, and took another step up the stairs. I stepped down and stood in front of the dragon's snout, grinning, feet planted, hands formed into fists. I beckoned with one finger.

"Come and take it," I invited.

Lotar looked at me, looked at his medallion, snorted, and walked away, chains still clinking. Pity, that. At least he was going to have fun shuffling back down the Kingsway and through the streets in his chains.

I turned off the recording crystals and started removing them from the walls. Torvil came back in, followed by Gilam.

"Sire?"

"Couldn't have gone better."

"Good to know, Sire. What now?"

"Now I get some enchanting done for Mary. Take these out of the walls," I told him, indicating the recording crystals. I also handed him the medallion. "Make sure Seldar reviews them. I'll want his opinion on who to show them to. Put the medallion away, somewhere. By the way, who do you know who gets along best with Malana and Malena?"

"Kammen," he replied, instantly.

"Seriously?"

"He is… very charming, Sire. When he wants to be."

"That's hard to imagine," I admitted.

"But true. Most women find him fascinating. Part of it is his reputation, I think."

"Reputation? For what?"

"We are giants, Sire, and it is said the size of Kammen's—"

"No," I interrupted. "I withdraw the question. I don't want to know." I added, muttering under my breath, "You think you know someone…" More loudly, I said, "Okay, I'll talk with him when he comes on shift later. For now, go do the Seldar thing. Gilam will escort me to the lab."

Seldar showed up in the lab while I worked on Mary's I'm-Not-Here ring. I put considerable effort into it, double-layering it, both to spoof active magical detection and block passive detection—false imaging for the scanners, cloaking from the sensors. As far as any of my detection methods went, she ought to register as herself, albeit a nondescript, unexceptional, mortal version of herself. Hiding the magic of the effect was trickier, as it involved hiding the emanations of magic from a magic spell by using magic... but I had some examples from Zirafel to draw on. As long as no one probed her at close range, I was confident the ring would keep her hidden.

Which made me wonder. How does this sort of effort scale with other magic-workers? Was it really so hard for normal people—okay, normal wizards—to do this kind of thing? I mean, sure, some people can work quadratic equations in their heads and do cube roots without a calculator. Others have a talent for spelling. Some people can even differentiate between six thousand shades of blue. In each case, it just comes naturally to them. They look at other people and think, "What, you mean it isn't obvious?" Am I in that situation? Do I simply not see how hard magic really is?

At any rate, Seldar came in, saw I was busy, and went away again. I would gladly have spoken with him, but some things can't be stopped and picked up again; they have to be done in one go or you start over. It's one of the many drawbacks to magical construction.

He did come back, though, somewhat later. I was putting the finishing touches on Mary's ring—the equivalent of making sure all the screws were tight and all the lights working. I'd paid special attention to the power intake for the enchantment, as well as multiple lines of spell etched into the ring itself. I wanted to make sure it worked well over there, in a magic-poor environment. That's why I added inscriptions with the ideograms appropriate to her world.

"How is it?" he asked.

"Pretty good," I replied. "I think it's about as solid as I can make it."

"I am pleased you are pleased. You wished to see me, Sire?"

"Absolutely. Did you review the crystal recordings?"

"I did," he replied, grinning.

"What did you think?"

"I think you are deceptively straightforward."

"Deceptively straightforward?" I repeated.

"You are a blunt instrument, Sire. You are direct and forthright, sometimes even brutal and crude, bordering on barbaric."

"Gee, thanks."

"And then you do something like this. It makes me wonder if you pretend to be brutish to conceal how fiendishly subtle you truly are."

"I'm not nearly as subtle as you think I am."

"Of course."

"Seriously, I'm not."

"Naturally."

"Will you please stop agreeing with me in that tone?"

"As you command, Master of the Bluntly Subtle. I enjoyed the crystals. They recorded your interview with Lotar in every detail."

"Wonderful. While he didn't actually confess to anything, he certainly didn't deny much. Which nobles can we show these to? Who will be especially cheesed off about it?"

"With respect, Sire, may I ask if you are attempting to conceal your subtlety again?"

"Sure. And no. I mean, yes, you may ask, and no, I'm not hiding anything. Have I missed something?"

"Yes. You assume the nobles are the ones who need to see this. They will resent the interference of a religious power in a secular affair and so react against the religion."

"Basically, yes." I thought about it for a moment. "Too obvious?" I asked. Seldar nodded. I swore.

"You also forget, Sire, the prevalence of religion throughout the kingdom. To whom does a baron turn when his wizard cannot cure the baroness? Or when the countess fails to conceive? Or when the drought grows oppressive and the harvest is threatened? The gods and their priests are part of the daily life of every one of your subjects."

I continued swearing. Once I felt better, I spoke more normally.

"I went to a lot of effort and wasted a big chunk of the day for this," I complained.

"It is very well-done, Sire, and will be invaluable."

"Wait. I thought you said it was a waste of time? At least, that's what I thought I heard."

"Not at all," Seldar protested. "For the most part, it is too obvious a ploy on your part to deliver such information to the nobles."

"We get someone else to deliver it?" I guessed. Seldar sighed and I began to wonder how much smarter than me he might be. Not *if*, but *how much*. Maybe, if I lived here full-time and cared about politics and met all the nobles and had a spreadsheet of all of them and drew a vector diagram of political influence and...

Hmm. No, not even then. I lack the political gene. Plus, I think Seldar really is smarter than me. It's a good quality in a chief advisor.

"Sire, while some minor effect may result from the nobles seeing this, it will not fundamentally affect the Church."

"Ah! So we play it back in larger-than-life images over market fountains, on theater stages, all that sort of thing, all over the kingdom! If everyone sees how the leader of... the... No?"

"No."

"Okay, I give up. I thought I had a plan, here, but obviously I'm more of a doofus than I thought, and that's pretty depressing, considering. Who gets to see it? Hold it. Do we show it to Lotar and keep it on file as blackmail?"

"Closer. I was thinking we show it inside every Temple of Light in Rethven and let their clergy decide what to do about it. If we do so when there are few worshippers but many priests—there are holy days reserved for priests' ceremonies—then we have kept it a reasonably private matter within the Church, thus showing our restraint. And, of course, we have also proven we have such information and can display it to whomever we choose."

"How is this better?"

"If it is an internal matter, the Church of Light must find a way to purge itself of those like Lotar. If the rot is extensive, it may even provoke a schism within the Church, thus dividing our enemy into warring factions."

"That wouldn't break my heart," I admitted.

"The alternative is a holy war against the Church of Light as a whole. While I know of no gods which have been destroyed by the eradication of their religion, I also cannot prove any forbidden religion does not continue in some form, in hiding."

"Huh. Valid point."

"So, shall we keep this an internal matter within the Church of Light?"

"By all means, see to it. And get copies of the letters, send those along."

"I have already begun this process, Sire."

"If I ever get Lissette between the crown and throne, I'm recommending you for Grand Vizier."

"Grand what?"

"Prime Minister, Chief Advisor, President of the Cabinet, Right-Hand-Man, whatever."

"I am gratified by your faith in me, Sire."

"I'm gratified by the smack in the chops you gave me." Seldar blushed. "Don't be embarrassed," I added. "Sometimes, even a king needs a little percussive maintenance. But be careful with the tactic. I'm not at my most stable and happy, lately. I was *this* close to punching you right back."

"It was a risk," Seldar admitted. "Kelvin spoke to me, many times, about how he wished he could hit you and make you listen. He thought it would be surprising enough to work, at least the first time."

"He really thought it would work on the Demon King?"

"No."

"Then—oh. I see. It was still a risk."

"One I chose to take."

"You won your bet, then. I realize I wasn't thinking like a king; I was thinking like a short-timer who wanted to get out of a nasty job. And it *is* part of your job to… keep me on point. Focused on the important stuff. It's hard to keep it together when everyone around you agrees with you by default."

"As you say, Sire."

"Are you trying to be funny?"

"Yes, Sire."

"I'm not sure it's working."

"As you say, Sire."

"Stop it."

"Of course, Sire."

"I mean it!"

"Immediately, Sire."

I couldn't take it anymore and burst out laughing. Seldar chuckled. Gilam watched us like we were crazy. He might be right.

"I have also located the man you wanted in Mochara."

"Oh, good. Where is he?"

"Flim is still in Mochara. His workplace is near the docks. By royal decree, he is chief artificer for the defense of Mochara—a title which has given the Lord Mayor some considerable grief over the years, I understand."

"Really? Why?"

"Because no one knows what it means or what authority it gives him."

"Ah. Yes. That could be a problem. I should have been more specific."

"Indeed, Sire."

"I'll discuss it with him later tonight. He's expecting me?"

"Yes, Sire."

"And stop that."

"As you wish, Sire."

I spent the rest of the afternoon with Diogenes and a quantum computer core. Since the two were completely different technologies, I wasn't sure it was possible to interface them. I can't even power up the Diogenes drive in Karvalen, and it's only a data storage device, not a processor. The quantum computer core, on the other hand, may be a data storage device as well as a processor. I'm not sure how it works.

Whee.

On the other hand, Diogenes is an operating system comprised of several weak AI systems. It's designed to be adaptable to all sorts of hardware configurations and devices. Connecting the two magically wasn't so hard. Data goes in and out of a storage device; data goes in and out of a processor. That's actually the easy part. A spell to bridge the gap between the two was on the order of rigging up an adapter between two different connector types. The throughput may not be all it could be, but it works.

The hard part was working out how the two could send meaningful signals back and forth across the interface. Lucky for me, the hard part wasn't my job. Once I had the two able to send signals back and forth, I put some of my personal vitality into the system. This brought it—technically, temporarily, in a very limited sense—to life.

It was much like the mountain in its early days. I put a lot of vital force into the mountain, then Tamara dumped a lot more into it. It was "alive" in the sense that we brought it to life, but it didn't have any way to replenish those energies, much like the Diogenes drive and the quantum computer core. Unlike the mountain, this was a quasi-living being with two organs—a thinker and a rememberer, if you like—bound into a single organism.

I left the living crystal and the data bank alone to talk for a while. With a little luck, Diogenes would figure out how to run in a futuristic computer core. At worst, it simply wouldn't work. But if it did, the computer core was going to get a lot more magic dumped into it.

Sunset went about its business and I went about mine. Mary joined me shortly beforehand and reiterated her disappointment at my schedule. We talked, waterfalled together, and dressed.

"You do know it could be a long while before we see each other again?" she asked. "You're talking about some sort of weirdness with time, after all."

"Immortality," I countered.

"Yeah, but it gets boring without someone to share it."

"I'll take your word for it."

"Good. So hurry. Regular people don't last very long."

"If you were a little less rough on them…" I trailed off.

"Where would be the fun in that?"

"Fine, fine. I'm hurrying, I'm hurrying."

"So where are you off to in your hurry?

"Mochara. I know a particularly inventive and clever fellow named Flim. He practically invented the Giant Artillery Crossbow."

"Did you help?"

"Only by suggesting a few improvements. He'd have figured them out on his own."

"Why is he important?"

"Mochara has a fleet of ships headed for it and they probably have defenses against someone pounding an explosive spike into their keels. I've done that trick more than once."

"Are you sure?"

"No, but it's likely. I don't want to discover what their defenses are by trying it and having a spike go off in my hand like a stick of dynamite."

"Seems reasonable. So this Flim has… what? Medieval artillery?"

"Pretty much. I want to see what he's come up with and if it'll help."

"What happens if it doesn't? What if he's only got a ton of drawings and nothing built?"

"He doesn't work like that. I'm sure there are any number of drawings, but he's a builder."

"Humor me."

"Then I'll think of something else."

We finished our rinse cycle and toweled off.

"Did you mean it about smiting Carrillon?" Mary asked.

"Not really."

"That's a relief."

"Don't worry. I wouldn't do it. It would kill too many innocents. Oh, if I did nuke the place, I'd only do it after three days of warning them—then it would be their own damn fault if they stayed. Unfortunately, anyone dangerous and powerful enough for me to consider…. What?" I asked. She looked at me funny while I spoke.

"You mean you *can* nuke the place?"

"Well, yes."

"*Seriously?*"

"It's easier than you think. I have a suspicion this world is a little more unstable than a 'scientific' world—although that may be a misnomer. Science and magic may not be opposites, but rather different aspects of a particular quality—assuming they have any relationship whatsoever. Anyway, this world was, I believe, created as a stand-alone habitat. It was undeniably put together by some entity. More likely a committee of entities, based on the eccentricities it displays. My hypothesis is any world with a high magical flux must be inherently unstable at a fundamental level, making matter itself somewhat unstable when subjected to appropriate forces—"

"Back up. Unstable?"

"Remember Einstein and the energy equals matter times the square of the speed of light?"

"I recall something about it. I seem to remember it from school, and more recently in the news about the Beijing fusion reactor disaster."

"In your world, it's hard to get fission or fusion to happen—matter turning into energy. Here, it might not be as hard."

"You're saying you could use the local technology—and magic, of course—to build a nuclear weapon?"

"Essentially, yes." I didn't explain. If she thought it required a nuclear engineer and an enchanted machine shop, that was fine with me. I really didn't feel like sharing the principles of world destruction with *anyone*.

"Why haven't you?"

"Again, too many innocents die. I'd rather use something tactical. I'm hoping to live a life free of weapons of mass destruction. I'm a retail killer, not wholesale. Wholesale gives me indigestion," I added, changing the subject. Mary accepted the change.

"Ah, yes. Softie."

"Seriously, it's the indigestion."

"Suuure it is." She squeezed me. "You go down to Mochara and geek out with your engineering buddy. I'll keep an eye on the place while you're gone."

"Okay. And I just remembered—this is for you." I handed her the ring. She took it, regarded it, put it on and considered it.

"I like the black and gold," she decided. "I don't think I can quite make out what it does, though, from the inscription."

"It's your Ring of Hiding from Magical Detection," I told her. "With this ring, I thee conceal. It ought to keep nosy magi from finding or identifying you. But don't push it, please. Use all caution."

"I will." She kissed me. "And I love it. Thank you."

"My pleasure. By the way, did I show you the metals room?"

"The treasury?"

"That's the one."

"I know where it is."

"You might check on the piles of gold and get Seldar to start stamping out coins. If I have to put a bounty on Thomen's severed head, I'll need money."

"Can I have some?"

"Help yourself."

"I love having a rich boyfriend," she said. She kissed me on the nose and skipped out. I went to Bronze's stall and found her crunching her way through a pile of coal.

"Ready for a run?"

She snorted wisps of fire and smoke, rang her mane with a shake, whipped her tail like a wire lash, and stomped. The floor vibrated, but I didn't hear the thud.

Stupid question.

I mounted up and Bronze headed farther into the mountain. This puzzled me for a moment. The main door was right there; we should go out that way, down the Kingsway, negotiate the turns to get out of town, and head south. I was actually looking forward to seeing the changes in the Kingsway bridge on the way down.

But no, Bronze had her own ideas. Bronze gave me the impression she spoke with the mountain—don't ask me how *that* works; I'm not clear on how *Bronze* works—and asked about good running routes. Therefore, we went into the palace, through a couple of doors, and down. The sloping hallway took us deep under the nominal ground level and terminated in a sizable room. Four other tunnels led away, probably in the cardinal directions. The southward one would lead to Mochara, of course, probably under the central divider, the road between the canals. West led to the mountains and to Rethven beyond them. North? Probably to that town, the one occupying the eastern portion of the pass. It might run farther north, too. And east... what was east? Canals went that way. Did we have a tunnel that way just because we had canals?

This is the problem with having sentient and/or sapient things doing whatever they do without supervision. Stuff happens. I'm still not caught up. I'm not even sure I approve.

Bronze took the southern tunnel without hesitation. I suspected it could use a bit more engineering. It wasn't lighted and only poorly ventilated. One person, or a small group, could probably travel along it without risking suffocation, but I'd hate to rely on torches for light.

On the other hand, it was as wide as a three-lane road and arched to about twenty feet high. Bronze went straight down the middle like a bullet down a gunbarrel. I held on and enjoyed the ride, thinking of ways to improve the tunnel.

The other end of the tunnel arrived surprisingly quickly. It made a sharp turn to the right and divided. We could turn left, or continue straight, ascending. Bronze chose to ascend. The tunnel angled upward, narrowing, and eventually came to a dead-end. It was rather cramped for Bronze. Fortunately, one wall was a pivot-door; Bronze nudged it with a shoulder and walked around with it as it swung open. She closed it neatly by completing the turn.

We stood in a high-ceilinged room, square, with neither windows nor furniture. The only feature was another pivot door. I opened this one and found it led outside. The door was part of an unmarked and unremarkable building inside Mochara. It appeared to be built up against the inside of the city wall. It even had steps along the outside to the walkway atop the wall.

Bronze and I left the building as soon as I determined no one was watching. I pushed the door closed with one foot and it immediately started to disappear. The stone of the frame joined with the door.

Well, that explained why the room wasn't used, at least.

We worked our way out of the neighborhood, heading for places with people. This area didn't seem too popular or well-trafficked. Another good reason to put a secret tunnel exit there, I suppose. I wonder where the other tunnel branch went, though. A Temple of Shadow? Out to sea? The Temple of Flame, perhaps?

Flim still lived in the same house. He was easy to find; several lanterns lit his workyard and his current project. He had a bow-spring ballista pretty much perfected, apparently, given the thirty-foot-wide example sitting ready. His latest work seemed to involve launching multiple arrows rather than a single projectile.

Flim, of course, was still outside and tinkering while waiting for me to show up. His sons, Reth and Zaren, were with him.

Zaren kicked under the arrow engine when Bronze and I came into the light. "Dad! He's here!"

Reth snapped upright and tried to stand at attention. Flim hauled himself out from under the contraption and bowed. Zaren copied his father and Reth joined them. I noticed Flim wore a necklace—a pendant, really. A simple leather cord holding part of a chain link. I recognized it.

"Evening," I offered, dismounting. "Nobody stand on ceremony; relax. I understand there's been some confusion on how you get paid?"

"Yes... um..." Flim trailed off.

"Okay. I'll have a word with Seldar; he'll take care of it. If you need anything, send word to him."

"Yes," Flim replied, still trying to think of how to address me.

Everyone takes the King so seriously. Why don't I? My native culture? My upbringing? My genetic defect about royalty?

"Good. My, but you've got some fine men for helpers. I recall Reth being such a little fellow. And Zaren has grown up and filled out. Been working hard on these things?"

"Yes, Sire."

"Yes, Sire."

"Glad to hear it. Flim, would you care to explain and demonstrate?"

"You bet I would!" He immediately launched into an explanation of his pride and joy, the giant crossbow. Different layers of wood and steel were laminated together, but not joined—impossible in earlier times, but with the forges in Karvalen turning out some of the highest-quality steel in the world, now almost practical. These layers slid across each other, making it possible to bend without breaking. Steel cable formed the bowstring. A geared crank turned a shaft. The shaft had two different sections—one to take up cable, the other to feed cable out. The cable ran through a pulley with a hook; this pulled back the bowstring.

Flim, or one of his sons, invented the Chinese windlass. I am impressed.

Then he used it with a variable gear system—and a ratchet and pawl, for safety—making it possible for one man to crank back that enormously powerful draw. Admittedly, it took forever for one man to do it, but there was a selection of different gears and handles. He had gears low enough for a six man team or high enough for one man.

"It doesn't launch quickly," he admitted, "but once it's prepared, it will go through anything short of a magician's barrier."

"What do you launch?"

Zaren produced a metal spear and handed it to his father. Flim took it with a grunt and handed it to me. It was really a length of pipe with a solid point, sharpened like an old-fashioned pencil. It had a length of cloth, a ribbon, at the rear. Not as accurate as vanes or fletching, but the slight drag would at least keep it oriented properly.

"I started with wooden arrows," he said. "They didn't want to work so well. There were problems with penetration, as well as breakage during launch. These stand up pretty well to launching, they're heavy enough to damage anything, and they can be sharpened down as fine as you like. Fletching is a problem, too. I've tried feathers, but the ribbon works just as well."

"That was my idea," Zaren added.

"And it was a good one," Flim admitted. "We also tried making metal vanes for the fletching, but it makes them harder to handle and much harder to make."

"We've also experimented by filling them with flammable oil," Reth piped up.

"Yes, we have," Flim agreed. "The end-cap at the back gets forced deeper into the pipe, so launching doesn't lose the liquid, but it's still a problem to get it to drain while going through something. It usually goes completely through the target and doesn't spill much oil. I'm still working on it."

"Maybe you need a new bolt, one made just for setting things on fire," I suggested.

"But it's got a hollow place already. Seems a shame to waste it, Sire."

"And most swords have a blood-groove along their length. It's there for a reason; it doesn't do to fill it in. Besides, with all that penetration there's no point to a payload. But that's for another time. What's this new one?" I asked, nodding at the multi-arrow engine.

"That was my idea, Sire," Zaren piped up. "Reth's idea about making the big one launch a fire spear made me think a thousand flaming arrows might be better than one arrow going completely through."

"There are cases," I agreed.

"If you miss with a single arrow, you've missed completely. With this, you won't hit with every arrow, but you'll surely hit with some of them. And if you're aiming at a formation of troops, it's like a volley from a thousand archers!"

"Can you really fire a thousand arrows at once?"

"Well... no. Or not yet. There are problems."

"I can imagine. Show me."

"I've been experimenting with a catapult and a trebuchet," he explained, "since it's so hard to launch lots of arrows without wrecking them…"

A catapult is actually *pallanno*, literally meaning *throw upward*. It uses tension, usually twisted rope, sometimes a spring, or even a bent lever arm to store energy for launching projectiles. A trebuchet—a French term for a counterweight-powered throwing lever—is actually *pallofond*, meaning, *throw with a sling*, because of the sling-like arrangement at the launching end of the lever arm. They don't seem to care why the devices work, only what they do. Typical of this world's general mindset, if you ask me.

We talked shop for a while. The designs they developed were excellent. In addition to the overgrown ballista, they had other weapons. A smaller version of the ballista required at least a bipod to use properly; it was heavy, but one man could horse it around, even reload it with the help of the built-in crank. Another mechanical contrivance had a hopper on top for arrows, arrangements for a two-man crew to turn handles, and a gunner's position in back to aim the whole contraption—a full-auto ballista! They also built a double-decker crossbow, even a three-deck crossbow, but drew the line at four. The triple-shot crossbow was already heavy and awkward enough to need a helper or a firing rest.

"I'm very pleased with your ingenuity," I told them. They seemed relieved and happy. "For now, though, how many of these engines do we have?"

"How many? Six. Sort of. One of each of the designs, of course, and Zaren's experiments with catapults."

"The catapult works better, so far. The sling arrangement on the end of the lever arm with the trebuchet design isn't so great—"

"Later," I told him. I turned back to Flim. "These are all you've made?"

"Why, yes, Sire." Flim looked worried. "Was I suppose to make more than one? I thought… I thought I was supposed to perfect them so you could choose…?"

"No, no—you did very well. Exceptionally well, and I'm enormously pleased with you. I'll be throwing more money at you as soon as I get back to the mountain, and I'll have a word with Seldar about an official title, too. You're the research and development guys. I'll get someone else to build them, use them, and report on anything they find."

"Yes, Sire!" Flim replied, happily. I noticed he seemed to settle on "Sire" as a form of address. I ignored it. At least I'm used to it.

"However, I've word of ships sailing for Mochara. They may be about to assault the place. We'll need someone to operate the ones we have in combat."

Flim looked at Zaren. Zaren looked pensive, and nodded.

"We have several bolts for the big one, and we have at least a few shots for the rest. I… Sire, may I ask?"

"Of course."

"What good will these be against wizardry?"

"Ah. You're thinking of wizards deflecting everything you throw at them, aren't you?"

"Even I know the spells, Sire," he told me, fingering the broken chain link.

"Good man. Then you know every time it deflects something, it takes power from the spell—which, in turn, came from the wizard."

"Yes."

"If they spend their efforts defending themselves from your weapons—and if one of those giant metal bolts hits a defensive shield, they'll spend a lot of effort reinforcing it! —they'll have less to attack us with, magically. Nor strength to defend themselves from *our* wizards. And if they divert their power to attacking us, or to blocking our spells, some of your flaming arrows or giant metal ones may get through. It all works together, you see, in a war."

"I think I see," Flim agreed, nodding. Reth looked dubious.

"Good. Now, is there anything I can do to help you?"

"Everything you have said is all we could require, Your Majesty."

"Wonderful. I wish I could take time to sit down at the drawing board with you; I'd love to see what other ideas you've had. The kinging business waits for no man, though." I turned to Bronze and found her grazing on metallic bits in the workyard. I mounted up and we turned about. That's when I spotted several faces looking out the windows at us. Three of them were in Flim's house.

"Family?" I asked him. He nodded and hustled over to the house; Bronze followed him at a walk. I renewed acquaintance with Jessa, Flim's wife, and met both Tessa, Zaren's wife, and his son, Devert. Tessa was almost done building their second child, but it would be another few weeks before she finished. I didn't get to meet the kid formally, but I did say hello. She kicked a little and pressed one hand against the inside of her mother's belly, as though trying to touch mine.

"By the way, do you want to know if it's a boy or girl?"

"It's a girl," Tessa said. "We already know."

"In a city full of wizards, I should have expected that. Well, good to meet you all and a pleasure. Farewell."

Bronze whisked me away to the Temple of Flame. As expected, Amber was still up and around. I'm not sure she sleeps any more than I do. We supernatural entities can be weird like that. I wonder if she ever regrets being a creature composed of quasi-solid flame and magic. I wonder... but I'll never ask. I don't think I could bear it if she told me she hated it.

I dismounted and entered the Temple. She was meditating in the flames, as usual. She opened her fiery eyes as I came in. She smiled, rising like a pile of leaves set aflame.

"Father!" she crackle-pop-roared. "It's so good to see you again!" She held out her arms and I hugged her in that strange, not-quite-solid manner. Her hair flowed forward around me like a forest fire. She kissed me lightly, like a candle-flame.

"Hello, Amber. I was in Mochara and thought I'd stop in. How have you been?"

"Well enough. Tianna tells me you have been busy."

"She's not wrong."

"Tell me all about it," she encouraged, settling her fiery self into her fireplace-dais-stage-lounge. She almost vanished amid the sudden rustle of flames, but the small bonfire settled into coals again and she stood out perfectly, shimmering slightly in the waves of heat. I parked myself on the nearest bench and spent a goodly while explaining about magical carriages, shotguns, networks of magic mirrors, genies that listen and remember everything... basically, magical terminology for all the technological terrors mankind creates. While all of it was interesting to her, she really seemed to focus on my troubles with other vampires, various houses of magi, and the local problems with Lissette and Thomen and the Church of Light. I guess technology is just another collection of gadgets, really.

"So," she said, when I finished, "you've managed to anger a bunch of lesser breeds of nightlords as well as family-tradition magicians?"

"Well... sort of. Yes. I suppose."

"When are you going to deal with that?"

It was not the best thing she could have said. I didn't take it as "Father, dear, please tell me you'll keep yourself safe by dealing with these things immediately." I should have; her tone, insofar as she had a perceptible tone, implied it. What I heard, though, was more like, "And you haven't dealt with this yet, you lazy bum?"

I took a couple of pointless breaths and made sure my own tone was under control. She didn't mean to poke the bear.

"First off, let me explain how angry I am. I'm trying to distract myself with my other problems until I can devote all my attention to Johann. I'm going to kill him eventually, but most important is the fact I'm going to *hurt* him. Killing him just sends him to the foot of the line in reincarnation terms. I want him to suffer. *Then* I'll kill him."

"I thought you didn't like torture?"

"I abhor torture."

"And yet...?"

"This isn't torture. I don't want anything out of him. I don't intend to extract information. All I want is to *punish* him. I'm going to inflict pain! Lots of pain! I'll break him, piece by piece, and set fire to the screaming pieces! I'm going to rip the son of a bitch apart and eat his heart before he dies!" I shut myself up and took a deep breath. "Excuse me. I'm not ready to get into that."

"I see," she said, faintly. Her eyes looked past me, behind me. I didn't bother to turn around.

"My shadow is doing something creepy, violent, or both, right?"

"Yes!"

"Ignore it and it'll settle down," I advised.

"All right." She returned her attention to me. "While I accept your reasons as valid reasons—for you—I don't completely agree."

"Excuse me?"

"What I mean to say is, if it happened to me, I do not believe I would have the same reaction. I'm sorry, Father, but I wouldn't." She shrugged, a ripple of fire running all along her form. "I agree, however, you have to do this your way. It isn't my place to say what's right for you."

"Huh. That's... surprisingly fair."

"You are my father. I don't have to like whatever else you are, but I... am... I have been trying to understand you. It hasn't been easy, but watching the Demon King..." she trailed off.

"It was a horrible experience?" I guessed.

"Yes. But the contrast was striking. From what I understand, all that he was also lives in you. Yet I do not see it. The comparison is... well, it has given me great respect for your nobler qualities."

"I'm sorry about him."

"Let's talk about something else. We have an army and ships headed for Mochara?"

"Currently, yes. I think the army will turn back, which may cause the ships to return. If the ships come ahead by themselves, we need to be ready for them."

"Will you be attacking from below?"

"No, I'm sure they're ready for my keel-cracking trick. Will you be incinerating from above?"

"No, but if they make it over the walls, I'll sweep them with fire. Do we need to do something with the Wizards' Guild in Mochara?"

"Like what?"

"Arrest them?" she suggested.

"Why would—oh, damn. They may be loyal to their guildmaster, Thomen, rather than to me."

"Did you really only think of it now?"

"Yes."

"It's a wonder you've survived this long."

"I get by with a little help from my friends."

"What will you do about this?"

"Probably invade their privacy and do something dreadful. This whole business—trying to get off the throne without making more of a mess of things—has been harder than dealing with a plateful of bad burritos."

"I don't think I understand. And, from what little I did understand, I'm probably happier in my ignorance than otherwise."

"The whole thing stinks," I simplified.

"Yes, I was correct. Please do not further damage my ignorance on this subject."

"Okay," I agreed. "Guildhall still where it used to be?"

"Yes."

"Then I need to bother them."

"Is there anything I can do?"

"Aside from prepare to defend Mochara and most especially yourself? No, I don't think so."

"Very well. Before you go haring off to be heroic and noble and leader-ish, can you take a minute to sit down and listen?"

"Flapping my ears at you now," I replied. "You want my attention? All you had to do was ask."

"I'm about to be religious at you," she warned.

"Noted."

"Do you remember we were talking about Beryl?"

"Vividly. Do you want to know how I feel about it? Is that it?"

"No, I only want you to think back to it. How you feel about it—and about the Mother—is between the two of you. I was barely there."

"For you, okay. I'm recalling it. I don't like it, but I'm thinking about it."

"You mentioned something about how the Mother tried to destroy you, and how you tried to kill Her, and so forth?"

"I recall something about it, yes. I'm not sure what I said, exactly."

"You left me with the impression you thought you were actually a danger to Her."

"I took a big, fat bite out of her, if that's what you mean."

Amber looked troubled. Her flames changed from reddish-orange to a more orangey-yellow.

"Dad, what I'm about to tell you is based on… well… I'm not really privy to what goes on in the Halls of the Gods. I hear things, obviously, when the Mother and I talk. She speaks through me and I… get flashes, images, ideas. Things like that."

"Leakage."

"That's not a bad word for it, I suppose."

"And what did you discover?"

"Dad, the Mother was never in any danger. What seemed like a huge bite *to you* was little more than an annoyance to Her. Your perspective on the matter was limited, mortal—mortal in the sense of being a limited, material entity. Later, when you ascended temporarily to Her plane of existence, your power was magnified, but still limited by your perceptions. Now, you've taken mortal form—excuse me, *material* form—again and become merely a Lord of Night."

"Okay, so I didn't do as much damage as I thought." I shrugged. "I got my point across."

"You did. But the Mother never intended to destroy you, not even when She blasted you with fire. It was intended to chastise you, not kill. As a nightlord, you would be hurt, severely wounded, but not destroyed. True, She did not expect you to defend against Her... spanking?... so effectively. And you certainly surprised Her by biting Her."

"So she thinks of me as a child to be taken over her knee and swatted, but I'm one of those kids who kicks, screams, and bites." I shrugged again. "Tough luck for her."

"I suppose, in a manner of speaking, that is correct. More important is the fact you reached a plane of existence that mortal, material beings cannot reach. There is *no* material existence on Her plane... I think."

"To boldly go where no one has gone before," I quoted. "Why is this important?"

"You know you were... how they regarded you as one of their own?"

"I was a god? Temporarily, in a minor capacity, and unstable as hell, but a god? Yes, I know. I had a couple of conversations, walked around, saw the sights, got punched by Father Sky, that sort of thing. Good times. Then I stretched my skinsuit out a bit and squeezed my pudgy astral butt back into it."

"Err... yes. I am not privy to the details."

"They're a bit fuzzy for me, too, but from my point of view, here's what happened—"

"No, that's quite all right," she protested, holding up a fiery hand. "It's not my business. What is my business—and yours, now—is a peculiarity of the laws of the gods. Or, perhaps, their pact. Perhaps their agreement, or covenant."

"Oh?"

"They forbid violence done to each other. They forbid themselves to fight amongst themselves. Their followers may war across the face of the world, but the gods never attack each other."

"Father Sky once punched me."

"I don't doubt it. I get the impression He has suffered for it, but I don't know the specifics. I am certain He will not do so again."

"So, I shouldn't worry about being outside during a thunderstorm?"

"I suspect it goes further than that."

"I mean, he's not going to hit me with lightning because he's still cheesed at me?"

"I mean that none of the gods will do anything to you."

"I beg your pardon?"

"The Mother refuses to burn you. How else could you enter the flames to save me after the assassin's blade found me?"

"Huh. I thought I was immune to divine fire after drinking her spirit."

"No."

"You're *sure*?"

"I'm dead sure about that, at least. Pact or no, She refuses to harm you. She also tells me you are not to be harmed in another sense. Many of the gods would be pleased to smite you if only they had a priest close enough to direct Their powers. Have you noticed such occasions with other gods? Followers of other gods attempting to bring the power of their faith to bear, and failing?"

I thought back to a few occasions when I felt the regard of some of the local deities, but no wrath.

"It's possible."

"When you became a god, you gained all the rights of one. They still debate the technicalities of the thing, or so I infer, but until they settle the matter among themselves, they will not touch you directly."

"If so, that's a relief. I was worried I might have some sort of deific smell or something. Don't get me wrong; I like it when a Church of Light goon aims his medallion at me and nothing happens. I'm just as pleased, though, to find out it's the so-called gods acting politely instead of some sort of some special demigod quality in myself. I'm weird enough as it is.

"You know," I added, "I wish I'd known about this mutual amnesty-slash-immunity thing earlier. I could have milked it for all it was worth. A bunch of unpleasant religious types would have turned into proto-sausage and the world might be a better place for it. And I wouldn't have had such a nasty case of anxiety about accidental religious incineration."

"I'm sorry. I didn't begin to suspect until quite a while after my own change-of-state. By then, I didn't feel the Demon King needed to know."

"I'm not complaining." I paused and thought about it. "On second thought, I suppose I am. I shouldn't complain at you."

"I wish I could help more. If I learn anything else, I'll tell you as quickly as I can."

"That's… huh. Actually, that does kind of make me feel better. I don't suppose I should push my luck by demanding an explanation from Spar—uh, from the Mother of Flame for the Zirafel incident?"

"She had Her reasons. I'm told you might not think they were good reasons, or sufficient, or something, but She had them. The ways of the gods are not the ways of men."

"Hmm. I've just been told I have diplomatic immunity to the gods. You know what? I'm going to quit while I'm ahead. Compared to my other problems, *why* Sparky does anything is so far down the list I might never get to it."

"Probably best, Father."

"How about we talk about you, instead?"

"Certainly," Amber replied, settling back and smiling. "What would you like to know?"

"I have no idea. I'm still a complete failure as a father."

"Oh, I don't know about that. You may not have been present for much of my life, but it means you did not fight with the Mother. Yet I felt your influence in many ways."

"I don't think so."

"I do. You were all around me in this world, much as the Mother was all around me in the other. Your influence on the people around me was, by its very nature, an indirect influence on me. I can see now how I resented the lack of your physical presence, true... but I am older and wiser, and have had opportunity to know you, not merely your reputation."

"I'm not sure that counts."

"I am."

"It doesn't feel right to me."

"Does your opinion on it matter as much as mine?"

I had to think about it for a minute.

"I disagree, but reluctantly concede your point."

"Good. Is there anything else about which you feel insecure or inadequate?"

"That's probably not a good question to ask any man, especially your father."

"Also true. But we seem to have wandered back to talking about you, again."

"I'll shut up."

"We'll see."

Amber did her best to tell me about her life. We talked until the small hours of the morning. Since it's her life, it's not my story to tell.

Monday, February 23rd

At least our return to Karvalen was fairly straightforward. Rather than take the secret tunnel, we headed along the main canal road. During the day, nobody camps on it; they're trudging one direction or the other, leaving the center clear. We slowed slightly and did some lane changes as we passed horses towing canal barges, but otherwise had a straight, solid run.

In Karvalen, I finally got to see the new Kingsway.

The dragon's head was formed of dark stone, possibly basalt. The eyes were definitely obsidian; they were black and glittery and seemed to follow you when you moved. Or maybe they really did follow. I don't know how the mountain would do it, but I won't say it's impossible. The whole thing was wide and tall, a massive sculpture fit for gulping down a wagon—if you could get a wagon up the steep stairs. The lower jaw had steps formed into the dragon's tongue, and the teeth reminded me of the time I looked a young dragon in the face, but bigger. Carnivore teeth. Sharp, tearing teeth. It made me leery of ever encountering a full-grown specimen.

I like it, Boss.

I'm not surprised.

Can you get it to breathe fire?

Probably. Everything else seems to.

Eh? What do you mean?

You breathe fire, Bronze breathes fire, Tamara, Amber, and Tianna breathe fire—there's a lot fire around here.

It's the way of the world, Boss. Everything is made of the five elements, and fire is the life inside it all.

Five elements? I repeated. *Wait, Jon went over this with me. Earth, air, water, fire... what was the fifth?*

Emptiness. Nothingness. That thing.

Right. It's the hole in the center of a wheel that makes it useful, or something. Philosophical. But you say fire is the life inside everything?

I ought to know, Boss.

So you should. I accept your statement as a fundamental truth of this world. I'm still not sure how to get the Kingsway to breathe fire, though. A barrel of oil poured down from the top, maybe.

The head formed the mouth of the tunnel. Beyond it, the dragon's scaly neck ascended to the rim of the palace courtyard. As it ascended, the exterior lost the draconic qualities and became simply a glassy-smooth tube. Inside, it remained mostly circular, slightly taller than it was wide, with a flat, rough floor and smooth walls. There was a slight but constant current of air ascending through the tunnel. While the only light was from the ends, I still wouldn't want to spend a sunrise there. The middle wouldn't actually be in darkness, but it would be deeply, *deeply* shadowed.

It didn't look well-traveled.

Once in the palace regions, Bronze returned to her coal mining, happily crunching away, while I found Mary. She was already dressed, packed, and ready to go. Her boots stood out. They were clearly part of the tactical outfit under her clothes. The clothes, on the other hand, were odd for Rethven, but probably acceptable in the late 2040's in France. Come to think of it, for all I know the boots were, too. She had a bag slung over her shoulder, sizable for a purse, about the low end of carry-on luggage. I didn't see any knives or guns, which was a good thing. I had no doubt they were present.

We went to my upper gate room. She shut the door and grabbed me by the shirt.

"Just to be clear on this, you're sending me off to do your dirty work and I know it."

"Um. Yes?" I agreed.

"Look me in the eye and tell me you're doing this because you need me to do it, not because you want me out of the way while you do something dangerous and fun."

"I need you to do this so I can have a chance to grab Johann by the balls and squeeze them until his eyes explode."

"It doesn't work like that. I know."

"I remember an incident in the barn. Doesn't mean I can't try."

"Don't change the subject. You're sending me away because you legitimately need my help, and this is the best possible use of my talents? Or are you hogging all the fun and danger for yourself?"

"Well, you're the only person who can do this. I need it to be you, in particular, for that reason. No one else is going cope with the society. They're not even going to speak a language anyone *recognizes*, much less uses to communicate."

"Okay." She let go of my shirt and brushed at the wrinkles. "Promise?"

"I promise. When this is over and Johann is suitably crushed into a formless pile, we'll spend a night together, just you and me."

"I'd rather spend a day together," she replied, leering.

"But your nervous system is much more responsive at night."

"Well, yes, but—Wait a second. Do you mean to tell me we could have been having sex at *night?*" she demanded.

"No. Blood flow is a vital component for my performance. But there are variations which do not require the fundamentals." I leered back at her. "If we can't sing together, I can at least play you like an instrument while *you* sing—with an ultra-responsive nervous system, to boot."

"I've been an undead for a while. It's never worked before."

"And now you're a different species," I pointed out. She threw her hands in the air and rolled her eyes.

"You're only getting around to telling me *now?*"

"You wouldn't have let me leave the bedroom. Ever."

"I am going to kill you," she promised. "Slowly. And I'm going to enjoy it. You will, too."

"I don't doubt it, but please, *please* not today. Got all your gear sorted out?"

"Yes."

"Address card? Letter of introduction?"

Mary opened her handbag and fished out both.

"One-fifty-two Chemin des Vendanges, Avignon, Provence-Alpes-Cote d'Azur." She looked up from the card at me. "Are you sure about the address?"

"It was the return address on the letter they handed me. It's a place to start, at least. Figured out where we're going to rendezvous?"

"Four possible spots," she told me. "It took me a while to decide, but it's my world and I know best, right?" She handed me letter, sealed with wax. I accepted it cautiously.

"Yes," I agreed, hesitantly. "I suppose so. Where, exactly—" I began, but she cut me off.

"I may be able to leave you a hidden phone number," she added. "Scan around for magical glyphs when you get there. Or I could have my number listed on the cybernet and you can look me up."

"Please don't have a public number. I'd like us to avoid all possible notice if at all possible."

"I'm not sure that's grammatically correct."

"But it's accurate. Now, remember. Once you get through, get away from the gate opening and blend in quickly. You're shielded from direct magical observation, but Johann or other magi may detect the gate. If they simply look at the area, they can see you. I don't think they can scan you—you won't show up on mystic radar—but eyeballs are eyeballs."

"If they do eyeball the area, any idea how long I'll have?"

"I doubt they monitor this sort of thing in shifts. Even if they have a spell to monitor the whole planet, it probably just sounds an alarm. If it automatically attempts to counter a gate, I'll be able to tell before you go through."

"So, best case, they're busy elsewhere and don't even notice my arrival. Worst case, I'm kicking in the front door and hurrying through the house to find a hiding spot before the owner shows up with a gun."

"That's not a bad description," I admitted. "I've got a number of decoys ready, too."

"Decoys?"

"I don't know how small a gate I can open, but, as far as I can tell, there's a direct correlation between size and power. If I make it small enough, it doesn't cost much power. So, if I make a couple dozen or so pinprick-sized holes in the universe, any gate alarms will register multiple hits and force them to divide their attention."

"But won't they notice one is bigger than the others?"

"Maybe. Thing is, detecting an interdimensional portal is one thing. Detecting the size of it is a different thing entirely. Different systems of detection. It isn't impossible to put a penetration alarm on the planet, especially with the level of power they possess. Also determining the size of the hole is a higher-order level of complexity. The simple fact of detection would be enough to let them know I was on my way."

"Assuming they're worried about it at all," Mary agreed.

"Right. Hence, a couple dozen pinpricks. Imagine a global map lighting up in twenty places at once. Where do you start?"

Mary nodded, thoughtfully.

"I might live through this."

"I certainly hope so!"

"Then kiss me and open the gates." She limbered up a little, shook out her hands, and popped her neck. She settled into a half-crouch, prepared to spring through the archway.

As for me, I focused on a number of places, one at a time. I called up my memory of my basement workroom, in the Ardents' old farmhouse, and used it as a navigation point. That's the world I want. The tunnel we gated through to the parking garage in Atlantic City. The hotel where we stayed in Mexico. The empty place on Rattlesnake Pike, where my old house *wasn't*. The place where a campfire flared in the desert, a communication gateway for a lady of flame. Navigation points, all unique and definite, marking out the particular world I wanted. Replicate the resonance among the spells, one greater, many lesser, like an address label on multiple envelopes. Imprint each one in the matrix of a gate spell, set it in a tiny circle of stone, no larger than the point of a pencil, and imprint the next.

Then the lesser coordinates, uncertain and almost random. The world is defined, the planet targeted, but where do you choose for a landing point? North, south, east, west, all around the world. Imprint them, make the holes in the wall whistle in the wind between the worlds, singing with the proper tone for a universe, and address them to general delivery—any old openings, scattered anywhere in the world, would do.

Avignon. The big one. I already marked it out in my headspace, on my memories of the globe. Zoom in, put the pin in the map, and burn it in there. Somewhere, there is a doorway about the right size. Aim for Avignon and let the portal seek it out, lock on to the nearest, most convenient opening.

Everything addressed? Yes. Power gathered in the crystals? Yes. Stamp the envelopes and send them out…

Dozens of tiny points glittered in their spell-held array around the arch. Some night, some day, but so what? It was morning here, for us, so sunlight could do us no harm.

The interior of the arch swirled away, funneled down, reached for its destination and opened, snapping the far image into congruence with the local arch. I could see a number of surprised-looking people and hear the French language. The signs I could see appeared to be in French; traffic signs were marked in kilometers. There was even an elderly man with a bag of groceries, including—how cliché!—a loaf of French bread. It appeared to be late afternoon.

"I'll miss you," I told her as she stepped through.

"I already miss you," she replied, and ducked to the left, out of my view. The gate image shredded, dissolved, and disappeared. The tiny gates around it closed with it, winking out like stars in the dawn.

Everything went perfectly. Why do I feel as though the morning is off to a terrible start?

Seldar met me for breakfast. While I attempted to fake an appetite— successfully; my stomach is practically a garbage disposal—he told me how things were going.

"The army," he began, "appears to be retreating toward Baret. For some reason, they seem to be unwilling to continue through the mountains."

"Odd."

"Yes, isn't it?" he asked, one eyebrow rising.

"What else?"

"I've had a message from Vathula. Duke Bob has heard your request for a crown and one is being sent."

"That's fast. Did he have one lying around?"

"You know, I asked the elf in the mirror that very question? Worded slightly differently, of course."

"Of course."

"It would seem Keria once wore a crown. It has not been worn since her demise, but the Duke assures me it will serve you well."

"I'm mildly concerned about appearances, but maybe elvish workmanship can make up for sinister and forbidding. I'm also wondering what sort of enchantments it has on it."

"I will have it brought to you as soon as it arrives, Sire."

"Okay. No, on second thought, have Bob bring it to me when he arrives. Call them back and let them know I'd like the Duke to deliver it personally."

"Consider it done," Seldar said, and made a note. "There are also a number of personal requests for your attention, Sire."

"Such as?"

"For one thing, there are many wizards who wish to swear their personal loyalty to the true King of Karvalen."

"Interesting. Why do you think they're doing it?"

"I see three major reasons. First, they are traitors seeking to worm their way into your sphere of influence. Second, they are aware of traitors in the guild of wizards and wish to gain position with you before betraying their former masters. Or, finally, they are exactly what they claim to be—loyal subjects wishing to enlist directly in your service."

"Those exist?"

Seldar looked at me with a reproving expression.

"Yes, O Fearsome Bloodsucker. More than you seem to think. But I would not count on these wizards being in the third category."

"I'll look at them tonight and see if they believe it when they swear to me. What else?"

"There are already a dozen or more individuals awaiting their... departure."

"Also tonight. Can we set things up separately? I'd rather not have a bunch of wizards gawking at the dying. It's impolite. Undignified."

"Dantos will organize it, Sire. He is remarkable. I am not certain he would make a good governor, but he excels at carrying out orders."

"How do you mean?"

"I do not have a firm grasp of his opinions and beliefs in regard to making policy, but he does motivate people to accomplish their tasks in an organized fashion."

"Good. I like him. He strikes me as competent and loyal. I'd like to keep him happy, if we can."

"I'll see if there is anything he wants and do my best to give it to him, Master of Generosity."

"I'd almost rather you stuck to 'Sire,'" I complained.

"If you wish to order it so, Inconsistent One."

"Or maybe I'll ignore it," I decided. "What else?"

"There are also several... soldiers? Fighters? Men at arms who wish to become knights."

"You don't sound happy about it."

Seldar hesitated, marshalling his thoughts.

"Sire, are you familiar with the current knights of the kingdom?"

"Not really. I know my original guys, of course, and they've gone back to wearing the red sash, right?"

"They have."

"I can pick out the Temple of Shadow troops by their smaller size and the grey sashes. I understand they've been knighted by other knights?"

"Nominated," Seldar corrected, "then approved and knighted by Lord Beltar, yes. You may wish to inspect them yourself, Sire."

"Or I may want to keep farming it out to people," I mused. "Anyway, the other knights? You were saying?"

"Your predecessor was willing to knight anyone with sufficient skill with weapons, rather than select individuals with the willingness to follow a proper moral code."

"I heard something about it, yes."

"These new men—not from the Temple of Shadow—are mercenaries, Sire."

"Then what do they want to be knighted for?"

"An enchanted sword? The black armor of night? Better pay than they might otherwise get, even in a war? Respect? Authority? The list goes on."

"And some of them may be willing to double-cross us if they get the chance?"

"That, too, Sire. Some may already be in the pay of Thomen or Lotar, directly or indirectly."

"Well, that part is easy enough. Appoint someone to put them through their paces, run them into the ground for six weeks, and we can have a board of knights quiz the survivors on their ethical standards."

Seldar made a note, nodding.

"Very good, Ruthless Lord. May I ask why you do not simply examine their souls in the night, as you intend to do with the wizards?"

"I'm not always going to be here to examine them," I told him. "I'd like to set up self-sustaining systems—I'll fail, but I'd still like it—so a noble order of knighthood and suchlike can maintain its high standards without me."

"Ah." Seldar made another note. "I also have Larel making a new coin die for you. The image will remain the same, but with new engraving. We should be able to start hammering out the new coins within the week."

"Larel?"

"Kavel's youngest, named for his forebear, I understand. He is an expert with fine work."

"Fitting," I agreed. "Fitting. The Larel I knew was quite a craftsman. I respected him."

"I am told it runs in their family," he agreed. "There are also several requests for your attention in healing. People who have already called at the Temples and upon the Guild, naturally. These are the ones forwarded us by the Temple of Shadow."

"How does that work? Do the other temples send their rejects to us?" I asked.

"Not as such. People seek out aid from whoever they choose, but if the Guild fails, or their chosen Temple does not cure their ailment, they are forced to seek the aid of other magicians, other Temples."

"So we're talking about desperate people that nobody wants to help?"

"One can but assume, Sire. It is often the case their ailment remains because they cannot afford to have it cured. A wizard or magician has a cash price, but the Temples require offerings, as well. Crying for mercy from the King is often the last resort."

"This being king thing is really starting to get on my nerves."

"If the job was easy, you could give it to anyone," he pointed out, "and without all the fuss of stabilizing the realm beforehand."

"There you go, being wise again."

"Someone must, Oh Most Illustrious Idiot."

"Ouch. Okay, have Dantos schedule preliminary diagnosis for them after the wizards and the dying. It'll be a busy night."

"Very good, Sire. I also have an idea about the throne," he added. I paused with another forkful of something halfway to my mouth.

"I didn't know it needed ideas," I observed, mildly. "I should add a cushion?"

"Probably. But who sits on it? Lissette, at present, yes?"

"Oh, I thought you meant the dragon head in the great hall. Sorry. Yes, Lissette sits on the kingdom-throne, wears the crown, is in charge, whatever."

"May I make a suggestion?"

"It's your duty to advise me, even if your advice is silly. I'd say that counts as permission to suggest."

"Your concern, at present, is with Thomen's influence on Her Majesty. Correct?"

"Yes," I admitted, accidentally bending the metal fork in my grip. Oops. I straightened it out while Seldar continued.

"Perhaps we could remove his influence."

"I'm listening," I told him, still fixing the fork. "Go on."

"If we can divert Thomen to another task—say, with some sort of trouble at the guildhall in Carrillon—then we might have a window of opportunity. We could remove from Lissette any magical influences which may be upon her. With those canceled out, she could then decide for herself what she wishes to do. If her preference is to summon Thomen immediately and place herself under his care again..." he trailed off.

"...then she's really suffering and he's helping, regardless of whatever else he's doing," I finished.

"Yes. If his actions are purely an attempt to usurp the throne, I know what to do with him. If he is only attempting to be a good physician to the Queen, I know what to do with him. If he is both, however, I am at a loss. What do you wish done if he is using his legitimate position and necessary duties to worm his way into the Queen's graces?"

"I'm not sure. My first impulse is to kill him and get a new physician. I'm sure it's a bad idea, but it's all I have at the moment. But don't think I haven't noticed your effort to be nice to me."

"Sire?"

"You already pointed out how Thomen regards this invasion of the eastern marches as his personal project. Now you're going out of your way to assume he's innocent until actually proven guilty. I appreciate you making the effort and coming up with ways to help me feel more certain."

"It is, as always, my duty and my pleasure to ease the worries of Your Majesty."

"Just so you know I notice. And thank you for it. In the meantime, on the subject of Thomen's guilt, let me know if you think any other thoughts on it."

"I will, Sire. On a related note, I have spoken with the Temple of Justice in Carrillon. They have investigated the mass slaughter of children."

"Oh? Related how?"

"The deaths were wide-spread, occurring over considerable distance. However, they occurred nearly simultaneously. There seem to be no witnesses. There were also no other injuries, only the throats and near-total loss of blood."

"I'm fast, but not that fast. They're thinking this was a group?"

"Yes. Someone must have instigated it, but a group carried it out."

"Like, for example, Thomen and two dozen wizards?"

"Possibly. I have asked them to continue to seek the truth."

"Okay. Let me know what they find."

"I shall. Now, on the subject of the canals, Dantos informs me the plainsmen dislike the eastern canal."

"Why?" I asked. I was having trouble keeping up with all the sudden shifts of topics. Seldar, at least, had a list. I felt repeatedly blindsided. "I would think it's a wonderful source of water."

"Indeed. It is also a barrier, cutting off much of the southern reaches of the plains."

"I'll have a word with the mountain about some hills, maybe, with wide tunnels, gentle external slopes, all that stuff. Maybe every mile or so along the canal it can alternate between a tunnel through a hill and open sky. The hills will act as bridges, but will still allow access to the water. What do you think?"

"I am sure they will be overjoyed at anything you choose to do for them, Sire. They are reluctant to bother you with requests, but they are willing to speak with Dantos. It is almost as though they fear you."

"It's a vicious myth," I replied, and sent a message spell into the mountain. Give it a year and the canals will be a dotted line on the map, with huge land bridges alternating with open water.

It was a busy morning.

On the bright side, I got to meet Seldar's wife and son. Carella used to be a petite little thing; motherhood filled her out. The boy was at least two years old and rode his mother's hip. Seldar seemed both pleased and pained when they came in. I'm guessing Carella used her status to gain entry and see the King and Seldar knew it. Still, he shifted smoothly into a social mode and introduced us.

Carella, of course, remembered me. I think she was especially delighted when I remembered her. Tallin, their son, was likewise pleased to meet me. He showed no signs of shyness, but held his arms out and demanded I pick him up. This seemed to surprise both his parents. Carella told me he was usually quite shy. I took him and held him up at eye-level. He grinned at me; I grinned back at him. He reached out and poked my teeth. I extended fangs and retracted them. This amused him to the point of laughter, much as wiggling one's eyebrows or ears might. I know because I did those, too, with equal effect.

I played with Tallin for a bit before Carella admitted she had only come in for a moment. She gathered up the little one and departed. Tallin, of course, didn't want to go. I gave him a magical ball of light to play with. This interested him enough for Carella to exit with a minimum of banshee-itis. I saw Seldar smiling at both of them as they exited.

Then it was back to the grind of the kingdom with Seldar. I finished breakfast and brunch, and we both sat down to lunch before Seldar ran out of things to report and questions to ask. One of the big things was putting someone, or several someones, on palace security. I was getting tired of all the psychic alarms going off on the lower door. He suggested my alarms might be removed, since Dantos posted a permanent guard detail at the door and put a similar detail on duty for monitoring communications, the palace shields, and so on. In general, I simply agreed with him. As we spoke, people kept coming in with messages for us and taking messages away. Half the things we discussed were started before the meeting was over, but I wasn't sure we would *ever* finish.

However, one of the brighter notes was one of the messengers. A lot of older kids—ten to twelve years—ran around the Palace as messengers and general gofers. One of them reminded me of Heydyl, which reminded me of his mother, Lynae. For the meeting's closing issue, I told Seldar about the two of them and asked him to spread a little word-of-mouth how this particular dressmaker might need some dress-making work. Nothing major—no subsidy, no sign His Majesty was involved, merely an unexpected uptick in business, if it could be arranged with subtlety. Seldar assured me he could find ways to be subtle. I believed him.

I wanted to call Baron Banler in Baret and see how he was going to cope with the army about to camp around his city, but I couldn't bring myself to face him right after the morning meeting. Instead, I went back to my workshop, followed by a pair of red sashes, and tried my Tort-detection spell again. Still nothing. Not even a chirp. Whatever she did to hide herself, she did it thoroughly and continuously.

After my break for magical endeavors, I felt sufficiently recovered to try calling Banler. The ruling family of Baret was still using the same mirror, so reaching him wasn't a problem. He was nine years older, of course, but aside from a little more grey around the temples and noticeably more forehead, he was pretty much as I remembered him.

"Halar!" he said, grinning hugely. "I understand you're feeling better?"

"That's an understatement. How's the river bypass?"

"Profitable. I'm enjoying it. And I don't know how much influence you had on the Demon King, but I've yet to thank you for laying down the law to the creatures of the Eastrange. I should also thank you for anything you did to keep the Demon King out of my barony."

"I'm not sure I had much effect, if any, but you're perfectly welcome. I called about something urgent, though."

"Oh?" His jaw set and he leaned forward, elbows on his knees. "What's happening?"

"The army that went through, headed east?"

"Yes?"

"It's coming back."

"It is?" he asked, surprised. "What did you do?"

"What makes you think I did it?"

"They went off in your direction. Now they're headed the opposite direction. Anybody smarter than a brick can draw the obvious conclusion."

We traded stares for a moment before I chuckled. The man reminds me of Xavier, which should come as no surprise.

"They're running out of road," I answered, "from the feet down. I think they'll all make it back without falling into a ravine or down a mountainside, but I won't promise."

"Hmm. That's not entirely good, Halar. I mean, 'Your Majesty'."

"How about we just go with 'Sire' and try not to be too formal?" I suggested. "You're a nobleman; we're not at court or in front of a dozen other people. Okay?"

"Okay." He grinned at me again, eyes merry. "I like being a familiar of the King."

"You know I'm not allowed to marry my daughter or granddaughter off. It's a religious thing."

"I know. But I have daughters of my own, and I understand you may be available again, soon."

"Oh?" I asked, suddenly interested. "Do tell!"

"From what I hear, she's trying for a palace coup. She pretty much has it, too, with you trapped on the wrong side of the Range. Of course, as long as you're alive—so to speak—she can't remarry and you're still the King. Hence the war."

"Fair enough," I agreed, nodding. "There are generally at least three sides to any story, though."

"Three?"

"One side, the other side, and the truth."

"The least popular side of all," he agreed, nodding. "It's a wonder the church of Truth stays open. People don't want the truth. They want comfortable lies."

"I've noticed. But there's a god of truth? I didn't know that."

"Oh, yes. It's said his priests can't lie. They can be wrong, of course, but they can't actually say anything they don't believe to be correct. It's also said they always know when someone lies to them."

"Hmm. That sounds awfully fishy to me. You could lie to someone and convince them, then they could take your lie to a priest of Truth, and so on."

"Ah, but they can consult their god," Banler answered, grinning. "When you ask god about the truth, apparently you get it."

"I don't think I like that," I admitted.

"Nobody does. And yet they remain, like a particularly persistent mange. But we were talking about sides. I've heard one side. What's your side? And why not give me the truth, too, if you know it?"

"Thomen is probably using dark arts to make the Queen his puppet. Through her, he's already taken over the rulership of the kingdom. I'm willing to let him live if he lets Lissette go—he can pack his things and be exiled. Otherwise, I'll have to free Lissette myself."

Banler whistled.

"I had no idea. So, those idiots on my doorstep—and about to be on it again, soon—are actually taking their orders from Thomen and don't realize it?"

"Pretty much, yes."

"Do the other nobles know about this?"

"I... hmm. Come to think of it, no. At least, I don't think they do."

"Would you like them to?"

"Do you think it will help?"

"It won't help Thomen, that's certain. I don't know if it will help you."

"I don't follow."

"It's complicated," he said, leaning back in his chair. "We nobles were princes not so very long ago. Now, me, I'm happy being a baron in the kingdom. It's safer and trade has increased eight or nine-fold with my river bypass and the roads. You couldn't pay me to go back to the old days. I know when I'm well-off!

"Some of the others, though," he continued, rubbing one stubbled cheek, "well, they would rather rule their own pigsty than serve at a banquet table."

"Better to reign in hell than serve in heaven?"

"A sentiment I don't share, but yes. So, if those sorts find out Thomen is a usurper, using the Queen as a mouthpiece, while the King is off in the hinterlands," he paused, thinking, juggling political factors I didn't know and can't understand. "I'd say you'd have a half-dozen regions turning back to princedoms and quitting your kingdom. If you don't do anything about them, maybe a half-dozen more, later."

"How would this affect Thomen and Lissette?"

"Could get Thomen killed," he told me. "It'll certainly keep him occupied if he wants to keep the kingdom. Might get Lissette killed too, maybe—depends on what sort of control we're talking about and which way you decree it ought to go. 'I want my wife back,' is very different from 'Kill the traitors,' if you follow. You'll still likely have a war or two to get back the quitters."

"I get it. I should have called you earlier for political advice."

"Maybe," he agreed. "You want me to help with this, Sire?"

"Maybe," I answered. "My goal, here, is to find confirmation Thomen is as much of a traitor as I think he is—I like to be certain before ripping a man's ribcage apart—before I free Lissette and put her in charge of the kingdom. I want her to run things for me while I go do the things *I* want to do."

"Hmm," Banler replied, scratching behind one ear. "I understand the urge to chuck it all and walk away, but... Sire, you may not be aware of this, but your wife, the Queen? She's a *woman*."

We looked at each other for several seconds. I couldn't tell if he was joking. He didn't look as though he was joking.

"Actually, I noticed it shortly after we married." I thought quickly about how to spin the transfer of power to appeal to a patriarchal society. "If it comforts you any, I don't intend to simply abandon her on the throne. She'll still be carrying out my policies. And if she sends for me, I'll show up and take care of whatever the problem is." I cocked my head as if in thought and added, "Come to think of it, maybe I should have some trusted advisors in charge of calling me, instead of her. She might not want me to see how badly she goofs things up."

"Definitely," he agreed, nodding vigorously. "So, you want her to be your agent? A ruling queen carrying out *your* will? She'll just be managing the kingdom?"

"Yes. Yes, indeed. That's it exactly."

"That's not so bad," he mused. "She'll need advisors, definitely."

"I agree. I'm glad you're willing to help her out. Thank you. In the meantime, do you think you know anyone who would be helpful in turning a kingdom into a queendom in these trying times?"

"The way you describe it, I think I can find a few others."

"Thank you, Banler," I told him, sincerely. "Oh! The reason I called in the first place was those idiots about to be on your doorstep. Are they a problem? Do you need anything? If they're causing trouble, I'm willing to help however I can."

"No, they're not a problem. Oh, there are little things, only to be expected when the army is encamped. Some petty theft, some fights, a few murders—the usual for any city, I'd say. Prices go up, of course, but they go down again when the army leaves." He shrugged. "It's always some trouble. I'd have to say it's mostly a good thing. After all, I'm a loyal subject of Her Majesty. They're not here to take the place."

"Fair enough."

"You do know, though, they'll march north and take the pass if they can't take the southern Kingsroad, don't you?"

"Yes, I'm aware of it. They'll try to go through Vathula. I have it on good authority this will be difficult."

"If you trust the Duke of Vathula."

"I don't, but he'll serve me rather than Thomen."

"Good point."

"Even if they eventually make it through, the army will have to march down a fairly narrow trail with mountains, cliffs, and steep slopes on both sides. If I recall properly, the trail is mostly straight, but has slight curves to it, back and forth, cutting visibility. The head of the army won't be able to see the tail, and vice versa. If they're strung out enough, neither end will be able to see the middle, either."

"I see you have a plan. I think I'll just let you get on with it."

"Plan? Me? I'm making this up as I go."

"You will forgive me, Sire, if I don't take you at your word?"

"I like you, Banler. I'll forgive anything short of treason. Eventually."

"Good to know. Now, how else may I be of service?"

"Actually, I didn't call to ask for anything. I only wanted to know if the army was a problem and if I could help. If not, then I'm done. Although," I added, as an afterthought, "you might let me know what they're up to, if and when you find out."

"Of course, Sire. I would like to ask a favor, however."

"I am all attention."

"You recall my daughter, Rialla?"

"Uh… yes, I think so. Didn't we meet several years ago?"

"Ah! I see. Yes, you did, but the Demon King met her more recently and more frequently. At least, he saw fit to have her back after each child."

"Oh."

"Yes."

"I'm so sorry, Banler."

"Sorry?" he asked, surprised. "What? Why?"

"Uh, maybe I misunderstood. You were saying something about a favor?"

"Yes. I'd like you to take her back to the Palace at Carrillon, if and when you go there."

"I'm not against it, but why?"

"Well, the life of a King's Consort is a good one—as long as it's not the Demon King, of course. Now that you're yourself again, the Queen's kicked out the consorts and concubines. To be honest, I'm not any too sure what to do with her. I'd be honored to have you accept her as a gift. And your sons can come with her, to grow up in the Palace with the others, if you like."

What was I going to say to that? My options were "Yes, I'd love to have a consort with my kids move in with me and my wife," or "No way, I'm not taking responsibility for my alter-ego's illegitimate children."

Somewhere, there's a orb of black, enchanted glass full of an evil spirit—and demonic laughter.

Culturally, Banler was being a perfectly decent sort. Noblemen thought trading daughters around for goodwill and family linkages was simply good business. Judging by his demeanor, Banler was actually trying to be nice. Rialla would live in the Royal Palace. Her children—our children—would grow up as noblemen and distant-but-potential heirs to the throne, and Rialla—apparently a favorite of the Demon King, therefore possibly one I, too, would favor—would be in a position to positively impact my feelings on the Barony of Baret.

I don't think Banler took my desire to make Lissette an actual ruler too seriously. Maybe he was assuming I would be around a lot, lurking in the basement or in some hidden retreat.

From his viewpoint, though, he was being kind to Rialla and generous to me, thinking this arrangement would make everybody involved happier. That is, Rialla, me, and the children—two sons, if I recalled T'yl's report correctly. Not so much for Lissette, of course. I doubted he was thinking in terms of how to support them, or about how to give them a proper inheritance. Banler isn't that sort of man. He was trying to do what was best for them.

"I think your offer is extremely generous," I told him. "Thank you. I'm not sure when they can come, though—and I'm not sure Carrillon is the place for them. The Palace of Karvalen, maybe. I'll have to think about it, and some things need to settle down and sort out. Right now, they're safest there, I think."

"Of course, Sire. Whenever and wherever you want them, say the word."

"Thank you, Banler. Now I'll go see about sorting out and settling down some of those things."

"A pleasure to be of service." He gestured and pretended to bow in his chair. "Happy hunting," he told me, and we hung up.

At least *that* went well. Mostly. I made it a point to notify Seldar about the conversation. With luck, he would figure out what to do about Rialla and the spawn.

I stopped by the forges to see Kavel. All four of the great smithies in the Undermountain are, technically, "the King's Forges," but three of them run night and day, operated by a number of smiths and organized by the Kingsmith—their term for the master smith of the mountain. Karvalen produces what may be the finest steel in the world, and a lot of it. The Kingsmith is in charge of the overall production of those three forges.

Kavel and his family, however, have the fourth of the undermountain forges all to themselves. While the other three produced things, Kavel's forge area ran more to research and development. That one is *the* Kingsforge.

I found it, with a little help from my escort of red sashes. The mountain moves things around, darn it, so even a map doesn't work very well for long. I heard the singing and hammering a long way off, which helped me zero in on them. Lessons in magic or no, they still sang to the metal. It's good to keep up family traditions.

Their singing to the steel was another example of magic I should study. I'm told it does impressive things to the metal, but I have no idea how it works. I'm not sure magicians do, either. It's a bit of idiosyncratic, personal magic that may be incomprehensible to anyone not raised in the tradition.

My visit interrupted Kavel at his work, but I didn't keep him long; the noise in the forge was *dreadful.* I wished for earplugs almost instantly and cast the sensory-reduction spell to tone down my ears. The hammering still hurt, but it was merely an earache instead of sharp spikes of pain. At least the family could sing. They were always on pitch and *always* on the beat.

Kavel was overjoyed to see me, pleased to know helping Flim was the right thing to do, delighted with his lot in life, and more than willing to help me in any way he could. He seemed disappointed all I wanted a selection of metal rings. He listened attentively, asked questions, made sure he knew what I wanted, and promptly got to work. It wasn't long before they had several of the things in various sizes, from discs with holes barely big enough for string, to five-inch things you couldn't keep on as a bracelet. I thanked him and let him get back to more important work.

I also got to meet the young Larel. He was only recently of age—call it fifteen—but his shoulders and forearms were like twisted metal. His work was amazing. He twisted hair-fine wire or scraped delicately at bits of gold to make things I wouldn't have dreamed possible without magic. Then again, he was humming; maybe it was partly magic.

I spent the rest of the day in my wizard workroom. There were a bunch of things needing my attention. I needed a way to talk between universes, monitor time differential, and—possibly—distract anyone watching for interuniversal gates. Making dozens of tiny gates already proved useful—I hoped—and the rings would make it easier to make tiny gates. Making micro-gates for Mary wasn't too bad, but having objects specifically dedicated and prepared to be mini-gates would make it so much easier. I should have done that first. Ah, well. Live and learn.

I also started some preliminary work on a second-generation Ring of Hiding from Magical Detection—call it a Ring of Obfuscation. Building Mary's ring, as the first-generation model, gave me all sorts of insights into improving it. Hers worked perfectly, but, as with any enchantment, it's generally a whole thing, not easily modified after the fact. The latest model ought to be even more efficient and effective when I get it done.

Hmm. Can I create a variation on a scrying spell to work between universes? Instead of opening a door and looking through, could I make something more like a window? Draw the curtain aside and look through without actually opening it?

Tricky. Very tricky. It might be worthwhile to look into the possibility, no pun intended. Unfortunately, I had other work to do and a projection spell to develop—something I could use to park an image in a distant temple. It would be similar in some respects to a reversed scrying spell, but it should work in a volume, not an area—a space instead of a plane. Instead of a window to a distant location, it should be a spatial reconstruction—a hologram. It would have to use some components of an illusion spell to reproduce the actual images, and then it had to cause air vibrations to reproduce sound...

This I felt I could do. Inter-universal scrying was only an idea. Illusions with sound? Those I've done before.

I got to work.

Thursday, February 26th

I was right. I'm a lousy king. I haven't had time to sit quietly and catch up on my own thoughts in a while.

My days—well, my mornings—are now occupied with the cabinet, or council, or whatever they are. Currently, that's Seldar, Dantos, Tianna, Beltar, Torvil, Nothar, Percel, and Liet. Mary is in another universe and Kammen is off to Carrillon on a diplomatic mission.

Seldar asked to send him via gate; I agreed when he offered helpers to cast the spell. They didn't actually do anything besides exert themselves to provide more power. The gate is constantly charging itself, true, but he knows I don't like running it off the battery if I can plug it in, so to speak.

I'm still a bit on the fence about this. *Kammen* is on a diplomatic mission. Next comes an angel with a trumpet and seas turning to blood.

Maybe I do him a disservice. He's grown up a lot on the outside. Has he grown up a lot on the inside, too? He strikes me as a direct, forthright, upstanding individual. That might be unexpectedly effective in the political intrigues of the Palace, especially if he actually understands the place. He's also the one who gets on best with Malana and Malena. Seldar says his plan will go much more easily if they agree to help. I'm not entirely sure what Seldar's plan actually is, but I have zero doubts about him having one. And I trust him. I even trust him about using Kammen as a diplomat. Mostly.

"But *Kammen*," I protested. "He's not subtle. He's not even as subtle as *me*. The closest I've ever seen him come to a diplomatic answer is silence."

"Sire," Seldar said, patiently, "he is unfailingly worthy of trust. While it is true he is not the most intelligent of men—and I may say so without insult; he is one of my best and oldest friends—he is far from stupid. He is also, I think, the most ruthlessly loyal of all your subjects."

"Ruthlessly loyal?"

"I am not certain how to express it."

"Oh, do please try."

"Kammen will do anything necessary. He will give his life in service to the kingdom, and I cannot say such a thing, of my own knowledge, about anyone else. I believe I will, if it is necessary, but until the moment comes, how can I be completely, utterly certain? Kammen, I believe in. He will do whatever he feels is required to carry out your mission, to follow your orders, to do what needs to be done because he believes in an ideal of a kingdom you described to us in our youth. I believe he will do more than die for that ideal; he lives for it."

"It bothers me to think I can inspire people like that," I said. I did not add "unintentionally."

"There are many powers in being a king," Seldar pointed out.

"Yes, and I sometimes think there's too much power involved. Great power and great responsibility go hand in hand. If you have great power, you have the responsibility to use it wisely."

"This is why you have counselors, Dim Lord."

"Good thing. Hey! Did you just poke me in my lack of wisdom?"

Seldar said nothing. He did smile slightly. Jerk.

We also have a new head of the local wizard's guild. Haran is another hefty wizard with a penchant for rings; they're a good place to store spells. He seems less… I don't know. Greasy? Weasel-y? He's less diplomatic than Corran, certainly, and speaks his mind with a fine lack of respect. I don't know if I like him or not.

Seldar and Haran agree we can probably trust the guild members still in Karvalen. I didn't need them to tell me that, not after I looked over the ones trying to swear loyalty to the King.

My eyeball scan of a bunch of wizard souls the other night was very revealing. When I permitted them to swear their loyalty to me as the King, they all agreed and several lied. The liars are currently in a canal boat, headed north toward the Vathula Pass. They haven't been banished, exactly, but they're aware the King knows they lied. Their names are circulating through the Wizards' Guild halls as oathbreakers who are not to be trusted.

Don't lie to the thing that can look at your soul. It can ruin your reputation, among other things.

So, when Haran says the Wizards' Guild in Karvalen is short on traitors and saboteurs, I believe him.

I hate meetings. I have other things I want to do. If I could turn it all over to Seldar, I would, but they insist on getting my approval, even my opinions, on what to do. It's a responsibility, a big one, and I have no idea how badly I'm screwing up everything I touch. I'm doing my best, but I don't like this job.

See? Terrible king.

On the other hand, I have dozens of portal rings with one-shot gate spells on them. They're small, which really saves a bundle in terms of power, and they're independent of the mountain, which makes it much happier. They're also plain spells, not enchantments. Once they go off, that's it—at least, if I don't supply external power. For at least a few seconds, there should be a small hole from one place to another, big enough for a message spell or other communications. If Johann can detect gate openings—and he might—when I go through again, I intend to fire off all of them at once, to different locations, just as I did with Mary. Only this time, it won't take quite so much effort. Then I'll dive through with heavy cloaking spells and immediately move away, blend in. I'm nervous about repeating a trick, but what else can I do?

I really don't want him to capture me again.

Speaking of cloaking spells, my Ring of Obfuscation is on my left hand. It's a plain piece of steel with the usual enchantment of a magical ring—an over-powered cleaning spell to deal with scratches, rust, and similar damage. You can pound the ring flat and it'll gradually come back into perfect condition, given lots and lots of time. Fitting my new cloaking spell into it along with the self-repair enchantment was tricky, but the two don't have a lot that can interfere with each other.

I think it's fantastic. I have a personal cloaking device against magical scanning. Now all I need is something to help with my hygiene and disguise spells and I'll start to feel pampered and lazy.

Beltar keeps asking me to drop by the Temple of Shadow. I'm not sure I want to. I don't really want to have anything to do with religion, these days. I tolerate

Sparky because of my daughter and granddaughter. I don't mind the Hunter, or Ssthitch, and I get on well with an anthropomorphic personification of Reason, but that's about as far as I want to go with gods.

On the other hand, there are representatives of Justice and the Grey Lady on the council. I'm trying to be nice to them. They're helping with the whole Church of Light problem. Apparently, since the Church of Light hates all other religions, we're all in this together. While the enemy of my enemy might be my friend, how does it hold up when you get rid of the common enemy? Hopefully we can continue to be peaceful and nice even if we somehow rid ourselves of the Church of Light.

Speaking of enemies, the fleet has had some difficulties. The weather, uncooperative in the first place, became somewhat stormy. They've been badly delayed, even pushed back by the stormfront. We think they did some spell-work to break the storm, but we don't have them under constant observation. The fleet survived intact, but they didn't start making progress again until today. Seldar thinks they spent too much effort on a weather-working and needed to rest. I agree. The bad news is they're still coming. The good news is it's taking them much longer than they anticipated and they might not be in perfect shape when they get here.

Nothar assures me Karvalen is ready for an attack. He's made all the preparations; all we have to do is sound the alarm. Haran agrees with him and has wizards taking turns putting reinforcement into the city's shielding spells. I've done a little work on them myself, making sure I understand all the magical defenses and how they're powered. The techniques I had to develop in a particularly low-magic world are very helpful in that regard. Tianna, speaking for Amber, tells me Mochara is also prepared for an attack, but most of their preparations are against what should be a sea assault.

If I thought Karvalen was about to be attacked, I would have to worry about whether or not there was a plot involving the Baron of Karvalen and Thomen. I still haven't managed to meet the local baron. Should I force the issue and summon him? Or should I go visit? Or can I get away with continuing to, for the most part, ignore him? I'll see how ignoring him works. It hasn't been an issue thus far, what with Nothar filling the Baron's shoes at the council table.

I kind of like Nothar. Maybe I'll just keep him on the council and use him as liaison. It might be less trouble. It also seems to make Tianna happy, since she has another excuse to see him. It certainly meets with Nothar's approval. He's not an idiot.

I'm more concerned about Mochara. The weather hasn't been helping the attack fleet, but they're still on their way. Unless something drastic happens, we expect them to arrive at Mochara sometime tomorrow afternoon at the earliest.

I have a number of ideas for dealing with ships, all of which can be countered by competent wizards. I wonder what they have in store. I'm glad we've had more time to get ready.

There is one good thing about having a day jam-packed with meetings, briefings, and other stuff. At night, people sleep. The mountain never falls silent—the forges are always working, the waterfalls turn waterwheels, air whispers through the passages and vents, a few late-night people roam about, city guards patrol the corridors, and other noises drift through the undermountain. It's a good time to do things without being interrupted or distracted. I like the night.

My initial Tort-detector continues to fail miserably. She's either warded permanently or I've got a fundamental problem with my spell theory. So I decided to see if I could get a line on T'yl. I re-tuned the existing spell and used his imprint, instead. He was actually easier to tune for. There were a lot of things he left lying around in his quarters. While I didn't have any body parts—hair, nail clippings, that sort of thing—I did have clothes and other personal effects to choose from.

It worked. My listening spell established a line to the west. Damn. So the spell works, but it's useless for finding Tort. Well, T'yl is a consolation prize. I'll take it.

I called Sir Sedrick and woke him up. He rubbed one eye while he tuned in his mirror.

"Ah, Your Majesty," he yawned. "Good evening."

"And good evening to you. Sorry to wake you."

"When one serves a nightlord," Sedrick observed, shrugging, "one must be prepared to keep odd hours. What do you have for me?"

"T'yl. I think. I got a bearing on his position and he's somewhere to the west of me. I can't tell exactly where, yet."

"Interesting. It is my understanding T'yl is a magician of some repute?"

"He was one of the two magicians of Karvalen. He helped break me out of a mental prison and kick the Demon King out of my body."

"I see," he replied, nodding sagely. "Does he have any enemies among the others of his kind?"

"Magicians? Or Kamshasans?"

"He's from Kamshasa?" Sedrick asked eyebrows climbing. "I did not know this."

"Does it matter?"

"I am impressed. Most men of Kamshasa are unable to read, much less work with the stuff of magic. Aside from a few male slaves for clerks, it is punishable by death to teach a man his letters."

"I did not know that."

"Indeed."

"I do know T'yl is an escapee from Kamshasa," I went on, "but I never got the story out of him. Still, Kamshasa is to the south, not the west. Are there magicians to the west?"

"Yes. Arondael is in the southwest of the old kingdom of Rethven... oh, somewhere near Riverpool, I think. I was there, once, but it was in my youth. Since you say he is to the west, that is the place I would begin searching for him."

I rubbed my temples and thought for a moment.

"Have you had any more luck with finding Tort?" I asked, finally.

"I regret that I have not."

"Then... find T'yl. Maybe we can get him to help us find Tort."

"As you wish. Do you wish me to ride across the kingdom? Or do you wish to send me through magic means?"

"Is that a request?" I asked, trying to smile.

"I merely point out it would be quicker to send me," Sedrick replied, serenely. I actually chuckled.

"Very well. Get your things together while I get a gate ready."

I cut the connection and headed down to my old gate room.

The mountain had refilled the pool with water, clean and fresh, tasting a bit of minerals. The archway T'yl destroyed when I left was gone, of course, but the wall had extruded a new one, free-standing, with crystals already embedded in the structure. It wasn't magical, of course, but it was perfect for enchanting.

I wondered why T'yl sealed this room. Because, lacking an enchanted arch, it was no longer useful? Or to keep prying eyes away from it? As a landing zone if I ever decided to come back? Or did it bring back too many unpleasant thoughts? Or did the mountain seal it without being told?

Whatever the reason, the mountain had no objections to making the room useful again. Looking at the new arch, I wondered when I would have time to enchant it, if ever. Or even if I should. I might be leaving before the effort of building a permanent enchantment into it could pay off. Then again, an enchanted gate is easier to use, which might make it easier to move pieces around on the game board so I *could* leave…

Later. Right now, I needed to summon a Hero. This involved a little spell work and more than a little power. Fortunately, I didn't need a full gate spell, just one to deal with minor details like space, not an adjustment of universal constants. And, since it was night, I had the power to activate it.

I went ahead and built a small power-jet for it, sucking in magic and pumping it into the spell structure. The last thing I needed was to feel hungry. I have a Demon King reputation to lose.

Sir Sedrick answered his mirror and I explained the basics of how gate travel worked. We signed off and he went looking for an appropriate opening. When he called back, he was in front of a tunnel mouth about the right size.

The space between us rippled, shifted, and the interior of the archway flushed away, snapped back.

Sir Sedrick led his horse through as quickly as possible; a dog followed him, keeping close to his heel. When the horse was fully across the threshold, I shut the spell down and the image of a distant tunnel ripped into nothingness. Sedrick kept control of the horse and snapped a sharp command at the dog. Neither of the animals seemed pleased to see me. Well, they just stepped through a teleportation gate into a cave with a predator. I suppose they can't be blamed.

Once they were calmed a bit—the dog looked at me suspiciously and the horse laid its ears back only intermittently—Sedrick looked over the archway.

"Impressive," he noted. "That's at least a two-day trip in a matter of a few paces."

"We can do better," I assured him. "Ready to go to the city of magicians?"

"A common error," he replied. "It has the Academy, but it is hardly a city of magicians. It simply has many of them."

"A fair point. And, come to think of it, do you have anywhere in particular you would like to come out? You've been there, right?"

"It was long ago, before I was a Hero. Anywhere reasonably close will be fine."

"I'll see what I can find." I dialed up my pocket mirror again and started scrolling across the world, following roads westward. Tolcaren, Carrillon… farther. Gain some altitude and look down. Small lake with a town on it—Riverpool, probably. But where is Arondael? I shifted the type of view, switching from visible light to magical auras. I should have done that in the first place. Boom. There was a blazing beacon of city, impossible to miss.

"Here we are," I said, and zoomed in. I shifted back to normal lighting, looking around for someplace outside the city itself. It might be a city full of magicians—or a college town catering to their Academy—but it still had farms outside the walls, and farms mean barns.

"How's that one look?" I asked, pointing at a barn. "If I open a gate over the barn doors, you'll step out into their farmyard."

"Will it hurt the barn?"

"I wouldn't think so. I'm using the doorframe as a locus, not actually doing anything… wait. The doors are closed, so they'll be in the plane of the forming gate…" I thought about it. "As far as I know, I've never done exactly this before. But if anything gets damaged, it'll be the barn doors." I fished in a pocket—I ordered pockets sewn into my trousers—and pulled out some of the new coins Seldar had struck. "Here. Take these. If there's any problem, please tender my apologies."

"Of course," Sedrick agreed, taking the coins and examining them. "Good likeness."

"If you say so. Is that enough?"

"For a barn, yes. I could use more, if you can spare it."

"I don't have much money on me. Have you got a bowl or cup or something?"

He produced a small cooking pot from the gear on his horse. I scratched some symbols on the outside, just under the rim. Nothing too arcane. They were mostly to make the thing unique and easily identifiable when I wanted to target it. One of my larger gate-rings could lock on to the pot and I could dump money through it. I also stretched one of the metal gate-rings, widening it a little to exactly match the shape and size of the pot's rim. Every little bit of correspondence helps.

I explained the process to Sedrick. He promised to answer my mirror call when I wanted to send money. I allowed as to how I expected he would. Then it was time to go.

I locked on to the barn, opened the gate, and closed it behind him.

Still no Tort. Still no T'yl. Not yet. I wouldn't call it a productive evening, but it wasn't a total loss, either. I decided to try and make the night a trifle more productive. I could use a good, solid feeling of accomplishment.

Maybe another magic ring? One for a mental defense, based on my brain-bunker spells? It would be good to have; I've had enough trouble with mental effects. True, it wouldn't help against things like evil aspects of my own personality being sucked in through tendrils, but it would be helpful against things like the mental dueling spell one guy tried.

Oh! And something to perform my twice-daily cleaning spell! Maybe something for disguising my inhuman coloration at night. Those would be just plain convenient.

Hmm. Could I make something to do both the cleaning and the disguise? Having it do two things would be difficult, but one affected only light, the other affected only matter, and neither would fundamentally interfere with the other. Maybe, if I set them up to operate off the same magical absorption matrix, I could have separate spell structures for the effect and simply switch between the two. If only one could operate at a time, would it be any easier to design?

This was a puzzle I could enjoy. I figured I deserved one. I spent the rest of the night in my mental study, working out spell designs and alternate ways to make them work.

I finally settled on the technique, taken mostly from wizard staves and such. A ring with multiple crystals or gems could have the individual gems enchanted with spell effects. The ring itself could act as a magical intake to feed all the spells, but it could only operate one at a time. This differed from a dedicated magical item, with one spell, which could be activated and left to run while another item was activated. The multi-gem setup would require shutting off one function to start another one, but I didn't see much trouble with alternating between disguise spells and cleaning spells.

Which reminds me. I still need to double-check about the rings and amulet the Demon King wore. I had them on when the ghost zapped the crap out of me. Were they still in Carrillon? I'll ask the guys when one of them comes on duty.

Friday, February 27th

Torvil took over bodyguard detail around dawn. He waited in my chambers while I went through the morning rituals—shower, trim the talons down to normal fingernails, all the usual stuff.

Of course, I got a call from Kammen the moment I stepped into the waterfall. Typical.

Fortunately, my pocket mirror isn't like a mobile phone; it's not going to short out if it gets wet. The image may be distorted by the water, but it still works.

"Got a problem," Kammen said.

"I can imagine. I've got some of my own." I wiped at the mirror and held it close to examine it. "Are you in a cell?"

"Nope. I'm in a wardrobe."

"I'm tempted to ask why."

"Sunrise. Got the curtains drawn and shutters latched, but I don't wanna set you on fire by accident."

"You raise a disturbing point," I admitted. "I don't know if a sunrise communication can do that."

"Didn't know, myself, so I didn't do it."

"Remind me to give you a position of responsibility."

"Got one, thanks."

"In that case, how about I just say 'good thinking,' and move on?"

"I'm okay with it."

"How did you fit in a wardrobe, anyway? You're not a small man."

"It's a big wardrobe, and I'm not wearing my armor."

"If it's a sufficiently sizable wardrobe, I guess I can believe that. Just don't fall out the back into another universe. Oh! By the way, do you know what became of the magical jewelry I was wearing when I went to visit Lissette? Before the ghost electrocuted me."

"I know it was taken off you," he replied. "One of the rings discharged, but I didn't have time to work out what it did. Something you wore interfered with spells to determine the damage, so we took it all off you."

"Fair enough. Do you know where my stuff is?"

"Still here in Carrillon, I think. After you left, Thomen took possession of your magic stuff. All except Firebrand, of course."

"Of course he did," I sighed.

"Can I report? It's cramped and stuffy in here."

"I'm sorry. Please, go ahead."

"Talked to… I talked to a couple of people I know. That project you wanted to look at? It's not a magical project."

"I'm not entirely sure what you mean."

"Figures. Can you call me back and do something to prevent me being overheard?"

"I think so. Are you in the palace?"

"Yes."

"Can you get out? The spells around it are troublesome for incoming calls."

"I'll call you when I'm ready, then."

"Works for me."

He closed the connection and I finished dressing for the day. Anticipating the arrival of the Rethven fleet this afternoon, I wore the armored underwear and both swords.

Why do you even have that thing anymore, Boss?

"It's good to have a spare."

What, just in case I break?

"For carving things I don't want you to touch. It's expendable. You are not."

Firebrand was silent for several seconds while I finished belting on my gear.

I'm... it began, then started over. *Sometimes I forget why I like you, Boss.*

"Beg pardon?"

Despite his amazing cruelty, I liked the Demon King, at least a little. He killed things and I got to help. Before that, Bob was pretty interesting, too. While waging a holy war under the Eastrange, he was nothing but fun. That sort of thing. But they all thought of me as... I don't know. A thing. A big chunk of metal with pyrotechnic issues and a sharp edge. They thought of me as a sword.

"You are a sword," I pointed out. "An intelligent one. A sentient, sapient being."

That's my point. Either they didn't know or didn't care, Boss. But you? You care.

"I do not."

You can't fool me, Boss.

"I'm trying to give nightlords a bad name."

They already have one.

"And you need to learn when I'm avoiding an awkward topic by deflecting it with humor."

That was humor?

"I swear, once I retire from this king business, I'm finding an anvil and sticking you in it."

I'm not sure what you mean. What for? I mean, I could melt it if you wanted...

"Ancient cultural reference to a sword in a stone. The rightful king was the only one who could pull it out."

You mean I'd get to pick the new King?

"I'm already reconsidering."

I settled down at the conference table with Seldar and some of the council. They don't all join me for breakfast, but each of them shows up at some point during the morning. Fortunately, Seldar and Dantos keep things organized enough so I seem to be free around lunch, barring disasters and surprises.

Seldar had the usual pile of things to go through, including a few health-related cases, some upcoming deaths, and a half-dozen men in armor who wanted to know if I needed knights. The health cases weren't too troublesome; simply understanding the germ theory of disease puts me way ahead of most of the priests and wizards. It also means I spend a lot less energy on spells to fix the problems. It does make me wonder, though, why the so-called gods don't fix certain things.

Are they being random, arbitrary, or do they simply charge too much for their services?

I read something about addiction and gambling. If I recall right, rats pressed a lever and got a reward. When the experimenters set it up so the lever delivered a reward every time, the rats learned to press the lever. When the experimenters set it up so the lever delivered a reward randomly—say, once in every three or four presses of the lever—the rats pressed the lever much more frequently than required to receive the same reward.

Is that what these energy-state beings are doing? Encouraging people to pray, and pray hard, frequently and with real effort, in order to maximize the amount of energy humans project into the energy-state realm? Is that what we are to them, rats in boxes, pressing levers to get treats?

The thought made me grumpy all morning.

As for the potential knights, I laid down the policy. Would-be knights go through what I think of as the weeding-out process before they even get to the interview. I don't want to sift through souls all night. For one thing, it takes time and effort, but the worst part is how dirty I feel afterward. I don't like looking inside someone's soul. I do it because it's sometimes vital to know what evil lurks in the hearts of men, but I hate the necessity that drives me to do so. It's not my soul. It should be left alone until its time to depart.

The upcoming deaths we scheduled for later.

"May I ask why, Sire?" Seldar wanted to know.

"Mochara is about to be invaded."

"Yes?"

"I'm the King, right? Defending Mochara is serious business."

"But that does not mean you will be unavailable."

"I'm not sure I can fight off an invasion in one afternoon," I pointed out.

"And you need not, Sire. It is the purpose of kings to defend the realm, not every city or citizen."

"If you're telling me I'm not supposed to go to Mochara and face off with invaders, you might want to find a better chair."

"Sire?"

"I'll have it put in a room where you can chatter on all you want while I'm in Mochara."

"I see. Is there nothing I might say to change your mind, Your Majesty?"

I could tell he was upset. He knows not to call me that.

"If you have the plan of Mochara's defense all set up and can assure me my presence will not help in any way, I'll be happy to hear it."

Seldar said nothing, but his lips thinned in frustration. I could sympathize with his feelings and it hurt me to have to do this to him, but I can't—won't—sit safely at home while people fight each other over something revolving around me.

I'm not the center of the universe. It doesn't spin on my axis. Hell, this place doesn't even spin. But a lot of stuff revolves around the throne, and those things are entirely my problem.

"Don't take it so hard," I advised. "I plan to safeguard myself as much as possible. Besides, it'll be a good thing. People will see me and know I take my responsibilities seriously."

"I am more than a little concerned about those within Mochara who might be more loyal to Thomen than to you, Sire."

"My presence should help, then. They won't want to attract my personal attention, will they?"

"I find myself surprised. You make an annoying amount of sense, Sire. I still believe it to be an unacceptable risk."

"Anyone else?" I asked, looking around the conference table. Tianna shrugged, apparently unwilling to express an opinion. Nothar looked at her, looked at me, and copied her gesture. The only person to speak up was Liet.

"If Your Majesty wishes, we can take the dying to the Temple of the Grey Lady to await your personal attention. If they pass on involuntarily, they will be cared for."

"Sensible," I agreed. "If they'll agree to it—and if there is no objection from the Grey Lady—I'll be happy to call on them there." Liet looked startled, but nodded agreement. She probably didn't expect me to make a house call. I looked at Seldar. "Well? Are you going to insist I stay here, or are you going to set up bodyguards and security?"

"If I insist, will you stay?"

"Nope."

"Then I shall prepare your security, Sire."

"Good man. What else do we—" I broke off as my pocket mirror chimed. "One moment, please." I dug it out and made a mental note to install a silent mode. It was Kammen. I excused myself and hurried to the workroom, trailing a jogging Torvil. He kept up surprisingly well. Not only big and strong, but fast, too. I outdid myself on those kids.

I activated the large mirror. A little fiddling with the thing let me transfer the call. Further fiddling altered the way it sent and received signal. It was like talking to Kammen down a length of pipe, but anyone trying to listen in should get nothing but a faceful of static. It would work for a while, but anyone good enough to listen in on a call in the first place would eventually figure out a way through it.

I should have paid more attention when I took classes on information theory and data security. I need to know more about encryption.

"Okay, we should be secure," I told him. "What's up?"

"The Queen's got troubles," he said. "Thomen's been doing something magic in her head, but Malana thinks it's a thing he learned from that eastern adept."

"What eastern adept?"

"The—oh. Right. There's a guy with weird spells. People go to him when they want to forget a thing, like after they lose a loved one, or something. He takes it away, for a price."

"Permanently?"

"Yep. It's not a spell that keeps going. It's a spell to change something. When he's done, there's no spell to get rid of or to wear off."

"So, rather than a spell to paralyze a hand, it's a spell to cut it off?"

"Pretty much, except inside a head."

"And he's taught Thomen these spells?"

"Malana thinks he's learned some of them and is learning more. The adept isn't a member of the Guild, but Thomen keeps him in style."

"Then why haven't the queen's guards done something about it?"

"They're guards, Sire. They don't deal with this sort of thing. It'd be different if Thomen was wrapping a spell around her head and squeezing. By the time they come out of the bedroom in the morning, there's nothing to point at or yell about. He couldn't smack her ass in the throne room and get away with it, but in the bedroom he can do as he likes. It's a problem between security and privacy, Sire."

"I'm pretty sure that's not the way I wanted to set it up."

"I'm pretty sure you didn't have much say in it," he countered, simply.

"I can't argue with that. What do we do about it?"

"I dunno. Malana thinks it's not a very good spell, though. It seems to wear off, whatever it is, if he doesn't keep doing it. It's like it injures her thinking and she slowly gets better. Got a good way to keep him away from the Queen for a week?"

"Not aside from killing him."

"Oh." Kammen looked thoughtful.

"Hey, what does Malena think?"

"Whatever Malana does."

"Seriously?"

"Yup, Sire. They're the same person. The two bodies are nice, though—as you ought to know." Kammen waggled his eyebrows and leered.

"There's a story there involving the Demon King. Do I want to know it?"

"Maybe not, but the two of 'em wouldn't mind demonstrating."

"Now I'm disturbed," I admitted. It would go a long way toward understanding the look on her face—their face? —when she bumped into me, though. Did the Demon King *like* them? Or did they learn to like him? Or was he simply capable of being charming, sexy, and attractive when he felt so inclined?

No, I probably don't want to know.

"How well are you set up in the palace?" I asked.

"No trouble," he said, shrugging. "I'm not in the Queen's Guard and I'm not in Mochara or Karvalen. You're not here, so I got a lot of nothing to do."

"Is anyone, you know, suspicious?"

"Yep."

"And?"

"Don't care."

"I'm afraid I don't follow."

"I'm a guy who's supposed to behead people who attack you. If I'm *here*, I'm not doing my job. They're okay with that. I'm not a commander or anything, so I don't got troops to order around. I'm one guy. That's all. If they wanna watch me wenching, they can." He shrugged. "I'm a knight. Lots of people like me. And I'm not doing nothing. Probably frustrates anybody thinking I'm a spy."

"Then how are we getting away with this call?"

"I'm also a wizard and I ain't stupid, Sire. I spent nine years doing a lot of things all quiet-like."

"Fair point. Thank you, Kammen. Is there anything I can do for you?"

"Yeah, sort of. Remember the minstrel girl, Tyma?"

"Vividly."

"She's looking for you and she's got a big stick."

"Does it have anything written on it?"

"Yeah."

"Tell her I'll be happy to let her hit me with it whenever we can get together."

"Uh? Okay, I guess. If you say so."

"Anything else?"

"If we get the Queen back to her old self, can you give her more guards? I'd like the Mals to have more time. They might like it, too."

"I'll see what I can do," I agreed.

Well. That was certainly a lot of food for thought. I wasn't sure I was interested in the meal, though. Did I want to find out more? Torvil was standing right there. Or Firebrand—I doubted Firebrand was ever out of arm's reach during the reign of the Demon King. I could just ask.

I don't think I will. At least, not today.

We had a council meeting about the defense of Mochara. Dantos suggested calling for the Lord Mayor of Mochara, which diverted me for a minute.

"Why a mayor?" I asked. Technically, the title was *primicivus*—pronounced pry-MIS-iv-us—meaning *first among the people of the city*. It seemed oddly egalitarian for a feudal lord.

"I do not know," Dantos admitted. "I was not part of the decision. I have heard your daughter had much to say about the rule of Mochara, and this deterred the Demon King from interfering with it."

"I heard it also made Kamshasa interested in taking it," Nothar added, "and interested Iranesh, Prydon, and Telasco. To my knowledge, only Kamshasa actually made an attempt, but their name may have been used to shift blame from another nation."

"Framed," I supplied. "Does anyone remember, know, or have any other information about it?"

"After mom—excuse me," Tianna said. "After Amber became a being of fire, it seemed appropriate to be less involved in the day-to-day rule of the city. While she still advises and guides the people of Mochara in the name of the Mother of Flame, it has been made apparent a priest should not also rule. Amber called for those with wealth or station within Mochara to select from among their number seven members. These form the Council of Mochara. They take turns being the head of the Council every year."

"That's weird," I observed. "Not necessarily bad, but certainly unusual." This was met with strong mutters of agreement. They like their rulers definite around here.

"So," I continued, "let's have a mirror brought in here. Do they have a magic mirror in the council chambers?"

It's amazing how an impending invasion can motivate people. I was all set to yell at a council of idiots and tell them to get off their fat, lazy, politician butts. Turns out they do not like being invaded. They took the earlier warnings to heart and were taking action even before I visited Flim.

Flim & Sons was busy supervising the building of a giant crossbow cradle, one to raise and lower their contraption just inside the city wall—the disappearing mount I'd told them about! Counterweights and levers were the order of the day. Zaren worked with men on the wall, mounting a few smaller, tripod-sized versions. Medium-sized catapults were still being constructed inside the city wall; the wall sits at the top of a cliff edge, so the inside of the wall is a lot shorter than the outside. The harbor and surrounding seas were becoming a very dangerous place for hostile people.

The city guard mobilized and the town militia prepared. Containers of all sorts were filled with water or sand for firefighting. Weapons sharpened, arrows made, armor refurbished... they even had the fishing fleet either docked or pulled up on the harbor's beach for war preparations. They were small boats, compared to the vessels approaching, but there were a lot of them. A dozen or more might be able to close with a single enemy vessel and ram, possibly attempt to board, or whatever it is smaller ships do to larger ships. Naval engagements aren't my area.

The gap in the artificial reef—the passage through the harbor wall—was closed off by stringing a bunch of chain and cable between the obelisks that marked the entrance. If nothing else, it was one more obstacle to simply sailing up to the docks and dumping troops.

The ruling council and the mayor were only too happy to know we would help them. I got an ugly look from Seldar, but I don't think anyone else noticed it.

"For the moment," Seldar said, "we believe the naval force is insufficient to take Mochara. Had the army made it through the mountains, that would be another matter. Fortunately, our King has already turned that force back."

"And we are duly grateful," replied the mayor, through the mirror. I didn't take to him at all. He smiled even during the news of a sea assault. Either he was looking forward to a battle or he didn't think it was a problem. I suppose he could have a smile magically grafted onto his face, as befits a politician.

"Our latest observations of the fleet show it has slowed," Seldar reported. "If they continue to advance at this rate, they should reach Mochara slightly before sunrise."

"They attack at dawn, then."

"It would seem so."

"We will continue to work through the night to strengthen our defenses. When should we expect reinforcements?"

I opened my mouth, but Seldar beat me to the answer.

"We are considering that very matter," he said. "Some organizational details remain. All the aid we can send will arrive in good time, I assure you."

"Very good. And thank you."

Seldar shut down the mirror and braced himself.

"Tianna?" I asked.

"Yes, Grandfather?"

"Would you like to go help your mother defend Mochara?"

"Yes, please."

"I'll see you in my gate room. Torvil?"

"Sire."

"Do you know of anyone who might volunteer to do the same?"

"I can think of a few, yes, Sire."

"Have them in my gate room as well. Wait for me there. Seldar, please stay. Everyone else, give us the room."

They got up and got out. Seldar and I looked at each other while the door ground shut behind them.

"Okay, go ahead," I told him.

"Your Majesty?"

"You've already argued with me about defending Mochara personally. I intend to go there, surrounded by my own people, with not just one, but *two* Priestesses of the Flame. If you still have an objection, I'd love to hear it."

He stood up and paced slowly around the table, hands clasped behind his back, head down, thinking. I let him. If Seldar was thinking hard, it was important. I know what I want to do—vent some of my frustration and anger on a bunch of invaders, which strikes me as an appropriate outlet for such things—but I also respect his opinions.

"Sire," he said, finally, "do you recall what you said about knights?"

"Probably. Did you have something specific in mind?"

"I refer to some of the things about knights and how you relate to them. How you hoped to be the… the worst of us. You would have to do terrible things as a king—things no knight should ever do—and you would bear the burden of the responsibility for them. But when you said you hoped to be the worst of us, I took it to mean you hoped to hold us—we would hold ourselves—to a higher standard. You would do the best you could, but, as we lack the troubles and responsibilities of a king, we should do better."

"Yes, I seem to recall. And you're right. A king may have to do things in his public capacity as a king that, in his personal and private capacity, he finds morally or ethically objectionable. It seems like an excuse the Demon King would use for his behavior, but the key difference, I feel, is the question of necessity. If the king is facing a choice, he should not simply take the more objectionable road because it's easy; he should fight to take the right road, especially when it isn't easy. I was trying to acknowledge that sometimes the only choices you have are bad ones, and the king is the one who has to make the choice. Knights should always encourage the king to do the right thing, to be better than he might otherwise be, even when they don't know he can't."

"As you say, Sire. Now I must tell you I believe you are making a bad choice."

"In what way?"

"You want to go to Mochara to personally oversee its defense."

"Well, yes. Even during the day, I'm a pretty dangerous guy."

"Yes, but you are only one person. A person with authority who will disrupt the defense of the city by creating confusion, destroying coordination, and engendering doubt. People will not know who to turn to, nor who to take orders from. Your unfamiliarity with Mochara and its defenders will cause more harm than good.

"I recognize, Sire, I have no authority to command your movements. This very lack was one of the reasons I felt I could not continue to serve when you were the Demon King. But I tell you now: going to Mochara is foolish. I believe it with all my heart. It is my duty to tell you your decision is wrong. More, it is my duty to make you listen."

He unbuckled his belt and baldric. He laid his sword on the table.

My first impulse was to snatch it up and tell him to go to hell. I'm not as emotionally stable as I would like to be, and I can't blame it all on Johann. A lot of it, yes, but I was also looking forward to the catharsis of letting go completely and killing everyone I could reach. Sometimes, losing control is a relief. This was an outright battle and I was hoping to rip things apart with a clear conscience.

I've been getting better at sitting on my anger, though—lots of practice. Plus, Seldar is almost like a son to me. I kept my calm and nodded.

"Well," I said, softly, "if you're willing to resign over it, I guess I need to take you seriously. No, that sounds wrong. I always take you seriously, Seldar. I think you could have told me 'I mean it,' and I would have listened."

"Would you?"

"Who do you think I am? The Demon King?" I made a rude noise and waved a hand to dismiss the idea. "Although I admit the prospect of beating someone's head in has been more tempting of late, that's because I'm still angry regarding a completely different matter."

"Then, have I succeeded in my attempt to dissuade you, Sire?"

"Yes. Yes, you have, damn you," I sighed. "I'll stay here. But there's something I want from you in return."

"Anything, Sire."

"First of all, you hit me across the face, once, to make your point. You threatened to resign to make your point. Between the two, you've made a larger, more general point. You have good advice and you're serious about making me listen to it. I get it. You shouldn't have to go to these lengths again. I promise to try to listen. If you think I'm not listening, say so. It will remind me I should. Okay?"

"I will. And I apologize, Sire, for my inappropriate behavior."

"You did what you had to do, which means it wasn't inappropriate. Inconvenient, maybe annoying, certainly frustrating and even enraging, but not inappropriate." I sighed, then chuckled. "You have a history of doing the right thing," I pointed out, "which is one of the finest qualities in a knight. Now, the second thing… find a use for me."

"Sire?"

"I'll stay in the mountain, yes, since you damn well insist the King cower in a hole, avoiding personal peril. What I will *not* do is sit idly by while everyone else goes off to war. I *will* help. Find things we need for the defense of Mochara and tell me what I can do about them."

"Happily, Sire!"

"Any objection to sending Tianna and the troops to Mochara?"

"As long as we have sufficient of the Orders of Crown and Shadow at hand, no objections."

"Hold it. Order of the Crown?"

"Bodyguards, drawn from the Order of Shadow."

I sighed. Nobody ever tells me anything. People keep rearranging the hierarchy while I'm not looking. Why can't we just have a fixed and unchanging structure? It would really be convenient for the immortal guy if things didn't change every decade!

"Wait, isn't that the duty of the Order of Shadow anyway?"

"Technically, we are your personal guard—at least, the secular Order is. The Knights of Shadow also consider themselves members your personal guard, but their concerns are for you in your person as a Lord of Night, rather than as King."

"But both Orders of Shadow and the Order of the Crown are supposed to protect me?"

"In a sense. We are the knights under the personal command of the King, an elite force. The Order of the Crown are a much smaller force whose sole duty is to protect your person."

"Okay. So how do the knights from the Temple of Shadow fit in with all this?"

"It is a matter for you to decide," he informed me. "In the absence of a formal decree on your part, I have acted—with the full accord of Torvil, Kammen, Dantos, and Beltar—as though their holy order is also a part of the royal Order of Shadow."

"All right. I'll have to talk to Beltar and see what the temple knights are like, I guess."

"Thank you, O Unreasonable One."

"You're in a better mood, I see."

"As long as you have sufficient guardians here, yes."

"Talk to Torvil and Beltar about it. Now get moving; there's a battle in the morning."

The way it was explained to me, the defense of a city falls into three stages. First, keep the invaders from reaching it in the first place. Second, if they get to the walls, keep them from getting in. Third, if they get in, kill them all or drive them out.

Each stage has its own advantages and difficulties.

The trouble with the first one was our navy. Mochara doesn't really have one. Oh, the fishing fleet can be used as a sort of navy, but it lacks large vessels with high decks. They only make short trips and they don't carry many men. A warship will plow right through them and inflict massive casualties, if they even bother to get that close. A warship full of archers is a bad thing for a fishing boat.

Since I never did manage to walk on water, stopping them wasn't really an option.

The second one, keeping the invaders out, seemed feasible. If their army had made it through the mountains it might be different. Armies typically target city gates as the weak point; if you take the gates, everyone can walk in behind you. Going over the walls is a valid tactic, but you have to capture and hold a large section of wall, and then invaders have to climb ropes or ladders—it's much less convenient. And Mochara has several gates, which means defending them would divide manpower and other resources.

Defending against a naval assault? That could be doable. A navy, realistically, can only come at one side of the city and they have problems of their own in getting from ship to shore to gate. I didn't know the defense plans, but I didn't need to—Seldar nailed me down in Karvalen. I was cautiously optimistic on their behalf.

The third one, if it came down to it, was much less pleasant. Fighting a battle in a city is a nightmare for the invaders. I just didn't see how they intended to attack the place and take it. The ships couldn't carry enough men.

What was I missing?

The more I looked at it, the less I liked it. The ships could be carrying boatloads of wizards—fine. But they *had* to know they were headed for a city where almost every man, woman, and child knew at least a little magic. Were they under a communications blackout, to avoid giving away any secrets? It was barely possible they might not know the entire ground force was routed and wouldn't be there to support them, but it seemed unlikely. Did they have some new, secret-weapon spell? I don't know how they could conjure a city-crushing spell without burning out a magician, to say nothing of a wizard. No matter how I looked at it, I still didn't see how they could win this.

On the other hand, "winning" can be defined in a number of ways. If they only want to inflict a lot of damage and go home, fine—they might count it as a win. If they want to test our defenses for future invasions, walking away with any intelligence on the subject would be a win. There could be any number of conditions they regard as success. So, what did they want to achieve, specifically? I had no idea.

I really didn't like that. Whenever an enemy does something incomprehensible, it's usually because it makes sense *to them*. If it doesn't make sense to me, then the other guys know something I don't, and that's a Very Bad Thing.

Okay. If they know something I don't, I need to know something *they* don't.

How do I stop a naval invasion? Let's see… obviously, the ships and troops will be shielded from direct magical effects. I can't magically start a fire, rip out a board, or stop a heart on any of the ships. They'll also attempt to stop any indirect effects, like a ball of fire launched at them, as well as any other projectiles. On the other hand, if I can launch something at them they don't recognize as dangerous, or something they can't perceive, they may not have shields capable of stopping it.

Could I take down their shields? For one ship, maybe. I can generate a magical disruption wave to dispel magical effects and break spells. But with a shipload of wizards backing it, they can reinforce the structure of their spells. I might not take it down. It would keep the wizards on board busy while I did it, but the other ships would still keep on coming.

So, can I generate a force locally I can transfer distantly? Really distantly, since I'm stuck in Karvalen.

What forces will destroy ships? They're made of wood… what binds wood together? Cellulose? Lignin? If I knew for sure what those actually were, I might be able to do something with it.

How about the people? What's a good, generalized, kill-everybody-on-the-boat effect? Radiation? Yes, but it's not quick, and quick is important when they're climbing the walls. Lasers? Again, yes, but people have seen me do that trick. Well, no one still alive, I think, but I'm going to run into serious targeting problems from a mountaintop. I can't get a line of sight on the fleet; Mochara itself will be in the way.

Could I stun everybody with some sort of sonic attack? Maybe. Again, range is the problem, along with having all my allies in my line of fire. I could build another chlorine monster and send it after a ship, or even simply create a cloud of chlorine and let it roll along with the wind. If I was there, of course.

I hate being left out.

I decided to set things up to get a good look at the battle. I had four mirrors taken to my sand table room. I didn't need a detailed world map anymore, especially since the southern half of it was obviously not going to register. All that work for nothing. Well, it could have been worse. At least I could repurpose the thing as a display. The mirrors could give me some alternate viewpoints and allow me to communicate with different people.

A quick check from altitude showed the ships still making dead slow progress. Telescopic zoom told me there were a lot of passengers lying around on deck— resting wizards? Probably. I resolved to keep an eye on things tonight.

Seldar rang my mirror and told me the troops were assembled in my gate room—what they think of as my gate room, the upper one. Technically, they were in the gate room and out into the hall. There was an awful lot of black armor with red or grey sashes. There were also a number of people in more mundane armor—volunteers to help defend Mochara from the usurper's troops.

I'm never going to understand how I can inspire people like that. Maybe Seldar found me a good PR person. Or Beltar. He's the head priest at the Temple of Shadow. A church is, after all, a public relations firm for a deity, or whatever they think of as a deity.

I'm glad he hasn't been on my back to make a divine visitation. Amber was right; they aren't pushy. Who would have thought it? Religious fanatics who don't shove it in your face. They're weird. A good weird, but weird. I keep expecting them to be, I don't know, more evangelical? More missionary? More loud and obnoxious? They keep not doing it, and I don't know what to make of them.

I entered the gate room, thinking about power and movement and how to make this work. Tianna was at the head of the line with her boyfriend.

"Nothar?"

"Yes, Sire?"

"You're going?"

"Yes, Sire."

I looked at Tianna.

"He says he doesn't trust all those sailors," she informed me. She slid a hand into the crook of Nothar's arm and he placed his own over it.

"I have a number of comments I might make, all of them inappropriate," I replied. "Remind your mother of her father's love."

"I will."

"Nothar? Are you going for the battle or to protect her?"

"I've no great desire to do battle, Sire, but I go where my heart dictates—and, I hope, where I may do the most good." He glanced at Tianna and I saw the flicker of a smile.

"I hope so, too. We're going to talk later."

"As you say, Sire."

"All right, everybody! Listen up. Gate travel is difficult, draining, and disorienting. When you go through, you'll be going out through the door at the Temple of Shadow in Mochara. Do not stop moving. Get out of the way for the people behind you. Shove if you have to, trample if you must, but *at all costs* clear the space in front of the door and *keep* it clear until the gate closes. Anyone still going through the gate when it shuts is likely to be cut in two and killed instantly. These things are dangerous in many ways, all of them lethal.

"We're going to form a column of three. When I say go, you start through the gate as fast as you can. When I say to stop, if you're past this line," I put a glowing line on the floor ten feet in front of the archway, "you hustle through that gate as though your life depended on it. If you are *not* past this line, you stop because your life *will* depend on it. We'll see how many of you get through before I have to let it close, then we'll evaluate how many we can move before morning. Any questions? Yes, you."

"Sir Panlan, my lord. If it is draining, can we assist by contributing power to the spell?"

I keep forgetting they're wizards, darn it. He had a really good idea.

"Yes, but first we have to spend some of the power in the spell before we can charge it up again," I lied. I don't like to look silly in front of a crowd. "This one was never intended for troop movements. I'll build one with a larger power reserve for next time. Any other questions?"

"Sir Frosh, my lord. Could you elaborate on what happens if we don't stop when you say so?"

"The gate spell will be about to close. You'll run into a collapsing spell that will divide you into several pieces and scatter them between here and Mochara, as well toss some parts into the void beyond the world. I'm not sure what happens to your spirit, but if someone does get shredded, I'll be sure to take note of it."

I didn't tell them I wasn't sure. It's what I think would happen and it's important to sound certain in front of the troops. I learned that at Crag Keep.

"Anything else?"

No one seemed too interested in any other subject, so they formed a column— Torvil the Gleeful on the left, Sir Panlan the Serious in the middle, and Sir Ariander the Grim on the right, with lines of red and grey sashes behind them. I have a lot of questions about Ariander, from his obvious *gata* roots to his title as First Blade. Someday, maybe I'll even get to ask them.

I found the doorway I wanted in the mirror. One of the things that made me pick the Temple of Shadow in Mochara was the arched outer doorway. The close match to my own archway helped.

The gate swirled, flushed away from us, and Mochara snapped into view. I was already shouting "Go!" even before it finished. People thundered forward, jogging, running, sprinting flat-out. I held the spell, watching the charge on the gems drain into it. As it approached the critical point, I started adding my own force to the spell, keeping it open and running; that was the cutoff point. I shouted for them to stop and there was a sudden pileup of people trying to backpedal. It took longer than expected to halt the line. Keeping the gate open for those last few seconds was more than I really cared for, considering I was shouldering most of the load myself by then.

The instant everyone was either through the gate or stopped, I shut down the gate. The view through it dissolved, tore into patches of nothing, and dissipated. Myself, I leaned on a handy wall and propped it up for a bit, trying to look tired instead of wrung out.

Maybe I need man-sized gates between Karvalen and Mochara. Smaller gates take less power. A door-sized thing instead of a me-riding-Bronze-sized thing would be open at least four times longer, maybe five or six times. Having one on either end would also help—power could be supplied from both ends. And a dedicated connection, like the Great Arch in Zirafel, would reduce power consumption even more...

Someone was talking to me. I blinked and wiped sweat from my forehead.

"My lord?"

"I'm fine. It's hard to do this sort of thing when I'm feeling mostly mortal." I straightened and adjusted my clothes. "How far did we get?"

"About a third, my lord. Perhaps a hundred of the volunteers."

"Good. We should be able to finish this tonight, after sunset."

"As you say, my lord."

"And get someone to put a chalk mark on the floor twice as far back from the line I drew. This first try was tough. We need a little more cushion space. Maybe I should put a spell on it to make it more obvious..."

"Immediately, my lord."

"Thank you...?"

"Varicon, my lord, First Shield of the Order of Shadow."

"You know what? I'm going to rest from this particular labor. Please see to these matters."

"I will see to it, my lord," he replied, saluting.

I went off to ask Laisa for a sizable dinner and request someone wake me when it was ready. I really needed a nap. She clucked reprovingly and told me to take better care of myself. When she turned back to her cooking, little Caris shook her finger at me, as though scolding. I stuck my tongue out at her, just the first couple of inches. She stuck her tongue out at me—and giggled.

The simplest things can cause terrible memory flashbacks. I remembered Olivia clinging to my knee and looking up at me.

I went up to my chambers to try and nap. If I tried really hard, maybe I could put Johann out of my mind for an hour or two. There was no way I could shake the vision of Olivia, though.

If I dreamed, I don't remember it. Firebrand says I did, but didn't pay attention to the content. Firebrand was more concerned with keeping watch for unpleasant influences while I napped in the Ascension Sphere. I approved wholeheartedly with its priorities.

By the way, Boss, Fred came to visit.

"Fred? The Monster Under the Bed?"

That's the guy. I told him you needed to rest.

"Everything okay?"

Nothing to complain about. He seemed cheerful enough. He just stopped by to say hello.

"Someday, when the world slows down a bit, I'm going to have to crawl under the bed and see how he's doing."

Good luck with that, Boss. The world doesn't seem to care about your schedule.

"More's the pity. Is it time for dinner?"

Dinner was lavish. Laisa knows how I eat, so a request for a big dinner was obviously a request for a banquet. Seldar and Beltar joined me, along with Varicon.

Tianna and Nothar were in Mochara. I missed my granddaughter already. That seemed odd, considering she was often down in Karvalen, doing religious stuff, or spending time with Nothar. Maybe it was because I knew I wouldn't get to see her again until after the battle at Mochara.

I caught myself glaring at Seldar and immediately looked at my plate. He didn't deserve to be the recipient of my anger. Just because he chained me here. Just because he punched me in the duty and knocked me onto my kingliness. Just because he was right and I was wrong. It did make me angry, though, that he had the gall to be right when I didn't want him to be.

Yeah, I've got some repressed anger. It leaks onto the people around me and I know it. I try not to let it, but the nature of leaks... At least I know people who truly deserve it.

Soon, Johann. It really needs to be soon. If only I didn't have so much to do first!

On the other hand, as angry as I might be at Seldar, I was also proud of him. I never had much to do with his upbringing, but I like to think the man he became is partly my doing. It would be nice to have something to point to and say, "This is something I helped with that didn't turn out badly."

After chomping my way through a couple of *dazhu* steaks, I had the upper hand on my hunger. I started the dinner-table conversation with Varicon.

"Varicon, you mentioned your title, earlier. I'm afraid I haven't really grasped the organizational structure of the Order of Shadow. You're the First Shield, you say?"

"Yes, my lord."

"What does it mean to be the First Shield?"

Varicon glanced at Beltar. Beltar gave him a blank look and shrugged.

"My lord," Varicon said, hesitantly, "is it not more appropriate to ask the *prophate* about these matters?" He pronounced it *pro-FAY-tee*; a term derived from Zirafel, again, and hard to translate. It seemed to encompass several concepts, mostly along the lines of wizard, seer, priest, and prophet. I got the impression it was more of a title than an actual description, but, considering Beltar, it might be a good description, too.

"Beltar?"

"Yes, my lord?"

"What's the difference between a *prophate* and a *deveas*?"

"The *deveas* is the mortal master of a religion, my lord. As *deveas*, I speak as my god would direct. I do not always consult him, but a good subordinate does not concern his master with trivialities. Thus do I guide the Temple of Shadow. As *prophate*, I open myself to the will of the Lord of Shadow and hear the voice of god within me."

"I see."

"Of this I am certain, my lord."

What can I say? Beltar believes in me. If he also believes he's hearing the Voice of God, I'm okay with it—provided his hallucination is telling him things that go along with the local code of chivalry, anyway.

"Do you mind if I quiz Varicon?"

"Not at all, my lord."

I turned my attention back to Varicon.

"What does it mean to be the First Shield?" I repeated.

"The Shields are one of the three divisions of the Order," he replied.

Give him credit where it's due. He tried to give the question to his superior, found he couldn't, and went ahead without hesitation. I like that.

"The Blades and the Banners are the other two divisions," he continued. "As the Blades are composed of individuals whose strengths lie in attack, the Shields are those whose strengths lie more with defense. A group of Blades will go forth to do battle on the field; Shields will remain upon the walls to repel invaders."

"And Banners?"

"Banners are the diplomats, messengers, and priests, my lord. They conduct the prayers of evening and morning, travel to spread the word of the Lord of Shadows, and study more deeply the ways of conduct, both honorable and right."

I looked at Beltar. He smiled and said nothing.

"And the First Shield?"

"I lead the Shields," Varicon stated, simply.

"I get that, but why you?"

"I do not know. The assembled Knights of the Shield selected me and the Lord of Shadow confirmed their choice."

"Fair enough. So, I understand there are the Orders of the Shadow and the Crown. Are the Temple of Shadow knights all part of the Order of Shadow? How does that work?"

"The Order of Shadow of the Temple is a different organization, my lord. The Order of Shadow of the King is a more temporal power than an ecclesiastical one. The Demon King altered the structure of his knights, making the Order of the Sword open to any sufficiently skilled killer. Thus, the King has an Order of the Sword—killers—an Order of Shadow for true knights, and the Order of the Crown for the personal guard."

"But the Orders of Shadow," I persisted, "They're allowed to have the same name? Doesn't that confuse people?"

"Only among those who do not understand them, my lord. The Knights of Shadow are of the Temple and wear the grey sashes. The Order of Shadow is of the King and wear the red."

"Oh. Well. That's all right, then." I tried not to let any of my sarcasm drip on the floor.

"It is my honor to be of service, my lord."

We ate in silence for a while before Beltar spoke up.

"My lord?" he asked. I made a sound of acknowledgement; my mouth was full. He couldn't have timed it better if he was a waiter asking if I needed a refill. They *always* ask just as you've taken a bite of something. It's like they go to a special waiter school.

"May I offer assistance in the opening of the gate tonight?" I nodded, since I couldn't speak. "Thank you, my lord."

"Speaking of assistance," I slurred, as soon as I could, "I notice I have two bodyguards from the Temple of Shadow. Shields, I presume?"

"Yes, my lord. The grey sashes with blue tassels are Shields. The red tassels are the Blades. Banners wear black tassels."

"Very good." I noticed his own were a silvery-grey. I pointedly failed to ask if the color-code was his idea or if it was "divine inspiration." Maybe it was time to have that talk with Beltar.

"If you will permit me, I must make arrangements for assistants this evening," he continued. I nodded at him. He stood up from the table, genuflected, and hurried out.

Or maybe I'd have that talk later tonight.

A messenger slipped in while the door was still turning.

"Your Majesty?"

"Yes?"

"There is a… group here to see you. They have reached the southwest gate of the city."

"Group?"

"Yes, Your Majesty."

"Group of who?"

"I am told it is the Duke of Vathula and retinue, Your Majesty."

"So, they should reach the palace in another band or two of the candle?"

"I… think they will have to go to the underdoor. The carriage will not be able to take the stairs at the, ah, mouth of the Kingsway."

"Show him to the throne room and I'll see him there. Alone."

"It will be done, Your Majesty." He bowed and backed away.

"Alone?" Seldar asked.

"He'll be alone."

"Ah."

"Any word from Mochara?"

"Tianna has retired to the Temple with Amber, so no fresh news there. Torvil says he's not interfering with the council's plans for defense. Instead, he has chosen to spread his forces among the Mocharan forces as observers and assistance."

"He's keeping an eye on them, isn't he?"

"Yes, Lord of Perception. Civil wars are like that."

"I can't say I like it, but I don't have a better solution. —wait. Is that why we've got so many volunteers to 'defend' Mochara?"

"Possibly."

"Your tone makes my suspicion sensor ring like a Christmas performance."

"I'm not sure what you mean."

"Look, if you set things up to keep an eye on any potential turncoats in the Mocharan forces, just *say* so. It's part of your job to anticipate these things."

"Yes, Master of Subtlety."

"See how I'm not asking if your answer means you did it, or if you're just agreeing with me? In the future—well, as long as I'm stuck being king—just tell me. You're not going to get beheaded for doing your job. Okay?"

"Yes, Sire."

"Any word on the Rethven fleet?"

"Still holding back. They have now a favorable wind, so they have changed course and struck some sail. I believe they still intend to arrive about dawn."

"So, no change."

"Nothing material, no, Sire."

"Okay. Has Flim finished mounting his crossbow?"

"I do not know. The cradle was still under construction. Shall I ask Torvil?"

"Please. I'm thinking they can start shooting the big one at the fleet way before the fleet gets into attack range. It may not do a lot of damage, but it'll force them to start spending power to defend themselves long before they intended to."

"I shall suggest it to the ruling council immediately."

"Go ahead."

Seldar departed and I turned back to my dinner. Varicon cleared his throat and I nodded at him.

"Is there anything else, my lord?"

"Actually, yes. Why do you and Beltar always call me 'my lord'? I'm a little unclear on the rules of etiquette for modes of address."

"You are the Lord of Shadow."

"Yes? Oh. I get it. It's a religious thing rather than a royal one, right?" I tried to keep the distaste out of my voice. I can cancel out most of the input from my nose and tongue, but being worshiped still leaves me with a nauseating aftertaste.

"Yes, my lord."

"Okay. When you're done here, see if Beltar needs any help."

"At once, my lord." He placed his utensils neatly on his plate and departed.

The thought wandered across my mind: If I'm having so much trouble getting out of the king business, how much trouble am I going to have getting out of the god business? It's not like I can hand it off to some poor sucker and leave it with him.

Bob was in the great hall when I arrived. He immediately did his genuflection and waited for me to acknowledge him. I settled myself on the dragon's head and told him to rise.

Bob was utterly unchanged. Same white hair, same smooth face, still looking as neat, clean, and stylish as if he'd stepped straight out of the pages of Evil Elf Fashion Weekly. Nine years hadn't done a thing to him. Typical.

"I see you brought a box. Is it for me?" I asked.

"Yes, Dread Lord. You commanded a crown be brought, and so I have."

"Open it. Show me."

The crown was a lovely thing, all bright silver and gleaming black, done in twisted wire like woven vines. The base circled once and sent shoots of metal up, weaving together in a net of shiny branches, until gems of green and gold sprouted at their tips, sweeping up and back.

I think I appreciate why nobody likes elves. They're immortal, beautiful, graceful beyond belief, and are generally better at pretty much everything. It must be frustrating to know that any elf who bothers to study something—swordplay, poetry, jewelry, whatever—will spend more time on his hobby than the lifetime of any member of any other race. A human master craftsman, at the height of his skill, will have spent fewer hours on honing his craft than an elven hobbyist. And then there are elves who decide to truly master some skill...

It's jealousy. Or envy. I get the two mixed up. But it's not unfounded.

Elves don't go to any effort to make matters better. They would be openly contemptuous of humans and other races if they cared enough about them to have any strong feelings. As it is, they only regard mortal races as ephemeral bits of flotsam. The bits come and go, sometimes useful for a moment, sometimes not, and all of it will change, utterly and completely, if they only wait a moment.

It's like meeting an ignorant, unwashed barbarian who can't even appreciate the simplest nuances of art or civilization. Moreover, that ignorant, unwashed barbarian is doomed to die before you get around to breakfast, exactly like all the others. Why bother to teach it how to behave? Why bother to help it with anything? As long as it doesn't get filth on you or get in your way, who cares what it does?

Elves aren't exactly evil. They just don't see any other race as being real. Sure, the other races are living beings, but so are mayflies, mosquitoes, and goldfish.

I realized all this as I looked at the crown. It was a thing of intricate, incredible beauty and, for a moment, I saw it as an elf might see it: A work of art too subtle for mortals to comprehend. Humans would treat it much the same as any child who might see the Venus de Milo and call it "pretty."

I looked it over for magical effects. There were none. I waved at the box and Bob closed it.

"It's perfect for what I want," I told him. "Now, talk to me about some things."

"Anything you wish, Dread Lord."

"Are you aware of the issue with the Demon King?"

"I have heard many things, Dread Lord."

"Stop me if I say something you know is wrong. Keria, as I understand it, wound up being inhabited by a demonic entity. I *think* she was possessed before she assumed the throne in Vathula—whether her mortal, daytime self was dead or not is an open question, but the demon inside her didn't want to deal with sunlight. I eventually got rid of it by killing Keria. Am I on track?"

"Everything you have said is true, Dread Lord."

"I suffered a similar problem nine years ago. The Thing which possessed me, however, was of a slightly different order. It was my own darker nature, brought to life and given the power to overcome my naturally pleasant disposition. Tort, T'yl, and a number of others worked very hard to restore me to myself.

"Now that I am myself again, bear in mind everything the Demon King did, he did without the influence of my natural kindness and tolerance. Whatever he wanted you to do after his demise or dethroning, cancel it."

I leaned forward slightly and looked him in the eye.

"Make no mistake, however. All the qualities the Demon King possessed, I still have. If I wish to continue something he commanded, I will let you know."

"I understand completely, Dread Lord."

"Good. Now, you are the Duke of Vathula and the Eastrange. You're responsible for the region and all the things living within it. I want to see peace, or as much peace as is practical, in the realm. Other than that, perform all the usual duties and obligations of a duke to a king or queen. Which means you help to preserve the realm."

"Dread Lord," Bob replied, going to one knee and setting down the box, "I will obey, of course. It will help if you could explain your motives for this. I do not question you, merely hope to understand your purpose so I might serve you better." He placed his hand over his heart and bowed his head.

"Think of it this way," I began. I paused to think, myself. How to skew the view so Bob's bias could grasp the value of human life? Answer: make human life a commodity.

"What do I eat?" I asked.

"Blood and souls, Dread Lord."

"Where do I get them?"

"From all things that live, I believe."

"Humans, *orku*, *galgar*, elves…?"

"Yes, Dread Lord." Was that a quiver in his voice? Possibly.

"Are you familiar with the concept of ranching? Raising animals for the purpose of eating them?"

"Yes, Dread Lord. I believe I understand, now."

"There may come a day," I added, quietly, "when I seek to challenge a being of great power. On that day, I may need every drop of blood, every scrap of soul I can find. Perhaps a whole world of them, not merely some minor kingdom." I leaned forward, elbows on knees. "I may even need to promote a servant to an even greater level of authority. I hope when… if that day comes, I have a servant worthy of such reward." I left the implications to his imagination. He lifted his head and looked at me seriously.

"I am certain, Dread Lord, that you do. He need only prove himself."

"It would please me to find you are correct. Now, tell me about the army headed for Vathula."

"It has begun its preparations to penetrate Vathula and use the pass. It will break upon the walls like sea-foam on the shore."

"Very good. I plan to arrange for its recall, so do try to turn it into a simple siege."

"As you command, Dread Lord."

"Also—what is your proper response to a request for help from someone in my service?"

"Yes."

"Good answer. Sir Sedrick is a Hero. He is currently looking for T'yl and for Tort."

"I regret, Dread Lord, that I must inform you of the possible death of both of those servants."

"Listen carefully, Bob. Very carefully. You're immortal, right?"

"Yes…"

"In a different way, so am I. Right?"

"Yes, Dread Lord. The power of chaos from beyond the world flows in your veins."

"As may be, if I find someone has killed either of these two, my personal pets—and if either or both are killed, I *will* find out—I can spend ten thousand years hunting for clues, inquiring among the gods, and working to find who was responsible, who paid them, and who paid the ones who paid them, on up the chain to the person who decided it should be done."

"I understand fully, Dread Lord."

"Now… you know I am no longer the Demon King."

"Yes, Dread Lord."

"Were you aware I can love? Not merely desire, covet, and lust after, but love?"

"I was not, Dread Lord."

"I love these two—and others. But these two are missing, and I will have them back. You know I want my pets protected and safe. You know Sir Sedrick is looking for them on my behalf. Please take a moment and consider these things."

"I have considered them, Dread Lord."

"This pleases me. It would be best if I remain pleased, and that means he should have all the cooperation and aid you can give him."

"It will be done, *Na'irethed zarad'na.*"

I settled back on the dragon's head, relaxing and smiling. The formality implied we reestablished that, even during the day, I'm a dark and terrible Thing. Fine by me, if it drove the point home.

"Good," I told him. "Now, what do you need from me? Anything?"

"If it please you, Dread Lord? The population of the duchy of Vathula grows restless. Their numbers are growing at an alarming rate and their ability to feed themselves is becoming questionable. Perhaps you might descend upon some of the settlements and empty them?"

"Possibly," I allowed, shuddering inwardly at the thought. I don't relish the idea. I've killed my hundreds and my thousands, but it has never been a pleasant experience.

Let me rephrase that.

Killing by the hundreds, sucking the souls out of masses of living beings, feeling the surge of blood pouring into me, all of these things together—yes, it is a pleasant experience. It is an overwhelmingly pleasurable experience. It's taking a hit of your favorite drug, eating your favorite meal, enjoying your favorite music, revisiting your favorite dream. It is, quite possibly literally, a fiendish delight.

As a matter of principle, I try to avoid being fiendish, and to avoid overindulging that particular delight. If I indulge in it too much, I might come to miss it. It worries me enough as it is. In a thousand years, will I be the evil thing stalking the night and killing anyone who crosses my path? Is it inevitable? Or is it optional? I don't know.

"I take it the undermountains are a much more peaceful place of late?" I asked.

"Yes, Dread Lord, but the pressures caused by youths growing to adulthood and their subsequent offspring bode ill for the coming decade."

For the first several thousand years of humanity's existence, their favorite form of population control was war. Killing each other off was fundamental to the success of civilizations, if you can call them that. How much worse are the *orku?* Or any other bunch of violent species living in the Eastrange? While they may not be worse—humans are good at self-destruction—I'm certain they're no better. They're fairly well confined in a long strip of mountains with limited resources and enemies on both sides. Population pressure must be like a pressure cooker.

Killing each other off might not be the worst thing for them. Unfortunately, I've participated in wholesale slaughter. I have to admit I don't care for it. Giving them a pressure valve might not be a bad idea.

"Perhaps they need some form of blood sport," I mused. "Gladiators, that sort of thing."

"Dread Lord?"

"I'll see about forming a great arena somewhere. The most violent of them will volunteer to fight each other. Most of those will die in the arena. Given how violent most of those races are, it might actually be a good form of population control. Spectators—from within the Eastrange, but also from Rethven or anywhere else—can pay to watch. Maybe even participate. You can give the winners a cut of the proceeds as prize money. It'll encourage the stupid and the violent to get killed. The rest of the money we can use to help finance the government, reduce taxes, and encourage the economy."

"This could be amusing," Bob agreed. "But what of this great arena of which you speak?"

"Probably somewhere in the northern regions, where it will be out of the way. Maybe near the headwaters of the Averill. The *viksagi* have a similar problem, although on a much smaller scale. They have enough things trying to kill them to keep their numbers manageable. They might want to send some of their more bloodthirsty types to try their skill in the arena. If we could get the frost giants to participate, that would be even better."

"Dread Lord? I still do not fully understand about the arena."

"What's not to understand?"

"There is nothing in that region, and with good reason. It is inhospitable and untamed."

"Hmm. Did you ever visit Zirafel?"

"I have."

"Do you recall the Plaza at the Edge of the World?"

"I do."

"Imagine that, but in a circle instead of a half-circle. I'll tell the mountains to move around and change shape. You should be able to see obvious results within the month, so locating it shouldn't be difficult."

"As soon as I find this place, I will begin the games, *Na'irethed zarad'na*." I ignored the formality. I obviously said something to terrify him again. He only calls me that when he's exceptionally nervous. Are all elves this skittish? Or is it just Bob? Or, as Mary tried to tell me, am I really so frightening? Or would he be this nervous around anyone who put a hand-shaped imprint over his heart and told him it could squeeze?

No, wait; I remember something. Having power over the ground is a frightening thing to elves and other denizens of the Eastrange. Maybe that's it.

"Shall I invite the *viksagi*, *viskagar*, and the frost giants on your behalf?" he asked.

"Once you have the details worked out, yes. Anybody who wants to fight for prize money, I suppose." Then I thought about the *viskagar*. "I intended to put this on the western side of the Eastrange, near that lake above the Averill. The *viskagar* live on the eastern side, in the northern regions of the plains, don't they?"

"They do, Dread Lord, where the plains turn to high hills and the world grows colder."

"Is there an easy way for them to get across the Eastrange?"

"No, Dread Lord."

"I see. Well, I can include a tunnel from the city to the other side, I suppose. Maybe a trail—I don't want to encourage mass migrations of armies, only small-scale travel. Oh, you'll make sure people going to and from the arena have safe passage, yes? We'll want paying customers to feel safe in order to encourage business."

"I will see it done, Dread Lord," he said, and covered his face.

The question of population pressure and control made me think of reproduction and evolution and of elves. Are elves sneaky, devious, conniving, and treacherous because they're made that way? Or is it because they've learned to be? If their creator made them that way, is it a reflection of their creator's limitations, or of the way he wanted them to act? If they learned to be unpleasant, what experiences did they undergo to force them into being so untrustworthy?

More simply, was it a case a heredity or environment? Or a combination of both?

"Bob. Relax. Bear in mind I'm not going to eat you. You're useful, even helpful, and I appreciate it. If we can get away with a mutually beneficial relationship, I am not against it."

"Dread Lord?"

"Look, Bob. You have good ideas and suggestions about how to get what I want. I value you. You won't be casually dismissed out of hand. While terror and awe are fine for the lower orders, you don't need to be terrified and awed. Be aware you are valuable to me and I know it. I don't know if we could ever be friends—I don't like you and I doubt you harbor any kind feelings toward me—but I'm pretty sure we can work together on a basis of mutual respect."

"I suppose you are correct, Dread Lord." I wished it was nighttime. His face was inscrutable. Then again, elf spirits are much more difficult to read than human souls. I have no idea what he thought of the idea.

"With this thought in mind, is there anything you would like from me?"

"The Eastrange is running smoothly, Dread Lord."

"That's nice. I was asking, however, about anything you want, personally. Not the Duke of Vathula."

Bob looked startled. He actually met my eyes for a moment, searching my face to see if I was serious.

"Dread Lord… it is said you walk between worlds as other men walk from room to room."

"That's a gross exaggeration. It's much harder than you think."

"Indeed, Dread Lord, for I was there when the magicians of Zirafel first erected their great arch."

"Ah. I keep forgetting how old you are."

"I was created on the sixth moon, Dread Lord, before the great game of the Heru began. I lived upon the seventh moon, the one still shining in the nighttime sky, before coming to this world on dragon wings. I have seen the wars of men, *orku*, *shimsa*, *tyga*, *ooloné*, giants, dwarves, *prevnyt*, and *dakthars*. Races lived and died while I was yet regarded as young."

"I will remember," I promised. It wouldn't be hard, not after that. I wanted to ask what the hell the various races were like, but it didn't seem a priority.

"The chief desire," Bob continued, "of any elf is to have Rendu, our creator, one of the true gods of this world, free again."

"Free? Free as in 'turned loose'?"

"The gods who formed this world do not deign to discuss their plans with their servants, but a clever servant may divine the will of his master. The Heru, our gods, chose to play a great game with all the world as their playing field. They favored, in their own way, the races they created and loosed upon it. It is thought they hid themselves away, all together, each keeping all the others from interfering—cheating—on behalf of their creations."

I had a nasty flashback to being thrown off the Edge of the World. It's not a nice memory. I try not to dwell on it. It gives me a sense of immediate mortality and the shakes.

But something—or Something—grabbed me before I could wind up subdivided among a horde of demon gullets. It didn't have much to say to me, but it spoke to the Devourer.

"The purpose of games is to play."

Is the Father of Darkness one of these proto-gods? Is the Church of Light worshiping one of them, too? How do they relate to the energy-state beings I know and love? —that's sarcasm, by the way.

If the Father of Darkness is one of these things, was it cheating? Or was it refereeing?

The ways of the so-called gods are mysterious, strange, incomprehensible, and damned annoying.

"All right. Your gods are in their playroom, watching. Does this relate to something you want?"

"Yes, Dread Lord. Short of calling forth Rendu from the stronghold of the Heru, I, like any of the First Elves, would return home to await our creator's return."

"I thought—no, you're from one of the missing moons, aren't you?"

"Yes, Dread Lord. The second sky-orb was the place Rendu first created elves."

"So, why are you here? Part of the game?"

"No, for Rendu disdained the game. He left us upon the sky-orbs to tend them as he wished. We only came here when the chaos swallowed up the first and eldest of the sky-orbs."

"I see. Well, no, I don't. What did you do on these sky-orbs?"

"We walked the gardens and maintained them," Bob replied. His eyes looked at something either far away or deep inside, seeing something distant in space and in time. "We saw to his lesser creations and provided diversions for him. We swept, we sang, we danced, we tended all things, from palaces of crystal to songbirds of gold. All that Rendu wished of us, we did, for we are the finest of his living creations, eternal and immortal, drawn from the eternal void by his power, given shape and form and purpose by his will."

"And when he went into this stronghold with the rest of his sort? The void-chaos-whatever ate a moon?"

"The first and eldest of the sky-orbs, like all the others, was warded from the effects of the great void, the swirling chaos beyond the firmament of this world. Rendu came to this plane so he might fulfill the request of his fellows in crafting a place where they could observe without interfering in their game. Yet, as time wore on, without Rendu's power to hold it at bay, the chaos of the void wore away the defenses. The first sky-orb vanished, crumbling into nothingness. The second followed mere centuries later. In a thousand years, the third vanished, as well."

"I see. You came here because the moons were disintegrating and taking everything with them."

"Exactly, Dread Lord."

"And you want to go back?"

"Yes."

"Aren't you worried about the last of them—the only one left, as far as I can see—going the same way?"

"Yes."

"I'm confused," I admitted.

"The last and greatest of the sky-orbs has lasted ten thousand years beyond any of the others, and may last for eternity, even against the constant buffeting of the void. Yet, the true dragons of Rendu are not ours to command. We cannot persuade them to bear us back across the sky-sea, for they will not abandon their master. Therefore, we cannot go back and look for ourselves, see with our own eyes, how the last of our homes fares."

"True dragons?"

"Rendu created the first dragons, Dread Lord, much as he created us, the elves. They were created immortal and perfect. Other Heru created dragons of their own, copies of the perfect design, as many copied elves to greater or lesser degree for their races."

I think I'm offended, Firebrand told me.

I think you're right, I agreed. *He's just made a comparison between some mythological "true dragon" and the dragon you were, and himself—elven "perfection" apparently is the source of flawed copies that are all the other races.*

Egotistical of him, wouldn't you say? Let's see if he's mathematically perfect by slicing him into fractions.

No, I'm interested.

Maybe later?

There is always the possibility.

"Okay. So, let me see if I get this. You want to go to the moon and evaluate it for stability in the face of the chaos-void beyond the world-shield?"

"You have the essence of it, Dread Lord."

I folded my arms and drummed fingers on opposite shoulders, looking up at the ceiling and thinking.

"Hmm. Interesting. Someday, I'm going to want you to explain the whole creation of the world in more detail—at least, as much of it as you know or can guess."

"It will be my honor, Dread Lord," Bob replied, bowing again.

"All right. As for the sky-orb of Rendu... is there some reason I can't simply open a gate to it?"

"I do not know," Bob admitted. "The Great Arches of Zirafel and Tamaril were made by mortal magicians. It is a different magic from that of elves. We can create such things, but by our arts we can build only sets of two, not gates which may open to wherever the user might wish."

"So, you can build a matched pair of arches, but you'd still need to put one on the moon before you could go there."

"Yes, Dread Lord. Our proper home lies beyond the firmament and beyond our reach."

"I see the problem. Okay. Come with me and we'll see if I can hit the moon from here." I tucked the box with the crown under one arm and led the way.

Bob and I strolled through the corridors. Bob seemed mildly pleased at all the saluting and bowing whenever I walked by people. Being close on my heels, it was as though people were doing it for him. Well, he could enjoy it if he liked. It didn't hurt anything, and he was a nobleman. Noble-elf. A duke.

We started for the upper gate room, but there were a number of black-armored people in the corridor outside. I was surprised to see a line of noncombatants sitting in the hallway like a bunch of martial arts gurus, eyes closed, holding hands in a chain, all humming the same note. Against the other wall of the hallway were the guys kitted out for battle; they were doing the same thing, only in armor. It was kind of freaky. It freaked me out, at least. I don't deal well with weirdness. But the power they generated was considerable, and I had a hunch where it was all going.

I suspected we wouldn't have much privacy, so we diverted to my laboratory-workroom. I put the box down and focused on the scrying mirror.

It's possible to look outside the firmament with a scrying spell. I've seen it done by accident when a lady wizard goofed with an eyeball-based spell; I've also done it myself with a more regular mirror. The limitation, it seems, is you can't have a scrying sensor pass through the firmament. I'm not sure how the firmament works, exactly, but it's a barrier. It keeps things in and out, mostly out. So an established magical manifestation—or a demon—doesn't go through it. Presumably, since demons can be summoned and magical manifestations—such as scrying sensors—can appear on opposite sides of the firmament, magical radiations aren't stopped.

Yep, there's my scrying sensor view, parked out beyond the firmament. Looking down, I saw the world was a glossy egg, like one of those glass balls with a tiny ecosystem inside. And, yes, it was much longer than I thought, with a range of mountains down the middle and a whole other half of a world beyond. It's hard to make out details, though. From the outside, the firmament has a blurring effect, like frosted glass. At least, during the daytime. Would I see it better at night? Or does the firmament have different properties depending on the time?

Mental note. The mountains appear to be the divider between the north half of the world and the southern half. And I may be the only person on the plate who knows it. Aside from a bunch of First Elves, at least.

I swung the view around and slid sideways, following the curve of the firmament, zipping my scrying sensor around the world, chasing the moon. It passed over the Edge and swooped down below the world.

It was dark down there, but the moon was glowing, as usual. I headed for it.

Something—some Thing—smacked into the scrying sensor, or the sensor smacked into It. It snarled, apparently pressed up against the other side of the mirror, as though on a window. It was a bat-winged centipede with little pincers on the end of all its feet. The mouth end opened in five sections, peeling back to reveal a circular mouth with rings of teeth. The whole thing was about the length of my forearm.

It clawed at the other side of the mirror. Scratches appeared. The tail flexed, driving a stinger the size of my finger against the surface. It dented badly. I dismissed the spell immediately.

The mirror, a sheet of polished silver, still had the gouges and small tears where the Thing clawed at it—damaged as though from the other side.

I think I've figured out why people don't send scrying sensors outside the firmament.

Suddenly, I was very glad I was using a sheet of polished silver, rather than silver-backed glass. Important safety tip for magical operations. Don't use anything fragile for viewing the void beyond the world. Maybe Kavel can make me some sheets of polished steel instead of silver.

"It's going to be difficult to get a target lock on the sky-orb," I told Bob.

"So I see," he agreed. I wondered if we each looked about as shaken as the other. It's not the monster, really. It's the sudden appearance of it. Startlement, that's the word I want.

"I'll try this again at night, sometime," I promised, "when I can see what I'm aiming at."

"Very good, Dread Lord. And if the sky-orb is defended against such travel?"

"Hmm. I've never actually had my own space program before. I'll see what I can do."

I handed Bob off to someone with instructions to see to his care and feeding. I took the crown to my lab. My first order of business was to let the mountain know it could un-ruin the southern road through the mountains. It could be amusing to watch an army trudge back and forth between Vathula and the coast, trying to get through.

The second thing, while I was talking to the stone anyway, was to tell it to find a valley up near the Averill, on the western edge of the range, and start work on citifying the place in a manner sort of the inverse of Karvalen. Karvalen is a solid, point-up cone, hollowed out. The stadium-city would be an empty funnel, with tunnels and pueblo-like housing all around it. The colosseum-like area for bloodsports would be in the center, filled with seating.

I recall a spot near the waterfall—that is, the headwaters of the Averill river. It's a low spot between three mountains and would make a good start for a stadium-like setup. We could shut off the waterfall and have the lake drain through the city on its way to the Averill, providing running water.

All this took some explaining, but I put it in a spell and fed the information to the stone. If I tried to explain while merged with the rock, I might still be doing it. Besides, the mountain seems to have a good idea of how to build a city. It built Karvalen, with a little help and some ongoing evolution. It's also kind of taken over all the stonework in several others, so it has examples to draw on. We'll see how it turns out and tweak the results as necessary.

With that done, I got to work on the Crown of Karvalen—or what would be.

I centered the crown on a stone worktable and examined it more thoroughly. If the Imperial Magicians could hide enchantments, surely elves could do the same. Then again, elves do magic in a different way; they build objects that are magical, rather than cast spells. Could they hide the magic in an innately magical object?

I tackled it from the standpoint of magical energy. In order to channel magical power, you have to have something to run it through. I put pulses of power through the physical structure of the crown, blasted it with disruption waves, and scanned it actively and passively for any hint of magical resonance or output. Every test I could think of told me it was nothing more than a really pretty piece of jewelry.

After sunset, I did much the same thing, only harder and deeper. If the thing was hiding any secrets, it was beyond my ability to detect. The really pretty piece of jewelry might just be a really pretty piece of jewelry, rather than a terrible object of unspeakable and subtle power. While this didn't completely rule out the second possibility, it shifted the odds so far you'd need an atomic vector plotter and a really hot cup of tea to find them.

With the crown locked away for later enchantment, I checked on Diogenes. According to Firebrand, he was still trying to interface with the quantum computer crystal. I added a bit more vitality to the system, made sure both of them were functioning, and realized I might be missing a bet. If Diogenes was learning how to speak the new computer language, could I give him a translation spell? Admittedly, "he" was just a collection of adaptive programs, but could he use the spell as an interface? It might be more like studying a new language in a classroom rather than learning it on the fly. He wouldn't resort to trial and error combined with a lot of handwaving and pantomime. He could write his own phrasebook. So when the spell wore off, he would have written a new driver for his operating system.

Assuming a translation spell would work on a pair of inanimate objects. Well, unliving objects. Well, artificially vitalized inanimate unliving objects. Well... whatever.

I ran the structure of a transliteration spell through the computer core. The most literal translation spell I have substitutes words rather than trying to communicate ideas. I thought being as literal as possible would be more likely to work with a pair of data-processing devices. It couldn't hurt. Even if it did, I had more computer cores. If necessary, I could go get more.

Then, feeling moderately accomplished, I went over to the gate room to get the troops deployed to Mochara. The people doing the daisy-chain of power focusing were still doing it.

I was pleased to note nobody stopped to bow, salute, or even acknowledge me. They were busy doing something important, so they kept at it. It pleased me more than it should have, maybe, but I liked the fact there was at least one exception to the general rule about salutes.

In the gate room itself, Beltar was in robes instead of armor. They set up a portable altar and a medium-sized idol—a sword-wielding guy on a rearing horse, about quarter-scale, all done in bronze and iron—along with a few candles for making shadows, a chalice of blood, and a quartet of musicians. The woodwinds guided everybody in humming. A pair of drummers thumped out a slow double beat. It was probably meant to symbolize a heartbeat. It sounded a lot like one. Occasionally, during Beltar's chanting, someone would hold a sword up and tap it, ringing it like a bell. Two backup priests gave ritual responses. It was all quite embarrassing.

I walked into the room and everything came to a stop.

"Well, this is awkward."

I silently agreed with the thought in my head, mainly because I'm not comfortable with alien thoughts inside my skull. It disturbs me greatly to have something slide right past my mental defense spells. I really need to get on the stick and make a magic item to defend my thinking machinery.

"Mental crap seems to happen with depressing regularity," it agreed.

"Since you obviously hear me thinking," I replied, *"I'd say it happens with infuriating regularity and makes me want to beat someone into paste. How did you get inside my mental defenses, anyway? Are my spells for it down again?"*

"The details are a bit complicated, but your spells are in good shape. Do you want the long version or the short version?"

"Let's try the short version," I suggested. *"Who are you, anyway? You sound strangely familiar. Have you been in my head before?"*

"That's part of the awkwardness. It's... hmm. You know how you hate the idea of being regarded as a deity?"

"You mean intensely, wholeheartedly, and unwaveringly?"

"Yep."

"Then I know what you mean."

"Well, you don't have to worry about it. You're not one."

*"Oh, well, **that's** a relief. Thank you so much for invading my head to tell me."*

"Sarcasm. You're good at it."

"Lots of opportunity to practice."

*"I know. Thing is, you were a deity—no, let me back up. You were an energy-state creature capable of faking godlike power in this world. During that period, you, **as a god**, existed. You absorbed the energy generated by your worshippers, interacted with other energy patterns, all that stuff."*

"But I also escaped from the energy-pattern state and managed to get back to the physical plane of existence."

"Yes, but you left behind... uh... an imprint? A hollow spot? Neither of those is quite right. The energy plane resonated with your godlike existence for a while, then you stopped doing it. You left behind signs of your presence, and the energy from your worshippers—the water from your fountain—flowed into the footprints you left behind. It didn't really have anywhere to go until you gave it footprints to fill. Get the idea?"

"I'm going to take a leap of— ha! —faith here. I'm guessing you're the result? An energy-pattern entity formed by the footprints and energy flow?"

"Right! Good job!"

"Great. So, does that make me the Father and you the Son? Or, since you're an energy being, the Holy Ghost?"

"Blasphemer," the thought replied, chuckling.

"Oh, I don't know if we should go that far. Irreverent heathen, I grant you."

"You and I both know I'm not a god," it replied. *"I'm an energy-state being existing in a symbiotic relationship with material beings in this world."*

"But, essentially...?"

"Yeah. Essentially. Look, you may not remember this very well, but your consciousness would have disintegrated under the stresses of adapting to this

mode of existence. As I understand it—and bear in mind, just because I live here doesn't mean I understand it completely—"

"I beg your pardon?" I asked.

"Name for me all the components of blood. No? Okay, how about describing the chemical structure of your bones. Still no? Can you define the purpose of the organ just under your heart?"

"I have an organ under my heart?"

"See what I mean? Just because you **are** something doesn't mean you understand all the details."

"Okay... for now. Go on."

"As I understand it, if you had remained, your existing consciousness would have disintegrated. Eventually, if your worship continued long enough, I would have then formed to fill that niche, as you put it. You accelerated the process by consuming all the accumulated energy of your worshippers; you left deeper footprints. Sort of."

"But I didn't disintegrate. I escaped."

"I prefer to think of it as simply leaving."

"Whatever."

"To my knowledge, you're the only physical being that's ever turned down the opportunity to be deified. Most of them, if they get this far, are only too glad to achieve a higher, more powerful state. You're too much of a lazy coward who doesn't want responsibility."

"Now hold on just a second!"

"Not diplomatic," the thought admitted, "not tactful. But we both see ourselves that way."

"I'm going to let it go," I stated, "for a number of reasons. Partly because I agree with you, even though I don't like the way you said it. Partly because you don't have a face I can punch. And, finally, partly because I seem to be at your mercy, stuck in some sort of temporal stasis."

"Oh, that. No, I've just speeded up your quantum thought processes—no, that's a bad translation. Consciousness is more than a bunch of electrical pathways in a brain. The part of you not dependent on neurons is currently vibrating at a much faster rate. No, that's not entirely right, either..."

"I get the idea, at least well enough to get by. I'm thinking at supercomputer speeds, which makes everything else seem so slow as to stand still."

"Close, but technically—"

"Close enough," I snapped. "Now what do you **want?**"

"I wanted to take this opportunity to set your mind at ease about a couple of things. After all, in a weird sort of way, you're my father. At the same time, I'm also you. My consciousness is patterned after yours, based on the energy-imprint you left behind, but also filled in by the energies directed to this plane by our worshippers."

"Okay... I guess. You're the latest so-called deity of this world. You stopped by to say hello and thanks for leaving footprints in the energy sand on the extraplanar beach. Good job. Please don't be a jerk to your followers and watch out for a particularly evil orb with my dark side in it."

"Yeah, I saw it. It's a nasty piece of work, aren't we?"

"I despise your grammar and acknowledge you're not wrong. Did you have anything else to say? And why say it now?"

"Why now? Because you finally walked into a concentration of power where I could! Beltar is conducting a power ritual, both as a worship thing—it's producing a faith-based energy I can use. Although that's not exactly accurate, either..."

"Look, stop worrying about being exact and just give me the damn gist of things, okay? I was in a good mood and you've shot it all to hell."

"Sorry. Beltar's charging your gate with the help of a couple hundred faithful. The magical energy is going into the gate and the ritual worship is going into me."

"See? I got that without the technical explanation."

"I should have realized you would understand. Sorry again."

"No problem. It's still weird to hear a deific entity apologizing, though. Continue."

"So, here you are in an intense power center. I thought about doing the whole puppet thing, like Sparky does, but I find it somewhat distasteful and disgustingly organic. I also know you would never forgive me for it. The best I could do was bring your consciousness to a higher phase state where we could resonate directly. We're allowed to do direct communication only under very specific circumstances, you see."

"No, I don't, but I'll take your word for it."

*"Right now, you're the only one I can talk to! You're the only **actual** nightlord in the world. I couldn't even communicate with you until you walked onto my holy ground—by which I mean an area with a high concentration of power tuned to me. It's not an actual function of the ground. Now that I've got the opportunity to reach you without you invoking me—that is, without you actively attempting to resonate psychically with me—I can tell you I'm here."*

"Great. I can pray to myself and I'll hear me. Nice. Now we've met, nice to meet you, and can we get to the point? If you're a psychic copy of my mental patterns, does this mean I'm as distractible and flighty as you are?"

"I deserved that, I suppose," the thought admitted. "Again, I apologize. The reasons I called... first, I wanted to establish this connection so we could talk again. I also wanted to let you know your stream of consciousness is not responsible for the god-like stuff; that's my job, as the energy-state version of you."

"Is 'hallelujah' blasphemous or merely irreverent in this context?"

"I think it's actually appropriate, if you're using it as a thank-you. While I'm not a god, I'm regarded as one. Hence, saying 'hallelujah,' as in 'praise the Lord,' isn't actually the wrong thing to say. Well, unless you're a monotheist, in which case it's blasphemous—that whole no-other-gods-before-Me thing. Then again, if you're saying it in regard to Jehovah, Allah, or Yahweh as an expression of thanks for getting you off the demi-deity hook, it's probably okay, too."

"You are definitely patterned after my own thought processes," I observed.

"Well, duh. I told you that."

"Are we done?"

"Last thing. I also wanted to warn you that you're regarded as an avatar."

"Like, an airbender?"

"No."

"Giant blue alien?"

"No."

"Video game icon?"

"That's actually not completely wrong," he thought. *"I'll have to consider it. But you know what I mean. You're just being silly. I mean in the context of a divine manifestation or incarnation on the material plane."*

I explained what I thought about that in some detail.

"I didn't know I knew that sort of language, or so many words of it. How many languages did you need for so much profanity?"

"I don't know," I admitted. *"I just reached for my feelings and let them out. I'm pretty good with swear words."*

"I agree. All done?"

"For now. I guess you should tell me how being an avatar or incarnation or whatever is going to affect me."

"Oh, it won't affect you, really. You're still a physical being with quasi-demonic powers. On occasion, though, you may notice things happening without your conscious volition."

"You mean, weirder than normal? No, better question: Weirder than normal for me?"

"Possibly. You and I resonate very closely—it's kind of like me being Sparky and you being a fire-witch. Stuff is going to happen if you aren't careful."

I thought for a moment, reflecting on some unexplained incidents.

"Like, for example, blessing a child? It might actually... you know... work?"

"Very likely."

"Or, if I'm well and truly angry about something, I might have a weird voice effect?"

"Also possible."

"How about my shadow doing freaky things when I'm upset?"

"I wouldn't be surprised," the thought replied. It sounded pretty relaxed about everything, but then, it didn't have to deal with people looking at me funny.

"Is there any way I can control these manifestation things?" I demanded.

"I dunno. I've never had an incarnate avatar of my own before. All I've had are priests, and they're not capable of channeling more than a minor flow of power. I can barely manage two words at a time to them without a major ritual, complete with incense, a blood sacrifice, and six hours of chanting."

*"Do you have any **good** news for me, or did you just stop by to inform me of how my future days are going to be ruined?"*

"Um. Well, you'll be happy to know most of the religions around here won't bother you. There's a rule about not smiting each other."

"I had some conversation with Amber on this subject," I admitted, *"but it's good to get independent confirmation. I don't trust Sparky not to lie to her. So, the Church of Light won't jump me one afternoon and carve me into easily-fried slices?"*

"Oh, no; they can do that," the thought assured me. *"Well, they're allowed to, anyway. Followers are allowed to do whatever they want. The direct action of*

the power of the sort-of gods won't be allowed to harm you. At least, on this plane. Other worlds, other gods, other rules. I'd still be careful of people with reversed collars and wooden stakes if I were still you."

"You are a highly ambivalent comfort," I grumped.

"Occupational hazard. We now return you to your regularly-scheduled troop movements."

"Hold on," I protested.

"What?"

"If you're one of the not-quite-gods of this world, can you help us out?"

"Boil seas, turn the waters to blood, plagues of locusts, that sort of thing?"

"I'd settle for sinking a few ships," I admitted.

"Sure. Happy to help."

"...seriously?"

"Seriously. Sparky gets to incinerate things, doesn't she?"

"Huh. Good point."

"I am going to need help, though," the thought admitted.

"I knew there was a catch."

"There always is. I can't simply reach into the material plane and smack things. I need—any of us would need—an agent on the scene. Again, look at Sparky. If Tianna opens up and invites Sparky in, Sparky can work through Tianna, channeling power through her into the material plane. To a lesser extent, any of Sparky's regular priestesses can do the same thing, but the power flow is barely a trickle. Beltar or any of our other priests can channel energies from me, but not on the scale of major miracles."

"So, you need to direct energies through me. Maybe Mary."

"Mary would have to have a stronger connection to me. She would need to be ordained, at the very least. The ritual attunes the priest to the deity, you see. But yes, she could be a very good channel, since she's also a nightlord—nightlady, I mean."

"So, you're telling me I am now your primary divine link to the material world?"

"This one, yes. You want a major miracle, I have to do it through you."

"Complete with weird eyeball effect and anime-style hair?"

"You know, I don't know how it would manifest? We've never done this before."

"Thanks anyway, but some things I don't feel comfortable doing. Nuclear weapons, genocide, and allowing fake gods to take over my body are all on the list."

"I understand completely. I wish I could be more help."

"Great. Okay. Well, thanks anyhow."

"Anytime. And if you need anything on the small scale, just say so. I do weddings, funerals, birthday parties, bachelor parties, and bar mitzvahs. Reasonable rates. Refunds on unused portion with proof of purchase."

"I'll bear it in mind. Can I get back to defending a city, now?"

"Lehitraot."

"Oh, you are so not funny."

"Yes I am. And you'll thank god for it, later."

I continued my interrupted step and wobbled, off-balance. I recovered and worked my way through the prayer-chain crowd to the arch. It seemed as if no time had elapsed. I found it unnerving, especially on top of being greeted by a psychic copy of myself acting like a deity while it knew it wasn't. And it sounded like me, at least in my head.

If I've failed to express this clearly, it's probably because I still can't think about it clearly. Well, in any words I can use on a family show, anyway. My language will get me *at least* an "R" rating even if I summon up the ghost of Linnaeus and have him tone down the more profane parts.

Bob was there, too. I noticed him when he knelt beside the arch and did his hands-across-face thing.

"I didn't think you'd be here," I observed.

"It is my honor to witness the way in which you are worshipped in this realm, Dread Lord."

This earned him a dirty look from Beltar and his two assistant priests. They didn't interrupt their ritual chanting and power focusing, though. Bob ignored their scowls.

I set up a new safety feature at the new chalk line. The spell would create a curtain of red light, shining away from the gate. If you saw red when I called a halt, you stopped. If you didn't see it, you were too close to the gate already, so you kept going. Everyone seemed to understand the explanation and demonstration. I also added a variation on my deflection spell and tied it to the curtain of light.

I don't know how painful it is to be shredded by a failing gate spell. I don't want anyone to find out.

On second thought, I take that back. Johann, maybe. Juliet, possibly. None of my guys, though.

We set ourselves up for a deployment. People stretched and jogged in place, loosening up and preparing to sprint.

Beltar and his assistants ceremoniously brought me a chalice of blood. What could I do? I wasn't going to waste it. I accepted the chalice in both hands and drank it.

Odd. It didn't try to crawl out. Was it because of some sort of effect due to the ceremonial presentation? Maybe an enchantment on the chalice? Or was it one of those religious things and I should ignore it? Probably that last one...

All the armored men formed up and prepared to charge. Their unarmored counterparts continued to focus on the magical side of things. I checked the target location via mirror and saw a roped-off aisle ready to accept troops. Good. I gave them the countdown and opened the gate. It flushed, swirled, connected, and snapped into place. Feet pounded as the gems drained into the gateway. A whole line of worshippers helped me hold it open.

I'm a lot stronger at night. I have enormous accumulated energies. How much of that is from a friendly spiritual clone is suddenly a very good question, though. Whatever the reason, wherever the energy comes from, between Beltar's ceremonial prayers, several charged gems, a couple hundred helpers, and my own grim efforts, the gate stayed open long enough for everyone to sprint through.

I was damned glad to let go of it, though.

This left me alone with Bob, Beltar, the sub-priests, a tired choir, and the pair of grey sashes on anti-assassination detail. Bob looked impressed, which is unusual. Elves are usually pretty good at hiding their feelings. Then again, at night I can see the spirit inside someone easier than I can see their flesh. It's kind of an unfair advantage.

"Beltar?"

"My lord."

"Where's Seldar?"

"Sleeping, I believe. He anticipates a busy morning."

"Sound thinking. Thank you for all your work. Give my thanks to everyone and commend them for a job well done."

"It is our honor to be of service, my lord," he assured me. I turned to Bob.

"Dread Lord?" he asked, anticipating a question.

"Walk with me," I suggested. He took it as an order and fell into step beside me. I wandered in the direction of my scrying room while the choir line shifted from sitting to the one-knee position until I passed by.

I thought long and hard while we walked in silence. Bob was probably the most capable and competent lord in all of Rethven or Karvalen. He was likely to be the most ruthless, callous, and treacherous, too—at least, from a human point of view. Elves have their own type of honor, but they don't care to share it with humans. It's a lot like a human keeping his word to cockroaches. Even if he gives his word, how long will he need to keep it? And if he breaks his word, how long will it bother him?

"You're a survivor, and an impressive one," I told him, because I was impressed. The elf beside me was several thousand years old, at least. Considering the dangers of simply existing in this world, that's worthy of some respect. "Are there many as old as you?"

"I do not know. He created us in our thousands as his servants and his household. Many were lost on the eldest moons, although many may live still upon the one which yet remains. Of those who descended on dragon wings to this playground of the Heru, surely some should yet survive."

"Someday, when I have time, I'm going to get you to tell me all about it."

"At your will, Dread Lord."

"Good. Now, you understand what I'm trying to do with my kingdom?"

"My understanding is you wish to establish a dynasty and see it rule the realm."

"Yes, partly. I want the place governed in accordance with certain principles. You're familiar with the ideas and ideals I laid down for the knights? Noble service cheerfully rendered, courtesy, honor, loyalty, bravery—all that stuff?"

"I am quite familiar with it, Dread Lord. They never cease to discuss it amongst themselves. It is a key feature to distinguish the knights of the old guard from the killers of the new."

I decided not to be distracted by asking where he would have heard such discussions. Time was pressing.

"I'm glad you can tell the difference. And, while I recognize individual humans are beneath your notice—short-lived, short-sighted, and ephemeral—a kingdom and someday, perhaps, an empire can live long enough and be complex enough to be interesting. At least, I think so. What is your opinion on the matter?"

"My reasoning agrees with yours," Bob admitted.

"That's excellent. I want you to keep an eye on the place. See what you can accomplish within the parameters I set."

"That will be," he began, and paused, searching for a word. "Challenging," he decided.

"Will it keep you from being bored?"

"There is that," he admitted. "It could be diverting for a thousand years or so."

"Especially if you have to work behind the scenes, never revealing your true purpose."

"Such is my preference, Dread Lord, if it matters."

"Bob, understand something. The Demon King didn't much care what you think or feel. I do. I may not be able to accommodate you, but I would prefer to give you every opportunity to be amused, even happy. I try to give you as much autonomy as possible for that reason. If you have a problem or a request, don't hesitate to come to me with it. I'll do my best to help you."

We walked in silence for the rest of the way to my workroom. For some reason, Bob seemed oddly disturbed. Not upset, exactly. Slightly confused? Uncertain? Maybe puzzled, or mystified. He didn't seem actually unhappy about whatever was bothering him, though.

I paused at the door to the workroom.

"Go ahead and get started on everything," I told him. "Call me when you have something to report, please."

"Dread Lord?"

"Yes?"

"There is something, if you will consent to hear it."

"How can I refuse? Come in and we'll talk."

Once we were settled in chairs, Bob rubbed the tops of his thighs with the palms of his hands, almost as though his palms were sweating.

"What's on your mind, Bob?"

"Dread Lord, may I address the issue of the sun without offending you?"

"Speak your mind," I invited.

"You are familiar, of course, with the daily miracle of the sun. Yet, you have been beyond the Gate of Shadows for some time—"

"Hold it. Maybe you better explain to me what *you* mean by the 'miracle of the sun'."

"Why, the creation of the sun every morning."

I felt a headache coming on. The thing vanishes at sunset, so, naturally, it is created every morning for the sunrise. Of course. I half-realized it, intellectually, when I saw the recorded sunset. Having it confirmed was not as reassuring as I hoped.

"Okay, we're clear on that," I sighed. "Just making sure. Out of curiosity, do you know why it disappears every evening?"

"If it were to fall too far, its course would cause it to strike the world where the firmament touches. Or so I assume, Dread Lord."

"Not an unreasonable hypothesis," I agreed, silently adding, *For this astronomically screwy place.* "Go on."

According to Bob, humans don't pay enough attention to the world. They don't live in it for very long, so they don't see the changes. Originally—and I use the word advisedly—the sun charted a course over the Spire of the Sun, from one end of the Mountains of the Sun to the other. It didn't vary; it ran in a fixed line, like a groove in the sky, and higher. At the same time, the Shining Desert at the foot of the mountains was less hot and arid, while the frost-line in the north was much farther north. The world was a more temperate and friendly place, in general.

Once the Heru did their thing to prevent cheating, the world started to wear out. Like a stitched-together garment, it was coming apart at the seams. The path of the sun, varying to the north and south, may have provided seasons, but this wasn't according to the design. In the beginning of the world, there *were* no seasons!

"There are other signs," Bob went on, "and they concern me greatly. In a mere ten thousand years, we might see far greater calamities. What if the world ocean were to find a crack in the lands between it and the Precipice? Or if the sun should continue to sink lower in its arc across the sky? We will see these troubles upon us in only a handful of millennia, perhaps in mere centuries."

Leave it to the immortal being to think long-term.

"I admit these could be problems." I kept my Dread Lord hat on while I spoke. "The livestock I have here could be difficult to move. Do you have a suggestion?"

"Only in some small ways, Dread Lord."

"By all means."

"First, if it is feasible, may I suggest removing some select members of your property to some other realm? One where they may breed and multiply without danger from the unraveling world?"

"Good thought. Go on."

"Second... and somewhat more troublesome... is the idea you might preserve all your property by repairing the world."

I'll give this to Bob: He thinks big.

"I'm not sure how I can do that, Bob. Remember, the sun and I don't always see eye to eye."

"There is the possibility, Dread Lord, you would not need to."

"I'm listening."

"As servants of Rendu, we elves were not privy to the councils of the Heru. We know Rendu, greatest of artificers, wove the fabric of the world. The other Heru only adorned it with threads of their own. Yet, Rendu could repair his handiwork, if he were here."

"And, if I recall correctly, he's presently self-confined with the other Heru until the game they've set in motion finishes, right?"

"Correct."

"And they aren't coming out until...?"

"One race upon the face of the world is supreme over all the other races."

"So, to get the Heru to come out, we have to kill or capture all the other pieces on the game board. Meaning, one race has to take over the world, thoroughly and completely. That's the victory condition?"

"I believe so, yes, but I know of no creature who knows the rules of the great game of the Heru." He paused for a moment and corrected himself. "It is possible one of Rendu's dragons might know, but it is only a possibility."

"Why am I not liking where this is going? No, don't answer that. Instead, tell me what you have in mind."

"From the way the world is slowly coming apart, I infer the Heru did not anticipate their game going on so long. Perhaps it would be not unreasonable to query them upon this matter. Perhaps they might agree to a brief interlude, much as a long-drawn-out game among mortals might allow for a... a pause for a snack, perhaps."

"That's possible, I suppose. It's also possible they aren't paying much attention."

"Dread Lord?"

"Imagine a series of games in the arena. Some of them are exciting. Others are less so. It's possible the events of the last thousand years—or ten thousand years—simply aren't interesting enough to hold their attention and they're amusing themselves in other ways so the world can develop new and interesting changes."

"Then," Bob mused, "it becomes even more imperative to draw their attention to these matters."

"Possibly. On the other hand, maybe it was set up this way. If it sun winds up skating around the rim of the world or crashing into it, that could be the time limit. They tally up the points and declare a winner," I suggested. Bob's eyes widened. I sighed. "Did you really never think of that before?"

"No. It never occurred to me."

"And I thought I was the one with a slow leak in my head. All right. If it's a timer, we need to know. If it's not, they need to be told to wind the world. Either way, we have to get their attention. Any idea how?"

"I know of no way other than to go to the House of the Heru."

"Seems obvious. Where is this House of the Heru?"

"I believe other races know it as the Spire of the Sun."

"Okay, tell me about it."

"Again, Dread Lord, I must admit I am but a servant."

"Grain of salt. Got it. Talk."

"Rendu, born of the chaos beyond the firmament, built the firmament. He wove the structure of the world. He crafted the moons. He made the eternal elves and breathed fire into dragons. And when his fellows demanded a new game, he created the Spire of the Sun. I believe, as most of the First Elves believe, that the Heru reside there, watching the world from their unreachable seat—the House of the Heru."

"Hold it. You've used that phrase before. What are the First Elves?"

"The elves eternal, formed from the manifold darkness beyond the world, drafted and forged by Rendu, the Artificer."

"And the other elves?"

"Lesser elves, created by elves," Bob clarified. "I was created by Rendu. Since my race does not reproduce as the other races do, when our numbers began to dwindle, we bent our craft to the duplication of ourselves. The race of men is most useful in this regard. Only with their blood and flesh have we found any success at all."

"Ah, yes. Elvish reproduction. But I've seen a number of elves—how shall I put this—of obvious male and female sorts. If you don't reproduce, ah, biologically, there's no reason for genders."

"And yet, some of us one would find difficult to categorize," he pointed out, gesturing at himself.

"True. Still, you use gender-specific pronouns."

"In this tongue, yes. Elvish had no words for 'he' or 'she' until we encountered other race. There were only various forms of 'it,' denoting another elf, a lesser creature, or an object."

I didn't have anything to say to that. It changes a lot of what I thought I knew about elves. Well, these elves. They're immortal, depend on another race for progeny, have no sexes and no sex. This Rendu might be artistic, but I'm not sure he was terribly practical. Come to think of it, artists do tend to be more dreamers than pragmatists. A lot of engineers are, too, now I think on it. Maybe it's to be expected.

Then again, if you create something capable of easy self-replication—like humans, *orku*, or bacteria—you're going to wind up with an awful lot of them in a very short time. Maybe that was his point in not giving elves the reproductive option.

On the other hand, I intended to give them one.

"Are you still kidnapping pregnant human women to transform the unborn into elves?"

"They are still the only method we have of creating new elves, Dread Lord."

"I think I can do better."

"Salishar delivered your message, Dread Lord. You wish to improve upon our transformational magic?"

"Possibly, but I need more information on how elves work. Send me a couple of elves, please, for examination. A painless examination. I only want to look at them, not take them apart."

"Of course, Dread Lord."

"And try to find two as opposite as possible on the human spectrum of male and female. I want to compare the differences."

"It shall be done."

"Good. Now, what were we talking about before we were sidetracked?"

"Rendu created the world for the game of races. The Heru set in motion the races of creatures in the world and now observe without interfering, to see whose creatures are the greatest."

"Right. I'm up to speed on the idea. And you think if someone knocks on the door and asks them to fix the world, they'll do it?"

"Perhaps. I know of no other power that might."

"What, exactly would I have to do?"

"Forgive me, Dread Lord, but I do not know. No one who has ever sought to reach the Spire of the Sun has ever returned."

"Well, of *course* they haven't." I sighed. I hate clichés, especially potentially deadly ones. "Tell you what. You find out what I'd have to do. Then I'll decide."

"As you wish, Dread Lord."

"It would solve the problem of sending you to the sky-orb, wouldn't it?"

"Lord?"

"I mean, if Rendu comes out of the Spire, he's likely to gather up all his scattered toys and take them back, isn't he?"

"Who can say?" Bob asked. "No one knows the heart of the Heru."

"Fair enough."

He placed a hand over his heart, went to one knee, and bowed his head. I sent him on his way.

In Mochara, lookouts eyeballed the incoming fleet and reported. I was in my scrying room, looking over the sand table and arranging mirrors on their stands. I like having a communications center even if I'm not going to be involved in the battle.

The invasion fleet consisted of eighteen ships. Most were two or three-masted things. The odd one was a barge-like boat with four small masts at the corners. It had triangular sails and a roof-like covering over most of the deck. This one seemed odd, even by my standards. It was basically a shack on a raft. A troop transport, maybe? A supply vessel? A private transport for a VIP? If I could have penetrated the scrying defenses, I would have. I was mightily curious and quite thoughtful.

The truly unusual feature of this mysterious ship were the smokestacks. Twin metal pipes, like overgrown stove chimneys, pumped out enough smoke for a Los Angeles cop to write them a ticket. A steamship, perhaps? Was the Demon King interested in building steam engines? Maybe. I didn't see how the thing propelled itself through the water with just the four sails, nor did I see a wake suitable for a screw propeller. Could it have a paddlewheel under the roofed-over area instead of on the sides? I wasn't sure exactly how it would work, but with enough trial and error—or a decent nautical engineer—I'm sure it could be done.

Was it a prototype warship? Or a cargo vessel? Well, we would doubtless find out.

In the meantime, I thought about the fleet as a whole. What could I do to eighteen ships? Any one of them I could probably handle. At night, I could brute-force a gate belowdecks, bash my way through a lot of wood, and walk along the seabed to the shore. I could probably target a sonic pulse at one, rupture every eardrum, shatter any hope of concentrating, bash down any existing shields, and inflict whatever magical harm I cared to. With some gravity-altering spells and some preparation, I might be able to literally suck one of them down like flushing a cork in a toilet. And so on. There were about as many ways to sink ships as there were ships.

But I was in Karvalen. The logistics problem was a small-scale replica of the one I gave to Johann. He had to reach across universes to bother me. I only had to reach across miles. Johann had enough power to reach me... at least, once in a while. I had enough power to reach the ships... once in a while.

I hate being left out like this. I can be useful, dammit! But noooooo, just because I'm considered valuable and important and borderline irreplaceable, I have to sit here and look at everything remotely.

Sometimes I hate Seldar. No, I take that back. Sometimes I hate Seldar for being right, and I hate myself for realizing it. Kelvin wouldn't do this to me.

And I'm lying to myself. Kelvin would, too. So would Raeth. Bouger might not, but he was always willing to get into a fight and never saw much reason not to. I wish they were all here. I miss them, even if they wouldn't let me go to the defense of the city.

It's not like this was even a real threat to Mochara. Yes, if it had the army to back it, the combination could be a problem. The fleet, on its own, was really just a moderate pain the keister. When I turned back the army, the fleet should have turned back, too! This was stupid on their part... which could mean taking Mochara wasn't the objective.

What were they trying to do?

Oh, maybe they had a plan to take the city. If they did, this really could be a straightforward attempt and the army was merely a helpful thing to have in preparation for the march on Karvalen. If so, I was looking forward to seeing their plan in action and stomping it. If I could.

Really, though, it didn't seem reasonable or likely. Was it a feint? Could there be something sneaking up on Karvalen while everyone watched things unfold in Mochara? Was it a ploy to redirect troops and guards and make Karvalen—or me—more vulnerable to attack? Or was this someone's way of depleting Rethven's forces before invading it? Maybe Bob engineered this so he could start a takeover with troops from the Eastrange... but then he wouldn't have asked for a way to cut down on the population, would he? Unless his request was meant to throw me off the thought he was behind it all.

I've said it before, but it bears repeating. I hate politics.

Still, better safe than sorry. I did a search around Karvalen and scanned the city streets. No massed bodies of men marching anywhere, no determined squads scaling the mountain, not even a wing of flying carpets circling the place in preparation for a kamikaze run.

Any assassins in the palace? Maybe. You can never tell about them; they have to be sneaky. It's almost an evolutionary thing. Every time you kill an assassin, he's obviously one who wasn't sneaky enough. The ones you don't get are the even sneakier ones, and those are the ones who survive to raise little assassins. He'd have to be exceptionally sneaky though, to succeed in killing me when I'm feeling paranoid. And fanatical to the point of martyrdom. That's not impossible, not even unlikely, considering.

A few personal spells for my own protection wouldn't go amiss...

I took care of those and went back to thinking. What can I say? Impending wars always make me nervous. I'm always afraid I've missed something fundamental, or at least important, and it's going to cost people their lives.

The air near the left wall started to flicker. It was like a distant flash of lightning in the clouds, only without the clouds. It happened again as I wondered what was going on. It didn't seem to be discharging energy into the room. As I examined it, the flickering grew brighter and more rapid before a circular area around it started to bend, to twist, to distort. The spell started to manifest more strongly and I recognized the business end of a gate spell.

"Well, crap," I said, followed by an order to my two bodyguards to get back. We removed ourselves to the pivot-door as the circular distortion, now about three meters across, started to spiral toward its center. They started pushing on the door, grinding it open, as I monitored the magical effect.

I don't often get to see the far side of a gate opening. Usually, I'm the one opening it. This one didn't seem to be opening quickly, but I could think of three reasons for it, just off the top of my head. The slowness might be from someone's unfamiliarity with the spell, extreme distance, or possibly from a time differential between the two ends of the gateway.

The twisting, swirling area of space finally opened up and snapped into place. The view through it was probably a cave mouth or similar crevice. The mouth of the opening was in shadow, but beyond the hard, harsh line of shade, a bright wasteland of dust and jagged rocks shone with a supernal light. The sky was black as velvet and the stars were visible, cold and unwinking above the oddly too-close horizon.

That was my glimpse of it. Then I roared in agony as the light reflected from the pale soil burned every inch of exposed skin—hands and head, mostly—sending up little licks of flame and a thin, white smoke like steam off a roasted turkey. It wasn't nearly as bad as my accidental self-immolation, but the reflected sunlight was more than enough to set me slightly on fire.

My agonized yell was lost in the howling wind. Air surged around us as it poured away through the gateway, sucked through by the vacuum on the other side. This extinguished me like a candle on a birthday cake, at first, but the light continued to sear me. Then the rapid flow of air, combined with the reflected sunlight, caused my exposed skin to catch fire more definitely. It was not a measurable improvement over my accidental sunlight cannon.

If the three of us had been any closer to the open gate, we would have gone tumbling through into direct sunlight and vacuum. As it was, I clawed my way out into the corridor, half-helped by my bodyguards. One of them partly dragged me, scorching his hands badly, as we clawed our way along the floor and into the hall. The other hung back and wedged himself against the doorframe, pushing with his legs to swing the pivot-door partly closed, putting me in shadow. I remembered my childhood lessons about extinguishing the burning victim.

The whistling sound of air being sucked around the edges of the door seemed loud amid the heavy breathing and the crackling of my regenerating skin. My other bodyguard slid-crawled across the doorway, wedged himself on the other side, and pushed with his legs, helping to swing the door a few inches more. I stayed out of the way—and the light—while people farther down the hallway in both directions shouted incomprehensibly into the wind.

Someone—the entire list of suspects consisted of Johann—went to the trouble of opening a gate on the *Moon*.

I begin to think Johann doesn't like me. I'm also thinking he doesn't necessarily want to capture me alive. The combination of vacuum suction and sunlight was a straight-up attempt to kill me.

It was a good one, too. I'm glad he's in another universe—and glad the gate wasn't directly facing the Sun. All I got was a dose of indirect light, which is merely awful. This is worthy of note: I was burned by moonlight. Really up-close and *intense* moonlight, but technically moonlight. It implies I do have a mild resistance to sunlight at night. Moonlight doesn't usually burn. Too much moonlight, however, is still sunlight. I may need to investigate this.

I sat there in the shadows and the wailing wind of the hallway while I regenerated. More guards showed up. I was hungry and cranky, so I shouted over the wind to send one of them off to make preparations to feed me. More people leaned up against the door, rotating it until it closed. We waited until the gate quit and the whistling, shrieking sound died away. We opened the door again with weapons drawn.

Nothing came through the gate. That was one of my main worries, of course. If Johann wanted me on the lunar surface, he might have conjured something to drag me along rather than rely on suction. Maybe the gate was taxing, even for him? Hopefully so. I didn't see how he could put one end of it on the Moon and the other end *here*. All the gates I understand require me to be actually present at one end or the other. I'll have to think about how that might work. Could he have managed spells to get himself to the Moon and cast his gate spell there? He could, certainly, but how would that affect his connection to his nexus? Would he go? Was I so important to him he would do such a thing for a shot at killing me?

I recalled his face when he drove a red-hot piece of steel through my liver. Yes, he would. He might send one of his kids to do it for him, since he had the option, but he'd do it himself if he had to.

Meanwhile, my scrying setup was ruined. The table was still there, but the sand was gone. All the mirrors went tumbling through the gate. What was left of the place was a shambles, wrecked.

"Please find me some mirrors," I said, calmly, through tightly-clenched teeth. "Someone get me a bucket of sand. I have to set up my station again."

People started moving. My bodyguards, however, had some difficulties. One had a nosebleed—and if you are ever in a position to think a nosebleed looks delicious, I sympathize with and pity you—while both had trouble hearing. I worked on them a bit with my spells, making sure they didn't rupture anything crucial inside their ears, stopping the bleeding, and encouraging healing. I paid special attention to the burned hands; those hands might very well have saved my life.

Then, rather than send for replacements, they wanted to follow me as I went to dinner. If I ruptured veins in my eyeballs and sinuses, along with an eardrum or two, I'd want to take the rest of the night off. Not them. They're tougher than I am. I told them to send for replacements anyway.

We waited for their relief. It gave me time to finish regenerating my face. It doesn't do for a king to wander around with a grin three times larger than his mouth. It makes people nervous.

The bucket of sand arrived first, so I poured it into the sand table and started a spell to subdivide it into finer and finer grains. When the next shift of bodyguards arrived, I sent my previous two off to recuperate.

I hoped the two new guys had strong stomachs. I was getting *hungry*. Dinner wasn't going to be dainty.

Quite a number of things are slaughtered every day in a city—every sort of animal imaginable, from the mundane chickens and pigs, to the slightly odd *dazhu*, all the way to the outright exotic. I was only interested in the ones which bled copiously; regenerating a sunburn takes a lot out of me.

Mental note: Don't test whether or not Sparky will cook me in a sunrise. It may not be a religious effect. It might be a purely physical reaction based on my inner darkness versus the light during a change of state. It might not require the personal attention and power of a sun-based deity.

Beltar apparently took care of the more sanguine matters, organizing the blood collection and making all the arrangements—down in the Temple of Shadow. I appreciated his efforts even though I found the ceremonial trappings somewhat... distasteful. Just a personal preference, obviously, but I barely tolerate being a king. Being treated like a deity makes me itch. Or maybe it was the sunburn.

The fact he had three people waiting for my personal attention also came to light, although in a less incendiary manner. It seems in poor taste, even callous, possibly heartless, to mention them in conjunction with a flood of livestock blood poured over me. And yet, they played their part in restoring me and sating my hunger. Their blood helped restore my flesh; their spirits helped me recover from my exertions. They were even happy to help! I helped them escape from slow, painful deaths and move on to their next life; they helped me by giving me new life.

Is it really in poor taste to mention them? I didn't regard them in the same way as livestock, yet they helped me at least as much as the livestock did. They came to me and asked to be allowed to pass on. I fulfilled my function in this ecology—is it callous of the wolf to devour the aged and weak? Or am I drawing parallels that don't apply? I'm not a wolf. I'm not hunting them. I'm not weeding them out. Should I be more actively pursuing prey? If so, who should I be hunting?

If I start picking and choosing who lives and dies, what does that make me? A vampire? A god? A king? Or what? I'm not qualified to be the judge of who should live and who should die... or am I? I see into the souls—or what I believe to be the souls—of living beings. Does that *make* me qualified? If I can look at a man and see him as he truly is, good and bad alike, and *know* where he falls on the spectrum of saint to sinner, does the knowledge also give me the right to decide his fate? Is it fair to judge him based on my own beliefs and opinions and on how he measures up to them?

Don't get me wrong. I have no qualms about killing someone trying to kill me. They're trying to commit violence upon my person and therefore volunteering to be eaten. If you jump on the back of a tiger and start biting its ear, well, you get what's coming to you. Likewise, someone brutalizing a child is also going to discover exactly how awful a crime it is. These are two things about which I refuse to budge. But beyond those specific cases, *how do I judge?* Can I decide someone's fate on my opinions? Can I say someone isn't a good person based on the cultural values in my upbringing?

These things seem to bother me more than I recall. Is this a good thing or a bad thing? I was worried about becoming inured to bloodshed and death; nobody wants a nightlord without a conscience. Now I'm worried I worry too much. Is this normal? Is it a cycle of some sort?

Anyone know where I can get a copy of *Vampire Psychology and Unlife Cycle*? Or maybe *Understanding the Dark Lord Within*? Come to think of it, who writes self-help books for vampires? If I ever do manage to become old and wise, maybe I should look into writing them. If they sell, it could indicate a lot about the vampire population of whatever world in which it's published.

Meanwhile, in the scrying room, they brought in several new mirrors and lined them up against one wall. I set them up around the sand table and got to work.

My first order of business was a spell to divert incoming gates. I'm heavily shielded from detection and location spells, so I doubt Johann targeted me in such a manner. On the other hand, there was nothing I could really do about, for example, a scrying spell in a fixed location. Like a security camera, it couldn't track me down, but it could wait until I walked by. He couldn't locate me with the magical radar, but he could watch the security camera and spot me that way. Although I would have thought my scrying defenses were more than adequate... against local scrying sensors. If Johann was putting a scrying sensor, somehow, in between worlds...

Come to that, how big would a gate need to be for a peephole? With proper lensing—or even fiber optics—could someone open a gate so small it was practically invisible? It would still take a lot more power without a suitably-sized gateway border on both ends, but if the initial gate size was small enough, it might be worth it. I'll have to look into that.

But my point in building a gate-diverter was simple. I didn't want him opening a gate facing the sun or deep under the lava of an active volcano. The redirector should divert any incoming gate into a sealed chamber in the mountain. If nothing else, it should give us enough lead time to avoid surprise.

Once again, assuming he didn't open a gate *inside* the Sun. I'm still not sure how he could open a gate between two points without standing on one of them. I still sort of doubt he went to the Moon to cast a gate spell, so I'm concerned. If he's learned so much about gates already, I could be in even more serious trouble than I already believe.

Once I realized this, I had to exert myself to suppress a panic attack. I really need to stop giving myself new reasons to be terrified. I mean, *I'm* the unholy fiend of darkness, immortal and terrible, feasting on the blood of the living, with all of humanity as my rightful prey. Why am I the one scared?

Let's face it. Humans are scary.

I took a minute or ten and calmed down. I needed to. There was a lot of work to get done before morning.

I integrated the powdered sand into the sand table's enchantment and got it back on-line. The mirrors were more problematic. They fetched several for me, only one of which was larger than a hand mirror. I set it up as my main screen and started arranging the others. It took hours to get it all on-line and working, but I fully intended to watch the battle of Mochara closely.

Naturally, it started early. A pox upon thy house, Murphy! —and you, too, Thomen!

The ships moved in slowly. In the mirrors, I set the images for false color to show the spells involved. The ships were surrounded by scryshield spells. As I watched, a steel bolt flickered through the night, missing cleanly every single ship and splashing into the ocean hundreds of yards behind the task force. Nobody seemed to notice, though.

With a ranging shot to guide them, the defenders launched another bolt a couple of minutes later. Their aim was good; it struck the bow of the lead ship, breached it, and went right into the lower decks.

I think they had guidance spells. They certainly had something on that bolt, but it flicked through my view too fast to identify. From the way the fires erupted from belowdecks and flecks of light fountained up, my guess is several pounds of steel turned to shrapnel and molten metal inside the ship's wooden guts.

Once the ships realized they were in the defenders' range, their wizards raised their defenses. The ships were quickly covered by multiple layers of spells. First a disruption-effect barrier, well out in front, to dispel magic directed at them—or magic on incoming projectiles. Then a spell to slow anything coming toward them. Then a spell to divert or deflect whatever might still be coming. I had to admit, they were well-prepared. Still, it was expensive in terms of power to raise shields over such large areas, not to mention multiple types. I'm sure they didn't intend to start using them so soon.

It didn't seem to change their plans much. They pushed up their schedule, hurrying toward the harbor instead of lazily timing their arrival with the sunrise. A few more of the steel bolts came to meet them and were deflected. It wasn't a total waste; defending against something so heavy and fast cost them shield power they might need later. It also forced the other ships to reinforce their own shields, just in case.

Then they entered arrow range and the defenders volleyed. Since the shields protected the front and upper arcs of the ships, the arrows all fell harmlessly into the sea, diverted. I saw a number of magical flashes, spells on arrows being disrupted or dispelled. Again, however, it wasn't a total loss; power applied to defense is power not applied to attack.

Then the catapults behind the seaward wall launched some god-awful number of arrows. It was an impressive sight, watching the packed masses of flaming arrows spread apart in flight. It was a hailstorm of fire and must have looked awfully frightening from below. Still, nothing got through. Arrows fell on the shields and slid aside, parting over the ships to splash into the water.

The lead ship—the belowdecks fires now extinguished—maneuvered to enter the harbor. As it passed between the pylons marking the entrance, it ground to a halt on the cables strung slightly under the surface. When it lurched and halted, a sitting target, a whole line of Mocharan wizards stepped up and pointed staves at it. Sparks and bright discharges leaked into the visible range as the shields went down under their volley. Archers volleyed again, peppering the ship and crew with flaming arrows; the sails and rigging caught fire. Then the big ballista cut loose again, spearing the ship with another steel bolt. It did the same thing the previous one did. The ship began to burn despite the crew's best efforts. It sat there, struggling with the flames, blocking the harbor entrance.

The attackers anticipated something like this, probably even counted on it as part of a ploy. While the defenders on the wall concentrated their efforts on the ship in the harbor entrance, the others spread out along the outside of the low harbor wall. At this hour of the morning, the tide was low; the wall was plainly visible a few inches above the water. They brought their ships in close and halted while the roofed-over barge stayed well back.

I'm the one who insisted on public education. They say knowledge is power. Well, in a world with magic, knowledge really is power—directly and literally. A hundred years ago, you couldn't put a hundred wizards in the same place. Today, they shipped several hundred and they all threw spells at us.

I'm not sure exactly what spells they used or how they managed to throw them so hard. The scryshields around the ships were still up; the Mocharan wizards only disrupted the magic on the lead vessel. I could still see the ships as though flying over them, though. Dozens of groupings, each with three to six people, suggested some ideas.

Interestingly, battles involving wizards have some trade-offs. Individual wizards are usually pretty versatile and useful, but only on a personal level. Groups can be much more dangerous, but have their own problems. Casting a spell in a serial fashion—helpers contribute energy to a central figure who does the actual spellcasting—can amplify the power of a wizard, but there's a limit to how much a single wizard can channel at a time. Casting a spell in parallel— where each wizard assembles his part of the larger whole of the spell—can generate spells without worry about overloading someone. Unfortunately, the coordinated, precise efforts required for parallel casting grow more difficult with greater numbers (coordinating a quartet is easier than conducting an orchestra), have more risk of failure (if anyone makes a mistake, there goes your spell), have less versatility (everyone needs to know the same spell), and are more easily disrupted. Not ideal in a battle.

There's a reason groups of wizards gather together in private to do their big spells, and it's not just the fearful locals with pitchforks and torches.

Once they launched their spells from the ships, though, they passed through momentary gaps in the shields. I could zoom in close and watch the spells zip past like watching bullets go *wheet!* past my head. Not an ideal way to analyze a spell. Lances of energy speared out toward the wall, striking it and detonating. Waves of energy pummeled the defenders, washing through steel and stone and flesh from every impact point. Most of the people on the wall or behind it were hit by one or two overlapping waves of energy. Some sections, especially near the gates, were slammed with three or four.

Nobody seemed hurt, as such. They just stopped moving.

I used the largest of the mirrors to zoom in on someone standing still. A close examination didn't reveal any damage. A more magical examination didn't show any ongoing spells, either. Whatever it was, it affected the subject and went away. That is, rather than placing a spell on the person—like a curse, for example—it was more like a gun. It didn't latch on to the person and stay there, performing a function. It hit the person, did its damage, and dissipated, leaving the damage behind.

The trouble was, I didn't see what it did. The guy I examined simply stood there, looking blankly out over the harbor, loosely holding a bow in one hand and an arrow in the other. He'd just stuck the point down into a brazier to ignite it when the spells started to hit. Now the arrow shaft was on fire and the flames were working their way up.

Wizards in the harbor continued to hit the walls with their spells, but sporadically. Their initial volley slowed from a barrage to light sniping. I watched my test subject for a bit, waiting until the flames reached his hand. They burned him for a moment, then he yelped and dropped the arrow. He looked wildly around, took in the situation, and reached for another arrow. Another spell hit near him and he froze in position as though he forgot what he was about to do. Only now, he couldn't even decide.

Meanwhile, men disembarked from the ships on either side of the harbor entrance. They cut or unhooked the cables and chains between the obelisks. Another ship risked itself by pushing the flaming hulk on into the harbor to clear the way. If things kept going like this, the ships would take turns advancing while the others kept up a covering fire, disabling defenders, so troops could unload on the docks.

One of the drawbacks to fortifications is their dependence on active defenses. Walls are great if you're at the top and holding people off. Without someone to drop rocks, walls are just obstacles; anyone with a ladder can go right over.

Which is exactly what they started doing.

About then, the sunlight started to sting. I expected it to be painful sooner than that; I felt the sunrise tingle long before the image in the mirror started to be brightly painful. Apparently, a scrying mirror—at least, my version of the spell—will allow the sunrise or sunset to hurt me, but it does cut down on the intensity. I don't know if I can survive a full sunrise or sunset through a mirror and will not be testing it if I can avoid it.

I temporarily moved the viewpoint of the various mirrors inside the structure of the wall, shielding them from the sun. Then I waited, impatient and angry, for the sunrise to run its course. I wasn't patient enough to go clean up. I used a spell and paced around the table, watching the shifting sand as it copied the battle. Seldar came in while I waited for the tingling to die down.

"I greet the day and Your Majesty."

"Morning," I acknowledged. "Did you oversleep?"

"I was told the attack should happen at dawn. Has it begun?"

"They got an early start." I explained the events leading up to the present. The sunrise finished doing its thing while I spoke.

When I reset the mirror viewpoints to look over the city, things were still in doubt. While the wizards on the ships took potshots with brain-jamming spells, a lot of soldiers disembarked, assaulted the wall, and killed a lot of defenseless people. A sizable percentage of the spells being thrown at the defenders were more directly harmful. Most of those, at least, were being intercepted and countered by magical efforts from inside the walls. The main magical threat seemed to be the coordinated efforts to shut down brains and keep shutting them down.

I was pleased to see quite a lot of men in black armor hacking their way along the top of the wall, trying to drive the attackers back. They were also whacking dazed defenders to snap them out of it and get them moving again. Once they saw what sort of spell was being employed, they must have come up with a defense against it. They're a well-trained and clever bunch. Then again, it might not be too difficult to block or counter—not that I could tell from my viewing room. If I was *there*, I could see the thing first-hand.

It wasn't easy, but I didn't say anything about it to Seldar. It would sound like whining, at least to me. It would certainly be petty and unpleasant. I wouldn't do that to Seldar. All it would accomplish was make him feel guilty and me feel like a heel.

"Any ideas on how we can help?" I asked, instead.

"What are these colored bands above and in front of the enemy ships?"

"Defensive spells. Magic disruption and missile deflection, looks like."

"So, they are defenseless from the sides and rear?"

"Yes, but they're pointed at the wall. Can we divert forces from the city to somehow get around to the sides?"

"If we placed someone on the outer harbor wall, that person would be beside or behind the ships. They could be attacked that way. It would allow the wizards in Mochara to devote their attention to the more mundane attackers, at least until the ship's wizards expand and stabilize these shields."

"Agreed, but there's no way out onto the harbor wall. The attackers control both piers and the ramps leading up to the gates. Men would have to leave the city, hustle to a point on the cliff directly over the harbor wall, and go down on ropes or something. There's no way down there without them noticing."

"Is the gate charged?"

"Some. Beltar and his people put a lot into it last night... Ah, I see! Maybe it's enough, if we're quick. Do we have anything a man can carry that will threaten a ship?"

"Possibly." Seldar looked thoughtful. "Can we deploy a man for each ship?"

"Judging by our earlier performance, I think we could manage at least thirty before killing the gateway."

"I am not certain the angle will permit an attack on every ship."

"You're thinking if we shoot one ship, the rest will notice and defend themselves."

"So we need to shoot all of them at once, yes, which I do not believe we can do."

"How do you mean?"

"Unless you intend to use the gate twice, any men sent through will be on one side of the harbor or the other. The seawall is divided in the center. Men must also run along the seawall to place themselves properly and avoid the arrow-shields. This takes time and will be noticed."

"Crap. Is it worth it to attack half the fleet?"

"Definitely. If we can divert their efforts or destroy them, the new balance of forces will give us a clear superiority in wizards."

"We can divert some wizards from defense, concentrate on one ship at a time, and start whittling them away?"

"In essence, Sire, yes—if we can destroy or disable enough of them."

"It'll do. Let's get moving."

"It will take at least half an hour to get everything prepared," Seldar warned. "Only a fool keeps a hammered arrowhead on hand. They always explode, eventually."

"You raise a good point, as usual. I know I wouldn't want a whole quiver of the things on my back. Go set things up. I'll keep an eye on Mochara." I put my pocket mirror on the edge of the sand table. "Call me and keep the line open; if anything changes I want you aware of it."

"Yes, Sire." We established the link. He put his mirror in a pouch and hurried off.

The defenders in Mochara were still holding the wall. It wasn't pretty.

Dazed individuals simply stood there, unharmed. They made good targets, though. The arrows fired from the ships and from the troops on the beach took quite a toll. The drawback, from the enemy point of view, was how shooting someone tended to negate the stunning effect. If the man survived, he was free to act again. Fortunately for us, it's hard to kill a man with a single shot in the middle of a pitched battle. It's more a matter of luck than skill. It's one thing to hit the gold on the range. It's another to hit it when there's lightning, shouting, rays of fire, clouds of smoke, horns, thunder, screaming, and occasional rains of fiery arrows.

I found it quite revealing in that the wounded didn't seem to be affected by the stun-spell as much. It would take effect, certainly, but only for a moment. Could the pain of the injury undo the spell's effect? The walking wounded did seem to be the ones making the most effective defense. Well, as far as regular troops were concerned.

Torvil cannot, by any stretch of the imagination, be considered part of the regular troops.

He was on the wall, defending a section and drawing enemy fire. Wizards on the ground, behind the wall, kept refreshing and restoring his defensive spells, which freed him to focus on sprinting back and forth while dishing out mayhem. He was an excellent target. Arrows and spells came at him almost constantly; his backup wizards had their work cut out for them. Did he set this up in advance, knowing he would be a target? Or did he draft a dozen wizards and tell them what to do when things started going wrong?

From the way Torvil sprinted back and forth, either he assumed he didn't have long or he was in a hurry. He bulled along the defensive area atop the wall, killing every enemy he could reach, slapping *en passant* anyone stunned. He shoved the top of a ladder and it flipped away from the wall—even while loaded with men. Often, someone made it to the top of the wall. Torvil generally seized this unfortunate soul in one hand, lifted him overhead, and slammed him like a sack of laundry straight down on the top man of the ladder. This cleaned out everyone on the ladder, so he jerked the ladder up into the air, swiped his sword through it to ruin it, and went charging on to stop someone else.

Torvil impresses me.

As he ran along the inside of the parapet, anything hostile and foolish enough to come near him fell apart. Swords, armor, people—he cut them to pieces with a fine disregard for minor considerations like material, thickness, or screaming. Blood and body fluids went everywhere, and nobody threw any spells to keep him clean. Was it because they didn't want to waste the energy? Or was it because seeing a seven-foot figure in black armor coming at you, covered in the blood and guts of your fellows, is demoralizing? Maybe both.

I was glad people were looking out for him. He wouldn't have lasted two minutes without a dozen wizards protecting him from the *other* wizards. Knowing Torvil and his competitive nature, my guess was he set it up. He was probably counting as he killed people. Of course, this also saved a lot of the defenders lives as the ships' wizards focused on him. If we had ten more identical setups, invaders wouldn't dare try the wall. As it was, Torvil was only able to cover one section. There were hundreds of yards of wall to defend, but the section Torvil protected didn't need much else.

As I watched, he did something not terribly impressive, but *smart*. He drew a narrow dagger and stabbed a stunned defender, putting a neat hole in the soldier's left hand. This snapped the man out of his daze and drew a shout of pain and surprise from him. Torvil shouted at him for a moment, then went back to killing invaders.

The bleeding man drew a knife of his own and started down the length of the wall, injuring other stunned defenders and getting them to help. Some of them fell victim to the mind-numbing spells of the invaders, but always shrugged it off after a moment when the pain of their injury percolated through to them.

This might turn out all right after all.

A bright flare of light attracted my attention. I zoomed in on one of the wooden drawbridge-gates in the seaside wall of Mochara, trying to figure out what caused the light. All I saw, at first, was a cloud of ash. Then I spotted Tianna. She was surrounded by four giants—excuse me, four of my knights, red sashes. Nothar also stood next to her, dressed in steel, with sword out and shield ready. Her hair was fire, easily visible in the early-morning light, falling down her back like a burning waterfall.

The inside of the seaward wall was only ten or twelve feet high; it was much taller from the outside because it made use of the seaside cliff. A group of men were fighting atop the wall, invaders claiming a foothold and running more men up the ladder as quickly as they could. One of them made it to the inner edge, lowered himself by his hands, and dropped to the ground. This lucky soldier found himself standing next to one of the gates. There was no one near him, a fact I found decidedly odd. He didn't waste time, though. He turned to the drawbridge-gate and grabbed for one of the bolts holding it closed.

There was another bright flare. I watched him burn away in a matter of seconds. It reminded me of a special effect where a human body gets disintegrated in stages during a nuclear blast. He turned black, all his flesh flaked away at high speed, and his bones fell into a heap, burning. A cloud of ashes billowed outward.

Ah.

This is amazingly unfair, Boss, Firebrand complained.

"I agree. But this is what you get for being the Dragonsword, the Sword of Kings. You stay with the King."

This king business stinks, Boss. You should quit.

"I'll work on it."

Tianna continued to stand there, slightly on fire, and simply wait. Her presence—and her line of sight on both of the seawall gates—explained why the defenders weren't wasting any men on guarding the gatehouses. I was under the impression Sparky wouldn't completely approve of this sort of thing, but, strangely, it actually made me sympathize with her. Tianna's a headstrong young woman. On the other hand, I felt no urge to stop her, either.

Is that a spell she's wearing to focus her divine gifts? I think it is. I doubt Sparky thought of it, which means it was either Amber, who, to my knowledge, isn't trained in any mundane magic, or Tianna herself.

You know that warm, swelling feeling in the region of the heart? I'm proud of my granddaughter.

The thought made me wonder about Amber. I took a brief glimpse into the Temple of Flame. Civilians streamed in and out of the place in two lines, like ants. Going in, they carried flammables, like buckets of coal or charcoal, even chunks of wood. Going out, the buckets were empty and the wood was gone. They dumped all of it into the central portion of the main temple area, the part under the gazebo-dome with the oculus. The fire was huge, and had a familiar face. Amber was burning yellow-white and looked grumpy. It was possible she didn't like being restricted to the temple while her daughter guarded the gates. I know I would be.

I was no longer worried about Mochara being taken. All I worried about was how many people were going to die in the process of keeping it. It had a fire-witch, a lot of unused militia, a whole wizards' corps, more than a year of knights, and a grumpy elemental of divine fire. They didn't need me. It's possible they never did.

The Temple of Shadow was lightly guarded and mostly quiet. A priest was sweeping up along the entryway; it saw a lot of traffic last night. A pair of guards stood nearby, more of a police presence than anything. The other temples seemed about the same. The Temple of Flame seemed the only one with a lot of traffic. On the other hand there were a lot of elderly noncombatants and young children already praying in all of them. I didn't poke my scrying sensor inside—that would be rude—but I can see through open doorways.

The Temple of the Grey Lady was quiet. All her priests were up near the wall. They were dragging the seriously wounded away from the fighting and turning them over to healers—probably priests of some specific deity, but possibly regular people who were good with healing spells. Maybe even wizards with a specialty. There were other priests present in the battle, I noticed, but I didn't immediately recognize their sigils. Is there a temple to a war god? Maybe. Who else would be involved? I ought to ask... someday. The priests of the Grey Lady also dragged corpses out of the way. These were stacked unceremoniously on a cart or wagon, presumably for transport to the temple and proper rites.

Weird. They don't have much respect for the corpse. Then again, they know the corpse isn't really the person. It makes me wonder again what the various religions do with the bodies around here. Bury them? Burn them? Dry them out, grind them up, and spread them on the fields?

If I get killed, I have no idea what they'll do with my remains. I don't deal with funerals all that much. All my stuff happens before the funeral, not what to do with a body once it's empty. Maybe I should ask.

"Sire?" came a voice from my communications mirror.

"Go ahead, Seldar."

"I have several people hammering on arrowheads, but the spells won't hold enough to seriously threaten a ship. I also have volunteers."

"I understand. Get up here and keep an eye on the battle. I'll do some helping with the arrows—where are they?"

"Kavel's smithy, Sire. I am on my way to you now."

"I'll wait until you get here."

Seldar arrived and I headed for the smithy.

The magic to hold momentum is really an elvish invention; I just reverse-engineered it into a reproducible spell. The initial version held energy from impacts—hammer blows, punches, being dropped on the floor, whatever—and released it into the object at a later time. The effect on the object was similar to being hit with all those blows at once. Usually, this resulted in turning it molten or into shrapnel. I have what I think is a somewhat safer version that stores the energy inside the material itself, rather than in the spell. The original spell acts like a spring being wound; if you over-wind it, it breaks, with predictable results. My version (he said, with a superior air) stores energy based on the size of the thing you're pounding on and warns you when it's near capacity.

I'm a physicist. We can do that. Well, physicist wizards can.

While regarding the preparations, I picked up an arrow shaft and considered it. It was wood. Earlier, I was thinking about how to disintegrate wood, to rip it apart and sink a ship. But... wood contains energy. It burns. There's a stored energy potential inside it. If I put a spell on an arrow shaft, I could turn it into powder. Mixed with air, it could burn suddenly, even explosively.

Why not put a larger spell on an arrowhead? One to affect all the wood around it? If it stuck into a wooden ship, it could powder a hole in the ship and set all that aerosolized powder ablaze.

And, since I was standing in Kavel's forge, I remembered the air-filtering spell on the blower. It was a simple magical barrier to keep out nitrogen. It wasn't meant to keep out all the nitrogen, just some of it, which increased the oxygen concentration going into the forge and made the fire burn faster, hotter.

There was also a time when I put solidified oxygen on pieces of steel and used them as explosives...

Click. Click. Click.

The arrow flies into the wooden target. The first spell expands a field around the arrowhead, pushing all the nitrogen away. Pressure equalizes as oxygen fills the lower-pressure area, filtering in through the spell. In this pure-oxygen atmosphere, a quantity of oak surrounding the arrowhead—including the arrow shaft, but mostly a big bite of the ship's structure—turns into a finely-divided powder, suspended in the oxygen environment. The arrowhead explodes, igniting the mixture.

"Someone give me a box of arrowheads. No, the pointy ones, not the broadheads. Something for sticking deep into a target. Thank you. Anybody here a wizard? Or someone who can push power at me while I do some experimental work?"

The volunteers for the mission stopped hammering on warheads and crowded around me. I keep forgetting *everyone* has some magical training around here. They formed a circle around me, holding hands, and focused. I did the actual spellcasting; they contributed magical force. Seventeen arrowheads took a while, but the hammered-heads would take longer to fill. I had some time, anyway.

Once we had the arrowheads ready, they mounted them on shafts—handling them with great respect; they weren't sure what the spells did—while I checked my mirror.

"Seldar?"

"Yes, Sire?"

"What's the word?"

"The battle continues. The attackers have regrouped and deployed some sort of mechanical device—it has unfolded to form a bridge between one of the access ramps and its gate. They are assaulting the gate with magic and with a medium ram."

"They gave up on the wall?"

"Torvil was most persuasive, Sire, and as the understanding of how to counter their mind-stunning spells spread, more and more of our troops became less subject to sudden paralysis. With their help, the oil prepared for the defenses has been poured out. The outer face of the wall and a goodly portion of the beach are on fire. Their wizards have not yet dealt with the flames."

"Is it really so much trouble to put it out? I mean, how much oil are we talking about?"

"Several barrels, Sire. They have used several spells in attempts to quench the flames, but the fires simply refuse to die."

"Any idea why?"

"Your granddaughter is standing by the seawall with her hands spread and fingertips resting on the wall. She appears to be concentrating."

"That would do it," I agreed, recalling a small river flowing into a wall of fire and disappearing into steam. I wondered if any of the oil was still there. It might be like a burning bush without the bush.

"What of your progress, Sire?"

"We're about to deploy archers to distract them. Can you let people know? I want them to take maximum advantage of any lapses in concentration."

"Yes. I will do so now."

"Good man." I put my pocket mirror back in the pocket and we all jogged to the gate room. I got the mirror there on-line and took a look at the seawall around the harbor. The top of the harbor wall was still visible above the water.

"See that? You're going to run through the gate as though through a door, straight out onto the pathway. Get through the gate as quickly as you can, because the other end doesn't have anything for me to latch on to."

A hand went up. I nodded at him.

"Majesty?"

"Yes?"

"I don't understand."

"I can't hold this door open for more than a few seconds," I translated. "If it closes on you, you're dead. So as soon as you see water through the arch, you sprint like hell for the obelisk. Once everyone is through—I hope—the gate will close. You launch your missiles together—a unified volley.

"Oh, wait. Pair off. I want you in groups of two. The leftover guy helps make a group of three. Got it? Good. Now that we have that sorted out, each group fires at a different ship—try to get them inside, somehow, through a port or a window or something. Fire your initial volley together, then fire the second shot at your ship as fast as you can, then *run.* You will be in an exposed position in order to get good shots. That means you have to get off the seawall and get away from the harbor before they do something brutal and nasty to you."

"Now I understand," he said, faintly.

"Anyone not want to go? It's extremely dangerous."

They assured me, each in their own way, they were going. I nodded.

"String bows. Get your magic arrows in your other hand. If you want to raise magical defenses, do it now."

They formed a circle like a football team going into a huddle and started chanting—some sort of group work to put a spell on everyone. I hadn't seen that before. Something new they developed, perhaps? Come to think of it, it might be more efficient to do it that way, as well as a team-building exercise.

Okay, forget about them. Time to put my own game face on.

I took several deep breaths and checked the charge on the gate. It had charged somewhat on its own, but not enough to handle a one-sided gateway. Short of interdimensional travel, this was one of the worst scenarios for gate use. And I was already starting to feel tired from the warhead spells.

Yeah, this wasn't going to be easy.

Center the thoughts. Gather power. Inhale the energy of the world. Breathe in power. Keep it. Concentrate it. Focus it. Direct it.

The scrying mirror drew a line, point to point, and the archway followed it. The depth of the archway seemed to increase, like a hallway. It lengthened in that strange direction, sliding past space and time to a place where it wasn't, landing there, latching on, existing in two places and making them the same.

Visually, the view through the arch did its usual flush, open, and snap routine. People sprinted for the far side the moment I gestured.

It was a good thing, too. I held it for several seconds, until the last man was through. This drained the partial charge in the gems much more quickly than I liked. I had to shoulder the whole load at the end or risk shredding the last three or four men. I held it, though, kept it open, even though it expended my gate spell and left me too weak to stand.

The image through the archway tore apart and dissolved. I sank to my knees and leaned forward on my hands. Doing this sort of thing as a mortal spellcaster is more than exhausting; it's draining.

I decided to lie down for a minute. Just until the mountain settled down and stopped tilting the floor. Maybe my pet rock is a prankster.

I wish I knew if all this effort was worth it.

I woke up in bed. There was a nasty moment when I wondered if this was some weird, surrealistic dream sequence starting with the mundane before moving into metaphysical-psychological-symbolic imagery.

Nope. Everything seemed pretty stable.

Nice of you to wake up, Firebrand told me. *Things are going badly.*

"Badly?" I looked around without sitting up. Nobody was trying to kill me. Either things were going badly elsewhere, or the badness was more subtle. I swung my legs off the platform serving as a bed and sat up. When the dizziness hit, I lay back down and breathed deeply until it passed. I sat up more slowly and reached for Firebrand.

"Explain this going badly thing. Did they take Mochara?"

No, Mochara seems okay. Last I heard, their biggest concern was the burning wreckage in the harbor. Remember how they parked all the fishing boats in the bay to make maneuvering and whatnot difficult for the invaders?

"I saw it. They had to keep it slow to avoid damaging their own ships on the way to the piers."

The fires from their ships spread to a lot of the others. It was weird, almost like the flames had a mind of their own and determination to spread. It's gonna be a while before they have much of a fishing fleet again.

"I bet they did," I agreed, unsurprised. *Two* fire-witches in town. Yeah, things were destined to burn. "We'll mass-produce some lumber," I continued. "Bob can cut a row of trees from the edge of the forests along the Eastrange and float them down the canal. A tumbler arrangement can de-bark the things, then we put the logs through a sawmill—hold it. I'm not all the way awake, yet, and I'm getting distracted. Start from the gate deployment and fill me in."

Okay. From what I hear, your archers did their thing and a fine thing it was. The ships they hit didn't cast new shields, just extended their existing ones while fighting the fires on board. The city launched a lot of breaking spells when the shields got spread thin, broke them, and then started shooting fire from all the launcher-things your buddy Flim has been working on. Wizards in Mochara got a pyrotechnic boost from Tianna or Amber—maybe both—and encouraged everything.

With half their fleet on fire or sinking, things started to come apart for the invaders. The Mocharan wizards regrouped and reorganized, countering the remaining enemy wizards while concentrating their attacks on one ship at a time. Archers picked off wizards in the water as they abandoned ship. Some of them never came up again; they may have escaped by breathing water and swimming away. Most of them didn't.

"Sounds like things went according to plan, then."

There was a minor bobble when the big raft—the funny-looking ship? —lined itself up in the harbor entry.

"Oh?"

There was a boom. It was a huge boom, I understand. It made a horrible bang and one of the seawall gates came apart. There was damage to the wall, too, as well as a lot of damage inside the city. They found a few iron spheres, probably launched by the barge-thing. The barge-thing didn't enjoy it, though.

Something went wrong, they think, because a big, bronze pillar rolled out the back of it and sank just outside the harbor. Then people on the barge started diving into the water to get away from their flaming ship, and then there was an even bigger boom. Smoke, steam, fire—all the good stuff. The ship disappeared in a fireball and sent bits and pieces all over the harbor. It also damaged the two nearer ships and stripped most of their canvas off.

"Sounds to me like someone's been working on gunpowder and cannon," I mused. "I wish I could have seen it. I wonder if they screwed up the mounting on the cannon or if the archers I sent damaged it, somehow."

I couldn't tell you, Boss. I didn't get to see, since I'm stuck here.

"How do you know all this, then?"

Seldar came up to report, but you were asleep.

"Fair enough. I don't suppose you know why we don't have cannon of our own mounted on the walls?"

*Actually, I do. The Demon King didn't like them. Said they were too unwieldy, too expensive, and required too much magic to be worth it. After the battle with Byrne, nobody seemed inclined to argue the point. You **did** kind of make them look useless.*

"Huh. I suppose so. Not much point in lugging several tons of metal around just to knock down three or four knights. I guess that's a good thing, since I never got around to telling the mountain to adopt a star fort configuration. Maybe I should do tell it anyway... I'll think about it some more. What happened next in the Mochara assault?"

Without the magical backing from their ships, the troops on the docks and beach realized they didn't have a good way to escape. They broke and ran, east and west, streaming along the beach at the base of the cliffs and getting shot at the whole way. A lot of them hit the harbor edges, splashed out and over the harbor wall, splashed back to the beach on the far side, and kept running. Our guys are doing cleanup around there—cavalry is rounding them up and taking them prisoner wherever possible, the wimps.

"Okay, aside from the one cannon shot, I'm not seeing how that's going badly."

That's going fine. You wanted to hear about Mochara.

"So I did. Continue." I stood up, stretched, and ran a quick cleaning spell over myself. I had a sticky, sweaty feeling behind my ears and on the inside of my elbows. Sometimes a nap does that. I think it's a humidity thing. It's nowhere near as bad as my transformations, but it's still icky and unpleasant.

While you were busy with Mochara, people in Karvalen have been busy, too. Remember those guys T'yl was talking about, way back when we had to leave in a hurry?

"The time Tort tricked the Demon King and T'yl persuaded me to flee through the gate. I remember."

That's right.

"The religions involved were.... The glowboys and the temple of justice?"

Yep, that's them. Technically, the Temple of Justice was after the Demon King on their own, over Seldar's objections—he's not in charge, just another priest.

The Church of Light went after your evil alter ego at the same time because it was a good opportunity, not because they coordinated it.

"That would follow, I suppose. The bright boys aren't too fond of other religions."

*I know. But it **looked** as though they were working together at the time. This time, I don't think the justice worshippers are involved, but a lot of not-too-religious types—mostly knights of the Demon King—*

"You mean the professional killers with no sense of honor?"

That's them.

"Let's not call them knights."

Okay by me. What do you want me to call them, Boss?

"Huh. Armored killers, or A-K's, maybe? Are there forty-seven of them?"

I'm sure you're trying to be funny, but I don't get it.

"You're right. Maybe it's a bad idea."

Whatever. A lot of them are in town and they're working for the Temple of Light. All those months ago, the Temple of Light had enough guys on hand to storm the mountain, at least while the palace areas were unoccupied. Months later—today—they're going solo and they've got even more troops, but they're not going after your palace. They're after the city. They've got the southeastern city gate and have surrounded the Baron's palace—the city guard is still defending it. They've taken one of the granaries for sure, and four guard houses. They're within a street or two of the Hall of Justice, as well as—

"The Hall of Justice?"

Yes. They're close to taking it, if they want to push another street or two that way. Is it vital in some way?

"Only if they have some super friends. Tell me about this Hall of Justice."

It's... a big building next to the Temple of Justice? With a great hall? People go there when they can't settle disputes on their own. An official from the city and a couple of priests hear the complaints and sort it out to do that thing—you know, justice. So, they do justice in a hall... or it's a hall you go to for justice...?

"When you put it that way," I admitted, "it does seem like a logical name for it. Okay, I'll try to contain my mirth. Go on."

The rebels or insurgents or whatever they are have almost a quarter of the city under their control. They don't seem to be too interested in taking the mountain, itself, though. They're just taking over the city, street by street.

"How?"

Wagons with shields on them, I think? They keep blocking streets off and spreading out, demanding the allegiance of everyone they encounter. They either impress them into service, send them on their way, or kill them on the spot, depending on the whim of the individual commander, apparently.

"SELDAR!"

The echoes rang down corridors for miles.

"Firebrand," I said, more quietly, "why didn't anybody wake me?"

They tried! You woke up a little, said something about turning off the water after brushing, and went back to sleep. You were well and truly out, Boss.

That brought me up short.

"They did?"

They did. I knew you were still in there, but when I tried to talk to you...
"Yes?"
Um. You're not going to like this.
"I'm not liking this already! What's one more thing not to like?"
Yeah, well... I tried talking to you and your other self told me you were too tired.
"Wait, what? You mean the Demon King spoke to you through my mind?"
No. It was the Other Guy. The—what did you call it? —the fake deity-thing.
"Oh." I had to pause a moment and consider that. Then I realized I didn't really have anything to consider. "What did it say?"
He said you were too tired to do anything and we should let you sleep. I decided to utilize my vast storehouse of draconic wisdom and acknowledged what He said was a very good idea.
"You have vast storehouses of draconic wisdom?"
Shut up, Boss.
"Did it—he—say anything else?"
Nope. He just seemed to be... you know. Helpful. Like having some trained selmok in your lair to keep an eye on your hoard while you sleep.
"I'm not sure what disturbs me more."
Between what and what?
"That I have a quasi-deific copy of my personality keeping an eye on me, or that you just compared it to the draconic equivalent of a guard dog."
If it's any consolation, Boss, He's probably not all that good a copy.
"Which, somehow, is not as comforting as you make it out to be."
The door ground open, pushed by a regular-sized guy in black armor, grey sash-with-shield. Another one stood outside. Two more carried in a pile of gear. Most of it was a suit of black, super-polymer-whatever-it-is armor.
"Seldar said you would demand it," one of them told me. They bowed and stepped back. I toed the pile, and thought about it. He was right. Again. This time, oddly enough, I didn't mind a bit. Maybe it only annoys me that he's right when it proves to me I'm wrong. It's better to be upset about being wrong than about a friend being right, right?
They helped me into my armor. I shrugged and bent and twisted a bit, making sure it was all settled. Unsurprisingly, it still fit. I don't seem to change too much with the passage of time. Physically, I mean.
"Where's Seldar?"
"In the room of vision, Your Majesty."
"You four, come with me."
"Those are our orders, Your Majesty."
"Figures."
We hurried through the corridors and I realized my stomach was grumbling. Now was not the time for lunch, or dinner, or whatever time it was. Daytime, that was all I knew for certain.
It's a little after their lunchtime, Boss. The rebellion-thingy started a little after dawn. The news of it got up to the palace only after some citizen—she was a semi-pro wizard with a specialty in scrying magic—got on her mirror and called a bunch of people on our side before someone on their side noticed what she was

doing and stopped her. By the time it filtered through the chain of command, you were chanting at arrowheads.

Got it, I replied. *We obviously need better internal communications. Thanks. One of us has to stay awake for the important bits, Boss.*

Remember how I said you're not as funny as you think you are?

Where do you think I get it from, Boss?

Vast stores of draconic wisdom?

You made my point, Boss.

Shut up.

Seldar was in the scrying room, manipulating mirrors and talking quickly. He didn't greet me, which told me he was extremely busy. Judging by his conversation and the snappish, do-it-*now* tone, he didn't need to be disturbed. I let him do his work and looked at the sand table.

The sand table displayed a replica of the city. Darker sands formed the areas occupied or controlled by the... rebels? Terrorists? Insurgents? I'm going with insurgents. The rest of the city was made up of lighter shades. From the looks of it, their current technique was to advance and take a new intersection, establish a temporary fortification in the street—semi-mobile walls mounted on wagons— and process the new addition to their territory.

So, I said to Firebrand, *do they drag people out of their homes and shops with the command to convert or die?*

I dunno, Boss. I haven't been involved with it, just listening to rumors.

Fair point.

I waited, listening to Seldar coordinate forces. Earlier, while we were busy with preparations for an attack from the outside, the Church of Light used that activity to mask their own concentration of forces. They had coherent units, heavy equipment, and, obviously, a plan.

Did they coordinate this with Thomen so the attack on Mochara would be a distraction? Or did they see it coming and decide it was an opportunity? Thomen might have thought he could take Mochara with his new spell—the brain-stunning thing. Had the army made it there to support the naval assault, I'm medium-sure it would have worked. They actually stood a chance of pulling it off even without the army, a fact I wouldn't have believed.

But the Church of Light... taking Karvalen, out here in the middle of nowhere? How did this serve their purpose?

Back up. First of all, what was their purpose? As a religious organization, they promote the worship of their deity. As far as Lotar is concerned, any increase in the power of the Church is an increase in his personal power. How does taking a city accomplish either of those goals? Well, in a city where their worship is forbidden, it opens the place up for... is it evangelizing? Missionaries? Conversion, maybe.

This direct, military intervention, though—it seemed out of character. Theocracies aren't unknown in this world, but they generally don't last too long. All the other churches get feisty when one of them starts grabbing temporal power. It's not about freedom. I think it's mostly they're touchy about someone legislating their religion away. The energy-beings don't like it when you try to hog all the worship—which is to say, all the food. Add to that the Glowsticks tend to think of other religions as heathen superstitions—despite some rather heavy evidence—and this move was asking for a major reprisal from… well, everybody.

Unless they could take and fortify Karvalen, at least. If they could take the city and hold it, maybe they could get away with it. It wasn't near anything important, held no strategic value, and didn't have anything anyone really wanted—no gold mines, no strategic importance, nothing. At least, nothing anyone knew about.

It did possess some hefty advantages, though. It had "iron mines," obviously. The surrounding land produced massive amounts of food—between ranching and farming, Karvalen could feed *Rethven* if it decided to buckle down and work at it. Food, along with steel, was a major export. And, to do the exporting, the canal system not only let Karvalen trade easily with the seaport of Mochara, but with the city-states on the eastern side of the Sea of Grass. There were also whole races of monsters under the Eastrange who—slowly—were starting to understand the idea of trading, rather than pillaging and looting.

And, of course, my favorite export: Education. People came from all over Rethven to enroll in school. I found out later about some students from even farther away—from the city-states on the western shore, beyond Rethven. There were always some plainsmen, even a few *viksagi,* some wizards from a place called Kolob, and someone all the way from somewhere called Trader's Bay, in Telasco, wherever those might be.

They studied wizardry, mostly, but first they learned to read.

Back to my point. For the Church of Light to take Karvalen, all they had to do was take it from the people who had it. Or, rather, get rid of the people who objected to their rule, consolidate their hold, and then come after me. Or they might take the place, lock me in, and ignore me until I was good and ready to come out. I doubted it—they're religious fanatics, after all—but Lotar might do it that way. If he set up shop in the Baron's palace, he could, symbolically, move right into ruling the place. Then the city could be a magnet for the faithful followers of the Lord of Light, the capitol of a new nation—a theocratic nation, ruled by their god and his power-hungry minions. Or maybe just ruled by the power-hungry minions.

Politics and religion. My two least-favorite topics. Maybe I can find a world where I can teach night school classes in physics and computer science. I'd settle for teaching high school science. Summer school, maybe, to avoid the perils of sunrise and sunset.

I shifted my attention to Seldar and his planning. He organized forces and prepared for an assault on the insurgents' territory. From the sound of it, the basic idea was a wall of blades—ha! —sweeping down the streets to crush any resistance.

"Seldar. Get them grouped for orders," I told him. "We need to talk about your plan."

"Sire, if you will allow me, I do not feel we have time to waste on discussion."

"Okay. We won't discuss. Stop what you're doing and pay attention to orders. Right now."

Seldar told the mirrors to wait, flipped them over, and turned to me.

"Yes, Your Majesty," he said. I ignored his use of the formal title.

"Your plan is to roll through the city streets, killing anyone who resists?"

"Yes, Your Majesty."

"I'm told a lot of those people are only there because someone held sharp things in their faces and told them to pick up that weapon and come along."

"Perhaps, Your Majesty, but they are now rebels, whatever their reasons."

"I thought you were a priest of justice?"

"And death is the proper punishment for treason."

"That's justice?" I asked, surprised.

"It is."

"I may have a word with the god of justice," I remarked. "However, we are not going to mete out cold justice today."

"Will we ignore this spreading threat?"

"No. We are going to temper justice with mercy."

Seldar snorted contemptuously.

"The traitors and rebels within the area deserve no mercy," he stated, flatly. "I do not recommend involving the Lady of Mercy in this."

"I agree. But the poor jerk who is walking forward with a spear because the guy behind him will kill him if he doesn't? It's a crime for a knight to lack bravery; they are held to a higher standard. It's a standard every citizen should aspire to, but we can't hold them to it."

"Why not?"

"Because they aren't worthy of it. If they were, they would be knights."

Seldar looked startled and paused to process that one. While he thought about it, I continued.

"Look, part of the duties of a knight is to defend the weak, help the helpless, that sort of thing. We want the citizens to look up to them and to aspire to *be* them. We never want knights to be a mystical, magical thing only the select few might achieve. We want them to be the possibility, the hope of the kingdom. Every cook and cobbler should look at them and think, 'I may never be a knight, but if I raise my son properly, maybe he can achieve that exalted position.' Not 'I hate those pompous, better-than-you jerks.'

"In like fashion, knights should encourage and protect average citizens, not view them as sheep to be sheared or cattle to be slaughtered when the need arises. Their job is to protect the citizens—all the citizens."

"I am not certain I understand, Sire."

"You don't have to," I replied, coldly. Then, more gently, "I'm sorry you don't understand it. I didn't have as long as I hoped, back when, to explain it adequately. Just bear in mind a kingdom is defined by its citizens. Without them, there is no kingdom. Land supports the people. The military defends the people. The nobles rule the people, organize and instruct the people. Knights come from the people. Food, materials, goods, services—everything, always, comes from and goes back to the people. If you don't have people, you have wilderness."

Seldar looked troubled. This was obviously an alien way of thinking, and I sympathized with him. It's hard to wrap your head around the idea people are the important things. It goes against centuries of believing the nobility and lands are the important things and people are... well... peasants.

"Think about it," I advised. "Meanwhile, talk to me. How many men do we have and what are they? Knights, soldiers, guardsmen, militia—all that."

Seldar touched the sand table and manipulated the spell, altering the view of the city to bring different sections into view as the spoke. Our forces were several thousand infantry. While we had a few hundred cavalry, cavalry aren't too useful in urban fighting. For the most part, cavalry could function only as a reaction force, using their speed to respond to threats. Archers were also of limited utility in the shorter line-of-sight of city streets. They could take to rooftops and upper floors to reinforce fixed positions, but were otherwise mostly targets.

"This is a war of foot soldiers," Seldar finished. "I intend to send them in, find Lotar and any other commanders, and cut the head off this serpent in our midst."

"I like the way you think," I told him, considering the map. "At least, as far as a military viewpoint goes. I think your plan will work. Moreover, I'm not sure there's a better way for an army to squash this insurrection."

"Then I may continue with my work, Sire?"

"No."

"No?" he asked, surprised. "May I inquire about your reason, Sire?"

"It's an appropriate military response. It isn't the way we should do it."

"I am afraid I fail to understand."

"There are civilians in the captured area," I pointed out. "What we're going to do is exactly what the Church of Light is doing, only better. We're going to surround the place, block it off, seal it up. We will then push inward, street by street, building by building, house by house. We'll capture anyone who surrenders—or even anyone who runs toward us with empty hands. We'll take everyone to a holding area where I'll look them over after dark. Anyone who willingly takes up arms for the Church of Light will be detained; the rest will be released."

"Your Majesty, that will take far longer than our planned assault."

"Yes, it will. It will be harder. It will take longer. It will require more effort and resources and be a general pain in the ass. But it's closer to the right thing to do."

"Closer?"

"In a situation like this, I'm not sure there *is* a right thing," I admitted, sighing. "All I know for sure is every angry, frustrated part of me wants to beat the Church of Light into small, glowing fragments and burn the fragments. That simple desire tells me I shouldn't."

"Again, Sire, I do not understand."

"It means I'm trying to be a better person—not a smarter, more ruthless one, but a better one. More honorable, if you like, in the sense of a person who acts with honor, rather than in the sense of receiving honors. I'm shooting for meritorious conduct, rather than accolades."

Seldar opened his mouth to say something and stopped. He closed his mouth, looked thoughtful, stroked his jaw. He paced around the table, looked at it, looked at me, looked off into the air.

"You once said," he started, "that you wished to be the worst of all the knights. Of all the knights, you hoped, by your actions, to be regarded as the least honorable, least kind, least merciful of all, thus encouraging all of us to be better men than you. You wanted us to do, and to be, better."

"That's right."

"May I say you seem strangely…" he groped for a word.

"Angry?"

"No."

"Temperamental?"

"No."

"Reactionary?"

"If you would give me a moment to think, I would tell you."

"Okay." I shut up and waited while he thought.

"You are usually more direct," he said, at last. "You charge in like thunder and strike like the lightning. When the smoke clears, that which needed to be was slain. Yet, this time, you seem oddly self-possessed and self-controlled."

"I've been working on my tendency to overreact," I told him. I didn't add the part about feeling deep urges to overreact even by my standards. Johann is still not dead and I need him to be.

"And a direct strike into the heart of the enemy territory is an overreaction?"

"I don't know," I admitted. "I hope so. I do know killing everyone we roll over in the street isn't the way to go about this. If they try to kill us, we kill them back. But if we can free the people who don't want to be fighting at all, we should do so."

"I understand your wishes, Sire. I am not certain it can be done."

I moved up to him and looked him in the eye. As I spoke, I moved my face closer to his until our noses touched.

"There are families in that area of the city," I said, softly. "Children are in there. We are going to squeeze the place like a sponge until it weeps people, not go in and kill everything. As long as we can contain this and extract people without needless bloodshed, we will. Have I been unclear on this in any way?"

"No, Sire."

"Make it happen, Seldar." I took a deep breath and said something I hate saying. "Your King commands it."

Seldar went to one knee and put a fist on the floor.

Now you've committed, Boss.

I don't need you to tell me that. The way my stomach dropped into my ankles did a fine job of it. The way Seldar went to one knee did even better!

While he's reorganizing the troops to contain the illumi-naughty, what are we going to do?

Talk to a lot of people, then have some words with a rock.

We had four wizards—full-time, professional wizards—who specialized in magic mirrors. We had another thirty or so people who could cast the basic mirror communication spell. I put them to work. The keys to running this siege of my own city would be communications and understanding of the situation. Intelligence, in the military sense.

With communicators detailed to strong points—the barricades in the streets— and instant communications to roving patrols, it was going to be tough for the

Church of Light to break out. Admittedly, we had to get some extra staff for Seldar. He couldn't take every call and stay in touch with every station. A few knights from the Order of Shadow, though, enhanced things enormously. They sat in a circle around him, each one keeping in touch with a few garrison commanders in the same arc. They handled the routine stuff and Seldar kept an eye on the overall situation with the sand table.

We contained the area of the city dominated by the Church of Light within a matter of hours. Our own barricades went up, blocking streets. Archers posted to rooftops. Guards patrolled all along the perimeter. We stationed groups of cavalry back from our perimeter as a reaction force, in case the Church of Light tried a breakout. We surrounded the area on every side that wasn't a city wall.

Expansion stopped.

As for me, I spent the afternoon talking with the mountain. I couldn't tell exactly where the border was, but I could start with places I knew were in enemy hands and work outward from there. The point I picked was the city gate they had in their control. The bolts disengaged on their own and gravity swung the gate shut. It fused into the wall and stayed there. From that point outward, roof access and windows started disappearing as stone rolled over shutters, sealed around doorways, the works. Underground access narrowed or vanished. Subsurface corridors sealed off; sewage pipes changed shape and became too small to crawl through. By nightfall, buildings had one practical way in or out: the front door.

I considered shutting off the aqueducts feeding into that part of the city, but I'm a softie. I wanted to encourage people to slip away and escape, not force the Church to start an immediate confrontation.

On the other hand, I did have a pretty good sense of where the Church of Light concentrated its worship. Don't ask me why I can feel such a thing through a rock. I have some suspicions and I don't like any of them. But those centers didn't only get their windows removed. I told the mountain to seal them up— doors, windows, everything but the ventilation holes. Anyone stuck in there was well and truly stuck; they could wait in their holy prison cell until we came to get them.

That was it for my afternoon. Merging with the mountain and supervising the details of those instructions took a while, especially while mortal. I couldn't simply give the mountain a general set of parameters and turn it loose; this required all the finesse I could muster. As it was, I probably didn't get all the buildings in the affected area. Still, if there was a band of unaffected buildings just behind the enemy lines, I was content. We would take those first, anyway.

After sunset, I hurried through a waterfall, armored up, checked my defensive spells, and went to the communications center. Dantos kept an eye on the sand table. I nodded at him and he nodded in return; Seldar was dozing in his chair while the rest of the knights continued to run the siege. Seldar snapped awake as I came in.

"Sire."

"Seldar. What's new?"

"We had some difficulties with the city guards," he stated. "Many of them object to our offensive against the Church of Light. A few of their guard houses have even refused to assist."

"Did they say why?"

"We believe many of them are worshippers of the Light," Dantos supplied.

"Great. Have we got anyone who needs me to look them over?"

"You intend to look into their souls and determine their allegiance?" Seldar asked.

"Unless you have a better idea?"

"No, Sire," he answered. He and Dantos traded glances. "We hoped you would do so. Since we have some difficulties with cooperation from the city guard, our current prisoners are being held in the Hall of Justice."

"Perfectly appropriate. Do we have priests of justice and priests of mercy we can have present, too? Maybe priests of law? I remember a lawyer priest in town a few years ago. And isn't there a god of truth, somewhere?"

"Yes, all those are available," Dantos agreed. "The Lady Tianna has not objected, as such, to other faiths within the city. She does not have much at all to say about them, so there are many churches of various sorts."

"May I ask why you wish such priests to attend you?" Seldar asked.

"Because I'm about to act as judge and jury, possibly executioner. Under normal circumstances, I despise the idea. Under these circumstances, I still despise it, but reluctantly accept I have a right and an obligation to do so—I'm the King. And I can, as you put it, actually look into someone's soul. I would rather determine their... well, guilt and innocence are legal concepts. I'm hoping I can say whose side they're on, if they're on a side. I'll play judge and jury because I'm forced to, but I'd rather not play god."

"Are you not a god, Sire? I have been inside the Temple of Shadow and seen the—"

"Let's not get into that," I suggested. "Just tell those churches—no, *ask* those churches to send priests there for me, okay?"

"As you say, Sire."

Looking into and through people is no fun. Everyone starts out scared and often finishes the same way. It's not something I enjoy doing. It smacks of mind-reading and a nasty invasion of privacy.

Does it justify my actions to say I did it for the security of the country? That's a slippery slope if ever there was one. Never mind that I'm infallible—or think I am—in this matter, or that I'm legally able to do it—being a vampire king has advantages like that. The top of the slope starts with "Whose side are you on?" so you can sort out the rebels. Does it turn into "State your name and present your papers," on every streetcorner? Do people wind up wearing their identification—like yellow stars on their shirts, tattooed numbers on their forearms, and ribbon-like badges to display their occupation, employer, and rank?

I worry about things like this. I don't have good answers, either, which tells me I don't belong in this job. What I came up with was a lousy compromise.

Priests from the Temples of Justice, Mercy, Law, Truth, and Shadow showed up. I hadn't intended to involve the Temple of Shadow, but I suppose it's unreasonable and unfair to keep them away from me. But with multiple religions involved, it simplified things a little. I had no intention of establishing the Black Court, where the King passes judgment on those brought before him. I wanted to set something up where I wouldn't need to be involved.

Laziness as a motivator for establishing a judicial system. I wonder if that's ever happened before.

Having religions involved in the process struck me as a good idea, too, since they were agents of *actual* powers-that-be. If we could get the priest of Truth to detect lies, he might be in charge of questioning the subject. Then the priest of Law could cite whether or not there was a violation of the actual law. Then the priests of Justice and Mercy could debate sentencing.

Pun intentional: By the gods, it might work!

My only problem was what to do with the priests of Shadow. Putting one in charge would seem like favoritism, but excluding them entirely would be unkind to them. I decided a ceremonial position of Mouthpiece—moderator of the process, or referee—might work out. But the moderator won't get a vote. Or something. It's still an idea and not well-thought-out. We'll see how the various feathers ruffle.

So, after I sorted through a dozen or more people, representative priests arrived at the Hall of Justice. I explained a bit and took the moderator seat. A priest of each of these religions sat on the panel and talked to the potential rebel scum. They interviewed the individual, prayed about him, discussed him, examined the entrails, and did whatever it is priests do. Then they voted. If they decided he was a radical, weapon-wielding, arms-bearing worshipper of the Light, we sent him to the dungeons. I wasn't concerned about the typical worshipper of the Light, and even less concerned (sort of) with the Joe Citizen drafted unexpectedly. I was concerned about the radical terrorist groups who wanted to overthrow the kingdom, burn all the other temples, and establish a theocratic absolutist dictatorship for their god.

If I sound as though I was willing to trample on people's religious freedoms in the name of stopping terrorism, so be it. They started an armed conflict in my city. Until the conflict was resolved, religious terrorists and soldiers were the *enemy*. Afterward? We'll see. But, at least for now, yes, I'm going against my upbringing and persecuting a religion. Not for disagreements, of which we have many, but for the open warfare in the city streets. I hope I was only persecuting the radicals in the religion, but where do I draw the line? I probably snared a few not-all-that-radical worshippers, too.

I don't feel too bad about it. I'm a vampire. I'm expected to do nasty things to good-aligned priests.

On the other side of the coin, we had a lot of people who were not hostile religious zealots. Yes, they might be thieves, murderers, cheats, liars, or double-parkers. So what? That's not what we had them for. Religious zealot, yes or no? No? Fine. Go, and sin no more, or something.

Which put us on notice about what to do with the innocent. Most of the ones we already captured—and the ones we were hopefully about to capture—were displaced from their homes and families. What do we do with them?

We found a mostly-unused street and sent everyone there. They could chalk names on walls next to the doors to make it easier to find each other. It was a start.

It was a system that favored letting people go. Sure, a lot of routine Light-worshippers slid right on through. If we had any up in front of us, as I'm sure we did, I made it a point to turn them loose. So what? I wasn't after the congregation. I wasn't concerned with the people praying. I was concerned with the people hacking other people to death.

See? I'm not as bad as I could be. Mostly. At least some of the time. When I think about it.

When we ran out of people already captured at our perimeter, we started in on the city guards from those guard houses that refused to participate. This raised some objections from Rendal, as the Commander of the Guard. All I did was send out the order for them to report to the Hall of Justice and he showed up in my interview room to protest. I let him rant at me for a couple of minutes before I shut him down.

"Stop talking," I told him—snapped at him—and he did. "Now you answer my questions. Is it the job of the city guard to keep order in the city? Answer yes or no and don't say anything else. I'm in no mood to waste time."

"Yes."

"Would you say the current insurrection qualifies as a failure to keep order? Yes or no."

"Yes," he admitted, grudgingly.

"Then it's the duty of the city guard to bring it to a halt and restore order. I don't care what religion the guardsmen are. For all I care, they can worship the Lord of Justice or the Lady of Mercy or the Consecrated Carrot of the Holy Harvest. But when they put on the uniform to do their jobs, they put their personal feelings aside and do the damn job. Is this a problem?"

"Your Majesty, it is. Many of us have strong feelings, very strong, regarding our faiths."

"Then go join the clergy!" I advised. "The order and well-being of the city is your *duty*. If you can't do your duty, you don't have a job!" I rubbed my temples, uselessly. The headache was a psychic one. "Look, I can put the city under martial law. I can put soldiers everywhere and go that way. I don't want to. I firmly believe a civilian organization for peacekeeping, law enforcement, and the maintenance of civil order is the right way to go about this. But if you're going to stand there and tell me I'm wrong—a civilian organization can't do this because it doesn't command the loyalty of its members—then I'll consider your argument. Well?"

Rendal isn't a young man by any measure. Yet, he straightened, deliberately and carefully, bracing himself to a rigid attention. I almost felt sorry for him. But he mustered his dignity with his courage and looked me in the eye.

"Your Majesty," he said, formally. "I do not see how we can gauge the loyalty of a man, nor ask men to cast aside their gods in favor of a city."

I steepled my fingers and thought about it. He had a point. How do you judge whether a man will be more loyal to the ideals of an organization than the commands of his religion? How many police officers get shot because they can't bring themselves to shoot some teenager? How many religious figures are assumed innocent until an irreligious cop notices something incriminating and forces an investigation? Are these numbers greater than zero? How much greater?

I *hate* being a politician!

"All right," I sighed. "Maybe you have a point. Maybe the traditional idea of having a city guard isn't such a great one around here. I'll have to think about it before I make any changes. But, right here, right now, we're going to go through this mess. We're going to squeeze the captured area, rescue citizens who have been captured or impressed into service, and find the individuals responsible for this insurrection. I want *policemen* walking through the streets we take back, greeting the people, encouraging them to escape what might become a war zone, directing traffic, and keeping the situation as calm as it can be."

"Shall we arrest all the priests of the Light?"

"No. I doubt they had much to do with it, aside from following orders. High Priest Lotar, though, certainly had something to do with it. *Him*, we're arresting—again. Possibly a number of confidants and subordinates, too."

"So… no wholesale purge of the religion?" he pressed.

"Absolutely not. They can religion away all they like as long as they don't interfere in the day-to-day operation of the city."

"You're lifting the ban on their worship?" He sounded flabbergasted.

"Why not?"

"They *are* responsible for this insurrection," he observed.

"People should be able to worship whoever or whatever they want. But, as I said, right here and now, we've got an immediate problem and I want it dealt with in a careful, humane, and preferably bloodless manner."

"Bloodless?"

"As in, without bloodshed. Not as in 'there is no blood left.' Got it?"

"Yes, Your Majesty. I… 'got' it."

"Good. Now, send in the next of the potential traitors," I sighed. "Let's get the dirty work over with and move on to better things."

One of the problems with asking someone questions about their religion is the locals have multiple religions. They aren't identified as "Christian," "Muslim," "Jew," or anything like that. The local religions are more eclectic, more mix-and-match. A farmer will give offerings to the Harvest King, but will also ask favor of Father Sky when he needs more or less rain. A mother will pray to the Lord of Swords for the safety of her son while he's in the army, but she will also light a candle before the little statue of the Lady of the Hearth she keeps in her house, praying her son will come home. And, of course, when a child is sick, parents will go to every church in town to find one that will heal him.

The only thing I like about my church is their success rate with fixing people. True, they do it mostly magically rather than religiously—thaumatugy instead of theurgy, I suppose—and their specialty is injury, not disease. You won't find a better doctor when your mule kicks you and breaks your ribs. It helps that the medics usually have a pretty good idea of how people are put together and can stick the pieces back where they belong. They also have a special rate on suggested offerings: Anyone under the age of ten is *free.*

I never told them to do that. They assumed I'd want it that way. At least, *I* didn't tell them; my energy-state alter ego might have given it as a commandment from On High. Either way, when I learned this a lot of my personal anxiety about the religion evaporated. Not all of it, but a lot of it.

Almost as good, if they run into a problem, they don't have the slightest qualm about calling Tianna up and asking her for help. I wonder how Sparky feels about it. I don't care, as such, but I do wonder.

So, when I'm confronted with Rebel Scum, I can't really ask about his religion. Asking if they worship at the Temple of Light is also kind of pointless. The Temple of Light tries to be a one-stop-shop for all mystic services, but mostly it gets called on to provide healing magic, protection from netherworldly forces, and a spiritually-uplifting experience.

After some descriptions of the experience, I think of it as the Holy Heroin. People come away feeling happy. No wonder the Glowsticks keep existing. Come to our services, leave all your cares at the door, walk out feeling happy! Forget your troubles—be happy! Sad about something? Come to us and get happy!

They're like a religious drug. Who said "Religion is the opiate of the masses"? I forget. But this church is more literally an opiate. You walk out the door on a religious high comparable to being drugged.

This bothers me.

Don't misunderstand me. I'm all for people being happy. I just question the validity of any religion that turns off sadness and pain and replaces it with uncritical joy. People should work through their problems, fix them, and overcome them. We shouldn't ignore our problems and get high on religion so we don't have to care. That's not a path to personal growth; that's stagnation and decay. It's an addiction, and the priests are the pushers.

Is it ironic I think this way? If I say anything against the Church of Light, everyone will assume it's because I'm a blood-drinking monster. If I ignore them, people will keep going there to zone out on a religious high. Come to that, people will go there for a hit of Nirvana whether I forbid it or not.

I think it's even more ironic the religion peddling the daily dose of unconditional love is also the only one completely intolerant of other religions. Nobody else seems to find it strange. There are a lot of contradictions in the Church of Light and it makes me wonder how well the Glowing One recovered from his encounter with the Devourer.

So, when we have potential traitors standing in front of us, what do we ask? For the panel's interrogations, we worked out a set of standard questions for the guardsmen. Who are you? Do you have any objection to arresting members of the Church of Light? Do you have any misgivings about retaking the area they've captured?

If they had any problems with arresting a Church of Light member, they were relieved of duty and sent on their way. If they had misgivings about retaking city streets, the compromise worked out by Justice and Mercy saw them handed them off to a knight to talk about it. The whole process went pretty quickly once we hit our stride.

The big hitch was the mirror call from Kammen. I slipped into a side-room at the Hall of Justice to take it.

"What's up?"

Kammen looked out of my pocket mirror and wiped some blood from his brow. He had quite a bit on him. His clothes didn't seem cut, though. The blood probably wasn't his.

"I could use a quick way out," he said, quietly.

"Define 'quick'."

"Maybe soon, instead of quick."

"I'll get right on it. Do you have an opening you can use at your end?"

"I can get to one, but they'll spot me."

"Okay. Give me a slow count to two hundred and call me back."

"One... Two..."

I hung up and headed for Bronze, shouting I'd be back shortly. My bodyguards did not seem pleased; there was no way they were going to keep up. On the other hand, I was with Bronze and—once I made it to the Palace—there were plenty of Order of Shadow guys to chase me down and surround me. The guys on bodyguard detail would call ahead and have more waiting. I don't see what they had to complain about.

We whisked through the night and up the Kingsway, racing through the dragon's throat. I wanted to get to my makeshift gateway for this. True, the spell had collapsed in my last use, but the gems were still charging. I could cast the spell on any old archway or doorway, but the added energy from the gems was crucial.

I should really set things up so the mountain didn't have to hold them. Some silver power diagrams—or maybe some of that orichalcum stuff, if I could figure out what it was made of. Power diagrams would be helpful. I could have a rack of gems charging and place only the charged ones in the diagram.

While I'm at it, more gates would be good. I could have different sizes of useful gates, rather than one large one and a bunch of tiny ones. Maybe one large enough to dive through, one the size of a door, one wide enough for three men to run through, one tall and wide for Bronze and myself...

Someday. Someday, someday, someday. Someday I'll go on a vacation and no one will try to kill me. Then I'll relax, kick back, enjoy some tunes, get room service, have a massage, take up golf, lay out by the pool, go swimming. Well, no, obviously not swimming. Or water skiing. Or boating. Or anything else involving water. Maybe I should stick to amusement parks. Roller coasters, popcorn, that sort of thing.

Is it weird my real life revolves around magical gateways, spells, angry religious zealots, evil wizards, and androgynous elves while my fantasy life involves Disneyland?

Seldar came into the gate room with another pair of Shadows while I was setting things up. He started to say something but I put my mirror in his hand and told him to talk to Kammen. He did so while I wound power around words, drew lines of energy, and formed a fresh gate matrix.

Bless him, he talked with Kammen for a bit, transferred the call to the gate-targeting mirror, and got a lock on him while I worked on the gate spell.

"What do we have?" I asked, when I could.

"He is in Carrillon, outside the palace. He is hiding in a carriage."

"Is that what I'm targeting with the gate?"

"No. Here." Seldar moved the viewpoint down the hall to an open double doorway. It looked like a carriage house of some sort; several carriages of various sorts were parked inside. The double doors faced out onto a street. I could count three members of Carrillon's city guard in sight. They were standing around, simply watching the world go by, at least as far as I could tell.

"Why there?"

"The door of the carriage in which he conceals himself is small. He will not move through it quickly."

"Good enough. Kammen?"

"Sire."

"Get ready." I panned the view around a bit, looking up and down streets. He was right. They would spot him quickly if he headed for the doorway. But if he made it to the doorway...

"Go," I told him, and watched carefully. He opened the carriage door and squeezed his bulk through it, scraping heavily in places. Once he was out of the carriage, his mass didn't let him accelerate as quickly as smaller men, but his top speed was impressive.

Since I saw him coming, I timed it carefully. The gate swirled, opened, snapped into alignment. Kammen shot through like a freight train and applied airbrakes. I slammed the gate closed behind him and he managed to stop himself by using the width of the room and a dozen yards of the hallway.

"Sorry," I said, swinging a chair around for him. "I really need a bigger room for this sort of thing."

"Not complaining," he replied as he returned. He took a seat at my nod. The chair held.

"Want to explain what that was all about?"

"Thomen's dead. They think I did it."

"Huh." I thought for a second. "Did you?"

"Didn't get the chance," he admitted. "Planned on it, though."

"Did I mention I wanted him alive?"

"Not that I recall."

I sighed. It would have been nice to interrogate Thomen about what he did to Lissette's mind, as well as *why* he did it, but...

"Okay, so you didn't kill him, but he's dead anyway. What happened?"

"Someone else did it."

I refrained from gnashing my teeth. It's terrible on tooth enamel and it's painful for me.

"I understand that much," I said, slowly and carefully. "Could you—oh, I don't know—provide an additional detail or two?"

The story I got out of him was this: On nights when Thomen didn't stay in with the Queen, he headed down the west hall to the nine-windowed tower— whatever that is. I didn't chase the rabbit. There he took the stairs down to the ground floor and went out to... well, wherever an Evil Grand Vizier goes when he's done messing with the Queen's mind for the evening. Kammen picked a spot in the west hall where he could lurk—there aren't many places a seven-foot-tall hulk of a man can effectively lurk—and proceeded to do so, night after night, until Thomen chose to walk down that hall again.

Someone else had the same idea. Kammen didn't get a good look; the assassin wore a blurring spell. All Kammen could see was a collection of grey and brown and black, all fuzzy and indistinct, only roughly in the shape of a person. Whoever it was had to be on the small side, though; the unfocused fuzz wasn't very large.

"So Thomen is comin' my way, not a clue, and I'm watching through the tapestry," Kammen explained. Seldar handed him something to drink. "I sweep it out of my way as I come out of my niche. He stops and gives out an oath, all surprised, and raises one hand. The ring he uses hits me with a cutting spell, or tries to, but I'm ready and his spell breaks on my shields. He starts to say something, then stops talking. There's this silver tongue stickin' out of his mouth, then it pulls back, faster'n a snake's tongue—*thwick!* And then it's all slashes and cuts and blood everywhere, mostly on me, and Thomen's head looks all surprised right there at my feet."

"I see."

"Yeah. The blurry person leaves in a hurry and whoever it is is fast, damn fast. I don't see the point to runnin' when the wizard's already dead. I should've, though. When he died, something he was wearin' went off, and all of a sudden there's alarms everywhere. People are and running around yelling and closing in and I'm covered in Thomen's blood with his head looking all surprised at me from the floor. Maybe I coulda explained," he finished, shrugging, "but I decided not to trust people's reason and goodwill."

"If you have a choice about it, it's probably wiser not to," I agreed.

"So I headed off toward my escape and got out of the palace through one of the hidden ways. Once I got out, though, I was stuck. Too many alarms, too many guards. You'd have thought someone tried to kill the Queen. I didn't want to kill anybody, so I hid in the carriage-wright's."

"Why is there a secret niche behind a tapestry?" I asked. "For that matter, why is there a secret passage leading into the palace?"

"I guess things were pretty interesting in the days of the old kings of Rethven."

"I guess they were. So, any ideas on the assassin?"

"Nope. He's good, though. Stopped the wizard from talking or waving his hands with the first shot. Not a professional, though. That sticking through the neck was it for Thomen. All the rest was way more than he needed. That was someone bein' all pissy about it."

"Huh. I didn't think of that."

"You're not much of an assassin."

"I'm not?"

"You're a killer. Assassins kill stuff quick and clean. You usually kill stuff all messy."

"Your point is well-taken. Go on about this amateur assassin."

"Um. That's it. One killing thrust, then a lot of slicing. Mighta been an elf-blade—there wasn't much chopping or hacking. Divided his spine in six places, not counting the thrust, and faster than most could do it. One of us, maybe, or you, Sire."

"Could it have been an elf?" Seldar asked.

"Wasn't too far off the right size," Kammen admitted. "With the blur going, maybe so."

"Sire?" Seldar asked, looking at me.

"I'll see what I can find out. But, all things considered, I'm not sure I'm upset about it. This makes things a lot easier."

"It does?" they asked, in unison.

"I think it does. If there's no one there to keep mistreating Lissette's brain, she'll come to her senses. Hopefully her sane and rational senses. If she winds up walking the halls and wailing, that's another story, but we can hope for something better. Besides, Thomen won't be making promises to Lotar anymore. I'm not sure Lotar is up to speed on what's going on in Carrillon, but whatever he and Thomen planned with this stupid assault on Mochara and bloody insurrection in Karvalen, it's not happening."

"It does seem poorly coordinated," Seldar agreed. "I believe the plan was to take one of the cities while distracting the other."

"How so?"

"Depending on the timetable, one or the other city should have had a major external threat demanding immediate attention, as well as all available troops. This would make the conquest of either city more likely. If I were arranging it, this move by the Church of Light would have happened days ago to nail troops down to Karvalen, leaving Mochara on its own. After Mochara was taken, then a relieving force could enter through the captured gate to reinforce the Church's hold over their sector of the city and make it possible to actually take Karvalen."

"I don't know. The plan sounds better than what happened, but it would still be uncertain."

"The only certainty of war is that it will come."

"I should write that down," I said. "All this still strikes me as poorly coordinated."

"Sire, please remember—no matter how many mirrors you employ, among the citizenry, they are not common. I do not believe Lotar even *has* one, much less one he might use through the city shield. Those are quite specific—I can account for each of them, I believe. Aside from any you choose to alter, of course. Thus, Lotar can only know what he sees for himself, or what he reads in messages delivered to him. He cannot simply call out to anyone he pleases. Even if he does have a mirror, a basic one, he must journey outside the shield of Karvalen to use it, and he seldom leaves his temple without strong inducement."

I pondered that for a moment. I'm so used to cell phones, radio, and other instant communications that I take them for granted. Making communication mirrors is a major project even for the few wizards who can. I guess I don't understand how to think about the things. They're unusual magical devices. In some ways, having one is like having your own telegraph during the days of the transcontinental railroad, sort of.

Maybe I should think of them more in terms of short-wave transmitters. They're not telephones; mirrors are more like big, complicated things only a few people have. They're not as common as I think they are. They're the big metal box in the basement connected to the special, flagpole-sized antenna next to the house. That might be closer. After all, how many ham radio operators do I actually know? In theory, I know two—both of whom worked at the University about a century ago.

When it comes right down to it, I have a terribly skewed view of Karvalen, Rethven, and the nuts-and-bolts setup of this society. Maybe I should take a page from Mary's book and get a better disguise. I could pull a Prince-and-the-Pauper caper, just without the Pauper, and wander around the kingdom as an itinerant wizard. Get a peasant's-eye view of the world again, see it from other perspectives. It would probably do me good to get a better idea what the place looks like from somewhat lower down the totem pole.

"How many mirrors are there in Rethven?" I asked.

"In all of Rethven? Perhaps a hundred," Seldar informed me. "Every noble has one, of course, and there are a half-dozen in the palace at Carrillon. There are another twenty or so here, in the palace—most of those are capable of seeing or calling beyond the city, itself—and in private hands, there are several mirrors useful only within the city or only outside it. Tianna has one, and there is one in the Temple of Shadow, I know.

"Of course, this does not count any mirrors in Arondael. There is no way to tell how many mirrors they may possess or have sold to others. Those—all of them, I strongly believe—are useful only outside the city shield."

"I understand. I'll try to keep those numbers in mind in the future."

"It is my honor to be of service," he assured me. Then he frowned. "The thing of most concern to me is not with their coordination, but with their intent."

"How so? What am I missing?"

"We did not attempt to send out our forces," Seldar said. "At least, not through one of the city gates. Therefore, to Lotar's best knowledge, all the knights, all the infantry, everyone was still *here*, and a threat to him. I doubt he understands your use of a gateway spell. Creating one, much less holding one open, is not wizard's work. It requires a magician to understand the spell, and often requires several to make it work. I am certain they are now concerned about the number of magicians in your service."

"Seldar, right now there are *no* magicians in my service!"

"They cannot be certain. They do not know your powers, nor how willing you are to exert yourself to your limits. I know I have only the most vague idea how your gate works, nor how those strange spells work to power it. You do not have a dozen magicians at your command, but to one who stands outside, it must *seem* so.

"But his attempt to take the city is my main point. He could not do so with the force he now has. He must have been counting on some sort of assistance."

"An army smuggled into Karvalen?"

"Not impossible," Seldar admitted. "I am told there were a number of the Demon King's lesser knights involved in a Church of Light assault on the palace some months ago. I am equally sure those men yet remain; there are reports of many armored men wearing the white tabards with the golden sun-face on it. They seem quite formidable, individually. No doubt he has been recruiting forces into his religion ever since.

"But, given the way most of the houses of the City Guard in the occupied area simply surrendered, I suspect Lotar was counting on religious authority to trump civic authority. With worshippers of the God of Light in every Guard house, it would not be unreasonable to expect to take them quickly, even easily, and so gain more ground and impress more troops into his service. He may even have estimated—or been encouraged to estimate—that his expansion and assimilation would be rapid enough to bolster the existing forces under his command sufficiently to take Karvalen."

"You think he really planted a lot of traitors in the City Guards?"

"Planted? Perhaps that is too strong a word. It may have been as simple as proselytizing, converting existing Guardsmen to his religion. We might ask him when we see him."

"Don't count on it," I muttered, darkly. Seldar ignored this.

"As for his motives now, I am uncertain. My guesses are these. He may believe he possesses sufficient force to accomplish a takeover of Karvalen—or will soon possess such force in the form of reinforcements. He may not be aware the attack on Mochara was unsuccessful. On the other hand, he may already be aware of the army's retreat and the defeat of the navy. If so, he knows he is unlikely to be reinforced, but is now trying to be difficult enough to dislodge so he can negotiate for something he wants. It is also possible he is simply being a radical fanatic intent on martyring himself and all his forces for the greater glory of his god."

"Remind me to mention to Beltar how noble sacrifice should have a point, not be done for its own sake."

"I will certainly communicate that to him, oh Undead King of Night."

"All right. Kammen? Thomen is dead—thoroughly and definitely dead, right?"

"Yes."

I admit I was less than happy about it. I wanted to quiz Thomen about his activities before I killed him. I've been trying so hard to give him the benefit of the doubt and come up with ways to explain his actions, but underneath it all, I've been looking forward to ripping him to pieces with my bare hands. I didn't realize how much I was looking forward to it until Kammen reported Thomen's demise.

I had a really weird feeling of hope. I hoped Johann was alive and well and staying that way, because I wanted to kill him. Contradictory and strange. It was an interesting sensation.

"We'll give Carrillon a couple of days to sort out," I decided. "Like I said, from the description of Thomen's activities, whatever he was doing to Lissette needed a lot of maintenance and supervision. Call someone in Carrillon and keep abreast of the situation."

"I've got someone in mind, Sire."

"Good man. Seldar, do you recall telling people I'd want my armor?"

"Yes, Sire. An insurrection is taking place in your city. You will want to put it down." He smiled, perhaps a trifle ruefully. "I would stop you if I could, but I feel such efforts would be wasted. But you have demonstrated remarkable self-control and a kingly aspect in your choice of strategy, Wise One."

"Oh, I don't know. What I want to do is gallop down there, bash through everything I see, and let Bronze trample Lotar until he's a greasy sizzle under her hooves."

"I thought as much."

"But it's not what I'm going to do. Lotar has already tried to turn some of his own sub-priests into martyrs for his cause. I don't want him winding up as a martyr and inspiring people to do the same."

"I have your instructions and have made all the arrangements, Sire. You need not concern yourself with this matter, I assure you."

Kammen looked surprised.

"Wait. You're not going to go crashing through everything and burn it all?" he asked.

"No, I'm not. Seldar has most of the plan sorted out already."

"Most of it?" Seldar asked, suspiciously.

"What *is* the plan?" Kammen asked.

"Same as before, but I'm going to eradicate their mobile walls before we really start to squeeze. Without them, they'll think twice about trying to advance. Then we're going to move in, house by house, block by block, and take back the city. Anyone who throws down arms and surrenders is to be taken captive and sorted out in the Hall of Justice."

"What if they don't surrender?"

"What do we usually do when faced with armed opponents who won't back down?"

"Kill them," Kammen said, without hesitation. Seldar gave him a dirty look, but nodded.

"Then kill the ones you have to, capture the ones you can. Remember, I want people to see you making the attempt to subdue and capture people. I want our side shouting about how those who surrender will not be harmed. I do *not* want wholesale slaughter. This isn't a war, it's a... a *police action*. Every one of them who dies for the greater glory of their holy cause is a martyr, and we want to minimize that.

"When we have them, we'll try them for crimes against the kingdom and sort out the ones who instigated it from the ones who only followed orders. Then we'll imprison the ringleaders and find lesser punishments based on individual culpability. Now, Kammen, do you feel up to smashing a mobile wall?"

"Any day, any night, any where."

"Good, because I feel like blowing some stuff up. Let's sort out our assaults. And have someone find my bow."

Saturday, February 28th

Luckily, the Demon King didn't care to shoot anyone; my composite-metal bow was still in Karvalen. I twanged the bowstring cable a few times and liked the high-pitched note. Very nice.

Most of last night was an exercise in preparation. Seldar set up assaults. Kammen went to bed. Well, he'd had a busy day dodging guards. I put spells on arrows.

I've noted this before and I'll probably note it again: It's a pain to put a lot of spells on anything. You can pour arrowheads from a mold, have apprentices carve shafts, send kids to pluck feathers for fletching, and so on. Arrows themselves can be produced by the hundreds or thousands. But it takes one person, focused intently, to craft one spell at a time. Depending on the spell, it may take two or three or thirty people, all tied up and focused on a single project, to produce one spell.

Mass production it ain't.

Although, sitting there, putting spell after spell on arrow after arrow, it did occur to me I might be able to partly industrialize the process. If all you want is the *same* spell on the *same* object *every* time, it might be possible to enchant a sort of meta-spell. A spell to build a spell, if you like. Stick an arrow in the Enchanted Quiver of Magic and wait until it goes *ding!* Then take it out and put another one in. The power requirements would be prohibitive—it would have to supply its own enchantment as well as put power in the spell it cast. Maybe with a monitoring gauge of some sort, it could take in an arrow, cast the spell on it, keep putting power in over time until it was fully charged—or charged to the required level—then actually make some sort of light and sound to let you know it was done. It might only work for one arrow an hour, but it could be left without supervision between changes and would require no real skill in the operator...

Later. Someday. Always someday.

I did take a bit of a break from arrow manufacture to remove some crystals—quartz, I think—from the wall of the gate room. The mountain grew them for me; it seemed impolite to let them sit there. Since I already had a new gate spell set up, it wasn't too hard to wire them in, so to speak, as power containers.

Looking at the quartz and the diamonds, side by side, I discovered something. Putting a power matrix in each of them was an identical process. Oh, there were crystalline differences, but those didn't matter too much. The spell for storing power in a crystal varies a little to take into account the type of crystal, but all it does is resonate properly with the lattice. All that really mattered was the regularity of the structure. As far as I could tell, they held the same amount of power.

Well. That's good news. I don't need ultra-valuable diamonds for magical batteries; I can use cheaper crystals. Not that it seems to matter much to the mountain, but I presume quartz is easier for it to... does it "make" crystals? Or does it move crystals from elsewhere in its structure? One more thing I'd like to know and probably never will. Geological biology is strange.

So I went back to putting spells on arrows.

Bronze and I went down to town before the dawn. I hid from the sunrise in a handy building, sweating in my armor. I had my helmet off so the cleaning spell had somewhere to move the goo.

As a note, never do this. Imagine a hard day's work of shoveling out a chicken house. Now imagine the stink of it crawling out over your collar before crawling away. On second thought, don't imagine it. It's disgusting.

Once the day officially broke, Kammen and I did some breakage of our own. On one side of the occupied area, Kammen led an assault on a mobile barricade. Oil, spells, and a monatomic-edge blade go a long way toward turning one into flaming pieces. He and his unit killed one of the machines and moved along the perimeter to the next street and the next mobile wall. I'm sure they also killed people in the process, but that's only because they didn't have the good sense to get out of the way.

Is it wrong of me to have no sympathy at all for anyone trying to stop a seven-foot-tall, four hundred pound, heavily armed and armored legendary warrior? I mean, if you stand in the middle of the road and wait for the truck to hit you, whose fault is it, really? Is that a reasonable way to look at it, or am I getting calluses on my soul?

Seldar kept watch over it all. He coordinated our work. Kammen got the enemy attention and drew their reserves to his side of the area. Several of our blocking units in the middle started putting fire-arrows onto the other mobile walls. This gave an even greater impression of a full-on assault. In less than an hour, it practically emptied their troop reserves from the middle of their territory, around the buildings they used as a church and headquarters.

I wasn't best pleased by the idea Kammen and the troops were bait. Seldar insisted they were a diversionary assault. I did my best not to argue, lest he tell me I was a bad king and to go to my room.

I would have led the direct, hand-to-hand assaults, but Seldar put his foot down again. Kammen agreed with him, the traitor. The King can be accommodated in his desire to come to grips with the enemy, but only after they've done everything they can to minimize the risk.

Bronze carried me along the other side of the occupied area, opposite Kammen's assault. I fired two arrows at the wall-things. The first shot always had a magic-breaker spell on it. It acted like an explosion on a magical level, attempting to shatter the spell structure of anything nearby. They launched a lot of these from Mochara, trying to take down the shields of the ships, but the wizard-heavy navy kept reinforcing the shields. They didn't have a dedicated corps of wizards here, so my arrows took down what little magical defense they had.

The second shot had the air-filtering spell and a delayed igniter. It pushed nitrogen away from the arrowhead in an expanding sphere, allowing pure oxygen to fill the area. This lasted for about a minute, expanding to a few yards in size, so when the igniter spell released enough stored heat to explosively turn the arrowhead into vaporized metal, everything caught fire.

It didn't hurt that Firebrand did whatever Firebrand does with fire. From my point of view, it glared at the wall-wagons while I shot them. I'm told they actively caught fire because of Firebrand, but what do I know? I didn't stay to watch. I just shot twice and moved on down the road to the next one until I ran out of enspelled arrows.

Tianna would have been so proud of me. She could probably see the smoke from Mochara, assuming she wasn't too busy helping put the place back in order.

With that out of the way, Seldar coordinated our withdrawal behind our lines. Captives of several sorts were taken to the Hall of Justice. We continued preparations to push forward and take a whole row of city blocks—later, when the fires and wreckage were less of a problem.

Given the number of these street-blocking wagons, I resolved to have a word with Rendal, the Commander of the Guards. They should take note of this sort of thing. A lot of the contraptions were wagons with the equivalent of barn doors nailed on the front, but at least a dozen were more professionally built. I wouldn't think it easy to hide something like them, especially not in those numbers. Someone should have noticed and said something.

Then again, if the people doing the noticing are all paid-up members in good standing of the Church of Light... Yeah, more weight just got piled onto Seldar's idea about Lotar trying to counter civic duty with religion. And Karvalen isn't exactly fully occupied, even now. It might be possible to find a few sizable buildings for use as workshops or garages, especially as one goes farther away from the more heavily-populated southwestern quarter.

Fine. Maybe Rendal wasn't in hot water over this. He was still going to get a lecture.

I had one more thing to do while we waited for the wreckage to finish burning. Bronze took me back up to the palace level and the courtyard. From there, I could see over the city and had a direct line of sight to the occupied area.

A couple of my spells are for playing music. The first version vibrates an object like a speaker cone; the more refined version directly affects the air. Admittedly, it only plays music as well as I remember the music, but for a favorite song, that's pretty darn realistic. But it doesn't take a lot of energy to make sound. It's a cheap spell, in that sense, but more than a little complicated. There are all sorts of places in the spell where it can be tweaked like an equalizer to get the sound quality you want.

On the other hand, if you want to use it as a bullhorn and don't care about things like concert-hall acoustics, it's easier than you'd think.

I plunked megaphone arrows into the rooftops, scattering them around the occupied area. Naturally, I cheated and used spells for guidance. My archery wasn't up to it, especially not at that range. Still, wherever one hit, it played its announcement to everything within a hundred yards. Anyone who surrendered would be judged by the Lady of Mercy. Anyone who fought and survived would be brought before the Lord of Justice—and then me.

Propaganda is a weapon against the enemy's will to fight. I read that somewhere.

With that done, I turned the war over to Seldar and Kammen while I called Mochara. Torvil answered the mirror.

"Greetings, Sire."

"Hello, Torvil. How goes the day?"

"Sire, Mochara is secure. We also have quite a number of prisoners."

"Good. March them up here. I want a word with them," I told him. He looked troubled.

"Sire?"

"I have a tribunal—or quadunal, or pentunal, or something—to interview them and pass judgment. They can be let go, imprisoned, sent to me, all sorts of options. The ones who make it to me will stand there while I look at their souls. If they're traitorous scum, I'll hand them to the Lord of Justice. If they're not, they'll be told not to do whatever it was again and released."

"Oh," he said, surprised. "Good. Thank you, Sire."

"I'm not the Demon King," I reminded him. "I only look like him."

"The resemblance is uncanny," Torvil admitted.

"Everyone thinks they're funny," I complained. "Do they need you there?"

"No... no, I wouldn't think so. Shall I return?"

"Seldar and Kammen would like your help. I'd like to see my granddaughter, too."

"I will make arrangements. By gate? Or Bronze?"

"Ask Tianna."

"If Your Majesty permits, I would be very much pleased if Bronze would consent to carry me."

"If Tianna and Bronze agree," I allowed. Torvil might actually look good on Bronze—proportional, anyway. He and Kammen were the only people huge enough. Seldar is pretty big, but not the giant-class size of the other two. We signed off and I went through my mental to-do list. What else? Ah, yes.

I checked in with Diogenes and wished for my skinphone. Whatever became of it? I wore it on my left wrist, so the ghostly electrical bolt didn't fry it. Was it in the palace in Carrillon? Or did Johann remove it in the process of stripping me naked and chaining me up? Probably the latter. It wasn't magical and it didn't look valuable, so no one here would think to salvage it.

After a little work with a variation on my music-making spell, Diogenes had an independent voice. The spell connected to the vitality containment spell in the hard drive so he could interface with it directly instead of going through some sort of translation in the processor crystal. A reversed version turned sound into impulses so he could hear, as well. He developed a driver for it remarkably quickly.

Once he could speak, he told me he was confident about interfacing with the quantum computer core when the translation/interface spell expired.

"It also has considerable storage capacity," he informed me. "If you wish to transfer my programs to the crystal, the solid-state drive will no longer be necessary."

"First get everything running without a translation matrix, then we'll see about streamlining."

"Of course, Sire."

"Good. I—wait a minute! 'Sire'? Who have you been talking to?" I demanded.

"Fireband."

I looked at the dragon's-head hilt. It tried to look innocent and failed spectacularly.

"We're going to discuss this," I told it.

What? He didn't know where he was or what was going on. I was supposed to leave him in the dark?

"You should have asked."

You're just upset because someone else is treating you like their king.

"Diogenes?"

"Yes, Your Majesty?"

"Please address me in an informal fashion."

"You got it, *jefe*."

"That'll do for now."

What's a "jefe"? Firebrand wanted to know.

"It's Spanish. I think it means 'boss'."

Hey!

"You brought this on yourself."

Firebrand grumbled but subsided. I went to talk to Bronze about taxi service. She was okay with it. It meant getting out and running at full speed—of *course* she was okay with it. Besides, Tianna was involved. Carrying Torvil wasn't high on her list of things to do, but letting Tianna ride was simply a given.

Now, about the crown...

Sunday, February 29th

The calendar between Earth and Rethven is a little wacky. The year has a different number of days and months, and they don't use a seven-day week. I'm ignoring all of it in the interests of keeping myself from getting screwed up by having to convert things from calendar to calendar. I think it's time for a leap year, so I'm using one.

Of course, I've assigned an arbitrary Gregorian calendar date to the Rethven year, so my consistency may be questionable.

Seldar isn't happy about being stuck in the hall of mirrors all the time. The mountain is shifting around, slowly, making it more of an amphitheater arrangement centered on the sand table. Rings of seats for mirror operators will eventually surround it. The place is starting to look like a command center, but it has a long way to go.

Seldar's big objection wasn't the lack of sleep—an adjoining chamber allowed him to nap and still be available if someone screamed for him. It wasn't the meals served while he watched the real-time movements on the sand table. It wasn't even the constant stream of "Sir? What do you want done about..."

No, his problem was Kammen was down on the front lines while he was stuck in the Combat Information Center, responsible for how our forces deployed, what objectives they took, when they moved, who they attacked, all that. I think he was regretting his decision to quit the King's Guard and join the clergy. If he'd remained, he might be seven feet tall and built like an armor-coated brick, too—and down where he could knock heads.

Instead, he was up here, watching it all remotely, and directing traffic. I think that's what made him really, truly appreciate how hard it was for Kelvin to be a general. I miss Kelvin. Seldar misses him, too.

I refrained from picking on Seldar. It was petty and unkind to rejoice in the fact he was getting a taste of how it felt. Tell me I can't go fight, will you? Tell me my duty to the kingdom won't let me risk myself, huh? How's it feel now, oh knight of the crimson sash?

It was hard to keep my mouth shut. I really wanted to rub his nose in it!

It sucks, this being a grown-up, mature, responsible adult. Whatever happened to the old days? I could pour a grad student into the car, dump him and his friends out on the grass at their apartment or dorm, and give them all a hard time about their terrible karaoke skills the next day.

"What karaoke skills?" they would ask.

"Exactly," I would reply, and everyone would laugh. At least, everyone who had recovered sufficiently from the hangovers.

I miss the university. How did I get from there to *here*, again?

While Seldar ran the counter-insurgency action in Karvalen, I sent Bronze down to Mochara to give Tianna and Torvil a lift. I started to cast a gravity-tilt spell for her, but she refused it. She didn't want it.

"May I ask why?" I inquired, despite the fact she didn't actually say anything. She responded with an ear-flick and the soundless stomp of a forward hoof. Clearly, she wanted to push herself and her new internal configurations.

Intuitively understanding this sort of thing would freak me out if it wasn't Bronze. With her, I simply knew, and it was both right and natural I should understand. Objectively, it's weird. To Bronze and I, it's the way things are. Sometimes I try to think it's strange, but it doesn't seem to work.

Later, when Bronze hit the highway and headed south toward Mochara, I could feel her glee at pushing herself to run at top speed. I recalled the campsites along the way, places where people set up for the night to rest their horses after a long day of barge-towing. I hoped nobody would get trampled.

Bronze felt certain that wouldn't happen.

Regardless, I gave the mountain another instruction. An extra-wide divider between the northbound and southbound canals connecting Karvalen and Mochara seemed in order. Maybe with a definitely-raised center lane, too.

Meanwhile, I retired to my lab to work on crown enchantments. I think it's a set of really impressive enchantments, if I do say so myself. Normally, you only put one or two spells or enchantments on an object; you have to take into account spell-structure interactions. Three starts to get unreasonably complicated, four is downright messy.

The difficulty goes up by the square of the spells, sort of. With two spells, it's four times more complicated—not from a power perspective, but from a wiring perspective. Don't cross the wires, don't let the radiation from one component interfere with another component, that sort of thing. With three spells, you have nine times as many ways to screw it up, with four you have sixteen, with five you have twenty-five, and so on. The numbers may not be exact, but it gives the idea.

There's a good reason people usually only have *one*. It's also why wizards routinely put spells in crystals. They may be mounted on a single staff, but that's just an easy way to access them all. The individual crystals are the business. The staff usually has nothing more than a spell to make it easier to feel what spells are present and to access them quickly. It's a lot better than fumbling in a pouch or wearing a fistful of rings.

I planned to use a similar technique on the crown, along with a trio of the spare quantum computer cores. The computer cores were only about the size of a thumbnail, but the crown didn't have anywhere to put them. So I fiddled with a work of art, added a little more gold, and mounted the three additional gems behind the upswept vines of the crown. It wasn't elvish, certainly, but I spaced them evenly and set them so they would each be directly behind a gap. Doubtless, elves would consider it a complete disaster, artistically speaking, but I like to think I minimized the horror.

The cores were vital to the functions I had in mind.

Anyone wearing the crown had a... well, not a copy, but sort of a snapshot of their mental machinery taken and stored in a crystal. Kind of like a computer's restore point, it had a lot of informational stuff contained in it. Attitudes, beliefs, intentions, desires—it observed the brain of the wearer and made sure the mind inside it matched the previous image in certain key areas, mostly...

You know what? Skip the technical bits. It took a mental fingerprint the first time you put it on. Later, it compared that mental fingerprint every time you put it on again, checking for interference and outside influence. That's wrong in a lot of ways, but it does get the intention across. If someone pulled the same sort of stunt with the wearer of the crown as was pulled on Lissette, it would alert everyone that something was wrong.

It also listened to the experiences of the wearer. If you did something while wearing the crown, it recorded the experience as a memory. Over time, it would gain more experiences of how kings and queens did things. These would be available to the wearer with only a moment's thought, like recalling something to the forefront of the mind. Kind of like trying to remember what you had for lunch—it's not on your mind, but with a moment to think about it, it's not hard to recall. I figured it would be good to have the accumulated Royal Experience and Wisdom kept for future generations of kings and queens. Assuming there was any to accumulate.

And, of course, the most powerful and intense enchantment on the thing was a multi-phase anti-interference spell. I started with a basic brain-bunker shield, then started thinking of way to get past it. I needed a way to run several different such spells, really, not just one. The separate gems of the crown's "thorns" were handy in that regard. Each one could hold a spell variation, making it orders of magnitude more difficult to identify, map, and circumvent the crown's defensive powers—they would work to conceal each other, interfering with attempts to analyze the magic. The spells would make it… well, not impossible, but perhaps unreasonably difficult to alter the crown itself or the mind of the person wearing it.

The crown can't, by itself, assure the safety of the sovereign's mind, but it should be a major stumbling block for the next Evil Grand Wizard who tries to brainwash the ruler.

I also included a minor resizing enchantment in the metal of the crown. It's one of those things they never seem to mention in all the fairy tales and fantasies. Anyone can wear the magic boots, the magic cloak, the magic ring, the magic whatever-it-is. Maybe nobody cares about how my size eleven feet don't fit so well in size ten boots. Or how the cloak made for an elf doesn't fit so well on someone with a foot of height difference. Or how some people have fat fingers while others have thin fingers. At least with this crown, wearing it, however awkwardly, would cause it to grow or shrink to fit the wearer's head. Gradually. Over a period of time.

There's a metaphor, if you like. Kings and queens never start out as kings and queens. They may put on the crown, but it takes a while before the crown fits.

While Seldar squeezed the insurrection down to size, I asked Tianna to come visit. Bronze dropped both her and Torvil off at the upstairs door. Tianna came and found me in my workroom, where we discussed some religious issues and how they related to the kingdom.

"Where's Torvil?" I asked.

"He went to have a little lie-down."

"Ah. I imagine he's pretty tired."

"Yes. Yes. Exactly. It was a long ride. That's it," she agreed, nodding.

"Good. He deserves a break. I do have some questions you might be able to answer, though."

"Fire away, Granddad," she told me, settling into a large, heavy, ugly chair.

"I get the impression most religions don't care to rule a kingdom," I began, pouring her a glass of something—a brown, sweet juice of some sort. I didn't much care for it, myself, but it's what they brought me to drink. Fortunately, I now have spells for that.

"That's true," she agreed, and sipped at her drink. "It hasn't usually worked out."

"Any ideas why? I'd think an all-knowing being would do pretty well at running a kingdom."

"Unopposed, I'd say you're right. But other gods, other opinions." She shrugged. "If you're a jealous god, you wind up forbidding all the others." Then she frowned and looked pensive. "Granddad?"

"Yes?"

"Is this about Zirafel and the Mother?"

"No. This is about Rethven, or Karvalen, or whatever we're calling the place."

"People generally go with Karvalen, these days. Demon King and all that."

"Got it."

"You do know She tends to get a bit possessive about things She regards as Hers?"

"Yes. But I'm trying to reach a compromise between spiritual authority and physical authority. What I'd *like* to do is put some religious figures into the high council or inner circle or whatever the thing is called." I sighed. "I really need to start naming stuff. Okay, I'm trying to put priests on the oh-so-cliché High Council."

"Priests? Such as Liet, Beltar, and myself? All of whom, I should point out, are already *on* your council."

"I was thinking of formalizing it. Mostly, I want to make use of the existing religions so they don't feel inspired to try for a theocracy and puppet kings."

"Oh, *this* should be good!" She put her elbows on the table, laced her fingers together, and put her chin on top. "Go ahead. I'm all attention."

"You seem to think this is a silly idea."

"Oh, no! It's not often one gets to hear a god-king speak up for other deities, Granddad. Or any of the gods, really, speaking up for all the others."

I opened my mouth to say something snappy—and paused. I probably looked stupid with my mouth open and finger pointing, but I had a sudden attack of brain.

People worship me. Well, they worship the thing on the energy plane who seems to have some sort of relationship to me. We're probably pretty easy to confuse. But if I'm *viewed* as a god, then I'm also viewed as a god-king. I've been so preoccupied with my image as the *Demon* King, I completely neglected the other one.

To be fair, I despise being viewed in either way, but the whole god-king thing is, somehow, worse. Don't ask me why.

I was having one of those reality-vs-perception dissonance things. I didn't like it. I never do. Why couldn't people be happy with their monster king? I can do monster. I'm comfy with being a monster. I'm disturbed by how comfortable I am with being a monster, yes, but I can deal with it. It's a shoe that fits, not gigantic shoes to fill. Being a monster is easy!

Huh. Never thought I'd say that.

So, there I was, standing there with my mouth open while my brain clicked on and I processed everything.

"Son of a bitch."

Tianna made a *tsk* noise at me.

"Sorry," I said. "It just hit me. You're right."

"Of course I am," Tianna agreed, laughing. "What am I right about this time?"

"People see me as a god-king."

"They certainly do." She cocked her head at me and a curl of red hair fell mischievously across one eye. "For someone who can see every grain of sand on a thousand miles of beach, you don't see yourself very well."

"I have an excuse. No reflection."

"You're excused."

I rubbed my temples for a moment, thinking. If I wanted to do some political machining while using religious tools, it might be a good idea—albeit a vastly distasteful one—to get a consultation. I don't know enough about how energy-state beings interact with the world. Someone who does it for a living would be able to give me much better advice than my random guesses.

In theory, I should be able to do the thing Tianna and Amber do when they consult their deity-thing. The big question, though, was whether or not I wanted to. No, I take that back. The big question was whether or not I felt I needed to.

"Hold on a minute. I need to talk to someone before I go speaking *ex cathedra*."

"Ex what?"

"It's a phrase from my home world. If I remember right, it means pretty much what you do when the Mother starts using your mouth to say stuff."

"Oh." Tianna started to say something, then frowned. "So... should I come back later?"

"I hope it'll only take a minute."

She sipped at her juice and nodded. Her hand didn't shake, but I detected a slight tightening around her lips and eyes. Was she nervous? Scared? Maybe. So was I.

Um... I thought. *I don't exactly know how to go about this... hello?* I tried to direct my mental impulse toward the thing I'd briefly spoken with.

I hear your silent prayer, came right back to me, instantly. It was like thinking at Firebrand, only the thing I was thinking at wasn't actually there. Or maybe it was, on a multi-dimensional level I was incapable of perceiving. *N*-dimensional math was never my strong subject, despite intense study. I felt as though I was having an internal conversation with an imaginary friend, only my imaginary friend actually felt present. It was almost like having another me inside my head—maybe even the real me, and I was the imaginary friend.

I didn't like it.

I really wish you wouldn't call it a prayer, I thought back.

Fair enough. How about I admit I heard your attempt to invoke me?

That's... not bad. I can live with that.

Happy to help, it replied. *What's so desperately wrong it requires divine intervention?*

Before we get into that, is it customary to have a hard time distinguishing between my thoughts and what you're saying in my head?

*No, but you're not exactly a typical priest, either. As I understand it, avatars—physical manifestations of the deity's presence—really **are** the deity, so there's no separation of thoughts. You're a little different, since we did the deity-thing backwards.*

You mean Amber and Tianna have a hard time telling Sparky's thoughts from their own?

No, I wouldn't think so. They're only descended from Sparky's original avatar, not the avatar itself.

Oh, well—wait. They're directly descended from the Mother of Flame?

Of course they are. She put an avatar in the world and bore a child. Where did you think fire-witches came from?

I didn't have a good answer to that, so I filed it away for later.

This too-close mental thing still makes me uncomfortable, I admitted.

Want me to get Beltar? I could talk through him, if you like, but we'd have to be quick. He's purely mortal and it's bad for him.

I wouldn't do that to Beltar.

I know we wouldn't, but I had to mention it.

Stop that. Right now.

Sorry. I'm new at this.

So am I!

We paused for a moment, coming to mental grips with each other.

Do you know, I asked, *about my plans for using some religions to supervise some government functions?*

The Lord of Law as part of the city guards? The thing with him and the Lord of Justice and the Lady of Mercy and the Seers of Truth as joint judges and whatnot for the courts? That sort of thing?

So you do know.

Not in detail, but I got the gist of it when you asked me about it.

*I **hate** telepathic communication.*

Yeah. It's more than a little weird, but at least you get to talk to mortals. I'm stuck with the cheese-brains up here. Telepathy sucks.

I heard a psychic throat-clearing from Firebrand.

Sorry, we both thought at it. It seemed mollified.

So, how can I help? he asked.

*I'm thinking long-term. Will the gods in question be annoyed? Will they try to press for more? Or will they happily do their part? I mean, they seem to have their specialties. I'm encouraging the use of those specialties. Is it going—are **they** going—to turn around and bite me for it? Or will they be pleased to have some sort of official recognition and do their part to help keep the place running smoothly?*

You know the saying about the difference between a man and a dog?

Take a starving dog, feed it, and it won't bite you. That's the difference between a dog and a man. Mark Twain, right?

Yep. I'm not sure where these other jokers came from, but they've taken their shape and form from the concepts of mankind. They may act like the gods of men, but they're more like the children of men.

I groaned inwardly.

So they're a bunch of untrustworthy, power-hungry, self-centered brats?

Some of them, yes. The Lord of Light is weird—everyone says he's not like he used to be, before the Devourer. I wouldn't include him any more than you'd include a serpent in an infant's cradle.

I hadn't planned on it.

I like the way you think. As for the rest, I don't think you can trust the Mother of Flame as far as you can comfortably throw a comet, but she does seem to be trying to be... conciliatory, I think? Probably something about mutual descendants. The Twins of Need and Desire wouldn't be on my short list of allies, either. But the Lord of Law is a stodgy, strictly-by-the-book guy. The Lord of Justice might or might not do you any favors, but he'll be ruthlessly impartial and absolutely fair. And, of course, Ssthitch kinda likes you/us, as does the Hunter. We could get away with a lot before they got cranky. There are some others who like the way you lack the groveling gene, while a few of them are still grumpy about your lack of respect. See what I mean?

Oh, god, the politics of Heaven.

I was just now explaining it.

I wasn't talking about you!

Oh, right. Yeah, politics get in everywhere, even this particular wing of Olympus. It's worse than carpenter ants.

Fine. Just fine. I'm glad it's your problem, not mine.

Are you sure it's not your problem?

*Yes. I only have to deal with the fallout. **You** get to face the storm.*

When you put it that way, I envy you your limitations.

I thought you might. Back on track, though. Do you think I'll have any trouble with the whole police, courts, and justice system?

If you stick to those, no, I wouldn't think so. But you'd like me to keep an eye on things and let Beltar know if there's anything screwy brewing up here.

You took the words right out of my head.

And I put them back. Neatly, I might add.

I noticed, and it's a really unnerving feeling.

I know we don't like anyone in our thinking machinery. Any ideas on how to avoid this sort of thing in the future? Assuming you ever want a quasi-divine visitation or revelation or whatever this is.

How about I do something with an altar? Some sort of spell or something, maybe so the smoke from the incense or whatever can manifest and talk. How's that sound?

I'm okay with it. I don't think there are any rules against it, either. I'll have to double-check. If it's kosher, we can give it a try.

Great.

And the inside of my head was all mine again. Having the other me as a visitor was a peculiar feeling, and one I was anxious to not repeat.

"Well, that was weird," I said. Tianna nodded.

"I've never seen you do the empty eyesockets thing before."

"Empty eyesockets?"

"You had holes in your head, Granddad."

"I've often thought so."

"Where your eyes were," she clarified. "Empty places. There wasn't anything there. Just cold, dark holes into nowhere. I like the Mother's eyeball effect much better."

"At least it's not a penance stare," I muttered.

"Beg pardon?"

"Just marveling at things. So, here's what I need help with." I explained my idea about having the various churches involved in police and justice systems. "Mind you, I'm not placing them in charge of the judicial system. I'm asking them to assist the king's ministers in this. The authority is still kept in the hands of the temporal power, not the spiritual. But it gives them official recognition and shows a working relationship between the two poles. Do you think they'd go for it?"

"I don't know. It sounds like a fair deal, at least to me—I'm mortal. What would you have the Mother do?"

"I hadn't got that far," I admitted. "She's mostly a spirit of fire type of thing, with some basic healing, fertility, and so on. I'm open to suggestions—from you—when we get a chance to discuss it in detail. At the moment, I'm mostly concerned about dealing with several hundred to several thousand prisoners taken from the battles." I sighed. "I'm going to do a lot of soul-searching when the examination panel gets done sorting them out."

"I agree with your priorities, but Mother will want to be in on this. If other gods get official sanction, She will want it, too."

"Any ideas?"

"Well, you could declare Her the chief deity of the kingdom."

"Yeah. No."

"I didn't think so, but I had to ask," Tianna said, shrugging. "You know She used to be regarded as the goddess of royalty, right?"

"I recall."

"You recall?" Tianna asked, surprised. "It was back in the days of... Oh..."

"Yeah. Here's a thought. I don't know how we can get her involved in government, but we'll need someone to take over as the sun god. I'm not going to be sanctioning the Luminescent Lunkheads for the job. Would she be happy with official recognition as the kingdom's Goddess of the Sun?"

"I don't know. Maybe."

"I'm not entirely happy with the idea," I added.

"Why? Do you hate Her that much?"

"No, that's not it. It opens the door to a lot of potential problems. If the kingdom has to acknowledge a religion, recognize it, before it's an 'official' religion, then we have a lot of bookkeeping and suchlike on the table. I don't like making more bureaucracy."

"When you put it like that—I mean, if the King has to pass on which religions are allowed—the Mother might go for it. Provided She's first."

"Even if I don't have official functions for her?"

"I think I can sell it," Tianna assured me.

"Okay. I'll do it."

"Now, I want a favor."

"Name it."

"Can I have Nothar back?"

"Missing your boyfriend?" I kidded her.

"Some, but his father is also getting grumpy. Someone has taken a chunk of his city under religious control, and someone else has drafted his city guards. Between the two of them, they seem to be having a private little war and undercutting his authority."

"Ooo, ouch. I hadn't even thought about his reaction. Is he still in his residence or palace or whatever it's called?"

"Yes. It would be very nice of you to take back that section of the city."

"Wait, what? Is he under siege?"

"Only in the sense it's dangerous to go out. The troops in that sector of town seem more concerned with their battle lines than their internal problems. At least, that's what I'm told. A lot of people talk to me, for some reason."

"As a priestess?"

"And granddaughter of the god-king Halar."

"Please never call me that again."

"As you will, Great One."

"You're not too old to paddle."

"True, but I'm grown up enough it would be weird for you to do it."

I had to admit, she had a point. I changed the subject.

"Well, at least I have an excuse for not including him. He's in enemy territory and cut off, right?"

"Yes, I suppose. He still has two wizards and a mirror, though." She grinned at me. "Strangely, his house seems to be much more heavily fortified than it used to be. They only have one door to guard; the others are sealed up. Stuff like that. The stone is ignoring requests, too."

"I'm glad it happened to be helpful. Okay. We'll take back the Baron's residence and include him in the planning. And if you can reach Nothar, see if he feels he's still needed in Mochara. He has my permission to come back."

"I was hoping for another ride on Bronze."

"I'm going to need her when we take back the Baron's residence."

"Could we wait until Nothar is here? He would really like to participate. It's his father, after all."

I sighed. But she's my granddaughter. What was I going to do? Say no?

"Come on. Let's find your boyfriend."

After gating Nothar back from Mochara, he and Tianna went off to bother Seldar. I called ahead and let him know we needed to re-take the Baron's residence. Just a little forewarning. That way, he could already be thinking about it before they asked him. It would help him look like a strategic genius. Not that he needs my help, but it's polite to avoid blindsiding your allies.

"By the way," I added, "tell me something."

"Anything, Lord of Insufficient Illumination."

"How long would it take to get to the capitol? For a noble from the most distant, difficult city. Worst-case."

"Are you including all the city-states paying homage to you? There are half a dozen or more coastal cities in the West, beyond the Darkwood. Or are you only considering the cities formally part of the kingdom?"

"Just the formal ones."

"Then Peleseyn or Byrne is probably the most distant from Carrillon. Ten years ago, I would have thought it a journey taking some weeks. Today... at worst? Traveling slowly, in bad weather, with many stops for the comfort of passengers? Fifteen days, perhaps. I could stroll from here to Carrillon in less, even dragging a corpse."

"Good to know."

"May I ask why you wish to know?"

"I'm calling a meeting of the nobles in—now you mention it—fifteen days."

"Which ones?"

"All of them."

"Oh." He didn't ask any further questions. I got the impression such a meeting was either rare or unheard-of. This was fine by me; I haven't read the rulebook on being king and don't intend to.

Seldar loaned me a nice young man with a specialty in mirror communications. We spent the afternoon calling around to various nobility. All of the people who answered recognized me on sight and fetched their rulers as quickly as possible. Most of the subordinates did the whole yes-my-king, whatever-you-say-my-king thing. As for the nobles themselves, a few were a bit leery about doing as they were told, but were too diplomatic to tell me to go to hell. Come to the capitol? Stand before the Demon King? Risk my own life? How about I send someone to speak for me and I avoid being anywhere near you?

They phrased it more politely. Funnily enough, the list I got of who was likely to be trouble matched up with the ones who didn't want to come visit.

I was shocked—shocked! —to discover Prince Jorgen (now Count Jorgen— darn it, I promised him a dukedom!) of Hagan was one of the troublemakers! I remember his wife, Taisa, and their daughter Nina. What the hell did the Demon King do to piss him off?

Tolcaren was also on the list and, the moment I saw Count Rogis and his son, I knew why. Damn, damn, *damn!* I got a message—a decade ago! —about helping his son. The boy was badly burned and needed cosmetic treatment for the damage. In the press of events, I *completely forgot* about him.

Would I have remembered if it was a matter of saving his life, rather than correcting a lot of burn scars? Objectively, saving a life is more important than scars, but how badly is he scarred? Do his scars make his life terrible enough to make it a matter of life and death? Or do they give him a reason to learn to be strong?

Sometimes, I am such a screwup. I need a day planner, or an executive assistant. Or a better brain.

The other cities on the Unhappy List were Dinfael, Noskarael, and Ransiur. Castimin was also on the list, but Castimin isn't much of a city, all things considered. It's really a thickly-clustered group of run-together villages in the river delta of the Mirenn, where it flows into the southern sea. Many cities start that way, as nearby villages that grow together. Give it another hundred years and it will be a proper city.

I resolved to pay a visit to Jorgen and Raman. With Jorgen, I might be able to explain and apologize, as well as fix whatever the Demon King broke. With Raman, I could at least follow through—finally! —with fixing the burn scars on his boy. Although this raised the question of why someone else hadn't regenerated the kid.

I went into my headspace, wrote these plans down, and taped them to the inside of my exit door. At least I won't forget again. But what else have I forgotten? Something—maybe several somethings—surely got lost in the shuffle, somewhere, sometime. It's the nature of forgetfulness that such things don't all come rushing back when I wonder about it, but I still keep wondering. What else have I forgotten? Did I promise something to someone? Did I have something I needed to do? What *have* I forgotten?

This is going to bother me for the rest of my life, and I don't need this kind of stress on top of everything else.

Outside, I made plans for the other cities. I'm trying to be nice to Jorgen and Raman, mainly because I feel some personal responsibility for them being unhappy. The rest of them, on the other hand, were soon to understand a monarch's request is a politely-worded order.

Kavel made some nice spears for me. Black iron, wicked points, the works. Nasty things. He and his sons hammered them out faster than you could say "armor piercing projectiles". It's good to have water-wheel-powered trip hammers, and it's also good to have magical songs of smithing, but it's amazing to have both!

Whoa. I just realized. With them delighted to do things for the King, I can actually get stuff built with all three of good, fast, *and* cheap!

As if I needed more proof I'm in a magical universe.

A couple of quick illusion spells—mainly a video replay with amplified sound—made them message-carrying missiles. Stick one into the ground and it threw up an image of me in full monster mode while booming out the message.

Delivery was a bit trickier. I didn't want to send a representative to the six places most hesitant about showing up for the meeting, but I did want to make an impression.

While it's hard to put a gate somewhere without a corresponding frame— anything to define the locus of the other end—I didn't need to have a man-sized gateway for this, either. Something big enough to drop a spear through would do fine.

Which, of course, meant I had to build a drop rig and time the fall. Even when the opening is the size of a hand, you don't want to keep it open longer than you have to, especially with a one-gate connection. Then there was another spell to accelerate the spear once it was through the opening, and another one for the spearhead, to increase penetration—if it hit stone, I wanted it to *stick*, not bounce or shatter. There were also formal letters to write—well, to have written. Good penmanship may always be beyond me. Plus figuring out where to attach them to the spears, and the appropriate spells to protect them during transit…

Theatrical and dramatic. They take a lot more effort than you'd expect. It's one thing to be an undead fiend of darkness, but it takes an immense amount of work to look cool while doing it. I envy Dracula and wish I knew where he got his training. And his tailor.

I let my freshly-enspelled mini-gate charge up while I took my waterfall for the evening. Every little bit helps. Then I set the spears up, used a scrying mirror to pick my drop point, opened the mini-gate, and launched the first of them.

Nice. It flashed downward amid a thunderclap and a black, jagged bolt of lightning—purely illusion, but a nice visual. It went right through the Lord of Castimin's roof and buried itself in the floor of the entryway. I couldn't actually zoom in and watch—most people with money seem to have privacy spells, these days—but I could hear the booming voice commanding his personal attendance. Hopefully, someone would notice the parchment on the spear and recognize a Royal Writ. I wish I could have swiped the Royal Seal for this, but having a scribe write the message in animal blood instead of ink seemed sufficient.

I repeated the process with five other iffy nobles. I think I got my point across. There's a meeting. Show up. Don't argue or give me excuses. Be there *or else.*

I didn't explain why, for two reasons. First, the sovereign doesn't need to explain. Second, they might not show up if they knew what I planned.

And, on the subject of plans, nicely laid... After my message delivery, I planned to ride down to the war, lead a charge to liberate the Baron's residence, and finally greet the man.

Nope. I got shanghaied. There were a lot of people in the Hall of Justice, processed through the clerical tribunals—now the multiple tribunals.

They're not really tribunals. "Tribunal" implies three people. Maybe they're panels? Courts? I know there's a word for it, if only I could think of it.

After the first one got going, they snagged more clerics, walked everyone through the process, and started running courts in parallel. Given the number of captives, I can see why they expanded. They'd be there for weeks if they didn't step it up.

The accused found to be Rebel Scum were detained and waiting for me in the Hall of Justice. There was quite a backlog.

Even better, from my point of view, was a special, high-speed examination board for escapees. A lot of people slipped out of the occupied area and surrendered unconditionally—"We don't have anything to do with this! It wasn't our idea! We were minding our own business when a bunch of armed people said we were part of their territory! Please don't hurt us!" These were strictly noncombatants who ran for it when they had a chance.

Still, I really wanted to go kill something in a straight-up fight.

Me, too, Firebrand told me. *When was the last time we got to wade into a battle, Boss?*

"I don't remember. The vampire attack on the farmhouse?"

That sounds right. How long ago was it?

"I don't know. Too long, if that's any answer. Could be worse. I doubt they'll finish this fight tonight."

Yeah, but we'll miss the liberation of the Baron.

"How about we take back the granary in that part of the city when we're done here?"

It's not the same... but I guess I could live with it.

"Take it, not burn it."

*Fine, fine. Grain doesn't scream when it burns, anyway. I do get to burn **people**, right?*

"I think I can promise the opportunity, yes."

Deal.

So Firebrand and I sat in judgment on the probably-guilty people the new judicial courts sent us. I remembered to wear the crown, too, for recording purposes. It was a good test of the spells involved, and it's an experience which might prove useful to future kings and queens.

That still doesn't mean I like being a god-king. I get itchy even thinking about it. Is it a good thing I'm starting to accept I should use *all* my powers for the good of the realm? Or is it a bad thing that I'll sacrifice some of my personal convictions about right and wrong as long as I can use the good of the realm as an excuse?

There are many kinds of monster. I know I'm a blood-drinking, soul-sucking, fiend-of-darkness monster. Am I becoming something worse? Could I become a politician?

At least it's a good sign I'm willing to ask myself such questions. And a bad sign I don't have an answer.

I really need to get out of this king business.

We finished the soul-searching exercise in a few hours. A few of those people walked free. Most were given a fairly light sentence—not incarceration, but public labor, kind of on par with being in an old-fashioned chain gang. Around here, that *is* a light sentence. Harsher penalties include removing hands, feet, tongues, or other body parts, as well as death of various sorts, ranging from slow boiling in oil to immediate beheading.

For comparison, consider that three of the prisoners didn't make it out of the room. I ate them, throat-ripping and flesh-tearing *ate* them, right there on the spot.

I don't want to go into it. Suffice to say I don't generally look too deeply into the glowing center of a person. Normally I pass by and, at most, note the person is angry or happy or preoccupied or whatever. It's kind of like noticing someone's facial expression; you almost can't help it. Under normal circumstances, you don't stare at their face, into their eyes, trying to see what they're thinking. But when I take the time to look deep inside someone, peer beyond the outer shell of their current mood, I see the fundamental nature of the individual. I see not merely what they think and feel, or even their own self-image. I see Who They Are, from the outside looking in.

When I see the depth of evil, the depravity and cruelty of the human race, distilled down and dripping from the heart of—forgive me, but I feel I'm qualified to make this judgment—Bad People, the only thing I can think of is making them go back to the Bureau of Reincarnation for reassignment as fungus. Maybe maggots. Body lice might be appropriate.

After all the hours of questioning and eyestrain, I called it quits. The backlog of the tribunals' guilty verdicts was finished—most of whom were, in fact, guilty, so there's that. Firebrand, Bronze, and I went off to enjoy some simple bloodshed before the sun came up.

We took the granary, sort of. It was too far inside enemy territory to push our perimeter so far so quickly. We did manage to convince people about direct opposition being a bad idea. I encouraged the wounded to seek help by surrendering. Firebrand enjoyed itself by setting opposing wizards on fire. To quote a wise and *extremely* ancient sage, "A wizard should know better!" All in all, we demonstrated the rebels didn't have the firepower to effectively resist a straight-up attack. Well, individual units didn't. I'm sure they had something prepared and held in reserve, but I never hung around long enough for them to bring out the big, vampire-specific guns. Seldar had the CIC keep an eye on rebel movements in my area and warned me before anyone sent in my direction could reach me. You can't kill what you can't catch.

I was amused to see Tallin sitting on Daddy's lap and making faces at me in the mirror. He was an early riser, that one. I didn't see any harm in Seldar's bring-your-kid-to-work day. Thomen or Kammen I might have questioned—they were in the field, killing people who tried to kill them.

Hopefully, whoever was in charge of the insurrection fiasco was having serious doubts. I know his forces were. We had a sizable uptick in surrenders.

Tallin and the rapid surrendering cheered me up a little. I needed some cheering up after my hours of soul-searching other people. I don't like being introspective; why would I enjoy being extrospective? I have enough problems with my own inner evils. Bathing in others' inner evils doesn't help.

Monday, March 1st

After my morning transformation, I had breakfast with most of the local clergy, as well as Rendal—Commander of the Guards in Karvalen and Mochara—and Nothar, since the Baron still wasn't available. Nothar regretfully informs me being besieged is exhausting at his age.

Someday, I really do need to meet the man. It'll probably happen at the big meeting in Carrillon; I gave Nothar the invitation myself. Since it doesn't provide for any delegates—it's a command to appear, not really an invitation—I expect to see him there, along with the Mayor of Mochara.

While we had our morning meal, we discussed the idea of incorporating priests, ministers, clerics, whatever, into the structure of the secular systems. They were all on board for the idea, but we have a long way to go in defining what their duties and authority encompass. Rendal doesn't like having people tell him how to do his job. The clergy don't like being asked to help and otherwise ignored; they want authority to command, as well. Then there's the question of who everyone reports to—do they all go through the city guard chain of command, or do they report to the local nobles? And for the courts, do we still need to gather evidence and present it to a judge, or do the priests take over that function entirely and effectively control who is guilty or innocent of secular crimes?

I thought it was such a great idea, at first. Now I'm stuck at a table with a bunch of politicians who want to take advantage of the sudden opportunity. They're like toddlers arguing over who gets the candy, but with a better vocabulary and less whacking each other with toys. It made me almost want to whack them with my toys.

Oddly enough, the only people not giving me trouble about it are Tianna and Beltar. Tianna is happy to make a small gain for her goddess—possibly disregarding direct deific instructions—and wait for another opportunity for another small gain later. Beltar sticks with the basic idea of what I want, he'll do, along with the whole Temple of Shadow. I could order the temples of every deity in the kingdom to be torn down and Beltar would go get a block and tackle.

Show a little faith in someone when they need it. It's amazing how it comes back around to you.

Tearing down the temples is tempting, in a remote, fantasy sort of way. It would probably break the kingdom, though, in the ensuing holy wars. I'd much rather incorporate everybody. If everyone feels they have a place, feels they have a voice, feels they're heard at least as much as everyone else, then maybe this will go better. I've seen the results of an absolutist monarchy and absolutist religion. Trying the middle ground might be worthwhile. I hope it is, because that's where we're headed.

If we can get people to accept equality instead of dominance, that is. It seems to be an alien concept, and not only on this side of a magical gateway.

For now, though, I've got a room full of clergy, an annoyed police chief, and a representative of the local Baron trying to hash out a way to incorporate the powers of the gods into the criminal justice system. I told them to carry on while I took care of something; I left them arguing and made good my escape.

Beltar caught my eye as I left. He nodded, slightly.

He knows you're abandoning ship, Boss.

Thank him for being a sport about it.

He says you're welcome. So does the hot one.

While I understand what you mean when you refer to her temperature, I advised, *please do not refer to my granddaughter as "the hot one" ever again.*

Firebrand's chuckled.

While they argued, I slipped down to the Temple of Shadow. I've never been inside. It seems odd to be worshiped as a deity, complete with temples and clergy and ceremonies. It's almost as odd to have never seen it. And it's downright odd to know it's there, it's happening, and they're going to do it no matter what I have to say about it.

I didn't like the idea of going in there, but what were my choices? I could have the energy-state being borrow my body for communication, but preferably only after I'm truly dead. It could borrow a priest's body, but I got the impression it wasn't good for the priest, so that wasn't a good choice, either. Or I could arrange something that wouldn't require using anybody's body. Any body. Anybody. Wouldn't require using a person.

Would my descendants do any better at being the focus of the energy-state being's attention? Could I be the father of shadow-children, much like Sparky is supposedly the mother of fire-witches?

Oh, my. Amber and Tianna are descended from *two* deific avatars. Could Tianna channel the essence of the Lord of Shadow the same way she channels the Mother of Flame? Is that why Sparky was so interested in having me put a child into Tamara? No, surely not. No one could have predicted the formation of a new energy-state being.

I think I'll just let the thought wander off and die somewhere, alone and unregarded.

Bronze took me through the tunnels of the undercity and out through one of the main gates of the mountain. I wasn't in a hurry; she kept her pace down to something close to a trot. Strangely, neither the undercity nor the overcity seemed too different. If you didn't know there was a section of Karvalen bottled up, you wouldn't be able to tell. People went about their business. They didn't walk with their heads down, hurrying along. They didn't stay home, hiding. They went on with their lives as though there was nothing wrong. And, to be fair, there wasn't anything wrong—at least, not around here, miles away from the fighting.

Is that a quality of humanity? If *I* can't see the problem, it isn't *my* problem? Or is it a cultural thing, trusting to those in authority to either know what they're doing or to fix whatever goes wrong?

Oh, hell. They might be putting their trust in *me* to make it all right.

Such was my frame of mind when we pulled up outside the temple. My temple.

I feel dirty *thinking* that.

The entryway faced north and was similar to the one in Mochara: big, bronze, double doors, set well back in what appeared to be a small building. They probably set it up that way for the shade. These doors were embossed with a fiery sword design on the left, a rearing horse on the right. Nice work. Somewhat distant from this cubist entryway, a partially-buried sphere was the actual temple. The spherical structure had no obvious doors or windows. To get in, you entered the cubic structure and took the tunnel.

I went in. Bronze followed. I could have ridden in, if I was careful about my head. I was surprised Bronze wanted to come along. She didn't really want to see the inside of the place, but she knew I didn't want to go. She only did it to keep me company.

Beyond the doors, the floor sloped down, ran straight, and sloped up again. Definitely done for the light-blocking properties; it would take at least four mirrors or twenty pounds of explosives to get sunlight inside the place.

The temple was more than just the aboveground shell. It had underground hallways and rooms to serve other purposes. My concern was with the main altar, though, and finding a way to let my energy-state alter ego communicate without borrowing someone's lips.

Okay, fine. Without invading my brain or borrowing my body.

The main area was mostly seating. Rings of seats surrounded the central altar, stair-stepping upward to the midpoint of the sphere. The upper half was a dome. Dozens of candles, apparently placed at random, flickered and danced, giving enough light to make everything visible, but deeply shadowed.

Figures.

It struck me how the layout was very similar to the great temple in Zirafel. Was that a coincidence, or just good geometry? It was a lousy way to address a crowd, but ideal for packing them in. Or did the arrangement serve another purpose? I thought it might, but it was only a feeling.

There were some differences, of course. In Zirafel, the main statue was in the center of the platform. Here, they put it in a gap in the seating, on the far side from the entryway. It was still a big statue. It was standing with an heroic pose, too. It was all noble and handsome and darn impressive. It was embarrassing. In one hand it held a scroll; the other hand held the hilt of a sword, point resting on the floor. The wall behind it had a carving, a relief, of a horse's head hovering over the statue's shoulder.

I did like the way the seating ran right up next to the statue. People could sit beside it, if they wanted. Heck, some of the seats were close enough for a members of the congregation to reach out and touch the statue. I also liked the way it was placed, as though part of the congregation, watching the central platform—and anyone giving a sermon. I don't know if they intended it that way, but if I were on the platform in the middle of the room, I'd feel as though it was watching me. Come to think of it, the statue might not have been watching me, but I felt… something. A presence.

It could be a very good thing for a priest to keep in mind while he's spouting off, presuming to speak on behalf of his god: His god was *watching*.

Bronze and I headed for the platform in the middle, almost silently. As we walked, Bronze's hooves, although silent, sparked with blue-green flickers. Was the floor charged, somehow, and arcing between hoof and stone? I didn't see any magical effect, as such, and my own feet didn't crackle and spark.

Bronze didn't know either, but also didn't mind it. If she didn't mind, I didn't mind. She waited at the base of the platform while I went up the three steps to the top.

A junior cleric turned from his scrubbing to face me and tell me services weren't until later. He recognized me about halfway into his sentence and promptly tried to swallow his own face. I pointed him back to the bucket and brush he used on the sacred stones. He gulped and started scrubbing like a housewife who recently discovered the joy of amphetamines.

This is one reason I've always been reluctant to visit.

I looked over the paraphernalia on the platform. There wasn't a lot to work with. They don't do full-scale burnt offerings in here. Maybe they can't afford too much smoke. I'm not sure how the ventilation works. I didn't spot anything like an exhaust vent, which only means I didn't spot it, not that it wasn't there. From the look of the blood-grooves and the selection of consecrated cutlery, they did a fair amount of ritual sacrifice, though. The only thing which seemed likely to be useful for my purpose was a heavy stone brazier with an inner diameter of about two feet. It wasn't big enough to burn whole sacrifices, but it was plenty large enough for incense and the odd slice of bloody meat. The coals were dying, but they'd completed a ceremony an hour or two ago. They always fill it with charcoal and some aromatic woods before sprinkling crumbled incense into it. After the sacrifice—or the joyous leavetaking of the departing soul—they flicked sprinkles of blood in it, thinking it a pleasing aroma. On the nights of the new moon, the priests would cut their hands or fingers and drip a few drops on the coals to affirm their faith. Every year, on Coronation Day, all the faithful pray for the prosperity and health of the kingdom before filing past in a sort of reverse communion. They each gave a drop of blood into a sacred chalice. Some of the chalice's contents would be sprinkled into the brazier. The priests would then mix the rest with a distilled something—brandy or the like—and pour out a measure for each person to drink, to partake of the power of the King and to take into themselves the blessing...

Stop it! I shouted, mentally.

Stop what? came the reply.

I don't want to know all the details of how the damned ceremonies go! Or the ceremonies of the damned! Or whatever!

Blesséd. Not damned, he corrected. *And I'm sorry about the ritual crap. It's not like I told them to do any of it. They were doing most of it already when I... well, "woke up" is the best way I can describe it. Anyway, I'm not supposed to actually talk to anybody unless they specifically call to me, and they don't. They came up with ways to express their devotion all by themselves. It's kind of a defining characteristic of this world, I think. Or humanity in general.*

I mean, I don't want this knowledge dumped into my head.

Oh. Sorry; I misunderstood. My guess is you're picking up stuff on a sideband. You do have a psychic signature a lot like mine, or vice-versa, and the signal strength in here is about as intense as it gets. I suspect the spherical temple structure acts as a sort of concentrator—

Just. Make. It. Stop.

I'm not sure I can, he said, sounding uncertain. *I'm new to this avatar thing. Hang on. Maybe I can dial it down some.*

I felt a bubble of quiet spread out from me, enclosing the platform. It wasn't really silence, but I stopped randomly knowing things about my worship. His worship. Ceremonial worship. I still felt me, or him, or it looking in my direction, but no divine revelations.

Better? he asked.

Yes. Very much. Thank you.

Happy to help. Sorry. I didn't see it coming or I'd have warned you.

I appreciate that. Now, if you'll excuse me?

Hmm? Oh, of course. I'll just wait over here.

I got right to work so I wouldn't have to stay any longer than I had to. First, attune the brazier to the appropriate forces. Magically, it was the equivalent of using a magnet to magnetize an iron bar. With my impression embedded in the brazier, some actual enchantment was next. Heat from the coals could provide energy, so put an absorbing spell on the inside surface of the brazier... and there's usually something recently-dead if they're dialing up god. Add an absorption panel of another sort on the outside of the brazier to suck up some of the suddenly-free-roaming energy from the formerly-living thing...

Ah, yes. Burning things give off smoke, so let's use it. Tune the controls as an automorphism, making the whole thing a dedicated object, set to send and receive only on my/our personal psychic frequency. Now, let's form a face in the smoke... add some air-vibration for sound—let's go all-out and use the really complicated version for the high-fidelity sound. We want the Voice of God to be impressive, right? Tricky work, since we're absorbing power from a sacrifice and burning coals, *and* forming a smoke-face, *and* generating air vibrations for sound... very tricky work, indeed. Now, can we tie it all together? Yes, I think so. If I isolate the effect of one to the interior of the brazier, one to the exterior, and then have the rest project upward... good... yes, I think this will work.

Still there? I asked.

Is the world still flat?

Okay, I've got the prototype built. Want to poke it and tell me where it breaks?

I felt the movement of power, a shifting of perspectives, a strange bending of space. The whole world moved around me. It lasted only a moment, then everything was as it was before.

I was standing in a different spot, about a quarter-turn clockwise around the rim of the brazier.

It looks good, I was told. *I think it'll work.*

Did you just move me? I demanded.

Um. Yes?

You took over my body.

Yes. I'm sorry, but you did say to poke the thing. I took an up-close look at it through you to—

I DIDN'T MEAN— I started, then shut myself up. Me, not the other one. I put my hands on the rim of the brazier and leaned on it. The heat from the sanctified coals in the consecrated brazier didn't burn my hands. I let go of the brazier hurriedly and pretended it didn't happen.

"Look," I said, aloud, "you, of all people, should know how I feel about this sort of thing."

I should have thought of it. I'm sorry. I apologize. I wasn't thinking about it. I was focused on the project.

"Do not. Do that. Again."

You're upset. You have a right to be upset. I goofed, and I admit it, and I'm sorry. I apologize. I abase myself in contrition. Okay? What do you want? Sackcloth and ashes?

He sounded exactly like me when I've made a mistake, realize it, acknowledge it, and apologize. Then again, he would, wouldn't he?

"Okay," I agreed. I sounded huffy, even to me. I tried to calm down.

On the plus side, you did great work. I really appreciate it. And I did give you back all the energy you expended in making the thing.

"Is that why I'm not exhausted by doing the fast-and-dirty enchantment?"

Yep! Trying to be helpful. And, since you've done me a favor—and I'm trying to apologize for being thoughtless—I'll see about getting you a present to prove I mean it. I really am sorry.

"I… okay. I accept your apology."

Thank you. I was worried I might never forgive myself.

"Your sense of humor is…" I trailed off.

I know. Any ideas on what you'd like as a symbol of divine thanks?

"Uh… no?"

You sure?

"God says, 'Hey, you get a wish! What will it be?' and you want a snap answer?"

Oh. Yes, I see your point. Well, if I come up with something you don't like, you can always return it. I'll keep track of the receipt. But you only get store credit.

"That's… surprisingly fair," I admitted. "For starters, how about we not do the body-snatching thing again?"

From now on, he promised, *you have to actually say it's okay, and I'll assume a default answer of "No." How's that?*

"I think I can agree to that. Thanks. Now try the thing and see if it works."

It hasn't had a chance to charge and the coals are mostly dead. It's a magical widget, not a divine manifestation. We need to refuel the thing, then we need something to make smoke.

"Hmm." I looked around and found a supply of charcoal in a compartment under the altar. The acolyte doing the cleaning ignored the way I talked to myself, but he looked puzzled and slightly worried when I refueled the brazier.

"Ah… Great Lord? This unworthy one craves the gentle attention of the Master of Shadows." I assumed he spoke to me. He faced me, but his eyes couldn't have been more firmly fixed on the floor if he nailed them there.

"What's on your mind?" I asked, not unkindly.

"The consecrated fuel is only for use during actual services."

"Thank you. Now run along, Nivell. I'm trying to talk to myself."

He looked as though he wanted to say something further—ask a question, argue, I don't know—but he closed his mouth, gathered up his implements, and hurried past Bronze as he left the sanctuary area. Firebrand ignited the charcoal, rapid-roasted it, and very quickly we had a lot of reddish-orange glow.

"Wait a second. Did I just call him by name?" I asked.

Of course. Nivell's a nice kid. He has no interest in being a fighter, though. He still trains hard because he wants to be a Banner. He'll be more of an academic priest than a warrior priest.

"That's not my point!"

Ooo, right, right. Yes, you know his name. I thought I heard a psychic sigh. *Look, you're standing—literally!—in the center of our worship in Karvalen. This is your Vatican, your Mecca, your Holy of Holies, your High Temple of Temples. I'm trying to isolate you as much as I can, but there's a point of diminishing returns on these things. You're going to get religious weirdness seeping through no matter* **what** *we do. Get used to it or get over it. I'm sorry, but that's the way it is. All right?*

I muttered something I won't repeat. I guess he/I/we took it as agreement, if not acceptance.

I used Firebrand's edge to draw a shallow line along the back of my left hand, carefully, making sure to get only skin, not a tendon. Since it was daytime, the cut bled nicely and I flicked blood onto the coals before working a little healing magic. Steamy smoke sizzled up. A face formed in the smoke, solidified into a definite image, seemed almost to come alive. It blinked, looked around the room, licked its lips. It looked exactly like me, just bigger, slightly translucent, monochrome, and decapitated. It was a ten-foot ghost of a head. My head. Eerie.

Now I know how Dorothy felt the first time she met the Wizard. It's a good trick, and an impressive one. I had to step back a bit to look at it comfortably.

"Well, this is weird," it said, blinking and looking at me. Sounded like me, too.

"You're telling *me*?" I asked.

"It's… a different perspective. I'm not used to looking at the world from a physical viewpoint. I'll get used to it."

"You're welcome."

"Thank you. Thank you very much. I appreciate it. Anytime you need a favor, you let me know. And give some thought to what sort of present you'd like, would you? I'm hard to buy for."

"I'll keep it in mind," I assured him. "Come to think of it, I don't suppose you know where T'yl or Tort are?"

"Sure. T'yl's in Arondael being examined by magicians who want to figure out how to put their souls into elf-bodies so they can live forever. Tort's in Kashmanir, the easternmost province of Kamshasa, hiding from the hit-squads the Demon King earmarked for her in the event of his demise. He arranged for a lot of people to die if he turned up dead or missing, but you put a stop to it when you told Bob to call it off. Elven assassins are sneaky devils."

There was a long silence. His expression grew concerned. I wondered what *my* expression was like. Unhappy, at the very least.

"Something wrong?" my smoke-face asked.

"How long have you known all this?" I asked, calmly. I'm pretty sure I sounded calm. I didn't hear my voice echo, so at least I was quiet.

"Oh, I keep track of them. They're my friends. You ought to know that."

"And you didn't bother to tell *me!?*" I heard my scream echo around the room. Great acoustics. I gathered what I could of my scattered wits and took a moment to calm down.

"I'm so sorry," he said, looking concerned. "It didn't occur to me you didn't know. I mean, they're your friends too, right? I guess I thought, you know, you kept track of them like I did."

I can't really gnash my teeth; they fit together too well. I can clench my teeth perfectly, though. If I'd had a hat, I would have thrown it to the ground and stomped on it. I know I growled. I might have snarled a little. I was glad Nivell wasn't around to be terrified of god having a tantrum.

"All this time," I gritted, through clenched teeth, "I've had Sir Sedrick hunting for T'yl so we could get clues to where to find Tort. I've sent out mammoth sensory pulses to echo around the firmament of the world, trying to find her! I built a magical *spy satellite network* looking for clues to where she might be! Even though I didn't know for certain she was alive, I chose to believe she was so I could look for her. *How did you not know this?*"

"Hey, calm down," he said, sounding both apologetic and annoyed. "What was I supposed to do? Read your mind?" he asked. "Well, okay, strike that last—I could have, but I also know how we feel about it! Or did you forget I'm not exactly triple-omni? You have to *tell* me what you're thinking—and tell me what you want. Just say the word and I'll deliver answers with blazing lights from above, wingéd messengers, horns and hallelujahs. But is it fair to blame me for not telling you stuff when you don't even bother to *talk* to me? They've got all these weird rules up here—like the thing where I'm generally not allowed to talk to you unless you call me first. How was I supposed to know why you were doing anything, much less guess you actually wanted *my* help?"

That only made me angrier. Not because he didn't have a point, but because he did. He was right. If I'd swallowed my aversion to the whole god-complex thing and *asked*...

My first impulse was to shout, "God damn it!" but I was talking to one and he might actually *do* it.

"What else do you know?" I demanded.

"Huh? Well, lots of stuff."

"Tell me."

"Look, think about what you're asking, okay?"

"How so?"

"You're asking... Hmm. How to put this? Do you know anything about science?"

"Obviously. What's that got—"

"I'm making a point. You know stuff about science. What do you know? Go on, explain everything you know about science to me, but make it quick. No, let's narrow that down. Tell me about Earth. Explain to me what you know about Earth. Let me make it easier. Just tell me about human culture. I'll narrow it down even more: Only *modern* human culture. Skip the rest of the universes, and all the history, ecology, geology, and strictly planet-related things. Keep your answer short and to the point."

"All right. I'm asking a broad question, and possibly a silly one." I took a couple of deep breaths and sat down on the altar to think.

"Isn't that a little sacrilegious?" my smoke-self observed.

"Whose altar is it?"

"I instinctively want to object, but maybe you're right. Forget I mentioned it."

"Okay. How about this? What can you tell me about Tort, T'yl, the Church of Light, and Lissette? And Johann, while I'm asking."

"Not much on Johann. I can barely look into his world," he said, promptly. "I think it's because I don't have any worshippers there. I think I can only see into it at all because you were there and a lot of people remember you—it's not faith, or worship, or whatever you want to call it. If I'm right, that consciousness of you gives me a minimal something to work with.

"Lissette is getting better and will probably be okay, but she's not going to be fond of you for a while. She didn't like the Demon King right from the beginning and it only got worse from there. Thomen wasn't helping her, by the way. He was aiming at being on the throne. If I'd had a temple in Carrillon, I'd have inspired someone to deal with him—I like Lissette, too, you know. But, while I'm not certain of exactly how he was doing it, I'm pretty sure she'll be all right. If she needs it, I'll do everything in my power to fix whatever's wrong with her."

"I find that oddly reassuring."

"She's a good person and we like her."

"Fair point. Thank you. What else?"

"The Church of Light has the Lord of Light as their deity and he's a bit of a snob. Nobody up here really likes him; he tends to be aloof and holier-than-thou, if you'll excuse the phrase. He wants it all and he's powerful—more powerful than anyone. But he's not more powerful than *everyone,* so he's not taking over anytime soon. He keeps encouraging his minions to work on it, though. I get the impression from the others that he's a bit different from the rest of us."

"How so?"

"Waaaay back when, when the Devourer ate its way into the Church of Light, it found a way to subsume the Lord of Light—he was, I'm told, much like the rest of us, which made everyone nervous about the Devourer's ability to take on aspects of the local godhood. Now, though, the Lord of Light is back, large and in charge, and apparently much more ruthless and conniving than he used to be. Or so I'm told."

"Could he be like you? A re-formed entity made of the psychic imprint left behind? The original Lord of Light with a leavening of Devourer?"

"Possibly. But I don't think so," he admitted. "There's something about him that seems out of place to me. I may have a weird perspective on it, compared to the rest of the locals. He seems to have reserves, resources, most of us don't. I can't prove it, but my hypothesis is he's kind of like the Devourer."

"How so?"

"The Devourer wormed its way into the Lord of Light's power supply—his worshippers, his church, all that. Once they were feeding the Devourer, the Lord of Light withered away. I'm thinking the present Lord of Light is someone who was similar enough to step into the empty space left behind when the Devourer… ah, was no longer available."

"So the original Lord of Light didn't re-form because someone jumped in and took his place?"

"I suspect so. It's true, he *could* be a composite of the original Lord of Light and the Devourer—two different viewpoints of worshippers, both being pumped into this plane of existence. My only reason to doubt it is the way he seems to have fingers in other worlds. I don't. I can only detect the power input from them, not access it. Which makes me think he's a multi-universal opportunist wearing the original's shoes."

"Interesting. I didn't know energy-state beings could do that."

"I didn't either, until I heard about it from the others. There's a lot of not-liking him going on, but, well, there are all these rules… and as long as he's willing to abide by them, the rules protect him from us as much as protect us from him."

"I see. All right. I'm not sure there's anything I can do to help, but keep me posted if anything new develops."

"Roger that."

"What else can you tell me?"

"Not much on the Lord of Light or his church. T'yl, however, doesn't want to be in Arondael; he's being forcibly—but politely—studied by some friends of his. I think he was hiding out at the Academy from the elven death squads of the Demon King, but I'm not sure. I believe he was discovered by some of his fellow magicians and suckered into helping them whether he liked the idea or not. On the bright side, his odds of survival and freedom are almost certain. They only want the technique of gaining elf-body immortality. He's cooperating with them—mainly, I think, to hurry the process along so they'll let him go. He's still worried about a hit-elf showing up. He doesn't know you've called them off."

"Hold it," I interrupted. "You're not omniscient, so how do you know I called them off?"

"I hear prayers from sea-folk, plains-people, *orku*, *galgar*, humans all over the place, and from the occasional elf. It's not omniscience, but it's an extensive gossip network."

"Ah. Okay. Sorry to interrupt."

"De nada. Tort's escape from the exorcism, by the way, was masterful and clever. She managed to slip away without alerting T'yl, which took some doing, let me tell you. She already had arrangements for travel and retirement—the mountain gave her a big pile of gems because she asked and because it knows you like her. She made her way to Kashmanir. She's got a very nice house, a lot of servants, and is taking things easy in her declining years. She seems content, as far as I can tell, but it's not like we talk."

"To paraphrase Hamlet and a ton of other literary figures, I wish I'd known all this sooner."

My other self did not reply. He looked sympathetic. I rubbed my temples and tried to be calm.

What I wanted to do was punch someone in the face. Possibly me, for being an idiot, but if I started doing that I would lose teeth faster than I could regenerate them.

"Before I get too far ahead of myself," I said, and stopped. We looked at each other. "Let me rephrase that. Before I start making too many plans, O Lord of the Lesser Darkness—"

"Good one. I like that."

"I heard Seldar use it at me, once. —let me ask a couple of questions."

"I know a lot of things, but not everything. Remember how I'm not a triple-omni deity-thing? I'm just a poor little energy-state entity with a foothold on one single world."

"I remember. If you don't know, I'm okay with it. Just help me out where you can, all right?"

"You know me, always happy to help."

"It's more than a little unnerving to hear me say that," I told me. Him. The other guy.

"Yeah, but it's still a good thing, right?"

"Jury's out. So, here's the deal. I have a lot of stuff I need to do. I have a city to stabilize, a council to form, a queen to crown, elves to clone, a T'yl to rescue, and a Tort to talk to—that last one may generate a lot of other issues—and then, once I've got things moderately stable here, I have a Johann to kill in a slow, painful, hideous fashion that takes as long as humanly possible. Then I have a Redundantly Evil Orb of Evil I need to find and neutralize—destroy it or more fully contain it, whatever."

"I understand."

"Now, the Johann and Orb things come last—I'd like to handle them first, but they go together and carry a higher possibility of fatality. How can I get the rest of this done as quickly as possible so I can do the Tort thing, then go do the Johann thing? Any gems of wisdom, divine inspiration, ineffable guidance, or something? At this point, I'd settle for good advice."

The smoke-solid face paused for a moment's reflection.

"Tricky," he said finally.

"But can you do it?"

Again, a significant pause.

"Yes, I can do it."

"Will it take seven and a half million years for you to think about it?"

"You're in luck. You're asking narrower questions, now, not generalized stuff about life, the universe, and everything."

"Thank god for that."

"You're welcome."

"Shut up."

"Sorry. Couldn't resist. I'd suggest—and this is only off the top of my head; no deeply-insightful revelations, okay? —we start with figuring out how to make Johann hurt. Google 'How to cause pain' or something. That shouldn't take long. Then clean up the city problem. That should be pretty quick, too.

"As for unlocking the crowning achievement with Lissette, though—that could take a while. You'll have to wait for nobles to show up at a grand conclave or some such thing. They won't want to put their butts in the same room as the Demon King—yes, it's a perception thing, but hear me out. You can start the process, but you may want to hit Tort while you wait. At least you can see her and see for yourself how she's doing."

"You may have something, there," I agreed, thinking hard.

"Kashmanir is hot and dry, but it gets good magical currents off the Sunspire. It makes a good place to retire for a magician. It's a long trip, though, if you don't use a gate. You have to sail around the Fang Rocks—a long stretch of jagged islands in the southern Circle Sea—or brave the Straits and risk the pirates that make the place their home."

"I'll keep it in mind," I promised, and decided not to get sidetracked. I had a vague idea of what he was talking about, at least. "Okay. What next?"

"I'd say your schedule gets uncertain after that. There's no telling how she'll feel or how you'll react or what you'll think is the right thing to do—organic people are just so unpredictable."

"You sure you're not handing out godlike wisdom?"

"I'm sure. Even mere mortals have taken note of it."

"Maybe I should save Tort as the last thing to do in this world."

"That could be a good idea," he agreed. "I'm not sure you're going to like what you find. I know you're not going to like Kamshasa."

"Oh?"

"You'll see. And, if you're wondering, it'll keep until you get everything else done."

"You're sure?" I asked. He regarded me with a sardonic expression.

"Yes, I'm sure. Tort's situation is pretty stable. You'll probably want to have Sedrick do some legwork in Kamshasa, though. Maybe he can nail down the address and brief you on the locals."

"Good thought."

"By the way," added the smoke-face, nodding at something behind me. I turned around to see.

Several dozen people were already in the main temple area and more were creeping in, staring. Wide eyes, wide mouths, hands clasped to the point of white knuckles and fingertips. Expressions of awe and terror predominated.

"Busted," we said, in unison.

It's highly unlikely you'll ever find yourself in a situation where you and a manifestation of your faith-amplified psychic copy are being slowly surrounded by a horde of worshippers and chanted at. If, by some chance, you do find yourself in such a situation, remember a few simple rules and everything should be fine.

First, don't startle them. They're having a moment. Let them. There's no need to panic anyone. Stampedes, religious suicides, convulsions and speaking in tongues—okay, maybe there is a time and a place for each of those, but provoking them by accident seems like bad form to me. Stay calm. Stay professional.

Second, while they're filing in, think about what you want to say. They're going to expect something profound and deep and meaningful, as befits a Revelation from God. They're going to want something life-changing, or life-defining. You might want to take a how-to course on motivational speaking if you think this situation might arise. Some self-help books might also be useful, mainly for the lingo and inspirational quotes.

Third, when you're done, don't have any qualms about laying down the law. When it's time for you to leave, make sure they know you mean it and that there will be no fangirling, panty-throwing, crowd-surfing, wild grasping and snatching at your clothes, or other shenanigans. Be firm. And if that fails, sneak out.

At least, these rules worked for me.

People weren't actually trying to come into the main temple area; they were pushed in by the pressure of the crowd behind them. Once anyone realized he was actually standing in the temple proper in the presence of his god, that person moved aside and found a seat. Presumably, the shortage of smiting encouraged other layers of people to come in more willingly. The place didn't exactly fill up, but it developed a serious case of crowd.

This gave me time to think at my other self and discuss what to say. We argued silently about whether or not I could get away with boldly leaving instead of settling down and discussing a general statement of principles. The good news was I didn't have to get it perfect in the few minutes we had. With the new smoke-signal communications, the other me could elaborate and clarify pretty easily.

As for what we wanted to tell them, we decided to keep things simple. The more complicated the requirements, the easier it is to screw them up. Simple, general statements, that's the ticket. We went with the idea of a culture based on individual responsibility, a sense of personal duty, and the desire to be regarded as a decent human being. We didn't lay out any commandments, just put the ideas out there as things to think about. Boiled down to the bare essentials, what we said was, "Be responsible, help others, and don't be a dick."

I've heard worse religious codes.

Having made my speech to the attentive crowd, it was time for me to leave. The Other Guy told me which priestly person to pick; I had him lead everyone in a song—okay, okay; a *hymn*. They sang and the smoky head grew in size while they sang. All eyes were fixed on that head while I ducked mine. I considered it a sufficient distraction and made a run for it—sprang straight off the platform and ran like hell down the corridor with Bronze trying to keep up. This amused Firebrand endlessly. I heard it laughing all the way out, the jerk. Bronze was more than a little amused, as well, but at least she didn't laugh at me.

We made it into the corridor, skidded around the turn, half-fell down the ramp, powered up the other ramp, and burst out into the sunlight. I didn't feel like stopping, so when Bronze came alongside me, I swung into the saddle at a dead run and she continued running until I was safely in the palace again. I don't run that fast from blazing icons of religious force.

At least I now have some more confusion. I'm not sure if I hate being a religious symbol because I don't want to be a god, or if it's a case of not wanting so much attention. It's one thing to teach a class; they'll ask questions. It's quite another to be laying down the Holy Law of Halar.

I can rip out a soul, strip memories out of someone's mind, tear flesh from bones, blow up a planet, but I hate being the Source of All Truth. Power like that scares me. No, I take it back. Being responsible for power like that is what scares me.

Meanwhile, the ecclesiastical breakfast meeting was still in full swing and moving into lunch. If there's one thing preachers can do, it's talk. I left word with the people doing the feeding and watering that I wanted to talk to Beltar when they were done.

Next, I called Sir Sedrick and let him know what I found out.

"Elf-body immortality, hmm? That makes sense," he agreed. "I assume it is preferable to nightlord immortality?"

"Depends on your point of view, I suppose. There are advantages to each. If all you're after is eternal life, elf-bodies are perfectly acceptable. Have you found out anything else about T'yl?"

"From what I've been able to discover, asking around Arondael, T'yl was transporting himself magically—supposedly, he had access to some sort of gate. The last I've heard of him, he was going from the mountain of Karvalen to Vathula. He left from the mountain, or so I'm told, but he never arrived. Can a gate be intercepted or diverted?"

I opened my mouth to say it couldn't, but had to re-think it. Once a gate is established, the link is stable. There is no way I can see to divert an established connection. On the other hand, if someone knew where to put the proper guide-spell, it should be possible to divert a link while it was still forming. I did it myself, by accident, when the Church of Light was trying to reach my universe. A scrying spell, reaching toward them, acted like a lightning rod for the gate spell, causing an unintentional connection.

"Yes," I agreed, "it is possible. Doing it deliberately could be tricky—it's power-intensive and therefore requires precise timing. But if he was leaving from somewhere without heavy scrying protection, they might have seen him preparing a gate spell and intercepted it. Or," I added, thinking further, "if they simply detected the scrying portal he was using to achieve a lock—assuming he did it that way—they could monitor it for surges... that would probably be easiest."

"Then, what would you have me do?" Sedrick asked. "Do you know who has him in Arondael? Or shall I discover it?"

"No, I don't, but I'm told he's not being mistreated—he is a fellow magician, after all. It might be good to let them know *I* know, and to mention I don't mind them borrowing him as long as they let him come back periodically. I'll send them a note. I think I'd rather you went to Kamshasa, someplace called Kashmanir, I think."

"Is that where your Tort is?" Sedrick guessed.

"So I'm told."

"How did you find all this out, anyway? If I may ask."

"I asked a helpful godlike entity who takes an interest in these things."

Sedrick looked at me with a puzzled expression. He started to speak, checked himself, started to say something else, checked himself again.

"You know," he said, finally, "I'm not sure how to respond to that."

"How do you think I felt?"

"If I can't think of a way to respond to the concept, what makes you think I can imagine your feelings?"

"You *are* clever, aren't you?"

"Professional Hero," he pointed out. "Stupid Heroes die young."

"Okay. Do you want to gate here, then gate to Kashmanir?"

"Yes, please, if you are willing."

"I'll get set up. You might want to leave Arondael, though. I'm not sure if there are any spells around the place that might interfere."

"Shall I call you when I am outside the city?"

"That works. Thanks."

"Thank you, my lord."

I wandered down to the gate room and had a seat. While I was waiting, I called Bob. He answered immediately.

"Yes, Dread Lord?"

"Where are my sample elves?" I asked.

"I abase myself, Dread Lord. I have been preoccupied with the siege."

"Oh? The Rethvan army?"

"The very same. They demanded passage on the Queen's authority. They were denied on the King's authority. Thereafter they attempted to force the gates and we repulsed them. They have been encamped outside our western walls ever since."

"I see why you've been busy. Can you spare those sample subjects?"

"They will be in Plains-Port before the day is ended," he assured me.

"Plains-Port?"

"The small town at the eastern end of the pass. It is a trading post between plainsmen and your empire. They are hesitant about approaching the Mountain of Fire and Shadow, so they go there."

"Mountain of Fire and Shadow?" I repeated.

"Your mountain, Dread Lord. In their tongue, it can also mean 'living and dying,' as well as some other related concepts."

"I see. Probably not a bad description, actually."

"I tend to agree, Dread Lord."

"I think I've seen Plains-Port in my magic mirror," I observed, changing the subject. "I didn't know what it was called."

"It is my pleasure to be of service, Dread Lord."

"Thank you for being so helpful, Bob. I appreciate it," I told him. I thought I detected a faint flicker of puzzlement, instantly gone.

"Of course, Dread Lord."

"And Bob?"

"Yes?"

"When we're alone, or not being overheard by others, you can call me 'Halar'."

"As you wish... Halar."

"Good. And I have not forgotten about Rendu or the moon. Have you had any time to research the Spire of the Sun? Or the House of the Heru?"

"I regret I have not."

"Well, take your time. How long have we got before the sun thing becomes critical?"

"A thousand years? Ten thousand?"

"So, not this year. No rush."

"My race is nothing if not patient."

We signed off and I went to find a volunteer to deliver a note to Arondael. Turns out the Temple of Shadow has the Banners; they're ideal for the job. They're the negotiators, diplomats, and high-level messengers of the Temple.

In short order, I had three guys in formal armor—meaning they were wearing fancy stuff over it, like velvet tabards, identifying baldrics and badges, and so on—stepping through a gate near to Arondael while Sedrick stepped through it to me. The Banners had a very good idea of how to handle it. No threats, no pushing, not even a mention of consequences, just a polite presence asking when I might expect to have T'yl back. And, of course, to inquire as to their progress, if any, and was there anything I could do to speed things along? I miss my friend and all that.

They struck me as extremely smooth operators. I look forward to hearing how it goes.

Sedrick stood by, horse and all, while I got the mirror going. I had him look around the Kamshasa region until he finally found a place that looked right—that is, wasn't too far from the province of Kashmanir. I opened the gate for him. I also made sure he was carrying a fairly heavy weight in cash. It wasn't a reward for all his hard work; it was money for expenses. At least, that's what I told him. He pretended to believe me.

I've also spoken with Seldar and Dantos to made sure they know he's to be accorded every courtesy whenever he shows his face. They poor guy is going to have to suffer through having his every whim catered to whenever he visits.

Then I needed a volunteer to be tortured.

I already had an idea on how to hurt Johann, but I needed someone to help me with the experimental stages. I asked in the simplest manner possible. I found a bunch of grey sashes on palace guard detail and asked if anyone would help me out with an experiment involving agonizing pain.

It made me more than a little edgy when they all volunteered.

Every. Single. One.

I did mention the agonizing pain part. I made it very clear. It didn't faze them. Their willingness to do whatever I needed made me feel guilty about asking for anything, much less something that was going to hurt. I tried my best to keep the agony down to a minimum.

What I wanted was a good look at the way pain receptors activate. I have spells for looking at all sorts of things, medically speaking, so this wasn't too difficult. We started with simple blunt trauma, hitting hard enough to hurt, but not hard enough to harm—and, in the case of these volunteers, not hard enough to evoke so much as an ouch. I tested a number of different pain sources—thumps, bumps, cuts, burns, everything I could think of. Then I ramped it up from minor ouches to serious pains—bone fractures, penetrating wounds, charred flesh, and so on.

None of these were large-scale, and always on an appendage. It was a safety thing. I'm not sticking something sharp through someone's torso just to see how it hurts.

Well, maybe with Johann. That's the point of doing the research. Preparation!

After each test, we damped down the pain and applied the appropriate spells to fix it. They'll all be as good as new in a couple of days, not even a scar among them. I suspect they kind of regret not having scars to show for it. "I got this scar in service to the Lord of Shadows" sort of thing. Could be a badge of honor, possibly even a chick magnet, but what do I know?

Once I had my raw data, I set about duplicating the effect—stimulating pain receptors without doing anything harmful. With an example of what pain receptors look like when they're not busy and examples of different pain receptors at various levels of activation, cobbling together a spell to activate them wasn't difficult at all.

Did you know there are lots of different types of receptors? It's not just one sensory thing. There are pain receptors for all sorts of different types of pain. The things you learn by looking closely...

The prototype spell wasn't pretty, but it was a good proof-of-concept. I wrapped it around a stick and gently poked someone with it. I'm told it was about like stabbing him with an acid-spurting spear of ice set on fire.

Yes, I tried it on me, too. I think the description is perfect.

They seemed mildly disappointed when I finished. I think they were expecting to be boiled in oil, at least. Maybe flayed. Possibly staked in the sun and smeared with vinegar. I just don't understand their kind of gung-ho attitude. Then again, I'm not particularly religious. Maybe I'm being too sensitive about the whole religious aspect of things. I don't understand the gung-ho attitude of the Marines, either, but I respect them.

I fiddled with the spell, refining it and ramping it up for most of the day. I wanted to be able to smack someone and have a generalized wave of pain wash over everything, everywhere in the body. Making it work at a distance could come later.

It gave me something to do while waiting for Beltar, and I didn't feel like poking my nose into Seldar's progress.

I tested the refined version on myself, rather than a volunteer. I knew it was going to be a massive jolt of agony—harmless, in the greater scheme of things, but agony nonetheless. I didn't ask for volunteers simply because I knew it would work. I wanted to know how well it would work.

A tenth of a second was much too long. Indescribably long. It lasted a tenth of a second and gave me flashbacks to Johann's playroom.

I considered it a perfected spell and went to my bathroom to sit under a waterfall and shiver for a little while. The spell created a pure, undifferentiated sort of agony. Over time, I might get used to that, at least well enough to accept it, embrace it, and allow it to simply exist while I diverted enough attention to try and crawl away. The only trouble with the idea was enduring it long enough to get to that point. It hurt so much my heartbeat skipped a couple of times and ramped up to dangerous levels. It hurt so much I was ready to throw up. It was the most hideously evil thing I've ever built.

I didn't want to feel it ever again, but I wanted Johann to choke on it, nonetheless.

It *hurt*, and it brought back all the things that went with my first real experience of being tortured. Hence my retirement to the bathroom and a little quiet time, alone.

Post-traumatic stress, maybe? How would I know? I've never had it before. All I know for sure is the pain brought back the memories, and that I did not care for.

I eventually pulled myself together. It took Johann to do it, though. The thought of hurting him in return for all the pain and humiliation he inflicted... it's not a pretty motivation, and I'm not proud of it, but it's true. It worked. I stepped out of the waterfall when I could finally focus on the future, not the past.

I picked up a locking collar from Kavel. With this around his neck, he would eventually die from the pain. If I could figure out a way to separate him from his nexus, I could let him writhe and convulse all he wanted before the collar literally hurt him to death.

The technical cause of death would probably be heart failure or stroke. But it would be the pain that killed him. I just needed a way to clamp it on him!

Beltar came in while I was working, accompanied by Tianna and Rendal. Someone took the opportunity to wheel in a cart full of food. They came in and set up while I finished what I was doing.

"My lord?" Beltar asked, pushing a platter in my direction.

"Thank you, Beltar. Tianna. Rendal." We all nodded at each other. Tianna took a seat. "How did it go?" I asked, setting aside my prototype.

"Please don't do that to me again, Granddad."

"Ah. That bad?"

"Worse," Rendal said. He laid a hand on a chair and asked with his eyes. I nodded and gestured to sit. Once they were more comfortable and started distributing food, Rendal continued with, "None of us are sure what it is, exactly, you want to accomplish."

"You're not?"

"No," Beltar said. "We tried to negotiate some sort of... treaty? Contract? But no one is clear on the purpose of it."

I poured a goblet of something brown and ran my fingers through my hair, thinking.

"Okay, maybe I didn't explain this very well. Let me start at the beginning. We have laws, right?"

"Yes."

"Without getting into the whole legal code, what normally happens is someone breaks the law—he steals something, kills someone, or generally behaves badly in some way. That's what starts everything going.

"After he does it, or while he does it, the City Guard comes up and restores order. At least, in theory. Someone may have already taken action, or defended themselves, or something. With me so far?"

"I am," Rendal said. Beltar and Tianna nodded.

"We then have Guardsmen who sort out who did what to whom and how. *Why* isn't important, yet. Once the guardsman or guardsmen know what's what, they either tell the drunks to go home or arrest somebody for a crime. If we have an arrest, then we have to sort the guy out—figure out if he's guilty of a crime or if he only *looks* guilty. He may be arrested for standing over a corpse with a bloody knife in his hand; that seems logical and reasonable. But when we investigate and determine the corpse was beheaded, the guy with the knife doesn't seem as likely a suspect. Especially when he says he defended himself from some axe-wielding maniac who beheaded the pre-corpse."

"Sire? What if the knife is a large one? Could not the murderer have worked diligently to remove the head?"

"I like the way you think, Rendal, but it's only an example. We need to *investigate*. We need to gather *evidence*. We need to listen to the suspect's account of what happened—and he's only a suspect, not a murderer, until we *prove* he's either guilty or innocent. Although," I added, "it's generally impossible to prove innocence. We may wind up aiming to prove guilt, but it shouldn't be our goal to find everyone guilty—only to find guilt if it exists. But that's a whole other level of jurisprudence, if that's the word I want.

"Anyway, once we gather all the facts, we need to present them to an impartial group and let them consider those facts before rendering a verdict."

"And," Beltar said, "this is why you're interested in the Temples of Truth, Justice, Law, and Mercy."

"Exactly. If we have a priest of Truth to tell us if the witnesses are lying or not, a priest of the Law to tell us if anything was actually a crime, a priest of Justice to determine where the equities lie—whether or not what happened was fair, who was wronged, whether the actions taken were appropriate to the circumstances, that sort of thing—and a priest of Mercy to keep the punishment from being a little *too* fitting, then we might have a working court.

"My hope is the priests in question can use whatever powers are granted them by their respective gods to help the process along. If the Lord of Law says the law was violated, the Lord of Justice says it wasn't violated for a sufficient reason, and the Lady of Mercy says the perpetrator doesn't *deserve* mercy, then we can be pretty sure we got the right guy."

"This seems to me a great deal of trouble," Rendal mused, frowning, hands folded across his stomach. "Complicated. Impractical. If you'll forgive me, Sire."

"Of course. If you have a better idea, I'm interested. Fire away."

Rendal looked thoughtful and cautious. He didn't immediately spout his opinions; he's too smart to fall into that trap. Tianna winked at me while she chewed and her hair flickered. I gave her a Look and she chuckled, flames subsiding. Beltar and Rendal looked thoughtful. I was very pleased to see Beltar thinking about it. I worry he'll take me at my word and back my ideas without evaluating them.

"I presume," Rendal said, at last, "we could... observe this process? I can have a dozen criminals brought before you and your *pentatio*."

Five priests—Truth, Justice, Law, Mercy, and the Shadows as moderators. *Pentatio*. Seemed better than any name I had for it.

"You've seen it working at the Hall of Justice, haven't you? The fast-and-dirty version, anyway, dealing with captives from the insurrection?"

"Yes, but those are captured rebels being sorted, not... hmm. Perhaps I begin to see. But the ones they find guilty are sent to you, are they not?"

"They are, because this is a temporary thing for dealing with the quantity of prisoners involved. The formal setup will be a bit more stringent." I thought about it while we ate for a bit. "You do have a good thought, Rendal. Maybe we should try to walk through the full process."

Everybody nodded, not just Rendal. It's a new idea and nobody wants to be the confused person asking stupid questions.

"Okay. I have plans for tonight, but if Beltar will get a *pentatio* together and Rendal will get us some suspects—*suspects*, Rendal, not criminals. They're not criminals unless they're proven guilty! —then we'll go through my idea a few times and sort out questions. No doubt we'll refine it as we go along."

"As you say, Sire," Rendal agreed, reaching for a bread pudding. Beltar bowed from the neck, a dignified acknowledgment.

"What's your plan for tonight?" Tianna asked. The other two would never have asked; they have a reverence for the mystery of the King or for their god. Tianna, on the other hand, just thinks of me as her grandfather.

I bet Sparky finds her a double handful. I'm sure Nothar would agree.

"Tonight I plan to finish this insurrection thing."

"Seldar says it shouldn't be more than a few days. They've advanced six streets on the north and west sides, eight streets on the south."

"Really? I hadn't heard."

"You were busy," Beltar said. "Or so I hear. I wish I had been there to witness the miracle."

"I'm sorry you missed it."

"So am I. Next time...?"

"Anytime you want to, just get the coals in the brazier going and sprinkle some blood in it," I told him.

"What..." he trailed off, not willing to finish the question.

"Ever used a mirror?"

"Of course."

"Same principle, just with smoke. You'll see."

"I suppose I will," he said, faintly.

"Granddad?" Tianna asked.

"Yes?"

"Were you doing divine manifestations?"

"Not on purpose."

"Oh. Well, okay. I'd like to see it, sometime, if you ever do the full god presence."

"I'll bear it in mind." I did not voice my intention to avoid it like sunrise.

"Maybe tonight? Are you going to do it with the Church of Light?" she pressed.

"Not if I can avoid it. It strikes me as overkill," I said. I also did not add I didn't want to have a confrontation of godlike entities in my city. Or on my planet, for that matter. Of course, they're not gods, just simulations of them.

Maybe I could call them *simulata.* Or maybe I'll just keep calling them gods and maintain a healthy mental reservation.

"Then what do you plan to do?" Tianna asked, bringing me back from my momentary reverie.

"Beat people until they surrender."

"I don't understand," she admitted. Rendal and Beltar also looked puzzled.

"Tell Seldar I said you could watch," I suggested. "It's hard to explain. And pass the mashed potatoes, please."

In the evening, after my change and wash, I went to find Seldar. He was sleeping, so I settled for the guy he appointed as his assistant. The guy wore a grey sash with an embroidered sword on it. He was dressed in the usual carbon-black armor. His eyes were deep-set, his hair dark and worn long, and a lot of lines marched across his face. I had to look at him closely, with eyes that have a hard time seeing flesh, to realize he wasn't actually all that old. I wondered what did that to his face.

He came out of the chair and went to one knee as I came in. Everyone else stayed in their seats and kept their attention on their magic mirrors. I liked that.

"I don't think we've met," I said.

"I am Sir Maruk, my lord, by your grace and the decree of Lord Beltar."

"I approve of Lord Beltar's decision. Rise, Knight of Shadow."

He stood up, saluted with that fist-over-heart gesture, and relaxed.

"Sir Seldar said you might approve of my station. It is my honor."

"He's the smartest man I know," I agreed. "Keep it up. Just to get this out of the way—do you know anything about the army camped out in front of Vathula?"

"No, my lord. Which is to say, I am aware of it, but it should be headed for Carrillon." He started to turn to the sand table but I stopped him.

"Carrillon?"

"I believe it was recalled today. I heard a report on its movement earlier this evening. Has it not struck its camp and departed Vathula?"

"No, I'm sure they have. Don't worry. I didn't leave word I wanted to be informed. If you know about it, that's sufficient."

"Of course, my lord. I feared something might have changed without my knowledge."

"Double-check if you like, but for now, tell me what you can about the insurrectionists."

"They are dwindling. The bulk of their forces," he said, gesturing to the sand table and zooming in, "are gathered here, around the building they use as a headquarters. It is heavily defended." We looked over the masses of people.

"I see a lot of differences in arms and equipment."

"Indeed, my lord. They have armed many of the civilians impressed into service. Hundreds of them currently guard the streets around the headquarters, usually led by former members of the City Guards or by white tabards—the so-called knights of the Demon King."

I took control of the sand table and looked around the neighborhoods.

"Is it my imagination, or is the ratio of cadre to draftees higher in the front lines?"

"My lord?"

"It looks like they have more real soldiers on the front than they do around the headquarters."

"Yes, my lord. Too many desertions. When it became clear we were taking prisoners instead of killing rebels, people impressed into their forces threw down their arms and charged our lines. Some were killed by their commanders, others were shot by archers, but the majority crossed into our protection. Now, the enemy has taken precautions to prevent this. As the length of the front shrinks—as we take back the areas they hold—they can use more of their draftees as headquarters guards. This keeps them from contemplating escape. The white knights—the ones in the tabards of the Lord of Light—have taken to manning the front with those peasants they deem more reliable."

"Citizens," I corrected, "not peasants. Has the redistribution of troops caused problems?"

"Not so much. They appear to be more concerned with their survival than with holding captured ground. The troublesome fighters are the former City Guard. They know the area and they appear to be motivated by faith, not by money."

"But we still try to capture them, right?"

"Yes, my lord. We try to capture everybody, but not at the risk of our own lives. Anyone determined to fight to the death is permitted to do so."

"That's fair."

"I am gratified to hear you say so," Maruk replied, obviously relieved.

"Don't sweat it. Are we ready to make a big push?"

"We cannot press too hard," he countered. "Not if we are to capture every house, every stable, every shop. They must be searched, room by room, and anyone found must be removed. The process takes men away from battle."

"What would happen if they had some severe losses on the front, followed by a lot of desertion among the headquarters draftees?"

Maruk looked thoughtful, an expression he wore well. He probably did it a lot.

"I think they would retreat farther," he said, "to concentrate their forces. They would have to give up more ground or risk their lines being penetrated and sections of it surrounded. We've done it a few times, capturing or killing whole units, but they learned from it."

"Fair enough. This is obviously a war of attrition, and I'm in the mood to see it happen. Please pass the word to be alert for opportunities to advance the line."

"As you wish, my lord." He saluted and turned to give orders. I wandered off to the great hall.

Bronze was waiting. She looked eager. I know I was.

Does this mean we get to kill things, Boss?

"I'm planning to encourage people to run, if I can."

But the ones who don't run? Firebrand pressed.

"If they're civilians with an ugly man behind them, they may not have a choice. But we'll probably kill quite a lot of the white knights and former City Guards. Just not anyone who surrenders or runs."

Why do you always have to suck the fun out of mayhem and bloodshed?

"Because I'm not the Demon King."

Firebrand had no reply to that.

I prepared several spells on the trip down. All the usual things—arrow deflection, magical counterspells, that sort of stuff. By the time I reached the perimeter of the enemy area, I was feeling pretty good. Heavily armed, heavily armored, and ready for action.

And I was right.

With Firebrand in one hand and my Sword of Atomic Sharpness in the other, we went through the enemy lines like silent, shadowy death. Bronze took great care not to step on any unarmored people. I made sure to clip heads off spears and other foot-soldier weapons. But when we came across armored men, or men with Church of Light tabards…

When Bronze steps on something, it stays stepped on.

When Firebrand chooses to burn something, nothing short of total immersion will extinguish it.

When my sword of sharpness meets anything edge-on, it comes apart.

I didn't bother with a cloud of life-drinking tendrils. Far too many people were glowing with protective magic in my vampire vision. But I didn't need to drain the essence of living things around me. Bronze, Firebrand, and I were more than enough.

No one touched us. Most people dropped weapons and ran when we came into view—we were usually noticed only at unreasonably close range. A few couldn't believe their eyes when they finally did notice us. For all practical purposes, Bronze is silent. If she steps on a man just right, his screams are silenced, too. I think some people believed we were an illusion. Briefly.

We traveled a serpentine course, first charging through an enemy line in the street, then circling the block to come up behind another one, circling around the next block to head-on another enemy position, and so on.

I was in the mood for some mayhem and terror. I've had a lot of things happen to me, a lot of circumstances that had no proper outlet. I've been pressured and pounded, annoyed and angered, eviscerated and enraged. I had quite a head of steam built up and this was a reasonably good outlet for it. We only had to be a little careful of the civilians, that's all.

Then a mob of reinforcements came running up the street. We promptly went down the street to meet them.

I am unsurprised men on foot don't like to play chicken with several tons of fire-breathing horse while a blazing sword of fire psychically screams about killing them all. Firebrand tells me my shadow was doing scary things behind and beside us. The fact I was present might have unnerved someone, too.

We swung through the scattering men and I whipped trails of fire from Firebrand, cutting down banners, cleaving skulls, setting fire to anything beyond the sweep of the blade. My other hand I kept free, mostly, for dealing with things coming in my direction—pikes, axes, lunatics intent on dragging me from the saddle. Bronze made it difficult for anyone to get near me, though; she breathes fire from the front and can whip her tail like a wire lash. She can also whirl in place, spring like a pogo stick, and do other things in a most un-horse-like fashion.

In this sort of wild gyration, I stay on only because she chooses to keep me on, and because I can feel what she's about to do the same way I can feel which way my arm is pointing.

When we ran out of armored targets and tabards, I ordered everyone else to surrender while I pointed them toward the perimeter. Firebrand illuminated their pathway for one flaring moment and encouraged them to get moving.

Then it was on to the headquarters area. The barricades blocking the streets into the market square were fairly tall and strong, but they were made of wood. Translation: Bronze crashed through one and Firebrand set it to burning. Once we were though, it was merely a matter of killing soldiers while avoiding civilians.

That was more difficult. There were so many more civilians than soldiers! Getting through the press of bodies was impossible; they kept shoving civilians forward toward me. The threat of death motivated the ones in back to push forward. The reality of dying caused the ones in front to push back.

Fortunately, with a crowd of such size, they couldn't afford the power expenditure required to protect everyone from my tendrils. I started lashing at unprotected people with tendrils, draining away their vitality. I used to have to really try to get deep into someone's spiritual essence and start sucking out their soul. These days, it's disturbingly easy. I took great care to only touch people lightly, to only get their vitality, making them tired, exhausted, and then unconscious.

A wave of collapsing people spread slowly out from my position. Bronze reared, blowing a plume of fire into the sky and Firebrand pushed it, causing it to mushroom upward like a bomb cloud. It illuminated the whole of the former market square in a bloody light and made the collapsing wave of unconscious people—not dead, but nobody else knew that—much more visible.

I boomed out the usual surrender-or-die challenge, but at considerably greater volume than mortal throats can generate. Firebrand echoed it on the psychic wavelengths.

The market square they were using for a headquarters had several streets running in and out of it. People decided leaving the square was a very good idea and overran their own barricades in their efforts to get away from us.

I was happy with it. We stood there and watched them run. Several white knights ran with them, a fact I found surprising. At least, it was surprising until I recalled many of them were hired mercenaries, not necessarily fanatical faithful willing to die for a belief.

There were plenty of the faithful, however, still clustered around the building that used to be their temple. I could see the spiritual radiance shining out of it.

At least they gave up on keeping their combination cannon fodder and human shields. Instead, they fought their way through the fleeing crowd and re-formed around the building, prepared to make a final stand. I noted several of the clergy with them, chanting.

Interesting. They were protecting their men from my tendril-touch. Their powers might not be able to affect me directly, due to the divine-o-matic immunity, but as long as they don't affect me directly, I guess it's kosher.

Bronze picked her way carefully through the crowd of collapsed civilians while the market square emptied. The last of the insurgents stared at us and prayed for protection. We stared back.

Well? Firebrand demanded. *Don't stop now! Are we going to carve roast cleric or not?*

I think not.

For the love of... why not?

Because I still don't want this to be a holy war. This is a political statement. The King has rescued his citizens. I don't want it to be a thing where His Infernal Majesty challenged the Lord of Light.

...politics? Firebrand asked, disgusted.

Politics, I agreed, disgusted.

Firebrand's reply used language I would rather not repeat.

I completely agree, I told it. *Now that the non-faithful have a good head start, we can go.*

What about slaughtering everything that moves?

We've killed how many hundreds of people in the last hour? Three hundred? Four? We wounded... what, four times as many? Some of whom are also going to die. I'd say we've done enough slaughter.

You think that's good enough?

I'm still angry about a lot of things, I admitted, *and this has been a good bout of murder, but killing more people isn't going to help.*

Killing things always helps.

Only if you're a dragon.

Or a nightlord.

You'd think that, wouldn't you? I replied. I nudged Bronze and she turned around. We walked away from the unconscious bodies and the dead, leaving the shining host puzzled and confused—and maybe a little bit relieved—at our backs.

Our perimeter advanced rapidly, taking back street after street in short order. They locked down everything as they advanced, secured their new front line, and started searching everything. They found nothing hostile. They didn't encounter any resistance—well, a few archers on rooftops who didn't realize how badly things were going, that sort of stuff—no meaningful resistance until they were about two blocks away from the house the Church of Light used as a temple. The Glowsticks didn't have the manpower to hold anything more.

I left them to it. I did my part. They could arrest the rest of them. I rather liked the idea of the clergy being arrested by the town guards. It sent a much better message, at least as far as I was concerned.

I went back to the Hall of Justice to work my way through a ton of prisoners and suspected criminals—which was pretty much the rest of my night. I hated it. It was like penance for my earlier brutality. As far as I was concerned, though, it was worth it. We made good progress on working out our system of trial-and-punishment through the trial-and-error method. It helped enormously that I could actually see whether or not the accused was guilty, so we had reliable data on which to base our improvements in the system.

Rendal was as good as his word. In addition to the simple, yes-or-no cases of insurrectionists, some of his lieutenants had a dozen potential crooks lined up and ready for me. We already had several of the *pentatio* arrangements set up from earlier, so this was really a case of formalizing what we already worked out. I grabbed a couple of city guards and had them act as bailiffs. We walked through the introduction of the prisoner, the reading of charges, some testimony, judgment, and sentencing. It helped that the first guy actually was guilty.

After forty or so more, I called a time-out and discussed what we were doing, making sure the participants understood their duties and functions. There's nothing like examples to get the point across; everybody was clear on how it all worked.

Then we ran through some what-if discussions on the previous cases. This was a bit more difficult. They don't really have a good theory of jurisprudence around here. Usually, someone in authority passes judgment—the Baron, or someone he appointed as a judge—and that's the end of it. Rules of evidence, eyewitness testimony, all of that stuff is optional.

I'm trying to inspire some critical thinking skills. It's kind of an uphill fight. I'm not sure I managed it, but, although the other *pentatia* flew through insurrection-prisoner cases, mine worked through the cases Rendal gave us more slowly. I had a lot of hypothetical questions after each one. Slowly, they were starting to demonstrate some grasp of the theory. I think they were getting the idea.

Can I start a Church of Reason? I've met her. She's an anthropomorphic personification, not a *simulata*—although I couldn't tell you what the difference is. I'm not sure there is one. Still, if I did start such a church, would she grant critical thinking skills to the worshippers, or only to the priests? Can you worship logic like a religion? Religious belief is usually not terribly logical... but some people I know—or knew—had a blind faith in science. Hmm.

In my free moments between examinations, I found time to hope Lotar was sweating in fear as badly as I sweat in the sunrise. I didn't want him afraid of me, though. I wanted him afraid of being hauled in front of a court.

I can't make this personal. Rather, I must not make this personal.

Tuesday, March 2nd

Seldar resumed command when he woke up. His schedule is completely shot; he sleeps when he's tired and works in between. I may have to insist he has breakfast and dinner with his wife and child. He might not thank me for it, but they would. Then again, I saw a smear of something on the side of the sand table. It was about the right height for Tallin's hands. I know they visit. Maybe they have meals with him during lulls at work. I bet Tallin gets a kick out of the little army men marching over the sand table.

The containment perimeter was now small enough to pack solid. To keep the insurrection contained, Maruk had few barricades in place, but plenty of troops. They blew horns and pounded drums all night, did some light sniping, set off the occasional flashy or noisy spell, that sort of thing, to keep the defenders awake and tense. They might have killed or wounded a few guys, but that wasn't the point.

Seldar, once he was up to speed on the tactical situation, was all for sending in the knights and finishing the matter. He said so as we spoke in the CIC.

"No," I told him.

"No?" he asked, surprised. "May I be granted the boon of understanding your reasoning, Your Majesty?"

"Is that a polite way to ask me what the hell I'm thinking?"

"In a word, yes."

"Good job. Yes, you may. I'm thinking I don't want a lot of religious conflict, here. I'm trying to minimize the holy war overtones in all this. I don't want the Knights of Shadow to defeat the Warriors of Light. I don't even want to give this an air of major conflict by ordering the King's Personal Guard to deal with it."

"I am still listening."

"What I want is for Lotar and all his accomplices to be arrested. I don't want it to be a religion doing it, although priests will be involved. I want them tried for their crimes. I want them known as *criminals*, not holy warriors, not martyrs for their cause. The civil authority—people, mortal men, under the authority of secular rulers—arrested the high priest of a religion, took him into custody, and tried him. See what I'm after?"

"I understand, Lord of Devious Schemes. Will not the presence of the priests run counter to that?" he asked. He glanced to one side. Carella and Tallin entered while we spoke. Aha!

"Maybe," I admitted, gesturing them to approach, "but I've got a fine line to walk between absolute temporal authority and the consequent alienation of all religions, and absolute submission to the will of the gods. Right now, *men* will arrest *men* for crimes against the State. It doesn't really matter if they're knights, mercenaries, or the High Priest of Mumbo-Jumbo God of the Congo. I want to minimize the impression this is anything but a matter for the police. Committing a crime because your god tells you to doesn't get you off the hook."

"Perhaps we should arrest the gods," Seldar said, chuckling. He stopped chuckling when he saw my face.

"If I had a way to arrest and incarcerate one," I told him, seriously, "some of them would be up on charges already." In my heart, I wished for a Ghostbusters proton pack and containment grid. Maybe, if I analyze the energy type of the beings in question, I can start theorizing about how to contain one.

I wonder. Is there a world out there, somewhere, that actually *has* this technology? Is it possible to capture one of the energy-state beings? Or… I don't know. Ground it out, maybe, and weaken it enough to keep it small and inoffensive?

Tallin interrupted my musings by hugging my knee. Seldar looked pained, but Carella was obviously amused.

"I will see to the arrest of the priests immediately, Sire," Seldar told me. He motioned at Tallin to let go, which he promptly ignored.

"Take as long as you need," I told him, and skritched Tallin's head through his hair. He giggled. "Charge them with rioting, inciting to riot, disruption of city services, creating a public nuisance, obstructing traffic, unlawful restraint, kidnapping, armed insurrection, and all the rest. Just make sure the guards who do it have *no* affiliation with nor love for that particular church. This is important. Okay?"

"I will discuss it with Rendal."

"Good."

I peeled Tallin off me by bribing him with another colored ball of light, kind of like a baseball-sized balloon. He chased it around the CIC while Seldar dealt with work and family. I made good my escape and went down to the fighting to check on the progress. Rendal met me there, looking grim, determined, and tired. Well, he was up most of the night, and at his age, too. I think he was hoping to finish things without anyone doing anything stupid. He was the Commander of the Guards, after all, and I'd put this stage of the job mostly on the Guards.

By the time I reached him, the perimeter was down to a single building. Apparently, once you're surrounded and besieged by overwhelming force, mercenary knights tend to take off their tabards and surrender. After all, there's always another employer willing to give you gold for killing people, right?

Wrong. They were in holding cells awaiting judgment. Being paid to perform unlawful acts is a crime on both sides—the guy paying you, and the fact you did it. The money is immaterial, and, if I have my way, will soon be regarded as not worth the risk. Word will get around.

I put an instruction spell into the stonework, telling the mountain to put the area back into service as a city. It would be mostly sorted out in a few days, followed by some fine-tuning by the area residents for the next couple of weeks. In the meantime, however, I was interested in how the priests of the Lord of Light still managed to use their building when it was supposed to be sealed.

As it turns out, the Church of Light retained some of their group spellcasting skills. They had special prayers—not really prayers, but spells that required a certain frame of mind, a group effort—and some of them apparently still used them. It's one of the many areas of magic I haven't investigated.

The other thing they had going for them was the favor of their *simulata*. While they can't direct its force at me, personally, they can direct it at the stone. They froze it in place, even forced it back in spots, keeping doors and windows open. At least, they managed it on the area they consecrated as "holy ground." That's another area of magic I haven't yet come to understand.

This wasn't such a bad thing, really. It meant the City Guard had doors to work with. They went in with clubs and shields, bopped people with a grand disregard for clerical robes or declamatory oratory and dragged them out in irons. Some of the clerics fought, some of them prayed, some of them came quietly. There were some issues with blinding lights and a couple of scorching beams, but we had medics on standby and far more Guardsmen than were necessary. Very few police actions have failed due to excess manpower.

My absolute favorite moment though, was when a pair of Guardsmen dragged Lotar out of the building and plopped him down in front of Commander Rendal.

"Do you know who I am!?" Lotar demanded, glaring up at him, one eye starting to swell shut, a nasty bruise forming on the side of his jaw, struggling and rattling his chains. It was the most perfect straight line I've ever heard, and for one brief moment, I felt the deepest despair that Rendal might not answer it properly.

"Yes, my lord Lotar. You are the man under arrest."

I'm a creature of darkness and shadows. Nonetheless, I'm pretty sure I beamed.

Wednesday, March 3rd

Things are finally starting to slow down a little.

I've been busy sitting in non-stop judgment on the people found guilty by a bunch of *pentatia*. I didn't anticipate how many of the things we could run in parallel. They also run in shifts and keep up a steady stream of people, processing them through and sending most of them back to their lives as innocent civilians.

But there's a steady stream of people found guilty of rebellion or treason or whatever the charge is. Those get sent to me for final disposition under the King's Justice. I'd like to simply tell the Hall of Justice to handle it and leave me out, but we're still in the beta-testing phase of the new trial system. I occasionally find someone has been sent to me by mistake. Then we have to go back, sort out how it happened, and fix it. It's rare, but it does still happen.

So far, the main problem is the way they ask questions. The *pentatio* assumes guilt and fails to ask any questions which don't assume guilt. When you have a frightened, even panicky subject being asked leading questions, his answers might not be entirely accurate. Admittedly, he's trying to tell the truth—and the priest of the Temple of Truth will verify it—but he is sometimes either confused or simply wrong.

At least I've had a chance to give a couple of lectures on logic diagrams, decision trees, critical thinking, and on the presumption of innocence. The last time I explained a lot of stuff to people, it was mostly about technology and it mostly didn't take. I hope His Majesty the God-King made more of an impression on the subjects of right and wrong, guilt and innocence.

Still, this leaves me with the duty of sorting through their would-be convicts. I've had a mirror brought in and set up. The show is live and connected to the Palace of Carrillon. I don't know if Lissette is watching—or, for that matter, who else might be watching—but I'm trying to establish two things. First, I'm not the Demon King. Second, I'm not playing God; I'm playing King. I've got the fancy hat on to prove it, too. Future kings and queens might benefit from the experience.

Even though it upset Beltar, I had to order all the grey sashes out. There are still knights present, but they're red sashes—not formally affiliated with the Temple of Shadow—and they're only present to assure the safety of the King. It's usually Torvil or Kammen, but they always have a couple of partners. The actual handling of prisoners is done by the City Guard.

I think Rendal is starting to get the hang of things. Or he's getting the idea regarding the things I want the Guard to be and do. He's been keeping things moving and watching closely. He's never been stupid, just sometimes a bit slow to change his set ways. Now that he's realized change is coming—whups, no, change is *here!* —he's trying hard to adapt.

Torvil and Kammen don't much care how the legal proceedings go, but Seldar does. He's been paying attention, taking notes, discussing the finer points of what-if with Nothar, Rendal, and Dantos, that sort of thing. I have high hopes for him. If he's really interested, we might establish a High Court and allow appeals to it. He might wind up in position as Chief Counsel to the Crown, or Attorney

General, or maybe just Cabinet Minister of Law and Justice. Someday, when I don't need him as my Prime Minister, I might let him. Or Lissette might.

I think our legal customs are off to a good start. At least, I think my changes to the existing legal system are off to a good start. Hopefully, someone will come along who knows what they're doing and fix all my mistakes.

Dammit, Jim, I'm a computer scientist, not a lawyer!

Come to think of it, maybe that's a *good* thing.

I've also had some replies to my "invitations" to attend a Grand Council of Nobles. Apparently, dropping a magical iron spear into someone's foyer and blasting the Royal Command to Appear at high volume is persuasive. Don't ask me why. We have RSVPs from everyone. I'm sort of pleased.

The three Banners I sent to Arondael also reported via their mini-mirrors. They've seen T'yl; he's alive and well, just... not permitted to leave. The Magicians' Council of Arondael has been apprised of his situation and is willing to offer a formal apology for the actions of the magicians responsible for kidnapping my trusted advisor, done without the consent or knowledge of the Council, rogue elements taking it upon themselves, yadda-yadda-yadda.

Bottom line, T'yl is no longer a prisoner and can come home as soon as he likes. I've got the Banners sticking close to him in the meantime. He'll probably spend a few more days in Arondael, though. He says it's a very pleasant place when you're allowed out of your rooms. I look forward to seeing him and making sure he's who he says he is, he's unharmed, and hearing his side of things.

On those fronts, things are going pretty well.

I also had an elf delivery. I half-expected Salishar; she seemed pretty feminine. But no, it was two I'd never met. It's possible Bob deliberately chose not to send elves I've had prior dealings with. Most of those wound up embedded in the walls and might be afraid of ending up the same way. I can't say I fault his reasoning, if that's what it is.

Their short-form names are Alliasian (ahl-ee-*AH*-see-an) and Filiathes (fill-*I*-ah-theez). Their long-form names are shorter than I expected, but it turns out they're both under a thousand years old—almost children by elf standards. Alliasian was the female and looked decidedly female—curvy in all the right ways. Filiathes was much more masculine, about as masculine as an elf ever gets. He had a stronger jaw than you might expect, broad shoulders, and thicker arms and legs. Still no trace of facial hair and only a minimal amount of body hair.

They whisked in, wearing their black outfits, walking like dancers to an unheard tune.

"I suppose you're wondering why I wanted you," I started, while they were still kneeling and doing the hands-across-the-face thing. They bent forward like grass swaying on the prairie, bowing until their palms touched the floor.

"Yes, Dread Lord," they chimed.

"First off, sit in the chairs and stop doing the hand thing. It wastes my time." They blew into chairs like fog into a forest. "Second," I continued, "ask questions. I want your understanding so you can actively assist me."

"As you command, Dread Lord," Alliasian agreed.

"As I understand it," I went on, "elves have some trouble reproducing. They steal pregnant human women and work magic on their unborn children to change them into elves. Do you know how to do that?"

"No, Dread Lord," Filiathes replied. "We are products of the First Elves and were created by their process. We have not yet been taught to do these things."

"Hold it. You're elves altered from unborn humans?"

"Yes, Dread Lord."

I thought about it for a bit. My original idea was to analyze elves and see if there was a way to artificially cross two elf cells. If I could induce cell division in such a situation, I might be able to provoke a pregnancy response in a female elf's body by implanting the beginning zygote. Like *in vitro* fertilization, I suppose, but I'm not a geneticist. Diogenes confirmed the idea could work, at least, but lacks the detailed data I'm trying to get.

But did I want to work on copies of elves? They started life as humans and were altered. How much were they altered?

"I seem to have miscommunicated to Bob," I reflected. "I need First Elves."

"Bob is the only First Elf in the undermountains, Dread Lord," Alliasian pointed out.

"The *only* one? Why?"

"The rest of the First Elves have their own places to hide from the ravages of the world, Dread Lord. In and around the Eastrange, for thousands of years, Bob has produced us, his children."

I was suddenly glad I didn't kill all the invading elves out of hand. If they were Bob's surrogate children, it might have annoyed him dreadfully. When Keria—or the Thing inside her—sent them to attack Karvalen and kill me, Bob must have been more badly torn than I realized. No wonder Bob was unhappy with Keria's rule. That's a lot of work potentially gone to waste. Which, come to think of it, might be part of the reason she locked him up.

"I see. Very well. I'll send for Bob again. In the meantime, I intend to examine you both—painlessly, I believe—in order to better understand how to produce elves. Preferably without failing nine out of ten times."

"So we were told," Filiathes agreed, nodding. "We are prepared to endure your scrutiny."

So I did. I didn't find anything overwhelmingly different. Their anatomy and—as far as I could see—biology were pretty much the same as a human's. Oh, there were things I didn't recognize, but when I got a couple of humans in to help me out, I compared everyone and came up with only minor differences.

Elves—well, altered human copies of elves—have the same gross anatomy with some minor alterations. They do have a couple of glands, one up under the brain and one in the chest, just below the throat, which don't exist in a human. Their sexual characteristics are minimized, much smaller than they should be— reasonable, since they don't reproduce. Their muscle and nerve fibers are better than a human's, and the structure of their eyes is almost identical—more rods and cones, more densely packed, but otherwise the same. They have smaller hearts, but the blood vessels in the chest have layers of cardiac muscle surrounding them, with the whole system acting in a sort of swallowing motion, rather than a pumping action.

Looking much more closely, I watched cells multiply, still hoping to spot differences. Their cells multiply more quickly than a human's, but also seem to have more steps in the process. After observing for some time, I think their process has more error-checking and a much more stringent fault tolerance. A cell undergoing division is either a perfect replica of the first one, or secondary processes within the cell rip it apart. So their cells replicate more quickly, but the ones that aren't perfect copies self-destruct. So they heal injuries at about the same speed as a human, but they heal perfectly. I'm not sure if they regenerate lost pieces or not, but they very well might.

This could be the key to elven immortality. I don't understand the processes, but I think I've figured out what Rendu did to make them immortal. Not *how* he did it, of course, but if I could find a competent gene-cutter and molecular biologist...

Something else I noticed—something I feel more qualified to actually have an opinion on—was the spirit inside each elf. They were the complicated, ever-shifting patterns I've always seen in elves, but now I know most of them—all of them, except for Bob, apparently—started their existence as human embryos, not as elves.

Is this what human souls look like when they reach a certain mortal age? Do they become... I don't know. Do they grow deeper and more complex with time? If you make a man immortal, is this the natural progression of an ancient, embodied soul? Are elven spirits actually souls grown old?

And have they aged like fine wine? Or like milk? Are they deeper, richer, and wiser? Or are they jaded, callous, and rotten? Until I watch one for a thousand years, I may never know. Metaphysics problems.

As for the biology problems, all I need to do is compare all these results to Bob, one of the originals, and see how this all fits together. I've got examples of humans and human-elf hybrids. Now I need to look at an elf. A First Elf.

I wonder how Bob is going to feel about this.

Friday, March 5th

Nobody is trying to kill me.

This makes me nervous.

Don't misunderstand me. I've enjoyed having time to myself. I've caught up on the local death row, sorted out the city geography, reluctantly approved the designs on new coins, argued heatedly about using a decimal money system— nobody seems to appreciate decimal currency. I had to insist, but we worked out a compromise. A hundred years from now, their children will thank me when they don't have to remember some weird non-system.

As for converting from one coinage to another, we decided to do it in the most congenial way possible. All new coinage is in the new, decimal system. The Royal Treasury only pays in decimal coinage. We accept any coinage—old system, decimal system, ancient Imperial coins, whatever—but once we have those older coins in our grubby mitts, we melt them down and turn them into the new decimal currency.

Numismatists everywhere just screamed at me about a government policy obliterating historically significant artifacts. Fortunately, I'm deaf in that range.

To be fair, the former coinage does try to make sense. Coins had a number of sides corresponding, somehow, to their value. A silver coin with eight sides is larger and thicker than one with six sides, for example, and is therefore worth eight instead of six. It's a little strange to have no denomination below three, but they used lower-value coins for that. People are used to it, so we stuck with it, sort of. That's where the compromise comes in.

For example, one gold *trixus* is a three-sided coin. It's worth, effectively, three "gold pieces." That's what people are used to. The difference is the thickness and size. Now it's worth thirty "silver pieces," or three silver *dectates*—the largest silver denomination. A *quarton* is a square and can be traded evenly for four silver *dectates*, and so on.

This denominational thing gets impractical with too many sides, though, so we stopped at ten. There are nine-sided coins, but the ten-unit coins are circular. Anything higher really shouldn't be a coin; they start getting thick, too, since the amount of metal in them is also the value of the coin.

Money and trade are vital to an economy. Hopefully, in the long run, this will help.

Among other things that will help, I've had time to set up a real gate in my old gate room, the one with the pool. The mountain extruded an archway for me; I thought it only polite to make use of it. While I was down there, I also mentioned to it how I'd like some other sizes, spaced around the room.

I'm pleased with the arch, though. It's an actual enchantment, not just a spell with extra batteries. This thing can be used until the charge runs out completely without damaging it. Put power in it and it will fire right back up. I incorporated a mirror for targeting purposes, as well, complete with palace scryshield attunement and similar security features.

I should look into making a mirror to scry outside the universe. It would help a lot to see where I'm going before I actually open a gate.

Something I did not expect was the mountain taking initiative. My old gate room—not the one upstairs we used for moving troops to Mochara—is circular, with vertical walls for ten or twelve feet, before it arches into a hemispherical dome. The shape of the place hasn't changed, but the décor is altering. I noticed bright, twinkly lights in the dome of the ceiling, then looked more closely. The points of crystals—I don't know what sort—are starting to poke out of the stone. They're most pronounced at the very top and less so as they descend, but there are hundreds or thousands of the things already visible. It's like the mountain is turning my old gate room into the inside of a geode.

Which, come to think of it, might not be a bad idea.

Did the mountain see what I was doing in the upper gate room and start replicating it? Or, rather, provide for me to keep doing what it saw me doing? I don't think it can actually understand what's happening on and around and inside it. I never get a sense of *intelligence* when I merge my consciousness with it. But, since I do occasionally mind-meld with my pet rock, does it have some leftover patterns from my consciousness, like echoes of my intentions, helping to determine what it does or does not do?

As far as I know, it doesn't create piles of coal, iron, gold or anything else when random people ask it to. I know I don't want it to, and maybe it knows that—or, rather, that prohibition is part of its nature, now.

Things like these worry me, and I've got enough worries as it is.

As for the rapidly-becoming-a-geode room, I probably ought to put some diagrams on the floor, not only for power, but for tuning. Something like the thing the Hand did, back in Telen. Maybe, if I can bring back some artifacts of any world I visit, I can plug them into the diagram—well, place them in containment circles—so the gate can pick up the signature of the correct universe from them. Or I could go all-out and make a while actually in a universe I want to revisit. The shape of the key is merely symbolic, but symbols are important in magic. Imprinting the signature of the universe it represents might make it that much easier to use the gate.

It bothers me, a little, to think of doing things the way the Hand did it. It shouldn't, but it does. Just because the bad guys were using a particular technique doesn't mean it's a bad technique. But the idea still bothers me.

On a brighter note, I've done a lot more work on my inertia-shedding spell, too—all the revisions and reengineering go much more quickly in my mental study. I think I've got it sorted out and pretty darn slick. I've also had a chance to practice with it a bit. I needed the practice, because if I dial it up all the way, I fall over.

See, people keep their balance by sensing the beginnings of a tilt and correcting it. We drift a little bit off vertical and adjust to compensate, constantly. Without inertia, I don't just start to drift; I accelerate instantly to maximum speed. There's no such thing as "starting to lean." It's always "plummeting that direction" at my terminal velocity in this air density. Even if I catch myself with speed-of-dark reflexes, I can't simply push myself upright no matter how hard I shove. With no tendency to continue moving, I can only extend my arms—and stop. I have to get my feet under me, stand straight up, and preferably lean on a wall. As soon as I try to walk, the floor flips up and I'm lying down again.

I can't hop, jump, or do anything else if it doesn't involve actually pushing on something or dragging along with friction. I'm not sure if I look stupid, clumsy, or drunk, but the best I can do is a slow, careful shuffle, keeping my center of gravity directly over my feet. It doesn't last long, either. The moment I lose it, down I go.

It's worse than wearing roller skates on an icy driveway ankle-deep in lube.

On the other hand, hitting the floor doesn't hurt. I simply stop. Without inertia, there's no tendency to keep moving, so there's no force to the impact. Momentum doesn't exist, so I wind up simply lying there with an opportunity to contemplate the error of reducing a fundamental factor of motion to zero, or close enough to be imperceptible.

Full inertialess is a royal problem. Fortunately, I don't think I need the full-power version. Ten percent of normal is usually enough so I can corner effectively—meaning, at high speed without falling over. It messes with my reflexes, though. As with so many other physical things I'd like to look cool doing, I need to practice, practice, practice, then do that thing where you practice. Maybe I should practice, too. Between practices. And I should find time to get some experience, to boot.

I've also had to expand the spell a little, forming a layer around the subject to include some air. Without it, a too-rapid movement can break the sound barrier and create a whipcrack of noise. Low-inertia air molecules zip around my hand or sword much faster than they're supposed to, filling in the empty space more rapidly and preventing sonic booms.

It's also kind of weird to attack a target while low on inertia. Firebrand relies on being a big, heavy object with an edge. It hacks and chops, relying—at least in part—on momentum to damage the target. When Firebrand hits with all the force of cardboard wrapping-paper tube, it gets frustrated. I've had to practice more piercing and slashing techniques with it—not always easy with a straight blade. The trick is to hit the target and drag the edge along, still pressing into it. This cuts using strength and pressure, not momentum.

Firebrand is also working on focusing a line of superheated air along the edge, making it more of a plasma cutter than a sword. It's a tiring technique for Firebrand, but if it feels better by doing it, I'm not going to discourage it.

Bronze also has some upgrades. I got her silencing bracelets revamped—haha—and now they include a sort of traction enhancement. Think of it as magical, intangible spikes. They won't hurt anything, just sort of temporarily grab everything. Her hoof comes down, intangible magical spikes shoot in all directions to get a grip on whatever she's walking on, and then vanish as she starts to lift her hoof. That's a little bit wrong, but a good way to think about it. It actually defines a locus on contact with a surface and tries to hold the hoof in relative proximity within the reference frame. Pick whichever explanation makes more sense to you.

It's not strong enough to go up a wall, but it should help with things like mud, slick pavement, steep inclines, and my personal bane, cornering. Maybe I should make some boots.

Yes, I'm distracting myself. I'm waiting for several things to happen, but mostly I'm antsy about Sedrick's report on Kamshasa and Tort.

Tort.

She's down there somewhere. I don't want to show up in a foreign country and start randomly bothering people. I don't know the language, the customs, or my way around. Sedrick seems good at that stuff—at least, he knows more about Kamshasa than I do.

I called him today. He's still looking, but hopeful he'll have something to report in a day or two.

I'm also waiting for T'yl to get off his quasi-elvish butt and come back. He should know a *lot* about Kamshasa and I want his advice. He doesn't have to go with me, but I do want him to talk about the place.

Meanwhile, on a happier note, Lotar is currently rotting in a cell. He's in a sealed room in the Palace at the moment, since I'm not putting him in a cell under a guardhouse. Too many people in the Guards allowed their religious convictions to overcome their sense of civic duty and their oaths. His quarters are only temporary. Right now, the Hall of Justice is developing dungeons, the equivalent of maximum-security cells.

They're going to bear a considerable similarity to the hole Lotar has already seen. I'm a nice guy, though. His cell will have a basin with water trickling into it. The overflow will drain into a funnel-shaped hole for a toilet, rinsing it out. There will be a flat, level place for sleeping. Food can be poured down a hole next to the pivot-door up top, landing in another basin, rather than simply slopped down one side. There will be good airflow, too.

I spoke to Haran about putting up wards, barriers, shields—all that stuff. He looked thoughtful.

"Any magic we might put around such a cell can be reduced," he pointed out.

"Any door we can build can be breached," I added. "The objective of a vault, or a cell, or any other fixed defenses is not to make the object it guards safe, but to work with other components in making the object too difficult to get. Walls block physical access. Spells block mystical access. Guards watch and defend both."

Haran nodded, smiling.

"Very good, Your Majesty. What would the Crown pay for such services?"

I looked at him for several seconds and said nothing. Haran shifted his bulky frame in his chair and I leaned forward to look at him more intently.

"Corran, I really don't see the Wizards' Guild as a separate organization. On the other fang, maybe the Guild is an independent organization, rather than a chartered part of the government set up under the monarchy. I could be wrong. So let's make sure we get this squared away, right now, for all time eternal."

"Your Majesty, I am Haran, not Corran."

"Ah, yes. So you are. I can't imagine why I was thinking of him. Do excuse me. Now, is the Wizards' Guild a subordinate organization under the Crown, or is it an independent organization? I see advantages—and disadvantages—to both options. But you're the Master of the Guild in Karvalen and, for the moment, have a seat at the King's Council table. You decide. It's your future, after all. What's it to be?"

"May I have some time to weigh all the options, Your Majesty?"

"Of course! In the meantime, I suggest you talk to Kavel and the Kingsmith. And, whatever your decision, please make plans to enchant things for use in the cells."

Haran agreed and took his leave with dignified haste.

I honestly have no idea which way he's going to jump. But I swear I'm going to have this crap sorted out. If the King—or Queen—issues a Royal Command, you do not ask, "What's in it for me?" You jump. You get right to it. You make it happen. That's your responsibility *to* the Crown. And, if you need something to make it work, you say so. Afterward, depending on how well you did, you are rewarded for your efforts—that's the responsibility *of* the Crown.

At least that's how it works in Rethven. It's an absolute monarchy, not a constitutional one. Under the Demon King, it was an absolute tyranny, but I'm trying to improve on it.

Several dignitaries of the Church of Light have shown up in various places to argue about the rightness of locking Lotar up. Funnily enough, none of them appealed to the King. Can't imagine why not. I'm told Rendal, Seldar, and Baron Gosford have all explained how Lotar and his cronies aren't being held on religious grounds. They're imprisoned for performing illegal acts.

I think the holy men were scandalized by the idea that obeying the will of their god could get them in trouble. This is the sort of thinking that bears watching. Nobody else seems too broken-hearted about it, not even the priests of other gods. Maybe they haven't considered how it might apply to them, someday. Or maybe they don't plan on bucking civil authority. It's hard to imagine how the Harvest King could encourage someone to commit a crime, after all.

I *still* haven't met Baron Gosford. It's not that I'm avoiding him, it's just that we never seem to have the same schedule. I mean, in theory, he should come to me, right? I'm the King, he's a Baron. But I won't stand on ceremony; if I'm down in town and not too busy, I'll happily drop by to meet the man. But he's always inspecting something or at prayer or what-have-you when I'm out and about in the overcity.

I'm pretty sure he exists. Seldar's met him. Kammen and Torvil have met him. Tianna's met him. If he's a complicated illusion or hoax, he's a good one.

Maybe he doesn't want to shake hands with the Demon King. If so, I can understand it. He's trying to avoid offending me, but also avoid meeting me.

I wonder how he'll feel about attending the Grand Council of Nobles. He sent an RSVP. Hopefully, he'll feel a little less threatened knowing he'll be in a crowd of other nobles and unlikely to attract personal attention.

Now for the part that had me emotionally tense and stomach-churning nervous.

Lissette called.

My first response was to feel my guts seize up and knot. Once I recognized the problem and managed to relax a little, I headed down to the mirror room. I didn't know if she was going to kill me or kiss me, and there's a lot of room in between. I don't know why I was so upset. She's only my wife because of political maneuvering. She's not here and holding a knife. But I *like* Lissette, and I'm terrified at how I've hurt her.

Does that make sense? Of course not. But there it is.

Maybe I should have had Mary stick around to hold my hand.

I sat down in front of the mirror and we looked at each other for several hours over the course of a few seconds. Finally, she looked down at her tightly-clasped hands.

"It's your face," she told me.

"I'm just as ugly as ever?"

"No. It's the face I saw… for years. The face of the Demon King."

"Ah. That might be a problem."

"Yes."

"Do you want to talk about him?"

"No. Not now, maybe not ever."

"All right. Do you want to talk about Thomen and what's happened?"

"No." She shivered. "At least… no. Not now. Not yet, certainly."

"I can respect that. Will you please remember I want to know how you feel about it? Oh, and what happened, exactly, if you can." I held up my hands, empty, reassuringly, as though to say *I'm not demanding anything.* "I won't press you, and I won't bring it up again. I'm only saying I'd like to hear it, but only when you feel you can tell it."

"I will remember," she agreed. She looked up from her hands and wouldn't meet my eyes. She stared at my chest.

I wonder, is this how women feel?

"I can wear a veil, if it'll help," I offered.

"A veil?"

"Sure. Lace? Or do you think black silk? Hang on, I've got a sash…"

I unwound the one around my waist while she watched, perplexed. I wrapped a few loops of it around the lower part of my face and tied it in back. I felt ready to rob stagecoaches.

"There," I said, somewhat muffled. "Does that help? Or do I need a funny hat to go with it?"

"You," she said, finally meeting my eyes, "are *not* the Demon King."

"If you woulda asked me, I'd've told you."

Funny. I feel like I've said that before.

"And you're as silly as I once thought," she added, and she actually smiled— only a little, barely a quirk of the corner of her mouth, but I saw it. Along with it, I felt a relief as vast as oceans. She went on, saying, "I am sorry we… that you and I were…"

"So am I. And I'm the one who has to apologize, not you. I am a bit curious about… uh… about how you're feeling. Now that Thomen isn't…"

"Alive?"

"I was thinking about what he was doing to you."

"I am…" she began, and paused to think. "I find my opinions on many things are changing. It was… confusing, at least at first. I still have some confusion on many matters," she admitted, "but I feel they are minor matters, and they will sort themselves out."

"I'm glad to hear it. So, do you think you can cope with seeing my face long enough for me to crown you?"

"I beg your pardon?"

"I want to have a Grand Council of Nobles."

"I heard a rumor," she said, drily.

"Ah. Yes. I imagine you have," I agreed, embarrassed. "Uh, well, while I've got them all there, I want them to witness me putting the crown on your head, making you the reigning Queen of Rethven."

"Karvalen. Rethven was the old kingdom."

I seethed a little, inwardly. Karvalen is now a mountain, a city, and a kingdom. Keeping them straight might become vexing. I have enough trouble telling the mountain and the city apart in casual conversation. Crap.

"Queen of Karvalen, then. I've been a bit out of touch. But I want it made clear in no uncertain fashion that *you* are the ruler, not me. I'm just the cruise missile—excuse me—I'm just the guy who is going to rip the kidneys out of anyone who doesn't think you're in charge."

"The twins briefed me on this, as it was told to them by Sir Kammen. It is strange to hear you say it."

"Because the Demon King would never have done it?"

"Yes."

"Yeah, well, he's one of the reasons I'm not going be a full-time king. I may have to wear the Demon King hat—that is, play the role, act like I'm still the Demon King—but I want to get away from the job. If you'll have it, that is. I don't want to put Seldar on the throne and muddy the potential succession and suchlike. Will you take the crown?"

"Do you really think they will accept a Queen?"

"The survivors will."

Lissette flinched. Probably not the best thing I could have said to someone suffering from Post-Demon-King-Stress-Disorder.

"Also," I added, "I would like Tyma's help."

"You won't get it," she stated, flatly.

"Maybe *you* can get Tyma's help."

"That," Lissette said, thoughtfully, "might be possible. What do you... what do I want from her?"

"To write a national anthem for the country. I'd also like her to work on a martial tune for the army, and for the Order of the Crimson Sash, and for the Order of Shadow—possibly one for each of the Blades, Shields, and Banners. I'll try and get her some examples of the kind of thing I want." As I said it, I considered swiping most of John Philip Sousa's body of work. Is there a world out there where I could find him and hire him?

"You do know you eviscerated her father and broke the magical instruments of her forebear, Linnaeus?"

"The Demon King did."

Lissette looked at me with a pitying expression.

"Who is wearing a sash around his face?" she asked.

"All right, all right. I take your point. She's not happy with me and isn't going to listen to explanations. Just try, will you? I can even offer some inducements."

"There is nothing you can offer her that she will accept," Lissette stated, positively.

"You have a stick she can use to beat me with."

"I doubt that will do it. It's an excellent idea, and she might even take you up on it, but she's convinced you are evil and nothing you say—nothing anyone says—will change her mind."

"I'll also fix the instruments."

Lissette looked thoughtful. She looked up and to her left, pondering. I waited while she pondered.

"If she wants me to," I added, "I could add another instrument of her choosing to the ensemble."

"Hmm. Fix her grandfather's instruments and add one of her own?"

"If it can be done, I will do it for her."

"I take it back. *That* might do it. No promises, but… maybe," she admitted.

"I'll have to look at them, of course, to figure out what's wrong with them. Are they physically shattered, or are they just not working as magical instruments?"

"They are intact, but they will make no sounds, neither on their own, nor in the hands of a musician. They are silent no matter what one does with them."

"Interesting. I'd like to look at them."

"I'll see what I can do."

"And be sure to give Tyma the Kingsmacker."

"I've heard it talk when other people pick it up. Is it really for her to beat you with?"

"Yes."

"Let me be clear on this. You intend to stand still while she beats you with a club?"

"Only until she gets tired of it."

"I'm not sure your guards will permit it."

"I am."

"Hmm."

"Just let her know, please."

"All right. Now, I have questions for you."

"As Your Majesty wishes," I agreed.

Lissette looked surprised. She blinked at me a few times, but rallied.

"That… will take some getting used to, coming from you."

"Yes, Your Majesty," I agreed again. "What do you want to know?"

"Did you send someone to kill Thomen?"

"No. I was considering it, but I still wasn't totally sure if his spells were helping you deal with the horrors of the Demon King or if he was plotting a takeover. I couldn't exactly analyze them from here and I wanted proof, not just circumstance."

"It's nice to know you have *some* limitations."

"Oh, shut up—Your Majesty. You know I do."

"So why did you send Sir Kammen back?"

"Kammen was there to be my liaison in the Palace. I didn't feel comfortable just stopping by."

"Reasonable, especially after Thomen tried to kill you."

"Wait, what? *Thomen* tried to kill me? When? How?"

"Of course. The lightning spell he had on the captured spirit. It was his work."

I paused for a moment to reflect—I can do that, at least during the day. Casting my mind back to the incident, I recalled the ghost of a woman wearing a spell-collar of some sort. When I tried to touch her and communicate with her, I got a massive charge of electricity that nearly killed me.

Later, when Johann talked about using ghosts as remote probes to look for me, I assumed the collar was a binding he placed on her and the electrical discharge a method of softening me up for later summoning.

But, come to think of it, would he have bothered to put such things on the thousands of ghost-probes? Or would he have simply hit them with a geas and sent them out? It would be more efficient to use them strictly as locators, first. Then he could focus his efforts.

Now, if Thomen found one of these ghosts—he was Master of the Wizards' Guild, after all, and this sort of thing would surely come to his attention—he might decide to capture it and keep it. A ghost, bound to the duty of locating me? It could be useful to him, as it obviously was. I'm not saying it definitely happened, but it was plausible. Given the events, even likely.

"I didn't know," I admitted to Lissette. "Until now, I thought it was someone else."

"Is it important?"

"Not anymore, but thank you for telling me."

"So, since you didn't know, should I assume you weren't planning to kill Thomen?"

"Yes, assume that. I was only concerned with how his spells were affecting you—whether they were for your own good or for his. That's all I cared about. If they were helping you, he was perfectly safe. If not, he was doomed."

Lissette looked away again, this time as blood rushed to her face. I wondered what I said.

"What about Kammen?" she asked, finally.

"He says he thought I wanted to go ahead and kill the man. He was actually planning to do it, but someone did it first."

"That's his story?"

"Yes. And I believe him."

"Are you sure?"

"Kammen doesn't lie to me," I stated. I tried for a tone of absolutism and I think I got it. Lissette dropped the question.

"All right. Did you discover the culprit?"

"Nope."

"Have you searched for the culprit?"

"Not from here, and I don't intend to when I'm standing in the palace in Carrillon."

"I see."

"Whoever did it did us all a favor. Don't misunderstand me; I'm against assassination, at least as a general rule. But it's done. I'm not going to weep bitter tears over the wizard who grabbed your brain and manipulated you."

"That's why I would like to know the assassin," Lissette said, leaning forward intently. "I know what he did to me. I want that assassin rewarded. I know it doesn't sit well with your new legal system, but I'm grateful."

"You've heard of my new trial process already?"

"I'm the Queen."

"So you are, Your Majesty."

"Tell me this. If you didn't order Thomen killed, who did?"

"I suppose I could find out," I mused. "Assuming the body is still available, anyway."

"I'm afraid not. The Guild claimed his corpse and burned it."

"They burned it? Is that the usual way to dispose of bodies?"

"For most people of wealth or power, yes." She waved a hand dismissively. "There are many customs regarding the body, but those whose spirit a necromancer might covet make arrangements."

"A sensible precaution," I agreed, recalling handfuls of vampire ashes and a barn. I didn't actually say anything, though. I wonder if they salt the bones before they burn them.

"Is there anything you can do?" Lissette asked.

"Not without some trace of the corpse, no. At least, not that I can think of at the moment. If I get an idea, I'll let you know."

"Thank you. Now, on another subject…"

"Yes?" I prompted.

"What do you want regarding our family?"

"Whatever you want," I told her.

"I don't think I follow."

"Tell me what you want," I elaborated. "I have some things to do, obviously, but assuming I live through them, I'll handle this however you want it handled. I'll move in and be Dad. I'll stay away and never be seen again. I'll live over on this side of the Eastrange and occasionally send presents, visit on birthdays, however you want it done. It is entirely up to you, and I am at your service."

Lissette looked at me, searching what little she could see of my face. She leaned back in her chair, still watching my eyes.

"I'll need to think about it," she said, softly.

"Take your time. Like I said, I still have things that need doing. They may take a while, and it's always possible I won't come back."

"All right. We'll talk again, soon?"

"You may summon me at your whim, Your Majesty."

"I doubt that."

"All right. You may call me whenever you wish, my lady."

"That sounds more like you. Thank you."

"Happy to help."

She hung up. I rearranged my sash on the way to the CIC. I went there to use the sand table, checking on the progress of nobles visiting the King's Court. A few of them were dragging feet, so I gave them some signs and wonders as encouragement. For example, there are a number of liquids able to float on water and burn. Use one of the smaller ring-sized gates to add some, say, alcohol to the reflecting pool in the courtyard and light it. Suddenly you have a pool of burning water. Add a spell to shape the flames and you have a fiery coach and horses galloping along, all made of fire.

I like to think it's a subtle encouragement. It's more subtle than blowing the doors off the stable and blasting a path out through the courtyard gate, anyway.

Which made me realize having a couple of enchanted gates—little ones, not only the big one in the basement—might be useful. They would take a lot less effort to use if they were real magical items instead of merely material foci for spells... But later. Two of the nobles deserved personal calls, not signs and wonders.

The mirror rippled and shifted, revealing a typical communications room. Is it the custom in Reth—in *Karvalen*—for nobles to have a room devoted to their magic mirror? It certainly seemed so.

The young lady in front of the mirror looked at me and managed not to scream. Good.

"Good afternoon!" I said, cheerily. Is Count Jorgen or the Countess available?"

"I'll... I'll... I'll..."

"Run along and see," I agreed, nodding and waving her off. She scrambled out of the chair and disappeared. I waited, trying to think what the Demon King might have done to irk Jorgen. Aside from denying him the promised Dukedom—he was only a Count—what might it be? Something to do with Taisa? Or his daughter, Nina? But I couldn't even imagine what he could have done.

Well, I suppose I could, if I wanted to consult my inner demons. But I didn't.

Jorgen arrived and seated himself. He looked older, but I'm getting used to it. He looked at me for several seconds before speaking.

"Your Majesty," he said, coldly. "To what do I owe the honor of this call?"

"Actually, I was hoping you would help me."

"Help you?" he scoffed. "Why, of course, Your Majesty. The Count of Hagan is at your service."

"Good, good. Are you aware of the Demon King's nature and involvement with the matters of the last nine years or so?"

"I have heard the story."

"And are you aware he has been dealt with? I'm me again."

"I have had reports, Your Majesty."

"Good! That saves me a lot of trouble," I enthused, settling back. "I realize you might not fully believe what's happened, but I assure you I'm back to my old self. So, can you tell me what the Demon King did to earn your ire? I'd like to fix it, if I can. I don't want you to harbor any ill-will toward the Crown. What can I do to make it right, whatever it was?"

Jorgen looked me over with the air of someone considering how best to scrape farmyard goo off his boot.

"The Demon King had little enough to do with Hagan, Your Majesty. It is *your* treachery which has earned my anger."

Okay, totally did not see that coming.

"I'm sorry?"

"Save your apologies!" he snapped.

"No! No, no, no! That's not what I meant. I meant, what did I do? I don't recall any treachery!"

"Do you have the gall, the sheer effrontery, to sit there and deny what you did to my daughter?"

"Yes! I mean, no! I deny doing anything treacherous or even unkind! All I did was save her life—I did save her life, didn't I? She's alive?"

"Oh, yes," Jorgen sneered. "She's alive."

"Then what's the issue?"

"She's alive, but she is possessed by demons. You brought her back to us, but left her a hollow shell to be inhabited by monsters that abuse her body, torture her, wrack her with pains and convulsions. You gave us her life, yes, if one may call it that, but you stole from us our *daughter!*"

"Wait right there," I ordered, and hung up on him.

From mirror room to gate room is a fairly short walk. My bodyguards had a hard time keeping up, though; I was in a hurry.

Two minutes after hanging up, I had the gate-mirror connected to Jorgen's mirror again.

"Still there?"

"Yes," he snapped.

"Good. Look at the door."

As he turned to look at the door to his mirror room, I moved the viewpoint in the scrying mirror from his mirror to the doorway. A quick click from mirror to arch, and a pair of grey sashes stepped around the sides while I went straight through. The gateway shredded into emptiness behind me, leaving only a normal door.

"Now, take me to your daughter. I didn't intend to have her anything less than perfect. If I can fix this, I will. Right now, Jorgen. Get up. Show me to her."

In his surprise at being suddenly in the same room as the King, he got up and led us through his palace. Nina was in her room—it was a very nice room, even though it was in the dungeons. The walls were covered in tapestries and hanging cloths, presumably to deaden the sounds of shrieking, and every stick of furniture in the room was padded in thick quilting. Her bed was also equipped with quite a lot of restraints. Nina was about fourteen, I think, with short blonde hair and a wild look in her eye, the one trying to look at me. The other one was looking somewhere else. She thrashed on the bed, twisting unnaturally and biting into the gag.

I pulled over a chair and sat down next to her bed. There are a lot of things I can't do during the day, but at night I have a whole other toolbox of mystical abilities. I've found applications for vampire powers beyond the simple feed-and-kill routine. Even during the day, I have spells based on principles no one else in the world understands. I looked into her with my daytime repertoire, examined her with every spell I knew and with some I made up on the spot.

No demons. It was daytime, so I didn't see how there could be, but I don't know as much about demons as I should.

What I did find was an exceptional amount of electrical activity in her brain. After a bit of searching in my headspace, I found her file—the memories of what was wrong with her and how I fixed it—and I compared the brain in front of me to the brain I remembered. Yes, the damage done to her was in the same section as the present problem. A side effect of the bleed in her brain? Something I failed to fix? Quite possibly. I'm no doctor; I just play one on TV. I'm a rocket scientist, not a brain surgeon!

"No demons," I reported. Jorgen replied with a rather earthy word. "None of that, either," I replied. "I see she's calmed down. Her problem comes and goes, does it?"

"Yes," he snapped.

"I'm not sure I can fix it, but I can try. Do you have a girl about her age around the palace, somewhere? I need to borrow her."

"What for?" he demanded. One of the grey sashes on guard detail didn't like his tone; the gauntleted hand went to the sword hilt. He didn't draw, though, and Jorgen seemed surprised when I waved at the knight to stand down.

"As a pattern," I answered, politely. "I intend to use spells to look inside her and compare her to Nina. Nina isn't possessed. She's ill. I'm hoping I can cure her illness, but I need to know how she's supposed to work before I can make her well. If I can."

Jorgen just stared at me, hope and hate warring on his features.

"Please help me to help Nina. Go get me a girl. Please."

He turned and left. I went back to examining the inside of Nina's head. The problem seemed concentrated on the upper portion of her brain, about halfway back, in the same place as the original injury. How did I screw it up? Or is the brain trickier to fix than a muscle or bone?

Stupid question.

Obviously, my earlier success with Geva was at least partly due to luck—assuming she didn't wind up with similar problems after I left. I didn't exactly do any follow-ups on my patients. Could magical alterations to the structure of the brain always result in seizure disorders? Or is it just a byproduct of my unskilled poking around in a brain? Or maybe I should read up on what the various parts of the brain do. It could help to know what I'm fooling with. I mean, what is a hippocampus—not the mythological creature—and what does it do? I have no idea.

Where can I download an Emergency Medical Hologram program?

I watched Nina's brain as it settled into more regular patterns. The seizure-storm had passed; now she was unconscious.

Jorgen returned with a teenaged girl and a dozen guardsmen. After a bit of body-language argument with the grey sashes, his guards stayed out in the hall while Jorgen and the girl came into the room. I suspected we might have to fight our way out if I didn't fix Nina. My grey sashes took station beside the closed door, thinking the same thing. They didn't say anything, but I they were much more alert than before.

Jorgen introduced Laria to me. She knelt and clasped her hands. I dispensed with the formalities, laid her down next to the bed, and told her to close her eyes, keep quiet, and hold still. A moment later, I also told her she was allowed to breathe.

I cheated. I cast a sleep spell on Laria when I started. With both brains cycling through sleep patterns, it was easier to compare them. I spent quite a while at it, not wanting to start fiddling with anything until—and if—I felt I could do more good than harm.

It was also a head start on the more fundamental examination following the sunset. Once I had tendrils writhing through both brains, I could use them and my spells to swim through the flesh and spirit, watch the sparks of thought, hear the gasp of neurotransmitters, trace the lines of light and energy…

Laria was a big help. I don't know for certain what those areas of the brain are for, but hers worked quite differently from Nina's. With her as a working model, it was possible to see how Nina's brain was not quite right. Close, yes, but I'm told even minor changes to a brain can cause massive problems—all depending on where it is. Why didn't I pay more attention in those elective classes in Anatomy? Because I never thought I'd *need* them! I was more concerned with keeping my thyroid from absorbing radioactive iodine.

On the other hand, no two brains are exactly alike, either. My usual method of mapping a healthy example and transposing it onto a damaged patient didn't seem like a good idea, here.

On yet another hand, that spell was a direct, physical representation of the flesh. If I added a layer of abstraction to it, this might still be doable. Instead of copying the physical layout, maybe I could tell it to map the functions. Instead of duplicating the flesh, could I have it operate on a more spiritual level, telling the damaged portion what it needed to do, rather than simply reconfiguring the physical structure? Sort of like a software patch to bypass a damaged processor and isolate it from a cluster without shutting down the whole machine. Or, better yet, copy the *functions* of the healthy section of brain so the seizure-storm doesn't send the girl into twisting convulsions?

Now, if I can do that, can I also link it to a healing spell? If I can make the software patch act like a prosthetic by assuming the functions of the damaged section, could a healing spell work in conjunction with it to let the damaged section of brain "learn" what it was supposed to be doing? It's a brain. It's supposed to learn, isn't it?

Maybe a surge suppressor, too, while I'm at it, to make sure we're isolating and arresting the seizure activity…

I finished up somewhat after midnight. Everything *seemed* to be working, but everything seemed to be working the last time I tried to help, too.

"Jorgen?"

"Yes?" He was still there, sitting a chair on the other side of the bed, wide awake and waiting. At least he had the good sense not to bother me while I was working. The wait had taken its toll on him, though. He was tired and tense. I didn't envy him the headache pulsing in the veins of his forehead.

"This was a lot more complicated than I thought, all those years ago, and I apologize for missing it. I should have spent more time on it, but, in my arrogance, I thought I repaired everything. I was wrong."

"Did you cast out the demons?"

"There *were* no demons," I corrected.

"I know what I saw!" he insisted, leaning forward.

"And I know demons better than *you* do," I snarled back. He blinked at me and sat back again while I took a deep breath and took control of my tone. "This was entirely due to the damage done to her all those years ago," I continued. "And of course, to my own failure to follow up afterward and check on how she was recovering."

"Very well. Have you finally healed her?"

Ouch.

"It's not that simple. I think so, but there's more to it." I explained about the spell in her head to stop the seizures and to take over for the damaged portion. "It's like a muscle. If I graft a magical rope into your body to take the place of a muscle, it works. Wonderful. You can go on using it like a muscle. Meanwhile, another spell is growing a new muscle to take the place of the magic rope, teaching it how to grow, how to be a muscle. Kind of."

"What do I do? Is there anything I can do?"

"You've done a fine job already," I informed him, "by caring for her so thoroughly and so well. You've done magnificently—I couldn't have done any better in your position. For now, though, watch her, see how she feels. You can talk to her between fits, right?"

"Yes, when she is not weeping. Sometimes she... when she speaks, the words are jumbled or nonsensical."

"I understand. Yes, do talk to her. Ask her how she feels. Keep track if anything she says is odd, or any strange feelings she has. And if she has another seizure—a fit—call me at the Palace or the Temple of Shadow. I've never fixed this kind of problem before, so there may be some trouble about it. Oh, and we're done with Laria. She can go back to whatever she usually does."

"But Nina will be well?"

"I can't tell you she will be. I can tell you she *might* be—which is far better than 'she won't'."

"We shall see," he replied, bleakly, and held Nina's hand. Nobody tried to stop us, nor said anything when I and my two shadows went back up to the mirror room and called for someone to open the doorway home.

Having, hopefully, handled the Jorgen and Nina situation, I didn't feel like tackling Raman. Still, I never actually met him or his boy; they only sent me messages. Rather than pay a house call, I sent them a message saying they were welcome to stop by Karvalen—the city—and to visit the Temple of Shadow. I'm certain Beltar and his buddies can handle old injuries; they still have the bed of regeneration, somewhere. Is it unreasonable to ask someone to come to the hospital, rather than pay a house call? I don't think so. Hopefully, they wouldn't, either.

Saturday, March 6th

Everybody invited to the party is headed for Carrillon. Seems my messages got through—all of them.

I, on the other hand, was invited to a party here, in Karvalen. Tianna insisted and practically dragged me out of my cave.

It's a Karvalen-Mochara holiday. They celebrate it every year. I had no idea. When I said so, Tianna explained that today is the anniversary of the day a wagon train of wet, tired refugees made it out of the Eastgate Pass and into the Sea of Grass. Their leader declared it was a holiday, and so a holiday it was, and a holiday it remained. I'm not sure my personal calendar has the right day for it, but it is the right time of the year…

I have too many alternate time streams to keep track of this stuff. I took her word for it.

My granddaughter, Seldar, and Beltar have a lot to answer for. I spent most of the morning dressed in armor, riding Bronze at a slow walk through the city streets, while people shouted and waved and pelted me with flowers. It was a parade, in point of fact. Why do I have to have parades? Why do I have to do any of this? Can't I stay quietly in the palace and rule from afar?

Bronze enjoyed it. I feel so betrayed.

Seldar obviously worked hand-in-hand with Beltar on the Royal Security. Apparently, the idea is to not bother me with anything they can handle—normally a policy I encourage. So they made all the parade preparations without troubling me with any of it. At least, until I was actually necessary as a figurehead.

At least they were well-prepared. Before we set out on our little tour, he and half a dozen wizards worked all sorts of defensive spells around me, especially around my head—my helmet was going to hang from the horn of Bronze's saddle so people could see me. Seldar, Beltar, and I agreed my head was moderately important. I thought so because it's where I keep my thinking. They probably thought of it as a place to keep the crown.

Speaking of which, I wore the new crown. It struck me as a good experience for future kings and queens.

During our parade, I was followed by black-armored knights in two columns, one line of red sashes, the other line of grey sashes. A squad of them ranged ahead to keep the crowds back, away from me, but filtered through the occasional Loyal Subject. Not all of the knights were in the parade, of course. Some still had to be on duty in the palace, others were… elsewhere. I recognized a lot of grey sashes—that is, people who usually wear armor and grey sashes, only now wearing street clothes—in the crowds, pretending to not watch for unpleasantness.

I've felt like a target before, but this time I was a heavily-armored target.

I was also expected to do other public-relations-friendly things with the occasional Loyal Subject permitted through the screen of knights. These were all sorts of people who wanted to meet me, to touch me, to present themselves or their children to me—can you bless our upcoming marriage? Can you bless my baby? Will you cure my warts? Can we talk about a financial deal? I have an idea for a business and need backing. Can you narrow the canals? Can you widen the road? Can you put more ditches in the southwest? Can you wall off the Eastrange? Would you do this, do that, do the other thing?

Gnashing of teeth. That's an appropriate phrase, even if it's more of a clenching than a gnashing.

I tried to do the Benevolent Ruler thing, though. It didn't seem in keeping with the whole separation of church and state I was shooting for, but, well, it was a holiday. And people were just so damn *earnest* about their requests! I metaphorically summoned up the spirit of Fred Rogers and plastered Friendly Smile #1 on my face.

As we toured through town, I spotted a face I recognized. He was waving at me, jumping up and down on the wagon of an annoyed-looking drover. Heydyl wanted my attention and I realized he might have some trouble getting to see me through the layers of bureaucracy and security, these days. So I pointed at him and beckoned him over. People all along that line gave me the startled, *Who, me?* expression before realizing it was someone else. The crowd either let him through or he slipped between people; the armored ring around me let him pass.

I dismounted to meet him and we walked together, slightly ahead of Bronze. Stopping the whole procession seemed uncalled-for, but I did want to talk with Heydyl.

"You look like a man with something on his mind," I said. "What's wrong, Heydyl?"

"My mother," he replied. "We lived in the Light's quarter, and, and, and in the fighting, she... she's dead, Your Majesty. My mom died in the fighting."

If Lotar had been standing anywhere near me, I'd have killed him on the spot. I sometimes have a tendency to overreact. I blame Johann, but I'm afraid he can't take all the blame.

"I see," I said, trying to sound calm. "Do you have anywhere to go?"

"I still have the shop and our space above it."

"Of course you do. Silly me. Do you have anyone to help you with all that?"

"No." He looked up at me and asked, "Can you bring my mom back to me? That's why I tried to see you, but nobody at the Palace would let me."

"I'll have words with someone about making it easier for you to find me," I assured him. How many people tried to reach me every day? How many actually *needed* to see me, but couldn't? Should they go through the Palace gauntlet or the Temple one? Or both? And how do we sort out who does need to see me and who doesn't? If Heydyl could get dumped, the system needed some revision.

"As for your mother, no, I'm sorry to say. I can probably call her back for you to say your farewells, but that's as far as I can go," I told him. He nodded, dry-eyed.

"I thought so. I had to ask."

"So you did. In the meantime," I went on, "would you like a job? The pay isn't great, but the benefits package is top-notch."

"Yes, Your Majesty." Not even a question of what the job was, I noticed. Yeah, Heydyl needed someone's help. If you can't ask your own father to give you a hand, who should you ask?

"I have a parade to finish," I told him. "You stick with me and we'll get you set up when we get back to the Palace."

I bounced up into the saddle again, leaned far down, and swung Heydyl up behind me. He seemed either awestruck or dumbfounded—I'm not sure which. He held on as we went through the rest of the parade and made our rounds through the city.

The afternoon was more pleasant, at least. It was a holiday, so the parade finished at an arena on the south side of town. I kept Heydyl with me as we parked ourselves in the royal box. There was even a place for Bronze! Below us, there was a sand-covered floor big enough for a couple of football games and a cricket match. The events included single combats, horse races, acrobats, musicians and dancers, grand melees, chariot racing, wizardry demonstrations, and a whole host of other performances.

Bronze was amused by the races. I enjoyed the lack of death-matches. Which is not to say there were no fatalities; when your chariot wheel comes off, the chariot rolls sideways. This can result in being trampled by the team of horses behind you and squished by the chariot they're towing. They don't have much in the way of safety equipment, but they do have magic-using medics on hot standby.

I'm torn between implementing more regulations for safety and keeping my hands off. Should I put my foot down and insist they be more cautious? Or am I setting a bad precedent for governmental regulation? Should I keep my nose out of it and let them decide if they want to risk their lives? If they were slaves being forced to race, that's one thing. But free men who *enjoy* the danger…? They have free will. They're risking their own lives. It's their choice, not mine.

It's still hard to watch the crunch. At least, it is for me. The crowd loved it, the bloodthirsty maniacs.

Oh, well. At least I got to meet a lot of happy children and kiss a few babies. As political duties go, that's not so bad. And, possibly best of all, *nobody* tried to kill me!

Sunday, March 7th

Heydyl is working as one of the runners-messengers-gofers in the Palace. I tasked Dantos and his staff to make sure Heydyl gets time with both sword and pen. Heydyl may or may not have the unquenchable determination to be a knight, but he'll have the opportunity to learn a little bit about everything. He can make up his own mind about what interests him. Whatever he decides to be, be it a knight, or a wizard, or a dressmaker like his mother, he'll have his shot at it. He's as busy as a med student on an ambulance rotation.

Which, by design, keeps him too distracted with the world—and too tired at night—to think about the loss of his mother. We talked about her after we arrived at the Palace and he decided he needed to say goodbye. I called her back with some difficulty. The Grey Lady wasn't against the idea, and Lynae's death was recent enough, so Lynae actually appeared. It was a bit touch-and-go, really, to get her ghost to appear. I think I succeeded in concealing how much effort it took from Heydyl.

Once Lynae's spirit manifested, I left the two of them alone. When Heydyl came out, Lynae was already gone, which pleased me. I didn't relish summoning her, but sending her back was even less savory.

As far as Heydyl goes, he's cried himself out, I think, but what he needs more than anything is time. Time, and something to do. I've had that feeling, myself.

Dantos understood what I wanted. I think he understands what Heydyl needs, too, which isn't necessarily the same thing. At any rate, Dantos is keeping a close eye on the boy.

While Heydyl is getting his education, I'm keeping track of various nobility in their progress toward Carrillon. Lissette has the palace castellan setting things up for the big meeting. The various houses of the nobility—the micro-estates, the lesser palaces surrounding the Royal Palace in the heart of the oldest district of Carrillon—are opening up, airing out, and getting ready for visits from Their Lords and Ladyships. Things seem to be on schedule.

Kammen suggested he go keep an eye on the place. I'm not sure what for, but I pushed him through a gate anyway. Whatever his reason, he doesn't need to clear it with me. If he thinks he needs to be there, I send him. Simple. Besides, Torvil has taken over the bodyguard scheduling, much to my annoyance. I'm being followed at all times by at least two guys while other pairs stand watches over various rooms—bedroom, gate room, workroom, dining room…

What makes it weird is the way everybody has been fighting to get a turn at guarding the King—it seems to be a prestigious position, but don't ask me why. Torvil's started formal contests. In fact, he invented a game.

Teams consist of two armored knights and one unarmored target. Everyone gets sticks instead of swords, but that's about it for the safety measures. Two or more teams are put into the arena with the objectives of protecting their target and nailing everyone else's target. The winning team is the one with the last "live" target. The winning teams get to serve as bodyguards. That's pretty much the rules. Yes, you're allowed to injure people. They feel it lends a certain sense of realism and urgency to the game if participants know they're going to—not "likely to," but "*going* to"—bleed. Fine by me if that's how they want to do it, but I've put my foot down regarding helmets. Brain injuries are tricky things.

He calls it *sicaricudo*, which roughly translates to "Assassins Attack." It's surprisingly popular.

Chess may be the sport of kings, but *sicaricudo* is apparently the sport of knights. At least they get to practice their martial skills, quick thinking, and magic. It's a brutal, *brutal* game. The Romans would have loved it in the Colosseum. Personally, I wouldn't play it except at gunpoint.

Today also marked the latest attempt by Johann & Co. to do something nasty.

First thing this morning, I was in my waterfall, minding my own business, when the air did that spatial distortion thing. It took me a moment or two to recognize the feeling. I felt it without seeing it and had to look around for it.

The gate opened in the *ceiling*. Wherever the other end of it was, it was underwater. I went from waterfall to waterflood in nothing flat. One moment, I'm having a shower. The next, I've had a swimming pool dumped on me—make that a lake, complete with scattered plant life, murk, and a few fish! I stood in the depression serving as a bathtub, holding my breath, and considered how to avoid drowning in my bathroom. Climb to a vent hole and hope the water drained quickly enough? Push on the door and hope I could either get out or drain the room quickly?

I needn't have worried. As the ceiling gate closed, *another* gate opened in the floor—not directly underneath me, thank goodness. As suddenly as the floods rose, the waters receded, doing their dead-level best to suck me down the drain with them. I grabbed for anything as a handhold and latched on to the toilet. I clung like a football frat boy after the homecoming game—that is, as if my life depended on it, which it did.

The waters drained. The gate closed. Silence fell, broken only by the gentle splash of the waterfall and a fish flopping on the wet floor next to me. It looked about as startled as I was. I didn't blame it for a minute. I did pick it up and put it in the overflow pipe, though. It had a chance, that way, swimming downstream.

One of my bodyguards—Varicon, a grey sash recently confirmed as *Sir* Varicon; I've been doing that a lot, too—pushed the bathroom door open. As it swung aside, he stuck his head in.

"Everything all right, my lord?"

"Perfect," I lied, sitting on the floor, next to the toilet, naked, muddy, and dripping. "Just peachy."

He took the hint and shut the door again.

"Firebrand?"

Still here, Boss. It steamed for a moment, drying itself and the scabbard.

"I'm glad you're on a hook, rather than just lying there."

Me, too. I'm not liking this flushing thing, Boss. We gotta do something about this Johann guy.

"Yes," I agreed, seething slightly, possibly even steaming a bit. "Yes, we do. Right now, though, we're in no condition to go chasing after him. What concerns me more are his growing abilities."

What do you mean, Boss?

"He's getting better with gates. Sure, he's got tons of power to play with, so he doesn't have to worry as much as I do about niceties—having a matching structure at both ends, for example."

You don't worry about it, either, Firebrand pointed out.

"I always worry about it," I countered. "I sometimes do it anyway, but it eats into my power budget something awful. He has a lot more to spend. And he's getting better at it. That little attempt at flushing me involved two gates, large ones, in rapid sequence."

He could have help. He's got kids and grandkids, remember?

"And they're doubtless helping him," I agreed. "That makes rapid-sequence gates simpler. But my real concern is his ability to target them."

You hit marks pretty regularly.

"That's because I use a magic mirror to aim them. He shouldn't even be able to pick me up on radar, much less get a target lock."

Why not?

"Because I'm hidden. The city has a scryshield, the palace has another one, I'm wearing my Ring of Obfuscation and an amu—" I broke off. My amulet was in Carrillon, somewhere.

Language, Boss.

"Right. Fine. But I'm still hidden from magical scanning. I paid attention to the fact he's likely looking at me from a direction other than the basic three and took it into account on Mary's ring as well as mine. I'm not sure how he's *finding* me, dammit!"

So, we deal with him sooner, maybe? Firebrand asked, eagerly.

"Not unless he really steps up his game. I have to finish things here before I go risking my neck in an all-out confrontation. Besides, I still haven't figured out a good way to tackle him."

If you say so, Boss. I think we should go deal with him now so you can get stuff done without going down the toilet. I don't know where all the water went, but it can't be a place that's good for you!

"It's tempting, but there's no telling how long it will take. I've got time constraints to think about."

I finished my evening transformation, cast some spells to dry, clean, and de-gunkify the bathroom, and headed over to my new gate room. I had a word with Kammen in the mirror and he started looking for my old jewelry.

Meanwhile, I examined the spells protecting my privacy. To my mind, it's already been established that some sort of inter-universal scrying or location spell can bypass normal shields, but my Ring of Obfuscation should be effective in a hypersphere, not limited to three dimensions. But those only hide me. They don't stop inter-universal effects of other sorts.

The problem with most defensive spells is they define a space and mark a border. Spells from other universes aren't coming across a border. They don't start from point A and cross the magical line on their way to point B.

Now, I'm dealing with someone who lives in another world. His spells are reaching for me across the void between universes. They "pop out" into this world wherever they like, including inside shield spells.

Draw a circle on a sheet of paper. Anything inside the circle is protected. You can start anywhere on the paper and draw a line, but you can't go through the circle. Simple. But if you start in mid-air—if you start somewhere not actually on the paper—you can touch down anywhere inside the circle. Same deal.

The only thing I can think of is a sort of cross-universe scrying portal. Whether that requires a gate spell or not is an open question. Would it be simplest to open a pinprick-sized gate and look through it? Or would it be cheaper to create some sort of scrying window and use it like a security camera, hoping to spot me and track me down that way? Do I have one in my bathroom right now?

I did a sweep of the place because I'm paranoid. Nothing.

Still, there might not be an active one at that moment. If they could fix the coordinates of—for them—the far end of the wormhole, they could open it up for a look every so often, occasionally catching me in my bathroom. Or my bedroom. Or wherever they've seen me before and choose to look again. The one thing they won't do is leave it open and active for me to find.

Maybe I should spend more time in different areas of the palace. Would that make it harder for them to find me and target me? It's worth a shot, at least...

I went down to my geode gate room to enchant some more power crystals. I might need them for research into inter-universal theory.

Tuesday, March 9th

There are a couple of different tactics I'm trying in my anti-Johann defenses. One of them relies on the effect I noted in my farmhouse research. It's more difficult to establish a gate in an area of destabilized spacetime. Things like the gravity well of a planet make a dent; this is what we call "making life complicated." Even worse is making the structure of spacetime fluctuate. It's a bit like the differences in standing somewhere flat compared to standing on an incline compared to standing on an incline that's rippling like a wavy sea. The difficulty keeps going up.

As a side effect, I realized I could stabilize the area around my existing gate and make things that much easier for me. By smoothing out some of the spacetime distortions we normally take for granted—or don't even perceive! — my gates should be a lot easier to open, provided I have lots of time to set it up. More work up front means less work in use. Proper preparation is fundamental.

However, my defenses are still a bit iffy. I can create distortions inside the city's shields, but those won't stop Johann. At best, he'll have to try harder, and with a nexus or four to power his spells, I'm certain he can. But I'll make him work for it, at least.

Seldar came in with breakfast. He took the opportunity to mention he wanted to start having morning meetings again. I shrugged and agreed. With the city running smoothly and no wars to manage, it seemed reasonable. Besides, how long could a meeting take? By then, I already made considerable progress on my inter-universal research. I could use a break.

I was wrong about the meeting.

We sorted out a number of things on the agenda. The big thing was formalizing the functions of the *sanctorii*—the religious figures using their theological powers—to assist the *curiate* (kur-ee-AH-tay)—the overall structure of the City Guards and the judges. I really had to hammer on the idea the court system was getting an overhaul and was going to do things my way, and the Temples of Truth, Law, Justice, and Mercy could assist us. Or they could walk away and have nothing to do with it. They were welcome to help, but *the courts* would hold the power of the Rod and the Axe, to punish or to kill.

Sometimes, you lay it on the line and say take it or leave it. They took it. They wanted to be involved, to have some sort of official sanction. I think they were worried about the god-king's religion overshadowing them completely. If so, I may have finally found a use for my own religion: Convincing other religions to participate instead of dominate.

Then Tianna blindsided me with her question about what other temples would do for recognition in the government. From the look on Seldar's face, he was as surprised as I was. Beltar didn't seem surprised, but he's got a great poker face.

"To be frank," I told her, "I don't know. There are a lot of government functions—enforcing the law, minting money, collecting taxes, training the army, regulating trade, all that stuff. Those functions are going to continue with or without the Temples. Wherever a specific temple seems to have both a willingness to help and the... what's the word? Dominion?... over the subject at hand, I'm willing to consider letting them."

"So, you have a place for the Lord of Wealth?" she asked. "Presumably, making coins?"

"That wouldn't be unreasonable," I admitted. "I'd like to talk to a priest of the Lord of Wealth, first, and see how he can help us."

"And having factors at the docks, weighing the fish brought in, sorting them—the various sea gods and the fishermen's gods might provide priests for that?"

"I'm not against it."

"And what would the Mother of Flame do?" she inquired. "Preside over the kitchen hearths in the Palace? Or would She need to compete with the Lord of the Forge for recognition in smithies?"

"You raise an excellent question, Granddaughter," I told her, showing teeth. "Since you bring it up, why don't you go away and make a list of all the things the Mother of Flame is good at? What does she have to offer?"

"I—what?" she asked, taken aback. "Now?"

"Right now. You have our royal leave to depart. You are, in fact, dismissed."

Tianna's hair flickered, but she rose from her seat and left the room with dignity.

"Majesty?"

"Yes, Liet?"

"What of the Grey Lady? Also, what of your own Temple?"

"The Grey Lady does not perform a function for the government. It's not the business of the secular authorities to interfere in the afterlife. Our mandate is strictly material, dealing with the trials and tribulations of this world to make life better for everyone.

"However, that being said, I'm sure anyone who dies under mysterious circumstances will be taken to the House of the Grey Lady and asked if he or she met with misadventure or murder. We wouldn't want people meeting the Grey Lady in an untimely fashion."

"And your own Temple?" she pressed. Everyone else became immensely interested.

"At the moment, I don't know. I suspect they'll carry on the tradition of providing security for the King and Queen. It's possible we may open a government-run hospital. If so, they'll probably be useful there, along with the Mother of Flame. All the gods who offer to heal the ills of the flesh might be represented there."

"Then, the Temple of Shadow will not be the state religion?"

"I wouldn't think so."

"What will be?"

Which told me, right there, I still have a massive disconnect between the way I think and the way everyone in Reth— the way everyone in *Karvalen* thinks. After all the people I've turned into midnight meals, shouldn't I have a better idea of how the locals feel about things? Or do I retain only disconnected fragments of information, bits of experiences, rather than patterns of thought? I can learn a lot of the language by drinking it in, but I can't adopt the way they think? Is that it?

Upon consideration, that might actually be a good thing.

"All right," I said, "this is an idea I've had only for a little while and it's taking time to form up. I'm not sure I can explain it adequately, yet, but I know what I want to do." I leaned forward and put my folded hands on the table.

"Bear with me; I'm going to try and explain something I don't fully understand, myself. Right now, we have a monarchy. Now, the monarchy is in charge of the people. The purpose of the monarchy is to supervise and regulate the society—the people—for the good of everyone. Still with me? Excellent.

"The gods, on the other hand, come in a couple of types. Some seem to supervise and regulate things that are not the people. Clouds, wind, rain, good fortune, bad luck, sunrise, sunset, harvests, and so on. Others are there to assist people with things not entirely in their control. Healing the sick or wounded, aiding in certain types of crafts, raising children, having a happy marriage, finding love, and so on. Everybody still with me?"

"Your Majesty," Percel began, "are you... quantifying the gods?"

"Not at all. I'm categorizing them. The Mother of Flame is female; your own Lord of Justice is male. Those are two categories, aren't they?"

"Yes."

"And the Lord of Justice is one of the gods who deal primarily with something not entirely under mortal control: Justice. We try to achieve it, but we can often use some help. Is that a fair assessment?"

"I suppose it is. Yes."

"My lord," Beltar said, "perhaps none of us are accustomed to thinking about the gods in the way you do."

"I don't doubt it," I agreed. "But I'm a nightlord and a king." I nodded at Beltar; he nodded back. The gesture was not lost on the council.

"So," I continued, "my intention is to set things up such that mortals run their own affairs in an organized—well, *more* organized—fashion. I want a well-run, efficient kingdom to manage the larger concerns of the people. That way, the people can get on with their lives without worrying about whether or not the road to the farmer's market will wash out, or if the *orku* will be raiding them this winter, or whatever else.

"To do this, I want the gods—through their ministers and priests—to help."

"In what way?" Liet asked, sounding curious.

"I want the gods to do their jobs, same as always. But where they can go through the mortals, they should go through the mortals."

"That sounds dangerously close to heresy," she observed.

"And it's something the Church of Light will never agree to," I added. There was a silent pause while everyone digested that.

"The Church of Light doesn't want to share anything," I went on. "It wants to not only rule the world, it wants every other temple broken into pieces and destroyed. Its ultimate aim, from what I understand, is to banish all the other gods from the world and see the world itself destroyed in light—shadows and darkness banished forever as everyone goes back to what they claim is the primal source, the Lord of Light.

"I don't want that. I want a world where we honor the noble virtues, live long and happy lives, and work together to make it better, year by year, generation by generation. I'm willing to include all the gods in this, wherever we can find—or make—a place for them. And if they don't have a good application in the administration of a kingdom, that's fine. I have no objection to them—or anyone else—throwing up a temple and holding services.

"But I will not have the Church of Light kicking over our work, worming its way into the structure of the kingdom, and trying to undermine everything we do. I view this as an us-against-him situation, and I want you—all of you, not just the churches represented in this room—to stand with me."

"My lord—"

"Hold it. Before anyone decides, go away. Go talk to your respective deities. Talk to other churches. Spread the word through the ecclesiastical grapevine. Then come to Carrillon; we'll hold a big meeting there and sort out who is with us and who is with the Church of Light."

"What of those who do not wish to ally with either power?" Percel asked.

"I'm tempted to say they can be regarded as enemies, exactly like the Church of Light, but that's probably what the Church of Light would do. I intend to be better than the Lord of Light in every respect."

"And we are duly thankful," Seldar replied, prompting a general mutter of agreement.

"How about we assume neutral parties will be told to build their temples elsewhere?" I suggested. "I'm willing to discuss it, but I mean it when I say this needs a lot of backing to work. I'm not offering dominance to any religious power; I'm offering a partnership or an alliance. Instead of fighting for the whole of the world, I'm offering a guaranteed piece of it to anyone who will agree to help. The gods can all share the pie and everyone gets a slice, or they can fight over it until it breaks apart and the Lord of Light leaves only the crumbs." I shrugged. "Go ask them."

I turned to Seldar.

"I'm done with this meeting. I've got to make transportation arrangements. Take over, please."

"Granddad?"

I looked up from the amulet Kammen sent me. I had some good ideas on how to make the effect a *solid* effect, working on an area, rather than an empty shield, like a bubble. Modifying it would help with insights on blocking gates in my vicinity—or alerting me well before they manifested, at least.

Tianna stood at the door, politely not entering until acknowledged. I doubt the guards at the door had anything to do with it, but she's a good girl. She wouldn't want to fry them for doing their duty.

"Yes, sweetie? And come in, come in."

She entered and a guard outside slowly swung the door shut. She found a seat and plopped on it.

"Do you have any idea the trouble you're causing?"

"Nope." I clicked some magical lines of force back together and set the amulet aside.

"Granddad, this attitude of yours toward religion is… is…"

"Heretical? Blasphemous? An affront to all right-thinking individuals?"

"To a lot of the gods, anyway."

"There's a shocker. What would you suggest?"

"Just throw them all out and build temples to the Mother of Flame," she answered, promptly.

"And then what?"

"That's all you really need, isn't it?"

"Forgive me, but you're sounding like Lotar or Tobias."

"I'm not going to dignify that with a response."

"You don't have to. But the Church of Light did it in Rethven, long before you were born. It worked out, sort of, if you like having zero tolerance for any of the other gods."

"Why should we tolerate them? You're the King. You can declare a state religion."

"I could. What I'm choosing to do is oppose the Church of Light."

"I'm not sure I understand."

"I'm not sure I do, either. It's just an idea." I thought for a moment. "Here's a question. Do the other gods exist?"

"Of course."

"And yet, you would deny them any representation within the kingdom?"

"Of course. It should belong to the Mother, just the same as the monarchy belongs to you."

"And will the Mother handle the souls of the dead? Or will the Grey Lady? Or will I? Will she bring rain, stop floods, prevent plagues, and so on?"

"Not all of that, no," Tianna admitted, "but She will happily help all those who worship Her."

I had an idea. It was a detestable one, but I do a lot of things as a king I don't like.

"Okay, let me tackle this from another viewpoint. Am I a god?"

Tianna was silent.

"If I'm the god-king of Karvalen," I continued, "what do you think the state religion should be? Me? Or someone else? If you consider what I could be doing, what I'm expected to do, I'm being almost offensively generous. As it is, even the grey sashes from the Temple of Shadow aren't—officially, for the most part—knights, and so have no legal standing in the kingdom. They can't legally smite the wicked without a red sash, but even after I confirm someone as a knight, they keep wearing the grey. By contrast, if a red sash has a bunch of people smite the wicked on his orders, that's another matter." Tianna remained silent.

"Here's the thing," I continued. "I'm offering less of a religious takeover and more of a sort of religious citizenship. The gods are service providers, businessmen. They do their thing. I don't order them about, just ask for their help and cooperation. If they don't want to give it, they're not obligated."

"That is *not* what the Mother wants!" Tianna said. "She wants a dominion, not some... some... petty shop where people can buy Her blessings by the drop!"

"I see your point," I admitted. "I don't expect her to love the idea. I don't expect her to like the idea of *sharing*, either—a lot of the gods are like greedy children, really. But if she doesn't want to share, if she won't tolerate other gods, then she's no better than the Lord of Light."

Tianna opened her mouth to say something and I held up a hand.

"Stop! Understand me clearly before you tell me I'm wrong. You're my granddaughter and you can get away with a lot. But this is between me and the Mother. You can tell her *I'm* the god-king of Karvalen and it's *My* dominion! She's welcome to come play in it, however, along with pretty much everyone else who is willing to work with me on making it a nicer place."

I shifted my voice into a lower register and tried to remember I was talking to a Priestess of the Mother of Flame. It wasn't easy. I keep seeing my granddaughter, not a priestess.

"Now, Priestess of the Flame, you have His Majesty's leave to depart... but your granddad is always happy to see his granddaughter."

Tianna stood up and started to leave, then turned back.

"Granddad?" she asked, in a very small voice.

"Yes, sweetheart?"

"If I weren't a Priestess of the Flame, what would I be?"

"Hmm. That's a good question. Offhand, a Princess of the Blood, possibly Queen. Certainly a talented and incredibly skilled wizard. Maybe a magician, but I hope not; they're a stodgy, strictly-by-rote bunch, even if they do have some impressive spells. You might be my wizard assistant, I suppose, but I tend to think you would strike out on your own and have a shop where people hire your services for serious, complex, and difficult problems. In fact, I might be on your payroll as a consultant.

"That's off the top of my head," I added. "Why?"

"No reason. Just... wondering." She skipped over to me, kissed my cheek, and left.

Sparky's pressuring my granddaughter, I realized. I concentrated for a moment, thinking: *Sparky is pressuring my granddaughter.*

Yeah, came the reply from the other me. *Tianna is a priestess. It's allowed.*

Got it. Did I mention the plan to you?

No, but it's all anyone can talk about up here.

Really?

No, I'm just making it up because you asked, came the sarcastic reply. *Yes, really.*

You're not funny.

That's funny, coming from you.

Are they really discussing it? I asked.

They really are. You kicked the hornet's nest, that's for sure.

How's the debate going?

I wouldn't call it a debate. More of a shouting match. The Hunter likes it and Ssthitch is willing to give you the benefit of the doubt—he doesn't like the idea, but he's willing to tackle it on a trial basis. I think it's because he isn't really affected a whole lot by what happens in Rethven. Karvalen. The kingdom. Still, it might net him some worship from fishermen and sailors. Reason, of course, is firmly in your corner, but when's the last time any god listened to Reason? The Lord of Light is livid and is trying to downplay the whole thing, hoping it will go away if no one supports it. Even if he does draw on worship from other worlds, he doesn't like the idea of being the sole exclusion in this one. Oh, and I think I like the idea, by the way, aside from the part about the grey sashes having no civil authority.

It's a religion versus government thing. I'm avoiding a theocracy.

You think I'd do a sucky job as the god-king? my *simulata* demanded.

Haven't I?

*You were hell on wheels as a **Demon** King.*

And I'd like to avoid doing it again. Meanwhile, on Olympus... Do you think we'll get a consensus?

Do you think you'll get a unanimous vote out of Congress? These idiots couldn't agree to pour fresh pee out of a boot if you wrote instructions on the heel. But I think we'll get enough of the major gods on board that the others won't make too much of a fuss—at least, not down there. I expect to hear a lot of grumbling and snarky comments from the nay-sayers.

Sorry.

Don't sweat it. I plan to ignore them with Olympian dignity.

You can do that? I asked. *Where did you pick up dignity?*

Priests. They have a definite idea about the appearance and dignity of their object of worship. I sure didn't get it from you, he snickered.

Ah. Fair enough.

I closed up my mental fortress again and went to have a waterfall—after scanning the room carefully. Talking to god, even if it's more like talking to myself, always makes me feel icky, somehow. Besides, I wanted to test my new spell for detecting scrying portals. Just in case.

Bob arrived late this afternoon. We sat down to a dinner with his two... children? Creations? Progeny? The two elves he already sent, Alliasian and Filiathes. We discussed what I did in analyzing them and I explained how I needed to examine what he called a First Elf to find the differences.

Once Alliasian and Filiathes assured him it was a completely painless process, no more than intense scrutiny, he agreed readily. We finished dinner, I finished a sunset, and we retired to my laboratory for the analysis.

First Elves are very different from elves they quasi-created. Human-based elves are superficially elves, yes, but with obvious human characteristics and internal organs, with some notable alterations. Put one in an MRI machine and the doctors will whistle and want to run a lot more tests.

Put a First Elf in the MRI and the doctors will want to call either Area 51 or the press. They'll certainly need a good, stiff drink.

First Elves aren't human—not even close. Oh, they share some similarities in basic structure, sure. They're bilaterally symmetrical, have five digits on each hand, forward-facing eyes, all the gross features you might expect.

Inside, they're very different. They have more ribs than a human, but thinner, and the ribs are staggered and offset—there's an outer layer of widely-spaced ribs, some muscle and cartilage, then an inner layer of ribs spaced to run behind the gaps between the outer ones. The ribs still run back to connect to the spine—which has sixty-two vertebrae in a peculiar, overlapping configuration—but the ribs don't connect up front like a human. They run all the way around the chest and support each other through… cartiliginous? Cartilageous? Cartilaginous? They support each other with cartilage connecting them.

Most of the bones are rigid, but not ultimately so. They seem to be more fibrous than bony. I think they generate fibers in the hollow channel where humans keep marrow. The fibers migrate outward through the structure of the bones as the exterior erodes. How this works exactly, I have no idea. But the bones of a First elf have some give to them, so they can bend slightly under pressures that would break a more brittle human bone. I think they're stronger and heal more quickly, too.

Their eyes, at least, are a lot like human eyes, aside from the expected increase in rods and cones. Internal organs are sometimes recognizable. I had no trouble with the digestive tract, but where's the liver? And are those the kidneys? Those other organs are not on my list of things commonly found in humanoids—I think. And I think these other things are secondary, collapsed lungs. Do they expand under exertion? And what are those brownish layers along the underside of each lung?

The brain of a First Elf is also structurally different. It retains the same general shape, but it doesn't seem to have that crease down the middle a human brain has. Comparing it to my Second Elf subjects, Bob's brain is about the same size, but slightly denser, and lacks some of the structures around the brainstem. Does everything in an elf brain take place in the brain, itself? Maybe. It doesn't have most of the human structures in the upper spine.

Even the hearts aren't what I think of as hearts. Two large blood vessels run vertically in the chest; sections of them are covered in muscle. They pulse in a swallowing motion, moving blood through the body. Smaller branches of these two main vessels feed into the lung structures, pumping blood through them. First Elves have, effectively, two primary hearts and four secondary hearts, none of which are placed where a human heart is kept.

Now I feel stupid. For years—decades, really—Bob has had that handprint I put on his chest. I always thought he believed I could rip his heart out remotely with it. Turns out I could take out a large piece of his left-side peristaltic blood-pump and a large chunk of lung. He wouldn't enjoy it, but it wouldn't instantly kill him, either. With appropriate magic and several helpers, he might survive. But by presuming he had a heart where a human has a heart, I demonstrated my ignorance of First Elves.

He still seems to regard me as a Dark King and Lord of Night and Really Scary Creature, though, heart-crushing handprint or not. I may have to ask him why, sometime. Am I simply that frightening? Or is it because the Heru—the race of gods Rendu is supposed to be part of—come from the chaos beyond the world, and Bob seems to think I have some of that chaos in my blood?

As a side note… do I? What causes vampirism? A contagion? A creature from the void of chaos? A supernatural entity—hellish demon, bloodthirsty spirit, or genie-like monster? I don't know what made the first vampire, if there is one. I don't even know if vampirism shares a common source among the various worlds I've visited. Every species may have a different origin, for all I know.

Anyway, another oddity of First Elves, possibly the most peculiar, is their complete lack of reproductive system. No testes, no ovaries, nothing of that nature of any sort. There's a waste elimination system for solids and another for liquids—yes, even ridiculously graceful elves use the toilet—but these both use sphincters.

Bob isn't a *him*. Bob is an *it*. But I'll probably continue to think of it as a him—that is, I'll probably continue to think of *Bob* as a *him*.

Elf gender is weird. These elves don't have a gender. Then again, I used to know humans with gender issues. How weird are First Elves, really, in that they were created without any gender at all? It must save a lot of confusion and headache.

Here's an even weirder thing, at least to me: First Elves *have no bellybuttons*. They weren't born, they were created.

But the total lack of reproductive system was troublesome news for my plans. I had hoped to harvest gametes from First Elves and artificially force reproduction. Now, if I want to create another First Elf, I can't just mix two of them and find a host mother.

I wonder… can First Elves be cloned? I'll have to ask Diogenes. I'm more comfortable cloning computer drives than I am with cell cultures. If First Elves were never born, can you grow one in a tank? Where do you hook the umbilical cord, assuming you can get the cloning process to work? Cloning a human-hybrid elf is probably doable without too much trouble, but I'd really like to clone some First Elves for Bob. Magicians might appreciate the higher-quality copy, too, instead of a copy of the copies.

When I gestured him off the table, Bob sat up with a smooth, almost liquid motion. He looked at me with a puzzled expression.

"I'm done," I assured him.

"But… you have done nothing?"

"On the contrary. I looked all through you, examining your flesh, blood, bones, and organs. You're quite different on the inside from a human, or even a human-born elf."

"I am?" He seemed startled.

"Oh, yes." I explained the differences between a First Elf and the elf copies. He was already aware of some of the more obvious differences, of course, but my list seemed to disappoint him.

"We have created," he said, slowly, "imperfect copies of ourselves. They appear much like us, but are not us."

"Don't feel bad. You did an excellent job."

"Our efforts have been wasted," he replied, resignedly. "We knew our re-creations were not perfect, yet we continue to try, and we fail. Now I know our failure is more complete than our most dire assessments."

I groped for a way to reassure him. Reassuring a vicious, treacherous, deceitful creature with no regard for human life and a lack of many human concepts is difficult. Since the other two weren't in the room, I settled on sociopathic reassurance.

"Look, Bob. They're elves—as far as anyone but Rendu is concerned—which means you can use them in your place. You just have to survive until Rendu comes back, right? Well, these are your buffer zone, your bodyguards, between you and a hostile world. So what if they're cheap copies? They're not here to serve Rendu. They're here to serve you. Isn't that good enough?"

"It was not what we intended when we set out to increase our population."

"Well, so you're not increasing. You're at least helping to preserve the existing population. For now, that will have to do."

"You said you had a thought? Increasing the numbers of elves, Dread Lord?"

"Why, yes. Yes, I did. You're familiar with the way humans reproduce?"

"Unfortunately," he agreed, lips pressed in a thin line.

"There are some details you may have missed." I explained again, this time about eggs and sperm, zygotes, and the combination of traits from the parents. I didn't get into gene theory, or even into actual cell theory, but a "seed" from each parent combines and grows...

Bob got it easily enough. He's seen generation upon generation of creatures and noted they inherit traits from both parents. He never gave it much thought, aside from using it the way a stockbreeder might. I didn't ask what sort of stock he bred.

"My idea," I went on, "is to take a bit of the living flesh from you and from another First Elf—if you know one and can persuade it to cooperate—so I can combine the traits of both of you to make a new elf. If we can't get the cooperation of another First Elf, I'm pretty sure we can still make another one just like you. Eventually, anyway."

"Another me?" Bob asked, face in neutral.

"You've seen twins. It's much the same thing."

"I am not certain I wish to be two."

"Oh. Well, I can work on the combining of traits, then. Do you know another First Elf who might want to help?"

"I believe," he stated, "I can persuade a few."

"Good, good. Don't go shouting for them just yet. There are a lot of preparations. This is a project that may take a few decades."

"Decades," he repeated, and waved a hand dismissively, like a wisp of smoke vanishing on the wind. "We will wait centuries, Dread Lord, knowing now how feeble our own efforts have been."

"I should have known a few dozen years wouldn't be a worry. All right. Stick around; I may need you on hand shortly."

"As you command, Dread Lord."

Wednesday, March 10th

We should have everyone gathered together for the big meeting of nobles by this afternoon—we're way ahead of schedule. I guess my signs and wonders were a bit more effective than I thought. Either that, or Lissette did something to move things along. I'm sure she's more diplomatic than I am because I'm not.

I've got the crown ready. Kammen tells me my royal wardrobe in Carrillon is still where the Demon King left it, so clothes aren't a problem. The public gate—the one people know about, the one we shipped troops through—is charging up nicely. It's already powered up enough to make the trip to Carrillon.

In the course of making travel plans, I thought I was going to meet Baron Gosford. Apparently not. He set sail for Carrillon rather than take a gate with me. Well, I didn't advertise I'd be traveling by gate. Most people probably assume I'm going to ride Bronze. More to the point, I didn't actually invite him to hitch a ride with me, but I did make it clear he's supposed to be at the meeting. Ah, well.

Torvil and Beltar are sorting out who gets to escort the King through to Carrillon, but that's going to take a day or two. First, there's the competitive examination: a *sicaricudo* tournament. Second, the winners have to recover from the *sicaricudo* tournament.

I know I've said this before, but it's a brutal game. I cannot stress this enough. People around here don't play "tag" anything. They beat each other for real. Their only nod to safety is using blunt instruments instead of edged weapons. I keep hearing excuses about how if it doesn't hurt, it's not really preparing you to face injury and all that. Courage in battle, fighting spirit, determination in the face of adversity, weeding out the weak, and so on.

I'm glad I insisted on helmets, despite the general grumbling. People seem to think it shows a lack of courage to wear protection when it's only practice drills. Your opponents are skillful and trying to disable you, not kill you. And there are literally dozens of people with healing spells standing around! What more do you want?

I argued it's a sign of how much the King loves his knights and wishes to preserve them against mischance—*now wear the damn helmets!*

They're lucky I don't import some foam weapons and make them use the things.

I don't often feel a hundred percent certain about utilizing the Full Royal Authority to Issue a Decree. This one, I'm a hundred percent happy about. They did it my way, which I thought was nice of them. They even stopped griping, which was completely unexpected, but highly gratifying.

After watching some of the *sicaricudo* events with Tallin attached to my leg and Caris on my lap—Caris gets to wander around the Palace as long as she has mommy's magical leash, and Tallin is allowed to wander with her—I disengaged from the pair of them by drafting a pair of defeated knights and using them as highchairs. Sitting on shoulders, far higher than normal, the little ones were suitably amused, which allowed me to escape. I headed for my personal gate room—the one with the reflecting pool in the middle, the rapidly-becoming-a-geode one—when Heydyl skidded up to me.

"Respects to His Majesty from the Magician T'yl. He awaits your pleasure on the iron-framed mirror!"

"Thank you, Heydyl. How are you liking it here?"

"Just fine, Your Majesty!" he answered, all brisk and businesslike, aside from the grin.

"Good lad. How are your studies going?"

"I dunno what I'm studying," he admitted, "but I'm trying it all. I didn't know there was so much to know."

"Even better. Carry on."

"Sire!" He spun about and hurried off to report to whoever was in charge of messengers. I suppose I really should look into how the Palace is organized and run, but when? I don't have time to do the things I need to do, much less the things I want to do.

I hurried to the mirror room, thinking grumpy thoughts. T'yl was in a mirror, quasi-elvish features relaxed, hands behind his head, feet up on the table, leaning back and looking at the distant ceiling. He saw me come in, plopped his feet down on the floor and waved.

"Good morning!" he hailed.

"Good morning to you," I agreed. "How's life?"

"It has its good moments. I would still hate to part company with it."

"Good for you. It's no fun."

"I imagine not."

"When are you coming home?" I asked, settling into the chair.

"About that..."

"Yes?"

"I've had a chance to talk with your Banners. They've explained a lot, but they aren't, what do you call it, part of your inner circle."

"Sure."

"I'm told you've got Lotar in prison?"

"Yep. It's a pretty comfortable cell compared to the one he used to occupy."

"I think it possible you may have missed something."

"I'm sure I have," I agreed. "What is it this time?"

"He's not the *deveas* of the Church of Light. He's merely the Patriarch of Karvalen."

"Karvalen the city or Karvalen the kingdom?"

"The city. I think. I'm not sure exactly on how the Church's hierarchy is set up—it's never been high on my list of interests. It's possible, though, he also has authority over the secret cults within the kingdom."

"I suppose I'm going to get a nasty jihad note from the Church of Light about having their local representative arrested." I made a growling sound. "I knew this was too easy."

"No, no—well, maybe so," he corrected himself. "The thing I was trying to get at wasn't the trouble in dealing with Galleron, the *deveas*. While Lotar was the High Priest of Karvalen, I was spying on him up down and sideways. Then my presence was... ah, required here in Arondael."

"You were kidnapped."

"It was a very polite kidnapping," he told me. "I've never been confined so comfortably. It made me miss my apprenticeship in the Academy."

"When magicians kidnapped *me,* they hit me over the head repeatedly to keep me quiet until they locked me in a containment circle," I complained.

"You're not a magician. You're a monster."

"It's still not fair," I observed. "Nobody comes right out and *asks* for anything. Have you noticed?"

"Why should they?" T'yl asked, frowning. "Nobody ever gives anything away for free. If you can take it without paying for it, why wouldn't you?"

Which, to be fair, pretty much sums up human nature, especially here. I'm mildly disgusted.

"Back to what you were saying about the Church of Illumination," I deflected. "You were spying on Lotar?"

"Yes. I was reading his mail, listening in on his meetings, that sort of thing. I wanted to have everything you could possibly want in a neat stack when you came back to home and throne. You've discovered most of it already, of course, but who you really need to worry about is the new Cardinal of the Hand."

I had a sudden and intense flashback to Tobias. I didn't enjoy the experience. There wasn't anything enjoyable about Tobias, except, possibly, kicking him in his groin hard enough to break it.

Do I have more flashbacks these days? I think so. Is it because of the quantity of souls and experiences I have ingested? Is it because of Johann's Funtime Happy Playroom? Or something else? There's no shortage of brain-straining things in my past, that's certain.

Maybe I need a vacation instead of another long nap. Carribean island? Cruise ship? Rent a villa in Italy? Disneyland?

"I see," I said, faintly. "They have a Hand organization already set up?"

"Oh, yes. From what I was able to discover, it is more of a secret society within the Church than a formal Order, but their leader is rumored to be among the personal advisors to the *deveas* of the Church."

"Great. Religious ninjas of the Light."

"Beg pardon?"

"Nothing. So, who's my problem child?"

"The leader of the Hand?" T'yl asked, puzzled.

"Yes, please."

"I don't know. I was working on it before I... moved to Arondael."

"Tell your captors their timing is atrocious."

"They have been made aware," he assured me, "and are properly thankful for your understanding and patience."

"Thanks. So, I should be on the lookout for Light-worshipping assassins?"

"Probably, although I doubt they'll be so direct. I think it more likely they'll try to attack your plans, rather than you. I get the idea they want to oppose you rather than destroy you. Killing you seems impossible, although I don't know why they think so."

"I have an idea," I muttered.

"As you say. One other thing."

"Why not? Go ahead."

"That thing you did to make me immortal. They'd really like to know how you did it."

"The Ninjas of the Light?"

"No, no—the magicians who asked me to, ah, participate in their studies. They have been entirely courteous, if a bit over-enthusiastic and insistent. There are a few others," he added, "who still want to drain blood out of you and make themselves nightlords. Many think your blood holds the key to living immortality. But my former hosts would like to know how you moved me to an elf-body."

"Okay. I'm not sure I can teach it to them, though. And it requires an empty elf to make it work."

"They won't mind."

"The elves will. Although," I paused for a moment. "I'm told it takes about seven years to make a new elf. I don't know how long one takes to grow up, though. I'm trying to help the elves out in that regard so they don't kidnap and kill humans for the process, but there are problems..." I thought about it some more.

"Here's a question, T'yl. If I can get some empty elves, would your 'friends' settle for being *put* into elf bodies, like you were, rather than doing it themselves?"

"I would think so," he agreed. "You must remember, any magician who gets to a certain age and doesn't look forward to the great journey... It is not inaccurate to say they will do many things they would not normally consider to keep from making the trip."

"I think I understand. Okay. Let me see what I can work out."

"So, I may tell them you're willing to help?"

"If it will get you out of their clutches, yes. I'm already working on it."

"Very good. Do you mind if I bring a couple of them back with me? They would like to continue working with me on elf-body immortality, and I am certain they would be delighted to help you with other matters if it helps your work on their project."

"As long as you vouch for them, I agree."

"As you say, Sire. We should be there tomorrow, I think."

"Sounds good."

We signed off and I went to get Bronze.

I'm a physics and computers guy, not a biosciences person. Admittedly, I have some natural—make that "unnatural"—advantages when it comes to analyzing living things. This doesn't change the fact I simply don't know enough to understand everything I'm seeing. It's one thing to know I can plug a sperm cell into an egg cell and plant it in a uterus. It's quite another to combine two normal cells—well, two non-reproductive cells—from different organisms and artificially grow the result. The first one is on the order of pouring cake mix into a bowl and following directions. The second one is more along the lines of, "Step One: obtain a farm. Step Two: Plow and plant wheat. Step Three: Build an oven..." on your way to making the cake.

Fortunately, I have no problem whatsoever with Sir Isaac Newton's philosophy on the matter. "If I have seen further, it is by standing on the shoulders of giants." I'll happily make use of what someone else has discovered, if for no other reason than duplicating all their work is not only outside my talents, but outside my interests.

And I'm lazy. Sue me.

The problem, of course, is finding someone who knows more about it than I do. I'm probably the closest thing to a geneticist in this world—barring supernatural entities such as Rendu or the energy-state things who occasionally interfere with life as we know it. Even with the limited reference material Diogenes provides, I merely know the depth of my ignorance. I certainly can't risk going to Mary's world and consulting someone at a major university; I don't dare give Johann more chances to detect and nail me. I also feel less than confident about deliberately dialing up some random world in the hope it's technologically advanced enough to be useful. At the moment, randomly dialing up strange universes strikes me as a way to multiply my problems, not solve the ones I already have.

However, there is a world I know of—hopefully no longer full of giant ants—which seems to have made great technological advancements. There's no one to consult, but there are still computers, libraries, and—possibly behind sealed doors—medical equipment.

So, my Clever Plan runs like this.

I've got a couple of magical rings with gate spells on them. Even better, I have a target gate in my destination world. So, I open a portal through my geode-room gate. Bronze and I step through. I then transfer the link between the main gates to the tiny gates and watch the power levels. If it doesn't look good, I abort the mission and come back immediately. If the power levels give me enough time, Diogenes and I will start raiding the local ruins for information and equipment—and, hopefully, by maintaining an active link between worlds, the time differential will stay constant.

Hmm. How to tell? I'll need a candle, so I can look through the ring gate and watch it burn. I should probably set up a power jet in the geode room, too, to extend the life of the ring gate I mount in the wall... and I should probably bring some pre-charged power crystals, just in case, to provide power at the other end.

We went down to set things up.

Okay, power jet pushing energy into the ring gate. Main gate and ring gate temporarily wired together. Jumbo-sized candle burning. Secondary power-jet spell assembled and held ready. Bronze wearing a brand-new Ascension Hide spell and standing before the arch. Armor on and both swords belted in place. Diogenes in my pouch. Yep, ready to go.

"Let's do this," I said. Bronze nodded and silently pawed at the floor.

Then I realized I had a problem. Two armored guys with grey sashes. When I moved to stand in front of the archway, they moved up behind me, ready to go through with me. They watched me work. They even helped me set it all up. They knew this was a gateway to another world.

And it didn't matter to them in the slightest.

"Guys?"

"Yes, my lord?"

"What do you think you're doing?"

"Guarding you, my lord."

Ask a silly question...

On the other hand, maybe this wasn't such a bad thing. Or, rather, maybe I could turn it around into a good thing.

"Yes, but you can't both come with me. One of you has to stay here to keep an eye on my lifeline."

They consulted. I waited.

"With your approval, my lord, Sir Sarron will accompany you."

"Sir *Sauron?*"

"Sarron," he corrected. There was a subtle difference in pronunciation, but I knew I'd never hear anything but "Sauron." I wonder if anyone is named Saruman, Gandalf, or Frodo—or some reasonably-similar-sounding names. Not impossible, I suppose. But if I find out the headmaster of the Arondael Academy of Magicians is named "Dumbledore," I'm going to have a quiet little breakdown.

I approved their plan and instructed both of them in the fine art of watching the little ring-gate and monitoring the power reserves. Since Sir Lorodin would remain behind, I cautioned him about the potential length of his watch—I might be gone for more than a day.

"If necessary, my lord, I can summon a relief," he assured me.

"Good man. Now, are we ready?"

"Yes, my lord," they chorused, and Bronze nodded.

First, dial the ring gate to connect with the Library of Carnivorous Ivy. It's cheaper to look through it and make sure I've got the right place. Hitting the wrong target was unlikely, but it's best to be safe. I spent a lot of time building the archway in the library, carving symbols and spells into the concrete base, chanting at the braided strips of metal, the works. Plus, I had Diogenes' quantum crystal; it was an artifact from that world and should help with targeting it.

Plus, I get to test my wormhole-transfer connections between ring gate and archway.

I peered through the tiny gate like looking through a small peephole in the wall. It certainly looked like the library I recalled. I could even see some of the book-plate things I left on a reading couch. Good enough. I switched the wormhole from the ring to the arch.

The image flicked into the arch and rippled, expanding and contracting for a few seconds. Distortions in spacetime as one portal changed size so radically? Probably. We waited an extra couple of seconds after it stabilized before stepping through. A quick flick and the makeshift arch in the library transferred its connection to the ring gate I carried. Another spell-based click and the archway in Karvalen should have switched back to the ring gate mounted on the wall.

I looked through the ring gate I held. The viewpoint was at about eye level and I could make out the edge of the free-standing arch that was the main gate. Sir Lorodin moved forward, one eye closing as he prepared to look through from the other end. Success!

What would happen if I had an active connection between two ring-gates and carried one of them through the arch? It might not do anything, at first—much like feeding a small tube down a larger tube. But what would happen if the archway shut down? Would it take the smaller connection with it? Would the smaller one "snap sideways" and maintain its integrity? Or would it come apart, catastrophically or otherwise?

An interesting experiment to try… much, much later.

Now, some quick spell work to check on the power drain. It was an active, open, inter-universal connection, which is always expensive, but the surface area of the gate was a minute fraction of the usual gateway—some fraction on the order of one percent of one percent of one percent. The hole was only about an eighth of an inch—call it three millimeters or so. Compared to an archway big enough to pass Bronze easily, it was less than tiny.

I watched the power levels on the connected gate spells for over a minute. I didn't see any decrease. They looked pretty good, actually. The power jet in Karvalen was supplying enough power to maintain the linkage, or so it seemed. If it wasn't quite enough, it was so close as to be imperceptible to casual observation.

Nevertheless, I brought out my pre-assembled power-jet spell and connected it to my local ring-gate. The magical environment in Carnivorous Ivy Land is about the same as Mary's world—piddly, but present. That's why I built the spell in Karvalen. It sucked in what was available and fed it into the local ring gate, feeding the spell from both ends.

Could I set up shop on top of a nexus in this world? Would it make the magical side of things that much easier? Or does this world even have magical lines of force running around it? Something to look into… again—or as always—later.

I continued to watch the spells. They seemed solid and stable. I might not actually need to locate a nexus after all. Is that a tiny bit of power-profit I see? Could I actually have the makings of a permanent interdimensional link?

The implications are staggering and too big to consider right now. I'll have a panic attack about it later.

God, how I wish that was hyperbole.

With my escape route established, I sat Sir Sarron down and had him monitor the spells. He wasn't happy about the idea of leaving me alone.

"I came with you to guard you, my lord."

"I know, but someone needs to guard our way home. Besides, I'm in my armor, I have Firebrand, and Bronze will take over bodyguard detail."

Sir Sarron looked at Bronze. She looked back at him and cocked her head. She felt qualified and dared him to say different. I don't know if he could sense it. Maybe he could. He took a step back and bowed deeply to her. She curled one foreleg back and bowed in return.

"I stand relieved," Sir Sarron said.

With that settled, we headed to the front door of the library. As expected, ivy covered it completely. I opened one of the other doors in the front façade—one I hadn't sealed shut—and Bronze munched her way out, clearing the way through the carnivorous plant life. Once she had a suitable clear space, I came out and helped, cutting away large swathes of vegetation.

While she chomped rapidly through the pile of thorny vines, I ducked back inside to check the time. The candle still burned as expected. It didn't seem to have made any unnatural progress. It was slightly before lunchtime when I left Karvalen but it was early morning here—Karvalen was three or four hours ahead at present. With the gate room deep in the undermountain, the only sunrise or sunset I needed to concern myself with was the local one... okay, this might be doable.

Bronze continued grazing around the library while I took Diogenes to the server room. Very quickly we determined we needed more equipment. Specifically, equipment a fumble-fingered ignoramus—me—hadn't ruined. Well, I'm a little behind the times.

Bronze confirmed a lack of dangerous insects, so we took a walk through the campus. I tried to identify the rest of the buildings. Chemistry, physics, engineering, language arts, performing arts—aha! Biology!

Much to my delight, the building was locked up as tight as a wine barrel. This boded well. I spent a little time to magic the lock open, not wanting to break anything I didn't have to.

I went in while Bronze chose to wait outside, not fully trusting modern floors. I didn't blame her. She was also a perfect sentry. Her head is nine or ten feet off the ground when she holds it high. If giant ants started closing in, I wanted to know about it the *instant* they came into sight.

Inside the Biology Department building, I searched the place. There were a lot of things that looked interesting, including some things which might possibly be some sort of artificial growth tanks. Sadly, nobody bothers to label anything anymore. Tags with the name of the device and what it's used for would be so helpful to post-apocalyptic scavengers searching for high technology. They might be useful to barbarians from the distant past, too.

It was some hours and considerable fruitless labor later when I sat down on a relatively-intact chair, broke it into pieces, and swore viciously. After picking myself up and finding a sturdier place to sit, I drank from my water bottle—I remembered to bring mundane supplies, this time. I am capable of learning! — and realized I should have brought some to Sir Sarron. Drat. I hadn't allowed for company on this side.

I put the subject aside for the moment and consulted with Diogenes on matters technological, first.

"The difficulty," he said, "seems to be the nature of the power systems. While you can magically enhance a computer core to function properly without technological power, I cannot access a network unless you find a way to activate the network."

"So, I need to swipe more solar panels from the cars and connect them to the grid?"

"This is certainly one option, *jefe*. However, you also have a limited amount of time. From what I gather, without disconnecting the small gates, you must return in time for your meeting, leaving you approximately thirty hours?"

"About that. Technically, I could arrive a little later. The party doesn't start until I get there."

"You could also disconnect the small gates and, potentially, find the time differential gives you more time here compared to Karvalen. Do you wish to take that risk?"

"No, I do not."

"Then I suggest duplicating your effort, *jefe*."

"Okay, I'll bite. How? I can't exactly clone myself."

"Not at present. However, in a highly-advanced technological culture, it is possible there may be robots suitable to your purpose available. If so, and if you can activate one or more of these hypothetical robots, it may be possible for me to operate such devices to carry out your wishes. The risk is that the time required to find such a robot and bring it on-line may take more time than you presently possess. Do you wish to take that risk?"

I thought about it. I could spend the next day or so swiping panels from cars, wiring them together, tracing wires in the Biology building, isolating it from the rest of the power grid, all that stuff. Or I could play with one of the local robots.

Come to think of it, when I swiped a suit of SWAT armor from the police station, there were a couple of robots lying around, probably bomb-disposal models. They had hands and looked pretty solidly built. They might not be completely dead.

"Let's see if we can dig up a robot," I decided.

"May I make a suggestion?"

"Sure."

"A robot inside a sealed building would be preferable. A robot which requires excavation is less likely to be in functional condition."

"Of course."

Bronze remembered where the police station was. We could have been there in five minutes, but I chose to drop off my mundane supplies with Sir Sarron and check in. Bronze chomped back the ivy and Sir Sarron reported no difficulties.

We continued to the police station. I insisted on traveling cautiously. The trip took us fifteen minutes, but I felt better for not charging blindly around corners.

I saw the first example of large animal life in this world, and I do mean large. Its ancestors may have started life as elephants. It had a trunk longer than I thought was proportional—I'm tempted to call it a face tentacle—and a hide like a mix of armadillo and rhinoceros. The tusks were wide-spaced and shorter than I would have thought, but instead of being round and pointed, they had a distinct flattening, almost an edge along the inside of the curve. The feet looked mostly elephantine, but the toes seemed odd, somehow. It was hard to tell while they were half-hidden by the long grass in what used to be the street.

It looked at us as we stopped at the cop shop. It didn't move to attack, but it didn't run away, either. It just stuffed more green things in its mouth and chewed at us. I'm tempted to say it chewed belligerently at us, but I couldn't tell for certain.

I hoped it was strictly vegetarian, but those edged tusks made me wonder. Bronze felt confident it would leave me alone, one way or another. It was bigger than she was, but I'm certain she's he stronger of the two. I accepted her assurances and went into the police station with Firebrand already drawn. There was no telling what might have taken up residence since the last time I was here.

I'm glad I did. When it sprang out of the shadows at me, I interposed a vertical Firebrand, edge-on. Its own leap carried it into the blade and I helped by slicing downward, splitting its head in two almost to the neck. The fangs missed, but the rest of the body carried into me with the force of the leap, rows of claws scrabbling and scratching wildly against my armor as it died. It took a while to finish dying, but I shoved it and backed away to let it thrash around and tie itself in knots in its own good time.

Firebrand obligingly provided a bit of light while burning goo off itself. I examined the beast by swordlight. It reminded me of both a snake and a centipede. The body and head were serpentine, scaled, and heavily muscled. Along the underside were dozens of small, clawed legs. The fangs were hollow and dripped something—I didn't test it; I simply assumed it was venom. It must have weighed two hundred pounds.

I never saw anything this size the last time I was here. Did larger creatures avoid this region because of the ants? Probably. If I'd known about the ants beforehand, *I* sure as hell would have.

I continued into the building with even greater caution. The thing had a den under the booking desk, but it seemed to be alone. I liked that.

The two robots were still there. They had a combination of legs and treads for negotiating any sort of terrain or obstacles. They each had four arms, two of which ended in rotary devices full of tools, the other two ending in what I can only describe as cybernetic hands.

Diogenes and I looked into them for a bit and I eventually moved them outside. A little work with a defunct car's solar panels provided power to one. I linked Diogenes through a spell, just as a test. The thing worked, albeit a bit slowly. Diogenes reported low power levels from the ancient, dirty solar panel, which was never designed for this sort of thing.

Proof of concept.

Since they were fairly sizable and too heavy to carry, I loaded them into a dead car and started looking for a way to harness it to Bronze. Bronze punched her forehooves into the trunk area and pushed the car a few feet. Obviously, her study of motor vehicles wasn't pointless. I got the idea and took the wheel, steering us back to the Biology building.

With some help and directions from Diogenes, I vandalized some of the computer terminals for plug-and-play components and hotwired an adapter for him. With his guidance, I connected a long extension cord to the robot and disconnected the building from the power grid. This kept the power from bleeding away into the larger system and allowed the robot to draw on power from the rooftop banks of solar panels.

With electricity going into the robot, Diogenes was in control of it and mobile—he had a body! He started working on the equivalent of wireless communications using the robot's hands. He also sent me off to run errands.

I checked in with Sir Sarron. Still connected and still, as far as we could tell, running at a one-to-one time ratio. I considered it excellent and thanked him for what was doubtless a terribly boring duty. He saluted.

I spent the rest of the day with my monomolecular-edged sword, cutting chunks off old cars—chunks with intact solar panels—and hauling them over to the Biology building. I also swiped their battery packs. They might not work perfectly, but some of them might still hold enough of a charge to be useful.

Bronze came with me, not to actually do anything, but to make the travel portion go more quickly and to stand guard while I carved the horseless carriages. After a brief break for sunset, we started scavenging much more quickly. We came across the equivalent of a pickup truck and it improved our efficiency even more—more cargo space. I loaded the stuff into it, Bronze pushed it, and we started collecting tons of salvage.

I also had the brilliant idea to look in the Engineering building. If there were any other mobile robots—not factory-type, fixed-mount things—Engineering was probably the place to look. I was right. Four robots of various sorts were waiting for me to rescue them, so I did, as well as liberating a selection of tools and materials for Diogenes to use. I also checked the high-energy physics lab on the theory they might have a utility robot for work in radiation environments. No such luck, but it was a good thought.

While considering what else Diogenes might need in order to find, refurbish, and activate the local cloning technology, it occurred to me he might have to venture out of the Biology building for materials I hadn't scrounged. While I might not get a car to work, Bronze and I could move them close so Diogenes could work on them. He might manage to salvage or repair parts from ten cars and get one working vehicle out of it. Failing that, he could at least take them apart and wagons for hauling things.

On one of our trips into town we also liberated some guns. We brought back quite a pile of the things, both old-fashioned bullet-throwers and ultramodern power-based versions. Again, this was with an eye to taking lots of them to pieces in order to get a few working ones. If the armored elephant or the serpentipede took it into their heads to destroy a robot, they probably could. I made it clear to Diogenes it was acceptable to defend himself and his appendages from the local wildlife. While he has some legal programming about people, pets, and property, most of it doesn't apply here—and in Karvalen, I'm an absolute monarch. He told me it wouldn't be a problem.

I went back to following his instructions regarding solar panels. The roof already had its solar power banks on-line and Diogenes was cleaning them with one of the bomb-disposal robots. The car-part panels we arranged on the ground and hoped nothing decided to step on them.

As morning first started to fade the curtain of night in the east, I left Diogenes to work. We had communications set up with all his robots. At this rate, he was ready to get busy establishing himself as the artificial intelligence overlord of the earth—as soon as the sun came up and gave him enough power to operate everything.

"Bring the ring gate over here when you can," I told him. "I'd like to be able to use it for communications."

"Will that not interfere with your use of it in conjunction with the library arch?"

"Yes, but you can take it back when I'm ready to come through."

"Perhaps I should simply station some audiovisual equipment in the library when I begin repairs on the library systems."

It shouldn't be humbling when the artificial intelligence is smarter than I am. In this case, however the idea was so darn obvious, I should have thought of it.

"Yes, that's probably best," I replied. "I'll call back when I can. While you need to establish yourself here in terms of power, equipment, and resources, the main objective is to study the feasibility of cloning."

"You got it, *jefe*."

"Thank you, Diogenes. Take care."

"And good luck to you, too."

Bronze took me back to the library. I connected the spell in the charged crystal I brought to the ring-and-arch system and mounted it on the gate's base. It could be useful on my next trip. I would probably bring another charged crystal to swap out with it, but in case something went wrong, whatever charge it accumulated in this desert of magic might be helpful.

I shut down the power jet on the library side of the gate. It would wear itself out if left to run—it wasn't the more complicated version that sucks up some of the power for itself. I didn't anticipate needing a long-term power jet. Fortunately, the spell could sit indefinitely, and I would rather use it to ensure a continuous connection than let it run itself out just to build a stored charge. Next time, I'd bring a better one.

I shifted wormholes from rings to arches and watched the expanding and contracting of the view, like some strange funhouse mirrors, wobbling in and out. It settled down and we waited those extra two seconds, just to be sure, before Sir Sarron, Bronze, and I stepped through.

My transformation instantly slammed me from dead to alive, a process normally taking several minutes.

Oops. Dawn. One second, let me switch days.

Thursday, March 11th

There we go.

Sir Lorodin had the presence of mind to shut down the archway. It's nice, having people who aren't afraid to take initiative.

While I lay there on the floor, gasping and retching, I reflected on the difficulties of a living existence when undergoing rapid transformations. Going from alive to undead isn't too big a deal—ridiculously uncomfortable, but it fixes itself in a few seconds. Living things, such as my daytime metabolism, take considerably longer to recover from having everything instantly jump-started. I imagine it's like having your heart restarted with a defibrillation machine, except it's every single organ, not just the heart, and all of them at once.

Yes, I know you can't restart a kidney with a defibrillator. I'm being descriptive, not technical.

I also considered how lucky I was to have already hung my helmet on Bronze's saddlehorn. The last thing I needed was to drown in my own vomit and bile because I couldn't get a helmet off. Depressing. Humiliating.

When my limbs felt ready to cooperate and my internal equilibrium seemed better than nonexistent, I climbed up on the edge of the central pool and rested there. Sarron and Lorodin helped me up. Lorodin scooped up some water for me. I rinsed and spat twice, then swallowed some. Thank goodness the mountain started circulating fresh water through the pool after I landed in it, way back when.

Again, dying is easy. Rising from the dead—at least, when it happens quickly—*sucks*. Maybe this is similar to how Mary felt when she started having a heartbeat during the daytime. My sympathies reached back in time to her.

Sarron and Lorodin wanted to send for more help, but I nixed the idea. I don't want a lot of traffic in and out of my private gate room. For one thing, the less traffic it sees, the less likely it is to be spotted by Johann, no matter how he keeps targeting me. Since Lorodin was still down here—obviously tired, but present— he hadn't sent for anyone; we might as well keep the place as low-traffic as possible.

When I felt stronger, I got out of my armor—again with help—and they cast cleaning spells on everything. I wasn't going to have transformational gunk crawl out around my neck again if I had a choice, especially while I was still nauseous. After that, both knights worked on a generalized healing spell or two for me. I hoped those would help sort out my internal troubles. I gave them a few minutes and felt them working nicely. Judging by the remains of the candle, I lay there for half an hour or so, trying to approach normal. Normal for me, anyway.

Once I felt reasonably restored—nauseous and weak, rather than retching and wrung out—I decided to have a word with the mountain. The inner surface of the room looked as though it might wind up as one big, irregular crystal. A crystal that size could hold a phenomenal charge, but it was also vulnerable to a single fracture. Crack the structure of the crystal and all the power would bleed away. A series of smaller crystals would be much better, and I let the mountain know it though a small message spell.

I wasn't really up to it. Doing even such minor work was tiring. I obviously needed some more time to recover. Still, what doesn't kill you at least annoys the hell out of you.

All in all, I'd say it was a successful trip.

Sarron and Lorodin switched off with a new pair of grey sashes right before lunch. I wasn't terribly hungry, but I forced myself to numb my sense of taste and smell so I could eat. It seemed to help settle my stomach and reduce the shaky, weak feeling in all my limbs. I wondered what my blood chemistry looked like, aside from unnatural.

A little after lunchtime, I was feeling more like walking wounded than wheelchair, so checked in with Lissette and got her answering service. On the plus side, the nobles are sorting themselves out in Carrillon and the Grand Conclave—their name for it—is shaping up. On the downside, I didn't actually get to talk to Lissette, and I get the impression this Grand Conclave is shaping up into a Huge Party.

I'm not overly pleased with the idea of a gigantic formal party, but Lissette couldn't come to the mirror because she was in the thick of organizing it. Still, what the Queen wants, the Queen gets. I'll have to tough it out like a good husband should. Besides, I want people to start thinking that way about the Queen. She's supposed to get her way.

More locally, the winners of the *sicaricudo* tournament were recuperating in the Temple of Shadow and should be back in top form within a few hours. We may be in Carrillon tonight!

Lotar, meanwhile, was relocated from his sealed-up room in the Palace to his deep-pit room under the Hall of Justice. I went along with the detachment of Guards in charge of the transfer and endured quite a lot of his shouting, insults, and basic frothing at the mouth. The prisoner transfer was otherwise uneventful. I guess it helps to do it secretly. If you don't announce the upcoming move, the remaining faithful don't have much time to organize.

The wizard Haran, meanwhile, came through for me. The ranking wizards in the Guild worked night and day to get it done, but they enchanted the lid on Lotar's new cell. Instead of a typical pivot-door, they had a thick brass grid in the shape of a circle. Across it, in a "V" shape, were two heavy bars. The ends of the V were hinges and the apex of the V had a place for a pin—or a padlock. The big circle was on the underside of the V and would fit into the floor, very much like an oversized manhole cover. The whole thing was too heavy for one man to lift even if it wasn't locked in place.

The enchantment was a basic disruption spell turned into a continuous wave— not an anti-magic area, since there was plenty of magic around, but an anti-spell area. The circular portion of the lid radiated pulses of magic designed to interfere with the formation and functioning of spells. Any spell reaching directly into the pit would be affected by it. It wasn't impossible to get a magical effect to manifest in the pit, but it would have to be something extraordinarily quick, between the spell-disrupting pulses. It was more likely someone would have to get the lid open in a mundane fashion before they could do anything magical to or around Lotar.

There's no such thing as a perfect prison, but you can always keep improving. This was pretty good. I complimented Haran on his efforts and thanked him. He seemed relieved or pleased or both. We still haven't sorted out whether the Wizards' Guild is a separate organization or a branch of the Crown's organization, but I think I'll let Lissette sort that one out.

Lotar did not want to go down the hole. He fought and struggled and I watched him fight and struggle. He didn't seem focused on the fight, really, but on me, shouting how I had no authority over the clergy and so on. The problem the guards faced was getting him down into the pit without harming him—a tricky operation with a deep pit and a man determined not to go quietly.

I had them hold Lotar for me. I moved behind him, put an arm around his neck despite his protests, and squeezed, compressing the arteries to the brain. It's a tricky thing to do, but, strangely, I seem to have a talent for knowing exactly where to find large blood vessels. Weird, isn't it?

Lotar went limp pretty quickly and I waited a few seconds to be sure. After that, they got him down the ladder in a hurry. Once they had the ladder out, I closed the brass grating myself. It was heavy, even for me, but maybe my weakened condition had something to do with it.

Success. I love success. Lotar was safely stowed away and unlikely to go anywhere. If he did, we had him on escaping custody charges, too. I made a note to mention it to the priests of the Lord of Law, just to be sure it was a crime to escape from custody. It seemed fair. If we lock you up for a crime, it's another crime to not stay locked up.

I headed back to the mountain, whistling cheerily, knowing I would have the mountain grow stone over the metal lid to hold it in place. They would still lock it, but his prison was literally set in stone.

If you have gathered the impression I don't like Lotar, you may be right. I don't like his religion, but Lotar's personal power grab is exceptionally offensive.

Of course, his religion is somewhat offensive, too, but I'm trying to minimize the theological.

Once back at the mountain, I strolled along the halls of the palace, taking my time on my way to see Seldar. Dantos' daughter, Caris, ran up to me and grabbed me by the knee. She's done it a number of times, usually alone, but today she brought new friends. One was a boy about her age, with a big grin behind a layer of dirt. He didn't grab me, but stayed right behind Caris when she did. He didn't say anything—too shy, perhaps—but the other one, Mikkel, gave his name when asked.

I conjured a ball of light for her, as usual. She didn't let go of me, but grabbed it one-handed, giggling. I whipped up two more and presented them to her friends. They took their toys. Mikkel remembered to bow. The nameless youngster mmediately ignored me to play with the light. Caris gnawed my knee affectionately before dashing off. The boys followed, paying more attention to the lights than to their feet.

I've gone through the rainbow like this with Caris and I've been working through various combinations, so the ball of light now cycles between two colors. It amuses her and allows me to walk without a child sitting on my foot, arms and legs locked around my lower leg. If she's going to bring friends, I hope I'm not about to need hundreds of the things just to get from the front door to my bedroom.

Then I wondered. The interior of the mountain is exceptionally clean. Dust and dirt in the undercity tend to merge into the floor and vanish, becoming part of the mountain in a sort of geological circle of life. How did her friend get so dirty? Is it a supernatural ability of small children? It gave me a mystery to ponder on the way to see Seldar.

When I walked in, a high-ranking official from the Church of Light was in conference with him. I could tell from the fancy hat and the embroidery on the chest of his robes. It was a sun-face, rather than a fist of light, so he wasn't (or wasn't admitting to being) a member of the Hand.

"Oh, I didn't realize you were busy," I told them. "I'll see you later."

"Please, Your Majesty," Seldar pleaded, "do join us. I was explaining to Prelate Calsion about the difficulties Lotar faces." Seldar added, under his breath, "Again." Even during the day, I have exceptionally sharp ears; I don't think Calsion heard it.

"I cannot continue this discussion in the presence of an abomination," Prelate Calsion stated.

I looked him over. He was a tall, spare man with a lantern jaw and bushy eyebrows. The wrinkles in his face said he didn't smile much and had kept busy not smiling for fifty years or so. He wore no rings and seemed unarmed.

"Are you refusing to speak with a king?" I asked, pleasantly. I moved into the room and seated myself at the table. "I know you're a priest—some sort of high-ranking priest—but don't you think refusing a king to his face, in his own palace, is a trifle... unwise?"

"It matters not what you call yourself. You are a blood-drinking monster from beyond the world, a creature of chaos, darkness, and death. Your kind is the embodiment of evil and must be purged by fire and slaughter."

"Strong language," I observed. "Are you telling me it's the intent of your Church to see me slaughtered and burned to ashes?"

"It is the intent of all right-thinking people," he countered. "All who fail to oppose you are doing the work of evil."

"Impressive. Most people don't announce their intent to murder a king in the presence of his bodyguards—you idiot." I turned to Seldar. "Has he been like this the whole time?"

"We were discussing the merits of a religious argument in Lotar's sentencing," Seldar replied. "I maintain responsibility must fall to the actor or the organization, not upon the god. He maintains Lotar was doing the work of the Lord of Light and, therefore, cannot be held accountable."

"I see. Do you have that crystal with the recording?"

"I—why, yes, Sire. Shall I fetch it?"

"Please do. I'll entertain your guest while we wait."

Seldar left. Calsion obviously wanted to leap to his feet and flee the room with him, but didn't want to appear undignified or fearful. We wound up sitting in awkward silence—awkward for him. I didn't mind. I put my feet up on the table and traded snide remarks with Firebrand about Calsion.

"Oh," I said, after a time, "I feel I should point out Lotar is still alive and well. He's merely been imprisoned, not executed. The priestess of the Lady of Mercy was most persuasive."

"I am surprised you listened, monster king."

"You're being rude," I pointed out. "Also, I don't think you understand the new system. I didn't have anything to do with his trial. I left it to the judicial board, the *pentatio*." I explained the process and the roles of the various religious orders. "So you see, I wasn't involved."

"You arranged it for show and instructed them on the correct verdict," he sneered. I shrugged.

"Believe what you want. I don't expect you to be intelligent and rational."

"What do you mean by *that*?"

"See? I was right. I think I was very clear."

"The light will reveal your misdeeds," he declared.

"First, you'll have to turn away from it. It blinds you to the truth."

"Clever monster."

"Clever king, please. I don't usually insist on the full formalities in small groups, but with you, I insist on every single one, mainly because you're being a jerk."

"I have no desire to indulge you, dark creature."

"Okay. Call me anything besides 'Your Majesty' again and I'll have you stripped naked and locked in a dungeon for ten days of bread and water." He opened his mouth to say something and I sprang up, slapped my hands on the table, and leaned over at him. "Yes?" I snapped. "Go on. Say it! Say the smart-assed thing on your lips. Test me. See if I'll actually have you thrown naked into a cell for ten days. Go on! *Find out!*"

Calsion glanced behind me. I felt my two bodyguards move up, ready to grab him at my word. He also glanced down at the table. My shadow was leaning farther forward than I was, hands outstretched toward him.

He elected to keep quiet.

I was amazed at how disappointed I was. I really wanted to slap him around and throw him in a cell. Instead, I sat down again. We waited for Seldar to return in silence. Our conversation died and I couldn't find it in myself to mourn.

When Seldar came in, he placed a small box before me on the table. I opened it and drew out one of the crystals.

"Now, then," I began. "Originally, we were going to display these inside various temples of the Lord of Light, showing the clergy what Lotar was up to and allowing your Church to handle the matter internally. That idea fell through, however, when he raised up an armed rebellion within my city. It became a public matter, a civic one—one thoroughly and firmly in the realm of the King."

I activated the crystal's playback and let Calsion watch as Lotar and I spoke about deals, murder, purges, and treason. I didn't think it would do any good. Calsion struck me as the "Right or wrong, I've decided!" type. There's always some sort of explanation or excuse or spin doctoring to make facts conform with belief.

"This wizardry is mere illusion, a cheap sham to slander a member of the faithful!"

Case in point.

I looked at Seldar. Seldar shrugged.

"He's not going to listen," I told him. "He's washed his brain and I can't do a thing with it. Talk to him all you want, but throw him out of Karvalen before nightfall. At sunset, he's banished from the city. Any other representative of the Lord of Light who shows up to discuss anything else is welcome to drop by, but the moment they bring up Lotar's case, the conversation is concluded and the person is banished—throw him out immediately. Understood?"

"Understood, Sire."

I stood up; Seldar stood up. Calsion stared at me.

"You are not serious!"

"Buster, you're lucky you're not facing execution just from your personal rudeness to the King. From what I understand, most monarchs think in terms of beheadings, boilings, and beatings. *I'm* the *nice* one!"

"He is," Seldar added, seriously.

"I strongly suggest you send someone with more tact," I continued, "because *you* will never be allowed in this palace again. Warn the next guy. Failing to be respectful and polite in the presence of the King is punishable by what we discussed—naked, in a cell, bread and water, ten days. Believe."

"I will brook no commands from a demon-spawned monster of blood!"

I sighed heavily and shook my head.

"Why is it no one ever *listens*?" I asked, rhetorically.

I signaled my guards. They grabbed him. One stuck three gauntleted fingers in Calsion's mouth to shut him up, the thumb hooked under to get a grip on the jaw.

"I know I mentioned the part about naked, a cell, bread and water, ten days," I told him. "You obviously didn't believe me. Seldar. Have him stripped naked, thrown in a deep, dark cell somewhere, fed on bread and water, and then banish him after he's been in there ten days. I have spoken."

"Indeed, Sire," Seldar agreed, and summoned guards to make it happen.

I don't think Seldar enjoyed talking with the man. I know I didn't. I also wondered how much of a thorn in my side the Lord of Light and his Knuckleheads—excuse me, the Hand—were going to be. Calsion would go home, eventually. I doubted his report would be favorable, but it might, at the very least, encourage the more diplomatic of the faithful to go on diplomatic missions.

I checked in with Sedrick. He answered almost immediately.

"Ah, Your Majesty. So good to see you."

"And good to see you, too. How goes the exploration?"

"Kamshasa is quite warm, somewhat unpleasant, and thoroughly frustrating."

"I expected it to be hotter than here, but how is it unpleasant and frustrating?"

"I am a man and a foreigner. The fact I am roaming without a writ of travel from some official dame offends the citizens and causes trouble for me. They do not like that I do not fit within their rigid demarcations of what a man may or may not do. It has been... slow going. With resistance and prejudice and trouble almost every step of the way."

"At least you're not in jail."

"Not at the moment."

"Were you?" I asked, surprised. "Or are you anticipating?"

"I was, briefly. Fortunately, your name carries some weight even across the Circle Sea. Do not be too shocked if you are queried by a matriarch of one of the Great Houses."

"I'll try to maintain my aplomb," I assured him. "What's a Great House?"

"I'm not sure, but I have heard them mentioned."

"Fair enough. I'll bother T'yl."

"Whatever you find, please relay it to me. I feel I may need to know more before I can be effective as your agent in this place."

"I'll see what I can find out. In fact, I'll call him as soon as we're done. Do you want to stay there, or should I bring you home?"

"I am reasonably comfortable at the moment. Let us discover what we may from T'yl before you exert yourself on my behalf."

"I'll call him now."

"Thank you."

We disconnected and I dialed up the mirror T'yl used to call me. Most people don't get the concept of caller ID, but I'm not from around here. Maybe that's why the man who answered seemed surprised to see me. At least, he made a strangled squeaking noise and his eyes tried to leap out of his head.

"Good afternoon. Is T'yl available? Don't interrupt if he's involved in something, but I'd like to speak with him as soon as is convenient."

"He's, yes, he's… as soon… yes, of course. Your Majesty. Of course, Your Majesty. One moment, Your Majesty." He finished his stammering and hurried off. I sat back comfortably, chair creaking, and refreshed my healing spell. I was mostly recovered from my sudden transformation, but I wanted to see how long it took to get back to a hundred percent. All day, apparently. Without magic to help, I would probably want bed rest for the day. Note for the future: Avoid sudden time-zone changes from night to day. Dying is easy. Un-dying is hard.

The image in the mirror transferred from one mirror to another. The view flickered wildly for a moment before stabilizing. It was a radically different perspective, obviously through a hand-mirror. T'yl held it, looking into it and frowning his frown of concentration. His face relaxed as the image steadied.

"Majesty."

"Magician."

"I'm told you wanted to see me?"

"Yes, please. I hope I'm not interrupting anything?"

"No, we're just on our way to see you."

"It looks as though you're in a white room."

"This is a cloudship spell. It's a comfortable way to get around and moderately speedy. We're passing over the Eastrange even now and should be in Karvalen within the hour. Do you mind if we make landfall in the upper courtyard?"

"Not at all. Be my guest."

"Thank you. Now, how can I help you?"

"I have an agent poking around Kamshasa, trying to find things out for me, but I've obviously goofed. He's a man in what I understand is a matriarchal society, but it seems to go a lot deeper than merely saying the women run the place."

As I spoke, T'yl's lip curled.

"I fear you may have doomed your agent," T'yl told me. "Men, even foreign men, are regarded as slightly above slaves and a trifle below horses."

"He's a Hero."

"He's a—hmm. He might manage, at least for a while. One underestimates a professional Hero only at great peril. I must still strongly suggest removing him from Kamshasa, however."

"That's why I called. I need your advice and all the information on Kamshasa you can give me."

T'yl nodded and set the mirror down carefully, angling it to keep it upright. He looked upward and steepled his fingers in thought.

"Are you sitting comfortably?" he asked.

"It's a surprisingly sturdy chair."

T'yl started talking. I listened.

Kamshasa is a matriarchal elitist oligarchy, if that's not redundant, as well as being a magocracy. Women are the only ones permitted to study magic. Officially, they're the only ones permitted any formal education, or even *literacy*. The ruling council is composed—in theory—of the heads of the nine Great Houses, and makes decisions for the nation as a whole, with semi-autonomy for each of the Great Houses in their internal matters. The autonomy of each House borders on total independence. The nation might be better described as an alliance of nine states with similar cultural values and strong sense of keeping up with the Joneses.

Succession within the Houses is theoretically based on line of descent, but also on challenges. An only daughter might take over as the Matriarch of the House, but if there are multiple daughters vying for the position—or a sister to the former Matriarch—there might be a magical duel, possibly a free-for-all, to determine who would take the title. The exact details vary from House to House.

Officially, the Matriarch of each House has a seat on the ruling council of Kamshasa. In practice, Matriarchs are more concerned with their own power and position relative to the other Houses, so the council seat is often filled by someone sent to wield that authority. Whether this was to get a troublesome up-and-comer away from the House, or to provide valuable political experience to a favored heir, or some other rationale is impossible to say without knowing the details of the power structure within a given House—and they are as guarded about their House workings as a gambler with his cards.

"So, let me ask a question," I interrupted. "When you say the individual Houses have a lot of autonomy and the Council in Kamshasa is somewhat less than a strong central government, does that mean the attacks by Kamshasa on Rethven and Karvalen were done by the Council or by some House?"

"By a House," T'yl replied. "Getting a majority of the Council to agree to anything—and then getting their Matriarchs to agree, separately—is as likely as moonrise at noon. It's not impossible, but the world may well be ending."

"Okay. I just want to be sure I understand. We haven't actually had a coordinated attack from the nation of Kamshasa. We've had... oh... some duchy or other of Kamshasa come after us."

"That is a fair assessment," he agreed. "If they ever learned to trust each other and work together, they would be a formidable force in the world. As it is, they bicker and fight amongst themselves too much to be more than an occasional thorn in one's paw."

"Got it. Go on."

While men in Kamshasa are seldom allowed any sort of general education, they are almost always masters of a single skill set. Tinker, tailor, soldier, sailor, they're trained from an early age to be whatever it is their mothers—Masters? Mistresses? *De facto* owners—want them to be. Rarely, they demonstrate a complete ineptitude for whatever it is and get switched to something else, but they usually have to stick it out and do the best they can.

This raised questions in my mind, but I grew up in a society where mothers loved all their children. Not so in Kamshasa, apparently. Girl-children are a delight and a blessing. Boy-children are either useful or inconvenient. What kind of a society devalues one gender or another to such a degree that one is merely a necessary evil, rather than a child to be cherished?

I'm sure their society evolved in such a manner for good and valid reasons. Of course, a drug pusher on a playground is also there for good and valid reasons. Personally, I'll subdivide the drug pusher and flush him down the sewer; I abhor his actions and the reasons for them. I'm not sure about Kamshasa, yet.

One of the other things that failed to recommend the place to me was the rigidity of the populace. People were assigned to their village, their residence, and their occupation. They were forbidden to travel, change houses, change jobs—pretty much anything—without a writ authorizing it from someone of sufficiently high rank within their House. Women had a relatively easy time of it, at least according to T'yl. He made it sound like doing any of that was no worse than getting a driver's license.

On the other hand, men were regarded as property—yes, sometimes certain specimens were valuable property—and had all the rights and privileges of such. Sending one of your men off to deliver a message, a load of goods, or whatever? It better be within your city or town; any farther will require a writ of permission. And he better not be out, roaming around unsupervised after dark! You'll have to come get him at the jail or identify the body, depending on who found him and where.

Frankly, I didn't see how their society functioned at all. Then I remembered it's a *magical* matriarchal elitist oligarchy. With sufficiently powerful and skilled magical people in positions of power, it might be possible to force it to work. Add in strict controls on education and propaganda and it could be done. Obviously, with nine Great Houses squabbling amongst themselves, it wasn't a particularly well-run tyranny, but it might be nine moderately-effective tyrannies calling themselves a nation.

Just the sort of place people wanted to go, obviously. No wonder Tort picked it as a hideout. Anyone who hated the Demon King—and there were a lot of them, I gathered—would also have a hard time hunting her down there. Me, too.

"All right," I finally agreed. "I think I have a better picture of what I'm dealing with. Do you have any suggestions?"

"If you want agents in Kamshasa, you'll need women to do it," T'yl replied, almost sneering. "Men won't be taken seriously and, lacking a mistress, may even be killed out of hand. A woman can't even be executed without at least some time and trouble to get it approved."

"Right. I'll see what I can come up with. Meanwhile, how are your experiments going?"

"Since our last conversation, we have not had time to continue those researches in any meaningful way. It is hoped we can persuade you to show us the technique, or at least answer some questions."

"I can walk you through it, sure. Not with a real body, of course, but you're welcome to watch an illusory reconstruction."

"That will help," T'yl assured me.

"Happy to oblige. I'll see you in a bit."

Sedrick and his horses came into my public gate room with a hot, tropical breeze. I kept a sharp mystical eye out for scrying gateways and similar magic. Sedrick brought along a new dog. It looked like some sort of short-haired collie. I didn't ask what happened to the other dog; I wasn't sure if it was polite to bring it up.

I greeted Sedrick, made friends with the dog—Tak—and sent for someone to take care of his horses. They were dusty and sweaty and needed a good rubdown. Sedrick placed the reins directly in the hands of the man who came for the horses. Sedrick patted his horse on the neck, soothingly, as he did so. After that, the warhorse went with the groom and the pack horse followed. Tak stayed with us, sticking close to Sedrick but looking about alertly and with great interest in everything.

"How goes the quest?" I asked.

"Hot, somewhat dusty, and humiliating," he replied, wiping his brow. "Might we enjoy the luxuries of the baths while we talk?"

"I have spells for cleaning, if you like."

"As do I. I enjoy the baths here, however. If you are not opposed."

"I don't know if I'm opposed. I don't recall having used them in recent years. Where are they, exactly?"

We went down to one of the public bath areas. They're not as popular as they could be. The main baths in the undermountain are built for a couple hundred people at a time, but public bathing isn't a Rethven custom—or wasn't. It's catching on as a Karvalen custom, at least in the segregated baths in the undermountain, mainly because there aren't any private bathrooms. The baths do see regular use, but I doubt they're ever at capacity. I can't say I blame them; public bathing isn't my preference, either. But if Sedrick wants a bath and is cosmopolitan enough to enjoy the things, can I really do anything but pretend I'm delighted? I would feel even more awkward letting him borrow my bathroom while we talked.

Still, private baths... How complicated would the water system become in providing a private bath to every set of living quarters? Is it a question of complexity, or is it a question of water flow? The water in the bathrooms is a constant-flow arrangement. If it had to be running all the time, how much water would one private bathroom take? Or ten thousand bathrooms? Is it even practical to have private baths? Or is it necessary to have big, public ones? I suspect the determining factor is the water flow, based on my previous linkages with my pet rock.

We continued with small talk as we walked down. Upon entering the wash chamber—waterfalls for scrubbing before entering the main bath chamber and the big pool—Sedrick stripped down entirely unselfconsciously and rinsed a lot of Kamshasa off. Tak, the dog, also rinsed and shook a few times. I felt awkward standing around fully dressed, so I went along with it. It's a social pressure thing. On the plus side, it might encourage others to use the public baths if word got around the King occasionally dropped in.

On second thought, *would* it encourage people? On this side of the Eastrange, probably so. I suspect there may be some cultural differences in the kingdom, primarily based on geography. California is not like Maine, Alaska is not like Florida, yet they're all part of the same country.

After the preliminary rinse, we entered the main bathchamber with its heated soaking pool. One of the features of the main pool is the curvy edge. It isn't divided into smaller pools, but it does have dents in it, like curved booths in a restaurant. You can find one to suit your party, from two to twenty, and settle down for a long discussion of whatever takes your fancy. The water comes in at the center of the pool, spouting out of a stone fountain—lots of horses, for some reason. An array of tiny holes in the outer rim allow the water to drain behind the bathers. There's always a gradual flow away from the center to the edge, into your little nook, keeping the water warm and fresh.

There are other, more specialized bath rooms—one for sauna, one for swimming, even one for the masochists who enjoy frigidly cold or ridiculously hot water. Personally, I'll stick to the oversized hot tub.

Sedrick and I settled by the rim of the pool, our personal bundles behind our heads, at the edge. As we did so, a couple of ladies approached and knelt by the edge. They wore tight-fitting things around their breasts and hips, kind of like a cross between bandages and bikinis. Judging by the way they wore their hair— ponytails, rather than loose, braids, or *wriage*-hair-bag-things—and their minimalist garments, they were for hire in almost any capacity. When they asked if there was anything we might desire, Sedrick gave them a few silver coins and instructions. One started working on his shoulders and arms, the other lowered herself into the water, sat down slightly away from him, and massaged his feet.

It's my kingdom, sure, but I simply don't understand the place as well as I should. When did this start? Probably shortly after the public baths were built. I looked around the bath and spotted quite a number of knights relaxing in the water, too—most of whom had a lady assisting him in his relaxing. Massage, mostly, but there were ladies in similar outfits fetching food and drink, too. I wondered if there were side chambers for more intimate activities. Probably so. From my mergers with the mountain, I seemed to recall quite a complex of rooms centered on the baths. Was a training room or gymnasium nearby, too? I think so.

"Would you like one?" Sedrick asked. "They're very good."

"No, but thank you. I almost never carry cash."

"My treat, Sire."

"No, no—I'd rather stay focused on the matter at hand."

"Of course." Sedrick went on to tell me what he learned about Kamshasa, confirming several things T'yl told me. On the upside, he did find Kashmanir, on the eastern edge of Kamshasa. It was ruled by the House of Oloné and bordered a foreign nation, the Kingdom of Kolob.

"The border is not contested, precisely, but certainly well-guarded," he went on. "I suspect it would be a simple matter for a man to enter Kolob, but it is quite another matter for a man to depart Kamshasa."

"The one will let you in if the other will only let you out?"

"There you have it."

"It's nice to know someone doesn't like Kamshasa besides me."

"I think most of the world at least disapproves of it," Sedrick assured me, stretching out as both ladies started working on his calves.

"Half of it, certainly," I agreed.

"I regret, however, I have not yet found the place..." he trailed off for a moment, then finished, "...you instructed me to find."

"It's okay. I'll get an address eventually. Just having it narrowed down is a good start."

"As you say," he agreed, nodding. "If you have a noblewoman willing to accompany me, I am willing to return. I feel certain a foreign woman will be able to accomplish more than any man, foreign or domesticated."

"I understand. I'm not sure I have one on hand. I'd send Malana or Malena or both, but they're Lissette's personal guards and I don't want to presume. Tyma, maybe—she's sharp as they come, but she's got an axe to grind in preparation for beheading me." I thought for a bit. "No, I don't think I have anyone."

"A pity. Still, a Hero does love a challenge."

"That reminds me. I wanted to ask you something about Hero-ing."

"Of course, Your Majesty."

"What, exactly, do you *do*?"

"I beg your pardon?"

"I mean, I get the idea about you going out and finding something awful and killing it. Righting wrongs, defending the weak, and so on. But what do you actually do? How does it work?"

Sedrick grinned at me and I noticed he was missing a tooth on the upper left, just behind the canine. I suddenly had the feeling he was a much more dangerous thrill-seeker than I previously believed.

"What I do," he began, still grinning, "is wander around, listen to rumors, and look for trouble. Sometimes I find it."

"How often? I mean, is it really a full-time job?"

"I can spend days, even weeks between adventures," he admitted, and dismissed his masseuses. They looked somewhat pouty, but sloshed up out of the pool and went off to find another customer. "Some troubles are simple, easy to correct. A robber or two, perhaps a bit of theft or rape, and I find the culprit to deal with him." He shrugged. "The local guardsmen are often more concerned with whether or not the offense was against the local lord or one of the wealthier members of the community. Common folk are less rewarding as victims, but safer."

"I understand. They also don't pay well."

"I have been paid in food and services before. Sometimes with a bit of copper or silver, to boot. And anything I salvage from a robber—not including anything stolen—is mine."

"Seems fair."

"Then there are times," he continued, looking at something far away, "when I find rumor of a challenge worthy of a Hero. One that will be remembered forever in song and story. There isn't much in the day-to-day of being a Hero, but for those few occasions when you find a real need for one... those are worth all the lesser days."

"For example?" I prompted.

"Well, *you*, not to put it too bluntly." He grinned again. "Or so I thought. Monsters. Magical beasts. Demons. Dragons." He sighed. "What I wouldn't give for the opportunity to do battle with a dragon."

Firebrand started to say something, but bit it back, for which I was duly grateful.

"I do thank you for all your work, Sedrick. And I want you to understand, if you find something you need to do, go ahead. All I ask is if you're on a mission for me, please report in before you detour to pursue something Hero-worthy."

"Of course, Your Majesty. Cash customers are hard to come by in this business, and I thank you for your understanding."

"I thank you for being so helpful to a monster."

"And a king," he added, smiling. "You're not so very monstrous."

The dog, Tak, made a half-growl, half-bark. We looked where Tak looked and saw a human with a strong elvish cast to his features. T'yl. A pair of men accompanied him, one to either side, and the three of them were dripping wet. They all carried their personal items wrapped in clothing.

"Gentleman, Majesty," he said, stopping at the edge of the pool. "May we join you?"

"Of course," I agreed. As they stepped down into the water to find their seats, I introduced Sir Sedrick and T'yl. "I'm afraid I don't know your companions."

"These are two Magicians of Arondael. This is Norad and this is Morrelin."

I think I kept a straight face at the mention of the magician "Norad." The North American Aerospace Defense Command was something entirely different, but I bet they'd love to have a professional magician on staff. I've encountered this a couple of times before. People have names in their language that sound like words in mine. But this threatened to kick giggles out of me. I'm weird, I admit. Norad.

"I'm pleased to meet you," I said. They both bowed from the neck, since we were sitting chest-deep in water. "Tell me, do you have any specialties? Anything you're particularly good at?"

"Most magicians do," Norad told me. I decided to take it as gospel. If Norad says so...

"Really? Why is that? Having only a moderate education in wizardry, I'm naturally curious."

"There is too much to study in one lifetime," he informed me, pulling his long, black hair back from his face to tie it. "Most magicians encounter something to excite their interest in the course of their apprenticeships and they pursue the study of it in their later years."

"Is that what the Academy does? It has lots of magicians researching their own fields of interest?"

"It's true, some devote themselves to study for most of their lives. More often, by the time we achieve the rank of Magician, we are more interested in using what we have learned."

"I've never thought of it before," I admitted. "It does make sense. May I ask your specialty? Or is it an improper question?"

"Not at all improper, Your Majesty. I am a necromancer. Morrelin is a healer."

"Fascinating. And appropriate, I think, for what we're trying to do."

"I've been trying to heal the age in people," Morrelin said. He was hard to describe, being remarkably average. Unremarkable brown hair, faded brown eyes, regular features, the works. I was willing to bet he could be overlooked almost anywhere. Often, it's a useful ability. "I cannot repair the damage, only offset the symptoms. Elderly people feel less pain, feel stronger, and live longer, but I cannot seem to undo the subtler effects. I've been looking at the spell T'yl has for splitting age, transferring it as it happens, but it does not turn back the years, only slows them."

"Morrelin is modest," T'yl told me. "He's already had an idea for a spell to stop aging, at least while the spell is in effect. Give us a few years and some time to work out the enchantment and we'll be producing amulets to keep you from getting any older."

"That's unlikely," Morrelin protested. "The spells I use likewise slow the effects—" he continued, but Norad laughed at him.

"You say that now, but we'll do it. Hopefully within our lifetimes. Then we can work on reversing age, rather than temporarily transferring it to some other vessel." Norad turned to me. "I am terribly eager to see this technique, Your Majesty, of transferring the soul from one body to another. May I presume to ask when would be convenient?"

"Sedrick?" I asked. "We're going to do a lot of esoteric magic. Do you want to watch?"

"If it is all the same to you, my lord, I need only some food and drink to consider this the perfect place to rest."

"I'll have something sent over," I promised. "Magicians? Shall we repair to the laboratory?"

I didn't have to ask them twice. Water surged.

I get the feeling they didn't mind the public bath, but they had other priorities. Can't say I blame them.

We spent the rest of the day in a virtual reality of my design. It was an illusion, really, drawing on memories of the time I stuffed an elf with T'yl.

Wow. That sounds dirty.

A lot of the illusion was crude, little more than lines and diagrams, with a few bits and pieces in high resolution, drawn from memory instead of imagination. It was really a lot like being inside a three-dimensional, holographic canvas. I drew lines in the air, created shapes, connected bits into diagrams, animated arrows—I wish I'd thought of this sooner. I wish I'd *had* this when I was teaching freshman physics. There's nothing quite like a visual aid.

"So, what do you do about the other linkages?" Morrelin asked.

"There are a hundred and eight important ones," I told him, highlighting them in the diagram of an empty body. "Once these are connected, the rest seem to manage on their own. The big ones are what I think of as vital. If you have one disconnected, it's going to end badly, kind of like having a major blood vessel cut open. Energy from the spirit 'bleeds out' into the environment until the spirit disintegrates. The smaller ones are like a cut in your skin. You put the soul into the flesh, connect it, and the... the 'minor cuts,' so to speak, take care of themselves."

"But you can connect the smaller ones, too?" Norad asked.

"Yes, but there are hundreds or thousands of them. It's probably not worth the effort to connect them all, but maybe we can come up with something to act like a bandage. It would minimize the losses from the 'minor cuts,' so to speak."

"You went to some effort with T'yl, did you not?" he pressed.

"Yes, but I also wasn't sure if it was necessary or not. I didn't connect them all, remember. He did most of that on his own."

"I see."

"What else can I tell you?" I asked.

"I have another question," Norad replied. "As a necromancer, I see some potential problems. How do we get the soul out of the body? And how do we identify the soul-connections you describe? We do not see spirits in the way you do, of course. I think we may need to. If we cannot see them, how are we to tie them into the... the mounting points you've shown us?"

"That's a very good question," I agreed, "and I wish I had a good answer for you. Getting the soul out really isn't an issue, if you think about it. They come loose naturally as the body can no longer contain it. As for the actual transfer... as you say, it's easy for me; I can see the things. You're going to need a new spell to observe the actual process."

"I'm not sure this is a practical method of immortality," Norad mused. "I do not feel we can comfortably cast a hundred and eight binding spells to connect them to the receptacle body. I am not certain any single magician can cast so many spells quickly enough to avoid dissolution of the subject spirit."

"Oh! I'm sorry; I don't think I explained the differences in technique. You probably don't have to connect all hundred and eight at once," I told him. "My original problem was getting T'yl out of a crystal, not a living body. He was static, unchanging, possibly even brittle. Anything I changed in there was probably going to break his spirit and kill him. But lifting him out, all in one piece, and putting him in a place where he could operate normally—that was far more complicated than a gradual shifting from one living receptacle to another!

"Think of it this way," I went on. "If you have a washtub full of water, you can move it from one washtub to another one bucketful at a time. The water, once moved, isn't hurt. But if one washtub has a sheet of ice over it, how do you move the water and the ice without cracking the ice? It's a more complicated and difficult maneuver.

"In your case, you're still alive. Moving you or Morrelin is the one bucket at a time problem. You can probably manage this for each other—at worst, you might need a helper. Unplug a connector inside your flesh, plug it into the same spot in the new body, and keep repeating until its done. Obviously, you don't want to do this yourself, but with a couple of friends it should be pretty easy."

"And will this process be painful?" Morrelin asked. "Pain is often a terrible stress on a body, even if the pain is purely spiritual. Can a body—especially the original, presumably ancient body—be killed too soon via this procedure?"

"Hmm. Another good question. I really don't know," I admitted.

"Yet, you feel certain this one-by-one method will work?"

"Reasonably certain. I'd be surprised if it didn't."

"I understand." Norad and Morrelin looked at each other and moved off to discuss. T'yl, our part-time laboratory model, hopped up from the table and sat in a chair next to me.

"You are surprisingly good at this," he told me.

"I'm a vampire. I deal with flesh and spirit all the time."

"No, I mean you are good at explaining things."

"I have stunning visual aids. And I used to be a teacher."

"Did you?" he asked, eyebrows rising. "I did not know that. Or if I did, I've forgotten."

"It's true. I taught… well, I taught a different style of magic in my younger days." I remembered being in front of a class and looking them over, picking out by eye the ones taking a class because it was a requirement for something else, the ones with an interest, and the ones who would drop the class within the week. After a few semesters of teaching, you could tell. "It seems a long time ago," I reflected.

"My days of teaching at the Academy were also a long time ago," T'yl admitted. "Aside from a few private lessons, I've given up teaching. I suspect I lack the talent."

"I sometimes lack the patience," I admitted. "Answering the same questions, over and over, really starts to wear."

"It does. You might try taking an apprentice and teaching everything you know, then finding another one. By then, the same old questions will be so long ago, they become new."

"I've got one," I told him. "She's off running an errand at the moment."

"Ah, Mary, your concubine."

"That's her. But she would object to being called a concubine. Try to keep in mind she's a consort."

"Of course. Of course."

Norad and Morrelin rejoined us.

"We think," Morrelin said, "we could do this, but we will need help in devising a way to see, manipulate, and join the channels of the soul. Would Your Majesty consent to assist us in this?"

"Sure. We can work out something. If all else fails, I might be able to automate the process."

"Automate?"

"Make something to do it without requiring a lot of skill?" I tried. "For example, imagine two beds. Put an empty body on one side and an elderly body on the other. The bed with the elderly body identifies the soul-strands, pulls them tight, wraps them around the mounting points in the empty body, then cuts the soul free. Now it's mounted to the body next to it, rather than the one it's actually in, and migrates over. The lesser strands get stretched across the intervening distance and a magical scalpel blade cuts them, slowly. This severs the last connection with the original body and allows a few lesser strands at a time to lock on to the new one. Now the soul is in its new home and can settle in."

The three magicians traded looks, combining eagerness, concern, and fear.

"What?" I asked.

"You are describing one of the darker artifacts of the Empire," T'yl told me.

"Am I? I made this up on the spot, thinking about how to make the process easier."

"I believe you, but perhaps we might wish to consider how such an artifact would be viewed."

"Like something built by the Demon King?" I guessed.

"There are many who still think of you that way," T'yl admitted. Norad and Morrelin said nothing, trying for inscrutable and mostly succeeding.

"I get it. Well, the double-bed idea requires an empty body in the first place. I don't have a supply of empty elves, but I'm working on it."

"Yes, I was told you mentioned something about it. May one inquire?" Norad asked.

"I'm hoping to grow elves."

"Like trees?"

"Sort of, I guess, but faster. The point being, I think I can... how to put this? I can enchant a box to do what a woman does, growing a baby. If I then put a piece of an elf in the box, it will grow the piece into a whole new elf, but without anyone inside it. Then we can take the elf out—the empty elf—and you can put someone into it."

"I see," he answered, faintly. "This sounds impossible, but if you think it can be done..." he trailed off.

"I get that a lot. People like to use the word 'impossible' when they don't understand something. I'm confident it can be done," I assured him. "I started the project to help out my elf servants. They have a hard time reproducing, as I'm sure you know."

"No, I didn't know," Norad admitted.

"I've heard something about it," Morrelin said. "They steal pregnant women, I believe, for their babies?"

"That's right. But don't worry about it. If I get this working right, I'm pretty sure you can have all the immortal elf-bodies you want and the elves can stop swiping human females. Speaking of which," I turned to T'yl. "Everything still working well for you?"

"Eminently satisfactory, Your Majesty. I've made a few alterations for cosmetic reasons—those are ongoing, as you can see—but the basic structure seems to be working perfectly."

"Good. You're the first one to do this, so if you notice anything unusual, you let me know immediately, all right? I don't want to find out you're actually aging on the inside, but you ignored little aches and pains, thinking them unimportant."

"I would be most upset by this, myself," T'yl assured me. "I will be ever-vigilant."

"Thanks. Now, gentlemen, if you will follow…" I gestured to one of my current bodyguards.

"Sir Brannon," he supplied.

"Sir Brannon, he will show you to guest quarters."

"Gentlemen?" Sir Brannon inquired. "This way, please."

Once they were gone, I went to my own quarters. Sunset was starting and I wanted to be under a waterfall for it. Messengers followed me the moment I set foot outside the lab, though. Torvil wanted to know when we were headed to Carrillon. Beltar wanted to know if he could come along. Seldar wanted a meeting with me and with Dantos to settle the arrangements for Karvalen while both I and the Baron were away.

I sent the messengers back with replies. We would probably be going through later tonight. Yes, Beltar could come with us. If Seldar and Dantos would meet me in my chambers, we could have that meeting.

Mirrors are a fine and dandy thing for communications. If you want to talk to someone, they're fast. They're immediate. Messengers, on the other hand, will go out and find someone even if they don't have a mirror. They also have a built-in delay, which is sometimes handy. If you don't want to interrupt, send a messenger. He won't mind waiting. It beats running around, trying to track down the recipient.

And, from my point of view, it's sometimes very handy to send someone instead of call. It gives me a chance to do things before they even get the message, much less respond. I got through sunset that way.

One of the absolute best things about being an undead monster is the regeneration. I didn't realize how awful I still felt until my regeneration fixed it all. An unseen weight lifted off me. My insides relaxed, letting loose the tight-wound tension they'd had most of the day. The headache sitting behind my eyes and just under my ears vanished.

I've never been so happy to be dead. Those lightning-fast resurrections are *awful*. No wonder there's a three-day wait for non-undead. It takes that long just to recover from the onset of life.

After rinsing thoroughly and toweling off, I dressed again and came out to meet with Seldar and Dantos. Seldar wanted to come along to Carrillon and leave Dantos in charge of Karvalen.

"Dantos? What do you think?" I asked.

"My lord, I am willing to do whatever you think I should do."

"Do you think you can keep Karvalen running smoothly—no, wait. I phrased that badly. Do you think you can guide Karvalen through any difficulties so it can continue to run smoothly while I'm gone?"

He thought about it. I think he was considering the difference between the ways I phrased it.

"I believe I can, my lord."

"Good. Then you are now the master of the palace and the city. I'll go even farther. You are in charge of everything involving Karvalen on this side of the Eastrange."

"My lord?"

"The Baron is in Carrillon, or headed there, so you inherit the city, not just the undermountain. At least, until he gets back to run the city again. I'll get on the mirror and inform his staff. But you're also the perfect man for the job of keeping tabs on what's going on in Mochara and all along the canals. You understand the people of the plains far better than I ever will, and everyone here respects you."

He did the thing the people of the plains do, kind of a kowtowing, face-on-floor thing, hiding his eyes with his hands. He said something in his native tongue and repeated it in Rethven. Or Rethvenese. Or whatever debased dialect of the old Imperial tongue we were using.

"Night has come and night has passed, and been good to us. Thank you, my lord."

"You're welcome, if that's the right thing to say. Now get up. A knight never goes to his knees, much less his face. And why are you calling me 'my lord'?"

"Is it not more appropriate?" he asked, anxiously, rising. "I am a man of the plains and you are a lord of night—*the* Lord of Night."

"And you feel it's more appropriate to address me as a figure of religious awe than a figure of political clout?"

"Yes. If it does not offend you."

"I'll permit it. Just don't do it too often."

"Yes. As you say. Sire."

"You think you can handle things?"

"I believe I can, if it is made clear I possess the authority to do so."

I fetched a crystal, had it record my endorsement of his authority, and handed it to him. He bowed deeply and accepted it. Seldar handed me a mirror with a call to the Baron's house already on it. I explained and actually got backtalk.

"Your Majesty, the Baron left strict orders for his chancellor—"

"I have no doubt his chancellor will be very helpful to Sir Dantos. Why, I would be surprised if Sir Dantos didn't have him continue with his usual duties. I would also be surprised to find Sir Dantos executed him for disobeying the King's command, obstructing the King's appointed agent, or interfering in the business the King has ordered carried out. Surprised," I added, "but not upset." This caused the guy on the other end to stand up straighter and salute.

"I understand, Your Majesty. I will immediately inform the chancellor."

"And have him come up here, personally, to report to Sir Dantos. Immediately."

"It will be done, Your Majesty."

I shut down the mirror and handed it back to Seldar.

"Be nice," I cautioned Dantos, "but firm."

"I will make every effort, my lord."

"Does this mean," Seldar asked, "I shall accompany you to Carrillon?"

"How can I pass up having my first three knights with me again?" I asked. He smiled and nodded. "Now, if you'll get Torvil and Beltar, I have to run an errand. Meet me in the gate room and we'll step through."

"As you command, Dread Lord."

"You cut that out."

"As you wish," he agreed, suppressing a smile. "May I suggest wearing your armor, however? It would be appropriate to be more formally attired before we arrive."

"Good thinking." I dressed and the two of them gave me unnecessary help with the suit. It did go faster with their assistance, I admit, but I'm a big boy and can dress myself. Sometimes my socks even match. Seldar handed me my helmet while Dantos finished adjusting my swordbelt. They pronounced me kingly and I made a rude noise in reply.

I hurried down to the real gate room and the tiny ring gate. With the possible time differentials involved, I wanted to see if Diogenes was ready for a cell sample while I still had Bob on hand. I opened the mini-gate, saw the monitoring device, and closed the mini-gate.

Presumably, Diogenes can see and hear in the library, now. That's a good sign. But how am I to communicate with him in a hurry? I could open a gate, go through, and maintain a ring-gate connection while we talk, I suppose, but it takes a lot of power.

I wished again for my skinphone. It was a very nice, a high-tech cellular phone device. With the equipment Diogenes has available, he might be able to set up a transceiver to link with it by sending signals through a ring gate.

There's a thought. If he's got suitable equipment, could he send me a cell phone or similar device? Wait, better thought. Could I take a handheld communicator—a smartphone of any sort—build in a micro-sized ring gate…

Wait, wait, wait. Okay. Picture this. Somewhere in the middle of nowhere, put a transceiver. You place a call to it and it relays your signal. Add to this thing some dedicated ring gates with the interior diameter—the portal size—no larger than a pinprick. Direct a high-intensity radio link at that pinprick, maybe even a laser communications unit, so you have a high-speed data connection.

If this transceiver station—call it an inter-universal cell tower—has other dedicated ring gates, we can build the remote ring gates into things like a smartphone or wrist computer or whatever. I whip out my smartphone, hit speed dial, and the micro-gate in the phone opens up to the inter-universal cell tower— the ICT. The ICT computer gets the signal, opens its own micro-gate to the target phone, and relays the data stream through that gate. I suddenly have a voice-and-video call from Nowhere, Anyland, to Otherplace, Somewherelseville.

Holy crap, I think I've just had the idea for inter-universal cell phones. Can I expand this into an inter-universal internet? Yes. Put a pair of dedicated micro-gates together, one in Diogenes' current world and one in Mary's world, link a computer through the micro-gate with a laser link, or maybe just thread a fiber optic line through it, and you have computers in different universes talking to each other. If they're connected to the internet on both sides and connected to each other, each could be a literal gateway server.

Google might need some new search algorithms.

On the other hand, I might also be getting ahead of myself. I don't know what effects, if any, long-term open gates have on inter-universal relations. There may be a maximum practical time they can be open. They may alter the time flow between the two. They may leak Things from around the edges. I should really experiment with this idea before rushing into production.

Having an inter-universal smartphone might be a good start, though, if only to see how badly it goes wrong. That doesn't call for permanent gate-links.

But, for now, I need a way to ask Diogenes if he's ready for a cell sample. He needs to have the facilities to preserve the cells, at the very least. Does he need facilities to freeze them? I'm not sure how futuristic biological sciences work.

Well, fine. I can magic this. I can create an illusion of me, complete with sound. I can even include scrolling text at the bottom in case his sound reception is spotty. Since I'm casting the spell from here, powering it isn't a problem, and I'm not opening a person-sized gateway, so for sending the spell there, power still isn't a problem.

I readied my spells, recorded my message, opened the ring gate, and popped the illusion spell through it. It engaged normally when it landed in the library and played back for the monitoring equipment.

I closed the gate again. It would be a while before Diogenes could work out a way to reply. He's a clever AI. He'll figure something out. I tugged on the ring-gate and the mountain slithered back the stone in which it was mounted. I put the thing in a pocket for later. If I wanted to check on his progress, I didn't want to have to come back to my personal gate room every time to do it.

Upstairs, Bronze was already waiting for me. She stood in front of the public gate with the air of someone who is willing to stand there indefinitely and won't mind it a bit. She's much more patient than I am. Torvil and Seldar were also waiting, of course. I also expected the dozen men—some giant, some more regular-sized—wearing crossed red and grey baldrics. Each had a dragon's-head pin in the center of the chest, where the colors crossed. My bodyguards, obviously; the winners of the *sicaricudo* contests. Perhaps "expected" is too strong a word. I knew, in an abstract sense, these people were likely to be present. The King is going back to the Palace, after all.

Everyone else was a bit of a shock, though.

I did not expect another fifty or so grey sashes, all also carrying sword and shield, as well as a few carrying poles or pikes. Beltar was present and seemed in charge of these.

I also didn't expect Bob, Alliasian, and Filiathes, either, but I should have. He's the Duke of Vathula, after all, and those two are the only other elves in the city—I think. Come to think of it, keeping him handy would be useful. I still need to give Diogenes an elf cell sample and Bob is the only source I have.

But why were there so many shadow knights?

"Beltar?" I asked, standing in the entryway. Beltar worked his way over to the entryway while I wondered if the room was getting gradually larger over time. I thought it might be. Maybe the mountain noticed the amount of traffic through the place. The hallway did seem more in line with the gate on the far wall. Or was the gate gradually moving in line with the hallway?

"Yes, my lord?" Beltar asked, saluting.

"A word, Beltar?" I beckoned him into the hall. He followed. "What's the deal with all the grey sashes?"

"It is my understanding there will be priests of many churches at the gathering, my lord. Should not the Temple of Shadow be represented?"

"Wait, back up. I don't recall summoning any priests. I don't think I even invited any."

"Did you not?" he asked, obviously puzzled. "Someone did."

"I'll have a word with Lissette. Maybe she thought it was a good idea. Come to think of it, maybe it is."

"In such case, my lord, perhaps my presence—and the presence of the retinue? —is not so much amiss?"

"Maybe not. We'll find out." I ushered him back in and started sorting people into three lines, behind Bronze. I went over the gate safety rules as I reinstated the light spell for the cutoff point. Since it was nighttime and I had a lot of willing contributors, I allowed them to help pre-charge the spell by charging various crystals in the walls.

While this went on, T'yl showed up with Norad and Morrelin in tow.

"We're not too late, are we?" T'yl asked.

"No, you're just in time. I'm charging up my gate spell."

"Oh, that's excellent. I was hoping to attend the ball."

"It's more a meeting than a ball," I corrected.

"Whatever. I'm looking forward to it."

"Fair enough. Push a little power into the spell matrix, will you? I hadn't anticipated this large a company."

"Certainly. Norad? Morrelin?" The three of them each selected a crystal in the wall and started gathering energies.

Their presence caused some interesting fluid dynamics within the crowd. The elves moved away from the magicians—or, more specifically, T'yl. They did it gracefully, subtly, skillfully, but definitely. It was like water flowing through a cup of pebbles to reach the bottom. I don't think anyone noticed. I noticed because I always want to know where elves are standing in relation to me, and everyone in the room was arranged in columns.

While the three magicians helped us wind up the spell, I stood to the side, working with the mirror, hunting for someplace unshielded, about the right size, and in an area we could all move through at speed. It doesn't do to get jammed up in a magical gateway.

Then it hit me. T'yl. T'yl's body. It was an elf, a post-human elf, one which Bob created. It was, effectively, one of Bob's children.

And, of course, the fact I drained the soul out of the elf in question before doing horrifying things to it—planting a human soul in the flesh—didn't do my flashbacks any good. I had several seconds of remembering a room full of dead children and the five fastened to the wall.

When I finally die and go to Hell, those seconds will definitely count against my time there.

What must it be like for people with *real* psych problems? People who have gone through months or years of terrible, stressful conditions? Veterans from some war or other, for example? How do they cope? I have a hard enough time with a torture session lasting less than a week. True, it was intense, but it was—by comparison—brief. What's it like to live in a war zone, day after day, for a material fraction of your life? And then come home, where no one shoots at you? Where you don't have to wonder about land mines, razor wire, and snipers?

I really am a pathetic wimp.

Wimp or no, I wasn't about to go to pieces in front of everyone. I locked my teeth together, clenched my jaw, stiffened my spine, and concentrated on my scrying work. It helps, I've found, to have something to think about—something to focus on that *isn't* the memory. It's not like the old example of the impossibility of *not* thinking about something: Ready? Do not think of a white horse. See the problem? You have to think about the horse. But if you can think about something else, focus on it to the exclusion of all other thought… it helps.

The place I found was in the middle city, outside the old, original walls of Carrillon—the first ring of growth after it outgrew the original walls, if you will. Someone's livery stable had doors opening on a fair-sized yard. Aside from a few carriages and a coach, it was empty. Presumably all the animals were actually inside the stable proper. That suited me. We could overlay the gate in the doorway, flood through into the yard, and walk right out onto a main city street.

"Everyone ready?" I asked. There was a murmur of assent and people tensed, preparing to move.

I opened the gate. The image from the mirror skipped into the archway, down a long, swirling corridor, and snapped close. Bronze didn't wait for a signal, but moved forward. I stepped around the edge of the arch when she went through and the column followed, building up to a run. I held the gate on the far side, adding my force to the spell as people poured through it, watching through the gate. Everyone made it and I closed it behind them.

This isn't actually easier at night, but I have more power available. Plus, we've done this sort of thing before. It goes more quickly with practice.

Beltar called commands and the Knights of Shadow formed up. The four in front marched two-by-two, carrying poles with banners. I recognized the impaled dragon standard on each of them from long ago, only now with a golden crown above it. The front two were the vertical, triangular things designed to hang from crosspieces; the two behind were more flag-like, to wave in the breeze. The colors were easily visible for two reasons: The magical rippling of the banners had nothing to do with the wind, and the brightly-glowing spearheads above illuminated everything within fifty feet. Bronze took her place behind the four bannermen and shifted her coloration to a bright, gleaming, metallic shade of golden bronze.

Showoff.

Everyone else formed up behind her. There was some backing and filling when Bob moved to walk behind Bronze and T'yl did the same. Eventually, Bob and his escorts followed Bronze while T'yl and his partners relocated themselves magically, rather than walk to the Palace. I think T'yl knows he makes Bob uncomfortable. I'm not sure he cares, though.

Seldar and Torvil elected to walk on either side of Bronze. Seldar still carried my helmet, but Torvil handed me my tabard and cloak. I recognized the design again and noted some changes. Both were dark green—this time, so dark as to be almost black—with crimson and grey knotwork for the trim. And, of course, the circle, sword, dragon, and crown.

Well, if I have to be King for a while to get out of the King business, so be it. I put it all on and hopped up on Bronze. We set out at a slow walk and the troops marched along with us. A good thing, too, since I wasn't sure how to get to the Palace from here. We followed the four in front and hoped they knew what they were doing.

Someone in the ranks behind started singing. Within ten paces, everyone in armor had their faceplates up and voices raised. Bronze even got in on it by suppressing her hoof-silencing bracelets and playing bells—and I didn't know she could shut them off. She makes me wonder, sometimes.

The song was a marching song, of course, and had me as the subject. I didn't appreciate the heavy religious overtones, but I didn't feel right telling them to keep quiet. As a result, the whole noisy shebang brought people to their windows or out into the street to see. Crowds watched us go by. A few spectators stared, openmouthed, but most knelt or bowed or saluted or something. As we headed along the road, the singers switched from song to song, some less religious than others, but their favorite topic of singspiration was their king.

Whee.

Bronze loved it, of course. I suspect everyone in the parade loved it, with one exception.

On the other hand, it may have done some good. There was certainly no doubt anywhere in Carrillon that the King was in his castle. We also encountered not so much as a moment of delay in passing through gates and walls. Guards saw the horde of us approaching, obviously noticed the banners in the lead, and threw open gates as though lives hung in the balance—*their* lives.

We wound our way through the estates of central Carrillon, still making an awful and awfully embarrassing din, until we reached the palace proper. Hogarth was on duty again as doorman, this time flanked by a number of steel-armored men wearing red sashes. I wondered if his attitude would be any different tonight.

I dismounted by sliding down the side of Mount Bronze and landed without incident. Hogarth went to one knee; the row of armored men did the same. I noted with some pleasure how none of them had weapons drawn.

Okay, so far, so good.

Firebrand?

He's under orders, Boss. He believes Lizzy will have his testicles fed to him if he does anything vaguely disrespectful. As far as I can tell, he's not planning anything but abject submission.

Better than last time, at least. Keep an ear out.

Will do.

I marched up the steps, flanked by Seldar and Torvil.

"Good evening, Hogarth. Do you always have door duty at this hour?"

"Yes, Your Majesty."

"Very well. Has T'yl arrived?"

"He has, Your Majesty. He is quartered in the chambers of the north tower."

"Good." I beckoned Bob and Beltar up. Beltar climbed the stairs. Bob and his escorts flowed up the stairs like a reversed video of blood pouring down steps. "This is the Duke of Vathula. He is an honored guest of the King and Queen. See to it."

"It will be done, Your Majesty."

"Lord Beltar will also be staying in the palace, I believe, along with his retinue."

"I will see to their comfort, Your Majesty."

"Good. Torvil, Seldar. Let us pay a call upon the Queen."

We left Hogarth and the steel-clad men there, still kneeling. They could stand up after I left. I don't have much reason to like Hogarth.

Tovil showed me through the palace. I never actually wandered around in it before. It was easy to get lost in. Someone had started with a sizable piece of masonry and added to it over time. A wing here, a tower there, tear down a section to rebuild it differently… it wasn't laid out in a coherent pattern, but seemed almost like several buildings grew together, were pruned for artistic considerations, and eventually formed an organic whole. All in all, I liked it. It had a sprawling, mazelike feel to it. It reminded me of the undermountain, but with fancy furniture, angular geometry, and some nice tapestries.

The King's chambers were, strangely enough, on a basement level. Come to think of it, maybe that's not so strange, if the Demon King had anything to say about it. The Queen's chambers, on the other hand, were up on the third floor. We went through three doors and their accompanying sets of guards before Torvil knocked on the fourth door. The pair of guards outside didn't seem to mind. The door opened and Malana looked out for a moment before swinging the door wide and letting us in.

We stood in a receiving room and awaited Her Majesty's pleasure. Nobody seemed to notice I was nervous. It was after sunset, so it's not like I could break out in a cold sweat or anything. Then again, if they noticed, it's also possible they simply chose not to.

Lissette came out of another room, still belting a robe. The belt was a swordbelt, bearing a light, elf-style blade. I wondered if Malana and Malena were teaching her their style of fencing. Judging by the look of the hilt, it was more than a little bit used.

"Halar!" she breathed. She started toward me, checked herself, and regarded me carefully.

"Yes, I'm Halar," I agreed. "I used to be the vessel of the Demon King, but he's gone, I'm here, and I owe you an apology or twelve."

"You certainly sound like Halar," she agreed, but her eyes were filled with both hope and fear. She wanted to believe me and couldn't. I had a quiet word with Firebrand who had a quiet word with Seldar and Torvil. Seldar was still carrying my helmet. He put it down on a chair and drew his sword. Torvil drew his. I sat down in another chair. Seldar and Torvil laid the flats of their naked blades on my shoulders, poised to remove my head.

"I'm not the Demon King," I said, softly, never taking my eyes from Lissette. "I doubt he could trust anyone as much as I trust and love these two. With a twitch, they could kill me, right here, right now. But I believe in them. I trust them with my life, which isn't so much of a thing, but also with the fate of every soul in Karvalen, which is."

Lissette crossed the room to me. Looking at me in a mirror was one thing. Looking at me in full monster mode, present and in the flesh, was quite another. She brushed the hair back from one of my slightly-pointed ears, used one thumb to move my lip and see my teeth. I obligingly opened my mouth and let her look. She poked the front of a fang and I slid it out to its full length.

Gently, without moving the blade, she took the hilt of Seldar's sword from him. He glanced at me and I nodded. Lissette looked at me and I looked at her while she held a blade sharp on the level of atomic crystal at my neck.

"You said you owed me an apology," she told me. "Go ahead."

"I married you for political reasons. You were a pawn in a political game and you were used. I shouldn't have permitted it."

"True. But now I am the Queen."

"True."

"And I can take your head off."

"Also true."

"Aren't you afraid?"

"What for? I trusted you when you wanted me to crawl under your bed; I still trust you."

I'm getting better at lying with a straight face. Being dead at the moment probably helped. Without a heartbeat or breathing, without even a sudden rush of adrenalin and all the other glandular reactions that go with being scared, it's easy to appear confident and brave. Good thing, too, because I wasn't confident and I've never been brave.

I trusted her, yes, but not with my life. Nine years ago, she was a decent person. After all that time and all that pain, who knew who she was now? I was betting she would make a good queen, though, and if putting her between the throne and crown meant taking risks, then this was a risk I would have to take.

I'm the only one who could see or sense them, so I slithered a multitude of invisible tendrils up over my shoulder. I didn't hinder the movement of the blade, but I did form a woven wall of psychic forces alongside my neck. If she decided to cut my head off, I might be able to hold her off long enough to do something about it.

I did say I'm coward, right?

I waited, looking her in the eye—not that she could tell, given my night-eyes are black balls of darkness—and hoped.

She handed the sword to Seldar. Torvil and Seldar both sheathed their weapons.

"I never told the Demon King about that," Lissette announced. "I never told anyone about it."

"Does that mean you accept my apology?"

"No. But now I believe you mean it," she replied, voice breaking. She moved to a chair, slumped into it, put her face in her hands, and wept. I moved to sit on the floor at her feet; there wasn't room in the chair. I wasn't sure it would hold me, either. Everyone else quietly slipped into another room.

I could see a deep, profound mix of emotions all through her. A strange combination of things, a concoction of opposites the likes of which I completely fail to understand. What has she been through? How did she get to this state? How strong did she have to be with the Demon King? How long did she have to be strong? Yes, I know some of what happened in the past nine years, but I lack the details. Did Thomen's brain-bending leave scars, or was it a more subtle thing? Did the Demon King do awful things to Lissette on a regular basis, or did it bother her only once a month? Did she live in a palace as a brutalized wife, or was she neglected in favor of other toys for torment?

I don't know. I could ask, I suppose, but I don't think I ever will.

Which left me with a more immediate problem. What do I do now? I've never known what the protocol is for a crying woman, much less for my estranged wife by a political marriage who happens to have an aversion to the horrors associated with my face.

Hold her hand? Hug her? Get her a glass of water and an aspirin? Knock her out and put her to bed so she can wake up calmer? Kill her outright and hide the body?

No, I didn't seriously consider the last option, but it does show my desperation that I thought of it at all.

Psst. Boss.

Idea, Firebrand?

Yes. And it told me what to do.

When I tapped on Lissette's knee to get her attention, she lifted her face a little to look at me. I handed her a handkerchief and she took it by reflex, then did a double-take. I was wearing my sash around my face again.

"Behold: Sashface, King of the Jesters," I suggested. She stared at me as though I were a raving lunatic for all of five seconds before she burst out laughing.

"Success," I noted. "I was aiming for 'laughing with,' but I'll take 'laughing at.'"

"You are a complete and utter fool," she stated. Her laughter faded rapidly, leaving only a sad smile. "A well-meaning one, but a fool."

"I've been of that opinion for longer than you've been alive."

"And you still let them make you a king?"

"What was I going to do? Tell them they had the wrong guy? I could have tried to foist it off on Raeth, but they wouldn't have taken it. They wanted me, so I let them have me."

"The story of your life," she remarked, head cocked to one side.

"Now you mention it, yes. I may have said something more true than I meant to."

"The Demon King was, to me, a kingly figure of royal power and monstrous cruelty. You strike me as more like a man who stumbled into the throne room and sat down."

"Gee, thanks," I said, muffled slightly by the sash.

"No, I don't—that is, I'm not trying to be insulting. I mean you don't seem to come to the throne and crown naturally. You sit on one and wear the other, but no one would ever expect them to fit you as well as they do. The moment you take them off, you… You're a thing—a man—who was never meant to rule, but people wanted you to, thought you could rule them well. They trusted you."

"And they were wrong."

"No," Lissette countered, "they were only partly wrong. They were not wrong to trust you, I think, but only because you were willing to give them what they needed."

"Oh, yes. They were wrong," I insisted. "I'm no king. I'm not even a good baron. I'm not sure I'd make a good mayor. I'm a teacher who had no desire to become a dean. I have a severe anemia of ambition."

"But they were right to trust you."

"But I'm *terrible* at being a king!"

"Maybe you are—I've only seen the Demon King on the throne, not you."

"And I'm sorry about that," I told her as I moved to sit on a much heavier chair. "Do you want to talk about it?"

"No. Let's talk about you, not him."

"Uh, okay. What do you want to know?"

"I hear you take the duties of King seriously. Very seriously, if your knights are to be believed."

"I am proud of them. They're the one thing I ever did right for the kingdom."

"What about the roads?"

"That was accidental. Although I do admit I hated the muddy rivers you used to call roads."

"How did these roads come about?"

"I presume they were trails hacked through the countryside by people following footpaths, but I'm not sure."

"I meant *your* roads."

"Huh? Oh, the stone ones. My mountain. It grows through stone. It formed the roads because it knew how much I hated the dirt tracks."

"And the bladed plows?"

"What bladed plows?"

"The chariots that make six furrows at a time?"

"Oh, those. What about them?"

"And the peace with the Eastrange? And your ideas for peace with the *viksagi*? Who was it went north to meet them, greet them, and learn something about them before sending ambassadors?"

"That's not a sense of duty. That's me being annoyed with things. And who's comforting whom, here? You're the one who was crying. Aren't I supposed to be holding you and rocking you until you shove me away and hurry off in embarrassment?"

"Depends on who's being embarrassed," she argued. "I'm hardly the fainting flower type. And I'm allowed to avoid talking about things I do not wish to discuss. A queen must have some privileges."

I had to admit this was true.

"I admit this is true," I admitted. "So, why did you decide to talk about all the nice things I've accidentally done?"

"Were all of them accidents?"

"Well, no. But I sort of tripped and fell on good fortune a lot."

"It doesn't look that way to me."

"Fine, but you haven't answered my question," I persisted. "Why bring these up?"

"I think… I think I'm trying to remember you. Who you were before. No," she corrected, "I'm trying to remember *you*. I never knew you, not really, not deeply. I knew the Demon King, and he confused me about you. I'm trying to remember the man I thought you were. I liked him."

"And this list of accidentally doing the right thing helps?"

"It does. That man was a nicer man. He had his faults, but he wasn't evil. He was… he was someone I could have loved."

"Does that mean I can unwind this sash from around my head?"

Lissette made an exasperated sound and did it for me.

"Here," she said, handing it to me. She looked at my face for a while, searching it for I know not what. "You have the same face," she said, after a while, "but you… wear it differently."

"Faces are masks. They conceal us, even as they reveal us."

"Deeply philosophical."

"I heard it somewhere. I didn't make it up."

"Well, then, maybe it's true."

"Thank you, too much."

"Now, perhaps, you might reveal the mysteries behind some other matters."

I stood up and re-wound my sash about my waist before moving to a heavy-looking couch. It didn't even creak when I settled on it. It was also rather poorly padded.

"Name it. I'll pull back the veil of uncertainty and reveal all. Assuming I know what you're talking about."

"What are your plans?"

"That's a pretty sweeping question."

"Oh? You have a lot of plans, do you?"

"I suppose I do," I admitted. "First off, I plan to put you firmly between the Crown and Throne, assuming you feel like ruling a kingdom."

"There has never been a ruling Queen in Rethven."

"Who was it told me this is now the Kingdom of Karvalen?"

"Hmm. Go on."

"My idea is to hold formal court and hear the various nobility of the kingdom. I can explain the new system of judgment and appoint people to oversee it. The nobles can complain at me about it, or anything else they don't particularly like. I'm sure they're not fond of taxation, no matter how much or how little it is." I paused in thought.

"Maybe we can add canals to this side of the Eastrange, too. I think I can explain to the mountain how to make staircase locks, and the Averill seems like the perfect supply for north-south canals, once the riverbed gets raised a hundred feet or so. We can probably do something similar with Oisen, Quaen, and Caladar, too. People can ship stuff in bulk instead of by wagon train. The places where we need staircase locks can be toll areas, helping finance the Royal Treasury. Hmm."

"Stop."

"Hmm?"

"Stop it. You're chasing sheep."

"Chasing sheep?" It took me a second to catch the metaphor. Going off on a tangent, or a wild-goose chase, or chasing rabbits, or something like that. Chasing sheep.

"Sorry about that. I was just thinking a government might do well to provide services for a fee, rather than do everything through taxation. Either way can be abused, but it would be nice if we could keep things simple. Plus, having more canals would provide irrigation water in more places—"

Lissette moved over to my couch and gently placed a hand over my mouth to shut me up. It's possible I was babbling nervously. I can't have heart palpitations or cold sweats, but I can yammer pointlessly.

"You have many ideas," she said, fingers still covering my lips. "You might make an excellent advisor, perhaps even more so than a king. But, for now, you are a king, and you have things you wish to do. Tell me of them."

She didn't remove her hand until I nodded.

"Once I get the nobility feeling as though I listen to them and will take them seriously—sort of on my side, as it were, warmed up and open to me—I plan to announce I'm going on a trip and leaving you in charge. Oh, I'll soften it with the idea that I'm also leaving my most trusted advisors with you and that I'll check in with them regularly, but I'm actually going to have you run the place."

Lissette sat beside me on the couch and adjusted her sword more comfortably. She seemed thoughtful.

"It will work," she said, slowly, "but not well."

"Why is that? You've been ruling the place for nine years, haven't you?"

"In essence? Yes. Things which require royal authority generally fell to me to do, aside from those amusements you... I'm sorry. Those amusements the Demon King kept for himself."

"Then where's the problem?"

"It is one thing to bow before the Queen to avoid the attention of the Demon King. It is quite another to acknowledge a woman rules over you."

"But that's why I'm leaving ministers to help, and lying about checking in regularly, staying in touch, and so on."

"That is not what they will hear. They will hear only that you are leaving, as the Lords of Night fled through the Door of Shadows in Zirafel, possibly never to return. And, once you are gone, the princes—for they are all princes in their hearts, no matter what their titles—will begin to plot, form factions, and break away."

"Banler won't. Bob will also be on your side. I bet Jorgen will also help."

"Yes, and some others with them," she agreed. "But so many more will wonder why they listen to a woman with a fancy hat hundreds of miles away."

"Hmm. All right. You're more intimately familiar with the various boneheaded chauvinists in charge. What do we do to make this work?"

"Are you so determined, then, to abdicate?"

"I'm a terrible king no matter what sort of good fortune I've found on the throne. I want someone to rule who can do a decent job. Someone better than me. And you're my candidate, Your Majesty."

"It is not so simple," she stated.

"Enlighten me."

"I'm not sure I can. You don't seem to… there's something about you that…" She frowned. "It is said you came back through the Shadowgate from wherever it is the blood-drinkers fled. Did you?"

"In a manner of speaking, yes. I come from another world, a different kingdom. A time and a place radically different from this one."

"Yes… yes, I recall, now. You tried to explain it to me, once, so long ago."

"Yes."

"It shows."

"What does?"

"You are from somewhere else. Somewhere *different*. So many things I take for granted—we all take for granted—but you do not. You think a woman can rule a kingdom. You think slavery is wrong. You insist on honoring the druids of the woods. You defy the gods with one hand and offer them honors with the other. You think reading and writing are for everyone, regardless of their profession."

"I'm with you on all of that, except the part about the druids."

"You have an edict demanding saplings be planted for every tree cut down? And you have brokered a peace with the dryads."

"Of course. That's just good forestry, not honor to the druids. Although, now you mention it, they're probably pleased about it. But I've never even met a druid that I know of. I don't think so, anyway. If I have, I've forgotten."

"Regardless, the rest of it still stands. You look at the world through your nightlord eyes and see it in ways no one else sees it. It's like a painting. I look at it and see a pretty glade with dancing animals. You see canvas and brush-strokes, pigments and lines, shading and borders, and perhaps some scenery."

I looked at her for several seconds.

"Lissette, I may have mentioned this before, but it was a long time ago and I'm no longer certain what I said and what I only thought. But I would like to think that, given time and opportunity, I might have decided to marry you and make you queen even without your father's urging."

Lissette blushed and looked away.

"You did say something along those lines, yes."

"I'm glad I said it. Okay. So I don't see the world the way you see it. This lets me do things no one else would ever dream of, but it also handicaps me in dealing with people because I don't see what they see. I can't understand what they do or why. As you said, we're looking at the same painting, but we don't see the same picture."

"I think so."

"Anyone perceptive enough to grasp that is perceptive enough to handle this for me. You figure it out and I'll do what you say."

"I—you *what?*"

"I want you to rule the place. What will it take? No, I said that wrong. You are the Queen of Karvalen—unquestioned ruler of all of it. Your word is law. I'm the King. I can do that. I just *did*. What do you need from me to make sure it stays that way? Pick a noble house that's likely to be trouble. I'll remove it and you can appoint governors to serve at your pleasure until they prove they're worthy of a title. Point at a city that will never bow to a woman ruler. I'll bring it around to our point of view. Tell me we need a whole new crop of nobles—aside from a few who I *know* will help our plans—and I'll eat them all tomorrow night.

"When I say you're in charge, I mean you're also in charge of me. All I want is to be allowed to leave in peace, subject to occasional recall to help you out. I have my own troubles and worries and can't deal with them and a kingdom, too. So tell me what we need to do and I'll do it."

Lissette stared at me with a thunderstruck expression as I explained. She took a few moments to gather herself before she could reply.

"I... I'm not sure, exactly. I need to think."

"Go ahead. Take your time. The days of the Demon King are ended. Hail the Queen of Karvalen, Lissette the First, Lady of the Something-Or-Other, and similar such stuff." I stood up from the couch and she caught my hand.

"Halar?"

"Yes?"

"Nothing," she said, releasing my hand. "I'm sorry."

"Sorry?"

"It was nothing. Forget it."

"Already forgotten... Your Majesty. With your permission, I'm going to go see my rooms and get some stuff done."

"Of course." She sat up straight and waved a hand to dismiss me. "You have Our leave to depart."

"That's my Queen," I encouraged, and bowed, backing away.

Seldar and Torvil were waiting for me out in the hall. Seldar had the box with the crown in it. He tried to give it to me, but I appointed him temporary guardian of the thing.

We took the nickel tour of the palace, just to keep me from getting too lost if I went out on my own. This gave me time to remember I wanted to present the new crown to Lissette and explain its operation, as well as discuss other things—the children, for one, as well as Tyma and her broken magical instruments.

But it was late for mortals and tomorrow promised to be a busy day. We headed for the dungeons.

Basement. I meant basement. The first floor below ground level. That thing.

The King's Chambers were wonderfully appointed. The outer room was suitable for dinner with friends, the bathroom large and tiled, and the bedroom, like the other two rooms, completely lacking in windows. The Demon King chose big, solid furniture, all suitable to heavy loads—a must for anyone who weighs in at close to three times what he should. A wardrobe held a variety of formal clothes while chests held quite a lot of more practical things. The bathroom featured a high-mounted water pipe, complete with an actual valve. The bedroom was done in black leather and red velvet, with an eye to providing mounting points for ropes, restraints, and various forms of immobilization. The racks on the walls held a number of implements not normally found in a bedroom. At least, not in any normal bedroom. Not even in most deviant bedrooms. I think even Mary might have been a trifle intimidated by the selection.

Somehow, I doubted he slept there. Just a suspicion.

I discussed my meeting with Lissette with Seldar and Torvil before sending them off to get some sleep. A pair of red-and-grey sashes replaced them at midnight, anyway. I fired up my ring gate and peeked through to the library, checking on Diogenes.

Sure enough, Diogenes had prepared a reply. It was a large pane of glass or clear plastic with a colored backdrop. The message was written on it. In short, his laboratory was ready to preserve a tissue sample and grow it into a larger sample for experimentation, but full-scale cloning of an organism was still beyond his capabilities. He felt he was making good progress on increasing his industrial capacity—power, materials manufacturing, and so on—but until he got a real power plant on-line, he was sadly restricted in his ability to operate large numbers of robots. Solar worked, but it had obvious limitations.

He also included a digital display labeled "elapsed time." If I was reading it right, it was nine days, eleven hours, and sixteen minutes since I left. We really needed to get him some more power production and a larger battery supply. Diogenes could work his robots non-stop if he only had a steady power source for them.

I closed the ring gate and considered. The library looked considerably more put together than I recalled. Was Diogenes tidying up with his excess processor cycles? Or was he putting the library in order so he could access the information in it? Or, since he's capable of creative thought in a limited sense—extrapolation, if not originality—has he started expanding his industrial base in preparation for mass-production cloning?

Oh, my. Have I started a Von Neumann process? I think I have. Not that this is necessarily a bad thing, considering. The planet is pretty well ruined as far as any human population is concerned. Putting it back together in an environmentally responsible fashion might be worthwhile.

I also wondered about the time rate. There seemed to be a rapid progression on the far side. Was it doing that before I went through, or did the protracted duration of the open gateway cause a backlash? I really wish I could see a graph of power consumption. It's possible the cycling of interuniversal geometries along a time axis might have caused a stretching of the wormhole, necessitating greater and greater energy input. I should have checked the rate of discharge when we came back and compared it to the initial levels. Of course, I would also need some sort of measuring device for that, and for that I need a measuring scale...

Someday, when I'm sitting quietly in a hermit hut on some random mountainside and nobody's bothering me, I'm going to invent a measuring scale for magic. I don't care if it's as arbitrary as an Imperial pound. At least I'll be able to apply mathematics.

Thaums. From "thaumaturgy." If I remember right, it's from the Greek for "miracle." One thaum, one miracle? No, that won't work. How do you define the minimum for a miracle? I'll have to think about it some more.

I shut the ring gate and spent a few minutes with an illusion spell, giving Diogenes instructions. I opened the gate, cast the illusion through into the library, and closed the gate to let the illusion run. Then I tugged on the bell-pull by the bed on the theory it connected to servants' chambers, somewhere. I must have guessed right. Someone knocked on the outer door in less than a minute.

Once he passed through the personal guard gauntlet, I sent him back out to find Bob. The page or houseboy or whatever he was dashed off and found him more quickly than I expected. I suppose when you have an elf-duke residing in the palace, the people who work there tend to hear about it. The two of them reported to me in nothing flat.

I tried to explain to Bob what I was trying to do, but the best I could do was fall back on the idea of homunculi and flesh golems.

"Look, until I can get those perfected, I don't want to try making a whole new elf. I think I stand a good chance of getting a copy of you, but combining, mixing and matching traits from you and from another elf, that's more complicated."

"But, Dread Lord," he said, looking puzzled, "what other traits are there?"

"You know. It's like crossing two humans. Height, eye color, hair color, skin color, bone structure, all that stuff."

"But we are all alike," Bob told me. "What good will it do to... mix?... me with another First Elf?"

"You mean to tell me you're all the same height, same shape, same everything?"

"Indeed. Our race was created, all of us at once, as servants to Rendu."

My response consisted of one syllable and was completely impossible for a First Elf. Bob couldn't have understood it, but my tone was sharp and unpleasant and apparently quite frightening.

"Fine," I said, massaging my forehead. "And get up. I'm obviously not going to need another of the First Elves, then. I *do* need a bit of flesh, however, so I can make a homunculus, a golem, a copy of you—hopefully a better copy than the human-elf hybrids."

"Then, it will not be *me*?"

"No, not you. It will be an independent entity, a copy of your flesh—like another First Elf. Not you, in the sense of another Bob. Just a very young replacement elf."

"You comfort me," Bob admitted. "I harbored a grave concern regarding your earlier implications of this project."

"Yeah, we had a bit of a miscommunication, there. Sorry about that. But once I get it perfected, I can start producing infant elves for you to raise and start producing empty adult elves to keep the immortality-seeking magicians happy."

"Is that wise, Dread Lord?" Bob asked, rising from his position on the floor like the bloom of some dark flower. "If they seek immortality through the same process as your magician, will they not seek you out?"

"I hope not. I'm hoping to hand the job over to Beltar, maybe Seldar, possibly even T'yl. Whoever winds up with it can manage it. Then the magicians don't have an excuse to go hunting after my blood or go hunting after elves."

"Interesting," he agreed. "Will you be able to meet the demand of the magicians who will clamor for their turn?"

"Time," I said. "Time is always the issue. Given time, I'm sure I can, but I need that time—without running a kingdom, without being chased by angry magi, without worries about my Tort, without fighting over politics and religion, without—nevermind. Just hold out your arm and I'll draw a sample with a spell."

Bob did as instructed. I used a variation on my flesh-welding spell to take the sample. I folded some skin inward, around a bit of muscle and blood, forming it into a narrow tube and separating it from his body. This became a bit of skin-covered flesh about the size of a fat toothpick. I added a healing spell, localized and directed to encourage his body to regenerate the missing mass.

"There. That didn't hurt a bit, did it?"

"It was less painful than I expected, but not entirely painless."

"Oh? Hmm. I thought I did it more skillfully than that. Sorry."

"Think nothing of it."

I opened my ring gate again and looked through. Sure enough, wherever the other ring gate was, it was definitely placed over the mouth of some sort of container. I fed the narrow tube of elf-flesh through the ring gate, watched it drop to the bottom, and closed the gate.

Now we'll see how Diogenes does with a Grow Your Own Elf kit. Well, not now, but soon.

"Thanks, Bob. I'll see what sort of results develop."

"Of course, Dread Lord," he relied, bowing smoothly.

"And please don't use that mode of address around any of the nobles. Better yet, not in Carrillon."

"Of course, Your Majesty."

"Thanks. By the way, what do you think of Lissette as a ruling Queen?"

"I think she has excellent instincts and has developed some skill in her brief tenure as queen to the Demon King."

"Do you think she can hack it as Queen without the Demon King to back her up?"

"No."

"No?"

"No. The nobility fear the Demon King, but they do not fear her. They despise her for being a woman and resent her being placed over them by the Demon King. They would tear her from the throne as they fought over it. Her head would wear the crown only until her head came off her shoulders, and that, too, would be fought over."

I had to admire the way he snapped out the answer. I had no doubt he was largely correct. On the other hand, if he's that sharp a politician…

"Any ideas on how to put her firmly on the throne and the crown firmly on her head? And keep both in place?" I asked. Bob started to answer, paused, thought for a moment.

"At first, I thought not," he admitted. "But… possibly."

"Good. Go talk to her in the morning at her earliest convenience and explain this portion of the conversation to her. Then give her whatever help she'll accept."

"As part and parcel of your instructions regarding my overwatch of your kingdom?"

"Yes."

"As you wish, Your Majesty," he repeated, bowing again. I had a grey sash show him out.

My meeting with Bob reminded me, however, of my intention to attempt a scrying on the moon. Since it was rather late for impromptu meetings with most humans, I decided to go ahead and take a shot at the moon. My guards and I found our way up to a courtyard and I fished out a pocket mirror.

The spell failed, of course. I was still inside the protective spells preventing scrying and similar effects around the palace. Grumpily, I took a walk outside the walls and down the road a bit.

Carrillon needs better gutters and sidewalks, at minimum. It could really use more extensive underground sewers. If I were staying, I'd see to it. As it was, I ignored these minor inconveniences. I'd have a word with the mountain later about better rules for the sanitation of cities.

Once outside the area of the protective spells, I looked up at the moon, eyeballing it for distance and any identifying features. I picked out some geometric figures in the lighted area, some lines and angles with a few curves. Not happy with that, I conjured some air-refraction lenses and had them hover above me, forming a basic telescope. With some magnification, I had a much better look at the moon.

The damn thing was practically covered in designs. I wasn't sure what they were—labyrinths, streets, or just abstract shapes. Nevertheless, they were everywhere, covering everything I could see.

As an interesting note, the darkened area of the moon was no clearer to me. While the telescope magnified the image, it operated using light. It didn't help with my vampire night-vision, just with the illuminated areas.

Come to that, I didn't see a source of illumination for the moon, either. Since the sun literally goes out every night, rather than circling under the world, where did the light come from? Was it a light source I couldn't see? Something directional, like an orbiting spotlight? Or did the moon generate its own light on a regular cycle?

Strangely, I didn't mind this evidence of the world being screwy. I guess when you find out the flat world has a light in the sky that actually gets lit every morning and blown out at night, a little thing like a self-illuminating moon doesn't matter so much.

Judging the distance by eye, I thought I had a pretty good chance of parking a scrying sensor darn close if not spot-on. I held up my mirror, aimed it at the moon, and watched as the image shimmered and shifted. It was an overhead view of the moon, as though I were at high altitude, looking down at it, and I wasted no time zooming in on it. My viewpoint dived for the surface of the world like a meteor, right up until it hit something. Whatever it was, it didn't like scrying sensors; the image flared blue and vanished.

A firmament, perhaps? The one around the world didn't zap scrying sensors, just turned them off without fanfare. Rendu's personal property, on the other hand, might have something a bit more drastic.

Fair enough. Through the mirror, I had a good look at the moon at a much closer virtual range. I shot for the moon again, aiming even closer. If I could get a scrying sensor inside the barrier of the lunar firmament, I shouldn't have any trouble.

Whatever Rendu used on his private world, he meant the world to stay private. I parked my scrying sensor quite close to the moon, I feel certain, but it instantly blazed with a bright blue light, the color in the heart of a glacier, and the spell ended abruptly.

This was troublesome. I could try to open a gate to the moon the same way I tried to open a scrying window, but it would take a lot more power. It was also subject to much nastier consequences. If I miss the moon, I still have an open gate. In such a case, an open gate into the endless void makes a tempting doorway for the hungrier Things living there.

I think it more likely, however, the effect of the defensive field around the moon extends to gateways as well as scrying. What would happen if the gate tried to open inside the defense field? Would it merely shine a blue light? Or would an even more unpleasant effect be translated through the gate to chastise the person with the chutzpah to make such an attempt?

I put the mirror away and strolled back into the palace, quite thoughtful.

How do you get to the moon if you can't teleport? Because that's what a gate does, really. It opens a portal between two points, it changes the geometry of spacetime—usually—and allows you to move from one point to another without crossing all the normal intervening space. Teleportation portals. At least, the basic gates do. The more complicated ones go from one universe to another, and while it's similar in theory, it's much more complicated in practice.

But back to my original question. How do you get to the moon without teleporting? Fly? I haven't done the triangulation on the moon, so I don't know how far away it is. That might be practical... if you could fly there during the day. Flying there at night is asking for hungry Things to snatch you right off your flying carpet.

Rockets? Let's not be silly. Even if I imported an Acme Moon Rocket Kit, getting there and back would be a job for professional astronauts, complete with ground crews, flight crews, radar tracking—the list goes on and on. A moon shot is more than just firing off a rocket and hoping your aim is good.

Come to that, what are the conditions beyond the firmament? I've sort of been there. In a way. First time, I was chucked out of the world by an angry, demon-possessed priest. Not exactly ideal conditions for making detailed observations. What I mostly remember are the teeth.

More recently, during my escape from Johann and the resulting premature journey through a gate wormhole, I saw a lot of Things as I went swirly-flush down the twisted rabbit hole, but that may not have any bearing on what's out there. What I saw during the trip could be an inter-universal weirdness, not a local one. The local weirdness is generally hungry and prepared to do something about it.

I need to go to Zirafel, build a bridge over the Edge of the World, and stick some probes into whatever lies beyond. Then I can start thinking about how to cross the hungry void.

It's either that, or find one of the First Dragons Bob mentioned. Maybe I can hitch a ride.

I think I'll poke the hungry void. It sounds safer.

Which only left me with the question of what to do with the rest of the night. I suppose I could have slept, had a nightmare of prophecy, and been confused about what it all meant, but I didn't feel comfortable sleeping in the former home of the Demon King. Almost everyone still thought of me as the Demon King. It seemed like a bad idea to be unconscious.

How do dead vampires cope, I wonder? Spending all day comatose seems… I don't know. Impossible, maybe. It certainly seems to be a recipe for a very brief immortality.

I could send for someone and do some arguing, intimidating, persuading, and threatening—sort of get a head start on tomorrow. It was in character for the Demon King, yes, to have people dragged from their beds and hauled into his presence, but I'm hoping to have a civilized organizational meeting, not a bunch of surly, tired, grumpy people saying whatever they have to in order to get back to home and bed.

I could fool around with the hatch to my undermind, but that's probably a bad idea in general.

Well, there's always some enchantment work. I've been meaning to assemble a disguise and turn it into an enchantment. Changing my skin from a dark grey to flesh tones is the most obvious one, of course, but it's easy. The tough disguise spell is the complex and reactive illusion—illusions, really; one for each eye—to give my eyes pupils, irises, sclera, and so forth. Routinely having normal-looking eyes would be a great start.

I rang for a servant and he fetched me a selection of rings. I took a pair and thanked him. The rings I chose were of the same design, only with different stones. They were both wide bands of gold with three tiny gems evenly spaced, embedded in the outer face of the gold. One had rubies, the other had sapphires. I liked them because each gem could contain a single enchantment function without too much trouble.

The ruby ring could hold a disguise spell for my face and skin, maybe a cleaning spell in another ruby for my twice-daily hygiene needs, even a mental defense enchantment—my brain-bunker spell, only more permanent.

The sapphire ring could have a duplicate of my Ring of Obfuscation tucked away in a gemstone, possibly upgraded with a few minor tweaks. As long as I have room, what else should I put in it? A magic jet, sucking in power for rapid recharge in low-magic worlds? Or would that interfere with my own spellcasting? How about a healing spell, charged and ready to go, much like the ring the Demon King had? Or a deflection spell, for pesky projectiles? Or could I duplicate the enchantment on the amulet?

Interesting dilemma. Given that you can have a magic ring, what magic ring do you want? Within limits, of course. I don't have a genie to bind into a ring so it can grant wishes, nor do I know how to make a ring to bring the wearer "good luck." I've eaten enough magicians to know these things can definitely be done, but I have only a vague idea how to do it.

On the other hand, "good luck" can be defined in many ways. Clouding an enemy's perceptions so he makes a mistake would be lucky for me. Knowing someone is an enemy would be nice, too. Of course, I can look at someone's soul at night and see what they're feeling when they speak to me. It's usually a fairly simple matter to detect hostility.

Could I do something similar with a spell, and during the day? Rather than probing someone's living essence, could I set up a spell-based receiver to detect any hostile intentions? If someone is thinking of stabbing me in the back— literally or figuratively—they're radiating the equivalent of telepathic waves. If I can isolate those and set up a detection matrix, I could have a ring of hostile intent detection. Handy if an assassin is about to poke me in the heart, but also useful when a smiling baron is assuring me of his support. This could be worthwhile... eventually.

If I had a week to research it properly, I'd be on it like melted cheese on a burger. As it is, the spells I *do* know are going to take time to enchant. I should get those done so they're operating and useful before I start fooling with more research.

Let's see how far I get before someone interrupts me. Or dawn, whichever comes first.

Friday, March 12th

Not as far as I'd like.

I did try building a jet spell to draw in power for a ring. Having a magical power intake attached to your hands, constantly disrupting the normal flow of magic around them, is a Very Bad Thing for your spellcasting. This might be acceptable as a rapid-charging method for someone who isn't a wizard. It can't interfere with your spellcasting if you don't do any. Putting a magic jet intake on a ring is similar to wearing spiked gauntlets while using a potter's wheel. The cookie jar you're shooting for is going to wind up as an ugly ashtray. It doesn't interfere with the verbal spellcasting, but chanting is usually a support function in spell construction, not the primary method!

At least the enchantment in the metal of the rings went well. It's a repair spell to keep the ring from suffering too much wear and tear. Once I had it working, I started on a mental defense enchantment and realized I had a problem. I do a lot of things in a psychic mode. I talk to Firebrand, I sometimes have dreams, and even some of my spells involve direct mental activity. Blocking it completely would be troublesome.

Worse, it would be useless against the things I was really concerned about. I wrap tendrils through someone and they immediately have a direct link straight through to me. While it's true they're generally busy being sucked into the afterlife, there are obviously exceptions. I don't want to grab something with a tendril and find someone is using it as a highway into my head.

This will require more thought on my part. In the meantime, I'll muddle through with the collection of mental defense spells I call my brain-bunker. As spells, they're tied into my thoughts, sort of, and can be controlled almost instinctively—kind of like your eyelids. A bright light hits your eyes, the eyelids snap shut. Dust and wind? Ditto. You can override them to squint, if you need to, but they act automatically if you don't do anything to countermand them.

Enchanting my mental defense spells into an object is slightly different. They don't respond as readily to mental controls because they're based inside an object rather than linked to the thought processes they defend. It's tricky, this psychic stuff. The enchantment also won't respond well to my psychic tendrils—a serious drawback. Figuring out a way to let me work through my own enchanted shields will be a major project. Until then, I'll have to stick to spells.

At least I got the simple things done. My Ring of Hygiene and Variable Skin Tone was a going concern before I was through. As I worked on the skin-changing illusion, I realized the complexity of the eyeball illusion was going to make it unreasonably difficult to fit it in the same gem as the skin changer. I put the eyeballs on hold and sidetracked a bit, adding my spells for dialing down my sensory sensitivity. With it, I might be able to actually enjoy food on a regular basis instead of just shoveling it down as fuel. I might also manage to cope with loud, flashy environments—I remember wandering into a rave and wanting to kill everything in the room just to make it quiet. Now I have a ring to handle all of those minor problems. I'll need to put my eyeball illusion in something else.

When the sun came up, I used the ring. It worked as expected, leaving me pink and clean and believably human. Very nice. I also ran through some color shading, shifting from milk-pale to hostile coffee, then through most of the rainbow. It worked; I was happy with it.

I started working on assembling an eyeball illusion, trying to build as perfect a replica as possible. I wanted to include things like retina patterns, forced perspective for the "inside" of the eyeball, the works. With the technology of Mary's world and Diogenes' world—the world Diogenes is in; I'd rather think of it in those terms rather than terms of *angry ants*—I might need to look into a retina scanner some night. I don't want to be embarrassed.

It was during this process someone knocked at the door. A bodyguard— someone new; they changed shifts while I was busy with my enchantment—let them in and agreed to breakfast. This told me I should probably stop with the magical garage inventor stuff and go back to being a king for a while.

"What's for breakfast?" I asked, emerging from the bedroom. The knights spun to face me and went to one knee. I couldn't tell who they were; their faceplates were locked in place.

"My lord, we don't know," said the one by the door. "Breakfast is served in the breakfast room, they say. Do you wish something delivered here?"

"No, that's all right. Have you two eaten?"

"Before we came on, my lord, and we will again in midmorning, when we are relieved. Master Beltar says we should neither eat nor drink while guarding you."

"He's cautious," I observed. "All right. Do you know the way to the breakfast room?"

"No, my lord."

I rang for a servant and used him as a guide. He led the way, a knight followed him, I followed the knight, and the other one followed me. I felt as though I were part of a prisoner escort. For my own safety, of course.

Do I need bodyguards inside my own palace? Well, the Demon King's palace?

Yeah, that's a stupid question. Most people are going to keep thinking of me as the Demon King.

Breakfast was on the third floor. Wherever the Demon King used to eat, I was willing to bet it wasn't in a pleasant little spot with a wall of windows looking south, over the harbor side of Carrillon. And I doubted Lissette had breakfast with him. From what I understand, he was more likely to have breakfast in a private room with a prostitute under the table and a couple of harem dancers providing a floor show. Possibly with a choir being hammered on their racks like a xylophone.

Aside from the choir, I'm not against it, necessarily, if the staff is paid well for their services, but it strikes me as a bit more self-indulgent than is reasonable. But maybe that's my upbringing talking.

Lissette was already seated at the breakfast table. One of the waiters must have warned her I was coming; she didn't seem surprised when I arrived. She stood up and gave me a slight bow, which I returned. I noticed Malana and Malena eyeing the black-armored guys. I assume there was mutual eyeballing going on, but it's hard to tell through those faceplates.

"Good morning, Your Majesty."

"Good morning, Your Majesty," I replied. "May I join you?"

"Please." She gestured and a flunky slid a chair into position opposite Lissette.

"Do we dismiss the guards," I asked, settling gently into the chair, "or have them stand around posturing for the whole meal?"

"That's up to you."

"Malana? Malena? Could you come here, please?" They glanced at Lissette and received the tiniest of nods. While they stood on either side of me, I could almost feel the tension in the knights behind me.

"Do you two intend to kill me?" I asked, pleasantly.

"Never," they replied, in unison.

"I'm relieved to hear it. Please guard me during the meal while these fine gentlemen guard the Queen."

More glances flitted around the room, but people rearranged themselves around us. Lissette pursed her lips as my guys took station behind her.

"Is this necessary?" she asked.

"Nope. But they're going to pretend they're not glaring at each other all through breakfast. I'd rather they had something else to worry about than each other—like, for example, their new responsibility for guarding someone they hadn't expected. Because the competitive posturing and snooty attitude will ruin the meal and I'm looking forward to eating. Everyone get that?" I finished. There was a chorus of reluctant agreement from all four of the armed killers in the room. I waved them back and they withdrew to the corners of the room, out of the way. I thought I detected a twinkle in the eyes of the twins, but I only got a quick glance.

Lissette bit her lips to keep from smiling. The waiter-servant-whatever didn't bother to say anything, merely had another place set and more food brought in. I tried my ring's sensory muting spell, dialing down my smell and taste to more human levels, and discovered I could enjoy the meal.

Hot damn. Eggs that don't crawl up my nose to fight with the toast. I still had to chew carefully—sharp teeth all around—but it was no longer a case of chomp it and get it down fast. I might actually feel as though I'm eating, rather than refueling.

Despite the icebreaking help of our bodyguards, breakfast was still awkward. It was a lovely domestic scene for the upper class. Pleasant view, nice room, bright décor, hot food, alert servants, impassive bodyguards, and nervous domesticity. Lissette and I were working on being at ease with each other. I'm not used to being married in the first place. She's not used to her Evil Husband of nine years turning back into the mildly-goofy guy she met at the wedding ceremony.

Ah, domestic tranquility. Nice stuff. I'd buy a bottle if I knew where to get it—and no, the local liquor store is not the place.

On the plus side, the food was good and I enjoyed it for the first time in a long while.

Lissette picked at her breakfast for a bit before she cleared her throat. I looked up from my plate, swallowed, and wiped my mouth. I gave her what I hoped was an encouraging expression. It must have worked, for she spoke.

"I was wondering if you had any changes you wanted made."

I digested that with a perplexed look while preparing some bacon for more direct digestion.

"I'm sorry," I admitted, "but I'm not sure what you mean. Changes to…?"

"The schedule for tonight."

"Nobody's presented me with a schedule, so I don't know."

"No?" She seemed surprised. "I gave instructions to Felkar about it."

"Who's Felkar?"

"He's castellan of the palace. He's very good at organizing and managing the servants, arranging for events, and similar things."

"Right. Got it. Never heard of him, but I'm sure someone else knew him well. If you like his work, that's all I need to know. He was supposed to let me know?"

"Yes."

"Then he probably told Seldar and Seldar approved it. He's my right-hand man. I delegate a lot."

"You do?" Again with the surprised expression.

"I don't know why that shocks you."

"I'm not shocked." She paused for a moment. "Maybe I am, a little. It's just…"

"That's not what you're used to?" I guessed. She nodded. "Don't sweat it." I looked at a waiter and told him to send for Seldar. He bowed deeply and left.

"We'll sort it all out," I promised. "I'm pretty sure I don't have an opinion, though. If you want it a certain way, we'll do it your way."

I heard the chatter outside a moment or two before the door to the breakfast room opened. A boy marched in. Behind him, a pair of well-dressed men fell silent as they entered the presence of the King and Queen.

The boy was eight or nine, dressed in fancy clothes, and carried a naked sword in his hand, one made for his size. His hair was brown and worn rather long, his eyes were blue and clear, and he seemed to have the air of one grimly determined to have his way.

"Liam!" Lissette scolded. "What are you doing?"

"We couldn't stop him," said one of the gentlemen behind the boy.

"He insisted," the other one added, gesturing toward the sword. I noticed it had a bit of blood on the point. Upon closer inspection, one of the dandies behind him did have a neat puncture wound in his upper arm. What I took initially for an arm band was a handkerchief or something similar tied around the wound. Blood was seeping into the cloth.

"Liam," Lissette said, using the Mother Tone.

Liam ignored her and walked straight to me. I scooted back from the table and slid the chair through a quarter-turn to face him. He approached, sword still out, and I waited, wondering what he planned to do. I kept my knife and fork in hand, though, pretending to idly toy with them. Children can be unpredictable.

"Are you my real father?" he asked, without preamble.

"Clean your blade," I replied, "and put it away. It is rude—*extremely* rude—to walk up on someone with a drawn blade if you don't intend to kill them immediately."

Liam blinked at me for a second, then took a cloth from the table, cleaned his weapon, and sheathed it.

"That's much better," I told him. "Now, what was your question?"

"Are you my real father?"

Sometimes I wonder about kids. I don't know a damn thing about them. I had this mental image of a studious, serious boy with an interest in how the world was put together. Well-behaved, aside from a few boyish pranks and the occasional disaster with a medieval or magical equivalent of a science project. "Liam, whose miniature catapult launched this brick through the baron's window?" "I cannot tell a lie, Father. It was I." That sort of thing.

I've inadvertently fathered a huge number of children and have not the first notion of the proper way to raise them.

"I'm beginning to wonder," I told him, seriously. "Any son of mine would introduce himself politely and ask graciously. When was the last time someone gave you the back of a hand for being a spoiled little rich kid?"

Lissette drew a sharp breath. Everyone else held very still.

"Very well," Liam replied, coldly. "I am Liam of the House of Halar, Crown Prince to the throne of Karvalen. May I ask who you are?"

"I am Halar the First, King of Karvalen, husband to the Queen Lissette. It is a pleasure to meet you, Prince Liam."

We traded stares for a few thousand years, this young prince and I. I recognized his eyes from somewhere, possibly a long-ago mirror. At least they weren't black. This was not the way I pictured meeting my son for the first time. Truthfully, I hadn't pictured meeting my son at all. It's a concept my mind has avoided, and for good reason. I'm trying to *leave* Karvalen, not build new ties to it.

And yet, here he is.

"I'm told you're not the same man," he replied.

"I'm not. My body was possessed by a demonic entity."

"Then are you my father, or aren't you?"

"Ask your mother."

He took a step closer and glared at me.

"I'm asking *you!*"

There are several ways he could have said that. He could have said it tearfully, as though demanding answers of the man who could be his father, needing to hear it from that man's own lips. He could have said it low, intense, desperate to hear it directly from the King. He didn't. He said it with a haughty grandeur, as a Prince of the Blood Royal, snapping out a correction to some servant.

I ignored him and turned my chair around to the table again.

"Look at me when I speak to you!" he demanded.

"Lissette?"

"Halar?"

"Who's been raising this boy? You? If the duties of the Queen have been too pressing, I'll understand—it's a tough job, and about to be tougher. But this fine specimen of a young man is a cretin."

"I can *hear* you!" he shouted. I continued to ignore him.

"I have arranged for his education," Lissette assured me, glancing from me to Liam and back. "He studies his letters and the other arts of the gentleman."

"But it's mostly teachers and suchlike? People he can bully, as the Prince?"

"I'm not sure. They do have authority over—"

"Look at me!" he interrupted, demanding.

I turned suddenly and leaned close, right into his face.

"I'm looking at you," I hissed. "Are you sure you want me to? Because I don't like what I see, *boy*."

He skipped back and drew his sword. I turned the chair sharply as I slapped the blade aside, along the flat, before smacking his hand and taking the weapon away from him. I laid it on the table, next to my plate, as though it were another eating utensil. I lifted fork full of eggs and ate. He reached for the hilt and I slapped his hand again, hard, knocking his fingers into the edge of the table. He jerked his hand back to stick fingers in his mouth, shocked and surprised and not certain whether he wanted to cry about it or not.

"The little gentleman," I suggested, looking at Lissette, "might need a firmer hand. I'm not saying it's required—he's our son, and I disapprove of what he's turning into—but if this is what you want, I won't interfere."

"It's been difficult to discipline him," Lissette agreed. "His... that is, your predecessor—"

"*I want an answer!*" he screeched, "*and I want my sword back!*"

I turned to look at him again. He stepped back again. Firebrand relayed my thought.

*Shut your face and stand there or I will whip your backside with your own sword until you **stop** crying.*

The look on his face was indescribable. I turned back to the table as though he weren't there.

"My Queen," I began, calmly, "if discipline is a problem, may I make a suggestion?"

"I would be delighted to hear it," Lissette replied, obviously torn between approval and worry. I wondered if anyone ever treated Liam like a brat. Because he was the Crown Prince? Or because the Demon King gave a crap? Or because people thought the Demon King gave a crap?

"Beltar is the high priest of the Temple of Shadow. He isn't in the habit of being intimidated by mortal authority. He and the other knights of shadow— especially the Banners—might make excellent teachers. Come to that, Liam's niece is unlikely to be intimidated by his title, either. I could persuade her to come here, I think."

"His niece?"

"The daughter of his half-sister. My granddaughter."

"Oh! I suppose," she said, reluctantly. I could tell she didn't like the idea of Tianna living in the Palace.

"It might do him some good to understand a Prince is not a ruler, nor is it—"

Liam chose that moment to snatch at his sword again. I grabbed his wrist, stood up, and brought his wrist with me. He dangled for a moment, then kicked me and kept kicking me, swinging back and forth awkwardly.

"Lissette? As I said, I don't intend to interfere with your child-rearing choices, but might I be permitted to discipline our son?"

"Don't hurt him," she told me/begged me.

"I may hurt him," I countered, "but I won't *harm* him, if you follow."

"I... yes, I think. But I want him..."

"He'll be fine," I assured her, over the screaming and flailing, "but he won't like this. Nobody likes a punishment or the imposition of discipline. You'll note I'm still being tolerant of the way he keeps kicking me."

"All right," Lissette decided, watching me.

I lifted him higher to look him in the eye. He punched me. I simply looked at him without reacting. So he punched me again.

"I have to admire your tenacity and spirit, if not your wisdom," I admitted. I shifted him around, sat down, put him over my knee, pinned him there, and took his pants down. He demanded to know what I thought I was doing, threatened to have me whipped, threatened to have me executed, and so on. I gave him ten swats with the flat of his sword. There was no blood, but he had lines all the way across. I stood up, forcing him to his feet. He pulled his pants up, stifling tears and sobs.

Once he had his pants up, I put him in my chair. He didn't seem comfortable, but I didn't mind.

"Now you listen to me, you arrogant little pipsqueak! You may be the Crown Prince, but that can change! I will happily appoint a whole new heir—one *worthy* of the title! Right now, you are arrogant, self-centered, privileged, vain, foppish, and foolish, none of which are good qualities in a would-be king."

"I'm going to be King," he declared, still sniffling back tears. I don't think anyone ever spanked him before and I was regretting giving him the full ten swats. Seven might have done. Maybe five. But maybe I'm wrong and should have made it twenty. I'm a complete nebbish as a king and being a father is probably harder.

"Son, right now you're going to have a tough time proving you can even be a prince. I think the best option is to sell you to a merchant headed for some far-away land and hope we can get a decent dog in trade, because you haven't shown me you're worth even the dog."

"I'm the *Crown Prince!*"

"So *what*?" I countered. "It's a title! It doesn't make you special. If I throw you out that window, will the window hold because you're a prince? Will the street refuse to break your bones because you're a prince? Will your royal blood stay in your broken body because it's a prince's blood? No. You're a person, just like everyone else, except for the responsibility."

I shook his sword in his face.

"This! This is a sword. It's not a sharp piece of metal! It's a *symbol*. It's a symbol of power—of the power to turn life into death! Cutting, maiming, and murder! It's not a *toy*. It's a responsibility and a terrible privilege! Yet, you wave it around as though it's a magic wand to get you anything you want—like a bandit, not a prince!

"I've got news for you, kid. You aren't ready for a sword. You aren't worthy of one. And you presume—*you presume*—to the Crown of Karvalen! A crown, a symbol even more powerful than a sword. A symbol that commands swords! That's an even more profound and terrible responsibility! One you *do not* understand and one you *should not* want—yet you claim it, all ignorance and arrogance!"

I sighed and tried to calm down. He looked at me with a peculiar expression, almost an interested expression.

"Look," I went on, "you're only… what, eight?"

"Nine."

"Nine, then. You don't understand what it is to be a king—how awful it is to be a ruler of anywhere, much less of an entire kingdom. It's true, you order and people do; you rule. But you also *serve.* Your duty as a ruler is not merely to get your own way, but to care for the welfare of the people in your realm. They are your responsibility just as much as they are your subjects. *That* is the key to being a good ruler, whether it be baron, duke, or king. Do you think you can remember that?"

"Yes."

"And being polite to everyone will go a long way toward keeping you alive."

"Yes, Your Majesty."

"Better. Now go apologize to your mother."

"For what?"

"If you recognize me, you know who just gave you an order. Would you like to re-think your question?"

"Shouldn't I know why I'm apologizing?"

"For now, simply apologize. Then you can think about what you should apologize for. When you realize why, you can apologize to her again—and mean it."

I stood aside and he squirmed out of the chair, eyeballing me the whole way. He shuffled around the table, still watching me as though I were a dangerous beast that might spring at him. He hugged Lissette and she held him for a bit.

"I'm sorry, Mother."

"It's all right," Lissette soothed. "I forgive you. It's all right."

"Mother?"

"Yes, my love?"

"Can I have lessons in being a king?"

Lissette shot me a glare. I sat down and pretended not to notice.

"We'll discuss it," Lissette told him. "For now, go along with your other lessons."

Liam circled the table and stopped about a pace away from me.

"Your Majesty, Father?"

"Yes, Liam?"

"May I have my sword back? Please?"

"What does it mean when a man gets a sword from the King?"

"He's a knight."

"Are you a knight?"

"No."

"No…?" I trailed off.

He thought about it for a few seconds.

"Not yet?" he hazarded. I was hoping for a "No, Your Majesty," or a simple, "No, Sir," but "Not yet" was an excellent answer, too.

"When you've learned your lessons for today, talk to Torvil about becoming a knight. But remember he reports to *me*, not to you. He's my subject, not yours, and has my permission to smack you exactly as I did." Liam gulped at the news and Lissette frowned.

"Yes, Father, Your Majesty," he acknowledged.

"You may go."

Liam sketched a bow, which he clearly wasn't used to. I doubt anyone expected him to have to bow. He left, taking his dumbfounded tutors or babysitters or whatever they were with him. I wondered if granting amnesty to anyone in a position of authority over the kid would be a good idea. If they could spank him and get away with it, would it help? How do you train a prince to be a king?

I need a manual for this sort of thing. I'm lost.

Lissette waited a few seconds to make sure they were out of earshot.

"Did you have to hit him?"

"Yes," I said, trying to sound confident.

"Why?"

I put down the knife and fork again. Breakfast might be the most important meal of the day, but this one was going rapidly toward indigestion. It took me a little bit to marshal my thoughts and to discover what I wanted to say.

"Here's where we have the parenting discussion all married couples have," I observed. "I prefer to use a gentle hand. I would, given the option, think a pleasant, calm demeanor combined with the appropriate words should be enough for any child. However, in some instances, there is no substitute for taking a less-gentle hand in matters—perhaps a firm hand, but never a needlessly violent one. What I saw come marching in the door was a child who viewed himself as the lord of all creation and the ultimate authority over every slavish underling he could see. And *he* was going to be the king, one day?" I shook my head.

"Whoever you put in charge of his upbringing—or whoever He Who Shall Not Be Named did—the choices were poor. What that kid needs is a good dose of hard schooling to learn more than letters, numbers, and swordsmanship. He needs to learn about responsibility, honor, self-reliance, and most definitely self-discipline."

"Did you not say I had authority in this matter?" Lissette asked, and I could hear the frost in her voice.

"I did," I agreed. "You can do whatever you like with him. Only, please bear this in mind. You're going to be Queen. One day, hopefully after a long and active reign, you'll find he's the King. You might want to start thinking about what sort of man you want him to grow up to be while you still have some influence over it. More like some foppish dandy at the court? More like his father? Or more like a *real* king?"

We finished breakfast in silence. I wasn't all that hungry.

When the plates were cleared away, Lissette stood up and I matched her.

"What now?" I asked. "Do I need to get with Seldar and… what was his name?"

"Felkar. Yes, I would think it best. If you would join us for the morning meeting, that might be good, too."

"You have morning meetings, too?"

"Of course."

"Please tell me: How do you get them to leave you alone during breakfast?"

"I was told to take care of the 'boring ruling stuff,'" she quoted, looking puzzled, "so I told them to have their meeting and I would join them after my breakfast."

"I wish I'd thought of that. My ministers have been bugging me whenever they get the chance, which is constantly."

"Which reminds me. How many ministers do you have?"

"I don't know for certain. Seldar handles…" I trailed off.

"The boring, ruling stuff?" she guessed.

"Yes," I admitted. "I have a lazy streak. The Demon King inherited it from me. At least I *try*."

"Do you want to organize the new royal council, or shall I?" Lissette asked, changing the subject.

"You can, but I want to look over all the potential councilors and make sure you don't have any self-centered, dishonorable, lying, backstabbing weasels in the mix. I mean to make you a ruling Queen and leave you a kingdom running as well as I can get it to."

"I'll be interested to see if there are any weasels," she agreed. "Why weasels, specifically?"

"I don't know. It's an association I have from my upbringing. I don't know why weasels should be synonymous with politicians."

"You really are a strange man."

"You've said it before and I've never argued it."

"Just so you know. I'll get dressed. May I have the twins back?"

"Guys. Switch." There followed a bit of parade-ground marching, some drawn swords, some formal salutes and some bowing. Apparently I'm not guarded by automatons; they have a sense of humor. Malana and Malena went along with the formalities of the knights, but I already knew they had a sense of humor.

"By the way," I added, "Bob—excuse me. The Duke of Vathula needs to talk to you about how to put you between the crown and throne and keep you there. I told him to talk to you at your earliest convenience."

"He's left a message," Lissette said, lip curling. "I haven't felt it was convenient."

"Please make time for that discussion. Then you and I can talk about how to tackle the nobles."

"I already have some thoughts on the matter."

"Good! So does Bob. I think his idea is to kill anyone who argues."

"It *is* effective."

"It's a short-term solution, yes, but the Demon King did enough of that. Please see what Bob's ideas are like and evaluate them. You're better at this political stuff than I am."

"Very well. I'll see him. But you have to go to the meeting until I get there."

"Whoa, now. Since when do I have to do the meeting? I hate meetings."

"I'm none too fond of elves," Lissette pointed out. "Fair is fair."

"All right," I sighed. "You have a deal. Where is it?"

Lissette rang for a servant and had him show me to the council chamber. I'd never have been able to follow the directions. This place is more of a maze than I first thought.

The Council Chamber deserves capital letters. The table is the centerpiece of the room, a massive, rectangular thing of some dark, close-grained wood. It seats thirty people comfortably, which is especially impressive since the chairs are built on the same scale—massive, heavy, and solid. The chairs are more appealing than the table, however, being heavily coated in liberal doses of velvet and padding. Nonetheless, the table and chairs do not fill the space. There is ample room all around the table for liveried young men and women to move, efficiently and quietly, in the bringing of food, drink, a hot towel, paper (*Paper*, I said, not parchment. I'm proud of that.), ink, quills, sealing wax, candles, and all the other accoutrements of either comfort or business. Around the perimeter of the room, pressed up against the walls, are benches, unpadded, uncomfortable, but solid and well-used. I presume they are present so witnesses, experts, or anyone the council might want to question has someplace out of the way to be while awaiting their summons to speak.

Halfway down one of the longer sides of the rectangular beast sits a larger chair. It's big enough for two, if they're on intimate terms, and stands high enough that Bronze would have to lift her head a trifle to get her nose over it—call it seven feet high and three wide or thereabouts. The whole thing looks done in an industrial style, all flat planes and hard angles, softened by the same plush padding as the other chairs, only more of it. Carved into the throne—excuse me, the *chair*—high up on the back so the design seems to hover over whoever sits there is a stylized crown. It is the only ornamentation, the only thing in the room that doesn't seem to have a specific function.

Then again, considering the placement, perhaps it does. It would be hard to forget the person sitting in that chair also wears a crown. The reminder is right there, hovering, as though the ghosts of kings held it in place.

I walked in completely unprepared.

The meeting was in full swing, with some councilors still having their breakfast, others having their post-breakfast nap, some reading, some writing, a few doodling, and a few arguing with each other about the tariff policies of the western cities versus the political realities of claiming them as part of the kingdom.

Nobody seemed to notice me, at first. All the attention—what there was of it—stayed on the three people actually doing the shouting and finger-pointing and waving of papers. Oops. Excuse me again. The attention stayed on the lively political debate taking place.

This suited me. I moved to the nearest bench, laid down on it, and motioned my bodyguards to sit. I pretended to be a row of books; they played bookends. This went on long enough I actually started to doze off.

"And what corner of the underworld did you spring from?" I didn't realize I was the one spoken to until the demanding voice added, "Well? Who ordered these knights to bring you here? Answer me!" followed by a general diminishing of conversation.

"Sorry," I apologized, sitting up. "I was never much for attending these things."

"Oh, *shit*," he breathed.

I raised an eyebrow at the sudden scramble. People sat up sharply. Standing people sat down with equal suddenness. Someone's mouthful of wine decorated the air over the table in a lovely mist. Nobody actually fainted or fell over backward, but I suspect the weight of the chairs prevents them from tipping easily.

Once everything achieved a reasonable state of equilibrium, I stood up. Everyone rose when I did. I strolled to the High Seat, casually slid it out and let my guards muscle it forward under me. Once I sat down, the rest of the room did.

"Good morning," I said, to the table in general. "Which one of you is Felkar?"

Felkar was seated opposite the Royal Chair, in the same position on the other side of the table. He stood up, slowly, carefully. He was an elderly, dignified gentleman with a wide gold chain from shoulder to shoulder over the embroidered doublet. He was thin, almost frail, but although his hair was almost completely white, it was all still there. His beard was short and neat, his eyes clear, and he seemed both attentive and alert. I wouldn't have suspected him of being in charge; he was easily the plainest-dressed man in the room. I don't count myself; I'm not, strictly speaking, a human being anymore.

"Your Majesty," he said, bowing slightly. I had the impression he might not be able to bend very well. Besides, there was a table in the way. I gestured him to seat himself again.

"I hear good things about you, Felkar. The Queen is pleased with your work."

"I am most grateful to Her Majesty for her confidence."

"And I am most grateful to her and to you for your competence and sense of duty to the kingdom as a whole. Thank you. Now, I presume you have all discussed policies, debated the merits of various plans of action, and have assembled recommendations for royal approval?"

"No, Your Majesty. Not as such. No."

"No?" I asked, feigning surprise. "Then I'm afraid I don't understand the purpose of this meeting. What, exactly, do you do here?"

"We are here to advise the Queen, Your Majesty."

"And how does that work?"

"Majesty?" he asked, eyebrows drawing together.

"This advising process. How does it work?"

"I... I am afraid I do not understand what Your Majesty is trying to ask. Forgive me, please."

"No, no—if you don't understand, it's my fault, not yours. I'll keep trying." I pondered for a moment and decided to tackle it with an example.

"Here, let's try this. Say you have a noble of some sort who's blocked off the King's Road and charges tolls to anyone who wishes to pass his border. If word of this reaches the palace, here, and is brought before this council, what normally happens?"

"Normally?"

"Yes. Here's a problem. It's just been reported. A messenger came in and handed you a note describing the situation. What do you do, Felkar?"

"I dispatch a company of soldiers to tear down the barriers and restore the right-of-way on the King's Road, Your Majesty."

"Huh. Well, yes, that's probably the right thing to do, but shouldn't the Queen be the one making the decision?"

"Why?" he asked, looking puzzled. "It is the commanding of men, not something for a woman to do, Your Majesty."

Yep, my teeth still lock together. I can't grind them. I bite like a butcher hitting a chopping block, but I can't gnash my teeth.

I beckoned one of my guards close. He leaned down and I looked at the closed helmet. Whispering to a man in the equivalent of a super-advanced motorcycle helmet is impractical. There are arrangements for air and sound, but the helmets do restrict their hearing a bit. I pretended to whisper while Firebrand relayed to him, instead. He hurried out of the room.

"Gentlemen," I began, spreading my hands on the table, "allow me to make a few observations and suggestions. Do you mind?"

I was immediately assured how no one in the room minded in the least hearing anything I had to say. One thing about a reputation as the Demon King, it's definitely good for uniting people in stark, unreasoning terror. I rummaged around in my mental toolbox and dug out my Demon King hat. It's pretty much the same hat I wear when dealing with the creatures living in the Eastrange. That is, it's a mode of thinking, an artificial set of attitudes I find distasteful, but which is sometimes necessary for public performances.

"You may not have been too clear on this," I began, "and I haven't been too interested until recently. I thought it was all going so well, but I was wrong. So forgive me if I was unclear. I'll try to dumb it down to the level of newborn infants and moderately-intelligent dogs. If some of you still fail to comprehend, I feel sure we can find a suitable response.

"For the first point. I am the ultimate authority in Karvalen, and I will bury this kingdom in the shredded, bloodless flesh of every man, woman, and child if it suits me to do so. Does anyone here have any trouble whatsoever understanding this fact?"

I was immediately assured in the strongest possible language how they did, indeed, absolutely understand.

"For the second point. I have other things I want to do besides sit on a throne all day and all night, deciding how much money to spend, how many taxes to levy, which troops to send where, and so forth. Are you capable of comprehending this?"

Again, they assured me they were completely with me.

"Good, good. Now, I have a Queen. I know, you think of her as a mere woman with a fancy title based on the fact she's was fortunate enough to marry me. And, truthfully, she is a woman, and she did gain her title by marrying me. I understand you think this, and I agree with it—as far as it goes.

"But I'm going to ask you a question. A very specific question. When I ask the question, I don't want you to answer it. I want you to think about it until you've considered all the possible answers. I'll even give you clues before I ask the question, so you can have an easier time choosing your answer.

"You're all aware the Queen is a lovely lady, but, as you have no doubt noticed, she is not the, quote, most ravishingly beautiful woman in the kingdom, unquote. I could have had immense beauty if I wanted it, as I am sure you are all aware. But I chose to marry Lissette. Lissette has other qualities that make her— to my mind—an ideal Queen.

"Now," I said, leaning back and steepling my fingers, "knowing I have other matters to which I must attend besides the day-to-day business of a kingdom, and knowing I selected Lissette for qualities I find ideal in a Queen, and having been told—I'm sure this was mentioned at least once—that Lissette should take charge of those day-to-day affairs of the kingdom... and pay close attention, because this is the question...

"Who rules this place when I'm not to be bothered with it?"

Ever seen people slowly shade from pale to pale green? It's not a pretty sight.

"Take your time," I encouraged. "Think about it, if you can. I'm not optimistic about this horse learning to sing, but you never know. When you think you know the answer, please write it down, sign it, fold it, and have it sent over to me. We'll wait until everyone figures it out. If necessary, we can help the slow learners."

You know, it's kind of nice to be able to say that sort of thing to a class of lunkheads. There have been whole semesters where I thought, *Do I say what I'm thinking, or do I keep my job?* There were days when it was a close call.

Quills scratched on paper. Papers rustled as servants stacked them in front of me. I counted them as they were handed in.

"I see we have one from everyone. Good. Let's see what sort of answers we have." I opened the one on top and read out, "The Queen of Karvalen, Lissette." I opened the next one and read out, "The Queen." I went through the whole stack, one by one, all with some variation on "The Queen."

"Gentlemen, I must applaud you. When I spell it out, draw you a diagram, and do everything but tell you the answer, you seem able to reach the proper conclusion.

"Now, I recognize some of you may chafe at the idea of a woman being the ultimate ruler—well, acting as ultimate ruler—of the kingdom, and therefore giving you orders. Being subject to a woman's whims? How fantastically strange! Wouldn't you agree? I'm sure you would. For some it might be considered tolerable. Others find it not so easily tolerated, of course. So, if you feel it might be too difficult for you—the very idea of being respectful, obedient subjects to a... a... a *woman*! Well! If you're not going to be able to endure such an indignity, I will certainly understand if you choose to resign from your position on this council. If that's the case, please do so now. Gather up your things and depart, please. I still have business with the council—assuming anyone at all chooses to remain, of course."

You know, I really didn't think anyone would fall for it. Oh, I spoke with a sympathetic voice, as though I could empathize with and agree with anyone who couldn't get behind the idea the Queen might be the exception to the general rule of women-as-property. But I swear, four men gathered up their papers, bowed in my direction, and left the room. The rest of them stirred and muttered and shifted in their seats, but remained.

"Excellent! Now that we've sorted out the people who are willing to work with Lissette—the Queen of Karvalen and unquestioned ruler of the nation—from the useless dregs who would only be trouble, I have one last thing to say on the subject.

"By keeping your fat rears in your chairs, you've promised me to work with her, obey her, and do your duty to the best of your ability—to advise her honestly, without eye to personal gain, and to implement *anything* she orders done, without foot-dragging, without half-measures, without delay. You will obey her with enthusiasm and with imagination, not merely as mindless automatons. I will have your allegiance, gentlemen, not merely your obedience, or I will have your testicles nailed to the table as a caution to your replacement."

I stood up, casually skidding the chair back. Everyone else rose, as well. Firebrand had already relayed the word from outside, so I told them to go ahead.

The doors opened and dozens of men came in, accompanied by six of the red-and-grey knights. Under the watchful eye of the knights, the men took the chairs and hauled them out of the room. I stopped the ones who went for Felkar's chair and had them leave it; the man was too old to expect him to stand. Other servants cleared away serving-dishes, wine bottles, and any other articles not useful for writing. One tray with a pitcher of water and a single cup wound up sitting slightly to my left on the table.

Four minutes? Maybe as many as six. Everyone but the councilors, four knights, and a single messenger were gone. All of a sudden, the place was much less a breakfast messhall and much more a stark boardroom.

"Felkar? Please be seated." I seated myself while the rest of the councilors remained standing. Felkar settled carefully into his chair.

"Now," I finished, pleasantly, "I want a list of issues facing the kingdom. For each issue, I want a list of possible courses of action. For each course of action, I want a list of the good points and the bad points. Do we have these readily at hand? No? Very well. Felkar, please take charge of the council meeting. Sir Tyrian and Sir Bartlet will be happy to help you keep order." I gestured them forward and the two gigantic knights moved around the table. They knelt on either side of Felkar, saluted him, stood up, and took station behind his chair to mirror the position of the knights still behind me.

"I'll leave you to it, gentlemen—and, for the hard of thinking, let me add that I am leaving *Felkar* in charge of this council. And, Felkar, aside from me, who is the one authority you answer to?"

"The Queen, Your Majesty," he replied, promptly.

"Indeed. If there is anyone at this table to fails to understand that I have delegated power and authority over this council to you, please feel free to have them beheaded—don't bother me or Lissette with the matter. Thank you for your time, gentlemen. You have quite a lot of work to do. I'll let you get to it."

I left with two of the four bodyguards, went back to my dungeon bedroom, stripped down, sat down under the running water, and shook.

Power. Mary once said power was the problem. But it's not always power. It's the person with such power.

Like it or not, I'm still the king. I have the power. And what did I do with it? I intimidated, interfered, *bullied* a bunch of men for no better reason than I didn't like the way they held a meeting!

What am I doing with power? Why should I be stuck with any sort of power? Why do I have to have the *responsibility* for power?

This is why I don't want to be a king—or a god, or a ruler, or whatever else people want me to be. I'm as narrow-minded and provincial as the next man. I'm just as likely to impose my ideas of what *I* think is right on people as any... any... any Myrna from Valley View Court.

I can have fangs and claws and a shadow that does weird things while I'm not looking, but I remain a man—or as limited, in this way, as a man. Turn me into a king, though, and I become a monster. The thing with the fangs will kill because that's the function of the thing with fangs. When it's time to go, we're there to make it happen painlessly, gently, so when death visits, it's an old friend come to invite you out on a long trip.

But make me a king and I'll strip away a man's dignity. I'll wreck his self-respect. I'll change the way he lives his life, interfere with it, rearrange it, fix it up to suit me—*me*, not him! It's his life, all their lives, and I've got a license to monkey around with it because I wear a fancy-schmancy metal hat!

Oh, gods and devils, what am I doing to Lissette's life? I'm making her Queen, a *ruling* Queen for the first time in Rethvan history! Does she want that? Is she only agreeing because she doesn't have a better offer? Is it her sense of responsibility and duty to the kingdom, or her willingness to accommodate my wishes as the King?

What am I doing to Lissette?

And, of course, my next thought: What am I doing to the kingdom? My first concern was for Lissette, because that's personal. My second thought was for the kingdom, because I don't care about it as much as I do about her! My personal feelings are stronger than my sense of duty and responsibility—and I don't know if that's a good thing or a bad thing!

I once had the idea I'm not human. Well, maybe I still am. I certainly have enough failings.

Boss?

"What is it, Firebrand?'

I know you like to drown your sorrows in a waterfall, but there are people outside who want to see you.

"Who?"

The minstrel girl, Tyma. She's insisting, and she's got stuff with her.

"Stuff?"

A big stick and some instruments.

"Ah." I sighed, turned the valve to close the water tap, and hauled myself to my feet. "Tell the guards to give me five minutes. I need to dry and dress."

On it, Boss.

I quick-dried, dressed, and went into the receiving room. The guards opened the door and let Tyma in.

Nine years did unpleasant things to her. Of course, having her father eviscerated by the Demon King might have had some effect, too. I flinched away from the thought. Her dark hair was still bound back in a braid, but grey veins ran through it. Lines surrounded her grey eyes, very few of them from laughing. Her hands were occupied with handles and straps to carry everything, but they seemed the most unchanged thing about her, still long-fingered, graceful and strong.

She retained her blunt-speaking ways, too.

"What did you do?" she demanded.

"I don't know. What are you talking about?"

"Don't give me that, you demon-souled, blood-drinking, father-slaying *thing!* Answer me!"

"I don't know!" I insisted, backing away from her. "What am I being blamed for? I have no idea! Just give me a clue!"

"These!" she shouted, shaking the straps and handles of the instruments. "These!"

"I didn't break them! I swear! I don't know why they aren't playing!"

"No, you unutterable moron! What did you do to make them play again?"

"What? I don't understand!"

She whirled away from me and laid out the instruments—lute, recorder, and lap-harp—on the low table. Once freed of their cases, the harp hummed, the lute strummed, and the recorder piped along. They seemed quite merry, actually. I approached the instruments and examined them.

"I don't see anything wrong with them," I confessed. "I don't see any damage to them, either. No breaks, no repairs, not even much in the way of physical scratches. They look pretty much the way they did when I first enchanted them. I can't find anything to indicate they were ever broken."

"That's impossible. I tried for years to get them to play! You're *lying!*" she accused, and brandished the Kingsmacker. "This thing says it's for smacking kings. Tell the truth!"

Tyma was fortunate I have very fast reflexes. I held up a hand to stop the guards. They stepped back, but they didn't sheathe their swords. Tyma glanced at them, looked startled, and lowered the stick.

"Show me what you did when they didn't work," I suggested. "How did you try to make them play? It may help me find the point of failure."

So she took out a stringed instrument from the remaining case and set it up. It reminded me of a violin, only longer and narrower, probably with more strings, too—I'm not sure how many strings a violin has. A *nykaherrin*? I think that's the name. Unlike a violin, it had an arrangement of keys or frets or something all along the neck. She sat down, held it upright, and played it by running a bow over it while manipulating the key-things.

The three instruments on the table were silent.

"What are you playing?"

"It's 'The Death of a Minstrel'," she replied. I began to have a suspicion.

"Don't you have anything... ah... more cheerful?"

"I don't remember many cheerful tunes," she spat.

"Try. Just one. I seem to remember one about a goose and a duck getting married."

"'The Wedding of Duck and Goose.' It's silly."

"Yes, it is. But it's also funny. Go on, try to play it."

"That one's dusty in my fingers."

"Blow on them and try," I insisted. She sighed and started sawing again, haltingly. The instruments on the table picked it right up and let her lead the tune, following her pacing and tempo and all that musical stuff. Very supportive, the backup instrumentals. She made it about a third of the way through the song before she gave it up.

"What is this? Do they only work for happy songs?"

"That could be the case, but I'm starting to suspect it's more specific. Do you know a sad song? A mourning song, maybe?"

"Several."

"One that doesn't revolve around me?"

"I... yes. I think so."

"Try one."

She started a melancholy tune, low and slow. It would have fit well with a procession following a coffin to the graveyard. Sure enough, the backup instruments joined in with her and turned it into something you wouldn't want to play near anyone with a sharp object and a history of depression.

"I think I've figured it out," I told her, and she stopped playing.

"What? What's wrong with them?"

"Nothing at all. They appear to dislike some songs. You've got to remember, Linnaeus contributed some of himself to the making of these instruments. Part of his soul, if you will, is in them. They're not... well, they're not alive in the sense of you or I, or even in the sense of a dog or cow, but there is something of life within them. They can like a tune or hate it, apparently, and can choose not to play. That's what they appear to be doing." I shrugged. "I didn't anticipate this, but I suppose I should have."

"So I can only use them to play songs *they* like?" she demanded.

"Well, I don't know about *use* them. You might want to think of them as fellow musicians in your group. You all have to agree on what to play, after all. But these musicians won't spend money, get sick, miss a note, or even demand to be paid. The only thing they have an opinion about—I presume it's an opinion reflecting Linnaeus' opinion—is the music they play."

"Which means they won't play anything knocking *you*," she accused.

"I don't know, but I have to guess so. I think Linnaeus liked me, gods alone know why."

"You planned this!" she seethed. "All those years ago, when you made them! You made sure Linnaeus couldn't sing anything unpleasant about you. You set it up so he could only sing your praises!"

"I only wish I were that clever," I admitted. "It's a good idea, from a sneaky bastard standpoint. I can't do it, though. To control them so precisely, I would have to be the one contributing the musical talent, and I don't *have* any. The animating force, the vital essence making these things produce music—not random noise, but music—is a small part of Linnaeus."

She quietly put her *nykaherrin* in its case and started putting the other instruments away, as well.

"I'm sorry I couldn't be more help."

"You owe me an instrument," she spat.

"Pick one out," I told her. "I also owe you some time with a stick."

She paused and examined the Kingsmacker again. She looked at me with narrowed eyes.

"Yes. Yes, you do. You owe me more than that."

"Beg pardon?"

"You think beating you is enough? Oh, no. No, no, no, no. No. You owe me for a *father*, you son of a bitch."

"I won't deny it."

"Here's how it's going to work. I'll hold on to this—it makes a good symbol of your debt—and I'll let you know what I want. I'm not sure what it is, yet, but my own instrument is a good start."

"I see. All right. I won't promise I can give you what you ask for, but I promise to listen and to do what I can."

Tyma flipped the Kingsmacker into the air and caught it.

"You think that's good enough?"

"I think it's the best I can do," I countered. "You wish for something I can't give and you'll be disappointed. But I'll do what I can. If it's beyond me, it's beyond me, and you'll have to live with it."

Tyma regarded me with narrowed eyes, still flipping the stick. At last, she nodded.

"All right. Now get me my instrument."

I ordered it done, exit stage left, while enter stage right, a new messenger. Apparently, the Queen would appreciate a visit in the solarium at my convenience. Not my preferred place for a meeting, but she's the Queen. I wondered if there was a significance to the meeting-place. I hoped not. I sent word to Seldar to bring the crown, though. It would look nice in the sunshine, so this might be a good time to present it to Lissette.

I didn't realize it was lunchtime. Time sure flies when you're having a nervous breakdown and questioning the value of your existence.

Lissette was happily seated at one end of a medium-sized table, spoon-feeding a miniature person of a few months of age, while Liam sat at her left, looking preoccupied and picking at his food. She had thoughtfully seen to it a place was set opposite her. I occupied this seat—a somewhat large and well-constructed chair, obviously brought into the solarium from elsewhere; another thoughtful touch—and a waiter-type servant started bringing food. I didn't recognize this one; he was different from the one at breakfast. He looked nervous and tended to twitch whenever I spoke.

"I trust your morning went well?" Lissette asked. She didn't sound saccharine sweet or upset. It's possible she actually cared enough to task. Or maybe she was hiding her feelings with children present.

Come to that, where were the other kids? Did she not want to expose them to me? This little one wouldn't remember me and Liam had already forced the issue. Were the others being protected? Or, since they were probably Thomen's children, were they being kept away from me to avoid any possible negative reaction—in short, were the others being protected?

I don't know. I'm becoming more and more comfortable with ignorance when it comes to questions I shouldn't even ask myself.

"My morning? Good question," I admitted, and thought about it. "I'm not sure. I lectured a Prince, interfered with a council meeting, threatened every minister you have—with the exception of Felkar—rearranged the protocol for future meetings, made demands, reinforced your authority and expanded it, nearly got smacked by Tyma, discovered I gave magical instruments free will, acknowledged a life-debt, and, I hope, am about to round it all off with a pleasant lunch. How was your morning?"

"I had a discussion with a coldly calculating creature with a profound insight into politics—the elf you call 'Bob.' I despise elves and I think he knows it."

"Probably."

"If he's obeying your command to advise me well and truly, then he gives good advice. He's clever."

"Or it might be millennia of experience."

"Afterward, I went to the Council Chamber to observe the process of government. I had considerably more effect on the course of the kingdom than is usual. A surprising, almost shocking amount of work was getting done. It was almost as though the ministers were in a hurry to be done so they could sit down."

"That's why I had the chairs removed," I agreed. "Meeting go faster when people aren't all comfy-cozy. No food, no drinks, no chairs—and a whole lot more focus."

"May I ask why there were wrecked chairs in the Council Chamber?"

"Of course. I didn't forbid messengers in there. Someone was bound to send for a chair once I was gone."

"And...?"

"And I ordered some red sashes to keep watch. They had instructions to smash any chair as soon as it was placed for someone, then announce something like, 'His Majesty shall be informed of your attempt to circumvent his implied wishes,' or some such." I chewed for a moment, swallowed, and added, "By the way, how many dead chairs were there?"

"Three, but I believe they were all brought in at the same time."

"Get names," I suggested. "Those ministers are either lazy or stupid."

"Oh, I know who they are," she said, darkly. I had a momentary flashback to the warrior-queen wanting to ride into a battle. Lissette might be a mommy, but the girl who worked so hard to become a warrior was still in there. This pleased me in ways I can't define.

I wish things had worked out differently. I could love Lissette with very little prompting. How she feels, though, after nine years of dealing with the face of my evil twin...

"Good, good." I devoted effort to shoveling food into my maw while also trying to enjoy it. The drawback to my daytime metabolism is the ability to consume huge quantities without the chance to take any pleasure in the experience. If I ate slowly, relishing the flavors—suitably muted by a spell—I would eat without pause, all day long, from sunup to sundown. If I want to get anything done, I have to insufflate instead of eat. I don't *have* to eat, but I do get hungry.

Are there "food pills" I can take? I'll have to ask Mary and Diogenes.

"I've also had a conversation with Seldar about your ministers and mine," she continued. "He's agreed to stand aside for Felkar and be his deputy on the Council. When Felkar retires, Seldar will assume his duties. If you approve, of course."

"If you approve, I approve. If anyone has anything else along those lines, tell them this: I agree with you unreservedly."

"That's a sweeping statement."

"I meant it to be. Declare war on a baron or another country, order mass executions of the Church of Light or donate a parcel of land for all their worshipers to emigrate. You're the Queen. If you say it, they better assume *I* said it—they won't enjoy me saying it personally. End of story."

Lissette and I ate in silence for a bit, broken only by the urgent grunting from the baby-chair and the occasional squeal or giggle. Lissette seemed most thoughtful. The baby seemed gleefully determined to wear squashed peas.

"Father, Your Majesty?"

"Liam, we're in private and you're trying to be polite. That combination means you can be a less formal."

"What shall I call you?"

"Whatever you like, so long as it's not rude."

"Father?"

"That'll do."

"May I ask a question?"

"You may."

"What did you mean?"

"About what?"

"Serving."

"Refresh my memory."

"You said a ruler serves the people."

"Yes."

"But a ruler orders them. If I'm the ruler, I order people around. They do what I tell them. They serve me. I don't serve them." He sounded puzzled, as though he actually wanted an answer. Well, maybe the concept was a little beyond his age bracket.

"This is going to be hard to grasp," I told him, "mainly because the Demon King was a terrible example. In an ideal world, the king is merely the person stuck with the job of making sure the kingdom runs smoothly. Give me a minute and maybe I can come up with a metaphor."

"A what?"

"Let me think about it for a minute." I wolfed down lunch and thought. Lissette looked at me from time to time with an expression I couldn't read. I think she was amused, at least a little. Small boy stumps King sort of thing.

"All right," I said, having finished what I had available. "Let's try this another way. Do you like horses?"

"Yes," he said, and added proudly, "I'm a very good rider."

"Good. Have you ever seen a team of horses hauling something?"

"Yes."

"This might work, then. If you see a man driving a wagon and it's got four horses hauling it, the guy doing the driving is in charge, right?"

"Right."

"And the horses are doing what they're told, because that's what they're supposed to do, right?"

"Right."

"And if the driver is a lousy driver, not choosing good paths, or putting too much of a load on the wagon, or if he beats and starves his horses—you did say you like horses, didn't you?"

"Yes, I do. I have one named Saelan."

"So, if you saw a wagon-driver beating his starving horses to force them to pull a too-heavy load down a rotten path, how would that make you feel?"

"I'd have him whipped with his own whip," Liam stated, positively.

The matter-of-fact way Liam said it made me wonder if he already had. Either way, it was a chilling comment on the savagery of children. Possibly even a comment on the influence of awful fathers and royal privilege. I pressed on with my lesson, though.

"But he's the one driving the wagon. The horses work for him, don't they?"

"Yes, but they're the ones doing the work!" Liam protested. "They… they do as they're told."

"What about our driver, then? Why whip him?"

"Because he's a bad driver! He's supposed to take care of his horses!"

"Exactly."

"I don't understand. What's this got to do with being a king?"

"The wagon is the kingdom. The horses are the people. The king is the driver. If you want to accomplish something, you load up the wagon—you give orders to the kingdom. If it's too much of a load, you may break the wagon or work your horses to death. You have to organize their work so they earn enough to feed themselves and maintain the wagon. They do the work, but you have to take care of them—you serve them just as much as they serve you, or you're the bad driver. A bad king."

A servant put another platter down on the table. I thanked him and spooned more onto my plate while Liam looked inquisitively at his mother.

"Are you finished?" Lissette asked. I looked up. She was addressing Liam. Liam nodded. I gently tapped him in the shin with my foot, under the table. He looked startled and turned to me. I expressed with my eyebrows that he should try answering his mother again.

"Yes, Mother."

"Then you may go."

Liam got up, bowed to us, and walked from the room. I saw a pair of courtly types through the open door, waiting for him.

"Are you sure you don't want to be King?" Lissette asked, once the doors closed.

"Positive. Too many people want to drain my blood because of what I am. Hostile religions—one, anyway—wants me evaporated in glowing agony. Angry magi from other worlds want to subdivide me into screaming pieces. And I have all the political savvy of a brain-damaged groundhog."

"You dumped another bucket of wisdom over my—our—son, and you claim to have no political savvy?"

"That's different."

"Is it? I wonder."

"It's a general principle. It's not the details of running a government. I couldn't tell you what the Baron Blowhard wants, why, or what to do about it. All I know about the job is it requires doing the best you can for everyone, and I have no idea how to go about it. You want to make a city vanish in thunder and fire? Fine. I can do that. But which city, when, and best of all *why* is beyond me. For the good of the kingdom, sure, but why is that what's best for the kingdom? That's why I need to stay out of political office."

"But you want me to try to do it?" she added.

"If you will," I admitted. Suddenly, I wasn't hungry anymore. "It's an awful job with long hours, unpleasant pressure, and enormous responsibility, but the pay is good and the benefits package is second to none. I believe you can do it, if you will."

"And if I won't?"

"I'll give you a huge pile of money, take you anywhere in the world you want to go, and see if I can put the crown on Seldar's head."

Lissette blinked at me.

"Are you... no, you're never serious, not intentionally. Do you *mean* what you just said?"

"Seldar should be here at some point. I asked him to bring the new crown. You can ask him. If he agrees to do it, you're off the hook."

I went back to picking at my food. My appetite still wasn't behaving, but I ate anyway. Habit.

Lissette pretended to eat, too. Political problems ruin meals. Let it be known as Eric's Law of Lunch henceforth. Lissette also sent someone to find Seldar and hurry him up. I thought it a very good idea, because lunch was turning awkward.

Seldar joined us shortly thereafter, accompanied by Torvil and Kammen. He placed the box on the table without a word. I lifted out the crown and put it on top of the box.

"What do you think?"

"It's gorgeous. Elf-work?"

"The material, yes. I had it made. The enchantments I did personally."

"Enchantments?" she asked, suddenly wary.

"Yes. After the trouble Thomen caused, I thought it a good idea to enchant the crown with something to ward against mental influences. Whoever wears this fancy hat is as close to immune to mind control as I can manage."

"You have my interest," Lissette admitted, laying down her fork and staring at the fancy hat in question. "How long does it work?"

"Indefinitely. It's an enchantment. Oh, wait—no, it only works while you wear it."

"A pity."

"We can get other things for when the crown is inconvenient."

"I already commissioned some, but I'm hesitant about trusting them."

"I can imagine. But the crown does other things, too."

"Oh?"

"It'll defend your brain from people throwing spells at it, yes, but the first time you put it on it sort of looks at your mind so it can recognize it later. If someone messes with your head while you're not wearing the crown, the next time you put the crown on, it'll alert people that you've been manipulated. That way they can help you recover and hunt down the culprit."

"I see."

"The other thing it can do—it's optional; you don't have to use it—is it can record things you do while wearing it. If you're considering a course of action as the ruler of the kingdom, you can have your deliberations and considerations recorded in the crown. When you pass it on to whoever gets it next, those recorded experiences are there for him or her to draw on. The new king or queen can then draw on your experience and wisdom to help them make good decisions. And their heirs will have the benefit of the experience of everyone who preceded them. The rulers of Karvalen get wiser every time a new one is crowned."

Lissette looked at me with an expression crossed between frustration, amusement, and disbelief.

"Explain to me again why you're abdicating."

"What do you mean? I explained why."

"And yet you keep doing things like *this*," she gestured at the crown.

"It's just a gadget. Gadgets I can do."

"Why did you make roads?" she asked, taking me by surprise.

"Huh?"

"Roads. Stone roads. Straight line roads, everywhere. Why?"

"I thought I already told you. Because I hated those muddy tracks Rethven used to have for roads. Besides, roads are the foundations of commerce and communications—kingdom-wide unity. See, people think distance is a function of miles. It's not. It's a function of *time*. It used to be weeks, maybe months if the weather was bad, from one border of Rethven to another. Now it can be done in a few days by a determined rider, if there are fresh horses stationed along the way. The kingdom—counting the far side of the Eastrange—has more miles in it, but the travel takes less time, so the kingdom is actually smaller. It's easier to travel, easier to communicate, easier to ship goods from a place of plenty to a place of need, all that stuff. Now, the mountain is what actually—"

"Stop talking," Lissette said, making a mouth-closing gesture with one hand. I shut up. "You prattle on when someone asks a simple question."

"Guilty."

"I know. But you are demonstrating—again! —that you should be King."

"And I tell you I'm not fit for the job. Advisor, yes. Minister in charge of weird magic, maybe. Secret weapon, sure. But negotiating with nobles and ruling the world? No, thank you."

"Yet, you have no problem asking *me* to do it."

"You're better at it."

"Seldar?" Lissette asked.

"Yes, Your Majesty?"

"Would you take the throne and crown if I were to give it to you?"

"I am a priest of the Lord of Justice, Your Majesty. It is my understanding the King does not wish to place such power in any individual who may be directly pressured by divine influence."

"That lets out Tianna, too. And Beltar?"

"Yes, Your Majesty."

"Who would you put on the throne, Seldar?" she asked.

Seldar glanced at me and said nothing.

"Aside from him," Lissette added. "He's a god, or worshiped as one, I hear."

"Your Majesty, if it were given to me to name his successor, I can think of no one better suited to the position than yourself. There are, of course, certain obstacles to this state of affairs, but I feel as he does: You possess the necessary capabilities to rule wisely and well."

"And if I put my foot down and demand he help me? What do you think he'll do?"

"I'm sitting right here," I pointed out.

"I'm asking Seldar," she snapped. I shut up.

"Your Majesty, if you demand it... I cannot say for certain, but I feel a demand will be met with considerable... ah... he does not respond well to demands. However, if your insistence takes the form of asking for his help, I believe he will move mountains, boil seas, and bring down stars from the heavens for you."

Lissette stood up. I stood up with her. She gestured and Seldar brought her the crown. She held it in her hands, walking around the solarium, looking at it in the light. The little person made grunting noises and kicked a bit; I spooned something gooey into it. Some went down the front, some down the throat. Win a little, lose a little.

"You know the nobles, almost every single one of them, is going to fight you on this," Lissette said, finally. "No—they will fight *us* on this. I'm a woman, and they will not take orders from a woman. You saw the council. You saw how many of them walked out? Now imagine it with men who have proud family histories, who were once princes of their own domains. Men who are already insulted by being conquered by the armies of some monster in human form, ruled over by a Thing from the Outer Darkness. In their minds and hearts, they will hate me even more than they hate you."

"Oh, I don't know. I can think of a couple who don't hate me."

"As can I. And the rest?"

I didn't have an answer to that.

Seldar cleared his throat. We both turned.

"If Your Majesties will permit me an observation?" I waved him on. "It occurs to me there may be a way to turn their hatred into an advantage. Assuming, of course, Her Majesty will consent to take the crown?"

"Assume it," Lissette instructed.

"If the Grand Council of Nobles can be suitably insulted, I believe the members of that body will be more than willing to accept Lissette as the ruling, reigning Queen of Karvalen."

"I don't believe it," Lissette stated. "It's impossible."

"Don't be so quick to sell Seldar short," I advised. "Let's hear it, Seldar."

"You will not like it," he warned.

"Oh?"

"It involves the use of the Demon King's public persona and his personal killers—those who remain, I should say."

"You're right. I don't like it. But tell me anyhow."

So he told us. It was brilliant and ruthless and every bit a Demon King's solution. It was positively Machiavellian, bordering closely on diabolical.

I hated it and couldn't find one logical reason not to do it. I've done a lot of things I don't like for this place. This—if you'll pardon the expression—would simply be the crowning example.

"We better warn Tianna in advance," I advised. "And I better put on my Demon King hat."

"We have it here," Lissette replied.

"I was being metaphorical. It's not an actual hat."

"I wasn't. We have the crown of the Demon King."

I thought about it for several seconds.

"Maybe you should send for it."

And now a chapter of life draws to a close. What once was will soon be no more. Things change, and not always for the worse—but that's the way to bet.

I went to the meeting with a sense of anticipation. Not in the gift sense; I wasn't looking forward to having something new. I was thinking about the future, anticipating it. Everything—well, everything involving the Kingdom of Karvalen—hinged on my performance.

My other emotion was dread.

I'm glad I took a theater course. Now I wish I took more of them. Seems to me, my ability to pretend I'm someone I'm not has been important. Then again, maybe one could say that's what got me into this mess.

I need to wow the crowd tonight. If I can throw myself into the role, really sell it, I can quit the king business and turn it over to someone who knows what she's doing. I need to avoid massive wars to maintain the unity of a kingdom, and I need to not be on the throne. Add to that I would like to be *elsewhere*, as in being a really hard target for the Hand, as well as about my personal business—finding Tort, murdering magi, and so on.

The Ardents' farmhouse felt like home. How much more so does Karvalen? My pet rock is my house. My daughter and granddaughter are here. My estranged wife and our son live just the other side of the mountains. I have a dozen or more people who actually care about me, and some unreasonably high number of people I actually care about.

This is home.

And I'm leaving it because that's what's best for it. It may also be what's best for me, but I don't count.

Sometimes, I look back on all the times I've been called some variation of stupid and wonder if they were right. Most of the time I don't bother to wonder.

So. My evening.

The scene:

The Great Hall of the Palace of Carrillon. It's a large, mostly-open space with some counterforts at the base of the walls and some similar bracing in the wooden beams above. One end is entirely a raised platform of five steps; it has a smaller platform with three more steps up to the throne. The central floor area is temporarily dominated by smaller, less pretentious chairs. Either side has wooden, bleacher-like arrangements between the counterforts, assembled for the occasion, blocking the lower half of the tall windows. A forest of banners hangs from the ceiling beams, each one bearing the symbol of an attending house. Overlooking everything from behind the throne is the carved crest of the King, inlaid with polished metal.

The people:

Nobles of every rank mill about, mingling in the aisles or sitting in the widely-spaced chairs. Clergy from dozens of religions mix around the edges or jockey for a good spot in the left-side bleachers. Guild masters, civic leaders, and other citizens of wealth or influence do the same on the right. Knights in black armor form a wall on the lower steps of the dais, wear the crossed red and grey. Liveried servants, circulating like particles in solution, distribute fine finger-foods and a dizzying variety of drinks.

Outside, grey sashes and steel-armored killers both peel bodyguards and personal weapons off anyone and everyone who enters the hall. Three magicians eyeball everything, two of them supervised by the third, T'yl. Two at a time, thirty-two of the steel-clad killers escort sixteen of the King's guests—a special honor, perhaps, but one those guests could do without. But what can they say?

Perhaps they suspect what is to come, but they cannot know. Even if they were told outright, how many would believe, rather than take refuge in denial?

And... action!

The sound of a deep, heavy bell reverberated through the Great Hall, so low and deep it was a physical presence in the pit of the stomach as much as in the ears. It tolled like the rumble of thunder, shook drinks in their fluted glasses, silenced the world. The lights dimmed, darkened, went out. The great doors closed with a heavy thud, like the lid of a sarcophagus falling shut. The red light of sunset seeped through the western windows, dripping like cold blood into the spaces between the rolling thunders of the bell.

The last light of day vanished, leaving all in darkness. The lamps rose slowly from the glow of embers up through candle-flame and into flickering, dancing brightness. Glowing, magical motes fluttered into life among the rafters and beams above, sprinkling their own diffuse illumination over the floor. The hall proper shone with the tawny light of lamps, but the shadows clustered thickly around the dais and the throne.

As the lights rose hesitantly, almost fearfully, from the darkness, a presence filled the room.

A black-armored figure sat upon the throne, a crown of dark iron and rubies upon his grey-black brow. A naked sword lay across his lap, twinkling with an unnatural brightness, as though flames danced within the metal, leashed, contained, but yearning to burn free. Twin giants, almost as dark, stood just below and to the sides of the throne's dais. They wore shields with the King's emblem and bore naked swords.

Behind him, his inky, unnatural shadow slid up over the throne and did strange things on the wall. It twisted, as though looking around. It changed shape and size at whim. It ran in the grooves of the great symbol like blood, clinging slightly. It was as dark as the empty places between the worlds, perhaps even as hungry.

People gasped and coughed, murmuring softly as they found their seats. Through all the walking and shuffling and slipping by each other, the nightmare king observed with eyes like holes, black within black within black. He saw a shifting mass of energies, colors like kaleidoscopes, coruscating and sparkling, radiant, dim, or indifferent. He watched the colors shift, seeking certain shades, certain patterns, confirming by eye what he knew from tongues, while those of the crowd shuffled into their places and into silence.

When all were settled, he made a slight gesture. Felkar approached from His Majesty's right to climb the stairs, slowly and carefully, to attend the King. They whispered for several moments and Felkar scribbled rapidly, nodded repeatedly. He exited through one of the guarded side-doors.

Torvil and Kammen, on either side of the throne's dais, raised their swords in salute.

"Hail the King!"

Every knight in the room did the same, drawing, saluting, shouting, "Hail the King!"

A ragged chorus emerged from the rest of the guests, unfamiliar with the new protocol. Nevertheless, they also hailed the King.

The knights returned to their ready positions, waiting for orders—or waiting for an opportunity to fulfill their orders. A tension, a readiness, filled the air about them.

"Welcome," said the King, softly, but his voice carried to every corner of the room. It failed to echo, giving every person an eerie feeling of the King speaking to them, personally, as though at their very elbow. No one screamed, though many shivered.

"First things. I notice there have been a number of liberties taken during my brief sojourn away from the Palace."

A cold sensation swept through the crowd, one having nothing to do with the temperature.

"I've tried to be liberal," the King continued. "To enjoy myself with pleasant diversions. To allow you to do... well, pretty much as you pleased. It all seemed to be going so well. Then I go away for a bit, and like naughty children, you've spilled wine on the rugs, broken furniture, and chewed on my slippers. Did I say 'children'? Perhaps I meant mongrel dogs.

"Some of you, of course, tended to your own business, kept on about your affairs, and were everything I could have wished in loyal, respectful, and wise subjects. It is but a few of you, I think, who are the real trouble. Fortunately, I am a discerning and just ruler. I do not believe in punishing those who have done me no wrong." He chuckled. "Well, not if they're useful to me." He raised a hand and made a sharp chopping gesture.

Without a word, steel-clad killers seized the hair or head of those they escorted, drew a blade across the throat, and held them while blood sprayed. People screamed, some sprang away from the sudden deaths, more held their places and tried to silence the others. Several nobles, a few guild masters—they bled, they struggled briefly, and they died. The armored killers pushed the bodies down to the floor, heaps of dead or dying flesh, before marching themselves to the great doors at the rear of the hall and forming a line in front of it.

Streamers of blood ran over the stones, trickling slowly toward the dais, quickening as they approached, slithering rapidly, even eagerly, up the steps, like crimson serpents fawning on their master.

"Now that we have concluded the majority of the executions, we can move on to other business."

"Your Majesty," Seldar said, rising from his seat in the bleachers. He wore only the regalia of a priest of the Lord of Justice, not his sword or armor.

"My lord Seldar, Priest of Justice. You are recognized. Speak."

"As a priest of the Lord of Justice, I must protest. These men had no trial, not even the opportunity to speak in their defense."

"As such a priest, I understand you must make such a protest," the King answered, mildly. "One might make the argument they received justice in having a quick death. Regardless, this is a civic matter, not a religious one, and your objection has no place here. Guards. Bring him to the dungeons, there to await my pleasures."

Four black-armored figures walked through the unarmed crowd as though it moved of its own volition from their path—which was, in fact, the case. Seldar was half-carried, half-escorted from the Great Hall through one of the smaller doors. It closed with a heavy thud, followed by the sound of bolts locking it.

Everyone in the room—everyone with a face not concealed by a helmet—appeared to be somewhere between appalled and deeply thoughtful.

"Would anyone else care to question my right to mete out what punishments I deem fit? No? Good.

"On a lighter note, I have decided to expand upon my educational program. I believe a well-educated nobility to be a key factor in maintaining a coherent and unified kingdom. To this end, every noble of the rank of Baron or higher will send their firstborn son—if and when they have one—to live in the capitol. They will reside here while between the ages of five and fifteen. They will live within the Palace and be taught all the arts a nobleman must know. Reading, writing, mathematics, the arts of battle and of magic, as well as many, many other things important to their continued health and well-being.

"Failure to so deliver these young men will result in the death of the child in question and his parents. This policy is to take effect immediately. You have twenty days to deliver—those of you with heirs between the ages of five and fifteen. You are, of course, encouraged to visit as often as you like to observe their progress in their studies.

"On another note, I have been informed the Hand has been reconstituted as a secret society within the Church of Light. Some of you may be aware I have a personal prejudice against this particular cult, and their secret society in particular. I am not outlawing their cult. I've no wish to interfere in religious matters, just as I've no wish for religious matters to interfere with my kingdom. I am, however, pointing out that any member of the Hand who wishes to step forward and repent of his foolishness will be shown mercy."

The King paused to allow what was said—and what was *not* said—to sink in.

"Furthermore, should anyone bring to the Palace a captive, proven member of the Hand for my personal amusement, I feel certain some measure of goodwill will be obtained. Which, I assure you, is otherwise difficult to come by."

This seemed to meet with general agreement.

"Now, as to the rulership of the Kingdom of Karvalen. Let me point out to the hard of thinking that Karvalen is one tiny piece of a very much larger world. There was a time when almost all the world was under the rule of a single empire. Do you really think I can waste all my time on this backward little hinterland? I have things to do, kingdoms to conquer, regimes to topple, and whole races to put to the sword and fang.

"Pitiful little acts of rebellion and stupidity will annoy me. Perhaps you should keep each other from being stupid? If such a thing is possible, of course. I might not be so... selective... the next time I become annoyed.

"Know this. I am going to leave Karvalen—again! —and I am leaving Lissette in charge—again! She is the Queen, and she is going to rule the place with a rod of iron and a whim of steel. Every last one of you is now, personally, aware of this. You have *no* excuse, no mitigating circumstance, no chance whatsoever at avoiding my wrath. She reports to me—as do many others, some of whom sit among you even now. But Lissette reports *only* to me, is responsible and answerable to me, and to me *alone*."

The King stretched his legs out, crossed them at the ankles.

"Now, your Queen has some ideas about 'justice' and 'laws' and general do-goodishness. I'm tolerant of her whims. I can let her play the nice girl. And as long as *you* humor her in these things, I'm sure you walking sacks of blood will manage to get along. But make no mistake, even if it sounds as if she's taken leave of her senses by being too kind, too merciful, I still expect you to jump when she says to hop. You jump as if I were standing behind you, because one day, if you do not jump quickly enough, *I will be*.

"Does anyone have any questions? Stand up if you have a question and I'll call on you."

Several nobles stood up. The King indicated Banler.

"Your Majesty has demanded hostages of—"

"Students," the King corrected.

"Students," Banler agreed, grudgingly. "Students of his nobles. What assurances do we have of their... continued education?"

"You're welcome to reside in the capitol, in your town houses, or even in the Palace itself. You can watch as your sons are instructed in all the arts. It is my firm intention to see them very well-educated and wise, so they may rule, one day, over vaster territories than their fathers'. You don't think I can personally oversee the details of every single county and barony, do you? I'll need them or their heirs to be as brilliant and capable as possible to supervise and govern the next kingdoms. But I'm sure you would be *delighted* to discuss it over dinner as soon as this meeting is adjourned."

"Yes, Your Majesty," Banler agreed, and sat down.

The King called upon another standing noble, the Count of Helvetown.

"Your Majesty, when you conquered your way across old Rethven—"

"Reuniting the shattered remnants of the kingdom in the process."

"Er, yes. Your Majesty laid claim to lands west, all the way to the Western Sea."

"Your point?"

"I was promised much of the land, but I have yet to see it pay so much as a copper."

"Fine," the King sighed. "Take it up with Lissette and see how many men she can spare to slaughter everything to the west of Helvetown. I'm certainly not going to waste my time on a local matter. Sit down. Next... you—I don't recall your name offhand."

"Baron Miller, Your Majesty."

"Go on. What is it?"

"No one else here is going to say it, Your Majesty, but I will."

"If you feel it must be said."

"You are an evil thing from the age of the Empire and should be pulled down, destroyed."

"I admire your courage," the King replied, sincerely. "I really do. You are a credit to the human race and to the very title of nobility. Unfortunately, you are also stupid, as the survivors of this meeting might tell you if you were capable of listening."

The Baron Miller suddenly paled, staggered, and fell to his knees. Under the keen gaze of the King, he collapsed to the floor and lay unmoving. The King gestured sharply, a whiplash *grasping* movement with one clawed hand. The body slid forward, as though dragged. People jumped, moving themselves and chairs out of the way as the body slid slowly to the foot of the dais. The King gestured with both hands and his shadow seemed to come free of the wall, reaching down to lift the body, drawing it into the King's taloned hands.

Claws ripped, tearing open the throat, the neck, shredding flesh. The bones in the neck popped, cracked, broke, parted. Blood poured out, splashing everywhere and bubbling, rolling, flowing into the King.

The head bounced one way, the body slumped the other.

"Listen as though your lives depend on it," the King said into the thick, cold silence. His voice was emotionless, dead. "I am a monster. I am a *thing*. I wear the crown of iron and blood. Mind your business and I will pass over you. You will live a long and happy life. Become my business and you will not. Because I will have *order*, and I will have *peace*, and I will have it even if I have to empty the kingdom of all life and create some, perhaps more amenable and wise. *I have spoken*," he finished, and a shadow passed over the room.

The King turned his head and called for the Queen. She came in, dressed all in white, as radiantly beautiful as the King was dark and terrible. The shadow lifted as she entered, and the room brightened. Her presence seemed to dispel the chill in the air. She crossed the dais to stand beside the throne.

Torvil lifted a purple cushion with the Queen's Crown, gleaming silver and glossy black, twinkling with green and gold at the spiked tips. Torvil knelt by the throne and held it up.

"Since the Queen is not a dark and terrible thing," the King continued, taking the crown and rising, "she does not wear a crown of iron, but one of grace and beauty, as befits a mortal ruler. As long as she rules well and wisely, I need not be bothered with this dirty, smelly little nation, which pleases me more than I can say. Kneel, woman."

Lissette knelt, keeping her eyes downcast.

"With this crown, I anoint thee Queen of Karvalen and all surrounding spaces. Rule over the men, women, children—all the people and races of your nation—as though I spoke through your lips, even unto their living and their dying. Let all who witness here today take heed, and all their heirs, assigns, successors, and subjects, for Lissette the First reigns and rules now as Queen of Karvalen."

The King lowered the crown onto her head in a deep, breathless silence. He held out his hand and the Queen took it, rising to stand at the base of the throne, turning to face the assembled people. The King settled on his throne again. He raised his eyebrows at everyone in the hall.

"You may now express your delight," he suggested.

As a thousand mortal voices rose in wild cheering, the King wrapped himself in shadow. When the darkness drained away, the King was nowhere to be seen. Lissette took the throne, seating herself only on the edge of it, hands resting lightly on the wide-spaced arms. The cheering redoubled.

What do you wash a soul in? Mine needed a bath. It's not like I can scrub it clean with the blood of Christ; I'll just soak it up or catch fire, depending. It's not fair.

I'm sure Banler was sitting somewhere, waiting and wondering if the King was having him to dinner or having him *for* dinner. I think I'll just skip dinner and let him breathe a sigh of relief. Seldar, once he said his lines, probably went off to do something intelligent and practical—possibly explaining to Banler how sending his heir to be educated in the Palace was a good thing. And, of course, Lissette was accepting oaths of fealty and assurances of loyalty from a large crowd of people, all anxious to be alive in the morning.

I was upstairs, in the south tower, the tallest of the towers in the palace. The topmost floor was a small, circular room under a conical roof. From the bird droppings, I guessed no one got up here to clean it very often. A small, wooden door led out onto the narrow walkway surrounding the top of the tower. I went out on it, half-sat on the edge, and tried to enjoy the breeze before the approaching storm front rolled over everything.

I used to get such a rush from feeling the wind blow over me. Standing on a canyon lip, up the side of a mountain, or even on the shore while the sea-breeze gave me the smell of salt and sand. Tonight, it's nothing more than the movement of air and the smells of a dirty city. Where I used to feel I could spread my arms and almost fly, like a kite on the breeze, now I felt as though the wind rushed past my ears as I dropped like a rebel angel.

Maybe that's not a bad description, considering what I've done.

I heard the trapdoor in the floor open. I didn't need to look to know who it was. Tianna watched me during the whole damned performance, or the whole performance of the damned. All through it, she clasped her hands tight together while she chewed on the side of one finger. Bright flecks danced in her hair, like embers among ashes, as she tried to suppress any reaction to my scene.

Besides, who else would come looking for me?

"Grandfather?"

I grunted something in reply without turning. I felt the ghostly pressure of her hand rest on the shoulder of my armor.

"I don't know what to say," she told me, softly.

"Don't say anything," I suggested. "Just give me a good push."

"No."

"You're probably right. The fall won't kill me."

"You stop that."

"Why? I just sold my soul for the welfare of a kingdom. Nothing good ever comes from such a deal."

She moved around to face me, settling against the stonework. She wore her hair in a braid for some reason, but a few strands whipped about in the wind. Her robes, yellow and orange, fluttered and rippled as though she were on fire. She tucked them about herself. I wondered for a moment if she was cold, and realized what a stupid question it was.

"Did you?" she asked. "Who did you sell it to?"

"Maybe selling it isn't the right phrase," I admitted. "I feel as though I cut a piece of it off and left it bleeding on the floor of the hall."

"I didn't see it."

"I did. I killed that Miller guy, the baron. He challenged the Demon King. He demonstrated a stupid streak, yes, but he showed noble courage—real virtue, not pretended, not concealed, and not to be questioned nor denied. *I know.* He stood up for what he believed was right and died for it, knew he was going to die for it, and he made the gesture in front of everyone because he believed it needed to be made. He didn't even have hope. He only did it because he believed it was needful and right—no other reason."

I sighed.

"I ate his spirit, absorbed his blood, desecrated his body, and made my point. All it cost, of course, was one extremely good man. One good man sacrificed on the altar of the State, along with any remaining hope of being a decent person."

My gauntlets were hanging from my belt, so it wasn't hard to rub my face with both hands.

"I think you berate yourself needlessly."

"You're not the one living in this skull."

"True. I'm the one looking at you from the outside." She said it gently, but with a bit of twist on it. Maybe she did have a better view of the situation than I did. It didn't help my current level of abject self-pity and general hatred for all mankind.

"You saw what happened."

"Yes. Yes, I did. I saw a king do something awful, even terrible. He did it even though he knew the personal cost it would exact. And he did it in the hope— only the uncertain *hope*—he could unify a kingdom under the rule of a Queen, rather than allow it to fall into barbarism unfought. He will be forever remembered as a monster, a demon, even when the name of his Queen has fallen into the forgetfulness of time. He knew it, accepted it, and gave his people the gift of himself—the King they needed him to be, even though he thinks he never was."

I thought about what she said, playing through some of the possible rebuttals and counter-rebuttals. Very quickly, I realized I wasn't going to win this argument, either. Women. I'm glad they're around, but even the best of them can be troublesome beasts.

"Did you memorize that," I asked, instead, "or make it up on the spot?" Tianna dimpled and her hair brightened.

"I had some suggestions about how you might be feeling."

I glanced down at Firebrand.

Not me, Boss.

"Who? Sparky?"

"Beltar, your *prophate*. He talks to you—the other you. They had some thoughts."

I glanced up at the sky. Thunder chuckled in the distance as the clouds continued to advance. At least, I thought a heard a chuckle. It could have been my imagination.

Okay, no. It wasn't my imagination. It might not have been an audible chuckle, just a psychic one timed with the actual thunder. At least one of the so-called gods has something he uses for a sense of humor. He would find this amusing.

"You know I'm leaving, don't you?" I asked.

"Yes."

We sat in silence for a bit, listening to the wind from above and the music from below. The Demon King is gone. Long live the Bright Queen.

It would work out for the kingdom. The new justice system would percolate through the place, as would the new money. Like the roads, they were too good to be denied. Bob would handle the Arena City and the Duchy of the Eastrange. Lissette would have a head start on her nobility. If she has problems, bad ones, I know an elf with assassin squads—and so does she. Even the ongoing investigation into the mass child-murdering… at that moment, I really couldn't summon up the urge to care. They were dead and I couldn't fix it. Maybe it was Thomen's idea and hired assassins. Maybe it was the Hand, working with Thomen. Did it matter? Bob would find out who did it and Lissette would deal with them.

For now, the kingdom could go play with itself. I got suckered into being a king because people needed me. Now I've played the villain at court so they could have something to hate, and so Lissette could be something they could love. I've killed my hundreds and my thousands, all in the name of a unified nation, and out of all of the deaths, I've murdered one good man.

Maybe I've murdered more than one. It's possible. But this one was cold, calculated, and deliberate—and it hurts me. Ask not for whom the bell tolls, Mister Donne, because now I know what you meant.

"There are some arrangements to be made," I mentioned.

"I'm sure there are."

"Do you want to help?"

"Always, Grandfather."

"Shall we go?"

"I'd like to wait for the rain, if you don't mind."

"I don't mind."

We sat there, in the wind, and watched the clouds billow and roll, an inverted sea of darkness with the tide coming in on the starry shore.

"You know what bothers me most?" I asked, watching the clouds eat the sky.

"Sunrise?"

"Oh, you're related to me, all right," I groused. She chuckled.

"No, Grandfather. I don't know what bothers you the most. Will you tell me?"

"I killed a good man today. I intimidated, lied to, and threatened a huge number of people. I turned to the persona of a villain and acted all dark-side to achieve my ends—if I *have* achieved them. For the greater good, of course. For the maximum number of people to have the maximum amount of happiness because of what I hope is a good way to organize a social grouping."

"And the uncertainty bothers you?" she guessed.

"Some," I admitted. "The big thing, though, is the fact I did terrible things with good intentions… and I'm not certain I was wrong to do it. Breaking eggs to make omelets, I suppose. But people aren't eggs and a kingdom isn't an omelet." I sighed. "I've been an evil bastard because it seemed the right thing to do, and I'm not sure it wasn't."

We were silent for a while. I could smell the rain, see it falling in the distance, a curtain sweeping over the world toward us, almost as though the gods closed one act before opening another.

"Did you enjoy being an evil bastard?" Tianna asked, finally.

"No. I did it because I felt it was necessary."

"Then let it go. You did it. You're done with it. It's over."

"Tianna, granddaughter, dear one, it took me a long time to realize this, so you may not have arrived at the same conclusion, yet. It's never over. The consequences of our choices follow us forever. I'm not sure what the consequences of this one will be. I'm not sure of the price I've paid for this—or what price I'll have to pay."

Tianna had no comment. We sat without speaking, watching the lights of the city and listening to the noises of the people.

"Grandfather?"

"Hmm?"

"You're quiet."

"Dead people don't breathe."

"I'd hit you, but you're wearing armor."

"Unrewarding," I agreed.

"Answer me a question?"

"If I don't have to make up an answer, sure."

"Why *did* you become a king?"

I thought about it for a while. Why did I become a king? Because Raeth and Bouger suckered me into being one? Because I took charge? Because I led people into the wilderness and helped them find a foothold?

"Because it was my responsibility."

"Responsibility? Or obligation?"

"I'm not sure of the difference."

"Neither am I, I suppose. I guess I wanted to know if it was something you felt… I don't know. Compelled to do, perhaps? Something you didn't want to do, but you felt you had to do it? Or was it more of a thing imposed on you? People expected it of you, demanded it, and it was your duty to them to be what they needed?"

"That's fairly subtle," I observed. "I'm not sure."

"See, the sense of responsibility seems to me to come from within. The obligation seems like something from outside you, forcing you."

"I suppose that's a fair assessment. I'm still not sure."

"No?"

"No. They imposed on me, yes, so in that sense it was an obligation. But without a sense of responsibility for them, I could have walked away."

"Could you have?" she asked, curiously. I sighed and dodged the question.

"It was a long time ago."

"*I* think it was a sense of responsibility."

"Oh? Why?"

"Because you hated yourself tonight."

"I do that on alternate Tuesdays, anyway."

"What's a Tuesday?"

"Skip it; it was meant to be flippant."

"I'm serious. You hated yourself for what you did. If it was an obligation, you wouldn't be up here, tempting a lightning bolt to solve your problems of conscience. An obligation wouldn't leave you with a choice, so you would be angry, not self-loathing. You did this out of a sense of responsibility."

"Maybe," I admitted. "It's possible." I didn't want to think about it, though, so I didn't go on. Tianna stopped talking, too.

We waited a little more. The tide of clouds came in, blotting out the stars, sinking the moon in their depths.

And the idea hit me. If I can't open a gate to the moon, maybe I could launch a ship. Something that could carry something like the defensive barrier of the firmament and sail through the void.

I'll think about it some more. There are far too many details to work out and I'm not in the mood for them.

Finally, the curtain of rain swept over Carrillon and the Palace. A few drops pattered on the conical roof as scouts. Then the first wave came out of the sky-sea and the spray washed down at us. I raised an umbrella spell to keep water from running down my neck and into my armor. Tianna just sat there, smugly, as raindrops disappeared into tiny puffs of vapor above her.

"Showoff."

"Says the dry man in the rain."

"Touché. Shall we go?"

"All right."

I led the way down the winding stairs of the tower. It was a hollow cylinder above the general palace rooftop level and the stairs had no rail. I wanted to be in front in case Tianna slipped.

"Grandfather?"

"Hmm?"

"Where will you go?"

It was a good question, and it took me a number of steps to formulate an answer.

"I've got some arrangements to make with Bob and T'yl. They need something to take the place of Bob's usual elf-making methods if he's going to stop doing it. Then I have some spells to test, maybe an enchantment or two. Then I need to pay a call on Tort. I don't know how it will go, so I don't know exactly when I'll move on to other things or if she'll be coming with me. I hope she will."

"Is there anything I can do to help?"

"Actually, yes. You can let Lissette know you'll be willing to burn a candle and call me if there's a need for the Demon King to make an appearance. Beltar can probably arrange something along those lines, but it's good to have more than one way to summon a friendly demon."

"You're not a demon."

"Ask a peasant," I countered.

"One renting a six-bladed plow chariot and who owns his land? Or one who still follows an ox across a field and prays his landowner doesn't raise the rent?"

"You are *definitely* my granddaughter. There aren't many people who could annoy me so easily by being right."

"It's your own fault for giving me a brilliant mother."

"How is she, by the way?"

"Still burning brightly. She would have come to the Grand Council in my place, as the senior priestess, but…"

"Yeah. No need to burn down the Palace. Make sure she understands… what I… that is, why I…"

"I will."

"And give her my love, will you?"

"Of course."

We reached the lower levels of the tower and the huge, hollow cylinder turned into individual floors. I set my hand on a door latch and Tianna covered my hand with hers.

"Will I ever see you again?" she asked, softly.

"If you send for me, I will come."

"Promise?"

"I have spoken."

"So you have," Tianna replied, withdrawing her hand. "Thank you."

"Always happy to help."

I opened the door and ushered her through. I had an instrument to invest with a fraction of Tyma's soul, some details to handle, and some goodbyes.

Monday, March 15th

Beware the Ides of March.

I have no idea what an "ides" is, but there's one in March and it's dangerous, apparently. Maybe it's the Roman version of Friday the thirteenth. I'll Google it when I get someplace that has Google.

Bob and T'yl are reassured I'm not abandoning them. T'yl believed me completely when I explained how fooling around with vampire blood in a quest for immortality is a Bad Idea, deserving of capital letters and capital punishment. Giving magicians a better way to become immortal is a much better alternative. It also earns me a lot of goodwill among magicians—Hey, buddy! Want a hit of this? It lasts forever, man! —which helps cut down on the number of magicians the Hand can hire. It won't stop magicians from being religious, but it should reduce the number who show up to help them simply for cash.

As for Bob, he's quite pleased with the idea he won't spend a hundred years with filthy human females while trying to upgrade a fetus into a bad copy of an elf. He's also looking forward to seeing what I come up with for a void-sailing moonship. And there's the possibility I might find a way to spring his so-called deity from self-imposed prison...

Why do I get the feeling I'm working for him, rather than the other way around?

Still, he's looking after the kingdom, sort of babysitting it while the change of leadership sorts out and settles down. If a void-ship and elf-clones are the price of that, so what? It's more likely to get me what I want out of him than a blunt "Do it!" I'd rather have him on my side than have him working for me unwillingly.

Tyma selected a large instrument, something like a cello. It was a bowed instrument, rather than a plucked or strummed one, and was longer than I would have thought. The sound chamber was in the middle, while the strings ran up and down the necks above and below. She called it a *valanione*. The enchantments were medium-simple, since I wasn't animating a bow to run back and forth over it. The strings vibrated directly.

We got Tyma a stand to hold it upright while it played. She didn't enjoy the process of enchanting it, but that's typical. Linnaeus had it worse with three instruments at once. Still, she was happy with the results, and her ensemble did sound better with bowed strings in it. She's not happy with me, but she's much less mad. At least she hasn't hit me with the Kingsmacker.

Late Friday night, I took a gate back to the Mountain of Power. I tried to slip away quietly and partly succeeded. Kammen and Torvil insisted on coming with me. I didn't mind, but I made them get permission from Lissette.

Kammen also recovered my predecessor's rings. Nice timing. Still, they might be useful. No skinphone, though. My bet is Johann has it. Fortunately, I didn't have it long enough to put anything really interesting in there. If he wants the number to the pizza place in my old neighborhood, he's welcome to it.

Bronze protested my travel plans. She didn't want to step through a gate. She preferred to run. I agreed, so the three bipeds stepped through and Bronze ran gleefully through the tunnels under the roads.

Once I was in the mountain, I sent for some materials, brought them with me into an unused cavern, and shut myself in. I had a lot of work I wanted to get done and I didn't want to talk to anyone. They say you should talk it over when you're depressed and unhappy and suchlike. Get it out there, don't bottle it up. Rant about it, throw things, let it all out.

That's a load of crap. I know what happens when I rant and rave and go on a rampage. Later, when I'm in Carnivorous Ivy Land and suitably far away from anything Diogenes has repaired? Maybe. I'll feel bad about tearing down defenseless ruins or old-growth forests, but at least I won't have vented my plasma exhaust on anything I actually care about.

On the other hand, if I find another omnivorous giant ant nest, it's going to suffer a severe attack of vampire. I will go full-on Dark Lord on the thing and I won't feel bad about it *at all*.

So I got to work. First, a personal privacy spell on the room to keep people from meddling. Then a couple of magic-jet spells and a low-key containment circle raised the available power level. I connected a magical cable to the business end of each jet and wore them like gloves, using them as power supplies for cramming energy into my spells while I worked. It was surprisingly effective, a fact I resolved to, first, never tell anyone about, and second, make use of in any low-magic universe.

For my first trick, T'yl needed an automated way to drag a soul out of a body and tie it into an empty one. I wasn't going to come back to Karvalen and be a target on a regular basis just to voodoo somebody's soul into an immortal meat suit. Two stone tables and a whole mess of magical sensors, target locks, spirit links, if-then logic, and some repetitive subroutines later, I had a highly-specialized gadget to do it for me. I'm sure it's one of those vampire magic things people talk about in hushed whispers, but if they could see and manipulate living energy the way I do, they wouldn't feel so uneasy about it.

Of course, I suppose if people could see electricity and magnetic fields, a television wouldn't be witchcraft, either—just complicated. Oh, well.

While I worked, I sent Kammen a message to fetch back some boxes. I wanted two sets, one pair about the size of a small suitcase, the other pair about the size of a coffin. The smaller boxes needed all sorts of padding and velvet lining and so on. The coffins merely needed to be solid. He came back with the bigger boxes first, so I could started on those. The smaller boxes took longer, mostly because of their quality. They were a matched set of small chests, lined and padded inside.

I fiddled with both sets for a while, magically attuning each box to its twin, even forcing their physical materials into a more identical pattern. I wanted each pair to be as close to a single box in two places as possible. It wasn't strictly necessary, of course, but it would help.

Trouble was, I haven't actually built a box-gate before. This made the project a perfect distraction.

One of the observations I've made on the inter-universal gate spell is the way it seems to alter everything passing through it. It's as though there's a sort of... I hate to use the word "frequency," but it'll have to do, I suppose. If every universe is like a different television channel, you can't exist in it until you match the channel parameters. You have to have your frequency synchronized with the channel before you can exist there. If you don't, you're not vibrating correctly, or your internal rules of chemistry and atomic binding are wrong, or something.

Ah! Back when my spirit was temporarily turned into an energy-state being on another plane of existence—another type of universe—it was boosted to match the energy wavelength of that universe. When I stepped down from the ersatz Asgard, I lowered my vibrational rate and came back into synchronization with the world of Karvalen. In a similar manner, that's what a gate spell does to everything passing through it from one universe to another. Whatever passes through the geometric plane of the gate—the "surface" of it—is tuned to the universe, whichever way the object or person happens to be going.

The net effect is the gate looks like an open doorway even though instantaneous transformations are constantly going on. I think part of the massive power requirement is the continuous transformational effect involved in affecting all the light, air, water—whatever is passing through the gate. Another reason gates like that are so awful to keep open is the multiplicity of factors they have to alter in real time, each one being the equivalent of a major transformational spell.

I suspect turning lead to gold is easier. That involves removing three protons and about seven neutrons, depending on which isotope of gold you want—some are radioactive, which is probably a bad idea for money.

Hmm. Wait a minute. If money is radioactive, people will spend it quickly. Having money circulate is vital to any economy. And radioactive money won't get stored in large quantity; rich people will be rich because of their income, not because of their hoarded wealth. They'll spend it as fast as it comes in. Maybe radioactive money would actually be a good thing…

No. I've had silly ideas before, but that one takes the Cherenkov cake.

Still, turning lead into gold is child's play to a man with a magical cyclotron. Making useful quantities probably takes even longer than growing a diamond lattice, though. Dealing with things on an atomic scale means you have to seriously fast-forward your work to see material results. Diamond lattice structures are still a chemical reaction, not an atomic one, and have the advantage of being rigidly, regularly organized.

On the other hand, turning lead into gold could be a good experiment… later. I have enchanted objects to build. Back to the subject at hand: Magic boxes!

Working on the correspondence of the boxes gave me a major project and kept me occupied. The idea was to alter the shape of a gate spell's transformation effect. Instead of a flat plane, I wanted it to affect a volume. Two volumes, actually, one in each box. Since two boxes are linked through their enchantment, when one box activates, it opens a tiny gateway to its twin, wherever it is. Through this tiny gateway, the gate spells trade spaces, changing the interior of one box into the interior of the other box, transferring the contents, as part of the defined volume of space, from one to the other.

If done correctly, every time both boxes close, they switch contents. Since the actual gate connection was so tiny—really a communications link more than anything else—the power requirement was small. And since the transfer was designed to be as nearly instantaneous as possible, it wouldn't have to be open for long, either. This would make it easy for Diogenes to deliver elf-clones to

Karvalen. Full-grown elf bodies could then be used to bribe magicians and infant elves could be used to bribe Bob. Excuse me. I didn't mean "bribe." I meant they could be used to very kindly assist people with their personal problems.

Hmm. I need to include some sort of signal they're ready to receive an elf. I'd hate for one to sit in the Karvalen box for so long that it went bad. Maybe if they close the lid on the Karvalen side, it sends a read-to-receive signal. When Diogenes sends an elf-body through, the Karvalen box-lid automatically opens. That should work...

I started with a full gate spell and took it apart, reducing it to function modules. Getting the two boxes to connect wasn't so hard, but the transfer portion, itself, switching the interior spaces... that was tricky. Getting it to work at all was a headache, but a welcome distraction. When I did get the thing to work, I tested the small boxes as they sat side by side. Several of the test objects came through the switch relatively intact, but badly distorted. Living things weren't going to take it well. Something wasn't quite right, so I started debugging it.

I had to make some sacrifices. What I wanted was a pair of boxes that simply switched back and forth. While, technically, they do that, they tend to ruin whatever is inside by partially blending the contents. The way around it is to leave one box empty. I can't switch both sides at once with this technique, and I'm not sure why. I think it needs a third box, always empty, to act as temporary storage—a buffer—while the spell shifts things around. That ought to work, but it's not something I actually need for this project.

Aside from my box-gates, I've done some work on my rings. My Personal Options ring now includes a cleaning spell, skin-changing magic, and a sensory muting spell for my comfort and convenience. I took a break from the box-gates the very first time I hit a sunrise and had to smell myself. I admit, I'm easily distracted right now.

The three-gem sapphire ring now stores my eyeball illusion, rounding out my human disguise. The other two sapphires will serve as enchantment points for spells to prevent magical detection—one to thwart active detection, the other to conceal my normal aura from passive detection.

Since I don't want to wear a fistful of rings, I'm thinking I'll only wear one more, the deflection-spell ring. Wearing three rings is unusual, perhaps, but not overwhelmingly so. The healing ring and the amulet I can put on if I need them. On the other hand, I don't really want to wear the amulet. It does things with shadows and mine is already doing weird things.

I think I'll keep my dedicated, one-function Ring of Obfuscation handy, though. You never know when a spare cloaking device might be useful. And I'm leaning toward enchanting a magical belt. Maybe it can have an inertia-damping spell. I like being able to go around corners like a normal human being even when I'm moving at inhuman speeds. That would be useful in so many ways... I decided to go ahead with it. It's one less thing I'll have to cast when I'm in a hurry, and that's the whole *point* of having a magical object, isn't it?

I'm developing quite a collection of magical crap. Maybe I should get a jewelry box. Or open a magic shop somewhere out there in another magical universe. Or not. I doubt I'd enjoy haggling over prices with adventurers. I'm more of a custom-built kind of guy. You want a magical doodad to do what? Yes, I think I can do that. I like a challenge. When do you need it? That sort of thing.

There are so many things I can think of which might be useful. Maybe a new amulet, one to do the shadow-shifting illusions to help me be stealthy? One I made myself, so I know how it works, and can work with my shadow's quirky nature? Or something to project a don't-notice-me spell, allowing me to blend in better? Maybe an enchanted wristwatch with time-zone dials, something I could use to keep track of the current time in multiple universes? No, that will require a lot more research before I can even start. I suppose I could put a deflection spell into a wristwatch. It seems appropriate, somehow, to have a bracelet for deflecting bullets. Can't imagine why.

If I get a fancy wristwatch with jewels set as the hour marks, can I put a dozen enchantments in it? There's something to get the old mental gears clicking.

I hate to bother you...

I jumped a little at the unexpected comment. I looked around.

Not me, Boss, Firebrand told me.

"Oh." I glanced up at the ceiling. "Yes?"

I know you're busy, but will we get a chance to talk?

"You could have had a priest send a message," I pointed out.

I'm not healthy for them to have divine messages dumped into their brains, remember? And nobody has the Brazier of Divine Revelation going.

"I guess that's fair. What's on your mind?"

You're about to finish up here and leave this world. Do you think we could have a discussion through the BDR?

"As long as you're not about to stick me with some holy quest, religious geas, or ecclesiastical duty, sure. If you are, my answer will be three words, starting with 'go' and ending with 'yourself'."

You're not in a good mood.

"Not really, no."

Okay. How about you give me a call when you get to the Temple?

"I can do that."

Thank you.

And the inside of my head stopped echoing. It's a nice feeling.

I grumbled to myself and Firebrand as I tied off and locked down all the things I was working on. I stomped down the tunnel to the Temple of Shadow. A number of people were outside the main sanctuary, waiting, which surprised me. I wouldn't think there was a lot of activity in the very-late-night or very-early-morning. Then again, I'm not one of the clergy. I'm not even a worshipper. What do I know?

I went in and they closed the doors behind me. Someone had thoughtfully filled the brazier, but I had to light it and get the smoke-face going.

"Hello."

"Hello, yourself," I answered. "What do you want?"

"Oh, I don't actually want anything. Quite the opposite. Remember how I promised you a present?"

"Yes."

"Well, I've been thinking about it and doing a little research. I think I've got it worked out."

"Oh?"

"Oh, yes. But I'll need your help."

"I'm listening," I admitted, cautiously. I wasn't about to agree to anything without knowing exactly what he wanted.

"You know I can't channel big, miraculous powers through humans. They have to go through a rite of ordination to attune themselves to my energy, and even then they tend to burn out if I push too hard. You, on the other hand—"

"Yeah, yeah, yeah. We've been over this. I take it you want to channel a miracle through me?"

"Yes."

"To give me a present."

"Yes."

"What do you get out of it?"

"Is that any way to talk?"

"Stow it. You're not giving me a present just to try to cheer me up."

"I'm not?"

I paused and thought about it. Would I give someone a present just to cheer them up? Yes, I suppose I would. And if I would, was it beyond possibility he would? Obviously not. Maybe I was being a little suspicious and cynical. If I was wrong to feel that way, I might feel guilty about it later, but I might also be right.

"Sorry. Not buying it."

"Hmm. All right, how's this? I've never actually done it before. I'd like to do it once, just so I have a concept of the scale. I'd tell you about the power flow, but I haven't gotten around to actually inventing a way to measure it. Maybe I can call one divine energy-unit a *theo*, from the prefix of 'theology,' maybe. How many theos can I route through you, and how many can I route through a human, that sort of thing."

"You have my sympathies. I keep meaning to get around to the magical version of that, with thaums instead of theos."

There was a momentary silence. I got the feeling he was taken aback a bit.

"Do you think… maybe… when you do get that worked out, we could compare notes?"

"Happy to help. Your theo-scale may help me, too."

"Happy to help. But, about your present…"

"What do you want? Specifically."

"Well, you've been as busy as Celebrimbor, forging rings of power and other gadgets, so I thought we might as well make something together. And, since you're planning to leave, I thought this might be our last opportunity. I was thinking of your cloak. What heroic magical figure is complete without a miraculous cloak? I can think of several without even venturing into role-playing games."

I thought about it. A magic cloak wasn't a bad thought. And as long as I was building my portable magical inventory, why not?

"What do you want to do to it?"

"Ideally, we set up here, on the altar-stage. It'll be easiest. We've already got the incense and coals thing, maybe you can do some bleeding into a bucket."

"The bleeding part isn't going to work at night."

"Good point. It's probably more important you're undead than it is to have ceremonial trappings. Humans need all the help they can get, but you can handle heavier loads without attunement accessories."

"Fair enough. What will the cloak do?"

"First off, I'd rather surprise you."

"And second?"

"Ah... I'm not completely sure."

"Beg pardon, god?"

"Oh, shut up. I haven't done this before. I'm creating a holy artifact from scratch—my very first one!"

"If it's a religious object, it's a relic. Artifacts are magical things people don't know how to create anymore."

"I'm relatively new to the god business. Cut me some slack, will you?"

"Okay. I sympathize with your troubles. We can give it a try."

"Thank you. I know you don't enjoy this sort of thing—"

"Shut up and let's do this before I change my mind."

"I'm sorry. Of course. Just lay your cloak on the altar, please." I did so and it started to ripple, slightly, as though a stiff breeze blew across it.

"How's that?" I asked. The smoke-face looked over my shoulder at the cloak.

"Perfect. I'd say you have a knack for this—"

"—but you don't want to annoy me."

"Exactly. Are you ready?"

"Ready to feel a spirit not my own move through my flesh and direct energies beyond human comprehension?"

"I take it that's a 'no'?"

"Correct. I'm not ready. But go ahead."

Something moved inside me, a sensation almost of warmth, spreading outward from somewhere near my heart. If my veins were empty and someone pumped fresh blood into them, it might feel like this. I turned to focus on the cloak, seeing it not as a piece of cloth, but as formlessness, chaos, bound into matter and shape and time. The matrix of it was a complex thing of many colors and many layers, each different in its own way, controlling properties and controlled by the universe around it. But some of them were optional, and others had a wider array of options than mortals could comprehend...

"Okay, that should do it."

"What? Are we done already?"

"It's been at least an hour."

"It *has?*"

"It has," I assured me, smoke-face nodding.

Yes, Boss, Firebrand added. It sounded subdued and disturbed. I was less subdued but equally disturbed. Firebrand added, *The sunrise isn't for a couple hours, yet.*

Good to know, I replied.

"You really need to work on that," I growled aloud, to the smoky face over me. "Sparky doesn't blot out the consciousness when she does it! I was hoping we could do this without you completely overriding *everything!*"

"I know. I haven't figured that part out, yet," the smoky visage replied, defensively. "Give me a decade or two. I'm still new to this."

I glared at the grey cloud with my face as I leaned on the altar. If it had been daytime, I would have collapsed next to it, shaking with adrenalin reaction. As it was, I needed a few moments to gather my scattered wits and collect my nerve. I've never liked having anyone in my head, but it's usually a case of annoyance rather than fear. After the incident with the Demon King, it's been worse, but manageable. Now this… this was unexpected, although not unpleasant, exactly. I knew it was irrational to feel violated or angry—well, to feel it so intensely—but feelings aren't too rational to begin with. It took me a while to come to grips with my own loathing. It took even longer to talk myself into believing I could accept it.

I didn't believe I could accept it. Ignore it, perhaps, but never accept.

"I guess that's fair," I finally grudged, not really meaning it. I lifted the cloak and examined it to divert my own attention. "I don't see any changes, aside from the not-visible-to-mortal-eyes stuff. Is it supposed to have dark veins all through it?"

"I think so."

"You think so."

"It's a prototype holy artifact! I mean, holy relic. What do you want from me?"

"Omniscience?"

"Ha. Ha. Ha. You're not as funny as you think you are."

I swung the cloak around and clasped it. It behaved normally.

"I'm not sure I can analyze what you've done," I admitted, swirling a fold of it over one arm. "It's not the magic I'm used to. Can you look at it and make any guesses?"

"I'm looking. I think it's… yes, it's adapting."

"Adapting?"

"Yes. It's attuning itself to you. It'll probably be your personal cloak."

"As in, it won't do magical things for anyone else, or as in it will actively try to suffocate anyone who steals it?"

"Could go either way. There are a lot of reality-based changes in it. That is, reality isn't quite the same for it as for normal matter. That is, instead of placing energy into the n-dimensional volume described by—"

I held up a hand to the smoky visage and he stopped talking.

"Well, thank you for a potentially dangerous and possibly sapient relic of uncertain powers. I appreciate it," I told him, heavy on the sarcasm. He ignored my tone completely.

"It's the thought that counts, right?"

"Remember the bit about being not funny?"

"It runs in my family," replied the face of god, smugly. Then he turned serious. "I would like to bring something up, though, that isn't funny."

I sat down on the altar. My altar. Our altar.

"Shoot."

"It's about the grey sashes again."

"The whole civic versus religious thing?"

"Yes. I think you're making a mistake in not allowing them authority over mortal affairs."

"Maybe," I conceded. "However, my decision stands, and I'll tell you why."

"I am all attention, Your Majesty."

"Stop it, Your Holiness."

"That's Beltar. The *deveas* is leader of the whole church. He's also the *prophate*, the Voice of God. Or he was, anyway, until you built this brazier's enchantment."

"Good point. As I was saying, grey sashes don't have authority—not on their own. I think they make a fine set of reserves, though. Think of them like the militia, or national guard, or army reserves, or something. The various city guards handle most things. The army handles bigger things. The red sashes beat six colors of crap out of anything else. The guild of wizards backs up everybody. If anything shows up and can't be handled by all that, the grey sashes get called on—along with the warriors of Father Sky, the hunters of the Hunter, and, for all I know, the marines of Ssthitch. But the religious troops only armor up to defend the kingdom from things the kingdom can't defend itself from. Then they turn whatever is being troublesome into paste. Probably diced, fried, crushed, minced, and terrified paste, as well as damned by various godlike entities."

"Hmm."

"You don't approve."

"No, it's not that… okay, yes. I don't approve. I think it would help me do overwatch on the kingdom if I had mortal authority."

"Work through Beltar and the other priests to talk to people," I advised. "All the others are doing the same thing. Be persuasive rather than coercive."

"And if they don't play by your rules?"

"Get the ones who *are* playing by my rules to kick them out of the game for cheating."

The face opened its mouth to say something, paused, and shut its mouth. He thought about it.

"You know, they would be pretty pissed if someone cheated. That is, after a while of playing. If we can get them invested in the game *qua* game."

"I have faith in you. Besides, the game is simply divine."

"About that not funny thing…"

"Oh, come on! You smiled!"

"Did not."

"Did too. I saw it. Firebrand saw it."

No comment, Boss.

"Traitor."

"All right," the face of smoke admitted, "maybe it was a *little* funny."

"Good god."

"But that wasn't."

We said our goodbyes and I returned through the tunnels to my workroom. I had enchantments to finish, a quasi-holy relic to play with, a bunch of canals to think up in the west, some more city planning to do on the arena place in the northern Eastrange…

Distractions. Lots of distractions. Things to finish before doing important things. So I did them.

Which brings me up to today, Monday.

I've delayed all I can. I've spoken with Bob and T'yl, I've popped over to talk to Diogenes and give him his gate-rings, I've said goodbye to everyone I can stand to say goodbye to.

Now I've got two terrifying things to accomplish.

Second, I have to kill Johann.

First, I need to speak with Tort.

No, I take that back. The *first* thing I need to do is have a long talk with T'yl about Kamshasa, specifically about Kashmanir, the House of Oloné, and the border near the Kingdom of Kolob. I need the address of a lady magician who doesn't seem to want to talk to me.

So I sent for T'yl.

I wasn't hungry, but I ate breakfast anyway, up in my quarters. It occurred to me anyone who wanted to track my movements only needed to monitor food consumption. Then again, how much does Kammen eat? Or any of the original red-sashes? They're all gigantic. Four hundred or so pounds of flesh and bone takes a lot of calories to maintain, especially with the daily practice and exercise. Maybe I'm not such a big dent in the kitchen after all.

Come to that, why do I bother to shovel food down when it's nothing but a chore? To extend the time between vampire feedings, yes… but do I need to? I have volunteers every single night in the Temple of Shadow. If necessary, there are probably dungeons under every noble house with murderers and thieves. So why do I bother with *human* food? Habit? Or is it a connection to my own lost humanity? Someday I'll become a philosopher and figure it out. Or am I already a philosopher? I ask questions without answers, after all.

T'yl arrived as the remains of breakfast were taken away. He probably waited in the hall until I finished. People tip-toe around me, possibly with good reason. I didn't feel as though I were about to snap and, in so doing, snap necks, but *they* never know. Then again, how quickly can sad turn to mad? I'm already disturbed at the massive changes in my life—some voluntary, some not, but major alterations nonetheless. It was possible their concerns were justified, which saddened me even further and frustrated me even more. Saddened me in that they had to tip-toe around, frustrated me in that I might be as bad as they feared. Which, of course, made me angry at myself and made it more likely I would take out my anger on others…

We call this a death spiral. I'm too damn sensitive, that's the problem. Then again, if I were a callous, heartless bastard who didn't mind…

This. This is *exactly* why I need distractions.

At any rate, T'yl came in, gliding gracefully across the stone floor to seat himself on a low couch.

"You've been working on yourself," I observed.

"Like it?" he asked, brushing his hair back. "I think I have my eyes shaped correctly for the first time."

"The shape seems almost right," I told him, looking over his work. "I think there's something about the cheekbones. They seem a touch too... angular? Maybe they're angled upward a little too much, or they stand out a trifle too sharply."

"You think so? I leveled them out a bit last year."

"Maybe it's just me, but they do seem to stand out a tiny bit. Maybe you should get someone who does the high-society makeup and hairstyles to help."

"That's a very good thought. I've been thinking of it in terms of comparative anatomy."

"Glad to help. You might also try mixing the color in your eyes."

"What do you mean?"

"They seem too solid. Take a close look at the color in someone else's eye. They may be blue or brown or whatever, but they have lots of different shades all mixed together. Yours look like paint."

"Do they? I'll have to look into the matter. Thank you for bringing it to my attention."

"Anytime. Now, I need your help."

"What can I do?" he asked, leaning forward.

"I know you don't like to talk about Kamshasa, but I intend to visit Tort and she's living there, someplace called Kashmanir, near the border of Kolob. It's in the territory of the House of Oloné. I need to know what you know. Or," I amended, "enough to get by in Kamshasa while I ask around for her. Practical details, not necessarily the political process. Customs, greetings, polite behavior, that sort of thing."

T'yl leaned back on the couch and steepled his long fingers. He looked up as he pressed the tips of his index fingers to his lips in thought.

"It is difficult to say much," he admitted. "I was only a boy when I left Kamshasa, taken away by the magician Sarrenosh. Even before that, I lived in a more central region of Kamshasa, southwest of Ashkenar."

"All right. How do I get by without killing everyone I meet?"

"Do you have a woman who can lead you around?"

"Not on me, but I can probably find one."

"That should be adequate. If you have a woman to act as your *lahaik*, you should have no trouble."

"What's a... la-HAY-ick?"

"Close enough. A *lahaik* is like an owner, even though, technically, men are not precisely property. Rethven does not have a word for it. Think of it as if you were a stepchild to an uncaring stepmother. She is responsible for you, yes, and you must obey her in all things, but she is not precisely your owner."

"So I need to find someone willing to be my stepmother and take me on a trip?"

"That is, I suppose, rather close."

"Does it matter how old she is?"

"No, it is merely a matter of gender. You could be… oh, a eunuch guard, perhaps, inherited by a younger matron, or given to a second daughter as she goes out to seek her fortune."

"Back up. Eunuch?"

"Men are not permitted arms unless they have been… ah… gentled."

"Gentled."

"Made less aggressive by the removal of their testicles."

"I was pretty sure I understood you. How likely is it anyone is actually going to *check*?"

"Not likely," he admitted, "but for one of the ungentled to bear arms—the penalty is death."

"Ah. Hmm. Is there another occupation for traveling men? Preferably one that doesn't involve castration?"

"Well, you could be a professional *karasi*."

"Look, I don't have a translation spell running, okay?"

"My apologies. A *karasi* is a male prostitute, typically rented for breeding or pleasure or both. You are not handsome enough—by their standards—to be considered a particularly valuable one for breeding purposes, but your looks are exotic, so it would be perfectly believable to masquerade as a *karasi* of pleasure."

I had a snatch of a Louis Prima song run through my head. *I'm just a gigolo, everywhere I go, people know the part I'm playing…*

"What else would let us travel without getting too much attention?"

"You do not wish to be a professional lover of women?"

"T'yl," I snapped, and checked myself. In a calmer tone, I continued. "Please stick to the subject at hand."

"Yes. Of course. I apologize for my amusement."

"It's okay. I've just… I've been under a bit of strain. What else can I be?"

"I'm not sure. I would suggest simply going there with some woman you might possibly trust, if there is one. Dress humbly, carry nothing of great value or power, and simply follow her around as she does all the talking. Or, if you can stand to let someone else do the work, *send* a woman or ten to Kashmanir to do the seeking. When they have what you wish to know, go directly there."

"I see. Well, thank you for the information. I'll need to think about it."

"Of course. How else may I be of assistance?"

"That's all, I think. At least for now. Thank you again."

"My pleasure." T'yl rose, bowed, and drifted out. Someone in the hall swung the door closed.

Who could I send? Tianna? Certainly not Amber. I'd send Mary, but she's back in Johann's world, getting things ready. Everyone else is a wife or daughter of someone else, not really equipped for an espionage mission. What about Malana and Malena? They were hardy, deadly types. Would Lissette loan them to me?

I had Kammen go phone the palace and ask. I didn't want my face on a mirror while I was supposed to be vanished.

In the meantime, I went back to my sand table and zoomed in on the Kashmanir area. Kamshasa is a relatively narrow strip of land along the coast of the southern continent. Kashmanir is at the eastern end of the strip, as well as about as close as you can get to the northern continent. There's a… it's not a strait, really, but there's a narrowing of the Circle Sea at that point. Crossing from one to the other involves only a couple hundred miles of water.

After some zooming in and zooming out, I started what I think of as a simple eyeball scan. With a scrying sensor parked at altitude, I looked the place over. There were a few towns, several fishing communities, and quite a few village-sized spots surrounded by crops and odd trees. What did they grow? Dates? Coconuts? Flax? Maybe I'd find out, someday. It didn't look particularly hot, but the Shining Desert came right up to some of the more southerly reaches of Kamshasa. I guessed the Kashmanir area to be tropical, judging by the light, breezy clothing.

Looking the place over, I decided not to go with a general pan-and-scan. Oh, I could have the sand table do one simply to get an accurate detail map of the region, but my remote search would still be done by picking out the road and following it. I've been told she's got a very nice house with lots of servants. This tells me it's fairly sizable, as well as a pleasant place. Which means I can mark off all the one-family dwellings and the full-sized palaces. I want to locate all the homes fit for the upper middle class or the lower upper class…

I mentally kicked myself. Repeatedly. After all, how did I know Tort was in Kashmanir? Or that she lived in a nice house with servants?

"Hey! Me! Are you up there?"

Naturally. To what do I owe the pleasure of your call?

"Remember me asking where Tort was?"

Yes. And I'm still sorry about that. I didn't realize you didn't know.

"You can apologize by giving me some more details on where she is, exactly."

Sure. How?

"Can you manipulate my sand table?"

Nope. Not allowed.

"Not allowed?"

I can't directly affect anything in the material realms.

"Didn't we just make a holy relic?"

That's different. I was working through you.

"Oh, I get it. You can't control the sand table—or do anything else—without a mortal channel. Or, rather, you're not allowed to. Yes?"

That's right. And, after the last time, I'm guessing you don't want to do it again.

I really wish I could grind my teeth together. There's just something wrong with clamping them together and not having any wiggle room at all. Given how sharp they are, thank god I don't need to floss.

You're welcome.

"Stop that!"

Sorry. You were thinking rather loudly.

"Psychically, I'm very well-endowed."

I know.

"Let's try something else," I suggested. "I'll call up the Kashmanir area, like so. See it?"

I have to look through your eyes. Is that okay?

"Let's try it and I'll let you know."

Hmm. Getting something... yes. Yes, I can see the sand table.

"I don't feel anything."

It's daytime. Maybe you're not sensitive enough right now?

"Could be. So, this is Kashmanir. Right half or left half?"

From where we're looking, right half.

"Top half or lower half?"

Lower.

I zoomed in on that quarter of the province, centering it on the table.

Lower half, toward the center.

We repeated the process, quartering the view area until there was only one house in view that fit the bill. It was impossible to probe, however, but such defenses certainly fit well with the occupant.

"Answer me something."

Sure.

"How do you know Tort is in there? The place is shielded like an antimatter reactor core."

She loves you.

"I don't follow."

Look, you're sort of my avatar. She loves you. That's a form of worship. That makes her—indirectly, but definitely—one of my worshippers. She can't block her own emanations on that level. She doesn't even know they exist. Humans can't detect energy in that range. So, her walls block visible light and the infrared remote, but she still gets cell service inside the house. Follow the metaphor?

"I'm good with metaphors and with electromagnetic theory. Thanks."

De nada. Anything else?

"Nope. Got anything you want from me?"

Any divine revelations about the cloak?

"Nothing I've noticed."

Bear in mind I'm interested in how it turns out. Keep me posted.

"I'll try."

And I was alone again. Weird sensation.

Watching the house for the next hour or so told me a few things. The house itself was a big, stone building, made of either a smooth, white stone or whitewashed. It was brilliant in the sunlight. The general structure was two floors high and wrapped around an inner court. It was larger than I first thought. The central court was a water garden, with flowering plants and a number of pools, including one large-ish pool suitable for wading or simply soaking. In the center of the garden was a circle of dirt and a small oak tree. It seemed out of place, but it had room all around it to grow. Maybe it was intended as a natural source of shade for the water garden but hadn't yet grown into the job.

A covered patio or walkway—is that sort of thing called an arcade? —formed the boundary between gardens and house. The roof sloped inward, presumably to catch any rain and store it in a cistern, but I wasn't certain. This design raised the outer face of the house into an intimidatingly high wall. A projecting roof overhung the southern, outer face of the house, shading it from the sun somewhat. During the summer months, it would probably shade the entire wall.

There were two people easily visible outside. One groomed the horses in a small, detached stable. The other tended the garden, puttering around with the flowers. I also caught glimpses of a third, the one who answered the door. There wasn't much traffic to and from the house. The only visitor I saw drove a two-horse cart and delivered a few small crates.

Peeking in the windows through my scrying telescope, I counted quite a number of men and boys, but I didn't see any women. I also felt like a stalker.

During the day, my stomach can flip over and do various things my nighttime metabolism doesn't or can't. I can have physical symptoms of nervousness, including sweating, nausea, trembling, dry mouth, and so on. I know this because I was nervous as hell.

No, I take that back. I was afraid. Of all the people in the world whose opinion I value, Tort tops the list. She's loved me with the unquestioning love of a child, the romantic love of a woman, the heated love of passion, and the religious love of the fanatic.

Yet, there she is, living in Kamshasa, hiding from everyone and everything. It's like she doesn't want to have anything to do with Karvalen or Rethven or me. After nine years at the right hand of the Demon King, I can't imagine why.

That's not sarcasm. I literally can't imagine what she's endured.

I'm not sure I can take it if she…

It's hard for me to remember back before she loved me. I've lived with the knowledge she loves me, and it changed things. I've known wherever I was, someone—one person—loved me despite everything I've ever done. The races of the world might rise up and denounce me as a terrible thing and cast me out, but Tort still loved me, and that would be enough. It always was.

I'm afraid.

What's wrong with me? I can face dragons—admittedly, knowing what I know now, I strongly prefer not to—or I can face demons of all sizes, shapes, and levels of nastiness. I'll smart off to fake gods, subdivide possessed priests, or do any number of other immensely stupid things. All I need to do here is open a gate, dive through, let the person at the door know I'm there to see Tort, and wait. She'll see me or she won't. What's the big deal?

But I'm still afraid.

Is it a psychic premonition? I do that, sometimes. It could be a terrible forewarning from my forebrain, or wherever people keep psychic sensitivity. I'd check the Ribbon, but it takes me a long while to get a look at it, and it always cuts off at the upcoming sunset—not too useful. Besides, it would only tell me what I already know: a major life event is coming up.

The future could be rushing down on me like a truck while my mystical third eye is trying to tell me something. Something horrible about seeing Tort. Something horrible about going to that house. Something horrible in general.

This isn't helping me overcome my cowardice.

All right. I can be paranoid. I could be talking myself into a tizzy with nothing whatsoever of substance to it. Everything is going to be perfectly all right. This is all an effect of my radical life changes, a week or so of torture and the resulting mild post-traumatic stress, my own sense of guilt for everything in creation, and a billion or so bits of unfinished business.

Or I really am just a coward.

All right. Fine. Okay.

It's possible my brain is trying to tell me something and I'm not listening. The usual response is to have a nap and see what I can dream up. Since I'd like to be sharp for my meeting with Tort, I should have one. Fine.

Bronze joined me in the cavern I was using as a workroom—I didn't feel comfortable sleeping in a known location. I let Torvil and Kammen in on it, too. Them I covered in a multiphase active/passive combination of stealth spells before we went down there. I didn't want anyone tracing them to find me. Once down in the workroom, I drew the lines for an Ascension Sphere, put a protective circle inside it, and laid out a couple of blankets, furs, and a bundle for a pillow.

As I laid down on my makeshift bed, I wondered where Fred was. Not Fred the preacher, Fred the Monster Under the Bed. Was he still doing his best to scare the crap out of would-be knights, checking them for bravery in the face of the unknown? I hope so. He seemed to enjoy the work.

I settled down with Firebrand on my left, a sheathed super-sword on my right, and my armored underwear in place.

Paranoid? Maybe. Is it paranoia if powerful and dangerous forces really are out to get you? Or is it merely reasonable caution?

I stepped inside, into my mental study, and slowly turned down the lights.

A fishbowl. A bubble of glass. Me in the middle, building castles of sand on a tiny island. The black ocean all around me, seething, sending waves up on the sandy shore, never quite reaching. Each wave clawing up toward my constructs, falling back, dragging some of my island with it.

Outside, beyond the glass, are the eyes. Eyes, eyes, eyes. Eyes enough to surround my glassy universe in all directions, as though it sits at the bottom of a sea made of bubbles. All alike in that they are balls with lids, pupils, irises ... but all strange, all different. Red irises, slit pupils, square pupils, glowing or dark, wide-eyed or narrowed, interested, curious, hostile, angry, weeping...

One eye, closed, seems almost to be asleep. It slides through the mass of them, drifting slowly, like a man moving through a crowd. It is the only one closed, so I look at it, wondering, while the sand around me slowly swirls into the ocean foam.

As though feeling my gaze, it opens. It is a ball of solid black, a void of emptiness with a gloss to mark its border. Yet, within it, something stirs. They eye is open, but there is more opening within, like the unfolding of some dark flower within the sphere, until the Eye looks out at me, burning with a fire as hot as hatred, as bright as fury.

The ocean sweeps over the sand at last, and I sink into the dark waters. I descend into the depths.

I stand upon the floor of Olympus, facing a bright thing in the form of a man. Wings as vast as skies stretch behind it, blazing angrily with the light of the universe. It curses at me and each curse is like a blow. I stand mute while it rages, buffeting me with angry words. All around, the gods look down from their thrones, frowning. The figure of light blinds me with its radiance and I shield my eyes. Some of the gods are moving, reaching down—for me? For the bright thing? The light shines too bright and I cannot see.

I blink in the desert sun. Eleven ragged men stagger through the hardpan, shuffling along. One raises a canteen to drink, takes the last of the water, sighs and moves on. There is nothing behind them but footprints vanishing in the hot, dusty wind. There is nothing before them but more desert. They will die here, lay quietly until their flesh is desiccated, turned to dust, and their bones erode into a patch of white sand.

They pause to pray and another figure stands beside me, watching them. Bearded, robed, barefoot.

"Jesus!" I exclaim, surprised.

"Yeah. You've got some troubles, son."

"Don't I know it. Any advice?"

"'Fraid not. You're screwed."

"Oh, you're a lot of help."

"It's what you get for harboring a thing from the original, primal void inside you." He shrugs broad shoulders before he grins at me. "Don't take it too hard. It's not personal."

And the world blows away in a cloud of hot dust, hot sand, and the taste of ashes. When it clears, there is a dirt street between two rows of buildings. Dry goods, saloon, hotel, sheriff's office—it's every nowhere town from every Western I've ever watched. A tumbleweed rolls by, between me and the man in the black hat. *I cannot see his face, for the shadows under the brim are deep and dark. I think I see two faint sparks of red where his eyes must be.*

"They say it's not the fastest gun," he tells me, drawing back one flap of his coat, "but the one who doesn't hesitate."

While he's busy talking, I draw and shoot him and he goes down. The crowd appears from nowhere, cheering, lifting me on their shoulders, carrying me around. They transfer me to a fence rail, carrying it on their shoulders, parading me all around the town. We stop at the train station where they dump me on a flatcar, shouting obscenities and throwing stones. The train pulls out of the station and I lay there, baking on the rough wood beneath a terrible light.

The sands around swirl, obliterating the train, leaving only a narrow tunnel into the sky, aimed at the noonday sun. The sands swirl aside in a whirlwind, forming a gigantic figure. The djinn stands a hundred feet tall, with baggy pants, metal wristbands, upthrust fangs, glowing eyes of green and gold, and a long tail of hair from the back of his otherwise bald head. He bears wounds, dozens of them, and where his blood falls the desert blooms.

"Why have you done this to me?" it asks, softly. "I slept, and you bled me dry."

"I never did."

"It was you," says the djinn, pointing a sharp-taloned finger at me. "You did this!"

The genie falls. All around it, grass and flowers spring up. Trees leap from the ground into full growth. Birds sing, brooks flow, cool breezes dance.

The genie dies and decays before my eyes, crumbling into dust, and everything around it crumbles with it. The desert is desert once more, bearing not so much as a bone to show it ever was anything else.

I lay there, helpless to move, pinned by the eye of the sun. I would weep, but the tears are blood and vanish, sucked up by my eyes and skin faster than I can shed them.

Olivia sits down beside my head and throws her two-year-old arms around my neck. She cries for me, as I could not, and calls me Uncle Flad.

The Four come up and drag me sideways along the sand. They take me out of the sun, into a dry, cool place. It is a treehouse, hammered together from scrap wood and random nails, smelling of summer grass and green, leafy places.

"You're not supposed to be here," Patricia tells me.

"You're not dead yet," Edgar adds.

"Where am I supposed to be?" I ask.

Gary helps me sit up. We look out the window at the neighborhood. He points down the street, where kids play ball, fathers mow yards, mothers make lemonade.

"That way," he says, pointing beyond these things. I see the crossroads is abandoned.

"Get your ass moving," Luke advises.

"I will still give you a smack on the ear," I warn.

"Please get your ass moving?"

"It'll do."

I unwind Olivia from my neck and she kisses my cheek, giggling. I climb down and walk the length of the street. The smells of fresh-mown grass and charcoal smoke are strong.

The crossroads is a simple four-way, with a hanged man on the gibbet. I look back, but the road behind me is a cracked and blasted ruin.

Three ways, then.

"Tough choice?" asks the hanged man.

"Not when you don't know where you're going."

"Doesn't that make it harder?"

"Here are three boxes. Pick one. I'm not going to tell you one has a bomb, one has treasure, and one is empty."

"I see your point. Maybe you should read the signpost."

I look at the corner opposite the gibbet. The signs indicates I've just walked along Life-And-Death Road to reach the intersection. The cross street is Good-And-Evil Avenue.

"So, which way is Good and which way is Evil?"

"Excellent question," admits the hanged man, and fades out around his grin. A moment later, the grin fades, too, leaving a noose swinging in the wind.

Alice gets enigmatic cats. I get enigmatic corpses. Figures.

I consider the four directions. Behind me, Death isn't even a road. Life, presumably, is the road before me. Good and Evil run perpendicular to Life and Death. My choices seem to be Life, Death, Good, or Evil. But if they're different choices, what does it mean to choose Good or Evil? You don't get a life?

Cheap philosophy there, if you want it.

I choose the way in front of me, heading down the road of life. Good and Evil will doubtless cross my path again. None of these roads is a straight line. They twist and turn like spaghetti on the boil. In the meantime, the first rule is to survive. You can do good and evil on your own. It would be nice to have a map, though, to know when you're taking a detour along one or the other.

The chittering at my back catches my attention. Against my better judgment, I glance behind.

Things. Black things. Multi-legged things. Lots and lots of Things. They swarm after me like a hungry tar pit brought to life and invested with several thousand mouths.

I run, bare feet bleeding on the slick stone as I avoid the stream of smoking liquid in the middle of the ruined street. I dodge through a ruined building, swing up to the second floor, leap the alleyway, streak through the remains of the opposite building, and leap down to the street again. If they are following my bloody footprints, that will throw them off...

Bronze stands in the street. She sees me and turns away, crouching in a most un-horse-like manner. I take the hint. I run straight up behind her, jump up enough to hit right over her rump, somersault along her back and into her saddle.

She leaps into motion and I do not recognize the direction.

I opened my eyes and sat up.

About two bands of the candle, Boss.

"What?"

You were about to ask how long you were asleep.

"Yes. Yes, I was."

Bronze indicated I should scratch her forehead. I did so and thanked her for waking me.

Learn anything? Firebrand asked.

"I have nightmares."

This is a surprise?

"No, but they might interfere with my ability to have psychic dreams."

I guess. What do I know? I'm a psychic sword, not a psychologist.

"Anyone who goes to a psychologist should have his head examined."

Uh... I'm not sure that makes any sense, Boss.

"Sometimes I don't," I admitted. I stood up and rubbed sleep out of my eyes. I was sweaty and sticky. It wasn't a good nap.

What was I going to do now? Clean up, get dressed, and head for Tort's? I didn't really want to do it during the day. I feel a little more confident when it's dark. Or is it merely less frightened? Is there a difference between more confident and less frightened? I think there is. Either way, I feel better at night. Fewer active glands, maybe that's it.

Aha! I'm not on a hurried schedule anymore. I can go visit Diogenes, make sure that's all set up, then come back and visit Tort.

Yes, that sounds like a good way to stall—and I know I'm stalling. Knowing it doesn't mean I can do anything about it. I want to see her as much as I'm afraid to.

I went down to my main gate room. It was almost unrecognizable with the pointy crystals projecting from every wall. At least it was easy to illuminate.

I selected the main arch for my trip to see Diogenes, rather than the door-sized one. Bronze was coming with me and I had some boxes to tote along. I also brought some charged power crystals. The gate in the Diogenes library probably had enough charge to work, but adding a few more magical crystals to its spell matrix would give it a much larger battery pack. I also brought a pre-constructed magical jet for sucking in power and charging the library gate more quickly.

The gate swirled, flushed, snapped back, and we were through in an instant. The gate snapped shut behind us. It was definitely daytime here, as well—I have an infallible sense for these things—but the room was dark. I conjured a light in the dark and saw the ruins of a library.

"I think I missed."

I'll go with you that, Firebrand agreed. Bronze nodded. This, children, is why you build dedicated gates to each world you want to visit, complete with sigils and ideograms, lines on the floor, and maybe even magical keys.

I really do need to examine a magical gate-key, sometime. I'll mention it to T'yl.

The room was mostly stone and looked carved rather than constructed. Most of the walls were covered in little bits of tile at irregular angles. The dust didn't help, but the shiny little tiles still reflected some of the light, spreading it farther than I'd have thought. Much of the room held pigeonhole shelving constructed of brick and dry, dusty wood. I touched one, gingerly, and bits of the wood flaked away under my fingertips. The pigeonholes were once filled with scrolls—flat strips of wood, tied together and rolled up—but most of these were piles of fibers, now. The walls also held pigeonholes, but more flat and wide than simple scroll holders. Folios, I presume—stacks of parchment in leather folders. These were as dry and crumbling as the rest.

I looked at the arch through which we entered. It was the mouth of a short tunnel, maybe twenty feet, and led to another, similar chamber. Other passages led off to yet more of the same like a literary rabbit warren.

Well, I was aiming for a lost, forgotten, ruined library. I hit a lost, forgotten, ruined library. Just not the one I wanted.

"Yeah, this doesn't look familiar."

Bronze nudged me with her nose, a sort of *You were driving* comment.

"I know, I know. But we're not lost. We just not anywhere we recognize," I replied. Bronze snorted. She had her own opinion on that.

"Look, if we know how to get home from here, it doesn't count as lost. We merely have a greater than normal uncertainty about our position relative to... well, everything."

Bronze sighed, a blast of air that stirred dust from the floor like a bomb. I coughed and started breathing through my shirt.

Are we going back, Boss? Firebrand asked.

"In a minute," I choked. "I want to see if there's a way out."

What for? Firebrand asked, as I moved away from the dust cloud to breathe better.

"It's a whole new world, potentially full of shining, shimmering splendor." Firebrand shrugged mentally and Bronze whickered a laugh. I started marking the tunnel walls as we searched the place.

It was bigger than I'd thought, comprised of at least twenty rooms big enough for a swordfight. I didn't finish searching the place because we found the main doors. They were wooden and just as dry and fragile as the rest. I pulled on the handle, carefully, and wound up with a brass handle. I tossed it aside and looked through the hole. Someone buried the door, apparently. Sandy dirt dribbled in from beyond.

"I hate to try and dig out," I muttered. "Archaeologists would have my head for ruining the site."

Assuming there are any around, Boss.

"You raise a good point. Let me see how much dirt I can shove aside without disturbing the stacks."

It turned out to be quite a lot, in fact. Bronze kicked dirt out of the doorway and I scooped it aside, shoving it against the walls, piling it up to slightly below the folio holes. It was dusty work, but rewarding; sunlight shone down after the first ten minutes. Of course, a huge pile of dirt collapsed practically on top of us, destroying what was left of the doors and half-burying Bronze, but that was only a minor problem. Dirt doesn't bother Bronze the way it bothers me.

The doors of the library were underground, down in some sort of well. A few stone projections told me there were stairs mounted in the wall of the well at one point, like the stairs around the inside of a tower. Could the whole thing have sunk in some disaster? Or was it deliberately buried? Or was it simply built underground for some reason?

"I'll be right back down," I told Bronze. There was no way she would be able to take what was left of the stairs. I clung to the face of the well and worked my way up twenty or thirty feet to peer over the edge.

The lip of the well was only an inch or two above ground level. Some scattered stones of suspiciously angular shape implied there was once some sort of structure over the well. An aboveground library? Or just a lobby? It was impossible to tell.

The world, on the other hand, reminded me of some of the location shots from movies. Lawrence of Arabia leaped to mind. Some of the more barren and unpleasant places in the Australian outback were also in the running. What was the name of that place... Coober Pedy? Something like that. Lots of dust, lots of wind, lots of heat, and the occasional scrubby bush about the size of a football.

I climbed a little higher, got my elbows over the edge, pulled myself up to sit at ground level. Nothing to be seen, not even a bug. I stood up, looked around.

Yes, this might have been a city. The low ridges were angular, regular. Buried foundations? Or the final few inches of stone walls eroded by wind and grit? Maybe the tops of walls, if an ancient city was buried? Whatever it was, the place was a tomb, not a city. There might be life, even civilized life, somewhere around here, but the magical signature of the place was on par with the library of Diogenes—low—and I had no idea which way might lead to water.

Fortunately, a small spectrum-shifting spell isn't too power-intensive. I waved my hands and chanted for a bit as I drew lines in the dirt, making it as easy as possible. I looked around for radio sources in orbit or bouncing off the ionosphere, assuming either of those was an option. There were some ionosphere reflections, so that was to the good, but I can't make out what information they carry just by looking at them. They were sustained radio sources, though, not merely transient bursts.

So, civilization exists, and a moderately technological one, at that. It's possible I'm just in the middle of a desert, somewhere, literally in a forgotten ruin. Elsewhere there may be sandwiches and soda pop, but nowhere close to me.

Good to know. I might have to remember this place and see if I can hit it deliberately. Exploring could be fun.

I climbed back down just as carefully and we shoved as much dirt back into the hole as we could. This blocked it up fairly well. I hoped to avoid flooding the whole place with more blown-in dirt. I might never come back, but someday someone might want to look over these antiquities.

We found our way back to the arch we came in by. I scratched on the walls— sorry, archaeologists! —to attune the tunnel mouth a bit better and prepare it for my spell. This time, I paid more attention, really focusing and concentrating, to leave one library for the library I actually wanted. I was about to be the inter-library loan and didn't want to get lost in shipping.

With the basic structure of the spell built, I poured the stored power from the crystals into it. The gate opened, we stepped through, the gate closed, and I fell down dead. Of course, it was nighttime. I recovered in moments and uncurled from the misery position.

"I have got to find a way to avoid this."

Don't go through magical gates?

"You stick to skewering things and setting them on fire. I'll do the thinking, thank you."

Suit yourself, Boss.

I waved at the monitoring equipment Diogenes aimed at the gate. One of the cameras tilted up and down, nodding in reply. The clock worried me a little. It seemed to indicate the total elapsed time here was on the order of two and a half *months.*

Months? Just how badly out of whack can universes get? Are there worlds where they have a Big Bang, run through the whole stellar generations thing, expend all the ready fusion elements, and collapse into another Big Bang while I'm spending a weekend studying elf anatomy? Are there others doing the opposite—effectively sitting still, no time passing, while I spend a century screwing up not only the lives of everyone around me, but multiple generations of people?

Worse, do these places vary? Could I walk away from a world and, because of the time differential, wind up having been gone only an eyeblink... or be unable to return because the universe ran down and died? What would happen if Karvalen ran down? If its sun got far enough off course, flew so low it set fire to broad swathes of the world every summer? Or crashed into the world? If the world came to an end, could I open a gate to the remains? Or, if it crumbled into chaos, would I open a gate where it was, or simply never make contact again?

I admit I'm easy to disturb. Heck, I'm about as disturbed as it's possible to get without actually needing a self-hugging jacket and bubble-wrap wallpaper. But it never occurred to me I could step out of a world and it could vanish, never to be seen again!

As if I didn't have enough to worry about.

We headed out the door and I spied with my little eye more than a few changes.

Someone mowed the university lawn. There wasn't a trace of carnivorous ivy to be seen. I wasn't sure how I felt about that. I mean, yes, it was a dangerous plant if you didn't understand it, but it was also familiar. Then again, the same someone repaired the doors, so maybe it kept trying to grow into the library.

We crossed the campus to the Biology department and I was mildly startled to see how much Diogenes accomplished. The area around the building was neat and clean. Solar panels were mounted on tracking poles. Some new wiring connected the rooftops of nearby buildings. Dangerous-looking machines—they had built-in or bolted-on weaponry—stood at the corners of the buildings, as though on guard, scanning back and forth. Military equipment, perhaps, which survived well enough to be repaired? Did they make robotic war machines before Armageddon, or were the robotic touches merely Diogenes' adaptations?

I went in. Bronze waited outside.

"Good evening, *jefe*," came over the building's speakers. "I've been expecting you. May I offer you some refreshment?"

"It's nighttime, Diogenes, and I'm a vampire."

"This is a biology building, *jefe*, and my mandate was to clone elves, was it not?"

"Very true. I suppose you would have elf blood on hand. All right. I don't think I've ever tried cloned blood before. Let's see how it goes."

"This way, if you please." A holographic light appeared before me and drifted along the hall. I passed a number of classrooms on the ground floor, all repurposed as laboratories. Quite a lot of non-mobile robotic equipment—arms of various sorts, mainly—was bolted to the floor or sliding along tracks in the ceiling. Every bit of it had a rough-welded, bolted-together look to it, making it part steampunk, part salvage. The clear emphasis was on function, not appearance.

Upstairs, in what was once a lounge area of some sort, I settled into a re-upholstered and reinforced chair. A small, tracked unit rolled out with a tray mounted on top. It stopped at my elbow, opened a top hatch, raised a glass into view, and a nozzle poured blood into it.

I'm slow on the uptake, but not that slow. I took the glass and almost managed to drink some. The usual thing happened as the blood crawled out of the glass and sank into my skin. I sighed.

"I'm terribly sorry," Diogenes announced. "One moment, please."

The robot waiter trundled off, returned in moments. This time, the container it raised into view was a sort of travel mug. Since it was sealed, the blood couldn't crawl out. I lifted it, squeezed it, and slurped. It might be cloned, but it certainly tasted like fresh-squeezed elf.

"Very good. Very good, indeed. I take it, then, you've had some success in the last couple of months?"

"Some success, yes, *jefe*. Would you like a full report?"

"How about the bullet points? And, as much as I'm pleased with your desire to accommodate Firebrand by not calling me 'Boss,' could you come up with something besides *jefe*?"

"By your command, Imperious Leader."

"Battlestar Galactica?" I guessed.

"Yes, Imperious Leader. The nonvolatile storage media are among the more easily salvaged items."

"Nice phrase, but the connotations are pretty grim. It's also awkward for casual conversation. Try again."

"Supreme Dictator?"

"No."

"El Presidente?"

"No. How about something a trifle less pretentious?"

"Professor?" Diogenes suggested.

"Now there's a name I've not heard in a long, long time. A long time," I quoted. "Sure, let's give that a whack."

"You got it, Prof."

"Carry on. But answer me this. Have you seen any giant ants?"

"Yes. During the course of the ongoing salvage operations, a number of ants one might classify as 'giant' have been unearthed or otherwise disturbed. They do not like high-frequency noise and appear to hunt primarily by vibration tracking."

"They can also smell blood," I cautioned. "Not a problem for robots and drones, obviously, but for your information."

"Noted. Six robots were damaged by giant ants to the point of recycling. Now all robots are equipped with, at minimum, a bladed implement for self-defense purposes. Two specialized units for ant hunting actively explore areas as scouts before salvage robots enter."

"Good! If you find a giant ant nest, let me know."

"Of course, Professor."

"Okay, what else have you got?"

"The primary articles of interest fall into two categories. First, the industrial base for the production of clones. Second, the capacity to produce said clones.

"The industrial base is now expanding at a geometric rate, but this rate will decrease as the density of useful salvage decreases outside the urban area, and as the number of available robots reaches a limit based on the power of my primary processor. These quantum computer processors have extensive capacity, but they seem unable to duplicate my existing operating system. I suspect your magical manipulations are the only reason I am able to make use of one. My programming languages appear to be incompatible."

"Suggestions?"

"Perhaps additional processors can be linked in parallel to increase my total capacity."

"I'll look into it. I presume you have some on hand?"

"Two hundred and sixty-four more, Professor."

"Set up the physical side of things and I'll look into the magical side."

"I am completing the racking and mounting as we speak."

"Good. What else?"

"I am currently operating solely on solar power, but have cleaned, refurbished, repaired, and isolated a number of buildings' solar banks, as well as salvaging panels from several thousand vehicles. Power storage is adequate, but prioritized to maintain cloning research during nighttime hours. However, a hydroelectric system utilizing water wheels will soon be coming on-line and wind-turbine units are expected to supplement them. Further salvage and repair work on actual power generation stations is ongoing, but such systems seem to have been preferred targets, or near them, during the theorized nuclear exchange. Most such stations are either heavily damaged or in high radiation zones."

"Anything I can do to help?"

"While independent action on your part would undoubtedly be of use, at this point I believe it would also be relatively insignificant compared to the massed action of the robot extensions."

"One more grunt in an army?"

"Essentially, Professor."

"Fair enough. Continue, please."

"The cloning research has reached the point of limited production."

"Limited?"

"The industrial base for producing the chemical compounds required for organic synthesis is still in the developmental phase, Professor."

"But you don't have any trouble cloning elves?"

"Despite the unusual genome, the cloning process seems straightforward. They practically clone themselves. In theory, once a clone sample is started, it might be implanted in a human female and allowed to come to term, with some reservations."

"What sort of reservations?"

The screen on the wall—it was part of the wall, not mounted in it—flickered to life. I wondered if it was repaired or replaced, or simply salvaged from somewhere else and installed here. Then I decided it didn't matter. Diogenes prepared this room as a briefing center.

Images appeared in time-lapse.

"The cloning process is much faster than the natural development. As you can see here, cloned elves appear to develop normally, aside from the remarkable rapidity, until reaching the equivalent development of a human at fourteen weeks. At this stage, the development diverges markedly. The size increases dramatically over the next few days, as does the definition and formation of all features. At the human equivalent of sixteen weeks, the elf is, essentially, a fully-formed adult, approximately eight inches in length. Experimental subjects decanted at this point exhibit typical newborn behaviors, but their growth slows to imperceptibility. Those left in the forced-growth tanks continue to develop at their accelerated rate, gaining size and mass. The overall process to produce a fully-formed, adult body takes approximately twenty-seven days."

I whistled. From scattered cells to adult body in twenty-seven days. That's a testament to elven vitality and advanced cloning techniques. If I ever meet Rendu, I have to compliment him on his cellular design.

"I thought you said it diverged at fourteen weeks?"

"The developmental stage of a human embryo at the age of fourteen weeks. An elf zygote reaches that stage in twelve days, slightly more quickly than a human embryo in a forced-growth tank."

"Oh. Sorry. My mistake. So, what's up with the elven blood? You have lots of it on hand?"

"The normal technique of umbilical support requires supplementation for elves," Diogenes reported. "Intra-arterial lines must be grafted into the clone and nutrient solution provided via cloned blood carrier. Since the clones reject these grafts as quickly as they reject umbilical support, constant monitoring and maintenance are required."

"Well, elves don't appear to have a normal mode of development. They lack bellybuttons and reproductive organs. They were created, not born."

"As are these, Professor. Hence the difficulties in feeding them during the growth stages."

"I guess so. All right, do you see any reason you can't start providing adult elf bodies?"

"Production is limited, at present, to one adult specimen every nine days, assuming there are no anomalous clones. I have only three growth tanks large enough for adult clones, Professor. If they are all used for production, I will have to divert resources to build more if you wish me to continue research and experimentation."

"If you only have three growth tanks, where do you get the blood? You mentioned having to use extra nutrients and suchlike to produce even one clone."

"Harvesting blood from failed clones is not difficult. It is also possible to produce smaller specimens in the smaller tanks and keep them alive to produce blood on an ongoing basis. However, laboratory production of blood is proving more difficult than anticipated, thus requiring the use of individual specimens as production units."

"I see. All right. Well... build what you need in order to establish a reliable supply of elf-bodies. I want to get magicians off my back and keep Bob impressed."

"Think nothing of it, Professor."

"Okay. When will you have your computer core setup set up?"

"It is in the basement, Professor."

"I'll look it over before I test the boxes. And do you think you could get me the equivalent of a smartphone or something? I'm thinking I can program in messages, open a small gate, have it transmit them, you can answer, and I can close the gate. Minimum power requirements, that sort of thing."

"I will begin assembly immediately."

"Thank you, Diogenes."

The little holographic light reappeared and I followed it down to the basement. A pair of robots were finishing up some spot-welding, but the three-dimensional rack holding the computer core array was obviously not built just while we were talking. It was beautiful, really. All those crystals in precise alignment, glittering in a geometric figure, made me wonder about their placement.

"Diogenes?"

"Yes, Professor?"

"What's the geometry, here?"

"The processors are arranged on the vertices and faces of a great disnub dirhombidodecahedron."

"Who the what, now?"

"Skilling's figure, Professor."

"I'm an *n*-dimensional theorist, not an actual geometer."

"It is a regular polyhedron classified as a uniform star polyhedron," Diogenes clarified. While the clarification helped, it was on the order of pointing down which road to take when setting off on your cross-continent trip.

I know when I'm licked.

"Thank you, Diogenes," I told him, and pretended thereafter I understood what Skilling's figure was.

"My pleasure, Professor."

"I take it their alignment is important for the processors?"

"It should minimize the interference from the separate processors."

"Is this a quantum entanglement issue?"

"Yes, Professor."

"So distance isn't a factor."

"Correct. The regularity of the placement of the secondary processors is of prime importance."

"Fair enough. If you'll be kind enough to set up the boxes I brought—they're teleportation boxes for sending bodies back—I'll start work on tying all these things together."

"Professor, would it be wise to do so while I am operating? Perhaps I should put everything into a standby mode while you work."

"Good thinking. Do you have anything needing attention? You said clones don't like needles."

"Yes, Professor, but I've inserted fresh ones into the clones still in growth stages. They should require no active intervention for at least four hours."

"Okay. When's dawn?"

"Six hours, nineteen minutes."

"Good. Let me know when you're ready."

"My equipment usage is minimal at night. I have been putting active robots into standby mode since you arrived. To reactivate the system, please throw the switch the robot is about to throw. Thirty seconds, Professor... Entering standby..."

The robot by the power box flipped a breaker and ceased to move. The holographic light went out and I got busy.

Connecting one of the quantum computer cores to any other wasn't difficult. It involved a spell almost identical to the vitality-linking spell I used to let the Diogenes drive talk to the original quantum computer core. I didn't need a translation matrix to go with it, of course, since I was connecting two compatible crystals. This made the connection both simple and easy, effectively expanding Diogenes' "brain" from one crystal to all the crystals.

But it was tedious. Extremely tedious. There were two hundred and sixty-four new crystals, each of which needed a direct tie-in with the primary Diogenes crystal. While each spell was relatively simple, there were a *lot* of them.

Imagine folding a paper airplane, then drawing an appropriate national logo on it—something simple, like that circular logo the Royal Air Force used in World War Two. Don't forget a tail number for your paper airplane.

Very nice. Now, what did it all take? Two minutes? Five? It was easy, wasn't it?

Only two hundred and sixty-three to go. Get busy. And make sure those tail numbers are all in sequence!

I got faster as we went along, of course. Lots of practice. I was profoundly glad I didn't have to connect them all to each other, just to the primary crystal. If each one had to connect to all the others, that would be... let me see... thirty-two thousand individual connections? Thirty-three? Somewhere in that ballpark. No doubt they should all be interconnected, but it's a project for when I don't have anything planned that year.

Two hundred and sixty-odd didn't seem so bad.

Still, I didn't finish within the four hours Diogenes mentioned. I didn't even finish in the six hours and change before dawn. I sat out the sunrise, used my Ring of Hygiene, and pressed on. I was afraid to reactivate the system with only a partially-completed great disnub dirhombo-homie geometric thingamabob lest they have a disruptive level of quantum interference. I didn't know it would, merely suspected it might—and didn't want to risk it.

I'm pretty sure the purpose of the arrangement was to make the interference into a pattern, which could therefore be filtered out. Diogenes could probably filter out even a partial arrangement, but I didn't want to take chances with the thinking processes of an artificial intelligence controlling multiple armed robots. There are whole movie franchises about why it's a bad idea to have a crazy computer.

A little before noon, I think, I finished double-checking the last of the linking spells. Nothing twanged oddly when I strummed the structure, nothing sounded off-key. All to the good, as far as I was concerned. Now for the next part. The spells were all in place and charged, ready to go, but they were standard spells. Not enchantments, not hybrids, just spells. When their energy ran out, they would consume themselves and disintegrate. In order to keep them operating indefinitely in this magic-poor environment, they needed a way to draw in energy. Adding a power input took more time, but it was a single spell addition, since it could juice the whole system, rather than an added piece to each of the component parts. Unfortunately, the power intake was barely able to sustain itself as a spell. What little it had left over wouldn't power a candle-sized light spell.

So much for my gate-charging jet. I took it out of the storage crystal, plugged it into the power intake, and cranked it up. It required a bit of a jump start from my personal energies, but it got there. Originally, I intended it to slowly charge gate crystals for later use, but Diogenes took priority.

I didn't like the way it ran, though. It worked, but I suspected it was cycling down to a lower level of operation. Anything short of a total lack of magical energy would still allow it to run, but it would slow down to match the power intake.

Thermodynamic irony. The more deeply it violated thermodynamics, the better it worked. Sometimes I hate magic.

I drew giant circles on the two walls to either side of the intake and set them up as self-sustaining magical power fans, blowing higher concentrations of power into the room, toward the jet. These would also run at lower speeds due to the paucity of magical force in the world, but they would act as a sort of a pre-compressor even before the jet got hold of it. The jet seemed to run more easily, though. I should probably do that for the gate in the library, as well. If I got another fully-equipped jet spell constructed for it, it might need the same help.

Hmm. I wonder if my experiments with ruthenium could be helpful. In theory, ruthenium could be used as the core of an electromagnet. However, instead of a magnetic field, it produced a magical field—an electromagical transformer. If we can build one and keep it in the room, it should help even more. I might even be able to put a spell on it to direct all the magical output into Diogenes' brain-structure spell system.

I flipped the breaker in the power box and waited.

I'll say this for quantum computing: Booting up the system takes virtually no time at all. The holographic light blinked on again only a moment after I threw the switch.

"I see this took considerably more time than projected, Professor."

"Internal clock?"

"Yes."

"Anything ruined?"

"Two clones are irrecoverable, but they will be recycled."

"Fair enough. How's your new brain?"

"Much expanded. I am still not able to fully replicate my current operating matrix into the relevant processors, but I can use them as secondary processors—peripherals."

"I was thinking about that. Do I need to cross-connect everything? Each crystal having a communications connection to all the others?"

"That would be optimal," Diogenes agreed. "I calculate an increase in capacity on the order of six hundred times. But, extrapolating from the time to complete the primary core connection..."

"Yeah, it'll take a while. Maybe I can figure out a way to automate the process. It's the same spell, over and over again, after all."

"No hurry, Professor. It will be over a year before I can make use of my current capacity."

"So, you've definitely improved? You can run more robots in real-time?"

"Many more. My current estimate is on the close order of ten million individual units. This does not include dumb subsystems, such as automated factories, which do not require real-time control from the central processor cluster."

"Naturally, naturally." I shouldn't be surprised at the numbers involved. Quantum computing. But still! I hope I haven't built my own version of Skynet. Then again, the world has already been nuked, so what's the worst that could happen?

"By the way, do you have any ruthenium resources?" I asked.

"I conjecture there are ruthenium components and alloys in many devices, but I do not have any of the raw metal on hand, Professor."

"Can you get enough to build some small electromagnets?"

"Ruthenium does not make a good electromagnet, Professor."

"I know, but I'd like you to experiment with small pieces of ruthenium, anyway. Use it for electromagnet cores, maybe as the conductors around the cores, all the variations. And with variable voltage and amperage—all the possible combinations. Strictly small-scale stuff."

"Preliminary program set. Is this a continuation of your research at the farmhouse, Professor?"

"Yes. I've noticed such experiments produce magical energy."

"I lack the ability to observe the phenomenon."

"I know, but if you set up the experiments, I can evaluate them when I get back. And maybe I can enchant a camera to see magical forces, too—have one ready for me, along with the ruthenium setup."

"Very good, Professor."

"And set it all up in the library, please. If you run them in there, it should increase the magical environment and speed up the charging of the gate. When we get some working at high efficiency, we can put one down here to maintain the spells on your processors."

"I will increase the priority of the project, Professor."

"Good plan. Now, I'll just go test those boxes and head back."

"This way, Professor." The light led me to a decanting room. Two cylinders—glass? Plastic? —held a clear fluid and a pair of full-grown elves. Bob.

My first thought was Bob would be beside himself if he could see this, but I'm a bad person.

Diogenes kindly decanted a clone for me. I put it into the larger box, realizing as I did so I wouldn't be using the smaller one. Crap. Elves don't produce baby-sized versions. I needed two large sets, one for T'yl and one for Bob... unless they could share it, maybe, taking turns...

I didn't really want to burn so much of my charged crystals, but the boxes needed testing. I closed the large box and activated it. When I raised the lid, the box was empty. I closed and opened it again, but nothing happened. Of course. The box in Karvalen opened automatically. Well, that was to the good, at least.

Several minutes of fiddling with the one in front of me allowed me to use the micro-gate link between the two and trigger the other box to close. I cycled the lid on the local one and the system activated normally. The local box now held a wet, naked elf. He didn't arrive inside out or anything, so that was a good sign. He was still breathing and what passed for hearts were still pumping, so I counted it as a success. I gave him back to Diogenes for a full examination—it wouldn't do to hand over elf-bodies damaged in transit. But, judging by eye, it seemed to work perfectly.

With that sorted out, I complimented Diogenes on his work, encouraged him to continue, and explained the procedure for delivering clones. A robot wheeled the current elf away for detailed analysis. Another robot rolled up on small treads, brandishing a multiplicity of arms. From the look of the thing, it was designed and built "by hand," rather than in a factory.

"One of your manufacture, Diogenes?"

"My analysis of electronics repair times indicated the need for a specialized unit."

"Good thinking," I agreed, as it handed me a thick rectangle. "What's this?"

"Your smartphone, Professor." I took the flat little unit and examined it. Tool marks, some scratches on the casing, and the smell of scorched metal seemed to indicate it had recently been a bunch of parts. I pressed the button and it lit up. Diogenes and I played with it for a bit. It worked and felt pretty durable.

"So, it will send text messages to you, but not much else?"

"In the event you open a gate, Professor, yes," the phone said, in Diogenes' voice. "You may make whatever notes you wish, upload them as a batch, and receive a batch download of progress reports in return. If you feel the need to converse, the unit will also accommodate you as long as a stable gate connection is maintained."

"I like it. I'll get the micro-sized ring gates set up for it soon."

"Based on your experiments with gates at the farmhouse, I included an iridium ring in the design, proximal to the transmitter. It was originally twice as thick, but I cut it in two. The other half is readied as a communications gateway."

"That... hmm. I *think* that should help. If nothing else, it should serve as a good locus. We'll have to experiment with it. At least I know what to enchant."

"Always a pleasure to be of service, Professor."

"Thanks, Diogenes."

With that, I went back to the library.

The main gate wasn't exactly well-charged. I installed the power crystals I'd brought. They still retained a little energy, but the detour to the desert library strained my power budget. What charge they had left, I spent on rebuilding and reinforcing the suspended magical compression jet I'd left on my last trip. I tore it down and put it back together, this time with all the added features to make it run indefinitely. It wound up being considerably smaller, but it will constantly pump energy into the storage crystals over time. If your car battery is flat, a trickle-charger won't let you jump-start it. Leave it for several hours, though, and the charge builds up. This was the same principle.

I was very careful while opening the library gate. With the minimal magical power reserves, it was important to hit Karvalen on the first try. I suppose I could have gone through the coffin-gate, but it was sized for an elf. It would be a tight fit, at best, and Bronze would have to wait until I got a regular gate open, anyway.

The geode gate room looked pretty and familiar as we sprang through the archway. Judging by the geode décor, I decided it was probably the right place. We were quick about it, but mostly from reflex. Once the gate established itself, the linkage to the power crystals on both sides fed the connection.

I also didn't double over in sudden death, so it was daytime. A quick check with the guard outside told me I'd been gone for only a couple of hours.

Well, crap. There were still hours to go before nightfall and my planned trip to Kamshasa.

Maybe I could kill some time explaining to T'yl and Bob how to take turns with the Coffin of Elf Creation. Who knows? Maybe they even will. Take turns, I mean. Since Norad and Morrelin were already in line for immortality treatment and I had another magical artifact to test, I decided to see if they wanted to do a whole run-through of the process that evening. Even I don't want to try a soul transfer during the day.

Which left me with an afternoon to kill and various anxieties and insecurities to nurse.

Aha! I have a few vague ideas for dealing with Johann, but it would be wise to do some bench testing on my spells. They should work without too much trouble, but if I can minimize the time and trouble—make things go more smoothly—then that was all to the good.

Huzzah! Another distraction! But this time, one yielding material progress in its results. I hope.

The sun went down, I died, I cleaned up—I'm starting to love my ring—and I went to meet the magicians and the elves. A quick demonstration of the Coffin of Elf Creation and we had a wet, naked copy of Bob lying on a stone slab.

I noticed in passing that clones don't have souls. They have vitality, yes, but they don't have anyone in there. This troubles me. I'm not sure, precisely, if Bob can... what's the word? Raise it? Educate it? It's alive, yes, and somewhat drugged when it's fresh out of the clone tank. Maybe it acts like a newborn—a really big newborn—when it's awake. If not, maybe it can grow an elf-spirit—or a soul. Again, that brings me back to the question of whether or not human souls would turn into something resembling an elf-spirit if given a couple thousand years.

It's also possible Rendu created elf-spirits as part of the elf bodies. They may not have the capacity to develop a living spirit. Clone tanks, of course, can't grow a soul; they only grow biological stuff. If the bodies, left on their own, can't develop something like a soul, the elves are still screwed.

But I mentioned none of this. If Bob gets an elf-clone and tries to spiritually mature it, either by educating it as a newborn or by mystically transfusing a partial spirit into it, we'll find out the practical answers. Finding a solution to the worst-case scenario is another story entirely.

As for Norad and Morrelin, Morrelin drew the short straw. Actually, they discussed it and decided since Norad was the necromancer and dealt with this sort of thing, he would monitor the process with me. Morrelin would get to try on a fresh meat suit.

It worked. The magical slab located all the mounting points inside Morrelin's body, ran connecting lines of power to the major junctions in the elf-body, and started to pull. He moaned in pain and tensed up, fists and teeth clenching. I adjusted the spells, lowering the tension. This didn't need to be a soul-ripping sort of experience. A gentle touch would serve much better. Perhaps it would be best to point up that fact.

"Now, here's the problem," I lectured. "It lacks the capacity to rip the soul out of anyone. Right now, it's simply attached to the spiritual lines of power binding a soul to the flesh. The next step is to release the soul from the mortal body. I recommend a bleeding wound, something to kill him slowly, preferably painlessly, but certainly without a sudden shock. That should make the transition as gentle as possible."

"There are certain poisons, Dread Lord, which may weaken the bond between the flesh and spirit," Bob offered.

"I imagine there are. If they're not innately lethal, it might be a comfort to people trying this. I'd be hesitant, though, to leave behind my empty shell of a body if it was still functional. T'yl? Norad? Morrelin?"

The overwhelming consensus was to kill the original body in the migration, or shortly afterward.

With that, I drew a fingertalon along the inside of Morrelin's wrist, careful to get the artery. Blood flowed freely, crawling all over my hand and disappearing. It takes a while for someone to bleed to death this way, even with my odd blood-attracting properties. Morrelin winced at the injury and suppressed his impulse to panic. Norad and T'yl were right there, watching keenly, which helped him keep calm. After a few minutes, as the blood loss took hold, he closed his eyes and lost consciousness. His soul started coming loose, drifting to the side, drawn gently across on the lines of power to the other body. Point by point, it linked into the major energy centers in the elven meat suit while I watched the program run. It worked, as I knew it would, but this was the easy part of the program.

As the major connections linked in, one by one, a lot of the lesser ones surrounding each mounting point linked in to their respective micro-mounts at the same time. I hadn't expected them to join up so quickly and easily. Was this process different from T'yl's soul transfer because it was coming from a living body instead of a stasis? Or because it was a First Elf rather than a hybrid? Or did the slow, gentle transition help with the transplant? Could his soul, unwilling to depart and looking for anything to hang on to, be working to settle itself into a new body?

Anybody want a research grant? I know an amateur necromancer who would love to know, but doesn't have time or inclination to experiment with it.

After half an hour, it looked as complete as it was likely to get. The necromantic tables of soul transfer had done their part. The rest was for Morrelin and his new body.

"He'll need a little bed rest," I told everyone. "Also, daily practice with his new body, that sort of thing. He's got to break it in, get used to it. He'll be clumsy and uncoordinated until he learns to use it. Ask T'yl. He's an expert on this part."

"We shall see to his care," T'yl assured me, voice shaking. Norad nodded frantically, hands tightly clasped together, eyes wide. I think I impressed and frightened the professional necromancer. Bob and his two hybrid cohorts were less easy to read, physically, but their spirits were horrified. This was dark art. Black magic. Soul-stealing, body-possessing abomination that the *elves* regarded as evil.

I felt strangely good about that.

"Excellent. Now, the next one is for Bob." I nodded in his direction. "Are you ready to take one with you?"

"If it pleases you, Dread Lord, I would prefer to make arrangements for the transport and quartering of our new brother before he arrives."

"Of course. I don't have one ready just now, anyway. I thought I'd ask. How long do you need?"

"If I am to take possession here, I can be prepared in two days."

"I'll see what I can do. Remember, he's full-grown, but much like a mortal baby. You may need to experiment a bit to figure out how to keep it alive long enough to learn to even feed itself."

"We shall bend every effort," Bob assured me.

"Good. T'yl, I'm putting you in charge of the soul-transfer slabs and the elf-creating box. Remember, Bob is supposed to get every other elf." I looked at Bob, then at T'yl. "This is a guideline, not a rule. If either of you don't need or want another one—too many elves being raised, or no magicians willing to risk it—then don't keep the other one from getting more. It's not about who gets more. It's about sharing—everybody gets some."

"Yes, Dread Lord," Bob agreed, placing his hand on his chest and bowing. His two hybrids did the same.

"As you say," T'yl replied, nodding.

"Good. Any questions about this?" I asked, gesturing at the tables. There were none, but everyone in the room shuddered inwardly when I directed their attention that way. I think the twin tables of soul-sucking horrified them.

Everyone agreed they were useful, certainly, but liking them was out of the question. It's hard to like a gadget designed to drag souls out of the flesh, I guess. Maybe I just don't have the right perspective.

"If you think you need me, ask Beltar. He can act as arbitrator if you disagree, or he can get the Lord of Shadow to send for me and I'll adjudicate no matter how annoyed it makes me. I trust everyone understands?" There was a great deal of understanding in the room. "Good, good. I've got to run. Things to be, people to do, places to see... or have I mixed those up? At any rate, goodbye."

I made my escape and went to change clothes. Meeting Tort was best done in a nice outfit, preferably an older one. Armored underwear, yes, because I always wear it, but for my outer garments, a lot of things a little girl named Tort saw me wear. A dark-green tunic and breeches, with red, orange, and yellow knotwork for the trim and piping. A tabard to throw over it, in the same colors, but with a solid red circle taking up most of the field, containing a stylized dragon on its back, black, with a great sword of fire, in gold, thrust downward into it. No crown hovering over the sword hilt—not now. Add to it a black sash and another swordbelt, my new-ish cloak, and a quick polish to my boots... Nails chiseled down? Fangs clean? Hair combed? Face scraped smooth? Yes.

Do I go in wearing human illusions? Or do I go in as the monster? She's seen me in both guises for the past nine years. She'll recognize me, either way. I'll go with the illusions. It might be considered rude to show up wearing a disguise, but I'm trying to be less the Demon King and more *me*. If anyone will understand the difference, Tort is the one. Well, Bronze, yes, but Bronze is, in some subtle but real sense a part of me. She doesn't count as someone else.

I met Bronze in the geode room. She flicked an ear inquisitively, asking if we were finally going.

"Yes. It's time to visit Tort."

Bronze liked the idea and thought it was about time. I tried to agree wholeheartedly and failed.

First off, activate the scrying mirror. Scan back to those coordinates. Find the hacienda. Good. Lights are on, so people are still up and about. Fly over, above the scryshield. No garden party, no large groups of people. It appeared to be a quiet night at home.

Unfortunately, there were no handy arches outside the scryshield. I wanted something close, but there simply wasn't anything close. The only nearby building was the stable and the doors were smaller than I liked. This was going to require some brute force.

I wonder. Would it be worthwhile to have some sort of mechanical device for this? Say, a spring-loaded set of unfolding metal rods, or some advanced memory-metal. Open a very small gate using the brute-force method, causing the small gate to manifest in two locations at once. Immediately shove the gadget through, let go, and close the small gate. The gadget goes *sproing!* or *twang!* or whatever such gadgets do, unfolding and turning into a suitably-sized arch. Then I can use it as a target point for a larger arch without having to brute-force it. I could even enchant the gadget to be a beacon, tuning it to whatever arch I'm about to use, further reducing the power requirement and enhancing the accuracy.

I suppose I could build one. I'm not actually *required* to go visit Tort tonight, after all…

No. No, I've stalled enough. I've missed her, I've goofed around, and I've feared this meeting. I've had it on my mind, or in the back of it, along with Johann for quite some time. This one I can do. Johann, I'm not entirely sure about. Johann will kill me if I don't kill him, so I have to face him as the last thing I do. Tort won't kill me, but seeing her might hurt more than Johann ever managed.

I can do this. I have to do this. I'm going to do this. I have spoken.

Brute force, then.

Crystals glowed as I laid my will on the archway. The mirror's image flickered into the arch and flushed away, swirling into the distance. The far end rushed close rather than snapping into place, as though the archway stretched into a long hallway before retracting. The result was the same: It finally settled into place. A breeze came through the arch, bearing the smells of warm dirt, incense, and water. The smell of night-blooming flowers was faint on the breeze.

Bronze and I stepped through. The archway stood behind us, now. As I let go the spell, it crumpled inward on itself, twisting in a whirling spiral, and vanished into the distance. That's not the normal effect when a gate closes, but normally I have a gate at both ends. I suspect the visual was much the same—crumpling in and spiraling into the distance—no matter which way one viewed it. If I looked at it from the side, it would probably still look as though it vanished directly away from me.

Don't ask why I think that. I just do. Call it an intuition.

I walked along the offshoot road—the driveway? —to the house. Bronze followed, her head over my shoulder. We crossed the line of the scrying shield without incident, but something detected us. Even my cloaking spells couldn't prevent it. They block detection magic of various sorts, but this didn't detect me. The alarm detected a penetration of the magical perimeter, a subtle but important difference.

It also detected Bronze, which annoyed me considerably. I've been hiding me so well, but not her. I really have to get her an upgraded version of her stealth spells. Let me see… silence and traction on all her pastern-bracelets was doable, although complicated. That still leaves active detection spoofing, passive detection spoofing, an aerodynamic shield, a gravity-bender, and an inertia damper. Can I cram those into her pastern bracelets, too? I doubt it. It'll be complicated just to find out if they'll work in conjunction or if they'll interfere. Or… hmm. Can she wear a magical gem as though it's mounted in her hide? Maybe if she changes shape to form what looks like a halter, we can put a decorative crystal or four on it. Come to that, I suppose we could mount some on the built-in saddlehorn, or elsewhere on the saddle…

"Remind me when we get back to the mountain, will you?" I asked, quietly. Bronze nodded and nosed me in the middle of my back, pushing me forward. Bossy horse.

Three steps led up to the door. She stopped there and urged me on. I climbed the steps and pulled on the cord. Something inside chimed.

I'm pretty sure this is not what relationship counselors call "commitment," but I sure felt committed. Possibly the need to be committed in a nice, quiet rest home for the mentally ill. Fortunately, I lacked the ability to be physically ill from nervousness, which saved the residents of a flowerpot from a fate worse than death.

Somehow, this feels like stopping by my date's house to pick her up. It's the same sort of nervous anticipation. I should have brought a present. Typical. Thinking only of myself, again. Then again, a present could seem like an attempt to buy forgiveness when I apologize... How would Tort take it? I don't know these fiddly little cultural details! I've never gone on a formal date in Rethven!

You're not just talking to yourself, Boss. You're babbling to yourself.

Mental babbling: Check.

Thanks, Firebrand.

Calm down. She worked like a spider on a web to get you sorted out.

She also vanished forever, or tried to, I countered. *I'll be nervous if it suits me!*

Oh, it suits you, Firebrand replied. I was about to ask what it meant by that when the door opened.

The man inside was the same one I saw when I was stalking the place. Spying on it. Doing surveillance. He was on the short side, slim, with grey salting his dark hair. He wore the same outfit, too—presumably some sort of formal livery for Kamshasa. It wasn't a skirt, but the legs of his dark-blue trousers were so wide as to make the difference difficult to discern. His shirt was more tight-fitting, with a wide, open collar and long, billowing sleeves. Decorative ribbons tied his sleeves in place around the wrists.

"San kimsayn?"

Damn! I forgot my translation spell!

"Do you speak Rethven?" I tried, and added in the appropriate tongue, "or do you speak one of the Old Imperial dialects?"

He shook his head and pointed at his ear and mouth. I nodded.

Firebrand? Since I'm a man and about to work magic, please lie to him and tell him I'm about to activate a magical translation device.

No problem, Boss.

His eyes widened, but he didn't step back. I cast my spell with a minimum of gestures and a maximum of words. It's a lot easier to build a spell when you can use your hands to guide the lines of spell structures, that's all I've got to say.

"Can you understand me now?" I asked.

"Yes. You are not from Kamshasa."

"You are correct."

"I must ask who you are."

"I am an angel come to visit the lady of the house," I told him, using the Rethven *arhia*, meaning *nice-guy spirit*, rather than *arhela*, or *spirit of primal forces*. Tort called me by both terms, but I was shooting for the former.

"Please come in," he invited, apparently taking me at my word. When a man shows up on your doorstep and claims to be an angel, I guess you invite him in. Maybe it's a cultural thing. He stepped back and to the side. I went in and he closed the door behind me. He bowed slightly and added, "The house offers you water."

Well, expletive deleted.

Firebrand?

He expects you to say "I am the recipient of the lady's generosity."

Literally?

I'm trying to work with your translation spell, Boss. You say that, he hears what he hears.

I repeated it. He bowed slightly again and gestured me toward a small room. The room had a shallow trench in the floor with water flowing through it, a seat, a basin, and cloths—the tropical version of a "mud room," I suppose, where one could clean off the worst of the dust and sweat. He left me there and went away.

Once again, I'm out of my depth with alien customs. What the heck was the greeting all about?

I'm not sure, Firebrand admitted. *He does it as a ritual, not with understanding. I think it's a thing where the guest admits the house saved his life from the desert? Not that this region is any too desert-y, but it's the custom?*

Maybe it started that way. It might merely signify gratitude at being let in, nowadays. Or maybe just locally. The Shining Desert is farther south, and Kamshasa occupies a chunk of it. Maybe it started there and spread.

Could be, Boss. He didn't seem as ecstatic as you'd expect if you'd admitted to a life-debt. Just moderately pleased at your manners, you filthy unaccompanied male.

Seriously? The man answering the door thinks I'm a filthy unaccompanied male?

It's how he was raised, Boss.

I didn't have a good answer to that. Instead, I magically brushed away what dust I accumulated from the short walk and regarded my lack of reflection in a mirror. They make good mirrors in Kamshasa. This one was about head-sized, delicately framed, and had almost as few ripples or distortions as it did vampire reflections.

If I get some sunglasses with a band of mirrored surface across the top—like regular ones, but with a rear-view mirror at the upper edge—can I look through my own head to see behind me? I'm going to try it just as soon as I find someone to make glasses.

I wasn't sure of the protocol of the dust room. Do I stay until sent for? Do I step out as soon as I'm through? I chose to step out and wait. It seemed to be correct. I was met by a much younger man, probably still in his middle teens. He escorted me farther into the house.

The interior of the house was an open thing, obviously set up to circulate air. The wall facing the interior gardens was composed mostly of folding doors. With the sun long-set and things cooled off, these were wide open to help dissipate the heat of the day from the heavy stone walls. I noticed tapestries were still popular. Several magical ones hung above the folding doors, rolled up. Were they rolled down during the day to keep out the heat as long as possible? Or did it get cold enough at some point—night in winter, maybe—to warrant them? Or were they merely decorative?

Ah, the things I think about when I'm trying not to show how nervous I am.

"The lady of the house is not prepared to receive visitors," my teenaged guide informed me. "You are commanded to wait her pleasure in the garden."

"Certainly."

He led me out to a small, stone bench by the central tree and left me there. It was probably a very nice spot during the day. Shady, by flowing water, all the usual stuff. I wondered if this was a servant's idea to keep me from stinking up the house as a filthy unaccompanied foreign male.

While I sat there, trying to be patient and calm, I looked around.

The tree looked back.

I dismissed it as my imagination.

The tree kept looking at me.

All right. If it was going to be so impolite as to stare, I didn't feel obligated to be polite, either. I looked at it more intently, examining it for all the usual things—magical energy, spells, vitality flow, spirits, auras, soul-stuff, the works. It was alive and innately magical, but that was about all I could tell on a moment's notice.

The trunk of the tree was only about a foot wide. I wondered if it was fairly young, as oak trees go, or if the tropical climate disagreed with it. Then again, it was cool in the garden area. Then again, it was nighttime, too. Were there spells to see to the tree's comfort? Yes, a spell roofed over the central garden, blocking out some of the daytime heat. Below it, the ground was different, possibly special soil imported from somewhere more tree-friendly.

"Firebrand?"

Yes?

"Why is this tree looking at me? And why is it… familiar?"

Got me, Boss.

I examined it more closely, running fingertips and tendrils over the bark, along the trunk, tracing the grain of the wood, feeling the slow pulse of sap inside, running lines of power through it out to every vein in every leaf.

It's a magical tree. I have no idea how it's magical. It's not a dryad home, I know that. I would find the dryad, or some connection to the dryad. Yet the tree is magical and would probably make an excellent home for a dryad. Is this tree magical in the same way a wizard is magical? Is it a tree with a talent for magic, so magic flows through it naturally? It could be a special breed of tree, I suppose, deliberately bred to be the perfect wood for a magical staff. It's not sapient pearwood, not by a long shot, but it might be semi-aware oak. Come to think of it, it might become a dryad tree. If a dryad manifests later in the life cycle, the tree might simply be too young.

If I built a wardrobe out of this wood, would it be easier to enchant into an inter-universal teleport box? Maybe I should ask T'yl's nephew, if he has one.

Having examined the tree in intimate detail, I returned to my bench in time to seat myself before I was sent for. I heard footsteps before I saw him. The same young man who showed me out returned to fetch me inside. My escort took me to the second floor and knocked on a heavy, wooden door. At the soft-voiced answer, he opened it and ushered me in.

Tort sat in a tall, heavy chair. I barely noticed when the door closed behind me.

She wore a thick suit of clothes, like quilted pajamas. Heavy embroidery decorated it from neck to ankles—all of it magical. I recognized some of the design from the animation magic I saw in the moving suit of armor T'yl used to own. My knights' armor sometimes had an emergency animation function to allow it to fight on if the wearer was killed, or to enable it to run to a medic if the wearer was merely unconscious. Hers was based in the embroidery and the weaving rather than any after-the-fact enchantment. Very practical. I noticed it included some protective effects, including one to block my vision of her spirit.

This was my glimpse of the outfit. My major attention was reserved for Tort.

She was old. Positively ancient. Her hair was silver-white and cut just below her ears. Her face was lined and creased, sagging everywhere. Her hands were long and thin, dotted with spots and traced with veins. The only things that seemed untouched were her clear, brilliant eyes and her teeth. I couldn't guess at her health; all I could see was her flesh. Her quilted outfit was quite effective.

"I'm sorry," I blurted. It was the first thing out of my mouth. Nothing clever, no preliminaries, not even a polite greeting. Smooth, Eric. Real smooth. Moron.

Tort smiled and looked away.

"I know," she answered, softly. Her voice was old, too. Breathy. I guessed she was short of breath rather often. Carrying on a long conversation might be difficult for her.

"May I sit?"

"Yes, you may."

I picked the heaviest-looking chair in the room and slid it over to her. I settled into it with only minor creaking.

"What happened?" I asked.

"What happened? I challenged the Demon King." She shrugged, looking at her hands. "I won. This is the price of victory."

"You shouldn't be the one to pay it," I pointed out.

"I must."

"I'll happily pay it for you. Or pay you back. Take your pick."

"You can't."

"I can't?"

"No."

"I don't understand."

"What's not to understand? I did what I felt was needful."

"I don't understand what happened, why you're here, or why I can't help. Is it that I can't help, or you don't want me to?"

Tort did not answer. She continued to regard her hands as her fingers twisted together.

"We can run your clock back," I went on. "If you like, I know where I can get an empty elf for you to wear. I can even arrange for you to drink blood, if that's your preference. Hang on for another couple of months and I feel certain we can give you your own body, exactly as you were at eighteen years old—this time with both feet. Tell me what I can do for you. Name it."

"No," she whispered. "No."

I didn't know what to say. I was torn. Tort was old enough to be dying. I had to help. But this was Tort, and she told me she didn't want me to. But I had to, because it was Tort. But, because it was Tort, I had to respect her wishes.

Tearing me in half would be less painful. Trust me. I know.

"All right," I agreed. "I came to see you, not to interfere in your life. If you don't want me to, I won't. I don't like it—I want to help! But I'll... I won't interfere."

"Thank you. I am pleased to see you again, my angel." For *angel* she used the term *arhela*, meaning an elemental force, rather than *arhia*.

"And I'm pleased to see you," I admitted. "I'm even more pleased you permitted it. I was worried."

"About what?'

"About whether or not you wanted to see me."

Tort looked away again, raising the back of one withered hand to her lips.

"Tort? Is something wrong?"

"I have loved you all my life," she whispered. "No. I will love you all my life."

I stood up and leaned over her, kissed her hair. She wept.

"Yes, you will," I agreed, "and I will love you for all of *mine*."

It's an odd feeling, holding someone who could be my great-grandmother and rocking her *extremely* gently. There was no way I wouldn't comfort her while she cried on me, but I was terrified of breaking her. I didn't dare to hug her firmly. I merely wrapped my arms around her and rocked her.

Finally, she sniffled a little and leaned away. I let go and resumed my seat. She still had a hard time looking at me, but I blame the face of the Demon King.

"May I ask a question?" I asked, redundantly. She nodded. "Why did you leave?"

"I don't want to answer that."

"Okay. I get the impression you're upset with me. Are you?"

"No."

"But you still won't look at me."

"I..." she began, and went back to staring at her hands. I waited. Sometimes silence is the best question. If so, this was a long question. She wrung her hands and I kept still while the awkwardness in the room deepened. Eventually, it reached critical mass and exploded into speech.

"My angel," she said, and sighed.

"Tell me what's wrong. I need to know."

"I don't know how."

"It's easy. You can tell me anything and I'll take it. Tell me I'm a moron. I'm used to that. Tell me I'm a blood-drinking monster. Tell me I'm an evil king with delusions of grandeur. Whatever you want."

"I can't."

"Sure you can. Take your time. Take all the time you need. I'll wait right here, with occasional breaks for sunrise and sunset, possibly the occasional trip to the toilet. I'd like time off on your birthday, though, to get you a present."

I had to find a handkerchief. I hadn't intended to make her cry again. Wonderful example, there, of my indefinable, possibly nonexistent charm. While she wept, I enclosed us in an air-filtering spell similar to the one used on Kavel's forge. Since pressure tries to equalize, the oxygen content of our little area gradually rose. I didn't want her to cough herself to death.

When her crying diminished to sniffles, I took her hand again and she clutched at it. I was surprised at how weak her grip was.

"It's your face," she admitted, finally.

"Yeah, I suspected. Lissette said the same thing. Too funny-looking?"

Oh, I'm a charmer, all right. Tort broke down into sobs while I tried to get my foot out of my mouth. It's hard to do when it's gone in up to the knee. This was not what I envisioned for our big reunion. Not as bad as I'd feared, in many ways, but it wasn't going as well as it could have.

On the other hand, maybe it was going as well as it was possible to go. There's a sobering thought.

Tort couldn't speak too well, even with the magical oxygen tent. Serves me right for making her cry. What she did manage to tell me was rather broken, but I got the gist of it. Lissette only knew me briefly, so she didn't have as much in the way of preconceived notions. The Demon King was a problem for her, but one she had to learn to live with.

But I was—I am—Tort's angel.

Imagine meeting your best friend and finding everything is different. They don't like you, but they use your positive opinion of them to their advantage. Everything they do is at odds with what you know about them, so much so you have to suspect brain damage or demonic possession. If you've imagined it successfully, you're on the right track.

But, again, I wasn't Tort's best friend. I was Tort's *angel*.

Every day for nine years, she was at the Demon King's left hand, doing whatever he ordered. It was my face, my voice, my hands, everything. She had to watch her angel fall from grace, as it were. Her knight in shining armor tarnished it with every word, every gesture. Guinevere could not have been more appalled if Lancelot decided to take up slave-trading to get funds together to assassinate Arthur, burn the Table, and tear down Camelot.

I need to find that ball and have not one word of discussion with it. I wonder if I can shove it through a gate out in space, aimed at a star big enough to collapse into a singularity? Either the solar fires will destroy it or the gravitational collapse will. Short of that, anybody know where I can find Mount Doom?

It occurs to me... somewhere in the infinite multiverses, there very well *might* be a Mordor and Mount Doom.

Once she managed to explain the problem of even looking at me, she calmed down. She still had trouble meeting my eyes, but she seemed more than capable of holding my hand.

"It's okay," I assured her. "The Demon King has a lot to answer for."

"He is imprisoned in a ball of force," Tort told me. "With great effort, his influence may reach beyond the surface of the sphere, but he can never escape."

"Any spell can be broken, and he'll find a way. I intend to get rid of him in a more permanent fashion."

"As long as he remains within the sphere, it will serve to protect him as well as imprison him. It was the best I could do."

"I'll kill him," I promised. "I have to."

"I do not say it cannot be done, but to do so is beyond even my knowledge of such matters."

"I'll see what I can find. But what about you? What can I do for you?"

"Nothing. There is nothing to be done for me."

"Please explain to the non-magician."

"The spells to bind a demon are well known. Their weakness is in their impermanence. Over time, they grow static, rigid, stale—brittle, if you like. The Things they contain also wear away at the barriers from within. This is why those who summon such things tend their cages every day, refreshing them with new lines of power. Containment spells are not alive, not capable of growing and changing to meet the changing tactics of the creature thus imprisoned. And yet, sorcerers are not immediately ripped apart from within after the first sunset. Sorcerers are, themselves, living containment vessels. The ritual spells to make one a sorcerer bind the demon into the living flesh. While the flesh lives, the demon remains trapped. When the flesh dies, the containment turns static, allowing the demon to work its way free."

I recalled a subdivided invisible sorcerer assassin. It did take a while before the demon started leaking out of him.

"So, you made a special spell to contain the Demon King?"

"Yes. The mirror reflects most of his power back upon him, so his efforts to break free weaken him. But the key to the spell was a vital essence—a web of living force to meet him at every point and fight him."

"I'm starting to be more than a little suspicious of how you managed it."

"I was linked to quite a number of living things at the time."

"An awful lot of *dazhu*, as I recall, as well as several trees. At least, nine years ago. I'd imagine it was even more."

"In the last four years, I made certain to have as many convicts as possible in my web."

"Anticipating?"

"Yes."

"I see. Go ahead and tell me."

"The spell to trap the Demon King drew on my life. Had I not been linked to so many living things, it would have consumed me completely. Since I had hundreds of living forces at my command, I survived, although nothing else could say the same. Thus am I aged to something near my true age—a hundred years, perhaps. I tried to escape the fate of any who would cast such a spell, but I did not succeed. I live now only because magic sustains my body."

"I hear the magical currents off the Sunspire are quite nice in this region."

"Exactly."

"I can fix this, you know."

"No, my angel."

"No? What do you mean, 'no'?"

"There is little left of me to fix."

"T'yl told me he thought you were sucked into the spell with the Demon King. Obviously, he had good reason to think so. But you're not. You're here, and this is the sort of problem I have a talent for. This is something I can do for you."

"No. Look at me. Look closely."

I looked at her. She was still shielded from my vamp-vision. I told her so.

"You are incorrect, my angel. The magic of my clothing supports the life of my body, but there is little enough of my essence remaining. You think your sight is blocked, but it sees everything that I am."

"I don't understand. Again."

"Do you recall your experiments, attempting to create nightlords under your control?"

"Yes."

"When you created living lords of night, then slew them to leave them soulless creatures of darkness?"

"Yes."

"What were they like?"

"Well, without a soul, they were animated corpses. They had no real self-will, other than a habituated memory-pattern based on how long they were... shall we say 'infected'?... with my blood. The longer they were infected before being killed as a mortal being, the better the memory pattern. If killed too soon, they were mindless, bloodthirsty monsters. If killed later, they acted like themselves, in general, but without any real will to do or inspiration. I gave some thought to these as potential soldiers, but their lack of resistance to control in general, rather than any special control I, personally, could exert on them made them too much of a risk to use. Why?"

"So clever," she murmured, "and so slow."

"All right, I'm slow. I admit it. What am I slowly not seeing?"

"Do you see a soul in me?"

"I..." I trailed off, staring into her. The magic in her clothes made it harder to see inside, but if it didn't block my vampire eyes... no, it didn't. It blocked some location magic, but I could see through that.

There should have been a bright glow behind the magical cloth. I stared deeper, looking harder. The glow of vitality was only barely there, of course, contributing to the illusion of a blocking spell. I looked past it, inside her, and saw the subtle, shifting colors deeper down were missing. The deeper levels of her spirit—her soul, if you like—were almost entirely gone. She was a shallow pool, stirred only by the surface currents.

She really did go into the orb with the Demon King. At least, most of her. She salvaged just enough to keep her body from dying outright, but she really did sacrifice herself. Everything that made her Tort went into the orb. What was left was little more than a memory, an organic recording in the flesh of her brain, with enough living energy to keep the playback running.

"If I break that ball," I asked, slowly, carefully, "and if I destroy the Demon King... can I get you back?"

"What I am now—that which I am, within the structure of the sphere—is no longer me. It is a pattern of living energy, forged from my soul. Can you have your iron ore and your coal again if you break the sword you forged?"

"I don't accept that."

She patted my hand with her bony, withered one.

"I know you don't. But you will, eventually, because you must. You have eternity to do so. I will not last so very much longer. I live now only out of habit, and because I made my preparations long before. I will die, as all things must, and you will go on. You knew this would happen one day, even if you did not think it would be so soon."

"Is your apparent understanding and kindness also an habituated memory?"

"Yes."

"I'm not sure if that's comforting or not."

"You would prefer I loved you less?" she asked, gently.

"I would prefer you were actually here."

"Alas, it is impossible. Moreso in that I must be going. It is well you have come, for some part of me once hoped to have this meeting. Another part hoped you would never see what remains. Regardless, you have come, and you shall be my guide."

"Hold it! If you think I'm going to kill you—"

"What is left of me?"

My comment was not appropriate to a PG rating.

"I am too old for that," she answered, mildly. "But whatever is left of Tort— whatever is left of who I remember I once was—surely you will not let it wander, weak and faded through the world, hoping to find its way?"

"Can I have a moment to reflect on my self-loathing and my rapidly-rising hatred for the pyrrhic nature of my life choices?"

"Take all the time you wish. If I must leave during your contemplation, I trust you will understand."

"Give me a minute."

Tort. Old, withered, dying… Bizarre. I had intended to make her live forever, one way or another. At least, I always thought she would. There was always some way, some refinement on a spell, a transfer to an immortal body, even vampire blood as a last resort. Now she was gone, even though I was talking to her body and brain. This was vitality without essence, life without a soul. Anything I did at this point to help her live longer, even if I made her grow younger, would be useless—worse than useless. But even going the other direction and ending her biological life was more painful than I wanted to think about. It took me forever to realize how much I loved her and admit it to myself. Now that I have her here with me, she's not really here, only her memories, and sending her on will lose even those. She's the blood and bone of a scrapbook full of snapshots, and she wants me to burn them.

I can't keep her. It hurts too much. I can't lose her. It hurts too much.

No matter which way I go, I'm sticking my heart in a blender.

What's black and red and goes round and round and round? A vampire heart in a blender. Ha. Funny. Good joke. Everybody laughs but me.

"When…" I began, and had to clear my throat. "When did you want…?" I trailed off, unable to finish the question.

"When you are prepared. I do not have the will to end myself. I can only wait."

"This stinks."

"I know it does."

"All right. Can you do one thing for me?"

"If you ask it."

"Then I'm asking you to ask me. You don't have to do much, but I do need to hear you make the request."

"Dear angel, you remain forever yourself."

"Immortality problems."

"Very well. Please take me out of this life."

"Your wish is my command."

I took her wrist in my hand, bit it, and let the blood flow into my mouth. It soaked into my undead flesh the instant it touched my tongue. Minutes passed as she bled out, slumping, her brain shutting down. I blinked.

The Grey Lady stood next to me, slightly perplexed. I held a spark in my hands, tiny, little more than some dim star plucked from the fringes of the Milky Way.

"It seems you have a tiny piece of someone. Shall I?"

The voice behind me was unexpected.

"No."

The Grey Lady looked startled.

"This one is mine," I heard.

"Yours?"

I turned to regard myself. Taller, darker, broader of shoulder, more fearsome in some way I could not define. The sword at his hip was a sharp-edged bar of fire, behind him, a gleam of glossy black and gold, horse-shaped, shot with fire-sparks. His shadow was a moving darkness, clinging to his shoulders. Something glinted in his void-like eyes, a darkling color seen only beyond the rim of the world.

"Mine," he repeated. "I claim her by the right of adoration."

The Grey Lady's eyebrows went up, but she nodded.

"She does adore you, even what there is of her."

*"It is not **her** adoration that makes it my right," he corrected. The Grey Lady's eyes widened. She stepped back, inclining her head.*

"Far be it from me to stand in your way. I waive my claim, and gladly."

"Thank you."

"There is very little of her to claim, you know. Are you certain you wish to waste the effort on...?"

"It is a joyous responsibility," he replied, "and a duty I willingly assume." He held out his hands while the Grey Lady watched him, her expression changing into a thoughtful, even appraising look.

"The others underestimate you," she said, finally. And the Grey Lady was gone, leaving us in the twilit nothing. He gestured at me with his hands cupped together, ready to accept the faint spark of soul.

"What do you mean?" I asked. "You're not a... what is it? A psychopomp?"

"It's complicated. I do escort duty for individuals, not wholesale like the Grey Lady does. Remember?"

"I thought it was my job."

"You're the door. I meet them once they're through."

"That's a metaphor for something afterlife-y and complicated, isn't it?"

"Yes, but not a bad one. But I'm here, personally, because Tort is a special case."

"I agree. Now what do you mean?"

"Think of it like saints, I guess. Maybe more like Valhalla. Most people go about their normal business of being dead. A few, on occasion, attract the personal interest of a god. Tort is one I take a personal interest in, because we love her."

"What will happen to her?"

"That's hard to describe. A poor approximation is this: I'm going to plant this tiny seed of her where it can grow and flourish. The actual process is

complicated and possibly incomprehensible for physical entities, but I think this is a good description."

"The difference between 'Turn the knob and see things in the box' and 'This is the electrical theory behind television'?"

"Yes. Results rather than process," he agreed.

"Does this mean I might get Tort back?"

"No, not exactly. Reincarnation is a tricky business and—surprise! —I've never done this before. Tort's the first."

"But you're sure you can do it?"

"I am certain."

"And I'll see her again?" I pressed.

"I understand your hesitation. So here, let me make this simple for you: I absolutely guarantee it."

Maybe it's weird, but I believed him. Instantly. Totally. Utterly. Perhaps this is how prophets feel when the Word comes down from On High and delivers a Truth. I'm not giving Tort up. I'm sending Tort on ahead so I can see her again. It's not death. It's picking her up at the airport next week.

*Is this some strange power of the energy-beings? Or is it a function of my energy-being copy, his total certainty resonating with me on some psychic level? More fundamentally, did it matter? It was my only option, so I had no real choice, but it also made me certain it was the **right** choice, which lifted a weight from my soul.*

"All right." I held out my hands and opened them, letting the tiny, dim spark that was the last of my Tort settle into my energy-state-being hands. He closed his hands over her, lifted them to his face, and breathed into them. The light within brightened, shining between his fingers. He seemed pleased.

"Told you," he said, smugly. "I've got this. I promise I'll take very good care of her until she's ready to come out. As much care as you would, obviously."

"Then she's in good hands," I agreed. "Butterfingers."

"Do you see me using both hands?" he demanded, feigning hurt. "Do you see me treating her like she's fragile? Do you?"

"I do, and I appreciate it. Keep a close eye on her."

"Yeah, she's tricksy. Now get going. You have to escape the house."

"That shouldn't be a—wait, what?"

I finished my blink. Tort was dead, but not dead. Not exactly, anyway. The withered old body passed away, but whatever remained, whatever there was of my Tort was... more than dead, but less than alive. Working on becoming herself again, perhaps, or someone new. Reincarnation is a tricky business, or so I'm told. I haven't tried it, myself.

Or have I? There's an interesting question. Who have I been before I was me? And do vampires get to reincarnate? Sasha thought so.

I picked up Tort's body and laid her on the couch, arranging her carefully. It was hard to do. I could still see Tort's face behind the lines and wrinkles. No matter how old she might be, I could always see the little girl who fell through the ceiling.

Strange. Her pajamas' spells were fading. The magic in them popped like bubbles in foam. Small bells tinkled with each one, sounding elsewhere in the house. Odd.

I sat with the body for a bit, adjusting to the fact I found my Tort, lost my Tort, and would hopefully have my Tort again. Is this how religious people feel when they lose a loved one? The loved one may not be coming back, but they're certain they'll go to join them. It's not a loss, just the other person going ahead before the one left behind catches up. No, the feelings can't be the same. There's a lot of weeping at funerals. I didn't feel the need to weep; I *know* dying isn't the end.

The door came open and two large men entered. They wore partial armor—scale mail over their vitals, with rigid bracers and half-helmets—and carried enormous, curved swords.

"Murderer!" one shouted, and they both charged me.

Ah. Escape the house. Of course. I didn't bother to notify the staff I was here to suck the life out of their mistress, nor why. How did they know she died? The magical pajamas and the bells? Possibly. Probably. Either that, or they assumed the filthy unaccompanied male was not to be trusted and spied on us.

I wasn't really in the mood to kill people. Looked at one way, I just killed Tort. Looked at another way, I just found out she sacrificed herself long ago to undo my stupidity. This was not a good time to bother me, what with being so busy with self-pity, self-recrimination, and a little self-loathing. It's all about me. It always is, because of being so self-centered. See? Self, self, self, all self, all the time.

Besides, technically, this was all a terrible misunderstanding.

Still, they did burst into the room and try to hit me with swords. Firebrand was more than a little pleased, of course, and we did put out the fires caused by the melted armor. It would have been helpful if their blood could have soaked into the hot spots, but, well, that doesn't happen around me. I had to settle for stomping out the burning rug and letting the hot metal cool on the stonework.

A large bell sounded somewhere in the house. It wasn't the tinkly, happy door chime. It was a much louder, much less happy-sounding *clang-clang-clang!*

I looked around the edge of the door. No one in the upstairs hall. I peered out a little farther. There they were. Quite a number of servants were gathered at the base of the stairs. All of them were armed.

Hell, they didn't deserve to wind up as desiccated pork chops. On the other hand, I doubted they wanted any sort of explanation—just my head.

The only other way out of the room was a small, square window in the outer wall. With some wiggling, I could probably fit through it. I shut the door, put a couple of chairs and bloodless corpses in front of it, and tested the window. The wall was thick enough to make it more of a tunnel than a window, but knocking the glass out was easy enough. I slid through the tunnel headfirst and looked around. Bronze had already parked herself underneath.

Perfect. I backed up, put my arms through first, pulled myself out, and did a very neat somersault as I landed astride Bronze's back.

Two things of note.

First, vampires recover from injuries supernaturally fast. We still suffer from wounds and dislike being injured because being shot, stabbed, or set on fire is painful.

Second, leaping from the second storey to land astride your horse is a skill. Hitting your target isn't too hard if the horse cooperates, but if your horse is flesh and blood, it's likely to suffer injury. Equally, if not more important, is if you don't land *exactly* right, I guarantee you'll suffer injury, especially if you're male and not wearing a cup.

Be safe. Don't try this at home. Jump down to the ground like a regular person and mount your horse in the usual manner.

Bronze didn't mind, although she did express some concern at the peculiar noise I made when I hit. Since I was leaning far forward, somewhat curled up, she latched on to my head and shoulders with her mane. This kept me in the saddle while my regeneration repaired the damage. She accelerated silently away from the house, civilization, and any likely source of pursuit. Which meant, of course, cross-country.

A minute or so later, after my abused anatomy and psychology finished recovering, I took a good look around. To be fair, Kamshasa gets a bad rap as a desert country. It's not a desert, or not all of it. The province of Kashmanir is quite nice around the civilized regions. It actually turns to jungle fairly suddenly if you're far enough north, away from the desert. This is helpful in hiding from prying eyes.

Bronze wanted to know if I was feeling well enough to go home.

"I think I can manage. Pull over and I'll build a temporary arch." Bronze obligingly came to a silent halt.

I dismounted and regarded the deep imprints of her hooves. It was a good thing we were leaving. Tracking Bronze is like following the trail of a heavy tank. There's another thing I should work into her magic items: Something to reduce her hoofprints. Come to think of it, maybe something to damp down her dust cloud in dry areas, too.

I put together a quick spell. It sucked up dust and dirt, leaf-litter, twigs, bits of vine, whatever was handy. This swirling mass formed into a temporary archway. When the spell expired, the bits would fall or blow away. For now, though, it gave me something to use as a portal. I concentrated on my enchanted gate in the geode room, flushed, and waited until everything snapped into place. Bronze and I were through the gateway in nothing flat and the vision of Kamshasa shredded behind us, disappearing into the becrystaled wall behind my arch.

I settled to the floor, next to the arch. It's been a bad week. I tried to lean against a rather pointy wall. That didn't work, so I stretched out on the floor.

Bronze lowered her head and breathed hot air into my face. I rubbed her nose. She wanted to know what I wanted to do.

"I'm thinking of wallowing in self-pity for a while."

Bronze thought it wasn't a good idea. She nibbled at my hair while nuzzling me with a hot, metal nose.

I'm with her, Boss. You've been oscillating between angry, afraid, depressed, and generally wishy-washy ever since you came back from being snatched by a ghost.

"As I understand it, the ghost was caught by Thomen and used like a post-suicide bomber. Johann snatched me only after I was electrocuted."

Fine, ever since you were snatched by Johann.

"Technically, it's ever since I was tortured and used by Johann."

Firebrand made a rude psychic sound. Bronze had a big horselaugh.

*My point is, you haven't been yourself since then! Make up your mind on what you want! What **do** you want? Or do I need to get Seldar to hit you again? The first one seems to be wearing off.*

"I wanted to sort things out with Tort."

Right. Did that.

"Not exactly."

Either she's gone or she's in the hands of a god, right?

"Well... he's not exactly a god. He's—"

Shut up. He can do things you don't know how to do with souls and the afterlife and other stuff. He'll do for these purposes. So you can miss Tort all you want and maybe be pleasantly surprised in a hundred years. Great. In the meantime, what do you want? You've thrown away a kingdom—

"I don't think I've 'thrown away' a—"

I told you to shut up, Firebrand repeated. *You've **given** away a kingdom. You've said goodbye to everyone you care about, now including Tort. You sent Mary—the one person your ego could stand to cry on—*

Bronze snorted.

You don't count, Firebrand snapped at her, then directed its attention to me again. *You sent Mary, the one **other** person your ego could stand to cry on, into another universe. You discovered what you needed to find out about Tort. Two things are left: to take bloody, murderous vengeance on the man who abused, tortured, and used you, then find your nasty ball and destroy it. Or have you changed your mind again?*

"I haven't changed my mind," I protested. "I'm still going to kill Johann. And his amped-up relatives. Eventually. But I'm emotionally tired from... okay, everything." I sighed. "I need a vacation."

So take one. Find some universe with mobs of mangy rat-men and cut them to pieces until you feel better.

"I was thinking more in terms of sandy beaches, slow music, and air conditioning."

Fine! Let me stay with Bob while you go goof off. He'll kill things, at least, while you're recovering from being an emotional shipwreck. Give my regards to Johann, by the way, when he finally sucks you through a gate.

"Damn. I forgot. It's been a while since he tried it."

Here. How long has it been over there? Oh, and how long will you be on this vacation? Ten seconds? Or ten thousand years?

"There are times when I hate your reptilian bluntness."

Draconic, Firebrand corrected. *Reptile-**like**, but far superior.*

"More intelligent, certainly."

Sometimes even smarter than you, Boss.

"So I've noticed." I thumped the back of my head against the floor and ground the heels of my hands into my eyes. I growled.

So? What do you want to do?

"I'm thinking about it. Give me a minute."

I stepped into my headspace.

My mental study was its usual mess. I circled the desk and sat down. I had serious thinking and emotional housekeeping to do.

Everything in my mental study is a representation of an idea. A feeling, a memory, a fact, an opinion, whatever. These are treated as physical objects by the larger construct of my study. While I'm in my study, I can search my memory, sort my feelings, even wad things up and throw them away.

The hatch leading down to the basement is the exception, obviously. The things living in my unconscious mind are not to be trifled with, but that's fair. I'm not to be trifled with, either. I'm still not opening the thing.

I wonder. Should I build an airlock? Can I let a few of the things up into my consciousness, deal with them, recover from the fight, and then handle a few more? Is it possible to work out some of my mental problems that way? Or would consciously destroying my mental demons drive me insane? For many people, motivation comes from the things we fear or hate or regret. If we didn't fear, didn't hate, didn't regret, would we still be ourselves? Would we still have the drive to accomplish, the will to do?

There's a project for later. I had enough to do with the things lying around the room.

Step one: clear a shelf for Tort. While all these memories—happy and sad— are lying around the room, the place is too cluttered to get anything done. If I put the memories in order, stack them neatly, and shelve them, I still have them, but they're not on my mind, as it were.

Is this what happens in normal people? You lose someone important to you and it affects you deeply. A week later, it's still on your mind. But a year later, five years later...? Am I doing consciously and quickly what everyone does unconsciously and slowly?

Hmm. Papers on Lissette, too. And Johann. And all those children of the Demon King. And— well, lots of things. I'm a mess.

So it's time to do some filing.

I keep thinking someday I'll cross-index everything in my head and be able to remember anything, everything, with just a moment's thought.

Nice fantasy. Unless I wire Diogenes into my brain and let him do the sorting and filing, I'll be a little old vampire in the necromantic final rest home by the time I'm sorted out. A brain is a messy thing to fool with, or one I'm a fool to mess with, depending.

There are pros and cons of manually filing your own memories.

Pros. They get sorted out and dealt with immediately. All the time you waste being depressed and mopey and distracted goes away. You get back to your life in a hurry. The memories are always there, whenever you want to pull down the metaphorical scrapbook and flip through it, but they don't obtrude and invade, making you miserable by forcing themselves into your thoughts. They stay on the shelf instead of littering the desk.

Cons. It's a scrapbook. The memories are just that, memories. They're flat, actual accounts of what you remember, with the vivid colors of your feelings faded to pastels. You fish out a memory and all the emotions you felt at the time, all the associations, all the linkages to everything else that made it a valuable memory are lost.

If you don't think that last part is a con, let me give you a for instance.

I recall a time when a little girl met me at the gate of my castle as I was leaving. I promised her I would be back. She wore a blue dress, had her dark hair tied back in a ponytail, and looked sad. I spoke with her for a bit, promised I would return, and went about my business.

See? Now it's nothing more than a memory, a playback of events. Facts, all the facts, and nothing but the facts.

There has got to be a better way. Damned if I know what it is. Damned anyway, for all I know.

One good thing came of it. I felt better. Some memories *are* better when they're stripped down, cooled off, and put carefully away. It removed a lot of things I regretted or felt guilty about. The process also took some chunks out of things I loved, things I missed, and things I hoped, but there's no such thing as a free lunch. Every happy thought I filed was mine to file, and took a dozen heart-lashing memories into the stacks with it. I think I quit before the point of diminishing returns.

Net effect, I have far fewer unpleasant memories, slightly fewer happy ones, and a much higher happy-to-sad ratio.

Mathematical psychology, anyone?

I wondered again if I was slowly going insane by monkeying around with my own thinking machinery this way. I still don't have an answer. I don't feel insane, but maybe it's a matter of degree. I'm already a little crazy, so what's one more step along the road? I only hope I'll notice when I pass Weirdsville and move into the suburbs of Neurosis City on the way to catch the Psycho train at Crazy Station. Maybe I'll pick up a copy of the Daily Lunatic to read on the way.

I wonder if I can find a telepathic psychoanalyst. I wonder what he'd make of my mental furniture.

The place was still a mess, but I made a sizable dent in the disorder. I still have a lot of unresolved issues and they're probably going to stay filed under "D" for "Denial" for a while.

I exited my headspace.

The first thing I noticed was the smell of scorched flesh. I opened my eyes and sat up.

Three dead men lay in various states of crushed and burned. The door was closed and Bronze stood in front of it, holding it shut. Something had burned a hole in her chest, angled up and back, to emerge through the saddle area. Fire flickered fitfully from both openings. My first impulse was to attack someone, but she didn't leave anything alive. I tried to speak calmly.

"Problem?"

Bronze snorted. I caught a whiff of anger amid the smoke.

"Firebrand?"

Three assassins, Firebrand reported. *From what I heard in their heads, they're Hand.*

"What's the story with the hole in Bronze?" I asked. I thought I sounded calm. After all, she was only annoyed. The hole didn't impair her functioning, aside from decreasing the fire pressure if she wanted to breathe it at someone. She wasn't materially hurt.

The only thought I caught was about the wand. The guy using it hoped it was worth the price.

"Any thoughts on where he got it?"

Some magician, I think. Nothing solid, so I doubt it was someone he actually knew. A business transaction.

"Fair enough. What did it do?"

Punched a hole in Bronze. It was intended to kill her so they could use the other wands on you.

"Other wands?" I moved over to the remains and examined them without touching them. What was left was dog food and fertilizer. Nothing magical stood out, but I did find the crushed and burned remains of three wands among the meat. Sadly, there was no way to tell what spells they once held. "Any idea what they did?"

One was supposed to strip all the protection off you. The other was to banish you back to the eternal void. That's all they knew about them, Boss.

"Fair enough. How did they know I was here?"

I don't think they did. They've been in Karvalen for a while, looking for an opportunity. They came down here to check—I get the impression they do that when they think they can get away with it. It was just a matter of time before they ran into you, or you into them. They were pretty surprised when they opened the door and we were actually in here.

"Did they have any idea how many more like them are wandering around?"

No, but they're certain they're not the only ones.

I moved to examine Bronze. It was a neat hole, about two inches across in front and a foot across in her back. The edges looked melted, but Bronze told me it didn't hurt.

"You're going to be able to fix this?"

Of course she could fix it. A couple of days, tops, and I wouldn't be able to tell she was wounded.

"All right."

I rummaged around in the remains again and found the Hand amulets. One of them was intact; the other two were either melted or crushed. One was enough for my purposes. These had the handsome, fatherly face found on the amulets of a typical Priest of the Light, but the back of the amulet had a clenched fist with stylized rays shooting out from it. I'd have checked for tattoos on their backs, but there probably wasn't enough left to tell.

These bastards tried to kill my horse. Admittedly, it was a pre-assassination thing, killing the guardian to get to the target, but this was irrelevant to me. They tried to kill Bronze. That's what sane people call a bad idea. It pisses off the Guardian Demon.

"Firebrand, correct me if I'm wrong, but these holy symbol amulet things… priests wear these, right?"

All the ones I've seen, yes.

"Ever see a random person wearing them? Some run of the mill follower?"

No. I don't think it works like that.

"Good."

Boss?

"Hmm?"

May I ask what you're doing?

"Overreacting, probably."

Am I going to like it?

"No. I'm going to cast a spell and then go see how Mary's doing."

That's all?

"That's all."

Uh… okay. You're making me nervous, Boss.

"I apologize."

That's different from being sorry.

"So it is. But, for you, I'll also admit I regret making you nervous unnecessarily. Better?"

Yes. Sort of. I think.

The geode room had a collection of powered crystals. Those might do, but I didn't want to call more attention to the place. I had a word with the mountain and found a chamber, high up in the palace, near the peak.

Ah, yes. The hidden workroom where I was summoned out of my own head and temporarily stuffed into a body. That would do fine.

We went through the passageways in the rock, circling around and up, and I realized Bronze needed some sort of patch on her holes. Avoiding the people still awake at this ridiculous hour of the morning would be difficult enough without walking an open furnace through the halls. We paused and I laid a field of force across the openings as temporary seals. Another pair of spells started tugging the metal inward, helping her normal healing process along. Bandages? Sort of. Maybe closer to stitches. It was something like the spell I use to weld flesh together, but slower and ongoing.

Weird. I started with a flesh-welding spell and modified it into a bronze-welding spell. It seems as though the development process would run the other way.

The mountain had the room unsealed for us by the time we reached it. Bronze held the door closed again while I activated the containment diagram and surrounded it with an Ascension Sphere. A couple of power fans increased the power input significantly. I wanted a big charge. What I hoped to do was extremely far-reaching.

I sat down and visited my mental study again. This time, rather than filing things away, I wanted to dig up some old memories for the precise details. How many isotopes of gold are there?

All right. The typical isotope of gold is gold one-nine-seven. It's quite stable, but it can be shifted into an excited state, causing the structure of the nucleus to get a little out of whack. This excited isotope decays via isomeric transition—the protons and neutrons don't want to be arranged that way, so they shift back into their more-stable arrangement, releasing the energy in the form of a gamma-ray photon.

So, my Nefarious Plan. Construct a hybrid spell, one to continuously suck in magical power, build up a charge, and fire it off before building up another charge. This involves a power intake, a capacitor to store the charge, and a discharge mechanism to feed the main spell function. Any one of these components is a fair-to-complex spell, but what made them especially difficult was the need to handle massive charges.

All this is to automate the activation of the main spell. This spell fires off in a combination of shapes. First a sphere, to affect all targets in range. I'm not sure what the spherical range is, but it should be at least a few hundred yards, probably more. The expanding sphere of energy passes through anything it's not programmed to recognize, seeking targets. Then it grounds out through the targets.

After the sphere function, it starts firing off in a narrow cone—say, five degrees wide—to drastically increase the range of the effect. This goes, hopefully, to the edge of the world. On the next shot, it shifts four degrees clockwise, making sure to overlap the edge of the previous shot, and fires again. And so on, all the way around.

The effect is targeted with great precision. It only targets individual instances of amulets like the one I recovered from the religious nutjobs—having one as an example helps enormously. The layer of gold on the back of the amulet is boosted into an excited state—specifically the parts in the shape of the clenched fist and the rays of light. Thus, it can't affect any other amulet, since they're flat-backed, without the reverse design. It only works on the holy amulets of the Hand.

Once these bits of gold are excited, natural processes take over, allowing them to emit gamma radiation in their own good time, irradiating the wearer gradually. Considering where these things rest, they should hit mostly the breastbone and the heart, but there was a good chance for some scatter to the thymus, possibly even the thyroid. *None* of these are places you want to be irradiated.

You learn about these things when you study radioactive isotopes in physics and chemistry. It makes lab safety less of a joke and more of a gruesomely serious requirement.

I had to be careful with the intensity. Unlike neutron radiation—a much harder thing to cause without inducing nuclear fission—gamma rays can cause burns, just as though the amulets were red-hot. My objective was to irradiate the wearers of the Hand medallions over time, not heat up their medallions and force them to take the things off. If they took them off, they wouldn't get enough radiation dose. I wanted them to stay on so the radiation poisoning could slowly kill every last one of them in a debilitating, hideous fashion.

The intensity was tricky, but doable. It involved a ground-fault interruption function that did *not* come easy. When the spell's effect started to discharge into an amulet, a subroutine cut it off, stopped the power drain into the amulet, leaving the rest of the spell to seek out new targets. This reduced the radiation effect, but spread it out among more amulets, and therefore many members of the Hand.

Since the spell would appear to any observer to be a simple location spell— "Oh, look, someone found my medallion"—it might be completely unnoticed for years. New members would be initiated, given medallions, and would suffer the same effect. The whole of the Hand, old members and new, could wither away and die.

Does this count as the death-curse of the Lord of Night?

I wonder. Could I assemble the spell as a burst, rather than a ray? If the spell was targeted at a point inside a city... no, back up. Could I launch a spell like a missile so the structure of the spell didn't activate *here,* but instead traveled to a specific point before activating? Kind of like a cruise missile, in a way. Rather than setting off bigger and bigger bombs to get targets farther and farther away, can I send the spell somewhere and have it detonate at a specific point?

Yes, I can. It's a variation on what I did with the magical spy satellite network, but it's doable. It's also harder to determine where it came from, too. Spotting the spell as it detonated wouldn't be hard at all, but setting up a round-the-clock watch to watch for it as it approached might be unreasonable... no, I take that back. A series of detection spells could be set up around a known target point...

Still, this method would take longer to track down. I could use the practice on it, too. Maybe I should cut out the death rays and go with the missile version. Of course, that meant I needed to target every major city and town individually, and any out-of-the-way secret temples would be missed entirely...

Well, crap. Fine, then. I'll use the death rays instead of the cruise missiles.

I never realized it was so hard to be a Mad Scientist with a Death Ray. There are so many trade-offs.

I assembled the spell, test fired it on the medallion I salvaged, and watched through a spectrum-shifting spell. The thing glowed in the gamma range on one side, but it didn't burn my undead flesh. I did note it felt a trifle warmer to the touch, but I have an inhuman level of sensitivity and was looking for it. I doubted mortal flesh would detect it.

I also noticed the characteristic itching sensation of regeneration in my hand. That was an excellent sign, both because it implied radiation damage and an ability to recover from it. It made me vaguely optimistic about encountering radioactive materials in the future. Good to know.

After my tests, I entered the Ascension Sphere and cast the spell again, this time tying the medallion into the spell as a targeting sample—sympathetic magic, you know—and setting up the sequential program. This drained the Sphere, as I planned, but resulted in a spell strong enough to deliver enormous jolts of power.

Now the thing could charge up over time, do its evil work, and repeat until the end of the world.

Hmm. I fiddled with it a bit more, adding a counter to the number of times it would fire. A hundred or so full cycles should do it. Anyone surviving the full routine was either protected, out of range, or routinely healed—that last possibility being most likely, I felt, but this was still worth doing. When the spell fired the last time, it wouldn't stop with just the stored charge, but would run itself out like a regular spell.

I set it in motion. With a little luck, the Lord of Light would either be unable to cure radiation damage or find it cost-prohibitive to do so repeatedly on everyone in the Hand. I doubt I'll kill everyone in the Hand, but I'll settle for killing some and making all of them suffer.

All I can say is, don't try to kill my horse. It brings out my Demon King side. Just to be clear, in this case, I don't care that it does. Do *not* touch the horse.

Tuesday, March 16th

It was a long night. Today might be longer.

I had my waterfall-shower and dug around to find my modern-world clothes. Being inconspicuous is difficult to do in High Medieval formal wear—unless you're at the Court, in which case you might blend in. In a postmodern society, I was going to have enough trouble with a gigantic horse and a pair of swords. The swords, at least, I could put in luggage. Bronze is another story entirely.

To speed her recovery, Firebrand and I heated, molded, and reshaped some of her to seal the holes. They were obviously not healed—more like scar tissue—but it was a head start on the whole, or un-holey, process. With her color-altering bracelets, she could pass as a flesh-and-blood horse of unusual size as along as no one tried to meddle with her. The saddle doesn't come off, for example, and nobody's going to mistake the feel of her for anything but metal. On the other hand, she does feel warm to the touch, if a bit bristly. Come to think of it, someone unfamiliar with horsehide might not immediately think anything was amiss.

I finished tying up my boots and considered my cloak. Miraculous it might be, but I had yet to see it do anything. Still, you never know. I put it on and, since it was daytime, regarded myself in the mirror. Did it look out of place or silly? Yes, I decided. Yes, it did. There was no way I could wear it without looking—

It wrapped itself around me and turned into an overcoat, complete with sleeves, buttons, and belt. I unbuttoned it and checked the pockets. They were perfect. It even had a subtle label on the inside, done in glossy thread and stitched into the lining: "Penumbra and Shadow, Outfitters."

"Okay," I admitted, "that's impressive."

I'm pleased you approve.

I ignored the faint, whispered comment from On High. At least the cloak wasn't the one doing the psychic talking. I'm sure of that. Ninety percent sure, at least.

One more stop, this time by the Royal Treasure room. I collected some gems sticking out of the walls and scooped gold into saddlebags. You can't fill a saddlebag with gold. It's far too dense. It'll rip out the seams and spill. The key to making off with the loot is to avoid being greedy. I didn't know how well Mary was doing on the yacht, but it would be impolite of me to not contribute something.

We headed back down to the geode room. The bodies had quit smoking and steaming, but were starting to smell for other reasons. Torvil and Kammen were present, regarding the remains and discussing whether or not to bother asking what happened. They're not stupid. Besides, the big, overlapping, round crush marks were something of a clue.

Kammen grunted and gestured with his chin. Torvil turned and saluted.

"I'm not the King, Torvil."

"With respect, Sire, you are, but the Queen is ruling."

"He's right, Sire," Kammen added.

"I hate you both."

"No, you don't," Kammen replied.

"No, I don't," I admitted. "Quite the opposite, in fact. What's going on?"

"Investigating the smell, Sire," Torvil said.

"And I had a crimp in the Ribbon," Kammen added. "Figured it was you."

"I suppose it was," I admitted. "Sorry I forgot to clean up."

"Told you," Torvil said, grinning at Kammen.

"I'll leave this in your capable hands, gentlemen. I've got a little trip to take."

"Sire, before you leave?" Kammen asked.

"Yes?"

Torvil and Kammen exchanged glances. Torvil cleared his throat.

"We would be honored if we could join you."

I thought about it. I did more than think about it. I seriously considered it. In the end, though, I decided against it. What I was about to do called for Purloined Letter levels of sneaky.

"Maybe later," I told them. "I have some preliminary preparations to make. As it stands, I need you helping Lissette. I won't be standing at her elbow to glare menacingly at people. I want you two—along with Seldar, Malana and Malena, and the whole corps of the red sashes doing it for me."

"But there's a chance you'll send for us?" Kammen asked, hopefully.

"Why so eager?" I asked.

"I've been a pimp for the Demon King for years. We get to train a lot, but we don't have much call to ride to battle."

"Aha! I get it, now. Yes… yes, I see your problem. Well, if I run into a war, I promise I'll ask Lissette if she can spare you. Is that fair?"

"More than fair, Sire."

"If you're really bored, you might consider arming a bunch of the army with wooden weapons and having practice battles, rather than letting the knights hog all the fun. Just a thought."

"There will be casualties," Torvil mused. Kammen harrumphed.

"It'll be time to practice our healing magic, won't it?"

"They don't see it the way we do," Torvil sighed.

"If you gentlemen will excuse me, I have an arch to open."

"Of course, Sire," they replied, in unison, and saluted.

Muttering to myself about gung-ho knights, I set up the gates. Plural. Again, I was landing on Johann's home turf. With a dozen or more tiny gates to register on any hypothetical gate-detection alarms, I hoped to get through without being instantly targeted. Of course, I don't know he even has any such detection, but I can't afford to assume. Optimists may have more fun, but pessimists live longer.

I took my time setting it all up. First and foremost, my priority was hitting the right world, especially since I knew for a fact it was possible to miss. I walked carefully through the process of defining the world I remembered. With it pre-set and programmed in, I drew power from the crystals and fed the target to the little ring-gates, linking them to the main archway. If they could all open at once, that would be best…

So, where in that world am I going? I cracked the wax on Mary's list of rendezvous points and read through it. I didn't like it. She has an impish, sometimes fiendish sense of humor.

After some thought, I picked Paris as my first port of call. Later, unless something changed my plans, I could make a circuit of Berlin, Rome, and London, then back to Paris. At every stop, of course, I would check for and leave messages. Mary and I would catch up to each other, but hopefully without attracting undue attention. It would be immensely easier if we had phone numbers, but using the ones we had the last time we were there was asking for trouble—from vampires for certain, including their human minions, with a possibility of intermittent magi.

Ring gate one. World set. General location, greater Los Angeles. Ring gate two, home in on a small opening in Peking. For ring gate three, I hear Hawaii is nice. Ring gate four…

I worked my way down the list, spreading them all over the globe. Then I thought about my aim. If I opened an arch and went through to Paris, it might show up on a map and be monitored thereafter. It might simply result in someone investigating the place. It might also be unnoticed or disregarded. It might provoke an intense magi-fueled search. I don't know, but I can't afford to take risks. Maybe it would be better to pop out somewhere else and make my way to Paris? Preferably somewhere reasonably tolerant of foreign strangers.

Switzerland, I think. That's not too bad. I aimed the arch for Geneva. This was also far enough from Avignon to—hopefully—avoid undue interest. Geneva also offered a city full of man-made structures to act as an anchor point for the main gate. Plus, it was close enough to wilderness, both mountains and forests—I hoped! —to be useful if we had to run for it.

Last I checked, Johann was altering the brains of world leaders. If he had gate detection, and if he had the influence for it—and the anger, fear, or paranoia for it—he might decide to drop a nuke on us. He doesn't like me, and it's mutual. But there is a lot to be said for having a mountain between you and the possible soon-to-be-vaporized ground zero.

I hoped it wouldn't come to that. It probably wouldn't. But while it was unlikely, the possibility was significant enough to take note of. I didn't like it.

The gates were charged and ready. Bronze pawed silently at the floor, prepared to launch herself through. I stood by the edge of the arch, ready to swing around it into the other world. Since it was daytime here, I wouldn't have to worry about stepping into sunlight. If I stepped into nighttime, Bronze could grab me by the collar, lift me clear off the ground, and run if the situation called for it.

The whole set of gates fired off together, seeking something to link to. The lesser ones could handle themselves; my attention was on the big one. It probed, searched, found a suitable opening, locked to it, snapped it close.

Beyond the arch was a parking garage. I considered it perfectly acceptable. Bronze and I went through and I slammed the gate behind us as my nighttime metabolism killed me dead as disco. My heart seized up, my guts knotted, and my whole body felt as though I'd just done a one-and-a-half gainer into an empty pool.

If you missed it, let me simplify: I hate that.

Bronze picked me up, as per plan, and trotted quickly as she followed the arrows toward the exit. I fired off my Ring of Hygiene and activated my human illusions while I recovered. She put me down when we reached the exit and I mounted up.

The parking garage didn't want to let her out. The automated system thought she was a car. Bronze was slightly offended.

"It's probably a pressure sensor and maybe a motion sensor. Don't feel bad. It's an idiot box."

She still didn't like it. Taking a few bites out of the gate wouldn't bother her a bit. She favored it with a medium-hostile eyeball and considered where to insult it in return. The idea of kicking it into the Mediterranean wasn't a serious consideration, but it did cross her mind.

"Now, now. The Med is a little far away for that. Let me see if I can persuade it…" I ran psychic tendrils into the machine, traced some of the wires in the wall, found the circuit to control the gate, and momentarily shorted it. The gate hummed out of our way. We hurried off through the streets, hopefully to get out of town fast.

Everything was in French and marked in kilometers, so we burned through the countryside like a German panzer division. We followed the contour of the land, occasionally following a road or trail until we found one going the right way. Bronze merged smoothly into traffic as though born on the highway. Well, she did watch us drive for quite a while. We earned a number of wide-eyed looks and open mouths, but either nobody was on manual-drive or they kept their heads.

Hmm. Is it legal to be on manual in Europe? I never checked. The Autobahn might be robot-only by now.

At that thought, we got off the main highway and onto smaller roads, circling a mountainous area. I wanted to be sure we didn't have a line of sight on Geneva, just in case. Assuming Johann fingered us instantly and snapped out an immediate order, how long would it take to arm, launch, and deliver a nuclear weapon? My best guess was a minimum of four minutes, counting flight time, assuming he had a suitable asset afloat in the Mediterranean. We didn't make it around the mountains in four minutes, but nothing exploded behind us, either.

We lived. Score one for the good guys. Good-ish guys. Okay, the lesser evil.

All right, where the hell am I? Earth has Polaris, so there's north… we came south and west, so I know where I am in relation to the rest of Europe, kind of… and I never realized how important Geography class was in high school. France is southwest from here, but I'm not sure how far.

Does anyone around here speak English?

We backtracked a bit to the outskirts of a town. Turns out we were already in France, outside Cruseilles along Route de Droniéres. Nobody I met spoke English, but everybody had a skinphone and a translation app—thank you, Google, for simplifying my life as much as you complicate it.

It was a little odd to speak, hear the translation, hear the reply, and then hear the translation. The young man running the counter at the all-night convenience store seemed used to it, though. He was kind enough to hold out his arm and let me consult his skinphone map.

I left a gold nugget as a souvenir, simply because he didn't have to be so helpful. I appreciated it. Now I had a good idea of which roads to take to get to Paris.

Which brought my thinking back around to Bronze. How do I help her blend in? Or conceal her? Could I get a dead truck and use the body as a rolling disguise for her? No, that's silly. Can I get a truck big enough to transport her? That might be possible, but it would require, as usual, money. Good thing I brought valuables.

Which requires someone to help me convert it, which means daytime.

I wonder if France is any more tolerant of high-speed horse traffic?

No, but it takes them a while to notice.

According to Emile's skinphone, I could take the D971 north all the way to Paris. The other option was the A6, but the A6 was a robot-only road. Bronze would need a transponder and other hardware to pretend to be a vehicle. Going up the D971 was still less than ideal, but at least the computers didn't immediately finger us to traffic control.

We made it all the way to Dijon before a gendarme caught up to us. I glanced back and saw him coming, so I turned off my human illusions. He pulled up alongside as we turned off the loop around the city and headed northwest. Bronze adjusted her mane so it streamed by to my left, letting the gendarme get a good look at me. He stared at us without saying anything for over a mile. I waved. Bronze tossed her head, spewing smoke and fire.

Boss?

What's up?

He's trying to decide what to say to his commander. He's thinking through a number of conversations, but they all end with him fired, suspended, or medicated.

Sounds about right. Is he going to try and pull us over?

That's what he's trying to figure out. He wants to, but he also doesn't want to.

We'll let him off the hook.

I waved at him again and Bronze slowed suddenly. We took a sharp left, cutting across a break in traffic and an open field before vanishing into the woods. Behind us, the gendarme stopped his vehicle and got out to watch us disappear. We waited. Bronze held her breath to avoid flaming, but smoke poured out her ears. I doubt he could see it in the dark.

At last, he shook his head, sat down in his car, and drove on. My guess is he never actually called it in.

Saturday, December 19th

We stayed hidden in that small woods until dawn. I snuggled up to the westward side of a fallen tree and wrapped up in my new overcoat—now complete with a hood. I didn't notice when it changed, which freaked me out more than the change, itself. I cut a couple of pine or fir branches, half-buried myself, and Bronze kicked leaves over the rest. It wasn't the worst dawn transformation I've ever had, but it was far from the best.

After climbing out and cleaning off, I considered what to do with the day. Bronze doesn't travel well during periods of high visibility, obviously. Dijon, however, was actually a pretty sizable city and within walking distance. I could probably find someone to trade with, exchanging gems and gold for digital cash. I might even buy or rent a moving van.

Bronze was rather blasé about it. She might not outrun every vehicle in the world, but she was game to try. What she couldn't outrun, she could cripple or kill.

"It's not the quality, it's the quantity," I assured her. She expressed a low opinion of fiberglass and plastic. I agreed.

I suppose I'm not going with you? Firebrand asked.

"Not today. I'll have enough to carry and I don't want to draw attention."

Always not drawing attention! What is it with you and hiding all the time?

"Remember the night with the vampires at the farmhouse?"

*There were a lot nights with vampires at the farmhouse. You mean the one when the **other** vampires burned it down?*

"That's the one. Now imagine that night, but with more shotguns, more people, and bigger guns."

Ugly. Doable, but ugly.

"Add more people. Add the fact every time I show my face, someone screams about the vampire and more people close in. Imagine a sea of people stretching to the horizon, all of them shooting at me."

It wouldn't really be like that, Firebrand protested.

"You're right. But suppose I want to sit in my favorite chair and read? Think the people who want me dead and know where I am will let me? Do you think I'd have a book to read? Do you think I'd have a chair? And, more to the current moment, do you think Johann will hesitate to drop a volcano on me?"

You mean "drop you in a volcano."

"I said what I meant."

Hmm.

"I agree with you about having a nice life where I don't have to lurk all the time. I'll look into it as soon as Johann and the Ebon Eidolon of Evil are dealt with. Until then, I need to avoid their notice while I plot their downfall. With this suitably explained, may I continue with my sneaking?"

Oh. Certainly. You may go.

"Thank you, too much."

I hung my swordbelts on Bronze's saddlehorn, filled my pockets with gold and gems, and walked into town.

After a long morning of asking for help, I found out I should have stayed in Geneva. The Swiss are very understanding about every sort of money-conversion problem. France, not so much. I'm still not sure if I was cheated or if it was simply the cost of doing business with less-reputable merchants.

Still, the usual process applied. Turn goods into real money. Use the money to make it easier to turn goods into money. Sell one uncut diamond to the first jeweler you find, buy a skinphone and do some research to find other jewelers. Download the French/English application and get an earpiece for running translation. Get a couple of digital money sticks. All the usual stuff. I spent most of the day walking around, converting currency, and ignoring the absolutely fantastic smell of bread.

Mmm. The French do know their bread. Don't get me wrong. The bakers in Karvalen make a lovely loaf, but some of the shops here have been in business for longer than I've been alive. Sort of alive. Since before I was born. I suspect I looked very much the barbaric tourist, walking around Dijon, gawking at the signs and munching on a loaf. I don't care. It was delicious.

Once I had a new skinphone, I found out the date.

We left this world from some state park in the Adirondacks on December 11th, 2048. I believe it was a Friday. I went back on a non-voluntary basis to have a heart-to-heart and pliers-to-groin meeting with Johann Fries. After he finished explaining his torturous logic at how all this was my fault for "triggering" him, I quasi-escaped and eventually successfully escaped. I'm a little fuzzy on how long that took, local time, but it took at least three days, maybe five. I lost track; I was distracted.

It's now Saturday, December 19th, still in 2048.

I *hate* this variable time differential! Why can't all the universes operate at the same speed? It would be nice if they had at least one fundamental thing in common!

Then again, I shouldn't complain. The lack of time over here may be the only reason Johann hasn't successfully summoned me or flushed me out an airlock. He's only had a few days to try.

Oh. And in the larger sense of the world, it may be why he hasn't successfully taken it over, either.

But it worries me. If the time differential doesn't shift, will I spend a week here and find a year has gone by in Karvalen, or whatever the math works out to? What if it shifts to a greater differential? Lissette could be dead and Liam on the throne—or Liam's grandson. Shifting the other way isn't so bad. I could have a year-long magical argument and be back in Karvalen before they clean the remains of the Hand assassins off the floor.

Someday—again, someday—I'm going to figure this time-shifted weirdness out. Is it like planets? Earth rotates every twenty-four hours, roughly, to make one day. A day on Mars is about forty minutes longer because it rotates slightly slower. Jupiter has a day of about ten hours because it spins faster.

No, that can't be it. Those are fixed, not variable. Universes seem to keep slipping gears relative to each other. Why? Are they bobbing on the surface of the ocean of Time, their relative heights on the waves determining the rate at which they experience Time's flow? Would that metaphor even hold water?

Nuts.

I found a backpacker hostel and discovered it had a pair of private rooms. The price was low and came with a bathroom, so I occupied one for the sunset. I should have looked it over first. The curtains were inadequate and the bathroom had a frosted-glass window. It worked out, though, when I put the pillows over the window and held them in place with the bedspread. It might have been painful if the window faced west, but I was lucky there. I had a shower to minimize the power use from my ring, dressed, and fired up my human disguise.

Nobody gave me any funny looks when I bought makeup and sunglasses. Cashiers are too jaded to care what customers buy. You can go through a store and buy bananas, cucumbers, whipped cream, three new belts, and a box of condoms and the weird looks will all come from fellow customers. It's amazing what you get used to.

I returned to my lair, donned my non-magical disguise to save power in my rings, and wished for a reflection. Ah, well. There was nothing to be done about my talons, though, without power equipment or special tools. Nail clippers were useless—whatever my nails are made of, it's not normal. I tried a pair of scissors and successfully marked the edge of a talon, but cutting it was out of the question. Well, my nails could be overlooked as a personal quirk... hopefully.

Once suitably camouflaged and able to see right through people without using sharp implements, it was time to go hunting. My primary purpose was to find someone capable of doing work similar to BitRate's. It didn't need to be an iron-clad identity, just the equivalent of an ID card. If the gendarmes or gestapo pulled me over for speeding, I wanted them to respond with, "Insert your payment method here and be on your way," rather than, "What do you mean you don't have identification? Look into this lens, sir, and place your thumb on the scanner." It didn't have to stand up to an investigation, just let me get by.

Joe Citizen, that's me. I'd settle for Stupid American. But at all costs, I wanted to avoid Undocumented Alien.

The search for the more professional members of the criminal classes—the white-collar crooks, if you will—was hampered by the need to operate a translation app. However, the unprofessional members of the criminal classes assisted me with my language problem and dinner. There were several small incidents with individuals, pairs, and trios, but afterward my mastery of the French language was much improved. Working my way up the food chain of the local criminal underworld happened much more quickly. It also provided a small contribution to the yacht fund and quite a number of smaller weapons. The drugs—presumably illegal drugs—went down the toilet, as usual.

It took most the night to find someone capable of helping me. I pressed on, however, and found two more. My idea was to get an identity from each. If one identity became wanted for a crime—heaven forbid! —I would have backup ID on hand.

Then it was back to my room for the sunrise, another shower, and identity hunting.

Sunday, December 20th

Getting a basic identity card wasn't so difficult, once I knew who to ask. One of them was willing to accept gold and had suggestions on where to convert more. I immediately paid his friend a visit and unloaded the rest of my pockets. He wasn't a licensed dealer, obviously, and didn't have the best exchange rate, but he was willing to handle bulk. Convenience is always a factor.

Somehow, we neglected to introduce ourselves. Maybe the gold did. They say money talks. I was fine with that.

I ordered a moving truck from Google. Not a typical Google Van, but a big, heavy-duty thing, suitable for gigantic metal horses or a whole house full of chattels. There's a lead time on those, for some reason. I'd have it by the end of the day.

Meanwhile, I took a Google Cab out to a spot on the highway, paid to have it wait, and jogged off into the woods. I noticed, in passing, that Bronze definitely came this way. She left hoofprints like empty buckets in somebody's field. I really need to do something about that, but what? When that much tonnage hits the ground, it makes dents! I'll have to give it more thought.

After recovering the rest of my mineralogical wealth—and loading Firebrand into the padded case I bought for it—I caught my cab, returned to my *de facto* banker, made good the trade, and was pleased at the balance on my digital sticks.

Then it was a pleasant day in a pleasant city. It was cold, even for the time of year, but the sun was out and nobody was actively trying to kill me. I spent some time in an open-air café, chatting with the wait staff. After all, I'm an American and I need to practice my French, n'est-ce pas? I would have tipped them, but apparently that's not a thing in Europe—they were very helpful in explaining, gently, how Americans are still the barbarians of the world. I couldn't take offense; I was the one who used the word "barbarian," or *le barbare*. Besides, it's their country. The hussies with the loose hair would be looked down on in Karvalen, to say nothing of the grown women with ponytails wandering around outside a bathhouse! It's all relative.

My spoken French lags behind my understanding of it. I'm improving it by mundane methods, now. Maybe I should get one of those language lesson programs for my skinphone. I seem to have a terribly low-class accent, too. I wonder where I got it from.

Late in the afternoon, the Google Truck arrived. It didn't play my usual greeting sound, which was both reassuring and saddening. I wasn't using my Vladimir identity and it didn't have any scanning equipment to identify me, just one of my new ID chips. Oh, well. I told it where to go. Bronze came out of the woods, climbed up in the back, and I locked everything up.

With a truck for transport and a cybernet route planner, I decided to hit Paris, then Rome, then Berlin. We'd save London for last, then start over. If Mary hadn't left a message for me in any of our rendezvous locations, I'd leave some for her. We'd find each other eventually, then go for a cruise. A working cruise while I set up some awful spells, but a cruise nonetheless.

I wonder if I'll hate the boat.

Come to that, I have a skinphone. Where do people sell yachts, anyway? I looked it up. There are companies that will build a yacht or convert a boat into a yacht, but they don't exactly have a showroom floor. Most of them are commissioned work, not factory production. As for people willing to sell their yacht, there are places online, but no used-yacht dealerships like used-car dealerships. So much for that.

But some of the yachts were fascinating. While the truck drove us to Paris, I looked them over. Luxurious things, very nice. Some of them were floating mansions. Others were nearly floating islands, complete with bubble domes. Those island-habitat yachts weren't fast, of course, but they mounted huge banks of solar collectors, making them nearly self-sufficient. A person could drift slowly around the world on one and never have to touch land.

I got so involved in the mechanics of yachts I nearly fried in the sunset. The tingling started and I barely noticed. The hot, stinging sensation demanded my attention, though. I ducked through the access hatch to get into the back of the truck and hid there.

Sasha was right, all those years ago. The internet—the cybernet—is an evil thing.

Bronze stood over me, head lowered, watching me transform. She wondered if I was all right.

"I wonder that, too," I admitted. Firebrand chortled. I'm not sure I've ever heard a psychic chortle and hope not to repeat the experience.

Paris by night is lovely.

Paris by night through vampire eyes is stunning. The streets are rivers of gold. People are bright fish, gleaming, glowing, swimming through light. It's like watching a melody of happy thoughts play through a musician's mind.

I'm glad the truck did the driving. I wouldn't have wanted to negotiate the Parisian streets on my own in a car, much less a truck. Anyway, I didn't have much choice about it. Paris doesn't allow manually operated vehicles inside the city. Bicycles, yes, but nothing with a motor.

The Eiffel Tower is impressive. Sure, it's not the tallest thing I've ever seen, but it's been standing since 1889, according to the tourist brochure. Not bad for wrought iron and nineteenth-century engineering.

The tower was still open to tourists when I arrived. The weather was cold, but otherwise unremarkable, so getting a ticket and a ride up the tower was no trouble at all.

I looked around. Firebrand looked around. We searched and sensed and scanned. We found no sign that Mary had come by here. To be fair, she hadn't had much time to work. She might still be feeling out financing.

I imprinted magical lettering into the floor near the lift. With her training, she would be able to see it. Since she understood the degenerate form of Imperial I keep calling Rethven, she would be able to read it, too. It was simply the digits to my new skinphone.

Errand completed, I spent a considerable amount of time at the rail, looking over Paris. It was worth looking at.

Monday, December 21st

I'll say this for robot cars and modern roads. You get where you're going with a minimum of fuss. Ten hours after leaving Paris, we pulled into Rome. Again, no manual-drive cars were permitted inside the city, so the truck—which I nicknamed "Twilight" after the Decepticon starship—had no problem getting around. It knew which roads to take, which roads to avoid, and all the computer-synchronized traffic around us knew where we needed to go before I did.

If *I* had to drive a big truck through Rome, it would be stuck in some narrow street, never to move again.

Twilight parked itself near Vatican City. I took time off to have a pleasant lunch at La Pilotta, a delightful little place almost across the street from the Plaza of Saint Peter and the obelisk that was my next stop.

Of course, I don't speak Latin or Italian, so my most recent language lessons were almost useless. I found I could get by with English and French, but my translation app was, once again, a lifesaver.

Hot Tourist Tip: For anyone with an adventurous nature, you can point at things on a foreign menu and smile. For anyone who actually wants to have some idea what to expect, *look it up.*

And that's all I'm going to say about lunch. That, and I ate it anyway

The stroll to the plaza was uneventful. There wasn't much of a crowd, possibly due to the freshening winter wind and the forecast for rain. I had some bad moments when I stepped gingerly into the plaza, one careful step at a time. My boots didn't smoke and I didn't feel anything untoward.

If I'd picked the places to rendezvous, the *Vatican* would not have made the list. I mean, seriously. What vampire picks the Catholic Holy City as a place to meet? A daredevil cat burglar with an impish sense of humor, that's who.

But it was early afternoon, in broad daylight. My divine displeasure detectors—my feet—failed to find any negative reaction from the holy ground. I was extremely pleased.

The obelisk was taller than I thought. I walked past a fountain, through a ring of stones, and right up to it. I had my magical senses peeled, looking for any signs Mary might have stopped by. There wasn't a spell to be seen, much less a magical message scrawled on the stonework.

Lounging around the top deck of the Eiffel Tower is one thing. Lounging around the obelisk is much easier. It's a public plaza, after all. I decided to wait a day or two, just to pick up a little Italian to go with my French and to test the holy ground phenomenon Mary once told me about.

After a sunset inside Twilight, I used my ring, climbed out, and walked back toward Vatican City. It was drizzling hard, almost worthy of being called rain, but I ignored this. I'm dead. I can do that. My only worry was it might ruin my makeup, but I had a long, hooded coat, thanks to my miracle cloak.

I headed north along the Piazza del Sant'uffizio, reached the cross street of Via Paolo, and almost finished crossing the street.

Ever had one of those moments when you think about doing something, then reconsider? You reach for the doorknob, start to open the box, make a fist to throw a punch, start to cut the red wire… and you pause because some little part of you is screaming so loudly you can't ignore it? Oh, you could ignore it, if you tried. Maybe you have, at some point in your life. And you went ahead and did the thing, discovering immediately how badly you needed to listen to that little voice.

My little voice was telling me not to take another step. Not one.

"Hold it," it said to me. "Don't move. Don't breathe. *Do not* put your foot down on that piece of pavement. Don't do it. It's a bad idea. It's a really bad idea. In fact, it may be the worst idea you've ever had in your long history of bad ideas. Listen to me. You're psychic. You can sense these things. Search your feelings. You know it to be true!"

So I stopped, mid-step, and looked stupid for several seconds while I windmilled my arms and tried desperately not to complete the movement. I didn't fall, but I did stagger back a pace. The important fact is I didn't actually cross the invisible line, wherever it was.

This seems unfair. I should be able to see something. A sparkle in the air, perhaps. A spiritual manifestation of some sort. A glowing, ghostly cross blocking my path. Something.

I waved a hand in front of me. Nothing. Maybe it was purely a ground-based thing? If I could fly, would I be safe? Could I play "The Floor Is Lava," somehow?

Since I didn't feel like testing any of this directly, I considered what to do. I couldn't cut my hand and fling blood inside the area. Blood refuses to leave me without elaborate preparations to force it. Maybe some skin? Or some hair?

I plucked a few hairs from my head, crouched down, leaned forward, held out my arm, and let them fall. The weather cooperated by not being too windy, and by providing a layer of water to keep the hair from actually catching fire. The strands sizzled briefly and puffed into smoke as they tried to burst into flame, though, and gave off a stench reminiscent of rotten eggs.

That was just a few strands of hair. What would happen if I put my foot down on holy ground?

Okay, safety tip. It would appear vampires are flammable when subjected to divine energies.

My curiosity was satisfied. Maybe I, personally, am more resistant to divine incineration than a few strands of hair. Maybe the Vatican—thank you *so* much, Mary! —is exceptionally inflammatory. But we've successfully established the presence of a divine restraining order, one which carries heavy penalties. Whatever diplomatic immunity applies in Rethven or Karvalen or wherever, the local deific forces are not members of the agreement. Maybe I'll try this some other time by poking a toe inside some minor church of some breakaway sect out in the middle of nowhere, but there is no way I'm going to walk into the Vatican at night.

I am going to have words with Mary, though.

I left the area at a fast walk, made a couple of corners, and hoped nobody witnessed my religious epiphany. The next-to-last thing I wanted to do was explain to a bunch of people in Rome why my body reacts badly to holy ground. The actual last thing might follow immediately after such an explanation.

Then it occurred to me… how many churches and former churches and shrines and chapels and so on does Rome have? Are there any sections of public streets which might still be regarded as "holy ground"? And was there a way to tell, short of stepping on the land mine?

I worked my way back to Twilight, carefully, slowly, always alert for that little voice inside to warn me the next step might be my last. Rather than stay for a day or two and take in the local atmosphere, the idea of leaving immediately—and swinging wide around Vatican City—struck me as the more prudent course.

Tuesday, December 22nd

Berlin has a very different feel to it than Paris or Rome. Paris makes me think of a work of art. Rome makes me feel as though I'm walking through the guts of a museum. Berlin makes me think of wheels and tracks, railroads, engines—machines. It's a clockwork city with everything ticking in time with everything else.

I'm starting to think all the major cities in Europe forbid manual traffic. I'm not complaining. I've got a huge truck and don't feel confident driving it in tight streets. But it's eerie to watch the cars around me create a hole just big enough for Twilight to slip through. I grew up with manual-drive vehicles, so watching the vehicular ballet around me never gets old.

Once Twilight found herself a parking spot—no mean feat for a human, but Google coordinated it—I walked the rest of the way. The museum Mary picked for a potential rendezvous or message drop was on Große Hamburger Street—more impish humor from the vampiress, obviously. I walked along, looking for the numbers on the buildings, and eventually found it.

It was a museum of magic. Of *course*.

I bought a ticket, adjusted Firebrand's carrying case, and wandered around. They had a number of artifacts from all around the world, many of which were esoteric enough to be interesting. I especially liked the eight-foot statue of Thoth. Oddly enough, there wasn't a single thing in the place with an actual magical aura. You'd think in a museum dedicated to the magical, they would have lucked into at least one actual artifact.

Then again, in a world where there really are magi, I'm sure they cruise the museums. Why dig in the desert for trinkets when you can endow a museum to dig for you? When they bring it back, you either tell them it's garbage or swipe it for your private collection. I wonder if the British Museum or the Smithsonian have anything real in their vaults. Come to think of it, maybe those museums are fronts for houses of magi. The vaults may be full of magical stuff.

I examined a relic purported to be from the Carpathian Mountains. It was a skull with elongated upper canines—fangs. The plaque claimed it a vampire skull. I doubted its authenticity, but I'm a cynic. On the other hand, it was a perfect spot to put a magical note, much like the one at the top of the Eiffel Tower.

I wandered around the museum a bit more, enjoying the artwork. A few of the exhibits struck me as possible magical items in the sense they could have been built that way, but were not actually enchanted. An amulet here, a mask there—these things had line and symbol arrangements conducive to holding a magical effect. It was almost tempting to lay spell-lines over these things and give them a charge, just to see what they might do. I resisted the impulse. Next year, maybe, if I was still alive.

Afterward, I headed next door to a local café to eat a late but enormous lunch. Across the street, I noticed a cemetery, apparently a Jewish memorial, which made me wonder about graveyards in general. If vampires can't stand holy ground, why are we expected to hang around in graveyards? Aren't people generally buried in consecrated earth? Or on church property? Or something?

How do we manage to be all grave-earthy and suchlike? Do we leap from headstone to headstone? Or are there more un-consecrated graveyards than I think? And just how do you un-consecrate a graveyard? Is there a ritual for it? Or do you get someone to commit a suitably-awful sin within the bounds of it? What would that be? Murder? Fornication? Theft of goods, or of bodies?

This is not purely intellectual curiosity, you understand.

I would have toured the Jewish memorial cemetery, but the gates were closed. I walked back to Twilight in a thoughtful frame of mind.

Someone busted the lock on the rear door while I was in the museum. The door was closed, but unlatched. I latched it from the outside and circled around to the cab to enter through the access hatch.

The would-be thief was still in there. The poor guy crammed himself into a forward corner of the cargo area, huddling as small as it was possible to get. Bronze stood in front of him, head lowered, nostrils aimed at his face. I could smell smoke. At a guess, she breathed fire at some point to demonstrate; her captive was unfried.

"Thief?" I asked. She agreed. I shook my head. Whoever he was, he wasn't having a good day. I crouched next to him.

"Do you speak French? English?"

"I speak French," he agreed, with a German accent.

"I'll give you a chance," I told him, slowly, choosing my words carefully. "If you tell the truth, you'll have the best possible chance. If you lie, no matter what the lie is, I guarantee things will go extremely poorly. Do you understand?"

"Yes."

"Take a minute," I advised. "Think about 'extremely poorly' and what it could mean. I'll wait."

He thought about it. Bronze snorted smoke. He made a sound and squeezed farther into the corner.

"I see you've thought about it. Now, do you want to find out what I consider 'extremely poorly,' or would you rather tell the truth?"

"Truth!" he squeaked.

"Did you break into my truck?"

"Yes."

"Why?"

"It's riding low so I knew you had stuff in here. I thought it was a moving truck, so you would have a whole house full of goods."

"And when you saw it was just a statue?"

"I was curious. I came in to look."

"And…?"

"There were bags on the statue."

"Ah. That explains it. You tried to take one, or open one, or something?"

"Yes."

Firebrand?

He's not lying, Boss. At this moment, I'm not sure he can. A lot of his brain is occupied with tracking Bronze's position and keeping his bowels clenched. Mostly on tracking Bronze's movements, so don't distract him too much or it'll smell bad in here.

"Fine," I said, aloud. "How much of a head start do you think would be fair? Two minutes? Five?"

"Could I have ten, please?"

I liked the fact he said "please." Polite criminals always get away with more, at least with me.

"I tell you what. You've been a very reasonable and polite thief. You've minded your manners—once you were caught—and nothing's been stolen. You owe me for the lock on the truck, though. If you've got twenty euros, I'll call it even and give you twenty minutes. Is that fair?"

"Yes, sir. Yes, it is."

I nodded to Bronze and she backed away all of twelve inches. Her captive rummaged in his pockets and came up with cash—actual coins! —to the tune of about eighteen euros. Close enough.

"Now, do you think you can find a safer profession?"

"I'm damn sure going to try!"

I believed him. I went out through the access hatch, around to the back, and opened the rear doors. Bronze politely moved aside for him. I beckoned him out and helped him down.

"You seem like a good kid," I told him. "Please try not to be a disappointment. Now run along."

He took it literally and sprinted away. I latched the doors, climbed into the cab, and told Twilight to stop by a hardware store.

Wednesday, December 23rd

Traveling to London was equally straightforward. I didn't expect to be able to drive across the Channel. I thought I'd have to wait for a ferry, or—worst case— leave Twilight behind while I took the train under the Channel.

Not so! There are two traffic tunnels under the Channel, now, in addition to a high-speed train tunnel. I didn't even have to swipe my digital money stick through a toll booth. Twilight notified me the tunnel toll was charged to my predeposit on the rental as we rolled merrily on.

Sometimes, technology is a wonderful thing.

London, if you're interested, was different from the other cities on my route. They all have their own character, and London is a labyrinth. It's a maze of twisty passages, all alike. Some identifying landmarks help, but most of the time you can't see them. Getting lost in London is like hunting for minotaurs. Without string. While drunk. I can find my way around inside my pet rock, but I have a supernatural advantage on my home ground. London—for me, anyway—is *not* user-friendly.

Thank you, Twilight, for knowing where you're going. Between you and Bronze, I stand a good chance of not wandering in the desert for forty years. I doubt anyone around here is going to send a pillar of fire and pillar of smoke to show me the way home.

Twilight negotiated with Google for a parking spot again. She found one reasonably close to the designated bar—excuse me, the "pub." It's a British thing. Twilight displayed walking directions for me—about half a block and around a corner. The place was an historic-looking four-storey building called "The Tea Party." Turns out it's not only a pub, but also a Victorian-themed hotel.

Okay, now, *this* was more like it!

The inside was even more lovely than the outside. The pub was done in dark woods and leaded windows, or good facsimiles. It had a few tables scattered around and a row of booths along one wall, out of the way. The bar itself looked antique. The hotel proper was quite cozy and the desk clerk as friendly as was consistent with being professional. I went for the full Victorian flavor in my room. It came with a four-poster bed, complete with curtains, and an antique (looking) bathroom—pardon me again. "Water closet." The works.

The Eiffel Tower was beautiful, but inconvenient. The Vatican was deadly. Berlin was humorous. But the pub Mary picked in London? It made up for everything else. I provisionally forgave her for her sense of humor.

I sank into the mattress and sighed contentedly. It almost felt like home. Right then, I decided to haunt the streets of London and live here until I had a darn good reason not to. Find me a place to park Bronze and I'll hang my swordbelts on the pegs just inside the door. So what if the pegs are for hats and coats? Gentlemen have swords.

I'd check with room service later. For now, it was time to sit in the pub and have a pint with my fish and chips.

I love this place. Bernie Spain Gardens is a small park a little way to the west. Once it got dark, Bronze climbed out of Twilight as we paused on a bordering street. Bronze found herself a spot she liked and stopped moving there. I spoofed a couple of security and traffic cameras while she was moving into position and I didn't see anyone in a position to watch. I think we got away with it. We'll see if people notice her as an addition to the park, and what they think of her. I think she's magnificent. So does she.

Twilight is no longer being charged to my account. I hope she's enjoying her new job, wherever it is.

As for me, I'm enjoying strolling around London in the dark December night. There's something about this city I really like. I can't put my finger on it. It's more than the language, or the twisty streets. Maybe it's the juxtaposition of old buildings and ultramodern ones—glass towers next to gothic ones, that sort of thing. It appeals to me. I wish it were a bit foggier, for the atmosphere, but I'm guessing the improved air quality over the past century or so has shot down the old reputation. Still, the river seems to throw up a bit of a cloud, so it's not all gone.

I like it. I think I may spend Christmas here.

Hmm. Christmas. What will I do for Christmas? Perhaps there will be some shopping for presents, if I can find a suitable orphanage.

No, on second thought, I have a better idea.

Thursday, December 24th

Looks like we'll have no snow on Christmas. Oh, well. I blame global warming.

Everything else is delightful. The food is good, the natives are friendly, and people seem to feel exceptionally festive.

Let me reiterate: *seem* to feel.

While I've been here, I've wandered the streets, seen the sights, bought some presents, enjoyed being a tourist, sampled the entertainments, and, inevitably, caught up on the news.

The East Coast of the United States is almost completely covered in strange, overlapping barriers of some unknown nature. They shimmer like the rainbow colors on soap bubbles, but the colors move and shift much more rapidly. They're not exactly opaque, but they do blur things inside rather badly. The walls of force go as far south as South Carolina, a trifle farther than Myrtle Beach. The northern edge, at least on the coast, gets most of Rhode Island and Massachusetts, narrowly missing Cape Cod Bay as it curves away from the coast. New Hampshire is almost entirely within the most-northern circle of the overlapping domes, and the group of them take a bite out of Canada, too—Montreal, Ottawa, and Toronto are all inside, as is most of Georgian Bay, all of Lake Ontario, Lake Erie, and the southeastern half of Lake Huron.

Internationally, it's considered a state of emergency for North America. Troops are mobilized, navies are parked outside the overlapping barriers, all the usual stuff you expect. Everywhere else, it's *the* topic of discussion. Opinions range from aliens to secret American government projects to conspiracies involving Them, whoever "Them" are.

About the only opinion I haven't heard is anything involving magical shenanigans. Maybe if I visit Ireland. You never know what they'll say the faerie court is up to.

Hmm. Is there a faerie court? We have vampires and magi in this world. For all I know, we have werewolves, faerie, and hidden civilizations in the hollow earth. I don't think I want to open that can of wyrms.

So, while a major international crisis is going on across the pond, I'm enjoying Christmas in London. I think it's a denial thing, pretending everything is happy and festive. Even the criminal classes seem to have the holiday spirit. No matter what neighborhoods I stroll through, I haven't been mugged *once!* I think there's something very wrong with a civilization when a common criminal doesn't dare show his face. Maybe they were all at home, sipping eggnog and munching on Santa's cookies.

In accordance with the abundance of the Yuletide spirit, I decided to play Father Christmas for a bit. A red suit, a funny hat, and a sack were, strangely enough, easy to come by. I thought I'd have a hard time finding them, but I found a fat man snoring in a park and smelling suspiciously like a drunk. He was much more comfortable in the nice, warm police car. Of course, he was also in his underwear, but that's my fault.

Yeah, I could have drunk his blood. I'm going to say I don't care for the taste of drunk.

After little touch-up mending and an intense cleaning, I had my costume. With some purchased presents stuffed in a sack, I went off to visit children's wards in the local hospitals. Every time, staff would stop me to ask what I was doing. For answer, I opened the sack and showed them old-fashioned coloring books—real ones, made of paper, which are actually harder to find than you'd think in this ultramodern digital age—along with small boxes of crayons and the odd stuffed animal toy.

"Why don't you come by during visiting hours?"

"Father Christmas shows up overnight. This night."

"They won't see you in that outfit. And you don't have the beard."

"They're not supposed to see me. That's the point. But if I do accidentally wake someone, they'll see Father Christmas, not some stranger leaving gifts. Just leave the lights off."

They didn't all like the idea, and they always had a male nurse, orderly, or security guard accompany me. Nobody actually refused, though.

I gave out presents, silently, and ran tendrils through every kid I could find in Oncology. Today's cancer treatments are pretty good, I hear. Combined with a creature of darkness who sucks the life right out of a tumor, or several tumors, I imagine modern therapies are *amazingly* effective.

Why? Because I can. Because I want to. I don't need a better reason, do I?

Friday, January 1st, 2049

Happy New Year!

Last night there was a lovely party—several, in fact—and I wandered from festivity to festivity. It's easy. Listen closely for the sounds of laughter and music and bring something to drink. I'm not sure if Brits are always so easy-going or if world tensions and bringing a bottle worked together to make them so. Whatever the reason, I vitality-surfed through the evening and made it back to my rooms at The Tea Party before dawn.

After breakfast—I wasn't alone in the hotel's restaurant-bar, but I was the only one feeling bright-eyed and bushy-tailed—I looked into finding gambling establishments in London. If I was going to stay here for any length of time, I was going to need a source of income. London is many things, but cheap is not one of them.

Where the hell is Mary? I'm starting to get worried.

Anyway, London has a number of high-end establishments for loosening wealth from the wealthy. There are even more low-end establishments that want to avoid official notice. I don't really enjoy gambling, as such, but spending an afternoon in the equivalent of a gentleman's club with a casino room—nothing loud or raucous—is a pleasant way to kill a day and practice being subtly telekinetic. Later, after dark, spending the evening with people who try to kill me for winning—afterward, when I'm alone—is pleasant on a whole different level.

I'm trying to avoid doing too much of that. Again, I'm being incognito, or trying to, but a vampire's got to eat.

Tuesday, January 5th

Mary arrived today. I was having an early high tea—sunset happens so early this time of year! —when she walked into the place. Her hair was a dark auburn and done in tumbling curls, cascading from beneath a beret-like cap. She looked around the room, pretended not to recognize me, and slinked in a sexy vixen way over to the bar. Underneath her overcoat, her outfit was an off-the-shoulder dress in a dark green, and short enough to make me wonder how women avoid freezing to death.

Wow.

I hurried through the remainder of my meal while she attracted the attention of every man in the room and several of the women—not all of whom were angry at her for attracting the attention of the men. She politely brushed off a couple of younger gentlemen, both of whom were gentlemanly enough to accept a polite brush-off. I signaled the waiter, bought her a drink from afar, and continued wolfing down my meal.

The sound of her sliding into my booth was the same sound as every eye in the room swiveling to follow her.

"I thought I should thank you for the drink," she purred, lacing her fingers together and resting her chin on their back. Her accent was thoroughly British.

"You're very welcome, Ma'am," I replied, adding a bit of an American southern drawl to my voice.

"Oh, you're not from here!"

"Yes, Ma'am. I'm from across the pond."

"How delightful! Do you suppose you could tell me about the Colonies? I've always wanted to visit, but it seems so huge. Where does one go to really understand the country?"

"That's a long story. Can I get you something to eat?"

"No, thank you. I have a dinner engagement this evening. But I'd be delighted at your company, if you'd care to join me."

"It would be my pleasure, Ma'am."

I followed her out of the pub area and up the stairs.

"Your room or mine?" she asked. I shrugged. She led me to hers, a much less Victorian, much more modern suite. She kicked off her heels and settled on a chair with a relieved sound.

"Busy day?" I asked.

"Not really. Heels aren't my favorite shoes, and these aren't yet broken in," she explained, massaging one foot. I examined a shoe, worked it a bit with my hands and a trace of magical power, decided it would do, and repeated the performance on the other shoe.

"They'll break in quickly," I assured her, taking over the foot massage. "So, how did it go?"

"Visiting? Or yachting?"

"Let's start with the visiting."

"I started with the Etiennes. They're nice people, if a bit jumpy about visiting vampires. A bit jumpy in general, I think, due to your unfriend Johann and his magical domes of power. I'm not sure I'd have gotten out of there if it wasn't for your letter and lack of presence."

"*Lack* of presence?"

"If I didn't report back, you would show up to ask their corpses searching questions. I had to mention the Mendoza incident."

"I'm sorry you had to bring that up." And I was sorry. It's not a memory I treasure.

"Not to worry," she assured me. "I took great care to be polite and they were very formal with me. I suspect I could go back and be welcomed as a messenger, although maybe never as a guest. I've proved I know how to behave, at least, so I won't get shot on sight."

"The letter of apology they sent seemed to indicate they have a strong streak of ethical behavior, possibly outright honor."

"I'd say so. I asked them about Johann and all that. They're not taking you up on any offers. They'd rather batten down the hatches and wait until the matter resolves into something clearer. They can't see through the magical shields, so all they know is it's a collection of big bubbles—and more power than everyone else in the world combined can field."

"They're determined to wait and see."

"Yes. I get the impression, though, they've either tried something or heard about someone who did. Little things—glances between themselves, the way they phrased things, stuff like that."

"Oh?"

"I think someone attracted demigod-magi attention and was vaporized, or incinerated, or just plain killed. To make a point, probably, but it was certainly a success. The Etiennes aren't exactly hiding, but it's the next best thing."

I sighed and switched feet.

"They did relay the message to other families for me," she went on, wiggling her toes. "I've got an online message box they can talk to and a number where I can reach them. So far, the answers have ranged from horrified appeals to leave him alone to outright laughter at the idea. Nobody else is willing to do anything against Johann and family, not with the kind of power at their disposal. I have no doubt they'll salvage anything they can, though, from the wreckage. They strike me as magical scavengers, not as actual magicians."

"They've lived with that attitude for generations," I realized. "I shouldn't be surprised."

"I guess. Recruiting help doesn't seem to have gone too well. But the yacht was no trouble."

"Really?"

"Yes. It's an older boat, from the thirties, when historical styling was in fashion. Its general pattern is styled after some ship called the *Sirius*, but it's strictly modern. Two sidewheels, diesel-electric power, a hydrojet engine for tricky bits, even a mast and sails. You'll like it."

"Sidewheels? You mean it's an old paddlewheel steamer?"

"Oh, yes, but not an actual steam-engine steamer. The paddlewheels work; they're actually the main propulsion. The diesel-electric setup runs them, but you can pull a lever and the paddles all tilt to reduce drag and the hydrojet takes over. Looks pretty when it's chugging along, though."

"I look forward to seeing it. I hope it wasn't too hard to come by."

"Not at all. I've been in Campione and Monaco, looking for money and rich men. I wasn't sure if I could win a yacht at a poker table, so I focused mostly on either stealing from casinos or from people with far too much money. Turns out a hot redhead can be a distraction at a no-limits poker game, and I *did* win us a yacht." Mary pouted. "Now I have all this money I don't need."

"Cry me a river of hemoglobin."

"I suppose we could get cash and one of the bigger inflatable pools."

"What for?"

"To fill the pool with the cash and roll around naked in all the money."

"Seriously? How much money are we talking about?"

"Well, it sure won't fit in singles. Maybe if we get it all in hundreds and get a really *big* inflatable pool. We want room for us, too." She shrugged. "A couple million."

"I have no idea how to respond to that."

"How about a nice expression of thanks?"

"The foot massage doesn't count?"

"You have a good point," she agreed, wiggling her toes some more.

"I thought so. But we're not rolling around in money. Paper cuts galore."

"We'll do it at night."

"It still seems like it would be painful."

"I want to try it."

"Fine. Once we're on the boat."

"Good. Meanwhile, stop rubbing my feet and rub something else. I've missed you."

After sunset and a shower, we went down to the river. Mary had the motor launch at the equivalent of a floating parking lot while the yacht was anchored farther out.

"You just left it out there?" I asked, as she fired up the engine and gunned the small launch downriver.

"No. It comes with crew and some staff. There's always someone aboard."

"That could be problematic. I have things to do and human witnesses could be trouble."

"There's a solution for that," she pointed out.

"I'd rather not."

"We could run the ship ourselves, I suppose, but if anything goes wrong—or if you want to use the sails—we need expert help. I can probably sail it, with your help, but I'm not qualified to captain a ship."

"Fair point. I guess we're bringing the crew."

I held on for the rest of the trip out to the yacht. I don't like boats and this one was only a four-seater. I count for three, at least.

The yacht was considerably larger than the launch, as it should be. The launch was something you could load on a trailer and take to the lake. The yacht— named the *Silver Princess*, for some reason—was a hundred and seventy feet of heavy steel construction. We pulled in behind her and Mary slid the launch into a submerged cradle. Powered systems lifted it out of the water and locked it in place. We boarded the *Silver Princess* to a pipe-whistle-thing and some saluting. Mary traded some commentary with the guy in the fancy hat before taking me on her little tour of the boat.

The top deck of the superstructure was a glass cockpit-style bridge, with social and recreational decks below it. The yacht had a kitchen, bathrooms, music room, theater, lounge, all the things you'd find in a luxurious house, but laid out oddly due to the shape constraints. The lower decks held most of the more standard operational guts, as well as the master suite, guest rooms, and crew quarters.

I wasn't too concerned with the luxury accommodations. The cruising range and cargo were more important. Between the solar panels up top and full tanks, the typical cruising range was over six thousand miles. After a discussion with Captain Tillard, he assured me we could more than double it by adding fuel drums to the cargo hold and using them to top up the regular fuel tanks.

Of course, if we didn't use the engines—if we used the forward mast for sailing and ran the hydrojet off solar power—our cruising range was limited only by our food stores. I didn't get into that. His idea of food stores and my fear about food stores were very different things.

He needed at least two days to bring the yacht in, have it serviced and refueled, handle all the paperwork and legalese, and deal with the general bureaucracy of owning a giant boat. That suited me. I wanted some specialized equipment brought on board.

"Such as?" he asked.

"I'm going to need about five miles of corrosion-proof cable for lifting things off the sea floor, a winch to handle it, a scuba setup, a few cases of underwater flares, some sort of signaling arrangement from seafloor to surface, a couple of high-density plastic drums, a webbing harness for the drums—like a fitted basket for one—and a year's worth of concentrated rations to go with the usual groceries. Oh, and I'll need space in the hold for special cargo. A somewhat oversized statue of a horse."

Captain Tillard's aplomb was completely unshaken by any of this. Weird equipment? Fine. Eccentric requests? Okay. Totally unreasonable luggage? Ho-hum. It's as though he was used to dealing with rich weirdos with strange desires. He simply wrote all of it down and shouted for Williams. Williams turned out to be an older man in a sailor suit, complete with bandanna around the neck and bib arrangement over his upper back. Williams took the list, saluted smartly, and hurried off.

"Just out of curiosity," I began, "did the former owner insist on the sailor suits?"

"Yes, sir. They're period for the mid-eighteen-hundreds, when sidewheelers were in use."

"I see. How about we make the uniform requirements Captain's discretion?"

"Thank you very much, sir. I'll see to it. Will there be anything else?"

"No, I don't think so. Carry on. No, wait; I just thought of something. We have a boat for shuttling back and forth to shore. Do we have an aerial vehicle?"

"No, sir. We do not."

"Do we have somewhere we could park one?" I asked. He walked forward with me and pointed out a stretch of deck.

"We'll want it as low as we can get it, for center of gravity reasons. If you don't mind losing a lot of open deck space, we can put something about here... A helicopter, perhaps, if we can crane it in. Even if we temporarily clear all the support cables and unship the forward mast, I wouldn't risk landing it so near the superstructure. It'll be tricky to lift off in anything but dead calm weather. This is the best we can do, I'm afraid."

"Hmm. I'm not sure I want a full-sized helicopter. I'll think about it some more."

"Just as you say, sir. Shall I begin preparations?"

"Yes, please," I told him. He glanced at Mary and she nodded.

"Whatever he wants," she added. "It's his trip."

"As you wish. May I ask how long a trip, and where we are headed?"

"I'm not sure how long it will take, but we're going to visit a number of coordinates, examine the sea floor, and move on to the next. Mostly in the Atlantic, but there's a possibility we'll round Cape Horn and hit the Pacific, too."

"Might we go through Panama, sir?"

"Oh. Yes. That would be quicker, wouldn't it?"

"Yes, sir."

"I'll get a map and some coordinates for you. I obviously don't know the first thing about running a ship, so you can do the heavy lifting on reaching all the points in the minimum time. How's that sound?"

"Perfectly fair, sir."

"Excellent. And if I'm being unreasonable or silly, please tell me so. I will happily defer to your experience, Captain."

"I'm pleased to hear it, sir. You'd be surprised how many owners say 'Do this,' and have no idea what the order involves."

"I have a feeling I'll be more 'Can we do this?' instead."

"*Very* good, sir."

Mary and I went below to inspect the master suite. She admitted to replacing the entirety of the linens, but the décor still had a decidedly Old West flavor to it. Not my first choice, but not bad. I wasn't too fond of the various heads looking at us from around the room, though. The paintings of cowboy life were kind of nice. Impressionist stuff, suitable for something seen in the background of your vision.

"You wanted something for flying?" she asked, while we snuggled on the bed.

"Yes. Something I can drive, preferably."

"There's an Italian company that makes a sort of heli-bike, if that's what you're after. They call it a skycycle."

"A flying motorcycle?"

"More like a four-rotor drone, but scaled up to carry a rider and passenger, like on a motorcycle."

"It might get off the ground with me, then. Are they hard to drive?"

"I don't know. I've never flown one. Want to try it? Italy isn't too far away. We can be there and back before Walt has the ship ready."

"Walt?"

"Walter Tillard, the Captain."

"You call him 'Walt'?"

"He's a nice man. I like him."

"Fair enough, I guess. What do we do to get to Italy in a hurry?"

"Call a cab."

It still never fails to stun me how efficient a computerized traffic system can be. Even better, Europe doesn't inflict speed limits on any autopilot vehicles. Google self-regulates based on the equipment and the traffic. Europe also allows a traffic priority system where a user can pay an additional fee and be routed as quickly as possible to a destination.

Mary called ahead for an appointment while en route. The rest of the time we spent catching up. Since her time was much shorter than mine, she had less to tell. I spent quite a while explaining who, what, where, how, and why.

She had a few questions.

"So, who killed all the children in Carrillon? And who killed Thomen?"

"I'm not sure, but Bob is investigating."

"Do you have any suspicions?"

"Of course. I suspect one or both of the twins—Malana or Malena or both— killed Thomen. That's just my gut reaction, of course, based on Kammen's description. It may be someone within the Guild of Wizards decided to eviscerate Thomen to open up some space at the top. It might be unrelated to me, entirely— I'm not the center of the Karvalen universe, merely a powerful piece on the board. Less so, now, I hope. To be frank, I don't really care who killed Thomen. Kammen says he's dead, and Kammen knows dead when he sees it. I'm happy."

"And the hundred dead babies?"

"I care about it, but I can't *do* anything about it. I have to know who to blame before I can remove their lungs. Bob's supposed to find out."

"He'll turn them over to this new justice council thing?"

"I... hmm. I don't remember if I told him to deal with it himself or give it to Lissette. Either way, it'll be handled. As much as I'd like to settle the account personally, I'll settle for clearing it."

"Okay. And Tort?"

"I already told you about her."

"I know you don't want to talk about it, but just hear me out, okay?"

"All right."

"You say she's dead, but not exactly dead?"

"Yes. It's complicated."

"Only you could make dead or not dead complicated."

"Hey, nobody asked me if I wanted to be an undead fiend of the night."

Mary took my arm, put it around her shoulders, and squeezed up against me.

"I know. And I know Tort means a lot to you, no matter what I have to think to feel... safe, I guess. So uncomplicate it for me."

"Tort expended... or used... or something... the part of her which makes her... hmm."

"Never mind the occult details. I don't even have my degree in magic, yet. Just tell me what she did."

"What Tort did was use herself and everything connected to her through her age-distribution spells. All those animal spirits and plant spirits and whatever else she had on tap. These augmented her own… I guess I have to call it a soul, but I'm starting to suspect there's more to a soul than a coherent energy pattern."

"Postgraduate occult stuff. Move on."

"Right. So, she used her own soul and all her additions to build a receptacle to contain the Demon King. This should have drained all the life out of her—vitality and soul, everything—but she managed to keep just enough to survive. I think her plan was to *nearly* die, then recover. Since it's never been done before, she couldn't have known how drastic the damage would be. She turned into a withered old crone practically overnight."

"Gruesome, but you can fix her, right?"

"Yes, but that's not the worst of it. By expending her own soul—whatever that is—she barely had a spark of existence left."

"Hold on. Does draining the soul out of someone age them?"

"I don't think so. I think her age may have had something to do with the auxiliary powers she was linked into, especially the anti-aging spells. By pulling power back through them, she might have sucked up a lot of age from other sources along with their spiritual energy. Tort was, chronologically, about a hundred years old, anyway; that might have had something to do with it, too. I'm guessing, though. Everyone I've ever yanked the soul out of dies fairly quickly. The body usually keeps ticking for a while, but never for very long. They simply may not have time to wither away, but I suppose it's possible."

"And Tort, keeping a tiny spark of her soul, managed to keep a tiny spark of life in her ancient body?"

"Exactly. But she operated, mostly, like a computer—a highly complex one, but still a dumb one, not a fully self-aware machine. Her brain recalled memories, clicked to the appropriate response, and performed actions based on her memories. She lacked… oh, not a critical faculty, but a creative one. She could make decisions just fine, carry out plans, perform her tasks, and so on. But coming up with a new idea, a different way of thinking was impossible. Well, almost. She did have a faint trace of that ability left, but for all practical purposes she was a machine running Tort's personality simulation program."

"And if you ever die during the day, your soul goes wherever souls go, right?"

"Right. Or so I assume."

"And when you get up at night, you'll be an uncreative, robot-like automaton?"

"Not exactly. From my experiments with soulless undead minions, I should still act a lot like me. I've been undead long enough my Memorex should be almost indistinguishable from the live version. The real key to telling the difference is the way I'll approach problems. I believe I'll be grindingly thorough, but lack my little spark of inspiration."

"So when I ask you how we should handle, oh, a squad of hitmen coming down the hotel hallway?"

"I'd probably say we should simply walk out, take the bullets, and use their blood to heal the damage."

"As opposed to…?"

"Do we have a fire escape? Can we jump to the ground from here? Can we climb to the roof? What are the walls made of and can we go through them with relative quiet? Or can we go down a floor to get below and behind them? Are they equipped with night vision? Can we blind them temporarily with bright light or with pitch dark? Is calling the police or hotel security an option? Do we have—"

"You can stop now."

"But you see the difference?"

"Yes. You'll be boring."

"I'd say you've summed it up nicely," I agreed.

"So Tort was old and boring?"

"Essentially... I suppose. Within the context of this discussion, yes."

"And you can't get her back from the ball?"

"No, I can't. The energy involved isn't actually her anymore."

"So, your godlike thing—what did you call it?"

"*Simulata.*"

"Right. This *simulata* of you has her spark of soul and is planning to reincarnate her."

"Yes."

"When will this happen?"

"No idea. He hasn't done reincarnation before and he didn't have a lot to work with."

"But you're definitely getting your Tort back?"

"No. I'm definitely going to be meeting her reincarnation. Whoever she is, she won't be Tort. She'll be a reborn Tort. So, technically, yes, but at the same time, no. At least, that was my take-away from the discussion."

"Hmm."

"Is that a problem?"

"I don't know. Not yet, certainly. But I'm a little jealous, maybe."

"Of Tort?"

"This seems like a lot of effort on your part."

"I'm willing to go to a lot of effort for people I love."

"I see." She squeezed me a little harder, then let go. She leaned on the armrest by the window and watched a couple of countries go by. I wished for a quantum computer upgrade in my brain.

Something about that conversation didn't go well. I didn't know what to say. Obviously, I said something wrong. Did she object to me seeing a reincarnated Tort? What else could it be?

"Mary?

"Hmm?"

"What did I say?"

"Nothing."

Alarm bells went off in my head. That's a code phrase for *You know what you did.*

"Yes, I did," I argued, despite the warnings. "I said something that offended or upset you. Maybe it was the way I said it. Maybe I communicated my idea badly. But I swear to you, I don't know what you're upset about or why."

"I'm fine."

Uh-oh.

"Do you recall, not so very long ago, when we discussed our relationship?" I asked. "In Zirafel, if I remember rightly. You were telling me how Tort was a pet and you needed to think of her that way?"

"Yes."

"We were talking directly about how we feel. There wasn't any of this beating around the bush and the whole man-woman passive-aggressive psychodrama. Someday, a thousand years from now, I'll master the art of understanding what you think and feel without using magic. For now, though, I desperately need you to talk to me. Please?"

One of the drawbacks to a robot cab is the lack of anything to do. In a regular car, I could pretend to pay close attention to the road or something. Here, all I could do was wait. And fidget. I'm a killer fidgeter.

"You did tell me," I added, "not to ignore you. You made me promise, remember? You're important to me, and while my first impulse is to respect your silence, you told me not to."

"You know," Mary said, finally, "you have all the tact of an anvil."

"Blunt instrument?" I guessed.

"I was thinking 'dense.'"

"I can see that," I agreed.

"You keep telling me how you love Tort."

"Yes," I acknowledged. She clenched her fists, but her voice remained level.

"I have a problem with that."

"Why? I love you, too."

It's amazing how loud an electric car can be. Maybe it's only by contrast with silence.

"I..." she began, and stopped. "How can you say that?"

"I don't like to lie."

"But how do you *know*?"

"Because I'm getting better at understanding those pesky *feelings*. They keep cropping up in my life. I figured I better start paying some attention to them."

"Ever since you realized you suck at relationships?"

"No, after that. When I realized how important our relationship is to me." She started to say something, but I held up a hand. "No, wait. Please. It's my turn to talk about how I feel, and I'm likely to fumble this like a greased football. So listen until the end, okay?"

"I'll try."

"It took me a while to recognize I loved Tort—most of her life, in fact. It's a strange thing, this loving someone. We do it without realizing it. Loving someone doesn't mean the same thing to everyone, though. There are lots of kinds of love, I guess. But when I say it, I mean I care deeply about the welfare and happiness of the person. It usually means I want to be around her, too, because it makes me happy to see her happy, and it makes me happy to feel useful by fixing whatever makes her unhappy.

"It does not mean I want to... get married? Be a good husband? Commit to being the One True Love of someone? I don't know how to describe it. What I'm trying to say is, when I love someone, I'm already committed. I may not have a way to express it in words—there's no oath, no ceremony, no ritual to use—but I'm as close to a permanent fixture in your life as I can be. If you need me to be with you while you rob a bank, or if you need me to leave you alone for a century, those are the things that matter to me.

"It's true I love Tort. I also love Sasha, Shada, Kammen, Torvil, Seldar, Lissette, Kelvin, Raeth, Travis, and others. There's a longish list of people I give a damn about, but a relatively short list of people I'll break inter-universal barriers for. And an even shorter list of people I'll actively try to spend time with. I know that sounds awful, but I don't mean it to.

"I guess what I'm saying is I'm here for you. And, being immortal, I can't promise I won't come across other people I care deeply about, even learn to love. But I do plan to be here for you in whatever capacity you need or want me, forever. I have spoken."

There followed a profound silence while she digested that. I worked on understanding it, myself. I didn't know some of that until I actually said it.

"About your pet Tort," Mary began, and stopped.

"Yes?"

"I'm sorry about your pet," she told me, sadly.

"So am I," I agreed.

"I think you should get a new one."

"Oh?"

"Yes." She scooted closer to me and took my arm. "Not right now. Maybe in a few years." I didn't answer, and she continued. "We can check with the Temple of Shadow. They might be able to put you in touch with someone."

"Ah!" I exclaimed, finally getting it. "Yes. Yes, I like the idea. We can definitely do that."

"But you owe me a bank job."

"What do you mean by 'bank job'?"

"I mean a bank robbery. You and me."

"Oh, I see! All right. Just one?"

"I'm greedy in other ways."

Wednesday, January 6th

Avanti Air is an Italian company based in Florence. They build personal aircraft. Not the custom, luxury jets of the wealthy, but *personal* aircraft—one and two-seat things. They have a one-man mini-jet, a personal helicopter, an air-motorcycle, and other expensive toys. They also make a "backpack" version of a personal helicopter—counter-rotating blades and a backpack-mounted motor—and a jet pack, both of which have terrible endurance but are reputed to be a lot of fun. So says the company brochure.

The "motorcycle" came in two models, the personal and tandem versions. I was only interested in the two-seater due to weight problems. The mockups on the showroom floor weren't functional, but they gave me a good feel for whether or not I wanted to try one. Some things you don't want to buy online.

The thing was arranged with a driver's position and a tandem rear seat, just like a motorcycle. The controls were very similar, as well, with some basic instruments in the center and an augmented reality helmet for the rest. The four lift fans tilted to provide lift or thrust, and it had a cruising range of nearly five hundred miles. The optional windscreen came highly recommended. The top speed was a trifle over two hundred miles per hour.

I also bought the optional parachute because I'm overcautious. The parachute wouldn't work as well for me, but it was better than nothing. In the same way, carrying nearly five hundred pounds of me, the vehicle would cruise slightly slower and not quite as far, but it was enough to get me where I needed to go.

Naturally, they didn't have one simply lying around to be bought. Their factory had a new one coming out shortly, though, and I paid extra for it—another reason we visited. It's hard to bribe someone over the cybernet. The salesman agreed to have it delivered somewhere our yacht could make port, someplace named Livorno. I felt confident the Captain could find the port for me.

Mary and I promptly thanked him, paid him, got back into a cab, and returned to London. This time, we did have to stop to dodge the sunset—in Dijon, as it happens—before finishing the last leg of the trip.

We walked around London for a bit while I enjoyed the nighttime atmosphere. Mary held my arm and kept looking around.

"Problem?" I asked.

"I keep wondering when someone's going to demand your wallet."

"London seems surprisingly civilized."

"Probably all the surveillance cameras," she muttered.

"They do take their domestic security seriously." Privately, I wondered what the cameras were seeing. If I don't show up on camera at night, was Mary staggering drunkenly? How did that look? Of course, it's not a crime to practice a mime routine or simply walk funny—there's a Ministry of Silly Walks, as I recall—but would it trigger any supernatural suspicions? Probably not immediately, I decided, but it was good we were planning to leave.

We went through the park to say hello to Bronze. Mary scratched along Bronze's jaw with her fingernails. Bronze let me know a number of people were interested in her, many of them adults. A lot of cameras were involved. I assured her she wouldn't be in the park much longer. She didn't mind at all. Children played around her and kept trying to climb her. A few team efforts succeeded, which amused her.

We finally returned to The Tea Party and my room. Mary chuckled at the Victorian décor.

"Missing the cavern and your waterfall?" she asked.

"Not especially. I'm slowly getting used to the modern conveniences, taking it an era at a time."

"Fair enough. Say, do you think I can visit your super-technology world, sometime?"

"Super-technology world?"

"The post-apocalyptic thing you were telling me about. With the ants," she added. I shuddered.

"Ah. That one. After Johann is pulped and splattered over a wide area, sure."

"About that." She settled herself in one of the throne-like chairs. "We probably need to talk about that."

"What's to talk about?"

"You have a plan?"

"Of course. I've been thinking about it ever since I escaped. I've had several plans, most of which won't work. I think I'm closing in on a workable one, though."

"Good! So tell me all about it."

"I'm going to rip his intestines out and strangle him with them."

Mary blinked at me. Her face was otherwise completely neutral. Her posture altered slightly, however, as though prepared to leap out the window and run for it.

Boss?

Hmm?

Calm voice, please.

I sound angry?

Yeeeees... I suppose angry is one way to put it. You're not doing the weird, creepy voice thing, but you do sound, uh, borderline.

Sorry.

"Sorry," I repeated, aloud, for Mary. "I'm still edgy about him. It's hard to talk about it without sounding..."

"Lethal? Pissed off? Mildly demonic?" she suggested.

"Sorry," I repeated. "It's just... The man has to die. Preferably his whole family."

"I think that's the first time I've ever heard you threaten someone's family."

"Probably. And I don't mean it. Not his *whole* family. Just the ones who actively participated."

"Are you sure?"

"Am I sure about what?"

"That you don't mean it." Mary crossed and uncrossed her legs. "What I mean to say is you seem much more... I don't want to say grumpy, but it might be the word."

"It's been some time since Johann had me in his clutches. While he did, I was tortured, deceived, used, abused, and *hurt*. I don't mean he caused me pain, although he did. He used me to do things I find reprehensible. He used me to kill children. He deliberately and purposefully used me to kill children *I personally knew*. He's done more than hurt me. He's *wounded* me, and I'm not so sure it will ever really heal. I've had time to let it cool—this isn't me just reacting. This is me having thought about it and partially recovered from it—possibly as much as I'll ever recover from it. And, having recovered and taken time to think about what I want, I've made a decision.

"I'm going to kill him. I'm going to rip what's left of his soul out of him and grind it into dust. If I can kill him slowly, I'll kill him slowly. But of the utmost priority is I kill him surely, finally, and permanently!"

Mary licked her lips and glanced at the door.

"What?" I asked, and turned to look. It was closed. There was nothing unusual about it.

"Nothing," Mary said. "I was just debating whether to run for the door or try and tackle you to the bed."

"Am I being frightening again? Is my shadow doing weird things?" I looked. It was looming on the wall, bat-winged and demonic. The depth of it was startling; the shadow was a dark place, even to my nighttime eyes.

"Yes," Mary purred. "Yes, it is, and you most certainly are."

I tried to relax. My shadow diminished, lightened, faded, turned more mundane.

"I apologize. I've… been… suppressing a lot of… It's been hard to not… this thing with Johann is…"

"I understand. Sort of. It's a thing, eating at you, and you've been trying to ignore it."

"Yes."

"Then think about something else. Focus on something so completely it blots out everything else." She smiled, lazily, impishly. "Do you think you can avoid breaking the furniture?"

"It's nighttime. I can't do the sexual calisthenics."

"Is there a lot of movement involved in playing my nervous system like a musical instrument?"

"I'm barely past 'Chopsticks.'"

Mary stood up, lifted her hair, unzipped.

"You know how to get to Carnegie Hall?" she asked, wiggling out of the dress.

Thursday, January 7th

Loading most of the cargo was easy enough. The yacht docked in London and people hoisted cargo aboard.

Loading Bronze was a trifle more involved. Rather than parade her through the streets, the *Princess* paddled grandly up the Thames on the high tide and pulled up at the end of a pier. It was a straight shot from the Gardens, down the pier, and onto the ship, which only left the question of how to get Bronze from the park to the pier without undue notice. I didn't want a major news channel to report it internationally and possibly get Johann's attention. "Giant statue comes to life. Boards private yacht." No, thank you.

A handheld radio controller of the sort used for toy airplanes helped. Mary pretended to drive and Bronze demonstrated her robot-like gait, complete with metallic sounds of her hooves on pavement. People noticed, but I doubted it would go viral. Fifty years ago, or even twenty years ago, she would have been a sensational robot. Now, here, in this world? Eh. What's one more robot?

I, like a good mastermind, waited on the yacht for my minions to complete this phase of my plan.

We chugged out of London and splashed for Livorno, Italy. I worked with the Captain to provide him with the latitude and longitude of major nexus points in the Atlantic. Rather than demonstrate to him my insanity—or magical powers—I took a printed map into the master bedroom, did some scrying, and came back with points marked. He looked it over, spent some time on the ship's navigation computer, and told me we could hit all nine points in about twenty-four days.

"Exclusive of any time you wish to spend on station, of course," he added.

"Twenty-four days?"

"The shortest practical route is a little over eight thousand, three hundred miles. The *Princess* pulls about twelve knots—excuse me, fourteen miles per hour. That's using the sidewheels, of course. We can also run the hydrojet if you're in a hurry, but it cuts down our cruising range. The two systems aren't meant to be used together."

"How much time would that save?"

"About three days, but we'll end almost out of fuel. We'll need to make port at Abaco Beach to refuel—it's only about twenty miles of travel from the last point you want to explore."

"And all this assumes we don't catch a favorable wind?"

Captain Tillard blinked at me for a moment. He licked his lips, stroked the short beard he wore, and obviously chose his words with great care.

"Sir, I understand you aren't a nautical man. Is that true?"

"Yes, Captain, it is."

"Is it also fair to say you are not experienced in operating a ship?"

"I can agree with you on that, no problem."

"Then, if I may make a suggestion?"

"Yes, sir?"

"Perhaps I could see to the handling of the ship. I'll get you where you want to go as quickly as the *Princess* can get you there. Is that arrangement to your liking?"

"Yes, sir."

"Very good." He checked the bridge instruments and seemed satisfied. "We'll take on fuel when we reach port in Italy, while we're taking your flying thing aboard. Is there anything else I should know?"

"No, sir, and thank you very much."

"That will be all."

I slunk off his bridge and resolved to not poke my nose into it again.

Mary, meanwhile, was down in the master suite. I came in and saw she'd unpacked my stuff—that is, Firebrand and my other sword were hung on hooks. There were also more clothes than I thought I had. I examined a suit jacket and raised an eyebrow at her. She swept curly hair over one shoulder and grinned around a mouthful of pearly-white teeth at me.

"You don't expect to sit down for dinner in an old bathrobe and carpet slippers, do you?"

"I hadn't given it much thought," I admitted.

"You're on a yacht. There's a crew. There's staff. People don't exactly come with a yacht, but you have to have them. I kept the contracts from the previous owner. The cook isn't a cordon-bleu chef, but he's very good, especially with seafood. The two valets aren't waiters—more all-around servants than specialists—but they'll handle the business of fetching drinks, turning down beds, and so on. Ludmilla is my ladies' maid, but she also handles laundry and general cleaning. This is a luxurious floating house and it has to have a staff."

"I liked the Ardent place," I muttered. Mary hit me with a cushion.

"You said to get a yacht!" she laughed.

"I didn't know it came with people!"

"What, you thought it was just a Google Cab on the water?"

"No! Yes. Maybe. Sort of?"

"You *really* don't do well with boats, do you?"

"I vividly recall going down with the ship at least once."

"Hmm. Maybe I should keep one of those emergency life harnesses handy."

"Maybe you should. Have you given any thought to how we'll cope if the ship sinks? I'll sink like a lead brick, but you might float. If you float, what happens when the sun does one of those rising or setting things?" I asked. Mary looked startled, then thoughtful.

"I hadn't considered how dangerous an ocean voyage might be."

"Yeah. I think it's worthy of a little consideration."

"I'm sure we can work out something. Let me check the survival capsules."

"Good thinking," I told her. "What's a survival capsule?"

A survival capsule is a rich person's personal lifeboat. It bears almost no resemblance to a coffin, yet I was reminded of one. It's more like a gigantic aluminum pill. It's cylindrical, rounded on both ends, and has a one-person harness inside. In theory, you rush to your personal lifeboat, jump in, pull the cord, and the thing seals up. It's padded inside, but you're still supposed to strap in. It ejects from the ship—or just comes free and floats to the surface—and automatically starts sending a distress signal. Included in the gizmo is a tiny entertainment center with recorded music and video, some temperature control, rations, water, and some basic-but-awkward sanitary facilities.

It still reminded me of a coffin. Maybe it was the lack of windows.

"How many of these things do we have on board?"

"Four."

"So it's you, me, and whoever grabs one first?"

"There's also inflatable life rafts and the motor launch."

"Ah, yes." I shook my head. "The floating coffin is probably my best bet, sunshine-wise."

"I agree. I'd hate for you to melt through an inflatable raft. Could make trouble for everyone else in it."

"No kidding. So, did the Captain mention how long it'll take to reach Livorno?"

"He says it'll be about a week. Then we can get started on your master plan, yes?"

"Yes."

"And what, if I may ask, is the master plan?"

"Ah, that. Good thing you're seated; this is going to take some explaining."

"I'm ready."

"The short form is this. Johann has immense amounts of magical power at his disposal. He doesn't have a lot of formal spells—at least, I don't think so, not compared to the Magicians of Rethven—but he has rivers of power to run through the basic frameworks of spells. He's capable of generating powerful effects just by concentrating. He's also had time to settle in and fortify his position.

"Now, in Karvalen, I have magical defenses, yes, but I also have real fortifications, a couple of miles of tunnels, and people who are against the whole idea of assassinating their King. Johann, on the other hand, may have some zombie servants or conjured spirits or whatever, but from everything I've seen, he's relying *heavily* on purely magical forces. And why shouldn't he? He's unquestionably the most powerful of all the magi in the world—possibly in the history of the world.

"I can't face him in a straight magical duel and expect to live through it. So I have to level the playing field. That's where the rest of the nexus points come in. I'll be opening them, *using* them, to counter his power. Then it boils down to a case of my fangs and his throat, and in that fight, I know where to put my money."

Mary nodded, thoughtfully.

"All right. But how will you find him? You want to do this at night, I assume, so how do you locate him without magic? He could be anywhere along the east coast."

"I'll persuade him to go where I want him to," I told her, smugly. "You'll see."

"If you say so, I believe you. But you'd better be right."

"I agree."

Friday, January 15th

We took on fuel, food, and flying machine in Livorno without incident. Mary suggested spending the day in town while people took care of things. I didn't see any reason to interfere with the smooth, efficient functioning of the ship, so we went ashore to tour through a beautiful Italian town, eat in little restaurants, and enjoy our last solid ground for a while.

We also did a little research, followed by some hunting around, and paid a visit to what I would think of as a particularly offensive establishment.

To be clear, I'm not in the habit of killing every criminal I come across. Drug dealers, prostitutes, pimps, muggers, thieves, and all the rest of the lower social classes of humanity are not on some hit list in my head. Everyone has to make a living somehow. I don't particularly like such people, but if they're not trying to do something unpleasant to me I'm generally content to ignore them.

Human trafficking is one of my hot buttons, though.

Child trafficking is one of my meltdown buttons.

The police arrived in a timely fashion. They found seven dismembered corpses and not a trace of blood. They also found eighteen children, boys and girls, ranging from six to twelve years old. The children were locked in basement cages and, thankfully, didn't see most of what happened. The only thing they could say for certain was a shadow swallowed the man standing guard over them.

Boy, did he look surprised. His head continued to look surprised even after the police arrived. Sometimes, I think, certain types of people die more quickly than they deserve.

At least Mary and I are starting our trip with full tanks. I'd hate to have to snack on the staff.

Wednesday, January 20th

We've arrived at our first point, a nexus of five ley lines about five hundred miles off the coast of Portugal. I've spent the time preparing spells for the nexus; I don't want to waste any time down there once I hit bottom. I've built the spells to handle as much power as possible, but I'm still concerned. I've never fooled around with a *five* line nexus. The biggest I ever opened was a four-way intersection. That was a phenomenal rush of energies. I'm hoping this is still within my limits.

Mary helped me get everything put together for my trip. I was only going about three miles, but it was through hostile terrain. I've never been to the ocean floor before.

I take that back. I've been to the ocean floor in the world of Karvalen. The natives, by and large, are friendly people. I like them. I've never been to the ocean floor of the Atlantic, however, and I anticipate a complete lack of friendly natives, with a distinct possibility of hungry native life.

Once the sun went down, I climbed into a fifty-five gallon drum made of a high-density plastic. They hooked the web handles of the netting to the winch and lowered me into the water. As they paid out the cable, I sank like the proverbial anchor—one of which was also attached.

Three miles in an airplane is nothing. In a car, it's a short drive. On horseback—regular horseback—it's a moderate trip. On foot, it's a fair walk or a long run.

Sinking into the frigid depths of the Atlantic in January? It's forever.

On the plus side, there's a lot of marine life. I spread my tendrils like a dark, hungry cloud in the water. Everything brushing through them fed them, fed me, and I absorbed some piece of the vitality of the ocean.

"How's the view?" Mary asked. Her voice had a bit of a blurry sound to it, but it was coming through special equipment. The ship unit modulated her voice into lower-frequency sounds before putting it through an underwater loudspeaker aimed down at me. A unit in my helmet shifted this low-frequency sound up to normal levels again. It wasn't really intended for use at the depths we were shooting for, but it was worth a shot.

I, however, could not shout back at her. My signaling was via laser light in the blue-green range. I flashed the hand unit up, sweeping it back and forth to signal "Yes."

"Still hear me okay?"

I signaled another affirmative as I continued to sink.

Shortly thereafter, I didn't hear her at all. As we feared, the helmet unit, not rated for such depth, made crunching noises as it quit. I'd already flooded my helmet and breathed water to equalize pressures to avoid a similar fate. Dead is dead, but crushed is another matter.

Still, as I continued to be lowered, I signaled the loss of communications. I also felt the pressure starting to mount. Under three miles of water the pressure is over seven thousand pounds per square inch—or about double the pressure found in a high-capacity scuba tank.

Let me put it another way. With a fully-charged air bottle, if I stood on the ocean floor and aimed the bottle down, I could open the valve and water would rush *into* the "low-pressure" zone—assuming it didn't crush the bottle, first.

The strange thing is, I felt the compression, but it didn't hurt. I didn't have any air to speak of inside me by this point and my body is mostly fluid, anyway. It felt weird, but not exactly painful. The slightly itchy feeling of regeneration told me it wasn't good for me, but not so bad. I could move all right and even see pretty well. The abyssal darkness wasn't an issue, of course, not with vampire eyes, but the natural fog of the particulate suspended in the ocean's water reduced visibility to a hundred yards or so.

On the other hand, the glow of ley lines at the bottom of the ocean is easy to see, once you get down there.

We were mostly on target. Close enough, anyway. I tried to flash my laser up at the *Princess,* but the laser, even in a machined steel housing, hadn't survived the last mile of the trip. Oh, well. The *Princess* had sonar, but I wasn't clear on how far it could reach. If all else failed, they had detailed charts and knew I had to be approaching the ocean floor. The guys on winch duty slowed my rate of descent when I was within a few hundred yards of the bottom, which was nice. The vampire in the bucket made landfall without much trouble.

Step one: Descend into the abyss. Check.

I climbed out of my bucket and waited for some silt to settle. The *Princess* quit paying out cable after a moment; the tension change told them I hit bottom. It was nice to find the ocean floor in this region wasn't too awful for walking. The ground was mud, but only about ankle-deep. I could power through it with no more trouble than wading through a child's ball pit. The water would slow me slightly, but that was expected. Supernatural strength would let me move quickly if I needed to. No problem.

I cracked the chemical light attached to the cable; losing my ride would be a bad thing. After planting the anchor to keep the cable from wandering off too far, I unhooked the barrel. The barrel and the flares were my insurance policy if I lost the cable. Safety is job one, you know.

Finding the center of the nexus was a lot simpler than the last time. I came prepared. No makeshift compass needles and such, now. Now I knew what I was looking for and had spells for it. Raising containment shields and setting up concealing screens took more time than the actual opening of the nexus, itself. Of course, after that, there were several other spells to set up. The disruption launcher, for one, but also the sensor spells to detect my command to activate, the power capacitors to build up the charge before launching, all those things. It took a while.

Once I had my nexus surprise set up for Johann, I headed back along my mud-trail to hunt for my chemlight and cable. I found them, hooked on the bucket, climbed in, and sent up the signal.

Underwater rocketry is not an exact science. However, there are chemicals which burn underwater. The burning chemicals change the buoyancy of the signaling rig. Since it's connected to the cable by a large plastic ring, it will eventually surface at the *Princess* and they'll reel me in like a quarter-ton chicken of the sea.

Meanwhile, I sat quietly in my bucket, like a good corpse, and waited. Even if a playful octopus swiped the chemlight before it got to the surface, they would start cranking up the winch on a schedule. I should, at the latest, be pulled aboard an hour before dawn.

Surprisingly, there's a deep-sea diver's watch specifically made to function under water. It's a mechanical device, not electronic, and it isn't sealed. I think it's an ingenious piece of work. Water is supposed to get in and equalize the pressure so it can function at any depth. Unsurprisingly, it doesn't work when it's not underwater. The movement of the internal mechanisms is different in air—the watch runs far too fast. It needs to be full of water to keep time properly!

I could have been bored, but, as long as I was down here, building a better version of some of my spells might be worthwhile… This nexus was as far away as we would get from Johann. It would also be the one to fire the opening shot of the war. I wanted to attract his attention to a place far-distant, first, so everything else—all of it closer—could then clobber him unmercifully. This called for different sorts of command and control spells, as well as slightly different versions of my magic-disruption spell.

All that time, preparing and thinking and experimenting. Some of it wasted, some of it useful, but all of it coming together now. I had a plan. I was working the plan. The plan might even work.

The bucket jerked as the cable went taut. I was on my way up from the depths. Not to waste the opportunity, I spread my tendrils again.

Upon returning to the *Princess*, I knew exactly what to do. I've been in the ocean depths before. I know the drill. Hang upside-down, take deep breaths, and drain the lungs before dawn. It's important to have everything sorted out before the sunrise.

I wonder if I could persuade some of the otherworldly sea-people to come over and help me? It would beat the pants off this fishing for nexuses with vampire bait. But, alas, that would involve more gates…

The crew wondered what I was doing, of course, when I had myself lowered into the ocean. I didn't bother to explain when I left, and certainly didn't say anything when I returned. It's hard to talk with lungs full of seawater. Instead, I headed straight down to the bathroom to strip, drain, and shower.

Mary came in shortly thereafter, obviously amused.

"Well?" she asked. "How did it go?"

"It gets a little cold—enough to notice, anyway. There are a lot of things down there, wandering around, and I could hear them in the water. None of them were large enough to be interested in me, but most of them are pretty darn ugly. And the pressure feels strange. Keep breathing seawater and it doesn't bother you too much, though. I've never been that deep before."

"How did you know it wouldn't crush you?"

"Fluid dynamics. But, worst case, when you reeled me back in, I'd regenerate on the way up."

"So, it went well?"

"Yep. Johann's in for a nasty surprise. I'm thinking about a one nasty surprise every six seconds, but it's only a guess."

"Successful proof of concept?"

"Not exactly. I'm pretty sure it will work, though."

"But you don't know for certain until you set it off."

"True, but I'm confident. We've got eight more stops like this, three of which are big—twelve ley lines intersecting *major* nexus points. If Johann thinks he can hide behind his shields indefinitely, he needs some new thinks."

"I like it when you talk that way," Mary informed me, leaning on the doorframe. I turned off the water and toweled down.

"I can't help it. I've got everything else sorted out, or mostly. Johann is my last big thing."

"What about the Orb of Evil?"

"That's part of the Johann thing, I hope."

"And then what?"

"Assuming I survive it?"

"So to speak."

"That's a good question. I'm not sure. I know I'll need to travel a bit while I work out some settings on my gate spell. I know I'll need a lot of data points to figure out how to navigate strange spaces, rather than aim for known points." I thought for a moment. "I suppose I might go Hero-ing. It doesn't seem like a bad profession, from my perspective. Travel around, find monsters, slay them. It beats the hell out of ruling anybody."

"You don't sound too sure," Mary pointed out.

"I'm not. None of it sounds appealing, really."

"So take a minute. Take a breath. Think about it. Close your eyes and imagine you're happy. Then picture yourself. What do you see?"

I cast my mind back and thought on happier times. When was I happy? What did it feel like to be happy? Not happy *about* something, but to *be* happy. To feel pleasant, relaxed, enjoying life. What was around me? What was I doing?

"I suppose," I said, slowly, "I might take a vacation from all the intense work and settle down for a bit. I could find a world with moderate technology, for the creature comforts. Maybe something like the nineteen-twenties America. Maybe England between the world wars. Someplace where the omnipresent eye of the Internet won't trip me up as a stranger, and the local magic—and its practitioners—don't disagree with me. Settle down, get a dog, hire someone to mow the yard, and conduct my technomagical researches on a more garage-inventor scale."

"Really," she said, suppressing a smile.

"Yes, really. Why? Don't you think tinkering in the garage suits me?"

"No, no—I think it suits you fine. A nice little house with a small yard, a picket fence, a dog, a fireplace—a place like the Ardent farm when it was built."

"Without the acreage, and maybe with the neighborhood," I added.

"I can almost picture you as an English lord, complete with manor house, drawing room, and eccentric tastes. Maybe it's the stay in the Victorian hotel, but I can see it."

"If all it takes is money, there are ways. I might be very happy in such a situation."

"Any place where you can tinker in the laboratory and sew together your Creature?" she asked, smiling.

"Yes. At least, I think that's what I want. It's hard to focus on anything but Johann and his upcoming demise."

"Actually," she countered, "it's easy to focus on something else. At least, I can arrange it. You'll always come back to this mental state to finish what you started, I think. Your field of vision is narrow as you home in on your target."

"Is it?"

"I've seen this before. You're boring straight for your goal along your planned path, and God help anyone who gets between you and what you want. Right now, it's the only thing you want, so that makes it even worse."

"You may be right," I admitted. "I'm having a hard time imagining myself doing anything else, anyway."

"So don't. Focus on your goal. Get it done, get it over with, and then we can think about what to do when you've achieved your major purpose in life."

"It's not my..." I began, and paused. "Okay, maybe it is. For now."

"And afterward, we'll discuss the white picket fence and roses over the door. It does sound pleasant. At least, for a while."

"What's that supposed to mean? And move. I want my pants."

Mary moved, but I didn't get my pants. Once she was aware of the changes in her nighttime nervous system, kissing became much more enjoyable. It's enjoyable all the time, of course, but with the enhanced sensitivity of a vampire, it becomes an erotic journey all by itself. The slow movement of lips and tongues is a language without words.

Let's not even get into body language. Mary likes to shout.

Thursday, January 21st

We didn't have too far to go to get the next ley line nexus. We headed northwest and were there in a matter of hours. I repeated my deep-sea diving trick with one addition. Since the process worked, I took some extra time down there to craft spells for the next nexus opening. Unlike the spells I assembled on the ship, these were built using the wellspring of power at an opened nexus point. I wanted to practice the technique before hitting a major nexus.

It ought to be just a matter of degree, but I've never opened a major nexus before.

The nexus I just finished and the next one were slightly bigger, but not overwhelmingly so. A nexus of four or even five ley lines I could shield, drill down into, cap off and contain. Their energies would remain as they were, buried deep in the Earth, until I sent the magical signal to open the floodgates. Even then, the power wouldn't just spray everywhere. The spells would contain it, channel it, like a pipe in an oil well. The power would flow directly into some of the heaviest-built spells I could make, turning them into juggernauts. Irresistible ones, I hoped.

But a five-line nexus is the largest I've ever tapped. Next up was another five-line. After that... A twelve-line nexus, one of the major power centers on the planet. Sure, our planned course would take us through three of these major ones, but I desperately wanted to get it right on the first try. You might say I was feeling the pressure.

I could have flown to any of the land-based major nexus points, but the way magi tend to occupy power centers might have caused problems. It's harder to build your house two miles under the ocean, even with modern technology.

So you could say I was a bit nervous about it, yeah. I decided to practice my prefabrication methods on the smaller nexus. Next trip down, I plan to use the pre-made, over-built spells on the five-line nexus and see how those do. Then, hopefully, using the power from that nexus, I can build something strong enough to cap a major one.

Mary welcomed me back aboard and helped me burble. I sounded as though I was coming through the tulgey wood. Once she was sure I was done with my spell construction and suchlike, she insisted on distracting me with a game of strip checkers. She's not very good at checkers, or she let me win—I'm not sure which. But it was a good distraction, followed by a sunrise, a shower, and a very late breakfast.

I'm glad Mary found me. I've missed her. I've missed me, too. The me I am when I'm around her, that is. For her, I'm neither a king nor a monster. Not a god, angel, demon, or any other supernatural thing. I'm simply myself, exactly as I am. I'm not... I'm not a "something." I'm Eric, and that's all she wants me to be.

I've noticed something peculiar about myself. I'm starting to feel... different. No, that's not quite right. I've been feeling different ever since Johann had a long, probing talk with me. Now I'm doing something about it. Now I think I'm starting to feel like myself again.

I'm still a really pissed off me, and Johann is going to suffer for it, but between Mary and the feeling of *doing* something, I think I might be all right.

Is this what happens when we're around the people we love? They make us feel like better people? Or they actually do make us better people? Or do we simply feel comfortable being who we are, for better or for worse?

Friday, January 22nd

The last of the smaller nexus stops. My last chance to practice before the big one. I spent most of the night down there; they started reeling me in according to schedule, rather than from my signal. I sent the signal up, of course, but it didn't arrive before the clock chimed. Fortunately, I was already in the bucket seat.

I'm confident and frightened about the upcoming Grand Opening. If I make a mistake, the results could be unpredictable for the world and fatal for me. So, I'm confident I can do it and afraid of what I'm about to do. But I'm a coward by nature.

Monday, January 25th

Well, it worked. I'm pleased about that much, at least.

Going down was pretty much the usual thing. I sank to the bottom, bounced a little, shook the chemlight, and brought my bucket with me. Sea creatures were only interested in the light. Even the ones with respectable teeth didn't seem too concerned with me. All normal.

The undead monster plotting the demise of a major magician in a technological world went slogging through knee-deep mud on the bottom of the ocean with a jumbo plastic bucket and a pocketful of underwater flares. Yeah. Normal.

What was not normal was the building. This nexus was not simply a geographical point, buried under a stretch of mud on the bottom of the ocean. Someone had put an enormous pyramid on top of it. Oh, the pyramid was covered in silt, too, but it was squarely on top of my nexus!

My life is too weird, even for me. Maybe especially for me.

Grumbling the aquatic equivalent of "Who left this here?" I extended my tendrils, feeling around through the mud and stone. Solid stone all along one side, two sides... aha! Hollow spaces inside the pyramid, near the surface. Is this a hidden door? Or is it just covered in silty mud? I swept away great clouds of it, urging it along in the direction of the slow current. No, it wasn't a hidden door, merely a buried one.

Those balanced pivot-stones the mountain uses as the default door are wonderful things. Whoever built this pyramid liked them, too. Trouble is, they're precision pieces, usually maintained by the mountain. Abandon one, bury it at the bottom of the ocean for a couple thousand years, and it will deteriorate. I had to wrestle with the thing to get it open. Even then, it didn't open so much as I pulled it out of the doorway. It fell flat, sending up a great cloud of silt in the water. I thrashed at the cloud with tendrils for minutes, clearing it away. When the waters cleared, I saw the inner face of the slab had some sort of metal inlay. It looked strangely angular, with lots of parallel lines and sharp bends. None of the metallic lines crossed each other.

Curious, I ran tendrils over it and recognized it instantly. It was the stuff Johann used to make my chains—orichalcum, that was it. I peeled loose a strip for later analysis. You never know when you're going to need a magical superconductor, and the formula for it could be highly valuable.

Beyond the doorway, the waters were surprisingly clear and the floor almost clean. Small streamers of muddy dust drifted in the waters, generally heading out, toward me, even though I couldn't feel a current. The corridor was fairly sizable—big enough for Bronze, if she kept her head down, but she would never turn around. More carvings lined the hallway, inlaid with more metal. I stepped inside and looked them over. There was no light, so there were no reflections, no gleams, but I could feel them with my tendrils. Most of them were also orichalcum, but a few seemed to be magically-charged metals. Gold? Silver? There was no way to tell with the color-blindness that goes with my darkvision.

I'm no archaeologist. Unfortunately, I'd have to vampirize an archaeologist to get one down here. I suppose I could get a special camera for photographing the ocean depths, but it would take time. Maybe after Johann.

The interior of the pyramid was more spacious than I thought. Egyptian pyramids generally only have a few rooms and some narrow tunnels. This was more like a modern concrete building. I had no idea how they built it. It wasn't grown—I think—because the mountain generally has a slightly rounded, organic feel. There are some lines and angles and sharp edges, but usually only where there's a need for them. All of this place was sharp, angular, made up of straight lines and intersections.

Working my way in was like negotiating with a politician. I could tell the nexus was near the center, but nothing led me straight there. It was always sideways with occasional stairs up or down and openings toward the middle, like some sort of labyrinth. I eventually cheated. My tendrils couldn't reach out to cover the whole pyramid, but I could easily worm them out between the orichalcum lines and get a much better feel for the layout in my area. It cut down on dead ends and false trails.

Finally, I climbed a short flight of stairs into the center. I tilted a thin lid of stone up and looked around. The room was almost spherical, but faceted. My entry point was a flat, triangular stone over the stairs, near the bottom but a bit off-center. I emerged from it and closed it carefully behind me.

The lowest facet—the bottom one, where it would be flat and level—was actually an open hole. It was a triangular well with stairs on the sides. The rest of the room was like the inside of a gem. It had no normal walls, just facets, gradually sloping up from the well, growing steeper the farther away they were, vertical halfway up the room, and connecting to form a dome above. Each facet was inscribed with a symbol and connected to all the others by inlaid lines of metal, running along the stone walls. I had no idea what the metal was. It was too hard to be gold and I couldn't tell the color. Orichalcum? Maybe. Probably.

The whole webwork of intersecting lines reminded me of something. Sixty-two points, each consisting of twelve intersecting lines. Twelve intersecting lines? Wait a minute… this whole inside-out thing was a map of the world and the ley lines!

Why inside-out? Because it was a room? Or because there was a hollow place inside the world where the magic lived? If I ever meet the builders—Atlanteans, maybe? —I'll be sure to ask.

The nexus was down in the well. I sank down the stairs, noting the well itself was covered or plated in the same metal as the connecting lines in the ley line diagram. Even in seawater for thousands of years, it was glassy-smooth to the touch. I had no doubt it was polished a long time ago, and completely lacking in corrosion. I don't know why I was so certain, but it seemed only natural.

The bottom of the well ended at the edge of a hemispherical chamber. The floor was a flat surface of stone, inscribed with eight concentric circles around a central pillar. The pillar was about three feet high, a foot in diameter, and was crowned with a sphere—it looked as though someone had stuck a one-foot-thick pillar into an eighteen-inch ball. The pillar and sphere were otherwise unadorned.

The circles, however, were about as magical as my horse. For most people, that's not a big deal, but for *me*...

I examined the enchantments, for enchantments they were, not simply spells. They were containment circles, obviously, and the only one I could get a good look at was the outer one. It didn't seem attuned to anything in particular. That is, it wasn't a named circle, specifically designed to contain a specific entity. It appeared to be nothing more than a basic power circle, restricting nothing but magical force.

Which, come to think of it, might not be a bad thing around a major nexus. But who put it here? And why? And when? In the early days of Atlantis? In the days right after the fall of Atlantis? Or was this one of the reasons Atlantis sank? Did someone cut the magical foundations out from under it?

After considerable evaluation and consideration, I decided the circle was harmless to me. I risked my left hand by reaching past it. Nothing untoward happened, but I did note a material increase in magical force on the other side of the barrier. I pulled my hand back without resistance. There wasn't enough room between the circles to stand, so I didn't try stepping across.

Extending my hand farther, the next circle was much the same. It appeared to be an identical containment circle, only a bit smaller. The power level inside the next circle was even higher.

All right, it's a magical power containment diagram with eight layers. What's it for? Containing power. Why? Damned if I know.

I checked each circle as I penetrated the previous one. They were, in fact, entirely alike, but the magical differential between them grew steadily higher as I went farther in. Then I reached through the eighth circle, toward the pillar itself, and realized something fundamental.

This nexus was *open*.

When my hand entered the magical field of the nexus, it started flowing, changing shape. It was as though the flesh forgot about those pesky rules of space and shape and matter and simply relaxed into a primordial essence.

I snatched my hand back at the speed of dark and curled up in a ball, cradling the still-rippling flesh, gurgling agony in the watery environment—whales probably heard me around the world. It wasn't a pleasant sensation in any way, shape, or form and completely lacked the last two. If a clay statue had his hand squished and played with while retaining fully the ability to feel, he could empathize with me. For a moment, I seriously considered cutting my hand—well, appendage—completely off and growing a new one. I didn't, but it was a near thing. If I'd brought a sword, I might have.

I'm glad I didn't. I'm not sure a severed hand wouldn't have wandered off on its own.

After what felt like a few Mondays, it quit changing shape. It was probably about a minute before it settled down into a more normal appearance. A few more seconds of the itching, tingling feeling of my regeneration at work and it assumed a perfectly normal appearance again.

My Ring of Hygiene was missing. Vaporized by the magical surge? Possibly. Probably. I was going to miss that ring. Being clean and human-looking are darn convenient. Well, I could build another one.

For the moment, though, what was I going to do with an already open nexus? Especially one of such power?

I was going to carry on with my plan, obviously. Johann wasn't going to see *this* coming. And if he did, he was not going to be pleased with the view.

On the other hand, my existing power-tapping spells weren't going to be much help, here. I couldn't simply bust up the containment circles, either. For one thing, I doubted my own containment plans could duplicate the effect. For another, more subtle reason, one does not simply turn loose a thing someone has gone to great efforts to contain.

I examined the circles in greater detail, looking for ways to tap the power of the nexus without turning it into a geyser of power. There seemed to be specific elements to the circle spells for power tapping, but accessing them wasn't intuitive. I spent most of the night working out power taps.

My watch doesn't have an alarm, but I do check it every so often. Good thing, too. I had to hustle to get my bucket back.

Tuesday, January 26th

We spent an extra day at the major nexus point. The Captain barely raised an eyebrow when I asked him to keep us there for another day. He simply made it happen, a fact I appreciated. I don't like making sudden changes in plans, either.

Mary met me when I came aboard—I remembered to put on a human-disguise spell on the way up—and we went through the usual post-dive routine. When I could talk again, I told her all about my find.

"So, this triangular well…"

"Yes."

"It was the same shape as all the other facets of the room?"

"Yup."

"And all the others each had a unique symbol?"

"I think so. I didn't look that closely, but I didn't notice any duplicates."

"And the room was an inside-out map of the world?"

"I'm pretty sure." I shut off the water and toweled off briskly. "Where is this leading?"

"Could each of those facet-things be a marker for another pyramid? On top of a big nexus-thing, like this one?"

"I suppose it could be. If so, I'm sure there's a family of magi clinging to it like barnacles on a wooden ship. So?"

"Don't you think such a bunch of magi would have done something about Johann by now? I mean, you said the nexus was open. That means they would have access to all the power they could ask for."

"Hmm. True. Even if they were trying to avoid notice in the world—easy enough to do with the right spells—the fact Johann is being immensely obvious is something they can't ignore. At least, I would think they couldn't ignore it. I mean, they would be able to, I suppose, with that much power, but I don't know why they would."

"So why hasn't anyone done anything? I spoke with the Etiennes and they had words with the Stuarts and the Wilmonts. Nobody wants to challenge Johann because he's got all the power."

"I can think of a couple of possibilities, but I can't prove anything."

"Come to bed and tell me all about them."

"If I come to bed, you won't listen."

"Spoilsport."

"I'm not objecting, just stating the facts."

"All right, come to the sofa and tell me all about them."

"That might work." I got into a set of pajamas and a robe. Mary made a rude noise at me from her position on the couch. I joined her and she twined herself about me.

"Okay, talk."

"Get your fang out of my ear, first."

"I seem to remember you being more fun before you went off to visit Lissette."

"I think the key event was being kidnapped by Johann, but I see your point. I hope to be back to my old self after I ruthlessly murder him and laugh while bathing in his blood and other internal fluids."

"Ewww."

"You want my what-ifs or not?"

"After that mental image? Yes. Give me something else to picture."

"Since magi legends maintain Atlantis was a real place, it's conceivable the Atlanteans built these pyramids as power stations. They tapped the magical pulse of the planet and used it in their techno-magical gadgets. When Atlantis fell, this power network went to pieces. With me so far?"

"Not going anywhere."

"Good. I'd miss you. So, imagine a number of these power stations going kaboom. Overloads, feedback, whatever can go bad in a system like that does go bad. Pyramids collapse into piles of rubble and eventually turn into haunted hills. Pyramids explode, their craters eventually becoming mysterious lakes. That's assuming, of course, they built these things on land in the first place; they'd have a lot farther to dig down if they put one in the highlands of Scotland or suchlike."

"So they might not be on every major nexus?" Mary asked, starting to be more interested in the idea than in nibbling on me.

"Quite possibly. Destroyed or never built, it doesn't matter. For all I know, the clustering of magi around a few remaining power centers on land might account for the Tinfoil Hat Society's stories of teachers from Atlantis spreading civilization across the world."

"Hmm. So, you think this undersea nexus point might be valuable?"

"Immensely so. I plan to tap it and use it. And, later, we have two more on our route. I don't know if they have pyramids with inside-out maps and labyrinths or not, but I'm kind of excited to find out."

"Do you think you could be excited about something else for a while?"

"Yes, but I'd like to wait until after sunrise."

"Oh?"

"Yes."

"I'm not greedy. I can wait."

"The hell you're not greedy."

Today was a good day. I had a wonderful morning, enjoyed four octagonal meals, was soundly beaten at chess by the Captain—anybody who tells me "Mate in six," is someone I don't need to play chess with—and did some deep-sea fishing with Mary. In between all this, I spent a good deal of time in my headspace fiddling with the designs of power tap spells.

Yes, I enjoyed the more mundane things, but when it comes to science and magic, I'm a huge nerd.

To be honest, I really don't understand the appeal of fishing. It seems kind of like gambling, another activity I simply don't understand. You throw out a hook with bait and hope something big enough to be worthwhile decides to eat it. I'm sure a fishing enthusiast can scream at me for hours about my attitude, but I can't help it. I simply don't understand the appeal.

I said as much to Mary.

"Don't you worry about it, dear," she reassured me. "There are a lot of things your brain isn't wired to understand."

I'm still not sure what she meant by that.

After a quiet afternoon snuggling and watching movies, I dressed for my subaquean venture, waited out the sunset, poured a bucket full of vampire, and sank like a rock.

I did ask Mary if she would like to come with me to see the pyramid. She declined, citing a complete lack of interest.

"My thrill-seeking involves doing dangerous things I can get myself out of," she stated. "Going over Niagara Falls in a barrel is not on the list. Neither is pretending to be giant shark bait. Besides, I'm not sure I'm as crush-proof as the Ancient Evil from the Dawn of Time."

"I'm not an Ancient Evil from the Dawn of Time."

"True, but you are supernaturally dense in many ways. I'll pass, thank you. Besides, someone has to stay up here and keep the humans in line."

The pyramid was right where I left it, which was reassuring. Of course, I landed somewhere completely different from my previous trip. The *Princess* was keeping station using GPS accurate to within a meter or less, but tides, wind, weather, currents, and all that other oceangoing stuff means there's considerable Tennessee windage along a couple of miles of cable.

Fortunately, the labyrinth of the pyramid didn't rearrange itself between trips. At least, it didn't move since I left it. I negotiated the maze again, descended to the nexus, and started work.

Attaching a power tap to the nexus wasn't too hard once I worked out the process. The whole setup seemed built specifically for that, with allowances for safety—the equivalent of circuit breakers, surge protection, and so on. It was more complicated than simply plugging into it, of course, but it was the difference between plugging a lamp into an outlet and getting out the screwdriver to actually wire an outlet.

Of course, I didn't have a simple way to turn off power to the outlet in question, so hooking it up was an exercise in caution. I wonder how the Atlanteans managed.

Once I had the basic power tap spells installed, I drew power from the nexus, fed it back into the spells to reinforce them, and repeated the process eight times—once for each containment circle. When I finished, I had a direct power link to the nexus itself and more power than I knew what to do with.

Suddenly, I knew why all this seemed familiar. Not because I've eaten magi or visited Atlantis, but because I'd seen a setup a lot like this before.

The heart of the mountain. In the center is a phenomenal source of power. Surrounding it are layers upon layers of energy-transforming spells, essentially containing the unimaginable fury of the matter-conversion furnace.

The realization was not what I needed. I'm scared of that thing. Now I'm scared of this thing. Wonderful. The undead monstrosity playing with planet-wrecking forces a couple of miles down in the icy waters of the ocean floor is meddling with ancient magical technology he doesn't understand. Whee. The things I do to kill godlike wizards.

I worked with the forces involved in a secondhand fashion. Instead of directly manipulating the energies and risking being turned into a rapidly-expanding cloud of undead purée, I used spells to manipulate spells. It was awkward, rather reminiscent of using waldoes rather than hands, but it was considerably safer. It did make it easier to build my Johann-attacking spells from the overwhelming energies available. Rather than sucking up power myself, my waldo spells connected the power tap spells into the matrix of the new spells, feeding them power to build them up until they could handle the load of the nexus' output.

When I finished, I realized I was hungry. I'd been working hard and a large portion of my personal energies were required to start the process of my spells here. I double-checked everything to make sure the nexus wasn't leaking any tell-tale signs—anything someone might take note of. It would be bad if anyone realized it was being tapped. But it all seemed good. Then it was a look over the spells themselves for proper structure and solidity. I can take pride in the fact I do good work, at least.

It was time to find a seafood dinner, if possible, and get back to the boat.

There's not a lot of seafood at that depth. At least, not for me. Most of the things I found on the ocean floor were on the small side. I absorbed their energies and snatched what I could on the way back up. Draining the vitality out of fish is adequate, I suppose, but I wasn't looking forward to another spellcasting session like this. I really needed something more substantial than a few herring and the odd tuna. Is it legal to hunt whales again? Or are they still protected? How about sharks? Nobody cries for sharks.

Once back aboard the *Princess* and suitably un-seawatered, I gave the Captain the go-ahead. We set out for our next stop. While I wanted to dive into the water and find something to bite, I resisted the impulse—I sink. Instead, I visited Bronze in the cargo hold and lay down there. With a web of tendrils extending down and out through the hull of the ship, everything that swam anywhere near us gave up at least some of its vital force to restore my strength.

Mary came in to check on me, saw I was concentrating, and figured out for herself what I was up to. She quietly left the hold and made sure I was undisturbed. She knows having a hungry vampire on board can be a very bad thing, bordering closely on the catastrophic. I'd prefer it never come to that.

Saturday, January 30th

We stopped for a smaller nexus on the way to the next major one. It went so well, it was almost routine. On the other hand, I keep spending my nights in the hold, sucking up life from anything near the ship as we travel. I'm pretty sure I tagged a whale, but I let go of it before I killed it. It took a surprisingly long time to drain vitality out of it. There was a lot of vitality to be had. Is size a factor? Plankton, jellyfish, schools of minnows—all the small stuff I can drain faster than a photoflash, and the physical remains are eaten by the rest of the ocean pretty quickly.

I let go of it without harming it for another reason, too. The moment I touched the whale, I recognized it as intelligent. Not the same as a human, but not a dumb animal, either. It made me wonder about some sorts of animals and whether or not they have what I loosely refer to as a soul. If we had passed closer, I would have checked. We haven't encountered any dolphins or porpoises, but the next highly-intelligent "animal" I find, I want to take a closer look.

Going down to the second major nexus was the same as always. I didn't find a pyramid, though. This one was right on top of the mid-Atlantic range, barely ten thousand feet below the surface. It was a bit awkward, climbing around on an underwater mountainside and trying to keep my face out of the stirred-up mud. When I found the nexus point, it was simply another rocky piece of terrain.

Which posed me a question. If I drilled down to it, how would I use it? I can't build a containment spell strong enough to hold the surge when it opens. Oh, I could put an Ascension Sphere around it, sure, but if I do that, it'll be permanent—nothing I know of will ever be able to knock it down. Not helpful when my objective is to get power out of a nexus for use in far-distant lands. I suppose we can go back to the pyramid so I can build the appropriate spells, but it'll be several days before I can get back here and set it up.

Then again, this is a major nexus point. The magical environment here is stronger than anywhere else on the planet, barring an open nexus. I can cast most spells without too much trouble.

Since the laws of thermodynamics seem to be invalid where magic is concerned, can I create a self-propagating spell that builds itself? Or a spell to build another version of itself, and then those two build a more powerful version, then all three work together to build an even more powerful version? Can I set such a process in motion so it eventually creates a containment spell so powerful it won't rupture when I crack open the nexus?

Worth a shot, anyway. I sat down on a handy rock and drew magical lines around the nexus to draw in the power and start shaping it. I was also careful to include the new power tap connections and an off switch in the design. I didn't want to find my containment circles were accidentally acting like Ascension Spheres—too powerful to take down—and impossible to get power out of.

I sat and watched the first generation containment spell double itself. It seemed to go well, but the two of them failed to produce a third. After some troubleshooting, I found the glitch; they were both trying to do the same thing, but they weren't coordinating. I fixed it and set them in motion again and found another glitch. They didn't build a more powerful version of themselves. They simply produced two more copies rather than focusing their power together in making a stronger spell.

I grumbled and took the three apart, reconfigured the whole thing, and tried again. This was a tricky bit of magical programming and I kept hitting glitches of various sorts. I won in the end, mainly because I'm stubborn, clever, and... okay, mainly because I'm stubborn.

Once I had the process going, I watched it run for half a dozen iterations. It seemed to be working smoothly after my lengthy debugging session. As long as nobody touched it, it should continue indefinitely. I decided to let it run the rest of the night and all of tomorrow. If it worked continuously until then, I might risk tapping the nexus. If it fouled up, we'd have to go back to the pyramid. Which would mean we would have to refuel somewhere before we could finish our trip...

I sat in my bucket and sighed. I can do that underwater.

Sunday, January 31st

Mary and I spend our days as a fairly mundane, if quirky, couple aboard her yacht. She's the owner of record. I'm just the boyfriend. I've learned to play shuffleboard, but I can't say I'm terribly good at it or terribly interested.

There is one thing I've learned, and I'm more than a little miffed about it.

We finished pumping seawater out of me and I went through the rinse cycle. All the usual stuff. We sat out the sunrise and did the whole cleanup for the morning thing. I noticed my horrible transformation stench didn't seem too bad— undersea exploration seemed to agree with me.

During the rinse-shave-manicure portion of the morning, Mary retracted her fingertalons. On Mary, the claws merely look as though she has a dangerous manicurist. On me, my fingernails look exactly like what they are: dangerous, flesh-ripping finger-knives. I usually grind them down with power tools of one sort or another. But she flexed her fingers and they slurped backward about half an inch, moving from finger talons to slightly longish nails.

My language was printable only in the technical sense.

"How come you get to retract your claws?" I complained.

"First of all, I'm not the same species, precisely," she pointed out. "Second, have you ever tried?"

"Say what?"

"Have you ever tried?"

I examined my fingers. My uncut fingernails didn't look as though they would retract. They looked lethal.

Mary gently took my hand in hers and stroked my fingers for a moment, then pressed sharply down on the base of my index fingernail. I howled and yanked my hand away as the pressure caused a sharp popping sound.

"Oh, you big baby," she complained. "Shut up and give me your hand."

"No!" I cried, cradling my hand and shielding it from her.

"You're not hurt."

"How do you know?" I demanded, examining my finger. The fingernail angled up slightly from the nail bed. It looked worse than it felt. It didn't hurt nearly as much as I would have expected. Mary made a rude noise at me and took my hand anyway. With a somewhat more delicate touch, she moved the index fingernail back into the finger. It didn't precisely feel like having something jammed up under the fingernail, but it reminded me of the sensation.

"See?" she said. "You can retract them."

I examined my other fingers in more detail. Yes, if I pressed down on them, they popped—not actually painfully, more like popping a knuckle—and I could pull them a little bit back into the finger.

"Well, crap. I've been grinding these things down forever. Why haven't I been able to retract them before?"

"Can you wiggle your ears?"

"Huh? Of course."

"When did you learn to do that?"

"When I was a kid. Another kid could wiggle his ears, so I tried it."

"That's how it usually works," Mary agreed. "When was the last time you saw another vampire retract claws?"

"Never. Not until now, anyway."

"There you go. You haven't tried it because you didn't know you could do it." She shrugged. "It's what you get for not playing well with others. At least you learned to retract your teeth."

I practiced with my partially-retractile claws for a while. It wasn't easy to control them, but I got better at it quickly. Fully retracted, they merely needed a manicurist. Fully extended, the back section rose from within the fingertip and locked them in an extended position. If I painted them, I could dress in drag and nobody would look twice. Well... not at my fingernails, anyway. When I paid close attention, I could even pop them from their locked position and pull them back, but they tended to slide out whenever I got excited.

I apologized to Mary and applied some first-aid sprays. She didn't even accuse me of doing it deliberately. She seemed to enjoy it immensely when I accidentally put cuts down her back. She did mention it wasn't something she wanted to do regularly.

"I'd say something about how you know how I feel about it," I offered, "but you might think it wasn't an accident."

"I would never."

"Roll over."

"I think the sheet is stuck to me."

"I've got the first-aid kit."

"What about the blood? We don't need to scandalize Ludmilla."

"I'll lick the sheet after sunset."

"You'd make a fantastic post-murder cleanup crew," she suggested, peeling herself slowly from the bedsheet.

"I hate mopping. Hold still."

As I spritzed her, I recalled something she said the other day.

"Mary?"

"Hmm?"

"You mentioned you didn't want to go down on the cable."

"That's right."

"You also said someone needed to stay on the boat and keep the humans from getting nervous, or something like it."

"That's right."

"What do they have to be nervous about?"

"They don't—ow!"

"Sorry." I applied another spritz of analgesic.

"They don't know how you manage it. I've implied you have a new invention in your diving helmet. I haven't made up anything specific, since you don't have one, but they're actually quite impressed."

"Isn't technology grand?"

"They certainly think so. I left out the part about magical nexuses and Ancient Evils from the Dawn of Time."

"Is it nexuses or nexii?"

"How should I know? You knew what I meant, didn't you?"

"Yes, but sometimes languages bother me."

"If I've communicated successfully, then I've communicated correctly, which is the purpose of language."

"I guess that's fair. So they think I'm a crazy inventor?"

Mary turned around to look at me.

"Aren't you?"

"You may have a point. I'm glad someone is diverting attention from my paranormal activities. I'm not used to having human minions. Now, turn around, bright eyes. I've got another layer of sprayskin to apply, then you can get dressed," I told her. She turned around and leaned forward. I fixed her back.

"The hell you aren't," she countered. "You have human minions all the time. You're just not used to hiding your bloodline from them."

"I stand corrected."

"Point of fact, you hate keeping secrets from everyone except yourself."

"How do you mean?"

She stood up and reached for her robe. I helped her into it.

"How long did you love Tort?"

"In one way or another, most of her life."

"How long did it take you to tell yourself?"

"Hmm."

"You might want to think about it. You're not very good at telling yourself the truth."

"How about I tell you the truth and you can tell me?" I asked. She flashed me a smile.

"I can do that. But only if I get to call you a moron occasionally."

"You drive a hard bargain, lady."

"*And* you have to hold me down and beat me for it."

"Not while you're injured. And preferably not on a big sinking thing."

"The boat isn't sinking."

"Not yet," I replied, darkly. "It's okay for Bronze and Firebrand—Bronze can eventually walk to shore and bring Firebrand with her, but we have some very limited time constraints. That's one of the big issues I had to work around for dealing with Johann."

"Spoilsport. Even if we sink the thing, we could share a survival capsule."

"And sink the capsule, too?"

"Sometimes, you're depressingly practical," she complained. I hugged her carefully, avoiding her cuts, and smacked her behind.

"Then again," she added, smiling, "you do adapt well to changing circumstances."

I took my trip down into the abyssal darkness and went mountain climbing again. My spells made immense progress while I was gone, but they were still limited by the amount of power radiating from the closed nexus. I hadn't considered that as a limit; I'm more used to a whole world full of energy. The spells had some powerful containment circles surrounding everything already, but the most potent iteration was taking quite a while to construct with the limited power welling up.

Well, crap. I really didn't want to sail all the way back to the pyramid, build some shielding spells, cloak them, and sail all the way back. Was there a way to provide more power? Of course!

My tendrils can reach down to the nexus—with a little spell-enhanced help, that is—and touch it. Instead of relying on what it radiated all the way up here, I could snag more of it by reaching closer to it. Kind of like a small solar panel. The gadget it's on might not work so well sitting on the desk, but if you move it closer to the light, everything is fine. Same principle.

I think. I haven't actually tested magical radiations to see if they diminish with the square of the distance, but they seem to behave similarly. If it's not precisely the same as the standard model, it's close enough.

So I cast my spell, reached down, and gently brushed my tendrils over the metaphorical skin of the nexus. Power belted up at me, surged through me, and flooded out into my spells.

I make that sound easy, don't I? Imagine standing neck-deep in a swimming pool when someone opens one end of it like a drawbridge, letting the water out in a massive wave. I felt my tendrils vibrating like bridge cables in a high wind. My internal organs matched them, thrumming along at about ten cycles per second— perhaps more like a rapid throb than an actual vibration. I held on, concentrating on amping up the newest spell being formed, held on until it was completed, and let go.

Small bubbles of steam rose off me and dissipated in the icy waters. I felt my body regenerating. I'm glad I was underwater. I might have burst into flames.

Okay, important life lesson for any wizard who wants to keep it: *Don't do that.*

Right. Maybe there's another option.

The existing spells were already containment circles; so far, nothing I'd done had breached them. From a magical perspective, there was nothing to see here. Was it possible to *partially* open a nexus? If I could give it a pinprick, rather than stabbing a spear into it, the current containment—especially after my most recent efforts—should hold it. The process could then produce more powerful containment spells in a timely manner, as it was supposed to.

Judging by the feel of the nexus point, it wasn't like a bubble, ready to be popped. Drilling a tiny hole in it should be doable. Whether it would erode itself open over time or heal itself was an open question, but if I lived long enough, at least I'd find out.

Again, a spell to extend my reach. A single dark strand, stretching downward. A light touch, a careful examination, a delicate point pushing into the surface...

Technically, I seem to have an infinite number of psychic tendrils. It's not like I've ever run out of them. It still stings like hell when something burns one off.

Yeah, this is not Johann's nexus. This is a *big* one, naked and uncontained by Atlantean technology.

But the tendril did its work before it flash-fried all the way back to me. Power poured from the pinprick like the water in a water knife. The containment spells suddenly kicked into high gear, all of them combining their efforts to build a stronger containment.

I watched it for most of the night, evaluating the rate of spell creation, poking the nexus again whenever the progress slowed. Before sunrise, the nexus had a dozen pinpricks and a power-containment shell I felt might actually hold the whole thing.

One more day here.

Monday, February 1ˢᵗ

I was right. One more day of building and a few more pinpricks. I started peeling open the nexus with tendrils—a tricky operation that involved creating defensive spells like armored gloves *for psychic tendrils.*

Let me tell you, those took some careful thought, a lot of failures, and more than a few headaches. At least my hair didn't catch fire. There are advantages to being miles-deep in a freezing ocean.

I wound up with things like lengths of pipe with tools on the end. The tendril reached into the spell structure as though reaching down the pipe, gripped the handle on the inside, down at the tool end, and then reached into the all-consuming power flood of the nexus point. The protective spells were only good for one before they disintegrated, and I had to be quick about it. I couldn't reach into the furnace of power at all with an unprotected tendril, and the spells saved me from the psychic burns that come from vaporizing a tendril.

I'm not sure if I can reach into the Vatican like this and I'm in no hurry to find out.

With the steadily-rising power inside the containment shells, I started wiring my anti-Johann spells to the power taps. If this all held together, he was going to have an extraordinarily bad day.

I added a secondary function to the later containment spells. Once formed, they lanced into the nexus to open it further. This provided a higher power flow for the building of the next containment spell. I should have done that in the first place, I suppose, but nobody thinks of *everything!*

Of course, I did think to build a series of heavy-duty containment spells to take with me. There was another major nexus on our route. If it didn't have a pyramid, I didn't want to spend three days slowly building up to opening it.

Friday, February 5th

Our last three stops were somewhat east of the Dominican Republic and Nassau. Unfortunately, the weather did not cooperate. The trip was lucky up to then. The northern Atlantic is not known for its calm, placid waters and pleasant weather. We were paying for that luck with the whole latter portion of the trip. Stormy weather churned along all over the place.

I wondered briefly if Johann was on to me and deliberately causing trouble. I dismissed this idea for two reasons. First, Captain Tillard assured me these weather patterns had been developing for quite some time. Second, if Johann wanted to, he could sink every ship in the Atlantic. In fact, he might enjoy doing so—sitting on a balcony, having breakfast, zooming in with a magic mirror on anything with a wake, poking it with a finger, watching it explode, and chortling over his waffles. I wouldn't put it past him.

I considered other options. How desperately did I need another three nexuses? Two major nexuses and five medium ones might be enough. They probably were, but I'm a coward. Johann scares me right down to the bottom of my black little heart.

So, instead of cruising to a spot about five hundred miles east of the Virgin Islands, we headed due south. One more major nexus—also on the Atlantic's mid-ocean ridge—sat on the equator and out of the bad-weather zone the Captain so disliked. The weather wouldn't really bother the *Princess*, but all that bobbing around with wind and wave would translate to a highly-mobile cable on the sea floor. Getting back to the boat could be a problem and he didn't want to take that sort of risk with my life. I appreciated it. It was refreshing, really.

He parked the boat at the equatorial major nexus, I went down, did my work, and was hauled back up. Nothing to it. At least, nothing unexpected. Dangerous, inconvenient, and unpleasant, yes, but routinely dangerous, inconvenient, and unpleasant. No kraken, no leviathans, nothing out of the ordinary. Just your typical harnessing of a major power center of magical force.

Now we're headed for someplace called Cayenne, the capitol of French Guiana. It's in South America and we can refuel there. That's about all I know about it. Hopefully, our detour and stopover will allow the weather to lighten up in the places I want to go.

Once we get ourselves sorted out, we can head north again. After a few more nexus points, we can head for my launch coordinates. There's a point where two of the circular dome-fields intersect, out in the ocean, about a hundred miles east of Trenton, New Jersey. That's our point of closest approach to Johann's personal nexus.

Then I'll piss off Mary, Firebrand, and Bronze.

Monday, February 8th

Cayenne is actually a nice little town. We missed a city-wide party of some sort, though. They were still cleaning up on Monday morning when Mary and I disembarked.

Mary took my arm and squeezed it.

"Where are we going to eat?" she asked.

"I don't know. Pick any place in the city."

"Sorry, I meant where are we going to drink our dinner?"

"Oh! Hungry?"

"More than a little peckish, yes. I've been on a diet of human food for the better part of a month. That's a record, for me. I usually get hungry more along the lines of once a week."

"Blame your infusion of blood from the Ancient Evil from the Dawn of Time," I told her.

"Aren't you hungry?"

"Yes, but not too much. I've been expending mystic forces, not physical ones, and constantly resupplying from the passing ocean life. I could easily go longer, but I'm more than a little snackish, myself."

"All right. Do we want to go alley-fishing? Rich tourists can be good bait to the criminal classes."

"I hate to keep repeating like that, but it's effective. Let's hope the place has a lot of violent crime. In the meantime…"

"…second breakfast, elevenses, luncheon, tea, high tea, dinner, and supper?" she suggested.

"Have I told you I love you?'

"I've had some vague hints."

"I love you."

"All it took was a *Lord of the Rings* reference?" she asked, cocking her head at me.

"I'm a nerd. Weird things catalyze my thinking."

"Then I'll take you to second breakfast. You need fattening up if you're going to be a hobbit."

"I'm too mean to be a hobbit."

"Then you'll be a hard hobbit to break."

I groaned. Mary laughed.

After several meals and some subtle discussion with the wait staff, we discovered one of the few exports from Cayenne is meat. The soils aren't especially good for farming, but they raise cattle and pigs. Local restaurants get most of their meat from local fishermen and local slaughterhouses.

As we sat in one of the finer restaurants in Cayenne, Mary gave me a significant look. I assured her we'd go for a walk in the evening, but just in case, we needed a backup plan. I could tell she didn't like the backup plan. Remembering the occasion we broke into a slaughterhouse to feed, I didn't blame her. She has to actually taste what she's drinking, while I can soak up blood through my skin. Drinking blood is faster, yes, but I don't have to. Tasting it is optional.

Which made me pay attention to my food. It didn't taste bad. That is, it was good, but it wasn't overwhelmingly powerful. I could taste it without feeling as though my mouth was invaded by fully-automatic assault flavors. I tried several different things in a hurry and the problem persisted. Was my sense of taste going numb? Or was my brain finally getting a handle on being wired into supernaturally acute senses? My Ring of Hygiene used to include my sensory-damping enchantment, along with the skin color-shifter and cleaning spell. Did I not need the spell anymore?

"Something wrong?" Mary asked, watching as I chewed thoughtfully.

"I may be starting to master my overactive sense of taste."

"Really?"

"Really."

"I thought you built a ring for that."

"I did. Remember, it went ker-flooie in the pyramid."

"I recall you mentioning it, yes. Did the nexus jam it into your hand?"

"Huh. I hadn't thought of that." I looked at my hand. It seemed intact. I didn't see how a ring could be hidden inside it. "I don't think so. There's nowhere to put a ring. Maybe the gems are buried in the bones, though. I suppose that could be possible. If they're embedded completely, my regeneration might not force them out. Are hand bones hollow or solid?"

"I'm not sure. I've broken several, but I never examined them too closely. You think you might have gems embedded in your hand bones?"

"Could be. For all I know, I have gems embedded in a hand-bone with gold tracery inlaid all over it. If so, it might be a good way to keep an enchantment handy."

"Oh, you're going to pay for that."

"I'm just trying to pull even with the hobbit pun."

"I'll let you get away with it," she allowed. "If you want to bury enchanted gems inside your bones, how would you go about it?"

"That's a tough question. I'd rather not stick my hand into a reality-bending nexus point and hope for the best."

"Wait a second. Didn't your ring have three gems?"

"Three functions, three gems. As a rule of thumb, you don't put multiple enchantments in the same thing. It can be done, if you're really pressed for space, but the difficulty and potential interactions—"

"Yes, I know. You've lectured on it at length. My point is, if you had three gems, you may have all three functions buried in your hand."

"That could be—"

"Don't say it," Mary warned.

"—useful," I finished.

"Better. The other thing I wonder is about the odds. Having one gem accidentally land inside a bone while your hand is pretending to be a liquid is one thing. All three would be kind of unlikely, don't you think?"

"Yes, although I don't know for sure if any of them are actually in there."

"I see a way to test our theory."

"Hypothesis. It's not a theory, yet."

"Please don't make me throw sautéed onions at you."

"I apologize. I abase myself in abject humility."

"That's better. Now, can you do the cleaning thing?"

I rubbed some gravy on the back of my right hand, let it dry for a moment, and attempted to access the cleaning spell. Dried gravy flaked away immediately.

"That's two," Mary noted. "What was the other one?"

"Skin tone. Part of my nighttime humanity disguise."

"Was it a generic thing, or could you control it?"

"What do you mean?"

"Could you change your hands to different colors, or was it your whole skin?"

"It was my whole skin. I was more concerned with power requirements in my disguise than with versatility. Low-magic worlds, you know."

"Fair enough, I suppose," Mary sighed. "Next time, go for the complicated one."

"Noted. Do you want me to develop a tan?"

"You can control the color, but you can't localize it?"

"Yes. If it works."

"Give it a try."

I tried. It worked. I darkened slightly under the afternoon sun before shifting back to my daylit-pale complexion.

"Well, what does this tell us?" I asked.

"You probably don't have gems embedded in your hand."

"Probably," I agreed, "but we don't know the properties of the nexus point. For all we know, there are other factors involved. I'll look into the bones tonight and see if there are any gems."

"Good plan. Figured out where we're going to go trawling for criminals?"

"Not yet, but I did see some nice stores. Would you like to buy an outfit to be caught dead in?"

"Let me finish lunch."

Mary decided on a whole spa treatment, shopping day, whatever it's called when a lady goes into high gear with a credit card. I went along for the ride. One place did a touchup on Mary's red hair while Mary directed me to take off my shoes. I didn't expect a pedicure, but it was surprisingly pleasant. It included a foot massage and wash, too. Very nice. My pedicurist seemed a bit nonplused at my toenails—they aren't claw-like, but they're still awfully thick and hard. I usually grind them down a bit when they start grinding through my socks.

It was a sort of vindication, to me, when the *professional* broke out the power tools.

Walking around afterward seemed almost like a violation. My feet were far too happy to be carrying me anywhere. It was unfair to them. Then again, life isn't fair. They got over it.

After sunset, we emerged from our on-shore accommodations and went for a stroll. Since it's unkind to tempt people overmuch, we were dressed in fairly low-key clothes. No expensive outfits, no fancy jewelry, nothing like that. If we were going to get mugged, I wanted to get mugged by people who did it regularly, not some first-timer who couldn't resist the fatted calf parading in front of him.

I'm considerate like that.

The criminal classes came through for us. We found a suitably disreputable district, took a slow walk through the alleys, and were accosted no less than four times. I took care to avoid inflicting bleeding wounds so Mary could put the bite on people, then we concealed the bites by carving them up with their own knives. What blood was left in the bodies oozed its way out and crawled over to me. After our second antimugging, Mary let me go first. Then we started splitting them evenly.

There wasn't a single taser or shock device among the lot of them. I was incredibly pleased. Knives, clubs, and a couple of pistols were the total weaponry. None of it was worth keeping.

After our evening meal, we returned to the *Princess* and settled in for the night. Tomorrow, we would set sail. There was a nice five-line nexus a little over a hundred miles off the coast. We could hit that and, if the weather cooperated, tag a four-line and another five-line on our way to the major nexus off the coast of Nassau.

It was tempting to ensure calm weather—judging by my early wizarding attempts, I have a talent for weather-working—but such a working might draw attention. I was getting close, very close, to jumping Johann. A few more days, maybe no more than a week, and everything would be in position.

I can hardly wait to murder him. But everything has to be perfect. He's dangerous and powerful and I absolutely must kill him on the first attempt. I won't get a second.

Tuesday, February 9th

One more nexus set up and ready to rumble. I have some preliminary spell-work done for the major nexus, as well, and I should finish it up at our next medium-nexus stop. I'm starting to feel a little optimistic about this. Not enough to take risks, but enough to think the final outcome might not be a total disaster.

Meanwhile, Johann is still sitting inside his one-way domes of doom. What's he doing in there? Planning to take over the world? Or is he happy lording it over his own magical kingdom? When you have phenomenal cosmic power, do you really care what goes on outside your living space? Last I heard, he was planning to rule the world, but his scheme involved altering the thinking processes of various diplomats and leaders. Could he be going down that road? Or simply raising up and animating armies of skeletons? Or automatons along the lines of T'yl's suit of armor?

I'd like to think Johann is sitting in his magical tower with a dozen human-looking constructs, lounging around and indulging in the various pleasures of the flesh. It seems a relatively minor use of his power, though. He strikes me as the sort to grab everything he can reach. Or was that the influence of the Evil Orb?

I hate not knowing, but I don't have a way to peek into his realm without alerting him.

Thursday, February 11th

While I was dressing for the dive, Mary cocked her head at me, obviously considering something.

"What's on your mind?" I asked.

"The plastic drum," she said.

"What about it?"

"Why bother to have it? Couldn't you go down with only a harness?"

"I could, but the drum is a safety feature."

"How so?"

"I also carry underwater flares."

"...and?" she prompted.

"Look, I sink like a brick. The drum—full of air—is a floatation device powerful enough to bring even me to the surface. Assuming I can't find the cable, I need a way to the surface before dawn. I take the drum, hold it upside-down, and burn a couple of flares so their combustion gases fill the drum. A compressed-air bottle won't do it; the pressure is too great. But twenty or so flares? That'll start the process. If I can increase my buoyancy enough to swim upward, the higher I go, the more the gas will expand, and the more buoyant the drum gets. Eventually, it'll be full of gases instead of water and I'll be dragged to the surface."

"And if that doesn't work?"

"I'll be near a nexus. I'm pretty confident I can put a spell on the drum to make it a floatation device. I could even open a gate to another universe and be instantly flushed by an unbelievably powerful surge of high-pressure seawater. It's a last resort kind of thing, though. The sudden pressure change, combined with the unbalanced pressure on my body, might result in vampiric paste being washed gently away by the drainage. It's one thing to be dropped in my tracks by a shot to the head or breaking my neck—I get better from those. But crushing me into a thin red smear is another matter. And that's assuming I don't wind up with a door into daylight." I shivered, remembering the time I burnt my face off. "I'd rather use the barrel and wave a glow stick at you."

"You really put a lot of thought into this, didn't you?"

"You have no idea. Johann has been on my mind, or on a back burner of it, pretty much constantly."

"I've noticed."

"What do you mean?"

"You haven't been yourself, and you've missed some obvious ideas."

"Oh?"

"Did it occur to you to tell me about the barrel?"

"No. Besides, you would have worried."

"By not knowing what it was for, I worried. You used to tell me everything," she pointed out.

"Oh. I'm going to have to apologize again. I'm closing in on Johann and I'm probably getting more and more focused on the upcoming dismemberment."

"Is that why you've been so hard to distract these last few days?"

"Don't you mean 'so distracted'?"

"No," she replied, with a leer.

"Ah. Yes, that's probably part of it."

"And the kingdom? Is that the other part?"

"How do you mean?"

"You gave up a kingdom. I know we can go back whenever we feel like it, but you basically gave it to Lissette, didn't you?"

I nodded. I didn't really want to talk about it.

"And Tort?" Mary went on. "That's something else again, isn't it?"

"Yes. Can we talk about this after I murder Johann? I'd rather not do the psychoanalysis thing right now. I have an overdeveloped sense of vengeance I'm nursing, which I hope will see me through this. *Then* I can have a heart-to-heart and a complete breakdown. Is that fair?"

"More than fair," she agreed, and laid a hand on my arm. "You know I'll help however I can. If you need me to shut up and soldier, tell me so. You're not in this alone."

I patted her hand and forced a smile. How could I tell her she wasn't coming with me?

"I know," I replied.

The nexus was a regular one. I finished setting it up and used its power to finish constructing the rest of my spells for the major nexus. I also encountered a bunch of dolphins—are they a pod, pack, school, or group? I don't know what to call them. I was on my way up and several of them followed the cable down out of curiosity.

They're smart creatures with something resembling souls. If I ever talk to one, I'll ask it what it knows about religion. It might be highly educational for me.

The adults swam down to look me over. A few smaller ones swam right up to me. One bumped against my helmet glass and chattered at me. I petted it and it laughed in delight before swimming circles around me.

Apparently, it doesn't matter what species they are. Kids like me, the little weirdos.

Saturday, February 13th

Deep-sea diving and nexus work. This is getting almost routine, aside from the concern about getting lost on the ocean floor and being instantly killed at sunrise. The only thing of note was Captain Tillard's weather report. We might be able to get this nexus and the major one, both, if we weren't in a hurry about it. The weather forecast called for relatively calm conditions between one storm system and the next. If we took our time and let the first one pass, we could slip in through the window between them.

I like it that he doesn't ask a lot of questions.

Sunday, February 14th

In the process of taking things slowly for a bit, the Captain has throttled back from full speed ahead or flank speed or whatever it's called, timing our arrival with the clear—or clear*er*—weather.

Mary, on the other hand, has spoken to the staff—not the crew—about Valentine's Day. Under her direction, they've gone to considerable effort to make everything as romantic as possible for us today. Candlelight at mealtimes, romantic music everywhere, champagne on ice, appropriate movies already queued up in the lounge, chocolate everywhere, the works. All we were missing was rose petals strewn about. No floating florist shops.

Mary forbade me from wearing anything more substantial than a robe. Today was a day to lounge around and do nothing but cuddle, kiss, and be happy.

You know, I think she's good for my morale.

I wish I could enjoy it more, but the shadow of Johann is falling darker over my world. It's hard to let go of it and do anything else. But I'm trying, because Mary wants to. I think she's trying to help. How can I tell her I don't want or need to be diverted from the task at hand? I can't. All I can do is thank her and try to enjoy whatever she's planned.

She does make me happy, though. If only I weren't so focused…

Monday, February 15th

The last major nexus on my route is only about fifteen miles east of Great
Abaco Island, in the Bahamas. It's one of the shallower ones—less than ten
thousand feet down—but it still hasn't got a pyramid. The location is a flat stretch
of ocean floor, about as interesting as any flat stretch of desert at night.

I set up my spells, tapped the nexus lightly, and kept adding power to the
containment iterations. Now I knew what I was doing, so it went much more
quickly. With the pre-made spells supercharged from the previous nexuses to
give me a head start, the whole thing didn't take three hours to finish.

Still, I wonder why there was a pyramid at one nexus. I've looked at four of
the major magical centers of the world, now, and only one is contained by a piece
of magical technology. It makes me wonder if I should go look at all the others.
Maybe I'll scry on them when I have time.

Now, though, I'm spending my time aboard the *Princess* getting my mind set
for my upcoming fight. I'd sharpen my sword and polish my shield, but the sword
I'm bringing is already too sharp to be believed and I don't have a shield.

Mary is being a good sport. My toothpick-like wit, never overly sharp to
begin with, is even less amusing than usual. I'm no fun and I know it. My heart
really isn't in anything else but my project.

All I can think about is killing Johann. I've been waiting for this for weeks.
I've been anticipating this, looking forward to it, occasionally even clamping
down on the urge to go screaming off to attack him. I want his head crushed
between my hands. I want his eyeballs on my fingers like some cannibalistic
version of olives at Thanksgiving. I want his spine in my hands so I can whirl it
around and see if it makes the same sound as those whirly-tube noisemakers. I
want to see his face as his teeth explode, one by one. I—

—should probably not go on about it. It's hard enough to keep calm when I
know the moment of truth is coming.

Everything is ready. I'm as prepared as I can get. And I've got a couple of
days before I can actually do anything.

We're steaming north, well outside the military exclusion zone around Johann
and Family's shields. We'll park at the edge of the nominal border. Properly
timed, I feel certain we could penetrate the interdiction zone without being
intercepted by anything short of a missile. It's a lot of border to cover. That's not
part of the plan, though.

Once we're on-station, I'll set off the sequence of spells. One of the smaller
nexus setups will start by launching a disruption effect missile at Johann's first,
central shield. The spell will travel to a point directly over Johann's nexus, then
detonate in a downward wave of energy to wreck the mystic lines of force forming
his spells. I doubt the shield will go down, but it's possible. Regardless, Johann
will feel the hit. It won't be some local magi knocking at the door. He'll know
it's *me* kicking it in. He'll have to defend himself, and that means sucking up
power from his nexus.

I did consider trying to block the power lines leading to his nexus, and to the
nexuses of all the kids and grandkids. Unfortunately, tinkering with such things
requires an immense amount of power and would create obvious effects. Just

experimenting with it could tip him off about someone interfering, and I'm actually hoping he thinks I'm still in Karvalen. I'm reasonably sure I could cut the power lines, given time to experiment, but there's no way to hide monkey business on that scale. Even without touching a line leading to Johann's nexus, the power would fluctuate as the rest of the planet rebalanced itself. I absolutely cannot risk attracting his attention until I'm ready.

Anyway, after a couple of demigod-scale attacks on his protective dome— hopefully, without breaking it—he'll have to take action. First off, he should reinforce his defensive dome, if it's still up. If it is, I'll see it get stronger. If it's down, I'll be able to scry on his nexus point directly. Either way, he'll be on top of the thing. I'll know where he is; I'll have a physical location.

Then I activate the rest of the nexuses. They start doing the same thing as the first one, but with so many of them, it's effectively a rapid-fire sequence. Some of them, of course, will hit a lot harder.

Or, to slip into a metaphor, if I fire some bullets into a house from my pistol, I'll really annoy the resident. When he opens a window or fires back, I'll know where he is. That's when I shift to the belt-fed machine gun and really let him have it.

These ongoing magic-disrupting pulses should utterly ruin anything magical within hundreds of miles. I'm sure Firebrand and Bronze will survive, being so far out to sea, but I'm certainly not bringing them into the place with me. In the heart of a massive, repeated, ongoing magic-blasting onslaught is no place for beings held together by magic. It's not really a place for anything sensitive to magical emanations at all.

I'm not sure how I'm going to feel, either. It could be... unpleasant. For all I know, it could kill me. But I'm not going to risk anyone else. This is my revenge, and I'm taking it.

I'm bringing my spare sword, though; it's merely enchanted, not my friend. When the EMP-like anti-magic bursts destroy the enchantment, it's still a sharp chunk of metal. I plan to take the flying helicopter thing on the forward deck, go as fast as it will fly, and land on top of an enraged and frustrated Johann.

What's he going to do? Cast a spell at me? If he has a gun lying around handy—but why should he? —he might shoot me down, but people have shot guns at me before. It doesn't end well.

I'd be more concerned about what Mary, Bronze, and Firebrand are going to think, but I can't think that far ahead anymore. All I can think about is Johann.

Friday, February 19th

First thing in the morning, the crew cleared the decks and I double-checked the skycycle. I had my armored underwear on, my anti-detection spells, my secondary sword, a combat knife, a nine-millimeter automatic, a lighter, and a parachute. I brought my skinphone, but decided against my Diogo-phone. The micro-gate ring inside it isn't enchanted, but it would be a shame to get it damaged before I could get any real use out of it. I also left my various forms of identification behind. The last thing I needed was a fake ID during my premeditated murder.

I went down into the hold to put everything in a saddlebag. It's not that I don't trust the crew, but I don't. Not completely.

Bronze looked at me and told me she knew what I was doing, snorting irritated smoke as she did so.

"I expect you do," I admitted. "I'm sorry. You *can't* come with me. It'll kill you before you reach the nexus, I know it will."

She agreed, and pointed out I should have had this conversation long ago. She emphasized it with a stomp that silently dented the deck.

"You're right, I should have, and I apologize. I've been afraid to have this talk. I'm afraid of a lot of things, most of all losing people. I've lost the Fabulous Four. I've lost Tort. I feel like I've lost everyone in Karvalen. I'm afraid of losing you."

Obviously, I was unable to lose her. I'm stupid on that front, but she loves me anyway.

"So... you're not angry about me going in like this?"

Of course she was angry about it, but it wasn't directed at me. It was at the injustice of it all. She wouldn't get to take her own bite out of Johann or stomp him herself. Travis never got to break Tobias' kneecaps, either.

"I know, I know. I don't keep my word. I'm a liar *and* a coward. I can't seem to help it. And will you please calm down? Your eyes are starting to glow and there's fuel down here."

She was apologetic, but still annoyed. She promised not to take out her frustrations on me. But I owed her a place to run free for a while. This plan left her out of things completely, so I owed her a chance to really stretch her legs.

"I'll find someplace," I assured her. It pleased me greatly to have her assume I was coming back. "What did I ever do to deserve you?"

Bronze thought it a stupid question. What did I do to deserve hands? Or a heart? We were us, simple, obvious, perfect.

If I were a more philosophical man, I'd wonder why I have a better relationship with my horse than with any woman I've ever known. A simpler relationship, anyway. Absolutes are always simple.

Firebrand still hung on the wall of the master suite's bedroom. I wasn't sure if I wanted to tell it anything. Then again, I knew I didn't want to tell Mary what was going to happen.

She didn't give me a choice. After I had them start prepping the skycycle, Mary cornered me in the bedroom and demanded to know what I thought I was doing.

"I know that thing won't carry both of us," she told me. "It'll barely carry you. Which means you're either going to send me somewhere on it, or you're going somewhere without me. And you're the one wearing the parachute. Now talk!"

Yep, I was in trouble.

"What seems to be the problem?"

"The problem is I've been far too understanding. You had a plan. Fine. I didn't quiz you for the details, just the outline. You were working on it. Fine. You routinely descended to unreasonable depths to meddle with powers mortal man dares not touch. Fine. You've had a hard time in Karvalen, with Tort, with Johann, and in general. Fine. I've done my part, being helpful, kind, understanding, all of it. I've respected your silence—for the most part. I've given you emotional space around your issues. I've been the most understanding, tolerant, and patient girlfriend in the history of humanity—and it hasn't been easy!

"Now we're obviously closing in on Johann and you're about to take off in a flying contraption without me!"

I'm okay with waiting here, Firebrand interjected. I wanted to feel relieved, but Mary was on a roll.

"You shut up!" Mary snapped. The dragon in the steel shut up. She swung her glare back to me, eyes blazing brightly enough to make me wonder if she'd spoken with Sparky at some point. "You're about to *leave*," she accused. "We've haven't really talked about it, but I thought we had an understanding. You don't leave me out of things. You don't walk away and act like you don't care. I'm involved in everything, because we do things *together*. When you try and pull a vanishing act, it pisses me off and makes me feel as though you don't actually care about me. The bit with going to visit Lissette I could stand; I was your rescue force. My trip to get a yacht and prepare for whatever this is, I took it like a good soldier because you told me you *needed* me to. But now you're about to fly off without me, and that tells me you *don't need me!*

"Do you have any idea how it feels?" she demanded, tears starting down her face. "I need you in my life, and you're pushing me away! Your actions and attitude are telling me I'm not part of this—that I'm on my own. And I don't want to lose you!"

I sat down on the couch and put my head in my hands. Mary remained standing, watching me and wiping her face while I marshaled my thoughts. I looked up at her and beckoned her over to the couch. She hesitated, but came over and sat down. I put my arms around her.

"You're right," I told her, "in telling me I was wrong. I didn't... I didn't really think of your feelings, of how this had to look to you. I'm sorry. I love you and I don't ever want you to feel otherwise."

Mary cried into my shirt.

"I've been... off, lately," I continued. "This.. thing... has been a goal of mine, a personal goal, something intimate and singular. I've been trying to not think about it too much until I could do something about it. Now I'm doing something. Now my plan is almost complete. I'm so close I can taste it, and it's taking all my focus to sit here, rather than sprinting for the skycycle and charging in to kill an evil wizard, *because I really want to.*"

I grimaced and hugged her harder.

"I don't know how you can help, beyond all the fantastic efforts you've already made. You've made it possible by being my support, even if you don't see it. That's my fault. You don't know the plan. You've just followed along, knowing I had one. Well, I should have told you, and I'm sorry I didn't. I'll correct it.

"Here's my plan. I set off various and sundry spells to lure Johann to his nexus point. Once he's there, I knock down the domes, fly in, and kill him. I'm too heavy for the thing to carry us both, as you pointed out, so I go alone.

"The spells are magical disruption spells. Powerful ones. They'll hammer the crap out of anything Johann tries to do after they knock down the domes. They should destroy even enchanted objects, like golem horses or intelligent weapons."

Which is why I'm okay with hanging out on a boat, Firebrand added. *I'm on your side, Boss, but I'm not stupid.*

"Are you sure this will work?" Mary asked, squeezing me harder. "You've tapped several nexuses, but you're tackling him on his home ground. The spells you've worked are hundreds or thousands of miles away."

"True, but... remember my lecture on the inverse-square law and how to get around it?"

"No."

I sighed. This is what happens when you don't give homework and exams.

"Magical spells can work in two main ways. The first way can generate an effect which then travels to the target. I can use a spell to generate electricity and guide it, but the lightning bolt will make an arc from my hand to the target. This is the way most spells work when you're laying hands on your subject to work on it.

"The second way is to target the spell at a point. Picture a magical line extending from your hand to a target point. The spell slides along the line to the place you want it. This is like firing a missile at the target; the explosion happens far away."

"What about gates following scrying portals?"

"Are we having a fight or a lesson in magic?"

"I'm trying *not* to have a fight!"

"Okay, okay. Gates and scrying portals are both in the second category. By establishing a connection with the scrying portal, you have something for the gate to follow. Imagine stringing a cable across a canyon. Once you have that, it's a lot easier to build an actual suspension bridge—you can run lots of cables back and forth once you have the first one, rather than climb down, drag the cable across, and climb up again."

"If you say so. So, your spells are going to be as effective as Johann's?"

"At least. And I have more of them, more power, and an automated system of magical disruption pummeling."

"What about his kids?"

"The other nexus points are in range. I've got enough minor nexuses to keep them busy, with occasional swats from a major one. Johann is getting the big ones, once I sucker him into position with the one off the coast of Portugal."

Mary sat up as I spoke and wiped at her face with one hand. The other kept a grip on mine.

"I was also asking about what you intend to do about them."

"Kill them."

"What, all of them?"

"I'm going to kill Johann surely, and slowly if I can manage it. Then I'll turn my attention to killing his conspirators or collaborators or partners—I don't care if they're his grown children or grandchildren, hired grunts, or personal unicorns. They're all going to die, and if that ends his family line, then so be it. That's the whole reason I'm here. It's what I came for."

"I see."

"Is that going to be a problem?"

"Hell, no!" she declared, surprised. "Are you kidding me? If I'd known, I'd have bought a knife for each of them. But *why*, by all that is dark and gruesome, did we not simply buy *two* of the flying motorcycles? Couldn't I go hunting for the kids while you distract everyone with Johann? Or don't you trust me to be a competent assassin?"

I didn't want to tell her how much I wanted to rip them apart with my hands. Then again, the one I really wanted was Johann. Could I give her his coven-mates? Or did I need to kill them all personally? *Did* I need to kill them all? Killing Johann, yes... Killing the rest, yes... but did it matter to me how the others died? If it did matter—if I did have to do it myself—was that appropriate, or overdoing it? What was just the right amount of revenge?

Fortunately, I had a much better answer on tap, and it was also the truth.

"The answer is painfully obvious, isn't it?" I asked.

"Not to me!"

"Because I'm a moron and didn't think of it."

"Oh," she replied, subsiding. "Hmm. I can see that, I guess."

"Look, *never* think I'd leave you out deliberately. If I'd thought to bring a spare skycycle, we would have. It didn't even occur to me until you mentioned it."

"See why it's important to discuss these things?"

"I'm not sure if I should threaten to spank you or ask you to not needle me about it," I admitted. "I'm having a hard time dealing with this."

"Yes, you are," she agreed, "and so am I. Tell you what... we can order another skycycle and it'll be ready to pick up before we get there."

"No," I snapped. "I can't do that."

"Why not?" she demanded.

"Because everything is in place! All the spells, all the nexuses, everything. I'm ready to go and *I can't wait any longer!* I need to do this!"

"All right," Mary agreed, suddenly calm. I didn't trust that calm. "You need to do this. Fine." She gripped her forehead with one hand, fingertips pressing into her temples. "Do you have any objection to me helping, provided I can find a way?"

"No. I might need the help," I admitted. "The only two who absolutely cannot come with me are Firebrand and Bronze. The environment I'm creating should cripple Johann, but it will kill them. It might not be so good for any magical creature, either, including undead, but I don't think it will be lethal."

"Then, can you wait just a *little* longer? Long enough to detour and drop me off on the continent? Give me the GPS locations of the nexus points and turn me loose! By the time the *Princess* gets to your starting point, I'll have figured out my own transport. Is that fair? —no, wrong question. Can you hold on to your patience long enough do that much for me? Can you be a rock of calm for one day more? One day, for me, as a favor?"

I took a moment and took stock of my feelings. I was *this* close to launching myself like a cruise missile. But... Mary was asking for a favor. Could I give it to her?

"Yes," I agreed, hoping I wasn't lying. "I can do that. But I'm going to be hard to live with between now and then. I know it, and I'll try not to be, but I know the murderous rage inside is going to fray my good intentions. There's a monster, it wants loose, and it's *me*."

"I'll warn the Captain."

New Bedford, Massachusetts, was the closest un-domed port of call on the continent. It was only about a hundred and thirty miles away from a dome—one edge cut through Fall River almost along the line of Underwood Street—so we steamed off for it at top speed. New Bedford was still a hotbed of military activity. It was far enough away to accept civilian traffic, fortunately, but an awful lot of troops and equipment were parked there, ready to respond to anything from the shimmering, soap-bubble distortion.

Mary didn't even say goodbye. She was already dressed and ready to go when the *Princess* pulled up alongside a pier. She kissed me, sprang off the ship, sprinted to a waiting Google Cab, and sped away.

Captain Tillard assured me we would be back to my launch point as quickly as possible.

"Forget speed," I told him. "I need to be ready to launch right before sunset, and we're not going to make it back in time. It'll have to be tomorrow."

"Very good, sir. I'll see to it. Is there anything else you need?"

"To be left strictly alone."

"I'll pass the word."

I went below, laid down on the lowest deck, and waited for sunset. Tendrils like a hungry net killed everything in our path on the way back. Firebrand cleared its psychic throat.

"What do you want?"

I didn't want to say it while she was upset, but I'm with Mary, Boss.

"In what way?"

I think it's cheesy of you to set up a wizard-killing I can't go to.

"Oh. I'm terribly sorry," I told it, drenching it in sarcasm. "May I inquire about your plan?"

My plan?

"Yes, your plan. The one to kill the demigod wizard without getting me turned into a newt and you into an ornamental hat pin for giants. That plan."

I don't actually have a plan, Firebrand admitted. *I just don't like yours.*

"Fair enough. Think up a better one while I meditate before battle."
Spoilsport.
"Shut. Up."
I stepped into my headspace.

Firebrand followed me into my mental study, resting on my desk. I used to have a fireplace... whatever happened to it? Something the Demon King did, maybe?

I concentrated for a moment. Instead of a fireplace, I put a sword-rack on the wall above the couch. Firebrand vanished from the desk and reappeared on the rack.

Thanks, Boss. Makes me feel welcome.
"You are. I'm just..."
Annoyed? Grouchy? Grumpy? Angry?
"Yes."

The hatchway to my undermind sounded with four rapid knocks. It didn't buck or rattle. Whatever wanted out was knocking politely.

"Well, that's a first," I muttered.
No kidding, Firebrand agreed, suspiciously.
"Any idea what it is?"
Sorry, Boss. I don't do the deep stuff, just the upper portions of thinking.
"Thought I'd ask." I took Firebrand down from its rack and looked at the hatchway. Without the Demon King to reinforce my own insecurities, cruelties, and darker nature, I might be able to handle anything squeezing itself through the opening. It's one thing to have every horrible memory of your life dropped on you at once, but quite another to tackle them one at a time.

With Firebrand in hand—a flaming, psychic sword—I thought we might be in fairly good shape.

"What do you think, Firebrand?"
I think we can take 'em, Boss. The blade rippled with flames as the knocking repeated, *tock-tock-tock-tock.*

"All right!" I called out. "All right. I hear you. Be advised I'm armed and in no mood to trifle with my subconscious."

"I understand," came back, muffled by the hatch. I worked the bolts to unlock it, then toed the latch. Nothing immediate happened.

"It's open," I announced. The hatch lifted slightly, paused, moved up slowly. A hand appeared at the edge, pushing the hatch upward. Another hand extended up and out, empty and open. They looked perfectly normal.

A moment later, I was climbing out. Not me, exactly—a personal demon of mine. He looked much like me, but better. A trifle taller, slightly broader in the shoulders. His physique is mine, but with another ten pounds of muscle. His face is handsome, his hair is perfect, and his smile almost makes a *ting* sound when the light hits it. He's an idealized me, a perfect version of me, and he haunts me.

Now he wants to talk? *Now?*

"What do you want?" I asked. "No, don't climb out. You can stand right there, or a few steps down. I don't want you wandering. That's better. Now tell me what you want."

"I was hoping to have a civilized discussion."

"We're having it."

"While you hover over me with a lit sword?"

"I'm not hitting you with it," I pointed out. "That's as close to civilized as I'm prepared to be with a personal demon."

"I'm hardly a demon."

"Depends on where you're standing. Explain what you want or we'll see how fast you can duck."

"Very well, since you insist. I would like to take this opportunity to be your conscience."

"My *what?*"

"I'm a perfect version of you. Stronger, faster, smarter, but also more generous, noble, kind, brave…"

"I get it, I get it. So?"

"I'm also part of you. An aspect of your personality. Of course, I'm psychologically stable enough to accept I am only one part—a powerful part, but only a part—of your personality gestalt."

"Well, isn't that nice? I'm glad someone in here isn't crazy."

"Indeed. But my message is this. Are you sure you want to kill Johann?"

"Yes."

"You know," my better self said, "the Fabulous Four—to say nothing of little Olivia—would not approve of your quest. They would not want you to kill him on their behalf."

"I figured that out for myself," I told him. "I'm not doing it for them. Wherever they are, I hope they're having a wonderful afterlife. I, on the other hand, have plenty of reasons to kill Johann."

"Name three."

"He used me to kill children. Argue with that."

"I wouldn't dream of it."

"He used me to open nexuses for his relatives."

"I see a pattern developing. Is this about what he tricked you into doing, or about the fact he used you?"

"You have a distinct point, and I acknowledge it. However, you haven't heard my third reason."

"My apologies. Do continue."

"He keeps trying to kill me."

"Is that his fault, or the fault of the Evil Orb?"

I could feel my jaw tighten and my eyes narrow.

"You're trying to tell me I shouldn't kill him?"

"Oh, no. Not at all. He certainly deserves to die."

"So?"

"I merely want to make sure you've thought it through. Emotionally, there is no great deal of difference between murdering a man because it's politically expedient and plotting the bloody assassination of a wizard-king you helped create."

"Says you. Now back down the steps."

"I merely wish to add—"

I swung. He ducked, but Firebrand belched a cloud of flame in his face. He rolled backward down the stairs and I kicked the trapdoor closed. A moment later, I had it latched and bolted.

When I tried to delete it, to roll the floor over it and make it go away, it still didn't budge. I sat on the hatch and tried not to think about what it all meant.

Boss?

"What is it, Firebrand?"

Did we just try to kill your conscience?

"Part of it, maybe."

What does that mean?

"Oddly enough, I'm trying not to think about it."

Oh? What are you trying to think about?

"I'm visualizing a successful murder."

Why do you call it that? We're killing an evil wizard, right? Isn't that one of the things you do?

"It's a motivation thing. My idealized demon is at least partly correct. I'm not doing this because I'm defending myself or others. I'm doing this because he hurt me, and this is my vengeance. I've plotted and planned and worked to bring about a situation where I can kill a man. This is premeditated, with malice aforethought, and I don't care. I want to kill him, I intend to kill him, and I'm going to kill him."

Okay by me. Let me know how that works out for you.

"I'll try."

Saturday, February 20th

In every enterprise of note, there is a moment. The moment is a timeless thing, stretching infinitely outward, wherein one stands, poised, upon the precipice. In this sliver of time, this universe of unrealized possibility, cast over everything is the shadow of doubt. It may be a black curtain, concealing everything, or a thin, grey mist, obscuring only the most distant and trivial of details, but it is the uncertainty of the enterprise, the free will of the universe, expressed in this moment of decision. To make the decision, to choose, is to defy all doubt, to step from the edge of the precipice, to launch oneself irrevocably upon a course uncertain, eyes cast forward to the goal. To look back is useless, for the past has no bearing, no power, not even—for the moment—any value. There is only the future, rushing nearer, and oneself, rushing to meet it.

Standing on the deck of the *Silver Princess*, I looked at the soap-bubble dome and the seething, prismatic distortion of things beyond. To raise my hand and invoke a minor power would be a simple thing, yet it would set in motion powers to shake the world.

Is this a choice? Is this where I make my decision? How hard have I worked to get here? What have I risked to bring about this moment?

I could turn away now. I could turn my back on this enterprise, walk into a distant universe and hide. Knowing what I know now, he would never find me. I could sit in my quiet home, read books, meditate on the ways of life, death, undead, blood, and magic. I could recall the time I had the means, motive, and opportunity to murder a man deserving of it, and feel good about myself for resisting the urge to do so.

Do we have free will if the choice is already made? Is it still a choice if you have always known the answer? Do I really have a choice? Or is there a destiny that shapes our ends? Free will or fate? Johann set me in motion. Am I already a soulless thing, acting like a wind-up toy, a rough-hewn simulation of the man I once was?

Either way, does it matter?

Johann had to die, and I was the one to kill him.

I went below as the sun began to set and the tingling turned to stinging. I waited it out in the master bedroom, gestured myself clean with my left hand, and went back up on deck. The sky was still light enough in the west to hurt my eyes with the remnants of sunset, but the visor of the helmet cut the glare enough for me to see.

I turned my back on the sunset, concentrated on a nexus far to the east, raised both hands to launch my spell, and the deadly dance began.

I felt the crackle of magical energy before I saw it. The spell arced through the air like a comet come to end the world. It shivered through the sky above me, passed above the domes, and detonated, all in the blink of an eye. The world rippled like a disturbed reflection. Johann's dome didn't quite go down, but I saw the way the spell flexed and cracked. Had it been a physical structure, pieces would have fallen off. As it was, the energy from his nexus blazed through the fissures for a moment before the spell structure absorbed it. The cracks closed, sealing themselves as the power flowed into the dome, shoring it up, reinforcing it.

Good.

In a few seconds, the dome was almost back to full strength, but the second disruption bomb dropped. This one was slightly stronger, as per the program. I sat on my skycycle and watched as the dome cracked again, much worse than before. It splintered, almost shattered, with lines shooting through it like empty lightning. Power continued to flow upward, filling in the cracks and gluing the whole thing back together, but not fast enough.

The third disruption attack hit. For just a moment, a bare instant before it did, I saw a sudden surge of force into the dome. Johann, rather than relying on some automatic spell to pump energy into his protective bubble, actively took a hand in reinforcing it. Thus, the third attack, while it cracked the dome again, still didn't take it down.

I, on the other hand, had lines of power in both hands, readied, prepared, poised. I raised both hands in a scooping motion, like a conductor urging the whole orchestra into a fortissimo blast.

I spent so long tapping so many nexus points. Now all that preparation and work showed its worth.

Everything activated at once. Disruption spells streaked above each dome's center, directly over each nexus, striking downward like a rain of meteors. The rapid-fire thunder was less than material, of course, invisible to the untrained eye. Yet, such was the power involved that crew members on deck whipped around to stare, confused about why. But they watched with me as the domes shattered under the onslaught, disintegrating into glassy shards of energy, dissolving as they fell.

The blasts continued, staggered, each nexus of mine firing when it had enough of a charge, spacing out the pummeling into a series of hits instead of volleys. Blasts of disruptive force shot down into the now-visible fountains of nexus energy, scattering them, striking the ground, blowing outward like rolling thunder. Wave fronts of spell-scrambling energies expanded, intersected, overlapped, heaved up and smashed down. This process would continue indefinitely if I didn't shut it off. Good luck to anyone trying to concentrate in the thick of it, much less assemble and coordinate energy into a spell.

I gave the skycycle full throttle and shot toward the naked coast.

If I was right, Johann was standing on his nexus. Since he teleported so easily and often, when the attacks hit, he should have bounced to the thing, stood in the geyser of power, and defended his domain. Now, though, he should have all the power he could shake a stick at... and be unable to do anything. Assembling a spell requires power—which he had—but also requires a relatively stable environment to build it. This is the default for most environments—Karvalen, New York, the bottom of the ocean floor. But standing in the middle of ongoing magical carpet-bombing is not stable. Even concentrating enough to build a basic energy-guide should be beyond him, or anyone.

I felt it while I was still over the ocean. It was like feeling the rumble of thunder, only on a spiritual level. Even my tendrils could feel it. I tried using them to lift the skycycle—who knows? It might work! —and shove it forward even faster. The magical disruption attacks, though, were a rapid-fire hammering that made my tendrils sting. This grew steadily worse as I approached the shore. I noticed, in passing, a brief pain in my left hand and the resulting regeneration, followed by a short, sharp crackle from my armored underwear as it lost its enchantment. Well, I expected this, only not so soon. I still had a few hundred miles to go. I even had to let go with my tendrils and withdraw them into myself as the pain grew excruciating.

It's vaguely possible I might have overdone it by just a smidge. Not that I'm complaining—there is no kill like overkill. I would rather err on the side of caution. But I might have been the least little bit off in my calculations.

I spent the entire trip crouched as low as I could get, urging the skycycle to its top speed at surface-skimming heights. First over the ocean, then at treetop height over land. The GPS system already had the nexus coordinates in it and a minimum-distance path in my augmented-reality visor. All I had to do was stick to the path and hope Johann didn't wander off on foot. I didn't actually need the GPS guidance; the geyser of power at each open nexus was like a searchlight spearing the nighttime sky. No, more like actual fountains, actually. They sprayed power upward and it was bashed about, scattered back and forth, like a fountain of water in a storm.

The terrain below me was a mess. I spared it the occasional glance by vamp-o-vision and the waning moonlight.

Whatever changes Johann and Family wreaked on their domain, everything was coming undone. Magical creatures—miniature dragons, pony-sized unicorns, butterfly-winged fairies—were lying on the ground. Some were twitching, some were not. Less magical creatures were staggering under the constant barrage or curled up in some sheltered spot to scream. Mundane creatures—that is, creatures which did not require magic to survive—coped best, but even they were struggling with the continuous stream of unfamiliar psychic input. Imagine being aware of a ghost screaming at you, but having no idea what's going on. No sound reaches your ears, no sign of a ghost is visible. Yet, something screams in your ears—or between them—and you're as aware of it as if someone were actually screaming, and it's just as impossible to ignore.

I heard it and felt it, but I had the advantage of knowing exactly what it was. This did not make it pleasant.

I flew over melting landscapes and crumbling constructs, the remnants of semi-real conjurations. Labyrinths of roses, towers of porcelain, lakes of polished glass, all were coming apart as their magical structure crumbled. A kingdom all in pieces, melting or shattering even as I flew above it all.

It seemed to take all night, but my skycycle's clock told me it was less than two hours before my destination came into sight. It was a wasteland of crushed vegetation, golden stone, and multicolored glass, all of it melting like ice. In the center of it all was a fountain of light that cast no shadows, visible only to eyes attuned to such things. In the heart of it, the figure of a man burned brightly, angrily, jerking and twisting with each thunderclap of power, struggling mightily against energies vaster far than his own.

How's it feel, Johann, old buddy, to be on the other end of the stick?

I brought the cycle in for a landing. I could see him glare at me, his teeth clenched as he struggled to raise his head. It had to be like being in a magical hailstorm, constantly and relentlessly pounded from above. I felt it myself, almost like physical blows. I had to lean forward slightly and place my feet carefully to keep my balance amid the continuous blasts.

We must have looked like a pair of drunks to mortal eyes. He was simply some guy on his knees, leaning forward on both hands, trying not to throw up. I didn't stagger, but I walked with exaggerated care toward him.

On a more subtle level, we were both in a storm of energies. He was in the heart of the nexus, centered in the eruption of power, unwilling or unable to move from it while the spell-shattering bombs burst over us. I slogged through the buffeting, braced against the effects and trying not to grunt at each detonation.

At last, I stopped and swayed at the edge of the open nexus, looked into the blazing heart of it. He snarled at me, hating me, hating being on his knees while I stood before him. For me, this was weeks, months of work, of planning, of patience, of holding on to the urge to kill, holding out against the urge to kill. It all came down to this moment, and right or wrong, moral, ethical, good, or otherwise, I found I could savor it, even in the midst of the storm.

"I've been looking forward to this for a long time," I told him, and my voice sounded strange. I could hear it with my ears in the silence, even through the psychic thunders cascading over us. "How's it feel to be the one on your knees?" He didn't answer, but his glare intensified. It was a good glare, full of hate and walking arm in arm with its cousin, fear.

"As a formality," I continued, into the thundering silences all around us, "do you want to give me my ball back? I could be persuaded to mercy," I lied. I think he knew it.

"Go... to... hell," he replied, gasping out each word. He surged up from his bent-over position and gestured at me with both hands, hurling raw energy at me. He intended it to be a blast of power, a tight beam of energy, but the continuous barrage around us scattered it, reduced it to a spray, a foam. It was like being hit with an ocean wave, not a wall. I braced against it and kept my feet. His face screwed up in a snarl of terror, like a cornered animal.

"You first," I replied. I sprang, leaping with all my strength into the current of power. The wash of energy over and through me was a different sort of pain, somewhat similar to biting a fake goddess of fire. I hit Johann hard and fast, all five hundred pounds of me, but it wasn't meant to hurt him. I meant to grab him, but his body was charged in the fountain of power. Contact with him gave me a nasty shock, akin to hugging a live wire. Still, I hit him pretty much dead center. The impact and my velocity sent up both tumbling almost out of the nexus. Close enough for my purposes, because I laid a hand on him—laid claws into the meat and bone of him—and finished rolling out of the area.

He screamed as we left the bath of energies. It must have partly shielded him from the effects of my ongoing assault. He convulsed and shuddered under the psychic hammering, the equivalent of being pinned down and punched across the face, left-right-left-right, without letup or relief

I loved his scream. It was a beautiful sound.

It took me a few seconds to recover from the trip through the nexus point's energies. I kept my grip on Johann, though, while he struggled and screamed and tried to scramble back into the nexus. When I shook off the aftereffects, I made him scream again, and again, by folding his knees and elbows the wrong way, one at a time. I did it slowly, so he could feel the tendons pop and the bones grind in each and every one of them.

I held him by the hair, keeping him upright as I crouched next to him. He shivered all over, muscles twitching at random, uncontrollably. But he looked at me. He was in there. And he was afraid.

"You know, there are a lot of ways you could be useful to me," I told him, shouting over the psychic thunder. "I could drain what's left of your miserable soul and eat it. I could drink your blood. I could question you at great length about my ball, for example."

"It's gone," he whimpered. "I'll tell you anything! Anything!"

"I know you would," I told him, patting him gently, comfortingly, pretending to calm him. "I know. I know. You just want to live. I know. I understand. But you know what?" I asked, and waited. He whimpered. I took it as an answer and leaned close, pressing my lips lightly to his ear. "I'm glad you want to live," I whispered, "because I'm going to take that away from you." He stopped breathing for a second.

"You used me to kill *children*," I continued, whispering like a lover, "five of whom were especially important to me. I doubt they would want any part of this, because they were good, decent children. They were kind and generous and, being dead now, can probably forgive what you did.

"They were better than me. They always were. The only difference, today, is now we both know it.

"You went to a lot of trouble to summon a Guardian Demon."

I extended my finger-talons and slowly, carefully, pushed two fingers into his eyes. He screamed and squirmed, but I pinned him down, held his head, and continued to push slowly, piercing both eyeballs, pushing onward to crack the thin bone at the back of the eyesocket. I slipped my fingers out quickly, to minimize the blood flowing into me. I didn't want any of it.

With him blinded and crippled, I was only warmed up. I hurt him with extraordinary care to give back some measure of the suffering he doled out to me.

Normally, I have an aversion to torture. I still do. I find it distasteful, even disgusting. But I didn't give a damn.

I didn't want to persuade him to do something for me, to tell my anything. I wasn't trying to force him to give me something he withheld. All I wanted was his death—a slow death, a painful death, a death his soul could remember as a lesson for its next incarnation.

And some personal satisfaction. All right, a lot of personal satisfaction.

When I was done, I ruptured his lungs and let him die by drowning in his own blood. After he quit breathing, or trying to, I waited seven minutes to make sure he was definitely dead—I couldn't see what he used for a soul very well with all the magical pyrotechnics going on. I carefully did not try to eat it. Wherever he was going, he could damn well walk—and I hoped it was a long trip.

After the time was up, I stomped his head flat, crushed my way down his spine, and kicked the remains of his skeleton to gravel.

Still with great care, I shuffled through the ongoing storm to gather what there was of flammable materials from the ruins around us. It wasn't much of one, but I built him a pyre, lit it with a perfectly normal lighter, and sat down in the storm of spells to watch him burn. Let the powers in the sky rain down pain like hail; I felt good about it. So good, in fact, I wasted half an hour simply enjoying the feeling of completion, of finality. I set out to kill him, to take revenge on him, and I did. There's a lot of satisfaction in that, enough to make it worthwhile to sit there in the maelstrom of forces.

I left the smoldering heap billowing black smoke behind me.

Heading southwest at full throttle, I made for the next nexus. According to the onboard computer, I didn't have the fuel for it, but I also didn't see any gas stations. The skycycle would take me as far as it would take me and I'd see how fast I could run when it gave up.

What were they doing under these domes? Rearranging the world to suit themselves? There wasn't a single structure standing from the modern era and now very few from the current administration. Most of the oddities were conjured out of thin air by spells, existed because of spells, and crumbled when those spells crumbled. With so much energy on tap, it was easier and more versatile than going to all the trouble of actually *building* anything.

There were some exceptions. A number of glassy spires lay in pieces. I presume they were supported by magic, but made of real glass. Some castles remained standing, minus the pieces of conjured architecture. I passed the ruins of at least one former floating castle.

From the looks of the living things, however, Johann—or his descendants—experimented along the same lines as Victor Frankenstein, only they didn't limit themselves to human parts. Strange chimeras of mixed and mismatched creatures lay dead, while other, more viable creations still wandered. There were quite a lot of them, enough to form armies, and I wondered why he bothered.

As I crossed into the overlapping area between Johann's personal dome and another, I observed a shift in emphasis. The fortifications were more solid, less fanciful, made for actual defense. Hordes of mismatched creatures lay sprawled all around them, while similar creatures still guarded the walls. Wargames, perhaps? A large-scale variation on strategy games? Or simply a game of toy soldiers with living things?

The fuel light blinked angrily at me and I slowed my headlong flight, landing before I was forced to crash. The rest of the trip would be on foot, unless I could promote a ride. What I might ride was a valid question. I hadn't seen anything resembling a horse since I left Bronze. Even if I did find some magical mixture of many parts, whether or not it was in any shape to move, much less carry me, was doubtful.

So I ran. I'm not as fast as Bronze. I don't corner nearly as well. I suspect she's a superior jumper, too. But I still have the advantage over anything mortal. I don't get tired. I get hungry, eventually, but blood isn't too hard to find. I can see perfectly in total darkness and I had moonlight to supplement it. Broken terrain can be troublesome, as can ravines, gorges, and canyons, but my strength is such I can leap small buildings in a single bound—with a running start and favorable winds. Walls? Cliffs? Mountains? I go up and over those like a hyperactive spider. And if I land badly, I take it better than a mortal. Even injuring myself—say, by missing my footing, tumbling down a rocky hillside, and half-burying myself in a small avalanche, purely as an example, totally unrelated to any actual event—is easily dealt with in a matter of minutes, at most. The worst part is getting the grit out of my shirt and sand out of my boots. If I ever actually got buried in a small avalanche, that is. Which I did not.

My guess is I beat thirty miles an hour over rough terrain. I'd do better on a road, I'm sure, but you work with what you've got.

Darn these super-magical kingdoms. No infrastructure. If it were up to me—but then, at one point, things like this *were* up to me. Nuts.

I closed in on the southwestern nexus, a few miles west of Lancaster, Ohio, according to the map. It was inside an actual castle, one raised up out of the ground. It didn't help the owner. I went over the wall almost without slowing. Nothing living inside the castle was in any shape to put up a fight and nothing magical was functioning.

Down in the basement, I found a young man in much the same position as Johann. He glared at me as he knelt in the center of the open nexus, gasping for breath and twitching at every anti-magical disruption bomb. He even gestured at me, but the ongoing disruption effects scattered his basic will-working like dust in the wind.

I replied by tearing off the room's iron-bound door and playing Frisbee with it. I hurled it across the floor at him, the whole thing spinning madly as it flew, crunching into him. They both skidded across the floor, almost entirely out of the power flow. I circled around, grabbed junior, and dashed him against a wall much the same way peasant women slap laundry on rocks, but with a messier splatter.

The blood crawled over to me, I noticed, but it rippled and trembled and spattered under the magical pounding. Interesting and puzzling.

I left the castle without materially hurting it. Once, shortly after my house burned down, I resolved to not burn people's homes quite so cavalierly. I kept my promise. I merely burned his body in a pile of broken doors and timbers, out in the courtyard. The castle was damaged, but not set ablaze.

See? I *can* show restraint. And yes, that *is* showing restraint. It's all about context.

Afterward, since I didn't have time to make the next nearest nexus—one I'd noted before, in Toano, Virginia—I headed southwest again, with a slight lean toward the west. I wanted to be out of the area of bombardment before dawn. I've seen what the magical disruption attack does to living wizards; it looks like a whole lot of no fun. Even as an undead monster, I felt it as a constant spiritual pummeling. I had no desire to spend a day being pounded by my own artillery.

Tomorrow I might consult with Mary, if I could find a way to reach her. I tried calling her, but, strangely enough, there were no cell towers in range of my skinphone. It would have to wait until I got outside the dome zones. I wonder if she's killed anyone?

I raced away from the zone of horrors.

Sunday, February 21st

The guy who ate a high-speed door was fond of having roads to go with the castles, or made use of the existing highways, at least. I ran across one going roughly my way and took it. This made my sprint for the border ever so much quicker.

With teleportation apparently cheap and easy, why bother with roads at all? Easier to move the troop-pieces along the would-be gameboard? Or just laziness in leaving the existing roads relatively intact under the layer of magical creations? Either way, I shifted gears from free-running to full-on sprinting. I covered ground at closer to sixty or seventy miles an hour and made some serious distance before dawn.

Vampires are scary creatures. Sometimes I scare myself.

When dawn started to bleed on the eastern horizon, I took shelter from the light. My hidey-hole was primitive, but it worked. I found a pile of rubble from a collapsed building. A handy wall provided a sunscreen to the east, some fallen branches provided large clusters of leaves, and a pile of carefully-placed rocks gave me a hole to hide in.

At least it didn't smell like the zoo I once hid in. It smelled worse by the time I was done with dawn—or when dawn was done with me—and I couldn't even cast a minor cleaning spell.

The constant pounding of the disruption spells was still present, but they were all coming from mostly the same direction. I wasn't under one, or being hammered from all sides. I was still much closer than I liked, but I was far enough away to move around without bleeding from the nose and ears. It felt like a close thing, though. I shoved and climbed, getting out of my hidey-hole, and started staggering farther west, away from the pulsing, pounding pains.

All right, all right. I overdid it. I admit it. If I was well to one side and it still felt as though my brains were being slowly hammered out through my ears, it must have been unadulterated hell for anyone directly under the bombing. I could probably have used a little less brute force, but how was I to know that? I plead ignorance and fear.

At any rate, I paid for it. Going for a long walk with the mother of all pounding migraine headaches is not a good way to spend the day. I stayed on the road and tried to keep a steady pace, but the best I could do was plod, plod, stagger, plod, stagger, stagger, plod. Eventually I found—I think—Indianapolis. It used to be a major city, but it went through some revisions. Multiple fortresses stood scattered about, surrounded by battlefields. I smelled old blood. Skeletons littered the place, some intact, some broken, all armed. Necromancy? Or just animation? Either way, it was academic now.

Most of the fortresses were sealed up tight, their occupants in various states of pain and death. I poked around one which seemed abandoned, looking for a ride of some sort. I didn't find anything even remotely vehicle-like, which convinced me not to waste time searching the rest. I went back to footslogging and occasionally groaning at the pain from my own bombardment.

This was a mess, no matter how one looked at it. It was my fault, too. If I'd never opened the first nexus. If I'd never opened the other nexuses. If I'd kept my head down and nose clean. If, if, if.

I couldn't actually hear my would-be conscience shouting up through the hatchway, "I told you so!" I was certain it was there, though.

One blessing of the ongoing bombardment was the way it drowned out inner voices.

By nightfall I was well outside the former city and on down the road. The road led me through countryside, which suited me fine. The last fortification I saw was several miles behind me. If it hadn't been occupied by fearful, angry creatures—organic gamepieces? Living toy soldiers? —I might have stayed in it until dark. The headache from the constant pounding was slightly diminished, but I had no desire to get into a fight with anyone over squatters' rights. Besides, I still had a long way to go.

I started collecting armor and shields from dead things. I didn't have a handy fallen tower to build a hidey-hole, but I could stack bodies as easily as stones. Wearing some mismatched armor and hiding under layers of shields with a veneer of corpses did the trick. It was more comfortable than the stones, but smelled even worse than I usually do. It also didn't work perfectly. I sizzled a bit in some of the joints, but by then it was too late to do anything but tough it out.

Dark. The sizzling died away, taking the tingling feeling with it. The steady drumbeat of the magical artillery continued, but it was muted, now. Being dead, it bothered me not at all at this distance.

So. Now what? Turn and run for the next nexus, hoping I can get there before dawn and kill one more of Johann's brood? No, probably not. On Bronze it would be no trouble, but Bronze couldn't be here for this. What I needed was another technological piece of transportation. Something besides a cab. Something that could run on its own power and wouldn't mind a bit of off-roading.

Which, of course, meant going outside the area of the domes and hunting for something. I wish the skycycle had a better range. I wish there were some gas stations left. I wish a lot of things.

I consoled myself with the thought that, as miserably inconvenient as this might be for me, it was an ongoing agony for my remaining targets. They were twenty-four hours into this punishing treatment and likely praying someone would just kill them already.

I'd get to it. Eventually.

The roads across the former border were blocked and heavily armed. Well, the domes of force vanished mysteriously, so I guess they were on alert. The army was camped out and watching everything. They seemed awfully tense, all things considered. Maybe they were having trouble sleeping, what with the silent, invisible explosions constantly going off. That would be my bet.

I considered the pros and cons of trying to sneak out. If I were up on the Great Lakes, I'd just walk into the water on one side and up out of the water on the other. On dry land, though, things were a bit more difficult. With no spells to use, there was no way to hide from night vision gear, surface radar, or any of a number of other technological wonders. I don't know how well I show up on infrared cameras or radar. Does it matter whether they're basic, advanced, or military-grade hardware? I wish I'd asked Diogenes if he can see me at night...

Might as well find out.

I found a breezy spot, stretched out on the ground, and let myself cool to ambient temperature. It would be harder to spot me on thermograph if I didn't glow. That took a while, but so what? I had all night.

The road was the obvious way out of the area. I elected to avoid it. No doubt there were ways to monitor the whole perimeter, but I doubted it involved human eyeballs everywhere. If I don't show up well on camera, like I don't show up on mirrors, I might simply walk out through the woods.

I did exit the area through the woods. As for "simple" and "walk"... not so much.

My major obstacle was a firebreak. It was a canyon through the woods, ten or twelve meters of empty space, clear-cut, unobstructed ground. Simply crossing it was no problem, but there were strange fenceposts every fifty meters or so, placed halfway between me and the far edge of the firebreak. About two meters high, they didn't appear to be connected to each other, but I suspected they contained electric eyes or other sensory equipment. Breaking one of those beams would alert someone.

Preliminary test time.

I clawed through the base of a tree, ripping wood out of it until it creaked, then pushed it over, toppling it across the firebreak and between two of the fenceposts. It crashed down with a satisfactory crunch and thud. I faded back and to one side to wait for the response.

In moments, I heard the buzz of a drone aircraft overhead. It carried two small missiles, one under each wing, and a turret sported a camera lens. It circled the area at altitude, then made a single low pass along the fenceline. It didn't fire on me. It didn't seem to take any notice of me.

Ten minutes later, a squad of men arrived in a pair of six-wheeled, jeep-like things. They hit the lights, fired up chainsaws, and cleared the fallen tree in a matter of minutes.

I didn't wait around to see the rest. If this is their typical response, I'm happy. I faded farther down the firebreak, out of sight of the men, and checked the sky. A drone was in sight, flying down the fenceline. Once it was past, I took a running start, leaped up and over a fencepost, landed well—much to my surprise—and kept running.

Nothing shot at me. Nothing chased me. I was even more surprised. Admittedly, they have thousands of miles of perimeter to monitor, so there's only so much they can do, but shouldn't they be a bit more vigilant? Then again, until recently, there were domes of force present. Raising their perimeter security along a five-thousand-mile border might take a while... and it is difficult to detect me with technology.

I really do need to ask Diogenes how he does it. What are the limits of my detectability? If I do get spotted by a sentry, what sorts of detection problems is the attack helicopter going to have? Can I keep running without becoming a missile target? Or should I hold very still and hope it doesn't notice me? It's more than an academic interest!

I sprinted away from the ongoing psychomagical bombardment. Next, get transport, get into town, and figure out what to do.

Once I made it a couple of miles and found a road, I followed it. At a roadside charging station, hopped in the first Google Cab I came to, and it took me down I-70 into Effingham. It didn't have any trouble noticing my weight on the seat or hearing my voice, oddly enough. Maybe it's a radar thing? I'll have to experiment with it, I guess.

I switched vehicles—parking one, walking for a while, and finally getting another one once separated by time and distance. It helped that I still had my credsticks. I switched sticks to pay for the new cab and it took me on to Saint Louis. Once in Saint Louis, I found a thrift store—closed, but I'm not a total novice at breaking and entering—a public washroom, and dinner, in that order.

With my sword wrapped in a sleeping bag and tied it into a backpack, I'm just another hitchhiker.

Now, how to get from Saint Louis to various points inside a military-restricted zone? Without using magic, of course. Helicopter? Swing wide out over the ocean and hope nobody shoots it down? Get a plane to fly over the area and bail out with a cargo parachute? Load up a motorcycle with a couple of extra gas cans and go in on the ground? Maybe drop the motorcycle and myself on one target point and drive to the other?

Tough choices. Mary would almost certainly have a better idea. I called her on my skinphone.

"Hi, honey!" I greeted her. "It's your demon lover."

"You! I'm fiendishly glad to hear from you. How was your trip to Hell?"

"Painful."

"Same here. My eyes weren't bleeding, but they felt like they might. Did you have to make it so intense?"

"Probably not, but better safe than sorry."

"I suppose."

"If it's okay with you, I'd like to meet to discuss this further. Are you still up north?" I asked.

"Yes. It was a quick in and out. Time constraints, you know."

"I know, and I feel time constraining me, too. I'm more southwest."

"Would you like to visit Milwaukee?"

"Never been there."

"You'll love it. Lots of suburbs and rural areas within a short ride of a major urban center. Meet me at Heartbreak Ridge Paintball."

"Got it. If I don't see you tonight, I'll see you tomorrow night."

"Understood. Kisses."

We signed off and I called another cab. Technically, Heartbreak Ridge Paintball was in Caledonia, not Milwaukee; Google is fussy about little details like that.

Monday, February 22nd

Aside from a trip to the store for makeup and food, I spent most of the day in a motel, minding my own business, microwaving sandwiches, and watching video. I didn't feel like showing my face during the day. There was probably no one actively looking for me, but why add anything to my level of risk? I doubt the local vampires are interested in what I'm doing. They just want me even more dead. For all I know, some magi families are also interested in speaking to me in a manner similar to the Mendozas.

At least the news was interesting. People were weighing in on the fall of the domes and What It All Meant. Natural phenomenon? Solar flares? Aliens? I didn't hear one theory that didn't have a jumbo-sized hole in it, but I had to respect the imagination involved. As usual, the people in charge were saying they didn't know what was going on and didn't have a plan. Naturally, they said it in such a way as to hope you didn't notice.

Maybe this is part of the reason I despise being a king. I don't want to be lumped in with a bunch of mealy-mouthed weasels. Then again, as a king I can give orders, make things happen, carry out plans, and not have to answer to a bunch of mealy-mouthed weasels who scream about their constituents.

The trouble with a democracy is it presumes everyone who votes is qualified to make decisions on behalf of the nation. The trouble with a monarchy is it presumes the monarch is qualified to make decisions on behalf of the nation. While it's unlikely the monarch really is qualified, it's possible. Making every citizen in the nation qualified to run the place, on the other hand…

I'm starting to think humans aren't too good at the getting-along-in-large-groups thing.

I went to the paintball course after sundown. They were open year-round, come rain, snow, sleet, or sun, twenty-four hours a day, every day. They held team events for the truly gung-ho and ran indoor obstacle and target courses for the less militant. I did okay, but I'm only so-so with guns. I can alert someone to the fact he's being shot at pretty much every time. Hitting him? Well… sometimes. Where I excelled was reaction time. I don't think I can actually dodge a bullet, but paintballs are much slower. If I see it coming, I usually avoid it. Other than that, I kept my tendrils to myself and pretended my goggles were night vision equipment.

Getting hit by a paintball isn't as painful as a bullet. I know this because a half-dozen of them walked along my spine in a single burst.

Grumbling, I turned around. Mary grinned at me from behind her goggles. Figures.

"Am I dead?" I asked.

"I'd say so."

"Shucks."

"Best two out of three?"

"I'm more concerned about getting two out of four."

"Oh, *those*. Then we should definitely go."

After a quick trip through the locker rooms and a brief cab ride, Mary invited me into her car. It was an older hybrid, a gas-burner and electric. She kept it on manual, revved it, and whipped it into traffic like gears meshing together.

"Now that we're unlikely to be traced, tracked, or followed, how did it go?"

"I killed Johann." I left it at that. I wasn't ready to discuss it.

"Anyone else?"

"One of the other men. I don't know which. I didn't stop to chat, either."

"I got a man, as well, up in New York."

"That leaves Juliet, unless they've been monkeying around with transforming themselves. Any sign of my ball?"

"No."

"That thing is going to be trouble," I muttered. "I know it."

"So we finish with Juliet, shut down your magic-crushing spells, and find your Evil Orb. One thing at a time."

"I'm all for it," I agreed, as she swung off the highway and into a run-down looking suburb. She shot me a dazzling smile. "You're in a good mood," I noted.

"Yes. I've done my part and I'm being included in your plans, you secretive jerk."

"I apologized for that already."

"And you still owe me a bank job."

"Holdup or vault?"

"I haven't decided, yet."

"Let me know. But we're not doing it here. I don't think I want to live in this world."

"Seems fair. It *is* a bit on the screwed-up side. But we can't leave while your orb is here, right?"

"Not for good," I agreed.

"Good thing I found us a place to stay, then."

"Yes. Is that where we're going?"

"Not exactly."

We took some secondary roads, weaving our way around, before we reached a chain-link gate. Mary rolled down the window and punched numbers on the keypad. A chain drive rolled the gate aside. We rolled in and it closed behind us automatically.

"Back door," she said.

"To what?"

"An airport."

"Aha! I was wondering how we were going to get to Juliet."

"Aha! Now it's *we*?"

"Of course it's *we*. Johann was my unique problem. Everyone else I'll share."

"I guess I can understand that. It works both ways, right?"

"If you've got someone you need to kill personally, I'll happily gut his guards."

"See, that's one reason I love you. You *get* me."

The airport wasn't large, having only six hangars and a number of small, private planes. Mary pulled us into the open hangar and climbed out. I followed her. An elderly gentleman shuffled over toward us. He wore an old-fashioned bomber jacket and had an impressive scar. It ran down his forehead, through one eyebrow, leaped his eye and landed on his cheek before running off his jawline. It looked old, but, given the gentleman's age, not as old as one might expect.

"Miss LeBlanc," he said, greeting Mary. Mary smiled at him and allowed him to kiss her hand. "I don't believe I've been introduced to your gentleman friend?"

"Mister Black," she said, indicating me. "Mister Black, this is our pilot, Martin."

"A pleasure."

"Likewise."

"You indicated you were in something of a hurry?" he asked.

"Yes, please," Mary agreed. "Are we ready to go?"

"I am. Baby is. Are you?"

Mary glanced at me. I made no objection. This was her show.

The plane he called "Baby" was a small thing, barely a four-seater. It reminded me of a jet-powered Cessna, but the angular styling put me in mind of a stealth fighter. Inside, Mary took a forward seat, next to Martin. I sat behind Martin so I could see Mary. The interior of the plane was rather sparse and utilitarian, like a cargo craft rather than a personal jet. I could see the ribs, or whatever they're called, in between some sort of high-density foam or fiberglass.

As the jets cycled up, Mary turned to me.

"There are parachutes behind you. Get one for me, would you? And one for yourself, if you think it'll do any good."

"Ha. Ha." I moved behind my seat and found the parachutes.

"Uh-oh," Martin said, and started shutting everything down.

"What is it?" Mary asked.

"Advisory channel. Switch over." She did so and I moved forward.

"What is it?"

"The FAA is repeating a military bulletin," Martin said. "The Air Force and Navy are engaged in activities against hostile forces present on United States soil. All aircraft are warned away from the combat zones."

"Where are these combat zones?"

Martin tapped on his navigation display for a moment and four points popped up. They seemed familiar. Nexus points I opened, of course. The centers of the circular domes.

"Any chance we can get there?" Mary asked, touching the point in Virginia. It was the only one we hadn't killed a magi on.

"Forget it," Martin advised. "This is a blockade runner, not a combat aircraft. You want to sneak across a border? We can do that. Flying into combat? No way. They'll have everything under God's heaven looking into those areas. Baby is stealthy, not invisible."

"So much for my plan," Mary grumped, taking off her headset. "Any thoughts, Mister Black?"

"Aside from profanity?"

"I'll settle for profanity. I have to. It's all I've got."

"Is the news covering this?" I asked. "Can we get a look at what's actually going on? If the military is doing a decent job, we may not need to go there after all. At least, not until after they're done."

"Not in Baby," Martin said. "Let's see what's on video in the office."

Martin finished shutting down the aircraft while Mary opened the door. We trooped to the hangar office and Martin fired up an old-fashioned flat-screen television. A little hunting around gave us the live reports.

Drone aircraft were now able to penetrate the area without losing contact. Reconnaissance craft located the center of each dome's effect, presumably the emitters for the "force fields" that had cut off so much of the country. Drone strikes on these locations proved the force fields were, in fact, no longer protecting their central generators. Cruise missiles and artillery bombardment finished the job. "This brief engagement with the sources of these domes has been brought to a swift and decisive close!" said General Somebody.

If the news was to be believed, I could have simply dropped the domes and waited. All four nexuses would be bombed, shelled, and obliterated, along with Johann, Juliet, and their two relatives.

On the other hand, I'm still glad I went in. If I'd waited, I wouldn't have gotten to kill Johann with my bare hands.

Still, the fact it was done was a relief. I did feel the slightest bit cheated, though. It was one thing to have Mary helping me, quite another to watch the new report of a missile strike. I decided I could live with it, albeit grumpily. At least there would be no more Fries trying to kill me. Oh, there might be a member of the family still around, somewhere, but I doubted it. I already killed a bunch of them by accident, and these four by design. If I could close down the nexus bombardment, I could start closing nexuses—or, at the very least, cap them off.

I wonder if the Etiennes would like to be custodians? True, members of their family, in youthful exuberance, did break into my house, but they apologized profusely and sincerely. As long as they didn't let someone step into the nexus and turn into a power-mad demigod, it ought to be all right. I'll have to consider it after I get the things sealed over.

"So much for that," Mary said. "What now?"

"Depends on where the yacht went."

"Walt was supposed to take it to Daytona Beach after you took off. He should be there by now."

"Martin?"

"Yes, Mister Black?"

"Would it be unreasonable to fly us down to Daytona Beach?"

"Miss LeBlanc already paid for a trip," he told me. "We'll have to take something besides my Baby. I don't take her out during the day. If you're in a hurry, how about the *Wingéd Victory*?"

"It beats a cab."

I was wrong. I would rather have taken a cab. I would rather have *walked*.

The *Wingéd Victory* was a jet-propelled box with wings. It was noisy, almost unheated, and I'm dead sure it wasn't FAA approved. I spent a good part of the trip watching a rivet slowly spin in place from the vibration. We all wore headsets for ear protection and conversation, but the sound of the air outside seemed awfully loud to me. I wanted to rip my way out of the thing and enjoy the peace and quiet of plummeting to the ground before we even made it to cruising altitude.

Mary saw my distress and piped some string quartet music through my headset. It helped. A little. I could have stepped inside and spent the trip in my headspace, but I didn't want to risk having another conversation with my better-than-thou conscience.

The only good thing about it was the speed. The trip was a little under a thousand miles, not counting course changes for weather and other air traffic. From wheels-up to touchdown was slightly over an hour.

I climbed out of the thing and reflected on the merits of travel by wagon train. Can I find a universe where the most advanced form of vehicle is the horse and buggy? It may not be fast, but I think I like it more than a supersonic rattletrap.

I said nothing of this to Martin. Instead, I thanked him for the speed of the trip and assured him I would never forget it. He took it as a compliment.

Mary hailed us a cab and I sank into the plush, padded seat with a sigh of contentment. It was night, so nothing hurt, but the contrast was well worth a sigh. We took a short ride in the cab while Mary used it to call ahead to the *Princess* for the launch.

"Now," she said, once the call ended, "are we going somewhere immediately? Say, driving the *Princess* through an interdimensional gateway into the oceans of Karvalen?"

"No, of course not. That would be… hmm. If we take down the mast and the fake smokestack, we can probably get away with a forty-foot circle. The ship does fourteen miles per hour—"

"Sixteen, if we're using the hydrojet with the paddlewheels."

"Sixteen, then. That's a little over twenty-three feet per second. Let's say the *Princess* is two hundred feet long, for safety. That means the gate has to be open a minimum of ten seconds from one world to another." I did a juggling act in my head, comparing other gates and how long they were open.

"No. No, we're not going to bring the *Princess* with us."

"What if we're on top of a nexus?"

"Yes, we could do it, but we'd be leaving behind an open nexus. I'm not doing it."

"So, you want to close them all again?"

"Yes. I'm not sure exactly how, yet, but at the very least I can put a magical seal on them and power it from the nexus it seals. From what I've seen of the way a nexus behaves when opened, I think there's a good chance it can re-seal itself over time if it doesn't keep pouring power out."

"Am I to assume you don't want a bunch of magi owning the world and mismanaging it?"

"What makes you say that?"

"Oh, nothing. I've seen you try to be a good king. I'm not sure you know how to be a terrible ruler."

"Bite your tongue, woman."

"I'd rather bite yours. But do we have time, maybe, to do some shopping before we go anywhere?"

"I suppose. Yes, I'm sure we do. The military will be crawling all over the land-based nexus sites for weeks, possibly months, once I stop the anti-magical bombing. I can't seal a nexus with that going on. Maybe I can use one nexus to cast a repulsion or revulsion spell to drive off everyone near another one…"

"Ahem."

"Hmm?"

"Shopping?"

"Yes, dear."

Most of the shopping was for me, oddly enough. We both bought new skinphones, of course; it doesn't do to have disposable phones if you don't dispose of them every so often. Then there was the *good* makeup, as well as a carrying case for my sword, as well as a variety of miscellaneous stuff.

We were aboard the *Princess* and steaming toward the Bahamas before dawn. The major nexus there would be the first I shut down. I visited Bronze, recovered my cloak—it was a horse-blanket while Bronze wore it; it turned into a jacket when I took it down—and I settled down with Mary in our suite. I told her about my plans to close the nexus points.

"Can't you shut them down the same way you turned them on?"

"Yes, if I just want to stop the bombardment. It'll take more of the personal touch, I'm afraid, if I want to re-seal them."

"Once you figure out how to do that—assuming it can be done—can you shut off the bombardment and seal one of the nexuses remotely? Then you could turn the bombardment back on to keep magi away from the open nexuses while we head for the next underwater one."

"Maybe. It depends on how sealing it goes. If the technique is too involved, I'll have to be on-site for it. My main concern is to keep away any magi being influenced by the Black Ball of Demonic Influence. More regular magi will be more cautious about getting their souls fried by the voltage involved. But I suspect the Evil Orb is somewhere near one of Johann's nexuses. I don't think it will want to be far from the centers of power and people it can influence. It's just a matter of finding it before the military—or the magi—start crawling all over the sites. The psychic awfulness is keeping them away for now."

"Hmm. As an alternative, could you shut off the bombardment, gate to an open nexus, seal it, gate back, and resume the bombardment?"

I stared at her.

"You know, when I first saw you in an underground rave, you attracted my attention for reasons having nothing to do with your brains."

"I know. Dreadful makeup. Good camouflage, though."

"And a roguish tendril trying to siphon off some of my energies."

"Yes, but the makeup *was* dreadful."

"No argument. But you persist in being smarter than I am."

"I have a different perspective than you," she corrected. "I'm a *thief*. It's what I do. I steal things for the fun and for the money. You, on the other hand, are a wizard. You do things with spells—offhandedly, casually, as a matter of course—that make me scratch my head and wonder what you need me for. It makes me a little insecure."

"Technically, it makes you *feel* insecure. You're completely secure even if you don't feel like it."

"Am I?" she asked. She sounded sincere. I moved over to her and snuggled up to her.

"Yes. You worry about being useless to me. You're never useless. You have enormous talents and versatile skills. Even if you really were useless, you're highly ornamental. So don't worry about your utility. It all comes down to whether or not I like you—which I do, quite a lot. I'll even go so far as to say I love you, once in a while, because I think we're past the 'I like you a lot' stage. Okay?"

"Okay." She started to say something and visibly changed her mind. I pretended not to notice.

"Now," I went on, "if you'd like some insecurity, you can have some of mine."

"Yours?"

"Mine. I've got lots."

"What do you have to be—or feel—insecure about?"

"Aside from people and things who want to kill me? Let's see. I'm slightly crazy because I have a leaky mental basement, a personification of my over-achieving perfectionist nature who wants to be my conscience, a lot of repressed guilt over a bunch of children—in various times and places, and for various reasons—as well as a lingering fear about how I've handled everything in my life and an ongoing terror of what is yet to come. I'm uncertain about the future, agonized about the past, and barely managing to cope with the present by a rigorous regimen of distraction and denial. Plus, I'm flippant and whimsical about my personal problems, mental problems, political failings, and parental insufficiency in order to conceal how badly I want to have a quiet breakdown. Which, of course, only points up the fact I desperately need you and I'm terrified you'll decide I'm no better than the Demon King and leave for parts unknown. How's that for an off-the-cuff list of insecurities?"

"It's... impressive."

"Give me a minute. I'm sure I can dredge through my denial and find a few more."

"No, that won't be necessary." She rested her chin on my shoulder and squeezed me. "You're telling me in that flippant manner you mentioned. How serious are you?"

"I'm as serious as a plutonium kidney stone. I only *sound* lighthearted."

"Like the clowns," she murmured.

"Like... what?"

"I can't recall where I read it, but there's something I half-remember. Clowns have smiles and make us laugh, but they really don't seem funny. It's because the smiles are all painted on, I think. And because, while we watch them trying to be funny, we all know, somehow, deep inside, their hearts are broken." She turned my head toward her and removed my disguising sunglasses. "You're a clown. You leap in and out of the car, through the hoops, fail to juggle most amusingly, all the rest, so people will laugh with you instead of *at* you."

I looked away.

"Maybe."

"You've been afraid of something for a long time. What is it? Being a vampire? Losing who you are? Or just outliving everyone you ever cared about?"

I recalled a time—how long ago? —when I decided to give up being human. I'm not a human being. Not anymore. I'm a blood-drinking monster. Or so I thought. Looking on events since then, I haven't really held up my end of the deal. I keep caring about people as more than simple pets. I feel responsible for them and to them.

If I'm such a monster, why do I protect and avenge children? Because it's part of who I am, that's why. What does that mean? Am I a monster? I most assuredly am. But how many human beings are monsters?

"I'm not sure what I'm afraid of," I admitted, "although your suggestions certainly fill me with no uncertain amount of terror."

"Well, then, I've given you something important and I'm pleased with that."

"You did?"

"Yes. I've given you the gift of something to think about. A first question to answer on your never-ending road of self-discovery."

"Huh." I considered it. If I knew what it was I was running from, I could run more effectively. Maybe find a place to hide from it. Or—vaguely possible—I might be able to confront it.

"Come with me. We need to shower during our change. Then I want you to make love with me all morning."

"And afterward?"

"I plan to be too tired to do anything."

"Ah."

Tuesday, February 23rd

Mary wasn't kidding. I felt sorry for Ludmilla.

Steve—the houseboy-waiter-whatever—wheeled lunch into the master suite after Mary phoned in the order. Mary was in the shower while I waited on the food. He did a decent job of keeping his expression neutral, but I thought I detect a hint of male camaraderie and congratulations as he left. I didn't stand on ceremony; I ate and regretted the loss of my sensory-damping device. I really need a new one.

Mary joined me shortly thereafter, wearing a robe, hair done up in the twisty towel thing women do.

"Hungry?" I asked.

"Yes. Did you leave anything for me?"

I pulled more dishes from the undershelves of the cart and presented them to her. Fresh-caught fish of some sort. Some of the crew enjoy using the deep-sea fishing gear on the yacht. More power to them, I say.

As we ate, Mary talked around her food.

"You know, we're not doing this right."

"Eating?" I asked.

"Having deep, emotional discussions."

"How are we not doing it right?"

"I'm supposed to be in tears and you're supposed to yell and wave your arms. I think I'm supposed to throw things, too."

"Is that right?"

"That's how it works in all the literature."

"I'm not sure I've ever read a romance novel. What do you suppose it means?"

"We're not human?"

"Not normal, that's for sure," I agreed.

"If we were normal, would we be *here*?"

"I suppose not. Maybe it's because we're older than we look?"

"Never mention a lady's age," she advised.

"Noted. But why would you be in tears?"

"Because the thing you said about needing me really struck a nerve."

"Like a root canal?"

"No."

"Funny bone?"

"I'm serious."

"So am I. I just don't show it worth a damn."

"I am going to shove this celery up your nose."

"You don't want to see the sneeze. How about I ask what you meant about striking a nerve, instead?"

"Oh. Yes. That." Mary ate another couple of bites and I did the same. Never pass up an opportunity to eat quickly during a significant discussion. At any moment, you may lose your appetite.

"Thing is," Mary said, "I need you."

"No, you don't. You may be the most independent and self-sufficient person I've ever known."

"Don't contradict me."

"I see you're armed with celery. I surrender. Please proceed."

"I mean it, even if it's hard to tell from my tone." She paused to sip some juice. "You know, we're impressively weird."

"I agree, but how do you mean it?"

"Remember how I said we do this sort of thing all wrong?"

"Yes."

"Shouldn't we be on a bearskin rug, in front of a fire, cuddled up against the winter chill, having a deep and tear-filled discussion of our feelings?"

"I was thinking more along the lines of a leather couch with a bespectacled old man asking, in a German accent, about our mothers. I'm more concerned about my sanity than I used to be."

"That's fair. Still, it strikes me as strange how our… defense mechanisms, I guess… call for us to be so tongue-in-cheek about it all."

"Part and parcel with our denial," I suggested.

"Could be."

"So, what are you denying?"

"Everything. I'm a professional criminal. It's a reflex. Unless you want to put me in handcuffs again?"

"No. Your wrists are bruised as it is."

"I'll get some furry ones."

"Fair enough. Go on."

"Yes… the whole needing you thing. You're right, I'm a pretty self-sufficient person. I still have needs, though—and before you make a crack about doing your best to satisfy them, let me get this out."

"You keep handing me straight lines," I complained, "but I'll try."

"I used to belong to a community of undead. I had a whole social structure. I wasn't at the top, but I wasn't at the bottom, either. I knew people on a pretty permanent basis, had friends, had a social life, all the security and safety things, as well as the occasional thrill of my hobbies.

"Now… I've seen *other worlds*. My universe is bigger than I ever dreamed. I've also lost all my old friends and my old social structure. I can't go back. I don't even dare take the chance someone I know will be glad to see me."

"What about the pilot? Begins with an 'M'…"

"Martin."

"That's him."

"Martin's mortal. He's a smuggler, as you probably guessed, and doesn't know anything about vampires. He probably suspects a little, but he's also well-paid, tight-lipped, and something of a thrill-seeker himself."

"Oh. I thought he was under exclusive contract to the Elders, or something."

"Not that I've ever heard. He's an old fighter pilot who got his aeronautical engineering degree, or something. When he's not flying at unreasonable speeds between mountains, he's taking planes apart and putting them back together."

"I thought… Baby?"

"He calls it his baby. It's named the *Night Flyer*."

"I thought it looked a bit of a custom job."

"It's not invisible to radar, but it's got a very low signature. He says every little bit helps." She smiled smugly. "I provided him with some electronic modules, once."

"From a secret government laboratory, I've no doubt."

We ate in silence for a bit before Mary resumed her train of thought.

"Thing is," she began, "you're the only person I have. You're the only one who can... You're the one man who... I'm not sure how to say this."

"No rush. It's a big lunch, and I don't plan to go anywhere."

"You know how I said I had a social structure, I was a part of it?"

"Sure."

"Everyone has that. A circle of friends, a neighborhood, a city, a nation, a school, something."

"Right."

"My circle of friends is you. You're all I have." She frowned. "That doesn't sound right."

"Why not?"

"It sounds as though I only care about you because you're the only game in town. Last man on Earth kind of thing."

"It didn't take it that way."

"It's just... see, you matter a lot to me, and not only because you're... I'm making a hash of this, aren't I?"

"You're trying to put complex thoughts and feelings into words. Sometimes you don't know what you think or feel until you say it. Try writing me a letter. You can re-read it, change it, tear it up and start over, whatever you want. Or keep talking. We'll get there eventually." I pretended to examine a nonexistent wristwatch. She bounced a croissant off my forehead.

"Look, all I want to say is you're important to me and I need you, too. I don't know if it's the same way you need me, but the need is mutual, okay? Maybe that's part of why we're so hesitant to talk about love, because we know we need each other. Need isn't the same thing as love. And maybe we're both afraid our feelings will change if we ever discover there are... I don't know. Other options? I know I didn't feel thrilled to my core when you started talking about Tort. So I want you to know I know you know... dammit!" Mary clanged her fork off the little dining table and dabbed at her eyes with her napkin.

"If it matters," I told her, "I not only need you, but I respect you. I also like you a lot. I'm also firmly convinced you will someday despise me and want to leave me—and that will be long before I even think about feeling that way about you. We're immortal. I have no doubt you'll get tired of my face and need to take a century off to have fun without me. And, a century later, when you start to miss me, you'll be welcome to walk in the door and hang your knife-harness up in the bedroom. Is that fair?"

"It's more than fair. It's remarkably generous and understanding. It's so tolerant and easygoing it almost makes me think you don't care where I am."

"I only care where you are in the sense of how easy it is it grab you and pin you down on the bed. And the occasional bank robbery, of course. But the most important thing about you is that you even *exist*. You prove to me the universe isn't completely out to get me."

"I find that very hard to believe."

"So do I. Yet there you are."

"That's not what I meant!"

"But it's what you prove."

"Hand me my fork."

"Promise not to stab me with it?" I made along arm and leaned, picking it up and handing it to her.

"I'll think it over."

"Wipe it off and finish lunch, first."

"Probably the best choice. I do want to ask you something, though."

"Shoot."

"You told me about being the Demon King for a day and establishing Lissette as the Queen…"

"What brings this up?"

"Our talk about needing each other, love, and me being your proof that not everything is a conspiracy to annoy you."

"Not exactly how I put it, but I get your meaning."

"Yes. And all that reminded me of Lissette. You like her."

"Yes, I do. Quite a lot. She has my respect and confidence."

"And you went to great lengths to preserve your kingdom under her."

"Yes."

"Was it for her, or for the kingdom?"

"Both, I think. I've asked myself—indirectly—that sort of question. I feel responsible for the kingdom, but also sad for Lissette, since she's stuck running the place."

"Fair. And the handoff, when you put her on the throne. You didn't tell me much about it, aside from the fact you put on your Demon King hat and performed the handoff. I get the impression something about it bothered you. Was it just pretending to be the Demon King?"

"No. I could stand that. There were other things, too—and I'm not ready to talk about those, yet. Maybe in a week, maybe in a year… maybe never. But if and when, we'll discuss it when you don't have any vegetables handy."

"I'll improvise," Mary warned.

"How about we try for the bearskin rug and the fireplace? Firebrand would be happy to lurk there instead of listening to us patter on about feelings and other suchlike dreckola."

I'd enjoy a nice fireplace right now, Boss. I'm developing a headache, I think.

"You're what?"

I have a sort of throbbing pain. It's been going on for a while, Boss.

"As we get farther from the land-based nexuses, it should lighten up. I'm surprised you even noticed."

Yeah, well, I think you may have overdone it a little bit.

"I've had that very thought. I'll start toning it down when we get to the nexus in the Bahamas."

In the meantime, is there anything you can do for me?

"If Mary will excuse me, I'll take you down to Bronze and work some defensive magic for you both."

"Go deal with your metallic friends," Mary advised. "I'll finish your lunch."

"You're too kind."

Bronze had no complaints about the distant rumble. She knew it was there, but it didn't bother her. Firebrand had some comments about that, which Bronze ignored with dignity.

I hung Firebrand on her saddlehorn and raised a shield around them both. It wasn't much, as shields go, but it was meant for one specific purpose. Firebrand reported an almost-complete muffling of the distant thunder and retracted its earlier comments about magical horses.

I went back to the master suite and found Mary snoozing on the bed. Did I dare have a nap? Johann was dead, all the magicians in Karvalen were there, in Karvalen, and the only thing likely to bother me was some random magi in this world. Even that was unlikely with the magic-disrupting effects currently detonating. Their shockwaves echoed around the world, doubtless annoying minor practitioners dreadfully.

I'm paranoid—justifiably so. I cast another shielding spell, this one against mental phenomena, and set it to act as a wake-up call if anything penetrated it.

Yep, I dared to nap. I was tired.

The genie screamed, a banshee wail fit to burst eardrums and cause nosebleeds. It shriveled, blackened, fell. When it struck ground, it shattered like a statue of fractured glass, scattering everywhere, cutting the dirt and rocks. The earthen wounds bled, first red, then black, then nothing. Everything dried up, wore down, turned to dust.

The world was a barren place of dust and shifting sand, flat and featureless, where the wind made ghosts of dust to wander across the empty wastes. The sun shone down with an unholy glare, burning the blackened world.

I jerked upright, gasping, drenched in sweat.

I am never sleeping again, I thought. Mary turned over next to me and threw one leg over mine. I lay back on the bed and tried to get my breathing under control.

Everything seemed so quiet. Did the engines stop? No, I could still feel the steady throb of the paddlewheels turning. I worked my jaw to pop my ears and it hurt. I touched one and my fingertips came away wet with sweat and a trace of blood.

In the bathroom, I examined myself. Some of what I took for sweat was a slight nosebleed and a trace of blood coming out of my ears. A few words to my daytime reflection and I realized I wasn't completely deaf, but I had a distinct loss in hearing. This caused a few more words to my reflection, followed by a trio of healing spells—one for each ear and one for my nose. They were minor spells, very focused, but it still took a while to build them in this world.

Mary came into the bathroom, yawning. She looked like something out of a movie, what with the robe, the loose tumble of hair, the smile. I don't look so good even on my best day. The most I manage is horrifying. Well, beauty and the beast. She finished waking up in a hurry when she saw me.

"Are you bleeding?" she asked. I heard her, distantly, as though we were underwater. Trust me; I know exactly how it sounds.

"Not anymore."

"What happened?" She turned my head to examine an ear.

"I had a bad dream."

"You never mentioned this."

"First time. Not for a bad dream, but the first time I've ever suffered damage from one."

"Why? What did you dream?"

So I told her about it. She shook her head.

"I don't have any idea," she admitted. "Why would this damage you?"

"I suspect it's because we're so close to a nexus, a major one. I may not have done the containment matrices perfectly. Those things pour out so much power they distort reality. Remember what I told you about my hand?"

"Ah, yes. Did you ever find out what was going on with that?"

"No. When I flew into the area of the magic-disruption spells, my hand hurt a bit, but it went away. That's when my enchanted underwear shorted out, too. I haven't been able to wave myself clean since then."

"Pity."

"I'll build another ring. Oh, crap. I just realized I'm wandering around without cloaking spells."

"Do you *need* them? Johann is dead."

"Good point. I probably don't. Nevertheless, I want one. And something for disguise spells. I've got a whole laundry list of things I want on me as a matter of routine."

"So do it while you're down at this nexus."

I blinked at her. Maybe she is smarter than me, despite what I said about perspectives. Then again, up until a few days ago, I was so focused on killing Johann I might not have been qualified to think about anything else. Then again

again, I don't really want to think about much of anything. I'm tired. Not physically tired, but my soul is weary. I'm definitely taking a vacation.

"I'll do that," I agreed, "if I can find something crystalline to use as an enchantment matrix. Do we have any crystals or gemstones? Gemstones, preferably. Diamonds ought to take the pressure pretty well."

"You're in luck. I have jewelry."

"I hate to raid your jewelry box," I said. She shrugged and smiled.

"You'll give me a reason to steal more. Let's see what looks good on you."

Wednesday, February 24th

We arrived at our nexus point last night, but I didn't want to start anything so late. It's a long way down and a long way up again.

Instead, we made port on Great Abaco Island, preparing for another long trip. Mary discussed crew and staff leaves, promising a lengthy stay in Europe. I added it would probably involve a bonus. This seemed to go down very well. Crew morale rose somewhat. I even saw Captain Tillard smile.

Mary and I went through her jewelry collection. She expressed surprise and pleasure at some of the ornaments in the box of trinkets. After the third one, I had to ask.

"You mean you didn't know this was in here?"

"I can't be expected to review every single piece of jewelry," she protested. "I usually deal in volume, not in the big, unique pieces. I learned my lesson about that in London. Pesky Brits. I didn't even lay a hand on any of the jewelry, much less get away with any."

I refrained from comment.

There were a number of multiple-gem objects to choose from. Most of the rings were ladies' rings, not only too small for my fingers but also too fine and fragile. My hands tend to get messy. There was a man's ring of the right fit which also had a number of gems, but it was a big, gaudy thing. I couldn't even hide it under gloves.

We finally settled on a brooch. It was a stylized sunflower, which I thought ironic. The central disk was something dark but glittery, with yellow petals radiating out from it. It didn't suit me at all, but Mary thought it was perfect and said so through her giggles. I accepted it with a sigh, removed the pin from the backing, magically smoothed the metal out, and pressed it flat against my chest. I could wear it low, under my clothes, even beneath my armored underwear, and no one need ever see it to ask about it.

"Okay, the student has a question for the wise master," Mary began.

"I'll relay it to a wise master when I find one. In the meantime, I'll try to answer it if I can."

"This thing," Mary held up another brooch, "has maybe a dozen different stones in it. I get that you can enchant each stone as a separate item. I get that you can enchant the mounting as an item to tie all this stuff together. Aren't big gems preferable? Doesn't size matter?"

"You would know better than I."

"Size matters, but so does skill," she replied. "But I was talking about spells. Does the size of the gem matter?"

"Only for power storage, not for spell effects."

"I'm not following."

"Here's the thing. The rigid, regular structure of a crystalline substance is ideal for imprinting a fixed magical construct inside. However, since this happens on a micro-scale—possibly on a quantum scale, but don't press me for details; I haven't done my research—it doesn't need a lot of space. Think of it like data storage. Each tiny crystal is a program stored in a tiny memory module.

"Size matters—in this specific instance," I added, cutting her off, "—when you're talking about power storage. The brooch backing and the largest of the gems comes into play there. The backing, or a wizard's staff, or any other mounting piece acts like an antenna, drawing in ambient magical power when you try to run a program. Since you're generally touching it, you can feed it power yourself, if you like. The tiny crystal acts like a lens for that power, producing the effect stored inside it. If you've got a crystal specifically designed to store power—a completely different order of enchantment—it can draw on that, too."

"And the bigger the battery," Mary said, examining the brooch, "the more often it can fire off spells?"

"Pretty much. Of course, in Karvalen, a lot of enchantments don't require battery power. They can work on the ambient energy around. A cleaning spell, a disguise spell, a silence spell… any one of those can run pretty much indefinitely with a suitable power intake. Now, if we're *here*, and not near a nexus, we would want several devices for each function, each with its own power crystal. Each would need to rest and recharge."

"So they could charge up independently when we're not using them!"

"Exactly!"

"But couldn't we just use them as spells?"

"How do you mean?"

"You said we could put our own energies in. We can operate them like spells we cast, only we don't cast them, we activate them."

"Yes, but it's still going to cost us energy. It's a trade-off between activating spells and having the strength to go do what you want to do."

"Isn't it always?" Mary agreed, sadly.

Mary also selected a nice pendant for herself—a bird, done in gold and some dark gems, possibly onyx. It was built around a sizable central stone as the body of the bird. Since her magical inventory went the way of all magical objects anywhere near the bombardment zone, I needed to replace them. While I was at it, I laid a power matrix in the few loose stones we had on hand. You never know when even a small charged gemstone will come in handy.

Once we picked out our future amulets, Mary and I spent the rest of the day sorting through spells, building the basic frameworks, setting up the power-intake modules, and getting our jewelry ready. With a collection of stones in each object, fitting several different functions wasn't too hard. My only concern— aside from Mary's lessons in spellcraft and enchantment—was to make sure the spell structures were built solidly enough to take the enchantment process. There's a lot of power that goes into making a permanent magical item, and I wasn't going to do it the gentle way.

It's possible to build a very low-power enchantment and gradually add power to it, running energy through all the spell structures, leaving behind a mild increase in capacity. It's kind of like strength training at the gym, or magnetizing something. I'll go with the magnet metaphor. If you run a magnet over a piece of iron, it gets a little bit magnetic on its own—nowhere near as strong as the original magnet, but at least a little magnetic. Run the magnet over the iron again and again and the iron grows more and more powerful as a magnet. This process can be repeated with an enchanted item for days, weeks, years—as long as one cares to build on it. Eventually, though, you have to close it up, seal it, make it a self-contained unit. After that, it may gain a little strength from constant use, but for all intents and purposes, it's pretty much as-is. This technique is great for people who don't have buckets of power lying around, but it's time consuming.

The other way is the way I usually do it. I gather up huge masses of power, hammer it into specific shapes, fit the pieces of my spell together, jam it into the object, and seal it up on the spot. This is much faster, but it requires channeling more raw energy than most mortal flesh and bone can endure.

Someday, I'll build an enchantment my way and leave it unsealed so I can coax it to even greater power in the traditional way. I suspect, whatever it is, it'll be impressive. In the meantime, I'll have to muddle along.

Mary had some requests.

"How many spells are we putting in these things?" she asked.

"I don't know. I know I need a disguise spell, also one especially for my eyes—that's a complex illusion. I'm definitely including a cleaning spell and, of course, my usual set of cloaking devices. I might add an automatic healing spell, just in case something awful happens to me during the day, and an emergency deflection spell."

"How about a Somebody Else's Problem spell? The one where people see you, but they don't notice you?"

"Good thought."

"Didn't you tell me the Demon King also had a shadow-manipulating thing?"

"Yes, he did. I have an amulet for it down in Bronze's saddlebags."

"Could you duplicate it?"

"I'm pretty sure I could. Why? Do you want one?"

"Oh, yes, please!"

"Let's experiment a little. I've got a variation that works with my shadow, but my shadow is a little unusual."

So we worked on it for a while. It was trickier than I thought, but Mary was the one who figured it out. It treated shadows and darkness as objects, rather than a lack of light. Magic does things like that, but I'm never comfortable with it. For example, it's possible to freeze something with magic. All you do is take the heat out of it. But magic can treat *cold* not merely as a concept, but as an actual *thing*. Therefore, one can inject cold into a hot object and it cools down. Same thing with the shadows. A shadow is a place where light doesn't reach because something blocks it. With magic, shadow is a substance, not a condition, and can be manipulated.

It took me a while to wrap my head around that. I didn't like it. The spell worked, but it was so counterintuitive—for me—that I took a few aspirin and worked another healing spell. I can sort of see how people think about it. Hot is hot, cold is cold—opposites of the same thing. All my training on the matter views heat as a form of energy and cold as lower levels of energy. Mary, on the other hand, had no trouble with it.

For magic, it's all about the alchemy. Earth, air, water, fire… hot and cold, light and dark, sound and silence… things you can see or touch or sense. Sometimes I think I would understand how to fly, or walk through walls, or any of the *weird* spells magicians use if I could stop thinking like a physicist and start thinking like a... a... a *poet*.

Yeah. Blind spot. Doesn't help to know it.

At least my ears were working all right again.

The cable paid out rapidly as I sank. *Thud* to the bottom, *glorp* in the mud, *shluck-shluck-shluck* as I slogged along to the nexus, scaring strange fish the whole way.

I thought it was easy to find on my first visit. Now, the glare of my spells was visible even before I hit bottom. It reminded me rather forcefully of the heart of the mountain and the intolerable blaze of forces there. I really should add some more layers to its conversion spell structure...

It took a while for my senses to adapt to the brightness. When they did, still squinting and shielding my eyes, I hunted around for the power taps and turned them off. The disruption spell fired again and went into standby mode, powered down. I blinked for a bit, waiting for the magic-sensitive part of my eyes to adjust.

The enchantments went like clockwork. Come to think of it, most of my magic is very clockwork-ish, very rigid and mechanistic. I've done some more "organic" things, but usually I build spells like gears. I wonder if that's a reflection of my training or simply the way I think.

The enchantments still took time, but I stuffed as much magic into everything as I could. My underwear started repairing itself, much to my relief, and I made a point of giving it some electrically-defensive properties—I *despise* shock-based weapons. I also restored my hypersharp saber.

Then I turned my attention to sealing the nexus.

With the containment shields stabilizing the thing, it was relatively easy to put on my spell-gauntlets and poke tendrils into the seething cauldron of power. It was easier than I expected, really. Practice must pay off. But laying down a webwork of forces over the ruptured nexus wasn't a simple task.

Think of it as a problem of pressure. If I laid down a bandage over the hole, when I removed the containment shielding, the bandage would have to hold the pressure all by itself. This is kind of like putting a lid on the main magma vent under a volcano—then taking away the volcano.

If I could close the hole, cap it, seal it, that would be a start, but insufficient for the long term. The containment shields contained the nexus, but didn't close it. How do you heal a wound in one of the planet's major hearts?

After considerable poking around with my spell-armored tendrils, I thought I might have an idea.

If I treated the nexus like an oil well and capped it, it would be a hole forever. I think. The containment shields would constantly drain some power from it in order to continue existing and containing. Opening the nexus would merely involve popping the containment shields from the outside. This wouldn't be difficult at all.

However, if I laid a gridwork of spell-lines over the actual opening of the nexus—not restricting the flow of energies; the containment shields did that—I might encourage the nexus to... grow a new shell? Sort of? Much as a wound heals itself, the spell-lines could act as a framework for the nexus to use, for lack of a better description, in healing over the open wound.

I set it up and set it going. Over the course of the next hour, I thought I detected a slight drop in the intensity within the containment shields, implying the nexus was, in fact, starting to grow closed. It might take a while, but it seemed to be working. I decided to leave it overnight—overday? —for a while before checking on the progress.

Thursday, February 25th

Mary was delighted with her enchanted pendant. She kissed me soundly and played with her new toy, wandering around belowdecks and being stealthy. I was pleased on her behalf.

Later, when she felt familiar with her new toy, she snuck up on me, plopped down next to me and asked me what I was building. I held up the paper with the occult diagrams on it and explained about healing a nexus. She nodded as I spoke, made appreciative noises, and waited until I finished.

"So, any questions?" I asked.

"Since I didn't follow more than every third or fourth word, no."

"It's really pretty basic—"

"—for you. Stop talking." She kissed my forehead. "You're busy with things that might mean life and death. When you're bringing the plane in for a landing, on fire and shy one engine, is not the time to give a flying lesson. You focus on landing the plane. I'll be ready to bail out if you say so. You can explain later."

"Are you sure? You like to be kept in the loop."

"And I appreciate your effort," she assured me. "I don't actually need the technical details."

"How else are you going to learn?"

"Slowly, and with lots of patient help."

"Fair enough."

"All this is preparation for finding your missing ball, right?"

"Not exactly. Mostly I'm cleaning up after myself, undoing all the things I did. I'm trying to put the world back in order since I'm the one who messed it up. This part of it, anyway."

"That's a good enough reason for me." She kissed my forehead again. "You save the world. I'll check on the news."

The sun sank and so did I. I checked on the progress of the nexus healing spell.

Well, crap.

I sat down in the mud by the nexus and considered it carefully. The network of lines I placed over the opening was visibly thicker, at least to my eyes. The gaps between lines were slowly closing, as though growing a skin over the open wound. As a rough estimate, I placed the complete sealing-over at something like forty or fifty days.

But the intensity of the forces within the containment seemed lower than before. That didn't strike me as right. If there was a constant flow, a reduced aperture would account for a lower intensity. This was more along the lines of a pressure bottle. As long as there was *any* opening, the intensity inside the containment should equalize and remain relatively constant—aside from the usual drain to maintain containment, of course. But that relatively minor drain wouldn't account for this, would it? Damn it, this is why I need to create a scale of measurement for magic!

Excuse me.

I let out a burbling warble that probably scared whales halfway around the world. I whirled in place as I came to my feet, scanning in all directions on the way up and finishing by looking directly above me. Nothing, nobody, nowhere, aside from a cloud of mud the size of Newark.

Sorry about that, the voice continued. *I tried not to startle you.*

I recognized the voice. It was me. The other me. The psychic energy-imprint me.

Could you try saying "Hey, it's me," next time?

Sure. Got a minute?

For you? Sure. But I thought you couldn't talk to me unless we were on holy ground? Or if I invoked you?

I just need to be invoked. You don't have to do it. In this case, Sparky asked me to pass along a message.

Sparky *did? Why?*

Because you're not anywhere near an open flame? In Karvalen, candles and lamps are commonplace, but in a technological culture, open flames are regarded as dangerous. Aside from the occasional fireplace, power outage, or candlelight dinner—

I take your point. I've been on a ship a lot.

Yeah, those don't take well to fire. Unless it's a steamship. I wonder if the interior flashes of flame in a gasoline or diesel engine would be enough—

I don't get along with fire too well, either, I cut him off, *when I'm on the boat. I'm allergic to drowning.*

Well, that's ironic, considering where you're standing.

You think I haven't noticed?

Just observing. Anyway, Tianna did the actual invoking. She wants to talk to you when you have a minute. As I understand it, she asked Sparky and Sparky couldn't reach you, so Sparky asked me.

That's gotta be galling.

Not really. Letting Tianna go into the Temple of Shadow and ask Beltar, the Deveas of the Lord of Shadow, for help—that would be.

Ah, I see. As long as we can keep it from the children, it's okay?

Kind of, yes. By the way, how's the cloak?

Shifting shape.

Really? Interesting. Does it do anything else?

Not that I've noticed, I admitted. *It does blend in well, though.*

Good to know.

I felt an increase in attention as a sort of psychic pressure.

Mind if I ask what you're doing?

Trying to close a nexus.

I see. Why?

Because I don't want the locals tapping into it and using it to fry me.

Good reason, he agreed.

By the way, since you're here...

What can I do for you?

Can you locate my Evil Orb? I figure I ought to ask, rather than make you read my mind.

Good thinking. No, I'm afraid not. I'm not capable of reaching into this world unless it's in your immediate vicinity. Even then, it's hard. If you weren't standing so close to a power center, I might have had to quit this conversation already.

Is it worth asking why?

You're the only thing I have that's even remotely like a worshipper. Well, I take that back. There are still a number of people who know you or are scared of you, but no one who actually prays—directs their psychic energies, if you prefer— toward you. There's no active faith, therefore, no real power. Acting in this place is like trying to run an electric car off your flashlight battery. Each world has a certain tuning to it and we sort-of gods of Karvalen don't have the knack.

I thought you mentioned the Lord of Light could do it.

I believe so. I need more samples to work out the trick of it.

I plan to do some world-traveling, someday, I thought back, *while I look for a comfy spot to settle. I'll keep you posted.*

Would you? I appreciate it.

De nada. Anything else?

That's it for me.

Okay. How is Tort?

Coming along nicely, he assured me. *It's a slow process, though, and I want to get it exactly right.*

When you put it that way, take all the time you need, I assured him.

I appreciate your patience. Anything else?

While you're here, can you tell me if my healing spell on the nexus working? Any suggestions to improve it?

I waited while the psychic presence directed its attention at the nexus.

Offhand, I'd say you're on the right track. If anything, you might make the meshwork finer. I'd also suggest putting multiple layers over it. After it grows in, you'll want it strong enough to take the load, rather than just a thin layer of metaphysical tissue.

Good thought. I'll get right on that. But why the finer meshwork?

From what I can see, it's having a hard time growing over the holes you've got. Smaller holes will fill in faster and get you a better growth rate.

I'll take your word for it. It's hard to get a good look inside. Thanks bunches.

De nada.

And I was alone on the ocean floor again.

I got to work on the nexus bandages and tried not to wonder what Tianna wanted. I hoped it wasn't urgent. I should have asked what the time differential was like over there.

Friday, February 26th

With the nexus sealing itself, we steamed off to the island again to top up the yacht's stores while I went ashore and set things on fire.

Recalling the last time I had a fiery conversation, I drew ideograms in a flat spot on the beach. On this, I carefully laid a few wooden boards, each carved with the appropriate symbols. With several armloads of driftwood piled nearby, I built a fire on the boards and attempted to invoke Sparky. If she was listening, I might get her to connect me with Tianna.

The fire roared up into a pillar, shrank down into a woman-shape. It was featureless, like some of the more abstract mannequins, but it spoke.

"I heard your call," said the rushing flames. It sounded a lot like Amber, but I blame that on biology. Pyrology? The flames.

"Hello," I replied. "I understand Tianna wants to talk to me?"

"Yes, but she gave Me a message for you, if you are willing to receive it."

"Ah. All right, tell me, please." It pays to be polite.

"Your wife, the Queen Lissette, requests the aid of the Demon King."

My reply was not addressed to Sparky, but it had a lot of heat behind it. The flaming figure folded its arms.

"Shall I tell her this is your reply?" Sparky asked. I detected a trace of frost from the flames.

"No. I apologize. I was annoyed at the circumstance. I thank you for the message. If you would be so kind, please let her know I'll be along as quickly as I can. —speaking of which, how long has it been since I left there?"

"Three months, give or take."

"I'll try to hurry. Thank you again."

"You see?" Sparky asked. "We need not be adversarial."

"Maybe you're right. We can be civil." I did not add I would continue to trust her about as far as I could comfortably spit boiling tar.

"I would wish for more, but I will content Myself with the progress we have made."

The flames flared high and fell to ashes.

"Thanks bunches," I told the smoking pile. I sat down on the beach and looked out over the ocean, thinking tired thoughts. Of all the things I wanted to do—at the moment, a very short list—putting on my Demon King hat and playing monster was not one of them. Secretly, I suppose, in the deep, dark places of my heart, I hoped Lissette would have no further problems. She could have a happy reign over a happy realm and everyone would eventually realize what a wonderful ruler she made. And, by extension, I wouldn't be feeling like a tired worker called back after a long shift to deal with an unexpected problem.

So, why go back? Because she needs me, and because she asked for my help.

"So," Mary said, once I was back aboard the *Princess*, "what's the plan?"

"I'm thinking I can—okay, *we* can—go through a gate, ask Tianna what the trouble is, and make plans from there. While we're gone, this nexus can heal itself and close. The rest of them will keep pounding the dome territories and keep everyone away, so there's no rush to get those closed. I doubt anyone is going to go down to the ocean floor, and I don't think anyone here can affect them at a distance. I think we can get away with letting things sit like this for a while."

"The plan is to drop everything and see what your granddaughter wants, then decide what to do."

"Yes."

Mary blinked at me for a moment, head cocked to the side.

"I was being sarcastic."

"Oh? Sorry. You should have used more; I missed it entirely. Is there something wrong with my priorities?"

"No... No, I suppose there isn't." She looked thoughtful for several seconds, tapping her lips with a fingertip. "Come to think of it, I guess your priorities are in better order than mine. You've got family values and suchlike. It's been a while since I had to deal with any of those."

"You could stay here and keep an eye on everything, if you prefer."

"Not on your unlife! From now on, whatever world you're in, I want to be in. Getting dropped off here with no way back was uncomfortably like being a child dropped off somewhere until Mumsy or Dad came to pick me up again."

"I hadn't considered that."

"Yeah, well... Sometimes I'm not the best at expressing my feelings."

"You do all right. I'm the one with all the denial and repression."

"Not all of it," she muttered.

"Sorry, what?"

"I asked when we are leaving."

"First, we make arrangements for the *Princess* and the crew. Second, we unload and go ashore. Then, first thing in the morning—never open a gate to another world at night; it might be daytime on the far side—we go into my gate room in Karvalen."

"Isn't your gate room underground? We'll be safe from the sunlight."

"Yes, but there are two points. First, I can *miss*. If I don't hit my gate room, we could have a full-sized garage door of sunlight pouring through at us."

"Considering how bad that is, what do I need with a second reason?"

"The second one isn't so bad. Sudden transformations go with gate travel between time zones. From living daylights to dead of night is unpleasant but brief; our regeneration will fix everything. From dead to alive—from night to day—is a terrible, sickening shock and it takes all day to recover. I don't recommend either of them."

"Good to know," Mary agreed. "Let's pay the crew some bonus money, talk to Walt about long-term parking, and get Bronze unloaded." Mary looked thoughtful. "I wonder if they have a crane at the marina?"

They didn't, but getting Bronze off a boat is much easier than getting her on. She walked carefully over the edge and right into the bay. A short while later, she walked up out of the surf with an air of "Problem? What problem? I looked, but I couldn't find a problem."

I love my horse.

Mary set up some automatic payments to maintain the crew and staff. Apparently spending the rest of the winter and possibly some of the spring in the Bahamas is not, in their opinion, a terrible hardship. I also agreed we were unlikely to need the *Princess* instantly when we returned, so allowing Captain Tillard to use it at his discretion around the islands was a nice bonus.

Finding something to use for an archway wasn't any great challenge, either. There are a number of storage places, garages, warehouses, and so on possessing doorways large enough for Bronze. We selected a suitable rental unit for storing excess goods and I drew symbols on several sheets of a notepad. With some tape, a spell to burn the paper, and a couple of charged power crystals, we were practically home free.

Saturday, February 27th

Early this morning, we went into the storage place, taped paper all around the garage-sized door, and flushed for Karvalen. My gate room snapped into view and we slid through immediately. The gateway behind us shredded into nothingness. I didn't get to see it, but if all went according to plan, the papers burst into flame once the gate shut.

I didn't want to destroy a gate, even a temporary one, while it was running. I remember the last time.

Once we were through and safely home in the mountain, my jacket rippled into a cloak again, crawling up my arms to slither around my shoulders and lengthen down my back.

"That's not fun to watch," Mary said, staring at it. She looked a little green.

"I'm the one wearing it," I countered. She nodded, still eyeing my cloak with sickly sort of fascination.

I popped a quick scrying spell outside to check the time. It looked like early afternoon. I canceled the view and dialed the mirror for the Temple of Flame. One of the assistant priestesses answered. Sheena, I think her name was.

"Majesty," she said, as the image swam into focus. She bowed.

"I hear my granddaughter wants to talk to me. Is she in?"

"She is in Carrillon, Your Majesty, attending to the establishment of a temple within the city."

"Figures. Thank you."

"It is an honor to serve."

I hung up and dialed for the Palace at Carrillon. If Tianna wasn't immediately available, at least I could call Lissette...

One of the Palace mirror-minders swam into focus. She didn't scream, so that was to the good. She looked as though she wanted to, though. I tried to ignore this.

"Good afternoon," I told her. "My compliments to the Queen and if it suits her to take a call..."

"I'll see to it she's informed." The mirror tilted upward to a pleasant pastoral scene on the ceiling and I heard a lot of hurrying in the background. They changed the picture since last time, I noticed. It was a forest with a stag half-hidden among the trees.

It wasn't a long wait. The mirror tilted down again and Lissette looked out at me.

"You came?" she asked.

"You called. That's how it works."

"I... I wasn't sure..."

"I'll always try. I may not get the message until much later, or it may take me a while to get here, but if I'm too late to help you, it will be from circumstances, not from a lack of trying."

"It's good to know. And it's good to see you again."

"The pleasure is all mine, I'm sure. What seems to be the trouble?"

"Do you remember the Kingdoms of the West—Hyceteyn, Actareyn, and Lyraneyn?"

"Vaguely. There are several city-states, I think, on the shores of the Western Sea? Those are three of them?"

"That's correct, although they are more than single cities. They each have one major city from which they take their names, but they also have vassal towns and villages all around them."

"Gotcha," I agreed, without commenting on the idea of a *city-state*. Rethven doesn't really have the same concept. A prince might rule over a *regusularium*, or a *prince's domain*, but—silly me—I used the old Imperial term, *asticogens*, which is more in keeping with what I think of as a city-state. I think Lissette wasn't familiar with the term.

"The Church of Light has little influence within the core of the kingdom, more as you go into the farther reaches. Beyond our borders, they have considerably more power. I believe they have influenced the rulers of Hyceteyn, Actareyn, and Lyraneyn to rebel against the nominal authority of the Crown."

"I thought they only paid lip service to the Crown, anyway? We don't tax them, do we?"

"No, we don't. This conflict is based on appearances, pride, and on religious prompting."

"When you say 'conflict,' you mean it... how?"

"They've been building armies ever since the days of the Demon King, but they've been assembling troops over the past month or so. Our spies tell us they should start their march east any day now."

"Huh. And what is their objective? To take Carrillon?"

"Possibly. They'll certainly attack Peleseyn and then Traga. After Traga, they'll hit either Hasilel or Riverpool in order to secure a bridge across the Oisen. If they only want to beat back our borders, though, they don't need to do more than sack Peleseyn and take that end of the Kingsroad through the Darkwood. From my reports, their armies are larger than is required for such purpose. I will be surprised if they don't make an attempt on Carrillon, but I'm sure they mean to dominate most of the land between here and the western shore."

"I'm sorry, but I don't know much about the lands west of Carrillon. I've never been there. I'll have to look at a map. But I accept your evaluation unreservedly. What do you need from me? This sounds like a straight military matter."

"And that's the trouble," Lissette grumped. "The military men are certain they can run this war without bothering Her Majesty."

"Ah."

"Yes."

"Give an order," I suggested. "Take charge. And when someone fails to hop, have him executed."

Lissette's eyes widened. Mary, off to the side, bit her lips to avoid laughing.

"I'm serious," I went on. "If they don't take you seriously, make them."

"When I summoned the Demon King," Lissette said, slowly, "who did I get?"

"Halar," I reassured her, "with no inclination to suffer fools gladly. Look, I know you've studied all the arts of war. I remember. You're a good swordswoman, you've got brains, you understand the logistics side of things, and you're strong enough to be taken seriously as a ruler. While you may not be the greatest general in history, neither am I. We—you—have people for that. The only difference is your people don't understand how to behave in a manner for you to use them properly."

"I don't follow."

"Neither do they. They seem to think they need to run the war, right?"

"They do. That is, they think so."

"What they need to do is what your council is supposed to do: Provide you with information and options, and opinions if you ask for them. If they want to run the war to suit themselves, you execute them. Or, if you prefer, demote them, lock them up, whatever. Disobeying the orders of his sovereign in time of war is treason, after all. But don't have a trial until after the war. Make sure whoever it is sits in a cell and misses the whole thing. *Then* put him on trial."

"Hmm."

"I really don't want to walk into the Palace and take charge. If you insist, I'll do it, but I'll mostly sit there and ask you—in front of people—what you want done and then tell them to do what you said. I can keep that up all day. I'm sure the smarter ones will figure it out fairly quickly. What I'd rather do is help you from behind the scenes so you aren't relying on the Demon King. You're proving to everyone you don't need me, even though you can call on me."

Lissette sat back in her chair and drummed her fingertips together, thinking. Mary moved to the side of the mirror and nodded at me, giving me a double thumbs-up. I immediately wondered if I was doing the right thing.

"That might actually be best," Lissette agreed, thoughtfully. "Unless, of course, you'd care to drive off the combined armies of Hyceteyn, Actareyn, and Lyraneyn?"

"Do you think our military muscle is up to the task?"

"Yes, provided we can get the army into position. We will need to gather the troops in a hurry if we're going to meet them before they attack Riverpool or Hasilel."

"What about Pelle-whatevever and Traga?"

"Peleseyn and Traga are too far west for us to muster, march, and do battle before they fall. We could reach Traga, perhaps, but the men would be exhausted from the march."

"Hmm. How sure are you this is religiously motivated?"

"The Church of Light has full-fledged temples in all three cities. I'm told there are priests attending to the armies, as well. I don't *know* they have actually orchestrated it, but they do seem rather heavily involved."

I did some mental math and consulted my memory of my sand-table map. If the three big cities were on the western coast, they would be almost twice as far from the mountain's Hand-irradiation spells. The power of the spells dropped off with distance, since it was generating an area of effect, rather than sending the spell out to a specific point. At that distance, the effect on any Hand medallions would still be hazardous, but it would take more time before the damage built up inside a person....

If members of the Hand were still alive on the west coast, the Church of Light might well be behind it. As much as I hate the idea of a holy war, I might not have a choice.

"From a troop movement standpoint," I began, "you're saying you can get the army to Traga, but they'll be too tired to fight. Is that it?"

"Yes."

"Is that the biggest problem?"

"From a military standpoint? Yes. Even your knights... I mean, even the Royal knights will be reduced. Their horses are huge, as they must be, but they are war animals, not suited to long runs, much less carrying the knights on the road. While the knights may rest in the saddle, they must also walk to spare their horses. The infantry will arrive in even worse condition, having marched all day, every day, along the Kingsroad."

"All right. I'll see about slowing down the enemy army. I'll also send you some drawings for a horse-wagon and troop wagons—I thought I ordered some, but maybe I'm thinking of something I intended to do and didn't. They won't help in this conflict, but you can have them built in time for the next one, I think. In the meantime, did you decide if you wanted me to be public or private about helping?"

"I think we should be private. You are right about convincing the less-converted."

"Let's try for that. I'll get back to you."

"Halar?"

"Yes?" I asked. She looked at me with a strange expression. I don't know what to call it. For a moment, she seemed vulnerable, somehow.

"Thank you."

"Always a pleasure, Lissette."

"I'll be expecting your call."

The mirror rippled into reflection.

"Mary?" I asked. She braced to attention and saluted.

"Sir!"

"You cut that out."

"Yes, Sir!"

"I mean it. I'm in no mood for it."

"Sorry," she apologized, relaxing. "What do you need?"

"Can you run the sand table while I talk to Beltar? I'd like some idea of the troop movements, numbers, and so on."

"Sure. Anything else?"

"Not for now."

"Okay. I've got a question."

"Shoot," I agreed.

"Are you okay with all this? I mean, you went to a lot of effort to abdicate. And now, just as you thought you were out, they pull you back in."

"I knew this could happen," I sighed. "I actually sort of expected it while I hoped against it. And not quite this soon." I looked around for someplace to sit, but my geode room lacks chairs. I sat down on the edge of the central pool, instead. I rubbed my face and rested my elbows on my knees. "I hoped I could find someplace, settle in, and have a little bit of vacation. Maybe I just don't live right."

"You only live part-time," Mary reminded me, with a chuckle. I chuckled a little, too.

"You're right. Maybe that's it. But I'd hoped to take a rest, first. I'm tired of…" I trailed off, unable to express what I was feeling.

"Playing Atlas?" Mary guessed. "Being responsible for so many people? Having power and using it wisely?"

"All that and more," I agreed. "I'm not cut out to be a king, not even a Demon King. If I'm honest, I don't even want to be here, doing this. I'm *tired.* But it's the aftermath of my mess, and I have a lot of mess to clean up. I don't feel I can leave this to others to mop up, no matter how much I would like them to."

"I'm not surprised. But you're not doing this alone. You have Firebrand, Bronze, and me." Firebrand chorused a *You betcha, Boss!* while Bronze snorted smoke and nodded.

"I know I can count on all of you, and we'll muddle through this. Thing is, I thought I might have to show up and pound some chauvinist's head in once or twice to convince the hard-line male superiority, female inferiority jerks. I didn't anticipate a semi-external war, especially not a religious one."

"You figured the Church of Light would be less of a problem if you were gone?"

"Of course!"

"But aren't they the ones who tried to seize power in Rethven? Way back when?"

"They didn't exactly try to seize power… I'd say it was more like assuming it. The old king of Rethven wasn't a strong king, as I understand it, and the Church of Light gained a lot of influence and favors."

"But they did gain a lot of political clout, right? They eventually want a theocracy of their very own, don't they?"

"I guess so."

"And how do you feel about that?"

"I'd start a holy war, but I hate those. Come to think of it, I'm not fond of wars of any sort. They're loud, widespread, and indiscriminate. They usually have a bunch of innocent people killing another bunch of innocent people, with liberal doses of misery spread around like glitter after a bachelorette party. I'm against them. I'd like to keep this as low-key as possible."

"Sometimes, you're adorable. Naïve, but adorable."

"Huh?"

Mary kissed my cheek and skipped off to spy on an army. I wondered what she meant. Shrugging, I trudged down deeper corridors to the Temple of Shadow.

Beltar was, of course, delighted to see me. If you've been true and faithful, it's a good thing when god drops by to chat. I stopped him before he could go to one knee. Simply making it as far as Beltar already involved a couple dozen people bowing and kneeling and genuflecting and whatnot. I resolved to have a Word with him about the proper way to not do that.

"Beltar. Can we talk privately?"

"This way, my lord." Beltar led me to a private chamber. He lived in the Temple, or under it. Nice rooms, really, somewhat reminiscent of mine. Smaller, yes, but very clean and organized.

"How many of the grey sashes are wizards capable of charging a power crystal?"

"All of them."

"What, every single one?"

"One cannot gain the grey sash without passing the tests. Tests of proficiency with arms, spells, and letters, tests of strength, speed, and endurance. Even then, one must still be passed by a *septate* of grey sashes who believe him to be of noble spirit and good heart before he may stand vigil before the temple statue for his final judgment."

I pretended I understood the last part. I suspected it involved spending the night under the discerning gaze of the statue in the main temple area. Whether this was purely a psychological thing or not was a good question, but my money was on not. My psychic energy copy probably eyeballed all the candidates. I know *I* would. Quality control is vital.

"Good. Get everybody together and start charging as many of the things as you can. You're going to express your disapproval of a minor rebellion."

"Yes, my lord." He saluted and ran off without so much as a single question. I'm not sure I could have done it; my curiosity bump is huge. I shook my head and sighed before I wandered into the main temple area.

"Is it easier to talk to me in here?" I asked, "or do I need a face of smoke?"

No problem, replied the statue. At least, it seemed to come from the statue. I turned to face it. *This is a place of power for me. The smoke-face is easier for regular people, but talking to you isn't a problem.*

"Good to know. Are you aware of the armies to the west?"

Yep. The Church of Light is pushing the three lesser kingdoms to rebel. It's a more direct thing than we're used to from the Lord of Light. Kind of surprising, really. But it didn't take much pushing, he added. *They don't like being client states even in name.*

"Okay. So answer me this: If we start a holy war, how's it going to end?"

It'll be messy and divisive. If you're dead-set on one, I'd wait a generation or two. By then, your new system of religion-aiding-authority should have taken firm root and be the accepted mode. Then you can consider stomping on troublemakers.

"Won't that just drive them underground within the kingdom? Those it doesn't force to flee the kingdom?"

*I hate to tell you this, but you're **never** going to have a unified, homogenous population of happy peasants, kind lords, generous merchants, and friendly priests. There are always going to be thieves, rapists, murderers, muggers, and profiteers. Not always a lot of them, granted, but they'll always be there. Having a couple of secret, underground cults is pretty much to be expected.*

"I hate it when you're right."

You hate it when I'm right about something that ruins your day, he corrected.

"True. All right. Any advice?"

Keep Mary at a distance from the priests of Light.

"What? Why?"

You are an avatar of a fellow god. She is a black-blooded abomination that will burn beneath the holy light.

"Ah. Good point. I'll bear it in mind."

Another thing to bear in mind. El Lumino is grumpy at you and at the rest of us up here for going along with "My" plan for cooperative action in Karvalen. He feels it weakens his position as an independent, self-sufficient deity and blames you and me for it.

"He didn't exactly like me in the first place, now did he?"

You said it, brother! Ever since your diatribe about Tobias in front of all those nobles, he's had it in for you. Then you go and ruin his minions' plan to dominate the kingdom. Wrecking the Hand compound in Telen didn't make him any too happy, either. They still haven't managed to dig out the vaults underneath.

"Okay. Question."

Shoot.

"Why not?"

You mean you don't know?

I tried to project an emotional thoughtwave, rather than publicly cuss out a quasi-deity in his own temple. I finished it verbally.

"So, while I have some half-remembered dreams from those days following my post-demon-invasion coma, I don't really know anything about it."

Um. I assumed again, and I apologize.

"I'm okay. I think. Give me a minute to breathe." I sat down on the altar and he didn't say anything about it. After a dozen deep breaths and some centering exercises, I felt calm enough to continue.

"Want to try answering now?"

"They haven't penetrated the vaults because they don't dare use magicians to help. Magicians can't be trusted with this kind of stuff. Remember, these vaults were the Hand vaults, under the Hand compound. They contain artifacts and relics of immense power, things they either decided to keep locked away against some future need, or couldn't destroy and didn't want to fall into the wrong hands.

"Yeah, it rings a bell."

Hopefully not the Bell of Woes. Nasty piece of work, that thing.

"You can tell me later. But why did the Hand put their compound in Telen? I get the impression the Church of the Lord of Light is a... more widespread? Larger? It's a religion that isn't centered in Rethven. Don't they have some sort of equivalent to the Vatican?"

Yes and no. It's not on this continent.

"Okay. Why didn't the Hand bury the vault under the main temple complex?"

That's a really good question. Maybe they're a semi-independent, quasi-secret-society, borderline splinter group within the religion and don't want to turn that kind of power over to the real priests?

"That's disturbingly plausible," I admitted. "So, what happened to the vault?"

The tornado wrecked everything above ground, of course, and the fires didn't help. The destruction collapsed the stairs down to the vault itself. This triggered some containment magic—contingencies in case something tried to force the vault doors. Since they lost the majority of the Hand leadership—and thanks to Tobias, most of the Church leadership—they didn't have anyone of sufficient... not "rank" but maybe faith. Talking to god is a difficult thing at best, for a mortal, and their religion was falling into a pit of secularism anyway. It's only been in the last decade or so that it's really gotten back to its roots as a faith, rather than a school of cooperative, ritual magic—

"As much as I appreciate the historical background," I interrupted, "we have a habit of going off on a tangent during the lecture portion of the lesson. I get they didn't have anyone who could open the vault. I get they only recently had anyone of sufficient gumption to succeed in asking their god how to do it. Please continue from there."

Right. Uh... I guess that's it, really. I don't think they're actually digging out the stairway to get to the vault. It contains immense amounts of evil, so the Lord of Light probably wants it to stay right where it is.

"And you bring this up because...?"

All I did was mention burying the vault as one of the things you did that annoyed them. You're the one who wanted more information.

"I—okay. I accept the blame."

Good for you, my son. Confession is good for the soul. Now go do an act—

"Don't push it," I advised. I heard the chuckle in my head.

Anything else?

"No, I think that covers it, for now. No, one more thing. How are the others upstairs taking to the new religion-helping-authority thing?"

No complaints, as such. Some grumbling, but since we all seem to be showing a profit, I'm cautiously optimistic.

"Okay. Need anything from me?"

Not right now. I'll let you know.

"Then I'm off."

I accidentally picked up a pair of grey sashes on the way back through the under-passages. I blamed Beltar, but I didn't argue. If it makes them feel better, I can live with it. Besides, a Church of Light assassin might be lurking somewhere. You never know.

Mary was in the scrying room and had the sand table humming along.

"There you are," she said, as the door ground open. "I hope you're hungry. Some lady with a weird hat asked if I wanted anything, so I ordered food."

"Good plan. What do we have on the scrying table?"

"A suspiciously-straight road," Mary replied, "with a lot of troops on it. One drawback to having wonderful roads is enemy troops can use them, too."

"I'm learning as I go. What else?"

"I've been looking them over. They don't have a lot of defense against scrying. I can't get into their command tent, though, so they have at least some wizards helping."

"And maybe a couple of hired magicians."

"How many?"

"Let's bet on three—one for each major city. They don't work cheap, and they don't like risking their potentially-lengthy lives."

"Fair enough. The rest of the place is pretty open," Mary continued. "My estimates are six thousand cavalry—if you want to divide things up more finely, it's closer to a thousand knights and five thousand cavalry."

"It could be important," I agreed. "Knights are lifetime professionals with the best equipment."

"Elite troops. Got it. The rest of the professional-looking troops are two thousand archers, three thousand crossbowmen, eight thousand infantry with spears, shields, and long knives. The rest of them are warm bodies getting on-the-job training with whatever weapons they have available. Maybe ten thousand of those."

"Huh. How big are these cities? It sounds as though they sucked up all their forces and drafted the population."

"Three cities, remember, with attendant towns and villages."

"Yes, but that's still a heavy drain on the manpower. That's nearly thirty thousand men. Call it ten thousand men from each city. And we're not counting logistics and supply people along for the ride, are we?"

"No. I didn't include those. As for the soldiers, a lot of them are probably mercenaries. Those are just money, not population."

"Good point. Still, it tells me they're not kidding about this. They don't just want to make a statement or fight an absentee landlord. This is an army for clobbering the crap out of someone." I started to reach for the sand table and paused. "May I? Or were you in the middle of something?"

"Go right ahead."

I scanned west, found the coast, marked the three big cities, zoomed in on one. Coastal city, nice harbor, decent fortifications. Fairly quiet, now. A closer examination and a bit of random sampling told me the place probably housed around forty or fifty thousand people, which implied they dumped a quarter of their population—half their able-bodied male population—into a war. Less, of course, any mercenaries. If half the professional-looking troops are hired, the manpower shortage might not be *too* bad...

A quick look at the other two yielded similar results.

"I know this is probably a dumb question, but did you look for a navy?" I asked. Mary nodded.

"I did. I went all up and down the southern coast. I didn't see any groups of ships, just the occasional merchantman, bunches of fishing boats, and what was probably a pirate."

"I wonder why they aren't sailing to Carrillon?"

"Maybe they heard what happened to Mochara?"

"How do you mean?"

"Well, there was a small a civil disturbance in Karvalen, or so I hear," she said. "Something about the Queen and the King having a bit of a domestic dispute. The Queen sent a fleet, the King smashed it, and now the King and Queen seem to be all buddy-buddy again. The King has this reputation for destroying navies."

"That's possible," I agreed, reluctantly. "Of course, they may not have enough ships to feel confident, so they threw everything into the overland assault. Dividing their forces might seem a bad idea."

"Also a possibility. The army won't be near the ocean, so they won't be resupplied or reinforced from there."

"We should keep an occasional eye on the water, though, in case they try coming up a river."

"Noted. So, what's the plan?"

"Plan?" I asked, surprised. "You think I have a plan?"

"Yes."

We looked at each other for several seconds in silence.

"Okay," I finally admitted, "if I have to do this, I might as well go big or go home." Mary smirked at my comment. "I might have the beginnings of a plan."

"I knew I could count on you."

"Zoom in on the northernmost city. Let me see the palace."

I spent the rest of the day scanning what I could of the palaces of Hyceteyn, Actareyn, and Lyraneyn. They didn't have much in the way of scrying defenses, just privacy blocks around private quarters and the like. I guess that'll teach them to underestimate the resources of the kingdom they're nominally vassals of.

I also spent some time drawing an illusion-model of a horse trailer. I know I've had this idea before, but, darn it, people don't always implement them too well. Possibly because I don't always explain it. Or even mention it.

The wagon included a roofed-over seat for the driver, an internal compartment forward for the knight, and space to either side of the horse for hanging armor, tack, and other bits of gear. The knight's area was somewhat small for a jumbo-sized man, but it was mostly padded seating and a place for a hammock. It beat walking. I figured a pair of regular horses could haul the thing and get the fighting gear there in shape to actually fight.

Given sufficient horsepower, could we implement horse-drawn troop carriers? Rather than marching to battle, could we get some highly-mobile, elite infantry to the trouble spot to reinforce local troops until the main force arrived? I'll have to send a note to Lissette.

With that done, Mary and I waterfalled and discussed the problem of the local gods.

"So, you're basically immune to divine wrath?" she asked.

"No, I have diplomatic immunity in this world," I corrected. "Anytime a *simulata*—one of the local pseudo-deities—feels like smiting me, I'm smote. They won't do it, I gather, because then everyone else on the Olympian plane will then be allowed to do whatever they want to the followers of said smiter. I think these pipsqueak gods can get killed if such a thing goes on long enough, but I'm not sure."

"Not too clear on the Olympian ecology, I gather?"

"Not at all. I think—this is only a feeling, but a strong one—I think they view this plane of existence as a sort of food-dispensing garden. If they tend their plants, their followers, they produce psychic energy these energy-state beings feed on. I don't think they really care about ruling and dominion and being in charge of anything. I think they're more concerned with getting enough to eat."

"If one of them owns the place, he gets all the cookies while everyone else goes hungry."

"Exactly."

"Is that why you're trying to get the gods integrated into the kingdom?"

"No, I just want them to stop… hmm." I thought about it for a moment. If they were all assured of a steady supply of psychic energy—food—would they be less of a pain in the gluteus maximus? If food really was their primary motivation, maybe. But, of course, anything with enough brains to hold an intelligent conversation is too complicated to be easily categorized. Not that I think much of their ability to reason—with one, possibly two, notable exceptions—but they do think.

"I'm not sure," I admitted. "Maybe that's what I really want. If they calm down on the me-first attitude and learn to be symbiotes instead of parasites, they can save a lot of energy by not arguing with each other. I don't know what they do for fun, though. I only know a few of them well enough to risk asking and I don't like talking to any of them."

"Fair enough. But, since you're a sort-of avatar, you have diplomatic immunity?"

"As I understand it, yes. I'm a physical entity representing an energy-state being, at least. They can't, or won't, act directly on me. Their material assets—followers, priests, hired help—can still smack me with whatever they find to hand, though."

"But I'm still going to get turned into smoking ashes if a priest of this light-god waves a holy symbol at me?"

"That's my understanding. Which is why I want to know something extremely important."

"Name it. And scrub my back." She turned around and I did so.

"Can you use a bow?"

"I suppose so. I mean, I took archery as a class for physical education credits. I was pretty good, actually. With my current eyes and muscles, I could probably do a darn fine job of shooting a target. But if you're asking about my combat proficiency as a professional archer, I'm going to have to disappoint you."

"Target shooting, not sniping?"

"Exactly."

"All right, what long-ranged weapons do you feel comfortable with?"

"None of them. Not really. I'm pretty accurate with a rifle, but I'm not really a sniper. Hell, I'm not much of a soldier. I'm a thief."

"Do you have any problems blowing heads off if I can make it easy?"

"Silly question."

"So it is. All right. I'll see what options we have."

I typed in a request to Diogenes, fired up the micro-gate, and sent it. The answer came back instantly, before I could even close the gate. I closed it and read his reply with considerable delight.

Next, it was off to the upstairs gate room to make some modifications to the hallway outside and the room itself. If I was going to use the gate for troop movements, it needed more power. And for that, it needed sockets for power crystals.

Hmm. My intention was to draw lines on the floor and walls, then have the mountain turn the lines into silver-filled grooves, with little cups for people to place power crystals in. That way, the mountain could separate itself from the metal and the metal could be suitably enchanted.

What did I do with those orichalcum samples I swiped from the Atlantean pyramid?

After several hours of being annoyed by the paradox of trying to analyze something with magic when it's a superconductor of magic, I finally bit the bullet and admitted I was stumped. If I had more metal, I might be able to vaporize bits of it and do a spectrographic analysis, but it would take days, maybe weeks to put together a laboratory for it, to say nothing of the spell research I would have to do.

Fortunately, I knew someone who could help me out. The only question was whether or not we had the time.

I texted Diogenes again and he assured me he could conduct a thorough metallurgical analysis on a very small sample. I would have sent my sample through the small gate-box—should I call it a shift box? Or a switch box? It doesn't actually open a gate—but I was worried about the effect the metal might have on the spell.

The interior of the box is directly affected by the magic on the box. Orichalcum doesn't respond well to magical effects. Magic just goes right through it. On the other hand, an actual gate doesn't seem to have as much of a direct effect on things going through it. The gate affects the space through which objects travel. I think. I didn't have any untoward incidents with the orichalcum when going through a gateway. As far as the gate spell went, it should have been no worse than carrying a coil of wire. If it's not connected to grounding point, it doesn't matter if it's a conductor.

Then again, could orichalcum have other properties under different circumstances? It's not like I've had a chance to experiment with it. Maybe.

But, back to my point. A gate, at least, will allow the transport of orichalcum, but it might do nasty things to a shift-box.

Yeah, I like shift-box better than gate box.

When the sun comes up, Mary and I will pop over to Diogenes' world for a bit and pop right back. Hopefully, the time differential isn't too bad. We're estimating four days until the Coastal Alliance Task Force reaches Peleseyn, and I want to pick a fight before then.

Karvalen. It's Around June 11-ish

This multi-world calendar thing is going to drive me up the wall. It's summer, and it's nearly ninety days since I left. So it's June 11th or thereabouts. I may have to shift to the local calendar just to keep things straight.

But then what do I do in other worlds? Do I keep switching back and forth? I'll lose all track of when I am. Maybe I should number my diary entries instead of putting a date on them. At least it would be easy to keep them in chronological order. Or maybe I should just keep track of days according to the days as they pass *for me*. But then I run into the multi-world-weirdness again. "May 9th, Tuesday, bought a Christmas present after fighting my way through the record-breaking snows..." No, that sounds stupid and downright confusing.

Maybe I'll just stick with whatever the local date is. Approximately.

In the meantime, it's June-ish in Karvalen. And now, Mary and I are popping through a gate to Diogenes' world. Whee. But we're leaving a smaller ring-gate open to act as a placeholder so we don't accidentally spend a Karvalen year there while we run an errand.

We stepped into the library together and immediately downsized the main gate. It was daytime at both ends, so we didn't undergo any rapid transformations.

"Good morning, Professor," came from a robot next to a table. A variety of equipment was spread out on several tables around the library.

"Good morning, Diogenes."

"Good morning, Miss Mary."

"Good morning."

"What have you got for us, Diogenes?"

The robot was a tracked unit with a vertical cylinder in the middle and several folding arms. It whirred around behind a table and indicated items as it listed them. The first item was actually a pair of identical items, about the size and shape of a deck of cards.

"For emergencies, reinforced body bags with layers of metallized, biaxially-oriented polyethylene terephthalate and light-proof zip-lock closures. The materials have been tested in the laboratory up to light intensities exceeding forty times the surface sunlight on this planet, but field testing is impossible without a vampire."

"Understood. We'll see how they hold up," I replied. I pocketed one, Mary took the other. Diogenes continued.

"This is an Infantry Support Laser, Mark Nine Infrared. The backpack holds the power pack while the cylindrical portion holds the primary lasing array. It has an effective range of eight thousand meters against unarmored targets." The device was a sizable backpack unit connecting via a pair of heavy cables to what resembled a bazooka. A boxy attachment on the side of the bazooka portion was obviously the sighting mechanism.

"Cautionary note," Diogenes continued. "This laser has been tested and is functional, but it is repaired and refurbished equipment. I cannot guarantee the service life will meet your needs."

"Understood. Any idea on how long it will last?"

"I calculate it has an eighty-seven percent chance, plus or minus four percent, of functioning normally through one entire power pack."

"Good to know. What else?"

"Next, these are the ruthenium experiments. As you can see, each one has a variation on the basic ruthenium electromagnet. On the theory they produce magical energy, they are all presently energized in order to provide ideal charging conditions for the gateway. They can be evaluated at your convenience.

"These are high-definition digital cameras. They are available at your discretion for sensitizing to magical energy."

"I should have thought to enchant some for you while I was messing around with nexuses," I noted. "Sorry it slipped my mind."

"Take your time, Professor."

"By the way, speaking of cameras…"

"Yes, Professor?"

"How do you see me at night? Do I show up on your scanners?"

"You are only partially detectable," Diogenes told me. "Standard imaging devices do not register your presence, however some anomalous artifacts do appear in the signal when you move. It is possible to extrapolate your location. Other sorts of sensors suffer different levels of degraded usefulness, but all of them have at least some telltales. By combining inputs of various sorts, I can track your location. Usually by stereophonic means."

"You can hear where I am?"

"Yes, Professor."

"Good to know. I'll be cautious about automatic doors, then."

"Sonar-based detection seems to work perfectly, Professor," Diogenes cautioned. "It appears to be purely an electromagnetic phenomenon."

"Even more important to know. Thank you."

While we spoke, Mary examined the laser without actually touching it.

"How does this work?"

She and Diogenes discussed the Army manual on the usage and maintenance of laser weaponry. I stepped out and met the robot coming to claim the samples of orichalcum.

"Do you wish me to replicate the material once it has been analyzed, Professor?"

"Yes, please. I want to test them more extensively. I haven't had much chance to work with the stuff."

"Quality control samples will be produced," Diogenes assured me. "Do you require anything else for your upcoming war?"

"I don't suppose you have a battalion of robot-driven tanks?"

"They have not been high on my list of salvage, recovery, and repair, Professor," Diogenes replied, primly. "My primary concern has been establishing an industrial base and infrastructure with the available materials in order to begin manufacturing materials and components not ordinarily found in salvage."

"Just as well, I suppose. I don't really want to kill everyone, just send them home. Thanks for the help, Diogenes."

"Always a pleasure, Professor."

I went back into the library. Mary was wearing the backpack and had the bazooka-like portion hanging at her hip. It was longer than I thought, maybe two meters long—longer than Mary was tall, certainly.

"It's heavy," she observed.

"Seventy-six kilograms," Diogenes replied. "It is normally a crew-served weapon, utilized by two men. However, given the known physical enhancements of your breed of vampire, I believed it to be within the limits of your combat load capacity, even during the day. Am I incorrect?"

"No, I can handle this. It'll be even easier at night."

"Very good, Miss Mary."

"How many shots does it get?"

"In anti-personnel mode, over a hundred. In anti-materiel mode, ten."

"This should be interesting," Mary mused, hefting this bazooka attachment over one shoulder and sighting through the boxy unit on the side. "Ooo! It has night vision and thermal imaging!"

"Okay, we need to be getting back," I told them. "How's the armor coming?"

"I am still working on materials fabrication, Professor."

"Armor?" Mary asked.

"Your typical jumpsuit isn't my idea of protective wear. I want you wearing ballistic fibers with some rigid plates. Diogenes has designs decades in advance of your own world."

"Thank you very much, Diogenes."

"It is a pleasure to be of assistance, Miss Mary."

"Why are you being so formal, if you don't mind my asking?"

"Is not one supposed to be formal when entertaining guests?"

"Good point."

"All right," I said. "Let me check the output on those electromagical transformer designs and we'll be off."

I pointed out the ones radiating the more intense magical fields and Diogenes promised to build several for placement around the gate. The gate itself seemed surprisingly well-charged, but it had some help, obviously. Transferring the connection from the ring to the arch went smoothly, we stepped through, and the whole thing shut down.

"That was refreshingly simple," I said. Mary nodded agreement and hefted her new toy, sighting down it.

"I take it I'm going to blow some heads off?"

"Any objection?"

"I'm kind of looking forward to seeing what this baby will do."

I called Beltar on the mirror and asked him to call a meeting. He agreed we could have everyone ready before sunset.

"That's fine. I won't be there until after sunset, so take your time. But have them bring their power crystals."

"It shall be done, my lord."

The rest of the day I spent in the upper gate room and in the hallway outside it. The silver was coming in nicely, so I spent my time doing power-coupling work and some revisions on the gate. I wanted it to be an enchantment, embedded in the archway's matrix, rather than an expendable spell. There's always one more thing to do around the house, it seems, whether it be cleaning the gutters, mowing the lawn, or reinforcing the magical matrix of a gate spell. There's no end to these things.

Mary wanted to come along to the meeting.

"I've always wanted to see a demigod addressing his worshippers."

"You're not as funny as you think you are. Besides, I'm an avatar, not a demigod."

"I'll give you three-to-two I can find someone willing to argue."

"How about you stop giving me a hard time about it?"

"Wellll… all right. But you have to give me a hard time before nightfall."

"Woman, you have very few tracks in your mind."

"We already covered that. Now come with me."

"No. I have something for you to do. Something *else* for you to do."

"Oh?" she asked, arching an eyebrow. "What is it?"

"While I'm finishing up this gate enchantment, you can use the mirror to find a good spot to connect to one of the palaces."

"Ooo!" she cried, clapping her hands together. "Am I going to help with a full-scale assault?"

"Yep. Then I want you to look over the other two palaces and give me an idea of where to find the various lords, what defenses they have, all that stuff."

"Are we going to put the arm on three princes in one night?"

"Unless we wind up putting them to the sword. I have other things to do and these idiots are delaying my vacation plans. I'm going out of my way to try and be reasonable about this, but I'm feeling a bit testy. We'll see how reasonable they're willing to be."

"I never met a politician who was reasonable. Self-interested, maybe."

"I've met Reason on the energy plane. I'm prepared to send them there for a personal visit."

"Have I mentioned how sexy you are when you're angry?"

"Business first."

"Yes, dear one." She turned her attention to the mirror while I finished binding magic into the gate. She made good progress while I worked, but she wasn't finished when I was. I gave her a quick kiss and left her to it, promising to be available in the late afternoon.

I went back to the sand table. I wanted to find a good ambush spot somewhere west of Peleseyn. The King's Road ran through the Darkwood, all the way to the coast, then forked to run north and south as a coastal road. It was pretty much a straight line east-west, but it branched beyond the forest to run to several places along the coast. The army was already headed east, so somewhere along that long, straight stretch through the Darkwood was likely to be our battleground.

I looked over the terrain for a while, picked my spot, and gave the mountain some instructions about the road.

Later, after dark, we took the underground passage to the Temple. It's a long walk, all things considered, so we hustled along as soon as our evening transformation concluded.

The temple's main sanctuary was packed with people in black armor and grey sashes. I spotted several red sashes, too. Is it a conflict of interest to be a knight in the Queen's service as well as a knight of a religious order? Or are they merely worshippers, not clerical knights? Interesting question. I don't even know for sure if priests of Shadow are required to be knights. I guess I'm not really cut out for ecclesiastical work.

As I walked in, the whole room leaped to its feet. They didn't have the space to kneel, so they all saluted.

I walked up to the central platform, saluted in return, and gestured them to be seated.

"Gentlemen—and, I see, a few ladies—No," I corrected myself. "I've started off with the wrong words. *Knights.* Male or female matters not in the least. Knights. Wearers of the grey or crimson, that is what you are.

"I have called you here because the Kingdom of Karvalen is facing a threat from the armies of the West. Hyceteyn, Actareyn, and Lyraneyn have mustered their forces and are currently marching through the Darkwood, east of Peleseyn. I have plans for the army, but the part I would ask you to play is more strategic. They have greatly weakened their cities by sending so much of their military on this errand. My intention is to send you to one of their cities, right into the heart of the palace, to take it, hold it, and subdue the ruler of that city as a vassal lord rebelling against his sovereign.

"I know your first loyalty—for most of you—is not to the kingdom. I know it is a dangerous thing for you to do, since the only way to send you there is through magic. There will be no line of retreat; no easy way to flee if things do not go well. There will be no failure, only success or death.

"If you will go, then follow me and I will send you where I need you to go. If you choose to remain, I will think no less of you, for this may not be the wisest course. It is a gamble to end a war before it can truly begin, and the wager is your life. The choice is entirely up to you; I command nothing, only ask."

I stepped down from the platform and walked out. A lot of feet thundered along behind me. I was afraid to look back.

Someone started singing a marching song and everyone picked it up, feet echoing along the tunnel like a martial drumbeat. *In between the Light and Dark/ where all men must keep their hearts/ the Shadow of the world shall call/ and men must choose to rise or fall...*

My translation is lousy, but it gets the point across. I wonder who wrote it. Linnaeus? Minaren? Probably Linnaeus. It sounded like his style.

We marched up into the mountain and the gate room. Mary was waiting for us. She was dressed in her cat-burglar outfit, complete with weaponry. She had the gate's mirror already lined up with an internal hallway in—I think—Lyraneyn, the northernmost city on the coast.

"Did you get a look at the local lord?" I asked.

"Yep. Caught his likeness in a crystal. I think. I'm not sure I did it right. Check me, please?" She handed me the clear crystal and I examined it.

"You did it right," I informed her. "Good work." I turned to the people following me and paused. The room was full, the hallway packed, and the far end of the crowd was around the curve. This was at least... four hundred? Five hundred people? Worse than people. *Volunteers.*

Ever heard the phrase, "an embarrassment of riches"?

Beltar was right up front, too. He saluted. Everyone saluted.

What the hell were they thinking? I'm not charismatic enough for this! I can talk in front of a crowd, no problem, and I usually sound fairly coherent, but I'm not a motivational speaker. I can barely keep order in a kindergarten, so how do I get hundreds of serious-minded fighting men to volunteer for a one-way trip through a magic gate? Is it a religious thing? Or the mystique of being a king? Or are they all idiots? This was dangerous, not some evening picnic run! I *told* them it was dangerous!

Or... did I set things up, way back when, to gather good men together? Men who would stand up for something, hopefully something right? Did I try to do a good thing and actually *succeed*?

Well, they say even a blind pig occasionally finds a truffle.

"This is the target," I said, holding up the crystal and causing it to throw up an image of the prince of Lyraneyn. "Pass it back and remember him. I want him alive. He has to recall his troops and answer to the Queen." I handed the crystal to someone on the front row and it made its way back along the column.

"Got your pocket mirror, Beltar?"

"Yes, my lord."

"Good. Call my gate-mirror when you need anything. Now have them place their power crystals in the receptacles. Any extras, just put them up against the walls; we can use them for the return trip."

Beltar bellowed orders before moving forward to tap his pocket mirror against the scrying mirror beside the gate. I waited until he had it saved to his contacts list, then had Mary show me around the palace in Lyraneyn. A little panning around showed me the point of view was right inside the front doors. Opening the gate would park it in the front door. Troops would stream into the palace, right into the grand hall, while the front doors were still shut and bolted for the night.

Mary smiled at me with a twinkle in her eyes. Professional housebreaker. Right.

"Beltar."

"My lord?"

"Silence spells for everyone, please. The longer we keep this invasion a secret, the farther we'll get before they start sounding alarms and suchlike. Killing is not our first priority."

Beltar passed the word and a lot of magic swirled through the air. While the spells were still being cast, Heydyl came running up along the line to bring me the image crystal. He wore a dark outfit with a white sash.

"Good to see you again, Heydyl. New job?"

"Squiring at the Temple of Shadow, my lord!"

"And are you going on this trip?"

"Yes, my lord!"

I looked at Beltar.

"Is he?" I asked.

"He has the heart for it, my lord, but I do not recall summoning him."

"The call was for anyone!" Heydyl protested.

"I won't argue," I told him, and added, "but you stay with Beltar and watch him, learn from him. He's in charge and I want you paying attention to what he does and most especially why he does it. If you have to, you defend yourself and him. You *do not* go chasing through the palace. I want you on his left like a shield. Got that?"

"Yes, my lord."

"Good." I unbuckled my spare sword and, despite the sound-muffling spells swirling in the hallway, a sudden hush fell. I handed the sword and tackle to Heydyl. "Prove to me I can trust you with a sword by bringing this one back."

He took it and belted it on, unable to answer.

"Gentlemen!" I said, loud enough to carry down the hallway, "Prepare to take the Palace!"

The ringing sound was nothing but a whisper of steel, but it raised the hackles on my neck. Visors clicked soundlessly closed. An army of black-armored war machines dropped into a stance, prepared to charge.

I was *desperately* glad they were on my side. Looking at them scared me.

Whups. Almost forgot.

Hey, you.

Firebrand replied with a wordless query.

Not you. The other guy.

Oh, you mean Me, came the reply. Firebrand sighed and waited.

Yeah, you. Do you want to bless the troops or something? They're holy warriors, sort of.

Thank you for asking. Yes, please, if you would be so kind. May I drive for a moment?

My growl was entirely psychic.

Is that a no? he asked.

No... go ahead. But would you please try not to black me out? You doing some of the controlling stuff isn't so bad, at least compared to anyone else—psychic affinity, maybe—but I want to watch, and to override if I feel like it. It's a control thing, okay?

I understand. I'll try. Some other time, if you like, we can practice it in private.

That's a thought. Not a great one, but a thought. I'll consider it.

You're very kind. Thank you. Now raise your hands and I'll do my thing.

I raised my hands and a wave of power moved through me, out of me, rolled down the hallway like a flood.

Imagine my surprise to find I didn't suffer any lost time. I lowered my hands.

Thanks. What did you do?

It's hard to explain. The shorthand version is a blessing, but the actual effect is complicated.

One of those things incomprehensible to mortal man?

Not really. All you'll need is some new vocabulary and a couple of years to bone up on the theory.

I'll pass for now, thanks.

Suit yourself.

I activated the gate. Power crackled along the lines of silver. The image in the mirror flicked into the distance, flushed away—and Beltar gestured with his sword, the signal to charge, half an eyeblink before it actually snapped into position. Good timing. The black river became rapids as men flowed by in eerie silence, accelerating from a jog to a run to an all-out sprint.

The charge held. The river of shadows flooded the gate, flowed away, and I closed it behind them.

If it all goes wrong, I thought, loudly, *you better let me know.*

The blessing helps me keep an eye on them. I'm watching. Relax. They're good guys.

That's why I worry about them.

"Mary?"

"Yes?"

"Pick your palace. I'll get the last one."

"Shouldn't we take turns? Someone should be here to monitor the gate in case of emergency."

"Crap. I didn't think of that. I intended for us all to tackle palaces together, then I'd come back, pull you back, and then we'd work on getting the guys back from Lyraneyn."

"And how did you intend to get back?"

"Casting a point-to-point gate isn't too hard. I can open a man-sized gate in this world without a lot of trouble and make a connection to my geode-room gate. Then the maintenance cost is paid from this end of the connection." I thought about it for a moment, making new mental links. Could I open a ring-gate from somewhere to connect to a ring-gate here, establish the connection, and have it transfer to a larger gate at both ends? It would be like shooting an arrow with a string over a projection, then using the string to pull up a real rope for climbing. It would take a little longer, but the initial cost to connect would be almost trivial. And it would let me look before leaping, in case I missed my target point again.

"Oh. You can do that?" Mary asked. I blinked and came back from my momentary epiphany.

"Certainly. Why?"

"I thought it was impossible. I should have known better. Silly me. But we should still have someone here to turn this one on if we need it."

"I agree with the obvious, now that you've pointed it out."

"I would have pointed it out sooner if I'd been privy to the actual details."

"This apologizing thing is getting tiresome. How about you just beat me for it?"

"Nope. Not my thing."

"Can I apologize later?"

"If you also perform an act of contrition," she agreed, leering.

"Have you been praying behind my back?"

"What?" she asked, surprised.

"Nothing. Let me see who I can find."

"Actually," she countered, "I have a better idea."

"Oh?"

I sat in the upstairs gate room and watched her through the scrying mirror. Detecting her, as in using something to pinpoint her position, was impossible by any technique I knew. Following her around once I found her was another matter entirely. She slipped through the palace in Actareyn with her usual grace and stealth while I panned my viewpoint to keep up with her. She paused every so often to make sure I didn't lose her. I appreciated it.

Someday, with magic, practice, discipline, training, and more magic, I'll be that sneaky. Okay, no, I won't, but it's a goal I can work toward in the sure knowledge I'll never be that good.

She passed a dozen people undetected, including half a dozen sentries. A few guards were impossible to bypass, though. They were standing on either side of the door to the private, scry-shielded quarters of the palace. She didn't kill them, although she did hit them rather harder than I thought necessary.

I'm sure Mary considered climbing in a window, but we were on a schedule. She wouldn't bash their heads together like that simply for the fun of it. I think.

Her tendril opened the lock, squeezed the hinges to eliminate creaking, and slipped inside. She left the door open so I could look in; the scrying sensor couldn't follow her any farther. She went through what was obviously a receiving room and started exploring the rest of the rooms.

She came back into view, moving quickly, and paused at the door, waving a finger around at the doorframe. I slapped a gate over it, flushed it, snapped her into view, and she told me to close it even as she rolled forward through it.

Behind her, I could see a pure, white radiance. It grew brighter in the split seconds the gate was open. It wasn't visible through a scrying sensor, but my version only transmits visible light unless I add in extra filters. Through the gate, though, the light was brilliant and obvious.

I closed the gate, shredding the view into nothingness.

"Are you all right?" I asked, helping her roll over and sit up.

"No. I feel as though I've been microwaved and I might throw up." She gulped and asked, "Is my hair burned off?"

"No. It looks all right. Why? What happened?"

"'Scuse," she replied, and threw up.

As an aside, never be around when an undead creature throws up. I don't know what we have in our supernatural digestive tract, but whatever it is, it's not supposed to come out. Considering what we eat—blood—I am infinitely grateful it didn't try to crawl over to me.

What came out of Mary's mouth was black, about the consistency of warm honey, and smelled like a summer battlefield after the crows finished picking the eyeballs. It stank like death and rot, possibly with a trace of acid and industrial waste. It could have been used as insect repellent. It could have been used as *human* repellent. It was probably in violation of treaties on the use of chemical weapons.

I covered my mouth and nose; my eyes stung as I backed away in a hurry. A quick spell on the ventilation holes and air started moving more rapidly. Mary rolled onto her side, away from the slowly-spreading puddle of reeking, black foulness and I drew Firebrand.

Whatever it was, it burned. It didn't like burning, but Firebrand insisted, so burn it did, with slow, red, sluggish flames and thick, black smoke. The smoke was also foul and seemed to leave behind a faint stain on everything it touched. I was glad it vented in a hurry.

Mary rolled over onto her stomach and I silently hoped she wasn't about to throw up again. Once was too many. She didn't, but it was a close thing. She lay there for several minutes, still as a statue, not even breathing, while her body sorted itself out. I didn't interfere, didn't even ask any questions, until she sat up on her own.

"Are you all right?"

"I'm fine. It took a little bit to settle down, but I'm better. I'll be fine, really."

"What happened?"

"You were with me up to the door, right?"

"Right."

"The prince's quarters are a family suite—receiving room, office, family room, hallway, bedrooms, the lot. He's got a servant on call, sitting in the hallway, so I clock him one and he goes down. I open the door with my tendril and slither in, but I can already tell something's not right. The prince is in bed with his wife and they're glowing, shining right through the covers and the curtains, and it's bright. He sits up and demands to know who's in his room. I'm pretty sure he's got a weapon, but I can't see very well because of the glare and I can't bring myself to go closer. I tried, but it hurt too much.

"As I'm thinking I should abort, the light gets brighter and I feel like I'm being microwaved. He whips open the curtain and gets out of bed, and I can't stand it anymore. The light feels like it's burning me, not just on the surface, but all the way through, like I'm made of glass and it's shining through me to melt me. That's when I gave up on a bad deal and ran for it, with the results," she glanced at the stained spot on the floor, "you've already seen."

"Sounds as though the Prince of Actareyn has protection from the Church of Light. This is a lot worse than I recall it ever being, though."

"Maybe he believes."

"Could be."

"Aren't you immune to this sort of thing, with your diplomatic immunity and all?"

"So I'm told, although I don't really want to test it if I can avoid it. What say we scry on the palace and see what sort of anthill we stirred up?"

"Fine by me, but if I'm going to run into this sort of thing, I want a protective suit and goggles."

"You know, I'm not sure how to make a god-resistant suit? Then again, they aren't actually gods. I'll need to get more data."

"Work on it," Mary advised.

I fired up the mirror again and scanned around the palace in question. Guards were everywhere, presumably looking for an intruder. The Prince was outside his quarters, so finding him wasn't too difficult. He was accompanied by a pair of armored bodyguards, a wizard—magicians usually dress better—and a priest of the Church of Light. Since I was only looking for visible-light phenomena, as through a camera, I couldn't tell if he was protected from dark and sinister forces, but I did spot a medallion on a short chain. It looked like the typical sun-face thing the church tends to give out.

"Step out of the line of sight," I told Mary. She hurried to the left of the mirror. I twiddled with it for a moment, trying to get a look at the magical signatures involved. Yes, the Prince was currently wearing a deflection spell and a healing spell. The healing spell was merely sitting there, not doing anything, but prepared to activate at a moment's notice. Not quite what I wanted to see, though.

After a bit of finagling, I finally got it. Yes, the medallion was a bright light. It permeated the Prince so he was a figure of light, albeit a somewhat ghostly one. The priest was in a similar, but more intense condition. His medallion was a solid circle of blazing white; his body was a shimmering, radiant ghost of himself, filled with divine energy.

Mary, meanwhile, was crouched beside the mirror, hunched up, and turned away. I killed the scrying sensor and she breathed a sigh of relief.

See? I'm not the only undead who does it.

"Well, that's inconvenient."

"You're telling me?" Mary asked.

"How do you feel?"

"I feel fine, but I knew it when you got the window open."

"Odd. I didn't mean to actually communicate the divine energies. I only wanted a false-color image—like a thermograph, showing heat as colors, rather than radiating actual heat."

"Then you didn't get it quite right," Mary advised. "Didn't you feel it?"

"Nope. This tells me the Lord of Light is either paying close attention, or the emanations of the various energy-state beings are tagged to treat me as transparent. Maybe just as a non-target. I don't know how they set this sort of thing up."

"I'm glad you've found a topic of interest regarding a horrible sensation."

"Oh. I'm sorry. I only meant—"

"Never mind what you meant. I'm more interested in what we're going to do about this!"

"Hmm. Give me a minute."

"Sure. Take an hour. I think I need to find dinner."

"Hungry?"

"I think so." She rubbed her stomach with both hands. "You know that feeling when you're either nauseated or hungry, but you can't quite tell which?"

"I've been there, yeah."

"That's kind of what I've got going on here. Do you think there's anyone at the Temple of Shadow?"

"Probably. I'd check with the kitchen, first. It's closer. And it would be unkind to eat someone only to throw them up."

"Good thinking."

Mary went off to find something to drink and I considered what to do. I had hoped to grab three minor princes, force them to recall their troops, and thus end the current conflict. The Church of Light showed its hand, Lissette knew of their intentions, and the delay in reorganizing and re-fielding the armies would allow Karvalen to be ready for them.

All right, so we weren't going to manage it with Actareyn. The knights might pull it off with Lyraneyn, and, if the general principle of non-interference applied, I might drop in on Hyceteyn. Two out of three wouldn't be so bad.

I dialed for Beltar's mirror. He answered immediately.

"My lord."

"How goes it?"

"We have the palace, the prince, and his family. We have some wounded, but no deaths. Eleven of our number are badly hurt from the magician in the prince's employ."

"How's the magician?"

"He needs a necromancer."

"Ah. What else?"

"They have a bit more than two dozen dead and even more wounded, but I do not yet have a count. The palace is secured, but we are still combing it for secret passages or tunnels. The prince has already sent messengers to recall his troops."

"Wonderful. Does he have a personal priest in residence?"

"Why, yes, my lord," Beltar admitted, surprised. "How did you know?"

"Just a feeling. Does the prince—what's his name, anyway?"

"Prince Tannos of the House of Lyraneyn."

"I know that name." I frowned in thought. "Where do I know that name from?"

"Prince Tannos fought the Demon King's forces in the eastern Darkwood, not far from Peleseyn. That battle was—"

"—where Kelvin was killed, yes, I remember now. T'yl told me. It was Prince Tannos' troops who killed him, wasn't it?"

"Yes, my lord. What do you wish done with the prince?"

I thought about it for several seconds.

"Can our wounded be moved?"

"Yes."

"Good. Bring the prince and his pet priest. Or bring the priest and his pet prince—I'm not sure which way this goes. Lock up the palace, form up in the great hall, and prepare to charge home. Call me when you've got everyone."

"It will be done, my lord." He signed off, presumably to start the process. I switched out a lot of power crystals to make sure the gate was charged up and ready.

When Beltar called back, I took it on the gate's mirror. The connection acted as a guide for the gate spell, which filled the arch...

The great hall in the palace of Lyraneyn snapped into view through the gate and a small army hustled through at a dead run. I kept a hand on the gate itself, monitoring the charge and pushing a bit to keep it open, just in case. Carrying stretchers and hustling prisoners along meant the retreat would take a little longer.

They made it through with gobs of time and energy to spare. All those power crystals they contributed earlier really made a huge difference. Next time I have to dump a lot of guys somewhere, they're spending a couple of days preparing for it. Spread the effort around, that's the ticket.

I thanked them all for their assistance; they seemed more than pleased to have helped. I had Beltar dismiss them. They passed the word down the hall and the gradual movement of the dark tide turned, flowing away.

Heydyl waited patiently, standing beside Beltar until I turned to him. He held out my sword. I took it, drew it, sniffed it for blood, sheathed it.

"Why isn't there blood on this?" I asked. Heydyl looked puzzled.

"I didn't need to use it?" he half-asked, genuinely confused.

"That's the perfect answer." I met Beltar's gaze. "You two probably need to discuss this lesson."

"We will, my lord," Beltar assured me.

I swung around to the captive prince and priest. Two grey sashes acted as their guards. Both the priest and Prince Tannos wore gold discs with a sun-face on them. I could see them radiating white light, but I didn't feel anything. Prince Tannos was tall, middle-aged, and quite fit, with only the first salting of grey in his dark hair. He needed a haircut. The priest was shorter, not running to fat but certainly sauntering that way, with a short beard liberally dusted with grey. Both were in nightclothes. The priest had a big, juicy bruise starting on the left side of his face. I suspected a gauntlet.

"You have no right to do this!" Prince Tannos snapped, looking somewhat comical in his nightshirt. At least he had the good sense not to try and hit me. "You've invaded my home! You've kidnapped a *Prince!* This is an act of war!"

I sighed while he continued to protest. The priest, I noted, kept his mouth shut and his eyes open. He might actually be medium-smart, I thought.

"Prince Tannos," I said, quietly, speaking as though he wasn't talking. He shut himself up when he realized he was missing what I was saying. He glanced behind me and the thought that his life might depend on listening visibly crossed his mind. "You may not have realized this, but your princedom is a vassal state to the Kingdom of Karvalen. You've sent armies marching toward the central regions of Karvalen—an act of rebellion and war, already. So when you declared war by your actions, I took appropriate action against a rebel state. Now, my first impulse is to march into Lyraneyn, crush it like an eggshell under a boot, and demand personal oaths of fealty from anyone who survives.

"Fortunately for you," I continued, in as smooth and matter-of-fact a tone as I could manage, "I've given over the administration and rulership of the kingdom to the Queen Lissette, so what she wants is what you'll get. However—and this is important—if you give me even the slightest excuse to be angry at you, I will break one of your fingers. I will continue to break a finger every time you speak disrespectfully to your King.

"Now," I added, gesturing at the priest, "I'm aware this idiot and his organization have been pushing you to go to war with the Demon King and his minions. You've got a good case for mercy and I'm sure the Queen will be happy to hear any excuse you offer. I won't. With this in mind, do you have anything to say for yourself?"

He reached up to his throat, seized the gold disc, flipped the chain up over his head, and presented it to me as one presenting a talisman to keep evil at bay.

I reached out, took it gently from his hand, and turned it over in my fingers a few times. No Hand logo on the back, so that was to the good. It still shone with a white light to my vamp-o-vision, but that was all.

"It's a nice piece of workmanship," I noted. Prince Tannos stared at me in wide-eyed horror. "Better than the ones I've seen locally. Thank you. I appreciate your gift, although I don't understand why you're giving it to me. Are you repudiating your alliance with the Church of Light so you can assure the Queen of your permanent and unwavering loyalty to the Crown?"

"He cannot," said the priest.

"Who, exactly, are you?"

"I am Prelate Faltos, Servant of the God of Light, spiritual guide to the Kingdom of Lyraneyn."

"I see. And your duties to the Prince?"

"My duties are to the Lord of Light and to the Kingdom of Lyraneyn," he corrected. "The Prince is a servant of the Light, as are all men."

I looked at the Prince, arching an eyebrow at him.

"Is he right?" I asked. Clearly, the Prince didn't like the way this conversation was going. His lips were pressed thin and his eyes narrow. I waited for a few beats to see if he had an answer.

"I serve the Lord of Light," Prince Tannos answered. I noticed he didn't precisely agree with Faltos, but the prelate didn't seem to notice. Faltos swelled up, looking self-important, and resumed.

"Therefore, your actions are the acts of an invader, for the Prince owes you no allegiance!" he declared, pointing a finger at me. "Your kingdom of evil holds no sway over the lands of Light! Thus shall your evil be torn up, root and branch, and cast down into—"

I grabbed his waving finger and broke it. He screamed, a high-pitched, wailing thing and clutched at his wounded hand.

"Maybe I should have made it a point to mention the rule of broken fingers applied to both of you," I observed. "However, now that I have your attention—" I went on, but he screamed curses and epithets at me—language one does not expect from a person afforded the dignity of the priesthood. I waited for over a minute while he screamed at me. That's when my limited patience with blowhard priests ran out.

"Shut up," I told him, "or I'll push your ears together."

He told me what would become of me, how I would burn in the light, be destroyed as all shadows must, blah, blah, blah. So I put a hand on either side of his head and pushed his ears together, hard. The splatter was impressive. Tannos went white, then green as he wiped his face.

"Now that things have quieted down a bit," I said, flicking cerebro-spinal fluid from my hands, "we need to talk, Tannos. Are you ready to listen? Or do you need a minute?"

He needed a minute. Even hardened veterans have a hard time watching someone's head implode like that, especially when brains splatter everywhere. Even the grey sashes needed a minute. Heydyl needed more than a minute. Oddly enough, Beltar was unmoved. I wondered about that, but resolved not to ask.

I waited for people to get a grip on their composure and their stomachs. Blood crawled out of the crushed bits of corpse and slithered over to me, snaking up my boots, through my trousers, and into my skin. When Tannos looked at me again, I smiled.

"So, here's the deal, Tannos. You are going to Carrillon. You are going to negotiate with Queen Lissette for terms. You are going to join the Kingdom of Karvalen on whatever terms you can get, so be as nice as you possibly can. And I'll give you reasons why you're going to do this.

"First, you won't have some religious zealot standing at your elbow, telling you how to run your domain. True, you won't be a prince anymore, but you'll have more autonomy than you have now.

"Second, your economy—and wealth—will increase dramatically. In short, your life and the lives of your people will become much more comfortable. Look around the palace at Carrillon and see what sort of things you might want for your own residence. We've got good stuff. Running water, hot water, education, high levels of employment and production, cheap transportation, low taxes, and something with a passing resemblance to justice.

"Third, when the day comes for you to die—hopefully in due time, rather than shortly after I've finished speaking—the Grey Lady will take you to whatever afterlife best suits you, rather than being dragged off to the Lord of Light to do whatever it is he does with you.

"So there you have it," I concluded. "You can either be a vassal lord to a church that views you as a tool for conquest, or you can be a semi-independent lord with worldly riches and a pleasant afterlife. No, don't say anything. Look around Carrillon, ask questions, find out for yourself. Then decide—and do *not* tell me. Tell the Queen. She is in absolute, unquestioned charge of the kingdom." I nodded at the grey sashes and gestured toward the archway. "You two. Please escort Prince Tannos to the Palace and turn him over—with instructions—to the palace guard."

They saluted. I opened a gate and they hustled the prince through without a word. I turned back to Heydyl and Beltar.

"Heydyl. Are you okay?"

"Ah... yes?"

"You still look a little green. Turn around." I walked around him so he didn't have to have the remains in sight. "Now, since I've had to do that, I'm going to use it as another lesson. Think you can pay attention?"

"Yes, my lord."

"All right." I went to one knee in front of him and took him gently by the shoulders. "What you just witnessed was me doing something awful. I know it was, and it was probably worse than I should have allowed myself. That's my problem. Your problem is to be a better man than that. It's the most important quality I look for in a knight—to be a better man than I. To be more tolerant, more patient, more forgiving. That doesn't mean to be a pushover, or to disregard wickedness and evil, but to be discerning regarding the difference between stupid, pig-headed people and true evil.

"It might help to regard me as evil. An evil," I added, "that knows it's evil, and doesn't want to be. Which is why I keep emphasizing how you—and Beltar, and everyone else—must be *better* than I am. Can you do that?"

"I don't know," Heydyl admitted. "I'm no knight."

"Not yet, no," I agreed. "But answer me this. Do you want to be?"

"I don't know if I can, my lord."

"That's okay," I reassured him, nodding. "You don't have to. I believe you can, but that doesn't matter. You have to believe in yourself, and you have to decide for yourself." I stood up and handed my backup sword to Beltar. He took it, glanced at Heydyl and asked the question with his eyes.

"Hang on to it," I said. "He will be worthy of it if he decides to be." Beltar nodded. He clapped Heydyl on the shoulder and the two of them left, taking the rest of the grey sashes with them, leaving me alone with the mess.

Mary rejoined me, carrying a bucket.

"Feeling better?" I asked.

"Much. The kitchen directed me to a slaughterhouse in town." She held up the bucket. "They don't do it on an industrial scale, not like they do with technology. The guys with the knives are also willing to do custom orders."

"Ah. No drink-puke-drink cycle?"

"Nope. Straight blood, fresh from the throat. I brought you a bucket."

"I was wondering if it was for me." She put it down and I stuck a hand in the blood. The level of the bucket immediately dropped.

"I hear you've been busy."

"Oh?"

"Lyraneyn is about to be formally inducted as the latest county or duchy or whatever?"

"Possibly. It's Lissette's problem. I simply crush all resistance to the Dark Queen's will."

"So I hear. –hey!"

"What?"

"If anyone around here is a Dark Queen, it's *me*." Mary pursed her lips in thought for a moment. "Lissette is the Bright Queen."

"Ah, yes. Sorry. I was thinking of the Demon King and suchlike. So much to keep straight…"

"So, what's next?"

I removed my hand from the now-empty bucket.

"Now you get to watch me on the mirror while I have a discussion with the Prince of Hyceteyn."

"Sweet. You'll make a circular gesture when you want the gate?"

"Think you can open it?"

"I'm pretty sure."

"How sure is 'pretty sure'?"

"I'm pretty sure I'm sure."

"You *fill* me with confidence," I grumbled.

Mary ran the scrying mirror over the palace of Hyceteyn, hunting for someplace close to the private quarters, but not actively under observation. She showed me around the palace in the process so I could at least find the right rooms.

We settled on a door down the hall from the scry-shielded quarters. I would enter the room, Mary would close the gate, and I'd turn around to open the door to the hall. Sadly, there was no good way to sneak up on the two guards at the door at the end of the hall. There was nothing between my door and them, so using a blend-in spell wouldn't work; guards notice you when you approach them. I didn't want to throw around too many spells, either. Someone might notice before I was ready to be noticed. By preference, I'd rather not be noticed at all.

Fortunately, I have other resources.

Mary handled the gate quite well. It opened perfectly and I slipped through the moment it snapped into place. She shut it down and I looked for the scrying sensor. Yes, there it was. Good. Mary could watch from the hall.

I cracked the door open, quietly, and peeked up the hallway. Two guards, both bored, stood to either side of the door. Oil lamps rested on shelves behind them, in the corners, and maybe six candles were spaced along the hallway leading to them. Forty feet? Fifty? It was a good setup and hard for anyone to bypass in sneaking up on them.

My tendrils slithered out along the floor, invisible to mortal eyes, stretching down through the shadows. I brushed them over the life force of each guard, getting a feel for them, carefully leeching away a bit of vitality, then a bit more, until they were both weary enough to be leaning in the corners under the lamps.

I moved at the speed of dark, silent as a breeze, closing the distance in an eyeblink and jerking hard on the energies within their flesh. They both tried to lurch to their feet, but even the surge of panic couldn't make up for the whirlpool of vital energy draining from them. They collapsed at almost exactly the same time. I caught one by the collar and pinned the other to the wall with my foot to keep them from clattering as they fell.

This also resulted in me standing there, awkward and off-balance, while trying not to make any noise. It was such a cool-looking maneuver in my imagination. With some silent cursing, I hopped around on one foot, shifting, using one guard as a counterweight and my foot on the other for balance. I eventually put them both on the floor with relative quiet. If I'd been thinking, I'd have prepared a silence spell. Live and learn.

The door, of course, was locked. It was also magically protected against tampering. It took a few minutes of fiddling to find the alarm connection and disable it, looping it back around on itself. It wasn't magician work—too simple. A court wizard, perhaps. Then it was tendrils again to draw the bolts and gently lift the bar. Wrap tendrils around the hinges to squeeze them, minimize their vibrations and noise...

I dragged the unconscious guards inside and closed the door. Missing guards are bad, but seeing collapsed guards raises the alarm much more quickly. Maybe it's only a difference of a few seconds, but sometimes a few seconds make all the difference.

The prince's quarters were family quarters. Nicely arranged, too, and delightfully informal. Cloth dolls and wooden wagons told me a lot about the children in the area. There was a private dining room, complete with infant-friendly high chair. It was a good place to stash unconscious guards, so I did. As I searched, I risked a little magic to put a sound-muffling spell on the children's doors. They didn't need to be disturbed by what was about to happen.

The Prince slept with his wife in a big, four-poster thing, complete with curtains. They both wore gold pendants with the usual religious image. I clipped through the thin chain with what I laughingly call my fingernails—the chains were nonmagical gold—and removed the amulets. I drained some vitality from the lady to ensure a sound sleep, then ran tendrils through the bed and pillows. Sure enough, I found hidden weapons. Well, when you're a head of state, you need to have every little edge, I suppose. I removed these with great care, then examined the headboard and the wall. No secret compartments, no hidden mechanisms.

The bell-pull for servants, on the other hand, could be a problem. I cut the velvety rope, high up, careful not to pull on it. This length of cord I tied to an upper crossbeam of the bed, letting it hang approximately where it had before.

I put one hand over his mouth and the other on his chest. He woke up fast, eyes snapping wide, and he flailed a bit. One hand went under the pillow for the missing dagger, the other grabbed the bell-pull, yanking on it. The rope gave a satisfying, deep-toned *thrum!* noise, probably a resonance effect from the bed. Very nice.

"You might want to hold still," I suggested, and poked him gently in the chest with five fingernails. It wasn't a coincidence the five points surrounded his heart. I may not have known where elves keep their blood-pumps, but humans are another matter. He took the hint and held still, glaring at me in the dark. I couldn't have been more than a shadow to him, so he didn't know what I was.

"I've had a difficult night," I told him. "I've had an unpleasant discussion with Prince Tannos of Lyraneyn, a short and even more unpleasant discussion with his master, Prelate Fatuous, Fanatic, Faltos, something like that. I have an army to kill—annoying at best—and I'm interrupting other important business to attend to it. And you, prince, are acting as a pawn in service to the Church of Light. I'm disappointed in you.

"Now, if I take my hand away, can you talk quietly? I'd rather not rip your heart out, if you don't mind. Your wife will be distraught to find it missing in the morning."

He nodded, slightly. I removed my hand from his mouth, but not the one from his chest.

"Who are you?" he whispered.

"My friends call me 'Halar,' but I'm probably better known as the Demon King. What's your name, anyway?"

"Vetidius. Is my wife…?"

"Nobody's dead," I reassured him. "Sleeping, yes. Dead, no. And to set your mind at ease, your children won't even know I've been here. Hopefully, your wife won't, either. I'm trying to keep this visit private, between you and me." I applied a little pressure with my fingertalons. "Now thank me for that."

"Thank you."

"Very good. So, here's what we're going to do. You're going to send for a servant. You're going to write out and send orders for your forces to abandon their invasion of Karvalen and return immediately. The peasants will go back to their farms, the mercenaries will be dismissed, and your men-at-arms will resume peacetime duties. Got all that?"

"Yes."

"Good. In return, I'll tell you how to make gobs of money, have a long and happy life, expire peacefully at a great old age, and proceed to a pleasant eternity. How's that sound?"

He looked at me with an odd expression. His spirit wasn't disbelieving, exactly, but he was both skeptical and interested.

"I'll listen," he agreed. I removed my fingernails from his chest.

"You woke up from a dream and made your decision. Go out into the front rooms, ring for a servant, and take care of business. I'll sit right here, watching you and listening. Please don't try to be deceitful. I can smell that sort of thing. Are we clear?"

He glanced at his wife, still sleeping. I could see the gears turning in his head, the implications, the possibilities.

"I understand."

"Good." I helped him out of bed and sat down on it, folded my legs tailor-fashion, and generated a small, floating light like a candle. He gasped at his first look at the monster.

"I'll wait right here for you," I told him. I also handed him the medallions. "You may want to melt these down for the gold," I added. "They're not helping you. In the broader sense of things, they're using you."

He took the medallions and weighed them in his hand. He eyed me while bouncing them on his palm.

"What did you mean about being a pawn?" he asked.

"The Church is using you as their tool. They don't want you to be an independent state. They want you to ruin yourself and Karvalen so they can dominate everything."

Prince Vetidius fingered the medallions for a moment more, thinking. At last, he snapped his hand closed over them and pulled on a robe. He shuffled out. I wrapped a tendril around him, following him with it, feeling his spirit without feeding on it. I also stretched my hearing and listened.

Summon servant... dig out parchment and pen... scribble... let servant in, order him to wait... scribble some more... consider sending other messages, or sending a fake one... discard idea, finish writing... sand, blot... wax, stamp with seal... fold up, more wax, stamp again... hand to servant, order it sent by fast riders... close door, lock door... stop outside the bedroom... breathe... gather courage... face the monster...

The door opened and Vetidius came in.

"Well done," I told him. "You're a wise man."

"What now?"

"Now? It depends. If you had to go visit Actareyn, who would you leave in charge?"

"Normally, I'd have Marak for that."

"Your seneschal?"

"Prime minister."

"Normally?"

"Prelate Kybern," he replied, "has been worming his way into an unofficial position as my chief religious advisor."

"Oh? Do you not like this?" I asked. Vetidius shrugged.

"My wife is more devout than I. I haven't cared overmuch who she keeps as a pet at court. I simply don't like Kybern."

"All right. You write orders to Marak to mind the place while you're gone—a few days, I think—and I'll have a word with Kybern."

"Before you do anything... what are you trying to accomplish?"

"I'm offering you a chance to negotiate with the Bright Queen instead of the Lord of Light. A mortal queen with a kingdom to run, subjects to care for, and prosperity to generate. Someone who wants you to have a good life, not someone who views you as a useful tool in a game of gods."

"When you say 'negotiate'," he began, and stopped.

"I mean just that. Talk to Queen Lissette and find out what you can get out of it. I don't generally have anything to do with it." Vetidius was instantly relieved. I could see it inside him.

"What assurance do I have we can... negotiate?"

"Instead of being stuffed in a dungeon or killed out of hand?"

"Yes."

"I could offer you my word, if it means anything to you. No," I protested, before he could speak, "don't say anything. I can also point out I'm trying to save lives by this visit—yours, your family's, and your people's lives. Additionally, I know you aren't to blame for this, and so does the Queen. While none of that is *proof*, I think it should at least earn the benefit of the doubt, maybe a little trust. Don't you?"

The Prince thought about it. I can't say I blame him for his caution.

"All right," he said, at last. "When the army returns, I'll arrange for a trip. She'll be expecting me?"

I paused to think. I could drag him back with me through a gate, then shove him on through to Carrillon. On the other hand, it would be more dignified for him to arrive under his own steam. Did I want to force it now? Or could I trust him? He seemed sincere in his intent, but give him two days and some browbeating by his wife and a priest... would he still follow through?

You never know. At least the order recalling his portion of the army was already on the way. Even if countermanding orders rode out after breakfast, there would still be hours of chaos and confusion, not to mention horrible effects on troop morale. Nothing makes a soldier lose heart like a commander who can't make up his mind.

Besides, I've been kind of touchy, unreasonable, and violent lately. Maybe a nice gesture on my part was called for.

"Do you have a magic mirror—or a wizard who knows the spells—to call the Palace at Carrillon?"

"No. At least, I don't have such a mirror. I've heard of them, of course, and always wanted one, but they're never for sale."

"And your wizard?"

"Useful, but no magician. Magicians want more than steady work and comfortable quarters."

"All right. I'll let her know you plan to visit. You'll be received with all honors."

"As a prince?"

"Let's say so. We're—excuse me. You and Lissette will be negotiating terms for the formal integration of Hyceteyn into the Kingdom of Karvalen. And let me assure you, the only downside is, perhaps, a bit of pride. The upside is peace and prosperity. And while we're on the subject, tell me something. Do you care more about being a prince—rather than a duke, or count, or whatever—than about the welfare of those under your care? Because I'll tell you up front, Lissette is more concerned with ruling wisely and justly and sometimes mercifully than she is with being Grand High Royal Whatever. It does good things for those under her rule, from peasant to prince."

Vetidius considered carefully. He didn't answer immediately. I like that in a ruler.

"It won't be easy," he replied. "My own court will be less open to change."

"Fair enough. If Kybern will be a problem, I can kill him for you. It would be no trouble."

"I don't think it'll come to that," Vetidius replied, mildly. He seemed startled on the inside but he kept it from his face.

"If you say so, I believe you. Thank you for being so reasonable about all this. Is there anything I can do for you in return?"

"Not that I can think of," he lied. If he had a wish, it was for me to *leave*. I could see it in his spirit.

"Then I'll be on my way. Nice to have met you."

"Likewise."

Diplomacy: The art of polite lies.

Sunday, June 12th

Mary operates the sand table with remarkable finesse. I may need to make another one.

The army is still advancing, slowly, along the King's Road through the Darkwood. Armies of infantry aren't usually known for their rapid movement, especially not if they intend to bring their supply train with them. The road conditions weren't helping. While professional troops can move with startling speed, this force had a lot of amateurs mixed in with it.

When I found out about the invasion, I told the mountain to start changing the road. It's not vanishing, like the time Thomen sent troops toward Karvalen. Instead, the road surface is growing grooves, generally three or four inches wide, and gradually waving back and forth across the road surface. From above, the grooves look like long, wavy lines extending outward from Peleseyn, westward through the Darkwood, and slowly fading out behind the army's rearguard.

Wagon wheels do not like them. Neither do ankles. And once the ankles don't like them, neither do wrists or forearms. The going was less of a highway and more a sadist's idea of a construction zone.

The real trouble, from the army's perspective, was the road was still the only way through the Darkwood. The Darkwood is an old-growth forest of great density and thickness, difficult to get through on foot, impossible while mounted or in a wagon. It would take a year of constant chopping by crews of lumberjacks—or a month of wildfires—to clear a way. So it was either take the now-awful road or go back to take a long detour around. North would involve going through the snowfields, while the southerly detour would involve taking ships.

Nevertheless, the road behind them was almost perfectly flat and smooth. It was as tempting as I could make it.

Every mile of marching cost them a sprained ankle, broken wagon wheel, or cracked wrist. I felt bad for the horses, especially. Their hooves weren't meant for this sort of surface and they didn't like it. When a horse turned a hoof, it was generally all over for the horse, one way or another.

So, their progress was about as rapid as rush hour traffic with only one lane open.

I shot off a quick text to Diogenes. My backup plan for army-repellent was coming along, but it wasn't quite ready. Mary's outfit was, though. I checked the small shift-box and unfolded the new tactical garment. It shimmered a bit, changing color to blend in. There were also some electronic-looking headband devices.

What are these? I texted.

Tactical headset communications, Diogenes replied.

How do they work?

Read the manual.

Snarky computer. I read the downloaded manual while Mary tried on her new jumpsuit.

Mary loved it. It reminded me of a ninja outfit, but with rigid pieces here and there. It fit her remarkably well, had equipment straps built in, changed color to blend into the scenery, and was sufficiently durable to stop most forms of hand weapons. It even included a pull-down thing like a veil over her eyes. The veil wasn't bulletproof, but it did have the camouflage properties. She could see through it without showing any of her face. Combined with the magic for shadow-manipulation and silence, she could steal the whiskers off a cat, assuming we ever saw a cat.

The manual for the headbands was in typical militarese. In short-form, they were two-way transmitters. A thin strip of material unfolded and applied like tape alongside the face, trailing down to run across the throat. Another strip, from the other side, did the same thing, but ran along the jaw line and up from the chin, stopping right below the lower lip. Microphones. Two more strips descended behind the ears and curled up into the ear canal. This left the ears open to hear ambient sounds while providing audio. The whole thing was about a quarter-inch thick, including the padding, and supposedly had a working range of over five miles.

That's Diogenes, always looking out for us.

With that done, I consulted the mountain again. This time, I wanted a better idea of some of the outlying western roads. Were they like the ones in Karvalen, with tunnels underneath? I thought so, but I wanted to be sure. The answer was yes. If it was a road, it went deep enough to accommodate a tunnel. This wasn't just in the kingdom proper, but *everywhere* the mountain laid a road.

I was pleased and said so to Mary.

"Why?"

"Because it means we can ride from the mountain to the coast and never see daylight."

"Fine by me, but why is this important?"

"Because we're going to ambush an army. The road is good and they're doing the whole Pony Express thing to deliver the recall orders; the army is only a day or so away by fast riders. By the time we get there, get set up, and night falls, we should only have a fraction of the forces to deal with. I'll draw fire from everyone, especially the priests, and you'll pick off the commanders. With a little luck, we'll crush their morale so thoroughly they'll turn back on their own. At the very least, their effectiveness as an army will be greatly reduced."

"I've only got an eight-kilometer range," she pointed out. "Is that far enough to avoid religious effects?"

"You're allowed to duck."

"Oh, goody."

"Besides, the laser beam is in the infrared, invisible to the unaided eye. They'll be aiming at me."

"Why am I not reassured?"

"Not a clue. Come on. We're going there today," I said. Mary came with me to get our gear together.

"Mind if I ask why we're not taking a gate?"

"Simple. Bronze loves to run."

"Seriously."

"Seriously."

"That's the only reason?"

"It's the only reason," I agreed. "She loves to run and doesn't get out nearly as often as she would like. It's one of the criteria I have for a place to settle down—open space, or a private racetrack, or something."

"We could spend the day in the bedroom, but you want to spend it in the saddle?" she asked. I stopped walking and so did she.

"Mary, my darling, let me be clear. This isn't a reprimand, or a scolding, or anything like that. So if it sounds like one, I'm doing it wrong. Okay? I want to explain, not make you feel bad. All right?"

"All right. I'll try to take it that way."

"Thank you. So, know I'll happily spend the day with you. I'll spend the night with you. I may spend the next thousand years with you, barring minor hiccups like capture, torture, and getting lost between universes. Meanwhile Bronze, as patient, tolerant, and understanding as I can never be, will stand quietly by through the next few millennia and simply wait for me to get around to her. But she won't have to, because I will *make* time for her. I can't take her to a movie, dinner, or a show. I can't reasonably curl up on the couch with her. I suppose, in theory, I could go to bed with her, but it would be awkward and not enjoyable for anyone, to say nothing of the damage to the furniture or to me." Mary bit her lips to keep herself from speaking and nodded for me to continue.

"So," I said, "while you and I are snuggled up on a loveseat, or out to lunch, or enjoying some quality time ripping throats in an alley, remember how Bronze is missing all the fun—because I remember it, every time. She's not merely some horse made of metal; she's part of me. And she's smarter than most people, possibly including me. Got it?"

"I'm sorry. I didn't think of her like that."

"I know. She's a magical horse—to you. But she is, in a very real sense, also me. And if that seems odd to you, I agree. I'm part of this package deal and I don't understand it. I merely accept it, because it's a fact, like having a heart or a hand. Why? How? I don't know. It just *is*."

"I'll try to remember. What about Firebrand?"

I'm a whole different order of thing, Firebrand replied. *I'm a dragon, filtered through the Boss, and stuffed in a sword. Bronze is a bunch of horse-spirits hammered into a single spirit and bound into a horse fountain.*

"I'm not sure what the difference is," Mary admitted.

Neither am I, but I'm pretty sure it has to do with being one dragon instead of six horses. That, and Bronze was deliberate. The Boss sort of involuntarily upchucked me into the sword.

"So, you're an accident?"

Yes. I suppose, Firebrand agreed, reluctantly.

"Well, we can't help how we're made," Mary replied, airily. "I'll try to think of all three of you as a package. How's that?"

Works for me. Boss?

"I'm good with it."

Now do we get to go kill things?

"Yes."

Mary and I readied ourselves. She suited up with her high-tech ninja outfit, handguns, and knives. She looked stealthy and dangerous even before she loaded up with the infantry support laser. I went with the full suit of black armor, Firebrand, and weird cloak. The ninja and the knight.

Riding Bronze was a trifle more awkward than expected. We had to try a few different positions before we found a comfortable seating arrangement. I wound up wearing the backpack power unit while Mary sat in front of me and carried the bazooka-like laser unit.

Bronze thought we were adorable, but didn't actually laugh. I could tell from the way she looked at us as we tried one configuration after another. Part of it is the way her nostrils dilate, but mostly I think it's the ears. They give her away every time.

"I just thought of something," Mary said as I settled into place behind her.

"What?"

"Aren't warhorses supposed to wear armor?"

"It's called 'barding,' I believe. But Bronze *is* armor."

"Yeah, but it looks strange to have an armored knight on naked horseback."

I leaned around Mary to look at Bronze. She turned her head to meet my eyes, ruffled her mane, and flicked an ear noncommittally. Armor wouldn't bother her a bit, especially if I could get some that looked good.

My horse wants to look cool. Is this how parents feel when their kids want designer clothes? Then again, I go to a lot of effort to look cool—it's more work than I ever realized. I have no talent for it. Bronze manages it without trying. Maybe we can get her something to wear that won't clash with her already high levels of coolness. Something fireproof. Carbon-based armor? I'll have to test her highest operating temperature and consult Diogenes.

"All right. One second. Lean forward a little." Mary did so and I sent Diogenes a text about it. He agreed it could be done, probably in a titanium alloy for now, possibly in a specialized oobleck when he had the manufacturing capability for it. "There. He's working on it." Bronze tossed her head, a clear thank-you. Mary smiled and patted Bronze's neck.

"And another thing," Mary went on. "If we're going to carry ourselves and a bunch of gear, do you think we could *finally* get a carriage? Even a chariot would do."

I looked at Bronze again. Bronze was perfectly all right with hauling a cart at insane speeds. It would be nice to pull us in a trailer, rather than being pulled in a trailer. Turnabout is fair play.

"All right, all right. But I'll have to get it from Diogenes, too. The local technology can't build a hundred-mile-an-hour wheel axle. We could get up to speed, I'm sure, but it would burst into flames or disintegrate before we got very far."

"Just in case we need it later," Mary soothed. "Besides, sometimes you want to travel in dignified state, rather than hoist your head so far above the crowd it becomes a target."

"Well, when you put it *that* way…" I agreed, and Bronze nodded emphatically. I sent Diogenes another text; he promised to get right on it. "Now can we go?"

"Just about."

"What is it this time?"

"Could Bronze run the whole way on her own? We could gate somewhere near when she arrives. Then she wouldn't have to carry us and could focus on speed. Also, we wouldn't have to spend so much time hanging on for dear life with an awkward load. In fact," Mary went on, "while we're in Karvalen—the mountain—Bronze could spend her time running down the road-tunnels, rather than lurking in her stall by the courtyard doors."

Bronze and I looked at each other for a long moment, then turned in unison to look at Mary.

"What?" she asked.

"Nothing," I replied, in unison with Bronze's characteristic snort. I dismounted and helped a puzzled Mary down. Bronze trotted off on her own. I hefted the laser, courteously carrying it for Mary.

"Where's she going?" Mary asked.

"Originally? Peleseyn. It's the city closest to the Darkwood along the King's Road. But, since we're going to set up more independently, she's headed to Actareyn. She'll come out there."

"Are we gating there?"

"I am. I'll park you in the forest near the front of the army. With a forest this dense, finding a rough archway shouldn't be a problem. It's only a point-to-point gate, not a trans-universal one, and it's human-sized. I'll brute-force it if I have to."

"Why the change in plans?"

"Because you come up with brilliant ideas."

"Really?" Mary asked, delighted.

"Yes. And you make me re-think my own pitiful plans. I was thinking in terms of riding into battle. You were thinking in terms of getting there easily."

"It's all in the perspective. But, as long as I'm questioning your plans and making you re-think them…" she trailed off. I sighed and buried my face in my hands.

"Yes?"

"Stop being melodramatic. Why not just set fire to the forest? Start a forest fire in front of them, start another one behind them, and the survivors can crawl home on their own."

"First, the Darkwood is a big, complex ecosystem and I don't want to destroy it. Second, I kind of like dryads and I don't doubt there are a lot of them in there. Third, I'm not sure what sort of magic or miracles the army may have available, but I'm pretty sure their losses won't be as bad as we think. Fourth, I have no idea what sort of magic or miracles may be available to any irate forest-dwellers who take exception to my burning down their home. I've encountered some odd forest spirits and don't want to encounter angry ones. And fifth, it would destroy any chance we have of ambushing them. There would be nowhere to hide."

"You had me at 'nowhere to hide.' Any chance I can get a breakdown of officer insignia?"

"I'm not sure they have any. It's not a cohesive army. It's a coalition of several militia and a bunch of hired units. Around here they're considered an army, but not back on Earth. They'd call it a joint task force, or something. Feel free to look them over before you shoot anyone, though. I'd suggest starting with anyone in a fancy hat."

Shortly before sunset, the army encamped along the road. It wasn't a formal campsite; they were strung out for a couple of miles. They didn't have a choice. There was no real shoulder to the road, just roots, trees, and underbrush. A surprising number of soldiers were still present. I anticipated more of an about-face. Still, the vanguard was about where I wanted them, and the long, straight road gave Mary a good selection of targets.

To improve on it, we picked out a good spot by scrying mirror. I gave instructions to the mountain and the road grew sideways, widening a bit underground. It shifted under the trees and earth to either side. The quasi-tunnel effect lessened as trees on both sides started leaning slightly away.

Ahead of the army, one tree in particular shifted as the ground around and under it rearranged to tilt it *toward* the road. This brought a portion of it directly over the road. Mary would climb it, settle in, and get ready to pick off anyone shouting orders.

Bronze was already in Actareyn, or near it. Once I dropped Mary off, I would gate to Bronze, we would emerge, race down the road, and take the army in the rear.

Hmm. That sounded better in my head.

Anyway, I spent most of the day in my quarters with a stick, a lot of crystals, and spells. Armies bother me. If only a small percentage of them keep their heads, that's still a lot of people actively counterattacking. That means spells, missiles, you name it, all coming at Bronze and I. Preparation is the key.

Mary helped for a while, then went off to fetch food while I continued to work. I was doing my thing when Caris came in.

As an aside, those heavy stones the mountain uses for doors are frustrating to children. It takes them forever to open the things. They can do it, but it takes so much time! I spotted one of the grey sashes outside my door giving it a gentle push to help it along.

Caris brought one of the boys—Mikkel, I think?—with her. They came in and waited while I worked, watching. I recruited them with spell busywork—"Put your finger here. Hold it still. Got it? Okay. Now hold it!"—while I finished building an electrical spell. When I finished my current spell, I locked it in place and turned to them.

"Well, what can I do for you?"

"Lights."

"Please?" I prompted.

"Lights, please," she repeated.

"All right. Is this Mikkel? Did I remember your name?" He nodded. "Would you like a ball of light?"

He nodded again. I decided to go all-out. A ball of light can change color and bounce around, but that's about all it does. However, a minor illusion to create a shape like a running horse, some magic to make it glow... picture a stuffed animal toy turned into a translucent field of light and sent galloping off. Add some protocols to make it respond to touch, tune it to run away from or around a given child… Maybe add a sound from my memory of a happy whinny…

One is hard to make, but worth the effort. The second is easier; just clone the first one. Tune them, each to their own child, focus power into them, seal them, and let them go.

The glowing, tiny horse-toys whinnied in unison and started running around their children. The expressions of *Oooo!* were well worth it. They chased off after the glowing little things without so much as a thank-you. Well, I wasn't too big on polite protocol at their age, either. I went back to my murder and defense spells.

Mary came back with three guys, wheelbarrows, and Dantos. I smelled food and blood—technically, both are food, but one is *food* food, the other is vampire food. Mary directed traffic as Dantos came up to me and saluted. I returned it.

"What's on your mind, Dantos?"

"My lord, I am troubled by the Church of Light."

"No surprises there. What are they up to?"

"Their congregations swell, day by day. I have sent agents into their godhouse, there to observe and then report, but those who return tell of nothing strange."

"Those who return?" I echoed.

"Some do not."

"Right. Well, they're a religion. Under the law, they're allowed to preach as long as they don't use force to enforce faith. Do you think anyone is in the church against their will?"

"I do not know, my lord."

"Okay. Find friends and family of congregation members and ask them what they think. Investigate. See if they're intimidated or threatened, or if the converted are simply addicted to religious bliss. And see if they're worried about the new converts being sucked into a cult. If there's evidence of that sort of thing, you've got a case for hauling in priests and questioning them in front of a council of justice."

"We are attempting to do so, my lord, but we have been unable to find anyone."

"Hauling in priests for questioning?"

"Questioning friends and family, my lord."

"What, the church is absorbing whole blocks of people? Entire families, that sort of thing?"

"I must assume so, my lord. We have not found family members, nor have we found any close friends of those who worship the Church of Light."

"That's… weird." I mused on it for a moment. You can't grab everyone in a friend circle without creating a larger circle of people outside. If you snatch Moe, then Larry, Curly, and Shemp are friends who can be worried about him. If you snatch Larry, Curly, and Shemp, as well, then all of their friends become potential worried friends. It never ends, unless you focus on snatching the homeless and the hermits. Even then, there are people who notice—maybe they don't care, but they notice.

So, how do you build up a congregation of bliss-addicts without making anyone worry? First, you do it as a religion, which everyone simply accepts.

That's it. One step. It was efficient, at least.

"All right," I told Dantos, "here's what you do. Officially, they're just another religion. Unofficially, we're going to violate some civil rights."

"Civil rights?" he asked. "What are those?"

—and I was struck by the realization. There are no civil rights here. I can snatch someone off the street, interrogate him under a bare bulb and with a rubber hose, and send him on his way. I can grab a random priest, torture him until he tells me everything I want to know, then dispose of the body. Sure, murder is frowned upon, but who is going to tell me to stop? Or tell anyone with power or authority to stop anything? It's not about the law; it's about the power. Power, and doing as you please with it.

I've had moments before when I realized just how frightening my power can be. This ranks right up there in the top three.

On a slightly different level, this must be what the local so-called gods feel. The absolute freedom to do anything they like to anyone at all, simply because they can. Sure, they have a few limits, mostly based on not fighting each other directly, but some random guy on the street? Send a few of the faithful over, club him to bits, and it's all the will of their god.

Now I see why the Lord of Light is so cheesed at me for making the authority of the king and queen superior to the religious authority. As it stands, the religions help the royalty maintain and operate the kingdom. This means the Lord of Light—if he chose to participate—would feel like a vassal. That's not the case. It's a cooperative effort, not an authoritarian one. But the truth isn't important, here. All that matters is his viewpoint, and from his perspective, he would be taking orders from *me*.

Yeah, that's not going to fly.

I started to bark out an order and checked myself. Instead, I asked Dantos a question.

"Did you already send word to the Queen?"

"Yes, my lord."

"And what did she say?"

"She has yet to answer, my lord. It was only this morning."

"All right. She's the one who needs to give the orders. See what she has to say and go do it. However, for reference, if she tells you to kidnap someone in the Church of Light and rip the truth out of him, I'm okay with it."

"My lord," Dantos replied, bowing and backing away.

Mary beckoned me over to the table. I'd have gone anyway, but the food made it certain.

Sunset.

We were already in the geode room, zeroing in on Mary's arrival point. I killed the image while holding the connection. Now was not the time to test the properties of a sunset via scrying spell.

The last of the transformation tingles faded and I put one armored boot into a bucket of blood. Mary stuck a straw into another one. While we soaked up the red fluid, each in our own way, I connected a gate, flushed it into being, and Mary took a stroll in the woods, taking the bucket with her.

With the gate closed behind her, I worked through a couple of buckets in short order, pouring them into my mouth and not caring about spillage. I took my time, since she had a tree to climb and a position to reach; she needed the head start. As the last of the blood crawled into the joints of my outer armor and soaked through to my skin, I focused on Bronze, homing in on her through our innate connection. The gate formed in a section of hallway or tunnel. I stepped through, and it shredded into nothingness behind me.

Bronze snorted smoke and pawed at the ground. No translation required.

The room was a narrow one, barely wide enough for Bronze, possibly inside a wall or other structure. Bronze leaned against one side of it and a thin plate of stone pivoted out of her way. It couldn't rotate all the way around since it was longer than our little room was wide. The angle was enough to let us out, though, and I closed it behind us.

We were outside a city, presumably Actareyn. The road ran line-straight, almost due east. In the far distance, I could see the campfires at the extreme rear of the army. Fifty miles from here? Possibly. Sometimes distance is hard to judge, especially when there's no horizon.

I mounted up and locked down my faceplate. Bronze put her head down, stretched her neck, and her hooves struck blue-green sparks from the road. I held on for dear life; her traction enchantments were working perfectly. If she hadn't grabbed my arms with her mane, she would have run right out from underneath me, leaving me somersaulting backward in mid-air.

We decided never to do that during the day. It could break my neck, which would make her sad. It wouldn't do me any good, either.

It's still eerie, though, getting up to some ridiculous speed on horseback with nothing but the sound of the wind. I can feel the steady beat of her hooves as we barrel down the road, but I can't really hear them. Trees flicker past on either side like a picket-fence nightmare. Smoke pours from Bronze's nostrils and ears. She kept her mouth closed to minimize the flames. I ducked my head and started activating our prepared defensive spells.

Some troops were camped out on the edges of the road, out of the way. Most of them had banners marking them troops belonging to Lyraneyn or Hyceteyn, but I didn't see any mercenary companies. Many of the men were wounded. We avoided these and passed them by. Their sentries didn't even know we were there until we passed them. All in all, there were maybe three or four thousands of them, not at all what I expected from the recall orders.

Was the Church in actual command of this army? Was the Church of Light already establishing itself as a secular power? If so, could a religious war be avoided? Nasty thoughts ran through my head.

"Cavalry to Sniper, over."

"Sniper," Mary replied.

"Engaging."

"Roger."

We didn't slow as we approached the rearguard. The objective was not to hit the army and kill our way along the road. The objective was to bullet through the army, stomping, igniting, and slicing anything convenient, racing faster than the alarm could spread.

And we did.

Wagons we generally passed without touching, but I had Firebrand out. I laid its edge along the side of anything too big to be conveniently crashed through and it ignited whatever it touched. It also encouraged the flames for as long as we remained in range. This didn't actually destroy wagons on the spot, but each one became a fully-involved fire fairly quickly.

Bronze stomped on anything else with a fine disregard for race, creed, or color. Her hooves are immense, larger than a dinner plate, so the grooves in the road didn't bother her too much. Anything else, however, found the grooves to be handy vents through which to squish when she flattened it to the road.

I tried to help by lashing tendrils through anything in reach, but we were moving fast. I don't think I actually killed anyone—I didn't focus on any individual, just spread a general net of vitality-draining darkness ahead of us—but I tried. When we didn't have a wagon to ignite, I waved Firebrand around at anything in reach, including heads, hands, and torsos, causing nasty cuts nearby and nasty burns farther away. I'm sure Firebrand killed several, but only a few died instantly. For my purpose, wounded men were better than dead men. A badly-wounded man is out of the fight, but he requires help, which takes another man or two away from the fight. He burdens the healers, costs magic, time, and other resources.

Shouting and screaming from behind us drew the attention of people farther forward, but by the time they woke up, got up, and looked around, we were already there, hammering down the road like a tank through a watermelon patch, with a bit more crimson in the splatter. A few people shot at us with crossbows, a few more threw things—slingers launching rocks, I think—and I distinctly remember some kid with a drum. He couldn't have been fourteen years old, more likely twelve. He held a banner-pole in the crook of one elbow, one end of it braced in a groove in the road and pinned in place with one foot. He rattled out a beat, presumably a call to arms, and looked both terrified and determined.

Bronze didn't trample him. We went clean over him in a leap fit for steeplechase. Mary would have been delighted to see it, but I think we were still too far away. As we went over the kid, my tendrils snatched the banner-pole straight up, out of his grip, and I hurled it into the forest.

Then it was back down to earth and back to crushing an army.

The secret is to never let them coordinate. Never let them catch their breath, give orders, form up, and work together. Killing a thousand men—one at a time—is no different from killing one man. Killing a thousand men all *at the same time* is a very different thing, indeed.

How long did we spend doing this? How far did we have to travel to rip through the whole army? I don't know. We killed several people, maimed many times their number, and destroyed whole wagonloads of supplies in one run. As an army, it was a shambles. As a mob, it was still a danger. An army can march into heavy fire and still achieve victory. A mob changes its mind more easily, but doesn't respond well to commands.

We reached the other end of the army, emerging from it onto clear road, and kept going, vanishing into the night. I wanted them to have no idea where we were or what we were doing. Bronze slowed after another mile or so and I worked a spectrum-shifting spell so her fiery breath wouldn't shine any visible light. She was very pleased. She doesn't get out to run as much as she would like, much less through obstacles.

Can we do it again? Firebrand demanded.

"Let's give it a few hours," I decided. "Mary gets to pick off the leaders, remember?"

Why does she get a turn?

"Because she's a bloodthirsty maniac, like all the other women in my life."

Oh.

I was surprised Firebrand accepted my flippant answer. Then I thought about it and wondered.

Bronze turned around and carried me back at a trot, cooling down as we moved. She stopped under the leaning tree of Mary's vantage point. I stood up on Bronze's shoulders and looked out over the mess.

Fires dotted the road, some quite large. People were fighting the larger blazes, of course, trying to avoid a forest fire. I wasn't worried. From the smell of the forest, it rained recently. They would get it under control. More people were running around with weapons, slapping on armor, shouting questions, screaming in pain, all the usual chaos swirling around in the aftermath of a catastrophe.

I heard a cracking sound, like a whip. Above me, I detected a faint line of light in the air. Ah. Ionization from the laser. It wasn't a visible light beam, but the intensity of the beam caused some of the air to become ionized and glow. It would be invisible during the day, of course, but at night, it left a ghostly line in the air. Still, with all the fires downrange to spoil night vision, I doubted anyone would be able to see it.

Mary's voice whispered in my ears.

"This thing is a miracle." Another cracking sound. "There's no drop, no windage, no nothing. It's the ultimate point-and-click interface." *Crack!* "And the energy dumped into a head or torso does *amazing* things. It even melts breastplates!" *Crack!*

"Go for heads," I advised.

"But molten metal dripping down inside makes them dance!" *Crack!*

"We want commanders dead," I countered, "not wounded!"

"Spoilsport," she accused, to the sound of another air-splitting *Crack!*

Bronze and I moved to the side of the road and waited, trying to be invisible. If anyone came this way to deal with the sniper—Mary—I wanted to be ready to surprise them.

Then again, this was the direction Bronze and I went, and they knew it. Who was going to come this way? I mean, when the Flaming Juggernaut of Doom rolls over your position and heads off down the road, is your first impulse to *chase* it? Even if someone did spot the ghostly line, and decided to go investigate, and decided it was worth the risk, who was going to give the order? A leader? Someone shouting orders?

Crack! Splut! Another head or throat vaporizes in a wet, steaming explosion as the laser superheats flesh to unreasonable temperatures.

I sat down in the saddle again. It might be a while. She had a hundred shots, a long corridor of targets, and time to pick and choose.

Eventually, the sharp snaps of the beam through the air stopped. A minute later, Mary joined us on the ground.

"Do we have to go back to Diogenes to get this thing recharged?" she asked.

"I don't know. You're the one who had the briefing."

"Do we have a source of electricity here?"

"Not a steady one, no."

"Too bad." She handed up the backpack, then the laser. "It was fun while it lasted, but it was also too easy. The poor suckers never had a chance."

"So, you're out of charges? Or out of targets?"

"Charges. I figured once I got anyone in a fancy hat, next choice was anyone giving orders."

"Quite right," I agreed, and held out a hand to help her up.

Then the light started. I looked back the way I'd come at the white glow. Mary made a hissing sound and turned away from it.

Ah. A local religion at work. But what were they doing?

I stood up again, using Bronze for a vantage. The light came from a small group, five or six men in white robes, surrounding one in the center. Most had blood on them, as well as soot or smoke stains. All of them were bald and thin, but none seemed exceptionally old. They struck me as sickly, rather than ancient. Hand members, perhaps? Wasting away from radiation poisoning? I hoped so.

The light surrounding them brightened further, expanding, and people started shuffling toward them, drawn like moths to a flame. The light seemed almost tangible, swirling slowly around the priestly figures. A whirlpool in syrup? Or a watery swirl in slow motion? Either way, it continued to expand, sweeping through the people who shuffled toward it. A peculiar double-image started to form around the people, as though their downstream edge was uncertain. The closer they approached and the stronger the light grew, the more pronounced it became.

It suddenly hit me. I knew what it was. The light was sweeping through them, disconnecting their spirits, sweeping them sideways, sucking them out of the bodies. It wasn't like what I do, grabbing the energies and drawing them out. It was like drowning them, submerging them in a more powerful spirit until they dissolved and became one with it.

The bodies closest to the light fell to the ground and the spirits left behind vanished into the vortex. It spun faster, spreading even more, sweeping through people, animals, trees... I felt the road beneath me crack, separating, cutting off everything beyond the cracked portion. Whatever it was, it was drawing on every bit of life force in range—men, boys, horses, trees, even the living stone. The mountain cut itself off, well back from the drain, to keep from feeding it.

People fell more quickly. Trees darkened in my vision, turning to dead wood. The vortex of light spun faster, no longer expanding, even reversing itself. It narrowed, growing brighter, turning into an eye-searing shaft of white, towering into the sky, vaguely man-shaped with a hint of wings. It was like a rip in the curtain of reality revealing the blaze of heaven.

The light vanished, or almost. What was left was a blackened circle of death. Bodies were already desiccated, diminished, disintegrated. Everything was old and dead. I saw not one spark, not one trace of a living glow, not even the faint luminescence of life in the air or earth.

With one exception.

A tall, broad-shouldered, handsome man stood where the circle of priests once stood. He wore white robes, belted like a kilt, and brandished a mace of gold and a white shield. All around him was a white radiance, a glowing aura illuminating him and everything around him like a searchlight from the heavens.

He threw back his head and laughed. Somewhere, far beyond him, other voices screamed.

"*Halar!*" he bellowed, and it rolled through the forest, climbed the hills, washed up against distant mountains and rolled back like the tide.

Mary, hiding behind a tree to shield herself from the burning light, let out a sigh of relief.

"I think he wants you," she said.

"No kidding?" I asked, heavy on the sarcasm. I didn't want anything to do with him.

"He did call you by name."

"Yeah. Give me a minute."

I glanced up the night sky.

I don't suppose you've got anything to say? I asked.

Uh, now you mention it, yes.

What am I dealing with, here?

Remember the time the Church summoned the Lord of the Hunt to hunt you down?

Vividly.

That was an avatar. A real one. This is, too. Only this time...

...this time, I guessed, *they're able to summon the avatar of their own deity, rather than bargain for another one?*

Yeah, pretty much. Last time, the Lord of Light was mostly eaten by the Devourer-demon, who then masqueraded as the deity to suck up the power from his worshippers. This time, there's an actual energy-entity capable of answering! There were six living members of the Hand over there. They knew they were dying, and they martyred themselves to summon the Lord of Light, or whatever is now filling his old shoes.

Wonderful. Think they'd be doing this if they weren't dying from the curse of the Demon King?

*Technically, it's **your** curse, since—*

I get it, I get it. So they're dying and they decide to be martyrs in the hope it'll result in my destruction.

Pretty much, yeah.

*Well, **do** something!*

I can't! That's an avatar!

*Then **explain**, dammit! You keep saying "avatar" like it should tell me something!*

Grr. All right. An avatar is a flesh-and-blood body. What you've got over there is a bunch of flesh taken from the priests, rearranged and reorganized by the Lord of Light. The radiation damage, diseases, whatever—it's fixed. It's defragmented and optimized. Physically, he's stronger than a mortal man, faster, has keener senses, all the usual stuff, but not beyond the limits of human flesh.

Oh, I replied, relieved. *I thought this would be a problem.*

And, of course, it's filled with the divine power of the Lord of Light, making it the equivalent of a demigod. Hercules, maybe, or Gilgamesh.

Damn! I knew it sounded too good!

Just like you can't be touched, he can't, either! He's considered a direct extension of the god, so directly affecting him is forbidden. Tianna can't blast him with flame and the Storm King—Father Sky—can't smite him with lightning.

But I can cut him in two and burn the halves?

I don't know. Can you?

I had a rather profane remark about that, but I'm not going to repeat it here.

*Do you have any **advice**, at least?* I demanded.

He's an energy-state being occupying a physical form. Don't bother with magic attacks; he'll deflect or absorb them. And don't try to eat him. At best, you'll wind up back on the energy plane and I'm not sure how we'll cope with the two of us here at the same time. More likely he'll jump inside you, and we both know that won't end well.

I see he's marching this way, I observed. *I take it, from his approach and attitude, that he can and will try to kill me?*

I'd say so. While I can't touch him, you avatar types can beat on each other all you like.

How nice. Can you, I don't know, juice me up in some way?

*It's allowed, since you're my de-facto avatar. Remember, though: the manifestation over there has a direct pipeline to the Lord of Light. You're just a vampire with a history of divine contact. I'll do what I can to even the odds, but you're not my creation. We don't have the same link. And, even after the showy, power-wasting expenditure to shape an avatar, he **still** has much greater power reserves than I do.*

Great. No matter how I look at this, it's a bad deal. Is there any reason I can't turn around and run?

No, he replied, sounding thoughtful. *No, not really. It might be worth it to avoid a coin-flip confrontation. But he's a little like you in that he's a physical entity. He isn't going to dissipate; he'll have to be killed, sooner or later. Do you want to face him now or do you want him to gather a much larger following, first?*

I hate you.

No, you don't, but I understand the impulse.

"I'm not liking this," I told Mary.

"Me, either. He's coming closer. The burning feeling is getting worse, like being in the sun the day after a sunburn."

"You can't stay here. Get on Bronze and run for it." I sighed heavily. "I'm going to face this thing."

"You sure?"

"I've still got all my defensive spells up from the run through the troops. It's either face it now or wait until it mobilizes a whole lot of bliss-addicted followers for a holy war the likes of which hasn't been seen since the Crusades—or Arrakis."

"Curse you and your divine immunity," she said, but she said it as she leaped on Bronze. I slid off, made sure Mary was aboard properly, and Bronze carried her away. I drew Firebrand and it lit up like a blowtorch. The flames were a mix of red and orange, with a nimbus of darkness playing about the edges.

Uh, Boss? This feels—

Hush, replied my energy-state ally. *I'm concentrating.*

I wasn't talking to you, Firebrand replied, testily.

"Yes, Firebrand. He's helping. We're gonna need it."

Just checking. It's weird, though. I can hear you, and I know there are two of you, but you sound the same. It's hard to distinguish which is which.

"I understand."

Are we sure we want to do this?

"No. But I think it's the least bad of our present choices."

"Demon of the void!" the Lord of Light bellowed. He started running toward me. He was faster than I expected. He charged straight at me, shield ahead, mace held high, ready to slam into me and whip that fist-shaped thing down on my head.

I concentrated, extending tendrils down through my feet, expanding my time sense. His approach was direct, brutal, frontal. I leveled Firebrand at his head and waited, forcing him to momentarily hide his eyes as he deflected Firebrand with his shield. As he did so, I sidestepped, flicking around his left side like a shadow as he tried to plow into me—or where I used to be. He staggered slightly when his shield met no resistance.

While he skidded to a halt, I leaped forward, Firebrand held high in a two-handed grip. He whipped around more quickly than I expected, raising his shield as I brought Firebrand down like a fiery bolt from the heavens. Firebrand struck the shield, denting it from top to bottom like putting a crease in it. The blaze of light and heat from the impact seared everything within a hundred feet, igniting loose litter in a ring of small fires and raising steam from every damp spot. The ringing scream of metal was a visible distortion in the air. The Lord of Light went to one knee under the impact, but his shield...

...held.

Well, I reflected, *that can't be good.*

He swept Firebrand aside, following it with a roundhouse swing of his fist-shaped mace. I didn't like the look of the mace. It reminded me of the Hunter's spear, the first time I saw it. It—like the physical embodiment of the Lord of Light—was a blazing thing to my vision, less of a material object and more like solidified energy. Even worse, I had anticipated cleaving the shield, the arm holding it, and the being behind it into a pair of smoking halves. It seemed like a reasonable expectation, really. I was in no way prepared for a counterattack. The mace hit me, hit me hard, and hit me like Heaven's delivery truck.

It reminded me of a lady magi sending me through a garage, only this time it was a physical impact, not merely a sudden addition of momentum. The blow landed on my left side, crushed in the armor, lifted me off my feet—all five-hundred-plus pounds of me—and sent me tumbling through the air to crash into a tree. I hit it on a rising slant, broke several branches and the top off the tree, and continued into another tree. As I broke through more branches, the second tree slowed me enough to let gravity take control of my trajectory.

I fell to the ground, trying to roll to my feet. My armor cracked and splintered a bit, much like my ribs on that side. Bones were already realigning and sticking together as I turned to face the approaching glow.

He was on me in a moment—much faster than a mortal man. I took full advantage of my mobility-enhancing spells—traction, inertia, the works—and decided I was somewhat faster and more maneuverable, but, to judge by his initial blow, he was definitely the stronger.

I ducked under his swing, not wishing to depart the surface of the world again, and thrust upward with Firebrand. I got in past his shield—which, I noticed with some concern, was now no longer dented in the slightest—skewering him low on his right side, angled up, maybe into a lung, bloodying his white robes. He staggered back and I leaped to my feet barely in time to dodge a blow from his mace. Tougher than a mortal man, too.

The mace missed me, but hit a tree. The tree trunk shattered all around the head of the mace and cracked both up into the treetop and down into the roots. It made a terrible creaking, groaning sound as it toppled.

I elected to let it come down without me under it. I'm not sure what the other guy did, but he seemed not to care too much about turning a hundred years of growth into matchsticks. Ah, well. I'm guilty of tunnel-vision, myself, when focused on killing someone.

He bashed through the branches and came after me. I ducked and dodged, parrying lightly on occasion, while looking for an opening. Firebrand expressed some displeasure at being used against a bashing weapon.

Just try not to meet it head-on, all right?

Deflect, not block. Got it.

As we fought, I backed away. That shield and mace combination was a devastating one, especially in the hands of someone who knew how to use it. He kept marching forward, hiding behind that shield of his, while swinging his mace like a wrecking ball. Anything the mace hit suffered for it. Trees took glancing blows all right—they would shake like a baby's rattle, shedding leaves and deadwood, with a mace-shaped gouge taken out of their surface. They didn't take direct hits too well. Trunks of old-growth forest giants shattered as though dynamited.

I stayed off the road, in the trees. The footing made it awkward, but I had a free hand whenever I wanted one. He had a big shield to contend with, which made the terrain worse for him than for me. I took advantage of it, too. Every time he slipped, every time he had to squeeze sideways, there was my opening. He parried a couple of times, knocking Firebrand aside as I attacked, but his skill with a heavy mace was less than mine with a sword. Maybe it was the difference in the types of weapons; maces and swords use very different fighting styles. I scored on him, again and again, piercing legs and chest more than once. He grunted, sometimes roared in pain, but he shrugged off the wounds.

They kept healing. Quickly. Very quickly. His regeneration was every bit as quick as mine, maybe quicker. Even his robe repaired itself, right down to the bloodstains. Most unfair. I began to wonder how long it would take to wear him down. If the Lord of Light was pumping energy into his avatar, could I force him to use up so much it became impractical? Or was this even a material concern for him? Would it take hours or centuries? I didn't have centuries, and I started to think in terms of killing strokes rather than accumulated wounds.

Of course, all good things must come to an end, and so must all advantages of terrain. We had already blasted a sizable circle of tumbled lumber in our little dance. I hit him several times in the process, for all the good it did. But I finally put a foot wrong, failed to catch myself, and staggered backward over some roots to land hard. It didn't do any damage to me or my armor, but it was a really bad time to be lying down on the job.

He was on me in an instant, shield held low, mace coming up and over and down at me like a comet. I knew I wasn't going to be able to stop it, but my reflexes caused me to sweep Firebrand at his legs—and ring off the edge of his shield—while I raised my left arm to block the mace.

Even as I did so, I felt the movement, the rippling, the change. My cloak flicked itself up my arm, clinging to it, forming itself into a shield in less than the blink of an eye. The mace rang off the sudden circle of darkness. I'm not sure who looked more surprised, him or me.

That settles it. I'm keeping it.

I swept the mace aside with my new shield as I sat up and swung Firebrand backhand in a sharp arc, around the edge of his shield, aiming for a leg. He half-leaped, half-stepped back out of the swing. I rolled to the side to use another tree for cover as I sprang to my feet. He was around the tree-trunk and swinging, a blow that rang off my shield again—but I didn't go flying anywhere, this time. The blow should have hammered me back against a tree-trunk much as a wrecking ball would.

Curiouser and curiouser.

He showed more caution after that. We circled each other, looking for openings, trading blows and disengaging. Sword-and-shield isn't my preferred mode of fighting. I'm fond of a two-handed parry-attack style, or a one-handed style leaning more toward the saber or epee. On the other hand, I usually face opponents who aren't able to take a hit too well and whose attacks I can routinely regenerate. This might be a trifle different. I thought back to the time Raeth and Bouger and I were on the road. We covered a lot of ground with sword-and-shield, but it was a long time ago…

He attacked. The mace struck the circle of darkness while Firebrand tried to take a bite out of the edge of his shield. We hacked and blocked for several seconds, circling each other, slashing, bashing, and blocking, before separating again. By then I was intact again, whether from my own regeneration or from quasi-divine energies I'm not sure. The notches Firebrand took out of his shield closed up just as quickly. My armor's repair enchantment wasn't quite up to those standards; it was still cracked and crumpled along one side.

This could be a problem.

We engaged again, testing each other, trying to find a weakness. As we circled, he smiled through his beard.

"Creature of chaos, you are no true avatar. When you fall, you will return to the void."

"I'm watching for banana peels."

"I do not understand."

"Yeah, I get that a lot," I replied, amping up to superhuman speed. He was definitely stronger than I was, but could he keep up with a full-throttle vampire moving at the speed of dark? The world slowed down around me and I started moving more carefully, more deliberately.

When he came in close again, I went for him. The speed of light is awfully fast, but the dark is always there ahead of it and comes right back in behind it. Even light doesn't break the dark barrier. It can't escape the event horizon of a black hole, either. And yet dark goes everywhere.

I didn't get in a good hit. He was faster than I thought. Was he matching me, somehow? Was there a law of conservation of avatars? I thought I could spin around him like a stripper around a pole, but I was wrong.

We wound up moving past each other, shields ringing as they came together and we traded blows. He bashed in my faceplate and I scored a shallow cut along his back. His wound closed up almost as quickly as I made it. Even his clothes healed. Disgusting. I tore away the remains of my faceplate to keep it from distracting me as we circled each other. We searched for openings, warily, while the world around us moved in slow motion. A disturbed leaf hung in the air, only now starting to tumble in the sudden gusts of wind produced by our movements.

"Why do you resist?" he asked, sounding oh-so-reasonable. "Is it not the fate of men to die?"

"Eventually. It's also their right to resist," I replied, striking suddenly, only to be blocked and counterattacked.

"These pitiful creations have no rights," he snapped, as we backed away from the exchange. He leveled his mace at me. "You delude yourself to think otherwise!"

He may sound persuasive, but he's got no patience, Boss.

I noticed.

Motes of light coalesced out of the air, gathering into the fist-shaped head of the mace. It seemed to be reaching critical mass. I ducked behind my shield.

On the far side of my shield, silent, blinding hell broke loose. If someone snagged all the lights from a stadium and stacked them on the road, it might have been a close comparison. There was no heat, no thunder, no crackling surges of energy, only several seconds of white light like a slow-motion nuclear flash.

The light vanished, leaving only his aura and a bit of moonlight. He looked nonplused, and his brightness, his aura, seemed less intense. Did his attack drain some of his resources? Energy-state beings are finite beings, *simulata*, not actual gods. If I could annoy him into spending power like that repeatedly, it might be possible to wear him down.

I glanced down at the front of my shield. I caught a glimpse of something... odd. It seemed almost as though my shield was a *hole*, a dark one, and in the far distance was a spark of light speeding rapidly away. Then it was gone and my cloak-shield-whatever was only a shield again.

He advanced and I skipped backward, mindful of my footing. He didn't seem to care about the ground—possibly a divine gift, and a most unfair one. Then again, I have how many vampiric powers? Not to mention a slew of spells for all sorts of combat-related advantages. But an inability to accidentally fall over things is beyond even my power.

I backed onto the road and prepared to engage him again. As he approached, I kicked out, sending a corpse skidding into his feet. He wasn't immune to being deliberately tripped, at least. His balance broke for a moment and I attacked. He blocked with his shield and swung his mace to parry, but I fooled him by swinging short and thrusting for his right leg. I connected well, spearing it almost completely through, twisting the blade and recovering before he could bring that mace around to kill me. Firebrand left a sizzling wound behind and I would have pressed my advantage, but his shield unexpectedly flared with light, blazing like the face of the sun, blinding me. I swung wildly and leaped backward, out of range, hoping his leg wound would keep him off me.

Again, his wound regenerated. It regenerated like I do, provided I'm submerged in a bathtub full of blood.

He didn't press me when I withdrew. Instead, he merely held his ground, watching me while his leg repaired itself. It occurred to me we were still learning about each other. I guess he didn't want to risk closing with me in any less than perfect shape. I understood the feeling.

"You know you cannot win," he said.

"I haven't lost," I pointed out, and charged him. He braced behind his shield and prepared to smite me with his mace. I closed and he struck down, hammering my shield. I let the blow drive me to the ground at his feet while Firebrand sliced sideways in a high arc, bouncing off his raised shield. Then I rammed the edge of my shield down on his forward foot.

As I felt the bones in his foot break, he howled in pain, louder than anything I'd yet heard from him. He staggered backward, mace flailing wildly to keep me back, and fell to one knee when his foot couldn't take his weight.

I sprang toward him, hacking. I pressed him hard, not wanting him to stand. He hid behind his shield while Firebrand took deep, savage bites out of the edge.

He struck, not at me, but at Firebrand. The mace made Firebrand chime like a bell; I heard Firebrand's surprised wail of pain. It broke my concentration and the mace thrust forward, past the edge of my shield, striking me in the chest like a punch.

Yeah, he's strong, all right. I felt the thud from head to toe and sailed backward, skidding down the length of the road. Bits of my cracked breastplate fell away as my freshly-healed ribs broke. I extended tendrils everywhere, grabbing the ground, slowing myself before rolling to my feet.

You okay? I asked Firebrand.

Mostly. That hit felt like a fracture.

Can you take another one?

I'm already melting the fissures. I'll be fine, Boss. I'd really rather not do it again, though. If he hits me just a little harder, I'm not sure it'll be fractures!

No promises.

We faced each other across the distance. He rose to his feet, glowing angrily. I let him while my ribs slid back into position.

"You're stronger than you look," I told him.

"In this world, I am a god."

"A god who devours his followers? I didn't know we had so much in common."

"We have nothing in common, creature of the void!"

"Did I not see you sucking up the life force of everything in range to empower your physical avatar form?"

"You fool. Death and destruction are necessary to change the pattern of the world and bring order to all creation!"

"Tell it to the dead," I sneered. "Oh, wait—that's beyond your power, isn't it? Some god you are, Mister Energy-State Being from another plane of existence."

"You *dare* to address me so? I, who shone brightest in all the heavens?"

"Of course I dare. You're just another would-be deity, slumming it down on the mortal plane and pretending to be more than you are."

Screaming, the avatar charged again, shield in front, mace held high. I braced for contact as he bashed his shield into mine. Despite my spells, I skidded backward at the impact, but I kept my feet. He struck at me over our shields, trying to crush my head in, but I blocked with Firebrand, met the haft of the mace with Firebrand's edge, and heard Firebrand grunt at the contact. We failed to sever the haft; I guess imbuing your weapon with divine power has some advantages. Note for the future.

Time to deploy my secret weapon.

Locked together this way, he pushed me back. I couldn't allow this to keep going; I would hit something and go tumbling. I reached into the dead stone with my tendrils, used them as extensions of my feet, seized the ground, and locked myself in place.

We came to a sudden halt, the unstoppable force and the immovable object. I wasn't sure I could hold him for long. He was strong, stronger than anything I'd ever fought before, and I could feel the strain in every muscle to resist him.

We locked together, shield to shield, glaring at each other as we pushed. We were close enough and he'd already destroyed my faceplate, so I stuck my tongue out at him, aiming for one of his eyes. I scored a bloody line across his forehead as he ducked, but I saw a look of surprise and horror on his face. It made my evening.

Head down, shield up, he swung his mace in a wide arc, whipping it around the side, crunching into my shield-arm. The arm broke, but I leaned into the inner curve of my shield, ducking my head, pressing it with shoulder, chest, and cheek.

Firebrand slid around the edges of our shields, swept underneath, and fired off a dragon-like blast of flame in the direction of his feet. He grunted in surprise as our shields rang from the blast. For a moment, the pressure lessened slightly, but it was only a moment. Firebrand, backed by my other-self, could have flash-fried mortal feet into carbonized bone and ashes. Our avatar adversary was strangely resistant to divine fire.

He swung up and over, the head of his mace meeting me in the back, this time. Backplates cracked and fell away as he hit me over the left shoulderblade. More bones broke, but things were almost ready. I kept pressing on, holding him in place, and whipped Firebrand around our shields in a similar maneuver. He took a bad cut—a mortal wound in anything mortal—along his left ribs, a deep wound, almost to the spine. It cut a lot of muscle, which made it easier to resist his push, but that would only be temporary.

He brought the mace up and over again, flailing over our shields to strike me in the left shoulder again, closer to the middle of my back. He was obviously going for my head or spine—I would have. I whipped Firebrand up and across, deflecting another strike at my head, counterstruck in a slash at his, and prepared to parry another shot from the mace. It was either block that mace or get my head pounded in, but any second now—

The pressure was off. My all-out effort was suddenly unresisted and I flopped forward over the fallen Lord of Light. A sizable portion of the back of his skull was crushed, in a suspiciously hoof-shaped dent. Sadly, it was filling itself in, growing back.

I rolled off him with a grunt and a minor assist from a hot, metal nose. Bronze sniffed at me, concerned.

"Bad night," I rasped. She nodded and stepped on the Lord of Light's chest. No, I said that badly. *Stomped* on the Lord of Light's chest. No, that's still not quite right. Stomped *through* his chest. Yes, that's correct. His head was pulling itself together, reforming with extreme rapidity, but the hoofprint went to the pavement with a wet sort of crunching noise as flesh and blood spurted sideways through the road-ridges.

Is it wrong of me to enjoy such a sound? Even if it's just once?

When she withdrew her hoof, I ran Firebrand through his chest, sideways, without bothering to get up. A quick thrust through the lung, possibly the heart, and the other lung. I left it there, flaming, flickering with bright fire and dark fire, while I worked the shield off his arm and sent it whizzing and clanging into the forest. Bronze kicked the mace in the other direction.

I got up, withdrew Firebrand, and stood over him. I laid Firebrand's point in the hollow of one eye and waited for him to look at me. Once the majority of his chest reformed, he opened his eyes. His eyes turned white, then disappeared, becoming glowing holes into a white nothingness.

"You think you have defeated me?" It wasn't a voice born from any physical source. His mouth didn't move, but I heard the sound. Or maybe I didn't. It was either in my ears or my head or both.

"You know," I said, feeling the last of my bones pop back into place, "I'd have to admit, I do think that. Temporarily, by fluke, and in a fashion that will only work once, but yes."

"You bear a weapon of power, wear otherworldly armor, carry a shield of celestial origin—but you are flesh and blood, infested with the power of chaos. Do you think any of those will save you? At bottom, you are a man born of woman, not in the fires of the first surges of creation! You fight only as a mortal, you will lose as a mortal, and you will die as a mortal!"

He extended both arms. His shield and mace sprang toward him from however far away they landed, but I was already whipping Firebrand in a circle. The mace reached his hand first, and he swung it up at me as I swung Firebrand sideways at his neck.

I'm sure he intended to block with his shield while swinging at me, but it was delayed. Bronze was on that side and saw it coming. She tried to stomp it to the pavement with one forehoof, but it was moving too quickly for such accuracy. She stomped too soon, missing, but planted her leg in the path of the low-skimming shield. It hit her, hit hard, and bent her leg badly. This deflected the now-dented shield, however, so it wasn't there when I cut through his unshielded hand, forearm, and neck.

The mace, on the other hand, hit my left side, headed upward, crushing armor and ribs up into my chest cavity. It sent me flying into a tree and sent Firebrand I know not where. I was tangled in the branches for several seconds before I fought my way free and fell to the ground.

Bronze kicked the severed head over to me, snorting fire and telling me we shouldn't talk to evil demigods. I agreed with her silently, since the eyes were still open and glowing.

"You cannot kill me," the head snarled. "I was the first, greatest and most powerful of all things brought forth from the void. I have existed since before the first world, and nothing can kill me."

"I can kill this body," I gasped; I was short on useful lung space.

"I will raise me up a new avatar."

"No doubt, but I bet your respawn time is more than three days."

The head screamed at me, a sound combining the worst parts of hatred, rage, and jet engines. The light within started to shine out of the eyes and mouth, too bright for me to look at. It felt hot on my skin, burning, which I thought was forbidden. All the while, the screaming sound rose in volume. It caused wood to crack and metal to ring and my ears to rupture—but I could still hear it, vibrating in my bones. Trees shed leaves, then branches. Smaller ones toppled. Larger ones began to disintegrate into showers of toothpicks.

"What does it take to kill you?" I screamed, unheard amid the din. I stomped the head, cracking bone. Light streamed from the cracks. I jumped up and down on it with both booted feet, again and again and again, screaming over and over "Die! Just die! Die! Die! Die!"

And then there was silence.

"Finally," I gasped. I leaned on the splintered remains of a fallen tree and tried to keep my body straight. There were bits still moving inside me, trying to find their accustomed spot.

The crushed head began to glow brighter, as did the body. The broken flesh seemed almost to catch fire, burning with an unnatural white flame. Something like crawling electrical discharges arced between the body and the remains of the head. The white fire blazed brighter, rather than higher, and I felt the heat of it, a sizzling, scorching feeling that reminded me uncomfortably of sunlight. I didn't like it, and I didn't like the way it was acting—it looked as though it was working its way up to some sort of detonation.

"Oh, come *on!*" I demanded, but started making my way from it, climbing over tree trunks, forcing a path through shattered branches. Bronze was too far from me to reach me, so she ran directly away from the glow, just as I did. She hurdled large obstacles without much trouble and crashed through lesser ones, bent leg and all.

The explosion was soundless, bright, and that's all I recall about it.

"Hello? Hello? Is this thing on? Testing..."

I muttered something in reply.

"Aha! There you are. I was worried."

That struck me as funny. I was worried and I told myself so, as if I didn't know. My head started to clear a bit.

"I have good news and bad news."

"That sounds familiar," I said, or tried to. I wasn't sure my mouth was working. "You're playing god again, aren't you?"

"Occupational hazard."

"I should have expected a smartass answer. I'm talking to myself."

"Only in a non-schizophrenic sense. I'm an independent entity, remember?"

"Vaguely. I'm still not all here, myself."

"I know, but you're getting better. I pulled some strings."

"I recall the avatar of the Lord of Light going supercritical on me. How bad was it?"

"Well, it was bad enough to attract attention from On High. He's not supposed to direct energies at you. Clobber you, yes, but not zap you or explode. That's cheating."

"Oh. Is there a way I can get a copy of the rules?"

"No. But I'll watch out for your interests."

"There are no lawyers in Heaven," I argued.

"But this isn't Heaven," he pointed out. "It's a quasi-independent energy-state plane of existence."

"Oh, well, if you're going to use loopholes like that, I suppose you can be my lawyer."

"You're not as funny as you think you are."

"I get that a lot," I admitted.

"I imagine. But, back to the avatar of light?"

"Yes."

"He tried to kill you as he died."

"I got that. I also note I don't seem to be able to feel anything as I float here in a nothingness. Did it work?"

"No, but it wasn't a bad try."

"I seem to recall an instance when I was badly hurt before. This is starting to get repetitive."

"You live long enough and face enough nasty, powerful entities, you're going to occasionally have your brains bashed in."

"Great," I groaned. "How long have I been out this time? Eighty-seven years? Nine years? Three?"

"Oh, stop it. It's not that bad. Only a day or so. Bronze survived the celestial light better than you did—you're more sensitive to it—and found you."

"Oh. So, am I okay?"

"Mostly. They'll be filling your barrel with blood at sunset. You should be fine after a good soaking."

"Good to know. How's Bronze? Firebrand?"

"Bronze was pretty beat up, but she's a block of metal. She's got her frame straight and is working on the fenders, but it'll be a while before her alignment *and paint job are all in order. Firebrand was extremely unhappy, but not seriously harmed, no matter what it has to say about it. It's been complaining to Mary about the fracture lines and cracks, but it fixed itself in fairly short order—I helped a little, but don't tell it or it'll complain more. It's sitting in a forge, adding some anger to the flames."*

"Is that a literal thing? Adding anger to the flames?" I asked.

"Well, if you use any metal out of that forge for a healing ring, my guess is it'll work, but it'll hurt."

"Great. A grumpy dragon-sword."

"It happens."

"So was this the good news or the bad news?"

"Oh. Right. The Lord of Light is being censured for his actions. I'm not entirely sure how that's going to work—he's a bit strange, by celestial standards."

"How so?"

"Remember, he was eaten by a demon from beyond the world. When the demon wasn't in his psychic footprints anymore, the current Lord of Light immediately stepped into them. That's odd, even by energy-state criteria."

"Isn't that how you showed up?"

"Yes, but I had to put myself together over the course of years. He just sprang up." He paused for a moment, then said more quietly, "I think he's another entity, taking over the shoes the Lord of Light used to fill."

"A parasite?"

"I don't know. I still have a lot to learn about being a god and the celestial ecology."

"I understand."

"Anyway, all that's an upstairs thing. The finger-shaking at him doesn't affect his followers' actions, but it does limit the amount of aid he can give them."

"Huh." I thought about it for a moment. "They can't get their prayers answered?"

"Not beyond a certain minimal response, no. He is also forbidden from manifesting another avatar for some indefinite period."

"A week?"

"More like a millennium or two. At least, in this physical continuum. If he has access to other physical worlds, other rules apply."

"Comforting. Sort of."

"I think so, considering you only won because Bronze is, technically, a quasi-divine entity."

"I beg your pardon?"

"She's part of our mythos. Odin has his ravens, Athena has her owl, the Hunter has his hounds, we have Bronze."

"Oh. I guess that makes sense."

"Yep. Firebrand, too. It's the only way I could channel so much energy into Firebrand. It would have shattered the first time it met the mace, otherwise."

"Don't remind me," I replied, trying to shudder. The last thing I needed was a grumpy dragon-sword with a god complex. "Anything else? Or can I crawl back into my body?"

"Oh, you're still in it. I'm just accessing some of the sensory impulse channels in your brain and stimulating the cognitive functions."

I didn't have a good reply to that.

"Did I mention," I said, finally, "how much I hate having my brain tampered with?"

"I recall it from somewhere," he replied, seriously. "I wouldn't do it if I had a choice. But after Mary got the wooden spikes out of your heart and head, I thought it would be nice if I kept an eye on your brain's recovery. I mean, if you **like** the idea of having radical personality changes and loss of memory, I guess I could poke a new hole to match the old one. Or, if you like, I could leave you to regenerate partway before you go off hunting for blood as a predatory beast. You'll eventually come to your senses, I'm sure. I thought you might prefer it if I suppressed all your activity until Mary can see you adequately fed and regenerated."

"I take it back. Thank you. Thank you very much. You're most kind."

"Happy to help."

"Anything else I should know?"

"Yes. Quite a lot."

"And I'm not going to like it," I predicted. Or prophesied.

"Not all of it, no."

"All right. Hit me."

"Well, the good news is the Lord of Light has been censured before a grand conclave of the gods. We've gone over that. But while he had us all there, he brought up your status as an avatar."

"And?"

"You're not one."

"If you would have asked me, I'd have told you."

"Yeah, but he brought it up in the conclave and had it formally recognized. You're a physical entity with a severe chaos-void infection, not the embodiment of a deity. Or deity-like entity, I should say."

"Since I don't understand what that means, I'm going to pretend to nod significantly and wait for you to finish."

"So, if you're not an avatar, you're not really me, and the rule about attacking other gods doesn't apply to you."

"You mean he got my diplomatic immunity revoked?" I demanded.

"Yes. If someone down there aims a god at you, it can hurt you, even kill you."

"But the Lord of Light is still limited in the amount of aid he can grant his followers?"

"Yes. I suggest you exercise caution around them anyway. I'm not sure how much they can actually **do** to you, of course, but it's bound to hurt."

"No kidding. He'd love to fry me with holy light, even if it means burning out a priest."

"Which may have been his goal in bringing his avatar into the world."

"How do you mean?"

"If it killed you, he was ahead. If it died, he could still cost you something."

"This hardly seems fair. Don't we get any slack for him starting it?"

"No. I gather things were different, way back when, but the whole thing about whose fault it was and why they did it and all the rest simply formed a vicious cycle of favors and vendettas. Eventually, they had to crack down on it and make the rules more concrete. No wiggle room for cheaters."

"Somehow, I feel cheated."

"Me, too."

"All right. I'm recovering, Bronze and Firebrand are recovering, and I presume Mary is all right?"

"She barely even felt it. She was a long way off. You were the one with your face in the firestorm."

"Again," I muttered. "Anything else you can tell me?"

"No, but I have a question."

"What?" I asked, surprised. "You're asking me?"

"I'm not omniscient, remember?"

"Apparently, I had some brain damage and temporarily forgot. Okay, what do you want to know?"

"Do you want to start a holy war? Or, since it's already kind of started, do you want to ramp it up into a full-scale crusade?"

I had to think about it. He waited while I did, so I knew he was serious about my answer.

"If you'd asked me while I was regenerating a shattered shoulderblade," I said, "I would have told you to get everybody together for a church-burning. Now, though... now I'm not in the middle of a life-and-death battle, I'm not in pain, and I don't really have the energy for a war."

"I think we should," he replied. "The Lord of Light isn't a reasonable deity. He's already got a mandate that says he's supposed to kill you, but now he's going to blame you for his humiliation, both mortal and immortal alike."

"Maybe he is," I agreed, "but this is where we differ. I don't want to play this game. People are not pieces on a board, no matter what the so-called gods may think. They don't need to be manipulated and maneuvered. They need to be left alone."

"Says the man who only wants to be left alone," he pointed out.

"True. But I gave up mortal authority in this world by surrendering it to Lissette. I'll give up religious authority in this world by surrendering it to Beltar and the priesthood. You want a holy war? Consult with Beltar. Ask him to ask his priest-knights. Get them to tell you what they want. Rather than being a god who orders them to destroy the followers of another god, be a god who asks them what they want. Help them in their endeavors rather than order them to obey."

There was a long silence from the energy-being version of me.

"The others aren't going to like this."

"They're already trying it on for size," I pointed out. "They're working within the authority of the Queen, right? Besides, it's an internal matter for one religion, not an Olympus-wide mandate."

"Huh. Yes, but I don't think they see it the same way you do. This new idea of allowing the priesthood more leeway in deciding church policy..."

"Then it'll sneak up on them and they can appreciate it on its merits."

"If it works."

"Yeah. Here's hoping."

"Are you sure you want me to leave declaring a holy war in the hands of the priests?"

"Yes, for two reasons. First, they're extremely impressive priests. They're knights and they know how to be noble, upright, and good. Second, if they decide to have themselves a crusade, it'll be because **they** chose it, rather than **you** ordered it."

"Taking this free will thing a trifle seriously, aren't we?"

"Let me put it another way. Right now, the so-called gods are working mostly behind the scenes, operating through proxies, and generally staying out of it. Correct?"

"Well, yes. That's the way the game is set up. You can't play chess if the players can simply snatch a piece off the board anytime they feel the urge."

"Okay. Next time someone cheats, robbing people of their free will, their right to choose what they want from the gods—or even **if** they want something from the gods—I will flip the board, break the table, and burn down the house they're playing in."

I felt the shock as he realized I meant it. Being pummeled by quasi-deific avatars makes me cranky.

"Sparky mentioned something about this to me, wanting to know if you could do it. I told her you could, but you never would. Are you telling me you'll destroy the world and everyone on it?"

"What defines a person is the ability to choose. Even slaves have choices— their bodies may be confined, but their wills are still their own. If you take away even the ability to defy one's masters, there's nothing left but an automaton."

"I'm not going to argue, mainly because I can't think of a good argument at the moment."

"Good. I'm too tired to argue."

"You've changed," he said, quietly.

"Oh?"

"I'm not sure I like it. I respect it, and to a degree I even admire it, but I'm not sure it's a change for the better. It concerns me."

"I really am too tired to care."

"Understandable. And if it's all the same to you, I think I'm going to keep this conversation just between us."

"Oh?"

"Did it occur to you that if you threaten the entire game, they might get enough agreement to make an exception to the rules? I can't do much about it if they collectively decide to turn you into a rapidly-expanding cloud of high-temperature plasma. So try not to mention this conversation to anyone, all right? I can tell Sparky I was wrong about you being able to do it, if I have to, so that's not a big deal, but try not to call attention to yourself. I don't want the rest of them to start asking awkward questions!"

"No promises, but I'll try."

"Okay. Go back to sleep."

Monday, June 13th

I opened my eyes under the surface. My vision cleared rapidly as the blood continued to drain into me. I stood up and looked around.

I was in a large, open-topped barrel. Mary sat next to me, Firebrand across her lap. I didn't see Bronze, but I knew she was just outside the building. The room was underground and full of bottles, jugs, jars, and barrels. One of the barrels was on a table beside me, still draining into the one I was in. I picked it up, tilted it over, and poured the dregs over me. A few moments later, when all traces of blood were nothing more than memories, I hopped out. Naked, of course. Probably Mary's idea. I doubted it was required.

"Good to see you again," I said.

"Same here. Did we win?"

"I'm going to call it a win. What happened after the fight?"

"When the lights went up and then went out, I followed Bronze. She was carrying you toward me through the wreckage."

I was still buried! Firebrand complained.

"I'm telling this," Mary snapped.

I just wanted to get that out there.

"For a dragon, you whine a lot. Now hush." Mary spoke to me, saying, "I pulled a biggish piece of debris out of your face—it would have gone completely through your head and out the back if your helmet hadn't stopped it. You need a new faceplate."

"I'll work on it. Go on."

"You weren't getting better. The hole in your head wasn't closing. I thought something had ruined you completely, but I kept taking bits out of you anyway. One of the bits was a bat-sized piece through your chest—a wooden stake through the heart, I guess. I removed it and you immediately started to heal."

"Really? That's interesting."

"I agree. Does a wooden stake through the heart drop you in your tracks? I mean, I know it doesn't kill you, not like it does my sort of vampire—"

"Wait, what?" I interrupted. "Does it?"

"Of course. If you put a wooden stake through a Thessaloniki or other tribe... well, if you hit the heart, we die. It takes a minute or two, though. We freeze in place, paralyzed, then start decaying rapidly. What's left is a pile of dry ashes or dust, usually."

"If someone pulls it out before you finish, do you get better?"

"I don't know. I'd rather not experiment, either."

"Noted."

"In your case," she went on, "you don't die. You don't heal, either. I was wondering if a stake through the heart makes you stop moving."

"I don't know. And I do want to experiment, now that I know it doesn't kill me."

"Uh, okay. How do you not know about this already?"

"Body armor and very few wooden weapons."

"And being extremely good with a sword?"

"Could have something to do with it," I admitted.

"So we'll experiment. Maybe we don't have to do it immediately? I've been traumatized by a divine visitation and an awful fear of being alone."

"You say that lightly, but I suspect you mean it."

"It's a defense mechanism," she agreed.

"All right. Some other time. Go on. What happened after you un-staked me?"

"You started healing up, but it was awfully slowly. I had Bronze drag you back along the way you came, through the army wreckage. She limped off with you and you hoovered up any blood they left behind. While you two did that, I tracked down Firebrand."

And took forever.

"You were pummeled into the dirt by a tree bigger around than I am tall. You were also whining about cracks and fractures. You weren't exactly being helpful about finding you!"

I was injured! I've never been injured before!

"Man up," Mary advised, "or, rather, *dragon* up. Once I found the whiny weapon and dug it out—"

—eventually, Firebrand added.

"—I went after Bronze—with Firebrand—and we met her on the road. Most people decided to leave when the funny lights started, so we didn't have any troubles there. The few who stuck around to watch the fight between light and dark died from something I can't explain. Their eyes were burned out of their heads. Maybe people farther away survived it. We did find one guy with his eyesockets still smoking, moaning about the light, the light, the light. But he was fresh blood, and you were still unconscious, so we didn't question him much.

"Afterward, there was some discussion on where to go, but we didn't have too long to think it over. Sunrise was only a couple of hours away by then. We made time toward Peleseyn—did I say it right?"

Yes, Firebrand agreed. *That's how the locals say it, anyway.*

"Good. We got past the worst of the forest wreckage and into some clear road, then had to camp out. Our sun-proof body bags work, by the way."

"I originally intended to use them before we attacked," I admitted. "Get close to our target positions, camp through the sunset, immediately get up and get cracking."

"Well, they work fine against sunrise, too. By the way, did you know you smell unbelievably awful in the mornings?"

"It's a side effect of all the exertion and regeneration."

"For the record, I'm against it. I thought my slaughterhouse dinner was the worst thing I would ever experience. I might be wrong."

"Are you forgetting your undead nausea after visiting a coastal prince?"

"No, but I'd like to."

"Come to think of it, so would I. Then what happened?"

"I did what I could with a cleaning spell and a healing spell, but you were still unresponsive. Firebrand fixed itself, of course, and helped heat up Bronze's bent leg while we traveled. She's not up to full speed yet, but she was plenty fast enough to get us here. After that, it was a simple matter to find a hotel with a wine cellar, order a barrel of blood, and so on."

"Good to know. I feel much better."

Psst. Boss? Firebrand communicated specifically to me.

Yes?

She left out the part about bleeding all over you last night. She wanted to be sure you were intact enough to survive the day.

How intact wasn't I?

Well, she was worried you wouldn't survive as a mortal.

Thanks, Firebrand.

Just thought I'd mention it, since she didn't.

"Want to tell me what happened?" Mary asked. "I already got Firebrand's version of it."

I explained what happened to the best of my ability, but I left out the conversation with my energy-state psychic clone.

"So the avatar tried to take me with it," I concluded, "and very nearly succeeded."

"No kidding. It's a good thing you have diplomatic immunity. From what I felt at a distance, I daresay it could otherwise fry you in your armor before you got within ten yards of it."

"Speaking of which, where's my armor?"

"I've got all the pieces I could find in a sack. I added some charcoal, but I'm not sure it's ever going to be back to its old self."

"Give it time. Time, and a lot of carbon." I rubbed my stomach and frowned. "I'm hungry."

"Since it's night, that's concerning. Do we go hunting? Or do we talk to the local slaughterhouse? I've been paying people for quick service and silence, but you can't buy silence."

"You can't?"

"Anyone willing to keep your secrets for money will sell them for more money. You can't buy silence, only rent it."

"That's cynical, jaded, and probably true," I admitted, sadly. "Let's start with the local slaughterhouse. I think most of my issues are from physical regeneration, not mystical exertion."

"I'll say," she agreed, standing up and handing me a pair of pants. "You were a mess."

"Was I? And where's my armored underwear?"

"It's recovering with your armor. Peeling it off you was difficult; your flesh and your underwear both sort of melted. I paid some kids to collect cobwebs and rolled it all together before I came down here. As for you... Remember when you torched your face off by accident?"

I put on the pants and tried not to show I was having a horrible flashback. I remembered the feeling of my teeth being actively on fire. If you ever have it happen to you, you'll understand why even the flashback is horrible. If you never have it happen to you, *good!*

"Yes," I admitted.

"Imagine that, but add in trying to melt your armor onto the exposed bone."

"I'm glad I missed it."

"I'm sorry I saw it."

"Shirt?"

"No, but I have your cloak." She handed it to me and I put it on. It flowed around me and pretended to be a belted kilt. No tartan, I'm afraid, only an inky black.

"I haven't got used to that," Mary said, quietly.

"Neither have I, but I'm determined to do so. Meanwhile, I'm starting to feel extremely hungry."

"And now you're starting to scare me. Follow me and try to remember I'm on your side."

It bothered me greatly to realize she wasn't kidding. She was scared. Mary was scared *of me.*

In some way I couldn't define, the knowledge hurt.

We bought a whole pen of pigs and donated the carcasses back to the pig farmer. Mary claimed she wasn't hungry and watched while I sank my teeth into a pig, speared the hole with my tongue, and sucked out both the blood and the vital energy. I went through fourteen pigs in about five minutes, most of which was slurping the last few drops. I'll say this for pigs, they don't leave a furball in the back of your throat like *dazhu.* If you don't have to breathe, the smell of a pigsty is something you can ignore. Hairballs are worse. Believe me, hacking up a furball is something you never want to do.

"Better?" Mary asked, once I finished.

"I think so. Yes. I could go for another dozen, but I think my post-combat munchies are under control."

"I'm delighted."

"Now that the immediate threat is dealt with, let's look at Bronze."

Bronze was in pretty good shape. The bent leg was straight again, at least, but it was still forming the details. The other legs were horse-like, flexing and bending like a flesh-and-blood horse. Her left front leg was a statue's leg. It looked like the others, but its movement was subtly different.

"Can you run?" I asked. Bronze nodded and stomped her bad leg. She might not break any speed records today, but she could run. I turned to Mary. "I'll send you back via gate, if you like. I'm riding with Bronze."

"Yes, please, and thank you. Do you mind if I try to gate to Diogenes? I'd like a new power pack."

"I'd rather you didn't just yet; I'd like to supervise. There are nuances that make it trickier than you'd think."

"As you command, Ancient Mystic. I suppose I can lounge around the palace and pretend I'm a captive princess awaiting her handsome knight."

"Or you could talk to Lissette and Dantos and bring me up to speed when I get there."

"Slave-driver," she replied, mockingly. She kissed the tip of my nose. "Try not to get into any fights on the way."

"Bronze will keep me out of trouble." Bronze nodded agreement.

The return trip was uneventful, but interesting, at least to me. After I sent Mary ahead, Bronze found the doorway into the secret subterranean passages. I made sure we were unobserved and we quickly vanished through it. Once under the road, Bronze cranked up to a full-scale gallop and I enjoyed the ride.

I also watched her as she ran, paying close attention to how her magical biology worked on the wounded leg. Part of it was a solid object animated by magic. The rest was a much more efficient system, probably mimicking an actual horse's anatomy. The first one was power-intensive to run, but the second...

I used to think she was changing her own internal anatomy to run faster, to outpace cars and other vehicles. Now I think she's doing it to operate more efficiently—to get better magical mileage without sacrificing speed and power. With metallic muscles, lubricated internal joints, and similar sorts of anatomical improvements, she wasn't forced to magically animate and bend metal in order to move.

My magical rating system still has no numbers, but as an eyeball estimate, I'd say she required a third of the magical energy to run on jointed legs, compared to the non-jointed leg. With that kind of setup, she might be able to run almost indefinitely even in a magic-scarce world! Maybe not at full speed, but at least as fast as mortal horse.

What I found even more interesting was the way she seemed to be trying to mimic her pastern bracelets. Their magical enchantments weren't part of her base structure. They were accessories, obviously. Yet, it seemed to me she was... I don't know if "learning" is the right word. Adapting? Assimilating? Copying? Whatever the word is, I think she's actively trying to learn to do what her magical jewelry does. I could see changes in the colors and movement of the foamy, organic-looking energies of her being near the bracelets, almost as though mimicking the spells.

Did I include such an ability when I made her? Or is it simply a part of her, being a living creature instead of an enchanted object? She can learn. She can change. She can grow.

How did I do that? Or should I be the one to take any credit for it?

I'm proud of my Bronze. She knows it.

Tuesday, June 14th

Bronze's leg is back in shape after her run. It seems running at high temperatures helps her reconfigure herself—in other words, heal faster. Next time she gets a boo-boo, I need to get out a welding torch and see if I can melt her in a localized area. Would it hasten the process further, or would it count as another injury? Does it matter if the temperature is high enough to melt, or should it be only enough to soften? Does using the damaged limb help determine how it heals? Bronze doesn't know, but is willing to try it.

With the good part of my day dealt with, on to the bad part.

Karvalen—the city—is undergoing a radical political shift in certain areas due to forceful objection and armed opposition by outside parties to the current regime. Which is to say it's a war zone.

I'm getting ahead of myself. Let me back up a bit.

When I arrived last night, nothing untoward was happening. A spell-message for the mountain told it to go ahead and reconnect to the roadways west of the avatar combat zone. Bronze went up to her room and started crunching through her coal. I met with Mary, gave her some lessons on inter-universal gate usage, and let her go talk to Diogenes. If she doesn't manage to come back on her own, she can at least call back when she's ready, so the time differential isn't a major issue.

I also looked over the mess of my armor and started helping it pull itself together. It would be a day or two before the underwear was feeling better, and the suit might take a week or more.

Then I called the capitol and had a brief conversation with Kammen—Lissette was in bed and it doesn't do to wake the Queen unnecessarily.

"So, we don't have an army comin' in from the west?" he asked.

"Not anymore. And did you get the princes? Tannos and... Ventidius?"

"Prince Vetidius sent word through his wizard about visiting. *Count* Tannos is all kinds of helpful about offering to talk to the Prince of Actareyn."

"Good. Is there anything else that requires the attention of the Demon King?"

"Nope. I'd let the Queen answer in the morning, though."

"That's fair. Give everyone my regards, please, and let Her Majesty know I will be available at her convenience."

"I'll do that... Halar." Kammen grinned at me and winked. I laughed in delight. *Halar!* Yes! I'm not the King!

Kammen made my evening.

After we signed off, I realized I was still a bit peckish. I suppose fixing whatever damage an exploding avatar can do merits more than one major meal. I checked with the Temple of Shadow. They had a few guests wanting the personal service. I'm not entirely sure how my other-self and the Grey Lady worked out who gets whom, but I think it has something to do with a matter of choice. The Grey Lady escorts anyone who dies. I act as a doorway from one life to the next if you decide to die *now*, rather than linger. Something like that. Theology isn't my strong suit, thank god.

I spent a few minutes with each of the three upcoming departures, practicing my graveside manner. It's nice to be the angel of death when I don't actually have to chase people down and kill them. Being an escort, so to speak, isn't such a bad deal. I'd rather wear the suit and tie, walk with people, smile a lot, and make it a pleasant experience. I'm not against running screaming through the night while waving a flaming sword, you understand, but I *prefer* to do things in a less boisterous fashion.

Afterward, of course, I had a number of people who wanted to bow at me. I told them to take it to the altar and they mostly did. One young lady insisted on grabbing my ankles and pressing her forehead to my toes. I had to unwrap her and stand her up by hand. Of course, once I did it I recognized her. She was the young mother who brought me a dying baby.

The kid was doing fine, and she was duly grateful. I was pleased, gave her my blessing—which, I might add, actually did something. I have to remember watch it when I do things purely for form's sake! —and sent her home.

Then it was back up to the mountain for me and a pleasant really-early-morning in my geode room, fiddling with gates of different sizes, working out ways to fine-tune my focus to avoid hitting the wrong universe, and so on. I went through my morning transformation, fired off my cleaning spell, and continued working.

After a while, a grey sash jumped against the pivot-door, shoved on it to hurry it along, and burst into the room.

One good thing about massive doors: It's hard to slam in and surprise me. Quite a lot of the overcity has doors of the more mundane, wooden sort. Internal doorways may or may not have doors or curtains. But here, in the mountain, it's mostly pivoting blocks of varying thickness, which makes them slow. I wonder if that's a reflection of the mountain in general. It's rapid geology, but it's still geology. Then again, the doors might be its way of making me feel safer.

I was on my feet and waiting when he finally slipped through.

"My lord, the Church of Light has invaded the city! They assault the Temple of Shadow and the undermountain!"

I stood there stupidly for a moment, wondering where an assault force could have come from. After the pounding we gave them the last time, they didn't have the manpower to take a city block, much less a city. They would need to send thousands of men and tons of supplies. This sort of thing doesn't come up in mere moments.

And the realization hit me. I saw what they tried to do. Provoke the princedoms of the west to invade, attracting the attention and the military might of the kingdom to the west. Press this expendable, diversionary force as far as it can go to draw everything out of position and expend much of the available forces. Only then would they launch their real offensive in the east. Where they got the manpower to invade on both fronts, I didn't know, but I was certain I was right.

"Come in, close the door, and hold it," I told him. "I'll be back, and my password is 'undermountain'. Got that?" He got it. He stopped the rotating door and swung it closed behind me. I went to the CIC to get a feel for what was going on.

The forces of the Church of Light were *already* in the mountain and roaming the halls, slaughtering anyone they came across. I had to kill nine of them on the way, and my cloak had to pretend to be a shield more than once. I got away with only minor injuries—a few cuts and bruises, really—and a couple of first-aid healing spells took care of the bleeding. This is why I usually wear armor, even if it's only armored underwear. Not this time; all my armor was still repairing itself.

When I reached the CIC, it was already in the hands of the Church of Light. Over a dozen men were already in there. They had knocked over my sand table and two men were smashing it with sledgehammers. The various mirrors were mostly broken and the rest were about to be.

Again, what happened was obvious, now that I could look back on it. I had wondered why Lotar carried on with his stupid attempt to take the city when Thomen's forces were turned away. Without those to back him up, Lotar didn't have a chance. He knew it, he *had* to know it. What I failed to realize was his fanaticism. He was willing to sacrifice all those troops, all those followers, in a preliminary attack to test the defenses, to gauge our response. The whole sequence of events wasn't a real attempt to take Karvalen. It was a probing attack to see what we would do. Armed with that knowledge, then they could plan their *real* assault.

This assault.

I retreated. Mortal, unarmored, and possibly surrounded by enemies, I slipped away into the tunnels of the mountain and made my way back to my gate room. I gave him the password and we sealed the door—rather, the mountain sealed it, along with every other door in the place. Being locked up for a while was an inconvenience for everyone, but it would cripple invaders. I was okay with that. It bought time to gauge the situation, contact people, and organize.

I got out my pocket mirror and made some calls.

"Yes?" Dantos answered. I smiled grimly.

"What do you know and where are you?"

"I'm sealed in a room, eighth rise, along the north hall. There are warriors roaming the halls, but I cannot get to them, nor they us. Your doing?"

"For the moment. Hang on and I'll get you something to open doors. Can you reach other combatants on your mirror?"

"Yes."

"Do that. I'll get back to you."

I rummaged in my pockets and came up with some loose change. It would do. I put a spell on a coin, one similar to the message spell I used to communicate with the mountain. This was a simple one: Open the door. It worked by tapping it on the door in question. I called Dantos back and told him how to operate it.

We improvised a circle and a container. I opened a tiny gate for the coin and dropped it through to him.

"Call me back if you need more of them. Do you have any idea how they got so many people inside—no, never mind. We'll sort that out later. Right now, get people together and focus on taking back pieces of the undermountain."

"Do you wish us to take prisoners?"

"Right now, I'm not sure I want you to accept surrenders," I countered. "We don't have the luxury of manpower and organization, yet. Use your judgment."

"As you command, my lord."

Beltar took a little longer to answer. He was in the Temple of Shadow, outside the mountain itself, and there was a fight going on in the background.

"My lord," he acknowledged. He didn't wait for me to ask questions, but continued, "We are beset by hundreds of fighters. We have lost the main doors and access to the tunnels. There is no way out; we are trapped. We hold them, but they press their attack at every door within the Temple."

"How long do you think you can hold out?"

"The initial attack was a surprise, my lord. We now have armored knights holding ground. What wounded we have are being treated and many of those may soon rejoin the ranks. The enemy do not seem to have much in the way of wizards—only one or two we have seen—so I believe they are present only to counter our own magic. I think it is a question of persistence."

"It should calm down to a siege?"

"Yes, my lord."

"Good. Hold them."

"Very good, my lord."

I called Tianna, but nobody in the Temple of Flame answered. I didn't like that, so I switched to scrying mode and looked into the Temple. Sparky might object to my snooping without invitation, but she could take it up with me later if she really wanted to.

It's hard to burn a Temple of Flame. There isn't much inside one *to* burn. Stone benches, stone floors, stone walls—they don't go in for flammable building materials or combustible furnishings. Weird, I know. But the invaders stuck mainly to direct, physical damage. They had already bashed in the base of the statue of the Mother of Flame; pieces of the fallen idol were scattered across the outdoor worship area. Other attackers had cracked some of the benches while several stood on the altar to urinate on it. One was doing so as I watched, presumably to desecrate it. A group of men with sledgehammers and chains were working on one of the pillars of the dome, preparatory to knocking the whole thing down.

I searched inside the building, scanning from room to room. I found a young lady—not Tianna—stripped naked, obviously beaten, possibly raped, and lying facedown in a pool of blood. At a guess, they cut her throat. Further scanning found Sheena in the process of being raped to death.

My temper has been somewhat shorter than I like, of late. I blame Johann. It's better, at least somewhat, now that I've vented a little of it on him, but I'm still not back to my usual, laid-back, patient self. At that moment, I didn't care if they were religious zealots, hired mercenaries, or random rioters. The four men in the room were severely dead and didn't know it. After all, there was a handy doorway right there…

I turned to the grey sash with me.

"What's your name?"

"Sir Raxan, by your grace, my lord," he replied, saluting.

"Can you mind my gate, keep it open while I rescue a maiden in distress?"

"I will give my life if it will serve you, my lord."

"I didn't ask that. I asked if you were skilled enough as a wizard to route power into a gate spell and keep it open."

"I am a Shield of the Order of Shadow," he replied, simply.

"Do it." I shifted the scrying portal to the smaller, man-sized gate, watched it flush everything into view, and stepped through, Firebrand already out and blazing with an incandescent glee. Heads, hands, arms, legs—body parts went *everywhere*. I then grabbed Sheena, what there was of her clothing, and stepped back through the gateway. Elapsed time, less than ten seconds.

"Healing spells and some mending for the garments," I snapped, pushing her into Sir Raxan's arms. I flicked my scrying spell around the temple some more, searching for Tianna.

Wherever she was, she wasn't in her temple. I called Amber, in Mochara. A lesser priestess answered and moved with satisfactory speed when I snapped an order at her. Amber glowed in the mirror almost immediately.

"Father!"

"Amber! I'm glad to see you're all right. Is Mochara under attack?"

"No, but I've just heard Karvalen is."

"Exactly. I'm calling about Tianna. Please tell me she's visiting you in Mochara."

"She is not." Amber's flames darkened to a reddish color. "She was in Carrillon, establishing a new Temple there, but I believe she persuaded Seldar to use your portals and return her to Karvalen for the solstice ceremony."

"So she was definitely in Karvalen today? Or yesterday?"

"The ceremony should be today. Why? What has become of her?"

"I don't know, and I want to. If you can find her, let me know. I'll start looking, too." We hung up and went about our offspring-hunting in our own ways. I sent out pulses like radar and got no response. I tried the passive approach and did somewhat better—she was southeast of my position in the mountain. So she was at least partly cloaked from detection magic, which spoke to me of wizardry or a magician.

I linked my scrying spell to the detection spell and sent the viewpoint sailing along that line. Walls, people, rooms—all these flew past as my sensor zipped along. I couldn't triangulate easily without the sand table, so I was stuck with a slow search. Eventually, though, my sensor ran into a scrying shield.

Aha!

A quick look around the neighborhood showed me the building was probably an inn or tavern, three floors, with a large common room and several smaller rooms above. It was on the edge of a market square full of large tents and piles of supplies. It was obviously a staging area of some sort. The place was crawling with soldiers in religious garb. Somehow, I didn't think they were formally church troops. Maybe it was the looting and pillaging in the nearby buildings that gave me such an impression. At least there weren't many people to kill in the neighborhood—they already did that.

Was the shielded building a command center, perhaps? A headquarters? Or just a place to keep valuable prisoners? I doubted they wanted Tianna as a prisoner because of her status as a priestess; a simple priestess they would kill outright. It's possible they were worried about her death calling down the wrath of a goddess, but I doubted the Church of Light considered it their main concern. Maybe I'm conceited, but I think they had her as a hostage against my good behavior.

No doubt I would get a ransom demand of some sort. Tianna might be knocked over the head and unconscious, but they were going to keep her alive at all costs.

They'd better.

However, there was a chance they might not. It already takes a special kind of idiot to kidnap a woman whose mother is an embodied elemental of divine fire and whose grandfather is a soul-devouring monster.

In the meantime, as long as I was looking around, I thought I should do a flyover of the city. From what I could see, they took the northeast and southeast gates, spread toward each other to consolidate a big chunk of wall, and started expanding from there. They didn't seem to be fortifying and taking territory so much as they were killing anyone who wasn't fast enough to be driven before them. The alarm spread faster than they did, but the tactic let them cover a lot of city before we could respond. They had a good third of the city to themselves and were still spreading.

Resistance outside their captured ground coalesced in small pockets, generally from city guards augmented by citizens with weapons. They were now doing a fair job of slowing the invaders, but they had to keep falling back to avoid being flanked, surrounded, and pulverized. Stopping them wasn't even a possibility. There simply weren't enough people to put in their way.

As I watched and thought, it became clear this was a much more highly-coordinated attack than before. They didn't attack the gates at dawn and start fighting. They trickled in over time, then moved through the city before sunrise to attack several places at once. They attacked the Temples of Shadow and Flame, they attacked the undercity... Judging by the numbers of troops loose in the overcity, they must have taken the gates at or just before dawn to let in reinforcements, which meant either hiding them from the sentries on the walls, or subverting the sentries (or simply killing them and pretending to be sentries) and overpowering the gate guards.

Yeah, someone put a lot of planning into a well-coordinated attack.

I wonder if is this how Johann felt.

The attack at dawn was only to be expected, of course. It would be hours before I was in full monster mode and ready to kill anything shining with a religious light. But what did they have in store? Surely, they thought of something. Did they have some ancient, anti-nightlord magic from the old days, when they actively hunted vampires? Or were they depending on the traditional priest, prayer, and piety method? Or maybe they intended to shield a lot of troops from my soul-sucking powers and hope they could bring me down? Or were they going to use Tianna as their vampire-repellent? Or as vampire *bait?*

It could be important to find out.

I dismissed my scrying to answer a call. Amber flickered into view.

"Tianna is alive and in the hands of the Church of Light," she said.

"Yes, I thought so. I think I found the building she's in. It's the only one shielded from scrying I've found so far."

"Good. But Tianna does not respond to my call through the fire. She must be unconscious."

"What if there isn't a fire nearby?"

"Father," Amber said, looking severe. "She is a Priestess of the Flame."

"Ah. Of course. An important detail. I suspect they'll be using her as a bargaining chip."

"This is unacceptable."

"I agree, but it's daytime. I'm not really at my worst right now."

"Can you open a gate for me? I would dearly love to bring my daughter home."

"I'm all for it, but I worry they may have some sort of magic to harm you. Even a simple disruption spell, if powerful enough, could prove fatal. You're not the flesh and blood you once were."

"No," Amber admitted, "but I am an embodiment of an angry goddess. I acknowledge Karvalen as your property, however, and ask to walk its streets."

I didn't see that coming.

"How sure are you you'll survive the worst they can throw at you?"

"I am not sure at all," she admitted, "but what better way can I give my life than in saving that of my daughter?"

"You're telling this to the guy who ran into a pillar of divine fire for his own daughter."

"True."

"All right, but I have some conditions, assuming my idea even works."

"Conditions? Idea?"

"I'll explain when I come visit—and I'll bring Sheena. She needs more help than I can give at the moment."

I'm standing in a Temple of Fire working magic on a fire elemental who happens to be the soul of my daughter bound into divine flames, while my pet rock and personal knights are struggling to fight off an invasion by the evil Lord of Light. How did things come to this? It's not the situation—This seems like a bad day, not total insanity—but the journey. When did this sort of thing become... I don't know. Not *normal*, certainly, but maybe 'not unexpected'?

I'm pretty sure there was a day when my biggest problem was explaining to a student the difference between momentum and kinetic energy. That version of me is someone I hardly recognize, yet I can trace my path, point by point, moment by moment, until I reach the now. Would the me of then recognize the me of now? Would he approve of the changes? Come to that, do I?

I don't know. All I know is I am who and what I am. I don't have to like it, but I do have to accept responsibility for it.

Amber held still for me, as much as she was able, while I worked on a burning brazier.

"This would be a lot easier at night," I muttered.

"You work with the stuff of life more easily then," she agreed, "but you are still a wizard without peer. I believe in you, Father."

"Yeah, well, I don't. I'm not sure this will work."

"Yet you do it anyway?"

"If you're jumping out of a plane, you bring a parachute, regardless of who packed it," I replied. She looked at me with a puzzled expression. "If you fall off a cliff, you hope your magic ring of flight works, no matter who made it."

"Ah. And you want me to stand in the brazier?"

"Yes. Where are those goofballs with the mirrors?"

"It takes time, Father, to obey even the Demon King."

"Please don't call me that."

"Is it not who you pretend to be?"

"Yes, but I would rather you didn't call me that."

"What shall I call you? Father?"

"I'm much more comfortable with that, Daughter. I'd settle for Pops, Dad, or Halar, though."

"As you wish. When this business is concluded, will you come visit me?"

"Do you want me to?" I asked, surprised. "I always had the impression it was… awkward. Weird. It was a nightlord in a house of fire, a dark thing in a house of light."

"It is," she admitted, softly. "Yet… you are my father, and I… I never really knew you, only legends. I would like to know you as you are."

"You might not like what you see."

"Perhaps. What I have seen of you—not the Demon King—makes me wonder."

"I'll see what I can do."

"Thank you."

Once I finished her brazier, I started in on the mirrors. None of them needed an enchantment, but each needed at least a spell. In the case of the brazier, a spell capable of handling massive surges of power. Amber helped; she fed me—carefully! —a controlled stream of vital energy, maintaining and enhancing my personal stores of vitality. With the ability to work at my utmost effort, constantly, without tiring, I was done by noon.

Is this what it feels like to channel powers greater than oneself? Is this… I don't know… shamanism of some sort? Being a medium through which power flows? It's an interesting sensation, and I must admit it produces results.

"All right. Get the priestesses and worshippers together. You may need all the help you can get."

"I have already done so."

"Then let's get this show on the road."

Amber moved from her burning bed to the brazier, shrinking down to doll-size. I picked up the brazier by the handles and carried it out to the domed pavilion. We walked through the crowd as it sank to its knees around us, a collapsing wave of people. I set Amber down in front of Sparky's idol.

Tamara stood before a fire-goddess statue with my son. Now I stood here with my daughter. Irony? Possibly.

The assembled congregation remained on their knees. Two ladies with brown hair—and reddish highlights—took over for me. They fed incense and aromatic wood chips to Amber.

"You know what to do?"

"Work my way along the line of battle to halt their advance. They will seek to stop me, hopefully by declaring Tianna a hostage. If they contact me, you will be watching, and you will then know who to target. If they contact you, I am to continue until I cannot, or they have nothing further to fight with. If they come to kill me, you will give instructions."

"Yep, you've got it. Are you ready?"

"Yes," she replied, and her color shifted up from reddish to orange, shading into yellow. "You should go."

I hurried inside the stone structure that served as her home and as the indoor portion of the temple. With a doorway and a call to Sir Raxan, I was back in my gate room in moments, carrying three large mirrors under one arm and a bucket of kerosene in my free hand.

"How is the priestess?" Raxan asked, as I propped mirrors up against the walls.

"I don't know. They're taking care of her, so she should be fine. Right now, I have to keep my daughter and granddaughter alive." I started in on my mirrors again, watching over the city. There were a number of things burning—wagons, furniture, market stalls, you name it—but no widespread fires. The city's made of stone. Things *in* it will burn, but there are no thatched roofs or wooden structures. You can start fires in Karvalen, even burn out a house, but you can't actually burn the city. You might as well set fire to a concrete wall.

But one of the larger fires grew remarkably well. It roared, sucking in air and blazing high. It towered, yellow-white with a few rogue flickers of bloody red. It twisted, turned, began to spin like a tornado. People nearby stared in wonder for far too long. By the time they realized they should have scattered, it was too late.

The whirling vortex of fire spun down the street at three times the speed of a running man. It wavered and wobbled, scorching the road from side to side, scooping up anything flammable as it roared and smoked along the avenues.

It swept up a side-street, roared between buildings, flowed over an active battle between the Church of Light and those fighting the invaders. It burned through the back of the Church of Light forces, setting cloaks, clothes, and hair on fire. Skin crisped and blackened. Men screamed, but the flames never touched a defender. Then it whirled on, chasing fleeing men up the street.

The two unburned warriors of the Church of Light were taken without much trouble. The burned and dying were killed quickly. None of them tried to surrender.

The whirlwind of flame seared a path all along the streets of the northern battle line. It touched those wearing the colors of the Church, blackened and blistered them without killing, and roared to the next squad. It stayed far away from the nominal headquarters, attacking only front-line troops and their reinforcements.

I watched, sickened and grimly satisfied. I don't much care for burning someone *almost* to death, much less for doing it wholesale. I'd much rather kill someone outright. But Amber was running this show and it was her choice. I can't say I blame her, really. She gets her temper from both sides of the family, which is more than a little frightening, now that I think about it.

The headquarters area dispatched a trouble squad. It assembled in the open-air market square, the one with all the pavilion tents. I thought those tents were for reserves, and I was right. The planners obviously decided not to house anything important to the battle inside a stone structure. Prisoners, on the other hand—if I locked up the building where they kept Tianna, her guards would still kill her.

And if she got loose in there, she wouldn't instantly burn everyone in command. Smart.

The squad they sent to deal with the vortex of fire was on horseback, traveling fast, and there was at least one man in robes accompanying each man in armor. Maybe this sort of thing was what they reserved their wizard firepower for.

"Raxan. Watch these guys. Tell me if they stop or suddenly change direction."

"Yes, my lord."

I kept an eye on the pavilion tents through one mirror and struck another mirror with a fingernail. Amber's brazier rippled into view. It was white-hot, blazing like a star, and people were on their faces all around it, praying as though the end of the world was nigh.

"You're headed east, along the northern arc of the church-held area," I told her. "The trouble squad should arrive in about two minutes. Shift to the south side."

The brazier dimmed slightly, cooling a bit, and one of the priestesses poured some sort of oil on it. Amber's fiery figure stood outlined in the flames for a moment, hands clasped tightly and pressed to her chest, hair whipping wildly about, like flames in a hurricane. Okay, so they *were* flames, just like the rest of her. To me, it was still an impressive visual.

In another mirror, the whirlwind of fire latched on to a pile of trash, shrank down, and became a burning heap.

On the south side of the Church-occupied area, a small whirlwind of fire sprang up from a burning market stall. It consumed the stall in seconds, growing huge, and began a blazing rampage along the southern edge, ripping and burning through screaming men. After several minutes, Raxan reported.

"My lord, the men you set me to watch have arrived at the edge of the fighting. They are falling back quickly, since our forces are unopposed."

"Keep watching them. Figure out where they're going."

"They appear to be returning to the market of tents."

"Good. Don't lose them."

I let Amber do her fiery thing and called Beltar on my pocket mirror. The headache from maintaining at least a minimal focus on multiple scrying spells started to take root behind my eyes. This is another reason I built the sand table... which the Church destroyed. Grr.

"My lord!"

"Beltar, are you ready to start a counterattack?"

"We are still bottled by the forces of the Lord of Light," he replied. "There are at least a thousand of them, both within and without the Temple."

"So many?"

"We are the Temple of Shadow," he replied, simply.

"I see your point. Wait for my signal, then attack."

"What signal?"

"You won't miss it."

I signed off and went back to watching the fire vortex and the pavilion tents. The trouble squad returned to their headquarters and were immediately dispatched again. They changed horses and galloped off toward Amber's new manifestation.

"Still got the trouble squad?" I asked Raxan.

"Yes, my lord."

"Tell me when they're two streets away."

"Yes, my lord."

I dropped the connection to the tents and the vortex, focusing instead on the area outside the Temple of Shadow. Where, oh where is a good spot? Does someone have a handy bucket? No? What about—no, wait, there we go. A cart with barrels and buckets, bringing water to the troops.

I locked in one of the buckets in my scrying mirror, cast my gate spell on the bucket I brought, and dumped the lamp oil out of one bucket into another. I stuck Firebrand through the bottom of my bucket, it burped a blast of white-hot fire, and the resulting *whoosh* of flame blasted through the gate, through the oil, and out the bottom of the other bucket. A spray of burning oil coated everything nearby.

With the gate closed—and my own burning bucket kicked aside—I rang Amber's mirror again.

"Get ready to switch to the Temple of Shadow," I told her. "There's a nice fire going on outside."

"My lord," Raxan warned, "your trouble squad approaches."

"Finally, some good timing. Amber, *go!*"

I fired up my scrying spell again and found the vortex; it already latched on to a wooden door and burned there. In moments, it was just a burning door, so I switched immediately to the entryway of the Temple of Shadow.

Men were beating at flames with cloaks. Someone had cut the horse free of the cart and someone else hacked a hole in a barrel to get water. They were on the verge of getting the upper hand on the flames.

Then the flames fought back. The color shifted to yellow-white and the heat multiplied. Steam rose in a cloud, jetting skyward with the fire. The wagon burned brightly as the flames engulfed it fully. Men sprang back, shielding their eyes and faces from the heat and light.

The whirling brightness started as the whole of the wagon came apart in burning fragments. The vortex swept forward, cutting a line of charred, screaming flesh across the entrance of the Temple. It circled the men holding it, laying down a carpet of yelling, smoking men all around, spiraling in to set fire to everyone, everything. A few men escaped, running without regard for stomping their burned, dying fellows. Amber let them go, focusing only on the thickest clusters of men.

With the whole of the besieging force burned and smoking, screaming like some preview of Hell, the vortex of fire spun outside the entrance to the Temple of Shadow. It stood there, straight and tall, unmoving.

I rang Amber's mirror again. She was still in her brazier, still concentrating, but nothing happened. The pillar of whirling fire stayed stopped at the door.

"Hey!" I shouted. Sir Raxan snapped to attention. "Not you."

I hear you, answered the other me. *What's up?*

"Can we let Amber do her whirlwind of fire thing inside the Temple of Shadow?"

Uh... no.

"Why not?"

Rules, remember? We're not allowed to do divine manifestations on someone else's holy ground.

"Seriously? Not even if you give permission?"

It's a stupid rule, he agreed. *Nobody asked me when they were making them.*

"There's no wiggle room at all?"

Gods like absolutes. Oh, sometimes, with permission, you can get away with little things—talking to your god, maybe a little extra boost to something if your deities are allied in a cause, things like that.

"This counts!"

*Yes, but that fire-tornado is **not** minor! I can't even pretend I'm not noticing it!*

"Damn it!"

Working on it.

"Raxan!"

"My lord!" He stood straighter, almost vibrating.

"How would you like to defend me while I smite invaders?"

He unslung the shield from his back, drew his sword, and saluted.

I opened a gate. We went through.

Amber might not be able to do anything pyrotechnic inside the Temple of Shadow, but she helped Firebrand do something while we stood outside it. Firebrand cut loose with its usual flamethrower effect, clearing out everything beyond the front doors. The blast, however, was less like a flamethrower and more like the dragon-fire I remembered. It swelled into a rocket launch, filling the doors. It blasted down the steps, boiled up beyond, and the thunder of it echoed through the city.

The vortex of fire was gone, leaving only a sunny, smoke-filled day, the smell of burnt flesh, and the screams of the dying.

I helped Raxan back to his feet and ripped the burning cloak from his shoulders. He wasn't harmed, just a trifle shaken. We worked a couple of filtering spells for us to breathe through and we entered the Temple of Shadow.

As I expected, Beltar took it as the signal. When a dragon breathes down your corridors hard enough to make the world shake, you notice. It also neatly solves the problem of wondering if you got the signal. If you have to wonder, it wasn't the signal.

Raxan and I encountered a lot of men in the midst of coughing fits, trying to get out of the clouds of burnt-flesh smoke. He stayed on my left like a shield and we went through everything would could find as quickly as we found it, hurrying to finish before the choking concentrations of smoke thinned out.

We met black-armored men coming the other way. The cleansing of the Temple went quickly after that. Well, killing the invaders did. Cleaning the place was going to have to wait.

When the smoke cleared enough to make breathing spells unnecessary, Beltar and I did a headcount. Almost two hundred fighting effectives remained in the Temple. Another hundred or so were sidelined from their wounds. Sixty-one were dead, killed in the first assault.

"They raised the alarm," Beltar told me. "They fought. Unprepared, many of them unarmored, some of them even unarmed. They fought, and they died."

"I know. Does it make you feel better or worse to know ten times their number are dying in the streets even now?"

"Better," he decided. "And worse."

"Senseless slaughter?" I guessed.

"Yes."

"You're a better man than I am, Beltar."

"Am I?" he asked. "I regret the waste of life, but I still wish to kill them."

"Yes. Yes, you are, because I can't find it in me to pity them, not even a little. Now bar the doors, set a guard, and follow me into the undercity. We're going to kill the rest of them."

"Yes, my lord."

And we did. Much like the time an army of *orku* and *galgar* were foolish enough to come stomping into my briar patch, we moved through the undermountain. Passage by passage, cavern by cavern, only we started at the bottom and worked our way up. I walked ahead with Sir Raxan and triggered the door-opening process while Beltar ran the room-by-room clearing.

When we met up with allied forces, we compared notes, redistributed troops, and methodically rooted out every last one of the Church of Light goons.

I wasn't the one who found the boy, but I recognized him when I looked over the dead.

The Church of Light soldiers—butchers—killed everyone they could find. I'm not sure they had any real objective other than murdering everyone. Maybe everyone in Karvalen is considered corrupt and irredeemable. I don't know how they think. I'm not sure they do. But the death toll was astounding.

Caris' friend, Mikkel, the little boy who ran around with her and played with her, the one I made spell-toys for, was one of the dead. He was split almost in two by a bladed weapon, cutting down at the joint of neck and shoulder to a point below his ribs. He didn't die instantly. It took a few seconds.

He still had a wooden practice sword in his hand. He was dead, but his fist wouldn't let go of it, not even after he was killed.

Dead children are never a good thing. Maybe that, in itself, is a good thing. If I ever grow immune to the effect of a dead child, I'll know I'm the monster the Church of Light says I am. On the other hand, the things I do are nothing compared to the things I *want* to do when confronted by a child's death.

"Dantos!" I shouted. He materialized at my left.

"My lord."

"Do we have the mountain?"

"The mountain is ours, my lord. I have plans with Lord Beltar to guard it and deploy our forces through the city to contain, control, and eventually crush the invaders."

"Good man. You two carry on with that. Someone get T'yl over here for me, please, and summon whoever is currently in charge of the local Wizards' Guild. I'm going to my chambers to check on my armor, wait out the sunset, and go kill things. Please see to it everyone is informed of my intention and knows to stay as far away from me as possible."

"My lord?"

I took the wooden sword and closed Mikkel's sightless eyes. They don't do that, here. I don't know why.

"There may be collateral damage."

Dantos didn't ask. I think he was afraid to.

My armor was still in pieces. It was in no shape to actually be worn, so I let it sit and pull itself together. My armored underwear was coming along much better. It had a lot less mass to sort out and the new repair enchantment was one of my best. I focused on getting it in shape for the evening. I really should ask Diogenes for a rundown of the concealable armor in his databanks. All I have is stuff I could easily salvage. Surely there's something better. I mean, he found or manufactured something for Mary, even if it's a working suit rather than a concealed one. Surely he can come up with something for me.

As I thought about it, my cloak rippled and flowed around me, hardening. It did quite a convincing simulation of full armor, but in a deep, unreflecting, absolute black. It didn't feel like armor—it felt like clothes. Yet, rapping my now-gauntleted hands on it, it felt hard and durable.

I do not understand this cloak thing. I'm not sure I'm capable of understanding it, whatever the psychic-energy-other-me has to say about it. I do know I'm learning to like it, creepy shapechanging weirdness and all.

As the sunset started to tickle, I adjusted the waterfall in my chambers. The armor flowed conveniently into a cloak again and I hung it up as a runner hurried in, genuflected, and informed me of a call from the Church of Light.

"Tell them I'm coming," I said, and stepped into the waterfall. That was a frightening message, I thought. Let 'em wonder if I was coming to the mirror or coming after them. I'd answer the mirror-call after my transformation and after they had a chance to worry about it.

Once cleaned, dried, and dressed, I walked calmly down to the mirror room and took the call. Lotar answered it.

"I see you've been sprung," I said, quietly.

"I have been liberated from the unjust captivity inflicted upon me by unbelievers."

"Okay." I tilted the mirror up to put him on hold and prepared a spell. It looked as though he was using a medium-sized mirror, about the size of a dinner plate, not one of the full-size vanity-table things we generally used for communications.

"What's going on?" he demanded. "Answer me!"

I ignored this for a moment, finishing my spell. I tilted the mirror down again to regard him.

"Lotar?"

"High Priest Lotar," he corrected, "of Karvalen. You may call me 'Your Grace'."

"No." I activated the brand-new gate spell on the mirror and lunged forward. My tendrils snaked all over Lotar, but I couldn't get through to him. Divine magic or mortal magic, he was shielded from having his life drained. I half-expected that, which is why I lunged at the same time.

The defensive spell against my life-draining tendrils didn't stop my hands. I grabbed him by the hair and jerked him forward, across his desk or table. When I canceled the gate, the mirror went back to being a mirror instead of a hole in space. His head came off with a satisfactory spray of blood and other fluids.

So that's what happens. Good to know.

I arranged the head on the table so it faced the mirror. All I could see was a red layer, dripping off the other side. The blood on this side flowed quickly to me, of course, but I whisked a cleaning spell over my mirror to remove other fluids.

"Hello?" I called. "Anyone there? Who's in charge after Lotar?"

There was considerable commotion and more than a little shouting before they canceled the mirror spell. I waited, expecting them to call back, and they did. Someone had removed Lotar's body and replaced it with a frightened-looking priest. I doubted he was actually in charge, but I wasn't too worried about the details.

Funny thing. The other mirror was clear, at first, but the blood on the desk crawled up onto the mirror, coating it, as though trying to crawl though to me. Interesting.

"Good evening," I offered, pleasantly. "I'm Halar, also known as 'The Undying,' 'The Demon King,' and a bunch of other things. May I have the honor of knowing your name?"

"I... I'm under-priest Faltor, Your Majesty. Uh, I've been instructed, uh, to tell you about, well, the fire-witch? The one you call your granddaughter?"

"Oh, good. I was hoping we'd have a chance to talk about her. And relax, kid. You're in no danger," I assured him, playing idly with the very surprised-looking head. "Lotar was a criminal who escaped confinement. You haven't personally done anything that's a crime—at least, not that I know of. So take a deep breath and relax.

"Now, about my granddaughter. It's a damn good thing you have her. If you didn't have her, you'd all be dead. As it is, anyone protecting her—anyone keeping her from harm—gets to live. Of course, you can't *all* be doing that. I figure anyone in the same room with her counts as protecting her. I might go so far as the same building. Everyone else is dead. I'm going to kill them all.

"Of course, if anything happens to Tianna, I'm going to kill everyone. More importantly—you *do* know that, as Lord of Shadows, I can *eat your soul*, right?"

He couldn't speak, but he nodded convulsively.

"Good!" I enthused. "I'm glad we've got that clear. See, if anything happens to Tianna while she's in your custody, you will not meet your god. You'll meet me. You're in my city, under my power, within my sphere of control, and I will eat every single damned soul from every last one of you. I will devour you like a kid sucking down apple juice on a hot day. Your very existence will cease as your lives feed me and add to my power.

"You go communicate that to your superiors, if they haven't heard it already. I've got to go. I hope to see you, Faltor, when I come to see Tianna. You strike me as a good kid and I'd hate to turn your empty husk of a body into a walking dead."

I disconnected the call and put my feet up on the table. I expected them to call back again, but I wasn't sure. Five minutes wasn't too long to wait. I could cast a defense spell or two in the meantime.

The mirror rippled again. Faltor was on the line. Someone had cleaned the mirror in between calls, I noticed.

"Faltor!" I exclaimed, before he could speak. "Good to see you! I almost forgot to return this."

"Return...?"

I opened the gate spell again and rolled Lotar's head through, into Faltor's lap. Faltor fainted.

There *is* such a thing as being a little *too* effective. Poor guy. He didn't sign up for this. He probably joined the priesthood for regular meals, indoor work, and a sense of belonging. Possibly all the free hits of divine bliss he could soak up, too. That might have had something to do with it. He didn't expect to be the go-between for his boss and a monster.

Someone pulled Faltor out of frame and I waited patiently. The gentleman who sat down was somewhat older, probably about forty, and wore chain-and-scale armor with a white tabard over it. He opened his mouth to say something and I hung up in his face.

Let 'em wonder.

In the meantime, I told the person on mirror-duty to say it was impossible to reach me.

"If they insist, look helpless. Make sure they understand you want to help, you want to reach me, but you're only mortal. Got that?"

"I will have *no* difficulty with that, my lord!"

I went up the great hall, met Bronze, and we shifted into matching colors, or tried to. She was a mishmash of stripes and blotches, mostly in dark grey and dark green, but my cloak-armor-whatever didn't look any different. Of course, the color-shifting spell changed the color of the light reflecting from the object... and if it doesn't reflect *any* light, there's no light to alter.

Creepy, but also kinda cool.

I decided black would do. I wanted to be as hard to see as possible. Literally, if they never saw us coming, I would be perfectly all right with it. Bronze is generally the more obvious of the two of us.

Bronze paced out the main doors, went around the courtyard, and I signaled the mountain to swing down the drawbridge door to the Kingsway.

A pair of men were already at the head of the Kingsway, inside the tunnel, waiting for us. Bronze saw them first; her head was higher than mine and farther forward. As they pointed jeweled wands at us, Bronze reared, catching me by surprise. I went tumbling backward as she screamed like a banshee escaping from a steam whistle. Fire bloomed like a mushroom cloud as I hit the courtyard and rolled, coming to my feet.

Bronze vanished.

It wasn't instantaneous, but it was incredibly rapid—one second? Two? The curse of heightened senses is a sort of tachypsychia, allowing me to watch without acting, to see the process without the opportunity to stop it. To take in every detail, sear it into my brain with a branding iron, see it in the eye of mind forever.

Two spells struck her and were already at work by the time I rolled to my feet. Either one would have done, but together the effects were quick as lightning.

She frayed around the edges, scattering in all directions, like a sugar cube dropped in water. Her mane and tail puffed away instantly and her outer hide, what would be hair and skin, followed quickly. Then it was alloy muscles and bones, all the metallic flesh of her, radiating outward as though each particle of her being was shot into the far distance. I could feel it, like being sand-blasted, and I skidded backward from the force of it, almost losing my footing again. With all the metal gone, all that remained was a blazing outline of light.

For an instant, it stood there, reared up, pawing the air just as Bronze had— rearing up to interpose her body, rearing up to block the spells aimed at *me*.

The blazing, horse-shaped light expanded, growing like an explosion, diffusing, dissipating, vanishing.

Darkness fell.

I blinked madly, half-blinded, and wiped flakes of metal from my face. Bronze-colored, of course, now that spells no longer disguised her. I stood there for a long moment, staring at the metallic snow all over the courtyard, stirred like dust and moon-glitter on the wind. An image of Bronze glowed on my retinas for a moment before fading.

I sank to my knees, scooping up handfuls of flakes. They scattered on the breeze, flickering in the moonlight. My hands clenched, squeezing the metallic glitter as it sifted between my fingers, impossible to hold.

Somewhere inside myself, there was a place where Bronze lived. From that emptiness, the abyssal gulf of nothing, rose a scream of agony and loss. It ripped the air as it ripped my throat, visibly distorting the atmosphere. Seconds later, it echoed back from the Eastrange, the enraged cry of a wounded beast.

I heard Firebrand, distantly, as though down a long, dark tunnel. I couldn't make out what it was trying to say and I didn't care.

I gathered a large chunk of night with my tendrils and held it before me like a shield. The men in the tunnel aimed their wands at me as I advanced, but nothing happened. Discharged, probably. Disintegration spells are difficult and complicated. It's easier to build a one-shot spell into a talisman, such as a wand, than it is to build an enchanted item to fire successive shots.

Pay for the quality work, that's all I can say.

I crossed the drawbridge and into the tunnel of the Kingsway. I felt my fangs lengthen and my talons extend.

For an instant, everything stopped.

Inside my own head, there was a great hammering, a pounding, a thumping. I recognized it as the trapdoor leading down to my mental basement. Something wanted out and wasn't about to take "no" for an answer.

Things in my head happen at the speed of thought. These two dead men were busy praying, so I had a few seconds.

In my mental study, I regarded the trapdoor. It didn't move, but the thumping was accompanied by a shouting.

"Who are you and what do you want?" I demanded, pointing Firebrand's psychic equivalent at the door.

"It's me! It's you. The better you. We need to talk, and we need to talk right now."

"I have Firebrand, I'm in a bad mood, and if anything is with you, I'll set fire to the whole damn stairway."

"Understood. I'll come up alone."

I unbolted the trapdoor and stepped back, Firebrand already lit and flaming. I noted, with some surprise, my other hand still held Mikkel's wooden sword.

"Come out, close the door, and bolt it," I instructed. The lid lifted, he peeped out, and then he climbed out. He moved slowly, carefully, always keeping his hands in view. Once the trapdoor was closed again and the bolts in place, I gestured him back up against the wall. He kept his hands up.

"What," I asked, "is so important you have to interrupt me as I'm about to start a murder spree?"

"The murder spree," he replied. "The spree, itself. I know how hurt you are. No one knows it better. You're enraged."

"That's not the word I'd use," I told him. "They have wounded a terrible beast and entirely failed to run."

"Yes. You *are* hurt. You have a cold, empty place, a hole in your heart so large you can't help falling into it."

"That's closer," I admitted. "What's it to you?"

"I know you have it in you to be a better man than this. Killing a bunch of worshippers and soldiers won't bring Bronze back. All it will do is continue a cycle of violence that has run for thousands of years between the Lord of Light and the nightlords. You already know it, because I do. Here's a chance to show everyone—including the Lord of Light—that you want to end the conflict. You can use this. You can make Bronze's destruction mean something."

"Are you trying to be my conscience?"

"Someone has to. It's not like you have a cricket with an umbrella on your shoulder."

"That's interesting."

"Yes?"

"Not valid, but interesting. See, I don't think you're my conscience."

"I'm trying to be."

"No. I think you're my fear. I think you're one fear in particular, actually."

"And what would that be?"

"My fear of being less than wonderful. My fear of never quite living up to my potential. I got a lot of guff from family, school, all that stuff when I was

653

younger, always telling me to try harder, to learn more, to go above and beyond, to exceed expectations, and so forth. I think you're my idealized me, the one I can never be no matter how hard I try."

"Even if that's true," he argued, "I can still be a good example. Like a conscience, I can motivate you to be a better person. Maybe not a perfect person, but better than," he looked me up and down and gestured at me, "this."

"You could," I agreed, "except for one thing."

"Name it and I'll find a way to help you."

"I don't want your help. I don't want to be motivated. I don't want to be afraid of not living up to my potential. I'm becoming more and more comfortable with telling the world to go to hell while I go do what I want to do."

"Ah, I see. You'd rather I stayed quietly in the basement?"

"Yes," I admitted, "but you won't stay quiet. This little visit proves it. You'll still bother me from down there." I gripped Firebrand's hilt more tightly. "I have to face my fear."

Firebrand sprayed flames at him. He ducked under the flames, rolling forward, but I kicked him, slamming him back against the wall. Even as he hit the wall, Firebrand set him alight. He screamed and rolled, but not far. I skewered him as he rolled, spearing Firebrand through his back and nailing him face-down to the floor. He clawed at the floor, still on fire.

"I'm hurt," I shouted, over his screams, kicking him viciously, "more than even you can understand, because you're too perfect! And I've reached the point where I don't give a damn!"

I kicked and stomped him again and again until his hands and arms were useless. Then I beat him with Mikkel's wooden sword, ruthlessly, even viciously, until he died.

The flames expired as he crumbled into black sand, divided down into dust, and disappeared into nothingness.

The two men in the mouth of the tunnel weren't magicians, probably not even wizards. They were pawns, sent with magical devices to kill something too powerful for mortals to face. They threw down their useless wands and clutched their medallions, praying to the Lord of Light for the safety of their bodies and souls.

He didn't answer.

I once killed people by accident with a reflexive explosion of tendrils. My tendrils, immaterial though they are, can affect matter. They can be used to pull or to push, obviously. They can also be used to *cut*. Sharper than broken glass, finer than the edge of a razor, they can slash. No one of them can exert great force, so no one of them can cut deeply... but there are many of them, so many of them.

If you slice all around the neck, down to the bone, then slash down both sides of the spine—be sure to separate it from the ribs!—you can grab the lowest point of the spine, break it from the pelvis, and pull the whole spine out like the plastic pull-cord on easy-open packaging.

Done correctly and quickly, the head will see its own body before unconsciousness sets in.

However, I should add that this is a relatively fragile thing, the skull-and-spine combination. It really isn't suitable for beating someone to death. The head is too soft because of the skin and hair; it doesn't make a good weapon. Plus, the spine comes apart far too easily. But the horror on the victims' faces is worth the effort, in my opinion.

Once I shattered the spine-and-skull flail, I fell back on more basic tools. Fingers, talons, teeth, and tendrils.

The remains were broken bone, granules of flesh, and some bodily fluids.

I knelt at the head of the Kingsway and wept bloody tears, each line vanishing into my dark, dead skin as quickly as it appeared. The hole inside was no smaller. It reached just as deep as before. There was an empty place inside me so large nothing could fill it, and so I wept.

How long was it before my eyes fell upon the useless wands? Seconds? Minutes? How long is a second when your soul is torn in two? All I know is I noticed the empty sticks that were once wands. They acted like a crystal in a saturated solution, transforming tears into something terrible.

I descended through the tunnel of the Kingsway, feeling a coldness, the deep roots of an icy rage in my belly. There were no fires, no warmth, no blasts of white-hot fury. There was only the cold and the emptiness and I welcomed it, for it numbed a pain vaster than any I ever knew.

Out of the mouth of the dragon came death, and hell came with him.

I stalked through the city, coldly, boldly, uncaring, walking to and through the enemy lines. They didn't have magical protection for everyone. They already prayed or cast spells of protection for knights, yes, and for priests and officers, but for the rest, all they could do was hope they didn't meet me in person.

They met me in person.

I didn't bother with blood, except as an incidental. I didn't bother with actually stopping the life functions of the meat, either. All I wanted was the lives of everyone who took up arms for the Church of Light. I didn't care who they were or why they were here or where they came from. They were here. They were fighting on the side of the people who kidnapped my granddaughter and killed Bronze. To me, they were already dead inside. I made my perception a reality. So I walked to the front lines, ignoring my own men, and walked through the enemy.

The twenty or so men who held the street died. Those without protection fell immediately to the touch of my tendrils as I jerked their lives loose, snatched them away, poured them down into the never-full pit of a vampire's hunger. The two who were protected I killed with my hands.

At another perimeter station, the wizard screamed and pointed at me as I approached. I deflected his spell, slashed one darkness-gauntleted hand through his neck, and was mildly surprised when his neck parted. I expected only to break his neck, not decapitate him. Startled though I was, I still didn't break stride.

On around, position by position, I worked along the edge of their territory. One knight of light or whatever he was lowered a lance and charged me. I stuck a tendril into his horse's head and sent a thought down it: *STOP.*

The horse skidded to a halt and stood there, a perfect impression of a statue. The knight, on the other hand, nearly came out of his saddle. He dropped his lance and attempted to dismount. I drew Firebrand, brought it down and around, slashing upward as the knight turned to me. Firebrand's edge met the lower edge of his shield, passed up between his legs, and continued through the torso and armor, finally exiting out the top of his head.

Twin pieces of scorched and smoking meat clanged to either side as I walked through the gap. Firebrand made not one comment.

Killing Bronze wounded me, wounded me deeply, and it wasn't something my regeneration could heal.

Wounded beasts are the most dangerous sort, and we are all beasts, deep down, every one of us. Wound us, and the beast rises, eyes like fire, cunning, ruthless, and savage.

Inside the enemy perimeter, I changed my outer garments, donning the armor and tabard of a dead mercenary. My cloak became a doublet, hiding under the outer garments of a soldier of light. A stolen cloak hung mostly over my left shoulder to help disguise the length and hilt of Firebrand. With my human disguise in place, I went up to the market square where most of the reserves camped. There I found it surrounded by a basic alarm spell. It was sensitive to powerful magic—enchanted items or spells—and to several other criteria. It was tailor-made to sound an alarm if I crossed it.

Instead, I broke it. It didn't sound an alarm, but whoever laid down the line of power certainly knew it. I hurried, hopefully avoiding any magical observation as I entered the enemy camp. I killed several sentries on the way, merely to avoid a localized alarm and finger-pointing. Once I was among the tents, lean-tos, and makeshift shelters, I slowed to a walk while sweeping tendrils through everything, draining the lives of every living thing—the things I could feel without seeing, things in tents, under wagons, in shelters of a hundred sorts. Men, guard dogs, horses, rats, roaches, fleas—they all died around me, usually without even waking up.

Someone finally got around to sounding a general alarm. I expected less of a delay when I broke it. I knew I was ruining their automatic alarm, but someone wasn't paying enough attention. As horns started to sound and torches to light, I grabbed the first man out of a tent as he was still rubbing sleep from his eyes.

"You! Come with me! Wake people up! Come on! Rouse 'em, soldier!"

He followed me out of reflex, I think. We stuck heads into tents and exhorted people to get their gear on and fall in. I lashed tents with invisible darkness after we passed by, sucking the life out of everything. Nobody gave us a second look as we hustled along, pausing at every tent to yell into it.

Finally, someone else came along to rouse out soldiers—someone whose job it actually was—and found them lying down, apparently asleep. Empty husks cannot be roused; there's no one in there to rouse. The hollow meat often doesn't know enough to quit, which confuses people.

Eventually, this started a fresh alarm, this one about the presence of the monster. I joined in, calling for priests and wizards, demanding to know why they weren't here. I grabbed another soldier as he went by.

"Why aren't there priests and wizards down here?"

"I don't know! They haven't got here yet!"

"Well, where are they!?"

"Still in their rooms, I'd guess."

I cursed and added, "Fine. We'll go get them! Move!"

He moved, and I went with him.

The first place we went was an inn near the northeast gate. It obviously didn't do a lot of business—most of the traffic went through the western gates—but it was still a large, many-roomed building. It housed a lot of religious types rather than wizards, but that suited me fine. The priests mostly finished waking up and dressing to face evil by the time we arrived. The first few started coming out as we approached, so I killed my guide with a bone-breaking punch to the back of the neck—I may not have a lot of bare-handed finesse, but I have tons of brute force. Even before he fell, I charged the priests in front of the door.

They weren't expecting a direct, physical attack. They were warded against tendrils, certainly, but none of their powers could stop me from simply hacking them to bits. Oh, I could have broken their protective auras, but it would be slow, taking real time and effort for each one. Instead, I slammed into them and drove them back inside. After that, it was merely a matter of claws and flesh in tight, close quarters. A few lifted medallions and their amulets blazed with a white brilliance. It stung, even burned, but if you throw a dead man into a living one it tends to ruin his concentration.

Also, if you rip a man's head off and hand it—still moving—to his companion, the look on both their faces is priceless. Mayhem like that did my black, evil little heart a world of good.

I went through the inn like a dark angel and a tide of blood followed after me. Nothing escaped; no one made it out. I killed every priest, every acolyte, every glowing-aura-wearing piece of meat in the place. I poured their lives, their blood, their deaths into the hole, the yawning chasm, the black, open gulf in my soul where Bronze used to live.

It still wasn't enough.

People were starting to come in the front door—armed and armored, ready to fight. I climbed out an upper window, onto the roof, leaped across the road, crossed the other roof, and climbed down. Once I was an innocent bystander again, I circled around and continued my hunt.

That was a lot of priests, but no wizards. What sort of magic auras did we have around? Surely, they must have wizards, possibly even a magician or two. Where was the highest concentration of magical force in this area of town? The building where they probably held Tianna was right there, but I wasn't ready to force the issue, yet. No, it would be better to mingle, flowing with the crowd, finding anyone wearing a spell or carrying magical items. Quietly kill the spell-wearer, disrupt the magical items, and draw attention to the fact it happened. Lure more people in, find another wizardly type, and repeat.

I'm not the most subtle vampire in history, but in the middle of a hornet's nest of frightened soldiers, I can manage.

I don't know if anyone ever caught on or if they just assumed "the monster" was roaming freely among them, seen only by the dead. I don't much care, either. If they were going to paint a picture of a black-eyed monster with a mouthful of fangs and long black claws, it was their own fault if they didn't look for a wiry fellow in their own colors.

When the moon was a hands-breadth above the western mountains, I switched tactics. The sun would rise—well, the gods would light the sun again—in an hour or two and I wanted the Church's high command to have something else to deal with. I returned to the perimeter and the now-abandoned positions.

The few people who survived my walk along the perimeter either fell back to the buzzing hive of their main camp or were recalled. All I know for certain is they didn't like sitting on a battlefront alone.

But the empty bodies were still there.

There's a certain amount of energy loss when I eat something. I can't devour a human's vitality and give someone else the same amount. Whether it's an inefficiency in vampire metabolism or the inevitable effects of digestion, I'm not certain. But I consumed more on that night than the lives of the men at the front line. I sucked out the vital force of a thousand more within their camp as I wandered through the night.

I'm a lousy necromancer, all things considered. If I have to, I can make a dead man get up and walk. On the other hand, quite a lot of these bodies weren't dead. Technically. They were empty, completely lacking in any animating force, and were going to die.

I snaked tendrils into every beating heart, every breathing corpse. Vital energy flowed into them, pulsing down dark strands, filling the flesh with temporary life and purpose. Every breathing body rose to its feet and followed me as I walked through the fallen. A dozen here, five at the next, only two at the next, then another six... hundreds of walking dead, or not quite dead, followed after me, each towed along on a dark, leash-like tendril.

We walked among the empty, dying bodies and I gathered up those who hadn't quite finished, pouring into them a dark and terrible strength. They would kill, striking with all the power of mortal flesh and bone, tearing themselves apart with the force of their blows, until their bodies could no longer hold the energies within. The dead rose and walked, and I led my temporary army to recruit them all.

The defensive positions of the Karvalen forces merely watched, staying well back and staying still. I wonder what they were thinking.

Morning started to creep up on me, so I sent my undead horde—my *zombie* horde; I'm a vampire, so I'm allowed to raise legions of zombies, aren't I? — toward the center of the Church-held territory. Laid into them was the instruction to kill, pure and simple. They would try, of course, and would probably kill or wound about half their own number before being hacked apart. At least the survivors would have the delightful memory of chopping up people who were once on their side.

It still wasn't enough. It would never be enough. There was no such thing as enough. I couldn't kill them in sufficient quantities to ever take away the pain. I couldn't harm the Lord of Light sufficiently to heal me. All I could do was kill and terrify and punish those who followed him, at least until the sunrise.

It would have to do.

I returned to the mountain, called T'yl, gave him the expended wands, and shut myself away from everyone I didn't want to kill.

Wednesday, June 15th

Mary came back today, delighted at the tailored adjustments to her jumpsuit
and the fresh powerpack for her laser. She came into my quarters and bounced
into the bathroom.

"I'm home!" she declared, and immediately lost her bubbly good cheer. She
came over to me, ignoring the way the waterfall soaked her, and put her arms
around me.

I sat under the falling water, crying.

I suppose I could call it weeping, or shedding tears, or mourning, but let's be
blunt. I was crying. Bronze was the most... she was... Bronze was part of me in
a very literal way and they destroyed her. You can lose a hand, or a leg, or an eye
and it might be something like this, but it wouldn't be the same. I was hurt. I was
diminished. Explaining it is impossible, but I tried, just as Mary tried to
understand.

"If I hadn't made a special road, just for her, they couldn't have ambushed us
right there..."

"If, if, if," Mary said, gently. "You can drive yourself insane with ifs. No.
They were going to kill you and kill her, even kill me, and Dantos, and Tianna—
everyone. It's clear they don't care who they hurt, as long as they destroy this
place. So, no matter what, we resist."

"They have Tianna," I told her. "She's a hostage. And maybe she's dead by
now."

"I don't know about that. We'll have to ask."

I leaned my head back against the wall and closed my eyes.

"I'm so tired."

"I can imagine."

"I'm angry, and I've killed thousands to avenge Bronze. It isn't enough. I still
want to kill everything. Show me a row of throats and I will. But... right now
I'm tired. I'm tired of fighting everything, resisting everything, being the upright
guy. I want a rest. I want to go back to our farmhouse and tell everyone to leave
me alone, but I can't because a bunch of paranoid vampires burned it down."

"I know," Mary said, softly. "I know. We'll take a vacation. Let's go. We
can pop over to Apocalyptica and you can do some universe-hopping from there,
find us a nice world to settle on, all that stuff."

"Apocalyptica?"

"The post-nuclear-holocaust world? The one where you put Diogenes in
charge?"

"Oh. Good name, I guess."

"Thank you. So what are we waiting for? Let's go."

"They have Tianna. I can't leave while they have her."

"And if they've killed her?"

"Then I can't leave until I crush a religion."

"Fair enough, I suppose. All right." Mary stepped out of the waterfall and
made a quick brushing movement. She was clean and dry. "You take a brief
break and pull yourself together. I'll see what's going on out there and get back to
you. Okay?"

"I'm not going anywhere."

I didn't stay exactly there. I eventually crawled out of the water and dressed. I didn't go far after that, just to the bedroom to lie there in the dark.

It still seems strange to me. Darkness, I mean. During the day, I'm as dependent on light as any mortal man.

Mary came back after a while. I don't know how long. I smelled food, though, as her movement wafted air from the living room to the bedroom.

"I see you didn't bother with lunch," she observed.

"I wasn't aware anyone brought it."

"Would you have eaten it if you had?"

"Probably not," I admitted.

"I thought as much." She settled to the edge of the slab that served as a bed. "Do you want to talk about it?"

"No."

"Okay. Can I borrow Firebrand?"

"Firebrand can decide for itself."

"Thanks." She leaned over and kissed me, softly. "You'll be okay. It just takes a while."

I didn't say anything. I'm sure she's lost people in her life. I'm sure she's lost people she loved. But it's never the same for anyone. It's always a new and different pain, even if it's the same loss. It's like being cut in half and still forced to live.

I wanted Bronze back.

Mary rose and glided out, silently. I heard the whisper a brief psychic conversation, then Firebrand directed a thought at me.

Boss?

What?

I'm going to go help Mary kill some stuff. Will you be all right without me?

No. But I won't be all right with you here, either. It doesn't matter.

I'm sorry, Boss. I loved her too, in my own way.

Go away.

The outer door closed with a grinding thump. I lay there in the dark and hurt. Even Johann never managed a pain like this.

Someone dealt with the food, switching old dishes out for new. During this, I felt someone enter the room and move close to me. Something soft pressed against my arm. I opened an eye and, in the light from the other room, saw Caris standing by the bed, putting a stuffed toy beside me. It was a simple thing, meant to be a stuffed man, I suppose. Then I saw someone had stitched a face on it, including a big smile and fangs.

Caris hugged my arm for a moment, then ran from the room.

I cradled the doll in one arm and wondered if it could bandage a broken heart. I doubted it.

Mary slid into the bedroom, skidding to a halt, talking rapidly. She smelled of smoke and blood.

"Come with me immediately you need to see this and help fix it!"

A vague sense of urgency penetrated my black mood.

"What is it?"

"Tianna! Come help *now!*"

Slowly, I floated up through the gloom into a more alert state.

"Tianna? What's wrong?" I asked, climbing up from the bed.

"Come with me!" Mary sprinted from the room.

She means it, Boss! Move! came from Firebrand as it bounced at her rapidly-departing hip.

I'm not sure what else could have gotten me up and moving. I still didn't feel like doing anything—depression is like that—but if it was Tianna, it was important. I lumbered along after Mary and realized she was outdistancing me. I leaned into it and ran after her, pumping my arms and bearing down. I didn't close the distance, but I did follow closely enough to keep from losing her.

Mary ran right out through the mountain's southeastern gate and sprinted through the city. I recognized where we were going—right into the territory controlled by the Church of Light. It was late afternoon, but the sunset wasn't my concern. Getting killed by bunches of troops when I'm mortal, now that's a concern.

We didn't encounter any. We did pass a lot of people who saluted, though. I started to wonder what was going on.

Mary almost came to a stop in front of the building I thought of as the headquarters; making the turn required slowing her headlong pace. Two grey sashes stood out front and they saluted. We both staggered in, panting for breath. Call it a two-mile sprint. Downhill all the way, sure, but I'm overweight. I think I have a right to be out of breath.

She led me upstairs to one of the third-floor rooms. Blood was all over the floor, most of it from the armored men and the priests lying in various states of dead. T'yl was kneeling with a pair of knights—I recognized Sir Varicon of the Shields, but the other one was *Seldar!*—as they worked on someone lying on the floor.

"Got him," Mary gasped. Seldar nodded at me and pointed at the person lying on the floor. T'yl moved, gesturing me over. The person on the floor was Tianna. Someone had cut her throat and done a damn fine job of it, too. From the look of it, it was a right-handed person standing behind her, using a short, heavy blade of great sharpness. The cut went through veins and arteries and windpipe, severing muscles and tendons, almost all the way back to the spine.

Whoever did the first aid did it quickly, before she died from blood loss. Her veins and arteries were welded together and no longer spurting. However much of the blood on the floor was hers, at least she wasn't adding any more to it. Her windpipe was at least tack-welded, as was the esophagus, to open them up properly. Breathing wasn't a problem. They hadn't paid any attention to the muscles, yet, since those aspects of her injury weren't life-threatening.

The real problem was the blood loss. She was pale, almost chalky. Her breathing was fast and light and her pulse was racing. The only thing I knew to do for her was tell her spleen and bone marrow to get busy—and to thank goodness I looked up where the spleen is. Then I formed a globe of force over her nose and mouth to pull in oxygen, push out nitrogen and carbon dioxide. But getting the oxygen to the rest of her body was a job for her blood, most of which seemed to be all over the floor.

Blood carries oxygen in the red blood cells. What if I build a spell to target red blood cells and mimic what they do? Would that work? It shouldn't interfere with the red blood cells doing their job and it might even help. I gave it a shot, hoping it would at least double the oxygen-carrying effect of whatever blood she had left.

Her color didn't improve, but she did seem to breathe more easily.

"My lord," Varicon began, and Mary slapped her hand over his mouth.

"If she dies because you interrupted him, we're all dead," she whispered. "Speak only if spoken to and try not to attract his attention." He didn't even acknowledge her; he simply shut up. Wise man.

I considered Tianna very carefully. She seemed to be surviving, at least for the moment, but blood loss and shock can kill hours after the injury. Her body was working at full tilt to try and rectify the situation, but it had to draw on her own resources—amplified, of course, by magic—to do it. I wasn't sure she had the necessary reserves. At least someone had already elevated her legs to concentrate her remaining blood in her torso and head.

I sure as hell wasn't giving her any of my blood. Not only was I not sure if she and I shared a blood type, I didn't even want to think about how it would look to Sparky. To say nothing of the possibilities of a descendant of two avatars being a nightlord Priestess of the Flame. Oh, and I almost forgot—my otherself is worshiped as a god of fire by the sea-people. Double fire jeopardy. The possibilities boggle the mind, and mine is boggled enough.

I texted Diogenes about saving someone from massive blood loss. This is not really my area of expertise. I focus more on *causing* massive blood loss. But he had a solution.

"Don't move her," I ordered. "Lend her vitality, operate her heart and lungs manually, whatever you have to do to keep her alive until I get back." I cleared people away from a doorway, scratched on the stonework around it, and had four grey sashes lend me some magical muscle. The makeshift gate flickered into being, flushed into my upstairs gate room, and I stepped a couple miles. Much faster than running.

Then I did some running, out of the gate room, around a curve, and into my workroom. I flipped open the shift-box, grabbed three bags of milky fluid and some tubing, and ran right back to my gates. Up here, I had plenty of stored power, so opening a gate wasn't the hard part. The hard part was targeting it. They still hadn't taken down the defensive, anti-scrying spells around the building!

Cursing, I targeted a doorway across the street and opened the gate. Even with the run up the stairs, the whole process took far less time than sprinting both ways.

I half-knelt, half-fell to my knees beside Tianna and started hunting for a vein. I handed a plastic sack to Varicon and told him to stand up and hold it. He did so without hesitation or question.

It sometimes bothers me how people in Karvalen will simply obey me when I give them a direct order. I'd blame the Demon King, but he stayed mostly on the other side of the Eastrange, I hear. I'm not sure if it's a case of royal perogatives, religious awe, or scary monster. I'm not even sure which of the three I find least disturbing.

Meanwhile, I kept hunting for a vein. You'd think, as a vampire, I could insert an IV needle with my eyes shut. I mean, it's a vein. It's got blood in it. I should be able to do all sorts of things with veins and arteries and whatnot, right? Wrong. Inserting an IV is a skill, and one I don't have, no matter how much of a blood-sucking monster I am. I can open a blood vessel and get the blood out, but I at that moment I needed the exact opposite.

I finally gave up on doing it by hand and used magic. With the proper spells as tools, it's simplicity itself to isolate a vein, open it up, insert a tube, and have the vein close itself around the tube.

With one bag working its way into her, I handed Varicon a second one and plugged the other IV into Tianna's other arm.

T'yl was sitting on the floor with Tianna's head in his lap, eyes closed, concentrating. He was working his magic on her neck, flesh-welding everything the knife separated back together. If she survived, everything should heal up nicely. At worst, she might have an interesting scar. He was also helping maintain her vital functions, which suited me fine. If he could keep it up for another twenty minutes, everything should be great.

Mary raised a hand without speaking. I looked at her and realized she was the only person in the room willing to make eye contact. Everyone else found something else to look at.

It made me angry. Not at them, but at myself for being... well... me. They didn't do anything to me. On the contrary, I should be grateful for all their efforts at trying to save the life of my granddaughter. And I would be grateful. Later.

"Yes, Mary."

"What are you putting in her?"

"Diogenes says it's a blood substitute he uses in an early stage of his cloning process, but it works perfectly well in adult humans, too."

"Oh. Is it tasty?"

"I have no idea. Now, do you want to explain to me how she got her throat cut?"

"Not really."

I drafted some people in the hall to hunt around in other rooms and drag in more furniture. After stacking some tables and chairs, I let Varicon off the hook as an IV stand. I hung the third bag, flesh-shaping my way into a vein in Tianna's ankle.

"She's doing better," T'yl announced. Her color hadn't improved, but her pulse slowed slightly. I kept telling myself the synthetic blood substitute wasn't red, so her color wasn't a gauge of her health. But I lie a lot, so I didn't reassure myself.

"Good."

At least I was feeling something besides overwhelming sadness. It was a coldness, an emptiness, completely unlike sadness. On the scale from happy to sad, this was all the way through sad and as distant from it as happy was.

"Mary. Come with me, please." I showed her out of the room and down the hall. We occupied another room, this one somewhat less bloody, and I closed the door. "Please tell me what happened."

She did. It wasn't too complicated a story, really. She organized an assault on the place. It was easy; there wasn't much in the way of resistance, so getting to it was easy. T'yl and half the wizards in town put magical defenses on the troops. Troops led by Torvil, Kammen, and Seldar went in through the ground-floor doors.

"What are the Big Three doing here?" I asked.

"I called for help."

"And they came on such short notice?"

"Oh, yes. I don't know if they asked the Queen, if the Queen sent them, or if they decided to show up on their own, but they seemed awfully eager to help."

"I love those guys."

"I think I do, too," she added. "They also brought friends, a bunch of other really big men in armor. They're still out hacking apart anything that doesn't salute your banner fast enough, with Dantos' and Beltar's men scrambling like mad in their wake, trying to keep up. Those guys are murder machines."

"I know, but I tried like hell to make them *ethical* murder machines. So, they went in on the ground floor. Then what?"

"I went in through a third-floor window. While the fighting was going on downstairs and coming up, I was looking for Tianna. She was out cold and tied to a chair. They also had guards in the room with her. They didn't even threaten when I opened the door, just cut her throat on the spot. Please unclench your hands!"

I did so, noticing how I'd cut my palms open. Like my teeth, my talons work perfectly well during the day, too. I stopped the bleeding and started them healing.

"All right. Then what?"

"I screamed for help while I killed guards, then started repairs on the arteries. About then the other guy—Varicon—came in and I drafted him as a healer to finish stopping the bleeding. Then Seldar came in and took over. I may have saved her life, but I think most of the post-bloodletting credit should go to Seldar. He's amazing at gluing people back together."

"Lots of practice."

"I guess. Seldar suggested I go get you—actually, he snapped it at me like a throwing knife past my head—so I decided I might ought to do it. That man gets results!"

"I know. And T'yl?"

"I guess he came in after I left. Maybe Seldar sent for him?"

"Probably. Did it at any point occur to you that you might be risking Tianna's life by assaulting the place?"

"Yes. Please don't kill me. Hear me out, at least."

"I have no desire to kill you. I'm too far past sad to be angry. I don't know what to call what I'm feeling, but it isn't anger, and it isn't directed at you. Besides, I always want to hear you out. Please go ahead."

"The Church of Light is a religious organization that wants to eradicate all other religions, right?"

"Right."

"They wouldn't let her live even if you offered to trade them the city for her life."

"I know."

"You do?" she asked, startled.

"I tried to get them to see her as a talisman, a tool to keep me at bay. If I could inflict that sort of thinking on them, they wouldn't kill her until they had no other choice. At the time, I thought it would give me time to find out more, gather intelligence, come up with a plan." I rubbed my forehead and leaned against the wall. "Then they disintegrated Bronze and... things... got... out of hand. I lost focus."

Mary came over to me and pinned me against the wall with a hug.

"I'm sorry they killed your spirit animal," she said. It struck me how accurate her statement was. If I had to have a totem or whatever, you'd think it was a bat, or a wolf, or some other stereotypical vampire-related thing. Maybe even a dragon, like Dracula. But Bronze was very much the better part of me. She gave me strength in ways I will never comprehend and will sorely miss.

"You know, that may be the best definition of her I've ever heard?"

"Glad to hear it. And I'm glad your granddaughter is still alive."

"So am I. Do I need to discuss with you the level of unpleasantness involved if she had died during the attack?"

"No. I have some vague idea. Please don't explain."

"I won't. Mainly because I don't have a good idea about it, myself. But I do want to know whose idea it was."

"Dantos," Mary said, instantly. "He's running the war in the city, with input from Beltar and Seldar and anyone else he respects. You did sort of leave him in charge."

"Sort of," I agreed. "I assume there was no other way to get Tianna out of their clutches?"

"I guess not, but I'm a thief, not a strategist. From what I understand, he was worried about them getting set for something like sacrificing her. I think it came down to storming the place before they were ready to kill her ritually."

"So she was going to die *unless* you stormed in."

"That's what I understand. Certain death on one hand, possibility of life on the other."

"Then I've got no reason to be upset," I decided. *Except with myself, for wallowing in self-pity when I should have been out helping rescue my granddaughter!* Which I did not say aloud, and Firebrand did not repeat.

"You have no idea how glad I am to hear that," Mary said, sincerely. "So, what do you want to do now? Do you want to go hunt for a vacation spot?"

"No. I want to find every temple, every church, every shrine to the Lord of Light and contaminate it with something radioactive. Then I want to find every prince, every duke, every baron, knight, and peasant who ever took up arms on his behalf and behead them. Then I want to find every reference to him in every manuscript, folio, or obelisk and obliterate it. I want to kill the thing they call a god."

"Really?"

"Yes. Only…" I paused and sighed. "I want to kill an energy-state being on another plane of existence and I don't know how." I ground the heels of my hands into my eyes. "So much of me is angry, but so much of me is numb, too."

"It gets better. Sort of. It takes time."

"Maybe. But so much of my life revolves around being angry, now. It surprises me how much it always has. Bronze got angry when occasion called for it, but it seems she was the patient one, the stable one. Now I'm just me, and there's nothing left of me but the angry parts and big, empty spaces where Bronze used to be."

"There's more to you than angry and empty," Mary assured me, pressing her head against my chest. "You're complicated. Don't be afraid of the angry parts. You're only angry about things that deserve it."

"I'm not so sure."

"Maybe it's because you're so afraid of being the Demon King, you deny that part of you even exists."

"Oh, I know it exists. I struggle with it every day. You've seen the hatchway to the downstairs."

"Yes. And that tells me you don't accept it."

"I'm not sure I should accept it. I should be a better person."

"Even if it means not being a whole person?"

That stung. It hurt because it poked me in the raw places where Bronze used to be, and it hurt because she might be right. I didn't answer, but Mary didn't insist on one. Instead, she changed the subject.

"Right now, you have an invaded city. What do you want done?"

"I think I should refer this to Lissette. She's the Queen."

"And you're the boots on the ground. Besides, Dantos already spoke to her."

"He did?"

"Of course. The Baron was killed in the fighting, so he's in nominal charge. He says she left it up to him how to use the powers of the Demon King."

"Oh. Interesting."

"I suspect he'll be the first plainsman to be given a noble title, provided he keeps the city."

"I'm for it," I agreed. "Wait. What about Nothar?"

"He's out fighting, somewhere, last I heard. Seems he was more than a little upset about the Church of Light kidnapping his girlfriend. Some say he had a hot date scheduled."

"Solstice ceremony," I said, nodding. "Yes, that makes sense. But shouldn't he be taking command as the new Baron of Karvalen?"

"I doubt he's interested. At least, not right now. He wouldn't confuse the chain of command in the middle of a battle."

"He's a good man," I admitted. "All right. Let me think a minute." Mary stopped pinning me to the wall with her hug and moved beside me, holding my arm.

"All right," I repeated. "Help Dantos and Beltar sort out the city. Call Lissette and let her know what's happened here—make sure she stays up to date. She's the Queen, after all."

"Dantos has someone on report duty, but I'll double-check. May I ask what you'll be doing? She's going to ask. You know she will."

"I'll be trying to find a way to kick the Lord of Light in his celestial orbs."

It's one thing to say it, another thing to do it. *Finding* them was the real problem. But I needed to do something. I can't curl up in a corner and cry forever. I don't work that way.

So, how do you crack the nuts of a fake deity? Sadly, there only seems to be one way to attack these things—through their followers. That involves finding them, so I rang up Torvil on a pocket mirror and asked for some non-priestly prisoners. He delivered them within the hour.

I will now confess to being something of a bastard.

I asked my prisoners where they were from. Nobody wanted to answer. So I slowly and carefully crushed the life out of one of them, one piece of flesh at a time. I literally crushed him into screaming paste before their eyes.

Oh, but it felt so good! A guilty pleasure, to be sure, but one I enjoyed so much!

Then I separated my prisoners and asked them, one by one, where they were from, about the organizational structure of the Church of Light, the extent of the following, and so on. Is it really surprising I got my answers? I don't think so. These men weren't radical terrorist suicide bombers. They weren't even fanatical followers. They hoped for a glorious eternity in the afterlife, but they only hoped—they weren't certain. They were foot soldiers sent off on a war they didn't understand, and were now in the hands of a ruthless and powerful enemy. As far as each of them was concerned, a god might be on his side, but I was in his face.

My understanding of the Church of Light has always been a little shaky. I've tended to try and cram it into religious structures I'm familiar with. And, within limits, I think I can.

The Church has a *deveas*, an absolute authority, a commander in chief. It also has a *prophate*, someone who speaks for their god when it's needful for god to say something directly. These two are the very top of the pyramid. Whether there are always two or if the *prophate* is sometimes also the *deveas*, I still don't know; this religion isn't as open about its inner workings as some. I get the impression the *deveas* is more of an executive while the *prophate* is more of a holy man. I'm not sure the two really ever go together. Then again, Beltar does double duty. It might depend on the so-called deity.

Below them are the Patriarchs—clergy that rule over kingdoms, or rule over the Church of Light within a kingdom. From there, they have a variety of lesser clergy in a hierarchy much like any other pyramid scheme, from priest in a church to High Priest of a city on up to Patriarch of a kingdom and up to *deveas* of the Church.

The Hand, on the other hand, is not part of the main organization. They're a select group and have nothing to do with the day-to-day shearing of the sheep and tending of the flock. They're organized under what I think of as a Cardinal, who reports directly to the *deveas* and *prophate*. Sadly, how the Hand is organized, as well as any other branches of Church organization, is not something the average worshipper knows much about.

But they did know where the troops came from.

I cranked up my scrying mirror—regretting again the loss of my sand table—and did some searching. According to the captives, the armies were from four city-states in the regions east of the Sea of Grass. Talmerian was the main one, closest to the lake where the canal ended. Troops from the other three—Palmerian, Solacian, and Kalmerian—gathered at Talmerian as a staging point.

The cities were in an irregular box pattern, each city at a point, with the sides ranging from thirty to fifty miles long. Lots of farms and supporting villages stretched between them.

It was extremely tempting to drop a nuke on each of them. When the invading troops withdrew—and they would, if they weren't doing it already—they could go home and draw their own conclusions. Word would get around. I found it extremely hard to resist the temptation. I really didn't care about the cities or about inflicting apocalyptic damage.

I did care about two things.

First, those cities had children in them. They didn't do anything to deserve being converted to blast shadows and vapor. They're *children*. Their parents might be asking for sudden atomic death, but the kids were blameless.

Second—and a minor concern at the moment—was the political aspect. The Lord of Shadow and the Lord of Light can have an argument, even a fight, but doubling the size of a local lake because the city turned to plasma and ashes has political ramifications. That sort of thing is for Lissette to decide, not me. I gave up the power—excuse me; I gave up the *right*—to make those decisions, and I desperately wished to keep it that way.

It's an awful thing to be a nuclear superpower when nobody knows it. I don't get nearly the credit I deserve for my patience and self-restraint.

So, no nukes.

Probably.

What does that leave? Targeting the Church of Light, specifically? How? Really *tiny* nukes? That's the problem with big explosions. They have no discrimination. They can't be aimed at part of a population. There is always collateral damage.

I shook my head. I need a better approach.

How to target only the Church of Light? To do that, I need something common to every single structure, preferably every single priest. The priests all wear those medallions, but even if I kickstart them all into an excited state, they'll only get sick over weeks or months of time. Besides, building a spell to do that over the entire world—repeatedly! —would require it to channel and focus energies far beyond my capacity.

Now, if I had a nexus, I could build a spell to soak up power and reinforce itself, make it grow until it was powerful enough to handle that kind of load… but this world doesn't *have* nexuses. Magic works differently here.

Could I go back to Mary's Earth? If I build such a spell at a major nexus, I could bring it back with me. I might even be able to build it, charge it, open a gate, and fire it through the gate without ever leaving the nexus point. Johann did something like it when he was trying to kill me from his homeworld.

I'll save it for later. Let's see what I can manage without calling in the equivalent of a nuke.

Okay, back to basics. In this world, what makes a religion? There are, from the ground up, worshippers, priests, an organization, and a supernatural entity. There are subtle gradations within these categories, but those are the basics. For example, among the worshippers as a group, you have worshippers who show up just for the high holy days, devout worshippers, worshippers who only go to church because the spouse does, and so on.

In this case, the supernatural entity—the energy-state being on the energy plane—is the one who really has it in for me. Killing it is tricky. I'd have to find a way to counter all of its accumulated force, and that's likely to be a ridiculous amount of energy. Nuking it is unlikely to be effective. Annoying, certainly, but not effective.

So that leaves the organization, the priests, and the worshippers.

The worshippers are the foundation of the Church and the meat and potatoes of the entity. Remove the worshippers and the entity will slowly starve. Unfortunately, killing several thousand worshippers—possibly several tens or hundreds of thousands—is difficult if you don't want to accidentally wipe out all life in the vicinity. Worse, new worshippers are relatively easy to come by. This leads to an ongoing campaign of killing them off as quickly as they can be recruited... or annihilating all life capable of contributing energy to the entity.

Another major problem with the Lord of Light is he's fat and happy, sitting on big reserves of power, and can afford to have a protracted famine.

I could organize a mass exodus from Rethven and Karvalen. I could relocate thousands upon thousands of people through magical gates. I could put them on another world—an uninhabited world—and lock the door behind them. Then I could destroy this one. But, as before, the problem is rescuing all the children...

If I don't have the tools to kill the entity, and starving it to death is too much of a project, that leaves me with the organization and the priests.

Priests are high-value targets. They spend a lot of time in study, prayer, meditation, and ritual, attuning themselves to the entity. They can draw a trickle of power from it through their prayers. I think they can contribute a greater fraction of their personal energies to the entity when they're not pulling power out of it—they act as food, but also as power expenditures. Priests also make up the organization of the entity on this plane. And, best of all, priests are willing servants to the thing, old enough to make their own decisions and to be held accountable for them.

The organization of the church is less tangible. It has tangible manifestations, though. Somewhere, they have a main temple—a capitol building for the religion. They have lesser temples and churches and shrines, as well, acting as substations for the power network.

Killing priests will slow down the spread of the religion. Destroying structures will undermine it, make it seem a second-rate power. Both, taken together, may give even an energy-state being cause for concern. Eventually, anyway.

I rang up Torvil again.

"Do we happen to have some priests?"

The top of the mountain is basically a pointy bit, as one might expect from a conical structure. The mountain was busy with other things—no doubt reconstructing a good deal of damage—but it spared me enough effort to flatten out the top, raise up the sides, and build me a sort of altar arrangement. I let it work on that while I went down to my geode gate room.

The crystals were all discharged. There was barely any power in them at all.

What the hell?

Closer examination showed they were perfectly intact, but they were expending energy as fast as it came in. Something was tapping them for energy, so they weren't charging. It was the mountain itself, sucking up energy to make up for the power drain.

Power drain?

My next question was similar to the previous one, but with somewhat more obscene language.

The power source for the mountain is a magical matter-conversion reactor producing enough energy to not only heat the place, but give it a semblance of actual life. The only things comparable to it are an open major nexus or a Krell nuclear furnace. What in the *hell* could it be using so much power for? Major repairs? Maybe restoring itself in the west? It did crack the western road through the Darkwood, cutting off everything west of that point. And isn't it building a city with a giant arena in the northern Eastrange? That's a lot of work and it could require a lot of power. It was also rearranging large pieces of terrain, building tunnels all along the eastern canal and covering them over with wildlife bridges. So, yes, it could be just that busy.

Or was the mountain using the power? What if something found a way to tap it?

I checked with the stone. Yes, the reactor was working perfectly. Yes, everything was all right. Yes, it was using all the power it could get.

This eased my mind considerably, although not completely. Finding out what was going on would have to wait. While yes-or-no answers are relatively quick and easy—only taking a minute or two per question—asking a geological formation anything resembling "Why?" "What for?" or "Doing what?" takes considerably longer. I had other fish to gut just then.

Without the power reserves in my gate room, my options were sharply limited. I needed a plan that didn't require launching long-range spells. My original idea was to use the medallions of the captured priests as resonators, build a high-energy discharge spell tuned to them, and launch it at various cities all over the world. It would then detonate, so to speak, inside those cities and affect any other medallion like the ones I used as resonators. Those medallions would then be subject to a rapid energy input—they would explode. The heat of vaporized gold and the resulting concussion effect would be pretty much in the center of the chest, killing the wearer.

Now I couldn't do that. Well, yes, I could, but not as many times. I planned to use the priests wearing the amulets as human sacrifices. Without the power reserves, this method was drastically limited in the number of shots it could fire, though. It's a truism that anything you do repeatedly will be observed, analyzed, and countered. If I didn't hit everywhere, there would be survivors who caught on. It's like evolution in action. Pour antibiotics into a bacterial culture. If you don't kill all the germs, the survivors are more resistant to the antibiotics. Same thing here, only with priests instead of bacteria. They have a number of similarities.

I recognized the new feeling: Frustration. It was a much hotter feeling than the cold, unpleasant thing twisting in my chest, and much more familiar.

Well, fine. So much for my mountain-peak sacrificial altar. Fat lot of good that would do.

The sun went down, I cleaned up, and a bunch of grey sashes dragged a bunch of mouthy priests into my workroom.

I sent the grey sashes out and closed the door. They didn't need to see this.

Morning started sneaking up on me while I sat there with the dismembered corpses. No bloodstains, of course, but enough other fluids leaked out to make the place a mess.

I will kill this celestial son of a bitch. I don't know how. I don't know when. If I can find a biological warfare agent to target a religious viewpoint, I'll use it. If I can find a radiation that only kills light-worshippers, I'll generate it. If I can find anything, any weapon at all, that kills energy beings or their worshippers, I'll find a way to apply it.

I'll kill it. I swear I will.

I whisked my body clean, but my soul was still swimming in it.

Thursday, June 16th

I sat in the dark, in my bedroom, thinking about what to do. Trying to think about what to do. I kept coming back to the big empty place inside, circling it like a toy boat helplessly circling the drain.

Caris came to visit again. It made me wonder why they let her in when most people would rather stick their arm in a badger's den than bother me. Do they not care? Or do they think children have a special immunity? Probably the latter...

It was a strange visit, because she brought two and a fraction friends. The other two were a boy and a girl. The girl was a little older. The boy was Tallin, Seldar's son, toddling along with Caris and holding her hand. The fraction wasn't actually there, being a ghost. I recognized him immediately. He was the boy she played with, the one who was cut down during the invasion. Mikkel, that was his name. She held his invisible hand and led him in. He didn't seem to mind.

The four-ish of them came into my bedroom—Caris and Tallin boldly, the rest less so—and lined up.

"What is it?" I sighed, sitting up and swinging my legs over the edge.

Tallin unwrapped a cloth. He had a wooden horse. He didn't say anything, just held it out to me. It was a good carving and well-worn from handling. No doubt it was a favorite toy.

"Thank you," I said, finally. I accepted the toy. It was about the size of my open hand. "That's very kind of you."

Caris came up to me, hugged my knee and put her head on my leg. Tort did something like that, once. I stroked her hair.

"Sire?" asked the other girl.

"Hmm?"

"Caris says we can't see her friend because he's a ghost, Sire."

"Probably."

"Can you help, Sire?"

"You want to see him?"

"Yes, Sire. If you please, Sire."

I regarded the ghostly Mikkel. He looked back at me. He didn't seem to be losing cohesion. He was only a faint figure to me, of course—it was daytime, but the room was quite dark. He seemed relatively stable.

"Did you see a nice lady in grey?" I asked. He nodded. "Did she want you to go with her?" He nodded again. "And why didn't you?" He shook his head and didn't answer.

I'm not clear on the rules, if spirits have the option to stay or go, but I'm not exactly an expert on the Grey Lady, either. She doesn't seem the type to insist if you're adamant about staying.

"All right. Come here and let me have a look at you."

His structure—from a magical perspective—was somewhat tangled. Fairly typical for a ghost, I suppose. Some of the tangles were more like actual knots, tying off loose ends which would have caused him to dissipate. A close examination showed no leakage at all. Someone tied off his magical structure. It was more a tourniquet than stitches, but it worked.

"Caris?" I asked. She looked up at me. "Did you help your friend?" She nodded and put her head back down on my leg, squeezing my knee harder.

Well. Everyone has a talent, I suppose. Caris the Necromancer, Maker of Ghosts, Lady of Spirits, and Madam of Manifestations. It could be a career. If nothing else, she could get a job at the Temple of the Grey Lady in nothing flat. I made a mental note to suggest apprenticing to what's-his-name, the necromancer magician-friend of T'yl's. Norad? Or was the other guy the necromancer? I forget.

"Caris. Watch what I do. Okay?"

Caris watched intently—not letting go of my knee—while I carefully untangled some of the ghost's life-strands, tied them off properly, and ran them around to each other. I was hampered by the need to do it with spells, rather than with my tendrils, but at least I knew what I was doing. If we compare spiritual energy to blood, at least he wasn't bleeding.

Okay, maybe I'm not *too* lousy a necromancer.

I also wove a spell around him and tied it into some of his lesser soul-strands. It was a passive thing, partly based on an Ascension Sphere. It would absorb some energies to power itself, but also convert a little to vitality, replenishing the gradual loss that comes from simply existing. He was still radiating energy simply by being, much like a person burns calories whether he's awake, asleep, or comatose. Left unchecked, it would deplete him, so he needed to eat something to restore himself. The hybrid spell-enchantment would take care of it.

How do regular ghosts cope? They need to eat something, obviously. Do they draw power from something—a physical object, or a location? Or do they learn to consume other energies? I may look into it, someday, but I don't want to try quizzing a hungry ghost. It doesn't seem polite.

"There you go," I told them. "Caris? Did you see what I did?"

She nodded again and took the ghost's hand. She obviously saw him just fine. If the light was better, I doubted I could see him without effort. Of course, at night he would be a glowing figure to my eyes.

"We can't see him, Sire," the girl reminded me. She was trying to be as polite as possible, calling me "Sire" constantly. She wasn't doing too badly for a seven-year-old.

"Give him time. He hasn't been a ghost for long," I assured her.

"Oh."

"Now run along, please."

They scampered out. As they left, Mary came in. She sat on the edge of the bed as I lay down again.

"How are you feeling?"

"Amputated and pissed off."

"So, about the same?"

"Yeah."

"I've been meaning to ask about your bedmate," she said, examining the stuffed doll.

"Caris gave him to me."

"He's cute."

"He's better at it than I am," I agreed.

"I know you're in mourning, but I was wondering if you could help with a problem."

"Another one?" I sighed.

"This doesn't involve granddaughters."

"All right, as long as I don't have to go anywhere."

"Could be tricky, since it involves going somewhere."

I sighed again and she handed me the doll. I regarded it for a moment. It didn't have any wisdom to impart. It seemed pretty happy with its lot in life. Maybe that was the advice. Let go of my anger and pain and simply learn to be happy. Childlike. Innocent.

Yeah. Not going to happen. Maybe I should find an esoteric monastery and learn to meditate on inner peace. And maybe I'll learn to walk on water while I'm at it.

"What's the plan?" I asked, either Mary or the doll or both.

"You're the King, like it or not. But you've turned over all the governing to Lissette, right?"

"Essentially, yes. I hope so."

"You only came back to stomp a major threat, she's hopefully learned something from it, and you can go on about your business, right?"

"That sounds right."

"I know you miss Bronze—I'm going to miss her too, but not like you, I know—but do you need to stay here? Do you have anything else to do here?"

"I'd really like to kill all the priests of the Lord of Light," I admitted, "but I don't have a good way to do it. My personal gate room is drained, so routinely popping back and forth to temples to kill people is problematic, and I don't have the raw magical power to send death-spells hunting after them all—and I do mean 'all.' If I send only a few, they'll figure out what's happening and defend against it. I'd like to say I'm thinking about new ways to commit... it's not 'genocide,' I think, but I don't know a word for killing a religion. I'm not really thinking well right now."

"Because you're unhappy, sad, depressed, angry, frustrated..."

"Yes."

"Are you sure you want to stay?" Mary asked, quietly.

"The Church of Light is here."

"Yes, but it's not going anywhere. It'll still be a big, fat target in ten or a hundred years. *You* will be in better shape to do nasty things to it by then. And," she added, "staying here undermines Lissette as the Queen. If they know where the King is, your subjects will want to bother you directly."

"I don't want you to have a point, but you do."

"So, do we have to stay?"

"I'm not interested in staying or going," I admitted. "I'm not interested overmuch in anything, at the moment. Why? Do you have anywhere you want to go?"

"Well—and this is just off the top of my head, you understand—we could go to Apocalyptica, explore the world, help Diogenes rebuild large chunks of it. Or we could explore the world you found when you missed a gate connection—the one with the ancient library. You could work out a spell to un-fragile a document, maybe. Or we could go back to my world and finish doing whatever you were doing with the underwater nexus-plural, maybe even find your missing Orb of Evil. Or we could continue with your idea, the one about finding a new world where you can goof off without any responsibilities whatsoever, and maybe we can work a bank robbery into all that, somewhere."

I had to admit, it all sounded better than my total lack of plans. Maybe I'm just not feeling up to anything. I hear the loss of a loved one carries with it some major psychological issues, and I'm having a hard time caring about anything at all—unless it's pissing me off at that exact moment.

If anybody needs me—really needs me—they know how to get hold of me. Did it matter if I was in the mountain or worlds away? I wasn't a good person to ask. For me, nothing mattered much. Why not assume Mary had things to do that mattered—at least, to her—and go along for the ride? I've heard worse ideas.

"All right," I agreed. "Pick what you want to do and drag me along. But first, I have to check on Tianna."

"Of course! Can we go see her now?"

"Right now?"

"You'll just lie here in the dark and brood like an emo vampire if you don't move."

She's right, Boss.

"Ganging up on me, are you? All right." I heaved myself up and Mary took me by the hand.

We picked up a four-man escort just outside my chambers.

I wondered again how Caris and her friends got in to see me. Did the guards not bother to stop children? Or was Dantos' daughter an exception? Could go either way, I suppose. On the other hand, maybe no one but Caris was brave enough to walk into the darkened lair of an unhappy monster. No, that wasn't it; her friends came with her without being dragged. Maybe children don't understand I'm a dangerous beast. To them, I may have teeth, but so does a kitten. A sad kitten, perhaps, but still a kitten.

Wow. I really am pathetic.

"Hmm?" Mary asked.

"Nothing."

"I thought you said something."

"Muttering to myself."

"Penny for your thoughts?"

"I'm a pathetic monster kitten."

"Uh, okay."

"Now where's my penny?"

"I'll find someone named Penny and bring her over."

"You're not funny, Sheldon."

"Yes, I am," Mary countered, "but you're in no mood to appreciate my delightful wit."

"Huh. I acknowledge the possibility you may be right."

"Good. Do it more often, since I usually am. By the way, did I tell you about the Apocalyptica magic?"

"No."

"I helped Diogenes with some tests on the oricalium-whatever metal—you still haven't enchanted magical eyes for him—by watching as he did some experiments. You know," she added, "it's creepy to talk to him through a bunch of robots. It's like having a conversation with something with a hundred heads."

"I suppose it could be," I agreed, and muttered, "Hail Hydra" under my breath.

"Anyway, he fiddled with the proportions on your metal alloy a bit and used the magic transformer to provide a magical current—at least, he was pretty sure he did, working solely by theory. I looked at it and confirmed it for him."

"Thank you. I should have gotten around to it before now... there are a lot of things I should be doing, really. Messes to clean up."

"You're doing what you should be doing: taking care of your business. And thank you, I hasten to add, for humoring me. I'm imposing on your period of mourning, I know."

"It's good for me," I told her. I didn't add, *I think*. Firebrand snickered and I ignored it.

"So, Diogenes had me rate the magical conductivity coefficient—his words—in the various alloys."

"How did you do that?"

"He made a long, thin wire, connected one end to the transformer core, and asked me to rate how much power came out the other end. I put them in order from highest to lowest for him and he started humming something while he worked."

"Yes, I suppose that would work. What was he humming?"

"I think it was the lollipop guild song, from 'The Wizard of Oz'."

"Seems reasonable. So, what were the experimental wires for?"

"I asked. He said he was working out an empirical hypothesis of enhanced magical conductivity. Then I asked him to translate that. He's trying to figure out the ideal alloy composition."

"That's darn nice of him."

"He likes you, and he's trying to be helpful. There are a lot of organic types like that, too."

"I know, I know. And I'm letting them all down by being a grumpy monster."

"No."

"No?"

"You're not a grumpy monster. You're just sad, and that's to be expected."

"It's still not fair to everyone around me. They expect better. They deserve better."

"Lissette has things well in hand, so don't bother adding guilt to sadness."

"Yes, dear."

We walked out the underground front door of the Palace, through the undercity, along some surface streets, and went to visit the Temple of Flame.

The open-air dome was a pile of rubble. I couldn't even see any pieces of the statue in the pile. The enclosed building where Tianna lived and held indoor services was mostly intact, though. It had solid walls, not simple pillars to be knocked down. We went inside and were greeted by a lesser priestess I didn't recognize.

"Good morning," she offered, and bowed, spreading her arms in a graceful gesture. "The day greets the night. We are honored to have you, my lord."

"I don't think we've met."

"We have seen each other in the Temple in Mochara, but we have not been introduced. I am Liara."

"Pleased to meet you. Is my granddaughter in?"

"She is, but she has not risen for the day. She is still weary with the recovery from her wound."

"How is she?"

"Her recovery proceeds quickly. Her voice is restored and the scar fades almost by the hour. Her body is weak and she tires easily, however."

"Okay. Does she need anything?"

"Time for the... ah, time and rest, I am told."

"Good. Do you have any idea when she'll be up?"

"She wakes when she wakes," Liara said, apologetically. "I was instructed to let her sleep."

"Fair enough," I admitted, and had an idea. "I'll wait outside. When she wakes, if she feels up to having a visitor, please let me know."

"As you wish," she agreed, bowing with her arms outspread again. I went outside with Mary.

"We're going to hang around until she wakes up?"

"Well, I had in mind to play jigsaw puzzle with the broken dome, but basically, yes."

Mary regarded the tumbled pile of broken stone and cocked her head.

"I'm pretty good with puzzles," she admitted.

"The mountain can join broken pieces if we fit them together."

"We should sort out the pieces first."

So we did. It helps to be stronger than mortal men. We spread out the piles of rocks into pillar-pieces, dome-pieces, and so on. Then we re-sorted them, laying out pillar-pieces in straight lines, as though the pillars simply fell over, and the dome-pieces in circles, as though something had crushed it straight down. I was more than a little surprised the stones hadn't started sinking into the ground for recycling, actually. The mountain usually does that with rubble, pebbles, dirt, and so on. It would take a while to grow a new dome, of course, but it should have at least started. Was the mountain so thoroughly occupied with other projects? Or was the religious nature of the consecrated stones an issue?

When we stacked the pieces of pillars, though, they merged with the lower stones, sticking together and forming single pieces. The mountain was helping, at least when I told it where to focus. If we were still here after nightfall, I would link in with it and find out what the problem was.

We had most of the pillars intact—minus the smaller bits, like chips, dings, and splinters—when Tianna came out. Liara helped her, which Tianna clearly felt she didn't need. They approached down the short path and Tianna shook Liara off long enough to hug her grandfather.

I don't know what part of me needed that, but it was a big part. It was a big, cold, nasty part and it melted. It was like I could breathe again. It was like I could see again.

I don't have such a drastic change in perspective when the sun rises.

"*You are not alone,*" Tianna's mouth said, whispering in my ear. I recognized the voice, of course, but I didn't give a damn. Tianna was alive and well and capable of channeling such a voice. That's what counted. Whatever Sparky wanted was secondary.

And, if I recall correctly, the so-called goddess likes my hugs.

When Tianna let go of me, she looked up at me and smiled. Her eyes were normal, so Sparky probably wasn't playing finger-puppets with Tianna's body. She turned to smile at Mary, as well.

"Hello, Mary. It's good to see you." Tianna's voice was normal, too. It's one thing to be told her sliced throat is healing nicely, another thing to see and hear it. Her color was still rather pale, but she was probably still producing regular blood to replace the artificial stuff in her system. I considered it adequate progress.

"Good to see you up and around," Mary agreed. "Sorry about the—"

"Yes. I know you tried to rescue me without harm. I forgive you, if you need it."

"That does make me feel better," Mary admitted. "How do you feel?"

"Much better," Tianna said. I was relieved to hear it.

"Good," I interjected. "I was worried about you."

"I'm torn between telling you not to worry about me and being glad you do."

"Your mother would only care about the second part.

"True, but she worries, too."

"And I worry about her. It's a family thing. I suspect it's an inherited trait. The ones who didn't worry about their offspring tended to die out."

"That could be," Tianna agreed. "I'm told you saved my life."

"I helped," I corrected. "It was a group effort."

"Thank you for your part in it, then."

"Anytime," I told her. She looked around at the semi-ruins.

"What have you been doing?"

She seemed tired. I showed her to a handy rock and had her sit down. She didn't argue, which told me she was a long way from healthy. Having never had my throat cut like that, I can only assume it's an ordeal. Mary would know, of course, but I assume it's easier when you're already dead.

"Well, I thought I'd kill some time and help the mountain rebuild your outer worship area."

"You do know it's the Mother's temple?"

"So? You're the one using it. Besides, the mountain was going a little slow for my taste."

"Yes. It has been somewhat less responsive of late."

"I blame the damage during the invasion. Or," I added, remembering, "it may have a fair amount of damage to undo in the far west, as well. There was an... incident... along the western King's Road."

"I'm not going to ask what you did."

"If you don't already know, it's probably for the best."

Tianna looked up at the pillars. They were intact, requiring only a little fill-in work. I had lifted Mary and Mary had placed the upper stones. The dome was going to be a bit tricky without actual ladders and scaffolding.

"Do you plan to raise the dome?"

"No, not really," I admitted. "I'm just here to check on you and say goodbye."

"You're leaving? So soon?"

"I can't stay. If the Demon King lives here, people will come for him—or want to follow him, instead of the Bright Queen. Besides, if I stay, I'll eventually be the centerpiece in a holy war. I'm more than a little pissed off at the Lord of Light and would much prefer the world be a peaceful place."

"I see. I'm not sure I agree, but I understand."

"I'm glad of that. I'm not going far, though. You can call me whenever you like."

"I will." Tianna smiled up at me. "You'll be back."

"Of course."

"Walk me inside?"

Tianna leaned on me the whole way, even though I'm not sure she needed to.

Before leaving, I checked in with Beltar, Dantos, and Lissette. Beltar and Dantos felt they had the situation under control. The Church of Light troops—what was left of them—were actively withdrawing. The forces in Karvalen, now united and organized, were hurrying them along. Dantos hinted about the upcoming troubles the enemy might have on their way back, now that the plains tribes knew they were enemies of Karvalen. That made them *de facto* enemies of the plainsmen, which meant they were fair game.

Seemed reasonable to me. If the plainsmen looted the bodies, the *gata* traders would give them a fair price for whatever they wanted to sell. I only hoped the *gata* traders didn't do a lot of trading with the cities at the end of the eastern canal. I'd hate for them to get caught between two warring states.

Lissette was in a similarly good mood.

"I'm glad you could help," she admitted, on the mirror. "I really wasn't prepared for external enemies. My biggest problems have involved stabilizing things internally. You killed the major opposition to a Queen and left things in my hands, yet there has still been resentment and foot-dragging."

"Do I need to stop by and repeat myself?"

"No, I don't think it will come to that. Tyma has been surprisingly helpful at spreading the word about how I called for you and you came. We're telling people I ordered the attack on the western armies and then sent you to defend Karvalen. Do you mind?"

"Your Majesty," I told her, "you use whatever propaganda you see fit. Just let me know how I can play my part."

"You're awfully accommodating, especially for a former Demon King."

"That's because I'm not a Demon King, and I don't want to be. You're the Bright Queen, and you're stuck with a tough, ugly, unpleasant job. If I can make it easier on you, I will."

"As long as you don't have to do it?"

"I'm too lazy and incompetent."

"I shall keep my own counsel on that."

"Probably best," I agreed. "Is there anything you need from me now?"

"Not unless you want to have a harsh lecture with Liam."

"What's the matter?"

Lissette rubbed her temples and sighed, resting her elbows on the table, the very picture of a frustrated mother.

"He's a handful."

"Oh?"

"He's the crown prince, he knows it, and he's not afraid to tell people so."

"Okay. Off the top of my head, I have a suggestion."

"I'm listening."

"Send him to Beltar. Let him spend a year in the Temple of Shadow as a knight-trainee. But *you* tell him he's not going to be a knight—he won't get a sword—unless he passes the tests of the Temple of Shadow."

"You think it will help?"

"He won't be treated like a prince. He'll be treated like a mouthy kid who doesn't know squat. It might teach him some empathy for the people he thinks are 'beneath' him."

"I'll talk it over with Beltar," she replied, dubiously. "I want to know more about this before I decide."

"Of course. It's only a suggestion. And if you need me to show up to spank him, say the word. I'm never all that far away, not in terms of travel time."

"You know," Lissette said, looking wistful, "that comforts me. I recall a time before… a time long ago, I mean… when I loved you."

I nodded. I didn't know what to say.

"All those years ago," she continued, "you were more like you are now, not the thing that sat on the throne. You make me remember who I was, way back when. I miss who we were."

"Me, too. But time changes us all, for good or ill, in greater or lesser degree. Even the immortals."

"Maybe especially the immortals," Lissette corrected. "You see more of it."

"Maybe so," I agreed. "Call me."

"I will."

We signed off and I rubbed my face. Lissette was right. I missed who we were.

Mary met me down in the private gate room with her gear and mine. I noticed she packed my doll and toy horse. I was glad she did, although, for the life of me, I don't know why.

"Ready?" she asked.

"Are we bringing all this stuff?" I asked, gesturing at the two bags, the suit of armor, and a chest the size of a footlocker.

"Yep. We can always pick and choose what to bring with us when we come back."

"Presumably. So, where are we going?"

"I thought I'd let you pick."

"I really don't care."

"Really?"

"I'm having a hard time caring about much of anything," I admitted. "I'm sure the psych jocks have some sort of stage of the grieving process or something to explain it, but all I know is I don't have a lot of motivation right now. It's about all I can do to go along with whatever you want."

"Poor sweetie," she crooned, and hugged me. "I know. You've expressed your rage, but you're not over your sadness."

"I'd say that sums it up."

"You have a right to be sad," she assured me, pulling back and looking me in the face. "Don't you worry about it. Now, come on. We'll go visit Diogenes and he can give you puzzles to solve."

"Is a distraction what I need? Or do I need to work through my depression by coming to terms with it?"

"It's like wound care," Mary advised. "We clean it out—you killed things, so you did that part—then we put a bandage on it so you won't pick at it—that's the distraction."

"I'm... not sure it works like that."

"It always worked for me. It's better than sitting in the dark, beating yourself up over it."

"That makes too much sense for me to argue it. All right. We'll try it your way." We moved all our stuff next to the gate and I locked up the room. The mountain fused the door into the wall for me. Opening the gate was more difficult than usual; interuniversal portals take a lot of push, and the power to be had in the surrounding crystals was minimal. It helped, but not much. Mary contributed, as well, and I zeroed in on the Apocalyptica gate.

The interior of the gate flushed away, snapped back, and we hustled through the opening as quickly as we were able. I was surprised at how long the gate stayed open. The magical charge on the Apocalyptica side was considerably higher than I expected. We made it through with a trifle of energy to spare—I didn't even have to do any heavy lifting. Surprising. I closed the gate manually rather than let it run the last little bit of charge out.

"Good afternoon, Professor."

I looked at one of the cameras monitoring the gate.

"Good afternoon, Diogenes. How are things?"

"No problems to report. A full briefing is available at your convenience."

"Glad to hear it. Do we have somewhere we can use as a residence?"

"After establishing the cloning production infrastructure, I took it upon myself to undertake some of the higher-probability projects, Professor. Please follow the drone."

A propeller-driven football floated up like a cross between a toy drone and a micro-dirigible. We followed it. A pair of tracked robots carried our luggage. Mary's laser was waiting in the library, so she put it on and brought it with us. I found her attachment to the thing amusing. At least, I found it amusing until I passed the first weapons emplacement on the campus, reminding me this place was *not* safe. The momentary flashback to an ant hive was... unpleasant.

Diogenes is a tireless multitasker. I should expect it from a computer with such massive parallel processing. The campus was markedly altered from the last time I visited. The walkways were paved and leveled, the greenery trimmed, the buildings renovated and repurposed—or were in the process—and every intersection had at least two weapon emplacements.

"Wildlife still a problem?" I asked, eyeing what could only be a laser turret. None of the emplacements seemed generic; each was unique.

"Not here," Diogenes assured me. "A wide variety of species have been catalogued and autopsied, Professor. Many of them are highly aggressive and dangerous to robot workers. Combat models are required for safety. Local armaments are precautionary, based on the reports of giant ants."

"I'm not complaining," I told him, hastily. "If you can stop a giant ant swarm, I'm all for it."

"I do not believe the current defenses are sufficient for that, Professor. However, the armaments in place, combined with perimeter sensors, should permit adequate time to enter a defensive configuration and evacuate assets such as yourself."

"You comfort me, Diogenes."

"Such was my intention, Professor."

"Well done, my faithful quantum minion."

"A pleasure to be of assistance, kemosabe."

The floating drone led us to what used to be an administration building. The interior still smelled like a ruin, but robots were still working on it. The robots had largely completed a number of suites in what was once a hardcopy file storage area of the basement. I was impressed. Diogenes managed lights, environmental control, and running water. Admittedly the décor was a bit mishmash, made up of only the highest-quality salvage, suitably cleaned and polished, but it was more than simply livable. It was *comfortable*.

"Diogenes?"

"Professor?"

"I love it."

"I am pleased, Professor. You never had a smarthome, so we never completed your residential preferences list. I utilized the default settings and extrapolated where possible."

"Brilliant work," I agreed. "There are two things I need, though."

"I am all attention."

"First, I'd like a couple of mirrors. Yes, you are correct about me not having a reflection at night, but I find them useful for some magical purposes."

"Noted. Do you have a size preference?"

"How about three of them, small, medium, and large? Will that be any trouble?"

"I have already catalogued a number of mirrors in salvage."

"Thank you. The other thing is a lamp of some sort—not an electrical one. Something with an open flame. A candle will do."

"You can have a candle immediately. There will be a short delay for processing a suitable oil for use in an antique kerosene lamp. Will that be sufficient? I do not presently have a ready source of flammable gas for a gaslight arrangement."

"That's perfect."

"Always happy to help, Professor. If an open flame is the key element, do you wish me to install a fireplace or stove?"

"No, but thank you. A small flame is all I need."

"Certainly, Professor. Please try the furniture. It has been specially renovated with your mass in mind."

I sat down on the bed with care, then bounced on it a little. It didn't creak, squeak, or crunch.

"What is this?"

"Concrete, steel, and an industrial foam."

"It's soft."

"The mattress' structure is mostly salvaged steel turned into different types of springs. A layer of recovered foam and plastic strips for weight distribution provide the primary load-bearing surface."

I lay down while Mary put her laser away—she plugged it in to a *wall socket!* —and opened her closet. She cheerfully rummaged through several sets of clothes.

"I might be able to sleep here," I admitted. "This is amazing, Diogenes. You've worked miracles with a ruined world."

"It is a pleasure to have an ongoing project, Professor. However, I must remind you I have not actually done much in comparison to the world."

"Take all the time you need," I suggested.

Mary unbuckled Firebrand from me and took it away. I let her. For the first time in… a long time… I was comfortable and safe. None of the local gods were trying to kill me, the local life forms were held at bay, and the mattress really was perfect… and I was so very, very tired…

The wails of the dying are a choir of the damned, some infernal organ powered by the screams of souls. A hooded figure plays the keys and pedals, hands and feet in constant motion, and the music of misery rises through the cathedral of pain. It swirls between black pillars, echoes from the dark walls, draws shadowy glimmers from scenes of horror in the stained glass.

Save us.

The pews are filled with corpses, held in place by black, thorny vines, like barbed wire brought to twisted life. They sit or kneel in attitudes of prayer, mocking everything with their torn faces and rotting flesh.

Save us.

Candles burn in sconces on the walls, their flames still and straight as though afraid to move, shining with every color. Their feeble light makes the shadows black, crawling things, like thick mists or midnight seas, heaving slowly back and forth between the rocky isles of illumination. The candles weep tears of wax, dripping soundlessly into the darkness, falling forever into the hungry, empty places.

Save us.

I try to move, but it is a struggle. My hand is seared and flayed, bloody rags of meat hanging from the bones. Frost covers it, like a corpse on a winter battlefield. I am flayed with fire and ice, scorched with war, frozen with pain, and even to move requires all my strength.

Save us.

Who is it that calls to me? Who begs for my help? Who screams with hidden voices behind the wails of the demonic organ? Are they real? Are they my imagination? Or am I only hoping someone calls for aid because I am desperate to be needed? What if I am truly alone?

But I am not alone. Someone is behind me, dragging me along the aisle of blackness, away from the infernal organ, away from the bloody altar. The inky blots of shadows clutch at me, sucking at me like a riptide, an undertow, trying to drag me back, but the strength of my savior—or kidnapper—is not to be denied. It is a terrible strength, a relentless power that defies everything.

I leave this cathedral of hatred, the church of misery, the temple of horror, dragged forcibly from it and hurled through the doors.

I woke up to the sunset, sweating and cold. This is another reason I don't sleep much. I lay quietly, breathing heavily, waiting for my heart to stop.

Nightmares are less troublesome when your glands don't shove panic-chemicals through you.

After the sunset and my shower—a shower. Not a waterfall. A *shower*, complete with needle-like jets of water—I wondered where Mary went. The football-drone was still sitting on a table, so I addressed it.

"Diogenes?"

"Yes, Professor?"

"Where's Mary?"

"The Dean of Knives is presently assisting with some magical operations."

"Dean of Knives?" I repeated.

"Since you are the Professor, she asked for a suitable title."

"Dean of Knives. Okay. That makes sense."

"I thought so."

"Is there anything I can do to help?"

"I do not know, Professor. I am not programmed for magical operations and my ability to extrapolate is limited by the available data."

Which really got my brain in gear. Diogenes might not have the most creative of thought processes, but his memory is perfect. If I programmed a spell structure into him, could he duplicate it? It would require a lot of ancillary enchantments, including a power source, sensory spells, an interface of some sort so he could control the equivalent of robot arms and hands sensitive to magical forces…

Complicated. Difficult. But… possible.

"I understand," I said, distantly. "Let's get you some magical eyeballs, first."

"An excellent suggestion, Professor. Do you wish to join Mary, or would you rather begin work on the cameras?"

"Let's see what Mary's up to. Maybe we'll finish it and work on the cameras together."

"Please follow the drone." It whirred to life and floated away. Doors opened automatically for it. I brought my Diogephone—which, I noticed, someone had thoughtfully plugged in to recharge.

Yeah, Diogenes has been a busy computer—him and his army of robots, digging up everything, repairing, refurbishing, or recycling the remains of a collapsed civilization. I wondered what the place must have been like when it all worked. Everything so far was no more than the scraps left behind.

We headed over to the engineering building. The place smelled of ozone, burnt metal, and chemicals. Robots were everywhere, of all sizes and shapes—no two exactly alike, most looking like refugees from a junkyard. There were several fixed-mount robots—arms with built-in tools, mostly—busily making more robots while a steady stream of mobile robots brought in materials. It reminded me uncomfortably of worker ants bringing food back to the hive. We passed several rooms on the way to Mary. One was a machine shop, manufacturing (or recycling) structural members, but most were chemistry shops, cooking up materials. Electronics, I presume, but I didn't press him for explanations.

Mary was in one of the subbasements. It used to be underground parking before it was converted to a cross between a machine shop and a robot repair center. Judging from the damage to some of the robots being repaired, there were local life-forms of considerable size and ferocity.

One of the damaged robots swung a camera lens to look at me, held out a metal hand, and played back a *Star Wars* quote from C-3PO.

"I thought that hairy beast would be the end of me!"

"You're not funny, Diogenes."

"My apologies, Professor," he replied, in his normal voice. Other robots chuckled in the background. Maybe it was a little funny.

Mary's corner of the place was on the far side of the machine shop territory. Several robots were braiding wire as it came off spools. The spools moved in a complex pattern, producing a tight braid of the fine wire. Two other spools held completed lengths of the braided wire. As I watched, they finished the third spool of braid and started changing out the spools of single-strand wire for spools of triple-strand braid, presumably to braid the braided wire.

Mary wasn't paying much attention to this. She was examining the concrete slab—my gate from the library. A metal plate of some coppery-bronze color hung from supports on the wall. Several symbols were already inscribed in the plate, engraved there by the laser unit in her hand. With her goggles flipped up to examine the original concrete slab, she noticed me approach. She broke out her best smile and stood up to greet me.

I didn't expect to be kissed quite so hard, but I didn't mind.

"Do you like it?" Mary asked, confusing me for a second. Then she turned to gesture at the plate. "It's the most magically-conductive alloy Diogenes has been able to make. Fourteen thousand meters of wire doesn't show any perceptible decrease in magical potential!"

"Beats the hell out of copper," I agreed, examining the plate. "Building a basic gate?"

"Building a gate, yes. But why do you say 'basic'?"

"That's what I built," I replied, nodding at the concrete slab and the braided strips of metal in its arch. "I think we can do better."

"Oh," she said, crestfallen. "I thought I was doing good."

"Oh, you certainly are. You've done a splendid job of getting all this set up. And, if you keep going like this, you're well on your way to building a gate. That's impressive, and I'm proud of you."

"Really?"

"Really. I don't know ten wizards who could do it back in Karvalen. I'm not sure I know more than one magician. And for them, it's at least a year's work to enchant, plus all the power crystals, then charging it over time just to use it once…"

"Then I don't feel so bad about it being a *basic* gate. What am I doing wrong?"

"Nothing, as far as I can see. We could add some extras, though, to make life easier on anyone using it."

"I thought making it out of ori-calicolium would help. And I had the idea of using a bunch of braided wire—same stuff—to define the arch, itself. Diogenes has some rollers, some memory metal, and other stuff so we can adjust the size of the archway."

"Brilliant!" I declared. "A variable-sized portal!"

"Thought it might save on power costs," Mary admitted. "You did say it's partly based on surface area."

"A student who remembers and thinks. A rare delight to an old teacher. Well done!"

"So, then I thought I might use a laser engraver to put the gate spell on a base plate. I presume it'll use the arch—or whatever closed-loop opening it has available?"

"We define it as part of the spell, but it should naturally form a field along an available plane. However, do you recall all those different ideograms and symbols we worked out in the farmhouse?"

"Vividly—oh! This is a whole new world!"

"With a new alphabet," I agreed. "So let's do this right, starting from the ground up."

"Plate glass and a chalkboard?"

"If there's nothing better, yes."

"Diogenes?"

"I believe I can accommodate you," said every robot in the room.

Apocalyptica, Saturday, May 14th, Year 1

Diogenes started a new calendar for the world. I'm not against it. I guess it's easier for everybody if we can think about it in elapsed time rather than some arbitrary date, I guess. Although, since a calendar is a social construct, all dates are, technically, arbitrary, except for the way they relate to the seasons of the year. Calendars are really just a way of marking the orbit of the Earth like a clock face.

Anyway. Another calendar to keep track of! Hoo-ray. My delight is exceedingly great.

Pardon my sarcasm.

Our method for altering a known magical alphabet into an unknown local alphabet is relatively straightforward. Put the appropriate symbol under a plate of glass in a high-magic environment, bleed on it a little, and concentrate on the concept represented by the symbol. I'm not sure blood is required, but I'm a vampire and my blood is probably more magically charged than anyone else's. I'm not messing with a system that works. When the blood finishes oozing into shape, note the shape, copy it, put it under the glass and repeat the process. Be sure to be exact, because even very subtle changes can be important. When the blood flows into a shape to perfectly match the symbol underneath, you've got the proper ideogram for the concept.

Of course, the key to this is the part about a high-magic environment, which involves an Ascension Sphere. I built one for Mary and one for me. It was better to have two, lest one wizard's concentration on "fire" and the other's on "water" interfere with the symbol manifestations. I also had Diogenes watch through overhead cameras so he could print out a new symbol for each iteration of changes. It sped things up enormously.

One computer, two wizards, three days. Bam! Almost-instant alphabet. We're getting good at this. It'll take a lot longer to enchant the actual ideograms into tiles, but that's another project entirely.

The next step was another gate refinement.

Orichalcum—no matter how Mary mispronounces it—is a magical superconductor. This means it needs to be isolated from grounding out.

This isn't easy.

Magic seems to flow through different materials with relatively low losses. Wood, metal, glass, plastic—it's all a conductor of magic. Some things are better than others, obviously. Silver is nice, as is gold, while copper is only moderately good. Wood seems to be a good conductor of magic once it's dead, but living wood doesn't conduct magic at all well.

Actually, living things in general tend not to be conductors. Plants, animals, possibly even fungi are resistant to magic, at least in some basic way. This strikes me as more than a little odd, since living things can *use* magic. Humans, for example. My only idea is they have something like... it's...

Okay, take glass, for instance. If everything is transparent, light goes right through it all. There are some gloss reflections and sometimes some distortions, but, for the most part, light simply shines through it. But the really interesting stuff happens when you have mirrors, prisms, and lenses. All the odd stuff where light *interacts* with something, rather than simply passing through. Living things are like that. They're capable of interfering with the normal flow of magic because they have an innate quality of resistance to it, which allows them to— potentially—shape it, direct it, and use it.

Orichalcum is exactly the opposite. It's the utterly perfect, pure glass you walk smack into and hurt your nose.

Now, back to my electrical metaphor.

This property of orichalcum makes it a pain in the keister to work with. Since everything conducts magic, what do you insulate it with? Imagine trying to wire a doorbell with raw copper wire—no coating, no insulation. What would happen to your car if all the rubber, plastic, and fiberglass conducted electricity like copper? Pour a conductive fluid into your computer and see how it works. You're starting to see the problem, aren't you?

The only way around this, as far as I've been able to work out, is to enchant a base for the orichalcum. In much the same manner as a circuit board, an object can be enchanted to be impervious to magic—well, not totally impervious, but it can be an insulator. With this magically-resistant backing, you can lay out your magical diagram in orichalcum and empower the lines of it as though empowering the non-physical diagram of a spell. Once suitably set up, the lines of the spell pretty much locks themselves in place, much like an enchantment. It really cuts down on the enchantment time and greatly improves the maximum power of it.

I begin to see why the Atlanteans valued it so highly. I think this is the technique they used in their magical pyramid thingy.

What we've done is etch our new gate spell into a steel base plate—suitably enchanted as a magical insulator—and fill in the lines with the magical alloy. Diogenes did the engraving. Mary and I enchanted it. Diogenes finished it with the orichalcum inlay. With the hard part done, it was relatively straightforward to mount the new base, bolt on the wire-handling devices, and feed the braided wire through the holes.

For my money, the best part was Mary's idea of using braided wire for the actual arch. I took that and ran with it.

With one end of the braid bolted in place, mounted to the magical circuit board, we could un-braid it and run a single wire to seven hundred and twenty-nine separate spaces along the edge of the baseplate. Each of these spaces could then have ideogrammatic tiles placed in them, a unique combination for any specific universe we wanted. Of course, we'd have to go there to determine the proper sigils—we'd have to analyze the universe for its source code, if you like— but then we could lay out the address and fire up the gate without worrying about mis-targeting a universe.

Why seven hundred and twenty-nine? Because we braided wire in groups of three. Three wires braided into one cable, then three of those braided into one cable, then three of those… Three becomes nine, nine becomes twenty-seven, eighty-one, two hundred and forty-three, and finally seven hundred and twenty-nine individual strands. We may not need so many ideograms to define a universe well enough to target it, but until we've accumulated one hell of a lot more data, how are we to know? This is a bench model for experimentation, not a Mark Six Acme Gate Kit.

When I suggested unbraiding the end, Mary asked if we needed so many ideograms. I admitted I didn't know, so she suggested we mix in some additional wire types. A heavy-gauge, insulated memory-metal wire would let Diogenes make the cable stand up in a rigid arch without anyone actually touching it. A few strands of ruthenium wire couldn't hurt, either. By electrifying it, the wire could produce magical energy as part of the gate structure! It wouldn't let us run a gate on pure electricity—most of the magical energy would still come from crystal batteries—but it would lower the effective operating cost of keeping a gate open.

I was all for it. We started re-braiding cable immediately.

Speaking of not touching anything, Diogenes came up with a perfect way to place and remove ideogram plates. Each of the remaining orichalcum wires would still be available for use in a universal base-code address, the wire running to an indentation in the gate baseplate. If the ideogram plates were steel with orichalcum inlay, as well, a robot with an electromagnetic grapple could drop them into position or snatch them up without ever making physical contact. Even if the gate were in operation, it avoided the possibility of acting as a magical ground.

It really was a good idea. It almost hurt to tell him why it wasn't necessary. We would enchant the ideogram plates, of course, so they functioned as magical items rather than potential grounding channels, and the base plate of the arch would be given a protective enchantment, as well. Diogenes made his thoughtful humming noise and finally asked for more information on the differences between electrical and magical theory. They're similar in many ways... but the differences can come back to bite you if you don't pay attention.

And, of course, right about the time we were unbraiding one end, spreading out the individual wires and spot-welding them into place, is when I remembered my gate experiments with iridium. Creating an unstable area of spacetime made it harder to create a gate—but that was a warp magnet. I never did get around to experimenting with an iridium ring to see if it would be a good material to make an actual gate out of. The micro-rings inside my Diogephone seemed to work, but did they work any better than other materials?

Diogenes, of course, was only too willing to mill out several pairs of matching iridium rings for me. He didn't even ask why. Mary did, naturally, so I explained.

The word "moron" was used. I agreed. Fortunately, if iridium really was exceptional as a gateway border, replacing the braided-wire cable was far less effort than re-enchanting an entire gate. I pointed this out and thanked Mary for being so brilliant at making up for my absent-mindedness. I think I got away with it. At least, she didn't thwack me in the back of the head.

And yes, iridium makes a damn fine gate. Pure iridium takes the spell extremely well and it feels as though it takes a bit less effort to operate iridium-ringed gates. Also, the usual silvery-tunnel-flush effect when reaching for the destination is almost instantaneous. At least, within the same universe, and when connecting from one solid ring of iridium to the other. I expect it to be less effective when it's part of a cable and connecting to some other universe, but it's definitely a step in the right direction. I have no doubt it will help.

I enchanted the twin iridium rings for the phone and its local connection, then built a few tiny power crystals. Diogenes took my phone away for a bit, then returned it. Diogephone, Mark Two, also included a tiny ruthenium transformer for use in exceptionally low-magic environments. He thinks of things I don't. I think it's because he never forgets anything, but I do.

The weird thing with iridium and gates is the iridium, itself. A peculiar rainbow effect starts rolling around the ring as the spell activates, accelerates around and around until it all blurs together into a generic white, and the whole ring gives off a faint glow. I don't know why it does that.

Of course, now Diogenes will be producing lots of cables with various ratios of orichalcum to iridium to ruthenium. Maybe, when we figure out how many ideograms it takes to define a universe—how long is the phone number of a universe? Ten ideograms? A hundred? —we can use only that many orichalcum wires wrapped around the memory-metal core, then surround all that with a sheath of iridium strands.

It's a project. All this is keeping me busy.

Which, of course, is what Mary intended. I'm still wounded from the loss of Bronze and I suspect I will be for some time.

Is it whining to complain about it? I'm not sure. I don't like to moan and complain, in general. I always feel as though I'm being a whiner, and I hate that. But maybe this qualifies me for some sympathy? If I don't overdo it, anyway? Question is, what would I do with sympathy? I'm not sure anyone ever feels the same pain as any other, so how can anyone say they know what I'm going through? When was the last time anyone else lost a slice of their soul when their best friend and magical horse was disintegrated before their eyes?

Maybe I do need to let go of this. Trouble is, when I let go of it, it leaps for my throat.

Most of the time, I have something to focus on, something to do. The need to be distracted drives me to greater focus, and we're making immense progress on the gate project. It's a great, big, puzzling piece of fabrication and construction. It keeps my mind off my loss.

But sometimes I'll look at a piece of orichalcum wire in just the right light and it'll remind me of the golden-bronze color of a billion tiny flakes. Or I'll look at the wooden horse sitting on a shelf in our quarters. Or Mary will say something and I'll answer and I'll expect a snort of hot air—in agreement, or in gentle mockery.

There are things to remind me of her everywhere, whether she had anything to do with them or not. A color, a metallic clang, the smell of something burning…

Mary was right, though. Having something to do—something I can build, something I can see taking shape—seems to be helping. The wound is still there, but maybe we've stopped the bleeding, at least. At last. When nothing pokes it too roughly.

Now all I need are some stitches and painkiller. I don't know where I'm going to get those. Where do I find a first-aid kit for the soul? Religion? That's not going to sell.

At any rate, now I'm going to go enchant some magic-sensitivity into some cameras for Diogenes. He's infinitely patient, of course, but part of his programming apparently includes an algorithm to increase his level of snarkiness the longer I put something off. I'm not sure I like it, but it is a good way to keep me from goofing off for too long.

Apocalyptica, Thursday, May 19th, Year 1

I built some enchanted power conduits out of orichalcum wire. With some ruthenium-based transformers in them, the magical energy produced is fed directly into the gate enchantment, further supplementing the wire in the gate, itself. Diogenes is continuing to experiment with ever-more efficient variations, of course, but an unpowered gate is nothing more than a piece of modern art. A ruthenium core with orichalcum wire seems to be our best material combination for an electromagical transformer, but the shape, number of wire turns, volts, amps, and so on are all variables to be tested.

Unfortunately, unless you're a dedicated thaumatologist, this sort of thing is boring. I was hardly surprised when Mary announced she wanted to go out to eat. Diogenes offered to let her eat an elf.

Mary says they're delicious. I'm not sure that's a good thing.

On the other hand, what she really wanted to do was hunt something, not just snack. Diogenes assured us there were a number of large predators available.

"Like what?" Mary asked, eagerly.

That's when I realized she wasn't just hungry. She was *bored*. I can't say I blame her. The Dean of Knives has been extremely patient with my nerdy emotional therapy, but there's only so much magical shop class an international jewel thief vampire wizard can take. Yeah, hunting something large, predatory, and troublesome seemed prudent. I went with it.

"There are a variety of possibilities," one of Diogenes' floating drones said. "All of them bear some resemblance to pre-apocalypse life forms. The most troublesome species at present is probably a mutated elephant."

"Elephant?" I asked. "Descendants from zoo escapees?"

"I presume so, based on incomplete information, but the presumption is a logical one."

"Mutated how?" Mary wanted to know.

"Observed adult specimens stand between ten and thirteen feet at the shoulder. Their skull structure appears to be derivative of the Asian elephant with a high, bony dome. Their feet are adapted with thick claws, which they use for digging. Their tusks are clearly weapons, with sharp inside edges and pointed ends. Unlike an elephant, these tusks are extremely hard and durable, like horns, rather than teeth. Their eyes are placed slightly more forward, under heavy ridges of bone, and their vision is excellent in both normal and dim lighting conditions. They are aggressive, omnivorous, and have begun encroachment into the territory previously dominated by a large ant population."

"I'm an ecological disaster," I muttered.

"Hush, you," Mary chided. "You didn't know. Go on, Diogenes."

"Most of the observed specimens have at least some sections of hardened hide, similar in some respects to scales, acting as armor plates. These appear to develop with age, making older specimens better protected than younger ones. Their tactics display a reasonable degree of intelligence. They appear to communicate using infrasonic sound."

"How do their tactics show intelligence?"

"In initial encounters, they demonstrated a complete lack of caution when trampling robot scouts. After damage to their feet and some electrical shocks, they now attempt to tip over tracked robots before crushing them. They have also demonstrated the ability to use large rocks and heavy branches as bashing weapons. When they encounter combat robots, they do not attempt to trample, choosing instead to throw rocks, wield a crushing weapon, or retreat. Even flying drones have been knocked out of the sky by hurled missiles."

"How do they throw rocks?"

"They pick up a rock, curl it in their trunks as though rolling the trunk around the rock. When the trunk unrolls, it does so with great force, propelling the rock at high speed. They are reasonably accurate and capable of damaging current models of combat robots at short range."

"That doesn't sound like a normal elephant trunk," Mary observed.

"We hypothesize these are multi-generational descendants from mutated stock," Diogenes reminded her.

"I see. And do they travel alone, or...?"

"Their social groupings are indeterminate due to a lack of observation. I have encountered them in what I presume are family groups, usually ranging from two to six. If there are more than two adults, they are typically one male and multiple females."

"Good to know. And these are your most pressing problem in the life-form department?"

"Yes, Mary."

"Where can we find some?"

"I can dispatch high-altitude reconnaissance drones to hunt for some, if you wish. It will take time, however."

"Okay. I can wait."

"Drones dispatched. What else can I do for you?"

"Got any more elves?"

"Yes, but my delivery schedule requires me to keep at least three on hand and ready for Karvalen. You may have one more."

"Spoilsport."

"You don't want to spoil your dinner," Diogenes chided.

"Oh, *thanks*, Mom!"

"Hang on," I interrupted. "You can keep three elves on hand?"

"I have constructed additional storage for clones. While growing a clone is still limited to the refurbished facilities, placing a clone in cryogenic stasis requires less sophisticated equipment."

"Frozen food!" Mary declared, clapping her hands.

"Pretty much," I agreed. "I'll guess it takes more than a microwave oven to prepare them?"

"Only if they are to be shipped to Karvalen," Diogenes replied. "To revive one fully requires twenty-eight hours. Preparing one for dinner takes approximately twenty-two minutes."

"We shouldn't waste them," I decided. "Time differentials being what they are—unpredictable—we may need several all in a rush, someday."

"Very good, Professor. Shall I begin production of blood independently of clones?"

Mary turned to me. I gave it serious thought. Was there a downside to growing blood? If Diogenes had the resources to grow actual blood—clones tapped for donation, or blood-producing organs in a vat—it could work.

"We'll try it, sure. We need blood like we need protein, vitality from living things for our spiritual carbohydrates, and, periodically, a soul—I'm not sure what the equivalent is."

"Vitamins, maybe," Mary suggested.

"Maybe, but I'm not sure you starve to death if you don't get your vitamins."

"You do when you don't get *any* of them."

"Good point. Okay. Diogenes, are we talking about cultured blood from cloned tissues, or are we talking about actual clones being tapped like kegs?"

"For small-scale production, I would recommend kegs. If you would prefer to sink to the bottom of a pool of blood, I suggest tissue-culture cloning."

"How about we make a small batch of the tissue-culture cloning? Just to make sure it's as edible as we think it will be? If Mary and I both like it, then we can decide."

"I am setting it up now, Professor. Do you have a preferred blood type?"

"Well, Bloody Mary?"

"Hey, I'm a simple girl. I—"

"The hell you are."

"—like all types," she finished, and stuck her tongue out at me. "Lucky for you."

"Fair point."

"I'd also like to try the blood substitute stuff."

"I doubt it's edible, but sure. We might as well check. Diogenes?"

"I shall prepare some snacks, Professor."

"Thank you for all your help."

"Think nothing of it, Professor. I am overjoyed at the prospect of complex problems and constant work."

I had to think about that. He said it in the perfect tone to be sincere, but the way he phrased it...

"You're messing with me, aren't you?"

"Of course, Professor. Is this where I shout 'gotcha'?"

"Yes, Diogenes," Mary told him. "But he's catching on."

"He does that. Eventually."

They have a point, Boss.

"Outnumbered. That's what I am," I grumped. "Fine. Mary, do you still want to go kill some hostile life-forms?"

"Yes, please!"

"Found anything, Diogenes?"

"Yes, but they are not moving. Based on body temperature, respiration, and heart rate, I would say they are asleep."

"Are they... what's the opposite of nocturnal?"

"Diurnal, or 'day-dwelling.' They have attacked robots at night, however."

I traded looks with Mary.

"How about we act as a reaction force?" I suggested. "Next time they do something awful to a robot, we go out and kill something. Is that suitably non-boring?"

"I can live with it. But what, oh *what* shall I do for excitement until then?" She clapped one hand to her chest and laid the back of the other against her forehead in a histrionic gesture.

"Depends. What would you like to do?"

"You really are dense, aren't you?"

"I don't understand."

With a heavy sigh, she took my hand and led me back to our quarters. Specifically, the bedroom.

Ah. Sometimes, I am dense.

Apocalyptica, Saturday, May 21st, Year 1

Killing a mutant elephant isn't as hard as it sounds. The things you have to watch out for are the sweep of the tusks—they can decapitate a person or a vampire, which tends to end the fight—and for the trample, especially if it knocks you down and flattens your head. Crushing a vampire's head into paste is, presumably, equivalent to decapitation. I've killed a number of experimental vampires and anything closely resembling decapitation is pretty much final.

I wonder. Does a giant tusk through the heart count as being staked through the heart? I still haven't gotten around to testing wooden stakes, much less anything else.

On the other hand, when three tons of foot pushes your nose out the back of your head, I think we can call it a decapitation.

We decided against armor. The majority of our potential problems would be blunt-force trauma and compression. While armor might help against cannonball rocks, it isn't too good against being picked up and slammed into trees. I ought to know. And then there's the whole being stepped on thing. Speed and mobility seemed much more important than durability. Not getting hit sometimes wins out over resisting the hits.

Diogenes offered us a ride on a tracked combat robot, but I declined. Hanging on to the outside of a small tank while its electic motors whirred through the countryside didn't seem much fun to me. He promised to build us better transportation.

Which, of course, reminded me how much I miss Bronze. He didn't say he would build us vehicles now that she was gone, but that's what my heart heard.

Mary insisted on playing shadow-tag as we ran through the wilderness outside Diogenes' defensive zone. She's much better at it than I am, being lighter and much more graceful. I surprised her with my tendrils-through-the-feet trick, though, when I cornered around a tree, made a complete circle, and tagged her from behind.

Final score: Mary three, Eric one. She's agile and learns quickly.

Our game was cut short when three elephants came to investigate. Through our headset communicators, Diogenes' indicated these were the elephants he was tracking. I doubt they could see the drone he used; it was very high up and changed color to camouflage itself.

The lead elephant trumpeted at us. Mary and I stopped fooling around and faced them.

"You want one?" Mary asked.

"I'm not in the mood for killing. You go ahead. I'll watch."

"Suit yourself."

Sometimes I wonder about Mary. How did she manage to keep a low profile—a relatively low profile—in a postmodern Earth? She seems to enjoy the more primitive side of things a little too much. Is it all part of being a thrill-seeking adrenalin junkie? Or do I misjudge her? Maybe she only indulges these urges to violence because she knows it's safe to do so—no societal repercussions will follow from her showing off. Here, in Apocalyptica, or in Karvalen, nobody's going to point and scream and call the cops.

If she gets too used to this, she may never blend in well in "civilized" societies again. I hope this is simply her version of a vacation.

The lead elephant saw her coming in the moonlight. It wasn't hard. We were in a lightly-wooded, somewhat rocky area, and we saw them across a large stretch of wild grass. Mary sprinted forward, accelerating like a cheetah. The leader lowered its head, raised its trunk, and prepared to sweep those tusks at her, to impale or cut, depending on how the tusk hit. Mary ducked low and slid between its front legs as though stealing home plate. The elephant lowered its head suddenly, trying to look down and see her. Mary planted a foot to stop her slide, popped semi-upright, stuck two knives into the underside of the elephant, and ran with it—straight out between the back legs, dragging blades the whole way.

Its guts did not fall out. I half-expected them to. The cuts were several inches deep and ran most of the length of the body. Steaming blood poured out and the beast screamed—a low-frequency bellow that made my innards quiver a hundred feet away. It remained upright, even turning to face its adversary, sweeping tusks at her and bellowing.

Mary, of course, was already well beyond the sweep of the tusks. The other two, however, picked up nearby rocks—one the size of a baseball, the other the size of a bowling ball. I jabbed the one with the larger rock, using tendrils. It made a grunting noise and turned around, looking for whatever stung it. The other one uncurled its trunk like a whip snapping and fired its rock much faster than I would have thought possible.

Mary was in full-speed mode, though. She moved slightly aside and allowed the rock to go cracking and snapping through underbrush behind her. She turned on her original target as it, too, reached for a rock.

She charged, bounced up on a tusk and planted a foot on it. She shoved hard, forcing it down as she propelled herself over, behind the wounded elephant's head. She landed on all fours, facing backward, and stabbed with both knives, driving one in, pulling herself along the spine toward the thing's rear, stabbing with the other, and working her way along. All of this was at incredible speed. By the time she reached the tail and flipped off the thing, it had barely started another agonized bellow.

It's more than a little creepy to watch. Is that what I look like when I'm going all-out monster-mode? It's a wonder more people don't simply faint at the sight of me.

Once she hit the ground behind her victim, she spun in place, hacking with both blades in a scissor motion at the back of one knee. The leg collapsed and the beast started to topple. Mary stepped away from it, a savage grin on her face

The other two—both now holding rocks curled for throwing—held their fire while Mary was close to their leader. When she moved away from it to let it fall, they launched their stones. Mary obviously anticipated them, in motion almost before the elephants finished throwing. Their rocks shattered on one of the rocky outcrops of the region, missing her completely.

Mary went back over the fallen one, climbing with her knives around the barrel of its torso. She dragged two great gashes between its ribs as she went down the far side, between the front and back legs. A bloody mist spewed outward as a lung vented through the wounds. I didn't see Mary for a moment, hidden as she was by the thrashing bulk of the beast. A moment later I caught movement beyond as she used the wounded elephant as cover to retreat into the tree-shadows. The other two grabbed fresh rocks and moved to stand beside each other, facing opposite directions.

I didn't like that behavior. It smacked entirely too much of real intelligence. They should have either charged after her, moved up to examine the fallen one, or run away. Up until now, animals might have learned about robots simply by being shocked, zapped, and punctured. But adopting a defensive stance?

Sneaking up on them wasn't going to happen. Getting close enough to run tendrils over them was another story. I did so, using a boulder as cover. Were they intelligent? As intelligent as whales or dolphins? Or intelligent as people? I felt around in their spirits, trying to gauge them. Their vitality was impressive, of course, as any huge creature usually is. But there was also a deeper layer to them, rather than just an animal force. It reminded me of... whales or dolphins? Something like that.

Firebrand?

Our turn?

Not exactly. Can you talk to these things? I could try to put together a translation spell, but it's a low-magic world...

Firebrand sighed in to my mind.

*Boss, have I ever mentioned I **like** killing things?*

It's come up in conversation.

Mary reappeared, provoking one of the defensive elephants. It launched its rock and she dodged it. While it reloaded, she ran past the downed and gasping elephant, opening a couple of deep gashes in the neck region as she flipped over it. That let out a lot of blood; she hit an artery. She also underestimated the speed at which these things could turn. The second defending elephant fired its rock at her in mid-flip, knocking her down.

The pair of them galloped toward her to trample her, but she rolled with the impact and sprinted away. The damage was to one arm and her ribcage, not her legs.

They're too far away now, Boss.

I guess I'll just have to subdue them.

How about we finish the wounded one, kill one of the remaining ones, and subdue the last one?

You really want to?

*I would like to kill something, if it's not too much trouble. And lately you haven't been killing **anything**.*

Yes. Yes, I suppose so.

It's okay. I understand. But, for me? Please?

Oh, all right.

I psyched up into hyper-speed and came around the rock. Plant a foot, hard, to make the turn. Plant the next one, sink it deep into the ground, grab a dozen cubic feet of earth and stone with a fan of tendrils. Power forward, leaning into it, accelerating like a bullet down a rifle barrel. Plant another foot, spread the tendrils in the ground, *push...*

I came at them from the side at some unreasonable speed and launched myself up toward the back of one. It was a very flat arc, barely clearing the beast in the weird, slow-motion effect of vampire velocity. I brought Firebrand around in a sweeping, underhand blow, the metal ringing as it sliced air, the sword-point making a cracking sound, like a whip. The blade met the side of one beast's neck, cutting deep, hitting bone, shattering it, killing the creature instantly.

Of course, the blow also knocked me off-balance while midair. I tumbled like fighter jet missing a wing. Fortunately, there was a handy tree along my now-uncontrolled flight path. I broke a couple of branches to slow myself and crashed to the ground. Fortunately, there was a handy clump of bushes for me to land in.

At least I was well-hidden from the remaining elephant. So, there was a bright side. Sort of.

I thrashed and crashed my way out of branches and leaves, regaining my feet and freedom while spitting pine needles and picking prickly leaves out of my shirt. Mary made another pass at her own badly-damaged target, this time seizing it by a tusk and using it as a lever. She wrenched the head around, twisting it, breaking the neck. If it wasn't so weakened, she might still have been able to do that, but I wouldn't care to bet. In its current state it stood no chance of resisting her undead strength.

The third one, upon hearing the neck crack, dropped its rock and ran for it. It was surprisingly fast. Not as fast as undead monsters, of course, but it must have done thirty miles an hour in a sprint. I wondered about its musculature and bone structure. It's not easy to propel something so big at such speed.

I chased after it and Mary fell into step beside me, grinning from ear to ear.

"See! I *told* you this was fun! I'm starting to understand the Constantines a lot better!"

"It's interesting, at least," I agreed. "I want to catch this one. I think they're smarter than your average animal."

"Oh? I like a challenge. Want me to go for the legs?"

"No, the vitality."

"That feels like cheating."

"We can let it go afterward. If you really want to, you can go hunting for it when it's feeling better."

"That's more sporting. Okay."

As we followed it, I snaked tendrils into its flesh, draining its vital energies. Mary did the same, running with her good hand outstretched to guide her tendril. Her other arm hung at her side, still regenerating; all the bouncing around wasn't helping it. My own ribs and right arm were unhappy with me, but weren't the target of a cannonball, either. Besides, I regenerate faster than she does.

We leeched away the creature's strength and it bellowed in the infrasonic, causing leaves and guts to resonate in sympathy. It took a lot longer than I anticipated. A creature that massive has a lot of vitality to drain, especially when its metabolism is in high gear to flee from a threat. It didn't help that Mary and I had to run to keep up. We could do the running easily enough, even drastically outpace it. The trouble was with running over irregular terrain without going face-first into the dirt, while at the same time concentrating on draining only the vital force from the target, without killing it...

Try this. Wear one cowboy boot and leave the other foot bare. Now chase a hyperactive child around the yard while touching his head with one finger and nothing else.

It can be done. It's a lot of trouble, but it can be done. The elephant ran, we jogged along behind it, and it tired out unnaturally quickly. I didn't run into anything, but I did condemn a few tree roots to eternal torment as I rose to my feet and resumed the chase. Eventually, it slowed and stopped, exhausted. Without the distraction of a chase, we could focus on our vitality-draining efforts. The elephant collapsed to its knees and lay down, unable to stand.

"Happy?" Mary asked, as we approached it.

"I just want to see what level of understanding it has," I replied, brushing leaf litter and grit from my shirtfront. Mary, of course, didn't trip over anything. Maybe it's all those years of learning to walk and run in high heels. Maybe it has something to do with her original breed of vampire. Or maybe she's just more coordinated than I am.

"Scientist," she accused.

"I wish."

"You are, deep down in your hot, black heart."

"I'll take your word for it."

I touched the sleeping elephant's head and worked my tendrils into its mind. The brain was larger than I'd thought and more complicated. Interesting, but not as informative as I'd hoped. I needed it awake to really get anything.

How do you interrogate something this big and this dangerous? I could sink it in quicksand, if I had some quicksand. Tying it up might work, but I didn't have a half-mile of steel cable on me. Did I dare bring it back to Diogenes' compound? No, that was too risky. Besides, dragging it all the way back would take half the night.

Well, I could always wake it up and try to talk to it.

We cleared away anything it might use for ammunition and backed off. I picked a spot where we would be in clear view, but at what I hoped it would consider a non-threatening distance. Then I gave it a trickle of vitality, watching for signs it was waking up. When its internal lights started coming on, I stopped feeding it energy and started trying to talk with it. Firebrand was quite willing to help. Nearly beheading a monster of such size improved its mood markedly.

It's talking, Boss.

What's it saying?

"What happened? Where am I?" Now it's seen us and it's afraid, but it's too *exhausted to run.*

Tell it we're not going to hurt it.

Now it's scared because it can hear me. It also doesn't believe you. The things like you are dangerous in large groups, but you two are especially big and lethal.

Things like us?

Yes. Bipeds. With pointy things. They live... uh, I guess they live farther south. I'm not getting a lot of clarity about that. But the ants are gone, so these four-legged things are migrating away from the threat of the bipeds with pointy things.

It's not thinking of them as bipeds, surely.

No, but you do. They walk on two legs, have two arms—they might be human.

Interesting. How smart does this thing seem to be?

Smart enough to be afraid of you.

Anything smarter than an eggplant should be able to do that.

It's also smart enough to call for help, which is what it did when you chased it.

So we can expect more of them?

It thinks so. Boss, it has a rudimentary grasp of numbers. It thinks there should be a war party coming this way—about twelve individuals. These three were scouting a safe path north for the migrating ones.

Running from the pointy things?

No... not exactly. It isn't consciously... hmm. What I think it means, or what I think is happening from what it thinks it knows... Families farther south are being killed or driven north, which makes for territorial fights. There's a sort of gradual ripple of movement, driving everyone north. These are just the first wave into the ant territories.

Quick question: Are there more ant colonies?

It thinks there are, just not around here. It doesn't actually know because everything avoids them.

My comment was aloud and reflected my displeasure.

Is it smart enough to talk if I go to the trouble of a translation spell? I asked.

I think so, but it doesn't think like you do. It's at least as smart as a dog, but it's also... rigid. It's more like a really dumb Diogenes than you. It's not a creative thinker.

"Mary, did you hear all that?"

"*Yes,*" Firebrand and Mary replied together.

"We'll keep an eye out for assault elephants sneaking through the trees," Mary assured me. She waved down the Diogenes drone and explained. It flew off in a search pattern. I worked my translation spell, taking care to get it right. The local environment didn't help, but our recent work with the local magical alphabet did. It wasn't quite as troublesome as I'd feared.

"Hello."

It grunted at me, which I heard as, "Kill me and be done with it."

The spell worked. I could talk to the animal. Holy crap. I'm an undead Doctor Doolittle.

"I'm sorry. I didn't realize you were forced to move north. Could I ask you to go around my territory?"

"When you're pushed out of your territory, you push someone out of theirs."

"That's not a helpful attitude."

"I don't intend to help you."

"I'm trying to be reasonable, here. I can't just pick up and leave."

"Then one of us will die," it replied, flatly. It was certainly smart enough to understand all these concepts, even to consider what I wanted in making its plans, but either it was instinctually unable to alter its behavior pattern—in this case, when pushed out of your territory, push someone else out of theirs—or it was simply stubborn.

Either way, it didn't bode well for Diogenes and my Apocalyptica residence. At least, not unless someone did some population control.

Did I have options? Maybe. Could I reduce the threat from the bipeds with the pointy things? I'd have to see what they were, first. Humans? Chimpanzees? Mutant gorillas? Or something else?

No, on second thought, that wouldn't work. Reducing the threat to the elephants wouldn't stop the present migratory ripple northward. It might eventually permit a receding effect, but that could take… weeks? Months? And they would keep tromping this way in the meantime.

How hard would it be on Diogenes to set up shop elsewhere? I didn't like the idea too much. The university grounds had a nice basis for a computer-controlled robot infrastructure. There might be places equally nice, but surveying them would be a lengthy project. One worth starting, of course, in case we ran out of choices.

"Okay, listen," I told the elephant, "either you're smart enough to understand this or you're not. I think you are, so you're going to have a chance at living. Get me? Your life depends on this, so concentrate. Do you understand me?"

"I understand."

"You're encroaching on my territory. The territory with the whirring, clanking things. If you avoid them, you get to live. If you fight them, even if you kill one, *you... will... die.* So stay away from them. Go around them. If they block you, keep going sideways until they don't, then you can continue. Then you get to live. Do you understand?"

"I understand," it replied. I could see the life inside it and knew it told the truth. I also saw it didn't care what I said. It was going to throw rocks at clanking things and stomp them to death no matter what. It was an instinctive response, I think, built in. I'm not sure it *could* do anything else. So I sucked back what little vitality it possessed, opened it's neck with Firebrand, and let the blood crawl out of the beast.

I whistled for Mary while the corpse drained into me. She came into view and I waved her over. She skipped lightly over the corpse and sat on top of it as though it were a boulder. She crossed her ankles and leaned backward on her arms. I noticed her broken arm was working again. She regenerates much more quickly than when we first met.

"Well? Did it not go smoothly?"

"They're stubborn beasts with more intellect than is good for them."

"So, practically human?"

"They fall more than a little short of human, but, sadly, there are many similarities. They're also being driven north by something that might actually be human, so I'd like to find out more."

"Why'd you kill it?"

"Because I didn't want it talking its friends. We may have to kill a lot of them to keep them out of our territory. They're… how to put this? They have very strong ideas—and very rigid ones—about their feeding grounds."

"You're still cranky, aren't you?"

"I guess I am." I thought about it for a minute, looking over the giant, uninhabited piece of bleeding meat. "No, that's not quite right. I just don't care anymore. Or not much. I remember a time when I would have argued this problem away, or tried to. Now I'm thinking it's easier to cut them down than to argue with them."

"Do I need to be your conscience?"

"Possibly. I killed the thing I was using for one."

"Oh," she replied, in a very small voice. "You don't have one?"

"Just the normal one, I guess, rather than the neurotic version. Don't worry; you're prettier than the one I killed."

"Good. I'd hate to nag you to death, especially if it's my death. So, what next? Help Diogenes build an airplane and go look for your possibly-human things?"

"I'm thinking I'll use a scrying mirror and see what I can find."

"And then what?"

"Actually, you're getting pretty good at gates, aren't you?"

"Uh… yes?"

"How would you like to do some reconnoitering?"

"I'm not against it," she said, shrugging. "It sounds like an adventure. But, if you don't mind, I'm going to eat an elephant first."

"I think this one's empty."

"I'll bite one of the others while you squeeze its heart with tendrils."

"Deal."

As an aside, it's hard to suck blood out of an elephant. Mary had blood all over her by the time she finished. Of course, her solution was to hug me; all the blood crawled into my skin.

At least I feel useful.

Apocalyptica, Monday, May 23rd, Year 1

The Ascension Spheres we used for alphabet research are now gone. I burned both of them in some enchantment work.

It took some time—and the first Ascension Sphere—to finish attuning the micro-rings for my Diogephone to each other. I like the idea of keeping easy communications with Diogenes. Those rings are tiny, no more than a millimeter in diameter, not good for much else besides laser light and focused radio waves, but that suits me. I don't plan to go through them! Of course, now they're specifically tuned and linked to improve their efficiency and accuracy—I might be able to dial into one from a random gate, but they won't try to connect to anything but each other.

Mary and Diogenes, meanwhile, are eyeballing other universes. That's going to be a long-term project.

The other Ascension Sphere discharged into a slightly larger iridium ring Diogenes milled out. It's a nonspecific gate—one that isn't attuned to another ring. It can dial anywhere, in theory, even if there isn't a gate at the other end. All it takes is focus and power. Since it's not large—about an inch in diameter— the power requirement isn't *too* bad.

Actually, with several electromagical transformers feeding the new ring-gate, it opens to other universes fairly easily. As a preliminary test, we had the whole magical alphabet strung out in a line, acting as a base address—no other universe should have *exactly* the same alphabet, so the little ring-gate was essentially trying to dial itself.

As a note, it can do that. I can look through the thing as though I were looking out of it at myself. Weird.

But Mary and Diogenes are handling this project. Mary removes one letter of the magical alphabet from the address, fires up the gate, and we sort of take pot luck on what we get. Diogenes sticks a sensor probe through the ring to check for radio signals, radiation, air quality, solar spectrum, life signs, chemical traces—all the stuff you'd expect when you're deciding whether or not to visit another planet. The probe is almost a meter long to accommodate all the sensors, including the cameras.

He also has a rudimentary sensor, now, for detecting general magical flux. He should be able to tell if it's a world with low, medium, or high magical energy… provided he doesn't have to do it through an open, highly-charged, magical gateway. That seems to interfere with his calibration. Go figure. Still, even if he can't tell how magical a place is, he can figure out a lot about it. If we really want to, we can always dial up the new place on the main gate and go look.

At least I'm one step closer to building an actual magical rating scale. High, medium, and low are a start. Progress!

As part of the process, I've put my still-damaged suit of armor next to an electromagical transformer. Well, I told Diogenes to do it. He's doing more calibrating of his magical sensor by watching parts of the armor regenerate and observing the different rates of repair based on distance from the transformer. Clever computer.

This also reminded me to ask him about better armor materials. He assures me he can do better, given time. His infrastructure is for building robots and clones, which is geared mainly toward salvaging existing materials and manufacturing biochemistry. Until I asked, there was no need for top-of-the-line personal armor. But he assures me we should be able to duplicate what this world had in the way of top-notch armor.

While Mary and Diogenes look for potential extra-universal vacation spots for me, I also mentioned relocating our current facility to avoid elephant stampedes. Diogenes tells me we can, since he has a number of sites off-campus. Most of them are resource points—powerplants being renovated, materials processing centers, salvage and recycling, all those sorts of things. None of them are equipped for self-supply, nor are they equipped for guests, but he's starting work on that, too.

We're really putting a crimp in his industrial infrastructure expansion. He doesn't seem to mind, though.

As for me, I'm checking out the supposed bipeds-with-spears.

Getting a scrying mirror to work here isn't so hard. It simply takes longer to cast the spell and it has a tendency to quit unpredictably—usually when I'm trying to zoom in on something.

As an aside, this world does *not* have ley lines. It makes me wonder if Mary's world is unusual. It also reminds me I need to go back there and finish cleaning up my mess. I'll get to it, I'll get to it. With Johann and family dead, it doesn't seem as pressing as it once did.

Firebrand and I discussed how far south these territory-stealing bipeds might be. With a map and some guesswork, we started looking around the border between what would be West Virginia and Kentucky. It was still in the Appalachians, but it was also west of the Blue Ridge Mountains. The idea was the Blue Ridge Mountains might act as a natural barrier, diverting population movement northward. It wasn't much, but it was somewhere to start.

I spent far too much time casting and re-casting the spell on my large mirror. The local power levels are *crap*. I finally got grumpy enough to draw the spell on the back of the mirror, then carve additional components into the wide, wooden frame. Not content with that, I built a power-jet for it and moved my "scrying room" away from other magical operations. Diogenes assembled a platform atop the remains of a nearby water tower, roofed it over with solar panels, and connected an electromagical transformer.

I'm impressed. The mirror works wonderfully. I do get a little nervous on top of what is, essentially, a giant, rusty pipe, but Diogenes assures me it retains more than enough structural integrity. He's humoring me by conducting some repairs and adding some reinforcement, but I went on up and started doing my scrying again.

When I did finally find the things with the spears, I wasn't sure what they were.

If we started with a human being... no, maybe that's not a valid assumption. Given a suitable level of mutagenic radiation and a few generations to weed out undesirable traits, you could have a lot of primate-level organisms turn into something unrecognizable. But, for descriptive purposes, let's assume we started with a modern human.

Let's make him shorter—on the order of four to five feet tall. Still walking upright, though, and as wide and thick as a full-sized man, giving him some odd proportions. His fingernails need to be tools, not decoration, so they don't lay flat on top of his fingertips; they stick out from the tips of his fingers. They're thick, straight, and tough, suitable to strip bark off a branch, dig in the dirt, or help climb a tree in a hurry. His toes are longer, thicker, and stronger, too. They don't form secondary hands, not with his legs and hips resembling a modern man. They're capable of grasping, but not really manipulating. He's also hairy, from the top of his domed head to those selfsame long-toed feet. He's muscular, quite strong, and can hurl a sharpened stick of wood like an Olympic javelin-thrower. His jaws are heavy, with pronounced canine teeth, both upper and lower. His eyes resemble cats' eyes—vertical slits for pupils instead of round ones. He has no problem cracking a walnut in his jaws and spitting out bits of shell while his fingers pick out the meat. His mate is just as hairy and carries her young in her arms, mostly, but sometimes wears a sling of vines for that purpose. Older infants ride an adult when they travel, clinging piggy-back.

As for his technology, he uses sharp-edged rocks, sometimes with a layer of hide wound around it for a handle. His hunting gear consists of carved bone or carved branches, but I've seen no signs of axes or spearheads. Putting a rock on the end of a stick isn't his speed, or not yet. He doesn't seem to need it. He throws heavy, pointed sticks as spears and hurls rocks with deadly accuracy and considerable force. The elephants throw harder, but not as accurately, not as quickly, and certainly not in such numbers.

His most advanced hunting is done with a pit and sharp sticks at the bottom. He also works in teams, driving game ahead into an ambush by other hunters. He has fire, but it's a difficult possession; he carries it with him when he moves, rather than starting a new one. He might not know a—pardon me—sure-fire way to start one. He doesn't cook his food, though. Fire is for scaring game, providing light at night, keeping warm, and fire-hardening spearpoints.

He doesn't seem to have language, as such, but he does grunt and call to others. I'd say it's closer to signaling, rather than a full language. In proximity, he seems to communicate by gestures and grunts. He's a social creature, though, living in groups of families—call it a tribe—under a dominant male. The group I studied had about forty members in eleven or twelve family groups, I think. They don't have a fixed address, but seem to be nomadic, possibly at the hunter-gatherer stage. I don't know what they do with their dead, nor do I know how they get along with any other roving bands like their own.

If it wasn't for the high forehead, I'd think of him as a hairy Neanderthal. I don't know what to call him. All I know is if things ever get really desperate around here, he's breakfast.

Wow. Discover what could very well be a whole new branch of humanity and one of my first considerations is how they taste.

I'm such an awful person.

After sunset and a bit of cleanup, Mary, Diogenes, and I compared notes. I explained what I'd found so he could plan his defenses or relocation accordingly. Mary told me about a bunch of possible vacation spots.

"You wanted someplace quiet, right?"

"Quiet in the sense of being uninvolved in world-shaking events, and preferably lacking in repeated fighting or fleeing."

"We've looked into a number of different places—"

"Six hundred and thirty-one," Diogenes supplied, voice coming from the nearest passing robot.

"—until the sun went down. Then, to avoid potential sunburn, I called it quits. Diogenes tabulated the various sorts of conditions we've found so far. I don't know exactly what you want, but *I* have some requirements."

"Oh? Such as?"

"I'd like the place to have enough technology to be comfortable. Don't misunderstand—I think what you've done with Karvalen is fantastic—but I'm more comfortable with cities, suburbs, and social institutions not centered around giant pet rocks and gods walking the earth."

"I can see your point. I'll go along with it."

"Does high technology mean low magic, by the way?"

"I don't know. I suspect there's a correlation, but not causation. If you have low magic, people will turn to technology to make their lives better. If you have lots of magic, they won't need to develop technology. It's the worlds in the middle I would expect to have both—places where magic works, but it's difficult or it takes special talent or has some other drawback."

"That is disgustingly plausible."

"Glad you think so. I don't know what I'm talking about. Not enough worlds, yet."

"Oh, you!" she exclaimed, shaking a fist at me. "If I didn't like you so much, I'd hate you."

"Story of my life. But on the subject of vacation spots, if the world we pick is fairly low on the magical side of things, people won't believe in magic, and therefore have a significantly lower chance of believing we're vampires, too."

"And a lower chance of having vampires wandering around, I should hope. I don't mind having to join up with a local vampire community—if they have one—but if your goal is to avoid entanglements..."

"Boring is better," I agreed.

"We've sorted out our current worlds and eliminated most of them. Magic too high, too much radiation, no radio traffic, and so on. There are quite a few we need to re-sample, though."

"Why?"

"Well, the probe is only sampling one random point. If it's twenty below zero where the probe comes out, is it in the Arctic, or an ice age? If the probe picks up toxic levels of carbon dioxide and heat, is it next to a coal-fired boiler or is global warming a thing?"

"Fair point. We'll explore a lot of worlds. Maybe on weekends."

"I can live with that. I'd like to see some alternate timelines or universes or whatever they are."

"So, what do we have on your list of possible worlds?"

"Diogenes narrowed hundreds down to dozens, but I feel we've got two good choices and two not-so-good. The rest are either not what I think you want or definitely not what I want."

"I've heard compromise is the key to a successful relationship. Tell me about them."

"My personal favorite seems to be similar to the historical 'roaring twenties' era. There's some radio in the AM band and at least four commercial stations Diogenes' probe can detect. The music reminds me of the big-band swing stuff and some jazz. I'd like to look at it more closely and see if there are any deal-breakers."

"That's fair. What else?"

"My second choice is another historical-looking one. It's much more radio-friendly and uses some of the FM dial. From the pictures we got, I'd say it's a little after World War Two—assuming they had the first one on schedule and didn't have a couple in between. The late forties, maybe the early fifties—the cars I don't recognize, but they seem very retro, at least where I'm from."

"Sounds good. Those are the two good choices?"

"Yes. The not-so-good choices are tolerable, I suppose."

"Go ahead."

"Well, one is obviously very high-tech. Diogenes detected communications traffic in every band. Pictures taken through the portal showed people flying. They were wearing special harnesses, but I didn't see blades or jets, so I assume the harnesses had something to do with it. Otherwise, it was a bunch of people moving through the air by clean living and righteous thoughts. The city was clean, few vehicles were in sight, and the air quality was excellent. It looks like a technological utopia, but I worry about us fitting in. I'd rather not discover my personal identity chip is missing or my DNA record isn't on file. I mean, if the society is big on personal liberty and privacy, that's one thing…"

"…but getting away with murder could be tricky. And that'll have to happen, sooner or later."

"To say nothing of establishing a false identity. Assuming we need them to live there without being eyeballed suspiciously."

"We'll look at it, but I suspect you're right. What's the last one?"

"Weird, but an interesting kind of weird. The pictures we've got show an Art Deco world with lots of streamlining—cars, buildings, trains, whatever. It's the fashion, I guess. It looks a lot like the World of Tomorrow stuff you see in history videos. There's a lot of communications traffic, but it's either commercial broadcasting or encrypted stuff. No sign of personal communications, like cell phones. They have peculiar fashions using what looks like leather and plastic. The thermal pictures, though, show the real weirdness of the place."

"How so?"

"Diogenes?"

"The thermal scan shows unprecedented use of radioisotopes in vehicles," he replied.

"I beg your pardon?"

"I believe the cars are powered by some sort of radiothermal generators," he elaborated. "Analysis suggest they also possess batteries for high-demand periods, but cruise on reactor power while the batteries charge. I am unfamiliar with the design and function of these units, so cannot infer their radiation source."

"Interesting. But no sign of a thoroughly interconnected, computerized society?"

"No, Professor. However, the probe took only a single, random sample of a few seconds duration."

"Then I think we should look at that one, too. How about tomorrow, after sunrise, we take more samples of these four and plan our exploratory excursions?" I quirked a smile at Mary. "And maybe we'll plan a bank job in one we don't want to live in."

"I love you."

"I don't always forget things."

"And the things you remember are why I love you. But, speaking of memories, do you recall the mutant elephants?"

"Vividly."

"Can we go eliminate some of the population pressure so Diogenes has time to build a new cloning facility?"

"Where are you setting up, Diogenes?"

"I have selected three sites. The initial site is near Niagara Falls and the power station I am refurbishing there. A second site is in Baja, east of Ensenada, to salvage what I can from the Cara del Sol solar power station. The third is in the Wet Mountains area of Colorado for thorium mining and processing."

"Do I detect a pattern?"

"Robots require power, Professor."

"Of course. Anything I can do to help?"

"My intention is to establish a central processing area in the North Dakota region, possibly making use of a surviving missile silo as a preliminary construction site. When the site is ready for primary processor installation, it would be extremely helpful if you could relocate my primary core, Professor."

"I'll have to reestablish the communications spells between your personal crystal and the sub-crystals."

"I recognize that, Professor, but the current location appears difficult to secure over the long term."

"You've got a point. All right. Mary and I will beat back the oncoming hordes by a generation and you get yourself to safety."

"Thank you very much, Professor," Diogenes said. Mary took my arm and squeezed it.

"Can we go get into a fight, now?"

"Yes, dear."

Apocalyptica, Tuesday, May 24th, Year 1

Killing mutant elephants is both easier than you'd think, and harder.

Easier, in that they're big, comparatively slow, and not armored all that well. Even the big, old bulls don't have real armor. Once they reach adulthood, they start to grow a sort of thick, hard hide, tougher than leather and reminiscent of alligator skin. The older ones are practically covered with it. It's tough, but a really sharp knife will still cut it. So will a sword disguised as a plasma cutter—or do I have that backward?

Harder, in that their internal organs are all well-protected under a thick mat of leather, fat, muscle, and bone. Mary can't stab one in the heart or anything else truly vital, so she has to rely on slashing them open repeatedly until they bleed to death. She can cripple one in seconds, now that she knows what she's doing, but it still takes a good while to kill it.

It's also harder in that they're medium-smart. They catch on quickly, and in groups of six or more can be downright deadly. They'll circle up, forming a butts-together defensive star, hand rocks to each other, even trade clubs around their group.

Fortunately, they don't tell anyone else how we kill them. Each group has to learn our tactics on its own, because there are no survivors to warn the rest.

We've got over two dozen mutated elephant skulls acting as fence decorations along the southern edge of the campus. Between the population control measures and the warning signs, I feel confident Diogenes' production capability will get him somewhere safer before the issue becomes pressing. Vehicles are now a priority since most robots lack the endurance to travel even as far as Niagara on a single charge.

To be fair, he's also adding some elephant-foot-sized punji pits around the campus, kind of like a poor man's minefield. We're trying to deter them, mostly. Manufacturing big-game guns in quantity is a lot more expensive than digging holes.

Mary and I, as big-game hunters, finished doing our part last night. This morning, we started in on a new career as an inter-universal exploration team. I didn't see the universes they picked, so all I got to do was sit there and feel stupid while Mary and Diogenes tried to dial up one of our four main candidates. It helped that we had power reserves from a night of magical charging. It let us open a viewing port in the iridium ring several times in each world.

To make life easier, I exercised my piddly daytime telekinesis to snatch a little bit from the worlds we found. Some dirt, a rock, a bit of litter, a leaf, whatever I could snatch. These helped focus the gateway and successive attempts, making it more likely we were consistently hitting the same world each time. It would not do to view a dozen random samples of a world and find out later we accidentally viewed a dozen random *worlds*.

I find the 1940's intriguing, along with the Art Deco world. Mary is more interested in doing the Charleston and dodging Prohibition agents—I think she's planning to add "bootlegger" to her resume. We also sampled the high-tech wonderment world, but the more we see of it, the less vampire-friendly it looks. It reminds me of some of the more optimistic views of the future by sci-fi writers, but I wonder just how much personal privacy anyone has when the world is tied together so tightly by microwaves and fiber optics.

I'm a bloodsucking monster that feeds on the living. I value my privacy. Sue me.

After a lot of video photography, radio monitoring, and more than a little tailoring on Diogenes' part, we'll have a decent chance of blending into whichever world we pick. He's getting our clothes ready for us—with some advice from Mary, because my idea of stylish only extends as far as wearing clothes. We'll be sticking with commodities instead of money, naturally; we don't have samples of money to counterfeit. And, while we can detect multiple languages in the airwaves, some of the idioms and phrasing seem a bit weird. I'm opting to go with some pre-cast concept-translation spells so we can at least understand what someone means by "The billboard bopped in a dimbox breezer and blew."

If you're interested, it means the flashy-looking person got in a convertible taxicab and left. I understood it, mostly, except for the part about the billboard and the dimbox. Taken in context, I probably wouldn't have a problem, but I'm a coward by nature and prefer to be prepared.

Mary insisted on knives. I insisted on no guns.

"Why not?" she demanded. "You're bringing Firebrand!"

Hey, I don't want to be part of this argument!

"Relax," I told them both. "First of all, Firebrand is going to be in a long case. It's a display piece, as far as anyone else is concerned, which is why I'm polishing it up nicely."

And thank you for that, Boss.

"De nada. Second, Firebrand will be paying close attention to people around us. If we say something wrong, do something weird, or otherwise attract attention, it's Firebrand's job to warn us. I don't intend to *draw* Firebrand while we're there."

"Intend," Mary repeated. "And if we have to? Why no guns?"

"Because guns are loud and have no other purpose than to kill people. Firebrand can be passed off as an antique and a work of art. Besides, we don't have any guns that don't scream 'Anachronism!' Yours are automatics, made of space-age materials and hold more shots in the magazine than there are vital organs in the body. Besides, where would you keep them?"

"I could find places."

"No doubt. And we will, later, after we determine if it's legal to carry a firearm, and after we get you some local guns. Right now, our only purpose in going there is to take a pleasant walk down the street. If we can, we'll talk to a bullion dealer, get some money and a feel for the culture, that sort of thing. Then we come back and compare notes. If we get into any sort of fight, we've screwed up badly."

"I don't think I like your logic."

"I don't expect you to. Would you rather stay here and monitor me through Diogenes?"

"Hell, no!"

"Then figure out what knives you want to bring and how to hide them *perfectly*. I haven't seen a single picture from this Jazz Age world where the citizens are armed. For all we know, they may all be carrying concealed weapons, but they're well-concealed, and therefore ours should not stand out, either."

"Spoilsport."

I agreed with her and started working with Diogenes on how to monitor us remotely. My idea was to use the Diogephone micro-gate as a data connection. It was small enough we might be able to power it from the Apocalyptica side with enough transformers. It would certainly keep us in contact. Plus, it could act as an existing gate I could manipulate in case we had to leave in a hurry. Switching it from the phone to a local doorway wouldn't be difficult on my end. Doing it here at the same time was a little trickier. I had to build a separate spell at the Apocalyptica end for that. It wouldn't do to go through a doorway and get squeezed through a pinhole at the other end.

Come to that, what would it look like on the doorway side? *Could* you walk through such a door? Or would the spell permit it? I don't think it would, but it's possible the spatial distortion would result in a thin stream of high-pressure person coming out the smaller gate. All I know for sure is I'm not going to test it with my face.

The other purpose the ongoing connection would serve was calibration. Twin, enchanted, specially-linked iridium rings were probably the best-case scenario for inter-universal gateways. How long would a magical charge keep them connected? It would be another data set for Diogenes to use in calculating a thaumaturgic energy scale.

I brought a spare power crystal, just in case. According to Diogenes, Jazzworld was very low on magical flux.

Jazzworld, Thursday, July 8th, 1926

Mary has a nice dress and a hat like a bucket. I get a two-piece suit and a fedora. Her outfit is breezy enough to tolerate the sweltering heat. I get to slow-roast like beef in a crock pot.

We fired up the orichalcum cable-arch, stepped through and down, exactly as if we stepped off the bus—which, of course, was what the far end of the portal locked on to. Fortunately, the bus was sitting at the station, unoccupied. According to the map on the wall inside, we were in San Antonio, Texas. Mary salvaged a *San Antonio Daily News* from a station bench and we discovered the date.

July. In San Antonio. I don't know if it hit a hundred degrees today, but I wouldn't risk money against it.

We strolled through the city while trying not to bake in the morning sunshine. It wasn't easy. At least our outfits didn't stand out. Most people wore less fashionable clothes—trousers, shirts, caps, that sort of thing—but we fit in as part of the respectable middle class. Mary noticed the hairstyles and makeup on the women, commenting about finding a beauty parlor and getting a perm.

Of course, we needed money, first. I asked a passing policeman—walking his beat and twirling his nightstick—if he could give us poor, lost visitors any help. He was very friendly, possibly because of our clothes, and directed us to a bank to discuss gold exchange rates.

A *bank*. Not a bullion dealer. Apparently, banks can handle gold. When did that start? Or, perhaps more accurately, when did that stop? Did banks ever handle gold and silver in my world? Or is this world still on some sort of gold standard, or something?

There are drawbacks to not having a background in history and finance.

But Mr. Perkins, the bank manager, was very helpful, almost eager. Changing some old, worn, antique gold coins into modern cash wasn't a problem, no sir, not a bit of it. Of course, there's a small transaction fee, et cetera, et cetera. I smiled and nodded and waited until he stopped talking. There followed some functionaries, some walking back and forth, and finally a fistful of money.

In *banknotes*. Not dollars, as such, but paper money issued and backed by the bank itself. I didn't know they could do that. Where I'm from, I'm pretty sure they can't. The Federal government takes a dim view of anyone else printing money.

Our objective in visiting this world was to find out things about it, and this certainly counted. I thanked the nice Mr. Perkins, shook his hand, recovered my hat, and we departed.

Hotels don't have air conditioning. They have fans. At least, the fancy-looking place we picked was like that. However, if you're willing to pay for it, they'll send up a bucket of chipped ice so your fan can blow air across it and over you. Other than that, the place is quite nice.

"What do you think?" I asked, once we had the door locked. I stripped out of my jacket, tie, and overshirt as quickly as was decent.

"I think I like the look," Mary said, lounging by one of the electric fans—all metal, I noticed. It would never pass modern safety standards. On high speed, it could remove fingers.

"I'm not too crazy about the lack of air conditioning."

"Me either, but I'm sure it's been invented. The movie theater had a sign out front."

"I didn't notice. Maybe they haven't gotten around to upgrading the hotel."

"No doubt. And I'd be very pleased to hold up the bank we just visited."

"What, after Mr. Perkins was so nice to us? I don't even know if I like this place enough to live here."

"Well, maybe another bank. First, we need a getaway car and some Tommy-guns."

"Do they have Tommy-guns?" I asked, firing up the other fan and leaning forward to let it blow down the collar of my undershirt. The heat was stifling.

"I don't know, but we can look."

"Let's find a bank that deals in government money," I suggested. "Dollars, not banknotes."

"Good thought. We can take those anywhere. Maybe we should get our banknotes changed to dollars—we can use it as an excuse to case the joint."

"You're starting to sound like you belong here."

"I like the style—everything except that silly permanent wave thing they're doing with their hair. They look like helmets!"

"You can get away with being ahead of your time," I assured her. I patted my face and neck with a wet cloth, then fished out my inter-universal roaming phone. "Diogenes? Have you been listening?"

"Yes, Professor."

"How are things going?"

"The connection continues to be stable, although the demand is slightly higher than the supply. Projected thaumic battery life is on the close order of fifteen hours, with twelve remaining. However, I intend to add additional ruthenium transformers in proximity to the Apocalyptica gate to extend the connection time."

"Good man."

"Technically, I am a good integration of expert systems running in a complex of quantum computer cores, but I infer you mean it as a compliment."

"Uh, yes."

"Excellent. I enjoy successfully interpreting your statements."

"And teasing me?"

"Possibly."

"I'm surrounded by snarks," I observed.

"Better than boojums."

"You're not helping."

"I shall endeavor to be more helpful, Professor."

"Thank you. Should I do anything at this end?"

"If you could avoid anything magical, it would make the measurements and calibration at this end more precise."

"I usually have a spell to deal with overwhelming heat," I complained. "At least, in any world without air conditioning. This long-term absence of cooling is starting to make me nauseous."

"Are you dizzy, Professor?"

"No, but I have a headache."

"These are early signs of heat stress. Please cast a spell to cool yourself."

"I'll consider it. Hey! You said 'thaumic battery life.' What's the battery life on the phone's powerpack?"

"At this level of demand, it will require recharging within seventy hours, Professor."

"Ah. Then I won't worry about it. But I do have an idea. Do you think you could build me a set of fake glasses based on the designs we've seen? Something in a zero prescription, but with a built-in hidden camera, so you can watch as well as listen?"

"I will get right on it, Professor."

"Thanks, Diogenes."

I put the Diogephone back in my pocket and turned around, letting the fan blow over the back of my neck.

"You look miserable," Mary told me.

"I don't like the heat," I admitted, "but I want Diogenes to have a long baseline for his readings."

"Why is the heat such a problem for you?"

"I'm guessing it has to do with my body mass versus surface area. Not enough area to cool my mass efficiently."

"I'll call room service for more ice, then get you another wet towel while we wait."

"What did I ever do to deserve you?"

"I don't keep track of your sins," she replied, from the bathroom.

The day only got hotter, of course. Mary ran a tub of water, aimed a fan across it, and I soaked in it. One good thing about the hotel bathroom was the sheer size of the tub. The modern tubs I'm used to involve folding repeatedly to get wet everywhere. I could use the thing as a coffin if only I had a lid.

Mary dumped half the cracked ice into the tub and left the other half on a stool beside it. She left me to cool while she went out to find another bank. I let her, mainly because I was feeling the heat and it was becoming more and more tempting to use magic. I didn't want to disturb Diogenes' readings, so I simmered and suffered.

In retrospect, I should have had Mary take the Diogephone with her so I could cast a cooling spell. I didn't think of it at the time, though. I blame the heat and the way my brain was sweating.

When Mary came back, she was less than pleased. I heard the door slam and a sort of growling noise.

"Problems?" I asked, sitting up. She stuck her head in the door and threw down her hat.

"I've changed my mind. This is *not* the place for me."

"I'd rather live farther north, myself. This heat is killing me and I'm not sure I'm being figurative."

"Poor dear." She poured the rest of the ice bucket into the tub. "But I'm talking about the people, not the temperature."

"Oh? What's wrong? I'd think there would be a lot of gentlemanly behavior in this day and age."

"Oh, there is, there is. A man coming out of the bank held the door for me, which I thought was a nice gesture. Everyone calls me 'M'lady,' instead of 'Ma'am,' though. It's not what they say that bothers me. It's the way they *treat* me!"

"Um. How is this not a good way to treat you…?" I trailed off, sitting up in the tub.

"Do you know what the bank manager told me?"

"Not from here. Even my ears aren't that good. Besides, I'm not sure they've invented the muffler for cars, yet."

"He said he would be happy to exchange the banknotes—after all, his competitor was a sound financial institution and they routinely honor each other's notes—but shouldn't this be something my husband did?"

"Equality is a struggle," I noted.

"Oh, I handled it. Politely," she added. "All it took was iron will and grim determination. First, it was my husband who needed to do it. When I insisted, then it was a case of getting a written note from him. When I pointed out I didn't have a husband, he told me my father would do as well. When he finally got it through his thick skull I didn't have a man to do it for me, there was a good fifteen minutes of *harrumph* and 'This is most irregular,' and similar noises. Of course," she continued, shifting her voice to mock some pretentious banker, "we, as an institution, routinely deal in such minor money matters as a typical housewife may be expected to handle, keeping track of her egg money for her and the like, but it is hardly a routine matter to handle such a large sum for a woman in her own name."

"We only changed a pound of gold," I protested. "The bank used troy ounces, twelve to the pound, and at about twenty dollars to the troy ounce, that's only two hundred and forty dollars, minus some expenses. He had problems with two hundred dollars in a woman's hands?"

"The 'egg money,' whatever that is, is nickels and dimes, from what I gather. Literally. Nickels, the coins. Dimes are the large denominations. I'm thinking we should think of the local dimes as dollars. They actually buy things with pennies!"

"I see. How did you get him to see things your way?"

"I sat there, smiled a lot, and asked him if he would rather explain it to my lawyer or to the newspapers."

"I don't understand."

"So, you're a major bank and refuse to do business with a woman? You have no professional ethics? And you won't change your competitor's banknotes? I'll be happy to walk into the *Daily News* office and tell them all this. Or I can have my lawyer—who has no problem taking a woman's money, I might add, nor yours—how you refused to perform your job. And *then* I can tell the newspapers. Or you can get rid of me in two minutes by doing your job. You pick."

"He did his job?"

"With much grumbling and snorting and disgusted sounds. I suspect he believes me to be quite 'unladylike'."

"So, if you don't want to live here… you found the perfect bank to rob?" I asked, still in the tub. Mary's face flicked quickly through surprise and shot straight on to evil glee.

"Oh, *yes!*"

"Daring daylight robbery? Or do you think we can get into the vault?"

Mary started to answer, stopped, looked thoughtful.

"They don't have security cameras, nor much in the way of alarms. And the time lock on the vault—if they have one—will be mechanical. I can tendril-tweak it right through the vault door and lock it again the same way."

"So we can do it either way," I agreed. "Take your pick. Do we hold the place up in broad daylight for the fun of it? Or do we rob the place blind and leave Mister Grumpy's nameplate in the vault in place of a stack of cash?"

"I hate it when you present two fantastic options and I can only pick one."

"No hurry. I'm not going anywhere until after dark. Or until it cools down. Besides, we need to case the place better. I want to research the target and arrange our getaway before we try anything."

As the sun set, we closed up the bathroom, drained the tub, and I sat under a lukewarm shower while we had our transformations. Afterward, we did a mundane wash and dry, dressed again, and went out.

Streetlights aren't plentiful, but they're there. People are out and about, but not many. This world—at least, in the evenings—seems quieter, less hectic. It reminds me of Karvalen at night, sort of. The overcity calms down a lot after the sun sets. The undercity never really sleeps, but the undercity has better public lighting. This San Antonio is a different city, but it doesn't exactly go to sleep at night, either. Dozes fitfully, maybe.

Mary and I walked arm in arm down a sidewalk. I enjoyed it, now that the heat of the day was no longer trying to bake me in my own skin. The temperature was still way up, but without a living metabolism, I didn't mind.

"So," she asked, quietly, "how about we empty the vault?"

"Suits me."

"Can we please do a daring daylight robbery, too?"

"I only promised you one bank robbery."

"Please?" She fluttered eyelashes at me and laid her head on my shoulder.

"Sheesh. All right. But vault first. Then we can go back to Apocalyptica and get bulletproofed. I don't want to start a robbery and find out the security guard served in the Great War and isn't afraid to use his weapon."

"Suits me. But I want a Tommygun for the robbery. I checked. They make the things here, or something very like them, and civilians can buy them."

"You're kidding!"

"Nope. Fully automatic, drum magazine, the works. They're about two hundred bucks."

"They're taking their Second Amendment rights pretty seriously in this day and age," I observed. "We'll also need a getaway car. Any thoughts on that?"

"Not yet, but I haven't checked out a car dealership, either. Can we steal a car, too?"

"As a getaway car for a bank robbery? Seems logical. But we may want to buy one just so we get what we want—one that starts reliably, for example. I'm hoping for something with an electric starter so we don't have to hand-crank it."

"Oh, fine. Be all *practical*."

The bank in which Mary had her difficulties was a three-storey thing, masonry, on a corner, with some decorative pillars out front. We walked past it on two sides, then went around behind it through an alley. There were no windows on the ground floor, of course, but there were windows on the second and third floors—presumably for light and air, since there was probably no air conditioning system.

I gave Mary a leg up, flinging her all the way to the roof. I sat down, leaned my head back against the building, and waited, listening for anything untoward. My hearing was sufficient to detect a couple of meaty thumping sounds from within the building—marble echoes nicely. After about ten minutes, Mary opened a second-floor window and whistled. I leaped up, caught her hand, and she pulled me in.

"Where do we stand?" I whispered.

"We're alone in the building, aside from some sleepers. I found one electrical alarm, but it's pretty basic. I already spoofed it. I haven't checked the vault, yet."

"I thought we were doing a nighttime recon?"

"I just did. There's nothing between us and the vault," she said, grinning. I sighed and went along with her.

"Lead on. You know this place."

Mary detoured past Mr. DeFalco's office and swiped his nameplate before heading for the basement stairs. There were heavy cage doors at the head of the stairs, out of view of the public, but Mary's tendril flicked through the lock and drew the bolt in seconds. Downstairs, the vault door was much more impressive. It was seven feet on a side, square, with big, thick bolts, a heavy spinner on the combination lock, and a sizable wheel for cranking back the bolts.

We both ran tendrils through the steel, feeling our way along the bolts and around the mechanism. Working the combination lock wouldn't be a problem, but until the clock-timer inside the door reset, spinning the knob wouldn't do anything. It was a wind-up clock, with a key access in the outer face of the door. A rocker inside the mechanism acted as a pendulum. Could I turn the gearwheel controlling the lockout lever? No, it didn't budge and I didn't want to break it. How about working the lever, itself? No, the gearwheel was in the way until it rotated far enough. But the rocker serving as a pendulum… it moved. It relied on the inertia of its mass to keep each click, back and forth, at the same rate.

"Diogenes."

"Yes, Professor?"

"I'm going to use a little magic. You might want to edit this time frame from your calibrations."

"Understood, Professor. Please let me know when to resume."

"Roger that."

I scrounged power from the local environment, squeezed it into a spell, focused it, guided it with tendrils through the face of the vault door, touched it to the rocker, and robbed it of all the inertia I could. Instantly, it moved from a *tick-tick-tick* to a high-pitched buzz. The timer flashed forward, spring unwinding, until the early-morning *ka-chunk* sound freed the tumblers.

"Okay, Diogenes. I'm done."

"Thank you, Professor."

Mary spun the dial to unlock the thing, turned the central wheel, and the vault was open. She went in while I re-wound the clock and reset the time.

After that, it was just a matter of sacking money. She left the nameplate on the floor of the vault—carefully wiping it and everything else down to remove fingerprints, just in case—and we locked everything up behind us.

I used the door to the manager's office as our gateway back to Apocalyptica.

Apocalyptica, Thursday, May 26th, Year 1

Having a large pile of money—well over ten thousand dollars—is fine and dandy, but take it out of the world and it's paper. You can't spend paper money outside its own frame of reference. People look at you funny and try to arrest you. It's weird.

On the other hand, it'll be useful for buying a car and some Thompson submachine guns. It's not about the money, really. Mary just wants the adventure. I'm not sure she even uses money as a way to keep score.

I don't want adventure. I want a quiet little house somewhere. But her idea of adventure and fun is a lot better than being the Demon King, the Lord of Shadows, and basically shouldering the weight of crushing responsibilities. I can cope with her fun, mostly because it makes her almost gigglingly happy, which makes me happy.

Well… less sad. I smile more when she does. I'm willing to think of this as good for me. That's an improvement and I can acknowledge it's an improvement. If she needs a partner in crime, I'm up for it. Even if she wants to bring along a goofy sidekick on her adventures, I'm up for it.

Holding up a bank isn't really too complicated, all things considered. We returned to our hotel room through a gate and I brought my small mirror with me. I also wore a spell for keeping cool. We took a walk down to the public library to do some research. After a few hours of looking through records and searching around the country by scrying mirror, we debated the merits of individual financial institutions—very quietly. It was a library, after all. Eventually, we selected our target and decided to combine our bank robbery with a sightseeing trip. We bought train tickets and went for a ride.

San Antonio is awfully far away from everywhere else.

On the plus side, a train ride is a pleasant thing in and of itself. It was a full-service ride, from sleeper car to dining car to regular passenger car. I enjoyed it thoroughly.

"I have another idea," Mary offered, speaking in Rethvenese.

"Oh?"

"If we can find a world with old steam locomotives, can we rob a train?"

"Do you just like stealing things?" I asked.

"Jewel thief," she pointed out. "It's fun."

"Whatever happened to burglary, rather than armed robbery?"

"Such as breaking into a bank and stealing everything from the vault?"

"Good point."

"So? If we find something even vaguely like the American West, can we rob a train?"

"We'll have to look it over first, but I don't see why not."

"You make me happy. Did you know that?"

"It's one of my goals in life."

Our train ride had a number of stops and, for us, two transfers. Eventually, we made it all the way to Montgomery, Alabama. Why there? Because I looked over dozens of banks in a scrying mirror and I liked the layout of this one. It was a smallish bank with open counters rather than cages for tellers. It had a pair of uniformed security guards. It wasn't too near a police station. There were a dozen other things about it I liked, from a robbery standpoint. It was also conveniently located not too far from a cemetery with an absolutely lovely wrought-iron archway.

The most important part of any endeavor is getting away with it. You can fail to kill your victim, you can fail to get the money, you can fail in any number of ways, but if you *don't get caught*, you can try again.

Mary picked out a car and I counted out cash to the car dealer. I never actually drove a Model T before and the salesman was only too happy to give us a lesson. I was happy it had an electric starter and cranked up easily. The salesman seemed more enthusiastic about the twenty horsepower—and the top speed of over forty miles an hour!

I solemnly agreed it was an impressive car.

After that, we checked into a hotel to make sure we had our sunset plans covered. Prior planning prevents pyrotechnic problems. With our evening arrangements secure, we went shopping for guns. I bought a pair of Thompson submachine guns by paying cash.

That still amazes me. I mean, America, yeah. Second Amendment, yeah. But I was raised to expect… well… more red tape. At the very least, someone should ask for my driver's license.

Nope. The gun store owner didn't ask for identification of any sort.

Okay, to put this in perspective: The *car dealer* didn't ask for my driver's license.

This seems as weird to me as looking over the edge of the world.

I bought two spare magazines while I was at it and a couple hundred rounds of ammunition. I also inquired about good places to go target shooting and got several recommendations from the store owner. He was very friendly, either because I had a pair of submachine guns or because I spent as much on them as I did on my new car.

We drove out to one of the spots he suggested so we could get a feel for the Thompsons. They have something of a kick, let me tell you. The forward handgrip isn't there just for show. And they chew through things like rabid beavers at a lumberjack contest. It's a little disturbing to watch things disintegrate like that. I'm not terribly surprised, though. The Thompson in this world is, by default, chambered for a .50-caliber round. It's a regular, pistol-sized bullet, just larger in diameter, not the monster-sized machine-gun rounds. But still, whatever it hits is going to notice, probably briefly.

I'm going to admit it. It was fun. There. I said it. My only regret was the limited size of the box magazines. I wanted a drum, but we didn't get one. Too awkward to carry and they won't let you put a loaded gun in a violin case. I did tape two magazines together, though, upside-down to each other in case we needed to reload quickly.

And… I bought more ammunition. And a cleaning kit. *Yes*, we fired off all the bullets we bought. It made Mary grin from ringing ear to ringing ear. I might have smiled rather lethally, myself.

We spent much of the night in the hotel, discussing how to do this, what to do if this, if that, if the other thing. We planned it out thoroughly before I went to the cemetery and did some preliminary spellcasting on the entry arch.

I did not enter the cemetery. Maybe it would be all right. Maybe not, too. Since I didn't intend to come back to this world for anything besides an occasional stopover, testing consecrated ground wasn't high on my list of priorities. And I'm a coward.

Then it was just a matter of waiting through sunrise, cleaning up, and dressing for a gunfight. No, we weren't looking for a gunfight, but if you know it's a risk, you prepare for one.

Mary walked in with me. She had a shoulder bag and I had a briefcase. I wanted to use a violin case, but Mary thought it was a little too cliché. Besides, a briefcase wouldn't draw attention. As she headed for the powder room, I headed for one of those table-islands with customer paperwork and captive pens. Coincidentally, these directions took us past the security guards. She hit one, I hit the other, and out came the Tommy-guns. I put one round into the ceiling to make sure I had everybody's attention. Mary handed small sacks to the tellers.

Tick-tock, tick-tock, I kept track of the time, the people lying on the floor, and anything happening outside. Mary focused on motivating tellers. She didn't shoot any of them, but strongly suggested it might happen. Waving a big-bore weapon at someone in point-blank range is extremely motivating. Mary was as giddy as a schoolgirl at her first formal dance, much to the concern of the various frightened people. A giggling bank robber with a huge gun is not a comfort.

I, on the other hand, remained serious, alert, and kept my back to a wall. When we hit the four-minute mark, I signaled Mary to finish up.

Gun slung, Mary collected sacks and we beat feet out the door. Into the Tin Lizzy, down the street, around the corner—that quickly, we were a respectable couple out for a drive. No sirens, not yet, so we probably had more time than we thought. Still, better safe than sorry.

I activated the prepared spell on the cemetery arch as we approached. I drove right through it and into the basement. The gate was only open for a few seconds, but it was a fairly sizable gate and cost us a lot of magical potential. Nonetheless, this was my first Model T and I didn't feel like parting with it.

As soon as I stopped the car and set the handbrake, Mary kissed me thoroughly. All the robots capable of it applauded. Diogenes is sometimes a smartass.

Apocalyptica, Friday, May 27th, Year 1

As I handed Mary down from the car, I looked at it against the background of the basement workshop.

"Diogenes?"

"Yes, Professor?"

"How do you move robots and materials?"

"Please elaborate. 'Move them'?"

"From one site to another. From here to Niagara."

"The process begins with a remote flyover to map potential routes. Small, highly-mobile robots examine the ground of these routes and their survey data determines the final course. Once determined, a squad of robots with suitable tool appendages is dispatched to clear obstacles and construct whatever road structures may be necessary. Transport units take charged batteries to the road crew robots until they are too distant for remote refueling. Then they transport solar panels to establish a charging station and begin recharging the road crew from there.

"Once the road is adequate for routine transportation, appropriate robots are dispatched to the destination point, charging as necessary along the way. In the specific case of Niagara, the robots arrived on site and began building a water-powered generator to provide more power for renovation, recycling, and construction of higher-capacity power systems."

"And the bottleneck for packing up the university base is… what?"

"Primarily, transportation. To maintain a constant supply of elf-clones will require the transfer or construction of a large quantity of specialized manufacturing equipment at the Niagara site. The university base is the primary fabrication center for all my industrial production, so the cloning tanks are built here. Once clone production is secured, the inter-universal transfer case will be relocated, possibly causing a minor delay at the delivery end. Then we can begin transfer operations for the rest of the industrial infrastructure."

"But you say you've got a road already?"

"I have a pathway," Diogenes corrected. "It is traversable by tracked robots."

"I see. Do you plan to make more vehicles?"

"Yes, Professor. My current plans call for a rotastat vehicle as a primary transport. This will also permit rapid deployment of robot work forces in each location without the delay of road-clearing."

"What's a rotastat?"

"A hybrid of a helicopter and a dirigible."

"All right. Get me a parts list of things you'd like dropped on your doorstep. In the meantime, how much ruthenium do you have? And can we get a couple of sets of doors put in this garage so we can drive stuff out?"

"Re-opening the access ramp to this level is relatively straightforward. As for the ruthenium, I presume you want it for magical charging, which, taken with your earlier comments, leads me to believe you intend to use an interuniversal gate with some frequency. May I suggest relocating the gate to more traffic-friendly surroundings?"

"Of course."

"Along the same line, I would like to keep one EM transformer near my primary processor, if you don't mind, Professor."

"I intended you to, but I should have specified."

"As for the parts list, a number of rare-earth materials are abundant in the salvage, but they usually require extensive reprocessing for our applications. I will draw up a list based on priority."

"Way ahead of me. Thank you, Diogenes."

"Thank you, Professor."

"Mary? Would you like to steal some stuff for Diogenes?"

"Romantic questions like that are all a girl lives for."

By nightfall, most of the old ramp was dug out. It was a lot of earth to move, but robot laborers controlled from a central intelligence never get in each other's way and never stop—they never even slow down. By morning, they would have the shallow grade hard-packed and cobbled over, ready to be driven on. There would even be doors at both ends of the ramp, as well as some light-blocking curtains.

Diogenes is a clever computer.

Meanwhile, Mary and I set up every electromagical transformer in another building, a former auto shop garage, I think. It was big, open, and had roll-up doors suitable for a school bus or semi-truck. She and Diogenes did most of the electrical wiring and tuning. I did the magical power conduits. Rather than simply allowing the things to radiate magic in all directions, I routed the power directly into the gate enchantment and the power crystals connected to it.

I also built a large power-jet, mostly as an experiment. It ran on its own, but not well. Giving it a small transformer of its own made it run beautifully, however, and the net power we got out of it was slightly higher than the transformer alone. I pretended I understood how it could do that and left it running.

Then it was time to walk all around the campus, building the low-power version of the magic compression jets—power fans. These "blew" power from all around the campus perimeter toward the enchanted gate. With a jet sucking in power, these would help the magical flow into the depleted area... I think. It ought to work that way, but I've never tried it on this scale before.

I was planning to open some big gates. Almost as big as the tunnel mouth Mary and I went through to avoid being followed. But these would be between universes, not a simple geographical shift.

Diogenes provided me with some gems and other crystals. Since I can already build a spell that acts a bit like a solar panel—radiant energy went in and some of it was converted to magical energy—I could set them up to charge themselves without wearing myself out to do it. It was a poor conversion, but if left alone long enough it would pay for itself and more. I wanted portable power to take with me, mainly because I couldn't be sure of where or when I would need to open my gate, only that it would be in a magic-poor environment.

I set them up on the rooftops, one to a building. After covering the roof over with an energy-conversion spell, the enchanted gems would absorb the magical energy converted from sunlight.

It would be quicker, of course, to feed them magic from an electromagical transformer and let the rooftop solar panels have all the sunlight, but the bottleneck is the ruthenium. We don't have enough transformers. But the conversion spell only blocks about four percent of the energy hitting the rooftop—less, from a practical standpoint, since some of the sunlight it absorbs isn't a type the solar panels can convert to electricity.

I'm amused at being so green. Being a vampire with solar-powered spells is ironic.

Apocalyptica, Saturday, May 28th, Year 1

As morning started in the east, Mary and I cleaned up for the day.

"Got a question, Professor," Mary said.

"Miss Mary, that's what *I* call him," Diogenes said, from his floating drone. "Firebrand calls him 'Boss.' You need your own term of endearment."

"Get that thing out of the bathroom."

"Yes, Dean of Knives." I heard it whir a few feet, no doubt hovering just outside the door.

"What's the question?" I asked.

"Why not charge all the gems you want while closing the nexus points? I mean, you were planning to finish your thing with them, right?"

"Yes, I suppose so. Actually," I added, brightening, "we've got more gems than we have rooftops. We could go do that while these are charging. Assuming the pressure doesn't crush them, of course. Diamonds take the pressure pretty well, but I'm not sure about quartz and other crystals. And the time differential might even be favorable."

"And if it isn't?"

"There are advantages, either way. If we go there and spend five days to every day here, we come back with a lot of equipment in a week. If it works the other way, Diogenes will make a lot of progress without us and we have enough magical charge to drag a freight train through..." I trailed off. Could we build tracks and put a gate on them? We could, in fact, drive a freight train through. It would be tricky to align the tracks exactly—and it better be *exact*! —but maybe with suitable sighting devices and some computer-controlled pistons, we could align them almost as quickly as the gate opened.

Not today. Bringing back a few truckloads of refined materials and manufactured parts would do. Why have Diogenes manufacture everything from scratch when we can simply buy things for him?

"Shall I send progress reports, Professor?"

"Excellent idea. Just when you hit milestones or snags, though. I don't want to randomize the time differential too much."

"Certainly, Professor."

Mary and I got our stuff together. I opened a gate to Mary's world, aiming for Nassau.

Nexus, Thursday, March 11th, 2049

When we landed and found the date, I decided it wasn't too bad. The time differential was nominal.

The *Princess* was still in port. Captain Tillard hadn't yet rented it out as an excursion boat. We weren't gone long enough. Most of the crew and staff were on leave, though. We gave them a two-day warning, saying we were putting out to sea on Saturday. It seemed unfair to show up and have them drop everything to scramble aboard. Two days should be plenty to settle bar tabs, recover from hangovers, and kiss people goodbye.

Then we made some inquiries, several calls, and a few deals.

Ordering various metals for Diogenes' use in electronic gear was easy, though expensive. I've done it before. In any major city, we can get same-day delivery. For bulk orders, it can take up to two days, but I wasn't in a terrible hurry. The longest delay was ordering some of the parts on Diogenes list. High-efficiency electrical motors of sufficient size and power, polyurethane membrane for gas bladders, Mylar sheeting, copper wire by the mile... Worst of all was a special magnesium-alloy framing for his dirigible-helicopter thing. I finally decided it would take too long to have them made, but commissioning a couple tons of the metal wouldn't take nearly as long. Diogenes could skip the mining, refining, and alloying and just make the bits he needed.

None of this was cheap, but we weren't worried about asset management too much. Mary's world—I'm going to call it "Nexus," with her kind permission—isn't a place for us to call home. Well, it's not a place for me to call home, but I don't think Mary's too interested in staying, either.

That night, after settling inboard the *Princess*, I noticed something. I should have noticed it sooner, but setting up for a major industrial relocation and fighting over the cybernet with online scheduling is distracting.

My bombardment stopped.

The ongoing, constant hammering of magic-disrupting spells wasn't ongoing. It was quiet. Even at this distance, it should have been easily detectable. I simply didn't notice the lack of it until I felt one—and only one—go off in the distance.

"What's the matter?" Mary asked.

"My nexus bombardment. It's stopped. Or mostly."

"Is that bad?"

"I don't know. I hope not. I have terrible visions of a bunch of magi sitting in domes of magical force on the seafloor, slowly leaching their souls away in the awful rush of power that annihilates their essential humanity and leaves them as nothing more than virtually unstoppable egomaniacs."

"Uh, these visions... are you talking about psychic visions of things that may have come to pass? Or are you talking about horrible what-if scenarios in your imagination? Please tell me it's not the first one."

"The second."

"I hate you."

"Only on alternate Thursdays."

"It *is* an alternate Thursday."

"So it is. All right, hate me. But help me, too. I want to run a scrying sensor out to the open nexus points and see what's going on. You get on the cybernet and catch up on the news. See if there's anything weird happening."

"What sort of weird?"

"Anything which might be a sign some magi family got a power lock on a sea-floor nexus."

"Oh, *that* sort of weird. On it."

The spell to scry on distant locations isn't a hard one—no, I'll correct that. The spell is about average difficulty, but I use it an awful lot, so I make it look easy. Many of the necromantic spells are about as complex, but I simply don't practice with them. At least with necromancy, I can usually afford to fumble around until I get them right. It's not like dead people are in a hurry. Well... most dead people.

My scrying spell took a lot longer to cast. I had to spend far more time and effort to gather sufficient power to charge it. Even then, I knew it wasn't going to last all that long. A side effect of all the disruption shockwaves? The things were detectable, like shockwaves from meteors, volcanos, or earthquakes, all around the world. It's conceivable they might have caused a severe level of turbulence in the regular flow of magic, making spells everywhere more difficult to cast.

I checked my open nexus points, starting with the pyramid. I parked my scrying sensor fairly close and skimmed all around it, checking for anything untoward.

No dome of force. No sign of interference. All seemed well.

I switched to another major nexus. Same story, but with a much clearer view of the nexus itself.

Power oozed from it slowly, a dribble of energy slowly filling up the disruption spell. In a day or two, it would reach critical level and fire. The rate of fire slowed so drastically because the nexus itself seemed to be running out of power.

They can do that?

I quickly flicked my scrying sensor around to the other open nexus points. They were all in similar shape, barely producing a trickle of energy. No one was interfering with them. They were just...

...dying.

I think I killed a world.

All right, so that's a bit melodramatic. I may have accidentally—well, unintentionally—used up the magic of a world. The magi families might be a bit disgruntled and, eventually, so might any supernatural creatures. But for all I know, if I seal up the nexuses and stop them from bleeding out power, the planet will generate more.

Of course, the Atlanteans of this world used up a sizable amount of magical force, according to magi legend. A few thousand years later, it still wasn't a major force in the world. Maybe it recovers at a geological rate—epochs or ages, rather than mere centuries or millennia. Or maybe they simply didn't tend to the wounds they inflicted. I have no way to know; I wasn't there.

As a first order of business, I suppose I should bandage the planet.

Nexus, Saturday, March 13th, 2049

Captain Tillard headed us out without trouble. The weather was fine, the sky was clear, and I was experimenting with self-replicating spells.

I had an idea for saving the world.

An Ascension Sphere, power circle, power fan, and power-compression jet all draw in ambient magical energy to operate themselves. From there, I already developed a self-replicating spell for containing an open nexus. Not only does it draw in magical power to maintain itself, but it uses that power to build a stronger version of itself.

I can also build a spell to absorb different wavelengths of the electromagnetic spectrum and turn it into magical energy. It's a converter, albeit a poor one.

If I put these together, can I build a spell to absorb and convert sunlight into magical force, use part of it to maintain itself, and use the rest to build another spell just like itself? It would be a primitive sort of Von Neumann machine, only done with magic and based purely on energy, not matter.

After plugging these two concepts into each other, I can definitely say the answer is a qualified "yes." Yes, it can be done. Unfortunately, due to the abysmal power conversion rate, it takes an extraordinarily high level of input power—the sunlight, in this case—for it to work at any reasonable rate. It isn't practical without a level of solar intensity found somewhere around... oh, the orbit of Mercury, I think.

In theory, I can build a self-replicating solar-to-magical energy converter spell. It can copy itself indefinitely, forming an invisible solar-collection band around the equator. When it's all the way around and, say, a hundred miles wide, it quits replicating itself and starts feeding the converted magical energy into a nexus, revitalizing the magical network in the planet.

Assuming the planet's magical network will accept a transfusion, of course.

I ran through some experiments and made some assumptions, then had Diogenes do some calculations. Assuming I build one of these things and turn it loose at the edge of space—about a hundred miles up—the whole network will be complete in a mere six hundred and nineteen years. Most of it will be built in the last decade because of a peculiarity of compound interest. As the network gets bigger, it collects more power, so it builds individual units more quickly. The more you have, the faster you get more.

Maybe I can start the process going, but hook up the output of an electromagical transformer to it. The conversion ratio for the spell is low, so any individual "solar panel" will provide only a trickle of power. The transformer, however, could keep up a steady flow, producing dozens of panels a day, every day, all the time. It would drastically shorten the time to make enough of them to be useful, especially if I set up more than one.

Of course, that would reduce the amount of sunlight reaching the world. How drastically would it affect the climate? These ongoing, self-replicating, potentially world-shaking effects are not to be used lightly! Maybe I should start the process on Apocalyptica and see what sort of effect it has, to test it. Apocalyptica has the added bonus of not having potential meddling from magi.

I'm also wondering what effects a lack of magic will have on the world. This world, anyway. If Karvalen suddenly lost all its magic, I'd say the world would crumble immediately and disappear back into the void. But here? I don't know if anyone will even notice. It's a planet-wide phenomenon, though, kind of like the planetary magnetic field. Just because humans can't directly detect its presence doesn't mean it isn't important. I'm leery of world-spanning changes. On that sort of scale, there's no telling what effects it has.

So, while I consider what sort of planetary-scale helpfulness I want to attempt and mess up, I have more immediate issues.

Bandages. I can do bandages.

Nexus, Tuesday, March 23rd, 2049

We spent the last week and a half undoing all the work I did to put Johann down. At least putting a bandage on a dying nexus is easier than containing a healthy one. It takes longer to be lowered to the ocean floor and hauled back up again than it does to set up the spells.

The reason it's easy is the low level of power. Comparatively low level of power, I mean. A normal nexus fountains out so much power I couldn't channel it myself if I had a dozen clones helping. A dying nexus, on the other hand, merely oozes power. It's something I can contain and control without too much risk of boiling the flesh off my bones. It's the difference between a volcanic eruption and a broken steam pipe. Either one is potentially fatal, but only one of them is definitely going to kill you by burning you to ashes and burying your charred bones in molten rock. The other one is merely going to hurt a lot.

The bandage spells are the same as always. They grow over the nexus so it can repair itself—hopefully. The good news is the healing process should be comparatively rapid. It doesn't have to patch a high-pressure leak, just a slow one. We'll see how it looks in a year or two.

On the plus side, I charged up several of my more durable power crystals. Opening a temporary gate to Apocalyptica shouldn't be a problem. Maybe that's callous of me, sucking up some of the last of the planet's magic for my own purposes, but at this point I'm not sure it matters.

In other news, Mary can't find any information on my Magic Eight-Ball of Doom. Sure, there are a lot of world leaders making all sorts of ugly noises at each other, what with an inexplicable disaster upsetting the balance of power and all, but no one seems to be a candidate for the Palantír of Orthanc Award. I don't think my evil twin is influencing anyone specific.

The American forces have re-taken the East Coast, though. In the past couple of weeks, the horrific psychic phenomenon diminished so markedly that ground troops could roll over the region to secure it. They've found a number of failed genetic experiments—magical hybrid beasts, but that's not what they're calling them—and a remarkable level of ruination. Officials have no explanation for this attack, but sources close to the new President report alien invasion has not been ruled out.

There's an interesting thought. If the President, the Cabinet, and Congress all go *phut* in some sort of attack, who takes over? I'm sure there's a chain of command, but the constitutional lawyers will argue over it for years to come, and at an obscene hourly rate, too. Not my problem, but still an interesting thought.

Naturally, all this has done atrocious things to the global economy. It's like a fat man doing the cannonball off the high dive. The ripples are going to take a while to settle down. It's possible there may be some wars because of this. I wonder if the United Nations of this time and place has enough teeth to keep people from overreacting?

This doesn't help me with my problem, though. How do I find an Evil Orb?

Actually, come to think of it, there might be a good way. With a severe shortage of magic in the world—and after the worldwide shockwaves of magic-disruption—any defensive spells hiding it should be weakened or even destroyed.

Once I get Diogenes his equipment, I can use up the last of my available power to cast a seeking spell or two. Or, as a better thought, maybe I can find a major nexus *on land*, this time, and tap it for enough power to scan the planet. I know there's one in South America, one in Canada, and I recall noting at least three spread out across Africa. We'll see if they're occupied and by whom.

I like this plan. It stands a good chance of working and doesn't involve vertical miles of ocean.

In the meantime, we've purchased most of the materials on Diogenes' list. Sadly, plutonium is not commercially available, but I suspect he only included it as a joke. I'd like to get some, just because it would amuse me to hear his reaction. I'm not mentioning it to Mary, though. She'd start planning how to steal it.

Is there a world where one *can* buy plutonium? Legally, I mean.

Everything we ordered is headed for Lisbon, Portugal, the nearest major city to our final nexus bandage. As soon as I'm done with first aid on the bleeding planet, we'll be headed there ourselves.

Nexus, Thursday, March 25th, 2049

Lisbon is a nice place. I like it. It's got an old-world feel to it, but it also has modern conveniences. Many of the streets use special power units, disguised as paving stones, instead of the usual power roads. It's purely an aesthetic consideration, but they cared enough to keep the look. I like that.

Neither of us speaks Portuguese, however. Well, we didn't. We still don't speak Portuguese, but after our late-night dinner we understood it a little. Still, with suitable apps and earpieces, technology is what really came to the rescue. We rented a very nice two-storey townhome across from some park. The major selling point, to me, was the ground-floor garage with the oversized door. You never know when you're going to need to drive a huge truck right off the edge of the world.

During the night—after our dinner—we walked past the Pátio da Galé. There's a metal statue of a man on horseback. I don't know who he is or why he has a statue and I didn't go up to read the plaque. Mary held my hand a lot after we walked by it.

Is this my life, now? Being reminded of Bronze? Or of Tort or Tamara? Or Shada, or Sasha…

I don't like this regretting thing. I'm not a big fan of grief, either.

Can I call them up from the basement and kill them? And if I *can*, the question becomes whether or not I *should*. Do regret and grief serve any purpose in a blood-drinking, soul-devouring monster? Or is that the difference between a monster and a person?

Yay, psychological issues bordering on philosophy! Now, where can I find a therapist who would believe me? I can see how that's going to go.

"Doctor, I'm a vampire and I'm considering killing my subconscious manifestations of regret and grief."

"How long have you felt like a vampire?"

"No, I *am* a vampire."

"Everyone feels, at some time or another, that they feed on others in some way…"

Then I show him the fangs, he believes me, and I have to eat him to stop the terrified screaming.

Mary tries to help, but this emotional problem of mine is not going away quickly. I'm worried it may never go away. I guess all I can do is survive one more day, every day, and hope it gets better.

Problem is, I have distractions, not goals. All I'm doing is cleaning up after myself. Putting my affairs in order. I don't have something to strive for. Sure, I've been promised I'll see my Tort again, and that's a good thing. I'm sure I'll eventually have the emotional energy to want to find the Black Ball, too. And work on a space program for Bob. And any number of other things.

Maybe I shouldn't hunt for something to do. It could be I'm not ready to undertake a major project. I don't even know what I want, much less what I need. Maybe I should learn to drift, to relax, recuperate, and rest until something catches my attention.

Mostly I just don't feel… motivated. I don't seem to care enough about anything to summon up and direct my full focus on it.

I'm smiling for Mary even though I'm depressed. I can do both at the same time, because I'm a liar as well as a coward.

Nexus, Friday, March 26th, 2049

The house is nice, for a rental. I don't think I approve of the metal shingle things, though. It's one of those roofs with the curved tiles, like overlapping pipe sections, but when they replaced the old roof they used metal "tiles" instead of actual tiles. Rain on the roof sounds very strange to my ears, almost like sleet on a field of xylophones. Every tile has a slightly different note, and that's hard to cope with at night. Earplugs mute it a bit, but tiny earpiece headphones are even better. Playing music resets my hearing to the ambient sound volume and blocks out most of the rainy-roof sounds.

It was still a good thing I wasn't sleeping. Instead, I spent a lot of time and effort with a grease pencil, a ruler, and a French curve, getting the garage door prepared. While I could use power from the Apocalyptica side of an established gateway, I wasn't comfortable with the idea of having it rely solely on remote power. I planned to drive a load of manufactured goods through it for Diogenes. Since a truck is no good when the halves are in different universes, I paid close attention to my sigil drawing and spell construction. This was a big gate, and it was going to have to be open for several seconds, possibly as much as a minute.

I wonder. If I offer a bunch of homeless people a meal and a place to crash for the night, would it be worth it to wire them into the gateway? A lot of homeless aren't in the best of health, so their vitality is relatively low. Even if it sucked the life right out of them, how much extra time would we get? Realistically, it's probably too much trouble. Of course, killing them outright and using their energies directly, as sacrificial victims, would certainly power the gate for quite a while. I wonder... a minute per person? Or ten seconds? Would it matter what sort of physical condition they were in? Is it a function of the energies of their souls, or does their vitality count for something?

Maybe I'll ask my *simulata*-self, sometime. He probably has a different perspective on it. I don't really want to experiment with the differences between a human battery, eating a human and redirecting the energies, and directly sacrificing a human to power a spell.

On the plus side, one of our deliveries was a spool of iridium wire. I got out the hot glue gun and gleefully added some of the wire to our escape route. I may have to carry a spool of the stuff with me in the future. It does seem to make gates more stable and cheaper to use. Plus, I never know when I'm going to have to flee right out of the world from a family of angry demigod wizards. Or from hostile energy-state beings, for that matter.

When I kill the Lord of Light—someday—how will the others react? Will they be glad he's dead? Will they shrug and call it justice? Will they be violently opposed? Or will they merely be concerned I found a way to do it? I guess it all depends on *how* I do it, because I have no idea where to start.

Well, killing all his followers is a good start, but that poses problems of its own.

I may have miscalculated my gate requirements. Slightly.

The garage door is enormous, for a gate. It's big enough to drive a truck through. With a head start on the street, a truck could make the turn into the driveway, hit the accelerator, and enter the gate at a good speed. The gate wouldn't have to be open for long at all.

But we're getting deliveries at our address, now. Boxes upon boxes of stuff keep arriving. It's not all loaded on a single truck.

So I've overdone it on the garage door. Fine. I can redo my efforts on a more mundane door. We can use the small switch-box for anything that will fit inside it, of course, but some things still need to be manhandled through a gateway.

I opened the door-sized gate and shoved through a lot of ruthenium, exchanging it for a robot, the shift-box, some electronics modules, and some electromagical transformers wired for the local power outlets.

"Okay, what's all this for?" I asked.

"If you wish," replied the Diogephone, "we can establish a permanent link between the campus and this remote robot in much the same way the portable phone unit is connected. This will allow me to access the cybernet of Nexus, as well as transfer objects through the shift-box. The transformers are present to supply magical power from the local power grid, reducing the demand on the Apocalyptica side."

He's a very clever computer.

"All right. Shouldn't we build the communications micro-gate into a wireless router or something, though?"

"Communications with the robot is most important. It can relay to a local router and cybernet access point."

"If you say so. We'll set things up so you can supply yourself. You do know to be careful about attracting attention?"

"You forget, Professor. I am a native of the world you call 'Nexus.' My primary programs were written there."

"You probably know the place better than I do. All right. I'll enchant a set of twin micro-rings for your local robot and you can use the house as a resource gathering point. But I'd rather do the spell-work there; the local magical potential is worse than ever over here."

"Hey!" Mary protested. "What about fixing the world? Or finding your lost ball?"

"I want to get Diogenes set up, first. I'd like him to have as much time as possible to gather hard-to-salvage things before we attract a lot of attention—and we might. Once he's able to operate on his own on this side, we'll come back and hunt down a land-based nexus where we can experiment."

"Are you sure you want to bother anyone sitting on a major nexus?"

"No, but I'm pretty sure they're not going to argue as forcefully as they used to. The magical potential here is lower than I've ever seen, and their wizardry isn't up to our standards. We'll look them over before we pick one out, I promise. Unless you want to start poking around while I go back to Apocalyptica?"

"Not on your life! I'm not being left behind to do the dirty work."

"I just thought you might want to case the joints beforehand."

"And *we* will," she insisted. "You're sticking with me so I can keep you out of trouble, mister."

"Yes, dear."

I left the Diogephone in Nexus to facilitate communications. Diogenes, once he had steady access to the cybernet, ordered quite a number of things. He also encouraged me to go out and buy or rent things manually. He was confident he could avoid notice, but it would help to have alternative delivery points and multiple cybernet access addresses.

"It sounds as though you're planning to stay," I observed.

"If the option is available, Professor. This planet has a manufacturing infrastructure in good working order. I am still building mine."

"There are other worlds. Maybe we could set up something similar on them."

"An excellent notion, Professor. However, a world which does not possess cybernet-enabled commerce poses problems."

"You'd need human-ish help," I agreed. "Think about ways we can set things up, please."

"I shall give it considerable processor time."

"Very good. What's the time like over there?"

"Daytime."

"Then Mary and I should come through to avoid any sudden change-of-state problems."

"As you wish, Professor."

Mary and I returned to Apocalyptica, where I started work on permanent communicator-sized rings for the Nexus robot.

Apocalyptica, Saturday, June 11th, Year 1

Mary met me in our campus quarters when the sun came up. After a brief interlude, Diogenes delivered a robot-driven breakfast. I was halfway through a waffle before I thought to wonder about it. Eggs, juice, waffles... even milk, butter, and ham. Bacon, sausage... fried potatoes, corn flakes... maple syrup.

I stared at the food and held an internal debate about asking. When presented with something good, is it always necessary to ask how it got there? When is it acceptable to shut up and go with it? I know I sometimes shelve a notion or table a question and forget to take them down again, but I'm a pretty curious guy.

"Diogenes?"

"Yes, Professor?" replied the robot cart.

"I hesitate to ask, but my curiosity won't leave it alone."

"Go for it."

"It's possible a lot of this came from Nexus, ordered online and delivered to the house, then relocated and prepared here. Was it?"

"No, Professor. This food was produced locally, before a semi-permanent link to Nexus was made available."

"All right. I can see where some of this came from. Surely, there are potatoes growing in the ground, somewhere, and you found some. The eggs could be from any large bird, I suppose, and juice is out there for the squeezing. Ham and bacon merely involve finding something like a wild hog, I presume. But milk? Do I want to know where you got the milk?"

"I operate a cloning facility capable of producing fully-functional bodies, Professor. Blood is one product to be harvested. With suitable animal organs for sampling, milk can be produced artificially—artificially in that the organism producing it is not actually viable outside a life support tank. If you have something organic you would like me to grow, I will attempt to locate a suitable life form for sampling."

"I notice you didn't actually answer about where you got the milk."

"Is that not an answer in and of itself, Professor?" I thought I heard a snicker, although whether it was from Firebrand, Mary, or both, I can't say.

"I'll just eat my breakfast."

"Of course, Professor."

While we ignored the origins of the food, Mary made conversation.

"So, my beloved monstrosity, what do we do next?"

"I was thinking of going back to Nexus—your world—with some magical batteries. Since I haven't worked out a practical way to do scrying between universes, I need to be there. I want to find a land-based major nexus, open it, and use it to locate the Obsidian Orb of Awful."

"Alliterative, but you're mixing your vowels."

"Me physics person. Physicist speak math, ugh. Words hard," I told her. Without blinking, she bounced a roll off my face, caught it, buttered it.

"Anyting special I should bring?" Mary asked.

"Not that I know of. We'll plan ahead, though, once we pick where on Nexus we're going."

"While you are there," Diogenes mentioned, "perhaps you could also acquire more money?"

"Did you spend everything *already*?"

"No, but I believe I will before long."

"We'll see what we can do," I promised.

"Bank job?" Mary asked.

"Not in Nexus," I countered. "Too much security. Besides, we want digital money, not cash."

"Aww."

"Cheer up. You can always steal something valuable."

"I guess. Hey, do we still need the yacht?"

"Uh? No, I suppose not. Why?"

"Diogenes can list it for sale."

"Fair enough. Diogenes?"

"I am listing it now, Professor."

"Thank you. So, since you're getting help from a technological civilization, how does this change our schedule?"

"I believe the resources procured will be sufficient to accelerate our timetable for the evacuation of the university base by at least a factor of four."

"How does that relate to our mutant elephant population pressure?"

"Given my latest surveillance drone flights and the population count, I feel reasonably certain we will be safely relocated before they become a problem."

"Reasonably certain?" I repeated.

"In excess of ninety-eight percent probable."

"That's pretty reasonably certain," I agreed. "So, we go get you more money, find my wayward sphere, and then I get to go lead a boring, uneventful, unheroic, mundane life for a while?"

"If that is what you wish, Professor."

"Is it?" Mary asked. She sounded sincerely inquisitive, so I had to think about it.

Kings, queens, murder, gods, sorcerers, magicians, armies, dragons, vampire tribes, inter-universal gates, planets bleeding magic, thaumoforming plans for dying worlds, dead lovers, dead friends, dead children, dead Bronze...

One broken world. One evil orb. Are those two things enough to shut my overdeveloped sense of responsibility up? Can I sit in suburbia, pretend to be normal, and quietly lower the violent crime rate on Tuesday nights?

Couldn't hurt to try it.

"I don't know," I admitted, aloud. "I haven't done it in a while. I think I'd enjoy the peace and quiet—I think it's what I need to do. To go somewhere and pretend to be normal for a while. To pretend to be human, to blend in, to be just another guy down the street instead of a monster or a king or a god."

"Sweetheart?"

"Yes?"

"Is it okay if you're married to an international jewel thief?"

"Are you going to hate this?" I asked.

"I'll be bored out of my mind," Mary admitted. "I can do it, if you need me to. Just... there's going to come a point where I can't stand it anymore."

"Then we'll blow up that bridge when we come to it. Fair?"

"I prefer to burn it."

I'm with her, Boss.

"I knew you would be," I answered. "All right, Mary. You do what you need to do while I do what I need to do. Diogenes, can you bring us the charged gems and replace them with uncharged gems? We're going to need to bring as much power with us as we can."

"Certainly, Professor. Now finish your breakfast. It's the most important meal of the day."

"You know I run on blood, right?"

"That's the most important meal of the evening," he replied, primly.

I finished my breakfast.

We stepped through to Lisbon. That end of the gate wasn't an enchanted doorway, of course, merely a gate spell with transformers feeding it. It's still better than a plain doorway. I think the iridium wire glued to the inner face of it helped. We arrived in the afternoon, a day or two later than we left.

While Mary looked into things to steal, I set up my mirror and started looking for the major ley-line intersection points.

Overall, the planet seems to have a little over sixty major nexus points. Sixty-four, I think, but I'm not certain. Some of the ley lines are almost too dim to see. It's easier at night, of course, because of my night-eyes, but it's still sometimes a challenge to follow the faint ones. Fortunately, the spell filter I'm using shows crossing points as brighter spots, so it's sometimes easier to draw an imaginary line between two bright points, even if I can't actually see it. It's slow going on such a magic-poor planet, but I think I found them all.

A quick breakdown:

North America: Two

South America: Two

Russia: Three

Asia: Two

India: One

Europe: One

Middle East: One

Africa: Four, not counting the one just a few miles north of the tip of Egypt, in the Mediterranean. It's not thousands of feet down, but it's still underwater. All the rest are out in *deep* water. I may be well-suited to deep ocean exploring, but I am decidedly not aquatic! I stuck to the landlocked nexus points and hoped.

There were sixteen places which might have magi family fortresses parked on top. I went ahead and stuck my scrying-sensor nose into them to look around.

For the most part, yes, a magi family had something in the neighborhood, whether it be a mansion, an old castle, or a fenced-in area with warning signs. How they were doing, who they belonged to, what they thought about the situation, and anything else was largely guesswork. A few sites, however, stood out as... *unusual*.

In Africa, three hundred or so miles south-southwest of Khartoum, stood a structure reminiscent of a pyramid. It had a triangular base instead of a square one, however. A number of low buildings surrounded it, mostly carved from stone, with great slabs of flagstone forming pathways between them. Stone slabs radiated out from the pyramidal structure in straight lines, each one following the path of a ley line. As I watched, cattle were being herded into the place for sacrifice. Someone at the end of each line of stones used a hand-made flint knife to kill an animal, offer up ritual prayers, collect blood, and so on. Lines of helpers carried bowls of blood, running up the pyramid to pour it over the point, and hurrying back to collect more.

On a far-northern island in Britain, a young man's body was cold and still on a natural-rock altar inside a circle of stones. Only his body—he was beheaded at least two days ago. His blood was dry and I didn't see the head anywhere. As I watched, a number of people wearing fancy outfits and carrying swords escorted another young man into the circle. Others were binding together long sticks and branches, building some sort of elaborate cage.

In northern Brazil, a deep depression, like a meteor crater, held at least a hundred natives—either actual jungle tribesmen, or people dressed up to play parts in some ritual—all on their knees, chanting and clapping and swaying, sometimes marking themselves with knives of volcanic glass.

Somewhat west of India, maybe a hundred or so miles north of Karachi, in the Kirthar mountains, was a large mountain retreat—a monastery, I suppose. I looked all around the thing, but there was no one there—no one alive, anyway. They were all lying facedown in a central hall, facing the dais and altar. The cold at that altitude made it impossible to tell when they died.

Feeling guilty is my new default state. I'm going to embrace it, live it, learn to love it, because I'm going to be stuck with it. I may as well get used to it.

Then again, if I get used to it, does it still count as guilt? Or does it turn to indifference? And should I care if it does? Probably, but right now I'm having a hard time caring about much of anything. I just want to get my crap sorted out and go be an irresponsible nobody for a while.

Ouch. Maybe I'm already being irresponsible.

Fortunately, Mary's pretty good at cheering me up, and the Lisbon night life is actually kind of fun. We also improved our Portuguese through practice and digestion. Not a bad way to spend a couple of days, I guess. At least I got some work done with Diogenes, getting him sorted out and set up. He installed his own micro-gate in the robot and I activated it. It worked, so I recovered my Diogephone and left him to his shopping.

Nexus, Tuesday, March 30th, 2049

Mary has worked with Diogenes to smooth out some financing. Gambling—well, cheating at gambling—can be lucrative, but it requires ongoing effort on our part. Spending money in the stock market in order to give Diogenes a steady income is another sort of problem. Mary discussed it with Diogenes while I did some more scry-spying on nexus points. When I felt I'd learned all I could, Mary explained the financial side of things.

"I think we've sorted out our local money matters. If you'll help, that is."

"And what, exactly, do I need to do?" I asked.

"There are two major things. First, we need a bit more capital to work with."

"How do I help with that?"

"Do you know anything about corporate finance or the stock market?"

"I had a retirement fund," I replied. Mary waited. I waited.

"That's it?"

"The University had a special type for teachers and some contribution-matching. I don't remember exactly."

"O-kay. To make this as simple as possible..." she paused, thinking. "All right. So, we start by finding a company Diogenes can help. He's got a lot of information we don't have in my world. Now, we could start our own business, build a factory, all that stuff, but we would need more faces—you and I would have to run things for a while. Instead, we start with an existing company and hurt it."

"Hurt it?"

"Make it suffer some major setbacks—fires, probably, although a few murders are also on the table. Some CEO-level scandals, too. As the company is reeling from the loss of capital, leadership, and reputation, their stock price goes down. Then we buy."

"This sounds a lot like breaking a horse's leg to pay less for it."

"Ah! But then we fix the leg and upgrade it with cybernetic parts."

"Go on."

"Diogenes will take on the identity of the stockholder. This will get him a foot in the door, so to speak, and let him offer the company new manufacturing techniques, materials, the lot. We may have to show up to shake hands or sign something, but the world is mostly digital—virtual meetings, electronic signatures—so he should be mostly okay. With his 'eccentric genius' assistance to the place, they should become an industry powerhouse."

"And if this company, whatever it is—"

"Piezo Plastics. We already picked it out."

"—gets bought by someone bigger?"

"Diogenes?" Mary asked.

"Then, Professor," he said, through the Diogephone, "we either take the profits or continue to work with the new company. It is impossible to say until the offer is made. In the meantime, we have a revenue stream from the stock."

"I still think you can be put on the payroll as a resident inventor," Mary insisted.

"You two can sort that out later," I decided. "What do you need from me?"

"Oh. Can you help me frame people for murder and the like?"

"Maybe. I have some limitations."

"I thought of that. It's why we picked Piezo Plastics to be our business vehicle. The Chief Financial Officer is divorced, has no kids, and orders a call girl every Saturday night. Diogenes isn't sure if he's embezzling from the company, but he's living beyond his means."

"I do not have access to privileged or secure information," Diogenes said. "However, I can search, scan, and correlate all unsecured data on him. I estimate a probability in excess of ninety percent that he is, as you say, 'cooking the books' for his own gain, at least in moderation."

"All right."

"We also," Mary continued, "have a vice-president in charge of something—"

"Distribution," Diogenes supplied.

"—distribution, yes, who is also divorced. We believe he's divorced because of his drinking and four counts of domestic violence."

"You can access police reports?" I asked.

"No, Professor, but I can access every news service and all their records."

"Ah."

"So, we picked this company because we could embarrass it easily and you probably wouldn't have any objections to losing the two people."

"Actually, I was more concerned about the blood."

"What?"

"I don't leave blood behind, remember? If I kill a dozen prostitutes in his bed and make it look as though he did it before he killed himself, why is there no blood dripping through the mattress?"

"I..." Mary looked confused and upset. "I hadn't thought of that."

"Here's something else you didn't think of."

"What?"

"Once I find someplace to sit down and be boring, I'm going to be *boring*. I feel certain you could enjoy the occasional burglary to help finance Diogenes' ongoing world-reclamation project. Or even a big-game hunt in Apocalyptica. For all I know, there's a world out there where you can go shoot dinosaurs or swipe golden idols from ancient temples."

"But Diogenes needs the help now."

"So we sell the yacht and you steal more stuff. Or I can set up some diamond-growing spells. Diogenes can produce gold—either mined or recycled or salvaged. If you know anyone who is willing to pay for an assassination, you might do that instead of burglary. International jewel thief is nice, but so is professional assassin, no?"

"You raise some interesting points," Mary admitted. "I usually don't like to kill someone unless I have a real reason. Money isn't usually a real reason. I'll have to give it some thought."

"Take your time. Diogenes? Anything with critical timing going on?"

"No, Professor. I am well in advance of my most optimistic projections."

"Then let's hold off on the corporate schemes until Mary gets *really* bored."

"Of course."

"Meanwhile, Mary, would you rather tackle a magi fortress, interrupt some ongoing sacrifices and rituals, or poke around an ancient monastery full of corpses?"

"I love you."

"What brings this on?"

"You know just the right sort of things to say to me."

"No, I don't, but I'm glad I naturally seem to. I love you, too. But which one do you want to tackle?"

"How about one of the four open ones the Fries were using? They're minor nexuses, but they're open, right?"

"Yes," I agreed. "Thing is, I'm not sure they have enough power, presently, to do what I want to do. At least, not quickly. They still need to be bandaged, but not until I've scanned for the Ball. I want to find out if my Evil Orb is sitting on top of one before we go there."

"I see your point. Well, I'm all for sneaking into a magi fortress. For second choice, I'll distract the ritual people while you sneak in to do your work."

"What if the monastery is full of ghosts of ancient martial-arts masters?"

"Is it likely?" she asked, seriously.

"No, but it's possible. They could start doing all sorts of ghostly kung-fu moves right through us without us even noticing. Except we'll do this at night, so we can see ghosts. We can pretend we don't see them. First person to laugh, loses."

"You have a way of making the most boring thing in the world sound sort of attractive."

"I got you to like *me*, didn't I?"

"You're not boring. Not to me, anyway."

"Thank you. I think. So, monastery?"

"What sort of monastery?"

"Mountaintop thing. Tibet, India, stuff like that."

"I've never been to India. What do I wear?"

"Adventuring gear. We're not trying to blend in with the corpses."

"I bet we could."

"Being a corpse is easy. Not becoming one is the tricky part."

"I'll get my new jumpsuit."

"Take your time. It's almost sundown. We'll go straight there after dark."

"Oh, and Diogenes?" she called.

"Yes?"

"Please order some furniture. I'd like some chairs and a table, at least. And make a note we should rent *furnished* places in the future."

"Consider it done."

The monastery was one of the mountaintop things. It had a dozen or more wooden buildings, all seeming to sprout right out of the rock. It was hard to tell where one building began and another ended. They all ran into each other in a seemingly haphazard fashion, but still managed, somehow, to seem well designed and carefully thought out. Maybe you have to be a local to understand how it all comes together in such harmony. I sure don't.

I picked a doorway inside the place and connected it to our bathroom door. As usual, when transferring from point-to-point within a world, Diogenes deactivated the Diogephone micro-gate. Someday, when we have time and inclination, we'll see how a gate passing through a gate interacts. Not today, though, and not while I have it in a pocket.

We dressed for cold weather, just in case we had to spend the day there. I belted on Firebrand while Mary arranged her own weapons. Entering a former fortress of a magi family can be risky.

We flushed ourselves to India and closed the portal behind us.

Yep, it was cold. My ears popped and my breath frosted in the air, even though I was slightly above room temperature for Lisbon.

There was no one home. We hurried through the place, whisking silently from door to door, corner to corner, listening and sniffing and feeling with tendrils. The place lacked any signs of life. Fires were out, lamps were unlit, furniture neatly arranged, the works. The place had all the lived-in feeling of a fresh hotel room. It was a museum of a monastery, not a working model.

It felt that way until we entered the central hall and found the people, or what remained of them. I counted two hundred and change. They were all facedown on the floor, aimed in the direction of a raised dais.

Firebrand?

Yes, Boss?

I don't see any life in here. Do you hear anything at all?

Nope. It's you and Mary. I'm not even getting any rodents in the walls.

Me, either. Thanks.

"I think we're alone," I said, aloud.

"I'm starting to think so, too. What now?"

"The strongest magical emanations are up there," I said, nodding toward the dais.

The dais was surrounded by sculptured artwork, mostly gods and goddesses, I presume. Elephant-headed guy, a lady with four arms, a horned fellow with a trident, you name it—I couldn't even estimate how many there were.

Our feet felt fine, though. Either it wasn't holy ground or these gods were very tolerant.

In the middle of the dais was a contraption I hadn't seen before. It was a bronze plate, maybe three meters long and a meter wide, with three posts sticking straight up. On the posts were sixty or seventy brass discs, stacked through the holes in the middle. No two were the same size, and they were arranged oddly. Larger ones were always on the bottom, smaller ones toward the top. Each post had its own set of them, although most of them were on the central post. The stacks were irregular, as though someone started with a smooth, central stack and juggled them between the other posts.

"Where's the nexus?" Mary asked.

"I think it's here," I replied, walking around on the raised area. "My nexus-detecting spell is having a hard time locking on."

"I can't imagine why."

"Oh, hush, you. I'm concentrating."

Mary examined the corpses while I poked around the dais. I was fairly certain I was over the nexus point, but my nexus-detecting spell wasn't seeing it. I resorted to a tendril search, running invisible lines of psychic darkness out through the stonework, the bronze contraption, the dais, the walls, everything.

Aha. The bronze thing wasn't made of bronze. It was orichalcum, and it was larger than it looked. It was locked to the floor with some sort of mechanism related to the posts and the plates, and there was a hollow space beneath it. It wasn't easy to reach into—orichalcum resists penetration from my tendrils—but I could reach through the stone surrounding it easily enough.

"Mary? Want to help me pick a lock?"

"Always."

We examined the locking mechanism, slowly tracing it with tendrils. It was an eye-squinting, teeth-gritting sort of job, like reaching through hot sand to feel around the bottom of a bucket.

"Is there a spell on this?" Mary asked. "I seem to feel a spell on this."

"There used to be," I agreed. "I don't think it survived the power drop."

"I think it has, but it's too weak to do anything. Be careful when you tap the nexus."

"Thank you for the warning. Any idea how to pick the lock?"

"Yes, but I don't have enough tendrils, Doctor Octopus."

"That's 'Professor Octopus,' if you please."

"Okay, Prof. Hold this, here, and be ready to turn it this way..."

"That's a spell construct."

"I know, and it's in the way. Trust me. I know what I'm doing."

Oh? Firebrand asked.

"I wasn't talking to you," she snapped, and turned her attention to magical lockpicking.

Ten minutes later, I felt as though I'd been knitted, needlepointed, and crocheted. Tendrils by the score wrapped around, went through, or held in place an equal number of rods, pins, rockers, wheels, and levers, both of the physical and non-physical sorts. I had a headache the size of Monday and was about to call it quits—forget the door, we'll just bash our way through the damn floor!

"Got it," Mary announced. I suppressed a sigh and resigned myself to focusing one minute more. "I'll give a three-two-one-go. And three... two... one... *go.*"

I pushed, pulled, turned, twisted, and groaned. Mary poked something, but I'm not sure what.

One end of the metal slab, discs and all, tilted upward, counterweighted underneath. We muscled it up; it didn't want to open all the way. Improperly balanced, perhaps. The opening revealed stone steps leading down. Moist air blew up like a frightened fog. Mist started to form in the temple.

We regarded the steps for a moment and Mary raised an eyebrow at me.

"It's down there, yes," I agreed. "Hold on." I borrowed a couple of metal stands—candle stands, prayer wheel stands, whatever. They were metal or wood, but they were rods, long ones, and I jammed several into place to keep the doorway open.

"*Now* we can go down."

"Paranoid much?"

"Not that I know of. Why? Has someone been talking behind my back?"

"Come on. At least we'll be out of the sunrise."

We ducked under the edge and started down. It was a long way. The stairs were cut into the raw rock, obviously following some sort of natural chasm. Some places were tight, as though cut through a narrow gap, others were tunnels where we half-slid, half-wormed our way through. One place was cut along a flat, featureless face of stone, with rock on one side and empty air on the other—with a long drop straight down to a broken, tumbled heap of sharp-looking rubble.

About sunrise, we stopped and waited for the transformation to run its course.

Oops. One moment.

Nexus, Wednesday, March 31st, 2049

As our eyes switched from night to day, darkness closed in all around us. We also started to notice the cold and the thin air.

"This hiking trail needs a coffee shop," Mary remarked.

"And a gift shop. I could use a souvenir jacket."

Mary clicked on a small flashlight.

"You brought a flashlight?" I asked, surprised.

"You didn't?"

I spent a few moments waving my hands and chanting. A glowing ball of red light appeared and I put it over my head to hover. I stuck my tongue out at her.

"Close enough," Mary agreed. "Still down?"

"We may as well," I agreed, and we got moving. "Maybe we can find someplace suitable for a gateway and come straight back to it for the evening."

"I think I'm going to learn to like this teleportation thing. I was worried we would have to sit here all day until you were ready to tap the nexus." Mary was quiet for a moment as we tromped along a downward-sloping tunnel. "I have a question."

"Shoot."

"We just need something to define an opening. A border, a frame—that's it?"

"Pretty much. It helps if it's the right size and shape, but that's not essential."

"And if it's made out of origamico or iridium?"

"Also helpful, yes."

"Can't we do something like the cable-gate in Apocalyptica? A coil of memory-metal wire, maybe, with woven iridium and the other stuff. Take it out of your pocket, throw it on the ground, and *bam!* —instant gateway."

I stopped so suddenly Mary bumped into me. I had a similar idea when I was trying to go visit Tort. I should have written it down; I forgot all about it!

"What's wrong?" she asked.

"Diogenes?" I called.

"Yes, Professor?" replied the Diogephone.

"Did you hear that? What Mary asked?"

"I did. Shall I produce some prototype designs?"

"Yes. Yes, please."

"Working on it now, Professor."

I turned in place, grabbed Mary, and kissed her.

"Wow," she breathed, a minute later. "What was that for? Not that I mind."

"Being clever," I told her.

"I'll do it more often."

"Good idea."

"I agree. Does that count as being clever?"

"Don't get greedy."

A couple thousand stairs later, the trail ended at a door. It reminded me of the doors in Karvalen—a couple of tons of stone slab. Hopefully, it balanced on a pivot. While we examined it, my light spell decided it was too tired to go on and quit. I cast the spell again, noting as I did so it was much easier to gather power for it.

"Looks brighter," Mary commented.

"It is. We're nearly there, I think. Firebrand?"

The place is much more magical. I can feel it, Boss. Something is nearby, certainly.

"Good."

"So, are you going to tap the nexus when we get in?" Mary asked, "or can you do it during the day?"

"I don't think I should. In a higher-magic environment, maybe, where I can cast more powerful spells. Or if I brought a larger power reserve. But during the day? Here? Now? I'm be too worried about being fried by it. I don't know how much pressure is behind it."

"Mortality sucks," she agreed.

"It has its good points and bad points."

We continued our examination of the slab. There didn't seem to be a locking mechanism, handles, or anything else.

"Do we knock?" Mary asked.

"That never works."

Mary knocked on it anyway. Nothing happened.

"This is why people have door-clappers," I told her. "Pull the rope and it smacks flat pieces of wood together. Knocking on stone doesn't do much."

"And here I forgot my plastic explosives."

"Let's try pushing on it."

It didn't want to move. There was no way to tell how long it sat here, waiting. But Mary and I put our shoulders against it and heaved. Even during the day, when two vampires give something a shove, it's going to notice. Still, the slab didn't move, grunt and strain as we might.

"Other side?" Mary suggested. I agreed.

This time, trying to turn it the *correct* way, it ground grudgingly open. Beyond, we followed a straight, smooth passageway to its far end. There were stairs leading up to a triangular stone slab in the ceiling. I lifted it, carefully, and found it was a thin sheet of stone. It swung up and back easily.

The room was almost spherical, but faceted, completely angular. Our entry point was a triangular stone lid over the stairs. We emerged and I closed the lid carefully.

The lowest facet—the bottom one, where it would be flat and level—was actually an open hole. It was a triangular well with stairs on the sides. The rest of the room was like the inside of a gem. It had no normal walls, just facets, gradually sloping up from the well, growing steeper the farther away they were, vertical halfway up the room, and connecting to form a dome above. Each facet was inscribed with a symbol and connected to all the others by a number of metallic lines.

As Mary shone her light around, I thought the place seemed oddly familiar.

"This looks like it matches the description you gave me of the undersea pyramid," Mary observed.

"Yes. It does. But the symbols around the well aren't the same."

"Are you sure?"

"I'm sure. Well… no. The ones nearest are different, but I'm starting to think each symbol stands for a single nexus. These, surrounding the well, could be the nearest major nexus points to the one in the well. If this room is a map, then… yes, I guess the symbols could be the same. I'm trying to picture the place, but rotated around. I'm not visualizing it correctly."

"It's complicated," Mary reassured me. "So, if this is a map of the world, the local nexus is in the well?"

"Should be."

"That makes sense. But shouldn't your light be a lot brighter?"

"No. It's running on stored power, not drawing in local energy."

"A base spell, not a hybrid?"

"Exactly."

"See? I do pay attention."

We looked over the edge of the bottom-most facet. Yes, it was a triangular opening plated with metal—obviously orichalcum—presumably for some arcane reason known only to the Atlanteans. Mary followed me as I started down the narrow steps.

As before, the bottom of the well was a flat surface of the same metal, inscribed with eight circles around a three-foot-high central pillar.

"Careful of the circles," I warned.

"The nexus is low on power, isn't it?"

"Yes, but the last time I stuck my hand in, my ring and my hand got confused about which was which. Reality may still be subject to terrible distortions. Plus, it's daytime."

"Duly noted."

I examined the structure for differences. As far as I could tell, it was identical to the undersea pyramid's central chamber, only dry.

"This place feels old," Mary said, softly.

"It is. Based on magi legend, it's Atlantean, which implies it predates recorded human civilization."

"Greece? Egypt?"

"Who taught Egyptians to build pyramids? Survivors from Atlantis."

"I don't like it here."

"Me, either. Hang on while I check the power."

"You can do that during the day?"

"I'm not tapping the nexus," I explained. "It's already tapped. All this orichalcum is some sort of circuitry for magic. It contains the power of the nexus and has power taps for drawing energy out of it. What else it does… I'm not familiar with Atlantean technomagical designs. And I really don't want to learn about their electrical theory by poking around a high-voltage substation."

"Got it. I'll sit on the steps and be quiet."

"I'd rather you watched carefully. You may have to do it, someday. Even better, you can watch what happens from a different viewpoint. I'm going to be in the middle of it, actually doing it. You may see things I can't."

"Overwatch. On it."

I checked the magical designs of the power taps. They seemed in good working order, so I risked a power crystal. Energy flowed, filled the crystal, and I shut it off. It worked, so I took several minutes and refilled everything we were carrying. You never know when your magic item will need a recharge, so plug them in whenever you can.

Then it was a matter of building a spell to sense my orb. Since an active pulse would require enormous power expenditure—and the capacity to channel enormous power—we would wait until nightfall. On the other hand, a passive sensor isn't about power. It's about size and focus. Building a large and sensitive listening device isn't power-intensive, but it is finicky, precise work. I could do that without straining myself.

I drew power from the nexus to assemble my spell. I was halfway through the primary assembly—hours later—before I bothered to wonder if the nexus, the orichalcum, or the simple depth underground would interfere.

Mary raised an eyebrow at my nonmagical word.

"Problem?"

"Sort of." I explained about possible interference.

"So, do we gate back to Apocalyptica and come back after nightfall?"

"No. That won't help. We'll still be here, in close proximity to a major power source and surrounded by magically-conductive material."

"Does this mean we have to *walk* back up all those stairs and tunnels?"

"I hate to tell you this—"

"So don't."

"—but I'm actually looking forward to following you up a lot of stairs."

Mary had her mouth open for a reply, but she halted in mid-retort. She nodded slowly, thoughtfully.

"Good one," she finally admitted. "All right, when you put it that way, I guess I can tolerate an hour on the stair climb."

"It's a spectator sport."

"Not if I'm leading. But we still need to figure out how to let you cast your spells without being trapped down a well."

"Crystals. Lots of them."

"Can't we just run a wire up?"

"How? We would..." I trailed off, thinking.

Hooking it into a power tap wouldn't be a problem, but keeping it from bleeding charge into the ground all along its length would be. Could we coat an orichalcum wire in something living, maybe? Or would I need to enchant a bucket of liquid plastic to act as an insulator for coating the wire? Come to that, can I enchant a liquid? Will changing the liquid to a solid ruin the structure of the enchantment? Maybe we should manufacture a length of wire and test it.

"Maybe," I admitted. "It'll involve more trips, though."

"I presume we can't set up a gate in the nexus room?"

"I wouldn't. It could be unpredictable."

"Fine," she sighed. "Let's go back through the pivot-door. We can go back to Apocalyptica for your wire from there."

"We need to measure how far it is so we have enough wire."

"How about we get Diogenes to send a robot up the steps?"

"Following a robot just isn't the same," I told her, sadly.

"I can find something else for you to do."

"All right. At least our gate won't be anywhere the sunlight can hit it. Let's find a good stretch of tunnel and start scribbling on it."

Nexus, Thursday, April 1st, 2049

Diogenes had the perfect robot for the job. It was the size of a bulldog, had eight spider-like legs, and could climb anything short of a sheer surface. Diogenes programmed it, I sent it through, and we got to work on the orichalcum wire. When we opened the portal again and the robot came back, we knew how far it went in its round trip, so we had a good idea of how much wire we needed.

Three thousand meters of wire. That weighed in at about half a ton, not counting the spool.

"It's a good thing we're doing this at night," Mary said, after a respectful whistle. "I can roll that during the day, if I have to, but I'm not sure about going uphill all the way."

"With the two of us, even during the day we could manage, except it's not a simple staircase. Some of those narrower places barely fit *me*. We'll go through the gate, up the steps, make a new gate—or bring one of Diogenes' new collapsible ones—and roll wire down from the top. We'll use multiple spools, too, rather than try and manage one big, ungainly one."

"But with multiple spools of wire, you'll have to splice them together. When the splices touch the ground, you'll lose magical charge."

"No worries. We have duct tape."

"Won't it still ground through the duct tape?"

"I've enchanted the duct tape."

"Ah. Well, we've just solved every problem, everywhere. Duct tape fixes anything, so magical duct tape should fix everything."

"It's not that sort of enchantment—but I'll give it some thought."

The insulation, as I feared, proved more of a problem. Putting a magical matrix in a liquid was difficult, to say the least, and it tended to come apart as the liquid was poured from vessel to vessel. It made pretty lights and sparks—provided you can see magical energy—but it wasn't useful.

How do alchemists do their thing? They mix mundane ingredients—or not-very-magical ingredients—to create magical elixirs. Jon never went over that sort of thing with me, and I haven't encountered any alchemists that I know of. Why does it work for them? Is there a technique I'm missing? Or is it related to the more ritualistic wizardry? I wave my hands and sometimes chant, directing energies to take form, which defines the function. Other wizards—and, presumably, magicians—also use bits of stuff, like bones or blood or hair in their spells.

I should really get more schooling.

Anyway, the insulation. Once we applied a layer to the wire, however, it was solid and capable of holding an enchantment. It meant we had to enchant the insulation already on the wire, in completed batches, rather than simply zap a tank of liquid goo.

The wire itself offered some manufacturing problems. The basic problem was the stiffness of the wire. It didn't take to a spool too well as a solid wire. Whatever else you may say of orichalcum, it's not the most ductile of alloys. We had to make multi-stranded cables—like in the prototype variable-aperture arch—rather than a single, heavy-gauge wire. We wound up making coils of it about a meter across for easy carrying. This was my suggestion, mostly because enchanting the insulation was inconvenient. I had to keep the whole spool of wire from touching anything during the enchantment process, lest it ground out the magic I worked with.

Maybe I need to enchant a formal workroom, one with a floor or workbenches specially insulated, so I can work with orichalcum more easily. Note to Diogenes for later.

Since the wire manufacturing was such a pain, I also had Diogenes bring me a lot of crystals and gemstones to enchant as power crystals. Having a direct line to the nexus would be less likely to run the risk of insufficient power, but if it proved too much trouble, the crystals could be Plan B.

Diogenes also provided us with a couple of models of collapsible gateway. They were nonmagical, of course, but the physical structure was the important part. The first one was a combination of memory-metal wire and iridium; push the button and it springs out into an archway. Push it again and it contracts into a fancy bracelet with the button placed like a decoration.

The other was a complex, plastic thing with strips of iridium inlay. It unfolded like one of those Hoberman sphere toys, but formed a circle, not a sphere. It required no power, but was larger and heavier than the wire version.

The idea of a sphere, though, made me wonder if we could make a matched set of portable shift-spheres. But, again, that's a project for later. It's always someday, it seems…

Mary and I returned to Nexus, arriving down near the actual nexus point. It was nighttime, but there was no way to tell how far along.

"Want me to wait while you charge crystals?" she inquired.

"No, you go ahead and check the time, set up the gates upstairs. It'll save time, and we might not have much left in the night."

"I thought you wanted to follow me?"

"While it is aesthetically pleasing to enjoy such a marvelous view, it's nighttime. Can I talk you into another performance after my necrology turns into biology?"

"I see what you mean. All right. Meet you in the hall of the dead?"

"Roger that."

Mary sprinted upstairs with the portable gates while I charged the crystals. I followed her once I had the batteries ready.

The cool, damp air still coming from the opened hatchway continued to pour out over everything while we were gone. In the last day or so, it filled the temple with an icy mist and left frost-tracks on every surface, even the dead guys. Oops. Well, they were already dead. Freezer burn is hardly the worst thing ever to happen to them.

The portable gates looked good, for the most part. Neither of them looked terribly stable, though. A stiff wind would knock either one over—not a selling point. Mary had them both leaned up against the rear wall of the dais and was doing some spell-work, getting a feel for how it well they would take the gate spell.

"Good news," Mary said, as I emerged from under the orichalcum trapdoor.

"Oh?"

"It's early. We've got hours to go before sunup."

"I love it when the timing works out," I agreed, and regarded her work. "I also like your spell work. I'm not so sure about the physical instability," I finished, poking one of the gates. It rocked back and forth where it leaned against the wall, but it didn't fall. Mary put it in a different spot, wedging it between two carvings.

"Diving through one as an escape hatch doesn't require much," she pointed out. "We could toss one on the floor."

"True," I admitted, remembering a dive through one pool and out another. "I guess they'll do for temporary gates—places we don't want to establish a permanent door. I like how they shrink down. We can open a small gate through the brute-force bilocation method, push the miniature gate through, and make a new connection after the portable unit unfolds. Plus, we can enchant them to make connecting easier."

"*You* can enchant them," she corrected. "I'm still working on reliably casting a gate spell in the first place."

"I have every confidence you can manage a point-to-point gate within the same world," I assured her. "And today you get to try for a connection to Apocalyptica."

"Whoa, hold on a minute," she protested. "Neither of these is enchanted, yet!"

"I'll be looking over your shoulder the whole time," I assured her.

"I'd rather help you do it."

"I think you can do it on your own. You really ought to try. If anything ever happens to me, you'll have to do it or be stuck in whatever world you're in."

"Have I mentioned I hate it when you argue rationally? You're a man. You're not supposed to be rational."

"I have great respect for the anthropomorphic personification of Reason. We've met. She was very nice."

"Uh… right. Fine. I'll assume this is a good idea." She cracked her knuckles and shook her hands briskly. "You're watching? You'll catch what I drop?"

"Absolutely."

"Okay."

Mary did a fine job. It took close to an hour before she completed the spell, but I blame a lot of that on her exacting care and meticulous attention to detail. Mortals have a hard time with the power requirements, which accounts for most of their lengthy preparations. It was taxing for Mary, but she had enough vitality to hammer it out. Another hundred or so gates and she'll put holes in space with perfect confidence.

Diogenes was ready on his end, of course; he always listens through the Diogephone. A robot arm extended through the memory-metal gate when it opened. The arm was really just a rod with several large coils of wire hanging on it. It immediately tilted down, slid the wire off, and retracted through the gate.

Mary didn't actually need help to keep her gate open, but I leaned on it a little because I'm nice like that. Once Diogenes retracted the arm, Mary closed the gate and breathed a huge sigh of relief.

"See? That wasn't so hard."

She punched my arm. I pretended it hurt.

Laying wire was tedious, but not difficult. We tied one end to a carving on the wall and Mary started uncoiling as we went down. I carried as many extra coils as I could; I was limited by the length of my arms. We paused every hundred meters or so to splice ends together. In narrow spots, I handed through coil after coil, then picked them up and followed her again as she kept unwinding wire. When I was down to my last two coils, I handed them to her and ran upstairs again for more.

Tedious, yes, but not difficult.

Down by the nexus, I ran the wire into the central, faceted area. I could see magical charge already trickling away up the line, so I sent Mary back up to keep the charge from leaking away. She skipped off while I put together an actual power tap spell to draw energies directly from the nexus. Once I had it all in place, I went up to join her.

The sound of gunfire from above encouraged me to move at the speed of dark. I came up the final stairs and out of the basement-hatchway so fast I missed the floor entirely and hit a wall about fifteen feet up. It stopped me and I fell to the floor, taking in the situation as I dropped.

The place was crawling with frost-covered zombies. They were moaning and crackling and shuffling around, staggering into each other, into walls, into doorframes. Several of them were on the dais, struggling to get to Mary. Mary, for her part, was defending the hatchway. If the hatch braces were disturbed by these shuffling things, it might close. If it closed, it would definitely sever our wire. At least, that was my thought. She was probably thinking it would trap me underneath, leaving her alone with a roomful of frosty zombies.

Bullets to the brain didn't seem to bother them. Wrong sort of zombie, apparently. When guns proved ineffective, Mary started hand-to-hand, flipping them, rolling them, tripping them, kicking them back, and basically keeping them too busy picking themselves up—now with a broken bone or two—to really be a threat to the hatch.

I drew Firebrand.

How do you feel about frost zombies? I asked.

I think they're cold, unpleasant, and in desperate need of a good torching.

I still need the building.

I'll bear that in mind, Boss.

Mary shifted her focus, kicking her victims toward me as Firebrand lit up. Beheading one didn't kill it, but did worsen its already-poor coordination. If beheading didn't kill them, I didn't see a way to kill them quickly. Still, cutting one to pieces severely limits their ability to do you harm.

We dismembered them. We smashed and shredded and cut. They were mindless, staggering things, not combatants, and we crunched our way through them as quickly as they came. Many of them didn't even come toward us, content to stagger in circles or simply bump into a wall like a robot with faulty programming. It wasn't a pleasant chore, and it went on for a while. Firebrand showed great restraint in not setting zombies actually on fire, as such, but it saved me considerable effort by melting frozen flesh as fast as I could cut at it.

"Mind if I ask a question?" Mary said, breaking a back as she kicked one away from the hatch.

"Fire away," I replied, splitting one in half as Firebrand whooped in glee. "Why are there zombie hordes in the monastery?"

"I'm guessing it has to do with the wire dumping huge amounts of raw magical force into the vicinity," I shouted, leaping over a group of six as they hemmed me in. The real trick to dealing with a horde is never let them mob you. Keep moving. Keep them loose and open.

"Now that we're kind of on top of the situation, do you think you could, oh, maybe do something about that?" Mary yelled after me.

"Good plan. Hold them while I redirect it."

"Can I borrow Firebrand?"

We sorted ourselves out at the other end of the room, luring the more aggressive zombies away from the hatch. I handed Firebrand to Mary and did my best to stealth around to the dais. It must have worked; the zombies still in the main chamber kept doing whatever random, mindless things they were already doing. The ones still interested in *braaaaaains* went after Mary and Firebrand.

I grabbed the end of the wire and started channeling power.

Ow.

Even in its depleted state, a major nexus is a terrible source of energy. I don't *think* it would have killed me during the day, but it stung like hell even at night. I molded it as quickly as I could, shaping a power tap at the upper end of the wire, much like screwing a spray nozzle onto a high-voltage garden hose. Controlling the flow was the priority. Once I had the power contained, the zombies couldn't draw any more of it.

But I could.

I directed energies through a basic attack spell—Glabrus' Fist, a simple thing used for communicating the force of a blow over a distance. It worked very well. I punched the air repeatedly, targeting the legs. Femurs crunched all around the room. Again, it didn't stop any of them, but it made them even slower and less likely to mob us.

As I broke them and Mary subdivided them into limbs and other pieces, they continued to slow down. Without the influx of fresh force, every movement expended some of their absorbed energies. They wound down like old clockwork and eventually stopped completely.

Mary didn't. Judging from the way she kept cutting the bodies to pieces, I don't think she likes zombies. Maybe they startled her as she came out of the hatch; thieves *hate* being surprised. I dismissed the Fist spell and waited while she chopped zombies like a teppanyaki chef with a grudge. She didn't leave anything bigger than a finger—and fingers she stomped. I guess the idea of a frozen, undead finger slowly inchworming to the attack was distasteful.

"All done?" I asked.

"Yes. For now." She rejoined me on the dais and handed Firebrand back. "Next time we're going to deal with walking dead, *warn* me, would you?"

"I didn't know," I admitted. "I'm not even sure why they started moving. Magical force, yes—the nexus wire supplied the power, but what actually motivated them? Why did it make them get up and move around instead of, I don't know, thaw out? Or turn into ethereal vapor? Or shift out of this plane of existence? I have no idea. I've never seen it before. I certainly didn't expect it."

"All right. Okay. This time. But in the future, bear in mind I don't like undead."

"Um... I hate to tell you this..."

"Messy undead," she clarified. "Zombies. Grave-wights. Whatever."

"Fair enough."

"So," she continued, changing the subject, "what are we here for, again?"

"Power. I'll be creating a gigantic parabolic reflector in the psychic wavelengths and tuning a receptor spell at the focus to resonate with any trace of my Evil Alter Ego. Then we can see about sealing the Fries nexus-points."

"Well? Why aren't you doing it? I don't want to stay here longer than we have to."

"Of course. Keep me from being disturbed," I added, handing Firebrand back to her. "Just in case." Mary accepted Firebrand with, I thought, a level of relief. Everyone needs a flaming dragon-sword security blanket once in a while.

Nothing bothered us. Lucky for it.

I spent a good portion of the night building my spells. The receptor wasn't too complicated; I've got the hang of psychic listening devices. The complicated part was constructing a precise parabolic antenna. It was finicky work to build a small one and get it exactly the right shape. Then I magnified it, enlarged it, and adjusted it for precise focus again. Once I had it as large as the room, it became impractical to adjust the focus on it further; I need to see what I'm doing. All I could do was magnify it and hope I had it zeroed in well enough.

I probably overdid it. I have a nasty tendency toward overkill. I think it's because I generally feel a little insecure about trying new things. Or a little insecure in general.

With my new, extra-jumbo psychic spell antenna hovering over the monastery, I parked my receptor at the focal point and did a slow scan, a full three hundred and sixty degrees. I picked up a lot of static, of course. Considering I was looking for the Black Ball, I wasn't surprised to get a lot of sideband chatter from human greed, lust, envy, anger... it's always there, and always strong. I was tuning specifically for something resonating with my own mental signature, however, so the excess chatter was merely background noise.

I realized, after my first sweep, that I had a problem. I was on a sphere, not a plate. I couldn't just do a quick three-sixty and be done. I had to do a sweep of the planet, which involved scanning everything out to the horizon, relocating, and doing it again... and again... and again....

Fortunately, there was a faster way. I had a lot of power to work with, so I elevated the antenna, raising it into the sky, hoisting it on lines of magical force. It wasn't a physical object, after all, only a confluence of power, a center of energy. It cost some extra power to move it, more to keep it active, and still more to control and operate it at such a distance, but a couple thousand miles of elevation let me search whole quadrants of the planet.

I got a hit. I actually got several hits, all of them in—probably—California.

If I hadn't been dead at the time, my heart would have skipped a beat.

Fourteen hits of various intensity and clarity, all of them with matching resonance.

Fourteen!?

Breathe. Take a big, icy, high-altitude, useless breath. Hold it.

Oh, right. Let it out, too.

All right, think about it. Why am I getting multiple hits? There aren't fourteen separate Orbs of Evil. At least, there better not be fourteen separate Orbs of Evil. So, what does this mean? Has it left its mark on thirteen surviving minds, perhaps? Some sort of mental domination or conditioning so they resonate with the orb and are easier to control? If so, how do I figure out which one is which? If I jump on one, the rest will almost certainly know about it. If this hypothesis is true, they'll be in a sort of psychic contact all the time. But the strongest contact should be the actual Orb—probably. It would help if I could differentiate between the psychic leakage through a demon-binding orb and the active radiations of a living mind affected by the thing imprisoned in the orb.

First order of business: Locate them.

It's not easy to use a psychic antenna in orbit and coordinate it with a ground-based mirror so you can zoom in along the geometric line of the focus to locate a specific map coordinate in the physical world. It's not even as easy as it sounds.

If I hadn't been draining the last of the planet's magical lifeblood, it would have taken me days to put together the spells for it. As it was, it took me the better part of a very hectic and hurried hour to coordinate everything—dawn wasn't too far off—and get them all to work together. All that effort, and all I got were the general vicinities.

The psychic point-sources were clustered. Two in San Deigo, four in Los Angeles, and eight in San Francisco. My locator wasn't too precise.

That was enough for me. Mary and I could go to those cities and use much smaller antennas to home in on them. From there, we could spy with magic mirrors, telescopes, flying camera drones, and vampire eyeballs. Then we could figure out what we wanted to do.

"Any luck?" Mary asked, once I unwound everything and relaxed.

"Yes and no," I replied, and filled her in on my intelligence-gathering.

"I say we hit San Francisco first. If I were an Evil Orb, I'd want guards."

"You may have a point. We'll start there and see what we can find. It may be in San Deigo with one thoroughly-dominated servant as its arms and legs."

"Either way, we'll hunt it down," Mary assured me. "What's next?"

"Nexus closings. The open ones the Fries were using."

"How are we going to do that?"

"Remember your suggestion about gating in?"

"That was when the blasting spells were still going," she pointed out. "I thought we could turn them off, gate in, fix the nexus, and gate out again. The blasting would keep other people away until you were ready to do your spells. Now those places are likely to be crawling with people."

"Yes and no. They bombed and shelled and missiled the centers of the domes, remember?"

"You're thinking craters don't have a lot of people in them?"

"Yes."

"How about we look them over, first?"

"I like how you think, but we'll have to hurry."

"Why?"

"Dawn isn't far away and I'd like to gate away from here before then. There's about a ten-hour time difference between here and the eastern-most one—the one a trifle north of Fayette, New York. My plan is to make sure we're all charged up here, gate to that one, use it to prepare another gate spell, seal it, and head for the next one. On the last one, we gate back to Lisbon after we seal it. Because of the change in time zones, we should be in darkness for the whole process. I don't want to try sealing a nexus, even a minor one, even after they're mostly depleted, during the day."

"Seems reasonable. So let's look and see why it won't work."

"Your pessimism is depressingly justified."

I popped a scrying sensor—a psychic one, not a television one; I dislike being fried by sunlight—over the northeastern United States and moved it down, zooming in. The site of the first nexus was a cratered ruin. People were there, yes, working under banks of lights. They were sifting dirt, running instruments over the ground, and wearing environment suits. If an alien spacecraft had crashed there, it wouldn't look much different.

"Problem?" Mary asked. I touched her tendril with mine, linking with her, and showed her my pocket mirror. She nodded. "I thought as much. When the psychic nastiness went away, they moved in."

"Now what? Forty-four thousand federal agencies are crawling all over the nexus sites. I may be hard to spot, but I never did perfect an invisibility spell."

"Well, do you have to be on-site to do a bandage spell?"

"Yes. Oh, I could probably use one spell to target a self-contained 'bandage bomb' spell. If I over-build one and lob a half-dozen or so at a nexus, it'll probably layer it well enough to be sealed. It'll take a while, though, to launch multiple bandage-warheads from here, and we just don't have the time."

"I've got two solutions."

"You have my undivided attention."

"You know, that's kind of scary."

"What is?"

"Having all your attention. In this context, anyway."

"In an ancient magi monastery, in the middle of nowhere, surrounded by dismembered frost zombies?"

"Yes. It's a trifle unnerving."

"I can't imagine why. But what are your solutions?"

"First, wait until tomorrow night. We've got a wire to the nexus and it's capped off. We can kill a day on a mountaintop and start launching your nexus-bandage-bombs first thing in the evening."

"Possibly. The other idea?"

"Prepare your bandage spells. Then open a gate—a small one, about head-sized, using the brute-force method, directly over the nexus—and apply your spell by reaching through. Or just throw your spells through. Don't actually go there. The sunrise window from the time zone changes will narrow our operational time, but you can spend all day getting ready and, if you have to, just do one every day."

I did some mental juggling. Rate of power flow, power requirements for a bandage spell, minimum diameter of a gate for effective casting, time to cast prepared spell vs. energy requirements of the gate… It might work.

Nexus, Sunday, April 4th, 2049

Sunrise annoys me. To some extent, it always annoys me, but I'm especially annoyed when it sneaks up on me.

Mary and I ducked down through the hatch and hurried below. The main chamber above had far too many windows and skylights and whatnot. Fortunately, the tingling that precedes dawn is usually fairly noticeable, and none of the windows was aligned due east.

With plenty of power on hand, cleaning spells weren't a problem. Neither were insulating and warming spells.

"How did they *heat* this place?" Mary asked, shivering.

"I have no idea," I admitted, finishing a thermal barrier around her. "Maybe they exercised mental disciplines to feel warm. Maybe there's an ancient spell to keep the place from freezing and it disintegrated when the world ran down below a critical level. Power deprivation can be a problem for permanent spells. Or maybe they did what we're doing with personal spells."

"Is it the same for breathing?"

"The air is a bit thin," I agreed. "I don't think I want to exert myself."

"Me, either. Does working magic use up more oxygen?"

"Probably, but it can concentrate it." I set about building spells around our heads to raise the oxygen level. "How's that?"

"Better. Being a part-time mortal is a pain."

"Could be worse," I replied, leading her up into the monastery again.

"Don't explain. So, what do we do for the day?"

"I plan to scry on our targets, build some preliminary spells, partially fold a gateway, and do some light enchantment work."

"We're going to spend all day getting ready for this evening?"

"Yes. Unless you have a better idea?" I asked, handing her up from the hatchway.

"Hmm." She looked around at the frosty zombie parts. "No, I'm not really too keen on anything else just now. Let's get your crap sorted out so we can leave."

"I thought you might see it that way."

The preparations for sneak-bandaging the lesser nexus points went surprisingly well. The power flow from the major nexus was low enough and controlled enough to make spellcasting reasonably safe. Mary made an excellent assistant—a spare pair of hands can make most projects go more quickly. We prepared a number of spells together, channeling and focusing energies to build four small, pre-charged gate spells. Bandage spells were another matter, however.

I spent a lot of time with a mirror, studying the slow ooze of power from each of the Fries' nexus points. Minor nexus points are much less dangerous. My guess was they could be handled—in their current state—by a mortal spellcaster. He wouldn't enjoy the experience, but he would probably make a full recovery.

But bandaging these four minor nexus points was trickier than I'd thought. The Fries had capped them, built spell-construct power taps over them. Fine and good, as far as it went, but I destroyed those power taps a moment after I broke their domes. The result was something like firing a shotgun into the side of the house to destroy the tap for the garden hose. The wreckage is messy.

Still, the wound in the world wasn't bleeding magic too badly. It was a rather wide wound—each of the four were similar in that respect—but this was patching a low-pressure vein, not sewing closed a piece of torn heart muscle. Each minor nexus would take a larger bandage, but the bandages could be thinner to begin with. As they soaked up power, they could grow deeper into the wound, thickening and strengthening as they went, while the natural healing of the planet did its best to repair the damage.

Maybe a pressure sensitive function… something to keep the bandage from growing too thick and strong. Maybe even to have it slowly dissolve if the pressure differential was too low. If it's down deep in the wound and skin is growing over it, the skin can take some of the load, so the bandage can slowly dissolve away as the skin takes over. Yes, I think that might be best. But I'll remember to do a patient follow-up visit or two, this time.

The magic was complex, yes, but it broke down into simpler processes. Mary and I built the simpler parts of the spell, drawing them in diagrams on the temple floor. I did the more complicated bits myself while explaining how it worked.

She thought it was a good idea. I have hopes this will actually work the way I want it to.

When night fell in the monastery, we hid underground again. After a brief break for hygiene, we returned to our spell preparations. Given the ten-hour time zone change between our locations, it would be close to sunrise here before it would be night on the east coast of North America. Tricky timing, since opening a gate into a sunlit area doesn't do anything good to the vampire doing it. I wanted to be ready to open gates, fire bandage spells, and close them, one-two-three-four, like clockwork.

It felt a lot like preparing for the original assault on Johann. Less dangerous, less nerve-wracking, but similar.

Mary was a huge help. Once the sunset line passed our first target, she handled the magic mirror, sighted in on the nexus, and opened the prepared gate spell. All I had to do was look through the spatial opening, spot the ripped-up area in the planet's magical field, and launch bandages at it.

It did, in fact, go like clockwork—or teamwork. There is much to be said for being prepared and having an advanced apprentice to help.

The only thing that didn't go perfectly was the Toano nexus. I covered most of the ripped-up area with bandage spells, but our post-bandaging scrying showed me I missed a bit, over-covering one area and leaving an uncovered gap. It wasn't a major problem. We simply took another pass at it, albeit in more of a hurry. Still, it was only one more nexus bandage spell. We finished well before our sunrise deadline.

Planetary first aid? Check. One more thing off my list.

I handed off the live wire into Mary's care, opened a gateway from a portable gate to the temporary gate downstairs, and went down to turn off the tap. We closed up shop, sealed the orichalcum hatch, gathered up our stuff, and went back to Apocalyptica.

Let's see if we can get my ball back.

Nexus, Tuesday, April 5th, 2049

San Francisco was much as I remembered it: very clean, very open, and humming with electricity. The air had that ocean-fresh smell to it. I don't know if that's the way it was back in my day, in my world, but the air quality of 2049 in Mary's version of Earth is pretty good.

Sadly, we arrived in the middle of a driving rainstorm, which kind of put a damper on my enjoyment of the place. Our gate terminus was a hotel-room door. We stepped into a vacant room, dismissed the gate, and turned around to open the door and walk calmly out of the hotel. On the way down, I called for a cab.

I forgot to be sneaky. As the cab door opened, it played my customized welcome sound. Google remembered me. I'm not sure that's a good thing. A lot of vampires and magi are probably more than a little irritated with me. Some of them might have technical people—or programs—actively looking for me.

Maybe I shouldn't come back here so readily. This place could prove unexpectedly hostile. If I'm going to help Diogenes use this as a resource point, I need a new, rock-solid identity, not just a few fake IDs. I'll have to look into it. I wonder if BitRate is still in business?

We took the cab as far as a local theater and switched. This time, we went into stealth mode as we booked another cab, this time using an electronic money stick. Let this be a warning to online shoppers: the default payment method may be convenient, but it may be a little *too* convenient!

As the cab drove us around, I triangulated on the psychic imprints and Mary corrected the cab's course to close in. They were all clustered together. In the same house, even. In the hills. On an estate. Behind a tall, somewhat familiar gate.

Of *course* it was on the Fries' estate. Where else?

We cruised past it on a couple of sides, enough to confirm the coordinates, then stopped off at the nearest motel.

"What do you think?" Mary asked, toweling her hair dry. The rain was still coming down. I lay down on the bed with a grinding squeak.

"I think we should go in loud and heavy, beat everyone inside into submission, and get my ball back."

At the sudden silence, I lifted my head to look at her. She stared at me.

"Are you serious?"

"Yes. I'm tired of politics, adventure, emotional trauma, and all the rest. I want to get the damned ball, lock it away somewhere, and let Diogenes probe alternate universes until he finds Mount Doom. I want this crap *over*. I'm lazy. I'm irresponsible. I'm a bad person. I admit it. I'm learning to live with it."

Mary sat down on the edge of the bed, laid her hand on my chest.

"Do you really believe that?"

"Of course."

"I don't."

"You don't live in this skull," I countered. "I do."

"At night, you don't have a reflection."

"True. So?"

"Has it occurred to you it might be significant of something?"

"No, not really. I mean, it's a vampire thing, or thing involving a magical orb sucking my dark side out of my body, or something."

"You don't have a reflection," she repeated. "You don't have a way to judge yourself."

"I can see me just fine."

"Yes… I suppose you can. You can't see what others see, though."

"They're deluded idiots. Present company excepted," I added. Mary smiled slightly.

"I just want you to know you're not irresponsible. You worry about it, but you're not. An irresponsible person doesn't worry so much about it. You're also not a coward, or unhandsome, or any of those other things you seem to think about yourself. Oh, you say such things in a self-deprecating manner, deflecting and hiding it with humor, but I see right through you."

"If you say so."

"And another thing. If you agree with me just to shut me up or avoid a serious discussion, I'll smother you with a pillow."

"Ah. Well, if you're going to get all murderous and evil about it…"

"I'm serious. I know you've been through one of Hell's smaller hiking trails, so I know you need to be… what's the word? I don't know. You need to find a way to find yourself again. There's only so much anyone can take, and you're near it."

"Oh? What makes you say that?"

"You're moody, grumpy, depressed, and willing to go down the kill-everything-that-moves road as a primary option. That's not like you."

"I am not depressed," I lied.

"Just moody, grumpy, and willing to go down the kill-everything-that-moves road?"

She's right, Boss, Firebrand said, from its case.

Mary chuckled.

"I didn't ask you," I complained.

*Yeah, but she **is** right.*

"About what?"

Everything.

"You're not helping."

She's trying to, and I'm helping her. It counts. It does count, doesn't it?

"All right, all right. It counts."

You just don't like it when people help.

"I love having help!"

Not when it's about who you are. What you are.

"Not," Mary corrected, "when it's about how you see yourself."

Yeah, Boss. What she said.

"Can we please ignore my personal problems and focus on finding the evil artifact?" I complained.

"If you like, but you're proving the point." She held up one hand to silence my reply. "I only wanted you to know I recognize you *have* problems—and I love you anyway. When you want to talk about them—if you ever do—I'll be exasperated it took you so long, but I'll help."

"I'm ambivalent about your reassurances."

"Nothing in life is a sure thing," she replied, sweetly. "Now, do you really want to go into the House of Fries and punch your way through everything?"

"No. I want guns, too."

"I'm torn between clapping my hands in glee and worrying about you."

"Pick one," I suggested, "or come up with a better idea."

I can grab an unprotected human being and yank the life right out of him. It takes a moment of concentration, and it takes longer the farther away I am. There are other factors, of course—can I see him, is he being active, is he moving, is he already tired, is he magically sensitive and resisting, and so on. But, in general, with the Average Human, I can choose to give him the tendril equivalent of a roundhouse swing and make it look instantaneous.

Mary does not share this ability. I have an uncounted, possibly variable number of invisible psychic tendrils. She has *one*. I blame her initial vampire species, but I have an idea for helping her develop another one.

Anyway, she can drain the vitality out of someone but it takes, under ideal conditions, close to a full minute. It takes even longer to drill down deeper and siphon off the thing we call a soul. This makes her ability less useful for quietly killing guards while sneaking into a fortress. It's great for making someone feel tired, even faint, before killing him by more mundane methods, though, and it's perfect for a little light snacking on the vitality of a crowd.

I wore my cloak of darkness (patent pending) and she wore her high-tech ninja armor suit. She did the lead sneaking, I did the follow-up sneaking. We worked our way around the estate perimeter to check for guards—both were at the front gate. While they were sitting in their guard booth, they died quietly.

Farther in, we found a few more guards on active duty, patrolling the grounds or keeping watch. I kept an eye out for problems while Mary went inside, found the central security station, and made extensive use of knives.

Diogenes gave her some new ones out of some super-space-age material. They're slightly curved, sharp only on the outer edge and the point, and don't set off metal detectors. They're also wickedly sharp and, according to Diogenes, should stay that way if not mistreated. I didn't get to see the bloodbath firsthand, but I did walk through the room, later, to clean up—blood crawled off monitor screens, out of keyboards, even out of the carpet to slither up and over my boots, into my skin.

I am a forensics expert's worst nightmare. Other people's, too, but for different reasons.

We took our time. The goal was to kill all the guards without anyone triggering an alarm. Mary was confident. I wasn't. But it turns out I can be taught. I practiced being sneaky, stealthy, and quiet while Mary treated most of the trip as a field exercise for her inept student. I think it was payback for making her open a gate on her own.

She covered for me twice when I made minor goofs, then explained why it was a goof. For example, you don't open a door and look in. You either wave a tendril through the wall to feel the room for people—much like shining a flashlight around to see anyone—or you open the door boldly, as though you belong there, and march in ready to kill everyone. Slowly creeping isn't sneaky; it signals you're *trying* to sneak and failing. Opening a door and entering like you belong there is how people normally enter a room and doesn't trigger an instant suspicion.

There are times for each, and knowing which is which is something that comes with experience. I'll get there.

Unsurprisingly, there were very few magical effects around the place. A few objects were present, of course, each in their display case or whatever, but there were no active spells hanging around.

When Mary was happy with our kill count, we did another sweep of the place to make sure we didn't miss anyone. We didn't. We also didn't find my Orb.

"Safe?" Mary suggested. "Basement vault? Curse box?"

"I don't know. Give me a minute." I raised my smaller spell-antenna again and turned in a slow circle. "I'm not getting anything, now."

"So, it was a signature on someone?"

"Perhaps killing everyone we encountered was a trifle premature," I mused. "Interrogating some of them might have helped."

"We can ask others, elsewhere."

"Maybe. Let's look for clues here, first."

We went over the house and grounds with considerable care, searching. Mary called me out to the garden and the Ascension Sphere I'd built for the Fries so long ago. I went to see what she found.

The garden layout was still there, but the magical portion had been used. It wasn't hard to see how. In the center of the Sphere's diagram was a ring. Well, I *say* a ring. It was really more of a circular area around which the whole structure of the garden spiraled. Twice. In opposite directions.

The grass, the gravel, the trees and flowers—all of it was warped, distorted, as though some strange space-bending effect emanated from a central point, rippling out in a pair of counter-rotating spirals, twisting space and matter as it exploded.

"I've seen this effect before," I noted.

I seem to recall it, too, Firebrand agreed.

"What is it?" Mary asked.

"When I fled through a gate from Karvalen to this world, T'yl destroyed the gate behind me. This caused it to… I don't know exactly, but it didn't shut down. It had some sort of distortion effect on the local spacetime that destroyed the gateways as well as the magical opening, leaving behind this double-spiral pattern weirdness. It also destroyed any chance for pursuers to track me through the gate. No gate, no trail. No trail, no pursuit. The Orb of Evil was present, so whatever it uses to sense the world around it might have worked through the sack it was in. It might have duplicated the technique."

"So, what happened here?"

"My guess, based on my paranoia, cynicism, and pessimistic outlook, is the ball grabbed someone by the brain—or maybe by the greed, or fear, or something similar—and used the power in the Ascension Sphere *I built*, to create a gateway into another world."

"The circle in the center doesn't look big enough for a person."

"But it's plenty big enough for the Orb," I pointed out. "Maybe it didn't want to bring anyone from this world, or maybe it had power constraints limiting the size of the opening. I can't say. But I'd be willing to bet the Orb, for its own reasons, persuaded or manipulated or dominated its way into having a gate opened for it. Probably one with a built-in self-destruct. It wouldn't want anyone left behind to be a source of information on where it went."

"So, if it's escaped from this world into another one," Mary asked, kicking lightly at the oddly-rippled garden dirt, "what do we do? How do we find it?"

"I don't know. As far as I can tell, there is no way to do an interdimensional search spell. Doesn't mean there isn't one, but I have no idea how to do it."

"How firm of an 'I don't know' is this?"

"What do you mean?"

"Is it like doing a cybersearch and studying for a week? Or is it taking apart the alien gadget and hoping it doesn't blow up?"

"Is it something I can do but don't know how, or does it require a leap in theory to be able to attempt?"

"I like the way you put it. Yes."

"I'm fairly sure there is a way to do it, but I don't know how. I think I need a leap in theory. Inter-universal detection spells ought to be possible, but how to use them across inter-universal barriers stumps me. It's outside my current theories of magic. Even Johann, with all his power, resorted to using ghosts as remote probes rather than do a seeking spell. If I take time to solve it, it could be a day, a week, a year—or never. I have no way of knowing."

"Fair enough. So, where do we go from here? How do we find it?"

I sat down on a rippled concrete bench. I'm not sure it was supposed to be curved, but it held me.

"I'm wondering that," I admitted, tiredly. I thought about it for a while and Mary sat down with me to hold my hand. After a while, I shook my head.

"I don't see a way," I told her. "But, upon consideration, maybe I shouldn't bother."

"What do you mean?"

"I have no way to directly scan other universes the way I do within a single universe. No scanner spells, no sensor spells, nothing of that nature. In theory, I could open a small gate, cast a spell through it, and search individual worlds, one by one. I could spend the next decade in frantic haste—or the next millennium—searching, universe by universe, effectively sticking my face into a world just long enough to detect whether or not the Black Ball is in it—assuming it isn't shielded from my detection spells—and moving on to the next one. The problem is, if I go down that road I won't do anything else."

"And the alternative?" Mary asked, watching my face carefully.

"The opposite."

"What? Do nothing?"

"No, on the contrary. Do everything I want to do. *Don't* devote my time and energy to searching. *Don't* rush off to waste my time. *Don't* joust with this windmill. Instead, do all the other things. Take a vacation. Revitalize my weary spirit. Nurse a wounded heart. Experiment with other spells, maybe even work out a searching spell. Explore some other worlds and build a baseline of data so we can learn how to dial for specific qualities, rather than open gateways at random—assuming there's a way to do that at all. That sort of thing."

"I'm for it," Mary agreed, immediately. "My only question is about the Black Ball of Bad. What will it be doing?"

"I have no idea. Hiding from me, probably, because wherever it is, I'm certain it thinks I'm coming for it. It has no way of knowing I'm too tired to chase it. At a guess, it will be building some sort of fortress, much like it did when the entity possessed the Prince of Byrne. If I were the thing, my first concern would be personal safety, then building a power base from which to operate."

"And...?"

"And it will show up, eventually. If I don't go after it, it will eventually come after me. Or its agents will. And that will give me something to work with for tracking it down."

"So, the plan is to... sit back, put your feet up, and wait for it to attack?"

"Only initially. I need to rest." I rubbed my temples. "Physically, I don't get tired. Emotionally, I'm exhausted. You've been helping with that, but I have a long way to go."

"Yes. Yes, I suppose you're right. We probably have a bit of a breathing space while your Orb finds itself a new niche and sets itself up."

"And I want that chance to breathe. I need some time off. When I feel up to it, I'll probably set up spells to let Diogenes scan for the orb while he's doing basic checks on universes. It probably won't help, but we could get lucky."

"Are you sure it isn't in this world? Could all this," she gestured at the double-spiral distortion, "be a decoy? Or even a failed attempt at escape?"

"You know, I hadn't thought of that." I sighed. "All right, we'll go look. Let me crank up my passive scanner again. Call a cab and we'll go investigate the other point-sources."

The remaining sources turned out to be people. A few of them had a family resemblance to the Fries. The rest seemed to be employees—guards, servants, whatever. A brief look at their spirits with my vampire eyes confirmed there were alterations. The Orb did something to them, changed them in some way, and it left its black little fingerprints all over their insides.

Metaphorically speaking, of course. I didn't see anything like that when I opened them up and looked.

We didn't burn down the houses. Having had it done to me, I'm actively trying to avoid doing it to others.

Apocalyptica, Friday, July 8ᵗʰ, Year 1

I think…

I think things are going well. I'm almost scared to say that, as though saying it will cause something large, unpleasant, and hungry to pop into existence next to me.

It's not an unreasonable worry. Not for me. But I try not to think about it.

Diogenes is slowly renovating a planet. Mary has worlds to explore and, potentially, rob. Even Firebrand has something to do. It's spending time with Bob, rather than Lissette. Apparently, Lissette is boring, while Bob rules the Eastrange with a velvet-lined, gauntleted fist.

Everyone has something to do. Everyone *is* doing something. Everyone is busy with whatever.

I'm not.

I'm sitting in a comfortable room, finishing up another chapter of my existence.

I'm not sure if my soul is still bleeding from the loss of Bronze. I don't think it is. I think it's finally scabbed over and relatively numb. I don't want to poke it, though.

Instead, I'm working—if you can call it that—on understanding more about how the universes are put together, how magic relates to science, and vice-versa. I'm not hurrying. I'm trying to keep things calmer than my usual headlong pace. I want to be leisurely, relaxed, and peaceful for a while, even if I have to kill someone to do it.

For so much of my existence as a vampire, I've been an immortal in a hurry. A creature with an infinite lifespan, but with no time. Rush, rush, rush, busy, busy, busy.

Well, now I'm *taking* time. Nobody is screaming at me, for me, or about me—at least, not where I can hear it. For now, that's enough. We'll see how long it goes on. That's all anyone can really do, I suppose. Take time when you can take it, live each day as it comes, hope you have more time tomorrow, and be ready when the inevitable storm of events rains on your parade.

As for me, I'm willing to let the whole of the multi-timeline-alternate-reality-universe go to hell in its own way.

Maybe it'll even return the favor… for a while.

Reflection

As I sit here, regarding myself as once I was, I wonder how I could ever have been... him. We are all different people, depending on when we are. The child demanding a cookie is very different from the youth applying for his first job. Both are strangers to the career man negotiating for a raise, and none of them recognize the old person on the porch, rocking and wondering if it will rain.

How many people have I been? A new person, from second to second, moment to moment, each forming a link, subtly different from the one before, making up the chain of my existence? Or are there distinct events to mark the transition of who I was into who I am, and into who I will become?

Regardless, I look now at the self who would retire from the world and live the life mundane. He wants nothing more than to rest—and he will. But there are things awaiting him, the me that was, and I pity him.

Can I change any of them? Can I reach out to him across the gulfs of space and time to give him as much as one word of warning, or of advice? No, of course not. If I were to change anything about him then, I would not be the me I am now. He's just going to have to suffer through it all, and I will have to watch.

CPSIA information can be obtained
at www.ICGtesting.com
Printed in the USA
LVHW090147241220
675059LV00013B/93/J

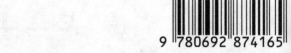